D1429229

3 GREAT THRILLERS

3 GREAT THRILLERS

JOHN LE CARRÉ

A SMALL TOWN IN GERMANY

FREDERICK FORSYTH

THE DOGS OF WAR

WILBUR SMITH

WILD JUSTICE

A Small Town in Germany first published in Great Britain in 1968
by William Heinemann Ltd
The Dogs of War first published in Great Britain in 1974 by
Hutchinson and Co. Ltd
Wild Justice first published in Great Britain in 1979
by William Heinemann Ltd

This edition first published in Great Britain in 1986
jointly by

William Heinemann Ltd
10 Upper Grosvenor Street
London W1

and

Octopus Books Limited
59 Grosvenor Street
London W1

ISBN 0 86273 328 6

A Small Town in Germany © le Carré Productions Ltd 1968
The Dogs of War copyright © Damsbrook Publications Ltd, 1974
Wild Justice © Wilbur Smith 1979

Printed and bound in Great Britain by
Collins, Glasgow

CONTENTS

JOHN LE CARRÉ
A SMALL TOWN IN GERMANY

Prologue

The Hunter and the Hunted

Ten minutes to midnight: a pious Friday in May and a fine river mist lying in the market square. Bonn was a Balkan city, stained and secret, drawn over with tramwire. Bonn was a dark house where someone had died, a house draped in Catholic black and guarded by policemen. Their leather coats glistened in the lamplight, the black flags hung over them like birds. It was as if all but they had heard the alarm and fled. Now a car, now a pedestrian hurried past, and the silence followed like a wake. A tram sounded, but far away. In the grocer's shop, from a pyramid of tins, the handwritten notice advertised the emergency: 'Lay in your store now!' Among the crumbs, marzipan pigs like hairless mice proclaimed the forgotten Saint's Day.

Only the posters spoke. From trees and lanterns they fought their futile war, each at the same height as if that were the regulation; they were printed in radiant paint, mounted on hardboard, and draped in thin streamers of black bunting, and they rose at him vividly as he hastened past. 'Send the Foreign Workers Home!' 'Rid us of the Whore Bonn!' 'Unite Germany First, Europe Second!' And the largest was set above them, in a tall streamer right across the street: 'Open the road East, the road West has failed'. His dark eyes paid them no attention. A policeman stamped his boots and grimaced at him, making a hard joke of the weather; another challenged him but without conviction; and one called 'Guten Abend' but he offered no reply; for he had no mind for any but the plumper figure a hundred paces ahead of him who trotted hurriedly down the wide avenue, entering the shadow of a black flag, emerging as the tallow lamplight took him back.

The dark had made no ceremony of coming nor the grey day of leaving, but the night was crisp for once and smelt of winter. For most months, Bonn is not a place of seasons; the climate is all indoors, a climate of headaches, warm and flat like bottled water, a climate of waiting, of bitter tastes taken from the slow river, of fatigue and reluctant growth, and the air is an exhausted wind fallen on the plain, and the dusk when it comes is nothing but a darkening of the day's mist, a lighting of tube lamps in the howling streets. But on that spring night the winter had come back to visit, slipping up the Rhine valley under cover of the predatory darkness, and it quickened them as they went, hurt them with its unexpected chill. The eyes of the smaller man, straining ahead of him, shed tears of cold.

The avenue curved, taking them past the yellow walls of the University. 'Democrats! Hang the Press Baron!' 'The World belongs to the Young!' 'Let the English Lordlings beg!' 'Alex Springer to the gallows!' 'Long Live Axel Springer!' 'Protest is Freedom'. These posters were done in woodcut on a student press. Overhead the young foliage glittered in a fragmented canopy of green glass. The lights were brighter here, the police fewer. The men strode on, neither faster nor slower; the first busily, with a beadle's flurry. His stride though swift was stagy and awkward, as if he had stepped down from somewhere grander; a walk replete with a German burgher's dignity. His arms swung shortly at his sides and his back was straight. Did he know he was being followed? His head was held stiff in authority, but authority became him poorly. A man drawn forward by what he saw? Or driven by what lay behind? Was it fear that prevented him from turning? A man of substance does not move his head. The second man stepped lightly in his wake. A sprite, weightless as the dark, slipping through the shadows as if they were a net: a clown stalking a courtier.

They entered a narrow alley; the air was filled with the smells of sour food. Once more the walls cried to them, now in the tell-tale liturgy of German advertising: 'Strong Men Drink Beer!' 'Knowledge is Power, Read Molden Books!' Here for the first time the echo of their footsteps mingled in unmistakeable challenge; here for the first time the man of substance seemed to waken, sensing the danger behind. It was no more than a slur, a tiny imperfection in the determined rhythm of his portly march; but it took him to the edge of the pavement, away from the darkness of the walls, and he seemed to find comfort in the brighter places, where the lamplight and the policemen could protect him. Yet his pursuer did not relent. 'Meet us in Hanover!' the poster cried. 'Karfeld speaks in Hanover!' 'Meet us in Hanover on Sunday!'

An empty tram rolled past, its windows protected with adhesive mesh. A single church bell began its monotonous chime, a dirge for Christian virtue in an empty city. They were walking again, closer together, but still the man in front did not look back. They rounded another corner; ahead of them, the great spire of the Minster was cut like thin metal against the empty sky. Reluctantly the first chimes were answered by others, until all over the town there rose a slow cacophony of uncertain peals. An Angelus? An air raid? A young policeman, standing in the doorway of a sports shop, bared his head. In the Cathedral porch, a candle burned in a bowl of red glass; to one side stood a religious bookshop. The plump man paused, leaned forward as if to examine something in the window; glanced down the road; and in that moment the light from the window shone full upon his features. The smaller man ran forward: stopped; ran forward again; and was too late.

The limousine had drawn up, an Open Rekord driven by a pale man hidden in the smoked glass. Its back door opened and closed; ponderously it gathered speed, indifferent to the one sharp cry, a cry of fury and of accusation, of total loss and total bitterness which, drawn as if by force from the breast of him who uttered it, rang abruptly down the empty street and, as abruptly, died. The policeman spun around, shone his torch. Held in its beam, the small man did not move; he was staring after the limousine. Shaking over the cobble, skidding on the wet tramlines, disregarding the traffic lights, it had vanished westward towards the illuminated hills.

'Who are you?'

The beam rested on the coat of English tweed, too hairy for such a little man, the fine, neat shoes grey with mud, the dark, unblinking eyes.

'Who are you?' the policeman repeated; for the bells were everywhere now, and their echoes persisted eerily.

One small hand disappeared into the folds of the coat and emerged with a leather holder. The policeman accepted it gingerly, unfastened the catch while he juggled with his torch and the black pistol which he clutched inexpertly in his left hand.

'What was it?' the policeman asked, as he handed back the wallet. 'Why did you call out?'

The small man gave no answer. He had walked a few paces along the pavement.

'You never saw him before?' he asked, still looking after the car. 'You don't know who he was?' He spoke softly, as if there were children sleeping upstairs; a vulnerable voice, respectful of silence.

'No.'

The sharp, lined face broke into a conciliatory smile. 'Forgive me. I made a silly mistake. I thought I recognized him.' His accent was neither wholly English nor wholly German, but a privately elected no-man's land, picked and set between the two. And he would move it, he seemed to say, a little in either direction, if it chanced to inconvenience the listener.

'It's the season,' the small man said, determined to make conversation. 'The sudden cold, one looks at people more.' He had opened a tin of small Dutch cigars and was offering them to the policeman. The policeman declined so he lit one for himself.

'It's the riots,' the policeman answered slowly, 'The flags, the slogans. We're all nervous these days. This week Hanover, last week Frankfurt. It upsets the natural order.' He was a young man and had studied for his appointment. 'They should forbid them more,' he added, using the common dictum. 'Like the Communists.'

He saluted loosely; once more the stranger smiled, a last affecting smile, dependent, hinting at friendship, dwindling reluctantly. And was gone. Remaining where he was, the policemen listened attentively to the fading footfall. Now it stopped; to be resumed again, more quickly – was it his imagination? – with greater conviction than before. For a moment he pondered.

'In Bonn,' he said to himself with an inward sigh, recalling the stranger's weightless tread, 'even the flies are official.'

Taking out his notebook, he carefully wrote down the time and place and nature of the incident. He was not a fast-thinking man, but admired for his thoroughness. This done, he added the number of the motor-car, which for some reason had remained in his mind. Suddenly he stopped; and stared at what he had written; at the name and the car number; and he thought of the plump man and the long, marching stride, and his heart began beating very fast. He thought of the secret instruction he had read on the recreation-room noticeboard, and the little muffled photograph from long ago. The notebook still in his hand, he ran off for the telephone kiosk as fast as his boots would carry him.

Way over there in a
Small town in Germany
There lived a shoemaker
Schumann was his name
Ich bin ein Musikant
Ich bin für das Vaterland
I have a big bass drum
And this is how I play!

A drinking song sung in British military messes in Occupied Germany, with obscene variations, to the tune of the *Marche Militaire*

I
Mr Meadowes and Mr Cork

'Why don't you get out and walk? I would if I was your age. Quicker than sitting with this scum.'

'I'll be all right,' said Cork, the albino cypher clerk, and looked anxiously at the older man in the driving seat beside him. 'We'll just have to hurry slowly,' he added in his most conciliatory tone. Cork was a cockney, bright as paint, and it worried him to see Meadowes all het up. 'We'll just have to let it happen to us, won't we, Arthur?'

'I'd like to throw the whole bloody lot of them in the Rhine.'

'You know you wouldn't really.'

It was Saturday morning, nine o'clock. The road from Friesdorf to the Embassy was packed tight with protesting cars, the pavements lined with photographs of the Movement's leader, and the banners were stretched across the road like advertisements at a rally: 'The West has deceived us; Germans can look East without shame.' 'End the Coca-Cola culture now!' At the very centre of the long column sat Cork and Meadowes, becalmed while the clamour of horns rose all round them in unceasing concert. Sometimes they sounded in series starting at the front and working slowly back, so that their roar passed overhead like an aeroplane sometimes in unison, dash dot dash, K for Karfeld our elected leader; and sometimes they just had a free for all, tuning for the symphony.

'What the hell do they want with it then? All the screaming? Bloody good haircut, that's what half of them need, a good hiding and back to school.'

'It's the farmers,' Cork said, 'I told you, they're picketing the Bundestag.'

'Farmers? This lot? They'd die if they got their feet wet, half of them. Kids. Look at that crowd there then. Disgusting, that's what I call it.'

To their right, in a red Volkswagen, sat three students, two boys and a girl. The driver wore a leather jacket and very long hair, and he was gazing intently through his windscreen at the car in front, his slim palm poised over the steering wheel, waiting for the signal to blow his horn. His two companions, intertwined, were kissing deeply.

'They're the supporting cast,' Cork said. 'It's a lark for them. You know the students' slogan: "Freedom's only real when you're fighting for it." It's not so different from what's going on at home, is it? Hear what they did in Grosvenor Square last night?' Cork asked, attempting once again to shift the ground. 'If that's education, I'll stick to ignorance.'

But Meadowes would not be distracted.

'They ought to bring in the National Service,' he declared, glaring at the Volkswagen. 'That would sort them out.'

'They've got it already. They've had it twenty years or more.' Sensing that Meadowes was preparing to relent, Cork chose the subject most likely to encourage him. 'Here, how did Myra's birthday party go, then? Good show was it? I'll bet she had a lovely time.'

But for some reason the question only cast Meadowes into even deeper gloom, and after that Cork chose silence as the wiser course. He had tried everything, and to no effect. Meadowes was a decent, churchy sort of bloke, the kind they didn't make any more, and worth a good deal of anybody's time; but there was a limit even to Cork's filial devotion. He'd tried the new Rover which Meadowes had bought for his retirement, tax free and at a ten per cent discount. He'd admired its build, its comfort and its fittings until he was blue in the face, and all he'd got for his trouble was a grunt. He'd tried the Exiles Motoring Club, of which Meadowes was a keen supporter; he'd tried the Commonwealth Children's Sports which they hoped to run that afternoon in the Embassy gardens. And now he had even tried last night's big party, which they hadn't liked to attend because of Janet's baby being so near; and as far as Cork was concerned, that was the whole menu and Meadowes could lump it. Short of a holiday, Cork decided, short of a long, sunny holiday away from Karfeld and the Brussels negotiations, and away from his daughter Myra, Arthur Meadowes was heading for the bend.

'Here,' said Cork trying one more throw, 'Dutch Shell's up another bob.'

'And Guest Keen are down three.'

Cork had resolutely invested in non-British stock, but Meadowes preferred to pay the price of patriotism.

'They'll go up again after Brussels, don't you worry.'

'Who are you kidding? The talks are as good as dead aren't they? I may not have your intelligence but I can read, you know.'

Meadowes, as Cork was the very first to concede, had every excuse for melancholy, quite apart from his investments in British Steel. He'd come with hardly a break from four years in Warsaw which was enough to make anyone jumpy. He was on his last posting and facing retirement in the autumn, and in Cork's experience they got worse, not better, the nearer the day came. Not to mention having a nervous wreck for a daughter: Myra Meadowes was on the road to recovery, true enough, but if one half of what they said of her was to be believed, she'd got a long way to go yet.

Add to that the responsibilities of Chancery Registrar – of handling, that is, a political archive in the hottest crisis any of them could remember – and you had more than your work cut out. Even Cork, tucked away in Cyphers, had felt the draught a bit, what with the extra traffic, and the extra hours, and Janet's baby coming on, and the do-this-by-yesterday that you got from most of Chancery; and his own experience, as he well knew, was nothing beside what old Arthur had had to cope with. It was the coming from all directions, Cork decided, that threw you these days. You never knew where it would happen next. One minute you'd be getting off a Reply Immediate on the Bremen riots, or tomorrow's jamboree in Hanover, the next they'd be coming back at you with the gold rush, or Brussels, or raising another few hundred millions in Frankfurt and Zurich; and if it was tough in Cyphers, it was tougher still for those who had to track down the files, enter up the loose papers, mark in the new entries and get them back into circulation again ... which reminded him, for some reason, that he must telephone his accountant. If the Krupp labour front was going on like this, he might take a little look at Swedish steel, just an in-and-outer for the baby's bank account ...

'Hullo,' said Cork brightening. 'Going to have a scrap, are we?'

Two policemen had stepped off the kerb to remonstrate with a large agricultural man in a Mercedes Diesel. First he lowered the window and shouted at them; now he opened the door and shouted at them again. Quite suddenly, the police withdrew. Cork yawned in disappointment.

Once upon a time, Cork remembered wistfully, panics came singly. You had a scream on the Berlin corridor, Russian helicopters teasing up the border, an up-and-downer with the Four Power Steering Committee in Washington. Or there was intrigue: a suspected German diplomatic initiative in Moscow that had to be nipped in the bud, a suspected fiddle on the Rhodesian embargo, hushing up a Rhine Army riot in Minden. And that was that. You bolted your food, opened shop, and stayed till the job was done; and you went home a free man. That was that; that was what life was made of; that was Bonn. Whether you were a dip like de Lisle, or a non-dip behind the green baize door, the scene was the same; a bit of drama, a lot of hot air, then tickle up the stocks and shares a bit, back to boredom and roll on your next posting.

Until Karfeld. Cork gazed disconsolately at the posters. Until Karfeld came along. Nine months, he reflected – the vast features were plump and lifeless, the expression one of flatulent sincerity – nine months since Arthur Meadowes had come bustling through the connecting door from Registry with the news of the Kiel demonstrations, the surprise nomination, the student sit-in, and the little bit of violence they had gradually learnt to expect. Who caught it that time? Some Socialist counter-demonstrators. One beaten to death, one stoned ... it used to shock them in the old days. They were green then. Christ, he thought, it might have been ten years ago; but Cork could date it almost to the hour.

Kiel was the morning the Embassy doctor announced that Janet was expecting. From that day on, nothing had ever been the same.

The horns broke wildly into song again; the convoy jerked forward and stopped abruptly, clanging and screeching all different notes.

'Any luck with those files then?' Cork enquired, his mind lighting upon the suspected cause of Meadowes's anxiety.

'No.'

'Trolley hasn't turned up?'

'No, the trolley has *not* turned up.'

Ball-bearings, Cork thought suddenly: some nice little Swedish outfit with a get-up-and-go approach, a firm capable of moving in fast ... two hundred quid's worth and away we all go ...

'Come on Arthur, don't let it get you down. It's not Warsaw you know: you're in Bonn now. Look: know how many cups they're shy of in the canteen, just on the last six weeks alone? Not broken, mind, just lost: twenty-four.'

Meadowes was unimpressed.

'Now who wants to pinch an Embassy cup? No one. People are absent-minded. They're *involved.* It's the crisis, see. It's happening everywhere. It's the same with files.'

'Cups aren't secret, that's the difference.'

'Nor's file trolleys,' Cork pleaded, 'If it comes to that. Nor's the two-bar electric fire from the conference room which Admin are doing their nut about. Nor's the long-carriage typewriter from the Pool, nor – listen Arthur, *you* can't be blamed, not with so much going on; how can you? You know what dips are when they get to drafting telegrams. Look at de Lisle, look at Gaveston: dreamers. I'm not saying they aren't geniuses but they don't know where they are half the time, their heads are in the clouds. You can't be blamed for that.'

'I *can* be blamed. I'm responsible.'

'All right, torture yourself,' Cork snapped, his last patience gone. 'Anyway it's Bradfield's responsibility, not yours. He's Head of Chancery; he's responsible for security.'

With this parting comment, Cork once more fell to surveying the unprepossessing scene about him. In more ways that one, he decided, Karfeld had a lot to answer for.

The prospect which presented itself to Cork would have offered little comfort to any man, whatever his preoccupation. The weather was wretched. A blank Rhineland mist, like breath upon a mirror, lay over the whole developed wilderness of bureaucratic Bonn. Giant buildings, still unfurnished, rose glumly out of the untilled fields. Ahead of him the British Embassy, all its windows lit, stood on its brown heathland like a makeshift hospital in the twilight of the battle. At the front gate, the Union Jack, mysteriously at half mast, drooped sadly over a cluster of German policemen.

The very choice of Bonn as the waiting house for Berlin has long been an anomaly; it is now an abuse. Perhaps only the Germans, having elected a Chancellor, would have brought their capital city to his door. To accommodate the immigration of diplomats, politicians and government servants which attended this unlooked for honour – and also to keep them at a distance – the townspeople have built a complete suburb outside their city walls. It was through the southern end of this that the traffic was now attempting to pass: a jumble of stodgy towers and lowflung contemporary hutments which stretched along the dual carriageway almost as far as the amiable sanatorium settlement of Bad Godesberg, whose principal industry, having once been bottled water, is now diplomacy. True, some Ministries have been admitted to Bonn itself, and have added their fake masonry to the cobble courtyards; true, some Embassies are in Bad Godesberg; but the seat of Federal Government and the great majority of the ninety odd Foreign Missions accredited to it, not to mention the lobbyists, the press, the political parties, the refugee organizations, the official residences of Federal Dignitaries, the Kuratorium for Indivisible Germany, and the whole bureaucratic superstructure of West Germany's provisional capital, are to be found to either side of this one arterial carriageway between the former seat of the Bishop of Cologne and the Victorian villas of a Rhineland spa.

Of this unnatural capital village, of this island state, which lacks both political identity and social hinterland, and is permanently committed to the condition of impermanence, the British Embassy is an inseparable part. Imagine a sprawling factory block of no merit, the kind of building you see in dozens on the Western by-pass, usually with a symbol of its product set out on the roof; paint about it a sullen Rhenish sky, add an indefinable hint of Nazi architecture, just a breath, no more, and erect in the rough ground behind it two fading goalposts for the recreation of the unwashed, and you have portrayed with fair accuracy the mind and force of England in the Federal Republic. With one sprawling limb it holds down the past, with another it smoothes the present; while a third searches anxiously in the wet Rhenish earth to find what is buried for the future. Built as the Occupation drew to its premature end, it catches precisely that mood of graceless renunciation; a stone face turned towards a former foe, a grey smile offered to the present ally. To Cork's left, as they finally entered its gates, lay the headquarters of the Red Cross, to his right a Mercedes factory; behind him, across the road, the Social Democrats and a Coca-Cola depot. The Embassy is cut off from these improbable neighbours by a strip of waste land which, strewn with sorrel and bare clay, runs flatly to the neglected Rhine. This field is known as Bonn's green belt and is an object of great pride to the city's planners.

One day, perhaps, they will move to Berlin; the contingency, even in Bonn, is occasionally spoken of. One day, perhaps, the whole grey mountain will slip down the autobahn and silently take its place in the wet car parks of the gutted Reichstag; until that happens, these concrete tents will remain, discreetly temporary in deference to the dream, discreetly permanent in deference to reality; they will remain, multiply, and grow; for in Bonn, movement has replaced progress, and whatever will not grow must die.

Parking the car in his customary place behind the canteen, Meadowes walked slowly round it, as he always did after a journey, testing the handles and checking the coachwork for the marks of an errant pebble. Still deep in thought he crossed the forecourt to the front porch where two British military policemen, a sergeant and a corporal, were examining passes. Cork, still offended, followed at a distance, so that by the time he reached the front door Meadowes was already deep in conversation with the sentries.

'Who are *you* then?' the sergeant was wanting to know.

'Meadowes of Registry. He works for me.' Meadowes tried to look over the sergeant's shoulder, but the sergeant drew back the list against his tunic. 'He's been off sick you see. I wanted to enquire.'

'Then why's he under Ground Floor?'

'He has a room there. He has two functions. Two different jobs. One with me, one on the ground floor.'

'Zero,' said the sergeant, looking at the list again. A bunch of typists, their skirts as short as the Ambassadress permitted, came fluttering up the steps behind them.

Meadowes lingered, still unconvinced. 'You mean he's not come in?' he asked with the tenderness which longs for contradiction.

'That's what I do mean. Zero. He's not come in. He's not here. Right?'

They followed the girls into the lobby. Cork took his arm and drew him back into the shadow of the basement grille.

'What's going on, Arthur? What's your problem? It's not just the missing files, is it? What's eating you up?'

'Nothing's eating me.'

'Then what's all that about Leo being ill? He hasn't had a day's illness in his life.'

Meadowes did not reply.

'What's Leo been up to?' Cork demanded with deep suspicion.

'Nothing.'

'Then why did you ask about him? You can't have lost him as well! Blimey, they've been trying to lose Leo for twenty years.'

Cork felt the decent hesitation in Meadowes, the proximity of revelation and the reluctant drawing back.

'You can't be responsible for Leo. Nobody can. You can't be everyone's father, Arthur. He's probably out flogging a few petrol coupons.'

The words were barely spoken before Meadowes rounded on him, very angry indeed.

'Don't you talk like that, d'you hear? Don't you dare! Leo's not like that; it's a shocking thing to say of anyone; flogging petrol coupons. Just because he's – a temporary.'

Cork's expression, as he followed Meadowes at a safe distance up the open-tread staircase to the first floor, spoke for itself. If that was what age did for you, retirement at sixty didn't come a day too early. Cork's own retirement would be from it to a Greek island. Crete, he thought; Spetsai. I could swing it at forty if those ball-bearings come home. Well, forty-five anyway.

A step along the corridor from Registry lay the cypher room and a step beyond that, the small, bright office occupied by Peter de Lisle. Chancery means no more than political section; its young men are the elite. It is here, if anywhere, that the popular dream of the brilliant English diplomat may be realized; and in no one more nearly than Peter de Lisle. He was an elegant, willowy, almost beautiful person, whose youth had persisted obstinately into his early forties, and his manner was languid to the point of lethargy. This lethargy was not affected, but simply deceptive. De Lisle's family tree had been disastrously pruned by two wars, and further depleted by a succession of small but violent catastrophes. A brother had died in a car accident; an uncle had committed suicide; a second brother was drowned on holiday in Penzance. Thus by degrees de Lisle himself had acquired both the energies and the duties of an improbable survivor. He had much rather not been called at all, his manner implied; but since that was the way of things, he had no alternative but to wear the mantle.

As Meadowes and Cork entered their separate estates, de Lisle was on the point of gathering together the sheets of blue draft paper which lay scattered in artistic confusion on his desk. Having shuffled them casually into order, he buttoned his waistcoat, stretched, cast a wistful look at the picture of Lake Windermere, issued by the Ministry of Works with the kind permission of the London, Midland and Scottish Railway, and drifted contentedly on to the landing to greet the new day. Lingering at the long window, he peered downward for a moment at the spines of the farmers' black cars and the small islands of blue where the police lights flashed.

'They have this *passion* for steel,' he observed to Mickie Crabbe, a ragged, leaky-eyed man permanently crippled by a hangover. Crabbe was slowly ascending the stairs, one hand reassuringly upon the banister, his thin shoulders hunched protectively. 'I'd quite forgotten. I'd remembered the blood, but forgotten the steel.'

'Rather,' Crabbe muttered, 'Rather,' and his voice trailed after him like the shreds of his own life. Only his hair had not aged; it grew dark and luxuriant on his little head, as if fertilized by alcohol.

'Sports,' Crabbe cried, making an unscheduled halt. 'Bloody marquee isn't up.'

'It'll come,' de Lisle assured him kindly. 'It's been held up by the Peasants' Revolt.'

'Back way empty as a church on the other road; bloody Huns,' Crabbe added vaguely as if it were a greeting, and continued painfully down his appointed track.

Slowly following him along the passage, de Lisle pushed open door after door, peering inside to call a name or a greeting, until he arrived by degrees at the Head of Chancery's room; and here he knocked hard, and leaned in.

'All present, Rawley,' he said. 'Ready when you are.'

'I'm ready now.'

'I say, you haven't pinched my electric fan by any chance, have you? It's absolutely vanished.'

'Fortunately I am not a kleptomaniac.'

'Ludwig Siebkron's asking for a meeting at four o'clock,' de Lisle added quietly, 'At the Ministry of the Interior. He won't say why. I pressed him and he got shirty. He just said he wanted to discuss our security arrangements.'

'Our arrangements are perfectly adequate as they stand. We discussed them with him last week; he is dining with me on Tuesday. I cannot imagine we need to do any more. The place is crawling with police as it is. I refuse to let him make a fortress of us.'

The voice was austere and self sufficient, an academic voice, yet military; a voice which held much in reserve; a voice which guarded its secrets and its sovereignty, drawled out but bitten short.

Taking a step into the room, de Lisle closed the door and dropped the latch.

'How did it go last night?'

'Adequately. You may read the minute if you wish. Meadowes is taking it to the Ambassador.'

'I imagined that was what Siebkron was ringing about.'

'I am not obliged to report to Siebkron; nor do I intend to. And I have no idea why he telephoned at this hour, nor why he should call a meeting. Your imagination is ahead of my own.'

'All the same, I accepted for you. It seemed wise.'

'At what time are we bidden?'

'Four o'clock. He's sending transport.'

Bradfield frowned in disapproval.

'He's worried about the traffic. He thinks an escort would make things easier,' de Lisle explained.

'I see. I thought for a moment he was saving us the expense.'

It was a joke they shared in silence.

2
'I could hear their screaming on the telephone ...'

The daily Chancery meeting in Bonn takes place in the ordinary way at ten o'clock, a time which allows everyone to open his mail, glance at his telegrams and his German newspapers and perhaps recover from the wearisome social round of the night before. As a ritual, de Lisle often likened it to morning prayers in an agnostic community: though contributing little in the way of inspiration or instruction, it set a tone for the day, served as a roll-call and imparted a sense of corporate activity. Once upon a time, Saturdays had been tweedy, voluntary, semi-retired affairs which restored one's lost detachment and one's sense of leisure. All that was gone now. Saturdays had been assumed into the general condition of alarm, and subjected to the discipline of weekdays.

They entered singly, de Lisle at their head. Those whose habit was to greet one another did so; the rest took their places silently in the half circle of chairs, either glancing through their bundles of coloured telegrams or staring blankly out of the big window at the remnants of their weekend. The morning fog was dispersing; black clouds had collected over the concrete rear wing of the Embassy; the aerials on the flat roof hung like surrealist trees against the new dark.

'Pretty ominous for the sports, I must say,' Mickie Crabbe called out, but Crabbe had no standing in Chancery and no one bothered to reply.

Facing them, alone at his steel desk, Bradfield ignored their arrival. He belonged to that school of civil servants who read with a pen; for it ran swiftly with his eye from line to line, poised at any time to correct or annotate.

'Can anyone tell me,' he enquired without lifting his head, 'How I translate *Geltungsbedürfnis*?'

'A need to assert oneself,' de Lisle suggested, and watched the pen pounce, and kill, and rise again.

'How very good. Shall we begin?'

Jenny Pargiter was the Information Officer and the only woman present. She read querulously as if she were contradicting a popular view; and she read without hope, secretly knowing that it was the lot of any woman, when imparting news, not to be believed.

'Apart from the farmers, Rawley, the main news item is yesterday's incident in Cologne, when student demonstrators, assisted by steel workers from Krupps, overturned the American Ambassador's car.'

'The American Ambassador's *empty* car. There is a difference you know.' He scribbled something in the margin of a telegram. Mickie Crabbe from his place at the door, mistakenly assuming this interruption to be humorous, laughed nervously.

'They also attacked an old man and chained him to the railings in the station square with his head shaved and a label round his neck saying "I tore down the Movement's posters". He's not supposed to be seriously hurt.'

'Supposed?'

'Considered.'

'Peter, you made a telegram during the night. We shall see a copy no doubt?'

'It sets out the principal implications.'

'Which are?'

De Lisle was equal to this. 'That the alliance between the dissident students and Karfeld's Movement is progressing fast. That the vicious circle continues: unrest creates unemployment, unemployment creates unrest. Halbach, the student leader, spent most of yesterday closeted with Karfeld in Cologne. They cooked the thing up together.'

'It was Halbach, was it not, who also led the anti-British student delegation to Brussels in January? The one that pelted Haliday-Pride with mud?'

'I have made that point in the telegram.'

'Go on, Jenny, please.'

'Most major papers carry comment.'

'Samples only.'

'*Neue Ruhrzeitung* and allied papers put their main emphasis on the youth of the demonstrators. They insist that they are mot brownshirts and hooligans, but young Germans wholly disenchanted with the institutions of Bonn.'

'Who isn't?' de Lisle murmured.

'Thank you, Peter,' Bradfield said, without a trace of gratitude, and Jenny Pargiter blushed quite needlessly.

'Both *Welt* and *Frankfurter Allgemeine* draw parallels with recent events in England; they refer specifically to the anti-Vietnam protests in London, the race riots in Birmingham and the Owner Tenents Association protests on coloured housing. Both speak of the widespread alienation of voters from their elected Governments whether in England or Germany. The trouble begins with taxation, according to the *Frankfurter*; if the taxpayer doesn't think his money is being sensibly used, he argues that his vote is being wasted as well. They call it the new inertia.'

'Ah. Another slogan has been forged.'

Weary from his long vigil and the sheer familiarity of the topics, de Lisle listened at a distance, hearing the old phrases like an off-station broadcast: *increasingly worried by the anti-democratic sentiments of both left and right ... the Federal Coalition Government should understand that only a really strong leadership, even at the expense of certain extravagant minorities, can contribute to European unity. ... Germans must recover confidence, must think of politics as the solvent between thought and action ...*

What was it, he wondered idly, about the jargon of German politics which, even in translation, rendered them totally unreal? Metaphysical fluff, that was the term he had introduced into his telegram last night, and he was rather pleased with it. A German had only to embark upon a political topic to be swept away in a current of ludicrous abstracts. ... Yet was it only the abstracts that were so elusive? Even the most obvious fact was curiously implausible; even the most gruesome event, by the time it had travelled to Bonn, seemed to have lost its flavour. He tried to imagine what it would be like to be beaten up by Halbach's students; to be slapped until your cheeks bled; to be shaved and chained and kicked ... it all seemed so far away. Yet where *was* Cologne? Seventeen miles? Seventeen thousand? He should get about more, he told himself, he should attend the meetings and see it happen on the ground. Yet how could he, when he and Bradfield between them drafted every major policy despatch? And when so many delicate and potentially embarrassing matters had to be taken care of here ...

Jenny Pargiter was warming to her task. The *Neue Zürcher* had a speculative piece on our chances in Brussels, she was saying; she considered it vital that everyone in Chancery read it *most* closely. De Lisle sighed audibly. Would Bradfield never turn her off?

'The writer says we have *absolutely* no negotiating points left, Rawley. None. HMG is as played out as Bonn; no support with the electorate and very little with the parliamentary party. HMG sees Brussels as the magic cure for all the British ills; but ironically can only succeed by the goodwill of another failing Government.'

'Quite.'

'And even more ironically, the Common Market has virtually ceased to exist.'

'Quite.'

'The piece is called *The Beggar's Opera*. They also make the point that Karfeld is undermining our chances of effective German support for our application.'

'It all sounds very predictable to me.'

'And that Karfeld's plea for a Bonn–Moscow trade axis to exclude the French *and* the Anglo-Saxons is receiving serious attention in some circles.'

'What circles I wonder?' Bradfield murmured and the pen descended once more. 'The term Anglo-Saxon is out of court,' he added. 'I refuse to have my provenance dictated by de Gaulle.' This was a cue for the older graduates to raise a judicious intellectual laugh.

'What do the *Russians* think about the Bonn-Moscow axis?' someone ventured from the centre. It might have been Jackson, an ex-Colonial man who liked to offer commonsense as an antidote to intellectual hot air. 'I mean surely that's half the point, isn't it? Has anyone put it to them as a proposition?'

'See our last despatch,' de Lisle said.

Through the open window he fancied he could still hear the plaintive chorus of the farmers' horns. That's Bonn he thought suddenly: that road is our world: how many names did it have on those five miles between Mehlem and Bonn? Six? Seven? That's us: a verbal battle for something nobody wants. A constant, sterile cacophony of claim and protest. However new the models, however fast the traffic, however violent the collision, however high the buildings, the route is unchanged and the destination irrelevant.

'We'll keep the rest very short, shall we? Mickie?'

'I say my God yes.'

Crabbe, jerking into life, embarked upon a long and unintelligible story he had picked up from the *New York Times* correspondent at the American Club, who in turn had heard it from Karl-Heinz Saab, who in turn had heard it from someone in Siebkron's office. It was said that Karfeld was actually in Bonn last night; that after appearing with the students in Cologne yesterday, he had not, as was popularly believed, returned to Hanover to prepare for tomorrow's rally, but had driven himself by a back route to Bonn and attended a secret meeting in the town.

'They say he spoke to Ludwig Siebkron, you see, Rawley,' said Crabbe, but whatever conviction his voice might once have carried was strained thin by innumerable cocktails.

Bradfield, however, was irritated by this report, and struck back quite hard.

'They *always* say he spoke to Ludwig Siebkron. Why the devil shouldn't the two of them talk to one another? Siebkron's in charge of public order; Karfeld has a lot of enemies. Tell London,' he added wearily, making another note. 'Send them a telegram reporting the rumour. It can do no harm.' A gust of rain struck suddenly upward at the steel-framed window, and the angry rattle startled them all.

'Poor old Commonwealth Sports,' Crabbe whispered, but once again his concern received no recognition.

'Discipline,' Bradfield continued. 'Tomorrow's rally in Hanover begins at ten-thirty. It seems an extraordinary time to demonstrate but I understand they have a football match in the afternoon. They play on Sundays here. I cannot imagine it will have any effect on us, but the Ambassador is asking all staff to remain at home after Matins unless they have business in the Embassy. At Siebkron's request there will be additional German police at the front and rear gates throughout Sunday, and for some extraordinary reasons of his own, plain clothes men will be in attendance at the sports this afternoon.'

'And plainer clothes,' de Lisle breathed, recalling a private joke, 'I have *never* seen.'

'Be quiet. Security. We have received the printed Embassy passes from London and these will be distributed on Monday and shown at all times thereafter. Fire Drill. For your information there will be a practice muster at midday on Monday. Perhaps you should all make a point of being available, it sets an example for the Junior Staff. Welfare. Commonwealth Sports this afternoon in the rear gardens of the Embassy; eliminating races. Once again I suggest you all put in an appearance. With your wives of course,' he added, as if that placed an even heavier burden on them. 'Mickie, the Ghanaian Chargé will need looking after. Keep him away from the Ambassadress.'

'Can I just make a point here, Rawley?' Crabbe writhed nervously; the cords of his neck were like chicken legs, stiffeners in the declining flesh. 'The Ambassadress is presenting the prizes at four, you see. Four. Could everyone sort of gravitate to the main marquee at quarter to? Sorry,' he added. 'Quarter to four, Rawley. Sorry.' It was said that he had been one of Montgomery's aides in the war and this was all that was left.

'Noted. Jenny?'

Nothing that *they* would listen to, her shrug declared.

De Lisle addressed them all, using as his focal point that middle air which is the special territory of the British ruling class.

'May I ask whether anyone is working on the Personalities Survey? Meadowes is pestering me for it and I swear I haven't touched it for months.'

'Who's it marked out to?'

'Well me apparently.'

'In that case,' Bradfield said shortly, 'Presumably you drew it.'

'I don't think I did, that's the point. I'm perfectly happy to take the rap, but I can't imagine what I would have wanted with it.'

'Well *has* anyone got it?'

All Crabbe's statements were confessions.

'It's marked out to me, too,' he whispered, from his dark place by the door, 'You see, Rawley.'

They waited.

'Before Peter, I'm supposed to have had it, and put it back. According to Meadowes, Rawley.'

Still no one helped him.

'Two weeks, Rawley. Only I never touched it. Sorry. Arthur Meadowes went for me like a maniac. No good, you see. Didn't have it. Lot of dirt about German Industrialists. Not my form. I told Meadowes: best thing is ask Leo. He does Personalities. They're Leo's pigeon.'

He grinned weakly along the line of his colleagues until he came to the window where the empty chair was. Suddenly they were all peering in the same direction, at the empty chair; not with alarm or revelation, but curiously, noticing an absence for the first time. It was a plain chair of varnished pine, different from the others and slightly pink in colour, hinting remotely at the boudoir; and it had a small, embroidered cushion on the seat.

'Where is he?' Bradfield asked shortly. He alone had not followed Crabbe's gaze. 'Where's Harting?'

No one answered. No one looked at Bradfield. Jenny Pargiter, scarlet in the face, stared at her mannish, practical hands which rested on her broad lap.

'Stuck on that dreary ferry, I should think,' said de Lisle, coming too quickly to the rescue. 'God knows what the farmers are doing *that* side of the river.'

'Someone find out, will they?' Bradfield asked, in the most disinterested tone. 'Ring his house or something will you?'

It is a matter of record that no one who was present took this instruction as his own; and that they left the room in curious disarray, looking neither at Bradfield nor at one another, nor at Jenny Pargiter, whose confusion seemed beyond all bearing.

The last sack race was over. The strong wind, whipping over the waste land, dashed pebbles of rain against the flapping canvas. The wet rigging creaked painfully. Inside the marquee, the surviving children, mostly coloured, had rallied to the mast. The small flags of the Commonwealth, creased by storage and diminished by secession, swung unhappy in disarray. Beneath them Mickie Crabbe, assisted by Cork the cypher clerk, was mustering the winners for the prize-giving.

'M'butu, Alistair,' Cork whispered. 'Where the hell's he got to?'

Crabbe put the megaphone to his mouth:

'Will Master Alistair M'butu please come forward. Alistair M'butu ... Jesus,' he muttered; 'I can't even tell them apart.'

'And Kitty Delassus. She's white.'

'And Miss Kitty Delassus, please,' Crabbe added, nervously slurring the final 's'; for names, he had found by bitter experience, were a source of unholy offence.

The Ambassadress, in ragged mink, waited benignly at her trestle table behind a motley of gift-wrapped parcels from the Naafi. The wind struck again, venomously; the Ghanaian Chargé, despondent at Crabbe's side, shuddered and pulled up the fur collar of his overcoat.

'Disqualify them,' Cork urged. 'Give the prizes to the runners up.'

'I'll ring his neck,' Crabbe declared, blinking violently. 'I'll ring his bloody neck. Skulking the other side of the river. Whoopsadaisy.'

Janet Cork, heavily pregnant, had located the missing children and added them to the winners' enclosure.

'Wait till Monday,' Crabbe whispered, raising the megaphone to his lips, 'I'll tell him a thing or two.'

He wouldn't though, come to think of it. He wouldn't tell Leo anything. He'd keep his head down and wait till it blew over.

'Ladies and Gentlemen, the Ambassadress will now present the prizes!'

They clapped, but not for Crabbe. The end was in sight. With a perfect *insouciance* that was as well suited to the launching of a ship as to the acceptance of a hand in marriage, the Ambassadress stepped forward to read her speech. Crabbe listened mindlessly: a family event ... equal nations of the Commonwealth ... if only the greater rivalries of the world could be resolved in so friendly a fashion ... a heartfelt word of thanks to the Sports Committee, Messrs Jackson, Crabbe, Harting, Meadowes ...

Lamentably unmoved, a plain clothes policeman, posted against the canvas wall, took a pair of gloves from the pocket of his leather coat and stared blankly at a colleague. Hazel Bradfield, wife of the Head of Chancery, caught Crabbe's eye and smiled beautifully. Such a bore, she managed to imply, but it will soon be over, and then we might even have a drink. He looked quickly away. The only thing, he told himself fervently, is to know nothing and see nothing. Doggo, that's the word. Doggo. He glanced at his watch. Just one hour till the sun was over the yardarm. In Greenwich if not in Bonn. He'd have a beer first, just to keep his eye in; and afterwards he would have a little of the hard stuff. Doggo. See nothing and slip out the back way.

'Here,' said Cork into his ear, 'Listen. You remember that tip you gave me?'

'Sorry old boy?'

'South African Diamonds. Consols. They're down six bob.'

'Hang on to them,' Crabbe urged with total insincerity, and withdrew prudently to the edge of the marquee. He had barely found the kind of dark, protective crevice which naturally appealed to his submerged nature when a hand seized his shoulder and swung him roughly round on his heel. Recovering from his astonishment he found himself face to face with a plain clothes policeman. 'What the hell—' he broke out furiously, for he was a small man and hated to be handled. 'What the hell—' But the policeman was already shaking his head and mumbling an apology. He was sorry, he said, he had mistaken the gentleman for someone else.

Urbane or not, de Lisle was meanwhile growing quite angry. The journey from the Embassy had irritated him considerably. He detested motor-bikes and he detested being escorted, and a noisy combination of the two was almost more than he could bear. And he detested deliberate rudeness, whether he or some one else was the object of it. And deliberate rudeness, he reckoned, was what they were getting. No sooner had they drawn up in the courtyard of the Ministry of the Interior than the doors of the car had been wrenched open by a team of young men in leather coats all shouting at once.

'Herr Siebkron will see you immediately! Now please! Yes! Immediately please!'

'I shall go at my own pace,' Bradfield had snapped as they were ushered into the unpainted steel lift. 'Don't you dare order me about.' And to de Lisle, 'I shall speak to Siebkron. It's like a trainload of monkeys.'

The upper floors restored them. This was the Bonn they knew: the pale, functional interiors, the pale, functional reproductions on the wall, the pale unpolished teak; the white shirts, the grey ties and faces pale as the moon. They were seven. The two who sat to either side of Siebkron had no names at all, and de Lisle wondered maliciously whether they were clerks brought in to make up the numbers. Lieff, an empty-headed parade horse from Protocol Department, sat on his left; opposite him, on Bradfield's right, an old *Polizeidirektor* from Bonn, whom de Lisle instinctively liked: a battle-scarred monument of a man, with white patches like covered bullet-holes in the leather of his skin. Cigarettes lay in packets on a plate. A stern girl offered decaffeinated coffee, and they waited until she had withdrawn.

What *does* Siebkron want? he wondered for the hundredth time since the terse summons at nine o'clock that morning.

The Conference began, like all conferences, with a résumé of what was said at a previous occasion. Lieff read the minutes in a tone of unctuous flattery, like a man awarding a medal. It was an occasion, he implied, of the greatest felicity. The *Polizeidirektor* unbuttoned his green jacket, and lit a length of Dutch cigar till it burned like a spill. Siebkron coughed angrily but the old policeman ignored him.

'You have no objection to these minutes, Mr Bradfield?'

Siebkron usually smiled when he asked this question, and although his smile was as cold as the north wind, de Lisle could have wished for it today.

'Off the cuff, none,' Bradfield replied easily, 'But I must see them in writing before I can sign them.'

'No one is asking you to sign.'

De Lisle looked up sharply.

'You will allow me,' Siebkron declared, 'To read the following statement. Copies will be distributed.'

It was quite short.

The *doyen*, he said, had already discussed with Herr Lieff of Protocol Department, and with the American Ambassador, the question of the physical security of diplomatic premises in the event of civil unrest arising out of minority demonstrations in the Federal Republic. Siebkron regretted that additional measures were proving necessary, but it was desirable to anticipate unhappy eventualities rather than attempt to correct them when it was too late. Siebkron had received the *doyen's* assurance that all diplomatic Heads of Mission would cooperate to the utmost with the Federal Authorities. The British Ambassador had already associated himself with this undertaking. Siebkron's voice had found a hard edge which was uncommonly close to anger. Lieff and the old policeman had turned deliberately to face Bradfield, and their expressions were frankly hostile.

'I am sure you subscribe to this opinion,' Siebkron said in English, handing a copy of the statement down the table.

Bradfield had noticed nothing. Taking his fountain pen from an inside pocket, he unscrewed the cap, fitted it carefully over the butt and ran the nib along line after line of the text.

'This is an *aide-memoire*?'

'A memorandum. You will find the German translation attached.'

'I can see nothing here that requires to be in writing at all,' Bradfield said easily. 'You know very well, Ludwig, that we always agree on such matters. Our interests are identical.'

Siebkron disregarded this pleasant appeal: 'You also understand that Doktor Karfeld is not well disposed towards the British. This places the British Embassy in a special category.'

Bradfield's smile did not flinch. 'It has not escaped our notice. We rely on you to see that Herr Karfeld's sentiments are not expressed in physical terms. We have every confidence in your ability to do so.'

'Precisely. Then you will appreciate my concern for the safety of all personnel of the British Embassy.'

Bradfield's voice came quite close to banter. 'Ludwig, what is this? A declaration of love?'

The rest came very fast, thrown down like an ultimatum: 'I must accordingly ask you that until further notice all British Embassy staff below the rank of Counsellor be confined to the area of Bonn. You will kindly instruct them that for their own safety they will please be in their residences—' he was reading again from the folder before him – 'Henceforth and until further notice, by eleven o'clock at night, local time.'

The white faces peered at them through the swathes of tobacco smoke like lamps through an anaesthetic. In the momentary confusion and bewilderment, only Bradfield's voice, fluent and decisive as the voice of a commander in battle, did not waver.

It was a principle of civil order which the British had learned by bitter experience in many parts of the world, he said, that unpleasant incidents were actually provoked by over-elaborate precautions.

Siebkron offered no comment.

While making every allowance for Siebkron's professional and personal concern, Bradfield felt obliged to warn him strongly against any gesture which might be misinterpreted by the outside world.

Siebkron waited.

Like Siebkron, Bradfield insisted, he himself had a responsibility to preserve Embassy morale and thus fortify the Junior Staff against strains yet to come. He could not support any measure at this stage which would look like a retreat in the face of an enemy who as yet had barely advanced ... did Siebkron really wish it said that he could not control a handful of hooligans? ...

Siebkron was standing up, the others with him. A terse inclination of the head replaced the obligatory handshake. The door opened and the leather coats led them briskly to the lift. They were in the wet courtyard. The roar of the motor-cycles deafened them. The Mercedes swept them into the carriageway. What on earth have we done? de Lisle wondered. What on earth have we done to deserve this? Whoever has thrown the rock through teacher's window?

'It's nothing to do with last night?' he asked Bradfield at last, as they approached the Embassy.

'There is no conceivable connection,' Bradfield retorted. He was sitting bolt upright, his expression stiff and angry.

'Whatever the reason,' he added, more as a memorandum to himself than by way of a confidence to de Lisle, 'Siebkron is the one thread I dare not cut.'

'Quite,' said de Lisle and they got out. The sports were just ending.

Behind the English Church, on a wooded hill, in a semi-rural avenue away from the centre of Bad Godesberg, the Embassy has built itself a modest piece of suburban Surrey. Comfortable stockbrokers' houses with open fireplaces and long corridors for servants they no longer have, hide behind the exiguous privet and laburnum of splendid isolation. The air trembles to the gentle music of the British Forces Network. Dogs of unmistakeably English breed ramble in the long gardens; the pavements are obstructed by the runabout cars of British Counsellors' wives. In this avenue, on each Sunday throughout the warmer months, a more agreeable ritual replaces the Chancery meeting. At a few minutes before eleven o'clock, dogs are summoned indoors, cats banished to the garden, as a dozen wives in coloured hats and matching handbags emerge from a dozen front doors, followed by their husbands in Sunday suits.

Soon a little crowd has gathered in the road; someone has made a joke; someone has laughed; they glance round anxiously for stragglers, and upwards at the nearer houses. Have the Crabbes overslept? Should someone give them a ring? No, here they come at last. Gently they begin the move downhill to the Church, the women leading, men following, their hands deep in their pockets. Reaching the Church steps they all pause, smiling invitingly at the senior wife present. She, with a little gesture of surprise, climbs the steps ahead of them and disappears through the green curtain, leaving her inferiors to follow, quite by accident, the order of succession which protocol, had they cared about such things, would exactly have demanded.

That Sunday morning, Rawley Bradfield, accompanied by Hazel, his beautiful wife, entered the Church and sat in their customary pew beside the Tills, who by the nature of things had gone ahead of them in the procession. Bradfield, though theoretically a Roman Catholic, regarded it as his iron duty to attend the Embassy Chapel; it was a matter on which he declined to consult either his Church or his conscience. They made a handsome couple. The Irish blood had come through richly in Hazel, whose auburn hair shone where the sunbeams touched it from the leaded window; and Bradfield had a way of deferring to her in public which was both gallant and commanding. Directly behind them, Meadowes the Registrar sat expressionless beside his blonde and very nervous daughter. She was a pretty girl, but the wives in particular were inclined to wonder how a man of her father's rectitude could tolerate such a quantity of make-up.

Having settled into his pew, Bradfield searched the hymnal for the advertised numbers – there were certain of them which he had proscribed on the grounds of taste – then glanced round the Church to check absentees. There being none, he was about to return to his hymnal when Mrs Vandelung, the Dutch Counsellor's wife, and currently Vice-President of the International Ladies, leaned over her pew to enquire in a breathy, somewhat hysterical undertone why there was no organist. Bradfield glanced at the little lighted alcove, at the empty stool with the embroidered cushion on the seat, and in the same instant he appeared to become aware of the embarrassed silence all round him which was accentuated by the creaking of the west door as Mickie Crabbe, whose turn it was to act as sidesman, closed it without benefit of a Voluntary. Rising quickly Bradfield walked down the aisle. From the front row of the choir, John Gaunt, the Chancery Guard, watched with veiled apprehension. Jenny Pargiter, upright as a bride, looked stiffly ahead of her, seeing nothing but the light of God. Janet Cork, wife of the cypher clerk, stood beside her, her mind upon her unborn child. Her husband was in the Embassy, serving a routine shift in the cypher room.

'Where the devil's Harting?' Bradfield asked, but one glance at Crabbe's expression told him that his question was wasted. Slipping out into the road, he hastened a short way up the hill and opened a small iron gate leading to the vestry, which he entered without knocking.

'Harting's failed to appear,' he said curtly. 'Who else plays the organ?'

The Chaplain, who found the Embassy a challenge but believed he was making headway, was a Low Church man with a wife and four children in Wales. No one knew why they would not join him.

'He's never missed before. Never.'

'Who else can play?'

'Perhaps the ferry isn't running. There's a lot of trouble about, I hear.'

'He could come the long way by the bridge. He's done it often enough. Can no one stand in for him?'

'Not that I know,' said the Chaplain, fingering the tip of his golden stole, his thoughts far away. 'But there's never been occasion to enquire, not really.'

'Then what are you going to do?'

'Perhaps someone could give a note,' the Chaplain suggested doubtfully, but his gaze had fixed on a baptismal postcard that was tucked behind a calendar. 'Maybe that would be the answer. Johnny Gaunt has a nice tenor, being Welsh.'

'Very well, the choir must lead. You'd better tell them at once.'

'Trouble *is* you see, they don't know the hymns, Mr Bradfield,' the Chaplain said. 'He wasn't at Friday's choir practice either you see. He didn't come, not really. We had to scrap it, see.'

Stepping back into the fresh air, Bradfield found himself face to face with Meadowes, who had quietly left his place beside his daughter and followed him to the back of the Church.

'He's vanished,' Meadowes said, dreadfully quietly. 'I've checked everywhere. Sick list, the doctor; I've been to his house. His car's in the garage; he's not used his milk. No one's seen or heard of him since Friday. He didn't come to Exiles. It was a special occasion for my daughter's birthday, but he didn't come to that either. He'd got engagements but he was going to look in. He'd promised her a hair-dryer as a present; it's not like him, Mr Bradfield, it's not his way at all.'

For one moment, just for one moment, Bradfield's composure seemed to desert him. He stared furiously at Meadowes, then back at the Church, as if undecided which to destroy; as if either in anger or despair he would rush down the path and burst open the doors and cry out the news to those who waited so complacently within.

'Come with me.'

Even as they entered the main gates of the Embassy and long before the police check cleared them, they could recognize the signs of crisis. Two army motor-cycles were parked on the front lawn. Cork, the cypher clerk on call, was waiting on the steps, an Everyman guide to investments still in his hand. A green German police van, its blue light flashing, had stationed itself beside the canteen, and they could hear the crackle of its radio.

'Thank the Lord you've come, sir,' said Macmullen the Head Guard, 'I sent the duty driver down; he must have passed you on the carriageway.'

All over the building bells were ringing.

'There's a message in from Hanover, sir, from the Consulate General; I didn't hear too well. The rally's gone mad, sir; all hell's broken loose. They're storming the library and they're going to march on the Consulate; I don't know what the world's coming to; worse than Grosvenor Square. I could hear their screaming on the telephone, sir.'

Meadowes followed Bradfield hastily up the stairs.

'You said a hair-dryer? He was giving your daughter a hair-dryer?'

It was a moment of deliberate inconsequence, of deliberate slowness perhaps, a nervous gesture before battle was joined. Meadowes at least construed it thus.

'He'd ordered it specially,' he said.

'Never mind,' said Bradfield, and was about to enter the cypher room when Meadowes addressed him once more.

'The file's gone,' he whispered. 'The green file for the special minutes. It's been gone since Friday.'

3
Alan Turner

It was a day to be nearly free; a day to stay in London and dream of the country. In St James's Park, the premature summer was entering its third week. Along the lake, girls lay like cut flowers in the unnatural heat of a Sunday afternoon in May. An attendant had lit an improbable bonfire and the smell of burnt grass drifted with the echoes of the traffic. Only the pelicans, hobbling fussily round their island pavilion, seemed disposed to move; only Alan Turner, his big shoes crunching on the gravel, had anywhere to go; for once, not even the girls could distract him.

His shoes were of a heavy brown brogue and much repaired at the welts. He wore a stained tropical suit and carried a stained canvas bag. He was a big, lumbering man, fair-haired, plain-faced and pale, with the high shoulders and square fingers of an alpinist, and he walked with the thrusting slowness of a barge; a broad, aggressive, policeman's walk, wilfully without finesse. His age was hard to guess. Undergraduates would have found him old, but old for an undergraduate. He could alarm the young with age, and the aged with his youth. His colleagues had long ceased to speculate. It was known that he was a late entrant, never a good sign, and a former fellow of St Anthony's College, Oxford, which takes all kinds of people. The official Foreign Office publications were reserved. While they shed a merciless light on the origin of all their other Turners, in the matter of Alan they remained tight-lipped, as if, having considered all the facts, they felt that silence was the kindest policy.

'They've called you in too, then,' said Lambert, catching him up. 'I must say, Karfeld's really gone to town this time.'

'What the hell do they expect us to do? Man the barricades? Knit blankets?'

Lambert was a small, vigorous man and he liked it said of him that he could mix with anyone. He occupied a senior position in Western Department and ran a cricket team open to all grades.

They began the ascent of Clive Steps.

'You'll never change them,' said Lambert. 'That's my view. A nation of psychopaths. Always think they're being got at. Versailles, encirclement, stab in the back; persecution mania, that's their trouble.'

He allowed time for Turner to agree with him.

'We're bringing in the whole of the Department. Even the girls.'

'Christ, that'll really frighten them. That's calling up the reserves, that is.'

'This could put paid to Brussels you know. Bang it clean on the nose. If the German Cabinet loses its nerve on the home front, we're all up a gum-tree.' The prospect filled him with relish. 'We shall have to find a quite different solution in that case.'

'I thought there wasn't one.'

'The Secretary of State has already spoken to their Ambassador; I am told they have agreed full compensation.'

'Then there's nothing to worry about is there? We can get on with our weekend. All go back to bed.'

They had reached the top of the steps. The founder of India, one foot casually upon a plateau of vanquished bronze, stared contentedly past them into the glades of the Park.

'They've kept the doors open.' Lambert's voice was tender with reverence. 'They're on the week-day schedule. My, they *are* going it. Well,' he remarked, receiving no admiring echo, 'You go your way, I go mine. Mind you,' he added shrewdly, 'It could do us a lot of good. Unite the rest of Europe behind us against the Nazi menace. Nothing like the stamp of jackboots to stiffen the old alliances.' With a final nod of undeterred goodwill he was assumed into the imperial darkness of the main entrance. For a moment, Turner stared after him, measuring his slight body against the Tuscan pillars of the great portico, and there was even something wistful in his expression, as if actually he would quite like to be a Lambert, small and neat and adept and unbothered. Rousing himself at last, he continued towards a smaller door at the side of the building. It was a scruffy door with brown hardboard nailed to the inside of the glass and a notice denying entrance to unauthorized persons. He had some difficulty getting through.

'Mister Lumley's looking for you,' said the porter. '*When* you can spare a minute, I'm sure.'

He was a young, effeminate man and preferred the other side of the building. 'He was enquiring *most* particularly, as a matter of fact. All packed for Germany, I see.'

His transistor radio was going all the time; someone was reporting direct from Hanover and there was a roar in the background like the roar of the sea.

'Well, you'll get a nice reception by the sound of it. They've already done the library, and now they're having a go at the Consulate.'

'They'd done the library by lunchtime. It was on the one o'clock. The police have cordoned off the Consulate. Three deep. There's not a hope in hell of them getting anywhere near.'

'It's got worse since then,' the porter called after him. 'They're burning books in the market place; you wait!'

'I will. That's just what I bloody well will do.' His voice was awfully quiet but it carried a long way; a Yorkshire voice, and common as a mongrel.

'He's booked your passage to Germany. You ask Travel Section! Overland route and Second Class! Mr Shawn goes First!'

Shoving open the door of his room he found Shawn lounging at the desk, his Brigade of Guards jacket draped over the back of Turner's chair. The eight buttons glinted in the stray sunbeams which, bolder than the rest, had penetrated the coloured glass. He was talking on the telephone. 'They're to put everything in one room,' he said in that soothing tone of voice which reduces the calmest of men to hysteria. He had said it several times before, apparently, but was repeating it for the benefit of simpler minds. '*With* the incendiaries *and* the shredder. That's point one. Point two, *all* locally employed staff are to go *home* and lie low; we can't pay compensation to German citizens who get hurt on our behalf. Tell them that first, then call me back, Christ Almightly!' he screamed to Turner as he ran off, 'Have you *ever* tried to deal with that man?'

'What man?'

'That bald-headed clown in E and O. The one in charge of nuts and bolts.'

'His name is Crosse.' He flung his bag into the corner. 'And he's not a clown.'

'He's mental,' Shawn muttered, losing courage, 'I swear he is.'

'Then keep quiet about it or they'll post him to Security.'

'Lumley's looking for you.'

'I'm not going,' Turner said. 'I'm bloody well not wasting my time. Hanover's a D post. They've no codes, no cyphers, nothing. What am I supposed to do out there? Rescue the bloody Crown Jewels?'

'Then why did you bring your bag?'

He picked up a sheaf of telegrams from the desk.

'They've known about that rally for months. Everyone has, from Western Department down to us. Chancery reported it in March. For once, we saw the telegram. Why didn't they evacuate staff? Why didn't they send the kids home? No money, I suppose. No third class seats available. Well sod them!'

'Lumley said immediately.'

'Sod Lumley too,' said Turner, and sat down. 'I'm not seeing him till I've read the papers.'

'It's *policy* not to send them home,' Shawn continued taking up Turner's point. Shawn thought of himself as *attached* rather than *posted* to Security Department; as resting, as it were, between appointments, and he missed no opportunity to demonstrate his familiarity with the larger political world. 'Business as usual, that's the cry. We can't allow ourselves to be stampeded by mob rule. After all, the Movement is a minority. The British lion,' he added, making an unconfident joke, 'can't allow itself to be upset by the pinpricks of a few hooligans.'

'Oh it can *not*; my God it can't.'

Turner put aside one telegram and began another. He read fast and without effort, with the confidence of an academic, arranging the papers into separate piles according to some undisclosed criterion.

'So what's going on? What have they got to lose apart from their honour?' he demanded, still reading. 'Why the hell call *us* in? Compensation's Western Department's baby, right? Evacuation's E and O's baby, right? If they're worried about the lease, they can go and cry at the Ministry of Works. So why the hell can't they leave us in peace?'

'Because it's Germany,' Shawn suggested weakly.

'Oh roll on.'

'Sorry if it *spoilt* something,' Shawn said with an unpleasant sneer, for he suspected Turner of a more colourful sex life than his own.

The first relevant telegram was from Bradfield. It was marked Flash; it had been despatched at eleven-forty and submitted to the Resident Clerk at two twenty-eight. Skardon, Consul General in Hanover, had summoned all British staff and families to the Residence, and was making urgent representations to the police. The second telegram consisted of a Reuter newsflash timed at eleven fifty-three: demonstrators had broken into the British Library; police were unequal to the situation; the fate of Fraulein Eick [*sic*] the librarian was unknown.

Hard upon this came a second rush telegram from Bonn: 'Norddeutscher Rundfunk reports Eick repeat Eick killed by mob.' But this was in turn immediately contradicted, for Bradfield, through the good offices of Herr Siebkron of the Ministry of the Interior, ('with whom I have a close relationship') had by then succeeded in obtaining direct contact with the Hanover police. According to their latest assessment, the British Library had been sacked and its books burned before a large crowd. Printed posters had appeared with anti-British slogans such as 'The Farmers won't Pay for your Empire!' and 'Work for your own bread, don't steal ours!' Fraulein Gerda Eich [*sic*] aged fifty-one of 4 Hohenzollernweg, Hanover, had been dragged down two flights of stone steps, kicked and punched in the face and made to throw her own books into the fire. Police with horses and anti-riot equipment were being brought in from neighbouring towns.

A marginal annotation by Shawn stated that Tracing Section had turned up a record of the unfortunate Fraulein Eich. She was a retired school teacher, sometime in British Occupational employment, sometime secretary of the Hanover Branch of the Anglo-German Society, who in 1962 had been awarded a British decoration for services to international understanding.

'Another anglophile bites the dust,' Turner muttered.

There followed a long if hastily compiled summary of broadcasts and bulletins. This, too, Turner studied with close application. No one, it seemed, and least of all those who had been present, was able to say precisely what had triggered off the riot, nor what had attracted the crowd towards the library in the first place. Though demonstrations were now a commonplace of the German scene, a riot on this scale was not; Federal authorities had confessed themselves 'deeply concerned'. Herr Ludwig Siebkron of the Ministry of the Interior had broken his habitual silence to remark to a Press Conference that there was 'cause for very real anxiety'. An immediate decision had been taken to provide additional protection for all official and quasi-official British buildings and residences throughout the Federal Republic. The British Ambassador, after some initial hesitation, had agreed to impose a voluntary curfew on his staff.

Accounts of the incident by police, press and even delegates themselves were hopelessly confused. Some declared it was spontaneous; a collective gesture aggravated by the word 'British' which happened to be exhibited on the side of the library building. It was natural, they said, that as the day of decision in Brussels drew rapidly closer, the Movement's policy of opposition to the Common Market should assume a specifically anti-British form. Others swore they had seen a sign, a white handkerchief that fluttered from a window; one witness even claimed that a rocket had risen behind the town hall and emitted stars of red and gold. For some the crowd had surged with a positive impulse, for others it had 'flowed'; for others again it had trembled. 'It was led from the centre,' one senior police officer reported. 'The periphery was motionless until the centre moved.' 'Those at the centre,' Western Radio maintained, 'kept their composure. The outrage was perpetrated by a few hooligans at the front. The others were then obliged to follow.' On one point only they seemed to agree: the incident had taken place when the music was loudest. It was even suggested by a woman witness that the music itself had been the sign which started the crowd running.

The *Spiegel* correspondent, on the other hand, speaking on Northern Radio, had a circumstantial account of how a grey omnibus chartered by a mysterious Herr Meyer of Luneburg conveyed 'a bodyguard of thirty picked men' to the town centre of Hanover one hour before the demonstration began and that this bodyguard, drawn partly from students and partly from young farmers, had formed a 'protective ring' round the Speaker's podium. It was these 'picked men' who had started the rush. The entire action had therefore been inspired by Karfeld himself. 'It is an open declaration,' he insisted, 'that from now on, the Movement proposes to march to its own music.'

'This Eich,' Turner said at last. 'What's the latest?'

'She's as well as can be expected.'

'How well's that?'

'That's all they said.'

'Oh fine.'

'Fortunately neither Eich nor the Library are a British responsibility. The Library was founded during the Occupation but handed over to the Germans quite soon afterwards. It's now controlled and owned exclusively by the *Land* authority. There's nothing British about it.'

'So they've burnt their own books.'

Shawn gave a startled smile.

'Well yes, actually,' he said. 'Come to think of it, they have. That's rather a useful point; we might even suggest it to Press Section.'

The telephone was ringing. Shawn lifted the receiver and listened.

'It's Lumley,' he said, putting his hand over the mouthpiece. 'The porter told him you're in.'

Turner appeared not to hear. He was studying another telegram; it was quite a short telegram, two paragraphs, not more; it was headed 'personal for Lumley' and marked 'immediate' and this was the second copy passed to Turner.

'He wants you, Alan.' Shawn held out the receiver.

Turner read the text once and then read it again. Rising, he went to the steel cupboard and drew out a small black notebook, unused, which he thrust into the recesses of his tropical suit.

'You stupid bugger,' he said very quietly, from the door. 'Why don't you learn to read your telegrams? All the time you've been bleating about fire extinguishers we've had a bloody defector on our hands.'

He held up the sheet of pink paper for Shawn to read.

'A planned departure, that's what they call it. Forty-three files missing, not one of them below Confidential. One green classified Maximum and Limit, gone since Friday. I'll say it was planned.'

Leaving Shawn with the telephone still in his hand, Turner thudded down the corridor in the direction of his master's room. His eyes were a swimmer's eyes, very pale, washed colourless by the sea.

Shawn stared after him. That's what happens, he decided, when you open your doors to the other ranks. They leave their wives and children, use filthy language in the corridors and play ducks and drakes with all the common courtesies. With a sigh, he replaced the receiver, raised it again and dialled News Department. This was Shawn, he said, S-H-A-W-N. He had had rather a good idea about the riots in Hanover, the way one might play it at Press Conference: it was nothing to do with *us* after all, if the Germans decided to burn their own books. ... He thought that might go down pretty well as an example of cool English wit. Yes, Shawn, S-H-A-W-N. Not at all; they might even have lunch together some time.

Lumley had a folder open before him and his old hand rested on it like a claw.

'We know nothing about him. He's not even carded. As far as we're concerned, he doesn't exist. He hasn't even been vetted, let alone cleared. I had to scrounge his papers from Personnel.'

'And?'

'There's a smell, that's all. A foreign smell. Refugee background, emigrated in the thirties. Farm school, Pioneer Corps, Bomb Disposal. He gravitated to Germany in forty-five. Temporary sergeant; Control Commission; one of the old carpet-baggers by the sound of it. Professional expatriate. There was one in every mess in Occupied Germany in those days. Some survived, some drifted into the consulates. Quite a few of them reverted; went into the night or took up German citizenship again. A few went crooked. No childhood, most of them, that's the trouble. Sorry,' Lumley said abruptly, and almost blushed.

'Any form?'

'Nothing to set the Thames on fire. We traced the next of kin. An uncle living in Hampstead; Otto Harting. Sometime adoptive father. No other relations living. He was in the pharmaceutical business. More an alchemist by the sound of it. Patent medicines, that kind of thing. He's dead now. Dead ten years. He was a member of the Hampstead Branch of the British Communist Party from forty-one to forty-five. One conviction for little girls.'

'How little?'

'Does it matter? His nephew Leo lived with him for a bit. Something may have rubbed off. The old man might even have recruited him then I suppose. ... Long term penetration. That would fit the mould. Or someone may have reminded him of it later on. They never let you go, mind, once you've had a taste of it. Bad as Catholics.'

Lumley hated faith.

'What's his access?'

'Obscure. His function is listed as Claims and Consular, whatever that means. He has diplomatic rank, just. A Second Secretary. You know the kind of arrangement. Unpromotable, unpostable, unpensionable. Chancery gave him living space. Not a *proper* diplomat.'

'Lucky bloke.'

Lumley let that go.

'Entertainment allowance' – Lumley glanced at the file – 'A hundred and four pounds per annum, to be spread over fifty cocktail guests and thirty-four dinner guests. Accountable. Pretty small beer. He's locally employed. A temporary, of course. He's been one for twenty years.'

'That leaves me sixteen to go.'

'In fifty-six he put in an application to marry a girl called Aickman. Margaret Aickman. Someone he'd met in the Army. The application was never pursued, apparently. There's no record of whether he's married since.'

'Perhaps they've stopped asking. What are the missing files about?'

Lumley hesitated. 'Just a hotchpotch,' he said casually, 'a general hotchpotch. Bradfield's trying to put a list together now.' They could hear the porter's radio blaring again in the corridor.

Turner caught the tone and held on to it: 'What sort of hotchpotch?'

'Policy,' Lumley retorted. 'Not your field at all.'

'You mean I can't know?'

'I mean you needn't know.' He said this quite casually; Lumley's world was dying and he wished no one ill. 'He's chosen a good moment, I must say,' he continued, 'With all this going on. Perhaps he just took a handful and ran for it.'

'Discipline?'

'Nothing much. He got in a fight five years ago in Cologne. A night-club brawl. They managed to hush it up.'

'And they didn't sack him?'

'We like to give people a second chance.' Lumley was still deep in the file, but his tone was pregnant with innuendo.

He was sixty or more, coarse-spoken and grey; grey-faced, grey-clothed owl of a man, hunched and dried out. Long ago he had been Ambassador to somewhere small, but the appointment had not endured.

'You're to cable me every day. Bradfield is arranging facilities. But don't ring me up, do you understand? That direct line is a menace.' He closed the folder. 'I've cleared it with Western Department, Bradfield cleared it with the Ambassador. They'll let you go on one condition.'

'That's handsome of them.'

'The Germans mustn't know. Not on any account. They mustn't know he's gone; they mustn't know we're looking for him; they mustn't know there's been a leak.'

'What if he's compromised secret Nato material? That's as much their pigeon as ours.'

'Decisions of that kind are none of your concern. Your instructions are to go gently. Don't lead with your chin. Understand?'

Turner said nothing.

'You're not to disturb, annoy or offend. They're walking on a knife edge out there; *anything* could tilt the balance. Now, tomorrow, any time. There's even a danger that the Huns might think we were playing a double game with the Russians. If that idea got about it could balls everything up.'

'We seem to find it hard enough,' Turner said, borrowing from Lumley's vocabulary, 'Playing a single game with the Huns.'

'The Embassy have got one idea in their heads, and it's not Harting and it's not Karfeld and least of all is it you. It's Brussels. So just remember that. You'd better, because if you don't you'll be out on your arse.'

'Why not send Shawn? He's tactful. Charm them all, he would.'

Lumley pushed a memorandum across the desk. It contained a list of Harting's personal particulars. 'Because you'll find him and Shawn won't. Not that I admire you for that. You'd pull down the whole forest, you would, to find an acorn. What drives you? What are you looking for? Some bloody absolute. If there's one thing I really hate it's a cynic in search of God. Maybe a bit of failure is what you need.'

'There's plenty of it about.'

'Heard from your wife?'

'No.'

'You could forgive her, you know. It's been done before.'

'Jesus, you take chances,' Turner breathed. 'What the hell do you know about my marriage?'

'Nothing. That's why I'm qualified to give advice. I just wish you'd stop punishing us all for not being perfect.'

'Anything else?'

Lumley examined him like an old magistrate who had not many cases left.

'Christ, you're quick to despise,' he said at last. 'You frighten me, I'll tell you that for nothing. You're going to have to start liking people soon, or it'll be too late. You'll need us, you know, before you die. Even if we are a second best.' He thrust a file into Turner's hand. 'Go on then. Find him. But don't think you're off the leash. I should take the midnight train if I were you. Get in at lunchtime.' His hooded yellow eyes flickered towards the sunlit park. 'Bonn's a foggy bloody place.'

'I'll fly if it's all the same.'

Lumley slowly shook his head.

'You can't wait, can you. You can't wait to get your hands on him. Pawing the bloody earth, aren't you? Christ, I wish I had your enthusiasm.'

'You had once.'

'And get yourself a suit or something. Try and look as though you belong.'

'I don't though, do I?'

'All right,' said Lumley, not caring any more. 'Wear the cloth cap. Christ,' he added, 'I'd have thought your class was suffering from too much recognition already.'

'There's something you haven't told me. Which do they want most: the man or the files?'

'Ask Bradfield,' Lumley replied, avoiding his eye.

Turner went to his room and dialled his wife's number. Her sister answered.

'She's out,' she said.

'You mean they're still in bed.'

'What do you want?'

'Tell her I'm leaving the country.'

As he rang off he was again distracted by the sound of the porter's wireless. He had turned it on full and tuned it to the European network. A well-bred lady was giving a summary of the news. The Movement's next rally would be held in Bonn, she said; on Friday, five days from today.

Turner grinned. It was a little like an invitation to tea. Picking up his bag, he set off for Fulham, an area well known for boarding houses and married men in exile from their wives.

4
Decembers of Renewal

De Lisle picked him up from the airport. He had a sports car that was a little too young for him and it rattled wildly on the wet cobble of the villages. Though it was quite a new car, the paintwork was already dulled by the chestnut gum of Godesberg's wooded avenues. The time was nine in the morning but the street lights still burned. To either side, on flat fields, farmhouses and new building estates lay upon the strips of mist like hulks left over by the sea. Drops of rain prickled on the small windscreen.

'We've booked you in at the Adler; I suppose that's all right. We didn't know quite what sort of subsistence you people get.'

'What are the posters saying?'

'Oh, we hardly read them any more. Reunification ... alliance with Moscow. ... Anti-America. ... Anti-Britain.'

'Nice to know we're still in the big league.'

'You've hit a real Bonn day I'm afraid. Sometimes the fog is a little colder,' de Lisle continued cheerfully, 'Then we call it winter. Sometimes it's warmer, and that's summer. You know what they say about Bonn: either it rains or the level crossings are down. In fact, of course, both things happen at the same time. An island cut off by fog, that's us. It's a very *metaphysical* spot; the dreams have quite replaced reality. We live somewhere between the recent future and the not so recent past. Not *personally*, if you know what I mean. Most of us feel we've been here for ever.'

'Do you always get an escort?'

The black Opel lay thirty yards behind them. It was neither gaining nor losing ground. Two pale men sat in the front and the headlights were on.

'They're protecting us. That's the theory. Perhaps you heard of our meeting with Siebkron?' They turned right and the Opel followed them. 'The Ambassador is *quite* furious. And *now*, of course, they can say it's all vindicated by Hanover: no Englishman is safe without a bodyguard. It's not our view at all. Still, perhaps after Friday we'll lose them again. How are things in London? I hear Steed-Asprey's got Lima.'

'Yes, we're all thrilled about it.'

A yellow road sign said six kilometres to Bonn.

'I think we'll go round the city if you don't mind; there's liable to be rather a hold-up getting in and out. They're checking passes and things.'

'I thought you said Karfeld didn't bother you.'

'We all say that. It's part of our local religion. We're trained to regard Karfeld as an irritant, not an epidemic. You'll have to get used to that. I have a message for you from Bradfield, by the way. He's sorry not to have collected you himself, but he's been rather under pressure.'

They swung sharply off the main road, bumped over a tramline and sped along a narrow open lane. Occasionally a poster or photograph rose before them and darted away into the mist.

'Was that the whole of Bradfield's message?'

'There was the question of who knows what. He imagined you'd like to have that clear at once. *Cover*, is that what you'd call it?'

'I might.'

'Our friend's disappearance has been noticed in a *general* way,' de Lisle continued in the same amiable tone. 'That was inevitable. But fortunately Hanover intervened, and we've been able to mend a few fences. Officially, Rawley has sent him on compassionate leave. He's published no details; merely hinted at personal problems and left it at that. The Junior Staff can think what they like: nervous breakdown; family troubles; they can make their own rumours. Bradfield mentioned the matter at this morning's meeting: we're all backing him up. As for yourself . . .'

'Well?'

'A general security check in view of the crisis? How would that sound to you? It seemed quite convincing to us.'

'Did you know him?'

'Harting?'

'That's right. Did you know him?'

'I think perhaps,' de Lisle said, pulling up at a traffic light, 'We ought to leave the first bite to Rawley, don't you? Tell me, what news of our little Lords of York?'

'Who the hell are they?'

'I'm *so* sorry,' de Lisle said in genuine discomfort. 'It's our local expression for the Cabinet. It was silly of me.'

They were approaching the Embassy. As they filtered left to cross the carriageway, the black Opel slid slowly past like an old nanny who had seen her children safely over the road. The lobby was in turmoil. Despatch riders mingled with journalists and police. An iron grille, painted a protective orange, sealed off the basement staircase. De Lisle led him quickly to the first floor. Someone must have telephoned from the desk because Bradfield was already standing as they entered.

'Rawley, this is Turner,' de Lisle said, as if there were not much he could do about it, and prudently closed the door on them.

Bradfield was a hard-built, self-denying man, thin-boned and well-preserved, of that age and generation which can do with very little sleep. Yet the strains of the last twenty-four hours were already showing in the small, uncommon bruises at the corner of his eyes, and the unnatural pallor of his complexion. He studied Turner without comment: the canvas bag clutched in the heavy fist, the battered fawn suit, the unyielding, classless features; and it seemed for a moment as if an impulse of involuntary anger would threaten his customary composure; of aesthetic objection that anything so offensively incongruous should have been set before him at such a time. Outside in the corridor Turner heard the hushed murmur of busy voices, the clip of feet, the faster chatter of the typewriters, and the phantom throb of code machines from the cypher room.

'It was good for you to come at such an awkward time. You'd better let me have that.' He took the canvas bag and dumped it behind the chair.

'Christ it's hot,' said Turner. Walking to the window, he rested his elbows on the sill and gazed out. Away to his right in the far distance, the Seven Hills of Königswinter, chalked over by fine cloud, rose like Gothic dreams against the colourless sky. At their feet he could make out the dull glint of water and the shadows of motionless vessels.

'He lived out that way didn't he? Königswinter?'

'We have a couple of hirings on the other bank. They are never much in demand. The ferry is a great inconvenience.'

On the trampled lawn, workmen were dismantling the marquee under the watchful eye of two German policemen.

'I imagine you have a routine in such cases,' Bradfield continued, addressing Turner's back. 'You must tell us what you want and we shall do our best to provide it.'

'Sure.'

'The cypher clerks have a dayroom where you'll be undisturbed. They are instructed to send your telegrams without reference to anyone else. I've had a desk and a telephone put in there for you. I have also asked Registry to prepare a list of the missing files. If there's anything more you want, I am sure de Lisle will do his best to provide it. And on the social side' – Bradfield hesitated – 'I am to invite you to dine with us tomorrow night. We would be very pleased. It's the usual Bonn evening. De Lisle will lend you a dinner jacket, I am sure.'

'There's lots of routines,' Turner replied at last. He was leaning against the radiator, looking round the room. 'In a country like this it should be dead simple. Call in the police. Check hospitals, nursing homes, prisons, Salvation Army hostels. Circulate his photograph and personal description and square the local press. Then I'd look for him myself.'

'Look for him? Where?'

'In other people. In his background. Motive, political association, boy friends, girl friends, contacts. Who else was involved; who knew; who half-knew; who quarter-knew; who ran him; who did he meet and where; how did he communicate; safe houses, pick-up points; how long's it been going on. Who's protected him, may be. That's what I call looking. Then I'd write a report: point the blame, make new enemies.' He continued to examine the room, and it seemed that nothing was innocent under his clear, inscrutable eye. 'That's one routine. That's for a friendly country, of course.'

'Most of what you suggest is quite unacceptable here.'

'Oh sure. I've had all that from Lumley.'

'Perhaps before we go any further, you had better have it from me as well.'

'Please yourself,' said Turner, in a manner which might have been deliberately chosen to annoy.

'I imagine that in your world, secrets are an absolute standard. They matter more than anything. Those who preserve them are your allies; those who betray them are your quarry. Here, that is simply not the case. As of now, the local political considerations far exceed those of security.'

Suddenly, Turner was grinning. 'They always do,' he said. 'It's amazing.'

'Here in Bonn we have at present one contribution to make: to maintain at all costs the trust and good will of the Federal Government. To stiffen their resolve against mounting criticism from their own electorate. The Coalition is sick; the most casual virus could kill it. Our job is to pamper the invalid. To console, encourage and occasionally threaten him, and pray to God he survives long enough to see us into the Common Market.'

'What a lovely picture.' He was looking out of the window again. 'The only ally we've got, and he's on crutches. The two sick men of Europe propping one another up.'

'Like it or not, it happens to be the truth. We are playing a poker game here. With open cards and nothing in our hand. Our credit is exhausted, our resources are nil. Yet in return for no more than a smile, our partners bid and play. That smile is all we have. The whole relationship between HMG and the Federal Coalition rests upon that smile. Our situation is as delicate as that; and as mysterious. And as critical. Our whole future with Europe could be decided in ten days from now.' He paused, apparently expecting Turner to speak. 'It is no coincidence that Karfeld has chosen next Friday for his rally in Bonn. By Friday, our friends in the German Cabinet will be forced to decide whether to bow to French pressure or honour their promises to ourselves and their partners in the Six. Karfeld detests the Market and favours an opening to the East. In the short term he inclines to Paris; in the long term, to Moscow. By marching on Bonn and increasing the tempo of his campaign, he is deliberately placing pressure on the Coalition at the most critical moment. Do you follow me?'

'I can manage the little words,' Turner said. A Kodachrome portrait of the Queen hung directly behind Bradfield's head. Her crest was everywhere: on the blue leather chairs, the silver cigarette box, even the jotting pads set out on the long conference table. It was as if the monarchy had flown here first class and left its free gifts behind.

'That is why I am asking you to move with the greatest possible circumspection. Bonn is a village,' Bradfield continued. 'It has the manners, vision and dimensions of the parish pump, and yet it is a State within a village. Nothing matters for us more than the confidence of our hosts. There are already indications that we have caused them offence. I do not even know how we have done that. Their manner, even in the last forty-eight hours, has become noticeably cool. We are under surveillance; our telephone calls are interrupted; and we have the greatest difficulty in reaching even our official ministerial contacts.'

'All right,' Turner said. He had had enough. 'I've got the message. I'm warned off. We're on tender ground. Now what?'

'Now this,' Bradfield snapped. 'We both know what Harting may be, or may have been. God knows, there are precedents. The greater his treachery here, the greater the potential embarrassment, the greater the shock to German confidence. Let us take the worst contingency. If it were possible to prove that by virtue of Harting's activities in this Embassy, our inmost secrets had been betrayed to the Russians over many years – secrets which to a great extent we share with the Germans – then that shock, trivial as it may be in the long term, could sever the last thread by which our credit here hangs. Wait.' He was sitting very straight at his desk, with an expression of controlled distaste upon his handsome face. 'Hear me out. There is something here that does not exist in England. It is called the anti-Soviet alliance. The Germans take it very seriously, and we deride it at our peril: *it is still our ticket to Brussels*. For twenty years or more, we have dressed ourselves in the shining armour of the defender. We may be bankrupt, we may beg for loans, currency and trade; we may occasionally ... reinterpret ... our Nato commitments; when the guns sound, we may even bury our heads under the blankets; our leaders may be as futile as theirs.'

What was it Turner discerned in Bradfield's voice at that moment? Self-disgust? A ruthless sense of his own decline? He spoke like a man who had tried all remedies, and would have no more of doctors. For a moment the gap between them had closed, and Turner heard his own voice speaking through the Bonn mist.

'For all that, in terms of popular psychology, it is the one great unspoken strength we have: that when the Barbarians come from the East, the Germans may count on our support. That Rhine Army will hastily gather on the Kentish hills and the British independent nuclear deterrent will be hustled into service. Now do you see what Harting could mean in the hand of a man like Karfeld?'

Turner had taken the black notebook from his inside pocket. It crackled sharply as he opened it. 'No. I don't. Not yet. You don't want him found, you want him lost. If you had your way you wouldn't have sent for me.' He nodded his large head in reluctant admiration. 'Well, I'll say this for you: no one's ever warned me off this early. Christ. I've hardly sat down. I hardly know his full names. We've not heard of him in London, did you know that? He's not even had any access, not in our book. Not even one bloody military manual. He may have been abducted. He may have gone under a bus, run off with a bird for all *we* know. But *you*; Christ! You've really gone the bank, haven't you? He's all the spies we've ever had rolled into one. So what *has* he pinched? What do you know that I don't?' Bradfield tried to interrupt but Turner rode him down implacably. 'Or maybe I shouldn't ask? I mean I don't want to upset anyone.'

They were glaring at one another across centuries of suspicion: Turner clever, predatory and vulgar, with the hard eye of the upstart; Bradfield disadvantaged but not put down, drawn in upon himself, picking his language as if it had been made for him.

'Our most secret file has disappeared. It vanished on the same day that Harting left. It covers the whole spectrum of our most delicate conversations with the Germans, formal and informal, over the last six months. For reasons which do not concern you, its publication would ruin us in Brussels.'

He thought at first that it was the roar of the aeroplane engines still ringing in his ears, but the traffic in Bonn is as constant as the mist. Gazing out of the window he was suddenly assailed by the feeling that from now on he would neither see nor hear with clarity; that his senses were being embraced and submerged by the cloying heat and the disembodied sound.

'Listen.' He indicated his canvas bag. 'I'm the abortionist. You don't want me but you've got to have me. A neat job with no aftermath, that's what you're paying for. All right; I'll do my best. But before we all go over the wall, let's do a bit of counting on our fingers, shall we?'

The catechism began.

'He was unmarried?'

'Yes.'

'Always has been?'

'Yes.'

'Lived alone?'

'So far as I know.'

'Last seen?'

'On Friday morning, at the Chancery meeting. In here.'

'Not afterwards?'

'I happen to know the pay clerk saw him, but I'm limited in whom I can ask.'

'Anyone else missing at all?'

'No one.'

'Had a full count have you? No little long-legged bird from Registry?'

'People are constantly on leave; no one is unaccountably absent.'

'Then why didn't Harting take leave? They usually do, you know. Defect in comfort, that's my advice.'

'I have no idea.'

'You weren't close to him?'

'Certainly not.'

'What about his friends? What do they say?'

'He has no friends worth speaking of.'

'Any not worth speaking of?'

'So far as I know, he has no close friends in the community. Few of us have. We have acquaintances, but few friends. That is the way of Embassies. With such an intensive social life, one learns to value privacy.'

'How about Germans?'

'I have no idea. He was once on familiar terms with Harry Praschko.'

'Praschko?'

'We have a parliamentary opposition here: the free Democrats. Praschko is one of its more colourful members. He has been most things in his time: not least a fellow traveller. There is a note on file to say they were once friendly. They knew one another during the Occupation, I believe. We keep an index of useful contacts. I once questioned him about Praschko as a matter of routine and he told me that the relationship was discontinued. That is all I can tell you.'

'He was once engaged to be married to a girl called Margaret Aickman. This Harry Praschko was named as a character reference. In his capacity as a member of the Bundestag.'

'Well?'

'You've never heard of Aickman?'

'Not a name to me, I'm afraid.'

'Margaret.'

'So you said. I never heard of any engagement, and I never heard of the woman.'

'Hobbies? Photography? Stamps? Ham radio?'

Turner was writing all the time. He might have been filling in a form.

'He was musical. He played the organ in Chapel. I believe he also had a collection of gramophone records. You would do better to enquire among the Junior Staff; he was more at home with them.'

'You never went to his house?'

'Once. For dinner.'

'Did he come to yours?'

There was the smallest break in the rhythm of their interrogation while Bradfield considered.

'Once.'

'For dinner?'

'For drinks. He wasn't quite dinner party material. I am sorry to offend your social instincts.'

'I haven't got any.'

Bradfield did not appear surprised.

'Still, you did go to him, didn't you? I mean you gave him hope.' He rose and ambled back to the window like a great moth lured to the light. 'Got a file on him, have you?' His tone was very detached; he might have been infected by Bradfield's own forensic style.

'Only paysheets, annual reports, a character reference from the Army. It's all very standard stuff. Read it if you want.' When Turner did not reply, he added: 'We keep very little here on staff; they change so often. Harting was the exception.'

'He's been here twenty years.'

'Yes. As I say, he is the exception.'

'And never vetted.'

Bradfield said nothing.

'Twenty years in the Embassy, most of them in Chancery. And never vetted once. Name never even submitted. Amazing really.' He might have been commenting on the view.

'I suppose we all thought it had been done already. He came from the Control Commission after all; one assumes they exacted a certain standard.'

'Quite a privilege being vetted, mind. Not the kind of thing you do for anyone.'

The marquee had gone. Homeless, the two German policemen paced the grey lawn, their wet leather coats flapping lazily round their boots. It's a dream, Turner thought. A noisy unwilling dream. 'Bonn's a very metaphysical place,' de Lisle's agreeable voice reminded him. 'The dreams have quite replaced reality.'

'Shall I tell you something?'

'I can hardly stop you.'

'All right: you've warned me off. That's usual enough. But where's the rest of it?'

'I've no idea what you mean.'

'You've no theory, that's what I mean. It's not like anything I've ever met. There's no panic. No explanation. Why not? He worked for you. You knew him. Now you tell me he's a spy; he's pinched your best files. He's garbage. Is it always like that here when somebody goes? Do the gaps seal that fast? He waited. 'Let me help you, shall I? "He's been working here for twenty years. We trusted him implicitly. We still do." How's that?'

Bradfield said nothing.

'Try again. "I always had my suspicions about him ever since that night we were discussing Karl Marx. Harting swallowed an olive without spitting out the pip." Any good?'

Still Bradfield did not reply.

'You see, It's not usual. See what I mean? He's unimportant. How you wouldn't have him to dinner. How you washed your hands of him. And what a sod he is. What he's betrayed.'

Turner watched him with his pale, hunter's eyes; watched for a movement, or a gesture, head cocked waiting for the wind. In vain. 'You don't even *bother* to explain him, not to me, not to yourself. Nothing. You're just ... blank about him. As if you'd sentenced him to death. You don't mind my being personal, do you? Only I'm sure you've not much time: that's the next thing you're going to tell me.'

'I was not aware,' Bradfield said, ice-cold, 'that I was expected to do your job. Nor you mine.'

'Capri. How about that? He's got a bird. The Embassy's in chaos, he pinches some files, flogs them to the Czechs and bolts with her.'

'He has no girl.'

'Aickman, He's dug her up. Gone off with Praschko, two on a bird. Bride, best man and groom.'

'I told you, he has no girl.'

'Oh. So you *do* know that? I mean there are some things you *are* sure of. He's a traitor and he's got no bird.'

'So far as anyone knows, he has no woman. Does that satisfy you?'

'Perhaps he's queer.'

'I'm sure he's nothing of the sort.'

'It's broken out in him. We're all a bit mad, aren't we, round about our age? The male menopause, how about that?'

'That is an absurd suggestion.'

'Is it?'

'To the best of my knowledge, yes.' Bradfield's voice was trembling with anger; Turner's barely rose above a murmur.

'We never know though, do we? Not till it's too late. Did he handle money at all?'

'Yes. But there's none missing.'

Turner swung on him. 'Jesus,' he said, his eyes bright with triumph. 'You checked. You *have* got a dirty mind.'

'Perhaps he's just walked into the river.' Turner suggested comfortingly, his eyes still upon Bradfield. 'No sex. Nothing to live for. How's that?'

'Ridiculous, since you ask.'

'Important to a bloke like Harting, though, sex. I mean if you're alone, it's the only thing. I mean I don't know how some of these chaps manage, do you? I know I couldn't. About a couple of weeks is as long as I can go, me. It's the only reality, if you live alone. Or that's what I reckon. Apart from politics of course.'

'Politics? Harting? I shouldn't think he read a newspaper from one year to the next. He was a child in such matters. A complete innocent.'

'They often are,' said Turner. 'That's the remarkable thing.' Sitting down again, Turner folded one leg over the other and leaned back in the chair like a man about to reminisce. 'I knew a man once who sold his birthright because he couldn't get a seat on the underground. I reckon there's more of that kind go wrong than was ever converted to it by the Good Book. Perhaps that *was* his problem? Not right for dinner parties: no room on the train. After all, he was a temporary, wasn't he?'

Bradfield did not reply.

'And he'd been here a long time. Permanent staff, sort of thing. Not fashionable, that isn't, not in an Embassy. They go native if they're around too long. But then he *was* native, wasn't he? Half. Half a Hun, as de Lisle would say. He never talked politics?'

'Never.'

'You sensed it in him, a political spin?'

'No.'

'No crack-up? No tension?'

'No.'

'What about that fight in Cologne?'

'What fight?'

'Five years back. In the night club. Someone worked him over; he was in hospital for six weeks. They managed to hush it up.'

'That was before my time.'

'Did he drink a lot?'

'Not to my knowledge.'

'Speak Russian? Take lessons?'

'No.'

'What did he do with his leave?'

'He seldom claimed any. If he did, I understand he stayed at his home in Königswinter. He took a certain interest in his garden, I believe.'

For a long time Turner frankly searched Bradfield's face for something he could not find.

'He didn't screw around,' he said. 'He wasn't queer. He'd no friends, but he wasn't a recluse. He wasn't vetted and you've no record of him. He was a political innocent but he managed to get his hands on the one file that really matters to you. He never stole money, he played the organ in Chapel, took a certain interest in his garden and loved his neighbour as himself. Is that it? He wasn't any bloody thing, positive or negative. What was he then, for Christ's sake? The Embassy eunuch? Haven't you any opinion at all' – Turner persisted in mock supplication – 'to help a poor bloody investigator in his lonely task?'

A watch chain hung across Bradfield's waistcoat, no more than a thread of gold, a tiny devotional token of ordered society.

'You seem deliberately to be wasting time on matters which are not at issue. I have neither the time nor the interest to play your devious games. Insignificant though Harting was, obscure though his motive may be, for the last three months he unfortunately had a considerable access to secret information. He obtained that access by stealth, and I suggest that instead of speculating on his sexual proclivities, you give some attention to what he has stolen.'

'Stolen?' Turner repeated softly. 'That's a funny word,' and he wrote it out with deliberate clumsiness in tall capital letters along the top of one page of the notebook. The Bonn climate had already made its mark upon him: dark dabs of sweat had appeared on the thin fabric of his disgraceful suit.

'All right,' he said with sudden fierceness, 'I'm wasting your bloody time. Now let's start at the beginning and find out why you love him so.'

Bradfield examined his fountain pen. You could be queer, Turner's expression said, if you didn't love honour more.

'Will you put that into English?'

'Tell me about him from your own point of view. What his work was, what he was like.'

'His sole task when I first arrived was handling German civilian claims against Rhine Army. Tank damage to crops; stray shells from the range; cattle and sheep killed on manoeuvres. Ever since the end of the war that's been quite an industry in Germany. By the time I took over Chancery two and a half years ago, he had made a corner of it.'

'You mean he was an expert.'

'As you like.'

'It's just the emotive terms, you see. They put me off. I can't help liking him when you talk that way.'

'Claims was his *métier* then, if you prefer. They got him into the Embassy in the first place; he knew the job inside out; he's done it for many years in many different capacities. First for the Control Commission, then for the Army.'

'What did he do *before* that? He came out in forty-five.'

'He came out in uniform, of course. A sergeant or something of the sort. His status was then altered to that of civilian assistant. I've no idea what his work was. I imagined the War Office could tell you.'

'They can't. I also tried the old Control Commission archive. It's mothballs for posterity. They'll take weeks to dig out his file.'

'In any event, he had chosen well. As long as British units were stationed in Germany, there would be manoeuvres; and German civilians would claim reparations. One might say that his job, though specialized, was at least secured by our military presence in Europe.'

'Christ, there's not many would give you a mortgage on *that*,' said Turner with a sudden, infectious smile, but Bradfield ignored him.

'He acquitted himself perfectly adequately. More than adequately; he was good at it. He had a smattering of law from somewhere. German as well as military. He was naturally acquisitive.'

'A thief,' Turner suggested, watching him.

'When he was in doubt, he could call upon the Legal Attaché. It wasn't everybody's cup of tea, acting as a broker between the German farmers and the British Army, smoothing their feathers, keeping things away from the press. It required a certain instinct. He possessed that,' Bradfield observed, once more with undisguised contempt. 'On his own level, he was a competent negotiator.'

'But that wasn't your level, was it?'

'It was no one's,' Bradfield replied, choosing to avoid the innuendo. 'Professionally, he was a solitary. My predecessors had found it best to leave him alone and when I took over I saw no reason to change the practice. He was attached to Chancery so that we could exert a certain disciplinary control; no more. He came to morning meetings, he was punctual, he made no trouble. He was liked up to a point but not, I suppose, trusted. His English was never perfect. He was socially energetic at a certain level; mainly in the less discriminating Embassies. They say he got on well with the South Americans.'

'Did he travel for his work?'

'Frequently and widely. All over Germany.'

'Alone?'

'Yes.'

'And he knew the Army inside out: he'd get the manoeuvre reports; he knew their dispositions, strengths, he knew the lot, right?'

'He knew far more than that; he heard the mess gossip up and down the country; many of the manoeuvres were inter-allied affairs. Some involved the experimental use of new weapons. Since they also caused damage, he was obliged to know the extent of it. There is a great deal of loose information he could have acquired.'

'Nato stuff?'

'Mainly.'

'How long's he been doing that work?'

'Since nineteen forty-eight or nine I suppose. I cannot say, without reference to the files, when the British first paid compensation.'

'Say twenty-one years, give or take a bit.'

'That is my own calculation.'

'Not a bad run for a temporary.'

'Shall I go on?'

'Do. Sure. Go on,' Turner said hospitably, and thought: if I was you I'd throw me out for that.

'That was the situation when I took over. He was a contract man; his employment was subject to annual revision. Each December his contract came up for renewal, each December renewal was recommended. That was how matters stood until eighteen months ago.'

'When Rhine Army pulled out.'

'We prefer to say here that Rhine Army has been added to our strategic reserve in the United Kingdom. You must remember the Germans are still paying support costs.'

'I'll remember.'

'In any event, only a skeleton force remained in Germany. The withdrawal occurred quite suddenly; I imagine it took us all by surprise. There had been disputes about offset agreements, there were riots in Minden. The Movement was just getting under way; the students in particular were becoming extremely noisy; the troops were becoming a provocation. The decision was taken at the highest level; the Ambassador was not even consulted. The order came; and Rhine Army had gone in a month. We had been making a great number of cuts around that time. It's all the rage in London these days. They throw things away and call it economy.' Once more Turner glimpsed that inner bitterness in Bradfield, a family shame to which no guest alluded.

'And Harting was left high and dry.'

'For some time, no doubt, he had seen which way the wind was blowing. That doesn't lessen the shock.'

'He was still a temporary?'

'Of course. Indeed his chances of establishment, if they ever seriously existed, were diminishing rapidly. The moment it became apparent that Rhine Army must withdraw, the writing was on the wall. For that reason alone, I felt that it would have been quite mistaken to make any permanent arrangement for him.'

'Yes,' said Turner, 'I see that.'

'It is easily argued that he was unjustly treated,' Bradfield retorted. 'It could equally be argued that he had a damn good run for his money.' The conviction came through like a stain, suppress it as he might.

'You said he handled official cash.' Turner thought: this is what doctors do. They probe until they can diagnose.

'Occasionally he passed on cheques for the Army. He was a postbox, that was all. A middle man. The Army drew the money, Harting handed it over and obtained a receipt. I checked his accounts regularly. The Army Auditors, as you know, are notoriously suspicious. There were no irregularities. The system was watertight.'

'Even for Harting?'

'That's not what I said. Besides, he always seemed quite comfortably off. I don't think he's an avaricious person; I don't have that impression.'

'Did he live above his means?'

'How should I know what means he has? If he lived on what he got here, I suppose he lived up to them. His house in Königswinter was quite large; certainly it was above his grade. I gather he maintained a certain standard there.'

'I see.'

'Last night I made a point of examining his cash drawings for the last three months preceding his departure. On Friday, after Chancery meeting, he drew seventy-one pounds and fourpence.'

'That's a bloody odd sum.'

'To the contrary, it's a very logical sum. Friday was the tenth of the month. He had drawn exactly one third of his monthly entitlement of pay and allowances, less tax, insurance, stoppages for dilapidation and personal telephone calls.' He paused. 'That is an aspect of him which perhaps I have not emphasized: he was a very self-sufficient person.'

'You mean he *is*.'

'I have never yet caught him in a lie. Having decided to leave, he seems to have taken what was owing to him and no more.'

'Some people would call that honourable.'

'Not to steal? I would call that a negative achievement. He might also know, from his knowledge of the law, that an act of theft would have justified an approach to the German police.'

'Christ,' said Turner, watching him, 'You won't even give him marks for conduct.'

Miss Peate, Bradfield's personal assistant, brought coffee. She was a middle-aged, under-decorated woman, stitched taut and full of disapproval. She seemed to know already where Turner came from, for she cast him a look of sovereign contempt. It was his shoes, he noticed to his pleasure, that she most objected to; and he thought: bloody good, that's what shoes are for.

*

Bradfield continued: 'Rhine Army withdrew at short notice and he was left without a job. That was the nub of it.'

'And without access to Nato military intelligence? That's what you're telling me.'

'That is my hypothesis.'

'Ah,' said Turner, affecting enlightenment, and wrote laboriously in his notebook *hypothesis* as if the very word were an addition to his vocabulary.

'On the day Rhine Army left, Harting came to see me. That was eighteen months ago, near enough.'

He fell silent, struck by his own recollection.

'He is so *trivial*,' he said at last, in a moment of quite uncharacteristic softness. 'Can't you understand that? So utterly lightweight.' It seemed to surprise him still. 'It's easy to lose sight of now: the sheer insignificance of him.'

'He never will be again,' Turner said carelessly, 'You might as well get used to it.'

'He walked in; he looked pale, that was all; otherwise quite unchanged. He sat down in that chair over there. That is his cushion, by the way.' He permitted himself a small, unloving smile. 'The cushion was a territorial claim. He was the only member of the Chancery who reserved his seat.'

'And the only one who might lose it. Who embroidered it?'

'I really have no idea.'

'Did he have a housekeeper?'

'Not to my knowledge.'

'All right.'

'He didn't say anything at all about his altered situation. They were actually listening to the radio broadcast in Registry, I remember. The regiments were being piped on to the trains.'

'Quite a moment for him, that.'

'I suppose it was. I asked him what I could do for him. Well, he said, he wanted to be useful. It was all very low-key, all very delicate. He'd noticed Miles Gaveston was under strain, what with the Berlin disturbances and the Hanover students and various other pressures: might he not help out? I pointed out to him he was not qualified to handle internal matters; they were the preserve of regular members of Chancery. No, he said, that wasn't what he meant at all. He wouldn't for a minute presume to trespass upon our major effort. But he had been thinking: Gaveston had one or two little jobs; could he not take them over? He had in mind for instance the Anglo-German Society, which was pretty well dormant by then but still entailed a certain amount of low-level correspondence. Then there was Missing Persons: might he not take over a few things of that kind in order to desencumber the busier Chancery officers? It made some sense, I had to admit.'

'So you said yes.'

'I agreed to it. On a purely provisional basis, of course. An interim arrangement. I assumed we would give him notice in December when his contract ran out; until then, he could fill in his time with whatever small jobs he could find. That was the thin end of the wedge. I was no doubt foolish to listen to him.'

'I didn't say that.'

'You don't have to. I gave him an inch; he took the rest. Within a month he had gathered them all in; all the end-clippings of Chancery work, all the dross a big Embassy attracts: Missing Persons, Petitions to the Queen, Unannounced Visitors, Official Tours, the Anglo-German Society, letters of abuse, threats, all the things that should never have come to Chancery in the first place. By the same token, he spread his talents across the social field as well. Chapel, the choir, the Catering Committee, the Sports Committee. He even started up a National Savings group. At some point he asked to be allowed to use the title "Consular" and I consented. We have no Consular duties here, you understand; that all goes up to Cologne.' He shrugged. 'By December he had made himself useful. His contract was brought forward' – he had taken up his fountain pen and was again staring at the nib – 'and I renewed it. I gave him another year.'

'You treated him well,' Turner said, his eyes all the time upon Bradfield. 'You were quite kind to him really.'

'He had no standing here, no security. He was already on the doorstep and he knew it. I suppose that plays a part. We are more inclined to care for the people we can easily get rid of.'

'You were sorry for him. Why won't you admit it? It's a fair enough reason, for God's sake.'

'Yes. Yes I suppose I was. That first time, I was actually sorry for him.' He was smiling, but only at his own stupidity.

'Did he do the work well?'

'He was unorthodox, but not ineffectual. He preferred the telephone to the written word, but that was only natural; he had had no proper instruction in drafting. English was not his native language.' He shrugged. 'I gave him another year,' he said again.

'Which expired last December. Like a licence really. A licence to work; to be one of us.' He continued to watch Bradfield. 'A licence to spy. And you renewed it a second time.'

'Yes.'

'Why?'

Once more Turner was aware of that hesitation which seemed to signify concealment.

'You weren't sorry for him, were you? Not this time?'

'My feelings are irrelevant.' He put down the pen with a snap. 'The reasons for keeping him on were totally objective.'

'I didn't say they weren't. But you can still be sorry for him.'

'We were understaffed and overworked. The Inspectors had already reduced us by two against my most strenuous advice. The allowances had been halved. Not just Europe was in flux. There were no constants anywhere any more. Rhodesia, Hong Kong, Cyprus. ... British troops were running from one to the other trying to stamp out a forest fire. We were half-way into Europe and half-way out again. There was talk of a Nordic Federation; God knows what fool gave birth to that idea!' Bradfield declared with utter contempt. 'We were putting out feelers in Warsaw, Copenhagen and Moscow. One minute we were conspiring against the French, the next we were conspiring with them. While that was going on we found the energy to scrap three-quarters of the Navy and nine-tenths of our independent deterrent. It was our worst time; our most humiliating time, and our busiest. To crown everything, Karfeld had just taken over the Movement.'

'So Harting took you through the act again.'

'Not the same act.'

'What do you mean?'

A pause.

'It had more purpose. It had more urgency. I felt it and I did nothing about it. I blame myself. I was conscious of a new mood in him and I did not pursue it.' He continued: 'At the time I put it down to the general state of intensity in which we were all living. I realize now that he was playing his biggest card.'

'Well?'

'He began by saying he still didn't feel he was pulling his weight. He had had a good year, but he felt he could do more. These were bad days; he would like to feel he was really helping to get things on an even keel. I asked him what he had in mind; I thought he'd just about swept the board by then. He said well, it *was* December – that was the nearest he ever came to referring to his contract – and he had naturally been wondering about the Personalities survey.'

'The what?'

'Biographies of prominent figures in German life. Our own confidential Who's Who. We prepare it every year, each of us takes a hand and contributes something on the German personalities with whom he deals. The Commercial people write about their commercial contacts, the Economists about the economists, the Attachés, Press, Information, they all add their bit. Much of the material is highly unflattering; some of it is derived from secret sources.'

'And Chancery edits?'

'Yes. Once again he had chosen very accurately. It was another of those chores which interfered with our proper duties. It was already overdue. De Lisle, who should have compiled it, was in Berlin; it was becoming a confounded nuisance.'

'So you gave him the job.'

'On a provisional basis, yes.'

'Until the next December, for instance?'

'For instance. It is easy now to think of reasons why he wanted that particular job. The survey provided him with a *laissez-passer* to any part of the Embassy. It runs across the board; it covers the whole range of Federal affairs: industrial, military, administrative. Once charged with the survey, he could call on whomever he liked without questions being asked. He could draw files from any other Registry: Commercial, Economic, Naval, Military, Defence – they all opened their doors to him.'

'And the question of vetting never crossed your mind?'

The self-critical note returned: 'Never.'

'Well we all have our moments,' said Turner quietly. 'And that's how he got his access?'

'There's more to it than that.'

'More? That's just about the lot, isn't it?'

'We not only have archives here; we have a Destruction programme as well. It has been running for years. The purpose is to keep Registry space available for new files and to get rid of old ones we no longer need. It sounds a somewhat academic project and in many ways it is; nevertheless, it happens to be vital. There is a clearly defined economic limit to the amount of paper Registry can handle, and to the amount of paper it will hold. The problem is akin to that of road traffic: we are constantly creating more paper than we can digest. Very naturally, it was another of those jobs we took up and put down as time allowed; it was also an absolute curse. For a while it would be forgotten; then the Office would write and ask for our latest figures.' He shrugged. 'As I say, it's very simple. We can't go on indefinitely, even in a place this size, building up more files than we destroy. Registry's bursting at the seams already.'

'So Harting proposed himself for the task.'

'Precisely.'

'And you agreed.'

'On a provisional basis. He should try his hand and see how it went. He has been working at it off and on for five months. When in doubt, I told him, he was to consult de Lisle. He never did so.'

'Where did he actually do this work? In his room?'

Bradfield barely hesitated. 'In Chancery Registry, where the most sensitive documents are kept. He had the run of the strongroom. He could draw whatever he wanted provided he didn't overplay his hand. There isn't even any record of what he did look at. There are also some letters missing; the Registrar will give you the details.'

Slowly Turner stood up, brushing his hands together as if they had sand on them.

'Of the forty-odd missing files, eighteen are drawn from the Personalities Survey and contain the most sensitive material on high-ranking German politicians. A careful reading would point clearly to our most delicate sources. The rest are Top Secret and cover Anglo-German agreements on a variety of subjects: secret treaties, secret codicils to published agreements. If he wished to embarrass us, he could hardly have chosen better. Some of the files go right back to forty-eight or nine.'

'And the one special file? "Conversations Formal and Informal"?'

'Is what we call a Green. It is subject to special procedures.'

'How many Greens are there in the Embassy?'

'This is the only one. It was in its place in Registry Strong-Room on

Thursday morning. The Registrar noticed its absence on Thursday evening and assumed it was in operation. By Saturday morning he was deeply concerned. On Sunday he reported the loss to me.'

'Tell me,' said Turner at last. 'What happened to him during last year? What happened between the two Decembers? Apart from Karfeld.'

'Nothing specific.'

'Then why did you go off him?'

'I didn't,' Bradfield replied with contempt. 'Since I never had any feeling for him either way, the question does not arise. I merely learned during the intervening year to recognize his technique. I saw how he operated on people; how he wheedled his way in. I saw through him, that's all.'

Turner stared at him.

'And what did you see?'

Bradfield's voice was as crisp and as finite and as irreducible as a mathematical formula. 'Deceit. I'd have thought I had made that plain by now.'

Turner got up.

'I'll begin with his room.'

'The Chancery Guard has the keys. They're expecting you. Ask for Macmullen.'

'I want to see his house, his friends, his neighbours; if necessary I'll talk to his foreign contacts. I'll break whatever eggs I've got to, no more no less. If you don't like it, tell the Ambassador. Who's the Registrar?'

'Meadowes.'

'Arthur Meadowes?'

'I believe so.'

Something held him back: a reluctance, a hint of uncertainty, almost of dependence, a middle tone quite out of character with anything that had gone before.

'Meadowes was in Warsaw, wasn't he?'

'That's correct.'

Louder now: 'And Meadowes has a list of the missing files, has he?'

'And letters.'

'And Harting worked for him, of course.'

'Of course. He is expecting you to call on him.'

'I'll see his room first.' It was a resolution he seemed to have reached already.

'As you wish. You mentioned you would also visit his house—'

'Well?'

'I am afraid that at present it is not possible. It is under police protection since yesterday.'

'Is that general?'

'What?'

'The police protection?'

'Siebkron insists upon it. I cannot quarrel with him now.'

'It applies to all hirings?'

'Principally the more senior ones. I imagine they have included Harting's because it is remote.'

'You don't sound convinced.'

'I cannot think of any other reason.'

'What about Iron Curtain Embassies; did Harting hang around them at all?'

'He went to the Russians occasionally; I cannot say how often.'

'This man Praschko, the friend he had, the politician. You said he used to be a fellow-traveller.'

'That was fifteen years ago.'

'And when did the association end?'

'It's on the file. About five years ago.'

'That's when he had the fight in Cologne. Perhaps it was with Praschko.'

'Anything is possible.'

'One more question.'

'Well?'

'That contract he had. If it had expired ... say last Thursday?'

'Well?'

'Would you have renewed it? Again?'

'We are under great strain. Yes, I would have renewed it.'

'You must miss him.'

The door was opened from the outside by de Lisle. His gentle features were drawn and solemn.

'Ludwig Siebkron rang: the exchange had orders not to put through your calls. I spoke to him myself.'

'Well?'

'About the librarian, Eich: the wretched woman they beat up in Hanover.'

'About her?'

'I'm afraid she died an hour ago.'

Bradfield considered this intelligence in silence. 'Find out where the funeral is. The Ambassador must make a gesture; a telegram to the dependants rather than flowers. Nothing too conspicuous; just his deepest sympathy. Talk to them in Private Office, they'll know the wording. And something from the Anglo-German Society. You'd better handle that yourself. And send a cable to the Association of Assistant Librarians; they were enquiring about her. And ring Hazel will you, and tell her? She asked particularly to be kept informed.'

He was poised and perfectly in control. 'If you require anything,' he added to Turner, 'Tell de Lisle.'

Turner was watching him.

'Otherwise we shall expect you tomorrow night. About five to eight? Germans are very punctual. It is the local custom that we assemble before they arrive. And if you're going down to his room, perhaps you would take that cushion. I see no point in our having it up here.'

Albino Cork, stooped over the cypher machines while he coaxed the strips of print from the rollers, heard the thud and turned his pink eyes sharply towards the large figure in the doorway.

'That's my bag. Leave it where it is; I'll be in later.'

'Righty-ho,' said Cork and thought: a Funny. Just his luck, with the whole ruddy world blowing up in his face, and Janet's baby due any minute, and that poor woman in Hanover turning up her toes, to be landed with a Funny in the dayroom. This was not his only grudge. The German steel strike was spreading nicely; if he had only thought of it on Friday and not Saturday, that little flutter on Swedish steel would have shown a four-bob capital profit in three days; and five per cent per day, in Cork's losing battle with clerical status, was what villas in the Adriatic were made of. Top Secret, he read wearily, Personal for Bradfield and Decypher Yourself: how much longer will *that* go on? Capri ... Crete ... Spetsai ... Elba ... *Give me an island to myself,* he sang, in a high-pitched pop improvisation – for Cork had dreams of cutting his own discs as well – *Give me an Island to myself, any Island, Any Island but Bonn.*

5
John Gaunt

The crowd in the lobby had thinned. The Post Office clock above the sealed lift said ten thirty-five; those who dared not risk a trip to the canteen had gathered at the front desk; the Chancery Guard had made mid-morning tea, and they were drinking it and talking in subdued voices when they heard his approaching footsteps. His heels had metal quarters and they echoed against the pseudo-marble walls like shots on a valley range. The despatch riders, with that nose for authority which soldiers have, gently set down their cups and fastened the buttons of their tunics.

'Macmullen?'

He stood on the lowest step, one hand propped massively on the banister, the other clutching the embroidered cushion. To either side of him, corridors, haunted with iron riot grilles and free-standing pillars of chrome, led into the dark like ghettos from a splendid city. The silence was suddenly important, making a fool of all that had gone before.

'Macmullen's off duty, sir. Gone down to Naafi.'

'Who are you?'

'Gaunt, sir. I'm standing in for him.'

'My name's Turner. I'm checking physical security. I want to see Room Twenty-one.'

Gaunt was a small man, a devout Welshman, with a long memory of the Depression inherited from his father. He had come to Bonn from Cardiff, where he had driven motor-cars for the police. He carried the keys in his right hand, low down by his side, and his gait was square and rather solemn, so that as he preceded Turner into the dark mouth of the corridor, he resembled a miner making for the pithead.

'Shocking really, all what they've been up to,' Gaunt chanted, talking ahead of him and letting the sound carry backwards. 'Peter Aldock, he's my stringer see, he's got a brother in Hanover, used to be with the Occupation, married a German girl and opened a grocer's shop. Terrified he was for sure: well, he says, they all know my George is English. What'll happen to *him*? Worse than the Congo. Hullo there, Padre!'

The Chaplain sat at a portable typewriter in a small white cell opposite the telephone exchange, beneath a picture of his wife, his door wide open for confession. A rush cross was tucked behind the cord. 'Good morning John then,' he replied in a slightly reproving tone which recalled for both of them the granite intractability of their Welsh God; and Gaunt said, 'Hullo there' again but did not alter his pace. From all around them came the unmistakable sounds of a multi-lingual community: the lonely German drone of the Head Press Reader dictating a translation; the bark of the travel clerk shouting into the telephone; the distant whistling, tuneful and un-English, that seemed to come from everywhere, piped in from other corridors. Turner caught the smell of salami and second breakfasts, of newsprint and disinfectant and he thought: all change at Zurich, you're abroad at last.

'It's mainly the locally-employed down here,' Gaunt explained above the din, 'They aren't allowed no higher, being German.' His sympathy for foreigners was felt but controlled: a nurse's sympathy, tempered by vocation.

A door opened to their left; a shaft of white light broke suddenly upon them, catching the poor plaster of the walls and the tattered green of a bilingual noticeboard. Two girls, about to emerge from Information Registry, drew back to let them by and Turner looked them over mechanically, thinking: This was his world. Second class and foreign. One carried a thermos, the other laboured under a stack of files. Beyond them, through an outer window protected with jeweller's screens, he glimpsed the car park and heard the roar of a motor-bike as a despatch rider drove off. Gaunt had ducked away to the right, down another passage; he stopped, and they were at the door, Gaunt fumbling with the key and Turner staring over his shoulder at the notice which hung from the centre panel: 'Harting Leo, Claims and Consular', a sudden witness to the living man, or a sudden monument to the dead.

The characters of the first two words were a good two inches high, ruled at the edges and cross-hatched in red and green crayon; the word 'Consular' was done a good deal larger, and the letters were outlined in ink to give them that extra substance which the title evidently demanded. Stooping, Turner lightly touched the surface; it was paper mounted on hardboard, and even by that poor light he could make out the faint ruled lines of pencil dictating the upper and lower limits of each letter; defining the borders of a modest existence perhaps; or of a life unnaturally curtailed by deceit. 'Deceit. I'd have thought I'd have made that plain by now.'

'Hurry,' he said.

Gaunt unlocked the door. As Turner seized the handle and shoved it open, he heard his sister-in-law's voice on the telephone again and his own reply as he slammed down the receiver: 'Tell her I've left the country.' The windows were closed. The heat struck up at them from the linoleum. There was a stink of rubber and wax. One curtain was slightly drawn. Gaunt reached out to pull it back.

'Leave it. Keep away from the window. And stay there. If anyone comes, tell them to get out.' He tossed the embroidered cushion on to a chair and peered round the room.

The desk had chrome handles; it was better than Bradfield's desk. The calendar on the wall advertised a firm of Dutch diplomatic importers. Turner moved very lightly, for all his bulk, examining but never touching. An old army map hung on the wall, divided into the original zones of military occupation. The British was marked in bright green, a fertile patch among the foreign deserts. It's like a prison cell, he thought, maximum security; maybe it's just the bars. What a place to break out of, and who wouldn't? The smell was foreign but he couldn't place it.

'Well, I *am* surprised,' Gaunt was saying. 'There's a lot gone I must say.'

Turner did not look at him.

'Such as what?'

'I don't know. Gadgets. All sorts. This is Mr Harting's room,' he explained. 'Very gadget-minded, Mr Harting is.'

'What sort of gadgets?'

'Well he had a *tea* machine, you know the kind that wakes you up? Made a lovely cup of tea, that did. Pity that's gone, really.'

'What else?'

'A fire. The new fan type with the two bars over. And a lamp. A smashing one, Japanese. Go all directions, that lamp would. Turn it half-way and it burned *soft*. Very cheap to run as well, he told me. But I wouldn't have one, you know, not now they've cut the allowances. Still,' he continued consolingly, 'I expect he's taken them home, don't you, if that's where he's gone.'

'Yes. Yes, I expect he has.'

On the window-sill stood a transistor radio. Stooping until his eyes were on a level with the panel, Turner switched it on. At once they heard the mawkish tones of a British Forces announcer commenting on the Hanover riots and the prospects for a British victory in Brussels. Slowly Turner rolled the turning needle along the lighted band, his ear cocked all the time to the changing babel of French, German and Dutch.

'I thought you said physical security.'

'I did.'

'You haven't hardly looked at the windows. Or the locks.'

'I will, I will.' He had found a Slav voice and he was listening with deep concentration. 'Know him well, did you? Come in here often for a cup?'

'Quite. Depends on how busy, really.'

Switching off the radio, Turner stood up. 'Wait outside,' he said. 'And give me the keys.'

'What's he done then?' Gaunt demanded, hesitating. 'What's gone wrong?'

'Done? Nothing. He's on compassionate leave. I want to be alone, that's all.'

'They say he's in trouble.'

'Who?'

'Talkers.'

'What sort of trouble?'

'I don't know. Car smash maybe. He wasn't at choir practice, see. Nor Chapel.'

'Does he drive badly?'

'Can't say really.'

Part defiant, part curious, Gaunt stayed by the door, watching as Turner pulled open the wooden wardrobe and peered inside. Three hair-dryers, still in their boxes, lay on the floor beside a pair of rubber overshoes.

'You're a friend of his, aren't you?'

'Not really. Only from choir, see.'

'Ah,' said Turner, staring at him now. 'You sang for him. I used to sing in choir myself.'

'Oh really now, where's that then?'

'Yorkshire,' Turner said with awful friendliness, while his pale gaze continued to fix upon Gaunt's plain face. 'I hear he's a lovely organist.'

'Not at all bad, I will say,' Gaunt agreed, rashly recognizing a common interest.

'Who's his *special* friend; someone else in the choir, was it? A lady perhaps?' Turner enquired, still not far from piety.

'He's not close to anyone, Leo.'

'Then who does he buy these for?'

The hair-dryers were of varying quality and complexity; the prices on the box ran from eighty to two hundred marks. 'Who for?' he repeated.

'All of us. Dips, non dips; it didn't signify. He runs a service see; works the diplomatic discounts. Always do you a favour Leo will. Don't matter what you fancy: radios, dishwashers, cars; he'll get you a bit off, like; you know.'

'Knows his way round, does he?'

'That's right.'

'Takes a cut too, I expect. For his trouble,' Turner suggested coaxingly. 'Quite right too.'

'I didn't say so.'

'Do you a girl as well, would he? Mister Fixit, is that it?'

'Certainly not,' said Gaunt, much shocked.

'What was in it for him?'

'Nothing. Not that I know of.'

'Just a little friend of all the world, eh? Likes to be liked. Is that it?'

'Well, we all do really, don't we?'

'Philosopher, are we?'

'Always *willing*,' Gaunt continued, very slow to follow the changes in Turner's mood. 'You ask Arthur Meadowes now, there's an example. The moment Leo's in Registry, not hardly a day after, he's down here collecting the mail. "Don't you bother," he says to Arthur. "Save your legs, you're not so young as you were and you've plenty to worry about already. I'll fetch it for you, look." That's Leo. Obliging. Saintly really, considering his disadvantages.'

'What mail?'

'Everything. Classified or Unclassified, it didn't make no difference. He'd be down here signing for it, taking it up to Arthur.'

Very still, Turner said, 'Yes, I see that. And maybe he'd drop in here on the way, would he? Check on his own room; brew up a cup of tea.'

'That's it,' said Gaunt, 'Always ready to oblige.' He opened the door. 'Well, I'll be leaving you to it.'

'You stay here,' said Turner, still watching him. 'You'll be all right. You stay and talk to me, Gaunt. I like company. Tell me about his disadvantages.'

Returning the hair-dryers to their boxes, he pulled out a linen jacket, still on its hanger. A summer jacket; the kind that barmen wear. A dead rose hung from the buttonhole.

'What disadvantages?' he asked, throwing the rose into the waste bag. 'You can tell me, Gaunt,' and he noticed the smell again, the wardrobe smell he had caught but not defined, the sweet, familiar, continental smell of male unguents and cigar.

'Only his childhood, that's all. He had an uncle.'

'Tell me about the uncle.'

'Nothing; only how he was daft. Always changing politics. He had a lovely way of narrative, Leo did. Told us how he used to sit down in the cellar in Hampstead with his uncle while the bombs were falling, making pills in a machine. Dried fruit. Squashed them all up and rolled them in sugar, then put them in the tins, see. Used to spit on them, Leo did, just to spite his uncle. My wife was very shocked when she heard that – I said don't be silly, that's deprivation. He hasn't had the love, see, not what you've had.'

Having felt the pockets, Turner cautiously detached the jacket from the hanger and held the shoulders against his own substantial frame.

'Little bloke?'

'He's a keen dresser,' said Gaunt, 'Always well turned out, Leo is.'

'Your size?'

Turner held the jacket towards him, but Gaunt drew back in distaste.

'Smaller,' he said, his eyes still on the jacket. 'More the dancer type. Butterfly. You'd think he wore pumps all the time.'

'Pansy?'

'Certainly not,' said Gaunt, very shocked again, and colouring at the notion.

'How do you know?'

'He's a decent fellow, that's why,' said Gaunt, fiercely. 'Even if he has done something wrong.'

'Pious?'

'Respectful, very. And about religion. Never cheeky or brash, although he was foreign.'

'What else did he say about his uncle?'

'Nothing.'

'What else about his politics?' He was looking at the desk, examining the locks on the drawers.

Tossing the jacket on to a chair, he held out his hand for the keys. Reluctantly Gaunt released them.

'Nothing. I don't know nothing about his politics.'

'Who says anything about him doing something wrong?'

'You. All this hunting him. Measuring him; I don't fancy it.'

'What would he have done, I wonder? To make me hunt him like this?'

'God only knows.'

'In his wisdom.' He had opened the top drawers. 'Have you got a diary like this?'

It was bound in blue rexine and stamped in gold with the Royal crest.

'No.'

'Poor Gaunt. Too humble?' He was turning the pages, working back. Once he stopped and frowned; once he wrote something in his black notebook.

'It was Counsellors and above, that's why,' Gaunt retorted. 'I wouldn't accept it.'

'He offered you one, did he? That was another of his fiddles, I suppose. What happened? He scrounged a bundle did he, from Registry, and handed them out to his old chums on the Ground Floor. "Here you are boys: the streets are paved with gold up there. Here's a keepsake from your old winger." Is that the way of it, Gaunt? And Christian virtue held you back, did it?' Closing the diary, he pulled open the lower drawers.

'What if he did? You've no call to go rifling through his desk there, have you? Not for a little thing like that! Pinching a handful of diaries; well that's hardly all the world, is it?' His Welsh accent had jumped all the hurdles and was running free.

'You're a Christian man, Gaunt. You know how the devil works better than I do. Little things lead to big things, don't they? Pinch an apple one day, you'll be hi-jacking a lorry the next. *You* know the way it goes, Gaunt. What else did he tell you about himself? Any more little childhood reminiscences?'

He had found a paper knife, a slim, silver affair with a broad, flat handle, and he was reading the engraving by the desk lamp.

'L.H. from Margaret. Now who was Margaret, I wonder?'

'I never heard of her.'

'He was engaged to be married once, did you know that?'

'No.'

'Miss Aickman. Margaret Aickman. Ring a bell?'

'No.'

'How about the Army. Did he tell you about that?'

'He loved the Army. In Berlin, he said, he used to watch the cavalry going over the jumps. He loved it.'

'He was in the infantry, was he?'

'I don't really know.'

'No.'

Turner had put the knife aside, next to the blue diary, made another note in his pocket-book and picked up a small flat tin of Dutch cigars.

'Smoker?'

'He liked a cigar. Yes. That's all he smoked, see. Always *carried* cigarettes mind. But I only ever saw him smoke those things. There was one or two in Chancery complained, so I hear. About the cigars. Didn't fancy them. But Leo could be stubborn when he had the mind, I will say.'

'How long have you been here, Gaunt?'

'Five years.'

'He was in a fight in Cologne. That in your time.'

Gaunt hesitated.

'Amazing the way things are hushed up here, I must say. You give a new meaning to the "need to know", you do. Everyone knows except the people who need to. What happened?'

'It was just a fight. They say he asked for it, that's all.'

'How?'

'I don't know. They say he deserved it, see. I heard from my predecessor: they brought him back one night, you couldn't hardly recognize him, that's what he said. Serve him right, he said; that's what they told him. Mind you, he could be pugnacious, I'm not denying it.'

'Who? Who told him?'

'I don't know. I didn't ask. That would be prying.'

'Often fighting, is he?'

'No.'

'Was there a woman involved? Margaret Aickman perhaps?'

'I don't know.'

'Then why's he pugnacious?'

'I don't know,' Gaunt said, torn once more between suspicion and a native passion for communication. 'Why are you then for that matter?' he muttered, venturing aggression, but Turner ignored him.

'That's right. Never pry. Never tell on a friend. God wouldn't like it. I admire a man who sticks to his principles.'

'I don't care what he's done,' Gaunt continued, gathering courage as he went. 'He wasn't a bad man. He was a bit sharp maybe, but so he would be, being continental, we all know that.' He pointed to the desk and the open drawers. 'But he wasn't bad like this.'

'No one is. Know that? No one's ever this bad. That's what mercy's about. We're all lovely people, really. There's a hymn about that, isn't there? One of the hymns he used to play, and you and I used to sing, Gaunt, before we grew up and got elegant. That's a lovely thing about hymns: we never forget them, do we. Like limericks. God knew a thing or two when he invented rhyme I will say. What did he learn when he was a kid, tell me that? What did Leo learn on his uncle's knee, eh?'

'He could speak Italian,' Gaunt said suddenly, as if it were a trump card he had been holding back.

'He could, could he?'

'And he learnt it in England. At the Farm School. The other kids wouldn't speak to him, see, him being German, so he used to go out on a bicycle and talk to the Italian prisoners of war. And he's never forgotten it, never. He's got a lovely memory, I tell you. Never forgets a word you say to him, I'm sure.'

'Wonderful.'

'A real brain he could have been, if he'd had your advantages.'

Turner looked at him blankly. 'Who the hell says I've got any advantages?'

He had opened another drawer; it was filled with the small junk of any private life in any office: a stapler, pencils, elastic bands, foreign coins and used railway tickets.

'How often was choir, Gaunt? Once a week, was it? You'd have a nice sing-song and a prayer and afterwards you'd slip out and have a beer down the road, and he'd tell you all about himself. Then there was outings, I suppose. Coach trips, I expect. That's what we like, isn't it, you and I? Something corporate but spiritual. Coaches, institutions, choirs. And Leo came along, did he? Got to know everyone, hear their little confidences, hold their little hands. Quite the entertainer he must have been by the sound of it.'

All the while they spoke, he continued to record items in his notebook: sewing materials, a packet of needles, pills of different colours and descriptions. Fascinated despite himself, Gaunt drew nearer.

'Well not only that, see. Only I live on the top floor, there's a flat up there: it should have been Macmullen's but he can't occupy, him having too many children, they couldn't have *them* running wild up there now, could they? We practised in the Assembly Room first, Fridays, see, that's on the other side of the lobby next to the pay office, and then he'd come on up after, for a cup of tea, like. Well, you know, I had a few cups here too for that matter; quite a joy to pay back it was, after all he done for us; things he bought for us and that. He loved a cup of tea,' said Gaunt simply. 'He loved a fire too. I always had that feeling, he loved a family, him not having one.'

'He told you that, did he? He told you he'd no family?'

'No.'

'Then how do you know?'

'It was too evident to be talked about, really. He'd no education either; dragged up really, you could tell.'

Turner had found a bottle of long yellow pills and he was shaking them into the palm of his hand, sniffing cautiously at them.

'And that's been going on for years, has it? Cosy chats after practice?'

'Oh no. He didn't hardly notice me really, not till a few months ago and I didn't like to press him at all, him being a dip, see. It's only recently he took the interest. Same as Exiles.'

'Exiles?'

'Motoring Club.'

'How recent? When did he take you up?'

'New Year,' Gaunt said, now very puzzled. 'Yes. Since January I'd say. He seems to have had a change of heart January.'

'This January?'

'That's right,' Gaunt said, as if he were seeing it for the first time. 'Late January. Since he started with Arthur, really. Arthur's had a *great* influence on Leo. Made him more *contemplative*, you know. More the meditating kind. A great improvement, I'd say. And my wife agrees, you know.'

'I'll bet. How else did he change?'

'That's it really. More reflective.'

'Since January when he took you up. Bang: in comes the New Year and Leo's reflective.'

'Well, steadier. Like he was ill. We did wonder, you know. I said to my wife' – Gaunt lowered his voice in reverence at the notion – 'I wouldn't be surprised if the doctor hadn't warned him.'

Turner was looking at the map again, first directly and then sideways, noting the pin-holes of vanished units. In an old bookcase lay a heap of census reports, press cuttings and magazines. Kneeling, he began working through them.

'What else did you talk about?'

'Nothing serious.'

'Just politics?'

'I like serious conversation myself,' Gaunt said. 'But I didn't somehow fancy it with him, you didn't quite know where it would end.'

'Lost his temper, did he?'

The cuttings referred to the Movement. The census reports concerned the rise of public support for Karfeld.

'He was too gentle. Like a woman in that way; you could disappoint him dreadfully; just a word would do it. Vulnerable he was. *And* quiet. That's what I did never understand about Cologne, see. I said to my wife, well I don't know I'm sure, but if Leo started that fight, it was the devil got hold of him. But he had *seen* a lot, hadn't he?'

Turner had come upon a photograph of students rioting in Berlin. Two boys were holding an old man by the arms and a third was slapping him with the back of his hand. His fingers were turned upwards, and the light divided the knuckles like a sculpture. A line had been drawn round the frame in red ball point.

'I mean you never knew when you were being *personal*, like,' Gaunt continued, 'Touching him too near. I used to think sometimes, I said to my wife as a matter of fact, she was never quite at home with him herself, I said, "Well, I wouldn't like to have his dreams."'

Turner stood up. 'What dreams?'

'Just dreams. Things he's seen, I suppose. They say he saw a lot, don't they? All the atrocities.'

'Who does?'

'Talkers. One of the drivers, I think. Marcus. He's gone now. He had a turn with him up there in Hamburg in forty-six or that. Shocking.'

Turner had opened an old copy of *Stern* which lay on the bookcase. Large photographs of the Bremen riots covered both pages. There was a picture of Karfeld speaking from a high wooden platform; young men shouted in ecstasy.

'I think that bothered him you know,' Gaunt continued, looking over his shoulder. 'He spoke a lot about Fascism off and on.'

'Did he though?' Turner asked softly, 'Tell us about that, Gaunt. I'm interested in talk like that.'

'Well, just sometimes.' Gaunt sounded nervous. 'He could get very worked up about that. It could happen again, he said, and the West would just stand by; and the bankers all put in a bit, and that would be it. He said Socialist and Conservative, it didn't have no meaning any more, not when all the decisions were made in Zurich or Washington. You could see that, he said, from recent events. Well it was true really, I had to admit.'

For a moment, the whole sound-track stopped: the traffic, the machines, the voices, and Turner heard nothing but the beating of his own heart.

'What was the remedy then?' he asked sofly.

'He didn't have one.'

'Personal action for instance?'

'He didn't say so.'

'God?'

'No, he wasn't a believer. Not truly, in his heart.'

'Conscience?'

'I told you. He didn't say.'

'He never suggested you might put the balance right? You and he together?'

'He wasn't *like* that,' Gaunt said impatiently. 'He didn't fancy company. Not when it came to . . . well, to his own *matters*, see.'

'Why didn't your wife fancy him?'

Gaunt hesitated.

'She liked to keep close to me when he was around, that's all. Nothing he ever said or did, mind; but she just liked to keep close.' He smiled indulgently. 'You know how they are,' he said. 'Very *natural*.'

'Did he stay long? Did he sit and talk for hours at a time? About nothing? Ogling your wife?'

'Don't say that,' Gaunt snapped.

Abandoning the desk, Turner opened the cupboard again and noted the printed number on the soles of the rubber overshoes.

'Besides he didn't stay long. He liked to go off and work night times, didn't he? Recently I mean. In Registry and that. He said to me: "John," he said, "I like to make my contribution." And he did. He was proud of his work these last months. It was beautiful; wonderful to see, really. Work half the night sometimes, wouldn't he? All night, even.'

Turner's pale, pale eyes rested on Gaunt's dark face.

'Would he?'

He dropped the shoes back into the cupboard and they clattered absurdly in the silence.

'Well he'd a lot to do, you know; a great lot. Loaded with responsibilities, Leo is. A fine man, really. Too good for this floor; that's what I say.'

'And that's what happened every Friday night since January. After choir. He'd come up and have a nice cup of tea and a chat, hang about till the place was quiet, then slip off and work in Registry?'

'Regular as clockwork. Come in prepared, he would. Choir practice first, then up for a cup of tea till the rest had cleared out like, then down to Registry. "John," he'd say. "I can't work when there's bustle, I can't stand it, I love peace and quiet to be truthful. I'm not as young as I was and that's a fact." Had a bag with him, all ready. Thermos, maybe a sandwich. Very efficient man, he was; handy.'

'Sign the night book, did he?'

Gaunt faltered, waking at long last to the full menace in that quiet, destructive monotone. Turner slammed together the wooden doors of the cupboard. 'Or didn't you bloody well bother? Well, not right really, is it? You can't come over all official, not to a guest. A dip too, at that, a dip who graced your parlour. Let him come and go as he pleased in the middle of the bloody night, didn't you? Wouldn't have been respectful to check up at all, would it? One of the family really, wasn't he? Pity to spoil it with formalities. Wouldn't be Christian, that wouldn't. No idea what time he left the building, I suppose? Two o'clock, four o'clock?'

Gaunt had to keep very still to catch the words, they were so softly spoken.

'It's nothing *bad*, is it?' he asked.

'And that bag of his,' Turner continued in the same terribly low key. 'It wouldn't have been proper to look inside, I suppose? Open the thermos, for instance. The Lord wouldn't fancy that, would he? Don't you worry, Gaunt, it's nothing bad. Nothing that a prayer and a cup of tea won't cure.' He was at the door and Gaunt had to watch him. 'You were just playing happy families, weren't you; letting him stroke your leg to make you feel good.' His voice picked up the Welsh intonation and lampooned it cruelly. "Look how virtuous we are. ... How much in love ... Look how grand, having the dips in. ... Salt of the earth, we are. ... Always something on the hod. ... And sorry you can't have her, but that's my privilege." Well, you've bought it, Gaunt, the whole book. A guard they called you: he'd have charmed you into bed for half-a-crown.' He pushed open the door. 'He's on compassionate leave, and don't you forget it or you'll be in hotter water than you are already.'

'That may be the world you've come from,' Gaunt said suddenly, staring at him as if in revelation, 'But it isn't mine, Mr Turner, so don't come taking it out of me, see. I did my best by Leo and I would again, and I don't know what's all twisted in your mind. Poison, that's what it is: poison.'

'Go to hell.' Turner tossed him the keys, and Gaunt let them fall at his feet.

'If there's something else you know about him, some other gorgeous bit of gossip, you'd better tell me now. Fast. Well?'

Gaunt shook his head. 'Go away.'

'What else do the talkers say? A bit of fluff in the choir was there, Gaunt? You can tell me, I won't eat you.'

'I never heard.'

'What did Bradfield think of him?'

'How should I know? Ask Bradfield.'

'Did he like him?'

Gaunt's face had darkened with disapproval.

'I've no occasion to say,' he snapped. 'I don't gossip about my superiors.'

'Who's Praschko? Praschko a name to you?'

'There's nothing else. I don't know.'

Turner pointed at the small pile of Leo's possessions on the desk. 'Take those up to the cypher room. I'll need them later. And the press cuttings. Give them to the clerk and make him sign for them, understand? Whether you fancy him or not. And make a list of everything that's missing. Everything he's taken home.'

He did not go immediately to Meadowes, but went outside and stood on the grass verge beside the car park. A veil of mist hung over the barren field and the traffic stormed like an angry sea. The Red Cross building was dark with scaffolding and capped by an orange crane: an oil rig anchored to the tarmac. The policemen watched him curiously, for he remained quite still and his eyes seemed to be trained upon the horizon, though the horizon was obscure. At last – it might have been in response to a command they did not hear – he turned and walked slowly back to the front steps.

'You ought to get a proper pass,' the weasel-faced sergeant said, 'Coming in and out all day.'

Registry smelt of dust and sealing wax and printer's ink. Meadowes was waiting for him. He looked haggard and deeply tired. He did not move as Turner came towards him, pushing his way between the desks and files, but watched him dully and with contempt.

'Why did they have to send you?' he asked. 'Haven't they got anyone else? Who are you going to wreck this time?'

6
The Memory Man

They stood in a small sanctum, a steel-lined tank which served both as a strong-room and an office. The windows were barred twice over, once with fine mesh and once with steel rods. From the adjoining room came the constant shuffle of feet and paper. Meadowes wore a black suit. The edges of the lapels were studded with pins. Steel lockers like sentinels stood along the walls, each with a stencilled number and a combination lock.

'Of all the people I swore I'd never see again—'

'Turner was at the top of the list. All right. All right, you're not the only one. Let's get it over, shall we?'

They sat down.

'She doesn't know you're here,' said Meadowes. 'I'm not going to tell her you're here.'

'All right.'

'He met her a few times; there was nothing between them.'

'I'll keep away from her.'

'Yes,' said Meadowes. He did not speak to Turner, but past him, at the lockers. 'Yes, you must.'

'Try and forget it's me,' Turner said. 'Take your time.' For a moment his expression seemed to yield, as the shadows formed upon his plain complexion, until in its way his face was as old as Meadowes', and as weary.

'I'll tell it you once,' Meadowes said, 'And that's all. I'll tell you all I know, and then you clear out.'

Turner nodded.

'It began with the Exiles Motoring Club,' Meadowes said. 'That's how I met him really. I like cars, always have done. I'd bought a Rover, Three Litre, for retirement—'

'How long have you been here?'

'A year. Yes, a year now.'

'Straight from Warsaw?'

'We did a spell in London in between. Then they sent me here. I was fifty-eight. I'd two more years to run and after Warsaw I reckoned I'd take things quietly. I wanted to look after her, get her right again—'

'All right.'

'I don't go out much as a rule but I joined this club, UK and Commonwealth it is mainly, but decent. I reckoned that would do us nicely: one evening a week, the rallies in the summer, get-togethers in the winter. I could take Myra, see; get her back into things, keep an eye on her. She wanted that herself, in the beginning. She was lost; she wanted company. I'm all she's got.'

'All right,' Turner said.

'They were a good lot when we joined, though it's like any other club, of course, it goes up and down; depends who runs it. Get a good crowd in and you have a lot of fun; get a bad crowd, there's jiving and all the rest.'

'And Harting was big there, was he?'

'You let me go at my own speed, right?' Meadowes' manner was firm and disapproving: a father corrects his son. 'No. He was not big there, not at that time. He was a member there, that's all, just a member. I shouldn't think he showed up, not once in six meetings. Well he didn't *belong* really. After all he was a diplomat, and the Exiles isn't meant for dips. Mid-November, we have the Annual General Meeting. Haven't you got your black notebook then?'

'November,' Turner said, not moving, 'The AGM. Five months ago.'

'It was a funny sort of do really. Funny atmosphere. Karfeld had been on the go about six weeks and we were all wondering what would happen next,

I think. Freddie Luxton was in the chair and he was just off to Nairobi; Bill Aintree was Social Secretary and they'd warned him for Korea, and the rest of us were in a flutter trying to elect new officers, get through the agenda and fix up the winter outing. That's when Leo pipes up, and in a way that was his first step into Registry.'

Meadowes fell silent. 'I don't know what kind of fool I am,' he said. 'I just don't know.'

Turner waited.

'I tell you: we'd never *heard* of him, not really, not as somebody keen on the Exiles. And he had this reputation you see '

'What reputation?'

'Well, they said he was a bit of a gypsy. Always on the fiddle. There was some story about Cologne. I didn't fancy what I'd heard, to be frank, and I didn't want him mixed up with Myra.'

'What story about Cologne?'

'Hearsay, that's all it is. He was in a fight. A night-club brawl.'

'No details?'

'None.'

'Who else was there?'

'I've no idea. Where was I?'

'The Exiles, AGM.'

'The winter outing. Yes. "Right," says Bill Aintree. "Any suggestions from the floor?" And Leo's on his feet straight away. He was about three chairs down from me. I said to Myra: "Here, what's *he* up to?" Well, Leo had a proposal, he said. For the winter outing. He knew an old man in Königswinter who owned a string of barges, very rich and very fond of the English, he said; quite high in the Anglo-German. And this old fellow had agreed to lend us two barges and two crews to run the whole club up to Koblenz and back. As some kind of *quid pro quo* for a favour the British had done him in the Occupation. Leo always knew people like that,' said Meadowes; and a brief smile of affection illuminated the sadness of his features. 'There'd be covered accommodation, rum and coffee on the way and a big lunch when we got to Koblenz. Leo had worked the whole thing out; he reckoned he could lay it on at twenty-one marks eighty a head including drinks and a present for his friend.' He broke off. 'I can't go any quicker, it's not my way.'

'I didn't say anything.'

'You're pressing all the time, I can feel it,' Meadowes said querulously, and sighed. 'They fell for it, we all did, Committee or not. You know what people are like: if one man knows what he wants ...'

'And he did.'

'I suppose some reckoned he'd got an axe to grind, but no one cared. There was a few of us thought he was taking a cut to be honest, but well, maybe he deserved it. And the price was fair enough any time. Bill Aintree was getting out: *he* didn't care; he proposed it. Freddie Luxton was already packed: *he* didn't care. He seconded. The motion's carried and recorded without a word being said against, and as soon as the meeting's over, Leo comes straight across to me and Myra, smiling his head off. "She'll love that," he says, "Myra will. A nice trip on the river. Take her out of herself." Just as if he'd done it specially for her. I said yes, she would, and bought him a drink. It seemed wrong really, him doing so much and no one else paying him a blind bit of notice, whatever they say about him. I was sorry for him. *And* grateful,' he added simply. 'I still am: we had a lovely outing.'

Again he fell silent, and again Turner waited while the older man wrestled with private conflicts and private perplexities. From the barred window came the tireless throb of Bonn's iron heartbeat: the far thunder of drills and cranes, the moan of vainly galloping cars.

'I thought he was after Myra to be honest,' he said at last. 'I watched out for that, I don't mind admitting. But there wasn't a breath of it, not on either side. Goodness knows, I'm sharp enough on *that* after Warsaw.'

'I believe you.'

'I don't care whether you believe me or not. It's the truth.'

'He had a reputation for that as well, did he?'

'A bit.'

'Who with?'

'I'll go on with the story if you don't mind,' Meadowes said, looking at his hands. 'I'm not going to pass on that kind of muck. Least of all to you. There's more nonsense talked in this place than is good for any of us.'

'I'll find out,' Turner said, his face frozen like a dead man's. 'It'll take me longer, but that needn't worry you.'

'Dreadfully cold, it was,' Meadowes continued. 'Lumps of ice on the water, and beautiful, if that means anything to you. Just like Leo said: rum and coffee for the grown ups, cocoa for the kids, and everyone happy as a cricket. We started from Königswinter and kicked off with a drink at his place before we went aboard, and from the moment we get there, Leo's looking after us. Me and Myra. He'd singled us out and that was it. We might have been the only people there for him. Myra loved it. He put a shawl around her shoulders, told her jokes. ... I hadn't seen her laugh like it since Warsaw. She kept saying to me: "I haven't been so happy for years."'

'What sort of jokes?'

'About himself mainly ... running on. He had a story about Berlin, him shoving a cartload of files across the parade ground in the middle of a cavalry practice, and the sergeant-major on his horse, and Leo down there with the handcart. ... He could do all the voices, Leo could; one minute he was up on his horse, the next minute he's the Guard corporal. ... He could even do the trumpets and that. Wonderful really; wonderful gift. Very entertaining man, Leo ... very.'

He glanced at Turner as if he expected to be contradicted, but Turner's face was without expression. 'On the way back, he takes me aside. "Arthur, a quiet word," he says; that's him, a quiet word. You know the way he talks.'

'No.'

'Confiding. Everyone's special. "Arthur," he says, "Rawley Bradfield's just sent for me; they want me to move up to Registry and give you a hand up there, and before I tell him yes or no, I'd like to hear what *you* feel." Putting it in my hands, you see. If I didn't fancy the idea, he'd head it off; that's what he was hinting at. Well it came as a surprise, I don't mind telling you. I didn't quite know what to think; after all he was a Second Secretary ... it didn't seem right, that was my first reaction. And to be frank I wasn't sure I believed him. So I asked him: "Have you any experience of archives?" Yes, but long ago, he said, though he'd always fancied going back to them.'

'When was that then?'

'When was what?'

'When was he dealing with archives?'

'Berlin I suppose. I never asked. You didn't ask Leo about his background really; you never knew what you might hear.'

Meadowes shook his head. 'So here he was with this suggestion. It didn't seem right, but what could I say? "It's up to Bradfield," I told him. "If he sends you, and you want to come, there's work enough." Well it worried me for a bit to be honest. I even thought of talking to Bradfield about it but I didn't. Best thing is, I thought, let it blow over; I'll probably hear no more of it. For a time that's just what happened. Myra was bad again, there was the leadership crisis at home and the gold row in Brussels. And as for Karfeld, he was going hammer and tongs all over the place. There were deputations out from England, Trade Union protests, old comrades and I don't know what. Registry was a beehive, and Harting went clean out of my mind. He was Social Secretary of the Exiles by then, but otherwise I hardly saw him. I mean he didn't rate. There was too much else to think of.'

'I get it.'

'The next thing I knew was, Bradfield sends for me. It was just before the holiday – about 20th December. First, he asks me how I'm getting along with the Destruction programme. I was a bit put out; we'd really been going it those last months. Destruction was about the last thing anyone had been bothering with.'

'Go carefully now: I want the fat as well as the lean.'

'I said it was hanging fire. Well, he says, how would I feel if he sent me someone to help out with it, come and work in Registry and bring it up to date? There'd been the suggestion, he said, nothing definite, and he wanted to sound me out first, there'd been the suggestion Harting might be able to lend a hand.'

'Whose suggestion?'

'He didn't say.'

It was suddenly upon them; and each in his way was mystified:

'Whoever suggested anything to Bradfield,' Meadowes asked. 'It makes no sense.'

'That's rather what I wondered,' Turner confessed, and the silence returned.

'So you said you'd have him?'

'No, I told him the truth. I said I didn't need him.'

'You didn't *need* him? You told Bradfield that?'

'Don't press me like that. Bradfield knew very well I didn't need anyone. Not for Destruction anyway. I'd been on to Library in London and spoken to them, back in November that was, once the Karfeld panic began. I'd told them I was worried about the programme, I was way behind, could I let it go till the crisis was over? Library told me to forget it.'

Turner stared at him.

'And Bradfield knew that? You're certain Bradfield knew?'

'I'd sent him a minute of the conversation. He never even referred to it. Afterwards I asked that PA of his and she was certain she'd put it up to him.'

'Where is it?' Where's the minute now?'

'Gone. It was a loose minute: it was Bradfield's responsibility whether he preserved it or not. But they'll know about it in Library all right; they were quite surprised later on to find we'd bothered with Destruction at all.'

'Who did you speak to in Library?'

'Once to Maxwell, once to Cowdry.'

'Did you remind Bradfield of that?'

'I began to, but he just cut me off. Closed right down on me. "It's all arranged," he says. "Harting joining you mid-January and he'll manage Personalities and Destruction," So lump it, in other words. "You can forget he's a diplomat," he said. "Treat him as your subordinate. Treat him how you like. But he's coming mid-January and that's a fact." You know how he throws people away. Specially Harting.'

Turner was writing in his notebook but Meadowes paid no attention.

'So that's how he came to me. That's the truth. I didn't want him, I didn't trust him, not completely anyway, and to begin with I suppose I let him know it. We were just too busy: *I* didn't want to waste time breaking in a man like Leo. What was I supposed to do with him?'

A girl brought tea. A brown woolly cosy covered the pot and the cubes of sugar were individually wrapped and stamped with the Naafi's insignia. Turner grinned at her but she ignored him. He could hear someone shouting about Hanover.

'They do say things are bad in England too,' Meadowes said. 'Violence; demonstrations; all the protests. What is it that gets into your generation? What have we *done* to you? That's what I don't understand.'

'We'll start with when he arrived,' Turner said. That's what it would be like, he thought, to have a father you believed in: values for their own sake and a gap as wide as the Atlantic.

'I said to Leo when he came, "Leo, just keep out of the way. Don't get between my feet, and don't go bothering other people." He took it like a lamb. "Right-ho Arthur, whatever you say." I asked him whether he'd got something to get on with. Yes, he said, Personalities would keep him going for a bit.'

'It's like a dream,' Turner said softly looking up at last from his notebook. 'It's a lovely dream. First of all he takes over the Exiles. A one man takeover, real Party tactics; I'll do the dirty work, you go back to sleep. Then he cons you, then he cons Bradfield, and within a couple of months he's got the pick of Registry. How was he? Cocky? I should think he could hardly stand up for laughing.'

'He was quiet. Not cocky at all. Subdued I'd say. Not at all what they told me he was like.'

'Who?'

'Oh ... I don't know. There's a lot didn't like him; there's a lot more were jealous of him.'

'Jealous?'

'Well, he was a diplomat, wasn't he. Even if he was a temporary. They said he'd be running the place in a fortnight, taking ten per cent on the files. You know the way they talk. But he'd changed. They all admitted that, even young Cork and Johnny Slingo. You could almost date it, they said, from when the crisis began. It sobered him down.' Meadowes shook his head as if he hated to see a good man go wrong. 'And he was useful.'

'Don't tell me. He took you by surprise.'

'I don't know how he managed it. He knew nothing about archives, not our kind anyway; and I can't for the life of me see how he got near enough to anyone in Registry to ask; but by mid-February, that Personalities Survey was drafted, signed off and away, and the Destruction programme was back on the rails. We were working all round him: Karfeld, Brussels, the Coalition crisis and the rest of it. And there was Leo, still as a rock, working away at his own bits and pieces. No one told him anything twice, I think that was half the secret. He'd a lovely memory. He'd scrounge a bit of information, tuck it away, and bring it out weeks later when you'd forgotten all about it. I don't think he forgot a word anyone ever said to him. He could listen with his eyes, Leo could.' Meadowes shook his head at the reminiscence: 'The memory man, that's what Johnny Slingo used to call him.'

'Handy. For an archivist of course.'

'You see it all differently,' Meadowes said at last. 'You can't distinguish the good from the bad.'

'You tell me when I go wrong,' Turner replied, writing all the time. 'I'll be grateful for that. Very.'

'Destruction's a weird game,' Meadowes said, in the reflective tone of a man reviewing his own craft. 'To begin with, you'd think it was simple. You select a file, a big one, say a subject file with twenty-five volumes. I'll give you an example: *Disarmament*. There's a real rag-bag. You turn up the back numbers first to check the dates and the material, all right? So what do you find? Industrial dismantling in the Ruhr, 1946; Control Commission policy on the allocation of shotgun licences, 1949. Re-establishment of German military potential, 1950. Some of it's so old you'd laugh. You take a look at the current columns to compare, and what do you find? Warheads for the Bundeswehr. It's a million miles away. All right, you say, let's burn the back papers, they're irrelevant. There's fifteen volumes at least we can chuck out. Who's the desk officer for disarmament? Peter de Lisle: put it up to him:

"Please may we destroy up to nineteen-sixty?" No objection, he says, so you're off.' Meadowes shook his head. 'Only you're not. You're not even half-way to off. You can't just carve off the back ten volumes and shove them in the fire. There's the ledger for a start: who's going to cancel all the entries? There's the card index; that's got to be weeded. Were there treaties? Right: clear with legal department. Is there a military interest? Clear it with the MA. Are there duplicates in London? No. So we all sit back and wait another two months: no destruction of originals without written permission from Library. See what I mean?'

'I get the idea,' said Turner, waiting.

'Then there's all the cross references, the sister files in the same series: will *they* be affected? Should they be destroyed as well? Or should we make up residuals to be on the safe side? Before you know where you are, you're wandering all over Registry, looking in every nook and cranny; there's no end to it once you start; nothing's holy.'

'I should think it suited him down to the ground.'

'There's no *restriction*,' Meadowes observed simply, as if replying to a question. 'It may offend you, but it's the only system I can understand. Anyone can look at anything, that's my rule. Anyone sent up here, I trust them. There's no other way to run the place. I can't go sniffing round asking who's looking at what, can I?' he demanded, ignoring Turner's bewildered gaze.

'He took to it like a duck to water. I was amazed. He was happy, that was the first thing. It tickled him, working in here, and quite soon it tickled me having him. He liked the company.' He broke off. 'The only thing we ever *really* minded,' he said with an unexpected smile, 'was those ruddy cigars he smoked. Javanese Dutch I believe they were. Stank the place out. We used to tease him about them but he wouldn't budge. Still, I think I miss them now.' He continued quietly: 'He'd been out of his depth in Chancery, he's not their sort at all, and the ground floor didn't have much for him either in my opinion, but this place was just right.' He inclined his head towards the closed door. 'It's like a shop in there, sometimes: you have the customers and you have one another. Johnny Slingo, Valerie ... well, they took to him too and that's all there is to it. They were all against him when he came, and they all took to him within a week, and that's the truth of it. He'd got a *way* with him. I know what you're thinking: it flattered my ego, I suppose you'd say. All right, it did. Everyone wants to be liked and he liked us. All right, I'm lonely; Myra's a worry, I've failed as a parent and I never had a son; there was a bit of that about it too, I suppose, although there's only ten years between us. Perhaps it's him being little that makes the difference.'

'Go for the girls, did he?' Turner asked, more to break the uncomfortable silence than because he had been preparing questions in his mind.

'Only banter.'

'Ever hear of a woman called Aickman?'

'No.'

'Margaret Aickman. They were engaged to be married, her and Leo.'

'No.'

Still they did not look at one another.

'He liked the work too,' Meadowes continued. 'In those first weeks. I don't think he'd ever realized till then how much he *knew* by comparison with the rest of us. About Germany, I mean, the *soil* of it.'

He broke off, remembering, and it might have been fifty years ago. 'He knew *that* world too,' he added. 'He knew it inside out.'

'What world?'

'Post-war Germany. The Occupation; the years they don't want to know about any more. He knew it like the back of his hand. "Arthur," he said to me once, "I've seen these towns when they were car parks. I've heard these people talk when even their language was forbidden." It used to knock him clean off course sometimes. I'd catch sight of him deep in a file, still as a mouse, just fascinated. Or he'd look away, look round the room, for someone with a moment to spare, just so he could tell them about something he'd come across: "Here," he'd say. "See that? We disbanded that firm in 1947. Look at it now!" Other times, he'd go right off into a dream, and then you'd lost him altogether; he was on his own. I think it bothered him to *know* so much. It was queer. I think he almost felt guilty sometimes. He went on quite a lot about his memory. "You're making me destroy my childhood," he says one time – we were breaking up some files for the machine – "You're making an old man of me." I said, "If that's what I'm doing you're the luckiest man alive." We had a good laugh about that.'

'Did he ever mention politics?'

'No.'

'What did he say about Karfeld?'

'He was concerned. Naturally. That's why he was so glad to be helping out.'

'Oh sure.'

'It was trust,' Meadowes said defiantly. 'You wouldn't understand that. And that was true, what he said: it *was* the old stuff we were trying to get rid of; it *was* his childhood; it *was* the old stuff that meant the most to him.'

'All right.'

'Listen: I'm not holding any brief for him. He's ruined my career for all I know, what there was left after you finished with it. But I'm telling you: you've got to see the *good* in him too.'

'I'm not arguing with you.'

'It did *bother* him, his memory. I remember once with the music: he got me listening to gramophone records. Mainly so that he could sell them to me, I suppose; he'd worked some deal he was very proud of, with one of the shops in town. "Look," I said. "It's no good Leo; you're wasting your time. I get to know one record so I learn another. By that time I've forgotten the first one." He comes right back at me, very fast: "Then you ought to be a politician, Arthur," he says. "That's what they do." He meant it, believe me.'

Turner grinned suddenly. 'That's quite funny.'

'It would have been,' said Meadowes, 'if he hadn't looked so darned fierce with it. Then another time we're talking about Berlin, something to do with the crisis, and I said, "Well never mind, no one thinks of Berlin any more," which is true really. Files I mean; no one draws the files or bothers with the contingencies; not like they used to, anyway. I mean *politically* it's a dead duck. "No," he says. "We've got the big memory and the small memory. The small memory's to remember the small things and the big memory's to forget the big ones." That's what he said; it touched me, that did. I mean there's a lot of us think that way, you can't help it these days.'

'He came home with you, did he, sometimes? You'd make an evening of it?'

'Now and then. When Myra was out. Sometimes I'd slip over there.'

'Why when Myra was out?' Turner pounced quite hard on that: 'You *still* didn't trust him did you?'

'There's rumours,' Meadowes said evenly. 'There was talk about him. I didn't want her connected.'

'Him and who?'

'Just girls. Girls in general. He was a bachelor and he liked his fun.'

'*Who?*'

Meadowes shook his head, 'You've got it wrong,' he said. He was playing with a couple of paper clips, trying to make them interlock.

'Did he ever talk about England in the war? About an uncle in Hampstead?'

'He told me once he arrived at Dover with a label round his neck. That wasn't usual either.'

'What wasn't—'

'Him talking about himself. Johnny Slingo said he'd known him four years before he came to Registry and he'd never got a word out of him. He was all opened up, that's what Johnny said, it must be old age setting in.'

'Go on.'

'Well that was all he had, a label: Harting Leo. They shaved his head and deloused him and sent him to a Farm School. He was allowed to choose apparently: domestic science or agriculture. He chose agriculture because he wanted to own land. It seemed daft to me, Leo wanting to be a farmer, but there it is.'

'Nothing about Communists? A left-wing group of kids in Hampstead? Nothing like that at all?'

'Nothing.'

'Would you tell me if there was something?'

'I doubt it.'

'Did he ever mention a man called Praschko? In the Bundestag.'

Meadowes hesitated. 'He said one night that Praschko had walked out on him.'

'How? Walked out *how*?'

'He wouldn't say. He said they'd emigrated to England together, and returned here together after the war; Praschko had chosen one path and Leo had chosen another.' He shrugged. 'I didn't press him. Why should I? After that night he never mentioned him again.'

'All that talk about his *memory*: what do you think he had in mind?'

'Something historical, I suppose. He thought a lot about history, Leo did. Mind you, that's a couple of months back now.'

'What difference does that make?'

'That was before he went on his track.'

'His what?'

'He went on a track,' Meadowes said simply. 'That's what I'm trying to tell you.'

'I want to hear about the missing files,' Turner said. 'I want to check the ledgers and the mail.'

'You'll wait your turn. There's some things that aren't just *facts*, and if you'll only pay attention you'll maybe hear about them. You're like Leo, you are: always wanting the answer before you've even heard the question. What I'm trying to tell you is, I knew from the day he came here that he was looking for something. We all did. You felt it with Leo. You felt he was looking for something. Well we all are in a way, but Leo was looking for something real. Something you could almost touch, it meant so much to him. That's rare in this place, believe me.'

It was a whole life which Meadowes seemed to draw upon.

'An archivist is like an historian; he has time-periods he's faddy about; places, Kings and Queens. All the files here are related, they're bound to be. Give me any file from next door; any file you want, I could trace you a path clean through the whole Registry, from Icelandic shipping rights to the latest guidance on gold prices. That's the fascination of files; there's nowhere to stop.'

Meadowes ran on. Turner studied the grey parental face, the grey eyes clouded with concern, and he felt the dawning of excitement.

'You think you run an archive,' Meadowes said. 'You don't. It runs you. There's qualities to an archive that just get you, and there's not a thing you can do about it. Take Johnny Slingo now. You saw him as you came in, on the left there, the old fellow in the jacket. He's the intellectual type, college and all the rest. Johnny's only been at it a year, came to us from Admin as a matter of fact, but he's stuck with the nine-nine fours: Federal Germany's relations with Third parties. He could sit where you are and recite the date and place of every single negotiation there's ever been about the Hallstein Doctrine. Or take my case, I'm mechanical. I like cars, inventions, all that world. I reckon I know more about German infringement of patent rights than any desk officer in Commercial Section.'

'What was Leo's track?'

'Wait. It's important what I'm telling. I've spent a lot of time thinking about it in the last twenty-four hours, and you're going to hear it *right*, whether you like it or not. The files get hold of you; you can't help it. They'd rule your life if you ever let them. They're wife and child to some men, I've seen it happen. And times they just *take* you, and then you're on a track and you can't get off it; and that's what they did to Leo. I don't know how it happens. A paper catches your eye, something silly: a threatened strike of sugar-workers in Surabaya, that's our favourite joke at the moment. "Hullo," you say to yourself, "Why hasn't Mr So-and-So signed that off?" You check back: Mr So-and-So never saw it. He never read the telegram at all. Well he must see it then, mustn't he? Only it all happened three years ago, and Mr so-and-So is Ambassador in Paris. So you start trying to find out what action was taken, or wasn't taken. Who was consulted? Why didn't they inform Washington? You chase the cross references, draw the original material. By then it's too late; you've lost your sense of proportion; you're away, and by the time you shake yourself out of it you're ten days older and none the wiser, but maybe you're safe again for a couple of years. Obsession, that's what it is. A private journey. It happens to all of us. It's the way we're made.'

'And it happened to Leo?'

'Yes. Yes, it happened to Leo. Only from the first day he came here, I had that feeling he was ... well, that he was waiting. Just the way he looked, the way he handled paper ... Always peering over the hedge. I'd glance up and catch sight of him and there was those little brown eyes looking all the time. I know you'll say I'm fanciful; I don't care. I didn't make a lot of it, why should I? We all have problems, and besides it was like a factory in here by then. But it's true all the same. I've thought about it and it's true. It was nothing much to begin with; I just noticed it. Then gradually he got on his track.'

A bell rang suddenly; a long, assertive peal up and down the corridors. They heard the slamming of doors and the sound of running feet. A girl was calling: 'Where's Valerie, where's Valerie?'

'Fire practice,' Meadowes said. 'We're running to two or three a week at present. Don't worry. Registry's exempt.'

Turner sat down. He looked even paler than before. He ran a big hand through his tufted, fair hair.

'I'm listening,' he said.

'Ever since March now he's been working on a big project: all the seven-o-sevens. That's Statutes. There's about two hundred of them or more, and mainly to do with the handover when the Occupation ended. Terms of withdrawal, residual rights, rights of evocation, phases of autonomy and God knows what. All forty-nine to fifty-five stuff, not relevant here at all. He might have started in half a dozen places on the Destruction, but the moment he saw the seven-o-sevens, they were the ones for him. "Here," he said. "That's just right for me Arthur, I can cut my mild teeth on them. I know what they're talking about; it's familiar ground." I shouldn't think anyone had looked at it for fifteen years. But *tricky*, even if it was obsolete. Full of technical talk. Surprising what Leo knew, mind. All the terms, German and English, all the legal phrases.' Meadowes shook his head in admiration. 'I saw a minute of his go to the Legal Attaché, a résumé of a file; *I* couldn't have put it together I'm sure, and I doubt whether there's anyone in Chancery could either. All about the Prussian Criminal Code and regional sovereignty of justice. And half of it in German, too.'

'He knew more than he was prepared to let on: is that what you're saying?'

'No it's not,' said Meadowes. 'And don't you go putting words into my mouth. He was being *used*, that's what I mean; he had a lot of knowledge in him that he hadn't done anything with for a long time. All of a sudden, he could put it to work.'

Meadowes resumed: 'With the seven-o-sevens there wasn't any real question of *destruction*: more of sending it back to London and getting it stored out of the way, but it all had to be read and submitted the same as everything else, and he'd been getting very deep in it these last few weeks. I told you he was quiet up here; well he was. And once he got tucked into the Statutes he got quieter and quieter. He was on a track.'

'When did this happen?'

At the back of Turner's notebook there was a diary; he had it open before him.

'Three weeks ago. He went further and further *in*. Still jolly, mind; still bouncing up and down to get the girls a chair or help them with a parcel. But something had got hold of him, and it meant a lot to him. Still quizzy: no one will ever cure him of that: he had to know exactly what each of us was up to. But subdued. And he got worse. More and more thoughtful; more and more *serious*. Then on Monday, last Monday, he changed.'

'A week ago today,' said Turner, 'The fifth.'

'Seven days. Is that all? My God.' There was a sudden smell of hot wax from next door, and the muffled thud of a large seal being pressed on to a packet.

'That'll be the two o'clock bag they're getting ready,' he muttered inconsequentially, and glanced at his silver pocket watch. 'It's due down there at twelve thirty.'

'I'll come back after lunch if you like.'

'I'd rather be done with you before,' Meadowes said. 'If you don't mind.' He put the watch away. 'Where is he? Do *you* know? What's happened to him? He's gone to Russia, is that it?'

'Is that what you think?'

'He might have gone anywhere, you couldn't tell. He wasn't like us. He tried to be, but he wasn't. More like you, I suppose, in some ways. Perverse. Always busy but always doing things back to front. Nothing was simple, I reckon that was his trouble. Too much childhood. Or none. It comes to the same thing really. I like people to grow *slowly*.'

'Tell me about last Monday. He changed: how?'

'Changed for the better. He'd shaken himself out of it, whatever it was. The track was over. He was smiling when I came in, really happy. Johnny Slingo, Valerie, they both noticed it, same as I did. We'd all been going full tilt of course: I'd been in most of Saturday, all Saturday; the others had been coming and going.'

'What about Leo?'

'Well, he'd been busy too, there was no doubt to that, but we didn't see him around an awful lot. An hour up here, three hours down there—'

'Down where?'

'In his own room. He did that sometimes, took a few files downstairs to work on. It was quieter. "I like to keep it warm." he said. "It's my old room, Arthur, and I don't like to let it grow cold."'

'And he took his files down there, did he?' Turner asked, very quiet.

'Then there was Chapel: that took up a part of Sunday, of course. Playing the organ.'

'How long's he been doing that, by the way?'

'Oh, years and years. It was reinsurance,' Meadowes said with a little laugh. 'Just to keep himself indispensable.'

'So Monday he was happy.'

'Serene. There's no other word for it. "I like it here, Arthur," he said. "I want you to know that." Sat down and got on with his work.'

'And he stayed that way till he left?'

'More or less.'

'What do you mean, "More or less"?'

'Well, we had a bit of a row. That was Wednesday. He'd been all right Tuesday, happy as a sandboy, then Wednesday I caught him at it.' He had folded his hands before him on his lap and he was looking at them, head bowed.

'He was trying to look at the Green File. The Maximum Limit.' He touched the top of his head in a small gesture of nervousness. 'He was always quizzy, I told you. Some people are like that, they can't help it. Didn't matter what it was; I could leave a letter from my own mother on the desk: I'm damn sure that if Leo had half a chance he'd have read it. Always though people were conspiring against him. It drove us mad to begin with; look in anything, he would. Files, cupboards, anywhere. He hadn't been here a week before he was signing for the mail. The whole lot, down in the bagroom. I didn't care for that at all at first, but he got all huffy when I told him to stop and in the end I let it go.' He opened his hands, seeking an answer. 'Then in March we had some Trade Contingency papers from London – special guidance for Econ on new alignments and forward planning, and I caught him with the whole bundle on his desk. "Here," I said. "Can't you read? They're subscription only, they're not for you." He didn't turn a hair. In fact he was really angry. "I thought I could handle anything!" he says. He'd have hit me for two pins. "Well you thought wrong," I told him. That was March. It took us both a couple of days to cool down.'

'God save us,' said Turner softly.

'Then we had this Green. A Green's rare. *I* don't know what's in it; Johnny doesn't, Valerie doesn't. It lives in its own despatch box. H.E.'s got one key, Bradfield's got the other and he shares it with de Lisle. The box has to come back here to the strong-room every night. It's signed in and signed out, and only I handle it. So anyway: lunchtime Wednesday it was. Leo was up here on his own; Johnny and me went down to the canteen.'

'Often here on his own lunchtimes, was he?'

'He liked to be, yes. He liked the quiet.'

'All right.'

'There was a big queue at the canteen and I can't stand queuing, so I said to Johnny, "You stay here, I'll go back and do a spot of work and try again in half an hour." So I came in unexpectedly. Just walked in. No Leo, and the strong-room was open. And there he was; standing there, with the Green despatch box.'

'What do you mean, *with* it?'

'Just holding it. Looking at the lock as far as I could make out. Just curious. He smiled when he saw me, cool as anything. He's sharp, I've told you that. "Arthur," he says, "you've caught me at it, you've discovered my guilty secret." I said, "What the hell are you up to? Look what you've got there in your hands!" Like that. "You know me," he says, very disarming. "I just can't help it." He puts down the box. "I was *actually* looking for some seven-o-sevens, you don't happen to have seen them anywhere, do you? For March and February fifty-eight." Something like that.'

'So then what?'

'I read him the Riot Act. What else could I do? I said I'd report him to Bradfield, the lot. I was furious.'

'But you didn't?'

'No.'

'Why not?'

'You wouldn't understand,' Meadowes said at last. 'You think I'm soft in the head, I know. It was Myra's birthday Friday; we were having a special do at the Exiles. Leo had choir practice and a dinner party.'

'Dinner party? Where?'

'He didn't say.'

'There's nothing in his diary.'

'That's not my concern.'

'Go on.'

'He promised to drop in sometime during the evening and give her her present. It was going to be a hair-dryer; we'd chosen it together.' He shook his head again. 'How can I explain it? I've told you: I felt responsible for him. He was that kind of bloke. You and I could blow him over with one puff if we wanted.'

Turner gazed at him incredulously.

'And I suppose there was something else too.' He looked Turner full in the face. 'If I tell Bradfield, that's it. Leo's had it. There's nowhere for him to go, is there? See what I mean. Like now, for instance: I mean I hope he *has* gone to Moscow, because there's nowhere else going to take him.'

'You mean you suspected him?'

'I suppose so, yes. Deep down I suppose I did. Warsaw's done that for me, you know. I'd like Myra to have settled there. With her student. All right, they put him up to it; they made him seduce her. But he did say he'd marry her, didn't he? For the baby. I'd have loved that baby more than I can say. That's what you took away from me. From her as well. That's what it was all about. You shouldn't have done that you know.'

He was grateful for the traffic then, for any noise to fill that damned tank and take away the accusing echo of Meadowes' flat voice.

'And on Thursday the box disappeared?'

Meadowes shrugged it away. 'Private Office returned it Thursday midday. I signed it in myself and left it in the strong-room. Friday it wasn't there. That was that.'

He paused.

'I should have reported it at once. I should have gone running to Bradfield Friday afternoon when I noticed. I didn't. I slept on it. I brooded about it all Saturday. I chewed Cork's head off, went for Johnny Slingo, made their lives hell. It was driving me mad. I didn't want to raise a hare. We'd lost all manner of things in the crisis. People get light-fingered. Someone's pinched our trolley, I don't know who: one of the Military Attachés' clerks, that's my guess. Someone else has lifted our swivel chair. There's a long-carriage typewriter from the Pool; diaries, all sorts, cups from the Naafi even. Anyway, those were the excuses. I thought one of the users might have taken it: de Lisle, Private Office . . .'

'Did you ask Leo?'

'He'd gone by then, hadn't he?'

Once more Turner had slipped into the routine of interrogation.

'He carried a briefcase, didn't he?'

'Yes.'

'Was he allowed to bring it in here?'

'He brought in sandwiches and a thermos.'

'So he was allowed?'

'Yes.'

'Did he have the briefcase Thursday?'

'I think so. Yes, he would have done.'

'Was it big enough to hold the despatch box?'

'Yes.'

'Did he have lunch in here Thursday?'

'He went out at about twelve.'

'And came back?'

'I told you: Thursday's his special day. Conference day. It's a left-over from his old job. He goes to one of the Ministries in Bad Godesberg. Something to do with outstanding claims. Last Thursday he had a lunch date first I suppose. Then went on to the meeting.'

'Has he always been to that meeting? Every Thursday?'

'Ever since he came into Registry.'

'He had a key, didn't he?'

'What for? Key to where?'

Turner was on unsure ground. 'To let himself in and out of Registry. Or he knew the combination.'

Meadowes actually laughed.

'There's me and Head of Chancery knows how to get in and out of here, and no one else. There's three combinations and half a dozen burglar switches and there's the strong-room as well. Not Slingo, not de Lisle, *no one* knows. Just us two.'

Turner was writing fast.

'Tell me what else is missing,' he said at last.

Meadowes unlocked a drawer of his desk and drew out a list of references. His movements were brisk and surprisingly confident.

'Bradfield didn't tell you?'

'No.'

Meadowes handed him the list. 'You can keep that. There's forty-three of them. They're all box files, they've all disappeared since March.'

'Since he went on the track.'

'The security classifications vary from Confidential to Top Secret, but the majority are plain Secret. There's Organization files, Conference, Personality and two Treaty files. The subjects range from the dismantling of chemical concerns in the Ruhr in 1947 to minutes of unofficial Anglo-German exchanges at working level over the last three years. Plus the Green and that's Formal and Informal Conversations—'

'Bradfield told me.'

'They're like pieces, believe me, pieces in a puzzle ... that's what I thought at first ... I've moved them round in my mind. Hour after hour. I haven't slept. Now and then—' he broke off. 'Now and then I thought I had an idea, a sort of picture, a half picture, I'd say ...' Stubbornly he concluded:

'There's no clear pattern to it, and no reason. Some are marked out by Leo to different people; some are marked 'certified for destruction' but most are just plain missing. You can't tell, you see. You can't keep tabs, it's impossible. Until someone *asks* for the file you don't know you haven't got it.'

'*Box* files?'

'I told you. All forty-three. They weigh a couple of hundred weights between them I should think.'

'And the letters? There are letters missing too.'

'Yes,' Meadowes said reluctantly. 'We're short of thirty-three incoming letters.'

'Never entered, were they? Just lying about for anyone to pick up? What were the subjects? You haven't put it down.'

'We don't know. That's the truth. They're letters from German Departments. We know the references because the Bag Room's written them in the log. They never reached Registry.'

'But you've checked the references?'

Very stiffly Meadowes said: 'The missing letters belong on the missing files.

The references are the same. That's all we can tell. As they're from German Departments, Bradfield has ruled that we do not ask for duplicates until the Brussels decision is through: in case our curiosity alerts them to Harting's absence.'

Having returned his black notebook to his pocket, Turner rose and went to the barred window, touching the locks, testing the strength of the wire mesh.

'There was something about him. He was special. Something *made* you watch him.'

From the carriageway they heard the two-tone wail of an emergency horn approach and fade again.

'He was special,' Turner repeated. 'All the time you've been talking, I've heard it. Leo this, Leo that. You had your eye on him; you *felt* him, I know you did. Why?'

'There was nothing.'

'What were these rumours? What was it they said about him that frightened you? Was he somebody's fancy-boy, Arthur? Something for Johnny Slingo, was he, in his old age? Working the queer's circuit was he, is that what all the blushing's for?'

Meadowes shook his head. 'You've lost your sting,' he said. 'You can't frighten me any more. I know you; I know your worst. It's nothing to do with Warsaw. He wasn't that kind. I'm not a child and Johnny's not a homosexual either.'

Turner continued to stare at him. 'There's something you heard. Something you knew. You watched him, I know you did. You watched him cross a room; how he stood, how he reached for a file. He was doing the silliest bloody job in Registry and you talk about him as if he was the Ambassador. There was chaos in here, you said so yourself. Everyone except Leo chasing files, making up, entering, connecting, all standing on your heads to keep the ball rolling in a crisis. And what was Leo doing? Leo was on Destruction. He could have been making flax for all his work mattered. You said so, not me. So what *was* it about him? *Why* did you watch him?'

'You're dreaming. You're twisted and you can't see anything straight. But if by any chance you were right, I wouldn't even whisper it to you on my deathbed.'

A notice outside the cypher room said: 'Back at two fifteen. Phone 333 for emergencies.' He banged on Bradfield's door and tried the handle; it was locked. He went to the banister and looked angrily down into the lobby. At the front desk a young Chancery Guard was reading a learned book on engineering. He could see the diagrams on the right-hand page. In the glass-fronted waiting-room, the Ghanaian Chargé in a velvet collar was staring thoughtfully at a photograph of Clydeside taken from very high up.

'All at lunch, old boy,' a voice whispered from behind him.

'Not a Hun will stir till three. Daily truce. Show must go on.' A hanging, vulpine figure stood among the fire extinguishers. 'Crabbe,' he explained, 'Mickie Crabbe, you see,' as if the name itself were an excuse. 'Peter de

Lisle's just back, if you don't mind. Been down at the Ministry of the Interior, saving women and children. Rawley's sent him to feed you.'

'I want to send a telegram. Where's room three double three?'

'Proles' rest room, old boy. They're having a bit of a kip after all the hoohah. Troubled times. Give it a break,' he suggested. 'If it's urgent it'll keep, if it's important it's too late, that's what I say.' Saying it, Crabbe led him along the silent corridor like a decrepit courtier lighting him to bed. Passing the lift, Turner paused and stared at it once more. It was firmly padlocked and the notice said 'Out of order.'

Jobs are separate, he told himself, why worry, for God's sake? Bonn is not Warsaw. Warsaw was a hundred years ago. Bonn is today. We do what we have to do and move on. He saw it again, the Rococo room in the Warsaw Embassy, the chandelier dark with dust, and Myra Meadowes alone on the daft sofa. 'Another time they post you to an Iron Curtain country,' Turner was shouting, 'you bloody well choose your lovers with more care!'

Tell her I'm leaving the country, he thought; I've gone to find a traitor. A full-grown, four-square, red-toothed, paid-up traitor.

Come on, Leo, we're of one blood, you and I: underground men, that's us. I'll chase you through the sewers, Leo; that's why I smell so lovely. We've got the earth's dirt on us, you and I. I'll chase you, you chase me and each of us will chase ourselves.

7
de Lisle

The American Club was not as heavily guarded as the Embassy. 'It's no one's gastronomic dream,' de Lisle explained, as he showed his papers to the GI at the door, 'but it does have a gorgeous swimming-pool.' He had booked a window table overlooking the Rhine. Fresh from their bathe, they drank Martinis and watched the giant brown helicopters wavering past them towards the landing-strip up river. Some were marked with red crosses, others had no markings at all. Now and then white passenger ships, sliding through the mist, bore huddled groups of tourists towards the land of the Nibelungs; the boom of their own loudspeakers followed them like small thunder. Once a crowd of schoolchildren passed, and they heard the strains of the Lorelei banged out on an accordion, and the devoted accompaniment of a heavenly, if imperfect choir. The seven hills of Königswinter were much nearer now, though the mist confused their outline.

With elaborate diffidence de Lisle pointed out the Petersberg, a regular wooded cone capped by a rectangular hotel. Neville Chamberlain had stayed there in the thirties, he explained: 'That was when he gave away Czechoslovakia, of course. The first time, I mean.' After the war it had been the seat of the Allied High Commission; more recently the Queen had used it for her State Visit. To the right of it was the Drachenfels, where Siegfried had slain the dragon and bathed in its magic blood.

'Where's Harting's house?'

'You can't quite see it,' de Lisle said quietly, not pointing any more. 'It's at the foot of the Petersberg. He lives, so to speak, in Chamberlain's shadow.' And with that he led the conversation into more general fields.

'I suppose the trouble with being a visiting fireman is that you so often arrive on the scene after the fire's gone out. Is that it?'

'Did he come here often?'

'The smaller Embassies hold receptions here; if their drawing-rooms aren't big enough. That was rather his mark, of course.'

Once again his tone became reticent, though the dining-room was empty. Only in the corner near the entrance, seated in their glass-walled bar, the inevitable group of foreign correspondents mimed, drank and mouthed like sea horses in solemn ritual.

'Is *all* America like this?' de Lisle enquired. 'Or worse?' He looked slowly round. 'Though it does give a sense of *dimension*, I suppose. And optimism. That's the trouble with Americans, isn't it, really? All that emphasis on the future. So dangerous. It makes them destructive of the present. Much kinder to look *back*, I always think. I see no hope at all for the future, and it gives me a *great* sense of freedom. And of caring: we're much nicer to one another in the condemned cell aren't we? Don't take me too seriously, will you?'

'If you wanted Chancery files late at night, what would you do?'

'Dig out Meadowes.'

'Or Bradfield?'

'Oh, that would be really going it. Rawley had the combinations, but only as a long stop. If Meadowes goes under a bus, Rawley can still get at the papers. You really *have* had a morning of it, haven't you,' he added solicitously. 'I can see you're still under the ether.'

'What would *you* do?'

'Oh, I'd draw the files in the afternoon.'

'Now; with all this working at night?'

'If Registry's open on a crisis schedule there's no problem. If it's closed, well, most of us have safes and strong-boxes, and they're cleared for overnight storage.'

'Harting didn't have one.'

'Shall we just say *he* from now on?'

'So where would he work? If he drew files in the evening, classified files, and worked late: what would he do?'

'He'd take them to his room I suppose, and hand in the files to the Chancery Guard when he left. If he's not working in Registry. The Guard has a safe.'

'And the Guard would sign for them?'

'Oh Lordy, yes. We're not *that* irresponsible.'

'So I could tell from the Guard's night-book?'

'You could.'

'He left without saying good-night to the Guard.'

'Oh my,' said de Lisle, clearly very puzzled. 'You mean he took them home?'

'What kind of car did he have?'

'A mini shooting-brake.'

They were both silent.

'There's nowhere else he might have worked, a special reading room, a strong-room on the ground floor?'

'Nowhere,' de Lisle said flatly. 'Now I think you'd better have another of those things, hadn't you, and cool the brain a little?'

He called the waiter.

'Well I've had a simply *ghastly* hour at the Ministry of the Interior with Ludwig Siebkron's faceless men.'

'What doing?'

'Oh, mourning the poor Miss Eich. That was gruesome. It was also very *odd*,' he confessed. 'It really was very odd indeed.' He drifted away. 'Did you know that blood plasma came in tins? The Ministry now say that they want to store some in the Embassy canteen, just in case. It's the most Orwellian thing I've ever heard; Rawley's going to be quite furious. He thinks they've gone much too far already. Apparently none of us belongs to groups any more: *uniblood*. I suppose it makes for equality.' He continued, 'Rawley's getting pretty cross about Siebkron.'

'Why.'

'The lengths he insists on going to, just for the sake of the poor English. All right, Karfeld is desperately anti-British and anti-Common Market. And Brussels is crucial, and British entry touches the nationalist nerve and maddens the Movement, and the Friday rally is alarming and everyone's very much on edge. One accepts all that wholeheartedly. And nasty things happened in Hanover. But we still don't deserve *so* much attention, we really don't. First the curfew, then the bodyguards, and now these wretched motor-cars. I think we feel he's crowding us on purpose.' Reaching past Turner, de Lisle took the enormous menu in his slender, woman's hand. 'How about oysters? Isn't that what real people eat? They have them in all seasons here. I gather they get them from Portugal or somewhere.'

'I've never tried them.' Turner said with a hint of aggression.

'Then you must have a dozen to make up,' de Lisle replied easily and drank some more Martini. 'It's so nice to meet someone from *outside*. I don't suppose you can understand that.'

A string of barges chased up river with the current.

'The unsettling thing is, I suppose, one doesn't feel that ultimately all these precautions are for our own good. The Germans seem suddenly to have their horns drawn in, as if we were being deliberately provocative; as if *we* were doing the demonstrating. They barely talk to us down there. A *total* freeze up. Yes. That's what I mean,' he concluded. 'They're treating us as if we were hostile. Which is doubly frustrating when all we ask is to be loved.'

'He had a dinner party on Friday night,' Turner said suddenly.

'Did he?'

'But it wasn't marked in his diary.'

'Silly man.' He peered round but no one came. 'Where *is* that wretched boy?'

'Where was Bradfield on Friday night?'

'Shut up,' said de Lisle crisply. 'I don't like that kind of thing. And then there's Siebkron himself,' he continued as if nothing had happened, 'Well, we all know *he's* shifty; we all know he's juggling with the Coalition and we all know he had political aspirations. We also know he has an appalling security problem to cope with next Friday, and a lot of enemies waiting to say he did it badly. Fine—' he nodded his head at the river, as if in some way it were involved in his perplexities – 'So why spend six hours at the deathbed of poor Fraülein Eich? What's so fascinating about watching her die? And why go to the ridiculous lengths of putting the sentries on every tiny British hiring in the area? He's got an obsession about us, I swear he has; He's worse than Karfeld.'

'Who is Siebkron? What's his job?'

'Oh, muddy pools. Your world in a way. I'm sorry, I shouldn't have said that.' He blushed, acutely distressed. Only the timely arrival of the waiter rescued him from his embarrassment. He was quite a young boy, and de Lisle addressed him with inordinate courtesy, seeking his opinion on matters beyond his competence, deferring to his judgement in the selection of the Moselle and enquiring minutely after the quality of the meat.

'They say in Bonn,' he continued when they were alone again, 'to borrow a phrase, that if you have Ludwig Siebkron for a friend you don't need an enemy. Ludwig's very much a local species. Always someone's left arm. He keeps saying he doesn't want any of us to die. That's exactly why he's frightening: he makes it so possible. It's easy to forget,' he continued blandly, 'that Bonn may be a democracy but it's *frightfully* short of democrats.' He fell silent. 'The trouble with *dates*,' he reflected at last, 'is that they create compartments in time. Thirty-nine to forty-five. Forty-five to fifty. Bonn isn't pre-war, or war, or even post-war. It's just a small town in Germany. You can no more slice it up than you can the Rhine. It plods along, or whatever the song says. And the mist drains away the colours.'

Blushing suddenly, he unscrewed the cap of the tabasco and applied himself to the delicate task of allocating one drop to each oyster. It claimed his entire attention. 'We all apologize for Bonn. That's how you recognize the natives. I wish I collected model trains,' he continued brightly. 'I would like to place *far* greater emphasis on trivia. Do you have anything like that: a hobby, I mean?'

'I don't get the time,' said Turner.

'*Nominally* he heads something called the Ministry of the Interior Liaison Committee; I understand he chose the name himself. I asked him once: liaison with whom, Ludwig? He thought that was a great joke. He's our age of course. Front generation minus five; slightly cross at having missed the war, I suspect, and can't *wait* to grow old. He also flirts with CIA, but that's a status symbol here. His principal occupation is knowing Karfeld. When anyone wants to conspire with the Movement, Ludwig Siebkron lays it on. It *is* a bizarre life,' he conceded, catching sight of Turner's expression. 'But Ludwig revels in it. Invisible Government: that's what he likes. The fourth estate. Weimar would have suited him down to the ground. And you have to understand about the Government here: *all* the divisions are very artificial.'

Compelled, apparently, by a single urge, the foreign correspondents had left their bar and were floating in a long shoal towards the centre table already prepared for them. A very large man, catching sight of de Lisle, pulled a long strand of black hair over his right eye, and extended his arm in a Nazi greeting. De Lisle lifted his glass in reply.

'That's Sam Allerton,' he explained in an aside. 'He really *is* rather a pig. Where was I? Artificial divisions. Yes. They absolutely bedevil us here. Always the same: in a grey world we reach frantically for absolutes. Anti-French, pro-French, Communist, anti-Communist. Sheer nonsense, but we go it time and again. That's why we're so wrong about Karfeld. So dreadfully wrong. We argue about *definitions* when we should be arguing about *facts*. Bonn will go to the gallows arguing about the width of the rope that hangs us. *I* don't know how you define Karfeld; who does? The German Poujade? The middle-class revolution? If that's what he is then we *are* ruined, I agree, because in Germany they're *all* middle class. Like America: reluctantly equal. They don't want to be equal, who does? They just are. Uniblood.'

The waiter had brought the wine, and de Lisle pressed Turner to taste it. 'I'm sure your palate is fresher than mine.' Turner declined, so he sampled it himself, elaborately. 'How very clever,' he said appreciatively to the waiter. 'How *good*.'

'All the smart definitions apply to him, every one, of course they do; they applay to anyone. Just like psychiatry: presume the symptoms and you can *always* find a name for them. He's isolationist, chauvinist, pacifist, revanchist. And he wants a trade alliance with Russia. He's progressive, which appeals to the German old, he's reactionary, which appeals to the German young. The young are so *puritanical* here. They want to be cleansed of prosperity; they want bows and arrows and Barbarossa.' He pointed wearily towards the Seven Hills. 'They want all that in modern dress. No wonder the old are hedonistic. But the young—' He broke off. 'The young,' he said, with deep distaste, 'have discovered the cruellest of all truths: that the most effective way of punishing their parents is to imitate them. Karfeld is the students' adopted grown-up ... I'm sorry. This is my hobby-horse. *Do* tell me to shut up.'

Turner appeared not to have heard. He was staring at the policemen who stood at intervals along the footpath. One of them had found a dinghy tethered under the bank, and he was playing with the sheet, swinging it round and round like a skipping rope.

'They keep asking us in London: who are his supporters? Where does he get his money from? Define, define. What am I to tell them? "The man in the street," I wrote once, "traditionally the most elusive social class." They adore that kind of answer until it reaches Research Department. "The disenchanted," I said, "the orphans of a dead democracy, the casualties of coalition government." Socialists who think they've been sold out to conservatism, anti-socialists who think they're been sold out to the reds. People who are just too intelligent to vote at all. Karfeld is the one hat that covers all their heads. How do you *define* a mood? *God* they are obtuse. We get no instructions any more: just questions. I told them: "Surely you have the same kind of thing in England? It's all the rage everywhere else." And after all, no one suspected a world plot in Paris: why look for it here? Mood ... ignorance ... boredom.' He leaned across the table. 'Have *you* ever voted? I'm sure you have. What's it like? Did you feel altered? Was it like Mass? Did you walk away ignoring everybody?' De Lisle ate another oyster. 'I think London has been bombed. Is that the answer? And you're just a blind to cheer us up. Perhaps only Bonn is left. What a frightful thought. A world in exile. That's what we are though. Inhabited by exiles, too.'

'Why does Karfeld hate the British?' Turner asked. His mind was far away.

'That, I confess, is one of life's unsolved mysteries. We've all tried our hand at it in Chancery. We've talked about it, read about it, argued about it. No one has the answer.' He shrugged. 'Who believes in motive these days, least of all in a politician? We did *try* to define that. Something we once did to him, perhaps. Something he once did to us. It's the childhood impressions that last the longest they say. Are you married, by the way?'

'What's that got to do with it?'

'*My*,' said de Lisle admiringly, 'you *are* prickly.'

'What does he do for money?'

'He's an industrial chemist; he runs a big plant outside Essen. There's a theory the British gave him a rough time during the Occupation, dismantled his factory and ruined his business. I don't know how true it all is. We've attempted a certain amount of research but there's very little to go on and Rawley, quite rightly, forbids us to enquire outside. God knows,' he declared with a small shudder, 'what Siebkron would think of us if we started *that* game. The press just says he hates us, as if it required no explanations. Perhaps they're right.'

'What's his record?'

'Predictable. Graduated before the war, drafted into the Engineers. Russian front as a demolitions expert; wounded at Stalingrad but managed to get out. The disillusionment of peace. The hard struggle and the slow build-up. All very romantic. The death of the spirit, the gradual revival. There are the usual boring rumours that he was Himmler's aunt or something of the sort. No one pays them much heed; it's a sign of arriving in Bonn these days, when the East Germans dig up an improbable allegation against you.'

'But there's nothing to it?'

'There's always something; there's never enough. Anyway, it doesn't impress anyone except us, so why bother? He came by degrees to politics, he says; he speaks of his years of sleep and his years of awakening. He has a rather Messianic turn of phrase, I fear, at least when he talks about himself.'

'You've never met him, have you?'

'Good God no. Just read about him. Heard him on the radio. He's very *present* in our lives in some ways.'

Turner's pale eyes had returned to the Petersberg; the sun, slanting between the hills, glinted directly upon the windows of the grey hotel. There is one hill over there that is broken like a quarry; small engines, white with dust, shuffle at its feet.

'You have to hand it to him. In six months he's changed the whole *galère*. The cadre, the organization, the jargon. They were cranks before Karfeld; gypsies, wandering preachers, Hitler's risen, all that nonsense. Now they're a patrician, graduate group. No shirt-sleeved hordes for him, thank you; none of your socialist nonsense, apart from the students, and he's very clever about tolerating them. He knows what a narrow line there is between the pacifist who attacks the policeman and the policeman who attacks the pacifist. But for most of us Barbarossa wears a clean shirt and has a doctorate in chemical engineering. *Herr Doktor Barbarossa,* that's the cry these days. Economists, historians, statisticians ... above all, lawyers, of course. Lawyers are the great German gurus, always have been; you know how illogical lawyers are. But not *politicians*: politicians aren't a bit respectable. And for Karfeld of course, they smack far too much of representation; Karfeld doesn't want anyone representing him, thank you. Power without rule, that's the cry. The right to know better, the right not to be responsible. It's the *end*, you see, not the beginning,' he said, with a conviction quite disproportionate to his lethargy. 'Both we and the Germans have been through democracy and no one's given us credit for it. Like shaving. No one *thanks* you for shaving, one one *thanks* you for democracy. Now we've come out the other side. Democracy was only possible under a class system, that's why: it was an indulgence granted by the privileged. We haven't time for it any more: a flash of light between feudalism and automation, and now it's gone. What's left? The voters are cut off from parliament, parliament is cut off from the Government and the Government is cut off from everyone. Government by silence, that's the slogan. Government by alienation. I don't need to tell *you* about that; it's a British product.'

He paused, expecting Turner to make some further interjection but Turner was still lost in thought. At their long table, the journalists were arguing. Someone had threatened to hit someone else; a third was promising to bang their heads together.

'*I* don't know what I'm defending. Or what I'm representing; who does? "A gentleman who lies for the good of his country," they told us with a wink in London. "Willingly," I say. "But first tell me what truth I must conceal." They haven't the least idea. Outside the Office, the poor world dreams we have a book bound in gold with POLICY written on the cover ... God, if only they knew.' He finished his wine. 'Perhaps *you* know? I am supposed to obtain the maximum advantage with the minimum of friction. What do they mean by advantage, I wonder: power? I doubt whether power is to our advantage. Perhaps we *should* go into decline. Perhaps we need a Karfeld? A new Oswald Mosley? I'm afraid we would barely notice him. The opposite of love isn't hate; it's apathy. Apathy is our daily bread here. Hysterical apathy. Have some more Moselle.'

'Do you think it's possible,' Turner said, his gaze still upon the hill, 'that Siebkron already *knows* about Harting? Would that make them hostile? Would that account for the extra attention?'

'Later,' de Lisle said quietly. 'Not in front of the children if you don't mind.'

The sun landed upon the river, lighting it from nowhere like a great gold bird, spreading its wings over the whole valley, frisking the water's surface into the light-hearted movements of a new spring day. Ordering the boy to bring two of his *nicest* brandies to the tennis garden, de Lisle picked his way elegantly between the empty tables to the side door. At the centre of the room the journalists had fallen silent; sullen with drink, slumped in their leather chairs, they gracelessly awaited the stimulus of new political catastrophe.

'Poor old thing,' he observed as they entered the fresh air. 'What a bore I've been. Do you get this wherever you go? I suppose we all unburden our hearts to the stranger, do we? And do we all finish up like little Karfelds? Is that it? Middle-class patriotic anarchists? How awfully dreary for you.'

'I've got to see his house,' Turner said. 'I've got to find out.'

'You're out of court,' de Lisle replied evenly. 'Ludwig Siebkron's got it picketed.'

It was three o'clock; a white sun had broken through the clouds. They sat in the garden under beach umbrellas, sipping their brandy and watching the diplomatic daughters volley and laugh in the wet, red clay of the tennis courts.

'Praschko, I suspect, is a baddie,' de Lisle declared. 'We used to have him on the books long ago, but he went sour on us.' He yawned. 'He was quite dangerous in his day; a political pirate. No conspiracy was complete without him. I've met him a few times; the English still bother him. Like all converts, he does hanker for the lost loyalties. He's a Free Democrat these days; or did Rawley tell you? That's a home for lost causes if ever there was one; they've got some *very* weird creatures over there.'

'But he was a friend.'

'You are innocent,' de Lisle said drowsily, 'Like Leo. We can know people all our lives without becoming friends. We can know people five minutes and they're our friends for life. Is Praschko so important?'

'He's all I've got,' said Turner. 'He's all I've got to go on. He's the only person I've heard of who knew him outside the Embassy. He was going to be best man at his wedding.'

'*Wedding? Leo?*' de Lisle sat bolt upright, his composure gone.

'He was engaged long ago to someone called Margaret Aickman. They seem to have known one another in Leo's pre-Embassy days.'

De Lisle fell back in apparent relief.

'If you're thinking of approaching Praschko—' he said.

'I'm not, don't worry; that's one message I have got.' He drank. 'But someone tipped Leo off. *Someone* did. He went mad. He knew he was living on borrowed time and he took whatever he could get his hands on. Anything. Letters, files ... and when he finally ran for it, he didn't even bother to apply for leave.'

'Rawley wouldn't have granted it; not in this situation.'

'Compassionate leave; he'd have got that all right, it was the first thing Bradfield thought of.'

'Did he pinch the trolley too?'

Turner did not answer.

'I suppose he helped himself to my nice electric fan. He'll need *that* in Moscow for sure.' De Lisle leaned even farther back into his chair. The sky was quite blue, the sun as hot and intense as if it came through glass. 'If *this* keeps up, I'll have to get a new one.'

'Someone tipped him off,' Turner insisted. 'It's the only explanation. He panicked. That's why I thought of Praschko, you see: he's got a left-wing past. Fellow traveller was Rawley's term. He was old chums with Leo; they'd even spent the war together in England.' He stared at the sky.

'You're going to advance a *theory*,' de Lisle murmured. 'I can hear it ticking.'

'They come back to Germany in forty-five; do some army service; then part. They go different ways: Leo stays British and covers *that* target, Praschko goes native and gets himself mixed up in German politics. They'd be a useful pair, those two, as long-term agents, I must say. Maybe they were both at the same game ... recruited by the same person back in England when Russia was the ally. Gradually they run down their relationship. That's standard, that is. Not safe to associate any more ... bad security to have our names linked: but they keep it up; keep it up in secret. Then one day Praschko gets word. Just a few weeks ago. Out of the blue perhaps. He hears it on the Bonn grapevine you're all so proud of: Siebkron's on the trail. Some old trace has come up; someone's talked; we're betrayed. Or maybe they're only after Leo. Pack your bags, he says, take what you can and run for it.'

'What a horrid mind you must have,' de Lisle said luxuriously. 'What a nasty, inventive mind.'

'The trouble is, it doesn't work.'

'Not really, does it? Not in *human* terms. I'm glad you recognize that. Leo wouldn't *panic*, that's not his way. He had himself much under control. And it sounds very silly, but he loved us. Modestly, he loved us. He was *our* kind of man, Alan. Not theirs. He expected dreadfully little from life. Pit pony. That's how I used to think of him in those wretched ground-floor stables. Even when he came upstairs, he seemed to bring a bit of the dark with him. People thought of him as *jolly*. The jolly extrovert ...'

'No one I've talked to thought he was jolly.'

De Lisle turned his head and looked at Turner with real interest.

'Didn't they? What a horrifying thought. Each of us thought the other was laughing. Like clowns at the tragedy. That's very nasty,' he said.

'All right,' Turner conceded. 'He wasn't a believer. But he might have been when he was younger, mightn't he?'

'Might.'

'Then he goes to sleep ... his conscience goes to sleep, I mean—'

'Ah.'

'Until Karfeld wakes him up again – the new Nationalism ... the old enemy.... Wakes him with a bang. "Hey, what's going on?" He saw it all happening again; he told people that: history repeating itself.'

'Was it really Marx who said that: "History repeats itself, but the first time it's tragedy, and the second time it's comedy?" It seems *far* too witty for a German. Though I will admit: Karfeld does make Communism awfully inviting.'

'What was he *like*?' Turner insisted, 'What was he really *like*?'

'Leo? God, what are any of us like?'

'You knew him. I didn't.'

'You won't interrogate me, will you?' he asked, not altogether as a joke; 'I'm damned if I'll buy you lunch for you to unmask me.'

'Did Bradfield like him?'

'Who does Bradfield like?'

'Did he keep a close eye on him?'

'On his work, no doubt, where it was relevant. Rawley's a professional.'

'He's Roman Catholic too, isn't he?'

'My goodness,' de Lisle declared with quite unexpected vehemence, 'What an awful thing to say. You really musn't compartment people like that, it won't do. Life just isn't made up of so many cowboys and so many Red Indians. Least of all diplomatic life. If *that's* what you think life is, you'd better defect yourself.' With this he threw back his head and closed his eyes, letting the sun restore him. 'After all,' he added, his equability quite revived, 'that's what you object to in Leo, isn't it? He's gone and attached himself to some silly faith. God is dead. You can't have it both ways, that would be *too* medieval.' He lapsed once more into a contented silence.

'I have a particular vision of Leo,' he said at last. 'Here's something for your little notebook. What do you make of this? One gorgeous winter afternoon. I'd been to a boring German conference and it was half past four and I'd nothing much to do, so I took myself for a drive up into the hills behind Godesberg. Sun, frost, a bit of snow, a bit of wind ... it was how I imagine ascending into Heaven. Suddenly, there was Leo. Indisputably, unquestionably, positively Leo, shrouded to the ears in Balkan black, with one of those dreadful Homburg hats they wear in the Movement. He was standing at the edge of a football field watching some kids kicking a ball and smoking one of those little cigars everyone complained about.'

'Alone?'

'All alone. I thought of stopping but I didn't. He hadn't any car that I could see and he was miles from anywhere. And suddenly I thought, no; don't stop; he's at Church. He's looking at the childhood he never had.'

'You were fond of him, weren't you?'

De Lisle might have replied, for the question did not seem to disconcert him, but he was interrupted by an unexpected intruder.

'Hullo. A new flunkey?' The voice was slurred and gritty. As its owner was standing directly in the sun, Turner had to screw up his eyes in order to make him out at all; at length he discerned the gently swaying outline and the black unkempt hair of the English journalist who had saluted them at lunch. He was pointing at Turner, but his question, to judge by the cast of his head, was addressed to de Lisle.

'What is he,' he demanded, 'pimp or spy?'

'Which do you want to be, Alan?' de Lisle asked cheerfully, but Turner declined to answer. 'Alan Turner, Sam Allerton,' he continued, quite unbothered. 'Sam represents a lot of newspapers, don't you, Sam? He's enormously powerful. Not that he cares for power of course. Journalists never do.'

Allerton continued to stare at Turner.

'Where's he come from then?'

'London Town,' said de Lisle.

'What part of London Town?'

'Ag and Fish.'

'Liar.'

'The Foreign Office, then. Hadn't you guessed?'

'How long's he here for?'

'Just visiting.'

'How long for?'

'You know what visits are.'

'I know what *his* visits are,' said Allerton. 'He's a bloodhound.' His dead, yellow eyes slowly took him in: the heavy shoes, the tropical suit, the blank face and the pale, unblinking gaze.

'Belgrade,' he said at last. 'That's where. Some bloke in the Embassy screwed a female spy and got photographed. We all had to hush it up or the Ambassador wasn't going to give us any more port. *Security* Turner, that's who you are. The Bevin boy. You did a job in Warsaw, didn't you? I remember that too. That was a balls-up, wasn't it? Some girl tried to kill herself. Someone you'd been too rough with. We had to sweep that under the carpet as well.'

'Run away, Sam,' said de Lisle.

Allerton began laughing. It was quite a terrible noise, mirthless and cancered; indeed it seemed actually to cause him pain, for as he sat down, he interrupted himself with low, blasphemous cries. His black, greasy mane shook like an ill-fitted wig; his paunch, hanging forward over his waistband, trembled uncertainly.

'Well, Peter, how was Luddi Siebkron? Going to keep us safe and sound, is he? Save the Empire?'

Without a word, Turner and de Lisle got up and made their way across the lawn towards the car park.

'Heard the news, by the way?' Allerton called after them.

'What news?'

'You chaps don't know a thing, do you? Federal Foreign Minister's just left for Moscow. Top level talks on Soviet-German trade treaty. They're joining Comecon and signing the Warsaw pact. All to please Karfeld and bugger up Brussels. Britain out, Russia in. Non-aggressive Rappallo. What do you think of that?'

'We think you're a bloody liar,' said de Lisle.

'Well, it's nice to be fancied,' Allerton replied, with a deliberate homosexual lisp. 'But don't tell me it won't happen, lover boy, because one day it will. One day they'll do it. They'll have to. Slap Mummy in the face. Find a Daddy for the Fatherland. It isn't the West any more, is it? So who's it going to be?' He raised his voice as they continued walking. 'That's what you stupid flunkies don't understand! Karfeld's the only one in Germany who's telling the truth: the Cold War's over for everyone except the fucking diplomats!' His Parthian shot reached them as they closed the doors. 'Never mind darlings,' they heard him say. 'We can all sleep soundly now Turner's here.'

The little sports car nosed its way slowly down the sanitary arcades of the American Colony. A church bell, much amplified, was celebrating the sunlight. On the steps of the New England chapel, a bride and groom faced the flashing cameras. They entered the Koblenzerstrasse and the noise hit them like a gale. Overhead, electronic indicators flashed out theoretical speed checks. The photographs of Karfeld had multiplied. Two Mercedes with Egyptian lettering on their number plates raced past them, cut in, swung out again and were gone.

'That lift,' Turner said suddenly. 'In the Embassy. How long's it been out of action?'

'God, when was anything? Mid-April I suppose.'

'You're sure of that?'

'You're thinking of the trolley? Which also disappeared in mid-April?'

'You're not bad,' Turner said. 'You're not bad at all.'

'And you would be making a most terrible mistake if you ever thought you were a specialist,' de Lisle retorted, with that same unpredictable force which Turner had discerned in him before. 'Just don't go thinking you're in a white coat, that's all; don't go thinking we're all laboratory specimens.' He swung violently to avoid a double lorry and at once a motorized scream of fury rose from behind them. 'I'm saving your soul though you may not notice it.' He smiled. 'Sorry. I've got Siebkron on my nerves, that's all.'

'He put P. in his diary,' Turner said suddenly. 'After Christmas: meet P. Give P. dinner. Then it faded out again. It could have been Praschko.'

'It could have been.'

'What Ministries are there in Bad Godesberg?'

'Buildings, Scientific, Health. Just those three so far as I know.'

'He went to a conference every Thursday afternoon. Which one would that be?'

De Lisle pulled up at the traffic lights and Karfeld frowned down on them like a cyclops, one eye ripped off by a dissenting hand.

'I don't think he *did* go to a conference,' de Lisle said cautiously. 'Not recently anyway.'

'What do you mean?'

'Just that.'

'For Christ's sake?'

'Who told you he went?'

'Meadowes. And Meadowes got it from Leo and Leo said it was a regular weekly meeting and cleared with Bradfield. Something to do with claims.'

'Oh my God,' said de Lisle softly. He pulled away, holding the left-hand lane against the predatory flashing of a white Porsche.

'What does "Oh God" mean?'

'I don't know. Not what you think perhaps. There was no conference, not for Leo. Not in Bad Godesberg, not anywhere else; not on Thursdays, not on any other day. Until Rawley came, it's true, he attended a low-level conference at the Buildings Ministry. They discussed private contracts for repairing German houses damaged by Allied manoeuvres. Leo rubber stamped their proposals.'

'Until Bradfield came?'

'Yes.'

'Then what happened? The conference had run down, had it? Like the rest of his work.'

'More or less.'

Instead of turning right into the Embassy gateway, de Lisle filtered to the left bay and prepared to make the circuit a second time.

'What do you mean? "*More or less*"?'

'Rawley put a stop to it.'

'To the conference?'

'I told you: it was mechanical. It could be done by correspondence.'

Turner was almost in despair. 'Why are you fencing with me? What's going on? Did he stop the conference or not? What part's he playing in this?'

'Take care,' de Lisle warned him, lifting one hand from the steering-wheel. 'Don't rush in. Rawley sent me instead of him. He didn't like the Embassy to be represented by someone like Leo.'

'Someone like—'

'By a temporary. That's all! By a temporary without full status. He felt it was wrong so he got me to go along in his place. After that, Leo never spoke to me again. He thought I'd intrigued against him. Now that's enough. Don't ask me any more.' They were passing the Aral garage again, going north. The petrol attendant recognized the car and waved cheerfully to de Lisle. 'That's your mede or measure. I'm not going to discuss Bradfield with you if you bully me till you're blue in the face. He's my colleague, my superior and—'

'And your friend! Christ forgive me: who do you represent out here? Yourselves or the poor bloody taxpayer? I'll tell you who: the Club. *Your*

Club. The bloody Foreign Office; and if you saw Rawley Bradfield standing on Westminster Bridge hawking his files for an extra pension, you'd bloody well look the other way.'

Turner was not shouting. It was rather the massive slowness of his speech which gave it urgency.

'You make me puke. All of you. The whole sodding circus. You didn't give a twopenny damn for Leo, any of you, while he was here. Common as dirt, wasn't he? No background, no childhood, no nothing. Shove him the other side of the river where he won't be noticed! Tuck him away in the catacombs with the German staff! Worth a drink but not worth dinner! What happens now? He bolts, and he takes half your secrets with him for good measure, and suddenly you've got the guilts and you're blushing like a lot of virgins holding your hands over your fannies and not talking to strange men. Everybody: you, Meadowes, Bradfield. You *know* how he wormed his way in there, how he conned them all; how he stole and cheated. You know something else too: a friendship, a love affair, something that made him special for you, made him interesting. There's a whole world he lived in and none of you will put a name to it. What was it? Who was it? Where the hell did he go on Thursday afternoons if he didn't go to the Ministry? Who ran him? Who protected him? Who gave him his orders and his money and took his information off him? Who held his hand? He's a spy, for Christ's sake! He's put his hand in the till! And the moment you find out, you're all on his side!'

'No,' said de Lisle. They were pulling up at the gate; the police were converging on them, tapping on the window. He let them wait. 'You've got it wrong. You and Leo form a team of your own. You're the other side of the wire. Both of you. That's your problem. Whatever definitions, whatever labels. That's why you're beating the air.'

They entered the car park and de Lisle drove round to the canteen side where Turner had stood that morning, staring across the field.

'I've got to see his house,' Turner said. 'I've got to.' They were both looking ahead of them, through the windscreen.

'I thought you'd ask me that.'

'All right, forget it.'

'Why should I? I've no doubt you'll go anyway. Sooner or later.'

They got out and walked slowly over the tarmac. The despatch riders were lying on the lawn, their motor-bikes stacked round the flagpole. The geraniums, martially arranged, glinted like tiny guardsmen along the verges.

'He loved the Army,' de Lisle said, as they climbed the steps. 'He really loved it.'

As they paused to show their passes yet again to the weasel sergeant, Turner chanced to look back at the carriageway.

'Look!' he said suddenly. 'That's the pair that picked us up at the airport.'

A black Opel had lumbered into the filter bay; two men sat in the front; from his vantage point on the steps, Turner could make out easily the multiple reflectors of the long driving mirror glittering in the sunlight.

'Ludwig Siebkron took us to lunch,' de Lisle said with a dry smile, 'and now he's brought us home. I told you: don't go thinking you're a specialist.'

'Then where were you on Friday night?'

'In the woodshed,' de Lisle snapped, 'waiting to murder Lady Ann for her priceless diamonds.'

The cypher room was open again. Cork lay on a truckle bed, a handbook on Caribbean bungalows lay beside him on the floor. On the desk in the dayroom was a blue Embassy envelope addressed to Alan Turner Esquire. His name was typewritten; the style was stiff and rather gauche. There was a number of things, the writer said, which Mr Turner might care to know about in connection with the matter which had brought him to Bonn. If it were convenient, the writer continued, he might care to call for a glass of sherry wine at the above address at half past six o'clock. The address was in Bad Godesberg and the writer was Miss Jenny Pargiter of Press and Information Section, presently on attachment to Chancery, She had signed her name and typed it beneath the signature for reasons of clarity; the P was written rather large, Turner decided; and as he opened the blue rexine diary he permitted himself a rare if puzzled smile of anticipation. P for Praschko; P for Pargiter. And P was the initial on the diary. Come on, Leo, let's have a look at your guilty secret.

8
Jenny Pargiter

'I assume,' Jenny Pargiter began, in a prepared statement, 'that you are used to dealing in delicate matters.'

The sherry stood between them on the glass-topped sofa table. The flat was dark and ugly: the chairs were Victorian wicker, the drapes German and very heavy. Constable reproductions hung in the dining alcove.

'Like a doctor, you have standards of professional confidence.'

'Oh sure,' said Turner.

'It was mentioned at Chancery meeting this morning that you were investigating Leo Harting's disappearance. We were warned not to discuss it, even among ourselves.'

'You're allowed to discuss it with me,' said Turner.

'No doubt. But I naturally would wish to be told how much further any confidence might go. What, for instance, is the relationship between yourselves and Personnel Department?'

'It depends on the information.'

She had raised the sherry glass to the level of her eye and appeared to be measuring the fluid content. It was an attitude evidently designed to demonstrate her sophistication and her ease of mind.

'Supposing someone – supposing I myself had been injudicious. In a personal matter.'

'It depends who you've been injudicious *with*,' Turner replied, and Jenny Pargiter coloured suddenly.

'That is not what I meant at all.'

'Look,' said Turner, watching her, 'if you come and tell me in confidence that you've left a bundle of files in the bus, I'll have to give details to Personnel Department. If you tell me you've been going out with a boy friend now and then, I'm not going to fall over in a faint. Mainly,' he said, pushing his sherry glass across the table for her to replenish, 'Personnel Department don't want to know we exist.' His manner was very casual, as if he barely cared. He sat impassively, filling the whole chair.

'There is the question of protecting other people, third parties who cannot necessarily speak for themselves.'

Turner said, 'There's also the question of security, If you didn't think it was important, you wouldn't ask to see me in the first palce. It's up to you. I can't give you any guarantees.'

She lit a cigarette with sharp, angular movements. She was not an ugly girl, but she seemed to dress either too young or too old, so that whatever Turner's age, she was not his contemporary.

'I accept that,' she said and regarded him darkly for a moment, as if assessing how much Turner could take. 'However, you have misunderstood the reason why I asked you to call here. It is this. Since you are quite certain to be told all manner of rumours about Harting and myself, I thought it best if you heard the truth from me.'

Turner put down his glass and opened his notebook.

'I arrived here just before Christmas,' Jenny Pargiter said, 'from London. Before that I was in Djakarta. I returned to London intending to be married. You may have read of my engagement?'

'I think I must have missed it,' said Turner.

'The person to whom I was engaged decided at the last minute that we were not suited. It was a very courageous decision. I was then posted to Bonn. We had known one another for many years; we had read the same subject at University and I had always assumed we had much in common. The person decided otherwise. That is what engagements are for. I am perfectly content. There is no *reason* for anyone to be sorry for me.'

'You got here at Christmas?'

'I asked particularly to be here in time for the holiday. In previous years, we had always spent Christmas together. Unless I was in Djakarta of course. The ... separation on this occasion was certain to be painful to me. I was most anxious to mitigate the distress with a new atmosphere.'

'Quite.'

'As a single woman in an Embassy, one is very often overcome with invitations at Christmas. Almost everyone in Chancery invited me to spend the festive days with them. The Bradfields, the Crabbes, the Jacksons, the

Gavestons: they all asked me. I was also invited by the Meadowes. You have met Arthur Meadowes no doubt.'

'Yes.'

'Meadowes is a widower and lives with his daughter, Myra. He is in fact a B3, though we no longer use those grades. I found it very touching to be invited by a member of the Junior Staff.'

Her accent was very slight, provincial rather than regional, and for all her attempts at disowning it, it mocked her all the time.

'In Djakarta we always had that tradition. We *mixed* more. In a larger Embassy like Bonn, people tend to remain in their groups. I am not suggesting there should be total assimilation: I would even regard that as *bad*. The A's, for instance, tend to have different tastes as well as different intellectual interests to the B's. I am suggesting that in Bonn the distinctions are too *rigid*, and too many. The A's remain with the A's and the B's with the B's even inside the different sections: the economists, the attachés, Chancery; they all form cliques. I do not consider that right. Would you care for more sherry?'

'Thanks.'

'So I accepted Meadowes' invitation. The other guest was Harting. We spent a pleasant day, stayed there till evening, then left. Myra Meadowes was going out – she has been very ill, you know; she had a liaison in Warsaw, I understand, with a local undesirable and it very nearly ended in tragedy. Personally I am against anticipated marriages. Myra Meadowes was going to a young people's party and Meadowes himself was invited to the Corks, so there was no question of our remaining. As we were leaving, Harting suggested we went for a walk. He knew a place not far away; it would be nice to drive up there and get some fresh air after so much food and drink. I am very fond of exercise. We had our walk and then he proposed that I should go back with him for supper. He was very insistent.'

She was no longer looking at him. Her fingertips were pressed together on her lap, making a basket of her hands.

'I felt it would be wrong to refuse. It was one of those decisions which women find extremely difficult. I would have been quite glad of an early night, but I did not wish to cause offence. After all, it was Christmas Day, and his behaviour during the walk had been perfectly unobjectionable. On the other hand it must be said that I had barely seen him before that day. In the event, I agreed, but I said that I would not wish to be late home. He accepted this provision and I followed him to Königswinter in my car. To my surprise I found that he had prepared everything for my arrival. The table was laid for two. He had even persuaded the boilerman to come and light the fire. After supper, he told me that he loved me.' Picking up her cigarette she drew sharply upon it. Her tone was more factual than ever: certain things had to be said. 'He told me that in all his life he had never felt such emotion. From that first day that I had appeared at Chancery meeting, he had been going out of his mind. He pointed to the lights of the barges on the river. "I stand at my bedroom window," he said, "and I watch every one of them, right through the night. Morning after morning, I watch the dawn rise on the river." It was all due to his obsession for me. I was dumbfounded.'

'What did you say?'

'I had no chance to say anything. He wished to give me a present. Even if he never saw me again, he wished me to have this Christmas gift as a token of his love. He disappeared into the study and came back with a parcel, all wrapped up and ready, with a label, "To my love." I was naturally completely at a loss. "I can't accept this," I said. "I refuse. I can't allow you to give me things. It puts me at a disadvantage." I explained to him that though he was completely English in many ways, in this respect the English did things differently. On the Continent, it was quite customary to take women by storm, but in England courtship was a long and thoughtful matter. We would have to get to know one another, compare our views. There was the discrepancy in our ages; I had my career to consider. I didn't know what to do,' she added helplessly. The brittleness had vanished from her voice: she was helpless and a little pathetic. 'He kept saying, after all it was *Christmas*; I should think of it as just an ordinary Christmas present.'

'What was in the parcel?'

'A hair-dryer. He said he admired my hair above everything. He watched the sun shine on it in the mornings. During Chancery meeting you understand. He must have been speaking figuratively; we were having a wretched winter.' She took a short breath. 'It must have cost him twenty pounds. No one, not even my ex-fiancé during our most intimate period, has ever given me anything so valuable.'

She performed a second ritual with the cigarette box, ducking her hand forward and arresting it suddenly, selecting a cigarette as if it were a chocolate, not this one but that one, lighting it with a heavy frown. 'We sat down and he put on a gramophone record. I am afraid I am not musical, but I thought that music might distract him. I was extremely sorry for him, and most reluctant to leave him in that condition. He just stared at me. I didn't know where to look. Finally he came over and tried to embrace me, and I said I had to go home. He saw me to the car. He was very correct. Fortunately we had two more days of holiday. I was able to decide what to do. He telephoned twice to invite me to supper and I refused. By the end of the holiday, I had made up my mind. I wrote him a letter and returned the gift. I felt no other course was open to me. I went in early and left the parcel with the Chancery Guard. I explained in my letter that I had given great thought to all he had said and I was convinced I would never be able to return his affection. It would therefore be wrong for me to encourage him, and since we were colleagues and would be seeing a lot of each other, I felt it was only prudent to tell him this immediately, before—'

'Before what?'

'The gossip started,' she said with sudden passion. 'I've never known anywhere for such gossip. You can't move without them making up some wicked story about you.'

'What story have they made up about you?'

'God knows,' she said uselessly. 'God knows.'

'Which Guard did you leave the parcel with?'

'Walter, the younger one. Macmullen's son.'

'Did he tell other people?'

'I particularly asked him to regard the matter as confidential.'

'I should think that impressed him,' Turner said.

She stared at him angrily, her face red with embarrassment.

'All right. So you gave him the bird. What did he do about it?'

'That day he appeared at Chancery meeting and wished me good morning as if nothing had happened. I smiled at him and that was that. He was pale but brave ... sad but in command. I felt that the worst was over.... Fortunately he was about to begin a new job in Chancery Registry and I hoped that this would take his mind off other things. For a couple of weeks I barely spoke to him. I saw him either in the Embassy or at social functions and he seemed quite happy. He made no allusion to Christmas evening or to the hair-dryer. Occasionally at cocktail parties he would come and stand quite close to me and I knew that ... he wished for my proximity. Sometimes I would be conscious of his eyes on me. A woman can tell these things; I knew that he had still not completely given up hope. He had a way of catching my eye that was ... beyond all doubt. I cannot imagine why I had not noticed it before. However, I continued to give him no encouragement. That was the decision I had taken, and whatever the short-term temptations to alleviate his distress, I knew that in the long term no purpose could be served by ... leading him on. I was also confident that anything so sudden and ... irrational would quickly pass.'

'And did it?'

'We continued in this way for about a fortnight. It was beginning to get on my nerves. I seemed unable to go to a single party, to accept a single invitation without seeing him. He didn't even address me any more. He just looked. Wherever I went, his eyes followed me.... They are very dark eyes. I would call them soulful. Dark brown, as one would expect, and they imparted a remarkable sense of dependence.... In the end I was almost frightened to go out. I'm afraid that at that stage, I even had an unworthy thought. I wondered whether he was reading my mail.'

'Did you now?'

'We all have our own pigeonholes in Registry. For telegrams and mail. Everyone in Registry takes a hand at sorting the incoming papers. It is of course the custom here as in England that invitations are sent unsealed. It would have been quite possible for him to look inside.'

'Why was the thought unworthy?'

'It was untrue, that's why,' she retorted. 'I taxed him with it and he assured me it was quite untrue.'

'I see.'

Her voice became even more pedagogic; the tones came very crisply, brooking no question whatever.

'He would never do such a thing. It was not in his nature, it had not crossed his mind. He assured me categorically that he was not ... stalking me. That was the expression I used; it was one I instantly regretted. I cannot imagine how I came on such a ridiculous metaphor. To the contrary, he said, he was merely following his usual social pattern; if it bothered me he would change it, or decline all further invitations until I instructed him otherwise. Nothing was further from his mind than to be a burden to me.'

'So after that you were friends again, were you?'

He watched her search for the wrong words, watched her balance awkwardly at the edge of truth, and awkwardly withdraw.

'Since the twenty-third of January he has not spoken to me again,' she blurted. Even in that sad light, Turner saw the tears running down her rough cheeks as her head fell forward and her hand rose quickly to cover them. 'I can't go on. I think of him all the time.'

Rising, Turner opened the door of the drinks cupboard and half filled a tumbler of whisky.

'Here,' he said gently, 'This is what you like; drink it up and stop pretending.'

'It's overwork.' She took the glass. 'Bradfield never relaxes. He doesn't like women. He hates them. He wants to drive us all into the ground.'

'Now tell me what happened on the twenty-third of January.'

She was sitting sideways in the chair, her back towards him, and her voice had risen beyond her control.

'He ignored me. He pretended to lose himself in work. I'd go into Registry to collect my papers and he wouldn't even look up. Not for me. Not any more. He might for other people, but not for me. Oh no. He had never taken much interest in work – you only had to watch him in Chancery meetings to realize that. He was idle at heart. Glib. But the moment he heard me come along, he couldn't work hard enough. He saw through me, even if I greeted him. Even if I walked straight into him in the corridor, it was the same. He didn't notice me. I didn't exist. I thought I'd go off my head. It wasn't right: after all, he's only a B you know, and a temporary; he's nothing really. He carries no weight at all, you only have to hear how they talk about him.... Cheap, that's what they say of him. A quick mind but quite unsound.' For a moment she was far above his grade. 'I wrote him letters. I rang his number at Königswinter.'

'They all knew did they? You made a display of it did you?'

'First of all he chases after me ... besieges me with declarations of love ... like a gigolo really. Of course, I mean there's part of me that sees through *that* all right, don't you worry. Running hot and cold like that: who does he think he is?'

She lay across the chair, her head buried in the crook of her elbow, her shoulders shaking to the rhythm of her sobbing.

'You've got to tell me,' Turner said. He was standing over her, his hand on her arm. 'Listen. You've got to tell me what happened at the end of January. It was something important wasn't it? Something he asked you to do for him. Something political. Something special you're afraid of. First of all he made up to you. He worked on you, took you by surprise . . . then he got what he wanted; something very simple he couldn't get for himself. And when he'd got it he didn't want you any more.'

The sobbing started.

'You told him something he needed to know; you did him a favour: a favour to help him along the line. All right, you're not unique. There's a good few others have done the same thing one way or the other, believe me. So what is it?' He knelt down beside her. 'What was it that was injudicious? What was it that involved third parties? Tell me! it was something that frightened the life out of you! *Tell me what it was!*'

'Oh God, I lent him the keys. I lent him the keys,' she said.

'Hurry.'

'The Duty Officer's. The whole lot. He came to me and begged me . . . no, not begged. No.'

She was sitting up, white in the face. Turner refilled her glass and put it back in her hand.

'I was on duty. Night Duty Officer. Thursday January the twenty-third. Leo wasn't allowed to be Duty Officer. There are things temporaries can't see: special instructions . . . contingency plans. I'd stayed in to cope with a rush of telegrams; it must have been half past seven, eight o'clock. I was leaving the cypher room . . . just going to Registry, and I saw him standing there. As if he'd been waiting. Smiling. "Jenny," he said, "What a nice surprise." I was so happy.'

The sobbing broke out again.

'I was so happy. I'd been longing for him to speak to me again. He'd been waiting for me, I knew he had; he was pretending it was an accident. And I said to him: "Leo." I'd never called him that before. Leo. We just talked, standing in the corridor. What a *lovely* surprise he kept saying. Perhaps he could give me dinner? I reminded him, in case he had forgotten, that I was on duty. That didn't bother him either. What a pity, how about tomorrow night? Then the weekend? He would ring me on Saturday morning, how would that be? That would be fine, I said, I'd like that. And we could go for a walk first, he said, up on the football field? I was so happy. I still had the telegrams in my arms, a whole bundle, so I said well, I'd better get along, post these into Arthur Meadowes. He wanted to take them for me but I said no, I could manage them, it was all right. I was just turning away. . . . I wanted to be first to go, you see, I didn't want him walking away from me. I was just going and he said, "Oh Jenny, look here, by the way . . ." You know the way he talks. "Well, a ridiculous thing has happened, the choir are all hanging around downstairs and no one can unlock the Assembly Room door. Somebody's locked it and we can't find the key and we wondered whether you had one." It seemed a bit odd really; I couldn't think why anyone should *want* to lock it in the first place. So I said, yes, I'd come down and open it; I'd just have to check in some telegrams for distribution. I mean he knew I'd got a key; the Duty Officer has a spare key for every room in the Embassy. "Don't bother to come down," he says. "Just give me the key and I'll do it for you. It won't take two minutes." And he saw me hesitate.'

She closed her eyes.

'He was so *little*,' she burst out. 'You could hurt him so easily. I'd already accused him of opening my letters. I loved him.... I swear I've never loved anyone ...' Gradually her crying stopped.

'So you gave him the keys? The whole bunch? That's room keys, safe keys—'

'Keys to all desks and steel cupboards; to the front and rear doors of the building and the key to turn off the alarm in Chancery Registry.'

'Lift keys?'

'The lift wasn't bolted by then ... the grilles weren't up.... They did that the next weekend.'

'How long did he have them for?'

'Five minutes. Maybe less. It's not long enough, is it?' She had seized his arm beseeching him. 'Say it's not long enough.'

'To take an impression? He could take fifty impressions if he knew what he was about.'

'He'd need wax or plasticine or something: I asked. I looked it up.'

'He'd have had it ready in his room,' Turner said indifferently. 'He lived on the ground floor. Don't worry,' he added gently. 'He may just have been letting in the choir. Don't let your imagination run away with you.'

She had stopped crying. Her voice calmed. She spoke with a sense of private recognition: 'It wasn't choir practice night. Choir practice is on Fridays. This was Thursday.'

'You found out did you? Asked the Chancery Guard?'

'I knew already! I knew when I handed him the keys! I tell myself I didn't, but I did. But I had to trust him. It was an act of giving. Don't you see? An act of giving, an act of love. How can I expect a man to understand that?'

'And after you'd given,' Turner said, getting up, 'he didn't want you any more, did he?'

'That's like all men, isn't it?'

'Did he ring you Saturday?'

'You know he didn't.' Her face was still buried in her forearm. He closed the notebook. 'Can you hear me?

'Yes.'

'Did he ever mention a woman to you; a Margaret Aickman? He was engaged to her. She knew Harry Praschko as well.'

'No.'

'No other woman?'

'No.'

'Did he ever talk politics?'

'No.'

'Did he ever give you any cause to suppose he was a person of strong left-wing leanings?'

'No.'

'Ever see him in the company of suspicious persons?'

'No.'

'Did he talk about his childhood? His uncle? An uncle who lived in Hampstead. A communist who brought him up?'

'No.'

'Uncle Otto?'

'No.'

'Did he ever mention Praschko? Well, did he? Did he ever mention Praschko, do you hear?'

'He said Praschko was the only friend he'd ever had.' She broke down again, and again he waited.

'Did he mention Praschko's politics?'

'No.'

'Did he say they were still friends?'

She shook her head.

'Somebody had lunch with Harting last Thursday. The day before he left. At the Maternus. Was that you?'

'I told you! I swear to you!'

'Was it?'

'No!'

'He's marked it down as you. It's marked P. That's how he wrote you down other times.'

'It wasn't me!'

'Then it was Praschko, was it?'

'How should I know?'

'Because you had an affair with him! You told me half and not the rest! You were sleeping with him up to the day he left!'

'It's not true!'

'Why did Bradfield protect him? He hated Leo's guts: why did he look after him like that? Give him jobs? Keep him on the payroll?'

'Please go,' she said. 'Please go. Never come back.'

'Why!'

She sat up.

'Get out,' she said.

'You had dinner with him Friday night. The night he left. You were sleeping with him and you won't admit it!'

'No.'

'He asked you about the Green File! He made you get the Despatch Box for him!'

'He didn't! He didn't! Get out!'

'I want a cab.'

He waited while she telephoned. '*Sofort*,' she said, *Sofort*,' come at once and take him away.

He was at the door.

'What will you do when you find him?' she asked with that slack voice that follows passion.

'Not my business.'

'Don't you care?'

'We never will find him, so what does it matter?'

'Then why look for him?'

'Why not? That's how we spend our lives, isn't it? Looking for people we'll never find.'

He walked slowly down the stairs to the hall. From another flat came the growl of a cocktail party. A group of Arabs, very drunk, swept past him pulling off their coats and shouting. He waited on the doorstep. Across the river, the narrow lights of Chamberlain's Petersberg hung like a necklace in the warm dark. A new block stood directly before him. It seemed to have been built from the top, beginning with the crane and working downwards. He thought he had seen it before from a different angle. A railway bridge straddled the end of the avenue. As the express thundered over it, he saw the silent diners grazing at their food.

'The Embassy,' he said. 'British Embassy.'

'*Englishe Botschaft?*'

'Not English. British. I'm in a hurry.'

The driver swore at him, shouting about diplomats. They drove extremely fast and once they nearly hit a tram.

'Get a bloody move on, can't you?'

He demanded a receipt. The driver kept a rubber stamp and a pad in his glove tray, and he hit the paper so hard that it crumpled. The Embassy was a ship, all its windows blazing. Black figures moved in the lobby with the slow coupling of a ballroom dance. The car park was full. He threw away the receipt. Lumley didn't countenance taxi fares. It was a new rule since the last cut. There was no one he could claim from. Except Harting, whose debts appeared to be accumulating.

Bradfield was in conference, Miss Peate said. He would probably be flying to Brussels with the Ambassador before morning. She had put away her papers and was fiddling with a blue leather *placement* tray, fitting the names round a dinner table in order of precedence, and she spoke to him as if it were her duty to frustrate him. And de Lisle was at the Bundestag, listening to the debate on Emergency Legislation.

'I want to see the Duty Officer's keys.'

'I'm afraid you can only have *them* with Mr Bradfield's consent.'

He fought with her and that was what she wanted. He overcame her and that was what she wanted too. She gave him a written authority signed by Administration Section and countersigned by the Minister (Political). He took it to the front desk where Macmullen was on duty. Macmullen was a big, steady man, sometime sergeant of Edinburgh constabulary, and whatever he had heard about Turner had given him no pleasure.

'And the night book,' Turner said. 'Show me the night book since January.'

'Please,' said Macmullen and stood over him while he looked through it in case he took it away. It was half past eight and the Embassy was emptying. 'See you in the morning,' Mickie Crabbe whispered as he passed. 'Old boy.'

There was no reference to Harting.

'Mark me in,' Turner said, pushing the book across the counter. 'I'll be in all night.'

As Leo was, he thought.

9
Guilty Thursday

There were about fifty keys and only half a dozen were labelled. He stood in the first floor corridor where Leo had stood, drawn back into the shadow of a pillar, staring at the cypher room door. It was about seven thirty, Leo's time, and he imagined Jenny Pargiter coming out with a bundle of papers in her arm. The corridor was very noisy now, and the steel trap on the cypher room door was rising and falling like a guillotine for the Registry girls to hand in telegrams and collect them; but that Thursday night had been a quiet time, a lull in the mounting crisis, and Leo had spoken to her *here*, where Turner stood now. He looked at his watch and then at the keys again and thought: five minutes. What *would* he have done? The noise was deafening; worse than day; not only the voices but the very pounding of the machines proclaimed a world entering emergency. But that night was calm, and Leo was a creature of silence, waiting here to draw his quarry and destroy. In five minutes.

He walked along the corridor as far as the lobby and looked down into the stair well and watched the evening shift of typists slip into the dark, survivors from a burning ship, letting the night recover them. Brisk but nonchalant would be his manner, for Jenny would watch him all the way till here; and Gaunt or Macmullen would see him descend these stairs; brisk but not triumphant.

He stood in the lobby. But *what* a risk, he thought suddenly: what a hazardous game. The crowd parted to admit two German officials. They were carrying black briefcases and they walked portentously as though they had come to perform an operation. They wore grey scarves put on before the overcoat, and folded broad and flat like Russian tunics. *What* a risk. She could revoke; she could pursue him; she would know within minutes, if she had not known already, that Leo was lying, she would know the moment she reached the lobby and heard no singing from the Assembly Room, saw no trace at all of a dozen singers entered in the night book, saw no hats and coats on those very pegs beside the door where the German officials were even now disencumbering themselves; she would know that Harting Leo, refugee, fringe-man, lover *manqué* and trader in third-rate artifices, had lied to her to get the keys.

'A gift of love, an act of love: how can I expect a *man* to understand that?'

Before entering the corridor, he stopped and examined the lift. The gold-painted door was bolted; the central panel of glass was black, boarded from the inside. Two heavy steel bars had been fastened horizontally for added security.

'How long's that been there?'

'Since Bremen, sir,' Macmullen said.

'When was Bremen?'

'January, sir. Late January. The Office advised it, sir. They sent a man out specially. He did the cellars and the lift, sir.' Macmullen gave information as if it were evidence before the bailies of Edinburgh, in a series of verbal drill movements, breathing at regulation intervals. 'He worked the whole weekend,' Macmullen added with awe; for he was a self-indulgent man and readily exhausted by work.

He made his way slowly through the gloom to Harting's room thinking: *these* doors would be closed; these lights extinguished, these rooms silent. Was there a moon to shine through the bars? Or only these blue lights burning for a cheaper Britain, and his own footsteps echoing in the vaults?

Two girls passed him, dressed for the emergency. One wore jeans and she looked at him very straight, guessing his weight. Jesus, he thought, quite soon I'm going to grab one, and he unlocked the door to Leo's room and stood there in the dark. What *were* you up to, he wondered, you little thief?

Tins. Cigar tins would do, filled with white hardening putty; a child's plasticine from that big Woolworths in Bad Godesberg would do; a little white talc to ensure a clean imprint. Three movements of the key, this side, that side, a straight stab into the flesh, and make sure the shoulders are clearly visible. It may not be a perfect fit; that depends on the blanks and the print, but a nice soft metal will yield a little in the womb and form itself to fit the inner walls ... Come on Turner, the sergeant used to say, you'd find it if it had hairs round it. He had them ready, then. All fifty tins? Or just one?

Just one key. Which? Which Aladdin's cave, which secret chamber hid the secret treasures of this grumbling English house?

Harting you thief. He began on Harting's own door, just to annoy him, to bring it home to an absent thief that *his* door can be fiddled with as well, and he worked slowly along the passage fitting the keys to the locks, and each time he found a key that matched he took it off the ring and dropped it into his pocket and thought, What good did *that* one do you? Most of the doors were not even locked, so that the keys were redundant anyway; cupboards, lavatories, washrooms, restrooms, offices, a first-aid room that stank of alcohol and a junction box for electric cables.

A microphone job? Was that the nature of your technical interest, thief? The gimmicks, the flex, the hair-dryers, the bits and pieces: was that all a lovely cover for carting in some daft conjuring set for eavesdropping? 'Balls,' he said out loud, and with a dozen keys already tapping against his thigh, he plodded up the stairs again straight into the arms of the Ambassador's private secretary, a strutting, fussy man who had borrowed a good deal of his master's authority.

'H.E. will be leaving in a minute; I should make yourself scarce if I were you,' he said with chilling ease. 'He's not awfully keen on you people.'

In most of the corridors it was daytime. Commercial Section was celebrating Scottish week. A mauve grousemoor, draped in Campbell tartan, hung beside a photograph of the Queen in highland dress. Miniatures of Scotch Whisky were mounted in a *collage* with dancers and bagpipes, and framed in plywood battens. In the Open Plan, under radiant exhortations to buy from the North, pale-faced clerks struck doggedly at machines for adding and subtracting. *Deadline Brussels!* A placard warned them, but the machines seemed unimpressed. He climbed a floor and was in Whitehall with the Service Attachés, each with his tiny Ministry and his stencilled title on the door.

'What the hell are you up to?' a sergeant demanded, and Turner told him to keep a civil tongue in his head. Somewhere a military voice wrestled gallantly with dictation. In the Typing Pool, the girls sat forlornly in schoolroom lines: two juniors in green overalls gently nursed a mammoth duplicator while a third laid out the coloured telegrams as if they were fine linen for going away. Raised above them all, the Head Girl, blue haired and fully sixty, sat on a separate dais checking stencils. She alone, scenting the enemy, looked up sharply, nose towards the wind. The walls behind here were lined with Christmas cards from Head Girls in other missions. Some depicted camels, others the royal crest.

'I'm going over the locks,' he muttered, and her look said 'Go over what you like, but not my girls.'

Christ, I could do with one, I'm telling you. Surely you could spare just one for a quick drop into paradise? Harting, you thief.

It was ten o'clock. He had visited every room to which Harting had acquired access; he had gained nothing but a headache for his trouble. Whatever Harting wanted was no longer there, or else so hidden as to require weeks of searching; or so obvious as to be invisible. He felt the sickness which follows tension and his mind was racing with unco-ordinated recollections. Christ: one single day. From enthusiasm to frustration in one day. From an aeroplane to the day-room desk, all the clues and none; I've lived a whole bloody life and it's only Monday. He stared at the blank foolscap pages of the telegram form, wondering what the hell to write. Cork was asleep and the robots were silent. The keys lay in a heap before him. One by one he began threading them back on to the ring. Put together, he thought; *construct*. You will not go to bed until you are at least aware of the trail you must follow. The task of an intellectual, his fart-arsed tutor brayed, is to make order out of chaos. Define anarchy. It is a mind without a system. Please teacher, what is a system without a mind? Taking a pencil he lazily drew a chart of the days of the week and divided each day into panels of one hour. He opened the blue diary. Re-form the fragments, make of all the pieces one piece. You'll find him and Shawn won't. Harting Leo, Claims and Consular, thief and hunter, will hunt you down.

'You don't know anything about shares by any chance?' Cork inquired, waking with a start.

'No, I don't.'

'My query is, you see,' he continued, rubbing his pink eyes, 'If there's a slump on Wall Street and a slump in Frankfurt and we don't make the Market on this run, how will it affect Swedish steel?'

'If I were you,' Turner said, 'I'd put the whole lot on red and forget it.'

'Only I have this firm intention,' Cork explained. 'We've got a bit of land lined up in the Caribbean—'

'Shut up.'

Construct. Put your ideas on a blackboard and *then* see what happens to them. Come on, Turner, you're a philosopher, tell us how the world goes round. What little absolute will we put into Harting's mouth, for instance? Facts. Construct. Did you not, after all, my dear Turner, abandon the *contemplative* life of the academic in favour of the *functional* life of the civil servant? Construct; put your theories to work and de Lisle will call you a real person.

Mondays first. Mondays are for invitations out. Buffet parties are favoured, de Lisle had told him in an aside at luncheon; they eliminate the pains of *placement*. Mondays are reserved for away matches. England plays the wogs. Away to a different kind of slavery. Harting was essentially a second division man. The minor Embassies. Embassies with small drawing rooms. The B team played away on Mondays.

'– and if it's a girl, I reckon we could get a coloured nanny, an Amah; she could do the teaching, up to O-level at least.'

'Can't you keep quiet?'

'Provided we have the funds,' Cork added. 'You can't get them for nothing, I'm sure.'

'I'm working, can't you understand?'

I'm trying, he thought and his mind drifted into other fields. He was with the little girl in the corridor, whose full unpainted lips faded so reluctantly into the feathery skin; he imagined that long appraising stare upon his nascent paunch, and he heard her laughing as his own wife had laughed: Alan darling, you're supposed to take me, not fight me. It's rhythm, it's like dancing, can't you understand? And Tony's such a *beautiful* dancer, Alan darling, and I shall be a little late tonight, and I shall be away tomorrow, playing an away match with my Monday lover. Alan stop. Stop! Alan please don't hit me! I'll never touch him again, I swear. Until Tuesday.

Harting, you thief.

Tuesdays were for entertaining at home. Home is a Tuesday: home is having people in. He made a list of them and thought: it's worse than Blackheath. It's worse than her bloody mother fighting for her fragment of power; it's worse than Bournemouth and seed cake for the minister; it's worse than black Sundays in Yorkshire and weddings timed for six o'clock tea; it is a custom built, unassailable preventive detention of vacuous social exchange. The Vandelungs (Dutch) ... the Canards (Canadian) ... the Obutus (Ghanaian) ... the Cortezanis (Italian) ... the Allertons, the Crabbes, and once, sure enough, the Bradfields; this happy band was mingled with no fewer than forty-eight accountable bores defined only by their quantity: the Obutus plus six ... the Allertons plus two ... the Bradfields alone. You gave them your *full* attention, didn't you? 'I understand he maintains a certain standard there.' Champagne and two veg *that* night. Plover's eggs paid for by the Russian taxpayer. His wife interrupted him: darling why don't we go out tonight? The Willoughbys won't mind, they know I loathe cooking and Tony *adores* Italian food. Oh sure, sure: anything to please Tony.

'– And if it's a boy,' Cork said, 'I'll take it on myself. There must be *some* facilities for boys, even in a place like that. I mean it's a paradise, isn't it, specially for teachers.'

Wednesday was welfare. Ping pong night. Sing song night. The sergeants' mess: 'Have a little something in that gin and whisky, Mr Turner, sir, just to give it bite. The boys say one thing about you, sir, and I'm sure you won't mind me repeating it, sir, seeing it's Christmas: Mr Turner, they say – they always give you the Mister, sir, it's not something they do for everyone – Mr Turner is tough; Mr Turner is firm. But Mr Turner is *fair*. Now, sir, about my leave ...' Exiles night. A night for worming an inch or two further into the flesh of the Embassy; come back little girl and just slip off those jeans. A night strictly for business. He studied the engagements in detail and thought: you really did work for your secrets, I will admit. You really hawked yourself, didn't you? Scottish Dancing, Skittles Club, Exiles Motoring, Sports Committee. Sooner you than me, boy: you really believed. I'll say that for you too. You really went for goal, didn't you? You kept the ball and you went through the lot of them, you thief.

Which left – since the weekends were not marked with anything but references to gardening and a couple of trips to Hanover – which left Thursdays.

Guilty Thursdays.

Draw a box round Thursday, telephone the Adler and find out what time they lock up. They don't. Draw another box round *that* box, measuring one and a half inches by half an inch and decorate the margins in between with sinuous snakes; cause their forked tongues to lick suggestively at the sweet Gothic curves of the letter T, and wait for the throbbing of a tormented head to be assumed into the waking drumbeat of the cypher machines. And the result?

Silence. Bloody silence.

The result is a Thursday shrouded in sexual mystery, tantalized by abstinence. A Thursday surrounded by meticulous entries written in a swollen, boring mayoral hand by a man with nothing to do and a lot of time to do it in. 'Remember Mary Crabbe's coffee grinder,' the worshipful mayor of Turner's home town in Yorkshire warned his fortunate biographer; remember to grind Mary Crabbe, you thief. 'Speak to Arthur about Myra's birthday,'

Mr Crail the Minister, well known throughout all Yorkshire for the inanity of his sermons, whispered in a benevolent aside; 'Anglo-German Society Buffet Luncheon for Friends of the Free City of Hamburg,' 'International Ladies Subscription Luncheon, Costumes of All Nations, DM. 15.00. Incl. wine,' the Master of Ceremonies proclaimed, puffing his Mess-Night capitals over the lined pages. And make a mental note to ruin Jenny Pargiter's career. And Meadowes' retirement. And Gaunt? And Bradfield? And who else along the path? Myra Meadowes? You wrecker, Harting.

'Can't you turn those bloody things off?'

'I wish I could,' said Cork. 'Something's up, don't ask me what. Personal for Bradfield decypher yourself. Following for Bradfield by hand of officer ... it must be his bloody birthday.'

'Funeral more likely,' Turner growled and returned to the diary.

But on Thursdays Harting *did* have something to do, something real; and not yet realized. Something he kept quiet about. Very. Something urgent and constructive; something secret. Something that made all the other days worthwhile, something to believe in. On Thursdays, Leo Harting touched the hem; and kept his mouth shut. Not even the weekly lie was recorded. Only last Thursday carried any entry at all, and that read: '*Maternus. One o'clock. P.*' The rest were as blank, as innocent and as unrevealing as the little virgins in the ground floor corridor.

Or as guilty.

All Harting's life took place that day. He had lived from Thursday to Thursday as others lived from year to year. What *kind* of meeting did they have, Harting and his master? What kind of relationship after all these years of collaboration? Where did they meet? Where did he unpack those files and letters and breathlessly recite his intelligence? In the tower room of a slate-roofed villa? In a soft, linen bed with a soft silk girl and the jeans hanging on the bedpost? Under the bridge where the train went over? Or in the crumbling Embassy with a dusty chandelier, and old father Meadowes holding his little hand on the gilded sofa? In a pretty baroque bedroom of a Godesberg Hotel? In a grey block on the new housing estates? In a coy bungalow with a wrought iron name and stained glass let into the door? He tried to imagine them, Harting and his master, furtive yet assured, the whispered jokes and the whispered laughter. Here: this is a good one the porno seller whispers; I hardly like to part with this myself. You do *like* it straight don't you? 'Well, it's nice to be fancied,' Allerton lisped. Did they sit over a bottle as they casually planned their next assault upon the citadel, while in the background the camera clicked and the assistant gently shuffled the papers? Give it me once more darling but gently, like Tony. You're not confident, dear, you haven't read the manuals and learned the parts of the rifle.

Or was it a hasty pick-up? A back-street encounter, a frantic exchange as they drove through the small alleys and prayed to God they had no accident?

Or on a hilltop? By a football field, where Harting wore the Balkan hat and the grey uniform of the Movement?

Cork was on the telephone to Miss Peate, and a note of awe had entered his voice:

'Stand by for seven hundred groups from Washington. London please pass and decypher yourself. You'd better warn him now: He's going to be in all night. Look dear, I don't care whether he's conferring with the Queen of England. This one's top priority, and it's my job to let him know so if you won't I will. *Ooh*, she is a bitch.'

'I'm glad you think that,' Turner said with one of his rare grins.

'I reckon she captains the team.'

'England versus the Rest of the World,' Turner agreed and they both laughed.

Was it with Praschko, then, that he had lunched at the *Maternus*? If so, Praschko could hardly be his regular contact, for *he* would not add the tell-tale P, that Harting, who covered his tracks so well; and would not lunch with Praschko in public either, after the trouble he had taken to sever his relationship. Was there, in that case, a middle-man, a cut-out, between Praschko and Harting? Or was this the day the system failed? Hold the line Turner, hold on to reason, for unreason will be your downfall. Make order out of chaos. Was this P the sign that Praschko proposed to see him in person, to warn him perhaps that Siebkron was on his trail? To order him – here was a chance – to order him *at any risk* and *at all costs* to steal the Green File before he ran?

Thursday.

He lifted the keys and swung them gently from his finger. Thursday was the day for meeting ... pressure day ... the day he was warned ... the day before he left ... the day of the weekly briefing and de-briefing ... the day he borrowed the keys from Pargiter.

Christ: had he really slept with Pargiter? There are certain sacrifices, General Shlobodovitch, which not even Leo Harting will make in the service of Mother Russia.

The useless keys. What did he suppose he would get from them? Entry to the coveted despatch box? Balls. He would have observed the procedure; Meadowes had even instructed him in it. He would know very well there were no spare keys to the despatch box in the Duty Officer's bunch. Entry to Registry itself then? Balls again. He would know at a glance that Registry was protected with better locks than these.

So what key did he want?

What key did he want so desperately that he imperilled his whole career as a spy in order to get a copy of it? What key did he want, that he made up to Jenny Pargiter and risked the disapproval of the Embassy – incurred it, indeed, if Meadowes and Gaunt were anything to go by. What key? The key to the lift, so that he could smuggle out his files, dump them in some hideaway on an upper floor and remove them singly and at leisure in his briefcase? Was that what the missing trolley meant?

Fantastic visions presented themselves. He saw the little figure of Harting sprinting down the dark corridor, pushing the trolley ahead of him into the open lift, saw the pyramid of box files trembling on the upper shelf, and on the lower shelf the accidental by-product: the stationery, the seal, the diaries, the long-carriage typewriter from the pool ... He saw the mini van waiting at the side entrance and Harting's nameless master holding the door and he said: 'Oh bugger it,' schoolboy-style at the very moment when Miss Peate came to fetch the telegrams, and Miss Peate's sigh was a statement of sexual abstinence.

'He'll want his code books too,' Cork warned her.

'He happens to be quite aware of the decoding procedure thank you.'

'Here, what's up then, what's going on in Brussels?' Turner asked.

'Rumours.'

'What of?'

'If they wanted you to know *that*, they would hardly use the person to person procedure would they?'

'You don't know London,' said Turner.

As she left she managed even in her walk – in her loping, English touch-nothing, feel-nothing, sex-is-for-the-lower-classes walk – to convey her particular contempt for Turner and all his works.

'I could murder her,' Cork said confidently, 'I could cut her nasty throat. I wouldn't have a moment's regret. Three years she's been here and the only time she smiled was when the Old Man creased his Rolls Royce.'

It was absurd. No questions; he knew it was absurd. Spies of Harting's calibre do not steal; they record, memorize, photograph; spies of Harting's calibre act by graft and calculation, not by impulse. They cover their tracks and survive to deceive again tomorrow.

Nor do they tell transparent lies.

They do not tell Jenny Pargiter that choir practice takes place on Thursdays when she can find out within five minutes that they take place on Fridays. They do not tell Meadowes that they are attending conferences in Bad Godesberg, when both Bradfield and de Lisle know that they are not; and have not done so for two years or more. They do not draw their balance of pay and allowances before they defect, as a signal to anyone who happens to be interested; they do not risk the curiosity of Gaunt in order to work late at night.

Work *where*?

He wanted privacy. He wanted to do by night things he could not do by day. What things? Use his camera in some remote room where he had concealed the files, where he could turn the lock upon himself? Where *was* the trolley? Where *was* the typewriter? Or was their disappearance, as Meadowes had assumed, really unconnected with Harting? At present there was only one answer; Harting had hidden the files in a cache during the day, he had photographed them at night in privacy, and, he returned them the next morning ... Except that he hadn't returned them. So why steal?

A spy does not steal. Rule one. An Embassy, discovering a loss, can change its plans, re-make or revoke treaties, take a dozen prophylactic measures to anticipate and minimize the harm that has been done. The best girl is the girl you don't have. The most effective deceit is the deceit which is never discovered. Then why steal? The reason was already clear. Harting was under pressure. Calculated though his actions might be, they had all the marks of a man racing against time. What was the hurry? What was the deadline?

Slowly, Alan; gently Alan; be like Tony, Alan. Be like lovely, slow, willowy, rhythmical, anatomically conversant, friendly Tony Willoughby, well known in the best clubs and famous for his copulative technique.

'I'd rather have a boy really, first,' said Cork. 'I mean, when you've got one behind you, you can branch out. Mind you, I don't hold with large families I will say. Not unless you can solve the servant problem. Are you married by the by? Oh dear, sorry I asked.'

Suppose for a moment that that furious private journey in Registry was the result of a dormant Communist sympathy re-awakened by the events of last autumn; suppose that was what had driven him. Then to what hasty end was his fury *directed*? Merely to the deadline dictated by a greedy master? The first stage was easily deduced; Karfeld came to power in October. From then on, a popular nationalist party was a reality; even a nationalist government was not impossible. For a month, two months, Harting broods. He sees Karfeld's face on every hoarding, hears the familiar slogans, 'He really *is* an invitation to Communism,' de Lisle had said ... The awakening is slow and reluctant, the old associations and sympathies lie deep and are slow in coming to the surface. Then the moment of decision, the turning point. Either alone, or as a result of Praschko's persuasion, he determines to betray. Praschko approaches him: the Green File. Get the Green File and our old cause will be served ... Get the Green File by decision-day in Brussels ... The contents of that file, Bradfield had said, could effectively compromise our entire posture in Brussels ...

Or was he being blackmailed? Was that the nature of the race? Must he choose between satisfying a greedy master or being compromised by an unknown indiscretion? Was there something in the Cologne incident, for example, which reflected to his discredit: a woman, an involvement in some seedy racket? Had he embezzled Rhine Army funds? Was he selling off tax-free whisky and cigarettes? Had he drifted into a homosexual entanglement? Had he, in fact, succumbed to any one of the dozen classic temptations which are the staple diet of diplomatic espionage? Girl, replace those jeans immediately.

It was not in character. De Lisle was right: there was a thrust, a driving purpose to Harting's actions which went beyond self-preservation; an aggression, a ruthlessness, a fervour which was infinitely more positive than the reluctant compliance of a man under threat. In this underworld life which Turner was now investigating, Harting was not a servant but a principal. He was not deputed but appointed; he was not oppressed, but an oppressor, a hunter, a pursuer. In that, at least, there was an identity between Turner and Harting. But Turner's quarry was named. His tracks, up to a point, were clear. Beyond that point they vanished into the Rhine mist. And most confusing of all was this; though Harting hunted alone, Turner reflected, he had not wanted for patronage ...

Was Harting blackmailing Bradfield?

Turner asked the question suddenly, sitting up quite straight. Was that the explanation of Bradfield's reluctant protection? Was that why he had found him work in the registry, allowed him to vanish without explanation on Thursday afternoons, to wander round the corridors with a briefcase?

He looked once more at the diary and thought: question fundamentals. Madam, show this tired schoolboy your fundamentals, learn the parts, read the book from scratch ... that was your tutor's advice and who are you to ignore the advice of your tutor. Do not ask *why* Christ was born on Christmas Day, ask whether he was born at all. If God gave us our wit, my dear Turner, He gave us also the wit to see through His simplicity. So why Thursday at all? Why the afternoon? Why *regular* meetings? However desperate, why did Harting meet his contact in the daylight, in working hours, in Godesberg, when his absence from the Embassy had to be the occasion of a lie in the first place? It was absurd: Balls, Turner, such as they are. Harting could meet his contact at any time. At night in Königswinter: on the forest slopes of Chamberlain's Petersberg; in Cologne, Koblenz, in Luxembourg or over the Dutch border at weekends when no excuse, truthful or untruthful, need be offered to anyone.

He dropped his pencil and swore out loud.

'Trouble?' Cork inquired. The robots were chattering wildly and Cork was tending them like hungry children.

'Nothing that prayer won't cure,' said Turner, recalling something he had said to Gaunt that morning.

'If you want to send that telegram,' Cork warned him, unperturbed, 'You'd better hurry.' He was moving quickly from one machine to the other, tugging at papers and knobs as if his task were to keep them all at work. 'The balloon's going up in Brussels by the look of it. Threat of a complete Hun walk-out if we don't raise our ante on the Agricultural Fund. Haliday-Pride says he thinks it's a pretext. In half an hour I'll be taking bookings for June if we go on at this rate.'

'What sort of pretext?'

Cork read out loud. 'A convenient door by which to leave Brussels until the situation in the Federal Republic returns to normal.'

Yawning, Turner pushed the telegram form aside. 'I'll send it tomorrow.'

'It is tomorrow,' said Cork gently.

If I smoked I'd smoke one of your cigars. I could do with a bit of soma just now, he thought; if I can't have one of *those*, I'll have a cigar instead. From beginning to end, he knew the whole thesis was wrong.

Nothing worked, nothing interlocked, nothing explained the *energy*, nothing explained itself. He had constructed a chain of which no one link was capable of supporting the others. Holding his head in his hand, he let the Furies loose and watched them posture in grotesque slow motion before his tired imagination: the faceless Praschko, master spy, controlling from a position of parliamentary impregnability a network of refugee agents; Siebkron, the self-seeking custodian of public security, suspecting the Embassy of complicity in a massive betrayal to Russia, alternately guarding and persecuting those whom he believes to be responsible. Bradfield, rigorous, upper-class academic, hater and protector of spies, inscrutable for all his guilty knowledge, keeper of the keys to Registry, to the lift and the despatch box, about to vanish to Brussels after staying up all night; fornicating Jenny Pargiter, compelled into far more sinister complicity by an illusory passion which had already blackened her name all over the Embassy; Meadowes, blinded by a frustrated father's love for the little Harting, precariously loading the last of the forty files on to his trolley; de Lisle, the ethical queer, fighting for Harting's right to betray his friends. Each, magnified and distorted, looked towards him, danced, twisted and vanished in the face of Turner's own derisive objections. The very facts which only hours before had brought him to the brink of revelation now threw him back into the forests of his own doubt.

Yet how else, he told himself, as he locked away his possessions in the steel cupboard and abandoned Cork to the protesting machines; how else, the minister would ask, breaking the seed cake on the little plate with his soft, enormous hand, how else do fancies multiply, how else is wisdom forged, and a course of Christian action finally resolved upon, if not through doubt? Surely, my dear Mrs Turner, doubt is Our Lord's greatest gift to those in need of faith? As he walked into the corridor feeling giddy and very sick, he asked himself once more: what secrets are kept in the magic Green File? And who the hell is going to tell me: me, Turner, a temporary?

The dew was rising out of the field and rolling on to the carriageway like steam. The roads glistened under the wet grey clouds, the wheels of the traffic crackled in the heavy damp. Back to the grey, he thought wearily. No more hunt today. No little angel to submit to this hairless ape. No absolutes yet at the end of the trail; nothing to make a defector of me.

The night porter at the Adler looked at him kindly. 'You were entertained?' he asked, handing him the key.

'Not much.'

'One should go to Cologne. It is like Paris.'

De Lisle's dinner jacket was draped carefully over his armchair with an envelope pinned to the sleeve. A bottle of Naafi whisky stood on the table. 'If you want to take a look at that property,' Turner read, 'I'll collect you on Wednesday morning at five.' A postscript wished him a pleasant evening at the Bradfields, and requested him in a facetious aside not to pour tomato soup down the lapels as de Lisle did not wish to have his politics misread;

particularly, he added, since Herr Ludwig Siebkron of the Federal Ministry of the Interior was expected to be of the company.

Turner ran a bath, took a tumbler from the basin and half filled it with whisky. Why had de Lisle relented? Out of compassion for a lost soul? Save us. And since this was the end to a night of silly questions, why was he being invited to meet Siebkron? He went to bed and half slept until afternoon, dreaming of Bournemouth and the spiky, unclimbable conifers that ran along the bare cliffs at Branksome; and he heard his wife say, as she packed the children's clothes into the suitcase, 'I'll find my road, you find yours, and let's see who gets to Heaven first.' And he heard Jenny Pargiter's crying again, on and on, a call for pity in an empty world. Don't worry, Arthur, he thought, I wouldn't go near Myra to save my life.

10
Kultur at the Bradfields

'You should forbid them more, Siebkron,' Herr Saab declared recklessly, his voice thick with burgundy. 'They are crazy damn fools, Siebkron. Turks.' Saab had out-talked and out-drunk them all, forcing them into embarrassed silence. Only his wife, a little blonde doll of unknown origin and a sweet, revealed bosom, continued to vouchsafe him admiring glances. Invalids, incapable of retaliation, the remaining guests sat dying under the sheer tedium of Herr Saab's diatribe. Behind them, two Hungarian servants moved like nurses along the beds, and they had been told – there was no doubt in Turner's mind – that Herr Ludwig Siebkron merited more attention than all the other patients put together. And needed it. His pale, magnified eyes were already drained of all but the last drops of life; his white hands were folded like napkins beside his plate, and his entire listless manner was that of a person waiting to be moved.

Four silver candlesticks, 1729, by Paul de Lamerie, octagonal based and, in the words of Bradfield's father, quite decently marked, joined Hazel Bradfield to her husband like a line of diamonds down the long table. Turner sat at the centre, midway between the second and third, held rigid by the iron bands of de Lisle's dinner jacket. Even the shirt was too small for him. The head porter had obtained it for him in Bad Godesberg for more money than he had ever paid for a shirt in his life, and now it was choking him and the points of the half-starched collar were stabbing the flesh of his neck.

'Already they are coming in from the villages. Twelve thousand people they will have in that damn Market Place. You know what they are building? They are building a *Schaffott.*' His English had once more defeated him. 'What the hell is *Schaffott*?' he demanded of the company at large.

Siebkron stirred as if he had been offered water. 'Scaffold,' he murmured, and the dying eyes, lifting in Turner's direction, flickered and went out.

'Siebkron's English is fantastic!' Saab cried happily. 'Siebkron dreams of

Palmerston in the daytime and Bismarck in the dark. Now is evening, you see: he is in the middle!' Siebkron heard the diagnosis and it gave him no comfort at all. 'A *scaffold*. I hope they maybe hang the damn fellow on it. Siebkron, you are too kind to him.' He lifted his glass to Bradfield and proposed a long toast pregnant with unwelcome compliments.

'Karl-Heinz also has fantastic English,' the little doll said. 'You are too modest, Karl-Heinz. It is just as good as Herr Siebkron's.' Between her breasts, deep down, Turner glimpsed a tiny flash of white. A handkerchief? A letter? Frau Saab did not care for Siebkron; she cared for no man, indeed, whose virtue was extolled above her husband's. Her interjection had cut the thread: once more the conversation lay like a fallen kite, and for a moment not even her husband had the wind to lift it.

'You said forbid him.' Siebkron had picked up a silver nutmeg grater in his soft hand and was gently turning it in the candlelight, searching for tell-tale flaws. The plate before him was licked quite clean, a cat's plate on a Sunday. He was a sulky, pale man, well-scrubbed and no more than Turner's age, with something of the hotelier about him, a man used to walking on other people's carpets. His features were rounded but unyielding; his lips autonomous, parting to perform one function, closing to perform another. His words were not a help but a challenge, part of a silent interrogation which only fatigue, or the deep cold sickness of his heart, prevented him from conducting aloud.

'*Ja*. Forbid him,' Saab assented, leaning well across the table in order to reach his audience. 'Forbid the meetings, forbid the marching, forbid it all. Like the Communists, that's the only damn thing they understand. *Siebkron, Sie waren ja auch in Hanover!* Siebkron was there also: why don't he forbid it? They are wild beasts out there. They have a power, *nicht wahr Siebkron*? My God, I have also made my experiences.' Saab was an older man, a journalist who had served a number of newspapers in his time, but most of them had disappeared since the war. No one seemed in much doubt what sort of experiences Herr Saab had made. 'But I have never hated the English. Siebkron, you can confirm that. *Das können sie ja bestätigen*. Twenty years I have written about this crazy Republic. I have been critical – but I have never been *hard* against the English. That I never was,' he concluded, jumbling his last words in a way which at once cast doubt upon the whole assertion.

'Karl-Heinz is fantastically strong for the English,' the little doll said. 'He eats English, he drinks English.' She sighed as if the rest of his activities were rather English too. She ate a great deal, and some of it was still in her mouth as she spoke, and her tiny hands held other things that she would eat quite soon.

'We owe you a debt,' said Bradfield with heavy cheerfulness, 'Long may you keep it up, Karl-Heinz.' He had arrived back from Brussels half an hour ago, and his eye was on Siebkron all the time.

Mrs Vandelung, the wife of the Dutch Counsellor, drew her stole more snugly over her ample shoulders. 'We are going to England every year,' she said complacently, apropos of nothing at all. 'Our daughter is at school in England, our son is at school in England ...' She ran on. Nothing she loved, cherished or possessed was not of an English character. Her husband, a shrivelled, nautical man, touched Hazel Bradfield's beautiful wrist and nodded with reflected fervour.

'Always,' he whispered, as if it were a pledge. Hazel Bradfield, waking from her reverie, smiled rather solemnly at him while her eyes regarded with detachment the grey hand that still held her. 'Why, Bernhard,' she said gently, 'what a darling you are tonight. You will make the women jealous of me.' It was not, all the same, a comfortable joke. Her voice had its ugly edge; she could be one of several daughters, Turner decided, intercepting her angry glance as Saab resumed his monologue; but she was not merciful to her plainer sisters. 'Am I sitting in Leo's place?' he wondered, 'Eating Leo's portion?' But Leo stayed at home on Tuesdays ... and besides, Leo was not allowed here, he reminded himself, raising his glass to answer a toast from Saab, except for a drink.

Saab's subject, miraculously, was still the British, but he had enriched it with autobiographical matter on the discomforts of bombing: 'You know what they say about Hamburg? Question: what is the difference between an Englishman and a man of Hamburg? Answer: the man of Hamburg speaks German. You know in those cellars, what we were saying? *Thank God they are British Bombs!* Bradfield prosit! Never again.'

'Never again indeed,' Bradfield replied, and wearily toasted him in the German style, looking at him over the brim of his glass, drinking and looking again.

'Bradfield, you are the *best piece*. Your ancestors fought at Waterloo, and your wife is as beautiful as the Queen. You are the best piece in the British Embassy and you didn't invite the damn Americans and you didn't invite the damn French. You are a good fellow. Frenchmen is bastards,' he concluded to everyone's alarm, and there was a moment's startled silence.

'Karl-Heinz, I'm sure that isn't very loyal,' said Hazel and a little laugh went up at her end of the table, originated by a pointless elderly Gräfin summoned at the last moment to partner Alan Turner. An unwelcome shaft of electric light broke upon the company. The Hungarians marched in from the kitchen like the morning shift and cleared away bottles and china with inconsiderate *panache*.

Saab leaned still further across the table and pointed a big, not very clean finger at the guest of honour. 'You see this fellow Ludwig Siebkron here is a damn odd fellow. We all admire him in the Press Corps, because we can't never damn well get a hold of him, and in journalism we admire only what we cannot have. And do you know why we cannot have Siebkron?'

The question amused Saab very much. He looked happily round the table, his dark face glistening with delight. 'Because he is so damn busy with his good friend and ... *Kumpan*.' He snapped his fingers in frustration. '*Kumpan*,' he repeated. '*Kumpan?*'

'*Drinking companion*,' Siebkron suggested. Saab stared at him lamely, bewildered by assistance from such an unexpected quarter. 'Drinking companion,' he muttered; 'Klaus Karfeld,' and fell silent.

'Karl-Heinz, you must remember *Kumpan*,' his wife said softly, and he nodded and smiled at her valiantly.

'You have come to join us, Mister Turner?' Siebkron inquired, addressing the nutmeg grater. Suddenly the lights were on Turner, and Siebkron, risen from his bed, was conducting the rare surgery of a private practice.

'For a few days,' Turner said. The audience was slow in gathering, so that for a moment the two men faced each one another in secret communion while the others continued their separate pursuits. Bradfield had engaged in a desultory cross-talk with Vandelung; Turner caught a reference to Vietnam. Saab, suddenly returning to the field, took up the subject and made it his own.

'The Yanks would fight in Saigon,' he declared, 'but they wouldn't fight in Berlin. Seems a bit of a pity they didn't build the Berlin Wall in Saigon.' His voice was louder and more offensive, but Turner heard it out of the dark that was beyond Siebkron's unflinching gaze. 'All of a sudden the Yanks are going crazy about self-determination. Why don't they try it in East Germany a little bit? Everyone fights for the damn Negroes. Everyone fights for the damn jungle. Maybe it's a pity we don't wear no feathers.' He seemed to be challenging Vandelung, but without effect: the old Dutchman's grey skin was as smooth as a coffin, and nothing would sprout there any more. 'Maybe it's a pity we don't have no palm trees in Berlin.' They heard him pause to drink. 'Vietnam is shit. But at least this time maybe they can't say we started it,' he added with more than a trace of self-pity.

'War is terrible,' the Gräfin whickered, 'We lost everything,' but she was talking after the curtain had gone up. Herr Ludwig Siebkron proposed to speak, and had put down the silver nutmeg grater in order to signify his will.

'And where do you come from, Mister Turner?'

'Yorkshire.' There was silence. 'I spent the war in Bournemouth.'

'Herr Siebkron meant which Department,' Bradfield said crisply.

'Foreign Office,' said Turner. 'Same as everyone else,' and looked at him indifferently across the table. Siebkron's white eyes neither condemned nor admired, but waited for the moment to insert the scalpel.

'And may we ask Mr Turner which section of the Foreign Office is so fortunate as to have his services?'

'Research.'

'He's also a distinguished mountaineer,' Bradfield put in from far away, and the little doll cried out with the sharp surprise of sexual delight. '*Die Berge!*' Out of the corner of his eye Turner saw one china hand touch the halter of her dress as if she would take it clean off in her enthusiasm. 'Karl-Heinz—'

'Next year,' Saab's brown voice assured her in a whisper. 'Next year we go to the mountains,' and Siebkron smiled to Turner as if that were one joke they could surely share.

'But now Mr Turner is in the valley. You are staying in Bonn, Mr Turner?'

'Godesberg.'

'In a hotel, Mr Turner?'

'The Adler. Room Ten.'

'And what kind of research, I wonder, is conducted from the Hotel Adler, Room Ten?'

'Ludwig, my dear chap,' Bradfield interposed – his jocularity was not so very hollow – 'Surely you recognize a spy when you see one. Alan's our Mata Hari. He entertains the Cabinet in his bedroom.'

Laughter, Siebkron's expression said, does not last for ever; he waited until it had subsided. 'Alan,' he repeated quietly. 'Alan Turner from Yorkshire, working in Foreign Office Research Department and staying at the Adler Hotel, a distinguished mountaineer. You must forgive my curiosity, Mr Turner. We are all on edge here in Bonn, you know. As, for my sins, I am charged with the physical protection of the British Embassy, I have naturally a certain interest in the people I protect. Your presence here is reported to Personnel Department no doubt? I must have missed the bulletin.'

'We put him down as a technician,' Bradfield said, clearly irritated now to be questioned before his own guests.

'How sensible,' said Siebkron. 'So much simpler than Research. He does research but you put him down as a technician. Your technicians on the other hand are all engaged in research. It's a perfectly simple arrangement. But your research is of a practical nature, Mr Turner? A statistician? Or you are an academic perhaps?'

'Just general.'

'General research. A very catholic responsibility. You will be here long?'

'A week. Maybe more. Depends how long the project lasts.'

'The research project? Ah. Then you have a project. I had imagined at first you were replacing someone. Ewan Waldebere for instance; he was engaged in commercial research, was he not, Bradfield? Or Peter McCreedy, on scientific development. Or Harting: you are not replacing Leo Harting for instance? Such a pity he's gone. One of your oldest and most valuable collaborators.'

'Oh Harting!' Mrs Vandelung had taken up the name, and it was already clear she had strong views. 'You know what they are saying now already? That Harting is drunk in Cologne. He goes on *fits* you know.' She was much entertained to hold their interest. 'All the week he wears angels' wings and plays the organ and sings like a Christian; but at weekends he goes to Cologne and fights the Germans. He is quite a Jekyll and Hyde I assure you!' She laughed indulgently. 'Oh he is very wicked. Rawley, you remember André de Hoog I am sure. He has heard it all from the police here: Harting made a great fight in Cologne. In a night club. It was all to do with a bad woman. Oh, he is *very* mysterious I assure you. And now we have no one to play the organ.'

Through the mist Siebkron repeated his question.

'I'm not replacing anyone,' Turner said and he heard Hazel Bradfield's voice, quite steady from his left, but vibrant for all that with anger unexpressed.

'Mrs Vandelung, you know our silly English ways. We are supposed to leave the men to their jokes.'

Reluctantly the women departed. Little Frau Saab, desolated to leave her husband, kissed his neck and made him promise to be sober. The Gräfin said that in Germany one expected a cognac after a meal: it aided the digestion. Only Frau Siebkron followed without complaint; she was a quiet, deserted beauty who had learned very early in her marriage that it paid not to resist.

Bradfield was at the sideboard with decanters and silver coasters; the Hungarians had brought coffee in a Hester Bateman jug which sat in unremarked magnificence at Hazel's end of the table. Little Vandelung was lost in memories; he was standing at the French windows, staring down the sloping dark lawn at the lights of Bad Godesberg.

'Now we will get port,' Saab assured them all. 'With Bradfield that is always a fantastic experience.' He selected Turner. 'I have had ports here, I can tell you, that are older than my father. What are we getting tonight, Bradfield? A Cockburn? Maybe he will give us a Cruft's. Bradfield knows all the brands. *Ein richtiger Kenner*: Siebkron, what is *Kenner auf Englisch*?'

'Connoisseur.'

'French!' Saab was outraged. 'The English have no word for *Kenner*? They use a French word? Bradfield! Telegram! Tonight! *Sofort an Ihre Majestät!* Personal recommendation top secret to the damn Queen. All Connoisseurs are forbidden. Only Kenner permitted! You are married, Mister Turner?'

Bradfield, having sat himself in Hazel's chair, now passed the port to his left. The coaster was a double one, joined elaborately with silver cords.

'No,' said Turner, and it was a word thrown down hard for anyone to pick up who wanted it. Saab, however, heard no music but his own.

'Crazy! The English should breed! Many babies. Make a culture. England, Germany and Scandinavia! To hell with the French, to hell with the Africans. *Klein-Europa*, do you understand me, Turner?' He held up his clenched fist, stiff from the elbow. 'Tough and good. What can speak and think. I am not so damn crazy. *Kultur*. You know what that means, *Kultur*?' He drank. 'Fantastic!' he cried. 'The best ever! Number one.' He held up his glass to the candle. 'The best damn port I ever had. You can see the blood in the heart. Bradfield, what is it? A Cockburn for sure, but he always contradicts me.'

Bradfield hesitated, caught in a genuine dilemma. His eye turned first to Saab's glass, then to the decanters, then to his glass again.

'I'm delighted you enjoyed it. Karl-Heinz,' he said. 'I rather think, as a matter of fact, that what you are drinking is Madeira.'

Vandelung, from the French windows, began laughing. It was a cracked, vengeful laugh and it went on for a long time, while his whole little body shook to the tune of it, rising and falling with the bellows of his old lungs.

'Well now, Saab,' he said at last, walking slowly back to the table, 'Maybe you will bring a little of your culture to the Netherlands as well.'

He began laughing again like a schoolboy, holding his knobbly hand to his mouth in order to conceal the gaps, and Turner was sorry for Saab just then, and did not care for Vandelung at all.

Siebkron had taken no port.

'You went to Brussels today. I hope very much that you had a successful journey, Bradfield? I hear there are renewed difficulties. I am sorry. My colleagues tell me New Zealand presents a serious problem.'

'Sheep!' Saab cried. 'Who will eat the sheep? The English have made a damn fine farm out there and now no one won't eat the sheep.'

Bradfield's voice was all the more deliberate. 'No new problem has been raised at Brussels. The questions of New Zealand and the Agricultural Fund have both been on the table for years. They present no problems that cannot be ironed out between friends.'

'Between good friends. Let us hope you are right. Let us hope the friendship is good enough and the difficulties small enough. Let us hope so.' Siebkron's gaze was on Turner again. 'So Harting is gone,' he remarked, laying his hands flatly together in prayer. 'Such a loss to our community. Particularly for the Church.' And looking directly at Turner he added: 'My colleagues tell me you know Mr Sam Allerton, the distinguished British journalist. You spoke with him today. I believe.'

Vandelung had given himself a glass of Madeira and was sampling it ostentatiously. Saab, sullen and dark faced, stared from one of them to the other, comprehending little.

'Ludwig, what an extraordinary idea. What do you mean, "Harting is gone"? He's on leave. I cannot imagine how all these silly rumours have got about. Poor fellow, his only crime was not to tell the Chaplain.' Bradfield's laughter was wholly artificial, but it was an act of courage in itself. 'Compassionate leave. It is not like you, Ludwig, to get your information wrong.'

'You see, Mr Turner, I have great difficulties here. For my sins, I am responsible for civil order during the demonstrations. Responsible to my Minister, you understand; and only in a modest capacity. But responsible all the same.'

His modesty was saintly. Put a ruff on him and a surplice and he could sing in Harting's choir any time. 'We are expecting a little demonstration on Friday. I am afraid that among certain minority groups the English are at present not very popular. You will appreciate that I don't want anybody to get hurt; anybody at all. Naturally therefore I like to know where everybody is. So that I can protect them. But Poor Mister Bradfield is often so overworked he does not tell me.' He broke off and glanced once at Bradfield, and then no more. 'Now I am not *blaming* Bradfield that he does not tell me. Why should he?' The white hands parted in concession. 'There are many little things and there are even one or two big things which Bradfield does not tell me. Why should he? That would not be consistent with his vocation as a diplomat. I am correct, Mister Turner?'

'It's not my problem.'

'But it is mine. Let me explain what happens. My colleagues are observant people. They look around, count heads, and notice that somebody is missing. They make inquiries, question servants and friends perhaps, and they are told that he has disappeared. Immediately I am worried for him. So are my colleagues. My colleagues are compassionate people. They don't like anyone to go astray. What could be more human? They are boys, some of them. Just boys. Harting has gone to England?'

The last question was spoken directly to Turner, but Bradfield took it on himself and Turner blessed him.

'He has family problems. Clearly we cannot advertise them. I don't propose to put a man's private life upon the table in order to satisfy your files.'

'That is a very excellent principle. And one we must all follow. Do you hear that, Mr Turner?' His voice was remarkably emphatic. 'What is the point of a paper chase? What *is* the point?'

'Why on earth are you so bothered about Harting?' Bradfield demanded, as if it were a joke of which he had tired. 'I'm astonished you even know of his existence. Let's go and get some coffee, shall we?'

He stood up; but Siebkron remained where he was.

'But of *course* we know of his existence,' he declared. 'We admire his work. We admire it very much indeed. In a department such as mine, Mr Harting's ingenuity finds many admirers. My colleagues speak of him constantly.'

'What are you talking about?' Bradfield had coloured in anger. 'What *is* all this? What work?'

'He used to be with the Russians, you know,' Siebkron explained to Turner. 'In Berlin. That was a long time ago, of course, but I am sure that he learnt a great deal from them, don't you think so, Mr Turner? A little technique, a little ideology perhaps? And *grip*. The Russians *never* let go.'

Bradfield had put the two decanters on a tray and was standing at the doorway waiting for them to go ahead of him.

'What work was that?' Turner asked gruffly, as Siebkron reluctantly rose from his chair.

'Research. Just general research, Mr Turner. Like yourself, you see. It is nice to think that you and Harting have common interests. As a matter of fact that is why I asked whether you would replace him. My colleagues understand from Mr Allerton that you and Harting have *many* things in common.'

Hazel Bradfield looked up anxiously as they entered, and the glance she exchanged with Bradfield was eloquent of the emergency. Her four women guests sat on a single sofa. Mrs Vandelung was working at a sampler; Frau Siebkron in church black had laid her hands on her lap and was staring in private fascination at the open fire. The Gräfin, consoling herself for the untitled company she was obliged to keep, sipped morosely at a large brandy. Her parsimonious face was lit with small red flowers like poppies on a battlefield. Only little Frau Saab, her bosom freshly powdered, smiled to see them enter.

They were settled, resigned to boredom.

'Bernhard,' said Hazel Bradfield, patting the cushion beside her, 'Come and sit by me. I find you *specially* cosy this evening.' With a foxy smile the old man took his place obediently beside her. 'Now you're to tell me *all* the horrors I am to expect on Friday.' She was playing the spoilt beauty, and playing it well, but there was an undercurrent of anxiety in her voice which not even Bradfield's tuition had taught her wholly to suppress.

At a separate table, Siebkron sat alone like a man who travelled by a better class. Bradfield talked to his wife. No, she conceded, she had not been to Brussels; she did not go often with her husband. 'But you must insist!' he declared and launched at once upon a description of a favourite Brussels hotel. The Amigo; one should stay at the Amigo; it had the best service he had ever encountered. Frau Siebkron did not care for large hotels; she took her holidays in the Black Forest; that was what the children liked best. Yes; Bradfield loved the Black Forest himself; he had close friends at Dornstetten.

Turner listened in grudging admiration to Bradfield's inexhaustible flow of small-talk. He expected no help from anyone. His eyes were dark with fatigue, but his dialogue was as fresh, as considerate and as aimless as if he were on holiday.

'Come along, Bernhard; you're just a wise old owl and nobody ever tells me anything. I'm just the Hausfrau. I'm supposed to look at *Vogue* and make canapés all day.'

'You know the saying,' Vandelung replied. 'What else must happen in Bonn before something happens? They can do nothing we have not seen before.'

'They can trample all over my roses,' Hazel remarked, lighting herself a cigarette. 'They can steal my husband away at all hours of the night. Day trips to Brussels indeed! It's quite absurd. And look what they did in Hanover. Can you imagine what would happen if they broke *these* windows? Dealing with that wretched Works Department? We'd all be sitting here in overcoats while they worked out who pays. It's *too* bad, it really is. Thank goodness we have Mr Turner to protect us.' As she said this her gaze rested upon him, and it seemed to him both anxious and inquiring. 'Frau Saab, does *your* husband travel all over the place these days? I am sure journalists make *far* better husbands than diplomats.'

'He is very true.' The little doll blushed unhappily.

'She means *loyal*.' Saab kissed her hand with love.

Opening her tiny handbag, she took out a powder compact and parted its gold petals one by one. 'We have been married one year tomorrow. It is so beautiful.'

'*Du bist noch schöner*,' Saab cried and the conversation disintegrated into an exchange of domestic and financial intelligence on the Saabs' newly-formed household. Yes, they had bought a plot of land up by Oberwinter. Karl-Heinz had bought it last year for the engagement and already the value had risen four marks per *quadratmeter*.

'Karl-Heinz, how do you say *quadratmeter*?'

'The same,' Saab asserted, 'Quadrate meter,' and glowered at Turner in case he should dare to contradict him.

Suddenly Frau Saab was talking and no one could stop her any more. Her whole little life was spread before them in an oriental tinkle of hopes and disappointments; the colour which had mounted so prettily in her cheeks stayed there like the warm flush of sexual success.

They had hoped that Karl-Heinz would get the Bonn *Büro* of his newspaper. Bonn editor; that had been their expectation. His salary would go up another thousand and he would have a real *position*. What had happened instead? The paper had appointed *den Flitzdorf* and the Flitzdorf was just a boy, with no experience and nothing and *completely* homosexual and Karl-Heinz, who had worked now eighteen years for the paper and had so many contacts, was still only second man and was having to make extra by writing for all the cheese-papers.

'Yellow press,' said her husband, but for once she quite ignored him.

Well, when that happened they had a long discussion and decided they would go ahead with their building plans although the *Hypothek* was appalling; and no sooner had they paid over the money to the *Makler* than a really terrible thing happened: the Africans had come to Oberwinter. It was quite awful. Karl-Heinz was always very sharp against Africans, but now they had actually taken the next door plot and were building a *Residenz* for one of the Ambassadors, and twice a week they all came up and climbed like monkeys over the bricks and shouted they wanted it different; and in no time they would have a whole colony up there, with Cadillacs and children and music all night, and as for herself, she would be all alone when Karl-Heinz was working late, and they were already putting special bolts on the doors so that she would not be—

'They talk fantastic!' Saab shouted, loudly enough for Siebkron and Bradfield to look round at him sharply; for the two men had drawn away to the window and were murmuring quietly into the night. 'But we don't get nothing to drink!'

'Karl-Heinz, my poor chap, we are completely neglecting you.' With a final word to Siebkron, Bradfield walked down the room to where the decanters stood on their bright-cut silver tray. 'Who else would like a nightcap?'

Vandelung would have joined him, but his wife forbade it.

'And take *great* care,' she warned the young Frau Saab in a dreadfully audible aside, 'Or he will have a heart attack. So much eating and drinking and shouting: it affects the heart. And with a young wife not easily satisfied,' she added contentedly, 'he could die easy.' Taking her little grey husband firmly by the wrist, Frau Vandelung led him into the hall. In the same instant Hazel Bradfield leaned purposefully across the abandoned chair. 'Mr Turner,' she said quietly, 'there is a matter in which you can help me. May I take you away a moment?'

They stood in the sun room. Potted plants and tennis rackets lay on the window sills; a child's tractor, a pogo stick and a bundle of garden canes were strewn over the tiled floor. There was a mysterious smell of honey.

'I understand you're making Inquiries about Harting,' she said. Her voice was crisp and commanding; she was very much Bradfield's wife.

'Am I?'

'Rawley's worrying himself to death. I'm convinced that Leo Harting's at the back of it.'

'I see.'

'He doesn't sleep and he won't even discuss it. For the last three days he's hardly spoken to me. He even sends messages by way of other people. He's cut himself off entirely from everything except his work. He's near breaking point.'

'He didn't give me that impression.'

'He happens to be my husband.'

'He's very lucky.'

'What's Harting taken?' Her eyes were bright with anger or determination. 'What's he stolen?'

'What makes you think he's stolen anything?'

'Listen. I, not you, am responsible for my husband's welfare. I have a *right* to know if Rawley is in trouble; tell me what Harting has done. Tell me where he is. They're all whispering about it; everyone. This ridiculous story about Cologne; Siebkron's curiosity: why can't *I* know what's going on?'

'That's what I was wondering myself,' Turner said.

He thought she might hit him, and he knew that if she did, he would hit her back. She was beautiful, but the arch corners of her mouth were drawn down in the frustrated fury of a rich child, and there were things about her voice and manner which were dreadfully familiar.

'Get out. Leave me alone.'

'I don't care who you are. If you want to know official secrets you can bloody well get them at source,' Turner said, and waited for her to rise to him again.

Instead, she swept past him into the hall and ran upstairs. For a moment he remained where he was, staring confusedly at the muddle of children's and adult toys, the fishing rods, the croquet set and all the casual, wasteful equipment of a world he had never known. Still lost in thought, he made his way slowly back to the drawing-room. As he entered, Bradfield and Siebkron, side by side at the French window, turned as one man to stare at him, the object of their shared contempt.

It was midnight. The Gräfin, drunk and quite speechless, had been loaded into a taxi. Siebkron had gone; his farewell had been confined to the Bradfields. His wife must have gone with him, though Turner had not noticed her departure; the cushion where she had sat was barely depressed. The Vandelungs had also gone. Now the five of them sat round the fire in a state of post-festive depression, the Saabs on the sofa holding hands and staring at the dying coals, Bradfield quite silent sipping his thin whisky; while Hazel herself, in her long skirt of green tweed, curled like a mermaid into an armchair, played with the Blue Russian cat in self-conscious imitation of an eighteenth-century dream. Though she rarely looked at Turner, she did not trouble to ignore him; occasionally she even addressed a remark to him. A tradesman had been impertinent, but Hazel Bradfield would not do him the compliment of taking away her custom.

'Hanover was fantastic,' Saab muttered.

'Oh not again, Karl-Heinz,' Hazel pleaded, 'I think I've heard enough of that to last forever.'

'*Why* did they run?' he asked himself. 'Siebkron was also there. They *ran*. From the front. They ran like crazy for that library. Why did they do that? All at once: *alles auf einmal*.'

'Siebkron keeps asking me the same question,' Bradfield said in an exhausted moment of frankness. 'Why did they run? *He* should know if anyone does: he was at Eich's bedside; I wasn't. He heard what she had to say, I suppose: I didn't. What the hell's got into him? On and on: "What happened at Hanover mustn't happen in Bonn." Of course it mustn't, but he seems to think it's my fault it happened in the first place. I've never known him like that.'

'You?' Hazel Bradfield said with undisguised contempt. 'Why on earth should he ask *you*? You weren't even there.'

'He asks me all the same,' said Bradfield, standing up, in a moment so utterly passive and tender that Turner was moved suddenly to speculate on their relationship. 'He asks me all the same.' He put his empty glass on the sideboard. 'Whether you like it or not. He asks me repeatedly: "Why did they run?" Just as Karl-Heinz was asking now. "What made them run? What was it about the library that attracted them?" All I could say was that it was British. Come on, Karl-Heinz: we must put you young people to bed.'

'And the grey buses,' Saab muttered. 'You read what they found about the buses for the bodyguard? They were *grey*, Bradfield, *grey*!'

'Is that significant?'

'It *was*, Bradfield. About a thousand years ago, it was damn significant, my dear.'

'I'm afraid I'm missing the point,' Bradfield observed with a weary smile.

'As usual,' his wife said; no one took it as a joke.

They stood in the hall. Of the two Hungarians, only the girl remained.

'You have been damn good to me, Bradfield,' Saab said sadly as they took their leave. 'Maybe I talk too much. *Nicht wahr, Marlene*: I talk too much. But I don't trust that fellow Siebkron. I am an old pig, see? But Siebkron is a young pig. Pay attention!'

'Why shouldn't I trust him, Karl-Heinz?'

'Because he don't never ask a question unless he knows the answer.' With this enigmatic reply, Karl-Heinz fervently kissed the hand of his hostess and stepped into the dark, steadied by the young arm of his adoring wife.

Turner sat in the back while Saab drove very slowly on the left hand side of the road. His wife was asleep on his shoulder, one little hand still scratching fondly at the black fur which decorated the nape of her husband's neck.

'Why did they run at Hanover?' Saab repeated, weaving happily between the oncoming cars, 'Why those damn fools run?'

At the Adler, Turner asked for morning coffee at half past four, and the porter noted it with an understanding smile, as if that were the sort of time he expected an Englishman to rise. As he went to bed, his mind detached itself from the distasteful and mystifying interrogations of Herr Ludwig Siebkron in order to dwell on the more agreeable person of Hazel Bradfield. It was just as mysterious, he decided as he fell asleep, that a woman so beautiful, desirable and evidently intelligent, could tolerate the measureless tedium of diplomatic life in Bonn. If darling upper-class Anthony Willoughby ever took a shine at her, he thought, what on earth would Bradfield do then? And why – the chorus that sang him to sleep was the same chorus which had kept him awake throughout the long, tense, meaningless evening – why the hell was he invited in the first place?

And *who* had asked him? 'I am going to invite you to dinner on Tuesday,' Bradfield had said: don't blame *me* for what happens.

And Bradfield, I *heard*! I heard you submit to pressure; I felt the softness of you for the first time; I took a step in your direction, I saw the knife in your back and I heard you speak with my own voice. Hazel you bitch; Siebkron you swine; Harting you thief: if *that's* what you think about life, queer de Lisle simpered in his ear, why don't you defect yourself. God is dead. You can't have it both ways, that would be too medieval ...

He had set his alarm for four o'clock, and it seemed to be ringing already.

II
Königswinter

It was still dark when de Lisle collected him and Turner had to ask the night porter to unlock the hotel door. The street was cold, friendless and deserted; the mist came at them in sudden patches.

'We'll have to go the long way over the bridge. The ferry's not running at this hour.' His manner was short to the point of abruptness.

They had entered the carriageway. To either side of them, new blocks, built of tile and armoured glass, sprang like night weeds out of the untilled fields, crested by the lamps of small cranes. They passed the Embassy. The dark hung upon the wet concrete like the smoke of a spent battle. The Union Jack swung limply from its standard, a single flower on a soldier's grave.

Under the weary light of the front porch, the lion and the unicorn, their profiles blurred with repeated coats of red and gold, fought bravely on. In the waste land, the two rickety goalposts leaned drunkenly in the twilight.

'Things are warming up in Brussels,' de Lisle remarked in a tone which promised little elaboration. A dozen cars were parked in the forecourt, Bradfield's white jaguar stood in its private bay.

'For us or against us?'

'What do you think?' He continued: 'We have asked for private talks with the Germans; the French have done the same. Not that they want them; it's the tug-of-war they enjoy.'

'Who wins?'

De Lisle did not reply.

The deserted town hung in the pink unearthly glow which cradles every city in the hour before dawn. The streets were wet and empty, the houses soiled like old uniforms. At the University arch, three policemen had made a lane of barricades and they flagged them down as they approached. Sullenly they walked round the small car, recording the licence number, testing the suspension by standing on the rear bumper, peering through the misted windscreen at the huddled occupants within.

'What was that they shouted?' Turner asked as they drove on.

'Look out for the one-way signs.' He turned left, following the blue arrow. 'Where the hell are they taking us?'

An electric van was scrubbing the gutter; two more policemen in greatcoats of green leather, their peak caps bent, suspiciously surveyed its progress. In a shop window a young girl was fitting beach clothes to a model, holding one plastic arm and feeding the sleeve along it. She wore boots of heavy felt and shuffled like a prisoner. They were in the station square. Black banners stretched across the road and along the awning of the station. 'Welcome to Klaus Karfeld!' 'A hunter's greeting, Klaus!' 'Karfeld! You stand for our self-respect!' A photograph, larger than any which Turner had so far seen, was raised on a massive new hoarding. '*Freitag!*' said the legend: Friday. The floodlights shone upon the world and left the face in darkness.

'They're arriving today. Tilsit, Meyer-Lothringen; Karfeld. They're coming down from Hanover to prepare the ground.'

'With Ludwig Siebkron playing host.'

They were running along some tramlines, still following the diversion signs. The route took them left and right again. They had passed under a small bridge, doubled back, entered another square, halted at some improvised traffic lights and suddenly they were both sitting forward in their cramped seats, staring ahead of them in astonishment, up the gentle slope of the market place towards the Town Hall.

Immediately before them, the empty stalls stood in lines like beds in a barrack hut. Beyond the stalls, the gingerbread houses offered their jagged gables to the lightening sky. But de Lisle and Turner were looking up the hill at the single pink and grey building which dominated the whole square. Ladders had been laid against it; the balcony was festooned in swathes of black; a flock of Mercedes was parked before it on the cobble. To its left, in front of a chemist's shop, floodlit from a dozen places, rose a white scaffolding like the outline of a medieval storming tower. The pinnacle reached as high as the dormer windows of the adjacent building; the giant legs, naked as roots grown in the dark, splayed obscenely over their own black shadows. Workmen were already swarming at its base. Turner could hear the piping echo of hammers and the whine of powered saws. A stack of timber struggled upwards on a silent pulley.

'Why are the flags at half mast?'

'Mourning. It's a gimmick. They're in mourning for national honour.'

They crossed the long bridge. 'That's better,' said de Lisle with a small grunt of satisfaction, and pushed down his collar as if he had entered a warmer world.

He was driving very fast. They passed a village and another. Soon they had entered the country and were following a new road along the eastern bank. To their right the tor of Godesberg, divided by tiers of mist, stood grimly over the sleeping town. They skirted the vineyard. The furrows, picked out by the mysterious darkness, were like seams stitched to the zig-zag patterns of the staves. Above the vineyard, the forests of the Seven Hills; above the forests, broken castles and Gothic follies black against the skyline. Abandoning the main road, they entered a short avenue which led directly to an esplanade bordered by unlit lamps and pollarded trees. Beyond it lay the Rhine, smouldering and undefined.

'Next on the left,' de Lisle said tersely. 'Tell me if there's anyone on guard.'

A large white house loomed before them. The lower windows were shuttered, the front gates open. Turner left the car and walked a short way along the pavement. Picking up a stone, he flung it hard and accurately against the side of the house. The sound echoed crookedly across the water, and upwards towards the black slopes of Petersberg. Scanning the mist, they waited for a cry or a footstep. There was none.

'Park up the road and come back,' said Turner.

'I think I'll just park up the road. How long will you need?'

'You know the house. Come and help me.'

'Not my form. Sorry. I don't mind bringing you but I'm not coming in.'

'Then why bring me?'

De Lisle did not reply.

'Don't dirty your fingers, will you.'

Keeping to the grass verge, Turner followed the drive towards the house. Even by that light, he was conscious of the same sense of order which had characterized Harting's room. The long lawn was very tidy, the rose beds trimmed and weeded, the roses ringed with grass-cuttings and separately labelled with metal tags. At the kitchen door, three dustbins, numbered and licensed according to the local regulation, stood in a concrete bay. About to insert the key, he heard a footstep.

It was unmistakably a footstep. It had the double imprint, slurred yet infallibly human, of a heel falling on gravel, and the toe immediately following. A cautious footstep perhaps; a gesture half made and then withheld, a message sent and revoked; but beyond all argument a footstep.

'Peter?' He's changed his mind again, he thought. He's being soft hearted. 'Peter!'

There was still no answer.

'Peter, is that you?' He stooped, quickly picked up an empty bottle from the wooden crate beside him and waited, his ears tuned to the lightest sound. He heard the crowing of a cock in the Seven Hills. He heard the prickling of the sodden earth, like the tingling of pine needles in a wood; he heard the rustling of tiny waves along the river's shore; he heard the distant throbbing of the Rhine itself, like the turning of an unearthly machine, one tone made of many, breaking and joining like the unseen water; he heard the mutter of hidden barges, the shoot of anchor chains suddenly released; he heard a cry, like the lowing of lost cattle on a moor, as a lonely siren echoed on the cliff face. But he did not hear another footstep, nor the comfortable tones of de Lisle's courteous voice. Turning the key he pushed open the door, hard; then stood still and listened again, the bottle rigid in his hand, while the faint aroma of stale cigar smoke rose lovingly to his nostrils.

He waited, letting the room come to him out of the cold gloom. Gradually, the new sounds began. First from the direction of the serving hatch came the chink of glass; from the hall, the creak of wood; in the cellar, a hollow box was dragged over a concrete floor; a gong rang, one tone, imperious and distinctive and from everywhere now, all about him there rose a vibrant, organic hum, obscure yet very close, pressing upon him, louder with every minute, as if the whole building had been struck with a flat hand and were trembling from the blow. Running to the hall, he charged into the dining-room, put on the lights with a single sweeping movement of his palm and glared savagely round him, shoulders haunched, bottle clenched in his considerable fist.

'Harting!' he shouted now, 'Harting?' He heard the shuffle of scattering feet, and thrust back the partition door.

'Harting!' he called again, but his only answer was the soot slipping in the open hearth, and the banging of an errant shutter on the poor stucco outside. He went to the window and looked across the lawn towards the river. On the far bank, the American Embassy, brilliant as a power house, drove yellow shafts through the mist deep into the elusive water. Then at last he recognized the nature of his tormentor: a chain of six barges, flags flying, radar-lights glittering above them like the blue stars nailed to the mast, was swiftly disappearing into the fog. As the last vessel vanished, so the strange domestic orchestra put aside its instuments. The glass ceased to chime, the stairs to creak, the soot to fall, the walls to tremble. The house settled again, ruminative but not yet reassured, waiting for the next assault.

Putting the bottle on the windowsill, Turner straightened himself and walked slowly from room to room. It was a wasteful, thinly built barrack of a place, built for a colonel out of reparation costs, at a time when the High Commission was stationed on the Petersberg; one of a colony, de Lisle had said, but the colony was never completed, for by then the Occupation had ended and the project was abandoned. A left-over house for a left-over man. It had a light side and a dark side according to whether rooms looked on to the river or the Petersberg; the plaster was rough and belonged out of doors. The furniture was equivocal, as if no one had ever decided how much prestige Harting was entitled to. If there was emphasis, it fell upon the gramophone. Flexes ran from it in all directions and speakers to either side of the chimney had been set upon pivots to assist directional adjustment.

The dining table was laid for two.

At the centre, four porcelain cherubs danced in a circle. Spring pursued Summer, Summer recoiled from Autumn, Winter drew them all forward. To either side, two places were set for dinner. Fresh candles, matches, a bottle of Burgundy, unopened, in the wine basket; a cluster of roses withering in a silver bowl. Over it all lay a thin layer of dust.

He wrote quickly in his notebook, then continued to the kitchen. It might have been confected for a woman's magazine. He had never seen so many gadgets. Mixers, cutters, toasters, openers. A plastic tray lay on the counter, the remnants of a single breakfast. He lifted the lid of the teapot. It was a herbal tea, bright red. Dregs of it remained in the teacup, staining the spoon. A second cup lay upside down in the plate rack. A transistor radio, similar to the one he had seen in the Embassy, stood on top of the refrigerator. Having once again noted the wavelengths, Turner went to the door, listened, then began pulling open cupboards, extracting tins and bottles, peering inside. Occasionally he recorded what he found. In the refrigerator half-litre cartons of Naafi Milk stood in neat order along the inside shelf. Taking out a bowl of pâté he gently sniffed it, testing its age. On a white plate, two steaks were set side by side. Strips of garlic had been threaded into the flesh. He prepared it on the Thursday night, he thought suddenly. On Thursday night he *still* didn't know he was going to defect on Friday.

The upstairs corridor was carpeted with thin runners of coconut matting. The pine furniture was very rickety. He pulled out the suits one by one, thrusting his hands into the pockets, then throwing them aside as if they were spent. Their cut, like that of the house, was military; the jackets were waisted, with a small pocket midway on the right side; the trousers were tapered and had no turn-ups. Occasionally, as he continued his search, he drew out a handkerchief, a scrap of paper or a bit of pencil, and these he would examine, and perhaps record, before tossing the suit aside and seizing another from the rickety wardrobe. The house was trembling again. From somewhere – it seemed this time to be from the very depths of the building – came the sound of clanking metal like a goods train braking, one place calling and another answering, ascending from floor to floor. Barely had it died before he heard another footfall. Dropping the suit he sprang to the window. He heard it again. Twice. Twice he had heard the solid tread of feet. Pushing back the shutter he leaned into the twilight and stared down at the driveway.

'Peter?'

Was it the dark that moved, or a man? He had left the lights on in the hall and they cast a patchwork of shadows on the drive. There was no wind to set the beech trees nodding. A man then? A man hurrying past the window on the inside? A man whose shape had flickered on the gravel?

'Peter?'

Nothing. No car, no guard. The neighbouring houses still lay in darkness. Above him, Chamberlain's mountain woke slowly to the dawn. He closed the window.

He worked faster now. In the second wardrobe another half dozen suits confronted him. Recklessly he dragged them from their hangers, struck at the pockets and cast them away; and then that extra sense warned him: go slowly. He had come upon a suit of dark blue gabardine, a summer suit but very much for formal wear, more creased than the others and set aside from them as if it were awaiting the cleaner, or tomorrow. He weighed it cautiously in his hand. Laying it on the bed, he felt in the pockets and drew out a brown envelope carefully folded upon itself. A brown OHMS envelope, the kind of thing they use for income tax. There was no writing on the outside and the flap had been sealed and ripped open. It was a key: a Yale key of dull, leaden colour, not newly cut but worn with age or use, a long, old fashioned, complicated key for a deep and complicated lock, quite unlike the standard keys which comprised the Duty Officer's bunch. A despatch box key? Returning it to the envelope, he put it between the pages of his notebook and carefully examined the remaining pockets. Three cocktail sticks, one with grime at the point as if he had used it for cleaning his nails. Olive stones. Some loose change, four marks eighty, made up in small denominations. And a bill for drinks, undated, from a hotel in Remagen.

He left the study till last. It was a mean room, filled with cartons of whisky and tinned food. An ironing board stood beside the shuttered window. On an old card table, piles of catalogues, trade brochures and diplomatic price lists lay in uncharacteristic confusion. A small notebook recorded the commodities which Harting was evidently pledged to obtain. Turner glanced through it, then put it in his pocket. The tins of Dutch cigars were in a wooden box; there must have been a gross of them or more.

The glass-fronted bookcase was locked. Crouching, Turner studied the titles, rose, listened again, then fetched a screw-driver from the kitchen and with a single powerful wrench ripped the wood so that the brass came through suddenly like a bone through flesh, and the door swung uselessly open. The first half dozen volumes were German bound and pre-war, heavily ribbed and gilded. He could not read all the titles precisely, but some he guessed; Stundinger's *Leipziger Kommentar zum Strafgesetzbuch; Verwaltungsrecht*; and someone else on the Statute of Limitations. In each was written the name, Harting Leo, like the name on the coathanger; and once he came upon the printed emblem of a Berlin bear over-written in a spiky German hand, very faint on the curves and very bold on the downstrokes '*Fur meinen geliebten Sohn Leo*'. The lower shelf was a medley: a Code of Conduct for British Officers in Germany, a German paperback on the flags of the Rhine, and an English–German phrase book published in Berlin before the war, annotated and very fingered. Reaching right to the back, he drew out a handful of slim, cloth-bound monthly newsletters of the Control Commission of Germany for the years forty-nine to fifty-one; some volumes were missing. As he opened the first volume the spine creaked and the dust rose swiftly to his nostrils. 'No. 18 Field Investigation Unit Hanover,' the inscription read, written out, every word, in a good clerical hand, very bold on the downstrokes and refined at the curves, in a black, powdery ink which only governments can buy. A thin line cancelled the title and a second title replaced it: 'No.6 General Inquiry Unit, Bremen.' Beneath it again (for Bremen too had been crossed out) he read the words: 'Property of the Judge Advocate General's Department, Moenchengladbach,' and beneath that again, 'Amnesty Commission, Hanover. Not to be taken away.' Selecting a page at random, he found himself suddenly arrested by a retrospective account of the operation of the Berlin airlift. Salt should be slung under the wings of the aircraft and on no account carried inside the fuselage ... the transportation of petrol presented high risks on landing and taking off ... it was found preferable, in the interests of morale if not of economy, to fly-in coal and corn rather than to make the bread in advance and deliver it ready-baked ... by using dehydrated instead of fresh potatoes, seven hundred and twenty tons could be saved on a daily ration of nine hundred tons for the civilian population. Fascinated, he slowly turned the yellow pages, his eye halting at phases of unexpected familiarity. '*The first meeting of the Allied High Commission was held on 21st September at Petersberg, near Bonn ...*' A German Tourist Office was to be opened in New York ... The festivals of Bayreuth and Oberammergau were to be resuscitated as swiftly as time allowed ... He glanced at the summary of minutes of the High Commission meetings: '*Methods of broadening opportunities and responsibilities of the Federal Republic of Germany in the field of foreign and economic activity were considered ... The wider powers for the German Federal Republic in the field of foreign trade, decided upon under the Occupation statute, were defined ... Direct German participation in two more international organizations was authorized ...*'

The next volume opened naturally at a page dealing with the release of German prisoners detained under certain arrest categories. Once again, he found himself compelled to read on: Three million Germans presently in captivity ... those detained were faring better than those at liberty ... the Allies faced with the impossibility of separating the wheat from the chaff. ... Operation Coalscuttle would send them down the mines, Operation Barleycorn would send them to the harvest ... One passage was sharply sidelined in blue ballpoint: *On 31st May, 1948, therefore, as an act of clemency, an amnesty was granted from proceedings under Ordinance 69 to all members of the SS not in automatic arrest categories, except for those who had been active as camp guards.* The words 'act of clemency' had been underscored, and the ink looked uncommonly fresh.

Having examined each, he grasped hold of the covers and with a savage twist wrenched them from the binding as if he were breaking the wings of a bird; then turned over what remained and shook it, searching for hidden matter; then rose and went to the door.

The clanking had begun again and it was far louder than before. He remained motionless, his head to one side, his colourless eyes vainly searching the gloom: and he heard a low whistle, a long monotone, resonant and mournful, patiently summoning, softly coaxing, eerily lamenting. A wind had risen; it was the wind for sure. He could hear the shutter again, slamming against the wall: yet surely he had closed the shutter? It was the wind: a dawn wind which had come up the river valley. A strong wind, though, for the creaking of the stairs was taut, and mounted its own scale like the creaking of a ship's ropes as the sails fill; and the glass, the dining-room glass, it was jingling absurdly; far louder than before.

'Hurry,' Turner whispered. He was talking to himself.

He pulled open the drawers of the desk. They were not locked. Some were empty. Light bulbs, fuse wire, sewing materials; socks, spare cuffs for shirts; an unframed print of a galleon in full sail. He turned it over and read: 'To darling Leo from Margaret, Hanover 1949. With fondest affection.' The script was clearly continental. Folding it roughly, he put it in his pocket. Under the print was a box. It was a square, hard box by the feel of it, bound in a black silk handkerchief, wrapped like a parcel and pinned upon itself. Unfastening the pins he cautiously drew out a tin of dull silvery metal; it must have been painted once, for the metal had the matt uneven texture of a surface scratched clean with a fine instrument. Loosening the lid, he looked inside, then gently, almost reverently, emptied the contents on to the handkerchief. Five buttons lay before him. They were each about one inch in diameter, wooden and hand-made to the same pattern, crudely but with the greatest care, as if the maker wanted for instruments but not for application, and they were pierced twice, generously, to admit a very broad thread. Under the tin was a German text book, the property of a Bonn library, stamped and annotated by the librarian. He could not understand it very well, but it seemed to be a technical treatise on the use of military gases. The last borrower had taken it out in February of that year. Certain passages were sidelined and there were small notes in the margin: 'Toxic effect immediate ... symptoms delayed by cold weather.' Training the light full upon them, Turner sat at the desk, his head cupped in his hand and studied them with the greatest concentration; so that only instinct made him swing round and face the tall figure in the doorway.

He was quite an elderly man. He wore a tunic and a peaked cap of the kind that German students used to wear, or merchant sailors in the First World War. His face was dark with coaldust; he held a rusted riddling-iron like a trident across his body, and it trembled dreadfully in his old hands; but his red, stupid eyes were turned downwards to the pile of desecrated books, and he looked very angry indeed. Very slowly, Turner stood up. The old man did not move, but the riddling-iron shook wildly, and the white of his knuckles shone white through the soot. Turner ventured a pace forward.

'Good morning,' he said.

One black hand detached itself from the shaft and rose mechanically to the peak of his hat. Turner strode to the corner where the cartons of whisky were stacked. He ripped open the top carton, pulled out a bottle, tore off the lid. The old man was mumbling, shaking his head, still staring at the books.

'Here,' said Turner softly, 'Have a drink,' and held the bottle forward into the old man's line of sight.

Listlessly he let the iron fall, took the bottle and held it to his thin lips while Turner charged past him to the kitchen. Opening the door, he shouted at the top of his voice.

'De Lisle!'

The echo carried wildly into the deserted street and outwards to the river.

'De Lisle!'

Even before he had returned to the study, the lights were going on in the windows of neighbouring houses.

Turner had pulled open the wooden shutters to let in the new daylight, and now the three of them stood in a baffled group, the old man blinking at the broken books and clutching the whisky in his shaking hand.

'Who is he?'

'The boilerman. We all have them.'

'Ask him when he last saw Harting.'

The old man did not immediately reply, but instead, waking again to the whisky, drank a little more, then passed it to de Lisle, whom he appeared instinctively to trust. De Lisle set it on the desk beside the silk handkerchief and quietly repeated his question, while the old man stared from one to the other, and then at the books.

'Ask him when he last saw Harting.'

At last he spoke. His voice was timeless: a slow peasant drawl, the murmur of the confessional, querulous yet subjugate, the voice of an underdog in the hopeless quest for consideration. Once he reached out his black fingers to touch the smashed beading of the bookcase; once he nodded towards the river, as if the river was where he lived; but the murmur continued through his gestures as if it came from someone else.

'He sells tickets for a pleasure cruise,' de Lisle whispered. 'He comes at five in the evening on the way home, and the first thing in the morning on the way to work. He stokes the boilers, does the dustbins and the empties. In summer he cleans the boats before the charabancs arrive.'

'Ask him again. When did he last see Harting? Here' – he produced a fifty mark note – 'Show him this – say I'll give it to him if he tells me what I want to know.'

Seeing the money, the old man examined Turner carefully with his dry, red eyes. His face was lined and hollow, starved at sometime and held up by the long cords of his shrivelled skin, and the soot was worked into it like pigment into canvas. Folding the banknote carefully down the centre he added it to the wad from his hip pocket.

'When?' Turner demanded. '*Wann?*'

Cautiously the old man began putting his words together, picking them one by one, articles in the bargain. He had taken off his hat; a sooty stubble covered his brown skull.

'Friday,' de Lisle quietly interpreted. His eye was on the window and he seemed distracted. 'Leo paid him on Friday afternoon. He went round to his house and paid him on the doorstep. He said he was going on a long journey.'

'Where to?'

'He didn't say where.'

'When will he come back? Ask him that.'

Once more, as de Lisle translated and Turner caught the half familiar words: *kommen ... zurück*.

'Leo gave him two months' pay. He says he has something to show us. Something that is worth another fifty marks.'

The old man was glancing quickly from one to the other of them, fearful but expectant, while his long hands nervously explored the canvas tunic. It was a sailor's tunic, shapeless and bleached, and it hung without relation to his narrow frame. Finding what he was looking for, he cautiously rolled back the lower hem, reached upward and detached something from his neck. As he did so he began murmuring again, but faster than before, nervous and voluble.

'He found it on Saturday morning in the rubbish.'

It was a holster made of green webbing, army issue, suitable for a three-eight pistol. It had 'Harting Leo' stencilled on the inside and it was empty.

'In the dustbin, right on top; the first thing he saw when he lifted the lid. He didn't show it to the others. The others shouted at him and threatened to kick his face in. The others reminded him of what they'd done to him in the war and they said they'd do it again.'

'What others? Who?'

'Wait.'

Going to the window, de Lisle peered casually out. The old man was still talking.

'He says he distributed anti-Nazi pamphlets in the war,' he called, still watching. 'By mistake. He thought they were ordinary newspapers and the others caught him and hung him upside down. That's who the others seem to be. He says he likes the English best. He says Harting was a real gentleman. He says he wants to keep the whisky too. Leo always gave him Scotch. And cigars. Little Dutch cigars, a kind you can't get in the shops. Leo had them sent specially. And last Christmas he gave his wife a hair-dryer. He would also like fifty marks for the holster,' he added, but by then the cars had entered the drive, and the little room was filled with the double wail of a police horn and the double flash of a blue light. They heard the shout and the stamp of feet as the green figures gathered at the windows, pointing their guns into the room. The door was open and a young man in a leather coat held a pistol in his hand. The boilerman was crying, wailing, waiting to be hit and the blue light was rolling like a light for dancing. 'Do nothing,' de Lisle had said. 'Obey no orders.'

He was talking to the boy in the leather coat, offering his red diplomatic card for examination. His voice was quiet but very firm, a negotiator's voice, neither flippant nor concessive, stiffened with authority and hinting at injured privilege. The young detective's face was as blank as Siebkron's. Gradually de Lisle appeared to be gaining the ascendancy. His tone changed to one of indignation. He began asking questions, and the boy became conciliatory, even evasive. Gradually Turner gathered the trend of de Lisle's complaint. He was pointing at Turner's notebook and then at the old man. A list, he was saying, they were making a list. Was it forbidden for diplomats to make a list? To assess dilapidation, to check the inventory of Embassy furniture? It was surely a natural enough thing to do at a time when British property was in danger of destruction. Mr Harting had gone on extended leave of absence; it was expedient to make certain dispositions, to pay the boilerman his fifty marks ... And since when, de Lisle wished to know, were British diplomats forbidden entry to British Embassy livings? By what right, de Lisle wished to know, had this great concourse of militia burst upon the privacy of extra-territorial persons?

More cards were exchanged, more documents mutually examined; names and numbers mutually recorded. The detective was sorry, he said; these were troubled times, and he stared at Turner for a long time as if he recognized a colleague. Troubled times or not, de Lisle appeared to reply, the rights of diplomats must be respected. The greater the danger, the more necessary the immunity. They shook hands. Somebody saluted. Gradually they all withdrew. The green uniforms dispersed, the blue lights vanished, the vans drove away. De Lisle had found three glasses and was pouring a little whisky into each. The old man was whimpering. Turner had returned the buttons to their tin and put the tin in his pocket together with the little book on military cases.

'Was that them?' he demanded. 'Were those the ones who questioned him?'

'He says: *like* the detective, but a little older. Whiter, he says: a richer kind of man. I think we both know who he's talking about. Here, you'd better look after this yourself.'

Tugging the holster from the folds of his brown overcoat, de Lisle thrust it without pride into Turner's waiting hand.

The ferry was hung with the flags of the German Federation. The crest of Königswinter was nailed to the bridge. Militia packed the bow. Their steel helmets were square, their faces pale and sad. They were very quiet for such young men and their rubber boots made no sound on the steel deck, and they stared at the river as if they had been told to remember it. Turner stood apart from them, watching the crew cast away, and he perceived everything very clearly because he was tired and frightened and because it was still early morning: the heavy vibration of the iron deck as the cars thumped over the ramp and pressed forward to the best berth; the howl of the engines and the clatter of chains as the men shouted and cast away, the strident bell that put out the fading chimes of the town's churches, the uniform hostility of the drivers as they rose from their cars and picked the change from their pigskin purses as if the men were a secret society and could not acknowledge each other in public; and the pedestrians, the bronzed and the poor, coveting the cars from which they were kept apart. The river bank receded; the little town drew its spires back into the hills like scenery at the opera. Gradually they described their awkward course, steering a long arc with the current to avoid the sister ferry from the opposite bank. Now they slowed almost to a halt, drifting down river as the *John F. Kennedy*, loaded with equal pyramids of fine coal, bore swiftly down upon them, the children's washing sloping in the wet air. Then they were rocking in its wake and the women passengers were calling in amusement.

'He told you something else. About a woman. I heard him say *Frau* and *Auto*. Something about a woman and a car.'

'Sorry old boy,' de Lisle said coolly, 'It's the Rhineland accent. Sometimes it simply defeats me.'

Turner stared back at the Königswinter bank, shielding his eyes with his gloved hand because even in that miserable spring the light came sharply off the water. At last he saw what he was looking for: to each side, like mailed hands pointing to the Seven Hills of Siegfried, turreted brown villas built with the wealth of the Ruhr; between them a splash of white against the trees of the esplanade. It was Harting's house receding in the mist.

'I'm chasing a ghost,' he muttered. 'A bloody shadow.'

'Your own,' de Lisle retorted, his voice rich with disgust.

'Oh, sure, sure.'

'I shall drive you back to the Embassy,' de Lisle continued. 'From then on, you find your own transport.'

'Why the hell did you bring me if you're so squeamish?' And suddenly he laughed. 'Of course,' he said. 'What a bloody fool I am! I'm going to sleep! You were frightened I might find the Green File and you thought you'd wait in the wings. Unsuitable for temporaries. Christ!'

Cork had just heard the eight o'clock news. The German delegation had withdrawn from Brussels during the night. Officially the Federal Government wished to 'reconsider certain technical problems which had arisen in the course of discussions'. Unofficially, as Cork put it, they had run away from school. Blankly he watched the coloured paper stutter out of the rollers and fall into the wire basket. It was about ten minutes before the summons came. There was a knock on the door and Miss Peate's stupid head appeared at the little trap. Mr Bradfield would see him at once. Her mean eyes were alive with pleasure. Once and for all, she meant. As he followed her into the corridor, he caught sight of Cork's brochure on plots of land in the Bahamas and he thought: that's going to be useful by the time he's done with me.

12
'And there was Leo. In the second class'

'I have already spoken to Lumley. You go home tonight. Travel section will attend to your tickets.' Bradfield's desk was piled high with telegrams. 'And I have apologized in your name to Siebkron.'

'Apologized?'

Bradfield dropped the latch on the door. 'Shall I spell it out for you? Like Harting, you are evidently something of a political primitive. You are here on a temporary diplomatic footing; if you were not, you would undoubtedly be in prison.' He was pale with anger. 'God alone knows what de Lisle thought he was up to. I shall speak to him separately. You have deliberately disobeyed my instruction; well, you people have your own code, I suppose, and I am as suspect as the next man.'

'You flatter yourself.'

'In this case, however, you were placed specifically under my authority, by Lumley, by the Ambassador and by the necessities of the situation here, and specifically ordered to make no move which could have repercussions outside the Embassy. Be quiet and listen to me! Instead of showing the minimal consideration that was asked of you, however, you go round to Harting's house at five in the morning, frighten the wits out of his servant, wake the neighbours, bellow for de Lisle, and finally attract a full-scale police raid which, in a matter of hours will no doubt be the talking point of the community. Not content with that, you are party to a stupid lie to the police about conducting an inventory; I imagine that will bring a smile even to Siebkron's lips, after the description you offered him of your work last night.'

'Any more?'

'A great deal thank you. Whatever Siebkron suspected that Harting had done, you have by now delivered the proof. You saw his attitude for yourself. Heaven knows what he does not think we are up to.'

'Then tell him,' Turner suggested. 'Why not? Ease his mind. Christ, he knows more than we do. Why do we make a secret of something they all know? They're in full cry. The worst we can do is spoil their kill.'

'I will not have it *said*! Anything is better, any doubts, any suspicions on their part, than our admission at this moment in time that for twenty years a member of our diplomatic staff has been in Soviet employment. Is there nothing you will understand of this? I will not have it *said*! Let them think and do what they like, without our cooperation they can *only* surmise.'

It was a statement of personal faith. He sat as still and as upright as a sentry guarding a national shrine.

'Is that the lot?'

'You people are supposed to work in secret. One calls upon you expecting a standard of discretion. I could tell you a little about your behaviour here, had you not made it abundantly clear that manners mean nothing to you whatever. It will take a long time to sweep up the mess you have left behind you in this Embassy. You seem to think that nothing reaches me. I have already warded off Gaunt and Meadowes; no doubt there are others I shall have to soothe.'

'I'd better go this afternoon,' Turner suggested. He had not taken his eyes from Bradfield's face. 'I've ballsed it up, haven't I? Sorry about that. Sorry you're not satisfied with the service. I'll write and apologize; that's what Lumley likes me to do. A bread and butter letter. So I'll do that. I'll write.' He sighed, 'I seem to be a bit of a Jonah. Best thing to do really, chuck me out. Be a bit of a wrench for you, that will. You don't like getting rid of people do you? Rather give them a contract.'

'What are you suggesting?'

'That you've a damn good reason for insisting on discretion! I said to Lumley – Christ that was a joke – I asked him, see: does he want the files of the man? What the hell *are* you up to? Wait! One minute you give him a job, the next you don't want to know him. If they brought his body in now you couldn't care bloody less; you'd pat the pockets for papers and wish him luck!'

He noticed, quite inconsequentially, Bradfield's shoes. They were hand-made and polished that dark mahogany which is only captured by servants, or by those who have been brought up with them.

'What the devil do you mean?'

'I don't know who's putting the finger on you: I don't care. Siebkron, I would guess, from the way you crawl to him. Why did you bring us together last night if you were so bloody worried about offending him? What was the point to that, for one? *Or did he order you to?* Don't answer yet, it's my turn. You're Harting's guardian angel, do you realize that? It sticks out a mile, and I'll write it six foot high when I get back to London. You renewed his contract, right? Just that, for a start. Although you despised him. But you didn't just *give* him work; you *made* work for him. You knew bloody well the Foreign Office didn't give a damn about the Destruction programme. Or for the Personalities Index either, I shouldn't wonder. But you pretended; you built it up for him. Don't tell me it was compassion for a man who didn't belong.'

'Whatever there was of *that* has worn pretty thin by now,' Bradfield remarked, with a hint of that dismay, or self-contempt, which Turner now occasionally discerned in him.

'Then what about the Thursday meeting?'

A look of sheer pain crossed Bradfield's face.

'My God you are insufferable,' he said, more as a mental note, a privately recorded judgement, than an insult directly intended.

'The Thursday conference that never was! It was you who took Harting off that conference; you who gave the job to de Lisle. But Harting still went out Thursday afternoons all right. Did you stop him? Did you hell. I expect you even know where he went, don't you.' He held up the gunmetal key he had taken from Harting's suit. 'Because there's a special place, you see. A hideaway. Or maybe I'm telling you something you know already. Who did he meet out there? Do you know that too? I used to think it was Praschko, until I remembered *you* fed me that idea, you yourself. So I'm going bloody carefully with Praschko.'

Turner was leaning across the desk, shouting at Bradfield's bowed head. 'As to Siebkron, he's rolling up a whole bloody network, like as not. Dozens of agents, for all we know: Harting was just one link in a chain. You can't begin to control what Siebkron knows and doesn't know. We're dealing with reality you know, not diplomacy.' He pointed to the window and the blurred hills across the river. 'They sell horses over there! They screw around, talk to friends, make journeys; they've been beyond the edge of the forest, they know what the world looks like!'

'It requires very little, in an intelligent person, to know that,' said Bradfield.

'And that's what I'm going to tell Lumley when I get back to the smoke. Harting didn't work alone! He had a patron as well as a controller and for all I know, they were the same man! And for all I bloody well know, Leo Harting was Rawley Bradfield's fancy boy! Having a bit of public school vice on the side!'

Bradfield was standing up, his face contracted with anger. 'Tell Lumley what you like,' he whispered, 'but get out of here and don't ever come back,' and it was then that Mickie Crabbe put his red, bubbling face round Miss Peate's connecting door.

He was looking puzzled and slightly indignant, and he was chewing absurdly at his ginger moustache. 'Rawley, I say,' he said and began again, as if he had started in the wrong octave. 'Sorry to burst in, Rawley. I tried the door in the corridor but the latch was down. Sorry Rawley. It's about Leo,' he said. The rest came out with rather a rush, 'I've just seen him down at the railway station. Bloody well having a beer.'

'Be quick,' said Bradfield.

'Doing a favour for Peter de Lisle. That's all,' Crabbe began defensively. Turner caught the smell of drink on his breath, mingling with the smell of peppermint. 'Peter had to go down to the Bundestag. Debate on Emergency Legislation, big thing apparently, second day, so he asked me to cover the jamboree at the railway station. The Movement's leaders, coming in from Hanover. Watch the arrivals, see who turned up. I often do odd jobs for Peter,' he added apologetically. 'Turned out to be a Lord Mayor's Show. Press, television lights, masses of cars lined up in the road' – he glanced nervously at Bradfield – 'where the taxis stand, Rawley, *you* know. And crowds. All singing rah-rah and waving the old black flags. Bit of music.' He shook his head in private wonder. 'That square is *plastered* with slogans.'

'And you saw Leo,' Turner said, pressing. 'In the crowd?'

'Sort of.'

'What do you mean?'

'Well the back of his head. Head and shoulders. Just a glimpse. No time to grab him: gone.'

Turner seized him with his big, stone hands. 'You said you saw him having a beer!'

'Let him go,' said Bradfield.

'Hey steady!' For a moment Crabbe looked almost ferocious. 'Well I saw him later, you see. After the show was over. Face to face sort of thing.'

Turner released him.

'The train came in and everyone started cheering pretty loud, and shoving about and trying to get a glimpse of Karfield. There was even a bit of fighting at the edges, I think, but that was mainly the journalists. *Sods*,' he added with a spark of real hatred. 'That shit Sam Allerton was there, by the way. I should think *he* started it.'

'For Christ's sake!' Turner shouted, and Crabbe regarded him quite straightly, with an expression which spoke of bad form.

'First of all Meyer-Lothringen came out – the police had made a gangway for him out of the cattle pens – then Tilsit, then Halbach, and everyone shouting like gyppos. Beatles,' he said, incomprehendingly. 'Kids mainly they were, long-haired student types, leaning over the railings trying to touch the chaps' shoulders. Karfeld didn't make it. Some fellow near me said he must have gone out the other side, gone down the passage to avoid the crowd. He doesn't like people coming too close, that's what they say; that's why he builds these damn great stands everywhere. So half the crowd charges off to see if they can find him. The rest hang around in case, and then there's this announcement over the blower: we can all go home because Karfeld's still in Hanover. Lucky for Bonn, that's what I thought.' He grinned. 'What?'

Neither spoke.

'The journalists were furious and I thought I'd just give Rawley a ring to let him know Karfeld hadn't turned up. London likes to keep track, you see. Of Karfeld.' This for Turner. 'They like to keep tabs on him, not have him talking to strange men.' He resumed: 'There's an all-night Post Office by the hall there, and I was just coming out when it occurred to me' – he made a feeble attempt to drag them into the conspiracy – 'that maybe I ought to have a quick cup of coffee to collect my thoughts, and I happened to look through the glass door of the waiting-room. Doors are side by side you see. Restaurant one side, waiting-room the other. It's a sort of buffet in there with a few places to sit as well. I mean sit and not drink,' he explained, as if that were a particular type of eccentricity he had occasionally met with. 'There's the first class on the left and the second class on the right, both glass doors.'

'For pity's sake!' Turner breathed.

'And there was Leo. In the second class. At a table. Wearing a trench coat, a sort of army looking thing. Seemed in rather bad shape.'

'Drunk?'

'I don't know. Christ, that would be going it, wouldn't it: eight in the morning.' He looked very innocent. 'But tired out and well, not dapper, you know, not like he usually is. Gloss, bounce: all gone. Still,' he added stupidly, 'Comes to all of us I suppose.'

'You didn't speak to him?'

'No thanks. I know him in that mood. I gave him a wide berth and came back and told Rawley.'

'Was he carrying anything,' Bradfield said quickly. 'Did he have a briefcase with him? Anything that could hold papers?'

'Nothing *about*,' Crabbe muttered, 'Rawley old boy. Sorry.'

They stood in silence, all three, while Crabbe blinked from one face to the other.

'You did well,' Bradfield muttered at last. 'All right, Crabbe.'

'*Well?*' Turner shouted. 'He did bloody badly! Leo's not in quarantine. Why didn't he talk to him, drag him here by the neck, reason with him? God almighty you're not bloody well alive, either of you! *Well?* He may be gone by now; that was our last chance! He was probably waiting for his final contact; they've dirtied him up for the journey out! Did he have anyone with him?' He pulled open the door. 'I said did he have anyone with him? Come on!'

'A kid,' said Crabbe. 'Little girl.'

'A *what?*'

'Six or seven years old. Someone's kid. He was talking to it.'

'Did he recognize you?'

'Doubt it. Seemed to look through me.'

Turner seized his raincoat from the stand.

'I'd rather not,' said Crabbe, answering the gesture rather than the exhortation. 'Sorry.'

'And you! What are *you* standing there for? *Come on!*'

Bradfield did not move.

'*For God's sake!*'

'I'm staying here. Crabbe has a car. Let him take you. It must be nearly an hour since he saw him, or thought he did, with all that traffic. He'll be gone by now. I don't propose to waste my own time.' Ignoring Turner's astonished gaze, he continued, 'The Ambassador has already asked me not to leave the building. We expect word from Brussels any minute; it is highly likely that he will wish to call upon the Chancellor.'

'Christ, what do you think this is? A tripartite conference. He may be sitting there with a caseful of secrets! No wonder he looks under the weather! What's got into you now? Do you *want* Siebkron to find him before we do? Do you want him to be caught red-handed?'

'I have already told you: secrets are not sacrosanct. We would prefer them kept, it is true. In relation to what I have to do here—'

'*Those* secrets are, aren't they? What about the bloody Green File?'

Bradfield hesitated.

'*I've* no authority over him,' Turner cried. 'I don't even know what he looks like! What am *I* supposed to do when I see him? Tell him you'd like a word with him? You're his boss, aren't you? Do you *want* Ludwig Siebkron to find him first?' Tears had started absurdly to his eyes. His voice was one of utter supplication. 'Bradfield!'

'He was all alone,' Crabbe muttered, not looking at Bradfield, 'just him and himself, old boy. And the kid. I'm sure of that.'

Bradfield stared at Crabbe, and then at Turner, and once again his face seemed crowded by private pains scarcely held at bay.

'It's true,' he said at last, very reluctantly, 'I am his superior. I am responsible. I had better be there.' Carefully double-locking the outer door, he left word with Miss Peate that Gaveston should stand in for him, and led the way downstairs.

New fire extinguishers, just arrived from London, stood like red sentinels along the corridor. At the landing, a consignment of steel beds awaited assembly. A file-trolley was loaded with grey blankets. In the lobby two men, mounted on separate ladders, were erecting a steel screen. Dark Gaunt watched them in bewilderment as they swept through the glass doors into the car park, Crabbe leading. Bradfield drove with an arrogance which took Turner by surprise. They raced across the lights on amber, keeping to the left lane to make the turn into the station road. At the traffic check he barely halted; both he and Crabbe had their red cards ready at the window. They were on wet cobble, skidding on the tramlines and Bradfield held the wheel still, waiting patiently for the car to come to its senses. They approached an intersection where the sign said 'Yield', and ran straight over it under the wheels of an oncoming bus. The cars were fewer, the streets were packed with people.

Some carried banners, others wore the grey gabardine raincoats and black Homburg hats which were the uniform of the Movement's supporters. They yielded reluctantly, scowling at the number plates and the glittering foreign paintwork. Bradfield neither sounded his horn nor changed gear, but let them wake to him and avoid him as they might. Once he braked for an old man who was either deaf or drunk; once a boy slapped the roof of the car with his bare hand, and Bradfield became very still and pale. Confetti lay on the steps, the pillars were covered with slogans. A cab driver was yelling as if he had been hit. They had parked in the cab rank.

'Left,' Crabbe called as Turner ran ahead of him. A high doorway admitted them to the main hall.

'Keep left,' Turner heard Crabbe shout for the second time.

Three barriers led to the platform; three ticket collectors sat in their glass cages. Notices warned him in three languages not to ask them favours. A group of priests, whispering, turned to eye him disapprovingly; haste, they said, is not a Christian quality. A blonde girl. her face chestnut brown, swung dangerously past him with a rucksack and well-worn skis, and he saw the trembling of her pullover.

'He was sitting just there,' Crabbe whispered, but by then Turner had flung open the glazed swing door and was standing inside the restaurant, glaring through the cigarette smoke at each table in turn. A loudspeaker barked a message about changing at Cologne. 'Gone,' Crabbe was saying, 'Sod's flown.'

The smoke hung all around, lifting in the glow of the long tube lights, curling into the darker corners. The smell was of beer and smoked ham and municipal disinfectant; the far counter, white with Dutch tiles, glinted like an ice wall in the fog. In a brown-wood cubicle sat a poor family on the move; the women were old and dressed in black, their suitcases were bound with rope; the men were reading Greek newspapers. At a separate table a little girl rolled beermats to a drunk, and that was the table Crabbe was pointing at.

'Where the kiddie is, you see. He was having a Pils.'

Ignoring the drunk and the child, Turner picked up the glasses and stared at them uselessly. Three small cigar ends lay in the ashtray. One was still slightly smouldering. The child watched him as he stooped and searched the floor and rose again empty handed; she watched him stride from one table to the next, glaring into the faces, seizing a shoulder, pushing down a newspaper, touching an arm.

'Is this him?' he yelled. A lonely priest was reading *Bildzeitung* in a corner; beside him, hiding in his shadow, a dark-faced gypsy ate roast chestnuts out of a bag.

'No.'

'This?'

'Sorry old boy,' said Crabbe, very nervous now, 'No luck. I say, go easy.'

By the stained-glass window two soldiers were playing chess. A bearded man was making the motions of eating, but there was no food before him. Outside on the platform a train was arriving, and the vibration shook the crockery. Crabbe was addressing the waitress. He was hanging over her, whispering and his hand was on the flesh of her upper arm. She shook her head.

'We'll try the other one,' he said, as Turner joined them. They walked across the room together, and this woman nodded, proud to have remembered, and made a long story, pointing at the child and talking about '*der kleine Herr*', the little gentleman, and sometimes just about '*der Kleine*', as if 'gentleman' were a tribute to her interrogators rather than to Harting.

'He was here till a few minutes ago,' Crabbe said in some bewilderment. 'Her version, anyway.'

'Did he leave alone?'

'Didn't see.'

'Did he make any impression on her?'

'Steady. She's not a big thinker, old boy. Don't want her to fly away.'

'What made him leave? Did he see someone? Did someone signal to him from the door?'

'You're stretching it old son. She didn't see him leave. She didn't worry about him, he paid with every order. As if he might leave in a hurry. Catch a train. He went out to watch the hoo-hah, when the boys arrived, then came back and had another cigar and a drink.'

'What's the matter then? Why are you looking like that?'

'It's bloody odd,' Crabbe muttered, frowning absurdly.

'What's bloody odd?'

'He's been here all night. Alone. Drinking but not drunk. Played with that kid part of the time. Greek kid. That was what he liked best: the kid.' He gave the woman a coin and she thanked him laboriously.

'Just as well we missed him,' Crabbe declared. 'Pugnacious little sod when he gets like this. Go for anyone when he's got his dander up.'

'How do you know?'

Crabbe grimaced in painful reminiscence: 'You should have seen him that night in Cologne,' he muttered, still staring after the waitress. 'Jesus.'

'In the fight? You were there?'

'I tell you,' Crabbe repeated. He spoke from the heart. 'When that lad's really going, he's best avoided altogether. Look.' He held out his hand. A wooden button lay in the palm and it was identical to the buttons in the scatched tin in Königswinter. 'She picked this up from the table,' he said. 'She thought it might be something he needed. She was hanging on to it in case he came back, you see.'

Bradfield came slowly through the doorway. His face was taut but without expression.

'I gather he's not here.'

No one spoke.

'You still say you saw him?'

'No mistake, old boy. Sorry.'

'Well, I suppose we must believe you. I suggest we go back to the Embassy.' He glanced at Turner. 'Unless you prefer to stay. If you have some further theory to test.' He looked round the buffet. Every face was turned towards them. Behind the bar, a chrome machine was steaming unattended. Not a hand moved. 'You seem to have made your mark here anyway.' As they walked slowly back to the car, Bradfield said, 'You can come into the Embassy to collect your possessions but you must be out by lunchtime. If you have any papers, leave them with Cork and we'll send them on by bag. There's a flight at seven. Take it. If you can't get a seat, take the train. But go.'

They waited while Bradfield spoke to the policemen and showed them his red card. His German sounded very English in tone but the grammar was faultless. The policeman nodded, saluted and they took their leave. Slowly they returned to the Embassy through the sullen faces of the aimless crowd.

'Extraordinary place for Leo to spend the night,' Crabbe muttered, but Turner was fingering the gunmetal key in the OHMS envelope in his pocket, and still wondering, for all his sense of failure, whose door it had unlocked.

13
The strain of being a pig

He sat at the cypher room desk, still in his raincoat, packing together the useless trophies of his investigation, the army holster, the folded print, the engraved paper knife from Margaret Aickman; the blue-bound diary for counsellors and above, the little notebook for diplomatic discounts, and the scratched tin of five wood buttons cut to size; and now the sixth button and the three stubs of cigar.

'Never mind,' said Cork kindly. 'He'll turn up.'

'Oh sure. Like the investments and the Caribbean dream. Leo's everybody's darling. Everybody's lost son, Leo is. We all love Leo, although he cut our throats.'

'Mind you, he couldn't half tell the tale.' He was sitting on the trucked bed in his shirt sleeves, pulling on his outdoor shoes. He wore metal springs above the elbows and his shirt was like an advertisement on the underground. There was no sound from the corridor. 'That's what *got* you about him. Quiet, but a sod.'

A machine stammered and Cork frowned at it reprovingly.

'Blarney,' he continued. 'That's what he had. The magic. He could tell you *any* bloody tale and you believed it.'

He had put them into a waste-bag. The label on the outside said 'SECRET. Only to be disposed of in the presence of two authorized witnesses.'

'I want this sealed and sent to Lumley,' he said, and Cork wrote out a receipt and signed it.

'I remember the first time I met him,' Cork said, in the cheerful voice which Turner associated with funeral breakfasts. 'I was *green*. I was really *green*. I'd only been married six months. If I hadn't twigged him I'd have—'

'You'd have been taking his tips on investment. You'd have been lending him the code books for bedside reading.' He stapled the mouth of the bag, folding it against itself.

'Not the code books. Janet. He'd have been reading *her* in bed.' Cork smiled happily. 'Bloody neck! You wouldn't credit it. Come on then. Lunch.'

For the last time Turner savagely clamped together the two arms of the stapler. 'Is de Lisle in?'

'Doubt it. London's sent a brief the size of your arm. All hands on deck. The dips are out in force.' He laughed. 'They ought to have a go with the old black flags. Lobby the deputies. Strenuous representations at all levels. Leave no stone unturned. *And* they're going for another loan. I don't know where the Krauts get the stuff from sometimes. Know what Leo said to me once? "I tell you what, Bill, we'll score a big diplomatic victory. We'll go down to the Bundestag and offer them a million quid. Just you and me. I reckon they'd fall down in a faint." He was right, you know.'

Turner dialled de Lisle's number but there was no reply.

'Tell him I rang to say goodbye,' he said to Cork, and changed his mind. 'Don't worry.'

He called Travel Section and inquired about his ticket. It was all in order, they assured him; Mr Bradfield had sent down personally and the ticket was waiting for him at the desk. They seemed impressed. Cork picked up his coat.

'And you'd better cable Lumley and give him my time of arrival.'

'I'm afraid H. of C.'s done that already,' Cork said, with something quite near to a blush.

'Well. Thanks.' He was at the door, looking back into the room as if he would never see it again. 'I hope it goes all right with the baby. I hope your dreams come true. I hope everyone's dream comes true. I hope they all get what they're looking for.'

'Look: think of it this way,' Cork said sympathetically. 'There's things you just don't give up, isn't there?'

'That's right.'

'I mean you can't pack everything up neat and tidy. Not in life, you can't. That's for girls, that is. That's just romantic. You get like Leo otherwise: you can't leave a thing alone. Now what are you going to do with yourself this afternoon? There's a nice matinee at the American cinema ... No. Wouldn't be right for you: lot of screaming kids.'

'What do you mean, he can't leave a thing alone?'

Cork was drifting round the room, checking the machines, the desks and the secret waste.

'Vindictive. Vindictive wasn't in it. He had a feud with Fred Anger once; Fred was Admin. They say it ran five years till Fred was posted.'

'What about?'

'Nothing.' He had picked a scrap of paper from the floor and was reading it. 'Absolutely sweet Fanny Adams. Fred cut down a lime tree in Leo's garden, said it was endangering the fence. Which it was. Fred told me: "Bill," he said, "that tree would have *fallen* down in the autumn."'

'He had a thing about land,' Turner said. 'He wanted his own patch. He didn't like being in limbo.'

'Know what Leo did? He made a wreath out of leaves. Brought it into the Embassy and nailed it on to Fred's office door. With bloody great two-inch nails. Crucified it near enough. The German staff thought Fred had snuffed it. Leo didn't laugh though. He wasn't joking; he really meant it. He was *violent*, see. Now dips don't notice that. All oil and how-d' you-do, he was to them. And helpful, I'm not saying he wasn't helpful. I'm just saying that when Leo had a grudge, I wouldn't fancy being the other end of it. That's all I'm saying.'

'He went for your wife, did he?'

'I put a stop to that,' said Cork. 'Just as well. Seeing what happened elsewhere. The Welfare Dance, that was. A couple of years back. He started coming it. Nothing *nasty*, mind. Wanted to give her a hair-dryer and that. Meet me up on the hill, that lark. I said to him, "You find your own hair to dry," I said. "She's mine." You can't blame him though, can you? Know what they say about refugees: they lose everything except their accents. Dead right, you know. Trouble with Leo was, he wanted it all back. So I suppose that's it: take the pick of the files and run for it. Flog them to the highest bidder. It's no more than we owe him, I don't suppose.' Satisfied with his security check, Cork stacked together his brochures and came towards the door where Turner stood. 'You're from the North, aren't you?' he asked. 'I can tell by your voice.'

'How well did you know him?'

'Leo? Oh, like all of us really. I'd buy this and that, give him a saucer of milk now and then; put an order in for the Dutchman.'

'Dutchman?'

'Firm of diplomatic exporters. From Amsterdam. Cheaper if you can be bothered; you know. Do you anything: butter, meat, radios, cars, the lot.'

'Hair-dryers?'

'Anything. There's a rep. calls every Monday. Fill in your form one week, chuck it into Leo and you get the order the next. I expect there was a bit in it for him: *you* know. Mind you, you could never catch him out. I mean you could check up till you were blue in the face: you'd never find out where he took his divi. Though I *think* it was those bloody cigars. They were really shocking, you know. I don't think he enjoyed them; he just smoked them because they were free. And because we pulled his leg about them.' He laughed simply. 'He conned the lot of us, that's the truth of it. You too, I suppose. Well, I'll be slipping on then. So long.'

'You were saying about that first time you met him.'

'Was I? Oh well, yes.' He laughed again. 'I mean you couldn't believe *anything*. My first day: Mickie Crabbe took me down there. We done the round by then. "Here," says Mickie, "just one more port of call," and takes me downstairs to see Leo. "This is Cork," he says. "Just joined us in Cyphers." So then Leo moves in.' Cork sat down on the swivel chair beside the door and leaned back like the rich executive he longed to be. '"Glass of sherry," he says. We're supposed to be dry here, but that never bothered Leo; not that he drank himself, mind. "We must celebrate the new arrival. You don't *sing* by any chance, do you, Cork?" "Only in the bath," I says and we all have a nice laugh. Recruiting for the choir, see: that always impressed them. Very pious gentleman, Mr Harting, I thought. Not half. "Have a cigar, Cork?" No thanks. "A fag then?" Don't mind if I do, Mr Harting. So then we sit there like a lot of dips, sipping our sherry, and I'm thinking, "Well, I must say you're quite the little king round here." Furniture, maps, carpet ... all the trappings. Fred Anger cleared a lot of it out, mind, before he left. Nicked, half of it was. *Liberated*, you know. Like in the old Occupation days. "So how are things in London, Cork?" he asks, "Everything much the same I suppose?" Putting me at my ease, cheeky sod. "That old porter at the main door: still saucy with the visiting Ambassadors, is he, Cork?" He really came it. "And the coal fires: still lighting the coal fires every morning, are they, Cork?" "Well," I says, "They're not doing too bad, but it's like everything else, it takes its time." Some crap like that. "Oh, ah really," he says, "because I had a letter from Ewan Waldebere only a few months back telling me they were putting in the central heating. And that old bloke who used to pray on the steps of Number Ten, still there is he, Cork, morning and night, saying his prayers? Doesn't seem to have done us much good, does he? I tell you: I was practically calling him sir. Ewan Waldebere was Head of Western Department by then, all set to be God. So then he comes on about the choir again and the Dutchman and a few other things besides, anything he can do to help, and when we get outside I look at Mickie Crabbe and Mickie's *pissing* himself. Doubled up, Mickie is. "Leo?" he says, "Leo? He's never been inside the Foreign Office in his life. He hasn't even been back to England since forty-five."' Cork broke off, shaking his head. 'Still,' he repeated, with an affectionate laugh, 'You can't blame him, can you?' He got up. 'And I mean, we all saw through him, but we still fell for it, didn't we? I mean Arthur and ... I mean everybody. It's like my villa,' he added simply, 'I know I'll never get there, but I believe in it all the same. I mean you have to really ... you couldn't live, not without illusions. Not here.'

Taking his hands out of his mackintosh pocket, Turner stared first at Cork and then at the gunmetal key in his big palm, and he seemed to be torn and undecided.

'What's Mickie Crabbe's number?'

Cork watched with apprehension as he lifted the receiver, dialled and began talking.

'They don't *expect* you to go on looking for him,' Cork said anxiously. 'I don't really think they do.'

'I'm not bloody well looking for him, I'm having lunch with Crabbe and I'm catching the evening flight and nothing on God's earth would keep me in this dream box for an hour longer than I need.' He slammed down the receiver and stalked out of the room.

De Lisle's door was wide open but his desk was empty. He wrote a note: 'Called in to say goodbye. Goodbye. Alan Turner,' and his hand was shaking with anger and humiliation. In the lobby, small groups were sauntering into the sunlight to eat their sandwiches or lunch in the canteen. The Ambassador's Rolls-Royce stood at the door; the escort of police outriders waited patiently. Gaunt was whispering to Meadowes at the front desk and he fell suddenly quiet as Turner approached.

'Here,' he said, handing him the envelope. 'Here's your ticket.' His expression said, 'Now go back to where you belong.'

'Ready when you are old son,' Crabbe whispered from his habitual patch of darkness. 'You see.'

The waiters were quiet and awfully discreet. Crabbe had asked for snails which he said were very good. The framed print in their little alcove showed shepherds dancing with nymphs, and there was just a suggestion of expensive sin.

'You were with him that night in Cologne. The night he got into the fight.'

'Extraordinary,' said Crabbe, 'Really. Do you like water?' he asked, and added a little to each of their glasses, but it was no more than a tear for the sober. 'Don't know what came over him.'

'Did you often go out with him?'

He grinned unsuccessfully and they drank.

'That was five years ago, you see. Mary's mother was ill; kept on flogging back to England. I was a grass widower, so to speak.'

'So you'd push off with Leo occasionally; have a drink and chase a few pussycats.'

'More or less.'

'In Cologne?'

'Steady, old boy,' said Crabbe. 'You're like a bloody lawyer.' He drank again and as the drink went into him he shook like a poor comedian reacting late. 'Christ,' he said. 'What a day. Christ.'

'Night clubs are best in Cologne, are they?'

'You can't do it *here*, old boy,' Crabbe said with a nervous start. 'Not unless you want to screw half the Government. You've got to be *bloody* careful in Bonn.' He added needlessly, '*Bloody* careful.' He jerked his head in wild confirmation. 'Cologne's the better bet.'

'Better girls?'

'Can't make it, old boy. Not for years.'

'But Leo went for them, did he?'

'He liked the girls,' said Crabbe.

'So you went to Cologne that night. Your wife was in England, and you went on the razzle with Leo.'

'We were just sitting at a table. Drinking, you see.' He suited the gesture to the word. 'Leo was talking about the Army: remember old so-and-so. That game. Loved the Army, Leo did, loved it. Should have stayed in, that's my feeling. Not that they'd have had him, not as a regular. He needed the discipline, in my opinion. Urchin really. Like me. It's all right when you're young, you don't mind. It's later. They knocked hell out of me at Sherborne. Hell. Used to hold the taps, head in the basin, while the bloody prefects hit me. I didn't care then. Thought it was life.' He put a hand on Turner's arm. 'Old boy,' he whispered. 'I *hate* them now. Didn't know I had it in me. It's all come to the surface. For two pins I'd go back there and shoot the buggers. Truth.'

'Did you know him in the Army?'

'No.'

'Then who were you remembering?'

'I ran across him in the CCG a bit. Moenchengladbach. Four Group.'

'When he was on Claims?'

Crabbe's reaction to harassment was unnerving. Like his namesake he seemed in some mysterious way to draw the extremities of his presence under a protective shell, and to lie passive until the danger had passed. Ducking his head into his glass he kept it there, shoulders hunched, while he peered at Turner with pink, hooded eyes.

'So you were drinking and talking.'

'Just quietly. Waiting for the cabaret. I like a good cabaret.' He drifted away into a wholly incredible account of an attempt he had made upon a girl in Frankfurt on the occasion of the last Free Democrats' Conference: 'Fiasco,' he declared proudly. 'Climbing over me like a bloody monkey and I couldn't do a thing.'

'So the fight came after the cabaret?'

'Before. There was a bunch of Huns at the bar kicking up a din; singing. Leo took offence. Started glaring at them. Pawing the earth a bit. Suddenly he'd called for the bill. "*Zahlen!*" Just like that. Bloody loud too. I said "Hoi! old boy, what's up?" Ignored me. "I don't want to go," I said. "Want to see the tit show." Blind bit of notice. The waiter brings the bill, Leo tots it up, shoves his hand in his pocket and puts a button on the plate.

'What kind of button?'

'Just a button. Like the one the dolly found down at the Bahnhof. Bloody wooden button with holes in it.' He was still indignant. 'You can't pay bloody bills with a *button*. Can you? Thought it was a joke at first. Had a bit of a laugh. "What happened to the rest of her?" I said. Thought he was joking, see. He wasn't.'

'Go on.'

'"Here you are," he said. "Keep the change," and gets up cool as anything. "Come on Mickie, this place stinks." Then they go for him. Jesus. Fantastic. Never thought he had it in him. Three down and one to go and then somebody cracks him with a bottle. All the blows; East End stuff. He could really mix it. Then they got him. They bent him over the bar backwards and just worked him over. Never seen anything like it. No one said a word. No how d'you do, nothing. System. Next thing we knew was, we were out in the street. Leo was on his hands and knees and they came out and gave him a few more for luck, and I was coughing my guts out on the pavement.'

'Pissed?'

'Sober as a bloody judge, old boy. They'd kicked me in the stomach, you see.'

'You?'

His head shook dreadfully as it sank to meet the glass: 'Tried to bail him out,' he muttered. 'Tried to mix it with the other chaps while he got away. Trouble is,' he explained, taking a deep draught of whisky. 'I'm not the fellow I used to be. Praschko had hoofed it by then.' He giggled. 'He was half-way out of the door by the time the button hit the plate. He seemed to know the form. Don't blame him.'

Turner might have been asking after an old friend. 'Praschko came often, did he? Back in those days?'

'First time I met him, old boy. And the last. Parted brass rags after that. Don't blame him. MP and all that. Bad for business.'

'What did *you* do?'

'Jesus. Trod gently, old boy.' He shuddered. 'Home posting loomed large. Bloody flea pit in Bushey or somewhere. With Mary. No thanks.'

'How did it end?'

'I reckon Praschko got on to Siebkron. Coppers dumped us at the Embassy. Guard got us a cab and we sloped off to my place and called a doctor. Then Ewan Waldebere turned up, he was Minister Political. Then Ludwig Siebkron in a dirty great Mercedes. Christ knows what didn't happen. Siebkron grilled him. Sat in my drawing-room and grilled him no end. Didn't care for it I must say. All the same, pretty serious when you think of it. Bloody diplomat tearing the arse off nightclubs, assaulting citizenry. Lot of fences to mend.'

The waiter brought some kidneys cooked in vinegar and wine.

'God,' said Crabbe. 'Look at that. Delicious. Lovely after snails.'

'What did Leo tell Siebkron?'

'Nix. Nothing. You don't know Leo. Close isn't the word. Waldebere, me, Siebkron: not a syllable to any of us. Mind you, they'd really gone for him. Waldebere faked him some leave; new teeth, stitches, Christ knows what. Told everybody he'd done it swimming in Yugoslavia. Diving into shallow water. Bashed his face in. Some water: Christ.'

'Why do you think it happened?'

'No idea, old boy. Wouldn't go with him after that. Not safe.'

'No opinions?'

'Sorry,' said Crabbe. His face sank beneath the surface, misted with meaningless wrinkles.

'Ever seen this key?'

'Nope.' He grinned affectionately. 'One of Leo's, was it? Screw anything in the old days, Leo would. Steadier now.'

'Any names attached to that?'

He continued staring at the key.

'Try Myra Meadowes.'

'Why?'

'She's willing. She's had one baby already. In London. They say half the drivers go through her every week.'

'Did he ever mention a woman called Aickman? Someone he was going to marry?'

Crabbe assumed an expression of puzzled recollection.

'Aickman,' he said. 'Funny. That was one of the old lot. From Berlin. He did talk about her. When they worked with the Russkies. That's it. She was another of those inbetweeners. Berlin, Hamburg, all that game. Stitched those bloody cushions for him. Care and attention.'

'What was he *doing* with the Russians,' Turner asked after a pause. 'What work was it?'

'Quadrupartite, bi-partite . . . one of them. Berlin's on its own, see. Different world, specially in those days. Island. Different sort of island.' He shook his head. 'Not like him,' he added. 'All that Communist kick. Not his book at all. Too bloody hard-nosed for all that balls.'

'And this Aickman?'

'Miss Brandt, Miss Etling and Miss Aickman.'

'Who are they?'

'Three dollies. In Berlin. Came out with them from England. Pretty as pictures, Leo said. Never seen girls like it. Never seen girls at all if you ask me. Emigré types going back to Germany. Join the Occupation. Same as Leo. Croydon airport, sitting on a crate, waiting for the plane, and these three dollies come along in uniform, waggling their tails. Miss Aickman, Miss Brandt and Miss Etling. Posted to the same unit. From then on he never looked back. Him and Praschko and another fellow. All went out together from England in forty-five. With these dollies. They made up a song about it: Miss Aickman, Miss Etling and Miss *Brandt* ... drinking song, saucy rhymes. They sang it that night as a matter of fact. Going along in the car, happy as sandboys. Jesus.'

He'd have sung it himself for two pins.

'Leo's girl was Aickman. His first girl. He'd always go back to her, that's what he said. "There'll never be another like the first one," that's what he said. "All the rest are imitations." His very words. You know the way Huns talk. Introspective beggars.'

'What became of her?'

'Dunno old boy. Fizzled away. What they all do, isn't it? Grow old. Shrivel up. Whoopsadaisy.' A piece of kidney fell from his fork and the gravy splashed on his tie.

'Why didn't he marry her?'

'She took the other road, old boy.'

'Which other road?'

'She didn't like him being English, he said. Wanted him to be a Hun again and face facts. Big on metaphysics.'

'Perhaps he's gone to find her.'

'He always said he would one day. "I've drunk at a good few pools, Mickie," he said. "But there'll never be another girl like Aickman." Still, that's what we all say, isn't it?' He dived into the Moselle as if it were a refuge.

'Is it?'

'You married, old boy, by the by? Keep away from it.' He shook his head. 'It would be all right if I could manage the bedroom. But I can't. It's like a bloody grease-pot for me. I can't make it.' He sniggered. 'Marry at fifty-five, my advice. Little sixteen-year-old dolly. Then they don't know what they're missing.'

'Praschko was up there, was he? In Berlin? With the Russians and Aickman?'

'Stable companions.'

'What else did he tell you about Praschko?'

'He was a Bolshie in those days. Nothing else.'

'Was Aickman?'

'Could be, old boy. Never said; didn't interest him that much.'

'Was Harting?'

'Not Leo, old boy. Didn't know his arse from his elbow where politics are concerned. Restful that was. Trout,' he whispered. 'I'd like trout next. Kidneys are just in between. If it's on the secret vote, I mean.'

The joke entertained him off and on for the remainder of the meal. Only once would he be drawn on the subject of Leo, and that was when Turner asked him whether he had had much to do with him in recent months.

'Not bloody likely,' Crabbe whispered.

'Why not?'

'He was getting broody, old boy. I could tell. Sizing up for another crack at someone. Pugnacious little beast,' he said, baring his teeth in a sudden grimace of alcoholic cramp. 'He'd started leaving those buttons about.'

He got back to the Adler at four; he was fairly drunk. The lift was occupied so he used the stairs. That's it, he thought. That is the sweet end. He would go on drinking through the afternoon and he would drink on the plane and with any luck by the time he saw Lumley he would be speechless. The Crabbe answer: snails, kidneys, trout and scotch and keep your head down while the big wheels roll over. As he reached his own floor he noticed vaguely that the lift had been wedged with a suitcase and he supposed the porter was collecting more luggage from someone's bedroom. We're the only lucky people in the place, he thought. We're leaving. He tried to open the door to his room but the lock was jammed; he wrestled with the key but it wouldn't give. He stepped back quite quickly when he heard the footsteps, but he didn't really have much chance. The door was pulled open from inside. He had a glimpse of a pale round face and fair hair carefully combed back, a bland brow furrowed with anxiety, he saw the stitching of the leather as it moved down on him in slow motion and he wondered whether the stitches cut the scalp the way they cut the face. He felt the nausea strike him and his stomach fold, and the wooden club buffet at the back of his knees; he heard the soft surgeon's voice calling from the darkness as the warm grass of the Yorkshire dales prickled against his child's face. He heard the taunting voice of Tony Willoughby, soft as velvet, clinging like a lover, saw his pianist's hands drift over her white hips, and heard Leo's music whining to God in every red timber tabernacle of his own childhood. He smelt the smoke of the Dutch cigars, and there was Willoughby's voice again offering him a hair-dryer: I'm only a temporary, Alan old boy, but there's ten per cent off for friends of the family. He felt the pain again, the thudding as they began slapping him and he saw the wet black granite of the orphanage in Bournemouth and the telescope on Constitution Hill. 'If there's one thing I really hate,' Lumley observed, 'It's a cynic in search of God.' He had a moment's total agony as they hit him in the groin, and as it slowly subsided he saw the girl who had left him drifting in the black streets of his own defiant solitude. He heard the screaming of Myra Meadowes as he broke her down, lie for lie, the scream as they took her from her Polish lover, and the scream as she parted from her baby; and he thought he might be crying out himself until he recognized the towel they had shoved in his mouth. He felt something cold and iron hard hit the back of his head and stay there like a lump of ice, he heard the door slam and knew he was alone; he saw the whole damned trail of the deceived and the uncaring; heard the fool voice of an English Bishop praising God and war; and fell asleep. He was in a coffin, a smooth cold coffin. On a marble slab with polished tiles and the glint of chrome at the far end of a tunnel. He heard de Lisle muttering to him in kindly moderation and Jenny Pargiter's sobbing like the moan of every woman he had left; he heard the fatherly tones of Meadowes exhorting him to charity and the cheerful whistling of unencumbered people. Then Meadowes and Pargiter slipped away, lost to other funerals, and only de Lisle remained, and only de Lisle's voice offered any comfort.

'My dear fellow,' he was saying, as he peered curiously downward, 'I dropped in to say goodbye, but if you're going to take a bath, you might at least take off that dreadful suit.'

'Is it Thursday?'

De Lisle had taken a napkin from the rail and was soaking it under the hot tap.

'Wednesday. Wednesday as ever was. Cocktail time.'

He bent over him and began gently dabbing the blood from his face.

'That football field. Where you saw him. Where he took Pargiter. Tell me how I get there.'

'Keep still. And don't talk or you'll wake the neighbours.'

With the gentlest possible movements he continued touching away the caked blood. Freeing his right hand Turner cautiously felt in the pocket of his jacket for the gunmetal key. It was still there.

'Have you ever seen this before?'

'No. No, I haven't. Nor was I in the greenhouse at 3 AM on the morning of the second. But how *like* the Foreign Office,' he said, standing back and critically surveying his handiwork, 'to send a bull to catch a matador. You won't mind my reclaiming my dinner jacket, will you?'

'Why did Bradfield ask me?'

'Ask you what?'

'To dinner. To meet Siebkron. Why did he invite me on Tuesday?'

'Brotherly love; what else?'

'What's in that despatch box that Bradfield's so frightened of?'

'Poisonous snakes.'

'That key wouldn't open it?'

'No.'

De Lisle sat down on the edge of the bath. 'You shouldn't be doing this,' he said. 'I know what you'll tell me; somebody had to get their hands dirty. Just don't expect me to be pleased it's you. You're not just *somebody*: that's your trouble. Leave it to the people who were born with blinkers.' His grey, tender eyes were shadowed with concern. 'It is totally absurd,' he declared. 'People crack up every day under the strain of being saints. You're cracking up under the strain of being a pig.'

*

'Why doesn't he go? Why does he hang around?'

'They'll be asking that about you tomorrow.'

Turner was stretched out on de Lisle's long sofa. He held a whisky in his hand and his face was covered in yellow antiseptic from de Lisle's extensive medicine chest. His canvas bag lay in the corner of the room. De Lisle sat at his harpsichord, not playing it but stroking the keys. It was an eighteenth-century piece, satinwood, and the top was bleached by tropical suns.

'Do you take that thing everywhere?'

'I had a violin once. It fell to pieces in Leopoldville. The glue melted. It's awfully hard,' he observed dryly, 'to pursue culture when the glue melts.'

'If Leo's so damn clever, why doesn't he go?'

'Perhaps he likes it here. He'd be the first, I must say.'

'And if *they're* so damned clever, why don't they take him away?'

'Perhaps they don't know he's on the loose.'

'What did you say?'

'I said perhaps they don't know he's run for it. I'm not a spy, I'm afraid, but I am human and I do know Leo. He's extremely perverse. I can't imagine for a moment he would do exactly what they told him. If there is a "they", which I doubt. He wasn't a *natural* servant.'

Turner said, 'I try all the time to force him into the mould. He won't fit.'

De Lisle struck a couple of notes with his finger.

'Tell me, what do you *want* him to be? A goodie or a baddie? Or do you just want the freedom of the search? You want *something*, don't you? Because anything's better than nothing. You're like those beastly students: you can't stand a vacuum.'

Turner had closed his eyes and was lost in thought.

'I expect he's dead. That would be very macabre.'

'He wasn't dead this morning, was he?' Turner said.

'And you don't like him to be in limbo. It annoys you. You want him to land or take off. There are no *shades* for you, are there? I suppose that's the fun of searching for extremists: you search for their convictions, is that it?'

'He's still on the run,' Turner continued. 'Who's he running *from*? Us or them?'

'He could be on his own.'

'With fifty stolen box files? Oh sure. Sure.'

De Lisle examined Turner over the top of the harpsichord.

'You complement one another. I look at you and I think of Leo. You're Saxon. Big hands, big feet, big heart and that lovely reason that grapples with ideals. Leo's the other way round. He's a performer. He wears our clothes, uses our language but he's only half tamed. I suppose I'm on your side, really: you and I are the concert audience.' He closed the harpsichord. 'We're the ones who glimpse, and reach, and fall back. There's a Leo in all of us but he's usually dead by the time we're twenty.'

'What are you then?'

'Me? Oh, reluctantly, a conductor.' Standing up, he carefully locked the keyboard with a small brass key from his chain. 'I can't even play the thing,' he said, tapping the bleached lid with his elegant fingers. 'I tell myself I will one day; I'll take lessons or get a book. But I don't really care: I've learnt to live with being half-finished. Like most of us.'

'Tomorrow's Thursday,' Turner said. 'If they don't know he's defected, they'll be expecting him to turn up, won't they?'

'I suppose so,' de Lisle yawned. 'But then they know where to go, don't they, whoever they are? And you don't. That is something of a drawback.'

'It might not be.'

'Oh.'

'We know where *you* saw him, at least, that Thursday afternoon, don't we, when he was supposed to be at the Ministry? Same place as he took Pargiter. Seems quite a hunting-ground for him.'

De Lisle stood very still, the keychain still in his hand.

'It's no good telling you not to go, I suppose?'

'No.'

'Asking you? You're acting against Bradfield's instructions.'

'Even so.'

'And you're sick. All right. Go and look for your untamed half. And if you *do* find that file, we shall expect you to return it unopened.'

And that, quite suddenly, was an order.

14
Thursday's Child

The weather on the plateau was stolen from other seasons and other places. It was a sea wind from March which sang in the wire netting, bending the tufts of coarse grass and crashing into the forest behind him; and if some mad aunt had planted a monkey-puzzle in the sandy earth, Turner could have hopped straight down the path and caught the trolley-bus to Bournemouth Square. It was the frost of November whose icy pipes encased the bracken stems; for there the cold had hidden from the wind and it gripped like arctic water at his ankles; the frost of a stone crevice on a north face, when only fear will set your hands to work, and life is treasured because it is won. The last strips of an Oxford sun lay bravely dying on the empty playing-field; and the sky was a Yorkshire evening in autumn, black and billowing and fringed with grime. The trees were curved from childhood, bent by the blustering wind, Mickie Crabbe's boyhood bent at the taps in the washroom, and when the gusts had gone they waited still, backs arched for the next assault.

The cuts on his face were burning raw and his pale eyes were bright with sleepless pain. He waited, staring down the hill. Far below to his right lay the river, and for once the wind had silenced it, and the barges called in vain. A car was climbing slowly towards him; a black Mercedes, Cologne registration, woman driver; and did not slow down as it passed. On the other side of the wire, a new hut was shuttered and padlocked. A rook had settled on the roof and the wind tugged at its feathers. A Renault, French diplomatic registration, woman driver, one male passenger: Turner noted the number in his black book. His script was stiff and childish, and the letters came to him unnaturally. He must have hit back after all, for two knuckles on his right hand were badly cut, as if he had punched an open mouth and caught the front teeth. Harting's handwriting was neat, rounding the rough corners, but Turner's was big and downright, promising collision.

'You are both *movers*, you and Leo,' de Lisle had said some time last night, as they sat in their deep armchairs. 'Bonn is stationary but you are movers. . . . You are fighting one another, but it is you against us. . . . The opposite of love is not hate but apathy. . . . You must come to terms with apathy.'

'For Christ's sake,' Turner complained.

'This is your stop,' de Lisle had said, opening the car door for him. 'And if you're not back by tomorrow morning I shall tell the coastguards.'

He had bought a spanner in Bad Godesberg, a monkey wrench, heavy at the head, and it lay like a lead weight against his hip. A Volkswagen bus, dark grey, Registration SU, full of children, stopping at the changing hut. Their noise came at him suddenly, a flock of birds racing with the wind, a tattered jingle of laughter and complaint. Someone blew a whistle. The sun hit them low down, like torch beams shining along a corridor. The hut swallowed them. 'I have never known anyone,' de Lisle had cried in despair, 'make such a meal of his disadvantages.'

He drew back quickly behind the tree. One Opel Rekord; two men. Registration Bonn. The spanner nudged him as he wrote. The men were wearing hats and overcoats and were professionally without expression. The side windows were of smoked glass. The car continued, but at a walking pace. He saw their blank blond faces turned towards him, twin moons in the artificial dark. *Your* teeth? Turner wondered. Was it your teeth I knocked in? I can't tell you apart. Trust you to come to the ball. All the way up the hill, they could not have touched ten miles an hour. A van passed, followed by two lorries. Somewhere a clock chimed; or was it a school bell? Or Angelus, or Compline, or sooty sheep in the Dales, or the ring of the ferry from the river? He would never hear it again; yet there is no truth, as Mr Crail would say, that cannot be confirmed. No, my child; but the sins of others are a sacrifice to God. Your sacrifice. The rook had left the roof. The sun had gone. A little Citroën was wandering into sight. A *deux chevaux*, dirty as fog, with one bashed wing, one illegible number plate, one driver hidden in the shadow, and one headlight flashing on and off and one horn blaring for the hunt. The Opel had disappeared. Hurry moons or you will miss His coming. The wheels jerk like dislocated limbs as the little car turns off the road and bumps towards him over the frozen mud ruts of the timber track, the pert tail rocking on its axle. He hears the blare of dance music as the door opens, and his mouth is dry from the tablets, and the cuts on his face are a screen of twigs. One day, when the world is free, his fevered mind assured him, clouds will detonate as they collide and God's angels will fall down dazed for the whole world to look at. Silently he dropped the spanner back into his pocket.

She was standing not ten yards away, her back towards him, quite indifferent to the wind, or the children who now burst upon the playground.

She was staring down the hill. The engine was still running, shaking the car with inner pains. A wiper juddered uselessly over the grimy windscreeen. For an hour she barely moved.

For an hour she waited with oriental stillness, heeding nothing but whoever would not come. She stood like a statue, growing taller as the light left her.

The wind dragged at her coat. Once her hand rose to gather in the errant strands of hair, and once she walked to the end of the timber-track to look down into the river valley, in the direction of Königswinter; then slowly returned, lost in thought, and Turner dropped to his knees behind the trees, praying that the shadows protected him.

His patience broke. Getting noisily back into the car she lit a cigarette and slapped the horn with her open hand. The children forgot their game and grinned at the hoarse burp of the exhausted battery. The silence returned.

The windscreen wiper had stopped but the engine was still running and she was revving it to encourage the heater. The windows were misting up. She opened her handbag and took out a mirror and a lipstick.

She was leaning back in the seat, eyes closed, listening to dance music, one hand gently beating time on the steering wheel. Hearing a car, she opened the door and looked idly out, but it was only the black Rekord going slowly down the hill again and though the moons were turned towards her, she was quite indifferent to their interest.

The playing-field was empty. The shutters were closed on the changing hut. Turning on the overhead lamp, she read the time by her watch, but by then the first lights were coming up in the valley and the river was lost in the low mist of dusk. Turner stepped heavily on to the path and pulled open the passenger door.

'Waiting for someone?' he asked and sat down beside her, closing the door quickly so that the light went out again. He switched off the wireless.

'I thought you'd gone,' she said hotly, 'I thought my husband had got rid of you.' Fear, anger, humiliation seized hold of her. 'You've been spying on me all the time! Crouching in the bushes like a detective! How dare you? You vulgar, bloody little man!' She drew back her clenched fist and perhaps she hesitated when she saw the mess his face was in, but it wouldn't have made much difference because at the same moment Turner hit her very hard across the mouth so that her head jerked back against the pillar with a snap. Opening his door he walked round the car, pulled her out and hit her again with his open hand.

'We're going for a walk,' he said, 'And we'll talk about your vulgar bloody lover.'

He led her along the timber path to the crest of the hill. She walked quite willingly, holding his arm with both her hands, head down, crying silently.

They were looking down on to the Rhine. The wind had fallen. Already above them, the early stars drifted like sparks of phosphorus on a gently rocking sea. Along the river the lights kindled in series, faltering at the moment of their birth and then miraculously living, growing to small fires fanned by the black night breeze. Only the river's sounds reached them; the chugging of the barges and the nursery chime of the clocks telling off the quarters. They caught the mouldering smell of the Rhine itself, felt its cold breath upon their hands and cheeks.

'It began as a dare.'

She stood apart from him, gazing into the valley, her arms clutching round her body as if she were holding a towel.

'He won't come any more. I've had it. I know that.'

'Why won't he?'

'Leo never *said* things. He was too much of a puritan.' She lit a cigarette. 'Because he'll never stop searching, that's why.'

'What for?'

'What do any of us look for? Parents, children, a woman.' She turned to face him. 'Go on,' she challenged. 'Ask the rest.'

Turner waited.

'When intimacy took place, isn't that what you want to know? I'd have slept with him that same night if he'd asked me, but he didn't get round to it because I'm Rawley's wife and he knew that good men were scarce. I mean he knew he *had* to survive. He was a creep, don't you realize? He'd have charmed the feathers off a goose.' She broke off. 'I'm a fool to tell you anything.'

'You'd be a bigger fool not to. You're in big trouble,' Turner said, 'in case you didn't know.'

'I can't remember when I haven't been. How else do I beat the system? We were two old tarts and we fell in love.'

She was sitting on a bench, playing with her gloves.

'It was a buffet. A bloody Bonn buffet with lacquered duck and dreadful Germans. Someone's welcome to someone. Someone's farewell. Americans I should think. Mr and Mrs Somebody the Third. Some dynastic feast. It was appallingly provincial.' Her voice was her own, swift and falsely confident, but for all her efforts it still possessed that note of hard-won dexterity which Turner had heard in British diplomatic wives all over the world: a voice to talk through silences, cover embarrassments, retrieve offences; a voice that was neither particularly cultured nor particularly sophisticated but, like a nanny in pursuit of lost standards, doggedly trod its course. 'We'd come straight from Aden and we'd been here exactly a year. Before that we were in Peking and now we were in Bonn. Late October: Karfeld's October. Things had just hotted up. In Aden we'd been bombed, in Peking we were mobbed and now we were going to be burned in the Market Place. Poor Rawley: he seems to attract humiliation. He was a prisoner of war as well, you know. There ought to be a name for him: the humiliated generation.'

'He'd love you for that,' said Turner.

'He loves me without it.' She paused. 'The funny thing is, I'd never noticed him before. I thought he was just a rather dull little ... temporary. The prissy little man who played the organ in Chapel and smoked those filthy cigars at cocktail parties ... Nothing there.... Empty. And that night, the moment he came in, the moment he appeared at the doorway I felt him choose me and I thought: "Look out. Air raid." He came straight over to me. "Hullo, Hazel." He'd never called me Hazel in my life and I thought: "You cheeky devil, you'll have to work for this."'

'Good of you to take the risk,' said Turner.

'He began to talk. I don't know what about; I never much noticed *what* he said; any more than he did. Karfeld I suppose. Riots. All the stamping and shouting. But I noticed *him*. For the first time, I really did.' She fell silent. 'And I thought, "Hoi; where have you been all my life?" It was like looking in an old bank book and finding you've got a credit instead of an overdraft. He was *alive*.' She laughed. 'Not like you a bit. *You're* about the deadest thing I ever met.'

Turner might have hit her again, were it not for the awful familiarity of her mockery.

'It was the tension you noticed first. He was *patrolling* himself. His language, his manners ... it was all a fake. He was on guard. He listened to his own voice the way he listened to yours, getting the cadence right, putting the adverbs in the right order. I tried to place him: who would I *think* you were if I didn't *know*? South American German? ... Argentine trade delegate? One of those. Glossy latinized Hun.' Again she broke off, lost in recollection – 'He had those velvety German end-bits of language and he used them to trim the balance of every sentence. I made him talk about himself, where he lived, who cooked for him, how he spent his weekends. The next thing I knew, he was giving me advice. Diplomatic advice: where to buy cheap meat. The Post Report. The Dutchman was best for this, the Naafi for that; butter from the Economat, nuts from the Commissary. Like a woman. He had a thing about herbal teas; Germans are mad about digestion. Then he offered to sell me a hair-dryer. Why are you laughing?' She asked in a sudden fury.

'Was I?'

'He knew some way of getting a discount: twenty-five per cent, he said. He'd compared all the prices, he knew all the models.'

'He'd been looking at your hair too.'

She rounded on him: 'You keep your place,' she snapped. 'You're not within shouting distance of him.'

He hit her again, a long swinging blow deep into the flesh of the cheek and she said 'You bastard' and went very pale in the darkness, shivering with anger.

'Get on with it.'

At last she began again: 'So I said yes. I was fed up anyway. Rawley was buried with a French Counsellor in the corner; everyone else was fighting for food at the buffet. So I said yes, I *would* like a hair-dryer. At twenty-five per cent off. I was afraid I hadn't got the money on me; would he take a cheque? I might just as well have said, yes I'll go to bed with you. That was the first time I saw him smile; he didn't smile often as a rule. His whole face was lit up. I sent him to get some food, and I watched him all the way, wondering what it was going to be like. He had that egg walk ... *Eiertanz* they call it here ... just like in Chapel really, but *harder*. The Germans were crowding the bar, fighting for the asparagus, and he just darted between them and came out with two plates loaded with food and the knives and forks sticking out of his handkerchief pocket; grinning like mad. I've got a brother called Andrew who plays scrum-half at rugger. You could hardly have told the difference. From then on, I didn't worry. Some foul Canadian was trying to get me to listen to a lecture on agriculture and I bit his head off. They're about the only ones left who still believe in it all, the Canadians. They're like the British in India.'

Hearing some sound she turned her head sharply and stared back along the path. The tree trunks were black against the low horizon; the wind had dropped; a night dew had damped their clothes.

'He won't come. You said so yourself. Get on with it. Hurry.'

'We sat on a stair and he started talking about himself again. He didn't need any prompting. It just came out ... it was fascinating. About Germany in the early days after the war. "Only the rivers were whole." I never knew whether he was translating German or using his imagination or just repeating what he'd picked up.' She hesitated, and again glanced down the path. 'How at night the women built by arclight ... passing stones as if they were putting out a fire.... How he learnt to sleep in a fifteen hundredweight using a fire extinguisher as a pillow. He did a little act, putting his head on one side and twisting his mouth to show his stiff neck. Bedroom games.' She stood up abruptly. 'I'm going back. If he finds the car empty, he'll run away; he's as nervous as a kitten.'

He followed her to the timber track, but the plateau was deserted except for the Opel Rekord parked in the lay-by with its lights out.

'Sit in the car,' she said. 'Never mind them.' For the first time she really noticed the marks on his face by the interior light and she drew in her breath sharply.

'Who did that?'

'They'll do it to Leo if they find him first.'

She was leaning back in the seat, her eyes closed. Someone had torn the cloth on the roof and it hung down in beggar's shreds. There was a child's driving wheel on the floor with a plastic tube attached to it and Turner pushed it out of the way with his foot.

'Sometimes I thought: "You're empty. You're just imitating life." But you daren't think that of a lover. He was a negotiator, an actor, I suppose. He was caught between all those worlds: Germany and England, Königswinter and Bonn, Chapel and the discounts, the first floor and the ground floor. You can't expect anyone to fight all those battles and stay alive. Sometimes he just served us,' she explained simply. 'Or me. Like a headwaiter. We were all his customers; whatever he wanted. He didn't live, he survived. He's always survived. Till now.' She lit another cigarette. The car was very cold. She tried to start the engine and put the heater on, but the ignition failed.

'After that first evening it was all over bar bed. Rawley came and found me and we were the last to go. He'd been having a row with Lésère about something and he was pleased at having come off best. Leo and I were still sitting on the stairs, drinking coffee, and Rawley just came over and kissed me on the cheek. What was that?'

'Nothing.'

'I saw a light down the hill.'

'It was a bicycle crossing the road. It's gone now.'

'I hate him kissing me in public; he knows I can't stop him. He never does it in private. "Come on my dear, it's time to go." Leo stood up when he saw him coming, but Rawley didn't even notice him. He took me over to Lésère. "This is the person you should really apologize to," he said. "She's been sitting alone on the stairs all evening." We were going out of the door and Rawley stopped to collect his coat, and there was Leo, holding it for him.' She smiled, and it was the smile of real love, rejoicing at the memory. 'He didn't seem to notice me any more. Rawley turned his back on him and put his arms into the sleeves and I actually saw Leo's own arms stiffen and his fingers curl. Mind you, I was glad. I *wanted* Rawley to behave like that.' She shrugged. 'I was hooked,' she said. 'I'd been looking for a fly and now I'd got one, feathers and all. Next day I looked him up in the Red Book. You know what that is by now: nothing. I rang up Mary Crabbe and asked her about him. Just for fun. "I ran into an extraordinary little man last night," I said. Mary had a fit. "My dear, he's poison. Keep *right* away from him. He dragged Mickie to a night club once and got him into *awful* trouble. Mercifully," she said, "his contract's running out in December and he'll be gone." I tried Sally Askew, she's terrifically worthy. I could have died' – she broke out laughing, then drew her chin down into her chest to copy the sonorous tones of the Economic Minister's wife: '"A useful bachelor, if the Huns are in short supply." They often are here, you know; there are more of us than them. Too many diplomats chasing too few Germans: that's Bonn. The trouble was, Sally said, the Germans were getting rather old school again about Leo's kind, so she and Aubrey had reluctantly given him up. "He's an unconscious irritant, my dear, if you know what I mean." I was absolutely thrilled. I put down the receiver and I shot into the drawing-room and I wrote him a great long letter about absolutely nothing.'

She tried the engine again but it didn't even cough. She gathered her coat more tightly round her.

'Cor,' she whispered. 'Come on, Leo. You don't half put a strain on friendship.'

In the black Opel a tiny light went on and off like a signal. Turner said nothing, but his thick fingertips lightly touched the spanner in his pocket.

'A schoolgirl letter. Thank you for being so attentive. Sorry for claiming all your time and please remember about the hair-dryer. Then a lovely long made-up story about how I went shopping in the *Spanischer Gerten* and an old lady dropped a two-mark piece into an orange-crate and no one could find it and she said it was payment because she'd left it in the shop. I delivered the letter to the Embassy myself and he rang up that afternoon. There were two models, he said, the more expensive one had different speeds and you didn't need an adapter.'

'Transformer.'

'What about colour? I just listened. He said it would be very difficult to make a decision for me, what with the speeds and the colour. Couldn't we meet and discuss it? It was a Thursday and we met up here. He said he came up every Thursday to get some fresh air and watch the children. I didn't believe him, but I was very happy.'

'Is that all he said about coming up here?'

'He said once they owed him time.'

'Who did?'

'The Embassy. Something Rawley had taken away from him and given to someone else. A job. So he came up here instead.' She shook her head in real admiration. 'He's as stubborn as a mule,' she declared. '"They owe it me," he said, "so I take it. And that's the only way I live."'

'I thought you said he didn't say things?'

'Not the best things.'

He waited.

'We just walked and looked at the river and on the way back we held hands. As we were leaving he said, "I forgot to show you the hair-dryer," So I said, "What a pity. We'll have to meet here next Thursday too, won't we." He was *enormously* shocked.' She had a special voice for him as well: it was both mocking and possessive and it seemed to exclude Turner rather than draw him in. '"My *dear* Mrs Bradfield—" I said, "If you come next week I'll let you call me Hazel." I'm a whore,' she explained. 'That's what you're thinking.'

'And after that?'

'Every Thursday. Here. He parked his car down the lane and I left mine in the road. We were lovers but we hadn't been to bed. It was very grown-up. Sometimes he talked; sometimes he didn't. He kept showing me his house across the river as if he wanted to sell it to me. We'd go all along the path from one little hilltop to another so that we could see it. I teased him once. "You're the devil. You're showing me the whole kingdom." He didn't care for that. He never forgot anything, you see. That was the survivor in him. He didn't like me to talk about evil, or pain or anything. He knew all *that* inside out.'

'And the rest?'

He saw her face tilt and the smile break.

'Rawley's bed. A Friday. There's an avenger in Leo, not far down. He always knew when Rawley was going away: he used to check in the Travel Office, look at the Travel Clerk's bookings. He'd say to me: he's in Hanover next week . . . he's in Bremen.'

'What did Bradfield go there for?'

'Oh God. Visiting the Consulates. . . . Leo asked me the same question: how should *I* know? Rawley never tells *me* anything. Sometimes I thought he was following Karfeld round Germany . . . he always seemed to go where the rallies were.'

'And from then on?'

She shrugged. 'Yes. From then on. Whenever we could.'

'Did Bradfield know?'

'Oh God. Know? You're worse than the Germans. It was in between. You want things spelt out for you, don't you? Some things can't be. Some things aren't true till they're said. Rawley knows that better than anyone.'

'Christ,' Turner whispered. 'You give yourself all the chances,' and he remembered he had said the same thing to Bradfield three days ago.

She stared ahead of her through the windscreen.

'What are people *worth*? Children, husbands, careers. You go under and they call it sacrifice. You survive and they call you a bitch. Chop yourself in bits. For what? I'm not God. I can't hold them all up on my shoulders. I live for them; they live for someone else. We're all saints. We're all fools. Why don't we live for ourselves and call *that* service for a change?'

'*Did he know?*'

He had seized her arm.

'Did he!'

The tears trickled sideways over the bridge of her nose. She wiped them away.

'Rawley's a diplomat,' she said at last. 'The art of the possible, that's Rawley. The limited aim, the trained mind. "Let's not get overheated. Let's not put a name to things. Let's not negotiate without knowing what we want to achieve." He can't . . . he can't go mad, it isn't in him. He can't live for anything. Except me.'

'But he knew.'

'I should think so,' she said wearily. 'I never asked him. Yes, he knew.'

'Because you made him renew that contract, didn't you. Last December. You worked on him.'

'Yes. That was awful. That was quite awful. But it had to be done,' she explained, as if she were referring to a higher cause of which they were both aware. 'Or he'd have sent Leo away.'

'And that was what Leo wanted. That's why he picked you up.'

'Rawley married me for my money. For what he could get out of me,' she said. 'He stayed with me for love. Does that satisfy you?'

Turner did not reply.

'He never put it into words. I told you. He never said the big things. "One more year is all I need. Just one more year, Hazel. One year to love you, one year to get what they owe me. One year from December and then I'll go. They don't realize how much they need me." So I invited Leo for drinks. When Rawley was there. It was early on, before the gossip started. We were just the three of us; I made Rawley come back early. "Rawley this is Leo Harting, he works for you and he plays the organ in Chapel." "Of course. We've met," he said. We talked about nothing. Nuts from the Commissary. Spring leave. What it was like in Königswinter in the summer. "Mr Harting has asked us to dinner," I said. "Isn't he kind?" Next week we went to Königswinter. He gave us all the bits and pieces: ratafia biscuits with the sweet, halva with the coffee. That was all.'

'What was all?'

'Oh Christ, can't you see? I'd shown him! I'd shown Rawley what I wanted him to buy me!'

It was quite still now. The rooks had perched like sentinels on slowly rocking branches, and there was no wind anymore to stir their feathers.

'Are they like horses?' she asked. 'Do they sleep standing up?'

She turned her head to look at him but he did not reply.

'He hated silence,' she said dreamily. 'It frightened him. That's why he liked music; that's why he liked his house ... it was full of noise. Not even the dead could have slept there. Let alone Leo.'

She smiled remembering.

'He didn't live in it, he manned it. Like a ship. All night he'd be hopping up and down fixing a window or a shutter or something. His whole life was like that. Secret fears, secret memories; things he would never tell but expected you to know about.' She yawned. 'He won't come now,' she said. 'He hated the dark too.'

'Where is he?' Turner said urgently. 'What's he doing?'

She said nothing.

'Listen: he whispered to you. In the night he boasted, told you how he made the world turn for him. How clever he was, the tricks he played, the people he deceived!'

'You've got him wrong. Utterly wrong.'

'Then tell me!'

'There's nothing to tell. We were pen friends, that's all. He was reporting from another world.'

'*What* world? Bloody Moscow and the fight for peace?'

'I was right. You are vulgar. You want the lines joined up and all the colours flat. You haven't got the guts to face the half tones.'

'Has he?'

She seemed to have put him out of her mind. 'Let's go, for God's sake,' she said shortly, as if Turner had been keeping her waiting.

He had to push the car quite a distance along the track before it started. As they careered down the hill, he saw the Opel pull out from the lay-by and hurriedly take up its position thirty yards behind them. She drove to

Remagen, to one of the big hotels along the waterfront run by an old lady who patted her arm as she sat down. Where was the little man? she asked, *der nette kleine Herr* who was always so jolly and smoked cigars and spoke such excellent German.

'He talked it with an accent,' she explained to Turner. 'A slight English accent. It was something he'd taught himself.'

The sun room was quite empty except for a young couple in the corner. The girl had long, blonde hair. They stared at him oddly because of the cuts on his face. From their window table Turner saw the Opel park in the esplanade below them. The number plate had changed but the moons were just the same. His head was aching terribly. He had not taken more than half his whisky before he wanted to vomit. He asked for water. The old lady brought a bottle of local health water and told him all about it. They had used it in both wars, she explained, when the hotel was a first-aid post for those who were wounded while trying to cross the river.

'He was going to meet me here last Friday,' she said. 'And take me home to dinner. Rawley was leaving for Hanover. Leo cried off at the last minute.'

'On the Thursday afternoon he was late. I didn't bother. Sometimes he didn't turn up at all. Sometimes he worked. It was different. Just the last month or so. He'd changed. I thought at first he'd got another woman. He was always slipping off to places—'

'What places?'

'Berlin once. Hamburg. Hanover. Stuttgart. Rather like Rawley. So he said anyway; I was never sure. He wasn't strong on truth. Not your kind.'

'He arrived late. Last Thursday. *Come on*!'

'He'd had lunch with Praschko.'

'At the Maternus,' Turner breathed.

'They'd had a *discussion*. That was another Leo-ism. It didn't commit you. Like the Passive Voice, that was another favourite. A *discussion* had taken place. He didn't say what about. He was preoccupied. Broody. I knew him better than to try to jerk him out of it so we just walked around. With *them* watching us. And I knew this was it.'

'This was what?'

'This was the year he'd wanted. He'd found it, whatever it was, and now he didn't know what to do with it.' She shrugged. 'And by then, I'd found it too. He never realized. If he'd lifted a finger I'd have packed and gone with him.' She was looking at the river. 'Not children, husbands or any bloody thing wouild have stopped me. Not that he would have wanted me.'

'*What's* he found?' Turner whispered.

'I don't know. He found it and talked to Praschko and Praschko was no good. Leo knew he wouldn't be any good; but he had to go back and find out. He had to make sure he was on his own.'

'How do you know that? How much did he tell you?'

'Less than he thought, perhaps. He assumed I was part of him and that was that.' She shrugged. 'I was a friend and friends don't ask questions. Do they?'

'Go on.'

'Rawley was going to Hanover, he said; Friday night Rawley would go to Hanover. So Leo would give me dinner at Königswinter. A special dinner. I said "to celebrate?" "No. No. Hazel, not a *celebration*." But everything was special now, he said, and there wasn't much time anymore. He wouldn't be getting another contract. No more years after December. So why not have a good dinner once in a while? And he looked at me in a frightfully shifty way and we plodded round the course again, him leading. We'd meet in Remagen, he said: we'd meet here. And then: "I say, Hazel, what the devil is Rawley *up to*, look here, in Hanover? I mean, two days before the rally?"'

She had a ready-made face for Leo as well, a frown, a heavy German frown of exaggerated sincerity with which she surely teased him when they were together.

'What *was* Rawley up to, then?' Turner demanded.

'Nothing as it turned out. He didn't go. And Leo must have got wind of that, because he cried off.'

'When?'

'He rang up on Friday morning.'

'What did he say? *Exactly* what did he say?'

'Exactly, he said he couldn't make it that night. He didn't give a reason. Not a real one. He was awfully sorry; there was something he had to do. It had become urgent. It was his boardroom voice: "Awfully sorry, Hazel."'

'That was all?'

'I said all right.' She was acting against tragedy. 'And good luck.' She shrugged. 'I haven't heard from him since. He disappeared and I was worried. I rang his house day and night. That's why you came to dinner. I thought you might know something. You didn't. Any fool could see that.'

The blonde girl was standing up. She wore a long suit of fitted suede and she had to pull tightly at the crutch to straighten the sharp creases. The old lady was writing a bill. Turner called to her and asked for more water and she left the room to get it.

'Ever seen this key?'

Clumsily he drew it from the official buff envelope and laid it on the tablecloth before her. She picked it up and held it cautiously in her palm.

'Where did you get this from?'

'Königswinter. It was in a blue suit.'

'The suit he wore on Thursday,' she said examining it.

'It's one you gave him, is it?' he asked with unconcealed distaste. 'Your house-key?'

'Perhaps it's the one I wouldn't give him,' she replied at last.'That was the only thing I wouldn't do for him.'

'Go on.'

'I suppose that's what he wanted from Pargiter. That bitch Mary Crabbe told me he'd had a fling with *her*.' She stared down at the esplanade, at the waiting Opel parked in the shadow between the lights; then across the river to Leo's side.

'He said the Embassy had got something that belonged to him. Something from long ago. "They *owe* me, Hazel." He wouldn't say what it was. Memories, he said. It was to do with long ago, and I could get him the key so that he could take it back. I told him: "Talk to them. Tell Rawley, he's human." He said, No, Rawley was the last person on earth he could talk to. It wasn't anything valuable. It was locked away and they didn't even know they had it. You're going to interrupt. Don't. Just listen. I'm telling you more than you deserve.'

She drank some whisky.

'About that third time ... in *our* house. He lay in bed and just went on about it: "Nothing *bad*," he said, "nothing *political*, but something owed." If he was Duty Officer it wouldn't matter, but he wasn't allowed to do Duty, being what he was. There was one key, they'd never miss it, no one knew how many there were anyway. One key he must have.' She broke off. 'Rawley fascinated him. He loved his dressing-room. All the trappings of a gent. He loved to *see*. Sometimes that's what I was to him: Rawley's wife.The cuff links, the Edward Lear.... He wanted to know all the backstairs things like who cleaned his shoes, where he had his suits made. That was when he played his card: while he was dressing. He pretended to remember what he'd been talking about all night. "I say Hazel, look here. *You* could get me the key. When Rawley's working late one night, couldn't you? I mean, call on him, say you'd left something in the Assembly Room. It would be *frightfully* simple. It's a different key," he said. "It's not like the others. Very easily recognized, Hazel." That key,' she remarked flatly handing it back to him. '"You're clever," I said, "You'll find a way."'

'That was before Christmas?'

'Yes.'

'What a bloody fool I am,' Turner whispered. 'Jesus Christ!'

'Why? What is it?'

'Nothing.' His eyes were bright with success. 'Just for a moment, I forgot he was a thief, that's all. I thought he'd copy that key, and he just stole it. Of course he would!'

'He's not a thief! He's a man. He's ten times the man you are.'

'Oh sure, sure. You were big scale you two. I've heard all that crap, believe me. You lived in the big unspoken part of life, didn't you? You were the artists, and Rawley was the poor bloody technician. You had souls, you two, you heard voices; Rawley just picked up the bits because he loved you. And all the time I thought they were sniggering about Jenny Pargiter. Christ Almighty! Poor sod,' he said, looking out of the window. 'Poor bastard. I'll never like Bradfield, that's for sure; but Christ, he has my full sympathy.'

Leaving some money on the table he followed her down the stone steps. She was frightened.

'He never mentioned Margaret Aickman to you, I suppose? He was going to marry her, you know. She was the only woman he loved.'

'He never loved anyone but me.'

'But he didn't mention her? He did to other people, you see. Everyone except you. She was his *big* love!'

'I don't believe it, I'll never believe it!'

He pulled open the car door and leaned in after her. 'You're all right, aren't you? You've touched the hem. He *loved* you. The whole bloody world can go to war as long as you have your little boy!'

'Yes. I've touched the hem. He was real with me. I made him real. He's real whatever he's doing now. That was our time, and I'm not going to let you destroy it; you or anyone else. He found me.'

'What else did he find?'

Miraculously, the car started.

'He found me, and whatever he found down there was the other part of coming alive.'

'*Down?* Down where? Where did he go? Tell me! You know! What was it he said to you?'

She drove away, not looking back, quite slowly, up the esplanade into the evening and the small lights.

The Opel drew out, preparing to follow her. Turner let it pass, then ran across the road and jumped into a taxi.

The Embassy car park was full, the guard was doubled at the gate. Once more, the Ambassador's Rolls Royce waited at the door like an ancient ship to bear him to the storm. As Turner ran up the steps, his raincoat flying behind him, he held the key ready in his hand.

15
The Glory Hole

Two Queen's Messengers stood at the desk, their black leather pouches hung like parachute harnesses over their regimental blazers.

'Who's Duty Officer?' Turner snapped.

'I thought you'd gone,' said Gaunt. 'Seven o'clock yesterday, that's what –'

There was a creak of leather as the messengers hastily made room for him.

'I want the keys.'

Gaunt saw the cuts on Turner's face and his eyes opened wide.

'Ring the Duty Officer.' Turner picked up the receiver and offered it to him across the desk. 'Tell him to come down with the keys. Now!'

Gaunt was protesting. The lobby swung a little and held still. Turner heard his silly Welsh bleat, half complaining, half flattering and he grasped him roughly by the arm and pulled him into the dark corridor.

'If you don't do as I say, I'll see they post the hell out of you for the rest of your natural life.'

'The keys aren't drawn, I tell you.'

'Where are they?'

'I've got them here. In the safe. But you can't have them, not without a signature, you know that very well!'

'I don't want them. I want you to count them, that's all. Count the bloody keys!'

The messengers, ostentatiously discreet, were talking to one another in awkward undertones, but Turner's voice cut through them like an axe: 'How many should there be?'

'Forty-seven.'

Summoning the younger guard, Gaunt unlocked the safe that was built into the corner and drew out the familiar bunch of bright-cut brass keys. Overcome by curiosity, the two messengers watched while the square, miner's fingers told off each key like a bead on the abacus. He counted them once and he counted them a second time, and he handed them to the boy who counted them again.

'Well?'

'Forty-six,' said Gaunt grudgingly. 'No doubt.'

'Forty-six,' the boy echoed. 'One short.'

'When were they last counted?'

''Tisn't hardly possible to say,' Gaunt muttered, 'They've been going in and out for weeks.'

Turner pointed to the shining new grille that cut off the basement stairway. 'How do I get down there?'

'I told you. Bradfield has the key. It's a riot gate, see. Guards don't have the authority.'

'How do the cleaners get down there then? What about the boilermen?'

'The boiler-room's separate access, now, ever since Bremen see. They've put grilles down there as well. They can use the outside stairs but they can't go no further than the boiler on account of being prevented.' Gaunt was very scared.

'There's a fire escape ... a service lift.'

'Only the back staircase, but that's locked too, see. Locked.'

'And the keys?'

'With Bradfield. Same as for the lift.'

'Where does it lead from?'

'Top floor.'

'Up by your place?'

'What of it then?'

'Up by your place or not?'

'Near.'

'Show me!'

Gaunt looked down, looked at the boy, looked at Turner and then back at the boy again. Reluctantly he dropped the keys into the boy's hand and without a word to the messengers led Turner quickly upstairs.

It might have been daytime. All the lights were on, doors open. Secretaries, clerks and diplomats, hastening down corridors, ignored them as they passed. The talk was of Brussels. The city's name was whispered like a password. It lay on every tongue and was stammered out by every typewriter; it was cut into the white wax of the stencils and rung on every telephone. They climbed another flight to a short corridor that smelt of a swimming-pool. A draught of fresh air struck them from their left. The door ahead of them said 'Chancery Guard Private' and the label underneath, 'Mr and Mrs J. Gaunt, British Embassy, Bonn.'

'We don't have to go in, do we?'

'This is where he came and saw you? Friday evenings after choir? He came up here?'

Gaunt nodded.

'What happened when he left? Did you see him out?'

'He wouldn't let me. "You stay there my boy and watch your telly, I'll see myself off the premises."'

'And that's the door: the back staircase.'

He was pointing to his left where the draught came from.

'It's locked though, see. Hasn't been opened for years.'

'That's the only way in?'

'Straight down to the basement it goes. They were going to have a rubbish chute till the money ran out so they put stairs instead.'

The door was solid and unrelieved, with two stout locks that had not been disturbed for a long time. Shining a pencil torch on to the lintels, Turner gently fingered the wooden beading that ran down the two sides, then took a firm grip on the handle.

'Come here. You're his size. You try. Take the handle. Don't turn it. Push. Push hard.'

The door yielded without a sound.

The air was suddenly very cold and stale; American air when the conditioners fail. They stood on a half landing. The stairs under them were very steep. A small window gave on to the Red Cross field. Directly below, the cowl of the canteen chimney puffed floodlit smoke into the darkness. The plaster was peeling in large blisters. They heard the drip of water. On the reverse side of the door post, the wood had been neatly sawn away. By the thin light of the torch they began their descent. The steps were of stone; a narrow strip of coconut matting ran down the centre. 'Embassy Club this way,' a very old poster ran. 'All welcome.' They caught the sound of a kettle bobbing on a ring and heard a girl's voice reading back a passage of dictation: 'While the official statement of the Federal Government describes the reason for the withdrawal as merely technical, even the most sober commentators ...' and instinctively they both stopped, heart in mouth, listening to the clear words precisely spoken in to the stairwell.

'It's the ventilation,' Gaunt whispered. 'It's coming through the shaft, see.'

'Shut up.'

They heard de Lisle's voice languidly correcting her. '*Moderate*,' he said.

'*Moderate* would be *much* better. Change *sober* to *moderate*, will you, my dear? We don't want them to think we're drowning our sorrows in drink.'

The girl giggled.

They must have reached the ground floor, for a bricked doorway stood ahead of them, and fragments of wet plaster lay on the linoleum. A makeshift noticeboard advertised vanished entertainments: the Embassy Players would present a Christmas performance of Gogol's *Government Inspector*. A grand Commonwealth Children's Party would be held in the Residence; names, together with details of any special dietary requirements should be submitted to the Private Office by 10th December. The year was 1954 and the signature was Harting's.

For a moment Turner fought with his sense of time and place, and almost lost. He heard the barges again and the chink of the glasses, the fall of soot and the creak of the rigging. The same throbbing, the same inner pulse beyond the register of sound.

'What did you say?' Gaunt asked.

'Nothing.'

Giddy and confused, he led the way blindly into the nearest passageway, his head wildly beating.

'You're not well,' said Gaunt. 'Who did that to you then?'

They were in a second chamber occupied by nothing but an old lathe, the filings rusted at its base. There was a door in the further wall. He pushed it open, and for a moment his composure left him as he drew back with a short cry of disgust, but it was only the iron bars of the new grille reaching from the ceiling to the floor, only the wet overalls hanging from the wire and the moisture pattering on the concrete. There was a stink of washday and half burnt fuel; the fire had set a red glow trembling on the brickwork; small lights danced on the new steel. Nothing apocalyptic, he told himself, as he moved cautiously along the gangway towards the next door, just a night train in the war; a crowded compartment and we're all asleep.

It was a steel door, flush against the plaster, a flood door deep below the water line, rusty at the frame and lintel with KEEP OUT done long ago in flaking Government paint. The wall on his left side was painted white at some time, and he could see the scratches where the trolley had passed. The light above him was shielded with a wire basket and it laid dark fingers on his face. He fought recklessly for consciousness. The lagged water pipes which ran along the ceiling chugged and gurgled in their housings, and the stove behind the iron grille spat white sparks which turned small shadows on and off. Christ, he thought: it's enough to power the *Queen Elizabeth*, it's enough to brand an army of prisoners; it's wasted on one lonely dream factory.

He had to fight with the key; he had to shake the lever handle hard before the lock would turn. Suddenly it had snapped like a stick and they heard the echo fly away and resound in distant rooms. Keep me here; Oh God keep me here, he thought. Don't change my nature or my life; don't change the place or move the path that I'm following ... There must have been a piece of grit beneath the door for it shrieked, then stopped and Turner had to force it with his whole body, force it against the water, while Gaunt the Welshman stood back, watching and lusting but not daring to touch. At first, fumbling for the switch, he saw only the darkness; then a single window thick with cobwebs come gloomily forward and it frightened him because he hated prison. It was high in the wall and arched like a brick oven and barred for security. Through its topmost panes he glimpsed the wet gravel of the car park. While he stood there watching and swaying, the beam of a headlight groped slowly along the ceiling, a prison spotlight searching for escapers, and the whole catacomb filled with the roar of a departing engine. An army blanket lay on the sill and he thought: you remembered to black out the window; you remembered the firewatching in London.

His hand found the light switch; it was domed like a woman's breast, and when he pressed it down it thumped like a punch against his own body and the dust rolled longingly towards him over the black concrete.

'They call it the Glory Hole,' Gaunt whispered.

The trolley was in an alcove beside the desk. Files on top, stationery below, all in varying sizes, nicely crested, with long and standard envelopes to match, all laid out ready to hand. At the centre of the desk, next to the reading light, square on its felt pad and neatly covered with a grey plastic cape, lay the missing typewriter with the long carriage and beside it three or four tins of Dutch cigars. On a separate table, a thermos and a quantity of Naafi cups; the tea machine with the clock; on the floor a small electric fan in two tones of plastic, trained conveniently upon the desk to help dispel the unfortunate effects of damp; on the new chair with the rexine seat, a pink cushion partially embroidered, by Miss Aickman. All these he recognized at a glance, dully, greeting them curtly as we greet old friends, while he stared beyond them at the great archive which lined the walls from floor to ceiling; at the slim black files each with a rusted loop and a rounded thumb-hole, some grey with bloom, some wrinkled and bent with damp, column after column in their black uniforms, veterans trained and waiting to be called.

He must have asked what they were, for Gaunt was whispering. No, he couldn't suggest what they were. No. Not his place. No. They had been here longer than anyone could remember. Though some did say they were Jag files, the Judge Advocate General's Department he meant, that's what talkers said and the talkers said they came from Minden in lorries, just dumped here for living space they were, twenty years ago that must be now, all of twenty years, when the Occupation packed up. That's all he could say really, he was sure; that's all he'd happened to hear from the talkers, just overheard it by chance, for Gaunt was not a gossip, that was the one thing they *could* say about him. Oh *more* than twenty years ... the lorries turned up one summer evening ... MacMullen and someone else had spent half the night helping to unload them.... Of course in *those* days it was thought the Embassy might need them.... No, nobody had access, not these days, didn't want it really; who would? Long ago, the odd Chancery officer would ask for the key and look something up but that was *long* ago, Gaunt couldn't remember that at all, and no one had been down here for years, though Gaunt couldn't say for sure, of course; he had to watch his words with Turner, he'd learnt that now, he was sure.... They must have kept the key separate for a while then added it to the Duty Officer's bunch.... But a while back now, Gaunt couldn't say when, he had heard them talking about it; Marcus one of the drivers, gone now; saying they weren't Jag files at all but *Group* files, it was a specialist British contingent.... His voice pattered on, urgent and conspiratorial, like an old woman in Church. Turner was no longer listening. He had seen the map.

A plain map, printed in Polish.

It was pinned above the desk, pinned quite freshly into the damp plaster, in the place where some might put the portraits of their children. No major towns were marked, no national borders, no scale, no pretty arrows showing the magnetic variation: just the places where the camps had been. Neuengamme and Belsen in the North, Dachau, Mauthausen to the South, to the East, Treblinka, Sobibor, Majdanek, Belzec and Auschwitz; in the centre Ravensbrück, Sachsenhausen, Kulmhof and Gross Rosen.

'They *owe* me,' he thought suddenly. 'They *owe* me.' God in Heaven what a fool, what a plain, blundering, clumsy fool I have been. Leo, you thief, you came here to forage in your own dreadful childhood.

'Go away. If I want you I'll call you.' Turner stared at Gaunt sightlessly, his right hand pressed against a shelf. 'Don't tell anyone. Bradfield, de Lisle, Crabbe ... no one, do you understand.'

'I won't,' Gaunt said.

'I'm not here. I don't exist. I never came in tonight. Do you understand.'

'You ought to see a doctor,' said Gaunt.

'Fuck off.'

Pulling back the chair, he tipped the little cushion to the floor and sat down at the desk. Resting his chin in his hand, he waited for the room to steady. He was alone. He was alone like Harting, contraband smuggled in, living like Harting on borrowed time; hunting, like Harting, for a missing truth. There was a tap beside the window and he filled the tea machine and played with the knobs until it began to hiss. As he returned to the desk he nearly tripped over a green box. It was the size of a narrow briefcase, but stiff and rectangular, made of the kind of reinforced leather-cloth used for bridge-sets and shot-gun cases. It had the Queen's initials just beneath the handle and reinforced corners of thin steel; the locks had been ripped open and it was empty. *That's what we're all doing, isn't it? Looking for something that isn't there?*

He was alone, with only the files for company and the stink of warm damp from the electric fire; and the pale breeze of the plastic fan and the muttering of the tea machine. Slowly he began turning the pages. Some of the files were old, taken from the shelves, half in English and half in a cruel Gothic script jagged as barbed wire. The names were set out like athletes, surname first and Christian name second, with only a couple of lines at the top and a hasty signature at the bottom to authorize their ultimate disposal. The files on the trolley were new, and the paper was rich and smooth, and the minutes signed with familiar names. And some were folders, records of mail despatched and mail received, with titles underlined and margins ruled.

He was alone, at the beginning of Harting's journey, with only his track for company, and the sullen grumbling of the waterpipes in the corridor outside, like the shuffling of clogs upon a scaffold. *Are they like horses?* Hazel Bradfield's voice inquired. *Do they sleep standing up?* He was alone. *And whatever he found there was the other part of coming alive.*

Meadowes was asleep. He would not for a moment have admitted it; and Cork would not, in charity, for a moment have accused him of it; and it is true that technically, like Hazel Bradfield's horses, his eyes were open. He was reclining in his upholstered library chair in an attitude of well-deserved retirement, while the sounds of dawn floated through the open window.

'I'm handing over to Bill Sutcliffe,' Cork said, loud and deliberately careless. 'Nothing you want, is there, before I knock off? We're brewing a cup of tea if you fancy it.'

'It's all right,' Meadowes said indistinctly, sitting forward with a jerk. 'Be all right in a minute.' Cork, staring down through the open window into the car park, allowed him time to collect himself.

'We're brewing a cup of tea if you fancy it.' he repeated. 'Valerie's got the kettle on.' He was clutching a folder of telegrams. 'There hasn't been a night like that since Bremen. Talk, that's all it is. Words. By four this morning they'd forgotten about security altogether. H.E. and the Secretary of State were just chatting direct on the open line. Fantastic. Blown the lot I should think: codes, cyphers, the whole bloody orchestra.'

'They're blown already,' Meadowes replied, more for himself than for Cork; and came to join him at the window. 'By Leo.'

No dawn is ever wholly ominous. The earth is too much its own master; the cries, the colours and the scents too confident to sustain our grim foreboding. Even the guard at the front gate, doubled since evening, had a restful, domestic look. The morning light which glistened on their long leather coats was soft and strangely harmless; their pace as they slowly walked the perimeter was measured and wise. Cork was moved to optimism.

'I reckon today might be the day,' he said. 'A father by lunchtime: how's that, Arthur?'

'They're never that quick,' Meadowes said, 'Not the first ones,' and they fell to counting off the cars.

'Full house, near as nothing,' Cork declared; and it was true. Bradfield's white Jaguar, de Lisle's red sports car, Jenny Pargiter's little Wolseley, Gaveston's shooting brake with the baby chair mounted on the passenger seat, Jackson's rugged Two Thousand; even Crabbe's broken down Kapitän, twice personally banished from the car park by the Ambassador, had crept back in the crisis, its wings bent outward like crooked claws.

'Rover looks all right,' said Cork. In reverent silence they duly admired its distinguished outlines against the fencing on the other side of the canteen.

Nearer at hand, the grey Rolls stood in its own bay, guarded by an army corporal.

'He saw him, did he?' Meadowes asked.

'Sure.' Cork licked his finger, selected the relevant telegram from the folder which he carried under his arm and began reading out loud, in a facetious, nursery-rhyme voice, the Ambassador's account of his dialogue with the Federal Chancellor ... '"I replied that as Foreign Secretary you had implicit trust in the many undertakings already given to you personally by the Chancellor, and that you had every confidence that the Chancellor would not for a moment consider yielding to the pressure of vociferous minorities. I reminded him also of the French attitude to the question of German reunification, describing it not merely as unsound but as downright anti-American, anti-European and above all anti-German –"'

'Listen,' said Meadowes suddenly. 'Shut up and listen.'

'What the –'

'Be quiet.'

From the far end of the corridor they could hear a steady drone like the sound of a car climbing a hill.

'It can't be,' Cork said shortly. 'Bradfield's got the keys and he –' they heard the clank of the folding gate and the small sigh of a hydraulic brake.

'It's the beds! That's what it is. More beds. They've got it going for the beds; he's opened it up for them.' In confirmation of his theory, they heard the distinct clank of metal on metal, and the squeak of springs.

'This place will be a Noah's Ark by Sunday, I'll tell you. Kids, girls, even the bloody German staff: Babylon, that's what it'll be. Sodom and Gomorrah, that's better. Here, what happens if it comes on while they're demonstrating? Just my luck, that would be, wouldn't it? My first kid: baby Cork, born in captivity!'

'Go on. Let's hear the rest.'

'"The Federal Chancellor took note of the British anxiety which he thought misplaced; he assured me he would consult his Ministers and see what could be done to restore calm. I suggested to him that a statement of policy would be very useful; the Chancellor on the other hand thought repetition had a weakening effect. At this point he asked that his best wishes be conveyed to yourself as Secretary of State, and it became clear that he regarded the interview as closed. I asked him whether he would consider reserving fresh hotel accommodation in Brussels as a means of ending uninformed speculation, since you were personally distressed by reports that the German delegation had paid its bills and cancelled its bookings. The Chancellor replied that he was sure something of that sort should be done."'

'Zero,' said Meadowes distractedly.

'"The Chancellor asked after the Queen's health. He had heard she had a touch of influenza. I said I thought she was over the worst but would make inquiries and let him know. The Chancellor said he hoped Her Majesty would take care of herself; it was a tricky time of year. I replied that all of us sincerely hoped that the climate would be more settled by Monday and he had the grace to laugh. We left on good terms." Ha ha ha. They also had a little chat about today's demonstration. The Chancellor said we weren't to worry. London are copying to the Palace. "The meeting,"' Cork added with a yawn, '"ended with the customary exchange of compliments at twenty-two twenty hours. A joint communiqué was issued to the press." Meanwhile, Econ are going up the wall and Commercial are totting up the cost of a run on the pound. Or gold or something. Or maybe it's a slump. Who cares?'

'You ought to sit the exam,' Meadowes said. 'You're too quick for in there.'

'I'll settle for twins,' said Cork, and Valerie brought in the tea.

Meadowes had actually raised the mug to his lips when he heard the sound of the trolley and the familiar trill of the squeaky wheel. Valerie put down the tray with a bang, and some tea slopped out of the pot into the sugar bowl. She was wearing a green pullover, and Cork, who liked to look at her, noticed as she turned to face the door that the polo neck had brought up a light rash at the side of her throat. Cork himself, quicker than the rest, handed Meadowes the folder, went to the door and looked down the corridor. It was their own trolley, loaded high with red and black files and Alan Turner was pushing it. He was in his shirt-sleeves and there were heavy bruises under both his eyes. One lip was cut clean through and had been summarily stitched. He had not shaved. The Despatch Box was on the top of the pile. Cork said later that he looked as though he had pushed the trolley through enemy lines single-handed. As he came down the passage, doors opened one after another in his wake: Edna from the Typists' Pool, Crabbe, Pargiter, de Lisle, Gaveston: one by one their heads appeared, followed by their bodies, so that by the time he had arrived at Registry, slammed back the flap of the steel counter, and shoved the trolley carelessly into the centre of the room, the only door that remained closed was that of Rawley Bradfield, Head of Chancery.

'Leave it there. Don't touch it, any of it.'

Turner crossed the corridor and without knocking, went straight in to Bradfield.

16
'It's all a fake'

'I thought you'd gone.' His tone was weary rather than surprised.

'I missed the plane. Didn't she tell you?'

'What the devil have you done to your face?'

'Siebkron sent his boys to search my room. Looking for news of Harting. I interrupted them.' He sat down. 'They're anglophiles. Like Karfeld.'

'The matter of Harting is closed.' Very deliberately Bradfield laid aside some telegrams. 'I have sent his papers to London together with a letter assessing the damage to our security. The rest will be handled from there. I have no doubt that in due course a decision will be taken on whether or not to inform our Nato partners.'

'Then you can cancel your letter. And forget the assessment.'

'I have made allowances for you,' Bradfield snapped, with much of his former asperity. 'Every kind of allowance. For your unsavoury profession, your ignorance of diplomatic practice and your uncommon rudeness. Your stay here has brought us nothing but trouble; you seem determined to be unpopular. What the devil do you mean by remaining in Bonn when I have told you to leave? Bursting in here in a state of undress? Have you no idea what is going on here? It's Friday! The day of the demonstration, in case you have forgotten.'

Turner did not move, and Bradfield's anger at last got the better of fatigue. 'Lumley told me you were uncouth but effective: so far you have merely been uncouth. I am not in the least surprised you have met with violence: you attract it. I have warned you of the damage you can do; I have told you my reasons for abandoning the investigation at this end; and I have overlooked the needless brutality with which you have treated my staff. But now I have had enough. You are forbidden the Embassy. Get out.'

'I've found the files,' Turner said. 'I've found the whole lot. And the trolley. And the typewriter and the chair. And the two-bar electric fire, and de Lisle's fan.' His voice was disjointed and unconvincing, and his gaze seemed to be upon things that were not in the room. 'And the teacups and all the rest of the hardware he pinched at one time or another. And the letters he collected from the Bag Room and never handed to Meadowes. They were addressed to Leo, you see. They were answers to letters he'd sent. He ran quite a department down there: a separate section of Chancery. Only you never knew. He's discovered the truth about Karfeld and now they're after him.' His hand lightly touched his cheek. 'The people who did this to me: they're after Leo. He's on the run because he knew too much and asked too many questions. For all I know they've caught him already. Sorry to be a bore,' he added flatly. 'But that's the way it is. I'd like a cup of coffee if you don't mind.'

Bradfield did not move.

'What about the Green File?'

'It's not there. Just the empty box.'

'He's taken it?'

'I don't know. Praschko might. I don't.' He shook his head. 'I'm sorry.' He continued: 'You've to find him before they do. Because if you don't they'll kill him. That's what I'm talking about. Karfeld's a fraud and a murderer and Harting's got the proof of it.' He raised his voice at last. 'Do I make myself clear?'

Bradfield continued to watch him, intent but not alarmed.

'When did Harting wake to him?' Turner asked himself. 'He didn't want to notice at first. He turned his back. He'd been turning his back on a lot of things, trying not to remember. Trying not to notice. He held himself in like we all do, sticking to the discipline of not being involved and calling it sacrifice. Gardening, going to parties. Working his fiddles. Surviving. And not interfering. Keeping his head down and letting the world go over him. Until October, when Karfeld came to power. He knew Karfeld, you see. And Karfeld *owed* him. That mattered to Leo.'

'Owed him *what*?'

'Wait. Gradually, bit by bit he began to ... open up. He allowed himself to feel. Karfeld was tantalizing him. We both know what that means, don't we: to be tantalized. Karfeld's face was everywhere, like it is now. Grinning, frowning, warning.... His name kept ringing in Leo's ears: Karfeld's a fraud; Karfeld's a murderer. Karfeld's a fake.'

'What are you talking about? Don't be so utterly ridiculous.'

'Leo didn't like that any more: he didn't like fakes any more; he wanted the truth. The male menopause: that is it. He was disgusted with himself... for what he'd failed to do, sins of omission ... sins of commission. Sick of his own tricks and his own routine. We all know that feeling, don't we? Well Leo had it. In full measure. So he decided to get what he was owed: justice for Karfeld. He had a long memory, you see. That's not fashionable these days, I understand. So he plotted. First to get into Registry, then to renew his contract, then to get hold of the files: The Personalities Survey ... the old files, the files that were due for destruction ... the old case histories in the Glory Hole. He would put the case together again, reopen the investigation....'

'I have no idea what you are referring to. You're sick; you are wandering and sick. I suggest you go and lie down.' His hand moved to the telephone.

'First of all he got the key, that was easy enough. Put that down! Leave that telephone alone!' Bradfield's hand hovered and fell back on to the blotter. 'Then he started work in the Glory Hole, set up his little office, made his own files, kept minutes, corresponded ... he moved in. Anything he needed from Registry, he stole. He was a thief; you said that. You should know.' For a moment, Turner's voice was gentle and understanding. 'When was it you sealed off the basement? Bremen wasn't it? A weekend? That was when he panicked. The only time. That was when he stole the trolley. I'm talking about Karfeld. Listen! About his doctorate, his military service, the wound at Stalingrad, the chemical factory –'

'These rumours have been going the rounds for months. Ever since Karfeld became a serious political contestant, we have heard nothing but stories of his past and each time he has successfully refuted them. There's hardly a politician of any standing in Western Germany whom the Communists have not defamed at one time or another.'

'Leo's not a communist,' Turner said with profound weariness. 'You told me yourself: he's a primitive. For years he kept away from politics because he was afraid of what he might hear. I'm not talking rumours. I'm talking fact: home grown British fact. Exclusive. It's all in our own British files, locked away in our own British basement. That's where he got them from and not even you can bury them any more.' There was neither triumph nor hostility to his tone. 'The information's in Registry now if you want to check.

With the empty box. There's some things I didn't follow, my German's not that good. I've given instructions that no one's to touch the stuff.' He grinned in reminiscence, and it might have been his own predicament that he recalled. 'You bloody nearly marooned him if you did but know it. He got the trolley down there the weekend they put up the grilles and sealed off the lift. He was terrified of not being able to carry on; of being cut off from the Glory Hole. Until then, it was child's play. He only had to hop into the lift with his files – he could go anywhere, you see; the Personalities Survey gave him the right – and take them straight down to the basement. But you were putting an end to all that though you didn't know it; the riot grilles queered his pitch. So he shoved everything he might need on to the trolley and waited down there the whole weekend until the workmen had done. He had to break the locks on the back staircase to get out. After that, he relied on Gaunt to invite him up to the top floor. Innocently of course. Everyone's innocent in a manner of speaking. And I'm sorry,' he added, quite graciously, 'I'm sorry for what I said to you. I was wrong.'

'This is hardly the moment for apologies,' Bradfield retorted, and rang Miss Peate for some coffee.

'I'm going to tell you the way it is on the files,' Turner said. 'The case against Karfeld. You'd do me a favour not interrupting. We're both tired, and we've not much time.'

Bradfield had set a sheet of blue draft paper on the blotter before him; the fountain pen was poised above it. Miss Peate, having poured the coffee, took her leave. Her expression, her single disgusted glance at Turner, was more eloquent than any words she could have found.

'I'm going to tell you what he'd put together. Pick holes in it afterwards if you want.'

'I shall do my best,' Bradfield said with a momentary smile that was like the memory of a different man.

'There's a village near Dannenberg, on the Zonal border. Hapstorf it's called. It has three men and a dog and it lies in a wooded valley. Or used to. In thirty-eight, the Germans put a factory there. There was an old paper mill beside a fast-flowing river, with a country house attached to it, right up against the cliff. They converted the mill and built laboratories alongside the river, and turned the place into a small hush-hush research station for certain types of gas.'

He drank some coffee and took a bite of biscuit, and it seemed to hurt him to eat, for he held his head to one side and munched very cautiously.

'Poison Gas. The attractions were obvious. The place was difficult to bomb; the stream was fast-flowing, and they needed that for the effluent; the village was small and they could chuck out anyone they didn't like. All right?'

'All right.' Bradfield had taken out his pen and was writing down key points as Turner spoke. Turner could see the numbers down the left side and he thought: what difference does it make about the numbers? You can't destroy facts by giving them numbers.

'The local population claims it didn't know what was going on there, which is probably true. They knew the mill had been stripped and they knew that a lot of expensive plant had been installed. They knew the warehouses at the back were specially guarded, and they knew the staff weren't allowed to mix with the locals. The labour was foreign: French and Poles, who weren't allowed out at all, so there was no mixing at the lower level either. And everyone knew about the animals. Monkeys mainly, but sheep, goats and dogs as well. Animals that went in there and didn't come out. There's a record of the local *Gauleiter* receiving letters of complaint from animal lovers.'

He looked at Bradfield in wonder. 'He worked down there, night after night, putting it all together.'

'He had no business down there. The basement archive has been out of bounds for many years.'

'He had business there all right.'

Bradfield was writing on his pad.

'Two months before the end of the war, the factory was destroyed by the British. Pinpoint bombing. The explosion was enormous. The place was wiped out, and the village with it. The foreign labourers were killed. They say the sound of the blast carried miles, there was so much went up with it.'

Bradfield's pen sped across the paper.

'At the time of the bombing, Karfeld was at home in Essen; there's no doubt of that at all. He says he was burying his mother; she'd been killed in an air raid.'

'Well?'

'He was in Essen all right. But he wasn't burying his mother. She'd died two years earlier.'

'Nonsense!' Bradfield cried. 'The Press would long ago –'

'There's a photostat of the original death certificate on the file,' Turner said evenly. 'I'm not able to say what the new one looks like. Nor who faked it for him. Though I should think we could both guess without rupturing our imaginations.'

Bradfield glanced at him with appreciation.

'After the war, the British were in Hamburg and they sent a team to look at what was left of Hapstorf, collect souvenirs and take photographs. Just an ordinary Intelligence team, nothing special. They thought they might pick up the scientists who'd worked there ... get the benefit of their knowledge, see what I mean? They reported that nothing was left. They also reported some rumours. A French labourer, one of the few survivors, had a story about experiments on human guinea pigs. Not on the labourers themselves, he said, but on other people brought in. They'd used animals to begin with, he said, but later on they wanted the real thing so they had some specially delivered. He said he'd been on gate duty one night – he was a trusty by then – and the Germans told him to return to his hut, go to bed and not appear till morning. He was suspicious and hung around. He saw a strange thing; a grey bus, just a plain grey single-decker bus, went through one gate after another without being documented. It drove round the back, towards the warehouses, and he didn't hear any more. A couple of minutes later, it drove out again, much faster. Empty.' Again he broke off, and this time he took a handkerchief from his pocket and very gingerly dabbed his brow. 'The Frenchman also said a friend of his, a Belgian, had been offered inducements to work in the new laboratories under the cliff. He went for a couple of days and came back looking like a ghost. He said he wouldn't spend another night over there, not for all the privileges in the world. Next day he disappeared. Posted, they said. But before he left he had a talk to his pal, and he mentioned the name of Doctor Klaus. Doctor Klaus was the administrative supervisor, he said; he was the man who arranged the details and made things easy for the scientists. He was the man who offered him the job.'

'You call this evidence?'

'Wait. Just wait. The team reported their findings and a copy went to the local War Crimes Group. So they took it over. They interrogated the Frenchman, took a full statement but they failed to produce corroboration. An old woman who ran a flower shop had a story about hearing screams in the night, but she couldn't say which night and besides it might have been animals. It was all very flimsy.'

'Very, I should have thought.'

'Look,' Turner said. 'We're on the same side now aren't we? There are no more doors to open.'

'There may be some to close,' Bradfield said, writing again. 'However.'

'The Group was overworked and understaffed so they threw in the case. File and discontinue. They'd many bigger cases to worry about. They carded Doctor Klaus and forgot about him. The Frenchman went back to France, the old lady forgot the screams and that was it. Until a couple of years later.'

'Wait.'

Bradfield's pen did not hurry. He formed the letters as he always formed them: legibly, with consideration for his successors.

'Then an accident happened. The kind we've come to expect. A farmer near Hapstorf bought an old bit of waste land from the local council. It was rough ground, very stony and wooded, but he thought he could make something of it. By the time he'd dug it and ploughed it, he'd unearthed thirty-two bodies of grown men. The German police took a look and informed the Occupational authority. Crimes against Allied personnel were the responsibility of the Allied judiciary. The British mounted an investigation and decided that thirty-one of the men had been gassed. The thirty-second man was wearing the tunic of a foreign labourer and he'd been shot in the back of the neck. There was something else ... something that really threw them. The bodies were all messed up.'

'Messed up?'

'Researched. Autopsied. Someone had got there first. So they reopened the case. Somebody in the town remembered that Doctor Klaus came from Essen.'

Bradfield was watching him now; he had put down his pen and folded his hands together.

'They went through all the chemists with the qualification to conduct high-grade research who lived in Essen and whose first names were Klaus. It didn't take them long to unearth Karfeld. He'd no doctorate; that comes later. But then everyone assumed by then that the staff were working under pseudonyms, so why not give yourself a title too? Essen was also in the British zone, so they pulled him in. He denied the whole thing. Naturally. Mind you: apart from the bodies there was little enough to go by. Except for one incidental piece of information.'

Bradfield did not interrupt this time.

'You've heard of the Euthanasia scheme?'

'Hadamar.' With a nod of his head Bradfield indicated the window. 'Down the river. Hadamar,' he repeated.

'Hadamar, Weilmunster, Eichberg, Kalmenhof: clinics for the elimination of unwanted people: for whoever lived on the economy and made no contribution to it. You can read all about it in the Glory Hole, and quite a lot about it is Registry. Among the files for Destruction. At first they had categories for the type of people they'd killed off. You know: the deformed, the insane, severely handicapped children between the ages of eight and thirteen. Bed-wetters. With very few exceptions, the victims were German citizens.'

'They called them patients,' Bradfield said, with intense distaste.

'It seems that now and then certain selected patients were set aside and put to medical uses. Children as well as adults.'

Bradfield nodded, as if he knew that too.

'By the time the Hapstorf case broke, the Americans and Germans had done a fair bit of work on this Euthanasia programme. Among other things, they'd unearthed evidence of one busload of "hybrid workers" being set aside for "dangerous duties at the Chemical Research Station of Hapstorf". One busload was thirty-one people. They used grey buses by the way, if that reminds you of anything.'

'Hanover,' Bradfield said at once. 'The transport for the bodyguard.'

'Karfeld's an administrator. Everyone admires him for it. Then as now. It's nice to know he hasn't lost the old touch, isn't it? He's got one of those minds that runs in grooves.'

'Stop stringing beads. I want the whole thing, quickly.'

'Grey buses then. Thirty-one seats and room left over for the guard. The windows were blackened from the inside. Where possible, they moved them at night.'

'You said there were thirty-two bodies not thirty-one –'

'There was the Belgian labourer, wasn't there? The one who worked under the cliff and talked to the French trusty? They knew what to do about him all right. He'd found out a bit too much, hadn't he? Like Leo, now.'

'Here,' said Bradfield, getting up and bringing the coffee over to him.

'You'd better have some more of this.' Turner held out his cup and his hand was fairly steady.

'So when they'd pulled him in they took Karfeld up to Hamburg and confronted him with the bodies and the evidence, such as they had, and he just laughed at them. Bloody nonsense, he said, the whole story. Never been to Hapstorf in his life. He was an engineer. A demolitions man. He gave a very detailed account of his work at the Russian front – they'd even given him campaign medals and Christ knows what. I suppose they did that for them in the SS and he made a great *spiel* about Stalingrad. There were discrepancies but not that many, and he just held out all the time against interrogation and denied ever having set foot in Hapstorf or possessing any knowledge of the plant. No, no, no all the way. For months on end. "Okay," he kept saying, "if you've got the proof, bring a case. Put it to the Tribunal. I'm not bothered; I'm a hero. I never administered anything in my life except our family factory in Essen, and the British have pulled that to pieces, haven't they? I've been to Russia, I haven't been poisoning hybrids; why should I? I'm a little friend of all the world. Find a live witness, find anybody." They couldn't. At Hapstorf, the chemists had lived in complete segregation, and presumably the desk-men had done the same. The records were destroyed by bombing, and everyone was known by his Christian name or an alias.' Turner shrugged. 'That seemed to be that. He even threw in a story about helping the anti-Nazi resistance in Russia, and since the units he mentioned were either taken prisoner *en masse* or shot to pieces, they couldn't get any further with that either. He doesn't seem to have come out with that since, the resistance bit.'

'It's no longer fashionable,' said Bradfield shortly. 'Particularly in his sphere.'

'So the case never reached the courts. There were plenty of reasons why not. The War Crimes investigation units themselves were near to disbandment; there was pressure from London and Washington to bury the hatchet and hand over all responsibility to the German courts. It was chaos. While the Unit was trying to prepare charges, their Headquarters were preparing amnesties. And there were other reasons, technical reasons for not going ahead. The crime was against French, Belgians and Poles if anyone, but since there was no method of establishing the nationality of the victims, there were problems about jurisdiction. Not material problems, but incidental ones, and they contributed to the difficulty of deciding what to do. You know how it is when you *want* to find difficulties.'

'I know how it was then,' Bradfield said quietly. 'It was bedlam.'

'The French weren't keen; the Poles were *too* keen and Karfeld himself was quite a big wheel by then. He was handling some big allied contracts. Even sub-contracting to competitors to keep up with demand. He was a good administrator, you see. Efficient.'

'You say that as if it were a crime.'

'His own factory had been dismantled a couple of times but now it was running a treat. Seemed a pity to disturb it really. There was even some rumour,' Turner added without changing the tone of his voice, 'that he'd had a head start on everyone else because he'd come by a special consignment of rare gases, and stored them underground in Essen at the end of the war. That's what he was up to while the RAF was bombing Hapstorf. While he was supposed to be burying his poor old mother. He'd been pinching the goods to feather his own nest.'

'As you have described the evidence so far,' Bradfield said quietly, 'there is nothing whatever which attaches Karfeld to Hapstorf, and nothing at all to associate him with the complicity in a murder plot. His own account of himself may very well be true. That he fought in Russia, that he was wounded –'

'That's right. That's the view they took at Headquarters.'

'It is even unproven that the bodies came from Hapstorf. The *gas* may have been theirs; it hardly proves that the chemists themselves administered it to the victims, let alone that Karfeld knew of it, or was in any way an accessory to –'

'The house at Hapstorf had a cellar. The cellar wasn't affected by the bombing. The windows had been bricked in and pipes had been run through the ceiling from the laboratories above. The brick walls of the cellar were torn.'

'What do you mean: "torn"?'

'By hands,' Turner said. 'Fingers, it could have been.'

'Anyway they took your view. Karfeld kept his mouth shut, there was no fresh evidence. They didn't prosecute. Quite rightly. The case was shelved. The unit was moved to Bremen, then to Hanover, then to Moenchengladbach and the files were sent here. Together with some odds and sods from the Judge Advocate General's Department. Pending a decision regarding their ultimate disposal.'

'And this is the story Harting has got on to?'

'He was always on to it. He was the sergeant investigating. Him and Praschko. The whole file, minutes, memoranda, correspondence, interrogation reports, summaries of evidence, the whole case from beginning to end – it has an end now – is recorded in Leo's handwriting. Leo arrested him, questioned him, attended the autopsies, looked for witnesses. The woman he nearly married, Margaret Aickman, she was in the unit as well. A clerical researcher. They called them headhunters: that was his life.... They were all very anxious that Karfeld be properly arraigned.'

Bradfield remained lost in thought. 'And this word *hybrid* –' he asked finally.

'It was a Nazi technical term for half Jewish.'

'I see. Yes, I see. So he would have a personal stake, wouldn't he? And that mattered to him. He took everything personally. He lived for himself; that was the only thing he understood.' The pen remained quite still. 'But hardly a case in law.' He repeated it to himself: 'But hardly a case in law. In fact hardly a case by any standards. Not on the merest, most partisan analysis. Not any kind of case. Interesting of course: it accounts for Karfeld's feelings about the British. It doesn't begin to make a criminal of him.'

'No,' Turner agreed, rather to Bradfield's surprise. 'No. It's not a case. But for Leo it rankled. He never forgot; but he pressed it down as far as it would go. But he couldn't keep away from it. He had to find out; he had to take another look and make sure, and in January this year he went down to the Glory Hole and re-read his own reports and his own arguments.'

Bradfield was sitting very still again.

'It may have been his age. Most of all, it was a sense of something left undone.' Turner said this as if it were a problem which applied to his own case, and to which he had no solution. 'A sense of history if you like.' He hesitated, 'Of time. The paradoxes caught up with him and he had to do something about it. He was also in love,' he added, staring out of the window. 'Though he might not have admitted it. He'd made use of somebody and picked up more than he bargained for.... He'd escaped from lethargy. That's the point, isn't it: the opposite of love isn't hate. It's lethargy. Nothingness. This place. And there were people about who let him think he was in the big league ...' he added softly. 'So for whatever reasons, he reopened the case. He re-read the papers from beginning to end. He studied the background again, went through all the contemporary files, in Registry and in the Glory Hole. Checked all the facts from the beginning, and he began making his own inquiries.'

'What sort of inquiries?' Bradfield demanded. They were not looking at one another.

'He set up his own office. He wrote letters and received replies. All on Embassy paper. He headed off the Chancery mail as it came in and extracted anything addressed to him. He ran it like he ran his own life: secretly and efficiently. Trusting nobody, confiding in nobody; playing the different ends off against each other.... Sometimes he made little journeys, consulted records, Ministries, church registers, survivor groups ... all on Embassy paper. He collected press cuttings, took copies, did his own typing and put on his own sealing wax. He even pinched an official seal. He headed his letters Claims and Consular, so most of them came to him in the first place anyway. He compared every detail: birth certificates, marriage, death of mother, hunting licences – he was looking for discrepancies all the time: anything to prove that Karfeld hadn't fought at the Russian front. He put together a bloody great dossier. It's hardly surprising Siebkron got on to him. There's scarcely a Government Agency he hadn't consulted under one pretext or another –'

'Oh my God,' Bradfield whispered, laying down his pen in a momentary gesture of defeat.

'By the end of January, he'd come to the only possible conclusion: that Karfeld had been lying in his teeth, and someone – it looked like someone high up, and it looked very much like Siebkron – someone had been covering up for him. They tell me Siebkron has ambitions of his own – hitch his wagon to any star as long as it was on the move.'

'That's true enough,' Bradfield conceded, lost in private thoughts.

'Like Praschko in the old days.... You see where we're getting, don't you?

And of course before long, as he very well knew, Siebkron was going to notice that the Embassy was making some pretty way-out inquiries, even for Claims and Consular. And that somebody was going to be bloody angry, and perhaps a bit rough as well. Specially when Leo found the proof.'

'What proof? How can he possibly prove such a charge now, twenty or more years after the crime?'

'It's all in Registry,' Turner said, with sudden reluctance. 'You'd do better to see for yourself.'

'I've no time and I am used to hearing unsavoury facts.'

'And discounting them.'

'I insist that you tell me.' He made no drama of his insistence.

'Very well. Last year, Karfeld decided to take a doctorate. He was a big fellow by then; he was worth a fortune in the chemical industry – his administrative talent had paid off in a big way – and he was making fair headway in local politics in Essen, and he wanted to be Doctor. Maybe he was like Leo; he'd left a job undone and he wanted to get the record straight. Or maybe he thought a handle would be a useful asset: Vote for Doctor Karfeld. They like a doctorate here in a Chancellor.... So he went back to school and wrote a learned thesis. He didn't do much research and everyone was very impressed, specially his tutors. Wonderful, they said, the way he found the time.'

'And?'

'It's a study of the effects of certain toxic gases on the human body. They thought very highly of it apparently; caused quite a little stir at the time.'

'That is hardly conclusive.'

'Oh yes it is. Karfeld based his whole analysis on the detailed examination of thirty-one fatal cases.'

Bradfield had closed his eyes.

'It is not proof,' Bradfield said at last; he was vey pale but the pen in his hand was as firm as ever. 'You know it is not proof. It raises suppositions I agree. It suggests he was at Hapstorf. It is not even half-way to proof.'

'Pity we can't tell Leo.'

'The information came to him in the course of his industrial experience; that is what Karfeld would argue. He acquired it from a third party; that would be his fall-back position.'

'From the real bastards.'

'Even if it could be shown that the information came from Hapstorf, there are a dozen explanations as to how it came into Karfeld's hands. You said yourself, he was not even engaged in research –'

'No, He sat at a desk. It's been done before.'

'Precisely. And the very fact that he made use of the information at all would tend to exonerate him from the charge of acquiring it.'

'The trouble is, you see,' Turner said, 'Leo's only half a lawyer: a hybrid. We have to reckon with the other half as well. We have to reckon with the thief.'

'Yes.' Bradfield was distracted. 'And he has taken the Green File.'

'Still, as far as Siebkron and Karfeld are concerned, he seems to have got near enough to the truth to be a pretty serious risk, doesn't he?'

'A prima facie case,' Bradfield remarked, examining his notes once more. 'Grounds for reinvestigation, I grant you. At best, a public prosecutor might be persuaded to make an initial examination.' He glanced at his telephone directory. 'The Legal Attaché would know.'

'Don't bother,' Turner said comfortingly. 'Whatever he's done or hasn't done, Karfeld's in the clear. He's past the post.' Bradfield stared at him. 'No one can prosecute him now, even with a cast-iron confession, signed by Karfeld himself.'

'Of course,' Bradfield said quietly. 'I was forgetting.' He sounded relieved.

'He's protected by law. The Statute of Limitations takes care of that. Leo put a note on the file on Thursday evening. The case is dead. There's nothing anyone can do.'

'There's a procedure for reviving it –'

'There is,' Turner conceded. 'It doesn't apply. That's the fault of the British as it happens. The Hapstorf case was a British investigation. We never passed it to the Germans at all. There was no trial, no public report, and when the German judiciary took over sole responsibility for Nazi war crimes we gave them no note of it. Karfeld's whole case fell into the gap between the Germans and ourselves.' He paused. 'And now Leo's done the same.'

'What did Harting intend to do? What was the purpose of all this inquiring?'

'He had to know. He had to complete the case. It taunted him, like a messed-up childhood or a life you can't come to terms with. He had to get it straight. I think he was playing the rest by ear.'

'When did he get this so-called proof?'

'The thesis arrived on the Saturday before he left. He kept a date-stamp you see; everything was entered up in the files. On the Monday he arrived in Registry in a state of elation. He spent a couple of days wondering what to do next. Last Thursday he had lunch with Praschko –'

'What the devil for?'

'I don't know. I thought about it. I don't know. Probably to discuss what action they should take. Or to get a legal opinion. Maybe he thought there was still a way of prosecuting –'

'There is none?'

'No.'

'Thank God for that.'

Turner ignored him: 'Or perhaps to tell Praschko that the pace was getting too hot. To ask him for protection.'

Bradfield looked at Turner very carefully. 'And the Green File has gone,' he said, recovering his strength.

'The box was empty.'

'And Harting has run. Do you know the reason for *that* as well?' His eyes were still upon Turner. 'Is that also recorded in his dossier?'

'He kept writing in his memoranda: "I have very little time." Everyone who speaks of him describes him as being in a fight against time ... the new urgency ... I suppose he was thinking of the Statute.'

'But we know that, under the Statute, Karfeld was already a free man, unless of course some kind of stay of action could be obtained. So why has he left? And what was so pressing?'

Turner shrugged away the strangely searching, even taunting tone of Bradfield's questions.

'So you don't know *exactly* why? Why he has chosen this particular moment to run away? Or why he chose that one file to steal?'

'I assume Siebkron has been crowding him. Leo had the proof and Siebkron knew he had it. From then on, Leo was a marked man. He had a gun,' Turner added, 'an old Army pistol. He was frightened enough to take it with him. He must have panicked.'

'Quite,' Bradfield said, with the same note of relief. 'Quite. No doubt that is the explanation.' Turner stared at him in bewilderment.

For perhaps ten minutes Bradfield had not moved or said a word.

There was a lectern in a corner of the room made of an old Bible box and long, rather ugly metal legs which Bradfield had commissioned of a local blacksmith in Bad Godesberg. He was standing with his elbows upon it, staring out of the window at the river.

'No wonder Siebkron puts us under guard,' he said at last; he might have been talking about the mist. 'No wonder he treats us as if we were dangerous. There can hardly be a Ministry in Bonn, not even a journalist, who has not by now heard that the British Embassy is engaged in a blood-hunt for Karfeld's past. What do they expect us to do? Blackmail him in public? Reappear after twenty-five years in full-bottom wigs and indict him under the Allied Jurisdiction? Or do they simply think we are wantonly vindictive, and propose to have our revenge of the man who is spoiling our European dreams?'

'You'll find him, won't you? You'll go easy with him? He needs all the help he can get.'

'So do we all,' said Bradfield, still gazing at the river.

'He isn't a Communist. He isn't a traitor. He thinks Karfeld's a threat. To us. He's very simple. You can tell from the files –'

'I know his kind of simplicity.'

'He's our responsibility, after all. It was us who put it into his mind back in those days: the notion of absolute justice. We made him all those promises: Nuremberg, de-Nazification. We *made* him believe. We can't let him be a casualty just because we changed our minds. You haven't seen those files ... you can't imagine how they thought about the Germans then. Leo hasn't changed. He's the stay-behind man. *That's* not a crime, is it?'

'I know very well how they thought. I was here myself. I saw what he saw; enough. He should have grown out of it; the rest of us did.'

'What I mean is, he's worthy of our protection. There's a kind of integrity about him.... I felt that down there. He's not put off by paradox. For you and me there are always a dozen good reasons for doing nothing. Leo's made the other way round. In Leo's book there's only one reason for doing something: because he must. Because he feels.'

'I trust you are not offering him as an example to be followed?'

'There's another thing that puzzled him.'

'Well?'

'In cases like this, there are always external documents. In the SS headquarters; with the clinic or the transport unit. Movement orders, letters of authority, *related* documents from somewhere else that would give the game away. Yet nothing's come to light. Leo kept on pencilling annotations; why no record in Koblenz? Why no this or that? As if he suspected that other evidence had been destroyed ... by Siebkron for instance.'

'We can honour him, can't we?' Turner added, almost in supplication.

'There are no absolutes here.' His gaze had not left the distant scene. 'It is all doubt. All mist. The mist drains away the colours. There are no distinctions, the Socialists have seen to that. They are all everything. They are all nothing. No wonder Karfeld is in mourning.'

What was it that Bradfield studied on the river? The small boats struggling against the mist? The red cranes and the flat fields, or the far vineyards that have crept so far away from the south? Or Chamberlain's ghostly hill and the long concrete box where they had once kept him?

'The Glory Hole is out of bounds,' he said at last and again fell silent. 'Praschko. You said he lunched with Praschko on Thursday?'

'Bradfield –'

'Yes?' He was already moving to the door.

'We feel differently about him now, don't we?'

'Do we? Perhaps he is still a communist after all.' There was a strain of irony in Bradfield's tone. 'You forget he has stolen a file. You seem to think all of a sudden you can look into his heart.'

'Why did he steal it? What was in that file?'

But Bradfield was already pushing his way between the beds and the clutter of the corridor. Notices had sprung up everywhere: First Aid Post this Way ... Emergency Rest Room ... No Children Allowed Beyond this Point. As they passed Chancery Registry, they heard a sudden cheer followed by a desultory handicap. Cork, white in the face, ran out to greet them.

'She's had it,' he whispered. 'The hospital just telephoned. She wouldn't let them send for me while I was on shift.' His pink eyes were wide with fear. 'She didn't even need me. She didn't even want me there.'

17
Praschko

There is a tarmac driveway at the back of the Embassy. It leads from the eastern part of the perimeter northwards through a settlement of new villas too costly for British habitation. Each has a small garden of great value in terms of real estate, each is distinguished from its neighbour by those cautious architectural deviations which are the mark of modern conformity. If one house has a brick-built barbecue and a patio of reconstituted stone, the next will match it with an external wall of blue slate, or quarried rock daringly exposed. In summer, young wives sun themselves beside minuscule swimming-pools. In winter black poodles burrow in the snow; and every midday from Monday to Friday, black Mercedes bring the masters home for meals. The air smells all the time, if distantly, of coffee.

It was a cold grey morning still, but the earth was lit with the clarity which follows rain. They drove very slowly, with the windows right down. Passing a hospital, they entered a more sombre road where the older suburb had survived; behind shaggy conifers and blue-black laurel bushes, leaden spires which once had painted donnish dreams of Weimar stood like lances in a mouldering forest. Ahead of them rose the Bundestag, naked, comfortless and uncomforted; a vast motel mourned by its own flags and painted in yellowing milk. At its back, straddled by Kennedy's Bridge and bordered by Beethoven's hall, the brown Rhine pursued its uncertain cultural course.

Police were everywhere: seldom could a seat of democracy have been so well protected from its democrats. At the main entrance, a line of school-children waited in a restless queue, and the police guarded them as if they were their own. A television team was setting up its arclights. In front of the camera a young man in a suit of mulberry corduroy thoughtlessly pirouetted, hand on hip, while a colleague measured his complexion; the police watched dangerously, bewildered by his freedom. Along the kerb, scrubbed as jurymen, their banners straight as Roman standards, the grey crowd obediently waited. The slogans had changed: *German Unity First European Unity Second: This is a Proud Nation Too: Give us Back our Country First!* The police faced them in line abreast, controlling them as they controlled the children.

'I'll park down by the river,' Bradfield said. 'God knows what it will be like by the time we come out.'

'What's going on?'

'A debate. Amendments to the Emergency Legislation.'

'I thought they'd finished with that long ago.'

'In this place, nothing is resolved.'

Along the embarkment as far as they could see on either side, grey detachments waited passively like unarmed soldiers. Makeshift banners declared their provenance: Kaiserslautern, Hanover, Dortmund, Kassel. They stood in perfect silence, waiting for the order to protest. Someone had brought a transistor radio and it blared very loud. They craned their necks for a sight of the white Jaguar.

Side by side they walked slowly back, up the hill, away from the river. They passed a kiosk; it seemed to contain nothing but coloured photographs of Queen Soraya. Two columns of students made an avenue to the main entrance. Bradfield walked ahead, stiff backed. At the door the guard objected to Turner and Bradfield argued with him shortly. The lobby was dreadfully warm and smelt of cigar; it was filled with the ringside murmur of dispute. Journalists, some with cameras, looked at Bradfield curiously and he shook his head and looked away. In small groups, deputies talked quietly, vainly glancing all the time over one another's shoulders in search of someone more interesting. A familiar figure rose at them.

'The best piece! My very words. Bradfield you are the best piece! You have come to see the end of democracy? You have come for the debate? My God you are so damn *efficient* over there! And the Secret Service is still with you? Mr Turner, you are loyal, I hope? My God, what the devil's happened to your face?' Receiving no answer he continued in a lower voice, furtively. 'Bradfield, I must speak to you. Something damned urgent, look here. I tried to get you at the Embassy but for Saab you are always out.'

'We have an appointment.'

'How long? Tell me how long. Sam Allerton wishes also; we wish together to have a discussion.'

He had bent his black head to Bradfield's ear. His neck was still grimy; he had not shaved.

'It's impossible to say.'

'Listen, I will wait for you. A most *important matter*. I will tell Allerton: we will wait for Bradfield. Deadlines, our newspapers: small fish. We must talk with Bradfield.'

'There's no comment, you know that. We issued our statement last night. I thought you had a copy. We accept the Chancellor's explanation. We look forward to seeing the German team back in Brussels within a few days.'

They descended the steps to the restaurant.

'Here he is. I'll do the talking. You're to leave him entirely to me.'

'I'll try.'

'You'll do better than that. You'll keep your mouth shut. He's a very slippery customer.'

Before anything else, Turner saw the cigar. It was very small and lay in the corner of his mouth like a black thermometer; and he knew it was also Dutch, and that Leo had been providing them for nothing.

He looked as if he had been editing a newspaper half the night. He appeared from the door leading to the shopping arcade, and he walked with his hands in his pockets and his jacket pulled away from his shirt, bumping into the tables and apologizing to no one. He was a big dirty man with grizzly hair cut short and a wide chest that spread to a wider stomach. His spectacles were tipped back over his brow like goggles. A girl followed him, carrying a briefcase. She was an expressionless, listless girl, either very bored or very chaste; her hair was black and abundant.

'Soup,' he shouted across the room, as he shook their hands. 'Bring some soup. And something for her.' The waiter was listening to the news on the wireless, but when he saw Praschko he switched it low and sauntered over, prepared to oblige. Praschko's braces had brass teeth which held doggedly to the grimy waistband of his trousers.

'You been working too? She doesn't understand anything,' he explained to them. 'Not in any damn language. *Nicht wahr, Schatz?* You are as stupid as a sheep. What's the problem?' His English was fluent, and whatever accent he possessed was heavily camouflaged by the American intonation. 'You Ambassador these days?'

'I'm afraid not.'

'Who's this guy?'

'Visiting.'

Praschko looked at Turner very carefully and then at Bradfield, then at Turner again.

'Some girl get angry with you?'

Only his eyes moved. His shoulders had risen a little into his neck, and there was a tautening, an instinctive alertness in his manner. His left hand settled on Bradfield's forearm.

'That's *nice*,' he said. 'That's fine. I like a change. I like new people.' His voice was on a single plane; heavy but short; a conspirator's voice, held down by the experience of saying things which should not be overheard.

'What you guys come for? Praschko's personal opinion? The voice of the opposition?' He explained to Turner: 'When you got a coalition, the opposition's a damned exclusive club.' He laughed very loud, sharing the joke with Bradfield.

The waiter brought a goulash soup. Cautiously, with small, nervous movements of his butcher's hand, he began feeling for the meat.

'What you come for? Hey, maybe you want to send a telegram to the Queen?' He grinned. 'A message from her old subject? OK. So send her a telegram. What the hell does she care what Praschko says? What does anyone care? I'm an old whore' – this too for Turner – 'They tell you that? I been English, I been German, I been damn nearly American. I been in this bordello longer than all the other whores. That's why no one wants me any more. I been had all ways. Did they tell you that? Left, Right and Centre.'

'Which way have they got you now?' Turner asked.

His eyes still upon Turner's battered face, Praschko lifted his hand and rubbed the tip of his finger against his thumb. 'Know what counts in politics? Cash. Selling. Everything else is a load of crap. Treaties, policies, alliances: crap.... Maybe I should have stayed a Marxist. So now they've walked out of Brussels. That's sad. Sure, that's very sad. You haven't got anyone to talk to any more.'

He broke a roll in two and dipped one half into the soup.

'You tell the Queen that Praschko says the English are lousy, lying hypocrites. Your wife okay?'

'Well, thank you.'

'It's a long time since I got to dinner up there. Still live in that ghetto, do you? Nice place. Never mind. Nobody likes me for too long. That's why I change parties,' he explained to Turner. 'I used to think I was a Romantic, always looking for the blue flower. Now I think I just get bored. Same with friends, same with women, same with God. They're all true. They all cheat you. They're all bastards. Jesus. Know another thing: I like new friends better than old ones. Hey, I got a new wife: what do you think of her?' He held up the girl's chin and adjusted her face a little to show her to the best advantage and the girl smiled and patted his hand. 'I'm amazing. There was a time,' he continued before either of them could make an appropriate comment, 'There was a time when I would have laid down on my fat belly to get the lousy English into Europe. Now you're crying on the doorstep and I don't care.' He shook his head. 'I'm truly amazing. Still, that's history I guess. Or maybe that's just me. Maybe I'm only interested in power: maybe I loved you because you were strong and now I hate you because you're nothing. They killed a boy last night, you hear? In Hagen. It's on the radio.'

He drank a Steinhäger from the tray. The mat stuck to the stem of the glass. He tore it off. 'One boy. One old man. One crazy woman librarian. Okay, so it's football team: but it isn't Armageddon.'

Through the window, the long grey columns waited on the esplanade. Praschko waved a hand round the room. 'Look at this crap. Paper. Paper democracy, paper politicians, paper eagles, paper soldiers, paper deputies. Doll's house democracy; every time Karfeld sneezes, we wet our pants. Know why? Because he comes so damn near the truth.'

'Are you in favour of him then? Is that it?' Turner asked, ignoring Bradfield's angry glance.

Praschko finished his soup, his eyes on Turner all the time. 'The world gets younger every day,' he said. 'Okay, so Karfeld's a load of crap. Okay. We've got rich, see, boy? We've eaten and drunk, built houses, bought cars, paid taxes, gone to Church, made babies. Now we want something *real*. Know what that is, boy?'

His eyes had not left Turner's damaged face.

'Illusions. Kings and Queens. The Kennedys, de Gaulle, Napoleon. The Wittelsbachs, Potsdam. Not just a damn village anymore. Hey, so what's this about the students rioting in England? What does the Queen think about that? Don't you give them enough cash? Youth. Want to know something about youth? I'll tell you.' Turner was his only audience now. "German youth is blaming its parents for starting the war." That's what you hear. Every day some crazy clever guy writes it in another newspaper. Want to hear the true story? They're blaming their parents for *losing* the damn war, not for starting it! "Hey! Where the hell's our Empire?" Same as the English I guess. It's the same horseshit. The same kids. They want God back.' He leaned across the table until his face was quite close to Turner's. 'Here.

Maybe we could do a deal: we give you cash, you give us illusions. Trouble is, we tried that. We done that deal and you gave us a load of shit. You didn't deliver the illusions. That's what we don't like about the English any more. They don't know how to do a deal. The Fatherland wanted to marry the Motherland but you never showed up for the wedding.' He broke out in another peal of false laughter.

'Perhaps the time has now come to *make* the union,' Bradfield suggested, smiling like a tired statesman.

Out of the corner of his eye, Turner saw two men, blond faced, in dark suits and suède shoes, quietly take their places at an adjoining table. The waiter went to them quickly, sensing their profession. At the same moment a bevy of young journalists came in from the lobby. Some carried the day's newspapers; the headlines spoke of Brussels or Hagen. At their head Karl-Heinz Saab, father of them all, stared across at Bradfield in flatulent anxiety. Beyond the window, in a loveless patio, rows of empty plastic chairs were planted like artificial flowers into the breaking concrete.

'Those are the real Nazis, that scum.' His voice pitched high enough for anyone to hear, Praschko indicated the journalists with a contemptuous wave of his fat hand. 'They put out their tongues and fart and think they've invented democracy. Where's that damn waiter: dead?'

'We're looking for Harting,' Bradfield said.

'Sure!' Praschko was used to crisis. His hand, drawing the napkin across his cracked lips, moved at the same steady pace. The eyes, yellow in their parched sockets, barely flickered as he continued to survey the two men.

'I haven't seen him around,' he continued, carelessly. 'Maybe he's in the gallery. You guys have a special box up there.' He put down the napkin. 'Maybe you ought to go look.'

'He's been missing since last Friday morning. He's been missing for a week.'

'Listen: Leo? That guy will always come back.' The waiter appeared. 'He's indestructible.'

'You're his friend,' Bradfield continued. 'Perhaps his only friend. We thought he might have consulted you.'

'What about?'

'Ah, that's the problem,' Bradfield said with a little smile. 'We thought he might have told *you* that.'

'He never found an English friend?' Praschko was looking from one to the other. 'Poor Leo.' There was an edge to his voice now.

'You occupied a special position in his life. After all, you did a great many things together. You shared a number of experiences. We felt that if he had needed advice, or money, or whatever else one needs at certain crises in one's life, he would instinctively seek you out. We thought he might even have come to you for protection.'

Praschko looked again at the cuts on Turner's face.

'Protection?' His lips barely parted as he spoke; it was as if he would prefer not to have known that he had spoken at all. 'You might as well protect a –' The moisture had risen suddenly on his brow. It seemed to come from outside, and to settle on him like steam. 'Go away,' he said to the girl. Without a word she stood up, smiled distractedly at them all and sauntered out of the restaurant, while Turner, for a moment of irrelevant, light-headed joy, followed the provocative rotation of her departing hips; but Bradfield was already talking again.

'We haven't much time.' He was leaning forward and speaking very quickly. 'You were with him in Hamburg and Berlin. There are certain matters known perhaps only to the two of you. Do you follow me?'

Praschko waited.

'If you can help us to find him without fuss; if you know where he is and can reason with him; if there's anything you can do for the sake of an old friendship, I will undertake to be very gentle with him, and very discreet. I will keep your name out of it, and anyone else's as well.'

It was Turner's turn to wait now, as he stared from one to the other. Only the sweat betrayed Praschko; only the fountain pen betrayed Bradfield. He clenched it in his closed fist as he leaned across the table. Outside the window, Turner saw the grey columns waiting; in the corner, the moon men watched dully, eating rolls and butter.

'I'll send him to England; I'll get him out of Germany altogether if necessary. He has put himself in the wrong already; there is no question of re-employing him. He has done things – he has behaved in a way which puts him beyond our consideration; do you understand what I mean? Whatever knowledge he may have is the property of the Crown. . . .' He sat back. 'We must find him before they do,' he said, and still Praschko watched him with his small hard eyes, saying nothing.

'I also appreciate,' Bradfield continued, 'that you have special interests which must be served.'

Praschko stirred a little. 'Go careful,' he said.

'Nothing is further from my mind than to interfere in the internal affairs of the Federal Republic. Your political ambitions, the future of your own party in relation to the Movement, these are matters far outside our sphere of interest. I am here to protect the alliance, not to sit in judgment over an ally.'

Quite suddenly, Praschko smiled.

'That's fine,' he said.

'Your own involvement with Harting twenty years ago, your association with certain British Government agencies –'

'Nobody knows about that,' Praschko said quickly. 'You go damn carefully about that.'

'I was going to make the very same point,' said Bradfield with a reciprocal smile of relief. 'I would not for a moment wish to have it said of the Embassy that we harbour resentments, persecute prominent German politicians, rake up old matters long dead; that we side with countries unsympathetic to the German cause in order to smear the Federal Republic. I am quite certain that in your own sphere, you would not like to have the same things said about yourself. I am pointing to an identity of interest.'

'Sure,' said Praschko. 'Sure.' His harrowed face remained inscrutable.

'We all have our villains. We must not let them come between us.'

'Jesus,' said Praschko with a sideways glance at the marks on Turner's face. 'We got some damn funny friends as well. Did Leo do that to you?'

'They're sitting in the corner,' Turner said. 'They did it. They're waiting to do it to him if they get a chance.'

'Okay,' said Praschko at last. 'I'll go along with you. We had lunch together. I haven't seen hiim since. What does that ape want?'

'Bradfield,' Saab called across the room. 'How soon?'

'I told you, Karl-Heinz. We have no statement to make.'

'We just talked, that's all. I don't see him so often. He called me up: how about lunch some time? I said make it tomorrow.' He opened his palms to show there was nothing up his sleeve.

'What did you talk about?' Turner asked.

He shrugged to both of them. 'You know how it is with old friends. Leo's a nice guy, but – well, people change. Or maybe we don't like to be reminded that they don't change. We talked about old times. Had a drink. You know the kind of thing.'

'Which old times?' Turner persisted, and Praschko flared at him, very angry.

'Sure: England times. Shit times. You know why we went to England, me and Leo? We were kids. Know how we got there? His name began with an H, my name began with P. So I changed it to a B. Harting Leo, Braschko Harry. Those times. Lucky we weren't Weiss or Zachary, see: they were too low down. The English didn't like the second half of the alphabet. That's what we talked about: sent to Dover, free on board. Those damn times. The damn Farm School in Shepton Mallet, you know that shit place? Maybe they painted it by now. Maybe that old guy's dead who knocked the hell out of us for being German and said we got to thank the English we're alive. You know what we learnt in Shepton Mallet? Italian. From the prisoners of war. They were the only bastards we ever got to talk to!' He turned to Bradfield. 'Who is this Nazi anyway?' he demanded, and burst out laughing. 'Hey, am I crazy or something? I was having lunch with Leo.'

'And he talked about his difficulties, whatever they may be?' Bradfield asked.

'He wanted to know about the Statute,' Praschko replied, still smiling.

'The Statute of Limitations?'

'Sure. He wanted to know the law.'

'Applied to a particular case?'

'Should it have been?'

'I was asking you.'

'I thought maybe you had a particular case in mind.'

'As a general matter of legal principle?'

'Sure?'

'What policy would be served by *that*, I wonder? It is not in the interests of any of us that the past be resurrected.'

'That's true, huh?'

'It's common sense,' Bradfield said shortly, 'Which I imagine carries more weight with you than any assurances I could give. What did he want to know?'

Praschko went very slowly now: 'He wanted to know the *reason*. He wanted to know the philosophy. So I told him: "It's not a new law, it's an old one. It's to make an end of things. Every country has a final court, a point you can't go beyond, okay? In Germany there has to be a final day as well." I spoke to him like he was a child – he's so damned innocent, do you know what? A monk. I said, "Look, you ride a bicycle without lights, okay? If nobody's found out after four months, you're in the clear. If it's manslaughter, then it's not four months but fifteen years; if it's murder, twenty years. If it's Nazi murder, longer still, because they gave it extra time. They waited a few years before they began to count to twenty. If they don't open a case, the offence lapses." I said to him: "Listen, they've fooled around with this thing till it damn near died. They amended it to please the Queen and they amended it to please themselves; first they dated it from forty-five then from forty-nine and now already they've changed it again."' Praschko opened his hands – 'So then he shouts at me, "What's so damn holy about twenty years?" "There's nothing holy about twenty years; there's nothing holy about any number of damn years. We grow old. We grow tired. We die." I told him that. I said to him: "I don't know what you've got in your fool head, but it's all crap. Everything's got to have an end. The moralists say it's a moral law, the apologists say it's expedient. Listen, I'm your friend and I'm telling you; Praschko says: it's a fact of life, so don't fool about with it." Then he got angry. You ever seen him angry?'

'No.'

'After lunch I brought him back here. We were still arguing, see. All the way in the car. Then we sat at this table. Right here where we are now. "Maybe I'll find new information," he said. I told him: "If you find new information, forget it, because there won't be a darn thing you can do: don't waste your time. You're too late. That's the law."'

'He didn't suggest by any chance that he already *had* that information?'

'Has he?' Praschko asked, very quickly indeed.

'I cannot imagine it exists.'

Praschko nodded slowly, his eyes on Bradfield all the time.

'So then what happened?' said Turner.

'That's all. I said to him: "OK, so you prove manslaughter: you're too late by years already. So you prove murder: you're too late since last December. So get screwed." That's why I told him. So then he gets hold of my arm and he whispers to me, like a crazy priest: "No law will ever take account of what they did. You and I know that. They teach it in the Churches: Christ was born of a virgin and went to Heaven in a cloud of light. Millions believe it. Listen, I play the music every Sunday, I hear them." Is that true?'

'He played the organ in Chapel,' said Bradfield.

'Jesus,' said Praschko, lost in wonder, 'Leo did that?'

'He's done it for years.'

'So then he goes on: "But you and I, Praschko, in our own lifetime, we have seen the living witness of evil." That's what he says. "Not on a mountain top, not at night, but there, in the field where we all stood. We're privileged people. *And now it's all happening again.*"'

Turner wanted to interrupt, but Bradfield restrained him.

'So then I got damned angry. I said to him, see: "Don't come playing God to me. Don't come screaming to me about the thousand year justice of Nuremberg that lasted four years. At least the Statute gave us twenty. And who imposed the Statute anyway? You British could have made us change it. When you handed over, you could have said to us: here, you bloody Germans, take over these cases, hear them in your own Courts, pass sentence according to your penal code but first abolish the Statute. You were party to it then; be party to it now. It's finished. It's damn well, damn well finished." That's what I said to him. And he just went on looking at me, saying my name. "Praschko, Praschko."'

Taking a handkerchief from his pocket, he dabbed his brow and wiped his mouth.

'Don't pay any attention to me,' he said. 'I get excited. You know what politicians are. I said to him, while he stared at me, I said, "This is my home: look. If I've got a heart left, it's here, in this bordello. I used to wonder why. Why not Buckingham Palace? Why not the Coca-Cola Culture? But this is my country. And that's what you should have found: a country. Not just a bloody Embassy." He went on looking at me; I tell you I was going crazy myself. I said to him: "So suppose you do find that proof, tell me what it's all about: to commit a crime at thirty, to be punished at sixty? What does that mean? We're old men," I said to him, "you and I. You know what Goethe told us: no man can watch a sunset for more than quarter of an hour." He said to me: "It's happening again. Look at the faces, Praschko, listen to the speeches. Somebody has to stop that bastard or you and me will be wearing the labels again."'

Bradfield spoke first. 'If he *had* found the proof, which we know he has not, what would he have done? If instead of still searching for it, he had already found it, what then?'

'Oh Jesus; I tell you: he'd have gone crazy.'

'Who's Aickman?' Turner said, ending the long silence.

'What's that, boy?'

'Aickman. Who is she? Miss Aickman, Miss Etling and Miss Brandt.... He was engaged to her once.'

'She was just a woman he had in Berlin. Or was it Hamburg? Both maybe. Jesus I forget everything. Thank God, eh?'

'What became of her?'

'I never heard,' Praschko said. His little eyes were roughly hacked in the old bark.

From their corner still, the clean faces watched without expression; four pale hands lay on the table like weapons put to rest. The loudspeaker was calling Praschko: the *Fraktion* was waiting for him to appear.

'You betrayed him,' Turner said. 'You put Siebkron on to him. You sold him down the river. He told you the lot and you warned Siebkron because you're climbing on the bandwagon too.'

'Be quiet,' said Bradfield. 'Be quiet.'

'You rotten bastard,' Turner hissed. 'You'll kill him. He told you he'd found the proof; he told you what it was and he asked you to help him, and you did that.'

'He's crazy,' Praschko whispered. 'Don't you realize he's crazy? You didn't see him back in those days. You never saw him back with Karfeld in the cellar. You think those boys worked you over? Karfeld couldn't even *speak*: "Talk! Talk!"' Praschko's eyes were screwed up very tight. 'After we saw those bodies in the field.... They were tied together. They'd been tied together before they were gassed. He went crazy. I said to him: "Listen it's not your *fault*. It's not your *fault* you survived!" Did he show you the buttons, maybe? The money from the camp? You never saw that either, did you? You never went out with him and a couple of girls to have a drink? You never saw him play with the wooden buttons to start a fight? He's crazy I tell you.' The recollection moved him to despair. 'I said to him, sitting here: "Come on, let's go. Who the hell ever built Jerusalem in Germany? Don't eat your heart out, come and screw some girls!" I said, "Listen! We got to get hold of our minds and press them in or we *all* go crazy." He's a monk. A crazy monk that won't forget. What do you think the world is? A damn playground for a lot of crazy moralists? Sure I told Siebkron. You're a clever boy. But you got to learn to forget as well. Christ if the British can't who can?'

There was shouting as they entered the lobby. Two students in leather coats had broken the cordon at the door and were standing on the stairs, fighting with the janitors. An elderly deputy was holding a handkerchief to his mouth and the blood was running over his wrist. 'Nazis!' someone was shouting, 'Nazis!' but he was pointing to a student on the balcony and the student was waving a red flag.

'Back to the restaurant,' Bradfield said. 'We can get out the other side.'

The restaurant was suddenly empty. Drawn or repelled by the fuss in the lobby, deputies and visitors had vanished in their chosen directions. Bradfield was not running, but striding at a long military pace. They were in the arcade. A leather shop offered black attaché cases in fine box calf. In the next window a barber was working up a lather on the face of an invisible customer.

'Bradfield, you must hear me: my God, can't I even warn you what they are saying?'

Saab was dreadfully out of breath. His portly body was heaving under his greasy jacket; tears of sweat lay in the pouches under his yellow eyes. Allerton, his face crimson under his black mane, peered over his shoulder. They drew back into a doorway. At the end of the corridor, calm had descended on the lobby.

'What who is saying?'

Allerton answered for him: 'All Bonn old boy. The whole bloody paper mill.'

'Listen. There are whispers. Listen. Fantastic what they are saying. You know what happened at Hanover? You know why they rioted? They are whispering it in all the cafés: the delegates; Karfeld's men are telling it. Already the rumours are all over Bonn. They have been instructed to say nothing; it is all a fantastic secret.'

He glanced quickly up and down the arcade.

'It's the best for years,' said Allerton. 'Even for this doorp.'

'Why they broke the line at the front and ran like mad dogs for the Library? Those boys who came in the grey buses? Somebody shot at Karfeld. In the middle of the music: shot at him from the window of the Library. Some friend of the woman, the librarian: Eich. She worked for the British in Berlin. She was an *émigrée*, she changed her name to Eich. She let him in to shoot from the window. Afterwards she told it all to Siebkron before she died. Eich. The bodyguard saw him fire, Karfeld's bodyguard. In the middle of the music! They saw the fellow shooting from the window and ran to catch him. The bodyguard, Bradfield, that came in the grey buses! Listen, Bradfield! Listen what they say! They found the bullet, a pistol bullet from an English pistol. You see now? The English are assassinating Karfeld: that is the fantastic rumour. You must stop them saying it; talk to Siebkron. Karfeld is terrified; he is a great coward. Listen: that is why he is so careful, that is why he is building everywhere such a damn *Schaffott*. How do I say *Schaffott*, for God's sake?'

'Scaffold,' said Turner.

The crowd from the lobby swept them outwards into the fresh air.

'Scaffold! An absolute secret, Bradfield! For your own information!' They heard him cry, 'You must not quote me, for God's sake. Siebkron would be fantastically angry!'

'Rest assured, Karl-Heinz,' the even voice replied, absurdly formal in the turmoil, 'your confidence will be respected.'

'Old boy,' Allerton put his head close to Turner's ear. He had not shaved, the black locks were tipped with sweat. 'What's happened to Leo these days? Seems to have faded all away. They say old Eich was quite a swinger in her day ... used to work with the scalphunters up in Hamburg. What have they done to your face, old boy? Close her legs too soon did she?'

'There's no story,' Bradfield said.

'Not yet there isn't,' said Allerton, 'old boy.'

'There never will be.'

'They say he bloody nearly got him in Bonn the night before the Hanover rally. Just wasn't quite sure enough of his man. Karfeld was walking away from a secret conference; walking to the pick-up point and Leo damn nearly got him then. Siebkron's chicks turned up just in time.'

Along the embankment the motionless columns waited in patient echelons. Their black flags barely lifted in the poor breeze. Across the river, behind a line of blue trees, distant factory chimneys puffed their smoke lazily into the drab morning light. Small boats, dabs of brilliance, lay marooned on the grey grass bank. To Turner's left stood an old boathouse which no one had yet pulled down. A notice on it proclaimed it the property of the Institute of Physical Exercise of the University of Bonn.

They stood on the bank, side by side. The palest mist, like breath upon a glass, drew in the brown horizons and filled the near bridge. There were no sounds but the echoes of absent things, the cry of lost gulls and the moan of the lost barges, the inevitable whine of unseen drills. There were no people but the grey shadows along the waterfront and the unrelated tread of feet; it was not raining, but sometimes they felt the moisture in the mist, like the prickling of blood upon a heated skin. There were no ships, but funeral hulks drifting towards the Gods of the North; and there was no smell but the inland smell of coal and industries which were not present.

'Karfeld is hidden until tonight,' Bradfield said. 'Siebkron has seen to that. They'll expect him to try again this evening. And he will.' He went over it again, rehearsing it as if it were a formula.

'Until the demonstration, Karfeld is hidden. After the demonstration, Karfeld will again be hidden. Harting's own resources are severely limited; he cannot reckon to be at large much longer. He will try tonight.'

'Aickman's dead,' said Turner. 'They killed her.'

'Yes. He will want to try tonight.'

'Make Siebkron cancel the rally.'

'If it were in my power I would. If it were in Siebkron's power, he would.' He indicated the columns. 'It's too late.'

Turner stared at him.

'No, I cannot see Karfeld cancelling the rally, however frightened he is,' Bradfield continued, as if a moment's doubt had crossed his mind. 'The rally is the culmination of his campaign in the provinces. He has organized it to coincide with the most critical moment in Brussels. He is already half-way to success.'

He turned and walked slowly along the footpath towards the car park. The grey columns watched him silently.

'Go back to the Embassy. Take a taxi. From now on there's to be a total ban on movement. No one is to leave the Embassy perimeter on pain of dismissal. Tell de Lisle. And tell him what has happened and put aside the Karfeld papers for my return. Anything that incriminates him: the investigation report, the thesis ... anything from the Glory Hole that tells the tale. I shall be back by early afternoon.'

He opened the car door.

'What's the bargain with Siebkron?' Turner said. 'What's the small print?'

'There is no bargain. Either they destroy Harting, or he will destroy Karfeld. In either case I have to disown him. That is the only thing that matters. Is there something you would prefer me to do? Do you see a way out? I shall inform Siebkron that order must be restored. I shall give him my oath that we had no part in Harting's work, and no knowledge of it. Can you suggest an alternative solution? I would be grateful.'

He started the engine. The grey columns stirred with interest, pleased by the white Jaguar.

'Bradfield!'

'Well.'

'I beg you. Five minutes. I've got a card to play as well. Something we've never mentioned. Bradfield!'

Without a word, Bradfield opened the door and got out.

'You say we have no part in it. We have. He's our product, you know that, we made him what he was, crushed him between all those words ... we ground him down into himself, made him see things no one should ever see, hear things that ... we sent him on that private journey ... you don't know what it's like down there. I do! Bradfield, listen! We *owe* him. He knew that.'

'All of us are owed. Very few of us are paid.'

'You *want* to destroy him! You *want* to make him nothing! You *want* to disown him because he was her lover! Because –'

'My God,' Bradfield said softly, 'if that were the task I had set myself I would have to kill more than the thirty-two. Is that all you wanted to tell me?'

'Wait! Brussels ... the Market ... all this. Next week it's gold, the week after it's the Warsaw pact. We'd join the bloody Salvation Army if it pleased the Americans. What does it matter about the names? ... You see it clearer than any of us: the drift. Why do you go on with it like this? Why don't you say stop?'

'What am I to do about Harting? Tell me what else I can do but disown him? You know us here now. Crises are academic. Scandals are not. Haven't you realized that only appearances matter?'

Turner searched frantically about him. 'It's not true! You *can't* be so tied to the surface of things.'

'What else is there when the underneath is rotten? Break the surface and we sink. That's what Harting has done. I am a hypocrite,' he continued simply. 'I'm a great believer in hypocrisy. It's the nearest we ever get to virtue. It's a statement of what we ought to be. Like religion, like art, like the law, like marriage. I serve the appearance of things. It is the worst of systems; it is better than the others. That is my profession and that is my philosophy. And unlike yourself,' he added, 'I did not contract to serve a powerful nation, least of all a virtuous one. All power corrupts. The loss of power corrupts even more. We thank an American for that advice. It's quite true. We are a corrupt nation, and we need all the help we can get. That is lamentable and, I confess, occasionally humiliating. However, I would rather fail as a power than survive by impotence. I would rather be vanquished than neutral. I would rather be English than Swiss. And unlike you, I expect nothing. I expect no more from institutions than I expect from people. You have no suggestion then? I am disappointed.'

'Bradfield, I *know* her. I know you, and I know what you feel! You hate him! You hate him more than you dare admit. You hate him for *feeling*: for loving, even for hating. You hate him for deceiving and for being honest. For waking her. For putting you to shame. You hate him for the time she spent on him ... for the thought, the dream she had of him!'

'But you have no suggestion. I imagine your five minutes are over. He *has* offended,' he added casually, as if passing the topic once more in review. 'Yes. He has. Not as much against myself as you might suppose. But against the order that results from chaos; against the built-in moderation of an aimless society. He had no business to hate Karfeld and none to ... He had no business to remember. If you and I have a purpose at all any more, it is to save the world from such presumptions.'

'Of all of you – Listen! – Of all of you he's the only one who's real, the only one who believed, and acted! For you, it's a sterile, rotten game, a family word game, that's all; just play. But Leo's *involved*! He knows what he wants and he's gone to get it!'

'Yes. That alone should be enough to condemn him.' He had forgotten Turner now. 'There's no room for his kind any more. That's the one thing we *have* learnt, thank God.' He stared at the river. 'We've learnt that even *nothing* is a pretty tender flower. You speak as if there were those who contribute and those who do not. As if we were all working for the day when we are no longer needed; when the world could pack up and cultivate its allotment. There *is* no product. There *is* no final day. This *is* the life we work for. Now. At this moment. Every night, as I go to sleep, I say to myself: another day achieved. Another day added to the unnatural life of a world on its deathbed. And if I never relax; if I never lift my eye, we may run on for another hundred years. Yes.' He was talking to the river. 'Our policy is that tide, taken at its three-inch flood. Three inches of freedom up and down the bank. That's the limit of our action. Beyond it is anarchy, and all the romantic clap-trap of protest and conscience. We are all looking for the wider freedom, every one of us. It doesn't exist. As long as we accept that, we can dream at will. Harting should never have gone down there in the first place. And you should have returned to London when I told you. The Statute has made a law of forgetting. He broke it. Praschko is quite right: Harting has broken the law of moderation.'

'We're *not* automatons! We're born free, I believe that! We can't control the processes of our own minds!'

'Good Lord, whoever told you that?' He faced Turner now and the small tears showed. 'I have controlled the processes of my own mind for eighteen years of marriage and twenty years of diplomacy. I have spent half of my life learning not to look, and the other half learning not to feel. Do you think

I cannot also learn to forget? God, sometimes I am bowed down by the things I do not know! So why the devil couldn't he forget as well? Do you think I take pleasure in what I have to do? Do you think he does not challenge me to do it? *He* set all this in motion, not I! His *damned* immodesty –'

'Bradfield! What about Karfeld? Hasn't Karfeld stepped over the line as well?'

'There are quite different ways of dealing with his case.' The shell had closed again around his voice.

'Leo found one.'

'The wrong one as it happens.'

'Why?'

'Never mind why.'

He began walking slowly back to the car, but Turner was calling to him.

'What made Leo run? Something he read. Something he stole. What *was* in that Green File? What were those Formal and Informal Conversations with German Politicians. Bradfield! Who was talking to who?'

'Lower your voice, they'll overhear.'

'Tell me! Have you been having conversations with Karfeld? Is that what sent Leo on his night walk? Is that what it was all about?'

Bradfield did not reply.

'Holy God,' Turner whispered. 'We're like the rest of them, after all. Like Siebkron and Praschko; we're trying to make our number with tomorrow's lucky winner!'

'Take care!' Bradfield warned.

'Allerton ... what Allerton said –'

'Allerton? He knows nothing!'

'Karfeld came in from Hanover that Friday night. Secretly to Bonn. For a conference. He even arrived and left on foot, it was so secret. You didn't go to Hanover after all, did you, that Friday night? You changed your plans, cancelled your ticket. Leo found that out from the Travel Clerks –'

'You're talking utter nonsense.'

'You met Karfeld in Bonn. Siebkron laid it on, and Leo followed you because he knew what you were up to!'

'You're out of your mind.'

'No, I'm not. But Leo is, isn't he? Because Leo suspected. All the time, in the back of his mind, he knew that you were secretly reinsuring against the Brussels failure. Until he saw that file, until he actually saw and knew, he thought he might still act within the law. But when he saw the Green File he *knew*: it really *was* happening again. He knew. That's why he was in a hurry. He had to stop you, he had to stop Karfeld before it was too late!'

Bradfield said nothing.

'What was in the Green File, Bradfield? What's he taken with him as a keepsake? Why was *that* the only file he stole? Because it contained the minutes of *those* meetings, was it? And that's what's drawn your fire! You've got to get the Green File back! Did you sign them Bradfield? With that willing pen of yours?' His pale eyes were alight with anger. 'When did he steal the despatch box, let's just think: Friday ... Friday morning he had his verification, didn't he? He saw it in black and white: *that* was the other proof he was looking for. He took it to Aickman.... "They're up to their old tricks, we've got to stop it before it's too late ... we're the chosen ones." That's why he took the Green File! To show them! *Children look*, he wants to say, *history really is repeating itself, and it isn't comedy at all!*'

'It was a document of the highest secrecy. He could go to prison for years for that alone.'

'But he never will, because you want the file and not the man. That's another part of the three-inch freedom, is it?'

'Would you prefer me to be a fanatic?'

'What he'd suspected for months, picked up in the wind of Bonn gossip and the scraps he got from *her*; now he had the proof: that the British were hedging their bets. Taking out a with-profits policy on the Bonn–Moscow axis. What's the deal, Bradfield? What's the small print *now*? Christ, no wonder Siebkron thought you were playing a treble game! First you put all your chips on Brussels and very wise too. "Let nothing disturb the enterprise." Then you hedge the bet with Karfeld and you get Siebkron to hold your stake. "Bring me secretly to Karfeld," you say to him. "The British also are interested in a Moscow axis." Very informally interested, mind. Purely explanatory talks and no witnesses, mind. But an eventual trade alignment with the East is not at all out of the question, *Herr Doktor Karfeld*, if you should ever happen to become a credible alternative to a crumbling coalition! As a matter of fact we're quite anti-American ourselves these days, it's in the blood, you know, *Herr Doktor Karfeld* ...

'You missed your vocation.'

'And then what happens? No sooner has Siebkron brought Karfeld to your bed than he learns enough to make his blood run cold: the British Embassy is compiling a dossier on Karfeld's unsavoury past! The Embassy already has the records – the *only* records, Bradfield – and now they're sizing up to blackmail him on the side. And that's not all!'

'No.'

'Siebkron and Karfeld have hardly got used to that little shock before you provide a bigger one. One that really rocks them. Not even Albion, they thought, could be that perfidious: the British are actually trying to assassinate Karfeld. It makes no sense of course. Why kill the man you want to blackmail? They must have been puzzled to death. No wonder Siebkron looked so sick on Tuesday night!'

'Now you know it all. You share the secret: keep it.'

'Bradfield!'

'Well?'

'Who do you want to win? This afternoon, out there, who's your money on this time, Bradfield? On Leo; or the cut-price ally?'

Bradfield switched on the engine.

'Cut-price friends! They're the only kind we can afford! They're the only kind we've got the guts to make! We're a proud nation, Bradfield! You can get Karfeld for twenty-five per cent off now, can't you! Never mind if he hates us. He'll come round! People change! And he thinks about us all the time! That's an encouraging start! A little push now and he'll run for ever.'

'Either you're in or you're out. Either you're involved or you're not.' He hesitated. 'Or would you rather be Swiss?'

Without another word or glance, Bradfield drove up the hill, turned right and vanished in the direction of Bonn. Turner waited until he was out of sight before walking back along the river path towards the cab rank. As he went there rose suddenly behind him an unearthly rumble of feet and voices, the saddest, deepest sound he had ever heard in his life. The columns had begun to move; they were shuffling slowly forward, mediocre, ponderous and terrifying, a mindless grey monster that could no longer be held back, while beyond them, almost hidden in the mist stood the wooded outline of Chamberlain's hill.

Epilogue

Bradfield led the way; de Lisle and Turner followed. It was early evening and the streets were empty of traffic. In all Bonn, nothing stirred but the mute, grey-clad strangers who swarmed the alleys and hastened towards the market square. The black bunting, becalmed, drifted in idle swathes over the ebbing tide.

Bonn had never seen such faces. The old and the young, the lost and the found, the fed and the hungry, the clever, the dull, the governed and the ungoverned, all the children of the Republic, it seemed, had risen in a single legion to march upon her little bastions. Some were hillsmen, dark haired, straddle-legged and scrubbed for the outing; some were clerks, Bob Cratchits nipped by the quick air, some were Sunday men, the slow infantry of the German promenade, in grey gabardine and grey Homburg hats. Some carried their flags shamefully, as if they had outgrown them, some as banners borne to the battle, others as ravens strung for market. Birnam Wood had come to Dunsinane.

Bradfield waited for them to catch up.

'Siebkron reserved space for us. We should enter the square higher up. We shall have to force our way to the right.'

Turner nodded, barely hearing. He was looking everywhere, into every face and every window, every shop, corner and alley. Once he seized de Lisle's arm, but whoever it was had gone, lost again in the changing mass.

Not just the square itself: balconies, windows, shops, every foothold and crevice was filled with grey coats and white faces, and the green uniforms of soldiers and police. And still they came, more of them, cramming the mouths of the darkening alleys, craning their necks for a sight of the speaker's stand, searching for a leader, faceless men searching for one face; while Turner peered desperately among them for a face he had never seen. Overhead, in front of the floodlights, loudspeakers hung like warnings from their wires; beyond them, the sky was failing.

He'll never make it, Turner thought dully; he'll never penetrate a crowd like this. But Hazel Bradfield's voice came back to him: *I had a younger brother, he played scrum half, you could hardly tell them apart.*

'To the left,' Bradfield said. 'Make for the hotel.'

'You are English?' A woman's voice inquired, teatime in a friendly house, 'My daughter lives in Yarmouth.' But the tide carried her away. Furled banners barred their path, dropped like lances. The banners formed a ring, and the gypsy students stood inside it, gathered round their own small fire. 'Burn Axel Springer,' one boy shouted, not with much conviction, and another broke a book and threw it on the flames. The book burned badly, choking before it died. I shouldn't have done that to the books. Turner thought; I'll be doing it to people next. A group of girls lounged on mattresses and the fire made poems of their faces.

'If we're separated, meet on the steps of the Stern,' Bradfield ordered. A boy heard him and ran forward, encouraged by the others. Two girls were already shouting in French. 'You are English!' the boy cried, though his face was young and nervous. 'English swine!' Hearing the girls again, he swung his small fist wildly over the lances. Turner hastened forward, but the blow fell on Bradfield's shoulder and he paid it no attention. The crowd gave way, suddenly, its will mysteriously gone, and the Town Hall appeared before them at the far end of the square, and that was the night's first dream. A magic baroque mountain of candy pink and merchant gold. A vision of style and elegance, of silk and filigree and sunlight. A vision of brilliance and Latin glory, Palaces where de Lisle's unplayed minuets pleased the plumper burgher's heart. To its left the scaffold, still in darkness, cut off by the screen of arclights trained upon the building, waited like an executioner upon the imperial presence.

'Herr Bradfield?' the pale detective asked. He had not changed his leather coat since that dawn in Königswinter, but there were two teeth missing from his black mouth. The moon faces of his colleagues stirred in recognition of the name.

'I'm Bradfield, yes.'

'We are ordered to free the steps for you.' His English was rehearsed: a small part for a newcomer. The radio in his leather pocket crackled in urgent command. He lifted it to his mouth. The diplomatic gentlemen had arrived, he said, and were safely in position. The gentleman from Research was also present.

Turner looked pointedly at the broken mouth and smiled.

'You sod,' he said with satisfaction. The lip was badly cut as well, though not as badly as Turner's.

'Please?'

'Sod,' Turner explained. 'Sodomite.'

'Shut up,' said Bradfield.

The steps commanded a view of the entire square. Already the afternoon had turned to twilight; the victorious arclights divided the numberless heads into white patches which floated like pale discs upon a black sea. Houses, shops, cinemas had fallen away. Only their gables remained, carved in fairytale silhouette against the dark sky, and that was the second dream, *Tales of Hoffman*, the woodcut world of German make-believe to prolong the German childhood. High on a roof a Coca-Cola sign, winking on and off, tinged the surrounding tiles with cosmetic pink; once an errant spotlight ran across the facades, peering with a lover's eye into the empty windows of the stores. On the lower step, the detectives waited, backs towards them, hands in pockets, black against the haze.

'Karfeld will come in from the side,' de Lisle said suddenly.

'The alley to the left.'

Following the direction of de Lisle's outstretched arm, Turner noticed for the first time directly beneath the feet of the scaffold a tiny passageway between the pharmacy and the Town Hall, not more than ten foot wide and made very deep by the high walls of the adjacent buildings.

'We remain here, is that clearly understood? On these steps. Whatever happens. We are here as observers; merely observers, nothing more.' Bradfield's strict features were strengthened by dilemma. 'If they find him they will deliver him to us. That is the understanding. We shall take him at once to the Embassy for safe custody.'

Music, Turner remembered. In Hanover he tried when the music was loudest. The music is supposed to drown the shot. He remembered the hair-dryers too and thought: he's not a man to vary the technique; if it worked before, it will work again, and that's the German in him; like Karfeld and the grey buses.

His thoughts were lost to the murmur of the crowd, the pleasurable growl of expectation which mounted like an angry prayer as the floodlights died. Only the Town Hall remained, a pure and radiant altar, tended by the little group which had appeared upon its balcony. The names rose in countless mouths as all around him, the slow liturgical commentary began:

Tilsit, Tilsit was there, Tilsit the old General, the third from the left, and look, he is wearing his medal, the only one they wanted to deny him, his special medal from the war, he wears it round his neck, Tilsit is a man of courage. Meyer-Lothringen the economist! Yes, *der Grosse*, the tall one, how elegantly he waves, it is well known that he is of the best family; half a Wittelsbach, they say; blood will tell in the end; and a great academic; he understands everything. And priests! The Bishop! Look, the Bishop himself is blessing us! Count the movements of his holy hand! Now he is looking to his right! He has reached out his arm! And Halbach the young hothead: look, he is wearing a pullover! Fantastic his impertinence: a pullover on such an occasion? In Bonn? *Halbach! Du toller Hund!* But Halbach is from Berlin, and Berliners are famous for their arrogance; one day he will lead us all, so young and yet already so successful.

The murmur rose to a roar, a visceral, hungry, loving roar, deeper than any single throat, more pious than any single soul, more loving than any single heart; and died again, whispering down, as the first quiet chords of music struck. The Town Hall receded and the scaffolding stood before them. A preacher's pulpit, a captain's bridge, a conductor's rostrum? A child's cradle, a plain coffin of boldly simple wood, grandiose yet virtuous, a wooden grail, housing the German truth. Upon it, alone but valiant, the truth's one champion, a plain man known as Karfeld.

'Peter.' Turner gently pointed into the tiny alley. His hand was shaking but his eye was quite steady. A shadow? A guard taking up his post?

'I wouldn't point any more if I was you,' de Lisle whispered. 'They might misunderstand you.'

But in that moment, no one paid them any heed, for Karfeld was all they saw.

'Der Klaus!' the crowd was calling, 'der Klaus is here!' Wave to him, children; der Klaus, the magic man, has walked all the way to Bonn on stilts of German Pine.

'He is very English, der Klaus,' he heard de Lisle murmur, 'Although he hates our guts.'

He was such a little man up there. They said he was tall; and it would have been easy enough, with so much artifice, to raise him a foot or so, but he seemed to wish to be diminished, as if to emphasize that great truths are found in humble mouths; for Karfeld was a humble man, and English in his diffidence.

And Karfeld was a nervous man too, bothered by his spectacles, which he had not had time to clean, apparently, in these busy days, for now he took them off and polished them as if he did not know he was observed: it is the others who make the ceremony, he was telling them, before he had said a word; it is you and I who know why we are here.

Let us pray.

'The lights are too bright for him,' someone said. 'They should reduce the lights.'

He was one of them, this isolated Doctor; a good deal of brain power no doubt, a good deal above the ears, but still one of them at the end of it, ready to step down at any time from that high place if someone better came along. And not at all a politician. Quite without ambition, in fact, for he had only yesterday promised to stand down in favour of Halbach if that was the people's will. The crowd whispered its concern. Karfeld looks tired, he looks fresh; he looks well; Karfeld looks ill, older, younger, taller, shorter.... It is said he is retiring; no, he will give up his factory and work full time on politics. He cannot afford it; he is a millionaire.

Quietly he began speaking.

No one introduced him, he did not say his name. The note of music which announced his coming had no companions, for Klaus Karfeld is alone up there, quite alone, and no music can console him. Karfeld is not a Bonn windbag; he is one of us for all his intellect: Klaus Karfeld, doctor and citizen, a decent man decently concerned about the fate of Germany, is obliged, out of a sense of honour, to address a few friends.

It was so softly, so unobtrusively done, that to Turner it seemed that the whole massive gathering actually inclined its ear in order to save Karfeld the pain of raising his voice.

Afterwards, Turner could not say how much he had understood, nor how he had understood so much. He had the impression, at first, that Karfeld's interest was purely historical. The talk was of the origin of war and Turner caught the old catchwords of the old religion, Versailles, chaos, depression and encirclement; the mistakes that had been made by statesmen on both sides, for Germans cannot shirk their own responsibilities. There followed a small tribute to the casualties of unreason: too many people died, Karfeld said, and too few knew the cause. It must never happen again, Karfeld knew: he had brought back more than wounds from Stalingrad: he had brought back memories, indelible memories, of human misery, mutilation and betrayal....

He has indeed, they whispered, the poor Klaus. He has suffered for us all.

There was no rhetoric still. You and I, Karfeld was saying, have learned the lessons of history; you and I can look on these things with detachment: it must never happen again. There were those, it was true, who saw the battles of fourteen and thirty-nine as part of a continuing crusade against the enemies of a German heritage, but Karfeld – he wished it to be known to all his friends – Klaus Karfeld was not, altogether, of this school.

'Alan.' It was de Lisle's voice, steady as a Captain's. Turner followed his gaze.

A flutter, a movement of people, the passing of a message? Something was stirring on the balcony. He saw Tilsit, the General, incline his soldier's head and Halbach the student leader whisper in his ear, saw Meyer-Lothringen leaning forward over the filigree rail, listening to someone below him. A policeman? A plainclothes man? He saw the glint of spectacles and the patient surgeon's face as Siebkron rose and vanished; and all was still again except for Karfeld, academic and man of reason, who was talking about today.

Today, he said, as never before, Germany was the plaything of her allies. They had bought her, now they were selling her. This was a *fact*, Karfeld said, he would not deal in theory. There were too many theories in Bonn already, he explained, and he did not propose to add to the confusion. This was *fact*, and it was necessary, if painful, to debate among good and reasonable friends how Germany's allies had achieved this strange state of affairs. Germany was rich, after all: richer than France, and richer than Italy. Richer than England, he added casually, but we must not be rude to the English for the English won the war after all, and were a people of uncommon gifts.

His voice remained wonderfully reasonable as he recited all the English gifts: their mini-skirts, their pop singers, their Rhine Army that sat in London, their Empire that was falling apart, their national deficit ... without these English gifts, Europe would surely fail. Karfeld had always said so.

Here they laughed; it was a warming, angry laugh, and Karfeld, shocked and perhaps the tiniest fraction disappointed that these beloved sinners, whom God had appointed him in his humility to instruct, should fall to laughing in the temple; Karfeld waited patiently until it died.

How then, if Germany was so rich, if she possessed the largest standing army in Europe, and could dominate the so-called Common Market, how was it possible for her to be sold in public places like a whore?

Leaning back in the pulpit, he removed his spectacles and made a cautious, pacifying gesture of the hand, for there were noises now of protest and indignation, and Karfeld quite clearly did not care for this at all. We must try to resolve this question in a pious, reasonable and wholly *intellectual* manner, he warned, without emotion and without rancour, as befits good friends! It was a plump, round hand and it might have been webbed, for he never separated his fingers, but used the whole fist singly like a club.

In seeking, then, a rational explanation for this curious – and, for Germans at least, highly relevant – historical fact, objectivity was essential. In the first place – the fist shot upward again – we had had twelve years of Nazism and thirty-five years of anti-Nazism. Karfeld did not understand what was so *very* wrong about Nazism that it should be punished eternally with the whole world's hostility. The Nazis had persecuted the Jews: and that was wrong. He wished to go on record as saying it was wrong. Just as he condemned Oliver Cromwell for his treatment of the Irish, the United States for their treatment of the blacks and for their campaigns of genocide against the Red Indians and the yellow peril of South East Asia; just as he condemned the Church for its persecution of heretics, and the British for the bombing of Dresden, so he condemned Hitler for what he had done to the Jews; and for importing that British invention, so successful in the Boer War: the concentration camp.

Directly in front of him Turner saw the young detective's hand softly feel for the partition of his leather coat; he heard again the little crackle of the radio. Once more he strained his eyes, scanning the crowd, the balcony, the alleys; once more he searched the doorways and the windows; and there was nothing. Nothing but the sentinels posted along the roof-tops and the militia waiting in their vans; nothing but a countless throng of silent men and women, motionless as God's anointed before the Presence of the Word.

Let us examine, Karfeld suggested – since it will help us to arrive at a logical and objective solution to the many questions which presently assail us – let us examine what happened after the war.

After the war, Karfeld explained, it was only just that the Germans should be treated as criminals; and, because the Germans had practised racism, that their sons and grandsons should be treated as criminals too. But, because the Allies were *kind* people, and *good* people, they would go some way towards rehabilitating the Germans: as a very special treat, they would admit them to Nato.

The Germans were shy at first; they did not *want* to rearm, many people had had enough of war. Karfeld himself belonged to that category: the lessons of Stalingrad were like acid in the young man's memory. But the Allies were determined as well as kind. The Germans should provide the army, and the British and the Americans and the French would command it.... And the Dutch.... And the Norwegians.... And the Portuguese; and any other foreign general who cared to command the vanquished:

'Why: we might even have had African generals commanding the Bundeswehr!'

A few – they belonged to the front, to that protective ring of leather-coated men beneath the scaffold – a few started laughing, but he quelled them at once.

'Listen!' he told them. 'My friends, you must listen! That is what we *deserved*! We lost the war! We persecuted the Jews! We were not *fit* to command! Only to pay!' Their anger gradually subsided. 'That,' he explained, 'is why we pay for the *British* Army as well. And *that* is why they let us into Nato.'

'Alan!'

'I have seen them.'

Two grey buses were parked beside the pharmacy. A floodlight touched their dull coachwork, and was moved away. The windows were quite black, sealed from inside.

And we were grateful, Karfeld continued. Grateful to be admitted to such an exclusive club. Of course we were. The club did not exist; its members did not like us; the fees were very high; and as the Germans were still children they must not play with weapons which might damage their enemies; but we were grateful all the same, because we were Germans and had lost the war.

Once more the indignant murmur rose, but he scotched it again with a terse movement of his hand. 'We want no emotion here,' he reminded them. 'We are dealing with facts!'

High up, on a tiny ledge, a mother held her baby. 'Look down, she was whispering. 'You will not see his like again.' In the whole square, nothing moved; the heads were still, staring with cavernous eyes.

To emphasize his great impartiality, Karfeld once more drew back in the pulpit and, taking all his time, tilted his spectacles a little and examined the pages before him. This done, he hesitated, peered doubtfully downwards at the faces nearest him and deliberated, unsure how far he could expect his flock to follow what he was about to say.

What then was the *function* of the Germans in this distinguished club? He would put it this way. He would state the formula first and afterwards he would give one or two simple examples of the method by which it could be applied. The function of the Germans in Nato was briefly this: to be *docile* towards the West and *hostile* towards the East; to recognize that even among the victorious Allies there were *good* victors and *bad* victors....

Again the laughter rose and fell. *Der Klaus*, they whispered, *der Klaus* knows how to make a joke; what a club that Nato is. Nato, the Market, it's all a cheat, it's all the same; they are applying the same principles to Market which they applied to Nato. Klaus has told us so and that is why the Germans must stay away from Brussels. It is just another trap, it is encirclement all over again....

'That's Lésère,' de Lisle murmured.

A small, greying man who obscurely reminded Turner of a bus conductor had joined them on the steps and was writing contentedly in his notebook.

'The French counsellor. Big chum of Karfeld's.'

About to return his gaze to the scaffold, Turner happened to look into the side street; and thus he saw for the first time the mad, dark, tiny army that waited for the signal.

Directly across the square, assembled in the unlit side street, the silent concourse of men waited. They carried banners that were not quite black in the twilight and there stood before them, Turner was certain there stood before them, the remnants of a military band. The oblique arclights glinted on a trumpet, caught the laced panels of the drum. At its head stood a solitary figure; his arm, raised like a conductor's, held them motionless.

Again the radio crackled, but the words were drowned in laughter as Karfeld made another joke; a harsh joke, enough to raise their anger, a reference to the decay of England and the person of the monarch. The tone was new and hard: a light blow on their backs, brisker, a purposeful caress, promising the sting to come, tracing like a whip's end the little vertebrae of their political resentment. So England, with her allies, had re-educated the Germans. And who better qualified? After all, Churchill had let the savages into Berlin; Truman had dropped atom bombs on undefended cities; between them they had made a ruin of Europe: who better qualified, then, to teach the Germans the meaning of civilization?

In the alley, nothing had stirred. The leader's arm was still raised before the little band as he waited for the signal to begin the music.

'It's the Socialists,' de Lisle breathed. 'They're staging a counter-demonstration. Who the devil let them in?'

So the Allies set to work: the Germans must be taught how to behave. It was wrong to kill the Jews, they explained; kill the Communists instead. It was wrong to attack Russia, they explained; but we will protect you if the Russians attack you. It was wrong to fight for your borders, they explained; but we support your claims for the territories of the East.

'We all know that kind of support!' Karfeld held out his hands, palms upwards. 'Here you are my dear, here you are! You can borrow my umbrella as long as you like; until it rains!'

Was it Turner's imagination or did he detect, in this piece of theatre, a hint of that wheedling tone which once in German music-halls traditionally denoted the Jew? They began to laugh, but again he silenced them.

In the alley, the conductor's arm was still raised. Will he never tire, Turner wondered, of that gruesome salute?

'They'll be murdered,' de Lisle insisted. 'The crowd will murder them!'

And so, my friends, this is what happened. Our victors in all their purity, and all their wisdom, taught us the meaning of *democracy*. Hurray for democracy. Democracy is like Christ; there is nothing you cannot do in the name of democracy.

'Praschko,' Turner declared quietly, 'Praschko wrote that for him.'

'He writes a lot of his stuff,' de Lisle said.

'Democracy is shooting Negroes in America and giving them gold beds in Africa! Democracy is to run a colonial empire, to fight in Vietnam and to attack Cuba; democracy is to visit your conscience on the Germans! *Democracy is to know that whatever you do, you will never, never be as bad as the Germans!*'

He had raised his voice to give the sign, the sign the band expected. Once more Turner looked across the crowd into the alley, saw the white hand, white as a napkin, fall lazily in the lamplight, glimpsed the white face of Siebkron himself as he quickly relinquished his place of command and withdrew into the shadow of the pavement, saw the first head turn in front of him, then a second, as he himself heard it also: the distant sound of music, of a percussion band, and men's voices singing; saw Karfeld peer over the pulpit and call to someone beneath him; saw him draw back into the furthest recess while he continued speaking, and heard, as Karfeld assumed his sudden tone of indignation, heard through all Karfeld's new anger and his high pitched exhortation, through all the conjuration, the abuse and the encouragement, the unmistakable note of fear.

'The Sozis!' the young detective cried, far out across the crowd. His heels were together and his leather shoulders drawn well back and he bellowed through cupped hands. 'The Sozis are in the alley! The Socialists are attacking us!'

'It's a diversion,' Turner said, quite matter of fact. 'Siebkron's staging a diversion.' *To lure him out*, he thought; *to lure out Leo and make him chance his hand. And here's the music to drown the shot*, he added to himself, as the *Marseillaise* began. *It's all set up to make him have a go.*

No one moved at first. The opening strains were barely audible; little, irrelevant notes played by a child on a mouth organ. And the singing which accompanied it was no more than the male chant from a Yorkshire pub on a Saturday night, remote and unconfident, proceeding from mouths unused to music; and to begin with the crowd really ignored it, because of its interest in Karfeld.

But Karfeld had heard the music, and it quickened him remarkably.

'I am an old man!' he shouted. 'Soon I shall be an old man. What will you say to yourselves, young men, when you wake in the morning? What will you say when you look at the American whore that is Bonn? You will say this: how long, young men, can we live without honour? You will look at your Government and say; you will look at the Sozis and say: must we follow even a dog because it is in office?'

He quoted *Lear*, Turner thought absurdly, and the floodlights were extinguished at one turn, at one black fall of the curtain: deep darkness filled the square, and with it the louder singing of the *Marseillaise*. He detected the acrid smell of pitch carried on the night air, as in countless places the sparks flickered and wheeled away; he heard the whispered call and the whispered answer, he heard the order passed from mouth to mouth in hasty conspiracy. The singing and the music rose to a roar, picked up suddenly and quite deliberately by the loudspeakers: a mad, monstrous, plebeian, unsubtle roar, amplified and distorted almost beyond recognition, deafening and maddening.

Yes, Turner repeated to himself with Saxon clarity, *that is what I would do if I were Siebkron. I would create this diversion, rouse the crowd, and make enough noise to provoke him into shooting.*

The music boomed still louder. He saw the policeman turn and face him and the young detective hold up a hand in warning. 'Stay here, please, Mister Bradfield! Mister Turner, stay here please!' The crowd was whispering excitedly; all round them they heard the sibilant, greedy hiss.

'Hands out of pockets, please!'

Torches were lit all round them; someone had given the signal. They rose like wild hopes gilding the sullen faces with belief, making mad dreams of their prosaic features, setting into their dull eyes the devotion of apostles. The little band was advancing into the square; it could not have been more than twenty strong, and the army that marched in its wake was ragged and undecided, but now their music was everywhere, a Socialist terror magnified by Siebkron's loudspeaders.

'The Sozis!' the crowd cried again. 'The Sozis are attacking us!'

The pulpit was empty, Karfeld had gone, but the Socialists were still marching for Marx, Jewry and War. 'Strike them, strike our enemies! Strike the Jews! Strike the Reds!' follow the dark, the voices whispered, follow the light, follow the spies and saboteurs; the Sozis are responsible for everything.

Still the music grew louder.

'Now,' de Lisle said evenly. 'They've drawn him.'

A busy, silent group had gathered round the raw, white legs of Karfeld's scaffold; leather coats were stooping, moon face flitting and conferring.

'The Sozis! Kill the Sozis.' The crowd was in mounting ferment; the scaffold was forgotten. 'Kill them!' Whatever you resent, the voices whispered, kill it here: Jews, Negroes, moles, conspirators, rejectors, wreckers, parents, lovers; they are good, they are bad, foolish or clever.

'Kill the Socialist Jews!' Swimmers leaping, the voices whispered; march! march!

We've got to kill him, Praschko, Alan Turner told himself in his confusion, *or we shall be wearing the labels again . . .*

'Kill who?' he said to de Lisle. 'What are they doing?'

'Chasing the dream.'

The music had risen to a single note, a raucous, crude, deafening roar, a call to battle and a call to anger, a call to kill ugliness, to destroy the sick and the unwieldy, the maimed, the loathsome and the incompetent. Suddenly by the light of the torches the black flags lifted and trembled like waking moths, the crowd seemed to drift and lean until the edges broke and the torches floated away into the alley, driving the band before them, acclaiming it their hero, smothering it with close kisses, dancing in upon it in playful fury, smashing the windows and the instruments, causing the red banners to flourish and dip like spurts of blood, then vanish under the mass which, cumbersome and murmuring, led by its own wanton torches, had reached into the alley and beyond. The radio crackled. Turner heard Siebkron's voice cool and perfectly clear, he heard the mordant command and the one word: *Schaffott.* And then he was running through the waves, making for the scaffold, his shoulder burning from the blow; he felt the survivors' hands holding him and he broke them like the hands of children. He was running. Hands held him and he shook them off like twigs. A face rose at him and he struck it away, riding the waves to reach the scaffold. Then he saw him.

'Leo!' he shouted.

He was crouched like a pavement artist between the motionless feet. They stood all round him but no one was touching him. They were packed in close, but they had left room for him to die. Turner saw him rise, and fall again, and once more he shouted, 'Leo.' He saw the dark eyes turn to him and heard his cry answered, to Turner, to the world, to God or pity, to the mercy of any man who would save him from the fact. He saw the scrum bow, and bury him, and run; he saw the Homburg hat roll away over the damp cobble and he ran forward, repeating the name.

'Leo!'

He had grasped a torch and smelt the singeing of cloth. He was wielding the torch, driving away the hands, and suddenly there was no resistance any more; he stood on the shore, beneath the scaffold, looking at his own life, his own face, at the lover's hands grasping the cobble, at the pamphlets which drifted across the little body like leaves in the gathering wind.

There was no weapon near him; nothing to show how he had died, only the crooked arrangement of the neck where the two pieces no longer fitted. He lay like a tiny doll who had been broken into pieces, and carefully put together, pressed down under the warm Bonn air. A man who had felt, and felt no more; an innocent, reaching beyond the square for a prize he would never find. Far away, Turner heard the cry of anger as the grey crowd followed the vanished music of the alleys; while from behind him came the rustle of the light, approaching footsteps.

'Search his pockets,' someone said, in a voice of Saxon calm.

FREDERICK FORSYTH

THE DOGS OF WAR

'Cry "Havoc" and let slip the dogs of war.'

WILLIAM SHAKESPEARE

'That . . . be not told of my death,
Or made to grieve on account of me,
And that I be not buried in consecrated ground,
And that no sexton be asked to toll the bell,
And that nobody is wished to see my dead body,
And that no mourners walk behind me at my funeral,
And that no flowers be planted on my grave,
And that no man remember me,
To this I put my name.'

THOMAS HARDY

For Giorgio, and Christian and Schlee
And Big Marc and Black Johnny,
And the others in the unmarked graves.
At least we tried.

PROLOGUE

There were no stars that night on the bush airstrip, nor any moon; just the West African darkness wrapping round the scattered groups like warm, wet velvet. The cloud cover was lying hardly off the tops of the iroko trees and the waiting men prayed it would stay a while longer to shield them from the bombers.

At the end of the runway the battered old DC-4, which had just slipped in for a landing by runway lights that stayed alight for just the last fifteen seconds of final approach, turned and coughed its way blindly towards the palm-thatch huts.

A Federal MIG-17 night fighter, probably flown by one of the six East German pilots sent down over the past three months, to replace the Egyptians who had a horror of flying at night, moaned across the sky to the west. It was out of sight above the cloud layer, as was the runway also hidden from the pilot's eyes. He was seeking the tell-tale flicker of the landing lights going on to bring in a landing plane, but the lights were out.

The pilot of the taxiing DC-4, unable to hear the scream of the jet above him, flicked on his own lights to see where he was going, and from the darkness a voice cried uselessly, 'Kill de lights!' They went out anyway when the pilot had got his bearings, and the fighter above was miles away. To the south there was a rumble of artillery where the front had finally crumbled as men who had had neither food nor bullets for two months threw down their guns and headed for the protecting bush forest.

The pilot of the DC-4 brought his plane to a halt twenty yards from the Super Constellation already parked on the apron, killed the engines and climbed down to the concrete. An African ran over to him and there was a muttered conversation. The two men walked through the darkness towards one of the larger groups of men, a blob of darkness against the darkness of the palm forest. The group parted as the two from the tarmac approached, until the white man who had flown in the DC-4 was face to face with the one who stood in the centre. The white man had never seen him before, but he knew of him, and even in the darkness, dimly illumined by a few cigarettes, he could recognize the man he had come to see.

The pilot wore no cap, so instead of saluting he inclined his head slightly. He had never done that before, not to a black, and could not have explained why he did it.

'My name is Captain Van Cleef,' he said in English, accented in the Afrikaner manner.

The African nodded his acknowledgement, his bushy black beard brushing the front of his striped camouflage uniform as he did so.

'It's a hazardous night for flying, Captain Van Cleef,' he remarked drily, 'and a little late for more supplies.'

His voice was deep and slow, the accent more like that of an English public school man, which he was, than an African. Van Cleef felt uncomfortable and again, as a hundred times during his run through the cloud banks from the coast, asked himself why he had come.

'I didn't bring any supplies, sir. There weren't any more to bring.'

Another precedent set. He had sworn he would not call the man 'sir'. Not a Kaffir. It had just slipped out. But they were right, the other mercenary pilots in the hotel bar in Libreville, the ones who had met him. This one was different.

'Then why have you come?' asked the general softly. 'The children perhaps? There are a number here the nuns would like to fly out to safety, but no more Caritas planes will come in tonight.'

Van Cleef shook his head, then realized no one could see the gesture. He was embarrassed, and thankful that the darkness hid it. Around him the bodyguards clutched their submachine carbines and stared at him.

'No. I came to collect you. If you want to come, that is.'

There was a long silence. He could feel the African staring at him through the gloom, occasionally caught a flash of eye-white as one of the attendants raised his cigarette.

'I see. Did your government instruct you to come in here tonight?'

'No,' said Van Cleef. 'It was my idea.'

There was another long pause. The bearded head was nodding slowly in what could have been comprehension or bewilderment a few feet away from him.

'I am very grateful,' said the voice. 'It must have been quite a trip. Actually I have my own transport. The Constellation. Which I hope will be able to take me away to exile.'

Van Cleef felt relieved. He had no idea what the political repercussions would have been if he had flown back to Libreville with the general in his entourage.

'I'll wait till you're off the ground and gone,' he said, and nodded again. He felt like holding out his hand to shake, but did not know whether he ought. If he had but known it, the African general was in the same quandary. So he turned and walked back to his aircraft.

There was silence for a while in the group of black men after he had left.

'Why does a South African, and an Afrikaner, do a thing like that?' one of the cabinet asked the general. There was a flash of teeth as the leader of the group smiled briefly.

'I don't think we shall ever understand that,' he said.

Further up the apron, also in the lee of a clump of palm, five men sat in a Landrover and watched the dim figures moving from the bush to the plane. The leader sat beside the African driver, and all five were smoking steadily.

'It must be the South African plane,' said the leader, and turned to one of the four other whites crouched in the Landrover behind him. 'Janni, go and ask the skipper if he'll make room for us.'

A tall, raw-boned, angular man climbed out of the rear of the vehicle. Like the others he was dressed from head to foot in predominantly green jungle camouflage uniform, slashed with streaks of brown. He wore green canvas jackboots on his feet, the trousers tucked into them. From his belt hung a water bottle and a Bowie knife, three pouches for magazines for the FAL carbine over his shoulder, and they were all empty. As he came round to the front of the Landrover the leader called him again.

'Leave the FAL,' he said, stretching out an arm to take the carbine, 'and Janni, make it good, huh? Because if we don't get out of here in that crate, we could get chopped up in a few days.'

The man called Janni nodded, adjusted the beret on his head and ambled towards the DC-4. Captain Van Cleef did not hear the rubber soles moving up behind him.

'*Naand, meneer.*'

Van Cleef spun round at the sound of the Afrikaans and took in the shape and size of the man beside him. Even in the darkness he could pick out the black and white skull and crossbones motif on the man's left shoulder. He nodded warily.

'*Naand. Jy Afrikaans?*'

The tall man nodded.

'Jan Dupree,' he said and held out his hand.

'Kobus Van Cleef,' said the airman and shook.

'*Waar gaan-jy nou?*' asked Dupree.

'To Libreville. As soon as they finish loading. And you?'

Janni Dupree grinned.

'I'm a bit stuck, me and my mates. We'll get the chop for sure if the Federals find us. Can you help us out?'

'How many of you?' asked Van Cleef.

'Five in all.'

As another mercenary, albeit of the air, Van Cleef did not hesitate. Outlaws sometimes need each other.

'All right, get aboard. But hurry up. As soon as that Connie is off, so are we.'

Dupree nodded his thanks and jog-trotted back to the Landrover. The four other whites were standing in a group round the bonnet.

'It's OK, but we have to get aboard,' the South African told them.

'Right, dump the hardware in the back and let's get moving,' said the group leader. As the rifles and ammunition pouches thumped into the back of the vehicle, he leaned over to the black officer with the Second Lieutenant's tabs who sat at the wheel.

'G'bye, Patrick,' he said. 'I'm afraid it's over now. Take the Landrover and dump it. Bury the guns and mark the spot. Leave your uniform and go for bush. Understand?'

The lieutenant, who a year ago had been a recruit with the rank of private and had been promoted for his ability to fight rather than eat with a knife and fork, nodded sombrely, taking in the instructions.

'Good-bye, sah.'

The four other mercenaries called good-bye and walked towards the DC-4.

The leader was about to follow them when two nuns fluttered up to him from the darkness of the bush behind the parking apron.

'Major.'

The mercenary turned and recognized the first of them as a sister he had first met months earlier, when fighting had raged in the zone where she ran a hospital, and he had been forced to evacuate the whole complex.

'Sister Mary Joseph? What are you doing here?'

The elderly Irish nun began talking earnestly, holding the stained uniform sleeve of his jacket. He nodded.

'I'll try, I can do no more than that,' he said when she had finished.

He walked across the apron to where the South African pilot was standing under the wing of his DC-4 and a watcher could have seen the two mercenaries in discussion for several minutes. Finally the man in uniform came back to the waiting nuns.

'He says yes, but you must hurry, Sister. He wants to get his crate off the ground as soon as he can.'

'God bless you,' said the figure in the white habit, and gave hurried orders to her companion. The latter ran to the rear of the aircraft and began to climb the short ladder to the passenger door. The other scurried back to the shade of a patch of palm behind the parking apron, from which soon emerged a file of men. Each carried a bundle in his arms. On reaching the DC-4 the bundles were passed up to the waiting nun at the top of the steps. Behind her the co-pilot watched her lay the first three side by side in the beginning of a row down the aircraft's hull, then began gruffly to help, taking the bundles from the stretching hands beneath the aircraft's tail and passing them inside.

'God bless you,' whispered the Irishwoman. One of the bundles deposited a few ounces of liquid green excrement onto the co-pilot's sleeve.

'Bloody hell,' he hissed, and went on working.

Left alone the leader of the group of mercenaries glanced towards the Super Constellation, up whose rear steps a file of refugees, mainly the relations of the leaders of the defeated people, was climbing. In the dim light emanating from the airplane's door he caught sight of the man he wanted to see. As he approached, the man was about to mount the steps in turn, while others destined to stay and go into the bush to hide, waited to pull away the steps. One of them called to the man about to go up.

'Sah. Major Shannon come.'

The general turned as Shannon approached and even at this hour he managed a grin.

'So, Shannon, do you want to come along?'

Shannon arrived in front of him and brought up a salute. The general acknowledged.

'No thank you, sir. We have transport to Libreville. I just wanted to say good-bye.'

'Yes. It was a long fight. Now it's over, I'm afraid. For some years at any rate. I find it hard to believe my people will continue to live in servitude for ever. By the way, have you and your colleagues been paid up to the contract?'

'Yes, thank you, sir. We're all up to date,' replied the mercenary. The African nodded sombrely.

'Well, good-bye then. And thank you for all you were able to do.'

He held out his hand and the two men shook.

'There's one more thing, sir,' said Shannon. 'Me and the boys, we were talking things over, sitting in the jeep. If there's ever any time ... well, if you should ever need us, you only have to let us know. We'll all come. You only have to call. The boys want you to know that.'

The general stared at him for several seconds.

'This night is full of surprises,' he said slowly. 'You may not know it yet, but half my senior advisers and all of the wealthy ones are crossing the lines tonight to ingratiate themselves with the enemy. Most of the others will follow suit within a month. Thank you for your offer, Mr Shannon. I will remember it. Good-bye again, and good luck.'

He turned and walked up the steps into the dimly lit interior of the Super Constellation just as the first of the four engines coughed into life. Shannon stepped back and gave the man who had employed his services for a year and a half a last salute.

'Good luck to you,' he said, half to himself. 'You'll need it.'

He turned and walked back to the waiting DC-4. When the door had closed Van Cleef kept the aircraft on the apron, engines turning, as he watched through the gloom the dim droop-nosed shape of the Super Connie rumble down the runway, past his nose and finally lift off. Neither plane carried any lights, but from the cockpit of the Douglas the Afrikaner made out the three fins of the Constellation vanishing over the palm trees to the south and into the welcoming clouds. Only then did he ease the DC-4 with its wailing and whimpering cargo forward to the take-off point.

It was close to an hour before Van Cleef ordered his co-pilot to switch on the cabin lights, an hour of jinking from cloud-bank to cloud-bank, breaking cover and scooting across low racks of altostratus to find cover again with another denser bank, always seeking to avoid being caught out in the moonlit white plains by a roving MIG. Only when he knew he was far out over the Gulf, with the coast many miles astern, did he allow the lights on.

Behind him they lit up a weird spectacle which could have been drawn by Doré in one of his blacker moods. The floor of the aircraft was carpeted with sodden and fouled blankets, which an hour earlier had been the wrappings of their contents. These contents of the bundles lay writhing in rows down both sides of the cargo space, forty small children, shrunken, wizened, deformed by malnutrition. Sister Mary Joseph rose from her crouch behind the cabin door and began to move among the starvelings, each of whom had a piece of sticking plaster stuck to his or her forehead, just below the line of the hair, long since turned to an ochre red by anaemia. The plaster bore in ball-point letters the relevant information for the orphanage outside Libreville. Name and number, if not rank. They don't give rank to losers.

In the tail of the plane the five mercenaries blinked in the light and glanced at their fellow passengers. They had seen it all before, many times, over the past months. Each man felt some disgust, but none showed it. You can get used to anything eventually. In the Congo, Yemen, Katanga, Sudan. Always the same story, always the kids. And always nothing you can do about it. So they reasoned, and pulled out their cigarettes.

The cabin lights allowed them to see each other properly for the first time since sundown the previous evening. The uniforms were stained with sweat and the red earth and the faces drawn with fatigue. The leader sat with his back to the lavatory door, feet straight out, facing up the fuselage towards the pilot's cabin. Carlo Alfred Thomas Shannon, thirty-three, blond hair cropped to a ragged crew-cut. Very short hair is more convenient in the tropics because the sweat runs out easier and the bugs can't get in. Nicknamed Cat Shannon from his initials, he came originally from County Tyrone in the province of Ulster. Sent by his father to be educated at a minor English public school, he no longer carried the distinctive accent of Northern Ireland in his speech. After five years in the Royal Marines, he had left to try his hand at civilian life, and six years ago had found himself working for a London-based trading company in Uganda. One sunny morning he quietly closed his accounts ledgers, climbed into his Landrover and drove westwards to the Congolese border. A week later he signed on as a mercenary in Mike Hoare's Fifth Commando at Stanleyville.

He had seen Hoare depart and John-John Peters take over, had quarrelled with Peters and driven north to join Denard at Paulis, had been in the Stanleyville mutiny two years later and, after the Frenchman's evacuation to Rhodesia with head wounds, had joined Black Jacques Schramme, the Belgian planter-turned-mercenary, on the long march to Bukavu and thence to Kigali. After repatriation by the Red Cross, he had promptly volunteered for another African war and had finally taken command of his own battalion. But too late to win, always too late to win.

To his immediate left sat what was arguably the best mortarman north of the Zambezi. Big Jan Dupree was aged twenty-eight and came from Paarl in Cape Province, a son of the impoverished stock of Huguenot extraction, whose ancestors had fled to the Cape of Good Hope from the wrath of Mazarin after the destruction of religious liberty in France. His hatchet face, dominated by a curved beak of a nose above a thin-lipped mouth, looked even more haggard than usual, his exhaustion furrowing deep lines down each cheek. The eyelids were down over the pale blue eyes, the sandy eyebrows and hair were smudged with dirt. After glancing down at the children lying down the aisle of the plane, he muttered '*Bliksems*' (bastards) at the world of possession and privilege he held responsible for the ills of this planet, and tried to get to sleep.

By his side sprawled Marc Vlaminck, Tiny Marc, so called because of his vast bulk. A Fleming from Ostend, he stood six feet and three inches in his socks, when he wore any, and weighed eighteen stone. Some people thought it might be fat. It was not. He was regarded with trepidation by the police of Ostend, for the most part peaceable men who prefer to avoid problems rather than seek them out, and was viewed with kindly appreciation by the glaziers and carpenters of that city for the work he provided them. They said you could tell a bar where Tiny Marc had become playful by the number of artisans it needed to put it back together again.

An orphan, he had been brought up in an institution run by the priests, who had tried to beat some sense of respect into the overgrown boy, and so repeatedly that even Marc had finally lost patience and at the age of thirteen laid one of the cane-wielding holy fathers cold along the flagstones with a single punch.

After that it had been a series of reformatories, then approved school, a dose of juvenile prison and an almost communal sigh of relief when he enlisted in the paratroops. He had been one of the 500 men who dropped onto Stanleyville with Colonel Laurent to rescue the missionaries whom the local Simba chief, Christophe Gbenye, threatened to roast alive in the main square.

Within forty minutes of hitting the airfield, Tiny Marc had found his vocation in life. After a week he went AWOL to avoid being repatriated to barracks in Belgium and joined the mercenaries. Apart from his fists and shoulders, Tiny Marc was extremely useful with a bazooka, his favourite weapon, which he handled with the easy nonchalance of a boy with a pea-shooter.

The night he flew out of the enclave towards Libreville he was just thirty.

Across the fuselage from the Belgian sat Jean-Baptiste Langarotti, engaged in his habitual occupation to while away the hours of waiting. Short, compact, lean and olive-skinned, he was a Corsican, born and raised in the town of Calvi. At the age of eighteen he had been called up by France to go and fight as one of the hundred thousand *appelés* in the Algerian war. Half way through his eighteen months he had signed on as a regular and later had transferred to the 10th Colonial Paratroops, the dreaded red berets commanded by General Massu and known simply as '*les paras*'. He was twenty-one when the crunch came and some units of the professional French colonial army rallied to the cause of an eternally French Algeria, a cause embodied for the moment in the organization of the OAS. Langarotti went with the OAS, deserted and, after the failure of the April 1961 *putsch*, went underground. He was caught in France three years later living under a false name and spent four years in prison, eating his heart out in the dark and sunless cells of first the Santé in Paris, then Tours, and finally the Île de Ré. He was a bad prisoner, and two guards would carry marks to prove it until they died.

Beaten half to death several times for attacks on guards, he had served his full time without remission, and emerged in 1968 with only one fear in the world, the fear of small enclosed spaces, cells and holes. He had long since vowed never to return to one, even if staying out cost him his life, and to take half a dozen with him if 'they' ever came for him again. Within three months of release he had flown down to Africa by paying his own way, talked himself into a war and joined Shannon as a professional mercenary. He was thirty-one when he flew out that night. Since being released from prison he had practised steadily with the weapon he had learned to use first as a boy in Corsica and with which he had later made himself a reputation in the back streets of Algiers. Round his left wrist he carried a broad leather strap, resembling for all the world the kind of strop used by old-fashioned barbers for honing their razors. It was held in place by two press-studs. In moments of idleness he would take it off, turn it over to the side unmarked by the studs, and wrap it round his left fist. That was where it was as he whiled away the time to Libreville. In his right hand was the knife, the six-inch-bladed bone-handled weapon that he could use so fast it was back in its sleeve-sheath before the victim had realized he was dead. In steady rhythm the blade moved backwards and forwards across the tense leather of the strop, already razor sharp, becoming with each stroke a mite sharper. The movement soothed his nerves. It also annoyed everybody else, but they never complained. Nor did those who knew him ever quarrel with the soft voice or the sad half-smile of the little man.

Sandwiched between Langarotti and Shannon was the oldest man in the party, the German. Kurt Semmler was forty, and it was he who, in the early days back in the enclave, had devised the skull-and-crossbones motif that the mercenaries and their African trainees wore. It was also he who had cleared a five-mile sector of Federal soldiers by marking out the front line with stakes, each bearing the head of one of the previous day's Federal casualties. For a month after that his was the quietest sector of the campaign. Born in 1930, he had been brought up in Germany through the Hitler period, the son of a Munich engineer who had later died on the Russian front with the Todt Organization. At the age of fifteen, a fervent Hitler Youth graduate, as indeed was almost the entire youth of the country after twelve years of Hitler, he had commanded a small unit of children younger than himself and old men over seventy. His mission had been to stop the columns of tanks of General George Patton, armed with one Panzerfaust and three bolt-action rifles. Not surprisingly he had failed, and spent his adolescence in a Bavaria under American occupation, which he hated. He also had little time for his mother, a religious maniac who wanted him to become a priest. At seventeen, he ran away, crossed the French frontier at Strasbourg, and signed on in the Foreign Legion at the recruiting office sited in Strasbourg for the purpose of picking up runaway Germans and Belgians. After a year in Siddi-bel-Abbès, he went with the expeditionary force to Indo-China. Eight years and Dien Bien Phu later, with a lung removed by surgeons at Toúrane (Danang), unable fortunately to watch the final humiliation in Hanoi, he was flown back to France. After recuperation he was sent to Algeria in 1958 as a top sergeant in the élite of the French colonial army, the 1st Regiment Étrangère Parachutiste. He was one of a handful who had already survived the utter destruction of the 1st REP twice in Indo-China, when it was at battalion size and later at regiment size. He revered only two men, Colonel Roger Faulques, who had been in the original Compagnie Étrangère Parachutiste when, at company strength, it had been wiped out the first time, and Commandant Le Bras, another veteran, who now commanded the Garde Republicaine of the Republic of Gabon, and kept that uranium-rich state safe for France. Even Colonel Marc Rodin, who had once commanded him, had lost his respect when the OAS finally crumbled.

Semmler had been in the 1st REP when it marched to a man into perdition in the *putsch* of Algiers and was later disbanded permanently by Charles de Gaulle. He had followed where his French officers had led, and later, picked up just after Algerian independence in Marseilles in September 1962, had served two years in prison. His four rows of campaign ribbons had saved him worse. Out in Civvy Street for the first time in twenty years in 1964, he had been contacted by a former cell-mate with a proposition – to join him in a smuggling operation in the Mediterranean. For three years, apart from one spent in an Italian jail, he had run spirits, gold, and occasionally arms, from one end of the Mediterranean to the other. Finally he had been making a fortune on the Italy–Yugoslavia cigarette run when his partner had double-crossed the buyers and the sellers at the same time, pointed the finger at Semmler and vanished with the money. Wanted by a lot of belligerent gentlemen, Semmler had hitched a lift by sea to Spain, ridden a series of buses to Lisbon, contacted an arms dealer friend and taken passage to the African war about which he had read in the papers. Shannon had taken him like a shot, for with sixteen years of combat he was more experienced than them all in jungle warfare. He too dozed on the flight to Libreville.

It was two hours before dawn when the DC-4 began to approach the airport. Above the muling of the children another sound could be made out, the sound of a man whistling. It was Shannon. His colleagues knew he always whistled when he was going into action or coming out of it. They also knew the name of the tune, because he had told them once. It was called 'Spanish Harlem'.

The DC-4 circled the airport at Libreville twice while Van Cleef talked to ground control. As the old cargo plane rolled to a halt at the end of a runway a military jeep carrying two French officers swerved up in front of the nose and they beckoned Van Cleef to follow them round the taxi track.

They led away from the main airport buildings to a cluster of huts on the far side of the airport and it was here that the DC-4 was signalled to halt but keep its engines running. Within seconds a set of steps was up against the rear of the airplane and from the inside the co-pilot heaved open the door. A kepi poked inside and surveyed the interior, the nose beneath it wrinkling in distaste at the smell. The French officer's eyes came to rest on the five mercenaries, and he beckoned them to follow him down the tarmac. When they were on the ground the officer gestured to the co-pilot to close the door, and without more ado the DC-4 moved forward again to roll round the airport to the main buildings where a team of French Red Cross nurses and doctors was waiting to receive the children and take them away to the pediatric clinic. As the aircraft swung past them the five mercenaries waved their thanks at Van Cleef up in his flight deck, and turned to follow the French officer.

They had to wait an hour in one of the huts, perched uncomfortably on upright wooden chairs, while several other young French servicemen peeked in through the door to take a look at '*les affreux*', the terrible ones, as they were called in French slang. Finally they heard a jeep squeal to a halt outside and the smack of feet coming to attention in the corridor. When the door finally opened, it was to admit a tanned, hard-faced senior officer in tropical fawn uniform and a kepi with gold braid ringing the peak. Shannon noticed the keen, darting eyes, the iron-grey hair cropped short beneath the kepi, the parachutist's wings pinned above the five rows of campaign ribbons and the sight of Semmler leaping to ramrod attention, chin up, five fingers pointing straight down what had once been the seams of his combat trousers. Shannon needed no more to tell him who the visitor was, the legendary Le Bras.

The Indo-China/Algeria veteran shook hands with each, pausing in front of Semmler longer.

'*Alors*, Semmler?' he said softly, with a slow smile. 'Still fighting. But not an adjutant any more. A captain now, I see.'

Semmler was embarrassed.

'*Oui mon commandant, pardon, colonel.* Just temporary.'

Le Bras nodded pensively several times. Then he addressed them all.

'I will have you quartered comfortably. No doubt you will appreciate a bath, a shave and some food. Apparently you have no other clothes; these will be provided. I am afraid for the time being you will have to remain confined to your quarters. This is solely a precaution. There are a lot of Press men in town, and all forms of contact with them must be avoided. As soon as it is feasible we will arrange to fly you back to Europe.'

He had said all he came to say, so he stopped. Raising his right hand to his kepi brim at the five rigid figures, he left.

An hour later, after a journey in a closed van and entrance by the back door, the men were in their quarters, the five bedrooms of the top floor of the Gamba Hotel, a new construction situated only five hundred yards from the airport building across the road, and therefore miles from the centre of town. The young officer who came with them told them they would have to take their meals on the same floor, and remain there until further notice. Within an hour he was back with towels, razors, toothpaste and brushes, soap and sponges. A tray of coffee had already arrived, and each man sank gratefully into a deep, steaming, soap-smelling bath, the first in over six months.

At noon an Army barber came, and a corporal with piles of slacks and shirts, vests, pants and socks, pyjamas and canvas shoes. They tried them on, selected the ones they wanted and the corporal retired with the surplus. The officer was back at one with four waiters bearing lunch, and told them they must stay away from the balconies. If they wanted to exercise in their confinement they would have to do it in their rooms. He would return that evening with a selection of books and magazines, though he could not promise English or Afrikaans.

After eating as never in the previous six months, since their last leave period from the fighting, the five men rolled into bed and slept. While they snored on unaccustomed mattresses and between unbelievable sheets, Van Cleef lifted his DC-4 off the tarmac in the dusk, flew a mile away past the windows of the Gamba Hotel and headed south for Caprivi and Johannesburg. His job too was over.

In fact the five mercenaries spent four weeks in the top floor of the hotel, while Press interest in them died down and the reporters were all called back to their head offices by editors who saw no point in keeping men in a city where there was no news to be had.

One evening, without warning, a French captain on the staff of Commandant Le Bras came to see them. He grinned broadly.

'Messieurs, I have news for you. You are flying out tonight. To Paris. You are all booked on the Air Afrique flight at 23.30 hours.'

The five men, bored to distraction by their prolonged confinement, cheered.

The flight to Paris took ten hours, with stops at Douala and Nice. Just before ten the following day they emerged into the blustery cold of Le Bourget airport on a mid-February morning. In the airport coffee lounge they made their good-byes. Dupree elected to take the transit coach to Orly and buy himself a single ticket on the next SAA flight to Johannesburg and Cape Town. Semmler opted to go with him and return to Munich for a visit at least. Vlaminck said he would head for the Gare du Nord and take the first express to Brussels and connect for Ostende. Langarotti was going to the Gare de Lyon to take the train to Marseilles.

'Let's stay in touch,' they said, and looked at Shannon. He was their leader, it would be up to him to look for work, another contract, another war. Similarly, if any of them heard anything that involved a group, he would want to contact one of the group, and Shannon was the obvious one.

'I'll stay in Paris for a while,' said Shannon. 'There's more chance of an interim job here than in London.'

So they exchanged addresses, *poste restante* addresses, or bars where the barman would pass on a message or keep a letter until the addressee dropped in for a drink. And then they parted and went their separate ways.

The security surrounding their flight back from Africa had been tight, for there were no waiting Press men. But someone had heard of their arrival, and he was waiting for Shannon when, after the others had left, the group's leader came out of the terminal building.

'Shannon.'

The voice pronounced the name in the French way, and the tone was not friendly. Shannon turned and his eyes narrowed fractionally as he saw the figure standing ten yards from him. The man was burly, with a down-turned moustache. He wore a heavy coat against the winter cold, and walked forward until the two men faced each other from two feet. To judge by the way they surveyed each other, there was no love lost between them.

'Roux,' said Shannon.

'So, you're back.'

'Yes. We're back.'

The Frenchman sneered. 'And you lost.'

'We didn't have much choice,' said Shannon.

'A word of advice, my friend,' snapped Roux. 'Go back to your own country. Do not stay here. It would be unwise. This is my city. If there is any contract to be found here, I will hear first news of it, I will conclude it. And I will select those who share in it.'

For answer Shannon walked to the first taxi waiting at the kerb and humped his grip into the back. Roux walked after him, his face mottling with anger.

'Listen to me, Shannon. I'm warning you ...'

The Irishman turned to face him again.

'No, you listen to me, Roux. I'll stay in Paris just as long as I want. I was never impressed by you in the Congo, and I'm not now. So get stuffed.'

As the taxi moved away, Roux stared after it angrily. He was muttering to himself as he strode towards the car park and his own automobile.

He switched on, engaged gear and sat for a few moments staring through the windscreen.

'One day I'll kill that bastard,' he murmured to himself. But the thought hardly put him in a better mood.

PART ONE
THE CRYSTAL MOUNTAIN

CHAPTER ONE

Jack Mulrooney shifted his bulk on the canvas and frame cot beneath the mosquito netting and watched the slow lightening of the darkness above the trees to the east. A faint paling, enough to make out the trees towering over the clearing. He drew on his cigarette and cursed the primeval jungle which surrounded him, and like all old Africa hands asked himself once again why he ever returned to the pestiferous continent.

If he had really tried to analyse it, he would have admitted he could not live anywhere else, certainly not in London or even Britain. He couldn't take the cities, the rules and regulations, the taxes, the cold. Like all old hands, he alternately loved and hated Africa, but conceded it had got into his blood over the past quarter century, along with the malaria, the whisky and the million insect stings and bites.

He had come out from England in 1945 at the age of twenty-five, after five years as a fitter in the Royal Air Force, part of them at Takoradi where he had assembled crated Spitfires for onward flight to East Africa and the Middle East the long way round. That was his first sight of Africa, and on demobilization he had taken his gratuity, bid good-bye to frozen, rationed London in December 1945 and taken ship for West Africa. Someone had told him there were fortunes to be made in Africa.

He had found no fortunes but after wandering the continent had got himself a small tin concession in the Benue Plateau, eighty miles from Jos in Nigeria. Prices had been good while the Malay emergency was on, and tin was expensive. He had worked alongside his Tiv labourers, and at the English club where the colonial ladies gossiped away the last days of empire they said he had 'gone native' and it was a 'damned bad show'. The truth was, Mulrooney really preferred the African way of life. He liked the bush, he liked the Africans who did not seem to mind that he swore and roared and cuffed them to get more work done. He also sat and took palm wine with them and observed the tribal taboos. He did not patronize them. His tin concession ran out in 1960 around the time of independence and he went to work as a charge-hand for a company running a larger and more efficient concession nearby. It was called Manson Consolidated, and when that concession was also exhausted in 1962 he was signed on the staff.

At fifty he was still a big, powerful man, large-boned and strong as an ox. His hands were enormous, chipped and scarred by years in the mines. He ran one of them through his wild, crinkly grey hair and with the other stubbed out the cigarette in the damp red earth beneath the cot. It was lighter now, soon it would be dawn. He could hear his cook blowing on the beginnings of a fire on the other side of the clearing.

Mulrooney called himself a mining engineer, although he had no degree in mining or engineering. He had done a course in both and added what no university could ever teach – twenty-five years of hard experience. He had burrowed for gold on the Rand and copper outside Ndola; drilled for precious water in Somaliland, grubbed for diamonds in Sierra Leone. He could tell an unsafe mine shaft by instinct and the presence of an ore deposit by the smell. At least, that was his claim and after he had taken his habitual twenty bottles of beer in the shanty town of an evening no one was going to argue the toss. In reality he was one of the last of the old prospectors. He knew that ManCon, as the company was known for short, gave him the little jobs, the ones in the deep bush, the wild hinterlands that were miles from civilization and still had to be checked out. But he liked it that way. He preferred to work alone; it was his way of life.

The latest job had certainly fulfilled these conditions. For three months he had been prospecting in the foothills of the range called the Crystal Mountains in the hinterland of the republic of Zangaro, a tiny enclave on the coast of West Africa.

He had been told where to concentrate his survey, around the Crystal Mountain itself. The chain of large hills, curved hummocks rising to two or three thousand feet, ran in a line from one side of the republic to the other, parallel to the coast and forty miles from it. The range divided the coastal plain from the hinterland. There was only one gap in the chain and through it ran the only road into the interior, and that was a narrow dirt road, baked like concrete in summer, a quagmire in winter. Beyond the mountains the natives were the Vindu, a tribe of almost Iron Age development, except that their implements were of wood. He had been in some wild places but vowed he had never seen anything as backward as the hinterland of Zangaro.

Set on the further side of the range of hills was the single mountain that gave its name to the rest. It was not even the biggest of them. Forty years earlier a lone missionary, penetrating the hills into the interior, branched to the south after following the gap in the range, and after twenty miles glimpsed a hill set aside from the rest. It had rained the previous night, a torrential downpour, one of the many that gave the area its annual rainfall of 300 inches during five soaking months. As the priest looked he saw that the mountain seemed to be glittering in the morning sun, and he called it the Crystal Mountain. He noted this in his diary. Two days later he was clubbed and eaten. The diary was found by a patrol of colonial soldiers a year later, used as a juju by a local village. The soldiers did their duty and wiped out the village, then returned to the coast and handed the diary to the mission society. Thus the name the priest had given to the mountain lived on, even if nothing else he did for an ungrateful world was remembered. Later the same name was given to the entire range of hills.

What the man had seen in the morning light was not crystal but a myriad of streams caused by the water of the night's rain cascading off the mountain. Rain was also cascading off all the other mountains, but the sight of it was hidden by the dense jungle vegetation that covered them all like a chunky green blanket when seen from afar and proved to be a steaming hell when penetrated. The one that glittered with a thousand rivulets did so because the vegetation was substantially thinner on the flanks of this hill. It never occurred to him, or to any of the other dozen white men who had never seen it, to wonder why.

After three months living in the steaming hell of the jungles that surrounded Crystal Mountain, Mulrooney knew why.

He had started by encircling the entire mountain and had discovered that there was effectively a gap between the seaward flank and the rest of the chain. This set the Crystal Mountain eastwards of the main chain, standing on its own. Because it was lower than the highest peaks to seaward, it was invisible from the other side. Nor was it particularly noticeable in any other way, except that it had more streams running off it per mile of hillside than the other hills to north and south.

Mulrooney counted them all, both on the Crystal Mountain and its companions. There was no doubt of it. The water ran off the other mountains after rain, but a lot of water was soaked up in the soil. The other mountains had twenty feet of topsoil over the basic rock structure beneath, the Crystal Mountain hardly any. He had his native workers, locally recruited Vindu, bore a series of holes with the auger he had with him, and confirmed the difference in depth of the topsoil in twenty places. From these he would work out why.

Over millions of years the earth had been formed by the decomposition of the rock and by dust carried on the wind, and although each rainfall had eroded some of it down the slopes into the streams, and from the streams to the rivers and thence to the shallow, silted estuary, some earth had also remained, lodged in little crannies, left alone by the running water which had bored its own holes in the soft rock. And these holes had become drains, so that part of the rainfall ran off the mountain, finding its own channels and wearing them deeper and deeper, and some had sunk into the mountain, both having the effect of leaving part of the topsoil intact. Thus the earth layer had built up and up, a little thicker each century or millennium. The birds and the wind had brought seeds, which had found the niches of earth and flourished there, their roots contributing to the process of retaining the earth on the hill slopes. When Mulrooney saw the hills, there was enough rich earth to sustain mighty trees and tangled vines which covered the slopes and the summits of all the hills. All except one.

On this one the water could not burrow channels that became streams, nor could it sink into the rock face, especially on the steepest face which was to the east, towards the hinterland. Here the earth had collected in pockets and the pockets had produced clumps of bush, grass and fern. From niche to niche the vegetation had reached out to itself, linking vines and tendrils in a thin screen across bare patches of rock, regularly washed clean by the falling water of the rain season. It was these patches of shimmering water amid the green that the missionary had seen before he died. The reason for the change was simple; the separate hill was of a different rock from the main range, an ancient rock hard as granite as compared to the soft more recent rocks of the main chain of hills.

Mulrooney had completed his circle of the mountain and established this beyond a doubt. It took him a fortnight to do it, and to establish that no less than seventy streams ran off the Crystal Mountain. Most of them joined up into three main streams that flowed away eastwards out of the foot hills into the deeper valley. He noticed something else. Along the banks of the streams that came off this mountain the soil colour was different, as was also the vegetation. Some plants appeared unaffected, others were non-existent although they flourished on the other mountains and beside the other streams. In general the vegetation was thinner beside the streams flowing off the Crystal Mountain than beside the others. This could not be explained by lack of soil, for there was plenty.

So there was something different about that earth, something that stunted plant life along the banks of the streams.

Mulrooney set about charting the seventy streams that took his interest, drawing his map as he went. He also took samples of the sand and gravel along the beds of the streams, starting with the surface gravel, then working down to bedrock.

In each case he took two buckets full of gravel, pouring them out onto a tarpaulin and coning and quartering. This is a process of sample-taking. He piled the gravel into a cone, then quartered it with a shovel blade, took the two opposite quarters of his choice, re-mixed them and made another cone. Then quartered that one, working down till he had a cross-section of the sample weighing two to three pounds. This went into a polythene-lined canvas bag after drying, the bag sealed and carefully labelled. In a month he had 1500 pounds of sand and gravel in six hundred bags from the beds of the seventy streams. Then he started on the mountain itself.

He already believed his sacks of gravel would prove to contain, under laboratory examination, quantities of alluvial tin, minute particles washed down from the mountain over tens of thousands of years, showing that there was cassiterite, or tin ore, buried in the Crystal Mountain.

He divided the mountain faces into sections, seeking to identify the birthplaces of the streams and the rock faces that fed them in the wet season. By the end of the week he knew there was no mother lode of tin inside the rock, but suspected what geologists call a disseminated deposit. The signs of mineralization were everywhere. Beneath the trailing tendrils of vegetation he found faces of rock shot through with stringers, half-inch wide veins like the capillaries in a drinker's nose, of milky white quartz, lacing yard after yard of bare rock face.

Everything he saw about him said 'Tin'. He went right round the mountain again three times, and his observations confirmed the disseminated deposit, the ever present stringers of white in the dark grey rock. With hammer and chisel he smashed holes deep in the rock and the picture was still the same. Sometimes he thought he saw dark blurs in the quartz, confirming the presence of tin.

Then he began chipping in earnest, marking his progress as he went. He took samples of the pure white stringers of quartz, and to be on the safe side he also took samples of the country rock, the rock between the veins. Three months after he had entered the primeval forest east of the mountains he was finished. He had another 1500 pounds of rock to carry back to the coast with him. The whole ton and a half of rock and alluvial samples had been carried in portions every three days back from his working camp to the main camp, where he now lay waiting for dawn, and stacked in cones under tarpaulins.

After coffee and breakfast the bearers, whose terms he had negotiated the previous day, would come from the village and carry his trophies back to the track that called itself a road and linked the hinterland with the coast. There, in a roadside village, lay his two-ton truck, immobilized by the lack of the key and distributor rotor that lay in his knapsack. It should still work, if the natives had not hacked it to bits. He had paid the village chief enough to look after it. With his samples aboard the lorry and twenty porters walking ahead to pull the lurching vehicle up the gradients and out of the ditches, he would be back in the capital in three days. After a cable to London he would have to wait several days for the company's chartered ship to come and take him off. He would have preferred to turn north at the coast highway and drive the extra hundred miles into the neighbouring republic where there was a proper airport, and freight his samples home. But the agreement between ManCon and the Zangaran government specified he would take it back to the capital.

Jack Mulrooney heaved himself out of his cot, swung aside the netting and roared at his cook, 'Hey, Dingaling, where's my bloody coffee?'

The Vindu cook who did not understand a word except 'coffee' grinned from beside the fire and waved happily. Mulrooney strode across the clearing towards his canvas wash bucket and began scratching as the mosquitoes descended on the sweating torso.

'Bloody Africa,' he muttered as he doused his face. But he was content that morning. He was convinced he had found both alluvial tin and tin-bearing rock. The only question was how much tin per rock-ton. With tin standing at about 3300 dollars per ton it would be up to the analysts and mining economists to work out if the quantity of tin per ton of rock merited establishing a mining camp with its complex machinery and teams of workers, not to mention improved access to the coast by a narrow-gauge railway that would have to be built from scratch. And it was certainly a God-forsaken and inaccessible place. As usual, everything would be worked out, taken up or thrown away, on the basis of pounds, shillings and pence. That was the way of the world. He slapped another mosquito off his upper arm and pulled on his tee-shirt.

Six days later Jack Mulrooney leaned over the rail of a small coaster, chartered by his company, and spat over the side as the coast of Zangaro slid away.

'Bloody bastards,' he muttered savagely. He carried a series of livid bruises about his chest and back, and a raw graze down one cheek, the outcome of swinging rifle butts when the troops had raided the hotel.

It had taken him two days to bring his samples from the deep bush to the truck, and another grunting, sweating day and night to haul the truck along the pitted and rutted earth road from the interior to the coast. In the wet he would never have made it, and in the dry season which had another month to run the concrete-hard mud ridges had nearly smashed the Mercedes to pieces. Three days earlier he had paid and dismissed his Vindu workers and trundled the creaking truck down the last stretch to the tarmac road which started only fourteen miles from the capital. From there it had been an hour to the city and the hotel.

Not that 'hotel' was the right word. Since the independence the town's main hostelry had degenerated into a flop-house, but it had a car park, and here he had parked and locked the truck, then sent his cable. He had only just been in time. Six hours after he sent it, all hell broke loose, and the port, airport and all other communications had been closed by order of the president.

The first he had known about it was when a group of soldiers, dressed like tramps and wielding rifles by the barrels, had burst into the hotel and started to ransack the rooms. There was no point in asking what they wanted, for they only screamed back in a lingo that meant nothing to him, though he thought he recognized the Vindu dialect he had heard his workers using over the past three months.

Being Mulrooney, he had taken two clubbings from rifle butts, then swung a fist. The blow carried the nearest soldier half-way down the hotel corridor on his back, and the rest of the pack had gone wild. It was only by the grace of God no shots were fired, and also due to the fact that the soldiers preferred to use their guns as clubs rather than search for complicated mechanisms like triggers and safety catches.

He had been dragged to the police barracks which were the nearest, and had been alternately screamed at and ignored in a subterranean cell for two days. If he did but know it, he had been lucky. A Swiss businessman, one of the rare foreign visitors to the republic, had witnessed his departure and feared for his life. The man had contacted the Swiss embassy, one of the only six European and North American embassies in the town, and they had contacted ManCon, whose name they had learned from the businessman, who in turn had looked through Mulrooney's belongings.

Two days later the called-for coaster had arrived from further up the coast and the Swiss consul had negotiated Mulrooney's release. No doubt a bribe had been paid, and no doubt ManCon would foot the bill. Jack Mulrooney was still aggrieved. On release he had found his lorry broken open and his samples strewn all over the car park. The rocks had all been marked and could be reassembled but the sand, gravel and chippings were mixed up. Fortunately each of the split bags, about fifty in all, had half their contents intact, so he had re-sealed them and taken them to the boat. Even here the customs men, police and soldiers had searched the boat from stem to stern, screamed and shouted at the crew, and all without saying what they were looking for.

The terrified official from the Swiss consulate who had taken Mulrooney back from the barracks to his hotel had told him there had been rumours of an attempt on the president's life and the troops were looking for a missing senior officer who was presumed to be responsible.

Four days after leaving the port of Clarence, Jack Mulrooney, still nursemaiding his rock samples, arrived back at Luton, England, aboard a chartered aircraft. A truck had taken his samples away for analysis at Watford, and after a checkout by the company doctor he had been allowed to start his three weeks' leave. He had gone to spend it with his sister in Dulwich, and within a week was thoroughly bored.

Exactly three weeks later to the day, Sir James Manson, Knight Commander of the British Empire, chairman and managing director of Manso Consolidated Mining Company Limited, leaned back in his leather armchair in the penthouse office suite on the tenth floor of his company's London headquarters, glanced once more at the report in front of him and breathed, 'Jesus Christ'. No one answered.

He rose from behind the broad desk, crossed the room to the picture windows on the south face, and gazed down at the sprawl of the City of London, the inner square mile of the ancient capital and heart of a financial empire that was still worldwide, despite what its detractors said. To some of the scuttling beetles in sombre grey, topped by black bowler hats, it was perhaps a place of employment only, boring, wearisome, exacting its toll of a man, his youth, his manhood, his middle age, until final retirement. For others, young and hopeful, it was a palace of opportunity, where merit and hard work were rewarded with the prizes of advancement and security. To romantics it was no doubt the home of the houses of the great merchant-adventurers, to a pragmatist the biggest market in the world, and to a left-wing trade unionist a place where the idle and worthless rich, born to wealth and privilege, lolled at ease in luxury. James Manson was a cynic and a pure realist. He knew what the City was; it was a jungle pure and simple, and in it he was one of the panthers.

A born predator, he had nevertheless realized early that there were certain rules that needed to be publicly revered and privately ripped to shreds; that, as in politics, there was only one commandment, the eleventh, 'Thou shalt not be found out.' It was by obeying the first requirement that he had acquired his knighthood in the New Year's Honours List a month before. This had been proposed by the Conservative Party (ostensibly for services to industry, but in reality for secret contributions to party funds for the general election), and accepted by the Wilson government because of his support for their policy on Nigeria. And it was by fulfilling the second requirement that he had made his fortune and why, holding twenty-five per cent of the stock of his own mining corporation, and occupying the penthouse floor, he was a millionaire several times over.

He was sixty-one, short, aggressive, built like a tank, with a thrusting vigour and a piratical ruthlessness that women found attractive and competitors feared. He had enough cunning to pretend to show respect for the establishments of both the City and the Realm, of commercial and political life, even though he was aware that both organs were riven through with men of almost complete moral unscrupulousness behind the public image. He had collected a few on his board of directors, including two former ministers in previous Conservative administrations. Neither was averse to a fat supplementary fee over and above director's salary, payable in the Cayman Islands or Grand Bahama, and one to his knowledge enjoyed the private diversion of waiting at table upon three or four leather-clad tarts, himself dressed in a maid's cap, a pinafore and a bright smile. Manson regarded both men as useful, possessing the advantage of considerable influence and superb connections without the inconvenience of integrity. The rest of the public knew both men as distinguished public servants. So James Manson was respectable within the set of rules of the City, a set of rules that had nothing whatever to do with the rest of humanity.

It had not always been so, which was why enquirers into his background found themselves up against one blank wall after another. Very little was known of his first start in life, and he knew enough to keep it that way. He would let it be known that he was the son of a Rhodesian train driver, brought up not far from the sprawling copper mines of Ndola, Northern Rhodesia, now Zambia. He would even let it be known that he had started work at the minehead as a boy, and later had made his first fortune in copper. But never how he had made it.

In fact he had quit the mines early, before he was twenty, and had realized that the men who risked their lives below ground amid roaring machinery would never make money, not big money. That lay above ground, and not even in mine management. As a teenager he had studied finance, the using and manipulating of money, and his nightly studies had taught him that more was made in shares in copper in a week than a miner made in his whole life.

He had started as a share-pusher on the Rand, had peddled a few illicit diamonds in his time, started a few rumours that set the punters reaching into their pockets, and sold a few worked-out claims to the gullible. That was where the first fortune came from. Just after the Second World War, at thirty-five, he was in London with the right connections for a copper-hungry Britain trying to get its industries back to work, and in 1948 had founded his own mining company. It had gone public in the mid-fifties and in fifteen years had developed worldwide interests. He was one of the first to see Harold Macmillan's wind of change blowing through Africa as independence for the black republics approached, and he took the trouble to meet and know most of the new power-hungry African politicians while most City businessmen were still deploring independence in the former colonies.

When he met the new men, it was a good match. They could see through his success story and he could see through their professed concern for their fellow blacks. They knew what he wanted and he knew what they wanted. So he fed their Swiss bank accounts and they gave Manson Consolidated mining concessions at prices below par for the course. ManCon prospered.

James Manson had also made several fortunes on the side. His latest was in the shares of the nickel-mining company in Australia called Poseidon. When Poseidon shares in late summer 1969 had been standing at four shillings, he had got a whisper that a survey team in central Australia might have found something on a stretch of land whose mining rights were owned by Poseidon. He had taken a gamble and paid out a very hefty sum to have a sneak preview of the first reports coming out of the interior. These reports said nickel, and lots of it. In fact nickel was not in shortage on the world market, but that never deterred the punters, and it was they who sent share prices spiralling, not investors.

He contacted his Swiss bank, an establishment so discreet that its only way of announcing its presence to the world was a small gold plate no larger than a visiting card, set into the wall beside a solid oak door in a small street in Zürich. Switzerland has no stockbrokers; the banks do all the investments. Manson instructed Dr Martin Steinhofer, the head of the Investments section of the Zwingli Bank, to buy on his behalf 5000 Poseidon shares. The Swiss banker contacted the prestigious London firm of Joseph Sebag & Co., in the name of Zwingli, and placed the order. Poseidon stood at five shillings a share when the deal was concluded.

The storm broke in late September when the size of the Australian nickel deposit became known. The shares began to rise, and, assisted by helpful rumours, the rising spiral became a rush. Sir James Manson had intended to start to sell when they reached £50 a share, but so vast was the rise that he held on. Finally he estimated the peak would be £115, and ordered Dr Steinhofer to start selling at £100 a share. This the discreet Swiss banker did, and had cleared the lot at an average of £103 for each share. In fact the peak was reached at £120 a share, before common sense began to prevail and the shares slid back to £10. Manson did not mind the extra £20, for he knew the time to sell was just before the peak when buyers were still plentiful. With all fees paid, he netted a cool £500,000, which was still stashed in the Zwingli Bank.

It happens to be illegal for a British citizen and resident to have a foreign bank account without informing the Treasury, and also to make half a million sterling profit in sixty days without paying capital gains tax on it. But Dr Steinhofer was a Swiss resident, and Dr Steinhofer would keep his mouth shut. That was what Swiss banks were for.

On that mid-February afternoon Sir James Manson strolled back to his desk, sat back in the lush leather chair behind the desk and glanced again at the report that lay on the blotter. It had arrived in a large envelope, sealed with wax and marked for his eyes only. It was signed at the bottom by Dr Gordon Chalmers, the head of ManCon's Department of Study,

Research, Geo-Mapping and Sample Analysis, situated outside London. It was the analyst's report on tests conducted on the samples a man called Mulrooney had apparently brought back from a place called Zangaro three weeks earlier.

Dr Chalmers did not waste words. The summary of the report was brief and to the point. Mulrooney had found a mountain, or a hill, with a peak some 1800 feet high above ground level and close to 100 yards across the base. It was set slightly apart from a range of such mountains in the hinterland of Zangaro. The hill contained a widely disseminated deposit of mineral in apparently evenly consistent presence throughout the rock, which was of igneous type and millions of years older than the sandstone and ragstone of the mountains that surrounded it.

Mulrooney had found numerous and ubiquitous stringers of quartz and had predicated the presence of tin. He had returned with samples of the quartz, the country rock surrounding it, and shingle from the beds of the streams surrounding the hill. The quartz stringers did indeed contain small quantities of tin. But it was the country rock that was interesting. Repeated and varied tests showed that this country rock, and the gravel samples, contained minor quantities of low-grade nickel. They also contained remarkable quantities of platinum. It was present in all the samples and was fairly evenly distributed. The richest rock in platinum known in this world was in the Rustenberg mines in South Africa, where concentrations of 'grades' ran as high as Point Two Five of a Troy ounce per rock ton. The average concentration in the Mulrooney samples was Point Eight One. 'I have the honour to remain, Sir, Yours etc ...'

Sir James Manson knew as well as anyone in mining that platinum was the third most precious metal in the world, and stood at a market price of 130 dollars a Troy ounce as he sat in his chair. He was also aware that with the growing world hunger for the stuff it had to rise to at least 150 dollars an ounce over the next three years, probably to 200 dollars within five years. It would be unlikely to rise to the 1968 peak price of 300 dollars again, because that was ridiculous.

He did some calculations on a scratch pad. Two hundred and fifty million cubic yards of rock at two tons per cubic yard was five hundred million tons. At even half an ounce per rock ton that was two hundred and fifty million ounces. If the revelation of a new world source dragged the price down to ninety dollars an ounce, and even if the inaccessibility of the place meant a cost of fifty dollars an ounce to get it out and refined, that still meant ...

Sir James Manson leaned back in his chair again and whistled softly.

'Jesus Christ. A ten-billion-dollar mountain.'

CHAPTER TWO

Platinum is a metal and like all metals it has its price. The price is basically controlled by two factors. These are the indispensability of the metal in certain processes that the industries of the world would like to complete, and the rarity of the metal. Platinum is very rare. Total world production each year, apart from stockpiled production which is kept secret by the producers, is a shade over one and a half million Troy ounces.

The overwhelming majority of it, probably over ninety-five per cent, comes from three sources: South Africa, Canada and Russia. Russia as usual is the uncooperative member of the group. The producers would like to keep the world price fairly steady so as to be able to make long-term investment planning in new mining equipment and development of new mines in the confidence that the bottom will not suddenly drop out of the market should a large quantity of stockpiled platinum suddenly be released. The Russians, by stockpiling unknown quantities and being able to release large quantities any time they feel like it, keep tremors running through the market whenever they can.

Russia releases each year about 350,000 Troy ounces on the world out of the 1,500,000 that reach the same market. This gives her between twenty-three and twenty-four percent of the market, enough to ensure her a considerable degree of influence. Her supplies are marketed through Soyuss Prom Export. Canada puts on the market some 200,000 ounces a year, the whole production coming from the nickel mines of International Nickel, and just about the whole of this supply is bought up each year by the Engelhardt Industries of the USA. But should the US need for platinum suddenly rise sharply, Canada might well not be able to furnish the extra quantity.

The third source is South Africa, turning out close to 950,000 ounces a year and dominating the market. Apart from the Impala mines, which were just opening when Sir James Manson sat considering the world position of platinum, and have since become very important, the giants of platinum are the Rustenberg mines, which account for well over half the world's production. These are controlled by Johannesburg Consolidated, who have a big enough slice of the stock to be sole managers of the mines. The world refiners and marketers of Rustenberg's supply was and is the London-based firm of Johnson-Matthey.

James Manson knew this as well as anyone else. Although he was not into platinum when Chalmer's report hit his desk, he knew the position as well as a brain surgeon knows how a heart works. He also knew why, even at that time, the boss of Engelhardt Industries of America, the colourful Charlie Engelhardt, better known to the populace as the owner of the fabulous racehorse Nijinsky, was buying into South African platinum. It was because America would need much more than Canada could supply by the mid-seventies. Manson was certain of it.

And the reason why American consumption of platinum was bound to rise, even treble, by the mid- to late-seventies lay in a piece of metal known as the motor car exhaust.

By the late 1960s the American smog problem had started to become a national issue. Words like 'air pollution', 'ecology', 'the environment', unheard ten years earlier, had jumped to every politician's lips and become the trendy, fashionable thing to be concerned about. The pressure was steadily mounting for legislation to limit, control and then reduce pollution, and thanks to Mr Ralph Nader the motor car became target number one. Manson was certain that the move would gain strength through the early seventies and that by 1975 or 1976 at the latest every American motor car would be fitted by law with a device for cleaning the exhaust fumes of their noxious gases. He also surmised that sooner or later cities like Tokyo, Madrid and Rome would have to follow suit. But California was the big one.

Motor car exhausts are composed of three ingredients, and each can be rendered harmless, two of them by a chemical process called oxidation and the third by another process called reduction. The process of reduction needs a substance called a catalyst, and that of oxidation can be achieved by either burning the gases at very high temperatures in excess air, or by burning them at low temperatures, such as exist in a car exhaust. Low-temperature burning also needs a catalyst, the same one as the reduction process. The only viable known catalyst is called platinum.

Sir James Manson could work out two things for himself. Although work was going on and would continue throughout the seventies on a car exhaust control device that relied on a catalyst of non-precious metal, no one was likely to come up with one that really worked before 1980. Thus a platinum-based catalytic exhaust control device would remain the only workable solution for a decade, and each device would need one tenth of an ounce of pure platinum.

The second was that when the United States passed legislation, as he felt it would have to do by 1975, requiring a control device that passed stringent tests to be fitted to all new cars from that year onwards, there would be a need for another one and a half million ounces of platinum every year. That was equivalent to doubling world production, and the Americans would not know where to get it.

James Manson thought he had an idea where. They could always buy it from him. And with the absolute indispensability of platinum in every fume control device established for a decade, and world demand far outstripping supply, the price would be nice, very nice indeed.

There was only one problem. He had to be absolutely certain that he, and no one else, would control all mining rights to the Crystal Mountain. The question was, how?

The normal way would be to visit the republic where the mountain was situated, seek an interview with the president, show him the survey report, and propose to him a deal whereby ManCon secured the mining rights, the government secured a profit-participation clause that would fill the coffers of their treasury, and the president would secure a fat and regular payment into his Swiss account. That would be the normal way.

But apart from the fact that any other mining company in the world, if advised of what lay inside the Crystal Mountain, would counter-bid for the same mining rights, sending the government's share up and Manson's down, there were three parties who more than any other would want to take control, either to begin production or stop it for ever. These were the South Africans, the Canadians and most of all the Russians. For the advent on the world market of a new massive supply source would cut the Soviet slice of the market back to the level of the unnecessary, removing from them their power, influence and money-making capacity in the platinum field.

Manson had a vague recollection of having heard the name of Zangaro, but it was such an obscure place he realized he knew nothing about it. The first requirement was evidently to learn more. He leaned forward and depressed the intercom switch.

'Miss Cooke, would you come in, please.'

He had called her Miss Cooke throughout the seven years she had been his personal and private secretary, and even in the ten years before that, when she had been an ordinary company secretary, rising from the typing pool to the tenth floor, no one had ever suggested she might have a first name. In fact she had. It was Marjory. But she just did not seem the sort of person one called Marjory.

Certainly men had once called her Marjory, long ago, before the war, when she was a young girl. Perhaps they had even tried to flirt with her, pinch her bottom, those long thirty-five years ago. But that was then. Five years of war, hauling an ambulance through burning rubble-strewn streets, trying to forget a Guardsman who never came back from Dunkirk, and twenty years nursing a crippled and whining mother, a bed-ridden tyrant using tears for weapons, had taken away the youth and the pinchable qualities of Miss Marjory Cooke. At fifty-four, tailored, efficient and severe, her work at ManCon was almost all her life, the tenth floor her fulfilment, and the terrier who shared her neat apartment in suburban Chigwell and slept on her bed, her child and lover.

So no one ever called her Marjory. The young executives called her a shrivelled apple, and the secretary birds 'that old bat'. The others, including her employer Sir James Manson, about whom she knew more than she would ever tell him or anyone else, called her Miss Cooke. She entered through the door set in the beech-panelled wall which, when closed, looked like part of the wall.

'Miss Cooke, it has come to my attention that we have had, during the past few months, a small survey – one man I believe – in the republic of Zangaro.'

'Yes, Sir James. That's right.'

'Oh, you know about it.'

Of course she knew about it. Miss Cooke never forgot anything that had crossed her desk.

'Yes, Sir James.'

'Good. Then please find out for me who secured that government's permission for us to conduct the survey.'

'It will be on file, Sir James. I'll go and look.'

She was back in ten minutes, having first checked in her daily diary appointments book, cross indexed into two indices, one under personal names and the other under subject headings, and then confirmed with Personnel.

'It was Mr Bryant, Sir James.' She consulted a card in her hand. 'Richard Bryant, of Overseas Contracts.'

'He submitted a report, I suppose?' asked Sir James.

'He must have done, under normal company procedure.'

'Send me in his report, would you, Miss Cooke?'

She was gone again, and the head of ManCon stared out through the plate-glass windows across the room from his desk at the mid-afternoon dusk settling over the City of London. The lights were coming on in the middle level floors – they had been on all day in the lowest ones – but at skyline level there was still enough winter daylight to see by. But not to read by. Sir James Manson flicked on the reading lamp on his desk as Miss Cooke returned, laid the report he wanted on his blotter and receded back against the wall.

The report Richard Bryant had submitted was dated six months earlier and was written in the terse style favoured by the company. It recorded that according to instructions from the head of Overseas Contracts, he had flown to Clarence, the capital of Zangaro, and there, after a frustrating week in a hotel, had secured an interview with the Minister of Natural Resources. There were three separate interviews spaced over six days, and at length, an agreement had been reached that a single representative of ManCon might enter the republic to conduct a survey for minerals in the hinterland beyond the Crystal Mountains. The area to be surveyed was deliberately left vague by the company, so that the survey team could travel more or less where it wished. After further haggling during which it was made plain to the Minister that he could forget any idea that the company was prepared to pay the sort of fee he seemed to expect, and that there were no indications of mineral presence to work on, a sum had been agreed between Bryant and the Minister. Inevitably, the sum on the contract was just over half the total that changed hands, the balance being paid into the Minister's private account.

That was all. The only indication about the character of the place was in the reference to a corrupt minister. So what, thought Sir James Manson, nowadays Bryant might have been in Washington. Only the going rate was different.

He leaned forward to the intercom again.

'Tell Mr Bryant of Overseas Contracts to come up and see me, would you, Miss Cooke?'

He lifted the switch and pressed another one.

'Martin, come in a minute, please.'

It took Martin Thorpe two minutes to come from his office on the ninth floor. He did not look the part of a financial whizz-kid and protégé of one of the most ruthless go-getters in a traditionally ruthless and go-getting industry. He looked more like the captain of the athletics team from a good public school, charming, boyish, clean-cut, with dark wavy hair and deep blue eyes. The secretaries called him dishy and the directors who had seen stock options they were certain of whisked out from under their noses or found their companies slipping into control of a series of nominee shareholders fronting for Martin Thorpe called him something not quite so nice.

Despite the looks, Thorpe had never been either a public school man, or an athlete and certainly not captain of the team. He could not differentiate between a batting average and the ambient air temperature, but he could retain the hourly movement of share prices across the range of ManCon's subsidiary companies in his head throughout the day. At twenty-nine he had ambitions and the intent to carry them out. ManCon and Sir James Manson might provide the means, so far as he was concerned, and his loyalty depended on his exceptionally high salary, the contacts throughout the City that his job under Manson could bring him, and the knowledge that where he was constituted a good vantage point for spotting what he called 'the big one'.

By the time he entered Sir James had slipped the Zangaro report into a drawer and the Bryant report alone lay on his blotter.

He gave his protégé a friendly smile.

'Martin, I've got a job I need doing with some discretion. I need it done in a hurry and it might take half the night.'

It was not Sir James' way to ask if Thorpe had got any engagements that evening. Thorpe knew that, it went with the high salary.

'That's OK, Sir James. I had nothing on that a phone call can't kill.'

'Good. Look, I've been going over some old reports and come across this one. Six months ago one of our men from Overseas Contracts was sent out to a place called Zangaro. I don't know why, but I'd like to. The man secured that government's go-ahead for a small team from here to conduct a survey for any possible mineral deposits in uncharted land beyond the mountain range called the Crystal Mountains. Now, what I want to know is this: was it ever mentioned in advance or at the time, or since that visit six months ago, to the Board?'

'To the Board?'

'That's right. Was it ever mentioned to the Board of directors that we were doing any such survey? That's what I want to know. It may not necessarily be on the agenda. You'll have to look at the minutes. And in case it got a passing mention under "any other business", check through the documents of all Board meetings over the past twelve months. Secondly, find out who authorized the visit by Bryant six months ago and why, and who sent the survey engineer down there and why. The man who did the survey is called Mulrooney. I also want to know something about him, which you can get from his file in Personnel. Got it?'

Thorpe was surprised. This was way out of his line of country.

'Yes, Sir James, but Miss Cooke could do that in half the time, or get somebody to do it ...'

'Yes, she could. But I want you to do it. If you look at a file from Personnel, or board-room documents, it will be assumed it has something to do with finance. Therefore it will remain discreet.'

The light began to dawn on Martin Thorpe.

'You mean ... They found something down there, Sir James?'

Manson stared out at the now inky sky and the blazing sea of lights below him as the brokers and traders, clerks and merchants, bankers and assessors, insurers and jobbers, buyers and sellers, lawyers and, in some offices no doubt, law-breakers, worked on through the winter afternoon towards the witching hour of five-thirty.

'Never mind,' he said gruffly to the young man behind him. 'Just do it.'

Martin Thorpe was grinning as he slipped through the back entrance of the office and down the stairs to his own premises.

'Cunning bastard,' he said to himself on the stairs.

Sir James Manson turned as the intercom broke the double-glazed, sound-proofed calm of the inner sanctum.

'Mr Bryant is here, Sir James.'

Manson crossed the room, switching on the main lights as he passed near the wall switch. Reaching his desk he depressed the switch.

'Send him in, Miss Cooke.'

There were three reasons why middle-level executives had occasion to be summoned to the sanctum on the tenth floor. One was to hear instructions or deliver a report that Sir James wanted to issue or hear personally, which was business. One was to be chewed into a sweat-soaked rag, which was hell. The third was when the chief executive decided he wanted to play favourite uncle to his cherished employees, which was reassuring.

On the threshold Richard Bryant, at thirty-nine a middle-level executive who did his work competently and well, but needed his job, was plainly aware the first reason of the three could not be the one that brought him here. He suspected the second and was immensely relieved to see it had to be the third.

From the centre of the office Sir James walked towards him with a smile of welcome.

'Ah, come in, Bryant. Come in.'

As Bryant entered Miss Cooke closed the door behind him and retired to her desk.

Sir James Manson gestured his employee to one of the easy chairs set well away from the desk in the conference area of the spacious office. Bryant, still wondering what it was all about, took the indicated chair and sank into its brushed suede cushions. Manson advanced towards the wall and opened two doors, revealing a well-stocked bar cabinet.

'Take a drink, Bryant? Sun's well down, I think.'

'Thank you, sir, er ... Scotch, please.'

'Good man. My own favourite poison. I'll join you.'

Bryant glanced at his watch. It was quarter to five, and the tropical maxim about taking a drink after the sun has gone down was hardly coined for London winter afternoons. But he recalled an office party at which Sir James had snorted his derision of sherry drinkers and the like, and spent the evening on Scotch. It pays to watch things like that, Bryant reflected, as his chief poured two fine old crystal glasses of his special Glenlivet. Of course he left the ice bucket strictly alone.

'Water? Dash of soda?' he called from the bar. Bryant craned round and spotted the bottle.

'Is that a single malt, Sir James? No thank you, straight as it comes.'

Manson nodded several times in approval, and brought the glasses over. They 'Cheersed' each other and savoured the whisky. Bryant was still waiting for the conversation to start. Manson noted this and gave him the gruff uncle look.

'No need to worry about me having you up here like this,' he began. 'I was just going through a sheaf of old reports in my desk drawers, and came across yours, or one of them. Must have read it at the time and forgotten to give it back to Miss Cooke for filing ...'

'My report?' queried Bryant.

'Eh? Yes, yes, the one you filed after your return from that place, what's it called again? Zangaro? Was that it?'

'Oh, yes, sir. Zangaro. That was six months ago.'

'Yes, quite so. Six months, of course. Noticed as I re-read it that you'd had a bit of a rough time with that Minister fellow.'

Bryant began to relax. The room was warm, the chair extremely comfortable, and the whisky like an old friend. He smiled at the memory.

'But I got the contract for survey permission.'

'Damn right you did,' congratulated Sir James. He smiled as if at fond memories. 'I used to do that in the old days, y'know. Went on some rough missions to bring home the bacon. Never went to West Africa, though. Not in those days. Went later of course. But after all this started.'

To indicate 'all this' he waved his hand at the luxurious office.

'So nowadays I spend too much time up here buried in paperwork,' Sir James continued. 'I even envy you younger chaps going off to clinch deals in the old way. So tell me about your Zangaro trip.'

'Well, that really was doing things the old way. After a few hours in the place I half expected to find people running around with bones through their noses,' said Bryant.

'Really? Good Lord. Rough place is it, this Zangaro?'

Sir James Manson's head had tilted back into the shadows, and Bryant was sufficiently comfortable not to catch the gleam of concentration in the eye that belied the encouraging tone of voice.

'Too right, Sir James. It's a bloody shambles of a place, moving steadily backwards into the middle ages since independence five years ago.'

He recalled something else he had heard his chief say once in an aside remark to a group of executives.

'It's a classic example of the concept that most of the African republics today have thrown up power groups whose performance in power simply cannot justify their entitlement to leadership of a corporation garbage depot. As a result, of course, it's the ordinary people who suffer.'

Sir James, who was as capable as the next man of recognizing his own words when he heard them played back at him, smiled, rose and walked to the window to look down at the teeming streets below.

'So who does run the show out there?' he asked quietly.

'The president. Or rather the dictator,' said Bryant from his chair. His glass was empty. 'A man called Jean Kimba. He won the first and only election just before independence five years ago against the wishes of the colonial power, some said by the use of terrorism and voodoo on the voters. They're pretty backward, you know. Most of them didn't know what a vote was. Now they don't need to know.'

'Tough guy, is he, this Kimba?' asked Sir James.

'It's not that he's tough, sir. He's just downright mad. A raving megalomaniac, and probably a paranoid to boot. He rules completely alone, surrounded by a small coterie of political yes-men. If they fall out with him, or arouse his suspicions in any way, they go into the cells of the old colonial police barracks. Rumour has it Kimba goes down there himself to supervise the torture sessions. No one has ever come out alive.'

'H'm, what a world we live in, Bryant. And they've got the same number of votes at the United Nations as Britain or America. Whose advice does he listen to in government?'

'No one of his own people. Of course, he has his voices. So the few local whites say, those who've stuck it out by staying on.'

'Voices?' queried Sir James.

'Yes, sir. He claims to the people he is guided by divine voices. He says he talks to God. He's told the people and the assembled diplomatic corps that in so many words.'

'Oh dear, not another,' mused Manson, still gazing down at the streets below. 'I sometimes think it was a mistake to introduce the Africans to God. Half their leaders now seem to be on first name terms with him.'

'Apart from that, he rules by a sort of mesmeric fear. The people think he has a powerful juju, or voodoo, or magic or whatever. He holds them in the most abject terror of him personally.'

'What about the foreign embassies?' queried the man by the window.

'Well, sir, they keep themselves to themselves. It seems they are just as terrified of the excesses of this maniac as the natives. He's a bit like a cross between Sheikh Abeid Karume in Zanzibar, Papa Doc Duvalier in Haiti, and Sekou Touré in Guinea.'

Sir James turned smoothly from the window and asked with deceptive softness, 'Why Sekou Touré?'

Bryant was in his own element, expounding his carefully acquired knowledge of political Africa, glad to be able to show his employer he did long hours of homework.

'Well, he's next best thing to a Communist, Sir James. The man he really worshipped all his political life was Lumumba. That's why the Russians are so strong. They have an enormous embassy, for the size of the place. To earn foreign currency, now that the plantations have all failed through maladministration, they sell most of their produce to the Russian trawlers that call. Of course the trawlers are electronic spy ships or victualling ships for submarines they meet offshore and re-victual with fresh produce. Again, the money they get from the sale doesn't go to the people, it goes into Kimba's bank account.'

'It doesn't sound like Marxism to me,' joked Manson.

Bryant grinned widely.

'Money and bribes are where the Marxism stops,' he replied. 'As usual.'

'But the Russians are strong, are they? Influential? Another whisky, Bryant?'

While Bryant replied, the head of ManCon poured two more glasses of Glenlivet.

'Yes, Sir James. Kimba has virtually no understanding of matters outside his immediate experience, which has been exclusively inside his own country and maybe a couple of visits to other African states nearby. So he sometimes consults on matters when dealing with outside concerns. Then he uses any one of three advisers, black ones, who come from his own tribe. Two Moscow-trained, and one Peking-trained. Or he contacts the Russians direct. I spoke to a trader in the bar of the hotel one night, a Frenchman. He said the Russian ambassador or one of his counsellors was at the palace almost every day.'

Bryant stayed for another ten minutes, but Manson had learned most of what he needed to know. At five-twenty he ushered Bryant out as smoothly as he had welcomed him. As the younger man left, Manson beckoned Miss Cooke in.

'We employ an engineer in mineral exploration work called Jack Mulrooney,' he said. 'He returned from a three-month sortie into Africa, living in rough bush conditions, three months ago, so he may be on leave still. Try and get him at home. I'd like to see him at ten tomorrow morning. Secondly, Dr Gordon Chalmers, the chief survey analyst. You may catch him at Watford before he leaves the laboratory. If not, reach him at home. I'd like him here at twelve tomorrow. Cancel any other morning appointments and leave me time to take Chalmers out for a spot of lunch. And you'd better book me a table at Wilton's in Bury Street. That's all, thank you. I'll be on my way in a few minutes. Have a car round at the front in ten minutes.'

When Miss Cooke withdrew, Manson pressed one of the switches on his intercom and murmured, 'Come up for a minute, would you, Simon.'

Simon Endean was as deceptive as Martin Thorpe but in a different way. He came from an impeccable background, and behind the veneer had the morals of an East End thug. Going with the polish and the ruthlessness was a certain cleverness. He needed a James Manson to serve, just as James

Manson would sooner or later on his way to the top, or his struggle to stay there in big-time capitalism, need the services of a Simon Endean.

Endean was the sort to be found by the score in the very smartest and smoothest of London's West End gambling clubs, beautifully spoken hatchet men who never leave a millionaire unbowed to, or a showgirl unbruised. The difference was that Endean's intelligence had brought him to an executive position as aide to the chief of a very superior gambling club.

Unlike Thorpe he had no ambitions to become a multi-millionaire. He thought one million would do, and until then the shadow of Manson would suffice. It paid for the six-room pad, the Corvette, the girls. He too came from the floor below and entered from the interior stairwell through the beech-panelled door across the office from the one Miss Cooke came and left by.

'Sir James?'

'Simon, tomorrow I'm having lunch with a fellow called Gordon Chalmers. One of the back-room boys. The chief scientist and head of the laboratory out at Watford. He'll be here at twelve. Before then I want a run-down on him. The personnel file of course, but anything else you can find. The private man, what his home life is like, any failings; above all, if he has any pressing need of money over and above his salary. His politics, if any. Most of these scientific people are Left. Not all though. You might have a chat with Errington in Personnel tonight before he leaves. Go through the file tonight and leave it for me to look at in the morning. Sharp tomorrow start on his home environment. Phone me not later than 11.45. Got it? I know it's a short-notice job, but it could be important.'

Endean took in the instructions without moving a muscle, filing the lot. He knew the score; Sir James Manson often needed information, for he never faced any man, friend or foe, without a personal run-down on the man including the private life. Several times he had beaten opponents into submission by being better prepared. Endean nodded and left, making his way straight to Personnel, an office which by chance Martin Thorpe had only just left. But they did not cross paths.

As his chauffeur-driven Rolls-Royce slid away from the front of ManCon House, taking its occupant back to his third-floor apartment in Arlington House behind the Ritz, a long hot bath, and a dinner sent up from the Caprice, Sir James Manson leaned back and lit his first cigar of the evening. The chauffeur handed him a late *Evening Standard* and they were abreast of Charing Cross station when a small paragraph in the Stop Press caught his eye. It was in among the racing results. He glanced back at it, then read it several times. He stared out at the swirling traffic and huddled pedestrians, shuffling towards the station, or plodding to the buses through the February drizzle, bound for their homes in Edenbridge and Sevenoaks, after another exciting day in the City.

As he stared a small germ of an idea began to form in his mind. Another man would have laughed and dismissed it out of hand. Sir James Manson was not another man. He was a twentieth-century pirate and proud of it.

The 9-point type headline above the obscure paragraph in the evening paper referred to an African republic. It was not Zangaro, but another one. He had hardly heard of the other one either. It had no known mineral wealth. The headline said:

'New *Coup D'État* in African state.'

CHAPTER THREE

Martin Thorpe was waiting in his chief's outer office when Sir James arrived at five past nine, and followed him straight in.

'What have you got?' demanded Sir James Manson, even while he was taking off his vicuña topcoat and hanging it in the built-in wardrobe. Thorpe flicked open a notebook he had pulled from his pocket and recited the result of his investigations of the night before.

'One year ago we had a survey team in the republic lying to the north and east of Zangaro. It was accompanied by an aerial reconnaissance unit hired from a French firm. The area to be surveyed was close to, and partly on the border with, Zangaro. Unfortunately there are few topographical maps of that area, and no aerial maps at all. Without Decca or any other form of beacon to give him cross-bearings, the pilot used speed and time of flight to assess the ground he had covered.

'One day when there was a following wind stronger than forecast he flew up and down the entire strip to be covered by aerial survey to his own satisfaction and returned to base. What he did not know was that on each downwind leg he had flown over the border and forty miles into Zangaro. When the aerial film was developed it showed that he had overshot the survey by a large margin.'

'Who first realized it? The French company?' asked Manson.

'No, sir. They developed the film and passed it to us without comment, as per our contract with them. It was up to the men in our own aerial survey department to identify the areas on the ground represented by the pictures they had. Then they realized that at the end of each run was a stretch of territory not in the survey area. So they discarded the pictures, or at any rate put them on one side. They had realized that in one section of pictures a range of hills was featured that could not be in our survey area because there were no hills in that part of the area.

'Then one bright spark had a second look at the surplus photographs and noticed a part of the hilly area, slightly to the east of the main range, had a variation in the density and type of the plant life. The sort of thing you can't see down on the ground but an aerial picture from three miles up will show it up like a beermat on a billiard table.'

'I know how it's done,' growled Sir James. 'Go on.'

'Sorry, sir, I didn't know this. It was new to me. So anyway half a dozen photos were passed to someone in the Photo-Geology section, and he confirmed from a blow-up that the plant life was different over quite a small area involving a small hill about 1800 feet high and roughly conical in shape. Both sections prepared a report, and that went to the head of Topographic section. He identified the range as the Crystal Mountains and the hill as probably the original Crystal Mountain. He sent the file to Overseas Contracts and Willoughby, the head of OC, sent Bryant down there to get permission to survey.'

'He didn't tell me,' said Manson, now seated behind his desk.

'He sent a memo, Sir James. I have it here. You were in Canada at the time and were not due back for a month. He makes plain he felt the survey of that area was only an off-chance, but since a free aerial survey had been presented to us, and since Photo-Geology felt there had to be some reason for the different vegetation, the expense could be justified. Willoughby also suggested it might serve to give this man Bryant a bit of experience to go it alone for the first time. Up till then he had always accompanied Willoughby.'

'Is that it?'

'Almost. Bryant got visa-ed up and went in six months ago. He got permission and arrived back after three weeks. Four months ago Ground Survey agreed to detach an unqualified prospector-cum-surveyor called Jack Mulrooney from the diggings in Ghana and send him in to look over the Crystal Mountains provided that the cost would be kept low. It was. He got back three weeks ago with a ton and a half of samples, which have been at the Watford laboratory ever since.'

'Fair enough,' said Sir James Manson after a pause. 'Now, did the Board ever hear about all this?'

'No, sir.' Thorpe was adamant. 'It would have been considered much too small. I've been through every Board meeting for twelve months, and every document presented, including every memo and letter sent to the Board members over the same period. Not a mention of it. The budget for the whole thing would simply have been lost in the petty cash anyway. And it didn't originate with Projects, because the aerial photos were a gift from the French firm and their ropy old navigator. It was just an *ad hoc* affair throughout, and never reached board level.'

James Manson nodded in evident satisfaction.

'Right. Now Mulrooney. How bright is he?'

For answer Thorpe tended Jack Mulrooney's file from Personnel.

'No qualifications, but a lot of practical experience, sir. An old sweat. A good Africa hand.'

Manson flicked through the file on Jack Mulrooney, scanned the biography notes and the career sheet since the man had joined the company.

'He's experienced all right,' grunted Manson. 'Don't underestimate the old Africa hands. I started out in the Rand, on a mining camp. Mulrooney just stayed at that level. So don't mock, lad, such people are very useful. And they can be perceptive.'

He dismissed Martin Thorpe and muttered to himself, 'Now let's see how perceptive Mr Mulrooney can be.'

He depressed the intercom switch and spoke to Miss Cooke.

'Is Mr Mulrooney there yet, Miss Cooke?'

'Yes, Sir James, he's here waiting.'

'Show him in, please.'

Manson was half-way to the door when his employee was ushered in. He greeted him warmly and led him to the chairs where he had sat with Bryant the previous evening. Before she left Miss Cooke was asked to produce coffee for them both. Mulrooney's coffee habit was on his file.

Jack Mulrooney in the penthouse suite of a London office block looked as out of place as Thorpe would have done in the dense bush. His hands hung way out of his coat sleeves and he did not seem to know where to put them. His grey hair was plastered down with water and he had cut himself shaving. It was the first time he had ever met the man he called the gaffer. Sir James used all his efforts to put the man at ease.

When Miss Cooke entered with a tray of porcelain cups, matching coffee pot, cream jug and sugar bowl, and an array of Fortnum and Mason Biscuits, she heard her employer telling the Irishman, '... that's just the point, man. You've got what I or anyone else can't teach these boys fresh out of college. Twenty-five years' hard-won experience getting the bloody stuff out of the ground and into the skips.'

It was always nice to be appreciated, and Jack Mulrooney was no exception. He beamed and nodded. When Miss Cooke had gone Sir James Manson gestured at the cups.

'Look at these poofy things. Used to drink out of a good mug. Now they give me thimbles. I remember back on the Rand in the late thirties, and that would be before your time, even ...'

Mulrooney stayed for an hour. When he left he felt the gaffer was a damn good man despite all they said about him. Sir James Manson thought Mulrooney was a damn good man – at his job at any rate, and that was and would always be chipping bits of rock off hills and asking no questions.

Just before he left Mulrooney had reiterated his view.

'There's tin down there, Sir James. Stake my life on it. The only thing is, whether it can be got out at an economic figure.'

Sir James had slapped him on the shoulder.

'Don't you worry about that. We'll know as soon as the report comes through from Watford. And don't worry, if there's an ounce of it that I can get to the coast below market value, we'll have the stuff. Now how about you? What's your next adventure?'

'I don't know, sir. I have three more days leave yet, then I report back to the office.'

'Like to go abroad again?' beamed Sir James.

'Yes, sir. Frankly, I can't take this city and the weather and all.'

'Back to the sun, eh? You like the wild places, I hear.'

'Yes, I do. You can be your own man out there.'

'You can indeed,' smiled Manson. 'You can indeed. I almost envy you. No, dammit, I *do* envy you. Anyway, we'll see what we can do.'

Two minutes later Jack Mulrooney was gone. Manson ordered Miss Cooke to send his file back to Personnel, rang Accounts and instructed them to send Mulrooney a £1000 merit bonus and make sure he got it before the following Monday, and rang the head of Ground Survey.

'What surveys have you got pending in the next few days or just started?' he asked without preamble.

There were three, one of them in a remote stretch of the extreme north of Kenya, close to the Somaliland border, where the midday sun fries the brain like an egg in a pan, the nights freeze the bone marrow like Blackpool rock, and the shifta bandits prowl. It would be a long job, close to a year. He had nearly had two resignations trying to get a man to go there for so long.

'Send Mulrooney,' said Sir James and hung up.

He glanced at the clock. It was eleven. He picked up the personnel report on Dr Gordon Chalmers, which Endean had left on his desk the previous evening.

Chalmers was a graduate with honours from the London School of Mining, which is probably the best of its kind in the world, even if Witwatersrand likes to dispute that claim. He had taken his degree in geology and later chemistry and gone on to a doctorate in his mid-twenties. After five years of fellowship work at the college he had joined Rio Tinto Zinc in their scientific section and six years earlier ManCon had evidently poached him from RTZ for a better salary. For the last four years he had been head of the company's scientific department situated on the outskirts of Watford in Hertfordshire. The passport-size photograph in the file showed a man in his late thirties glowering at the camera over a bushy ginger beard. He wore a tweed jacket and a purple shirt. The tie was of knitted wool and askew.

At 11.35 the private phone rang and Sir James Manson heard the regular pips of a public coin box at the other end of the line. A coin clunked into the slot and Endean's voice came on the line. He spoke concisely for two minutes from Watford station. When he had finished, Manson grunted his approval.

'That's useful to know,' he said. 'Now get back to London. There's another job I want you to do. I want a complete run-down on the republic of Zangaro. I want the lot. Yes, Zangaro.' He spelt it out.

'Start back in the days when it was discovered, and work forwards. I want the history, geography, lie of the land, economy, crops, mineralogy if any, politics and state of development. Concentrate on the ten years prior to independence, and especially the period since. I want to know everything there is to know about the president, his cabinet, parliament if any, administration, executive, judiciary and political parties. There are three things that are more important than all else. One is the question of Russian or Chinese involvement and influence, or local Communist influence on the president. The second is that no one remotely connected with the place is to know any questions are being asked, so don't go there yourself, and thirdly under no circumstances are you to announce you come from ManCon. So use a different name. Got it? Good, well, report back as soon as you can and not later than twenty days. Draw cash from Accounts on my signature alone, and be discreet. For the record, consider yourself on leave; I'll let you make it up later.'

Manson hung up and called down to Thorpe to give further instructions. Within three minutes Thorpe came up to the tenth floor and laid the piece of paper his chief wanted on the desk. It was the carbon copy of a letter.

Ten floors down Dr Gordon Chalmers stepped out of his taxi at the corner of Moorgate and paid it off. He felt uncomfortable in a dark suit and topcoat, but Peggy had told him it was necessary for an interview and lunch with the Chairman of the Board.

As he walked the last few yards toward the steps and doorway of ManCon House his eye caught a poster fronting the kiosk of a seller of the *Evening News* and *Evening Standard*. What was written on the poster caused him to curl his lip in a bitter sneer but he bought both papers. The news was not the headline, but was on an inside page. The poster said simply: 'Thalidomide Parents Urge Settlement'.

The story backed up the headline in greater detail, though it was not long. It recorded that after another marathon round of talks between representatives of the parents of the 400-odd children in Britain who had been born deformed because of the thalidomide drug ten years earlier, and the company that had marketed the drug, a further impasse had been reached. So talks would be resumed 'at a later date'.

Gordon Chalmers's thoughts went back to the house outside Watford that he had left earlier that same morning, to Peggy his wife, just turned thirty and looking forty, and to Margaret, legless, one-armed Margaret, coming up to nine years, in need of a special pair of legs, a specially built house which they now lived in at long last, the mortgage on which was costing him a fortune.

'At a later date,' he snapped to no one in particular and stuffed the newspapers into a wall-basket. He seldom read the evening papers anyway. He preferred the *Guardian*, *Private Eye* and the left-wing *Tribune*. After nearly ten years of watching a group of almost unmoneyed parents try to face down the giant Distillers for their compensation, Gordon Chalmers harboured bitter thoughts about big-time capitalists. Ten minutes later he was facing one of the biggest.

Sir James Manson could not put Chalmers off his guard as he had Bryant and Mulrooney. The scientist clutched his glass of beer firmly and stared right back. Manson grasped the situation quickly and when Miss Cooke had handed him his whisky and retired, he came to the point.

'I suppose you can guess what I asked you to come and see me about, Dr Chalmers.'

'I can guess, Sir James. The report on Crystal Mountain.'

'That's it. Incidentally, you were quite right to send it to me personally in a sealed envelope. Quite right.'

Chalmers shrugged. He had done it because he realized that all important analysis results had to go direct to the chairman according to company policy. It was routine, as soon as he had realized what the samples contained.

'Let me ask you two things, and I need specific answers,' said Sir James. 'Are you absolutely certain of these results? There could be no other possible explanation of the tests on the samples?'

Chalmers was neither shocked nor affronted. He knew the work of scientists was seldom accepted by laymen as being far removed from black magic, and therefore imprecise. He had long since ceased trying to explain the precision of his craft.

'Absolutely certain. For one thing there are a variety of tests to establish the presence of platinum and these samples passed them all with unvarying regularity. For another, I not only did all the known tests on every one of the samples, I did the whole thing twice. Theoretically it is possible someone could have interfered with the alluvial samples, but not with the internal structures of the rocks themselves. The summary of my report is accurate beyond scientific dispute.'

Sir James Manson listened to the lecture with head-bowed respect, and nodded in admiration.

'And the second thing is, how many other people in your laboratory know of the results of the analysis of the Crystal Mountain samples?'

'No one,' said Chalmers with finality.

'No one?' echoed Manson. 'Come now, surely one of your assistants ...'

Chalmers downed a swig of his beer and shook his head.

'Sir James, when the samples came in they were crated as usual and put in store. Mulrooney's accompanying report predicated the presence of tin in unknown quantities. As it was a very minor survey, I put a junior assistant onto it. Being inexperienced he assumed tin or nothing, and did the appropriate tests. When they failed to show up positive, he called me over and pointed this out. I offered to show him how, and again the tests were negative. So I gave him a lecture on not being mesmerized by the prospector's opinion and showed him some more tests. These too were negative. The laboratory closed for the night, but I stayed on late, so I was alone in the place when the first tests came up positive. By midnight I knew the shingle sample from the stream bed, of which I was using less than half a pound, contained small quantities of platinum. After that I locked up for the night.

'The next day I took the junior off that assignment and put him on another. Then I went on with it myself. There were 600 bags of shingle and gravel, and 1500 pounds weight of rocks, over 300 separate rocks taken from different places on the mountain. From Mulrooney's photographs I could picture the mountain. The disseminated deposit is present in all parts of the formation. As I said in my report.'

With a touch of defiance he drained his beer.

Sir James Manson continued nodding, staring at the scientist with well-feigned awe.

'It's incredible,' he said at length. 'I know you scientists like to remain detached, impartial, but I think even you must have become excited. This could form a whole new world source of platinum. You know how often that happens with a rare metal? Once in a decade, maybe once in a lifetime ...'

In fact Chalmers had been excited by his discovery, and had worked late into the night for three weeks to cover every single bag and rock from the Crystal Mountain, but he would not admit it. Instead he shrugged and said:

'Well, it'll certainly be very profitable for ManCon.'

'Not necessarily,' said James Manson quietly. This was the first time he shook Chalmers.

'Not?' queried the analyst. 'But surely it's a fortune?'

'A fortune in the ground, yes,' replied Sir James, rising and walking to the window. 'But it depends very much who gets it, if anyone at all. You see, there is a danger it could be kept unmined for years, or mined and stockpiled. Let me put you in the picture, my dear Doctor ...'

He put Dr Chalmers in the picture for thirty minutes, talking finance and politics, neither of which was the analyst's forte.

'So there you are,' he finished. 'The chances are it will be handed on a plate to the Russian government if we announce it immediately.'

Dr Chalmers, who had nothing particularly against the Russian government, shrugged slightly.

'I can't change the facts, Sir James.'

Manson's eyebrows shot up in horror.

'Good gracious, Doctor, of course you can't.' He glanced at his watch in surprise. 'Close to one,' he exclaimed, 'you must be hungry. I know I am. Let's go and have a spot of lunch.'

He had thought of taking the Rolls, but after Endean's phone call from Watford that morning and the information from the local newsagent about the regular subscription to *Tribune*, he opted for an ordinary taxi.

A spot of lunch proved to be pâté, truffled omelette, jugged hare in red wine sauce and trifle. As Manson had suspected Chalmers disapproved of such indulgence but at the same time had a healthy appetite. And even he could not reverse the simple laws of nature, which are that a good meal produces a sense of repletion, contentment, euphoria and a lowering of moral resistance. Manson had also counted on a beer drinker being unused to the fuller red wines, and two bottles of Côte du Rhône had encouraged Chalmers to talk about the subjects that interested him, his work, his family and his views on the world.

It was when he touched on his family and their new house that Sir James Manson, looking suitably sorrowful, mentioned that he recalled having seen Chalmers in a television interview in the street a year back.

'Do forgive me,' he said, 'I hadn't realized before ... I mean, about your little girl ... what a tragedy.'

Chalmers nodded and gazed at the tablecloth. Slowly at first, and then with more confidence, he began to tell his superior about Margaret.

'You wouldn't understand,' he said at one point.

'I can try,' replied Sir James quietly. 'I have a daughter myself, you know. Of course, she's older.'

Ten minutes later there was a pause in the talking. Sir James Manson drew a folded piece of paper from his inside pocket.

'I don't really know how to put this,' he said with some embarrassment, 'but ... well, I am as aware as any man how much time and trouble you put in for the company. I am aware you work long hours, and the strain of this personal matter must have its effect on you, and no doubt on Mrs Chalmers. So I issued this instruction to my personal bank this morning.'

He passed the carbon copy of the letter across to Chalmers who read it. It was brief and to the point. It instructed the manager of Coutts Bank to remit by registered mail each month on the first day fifteen banknotes, each of value £10, to Dr Gordon Chalmers at his home address. The remittances were to run for ten years unless further instructions were received.

Chalmers looked up. His employer's face was all concern, tinged with embarrassment.

'Thank you,' said Chalmers softly.

Sir James's hand rested on his forearm and shook it.

'Now come on, that's enough of this matter. Have a brandy.'

In the taxi on the way back to the office Manson suggested he drop Chalmers off at the station where he could take his train for Watford.

'I have to get back to the office and get on with this Zangaro business and your report,' he said.

Chalmers was staring out of the cab window at the traffic moving out of London that Friday afternoon.

'What *are* you going to do about it?' he asked.

'Don't know, really. Of course, I'd like not to send it. Pity to see all that going into foreign hands, which is what must happen when your report gets to Zangaro. But I've got to send them something, sooner or later.'

There was another long pause as the taxi swung into the station forecourt.

'Is there anything I can do?' asked the scientist.

Sir James Manson breathed a long sigh.

'Yes,' he said in measured tones. 'Junk the Mulrooney samples in the same way as you would junk any other rocks and bags of sand. Destroy your analysis notes completely. Take your copy of the report and make an exact copy, with one difference – let it show the tests prove conclusively there exist marginal quantities of low-grade tin which could not be economically mined. Burn your own copy of the original report. And then never mention a word of it.'

The taxi came to a halt, and as neither of his passengers moved the cabby poked his nose through the screen into the rear compartment.

'This is it, guv.'

'You have my solemn word,' murmured Sir James Manson. 'Sooner or later the political situation may well change, and when that happens ManCon will put in a tender for the mining concession exactly as usual and in accordance with normal business procedures.'

Dr Chalmers climbed out of the taxi and looked back at his employer in the corner seat.

'I'm not sure I can do that, sir,' he said. 'I'll have to think it over.'

Manson nodded.

'Of course you will. I know it's asking a lot. Look, why don't you talk it over with your wife. I'm sure she'll understand.'

Then he pulled the door to, and told the cabby to take him to the City.

Sir James dined with an official of the Foreign Office that evening and took him to his club. It was not one of the very upper-crust clubs of London, for Manson had no intention of putting up for one of the bastions of the old Establishment and finding himself blackballed. Besides, he had no time for social climbing and little patience with the posturing idiots one found at the top when one got there. He left the social side of things to his wife. The knighthood was useful, but that was an end to it.

He despised Adrian Goole, whom he reckoned for a pedantic fool. That was why he had invited him to dinner. That, and the fact that the man was in the Economic Intelligence section of the FO.

Years ago, when his company's activities in Ghana and Nigeria had reached a certain level, he had accepted a place on the inner circle of the City's West Africa Committee. This organ was and still is a sort of trade union of all major firms based in London and carrying on operations in West Africa. Concerned far more with trade and therefore money than, for example, the East Africa Committee, the WAC periodically reviewed events of both commercial and political interest in West Africa, and usually the two were bound to become connected in the long term, and tendered advice to the Foreign and Commonwealth Office on what would in their view constitute an advisable policy for British interests.

Sir James Manson would not have put it that way. He would have said they were in existence to suggest to the government what to do in that part of the world to improve profits. He would have been right, too. He had been on the committee during the Nigerian civil war and heard the various representatives of banks, mines, oil and trade advocate a quick end to the war, which seemed to be synonymous with a Federal victory in double time.

Predictably the committee had proposed to the government that the Federal side be supported provided they could show they were going to win and win quickly, and provided corroborative evidence from British sources on the spot confirmed this. They then sat back and watched the government on Foreign Office advice make another monumental African cock-up. Instead of lasting six months it had lasted thirty. And Harold Wilson, once committed to a policy, was no more going to concede his minions might have made a mistake on his behalf than fly to the moon.

Manson had lost a lot in revenue from his disrupted mining interests and the impossibility of shipping the stuff to the coast on crazily-running railways throughout the period, but MacFazdean of Shell-BP had lost a lot more in oil production.

Adrian Goole had been the FO's liaison officer on the committee for most of the time. Now he sat opposite James Manson in the alcove dining recess, his cuffs shot the right inch and a quarter, his face registering earnest intent.

Manson told him some of the truth, but kept the reference to platinum out of it. He stuck to a tale of tin, but increased the quantities. It would have been viable to mine it, of course, but quite frankly he'd been scared off by the close dependence of the president on the Russian advisers. The profit-participation of the Zangaran government could well have made them a tidy sum, and therefore more powerful, and since the despot was almost a puppet of the Russkies, who wanted to increase the republic's power and influence through wealth? Goole took it all in. His face was a solemn expression of deep concern.

'Damnably difficult decision,' he said with sympathy. 'Mind you, I have to admire your political sense. At the moment Zangaro is bankrupt and obscure. But if it became rich ... yes, you're quite right. A real dilemma. When do you have to send them the survey report and analysis?'

'Sooner or later,' grunted Manson. 'The question is, what do I do about it? If they show it to the Russians at the embassy, the trade counsellor is bound to realize the tin deposits are viable. Then it will go out for tender. So someone else will get it, still help to make the dictator rich, and then who knows what problems he'll make for the West? One is back to square one.'

Goole thought it over for a while.

'I just thought I ought to let you chaps know,' said Manson.

'Yes, yes, thank you.' Goole was absorbed. 'Tell me,' he said at length, 'what would happen if you halved the figures showing the quantity of tin per rock-ton in the report?'

'Halved them?'

'Yes. Halved the figures, showing a purity figure of tin per rock-ton of fifty per cent the figures shown by your rock samples?'

'Well, the quantity of tin present would be shown to be economically unviable.'

'And the rock samples could have come from another area a mile away, for example?' asked Goole.

'Yes, I suppose they could. But my surveyor found the richest rock samples.'

'But if he had not done so,' pursued Goole. 'If he had taken his samples from a mile from where he actually operated. The content could be down by fifty per cent?'

'Yes, they could. They probably would, probably would show even less than fifty per cent. But he operated where he did.'

'Under supervision?' asked Goole.

'No. Alone.'

'And there are no real traces of where he worked?'

'No,' replied Manson. 'Just a few rock chippings, long since overgrown. Besides, no one goes up there. It's miles from anywhere.'

He paused for a few instances to light a cigar.

'You know, Goole, you're a damnably clever fellow. Steward, another brandy if you please.'

They parted with mutual jocularity on the steps of the club. The doorman hailed a taxi for Goole to go back to Mrs Goole in Holland Park.

'One last thing,' said the FO man by the taxi door, 'not a word to anyone else about this. I'll have to file it, well classified, at the department, but otherwise it remains just between you and us at the FO.'

'Of course,' said Manson.

'I'm very grateful you saw fit to tell me all this. You have no idea how much easier it makes our job on the economic side to know what's going on. I'll keep a quiet eye on Zangaro and if there should be a change in the political scene there, you'll be the first to know. Good night.'

Sir James Manson watched the taxi head down the road and signalled to his Rolls-Royce waiting up the street.

'You'll be the first to know,' he mimicked. 'Too bloody right I will, boy. 'Cause I'm going to start it.'

He leaned through the passenger side window to see Craddock, his chauffeur, behind the wheel.

'If pisswilly little buggers like that had been in charge of building our empire, Craddock, we might by now just about have colonized the Isle of Wight.'

'You're absolutely right, Sir James,' said Craddock.

When his employer had climbed into the rear, the chauffeur slid open the communicating panel.

'Gloucestershire, Sir James?'

'Gloucestershire, Craddock.'

It was starting to drizzle again as the sleek limousine swished down Piccadilly and up Park Lane heading for the A40 and the West Country, carrying Sir James Manson towards his ten-bedroomed mansion, bought three years earlier for him by a grateful company for £250,000. It also contained his wife and nineteen-year-old daughter, but these he had won himself.

An hour later Gordon Chalmers lay beside his wife, tired and angry from the row they had had for the past two hours. Peggy Chalmers lay on her back looking up at the ceiling.

'I can't do it,' Chalmers said for the umpteenth time. 'I can't just go and falsify a mining report to help James Bloody Manson make more money.'

There was a long silence. They had been over it all a score of times since Peggy had read Manson's letter to his banker and heard from her husband the conditions of future financial security.

'What does it matter?' she said in a low voice from the darkness beside him. 'When all's said and done, what does it matter? Whether he gets the concession, or the Russians, or no one. Whether the price rises or falls. What does it matter? It's all pieces of rock and grains of metal.'

Peggy Chalmers swung herself across her husband's torso and stared at the dim outline of his face. Outside, the night wind rattled the branches of the old elm close to which they had built the new house with the special fitments for their crippled daughter.

When Peggy Chalmers spoke again it was with passionate urgency.

'But Margaret is not a piece of rock, and I am not a few grains of metal. We need that money, Gordon, we need it now and for the next ten years. Please, darling, please, just one time forget the idea of a nice letter to *Tribune* or *Private Eye*, and do what he wants.'

Gordon Chalmers continued to stare at the slit of window between the curtains, half-opened to let in a breath of air.

'All right,' he said at length.

'You'll do it?' she asked.

'Yes, I'll bloody do it.'

'You swear it, darling? You give me your word?'

There was another long pause.

'You have my word,' said the low voice from the face above her. She pillowed her head in the hair of his chest.

'Thank you, darling. Don't worry about it. Please don't worry. You'll forget it in a month. You'll see.'

Ten minutes later she was asleep, exhausted by the nightly struggle to get Margaret bathed and into bed, and by the unaccustomed row with her husband. Gordon Chalmers continued to stare into the darkness.

'They always win,' he said softly and bitterly after a while. 'The bastards, they always bloody win.'

The following day, Saturday, he drove the five miles to the laboratory and wrote out a completely new report for the republic of Zangaro. Then he burned his notes and the original report, and trundled the core samples over to the scrap-heap where a local builder would remove it for concrete and garden paths. He posted the fresh report, registered post, to Sir James Manson at head office, went home and tried to forget it.

On Monday the report was received in London and the instructions to the banker in Chalmers's favour were posted. The report was sent down to Overseas Contracts for Willoughby and Bryant to read, and Bryant was told to leave the next day and take it to the Minister of Natural Resources in Clarence. A letter from the company would be attached, expressing the appropriate regret.

On Tuesday evening, Richard Bryant found himself in Number One Building at London's Heathrow airport waiting for a BEA flight to Paris where he could get the appropriate visa and make a connecting flight by Air Afrique. Five hundred yards away in Three Building Jack Mulrooney humped his grip through passport control to catch the BOAC overnight Jumbo to

Nairobi. He was not unhappy. He had had enough of London. Ahead lay Kenya, sun, bush and the chance of a lion.

By the end of the week only two men had in their heads the knowledge of what really lay inside the Crystal Mountain. One had given his word to his wife to remain silent for ever, and the other was plotting his next move.

CHAPTER FOUR

Simon Endean entered Sir James Manson's office with a bulky file containing his hundred-page report on the republic of Zangaro, a dossier of large photographs and several maps. He told his chief what he had brought. Manson nodded in approval.

'No one learned while you were putting all this together who you were or who you worked for?' he asked.

'No, Sir James. I used a pseudonym, and no one questioned it.'

'And no one in Zangaro could have learned that a file of data could have been put together about them?'

'No. I used existing archives, sparse though they are, some university libraries here and in Europe, standard works of reference, and the one tourist guide published by Zangaro itself, although in fact this is a left-over from colonial days and five years out of date. I always claimed I was simply seeking information for a graduate thesis on the entire African colonial and post-colonial situation. There will be no come-backs.'

'All right,' said Manson. 'I'll read the report later. Give me the main facts.'

For answer Endean took one of the maps from the file and spread it across the desk. It showed that section of the African coastline with Zangaro marked.

'As you see, Sir James, it's stuck like an enclave on the coast here, bordered on the north and east by this republic and on the short southern border by this one. The fourth side is the sea, here.

'It's shaped like a match-box, the short edge along the sea coast, the longer sides stretching inland. The borders were completely arbitrarily drawn in the old colonial days during the scramble for Africa, and merely represent lines on a map. On the ground there are no effective borders, and due to the almost complete non-existence of roads there is only one border crossing point – here, on the road leading north to the neighbour country. All land traffic enters and leaves by this road.'

Sir James Manson studied the enclave on the map and grunted.

'What about the eastern and southern borders?'

'No road, sir. No way in or out at all, unless you cut straight through the jungle, and in most places it is impenetrable bush.

'Now, in size it has 7000 square miles, being seventy miles along the coast and 100 miles deep into the hinterland. The capital, Clarence, named after the sea captain who first put in there for fresh water two hundred years ago, is here – in the centre of the coast, thirty-five miles from the northern and southern borders.

'Behind the capital lies a narrow coastal plain which is the only cultivated area in the country, apart from the bush natives' tiny clearings in the jungle. Behind the plain lies the river Zangaro, then the foothills of the Crystal Mountains, the mountains themselves and, beyond that, miles and miles of jungle up to the eastern border.'

'How about other communications?' asked Manson.

'There are virtually no roads at all,' said Endean. 'The river Zangaro flows from the northern border fairly close to the coast across most of the republic until it reaches the sea just short of the southern border. On the estuary there are a few jetties and a shanty or two which constitute a small port for the exporting of timber. But there are no wharves, and the timber businesses have virtually ceased since independence. The fact that the Zangaro river flows almost parallel to the coast, slanting in towards it, for sixty miles, in effect cuts the republic in two; there is this strip of coastal plain seawards side of the river, ending in mangrove swamps which make the whole coast unapproachable by shipping or small boats, and the hinterland beyond the river. East of the river are the mountains and beyond them the hinterland. The river could be used for barge traffic, but no one is interested. The republic to the north has a modern capital on the coast with a deep-water harbour, and the Zangaro river itself ends up in a silted-up estuary.'

'What about the timber-exporting operations? How were they carried out?'

Endean took a larger scale map of the republic out of the file and laid it on the table. With a pencil he tapped the Zangaro estuary in the south of Zangaro.

'The timber used to be cut upcountry, either along the banks or in the western foothills of the mountains. There's still quite good timber there, but since independence no one is interested. The logs were floated downriver to the estuary and parked there. When the ships came they would anchor offshore and the log rafts were towed out to them by powered boats. Then they hoisted the logs aboard by using their own derricks. It always was a tiny operation.'

Manson stared intently at the large-scale map, taking in the seventy miles of coast, the river running almost parallel to it, twenty miles inland, the strip of impenetrable mangrove swamp between the coast and the sea, and the mountains behind the river. He could identify the Crystal Mountain, but made no mention of it.

'What about the main roads? There must be some.'

Endean warmed to his explanation.

'The capital is stuck on the seaward end of a short, stubby peninsula here, midway down the coast. It faces towards the open sea. There's a small port, the only real one in the country, and behind the town the peninsula runs back to join the main land mass. There is one road which runs down the spine of the peninsula and six miles inland, going straight east. Then there is the junction – here. A road runs to the right, heading south. It is laterite for seven miles, then becomes an earth road for the next twenty. Then it peters out on the banks of the Zangaro estuary.

'The other branch turns left and runs north, through the plain west of the river and onwards to the northern border. Here there is a crossing point, manned by a dozen sleepy and corrupt soldiers. A couple of travellers told me they can't read a passport anyway, so they don't know whether there is a visa in it or not. You just bribe them a couple of quid to get through.'

'What about the road into the hinterland?' asked Sir James.

Endean pointed with his finger. 'It's not even marked, it's so small. Actually, if you follow the north-running road after the junction, go along it for ten miles, there is a turn-off to the right, towards the hinterland. It's an earth road. It crosses the remainder of the plain and then the Zangaro river, on a rickety wooden bridge ...'

'So that bridge is the only communication between the two parts of the country either side of the river?' asked Manson in wonderment.

Endean shrugged. 'It's the only crossing for wheeled traffic. But there is hardly any wheeled traffic. The natives cross the Zangaro by canoe.'

Manson changed the subject, though his eyes never left the map.

'What about the tribes who live there?' he asked.

'There are two,' said Endean. 'East of the river and right back to the end of the hinterland is the country of the Vindu. For that matter, more Vindu live over the eastern border. I said the borders are arbitrary. The Vindu are practically in the stone age. They seldom if ever cross the river and leave their bush country. The plain to the west of the river and down to the sea, including the peninsula on which the capital stands, is the country of the Caja. They hate the Vindu and vice versa.'

'Population?'

'Almost uncountable in the interior. Officially put at 220,000 in the entire country. That is, 30,000 Caja and an estimated 190,000 Vindu. But the numbers are a total guess, except probably the Caja can be counted accurately.'

'Then how the hell did they ever hold an election?' asked Manson.

'That remains one of the mysteries of creation,' said Endean. 'It was a shambles anyway. Half of them didn't know what a vote was or what they were voting for.'

'What about the economy?'

'There is hardly any left,' replied Endean. 'The Vindu country produces nothing. The lot of them just about subsist on what they can grow in yam and cassava plots cut out of the bush by the women, who do any work there is to be done, which is precious little. Unless you pay them well, then they will carry things. The men hunt. The children are a mass of malaria, trachoma, bilharzia and malnutrition.

'In the coastal plain there were in colonial days plantations of low-grade cocoa, coffee, cotton and bananas. These were run and owned by whites, using native labour. It wasn't high quality stuff, but it made enough with a guaranteed European buyer, the colonial power, to make a bit of hard currency and pay for the minimal imports. Since independence these were nationalized by the president, who expelled the whites, and given to his party hacks. Now they're about finished, overgrown with weeds.'

'Got any figures?'

'Yes, sir. In the last year before independence total cocoa output, that was the main crop, was 30,000 tons. Last year it was 100 tons, and there were no buyers. It's still rotting on the ground.'

'And the others, coffee, cotton, bananas?'

'Bananas and coffee virtually ground to a halt through lack of attention. Cotton got hit by a blight and there were no insecticides.'

'What's the economic situation now?'

'Total disaster. Bankrupt, money worthless paper, exports down to almost nothing, and nobody letting them have any imports. There have been gifts from the UN, the Russians and the former colonial power, but as the government always sells the stuff elsewhere and pockets the cash, even these three have given up.'

'A real banana republic, eh?' murmured Sir James.

'In every sense. Corrupt, vicious, brutal. They have seas off the coast rich in fish, but they can't fish. The two fishing boats they had were skippered by whites. One got beaten up by the army thugs, and both quit. Then the engines rusted up, and they were abandoned. So the locals have protein deficiency. There aren't enough goats and chickens to go round.'

'What about medicines?'

'There's one hospital in Clarence which is run by the United Nations. That's the only one in the country.'

'Doctors?'

'There were two Zangarans who were qualified doctors. One was arrested and died in prison. The other fled into exile. The missionaries were expelled by the president as imperialist influences. They were mainly medical missionaries as well as preachers and priests. The nuns used to train up nurses, but they got expelled as well.'

'How many Europeans?'

'In the hinterland, probably none. In the coastal plains, a couple of agronomists, technicians sent by the United Nations. In the capital, about forty diplomats, twenty of them in the Russian embassy, the rest spread between the French, Swiss, American, West German, East German, Czech and Chinese embassies, if you call the Chinese white. Apart from that, about five United Nations hospital staff, another five technicians manning the electrical generator, the airport control tower, the waterworks and so on. Then there must be fifty others, traders, managers, businessmen who have hung on hoping for an improvement.

'Actually, there was a ruckus six weeks ago and one of the UN men was beaten half to death. The five non-medical technicians threatened to quit and sought refuge in their respective embassies. They may be gone by now, in which case the water, electricity and airport will soon be out of commission.'

'Where is the airport?'

'Here, on the base of the peninsula behind the capital. It's not of international standard, so if you want to fly in you have to take Air Afrique to here, in the republic to the north, and take a connecting flight by a small two-engined plane that goes down to Clarence three times a week. It's a French firm that has the concession, though nowadays it's hardly economic.'

'Who are the country's friends, diplomatically speaking?'

Endean shook his head.

'They don't have any. No one is interested, it's such a shambles. Even the Organization of African Unity is embarrassed by the whole place. It's so obscure no one ever mentions it. No Pressmen ever go, so it never gets publicized. The government is rabidly anti-white, so no one wants to send staff men down there to run anything. No one invests anything, because nothing is safe from confiscation by any Tom, Dick or Harry wearing a party badge. There's a party youth organization that beats up anyone it wants to, and everyone lives in terror.'

'What about the Russians?'

'They have the biggest mission and probably a bit of say over the president in matters of foreign policy about which he knows nothing. His advisers are mainly Moscow-trained Zangarans, though he wasn't schooled in Moscow personally.'

'Is there any potential at all down there?' asked Sir James. Endean nodded slowly.

'I suppose there is enough potential, well managed and worked, to sustain the population at a reasonable degree of prosperity. The population is small, the needs few, they could be self-sufficient in food, clothing, the basics of a good local economy, with a little hard currency to the necessary extras. It could be done, but, in any case, the needs are so few the relief and charitable agencies could provide the total necessary, if it wasn't that their staff are always molested, their equipment smashed or looted, and their gifts stolen and sold for the government's private profit.'

'You say the Vindu won't work hard. What about the Caja?'

'Nor they either,' said Endean. 'They just sit about all day, or fade into the bush if anyone looks threatening. Their fertile plain has always grown enough to sustain them, so they are happy the way they are.'

'Then who worked the estates in the colonial days?'

'Ah, the colonial power brought in about 20,000 black workers from elsewhere. They settled and live there still. With their families they are about 50,000. But they were never enfranchised by the colonial power, so they never voted in the election at independence. If there is any work done, they still do it.'

'Where do they live?' asked Manson.

'About 15,000 still live in their huts on the estates, even though there is no more work worth doing, with all the machinery broken down. The rest have drifted towards Clarence and grub a living as best they can. They live in a series of shanty towns scattered down the road at the back of the capital, on the road to the airport.'

For five minutes Sir James Manson stared at the map in front of him, thinking deeply about a mountain, a mad president, a coterie of Moscow-trained advisers and a Russian embassy. Finally he sighed.

'What a bloody shambles of a place.'

'That's putting it mildly,' said Endean. 'They still have ritual public executions before the assembled populace in the main square. Death by being chopped to pieces with a machete. Quite a bunch.'

'And who precisely has produced this paradise on earth?'

For answer Endean produced a photograph and placed it on the map.

Sir James Manson found himself looking at a middle-aged African in a silk top-hat, black frock-coat and sponge-bag trousers. It was evidently inauguration day, for several colonial officials stood in the background, by the steps of a large mansion. The face beneath the shining black silk was not round, but long and gaunt, with deep lines each side of the nose. The mouth was twisted downwards at each corner so that the effect was of deep disapproval of something. But the eyes held the attention. There was a glazed fixity about them, as one sees in the eyes of fanatics.

'That's the man,' said Endean. 'Mad as a hatter, and nasty as a rattlesnake. West Africa's own Papa Doc. Visionary, communicant with spirits, liberator from the white man's yoke, redeemer of his people, swindler, robber, police chief and torturer of the suspicious, extractor of confessions, hearer of voices from the Almighty, seer of visions, Lord High Everything Else, His Excellency President Jean Kimba.'

Sir James Manson stared longer at the face of the man who, unknown to himself, was sitting in control of ten billion dollars-worth of platinum.

'I wonder,' he thought to himself, 'if the world would really notice his passing on?'

He said nothing, but after listening to Endean, that event was what he had decided to arrange.

Six years earlier the colonial power ruling the enclave now called Zangaro, increasingly conscious of world opinion, had decided to grant independence. Over-hasty preparations were made among a population wholly inexperienced in self-government, and the events of a general election and independence were fixed for the following year.

In the confusion five political parties came into being. Two were wholly tribal, one claiming to look after the interests of the Vindu, the other of the Caja. The other three parties devised their own political platforms and pretended to make appeal through the tribal division of the people. One of these parties was the conservative group, led by a man holding office under the colonialists and heavily favoured by them. He pledged he would continue the close links with the mother country which, apart from anything else, guaranteed the local paper money and bought the exportable produce. The second party was centrist, small and weak, led by an intellectual, a professor who had qualified in Europe. The third was radical, and led by a man who had served several terms in prison under a security classification. This was Jean Kimba.

Long before the elections two of his aides, men who during their time as students in Europe had been contacted by the Russians who had noticed their presence in anti-colonial street demonstrations, and who had accepted bursaries to finish their schooling at the Patrice Lumumba University outside Moscow, left Zangaro secretly and flew to Europe. There they met emissaries from Moscow, and as a result of their conversations received a sum of money and considerable advice of a very practical nature.

Using the money, Kimba and his men formed squads of political thugs from among the Vindu, and completely ignored the small minority of Caja. In the unpoliced hinterland the political squads went to work. Several agents of the rival parties came to very sticky ends, and the squads visited all the clan chiefs of the Vindu.

After several public burnings and eye-gougings, the clan chiefs got the message. When the elections came, acting on the simple and effective logic that you do what the man with the power to extract painful retribution tells you, and ignore or mock the weak and the powerless, the chiefs ordered their people to vote for Kimba. He won the Vindu by a clear majority, and the total votes cast for him swamped the combined opposition and the Caja votes. This was aided by the fact that the numbers of the Vindu had been almost doubled by the persuasion of every village chief to increase the number of people he claimed lived in his village. The rudimentary census taken by the colonial officials was based on affidavits from each village chief as to the population of his village.

The colonial power had made a mess of it. Instead of taking a leaf from the French book, and ensuring that the colonial protégé won the first, vital election, and then signed a mutual defence treaty to ensure a company of white paratroops kept the pro-Western president in power in perpetuity, the colonists had allowed their worst enemy to win. A month after the election Jean Kimba was inaugurated as first president of Zangaro.

What followed was along traditional lines. The four other parties were banned as 'divisive influences', and later the four party leaders arrested on trumped-up charges. They died under torture in prison, after making over the party funds to the liberator, Kimba. The colonial army and police officers were dismissed as soon as a semblance of an exclusively Vindu army had been brought into being. The Caja soldiers, who had constituted most of the gendarmerie under the colonists, were dismissed at the same time, and trucks were provided to take them home. After leaving the capital the six trucks headed for a quiet spot on the Zangaro river, and here the machine-guns opened up. That was the end of the trained Caja.

In the capital, the police and customs men, mainly Caja, were allowed to stay on, but their guns were emptied and all their ammunition taken away. Power passed to the Vindu army and the reign of terror started. It had taken eighteen months to achieve this. The confiscation of the estates, assets and businesses of the colonists began, and the economy ran steadily down. There were no Vindu trained to take over who could run the republic's few enterprises with even moderate efficiency, and the estates were in any case given to Kimba's party supporters. As the colonists left, a few UN technicians came in to run the basic essentials, but the excesses they witnessed caused most sooner or later to write home to their governments insisting they be removed.

After a few short, sharp examples of terror, the timorous Caja were subdued into absolute submission, and even across the river in Vindu country several savage examples were made of chiefs who mumbled something about the pre-election promises. After that the Vindu simply shrugged and went back to their bush. What happened in the capital had never affected them anyway in living memory, so they could afford to shrug. Kimba and his group of supporters, backed by the Vindu army and the unstable and highly dangerous teenagers who made up the party's youth movement, continued to rule from Clarence entirely for their own benefit and profit.

Some of the methods used to obtain the latter were mind-boggling. Simon Endean's report contained documentation of an instance where Kimba, frustrated over the non-arrival of his share of a business deal, arrested the European businessman involved and imprisoned him, sending an emissary to his wife with the pledge that she would receive her husband's toes, fingers and ears by post unless a ransom was paid. A letter from her imprisoned husband confirmed this, and the woman raised the necessary half a million dollars from his business partners and paid. The man was released, but his government, terrified of black African opinion at United Nations, urged him to remain silent. The Press never heard about it. On another occasion two nationals of the colonial power were arrested and beaten in the former colonial police barracks, since converted into the army barracks. They were released after a handsome bribe was paid to the Minister of Justice, of which evidently a part went to Kimba. Their offence was failing to bow as Kimba's car drove past.

In the previous five years since independence all conceivable opposition to Kimba had been wiped out or driven into exile, and the latter were the lucky ones. As a result there were no doctors, engineers or other qualified people left in the republic. There had been few enough in the first place, and Kimba suspected all educated men as possible opponents.

Over the years he had developed a psychotic fear of assassination, and never left the country. He seldom left the palace, and when he did it was under a massive escort. Firearms of every kind and description had been rounded up and impounded, including hunting rifles and shotguns, which added to the lack of protein food. Import of cartridges and black powder was halted, so eventually the Vindu hunters of the interior, coming to the coast to buy the powder they needed to hunt game, were sent back empty-handed and hung up their useless dane-guns in their huts. Even the carrying of machetes within the city limits was forbidden. The carrying of any of these items was punishable by death.

When he had finally digested the lengthy report, studied the photographs of the capital, the palace and Kimba, and pored over the maps, Sir James Manson sent again for Simon Endean. The latter was becoming highly curious about his chief's interest in this obscure republic, and had asked Martin Thorpe in their adjoining offices on the ninth floor what it was about. Thorpe had just grinned and tapped the side of his nose with a rigid forefinger.

Thorpe was not completely certain either, but he suspected he knew. Both men knew well enough not to ask questions when their employer had got an idea in his head and needed information.

When Endean reported to Manson the following morning, the latter was standing in his favourite position by the plate-glass windows of his penthouse, looking down into the street, where pygmies hurried about their business.

'There are two things I need to know more about, Simon,' Sir James Manson said without preamble, and walked back to his desk where the Endean report was lying.

'You mention here a ruckus in the capital, about six to seven weeks ago. I heard another report about the same upset from a man who was there. He mentioned a rumour of an attempted assassination of Kimba. What was it all about?'

Endean was relieved. He had heard the same story from his own sources, but had thought it too small to include in the report.

'Every time the president has a bad dream there are arrests and rumours of an attempt on his life,' said Endean. 'Normally it just means he wants justification to arrest and execute somebody. In this case, in late January, it was the commander of the Army, Colonel Bobi. I was told on the quiet the quarrel between the two men was really about Kimba's not getting a big enough cut in the rake-off from a deal Bobi put through. A shipment of drugs and medicines had arrived for the UN hospital. The Army impounded them at the quayside and stole half. Bobi was responsible and the stolen portion of the cargo was sold elsewhere on the black market. The proceeds of the sale should have passed to Kimba. Anyway, the head of the UN hospital, when making his protest to Kimba and tendering his resignation, mentioned the true value of the missing stuff. It was a lot more than Bobi had admitted to Kimba.

'The president went mad and sent some of his own guards out looking for Bobi. They ransacked the town looking for him, and arrested anyone who got in the way or took their fancy.'

'What happened to Bobi?' asked Manson.

'He fled. He got away in a jeep and made for the border. He got across by abandoning his jeep and walking through the bush round the border control point.'

'What tribe is he?'

'Oddly enough, a half-breed. Half Vindu and half Caja, probably the outcome of a Vindu raid on a Caja village forty years ago.'

'Was he one of Kimba's new army, or the old colonial one?' asked Manson.

'He was a corporal in the colonial gendarmerie, so presumably he had some form of rudimentary training. Then he was busted, before independence, for drunkenness and insubordination. When Kimba came to power he took him back in the early days because he needed at least one man who could tell one end of a gun from the other. In the colonial days, Bobi styled himself a Caja, but as soon as Kimba came to power he swore he was a true Vindu.'

'Why did Kimba keep him on? Was he one of his original supporters?'

'From the time Bobi saw which way the wind was blowing, he went to Kimba and swore loyalty to him. Which was smarter than the colonial governor, who couldn't believe Kimba had won the election until the figures proved it. Kimba kept Bobi on, and even promoted him to command the Army, because it looked better for a half-Caja to carry out the reprisals against the Caja opponents of Kimba.'

'What's he like?' asked Manson pensively.

'A big thug,' said Endean. 'A human gorilla. No brains as such, but a certain low animal cunning. The quarrel between the two men was only a question of thieves falling out.'

'But Western-trained? Not Communist?' insisted Manson.

'No, sir. Not a Communist. Not anything politically.'

'Bribable? Cooperate for money?'

'Certainly. He must be living pretty humbly now. He couldn't have stashed much away outside Zangaro. Only the president could get the big money.'

'Where is he now?' asked Manson.

'I don't know, sir. Living somewhere in exile.'

'Right,' said Manson. 'Find him, wherever he is.'

Endean nodded.

'Am I to visit him?'

'Not yet,' said Manson. 'There was one other matter. The report is fine, very comprehensive, except in one detail. The military side. I want to have a complete breakdown of the military security situation in and around the president's palace, and the capital. How many troops, police, any special presidential bodyguards, where they are quartered, how good they are, level of training and experience, the amount of fight they would put up if under attack, what weapons they carry, can they use them, what reserves are there, where the arsenal is situated, whether they have guards posted overall, if there are armoured cars or artillery, if the Russians train the Army, if there are strike-force camps away from Clarence, in fact, the whole lot.'

Endean stared at his chief in amazement. The phrase 'if under attack' stuck in his mind. What on earth was the old man up to, he wondered, but his face remained impassive.

'That would mean a personal visit, Sir James.'

'Yes, I concede that. Do you have a passport in another name?'

'No, sir. In any case, I couldn't furnish that information. It requires a sound judgement of military matters, and a knowledge of African troops as well. I was too late for National Service. I don't know a thing about armies or weapons.'

Manson was back at the window, staring across the City.

'I know,' he said softly. 'It would need a soldier to produce that report.'

'Well, Sir James, you would hardly get an army man to go and do that sort of mission. Not for any money. Besides, a soldier's passport would have his profession on it. Where could I find a military man who would go down to Clarence and find that sort of information?'

'There is a kind,' said Manson. 'They are called mercenaries. They fight for whoever pays them, and pays them well. I'm prepared to do that. So go and find me a mercenary with initiative and brains. The best in Europe.'

Cat Shannon lay on his bed in the small hotel in Montmartre and watched the smoke from his cigarette drifting up towards the ceiling. He was bored. In the weeks that had passed since his return from Africa he had spent most of his saved pay travelling round Europe trying to set up another job.

In Rome he had seen an order of Catholic priests he knew with a view to going to South Sudan on their behalf to set up an airstrip in the interior into which medical supplies and food could be ferried. He knew there were three separate groups of mercenaries operating in South Sudan, helping the Negroes in their civil war against the Arab North. In Bahr-el-Gazar two other British mercenaries, Ron Gregory and Rip Kirby, were leading a small operation of Dinka tribesmen, laying mines along the roads used by the Sudanese Army in an attempt to knock out their British Saladin armoured cars. In the south, in Equatoria province, Rolf Steiner had a camp that was supposed to be training the locals in the arts of war, but nothing had been heard of him for months. In Upper Nile to the east there was a much more efficient camp, where four Israelis were training the tribesmen and equipping them with Soviet weaponry from the vast stocks the Israelis had taken off the Egyptians in 1967. The warfare in the three provinces of South Sudan kept the bulk of the Sudanese Army and Air Force pinned down there, so that five squadrons of Egyptian fighters were based around Khartoum, and thus not available to confront the Israelis on the Suez Canal.

Shannon had visited the Israeli embassy in Paris and talked for forty minutes to the military attaché. The latter had listened politely, thanked him politely and just as politely ushered him out. The only thing the officer would say was that there were no Israeli advisers on the rebel side in South Sudan, and therefore he could not help. Shannon had no doubts the conversation had been tape-recorded and sent to Tel Aviv, but doubted he would hear any more. He conceded the Israelis were first rate as fighters and good at intelligence, but he thought they knew nothing about Black Africa and were heading for a fall in Uganda and probably elsewhere.

Apart from Sudan, there was little else on offer. Rumours abounded that the CIA were hiring mercenaries for training anti-Communist Meos in Cambodia, and that some Persian Gulf sheikhs were getting fed up with their dependence on British military advisers and were looking for mercenaries who would be entirely their own dependents. The story was that there were jobs going for men prepared to fight for the sheikhs in the hinterland, or take charge of palace security. Shannon doubted all of these stories; for one thing he would trust the CIA like a hole in the head, and the Arabs were not much better when it came to making up their minds.

Outside of the Gulf, Cambodia and Sudan, there was little scope, and no good wars. In fact he foresaw in the offing a very nasty outbreak of peace. That left the chance of working as a bodyguard for a European arms dealer, and he had had one approach from such a man in Paris who felt himself threatened and needed someone good to give him cover.

Hearing Shannon was in town and knowing his skill and spees, the arms dealer had sent an emissary with the proposition. Without actually turning it down, the Cat was not keen. The dealer was in trouble through his own stupidity; a small matter of sending a shipment of arms to the Provisional IRA and then tipping off the British as to where it would be landed. There had been a number of arrests and the Provos were angry. Then there had been a leak in Belfast's apology for security organs, and the Provos were furious. The aim of having a bodyguard is primarily to scare off the opposition until tempers have cooled and the matter has been forgotten. Having Shannon giving gun-cover would have sent most professionals back home while still alive, but the Provos were mad dogs and probably did not know enough to stay clear. So there would be a gunfight, and the French police would take a dim view of one of their streets littered with bleeding Fenians. Moreover, as he was an Ulster Protestant, they would never believe Shannon had just been doing his job. But, the offer was still open.

The month of March had opened and was ten days through, but the weather remained dank and chill, with daily drizzle and rain, and Paris was unwelcoming. Outdoors meant fine weather in Paris, and indoors cost a lot of money. Shannon was husbanding his remaining resources of dollars as best he could. So he left his telephone number with the dozen or so people he thought might hear something to interest him and read several paperback novels in his hotel room.

He lay staring at the ceiling and thinking of home. Not that he really had a home any more, but for want of a better word he still thought of the wild sweep of turf and stunted trees that sprawls across the border of Tyrone and Donegal as the place that he came from.

He had been born and brought up close to the small village of Castlederg, situated inside County Tyrone but lying on the border with Donegal. His parents' house had been set a mile from the village on a slope looking out to the west across Donegal.

They called Donegal the county God forgot to finish, and the few trees were bent towards the east, curved over by the constant beating of the winds from the North Atlantic.

His father had owned a flax mill that turned out fine Irish linen, and had been in a small way the squire of the area. He was Protestant and almost all the workers and local farmers were Catholic, and in Ulster ne'er the twain shall meet, so the young Carlo had had no other boys to play with. He made his friends among the horses instead, and this was horse country. He could ride before he could mount a bicycle, and had a pony of his own when he was five, and he could still remember riding the pony into the village to buy a half-pennyworth of sherbet powder from the sweetshop of old Mr Sam Gailey.

At eight he had been sent to boarding school in England at the urging of his mother, who was English and came from moneyed people. So for the next ten years he had learned to be an Englishman and had to all intents and purposes lost the stamp of Ulster, both in speech and attitudes. During the holidays he had gone home to the moors and the horses, but he knew no contemporaries near Castlederg, so the vacations were lonely if healthy, consisting of long fast gallops in the wind.

It was while he was a sergeant in the Royal Marines at twenty-two that his parents had died in a car crash on the Belfast road. He had come home for the funeral, smart in his black belt and gaiters, topped by the green beret of the Commandos. Then he had accepted an offer for the rundown, nearly backrupt mill, closed up the house and returned to Portsmouth.

That was eleven years ago. He had served the remainder of his five-year contract in the Marines, and on returning to civilian life had pottered from job to job until taken on as a clerk by a London merchant house with widespread African interests. Working his probationary year in London he had learned the intricacies of company structure, trading and banking the profits, setting up holding companies and the value of a discreet Swiss account. After a year in London he had been posted as assistant manager of the Uganda branch office, from which he had walked out without a word and driven into the Congo. So for the last six years he had lived as a mercenary, often an outlaw, at best regarded as a soldier for hire, at worst a paid killer. The trouble was, once he was known as a mercenary there was no going back. It was not a question of being unable to get a job in a business house; that could be done, at a pinch, or even by giving a different name. Even without going to these lengths, one could always get hired as a truck driver, security guard or for some manual job if the worst came to the worst. The real problem was being able to stick it; to sit in an office under the orders of a wee man in a dark grey suit, and look out of the window and recall the bush country, the waving palms, the smell of sweat and cordite, the grunts of the men hauling the jeeps over the river crossings, the copper-tasting fear just before the attack and the wild cruel joy of being alive afterwards. To remember, and then to go back to the ledgers and the commuter train, that was what was impossible. He knew he would eat his heart out if it ever came to that. For Africa bites like a tsetse fly, and once the drug is in the blood it can never be wholly exorcised.

So he lay on his bed and smoked some more and wondered where the next job was coming from.

CHAPTER FIVE

Simon Endean was aware that somewhere in London there has to exist the wherewithal to discover just about any piece of knowledge known to man, including the name and address of a first-class mercenary. The only problem sometimes is to know where to start looking and whom to start asking.

After a reflective hour drinking coffee in his office, he left and took a taxi down to Fleet Street. Through a friend on the City desk of one of London's biggest daily papers he got access to the paper's cuttings library and gave the archivist his request for the folders he wanted to study. For the next two hours he pored over the file in the agency archives that dealt with every newspaper cutting in Britain over the previous ten years concerning mercenaries. There were articles about Katanga, the Congo, Yemen, Vietnam, Cambodia, Laos, Sudan, Nigeria and Rwanda; news items, commentaries, editorials, feature articles and photographs. He read them all, and paid special attention to the names of the writers.

At this stage he was not looking for the name of a mercenary. There were in any case too many names, pseudonyms, *noms de guerre*, nicknames, and he had little doubt some of them were false. He was looking for the name of an expert on mercenaries, a writer or reporter whose articles seemed to be authoritative enough to indicate the journalist knew his subject well, who could find his way round the bewildering labyrinth of rival claims and alleged exploits, and give a balanced judgement. At the end of two hours he had secured the name he was looking for, although he had never heard of the man before.

There were three articles over the previous three years carrying the same by-line, apparently that of an Englishman or American. The writer seemed to know what he was talking about and he mentioned mercenaries from half a dozen different nationalities, neither over-praising them nor sensationalizing their careers to set spines a-tingling. Endean noted the name and the three newspapers in which the articles had appeared, a fact which seemed to indicate that the writer was freelancing.

A second phone call to his newspaper friend eventually produced the writer's address. It was a small flat in North London.

Darkness had already fallen when Endean left ManCon House, and taking his Corvette from the underground car park, he drove northwards to find the journalist's flat. The lights were off when he got there, and there was no answer to the door bell. Endean hoped the man was not away abroad, and this was confirmed by the woman in the basement flat. He was glad to see the house was not large or smart, and hoped the reporter might be hard up for a little extra cash, as freelances usually are. He decided to come back in the morning.

Simon Endean pressed the bell next to the writer's name just after eight the following morning and a half a minute later a voice tinkled 'Yes' at him from the metal grill set in the woodwork.

'Good morning,' said Endean into the grill, 'my name is Harris. Walter Harris. I'm a businessman. I wonder if I might have a word with you?'

The door opened and he mounted to the fourth floor where a door stood open onto the landing. Framed in it was the man he had come to see. When they were seated in the sitting room, Endean came straight to the point.

'I am a business man in the City,' he lied smoothly. 'I am here in a sense representing a consortium of friends, all of whom have this in common: that we all have business interests in a state in West Africa.'

The writer nodded warily and sipped his coffee.

'Recently there have been increasing reports of the possibility of a *coup d'état*. The president is a moderate and reasonably good man, as things go down there, and very popular with his people. One of my business friends was told by one of his workers that the coup, if and when it came, could well be Communist-backed. Do you follow me?'

'Yes. Go on.'

'Well now, it is felt that no more than a small portion of the Army would support a coup unless the speed of it threw them into confusion and left them leaderless. In other words, if it were a *fait accompli*, the bulk of the Army might agree to go along in any case once they realized the coup had succeeded. But if it came, and half-failed, the bulk of the Army would, we all feel sure, support the president. As you may know, experience shows the twenty hours following the strike are the vital ones.

'What has this to do with me?' asked the writer.

'I'm coming to that,' said Endean. 'The general feeling is that, for the coup to succeed, it would be necessary for the plotters first to assassinate the president. If he remained alive, the coup would fail, or might not even be tried, and all would be well. Therefore the question of palace security is vital, and becoming more so. We have been in touch with some friends in the Foreign Office, and they feel it is out of the question to second a professional British officer to advise on security in and around the palace.'

'So?' The writer sipped more coffee and lit a cigarette. He reckoned his visitor was too smooth, too smooth by half.

'So the president would be prepared to accept the services of a professional soldier to advise, on the basis of a contract, on all security matters regarding the person of the president. What he is seeking is a man who could go down there, make a complete and thorough survey of the palace and all its security arrangements, and plug any loopholes in the existing security measures surrounding the president. I believe such men, good soldiers who do not necessarily fight under the flag of their own country, are called mercenaries.'

The freelance nodded several times. He had few doubts the story of the man who called himself Harris was some way from true. For one thing, if palace security was really what was sought, the British government would not be against providing the expert to advise on its improvement. For another, there was a perfectly capable firm at 22 Sloane Street, London, called Watchguard International, whose speciality was precisely that.

In a few sentences he pointed this out to Harris. It did not faze him in the slightest.

'Ah,' he said, 'evidently I have to be a little more candid.'

'It would help,' said the writer.

'The point is, you see, that HMG might agree to send an expert merely to advise, but if the advice was that the palace security troops needed extensive further training, and a crash course at that, politically speaking a Britisher sent by the government could not do that. And if the president wished to offer the man a longer-term post on his staff, the same would apply. As for Watchguard, one of their ex-Special Air Service men would be fine, but if he were on the staff of the palace guard and a coup were tried, despite his presence, there might be a question of combat. Now you know what the rest of Africa would think about a staffman from Watchguard, which most of these blacks regard as being linked to the Foreign Office in some way, doing that. But a pure outsider, although not respectable, would at least be understandable, without exposing the president to the sneer of being a tool of the dirty old imperialists.'

'So what do you want?' asked the writer.

'The name of a good mercenary soldier,' said Endean. 'One with brains and initiative, who'll do a workmanlike job for his money.'

'Why come to me?'

'Your name was recalled by one of our group from an article you wrote several months ago. It seemed very authoritative.'

'I write for my living,' said the freelance.

Endean gently withdrew £200 in ten-pound notes from his pocket and laid them on the table.

'Then write for me,' he said.

'What? An article?'

'No, a memorandum. A list of names and track records. Or you can talk if you like.'

'I'll write,' said the freelance. He walked to a corner where his desk, a typewriter and a stack of white paper comprised the working area of the open-plan flat. Running a sheet into his machine, consulting occasionally from a set of files beside his desk, he wrote steadily for fifty minutes. When he rose he walked over to the waiting Endean with three sheets of quarto paper and held them out.

'These are the best around today, the older generation of the Congo six years ago, and the new up-and-comers. I haven't bothered with the men who couldn't command a platoon well. Mere heavies would be no use to you.'

Endean took the sheets and studied them intently.

The contents were:

COLONEL LAMOULINE. Belgian, Probably government man. Came into Congo in 1964 under Moise Tshombe. Probably with full approval of Belgian Govt. First class soldier, not really a mercenary in full sense of the word. Set up Sixth Commando (French-speaking) and commanded until 1965, when he handed over command to Denard and left.

ROBERT DENARD. Frenchman. Police background, not army. Was in Katanga secession in 1961–62, probably as gendarmerie adviser. Left after failure of secession and exile of Tshombe. Commanded French mercenary operation in Yemen for Jacques Foccart. Returned Congo 1964, joined Lamouline. Commanded Sixth after Lamouline and up till 1976. Took part, half-heartedly, in second Stanleyville revolt (the mercenaries' mutiny) in 1967. Wounded badly in head by ricocheting bullet from own side. Flown out to Rhodesia for treatment. Tried to return by mounting November 1967 mercenary invasion of the Congo from the south of Dilolo. Operation delayed, some said as a result of CIA bribes, was a fiasco when it happened. Since lived in Paris.

JACQUES SCHRAMME. Belgian. Planter-turned-mercenary. Nicknamed Black Jack. Formed own unit of Katangese, early in 1961, and was prominent in Katangese secession attempt. One of the last to flee into Angola on defeat of the secession. Took his Katangese with him. Waited in Angola until return of Tshombe, then marched back into Katanga. Through the 1964/65 war against the Simba rebels, his 10th Codo was more or less independent. Sat out the first Stanleyville revolt of 1966 (the Katangese mutiny) and mixed mercenary/Katangese force was left intact. Launched 1967 Stanleyville mutiny in which Denard later joined. Took joint command after wounding of Denard and led the march to Bukavu. Repatriated 1968, no further mercenary work since then.

ROGER FAULQUES. Much decorated French professional officer. Sent, probably by French Govt., into Katanga during secession. Later commanded Denard who ran the French operation in the Yemen. Was not involved in Congolese mercenary operations. Mounted small operation at French behest in Nigerian civil war. Ferociously brave but now nearly crippled by combat wounds.

MIKE HOARE. British-turned-South African. Acted as mercenary adviser in Katanga secession, became close personal friend of Tshombe. Invited back to Congo in 1964 when Tshombe returned to power and formed English-speaking Fifth Commando. Commanded through bulk of anti-Simba war, retired in December 1965 and handed over to Peters. Well-off and semi-retired.

JOHN PETERS. Joined Hoare in 1964 on first mercenary war. Rose to become deputy commander. Fearless and totally ruthless. Several officers under Hoare refused to serve under Peters and transferred or left 5th Codo. Retired wealthy late 1966.

N.B. The above six count as 'the older generation' inasmuch as they were the originals who came to prominence in the Katanga and Congolese wars. The following five are younger in age, except Roux who is now in his mid-forties, but may be considered the 'younger' generation because they had junior commands in the Congo, or came to prominence since the Congo.

ROLF STEINER. German. Began first mercenary operation under Faulques-organized group that went into Nigerian civil war. Stayed on and led the remnants of the group for nine months. Dismissed. Signed on for South Sudan.

GEORGE SCHROEDER. South African. Served under Hoare and Peters in 5th Codo in the Congo. Prominent in the South African contingent in that unit. Their choice as leader after Peters. Peters conceded and gave him the command. 5th Codo disbanded and sent home a few months later. Not heard of since. Living in South Africa.

CHARLES ROUX. French. Very junior in Katangese secession. Quit early and went to South Africa via Angola. Stayed there and returned with South Africans to fight under Hoare in 1964. Quarrelled with Hoare and went to join Denard. Promoted and transferred to 6th Codo subsidiary unit, the 14th Codo, as second in command. Took part in 1966 Katangese revolt in Stanleyville in which his unit was nearly wiped out. Was smuggled out of the Congo by Peters. Returned by air with several South Africans and joined Schramme, May 1967. Took part in 1967 Stanleyville revolt as well. After wounding of Denard, proposed for overall command of 10th and 6th Commandos, now merged. Failed. Wounded at Bukavu in a shoot-out, quit and returned home via Kigali. Not in action since. Lives in Paris.

CARLO SHANNON. British. Served under Hoare in 5th, 1964. Declined to serve under Peters. Transferred to Denard 1966, joined the 6th. Served under Schramme on march to Bukavu. Fought throughout the siege. Repatriated among the last in April 1968. Volunteered for Nigerian civil war, served under Steiner. Took over remnants after Steiner's dismissal November 1968. Commanded till the end. Believed staying in Paris.

LUCIEN BRUN. Alias Paul Leroy. French, speaks fluent English. Served as enlisted officer French Army Algerian war. Normal discharge. Was in South Africa 1964, volunteered for Congo. Arrived 1964 with South African unit, joined Hoare's 5th Commando. Fought well, wounded late 1964. Returned 1965. Refused to serve under Peters, transferred to Denard and the 6th in early 1966. Left Congo May 1966 sensing forthcoming revolt. Served under Faulques in Nigerian civil war. Wounded and repatriated. Returned and tried for his own command. Failed. Repatriated 1968. Lives in Paris. Highly intelligent, also very politically minded.

When he had finished, Endean looked up.

'These men would all be available for such a job?' he asked. The writer shook his head.

'I doubt it,' he said. 'I included all those who could do such a job. Whether they would want to is another matter. It would depend on the size of the job, the number of men they would command. For the older ones there is a question of prestige involved. There is also the question of how much they need the work. Some of the older ones are more or less retired and comfortably off.'

'Point them out to me,' invited Endean.

The writer leaned over and ran his finger down the list.

'First the older generation. Lamouline you'll never get. He was always virtually an extension of Belgian government policy, a tough veteran and revered by his men. He's retired now. The other Belgian, Black Jacques Schramme, is now retired and runs a chicken farm in Portugal. Of the French, Roger Faulques is perhaps the most decorated ex-officer of the French Army. He also is revered by the men who fought under him, in and out of the Foreign Legion, and regarded as a gentleman by others. But he's also crippled with wounds and the last contract he got was a failure because he delegated the command to a subordinate who failed. If the colonel had been there himself it would probably not have done.

'Denard was good in the Congo, but got a very bad head wound at Stanleyville. Now he's past it. The French mercenaries still stay in contact with him, looking for a bite, but he hasn't been given a command or a project to set up since the fiasco at Dilolo. And little wonder.

'Of the Anglo-Saxons, Mike Hoare is retired and comfortably off. He might be tempted by a million-pound project, but even that's not certain. His last foray was into Nigeria where he proposed a project to each side, costed at half a million pounds. They both turned him down. John Peters is also retired and runs a factory in Singapore. All six made a lot of money in the hey-day, but none has adapted to the smaller, more technical mission that might be called for nowadays, some because they don't wish to, or because they can't.'

'What about the other five?' asked Endean.

'Steiner was good once, but deteriorated. The Press publicity got to him, and that's always bad for a mercenary. They begin to believe they are as fearsome as the Sunday papers say they are. Roux became bitter when he failed to get the Stanleyville command after Denard's wounding, and claims leadership over all French mercenaries, but he hasn't been employed since Bukavu. The last two are better; both in their thirties, intelligent, educated and with enough guts in combat to be able to command other mercs. Incidentally, mercs only fight under a leader they choose themselves. So hiring a bad mercenary to recruit others serves no purpose, because no one else wants to know about serving under a guy who once ran out. So the combat record is important.

'Lucien Brun, alias Paul Leroy, could do this job. Trouble is, you would never be quite sure if he was not passing stuff to French intelligence, the SDECE. Does that matter?'

'Yes, very much,' said Endean shortly. 'You left out Schroeder, the South African. What about him? You say he commanded Fifth Commando in the Congo?'

'Yes,' said the writer. 'At the end, the very end. It also broke up under his command. He's a first-class soldier within his limitations. For example, he would command a battalion of mercenaries excellently, providing it were within the framework of a brigade with a good staff. He's a good combat man, but conventional. Very little imagination, not the sort who could set up his own operation starting from scratch. He'd need staff officers to take care of the admin.'

'And Shannon? He's British?'

'Anglo-Irish. He's new; he got his first command only a year ago, but he did well. He can think unconventionally and has a lot of audacity. He can also organize down to the last detail.'

Endean rose to go.

'Tell me something,' he said at the door. 'If you were mounting an ... seeking a man to go on a mission and assess a situation, which would you choose?'

The writer picked up the notes on the breakfast table.

'Cat Shannon,' he said without hesitation. 'If I were doing that, or mounting an operation, I'd pick the Cat.'

'Where is he?' asked Endean.

The writer mentioned a hotel and a bar in Paris.

'You could try either of those,' he said.

'And if this man Shannon was not available, or for some other reason could not be employed, who would be second on the list?'

The writer thought for a while.

'If not Lucien Brun, then the only other one who would almost certainly be available and has the experience would be Roux,' he said.

'You have his address?' asked Endean.

The writer flicked through a small notebook that he took from a drawer in his desk.

'Roux has a flat in Paris,' he said, and gave Endean the address. A few seconds later he heard the clump of Endean's feet descending the stairs. He picked up the phone and dialled a number.

'Carrie? Hi, it's me. We're going out tonight. Somewhere expensive. I just got paid for a feature article.'

Cat Shannon walked slowly and pensively up the Rue Blance towards the Place Clichy. The little bars were already open on both sides of the street, and from the doorways the hustlers tried to persuade him to step inside and see the most beautiful girls in Paris. The latter, who, whatever else they were, mostly certainly were not that, peered through the lace curtains at the darkened street. It was just after five o'clock on a mid-March evening, with a cold wind blowing. The weather matched Shannon's mood.

He crossed the square and ducked up another side street towards his hotel which had few advantages but a fine view from its top floors, since it was close to the summit of Montmartre. He was thinking about Dr Dunois, whom he had visited for a general check-up a week earlier. A former paratrooper and army doctor, Dunois had become a mountaineer and gone on two French expeditions to the Himalayas and the Andes as the team medico.

He had later volunteered for several tough medical missions in Africa, on a temporary basis and for the duration of the emergency, working for the French Red Cross. There he had met the mercenaries and had patched up several of them after combat. He had become known as the mercenaries' doctor, even in Paris, and had sewn up a lot of bullet holes, removed many splinters of mortar casing from their bodies. If they had a medical problem or needed a check-up, they usually went to him at his Paris surgery. If they were well off, flush with money, they paid on the nail in dollars. If not, he forgot to send his bill, which is unusual in French doctors.

Shannon turned in to the door of his hotel and crossed to the desk for his key. The old man was on duty behind the desk.

'Ah, monsieur, one has been calling you from London. All day. He left a message.'

The old man handed Shannon the slip of paper in the key aperture. It was written in the old man's scrawl, evidently dictated letter by letter. It said simply 'Careful Harris', and was signed with the name of a freelance writer he knew from his African wars and who he knew lived in London.

'There is another, m'sieu. He is waiting in the salon.'

The old man gestured towards the small room set aside from the lobby and through the archway Shannon could see a man about his own age dressed in the sober grey of a London businessman watching him as he stood by the desk. There was little of the London businessman in the ease with which the visitor came to his feet as Shannon entered the salon, nor about the build of the shoulders. Shannon had seen men like him before. They always represented older, richer men.

'Mr Shannon?'

'Yes.'

'My name is Harris, Walter Harris.'

'You wanted to see me?'

'I've been waiting a couple of hours for just that. Can we talk here, or in your room?'

'Here will do. The old man understands no English.'

The two men seated themselves facing each other. Endean relaxed and crossed his legs. He reached for a packet of cigarettes and gestured to Shannon with the packet. Shannon shook his head and reached for his own brand in his jacket pocket, then thought better of it.

'I understand you are a mercenary, Mr Shannon?'

'Yes.'

'In fact you have been recommended to me. I represent a group of London businessmen. We need a job done. A sort of mission. It needs a man who has some knowledge of military matters, and who can travel to a foreign country without exciting any suspicions. Also a man who can make an intelligent report on what he sees there, analyse a military situation, and then keep his mouth shut.'

'I don't kill on contract,' said Shannon briefly.

'We don't want you to,' said Endean.

'All right, what's the mission? And what's the fee?' asked Shannon. He saw no time in wasting words. The man in front of him was unlikely to be shocked by a spade being called a spade. Endean smiled briefly.

'First, you would have to come to London for briefing. We would pay for your trip and expenses, even if you decided not to accept.'

'Why London? Why not here?' asked Shannon.

Endean exhaled a long stream of smoke.

'There are some maps and other papers involved,' he said. 'I didn't want to bring them with me. Also, I have to consult my partners, report to them that you have accepted or not as the case may be.'

There was silence as Endean drew a wad of French 100-franc notes from his pocket.

'Fifteen hundred francs,' he said. 'About £120. That's for your air ticket to London, single or return, whichever you wish to buy. And your overnight stay. If you decline the proposition after hearing it, you get another £100 for your trouble in coming. If you accept, we discuss the further salary.'

Shannon nodded.

'All right. I'll listen – in London. When?'

'Tomorrow,' said Endean, and rose to leave.

'Arrive any time during the course of the day, and stay at the Post House Hotel on Haverstock Hill. I'll book your room when I get back tonight. At nine the day after tomorrow I'll phone you in your room and make a rendezvous for later that morning. Clear?'

Shannon nodded and picked up the francs.

'Book the room in the name of Brown, Keith Brown,' he said. The man who called himself Harris left the hotel and headed downhill looking for a taxi.

He had not seen any reason to mention to Shannon that he had spent three hours earlier that afternoon talking with another mercenary, a man by the name of Charles Roux. Nor did he mention that he had decided, despite the Frenchman's evident eagerness, that Roux was not the man for the job: he had left the man's flat with a vague promise to get in touch again with his decision.

Twenty-four hours later Shannon stood at his bedroom window in the Post House Hotel, and stared out at the rain and the commuter traffic swishing up Haverstock Hill from Camden Town towards Hampstead and the commuter suburbs.

He had arrived that morning on the first plane, using his passport in the name of Keith Brown. Long since, he had had to acquire a false passport by the normal method used in mercenary circles. At the end of 1967 he had been with Black Jacques Schramme at Bukavu, surrounded and besieged for months by the Congolese Army. Finally, undefeated but running out of ammunition, the mercenaries had vacated the Congolese lakeside city, walked across the bridge into neighbouring Rwanda and allowed themselves, with Red Cross guarantees which the Red Cross could not possibly fulfil, to be disarmed.

From then on, for nearly six months, they had sat idle in an internment camp at Kigali while the Red Cross and the Rwanda government hassled over their repatriation to Europe. President Mobutu of the Congo wanted them sent back to him for execution, but the mercenaries had threatened if that was the decision they would take the Rwandan Army barehanded, recover their guns and find their own way home. The Rwandan government had believed, rightly, that they might do it.

When finally the decision was made to fly them back to Europe, the British consul had visited the camp and soberly told the six British mercenaries present that he would have to impound their passports. They had soberly told him they had lost everything across the lake in Bukavu. On being flown home to London Shannon and the others had been told by the Foreign Office that each man owed £350 for the air fare, and would receive no new passport ever again.

Before leaving the camp, the men had been photographed, fingerprinted, and had their names taken. They also had to sign a document pledging never to set foot on the continent of Africa. These documents would be sent in copy to every African government.

The reaction of the mercenaries was predictable. Every one had a lush beard and moustache, and hair left uncut after months in the camp, where no scissors were allowed in case they went on the warpath with them. The photographs were therefore unrecognizable. They then submitted their own fingerprints for another man's prints, and exchanged names. The result was that every identity document contained one man's name, another man's fingerprints and a third man's photograph. Finally they signed the pledge to leave Africa for ever with names like Sebastian Weetabix and Neddy Seagoon.

Shannon's reaction to the Foreign Office demand was no less unhelpful. As he still had his 'lost' passport he kept it, and travelled where he wished, until it expired. Then he took the necessary steps to secure another one, issued by the Passport Office but based on a birth certificate, secured from the Registry of Births in Somerset House for the standard fee of five shillings, which referred to a baby who had died of meningitis in Yarmouth about the time Shannon was born.[1]

On arrival in London that morning he had contacted the writer he had

[1] For a more detailed explanation of this procedure, which was used by a would-be assassin of General de Gaulle, see *The Day of the Jackal*, Hutchinson, 1971.

first met in Africa, and learned how Walter Harris had contacted him. He thanked the man for recommending him, and asked if he knew the name of a good agency of private enquirers. Later that afternoon he visited the agency and paid a deposit of twenty pounds, promising to phone them the next morning with further instructions.

Endean rang as he had promised on the dot of nine the following morning, and was put through to Mr Brown's room.

'There's a block of flats in Sloane Avenue called Chelsea Cloisters,' he said without preamble. 'I have booked flat 317 for us to talk. Please be there at eleven sharp. Wait in the lobby until I arrive, as I have the key.'

Then he rang off. Shannon noted the address from the telephone book under the bedside table, and rang the detective agency.

'I want your man in the lobby of the Chelsea Cloisters in Sloane Avenue at ten-fifteen,' he said. 'He had better have his own transport.'

'He'll have a scooter,' said the head of the agency.

An hour later Shannon met the man from the agency in the lobby of the block of service flats. Rather to his surprise the man was a youth in his late teens, with long hair. Shannon surveyed him suspiciously.

'Do you know your job?' he asked. The boy nodded. He seemed full of enthusiasm, and Shannon only hoped it was matched by a bit of skill.

'Well, park that crash helmet outside on the scooter,' he said. 'People who come in here don't carry crash helmets. Sit over there and read a newspaper.'

The youth had not got one, so Shannon gave him his own.

'I'll sit on the other side of the lobby. At about eleven a man will come in, nod to me, and we'll go into the lift together. Note that man, so you will recognize him again. He should come out about an hour later. By then you must be across the road, astride the scooter, with the helmet on and pretending to be busy with a breakdown. Got it?'

'Yes. I've got it.'

'The man will either take his own car from nearby, in which case grab the number of it, or he'll take a taxi. In either case, follow him and note where he goes. Keep on his tail until he arrives at what looks like his final destination.'

The youth drank in the instructions and took his place in the far corner of the lobby behind his newspaper.

The lobby porter frowned but left him alone. He had seen quite a few meetings take place in front of his reception desk.

Forty minutes later Simon Endean walked in. Shannon noticed that he dismissed a taxi at the door, and hoped the youth had noticed it as well. He stood up and nodded to the newcomer, but Endean strolled past him and pressed the summons button for the lift. Shannon joined him, and remarked the youth peering over his newspaper.

'For God's sake,' thought Shannon, and mentioned something about the foul weather lest the man who called himself Harris should glance round the lobby.

Settled into an easy chair in flat 317, Endean opened his briefcase and took out a map. Spreading it out on the bed he told Shannon to look at it. Shannon gave it three minutes and had taken in all the details the map had to give. Then Endean began his briefing.

It was a judicious mixture of fact and fiction. He still claimed he represented a consortium of British businessmen, all of whom did some form of business with Zangaro and all of whose businesses, including some which were virtually out of business, had suffered as a result of President Kimba.

Then he went into the background of the republic from independence onwards, and what he said was truthful, most of it out of his own report to Sir James Manson. The punchline came at the end.

'A group of officers in the Army has got in touch with a group of local businessmen, who are incidentally a dying breed. They have mentioned that they are considering toppling Kimba in a coup. One of the local businessmen mentioned it to one of my group, and put their problem to us. It is basically that they are virtually untrained in military terms, despite their officer status, and do not know how to topple the man, because he spends too much time hidden inside the walls of his palace, surrounded by his guards.

'Frankly, we would not be sorry to see this Kimba go, and neither would his people. A new government would be good for the economy of the place, and good for the country. We need a man to go down there and make a complete assessment of the military and security situation in and around the palace and the important institutions. We want a complete report on Kimba's military strength.'

'So you can pass it on to your officers?' asked Shannon.

'They are not our officers. They are Zangaran officers. The fact is, if they are going to strike at all, they had better know what they are doing.'

Shannon believed half of the briefing, but not the second half. If the officers, who were on the spot, could not assess the situation, they would be incompetent to carry out a coup. But he kept silent.

'I'd have to go in as a tourist,' he said. 'There's no other cover that would work.'

'That's right.'

'There must be precious few tourists go there. Why cannot I go in as a company visitor to one of your friends' business houses?'

'That will not be possible,' said Endean. 'If anything went wrong, there would be all hell to pay.'

'If I get caught, you mean,' thought Shannon, but kept silent. He was being paid, so he would take risks. That, and his knowledge, was what he was being paid for.

'There's the question of pay,' he said shortly.

'Then you'll do it?'

'If the money's right, yes.'

Endean nodded approvingly. 'Tomorrow morning a return ticket from London to the capital of the neighbouring republic will be at your hotel,' he said. 'You have to fly back to Paris and get a visa for this republic. Zangaro is so poor there is only one embassy in Europe, and that's in Paris also. But getting a Zangaran visa there takes a month. In the next-door republic's capital there is a Zangaran consulate. There you can get a visa for cash, and within an hour if you tip the consul. You understand the procedure.'

Shannon nodded. He understood it very well.

'So get visa-ed up in Paris, then fly down by Air Afrique. Get your Zangaran visa on the spot and take the connecting plane service from there to Clarence, paying cash. With the tickets at your hotel tomorrow will be £300 in French francs as expenses.'

'I'll need five,' said Shannon. 'It'll be ten days at least, possibly more depending on connections and how long the visas take to get. Three hundred leaves no margin for the occasional bribe or any delay.'

'All right, five hundred in French francs. Plus five hundred for yourself,' said Endean.

'A thousand,' said Shannon.

'Dollars? I understand you people deal in US dollars.

'Pounds,' said Shannon. 'That's 2500 dollars, or two months at flat salary if I were on a normal contract.'

'But you'll only be away ten days,' protested Endean.

'Ten days of high risk,' countered Endean. 'If this place is half what you say it is, anyone getting caught on this kind of job is going to be very dead, and very painfully. You want me to take the risks, rather than go yourself, you pay.'

'OK, a thousand pounds. Five hundred down, and five hundred when you return.'

'How do I know you'll contact me when I return?' said Shannon.

'How do I know you'll even go there at all?' countered Endean. Shannon considered the point. Then he nodded.

'All right, half now, half later.'

Ten minutes later Endean was gone, after instructing Shannon to wait five minutes before leaving himself.

At three that afternoon the head of the detective agency was back from his lunch. Shannon rang at three-fifteen.

'Ah, yes, Mr Brown,' said the voice on the phone. 'I have spoken to my man. He waited as you instructed, and when the subject left the building, he recognized him and followed. The subject hailed a taxi from the kerbside and my man followed him to the City. There he dismissed the taxi and entered a building.'

'What building?'

'ManCon House. That's the headquarters of Manson Consolidated Mining.'

'Do you know if he works there?' asked Shannon.

'It would seem he does,' said the agency chief. 'My man could not follow him into the building, but he noticed the commissionaire touched his cap to the subject and held the door open for him. He did not do that for a stream of secretaries and evidently junior executives who were emerging for lunch.'

'He's brighter than he looks,' conceded Shannon. The youth had done a good job. Shannon gave several further instructions and that afternoon mailed £50 by registered post to the detective agency. He also opened a bank account and put down £10 deposit in it. The following morning he banked a further £500 and that evening flew to Paris.

Dr Gordon Chalmers was not a drinking man. He seldom touched anything stronger than beer and when he did, he became talkative, as his employer Sir James Manson had found out for himself over their luncheon at Wilton's. The evening that Cat Shannon was changing planes at Le Bourget to catch the Air Afrique DC-8 to West Africa, Dr Chalmers was having dinner with an old college friend, now also a scientist and working in industrial research.

There was nothing special about their meal. He had run into his former classmate in one of those coincidental meetings on the street a few days earlier, and they had agreed to have dinner together.

Fifteen years earlier they had been young undergraduates, single and working hard on their respective degrees, earnest and concerned as so many young scientists feel obliged to be. In the mid-fifties the concern had been the Bomb and colonialism, and they had joined thousands of others marching for the Campaign for Nuclear Disarmament and the various movements that sought an instant end to empire, and world freedom now. Both had been indignant, serious, committed, and both had changed nothing. But in their indignation over the state of the world they had dabbled with the Young Communist movement. Chalmers had grown out of it, married, started his family, secured a mortgage for his house, and slowly merged into the salaried middle class.

The combination of worries that had come his way over the previous fortnight caused him to take more than his usual single glass of wine with dinner, considerably more. His friend, a kindly man with soft brown eyes, noticed his worry and asked if he could help.

It was over the brandy that Dr Chalmers felt he had to confide his worries to someone, someone who, unlike his wife, was a fellow scientist and would understand the problem. Of course it was highly confidential, and his friend was solicitous and sympathetic.

When he heard about the crippled daughter and the need for the money to pay for her expensive equipment, the man's eyes clouded over with sympathy, and he reached across the table to grip Dr Chalmers's forearm.

'Don't worry about it, Gordon. It's completely understandable. Anyone else would have done the same thing,' he told him. Chalmers felt better when they left the restaurant and made their separate ways home. He was easier in his mind, his problem somehow shared.

Though he had asked his old friend how he had fared in the intervening years since their undergraduate days together, the man had been slightly evasive. Chalmers, bowed under his own worries and his observation blunted by wine, had not pressed for details. Even had he done so, it was unlikely the friend would have told him that, far from merging into the bourgeoisie, he had remained a fully committed member of the Party.

CHAPTER SIX

The Convair 440 that ran the connecting air service into Clarence banked steeply over the bay and began its descent towards the airfield. Being intentionally on the left side of the plane, Shannon could look down towards the town as the aircraft overflew it. From a thousand feet he could see the capital of Zangaro occupying the end of the peninsula, surrounded on three sides by the palm-fringed waters of the Gulf, and on the fourth side by the land, where the stubby peninsula, just eight miles long, ran back to join the main coastline.

The spit of land was three miles wide at its base, set in the mangrove swamps of the coastline, and a mile wide at the tip, where the town was situated. The flanks along each side were also composed of mangrove, and only at the end did the mangroves give way to some shingly beaches.

The town spanned the end of the peninsula from side to side and stretched about a mile back down the length of it. Beyond the fringes of the town at this end, a single road ran between cultivated patches the remaining seven miles to the main coast.

Evidently all the best buildings were set towards the seaward tip of the land, where the breezes would blow, for the aerial view showed the buildings to be set in their own plots of land, one to an acre. The landward side of the town was evidently the poorer section, where thousands of tin-roofed shanties intersected with narrow muddy alleys. He concentrated on the richer section of Clarence, where the colonial masters had once lived, for here would be the important buildings, and he would only ever have a few seconds to see them from this angle.

At the very end was a small port, formed where, for no geological reason, two long curving spits of shingle ran out into the sea like the antlers of a stag beetle or the pincers of an earwig. The port was set along the landward side of this bay. Outside the arms of the bay, Shannon could see the water ruffled by the breeze, while inside the three-quarter-circle enclosed within the arms, the water was a flat calm. No doubt it was this anchorage, tacked on to the end of the peninsula in one of nature's afterthoughts, which had attracted the first mariners.

The centre of the port, directly opposite the opening to the high seas, was dominated by a single concrete quay without any ship tied up to it, and a warehouse of sorts. To the left of the concrete quay was evidently the natives' fishing area, a shingly beach littered with long canoes and nets laid out to dry, and to the right of the quay was the old port, a series of decrepit wooden jetties pointing towards the water.

Behind the warehouse there were perhaps two hundred yards of rough grass ending with a road along the shore, and behind the road the buildings started. Shannon caught a glimpse of a white colonial-style church, and what could have been the governor's palace in bygone days, surrounded by a wall. Inside the wall, apart from the main buildings, was a large courtyard surrounded by lean-to hutments of evidently recent addition.

At this point the Corvair straightened up, the town disappeared from view, and they were on final approach.

Shannon had already had his first experience of Zangaro the previous day when he had applied for his visa for a tourist visit. The consul in the neighbouring capital had received him with some surprise, being unused to such applications. He had to fill out a five-page form giving everything from his parents' first-name (as he had no idea of Keith Brown's parents' names, he invented them) and every other conceivable piece of information.

His passport, when he handed it over, had a handsome banknote idly lying between the first and second pages. This went into the consul's pocket. Then the man examined the passport from every angle, read every page, held it up to the light, turned it over, checked the currency allowances at the back. After five minutes of this Shannon began to wonder if there was something wrong. Had the British Foreign Office made an error in this particular passport? Then the consul looked at him and said:

'You are an American.'

With a sense of relief Shannon realized the man was illiterate.

He had had his visa in five minutes more. But at Clarence airport the fun stopped.

He had no luggage in the aircraft hold, just a hand grip. Inside the main (and only) passenger building the heat was overpowering and the place buzzed with flies. About a dozen soldiers lounged about, and ten policemen. They were evidently of different tribes. The policemen were self-effacing, hardly speaking even to each other, leaning against the walls. It was the soldiers who attracted Shannon's attention. He kept half an eye on them as he filled in another immensely long form (the same one he had filled the previous day in the consulate) and penetrated health and passport control, both manned by officials whom he took to be Caja, like the policemen.

It was when he got to customs that the trouble started. A civilian was waiting for him, and instructed him with a curt gesture to go into a side-room. As he did so, taking his grip with him, four soldiers swaggered in after him. Then he realized what it was about them that rang a bell in his memory.

Long ago in the Congo he had seen the same attitude, the blank-eyed sense of menace conveyed by an African of almost primeval cultural level, armed with a weapon, in a state of power, wholly unpredictable, with reactions to a situation that were utterly illogical, ticking away like a moving time bomb. Just before the worst of the massacres he had seen launched by Congolese on Katangese, Simbas on missionaries and Congolese Army on Simbas, he had noticed this same menacing mindlessness, the sense of power without reason, that can suddenly and for no recollected explanation, turn to frenetic violence. The Vindu soldiers of President Kimba had it.

The civilian customs officer ordered Shannon to put his grip on the rickety table, and then began to go through it. The search looked thorough, as if for concealed weapons, until he spotted the electric shaver, took it from its case, examined it, tried the 'on' switch. Being a Remington Lektronic and fully charged, it buzzed furiously. Without a trace of expression the customs man put it in his pocket.

Finishing with the grip, he gestured to Shannon to empty his pockets onto the table. Out came the keys, handkerchief, coins, wallet and passport. The customs man went for the wallet, extracted the travellers cheques, looked at them, grunted and handed them back. The coins he swept into his hand and pocketed them. Of the banknotes, there were two 5000 French–African franc-notes and several 100s. The soldiers had crowded nearer, still making no sound but for their breathing in the roasting atmosphere, gripping guns like clubs, but overcome with curiosity. The civilian behind the table pocketed the two 5000-franc notes, and one of the soldiers picked up the smaller denominations.

Shannon looked at the customs man. The man looked back. Then he lifted his singlet and showed the butt of a Browning 9 mm short, or perhaps a 765, jammed into his trouser band. He tapped it.

'Police,' he said, and kept staring. Shannon's fingers itched to smash the man in the face. Inside his head he kept telling himself 'Keep cool, baby, absolutely cool.'

He gestured slowly, very slowly, to what remained of his belongings on the table and raised his eyebrows. The civilian nodded, and Shannon began to pick them up and put them back. Behind him he felt the soldiers back off, though they still gripped their rifles with both hands, able to swing or butt-jab as the mood took them.

It seemed an age before the civilian nodded towards the door, and Shannon left. He could feel the sweat running in a stream down the spine towards the waistband of his pants.

Outside in the main hall the only other white tourist on the flight, an American girl, had been met by a Catholic priest who, with his voluble explanations to the soldiers in the Coast pidgin, was having less trouble. He looked up and caught Shannon's eye. Shannon raised an eyebrow slightly. The father looked beyond Shannon at the room he had come from and nodded imperceptibly.

Outside in the heat of the small square before the airport building there was no transport. Shannon waited. Five minutes later he heard a soft Irish-American voice behind him.

'Can I give you a lift into town, my son?'

They travelled in the priest's car, a Volkswagen Beetle, which he had hidden for safety in the shade of a palm grove several yards outside the gate. The American girl was shrill and outraged; someone had opened her handbag and gone through it. Shannon was silent, knowing how close they all had come to a beating. The priest was with the UN hospital, combining the roles of chaplain, almoner and doctor of medicine. He glanced across at Shannon with understanding.

'They shook you down.'

'The lot,' said Shannon. The loss of £15 was nothing, but both the men had recognized the mood of the soldiery.

'One has to be very careful here, very careful indeed,' said the priest softly. 'Have you a hotel?'

When Shannon told him he had not, the priest drove him to the Independence, the only hotel in Clarence where Europeans were permitted to stay.

'Gomez is the manager, he's a good enough sort,' said the priest.

Usually when a new face arrives in an African city there are invitations from the other Europeans to visit the club, come back to the bungalow, have a drink, come to a party that evening. The priest, for all his helpfulness, did no such thing. That was another thing Shannon learned quickly about Zangaro. The mood affected the whites as well. He would learn more in the days to come, much of it from Gomez.

It was that same evening that he came to know Jules Gomez, formerly proprietor and latterly manager of the Independence Hotel. Gomez was fifty and a *pied noir*, a Frenchman from Algeria. In the last days of French Algeria almost ten years earlier, he had sold his flourishing business in agricultural machinery just before the final collapse when one could not give a business away. With what he had made, he returned to France, but after a year found he could not live in the atmosphere of Europe any longer, and looked around for another place to go. He had settled on Zangaro, five years before independence and before it was even in the offing. Taking his savings he had bought the hotel and steadily improved it over the years.

After independence, things had changed. Three years before Shannon arrived, Gomez had been brusquely informed that the hotel was to be nationalized, and he would be paid in local currency. He never was, and it was worthless paper in any case. But he hung on as manager, hoping against hope that one day things might improve again, and something would be left of his only asset on this planet, to secure him in old age. As manager, he ran the reception desk and the bar. Shannon found him at the bar.

It would have been easy to win Gomez's friendship by mentioning the friends and contacts Shannon had who were former OAS men, fighters in the Legion and the paras, who had turned up in the Congo. But that would have blown his cover as a simple English tourist who, with five days to kill, had flown down from the north, impelled only by curiosity to see the obscure republic of Zangaro. So he stuck to his role of tourist.

But later, after the bar closed, he suggested Gomez join him for a drink in his room. For no explicable reason the soldiers at the airport had left him a bottle of whisky he had been carrying in his case. Gomez's eyes opened wide at the sight of it. Whisky was another import the country could not afford. Shannon made sure Gomez drank more than he. When he mentioned that he had come to Zangaro out of curiosity, Gomez snorted.

'Curiosity? Huh, it's curious, all right. It's bloody weird.'

Although they were talking French, and alone in the room, Gomez lowered his voice and leaned forward as he said it. Once again Shannon got an impression of the extraordinary sense of fear present in everyone he had seen, except the bully-boy army thugs and the secret policeman who posed as a customs officer at the airport. By the time Gomez had sunk half the bottle, he had become slightly garrulous, and Shannon probed gently for information. Gomez confirmed much of the briefing Shannon had been given by the man he knew as Walter Harris, and added more anecdotal details of his own, some of them highly gruesome.

He confirmed that President Kimba was in town, that he hardly ever left it these days, except for the occasional trip to his home village across the river in Vindu country, and that he was in his presidential palace, the large, walled building Shannon had seen from the air.

By the time Gomez bade him good night and weaved his way back to his own room at two in the morning, further nuggets of information had been culled. The three units known as the civilian police force, the gendarmerie and the customs force, although all carried sidearms, had, Gomez swore, no ammunition in their weapons. Being Caja, they were not trusted to have any, and Kimba, with his paranoia about an uprising, kept them without one round of ammunition between the lot of them. He knew they would never fight for him, and must not have the opportunity of fighting against him. The sidearms were just for show.

Gomez had also vouchsafed that the power in the city was exclusively in the hands of Kimba's Vindu. The dreaded secret police usually wore civilian clothes and carried automatics, the soldiers of the Army had bolt-action rifles such as Shannon had seen at the airport, and the president's own praetorian guards had submachine guns. The latter lived exclusively in the palace grounds, were ultra-loyal to Kimba, and he never moved without at least a squad of them hemming him round.

The next morning Shannon went out for a walk. Within seconds he found a small boy of ten or eleven scampering by his side, sent after him by Gomez. Only later did he learn why. He thought Gomez must have sent the boy as a guide, though as they could not exchange a word, there was not much point in that. The real purpose was different, a service Gomez offered to all his guests whether they asked or not. If the tourist was arrested for whatever reason, and carted off, the small boy would speed away through the bushes and tell Gomez. He would slip the information to the Swiss or West German embassy so that someone could begin to negotiate the tourist's release before he was beaten half-dead. The boy's name was Boniface.

Shannon spent the morning walking, mile after mile, while the small boy trotted at his heels. They were stopped by no one. There was hardly a vehicle to be seen, and the streets in the residential area were mainly deserted. From Gomez Shannon had obtained a small map of the town, a leftover from colonial days, and with this he tracked down the main buildings of Clarence. At the only bank, the only post office, half a dozen ministeries, the port and the UN hospital there were groups of six or seven soldiers lounging about the steps. Inside the bank, where he went to cash a travellers cheque, he noticed bed-rolls in the lobby, and in the lunch hour he twice saw pots of food being carried by a soldier to his colleagues. Shannon judged that the guard details lived on the premises at each building. Gomez confirmed this later the same evening.

He noticed a soldier in front of each of six embassies he passed, three of them asleep in the dust. By the lunch hour he estimated there were about a hundred soldiers scattered in twelve groups around the main area of the town. He noted what they were armed with. Each carried an old Mauser 7.92 bolt-action rifle, most of them looking rusted and dirty. The soldiers wore drab-green trousers and shirts, canvas boots, webbing belts and peaked caps, rather like American baseball caps. Without exception they were shabby, unpressed, unwashed and unprepossessing. He estimated their level of training, weapons familiarization, leadership and fighting capacity at nil. They were a rabble, undisciplined thugs who could terrify the timorous Caja by their arms and their brutishness, but had probably never fired a shot in anger and certainly had never been fired at by people who knew what they were doing. Their purpose on guard duty seemed to be preventive of a civilian riot, but he estimated that in a real fire-fight they would quit and run.

The most interesting thing about them was the state of their ammunition pouches. They were pressed flat, empty of magazines. Each Mauser had its fixed magazine of course, but Mausers only hold five shells.

That afternoon Shannon patrolled the port. Seen from the ground, it looked different. The two spits of sand running out across the water and forming the natural harbour were about twenty feet high at the base and six feet above the water at the tip. He walked down both until he reached the end. Each one was covered in knee- to waist-high scrub vegetation, burned brown at the end of the long dry season, and invisible from the air. Each spit was about forty feet wide at the tip, forty yards wide at the base, where it left the shoreline. From the tip of each, looking back towards the port area, one had a panoramic view of the waterfront.

The concreted area was at dead centre, backed by the warehouse. To the north of this stood the old wooden jetties, some long crumbled away, their supports sticking up like broken teeth above or below the water. To the south of the warehouse was the shingly beach where the fishing canoes lay. From the tip of one sand-spit the president's palace was invisible, hidden behind the warehouse, but from the other spit the uppermost storey of the palace was plainly visible. Shannon walked back to the port and examined the fishing beach. It was a good place for a landing, he thought idly, a gentle slope to the water's edge.

Behind the warehouse the concrete ended and a sloping bank of waist-high scrub, dissected by numerous footpaths and one laterite ride for lorries, ran back towards the palace. Shannon took the road. As he breasted the top of the rise the full façade of the old colonial governor's mansion came into view, two hundred yards away. He continued another hundred yards and reached the lateral road running along the sea shore. At the junction a group of soldiers waited, four in all, smarter, better dressed than the Army, armed with Kalashnikov AK 47 assault rifles. They watched him in silence as he turned right along the road towards his hotel. He nodded, but they just stared back. The palace guards.

He glanced to his left as he walked and took in the details of the palace. Thirty yards wide, its ground-floor windows now bricked up and painted over the same off-white wash as the rest of the building, the building was dominated at ground level by a tall, wide, bolt-studded timber door, almost certainly another new addition. In front of the bricked-up windows ran a terrace, now useless because there was no access from the building to it. On the first floor a row of seven windows ran from side to side of the façade, three left, three right, and one above the main entrance. The topmost floor had ten windows, all much smaller. Above these was the gutter and the red-tiled roof sloping away towards the apex.

He noticed more guards lounging around the front door, and that the first-floor windows had shutters which might have been of steel (he was too far away to tell) and were drawn down. Evidently no closer access to the front of the building than the road junction was permitted, except on official business.

He completed the afternoon just before the sun went down by making a tour of the palace from afar. At each side he saw that a new wall, eight feet high, ran from the main mansion towards the land for a distance of eighty yards, and the fourth wall joined them together at the rear. Interestingly, there were no other gates to the entire compound. The wall was uniformly eight feet high – he could tell by the height of a guard he saw walking near the wall – and topped by broken bottles. He knew he would never see inside, but he could retain the image from the air. It almost made him laugh.

He grinned at Boniface.

'You know, kid, that bloody fool thinks he has protected himself with a big wall topped with glass and only one entrance. All he has really done is pin himself inside a brick trap, a great big, closed-in killing ground.'

The boy grinned widely, not understanding a word, and indicated he wanted to go home and eat. Shannon nodded, and they went back to the hotel, feet burning and legs aching.

Shannon made no notes or maps, but retained every detail in his head. He returned Gomez his map, and after dinner joined the Frenchman at the bar.

Two Chinese from the embassy sat quietly drinking beer at the back tables, so conversation between the Europeans was minimal. Besides, the windows were open. Later, however, Gomez, longing for company, took a dozen bottles of beer and invited Shannon up to his room on the top floor, where they sat on the balcony and looked out through the night at the sleeping town, mainly in darkness due to an electricity breakdown.

Shannon was in two minds whether to take Gomez into his confidence, but decided not to. He mentioned that he had found the bank and there had been a job to change a fifty-pound cheque. Gomez snorted.

'There always is,' he said. 'They don't see travellers cheques here, nor much foreign currency for very long.'

'They must see it at the bank, surely.'

'Not for long. The entire treasure of the republic Kimba keeps locked up inside the palace.'

Shannon was at once interested. It took two hours to learn, in dribs and drabs, that Kimba also kept the national armoury of ammunition in the old wine cellar of the governor's palace, under his own lock and key, and had also transferred the national radio broadcasting station there, so that he could broadcast direct from his communications room to the nation and the world, and no one else could take control of it from outside the palace. National radio stations always play a vital role in *coups d'état*. Shannon also learned he had no armoured cars and no artillery, and that apart from the hundred soldiers scattered around the capital, there were another hundred outside the town, a score in the native township on the airport road and the rest dotted in the Caja villages beyond the peninsula towards the Zangaro river bridge. These two hundred were half the army. The other half were in the army barracks, which were not barracks in truth but the old colonial police lines four hundred yards from the palace, rows of low tin shanties inside a reed fence enclosure. The four hundred men constituted the entire army, and the personal palace guards numbered from forty to sixty, living in the lean-to sheds inside the palace courtyard walls.

On his third day in Zangaro Shannon checked out the police lines, where the two hundred army men not on guard duty lived. It was, as Gomez had said, surrounded by a reed fence, but a visit to the nearby church enabled Shannon to slip unnoticed into the bell-tower, run up the circular brick staircase and sneak a view from the belfry. The lines were two rows of shanties, adorned with some clothes hung out to dry. At one end was a row of low brick kilns over which pots of stew bubbled. Two score of men lounged around in various stages of boredom, and all were unarmed. Their guns might be in the hutments, but Shannon guessed they were more probably in the armoury, a small stone pillbox set aside from the huts. The other facilities of the camp were primitive in the extreme.

It was that evening, when he had gone out without Boniface, that he met his soldier. He spent an hour circling the darkened streets, which fortunately for him had never seen lamp lighting, trying to get closer to the palace.

He had managed a good look at the back and sides, and had assured himself there were no patrolling guards on these sides. Trying the front of the palace, he had been intercepted by two of the palace guards, who had brusquely ordered him on his way home. He had established that there were three of them sitting at the road junction halfway between the top of the rise from the port and the front gate of the palace. More importantly, he had also established that they could not see the harbour from where they stood. From that road junction the soldiers' eyeline, passing over the top of the rise, would meet the sea beyond the tips of the arms of the harbour, and without a brilliant moon they would not even see the water five hundred yards away, though undoubtedly they would see a light out there, if there were one.

In the darkness on the road junction, Shannon could not see the front gate of the palace a hundred yards inland, but assumed there were two other guards there as usual. He offered packets of cigarettes to the soldiers who had accosted him, and left.

On the road back to the Independence he passed several bars, lit inside by paraffin lamps, and then moved on down the darkened road. A hundred yards further on the soldier stopped him. The man was evidently drunk and had been urinating in a rain ditch by the roadside. He swayed up to Shannon, gripping his Mauser two-handed by the butt and barrel. In the light from the rising moon Shannon could now see him quite clearly as he moved towards him. The soldier grunted something. Shannon failed to understand, though assumed it was a demand for money.

He heard the soldier mutter 'Beer' several times, and added some more indistinguishable words. Then before Shannon could reach for money, or pass on, the man snarled and jabbed the barrel of the gun towards Shannon. From then on it was quick and silent. He took the barrel in one hand and moved it away from his stomach, jerking hard and pulling the soldier off balance. The man was evidently surprised at the reaction, not what he was accustomed to. Recovering, he squealed with rage, reversed the gun, gripped by the barrel and swung it club-wise. Shannon stepped in close, blocked the swing by gripping the soldier by both biceps, and brought up his knee.

It was too late to go back after that. As the gun dropped he brought up his right hand, crooked into a 90-degree angle, stiff-armed, and slammed the base of the hand under the soldier's jawbone. A stab of pain went up his arm and shoulder as he heard the neck crack, and later found he had torn a shoulder muscle with the effort. The Zangaran went down like a sack.

Shannon looked up and down the road, but no one was coming. He rolled the body into the rain ditch and examined the rifle. One by one he pumped the cartridges out of the magazine. At three they stopped coming. There had been nothing in the breech. He removed the bolt and held the gun to the moon, looking down the barrel. Several months of grit, dirt, dust, grime, rust and earth particles met his eye. He slipped the bolt back home, replaced the three cartridges where they had been, tossed the rifle onto the corpse and walked home.

'Better and better,' he murmured as he slipped into the darkened hotel and went to bed. He had few doubts there would be no effective police enquiry. The broken neck would be put down to a fall into the rain ditch, and tests for fingerprints were, he was sure, unheard of.

Nevertheless, the next day he pleaded a headache, stayed in and talked to Gomez. On the following morning he left for the airport and took the Convair 440 back to the north. As he sat in the plane and watched the republic disappear beneath the port wing, something Gomez had mentioned in passing ran like a current through his head.

There were not, and never had been, any mining operations in Zangaro.

Forty hours later he was back in London.

Ambassador Leonid Dobrovolsky always felt slightly uneasy when he had his weekly interview with President Kimba. Like others who had met the dictator, he had few doubts about the man's insanity. Unlike most of the others, Leonid Dobrovolsky had orders from his superiors in Moscow to make his utmost efforts to establish a working relationship with the unpredictable African. He stood in front of the broad mahogany desk in the president's study on the first floor of the palace and waited for Kimba to show some sort of reaction.

Seen close to, President Kimba was neither as large nor as handsome as his official portraits indicated. Behind the enormous desk he seemed almost dwarfish, the more so as he held himself hunched in his chair in a state of total immobility. Dobrovolsky waited for the period of immobility to end. He knew it could end one of two ways. Either the man who ruled Zangaro would speak carefully and lucidly, in every sense like a perfectly sane man, or the almost catatonic stillness would give way to a screaming rage during which the man would rant like someone possessed, which was in any case what he believed himself to be.

Kimba nodded slowly.

'Please proceed,' he said.

Dobrovolsky breathed a sigh of relief. Evidently the president was prepared to listen. But he knew the bad news was yet to come, and he had to give it. That could change things.

'I am informed by my government, Mr President, that they have received information that a mining survey report recently sent to Zangaro by a British company may not be accurate. I am referring to the survey carried out several weeks ago by a firm called Manson Consolidated of London.'

The president's eyes, slightly bulging, still stared at the Russian ambassador without a flicker of expression. Nor was there any word from Kimba to indicate that he recalled the subject that had brought Dobrovolsky to his palace.

The ambassador continued to describe the mining survey that had been carried out by ManCon, and the survey report that had been delivered by a certain Mr Bryant into the hands of the Minister for Natural Resources.

'In essence then, Your Excellency, I am instructed to inform you that my government believes the report was not a true representation of what was really discovered in the area that was then under survey, specifically, the Crystal Mountain range.'

He waited, aware that he could say little more. When Kimba finally spoke, it was calmly and cogently, and Dobrovolsky breathed again.

'In what way was this survey report inaccurate?' whispered Kimba.

'We are not sure of the details, Your Excellency, but it is fair to assume that since the British company has apparently not made any effort to secure from you a mining concession, the report they submitted must have indicated there were no mineral deposits worth exploiting in that region. If the report was inaccurate, then it was probably in this respect. In other words, whatever the mining engineer's samples contained it would appear there was more than the British were prepared to inform you.'

There was another long silence, during which the ambassador waited for the explosion of rage. It did not come.

'They cheated me,' whispered Kimba.

'Of course, Your Excellency,' cut in Dobrovolsky hurriedly, 'the only way of being completely sure is for another survey party to examine the same area and take further samples of the rocks and the soil. To this end I am instructed by my government most humbly to ask Your Excellency to grant permission for a survey team from the Institute of Mining of Sverdlovsk to come to Zangaro and examine the same area as that covered by the British engineer.'

Kimba took a long time digesting the proposal. Finally he nodded.

'Granted,' he said. Dobrovolsky bowed. By his side Volkov, ostensibly Second Secretary at the embassy but more pertinently the Resident of the KGB detachment, shot him a glance.

'The second matter is that of your personal security,' said Dobrovolsky. At last he secured some reaction from the dictator. It was a subject that Kimba took extremely seriously. His head jerked up and he shot suspicious glances round the room. Three Zangaran aides standing behind the two Russians quaked.

'My security?' said Kimba in his usual whisper.

'We would respectfully seek once again to reiterate the Soviet government's view of the paramount importance of Your Excellency's being able to continue to lead Zangaro on the path of peace and progress that Your Excellency has already so magnificently established,' said the Russian. The ocean of flattery caused no incongruous note; it was Kimba's habitual due and a regular part of any words addressed to him.

'To guarantee the continued security of the invaluable person of Your Excellency and in view of the recent and most dangerous treason by one of your army officers, we would respectfully once again propose that a member of my embassy staff be permitted to reside inside the palace and lend his assistance to Your Excellency's own personal security corps.'

The reference to the 'treason' of Colonel Bobi brought Kimba out of his trance. He trembled violently, though whether from fear or rage the Russians could not make out. Then he began to talk, slowly at first, in his usual whisper, then faster, his voice rising as he glared at the Zangarans across the room. After a few sentences he lapsed back into the Vindu dialect, which only the Zangarans understood, but the Russians already knew the gist; the ever-present danger of treason and treachery that Kimba knew himself to be in, the warnings he had received from the spirits telling him of plots in all corners, his complete awareness of the identity of all those who were not loyal and who harboured evil thoughts in their minds, his intention to root them out, all of them, and what would happen to them when he did. He went on for half an hour in this vein, before finally calming down and reverting to a European language the Russians could understand.

When they emerged into the sunlight and climbed into the embassy car, both men were sweating, partly from the heat, for the air conditioning in the palace was broken yet again, partly because that was the effect Kimba usually had on them.

'I'm glad that's over,' muttered Volkov to his colleagues as they drove back towards the embassy. 'Anyway, we got permission. I'll install my man tomorrow.'

'And I'll get the mining engineers sent in as soon as possible,' said Dobrovolsky. 'Let's hope there really is something fishy about that British survey report. If there isn't, I don't know how I'll explain that to the president.'

Volkov grunted.

'Rather you than me,' he said.

Shannon checked into the Lowndes Hotel off Knightsbridge as he had agreed with 'Walter Harris' to do before he left London. The agreement was that he would be away about ten days, and each morning at nine Harris would phone that hotel and ask for Mr Keith Brown. Shannon arrived at noon to find the first call for him had been three hours earlier that morning. The news meant he had till the next day to himself.

One of his first calls after a long bath, a change and lunch, was to the detective agency. The head of it recognized the name of Keith Brown after a few moments' thought, and Shannon heard him sorting out some files on his desk. Eventually he found the right one.

'Yes, Mr Brown, I have it here. Would you like me to mail it to you?'

'Rather not,' said Shannon. 'Is it long?'

'No, about a page. Shall I read it over the phone?'

'Yes please.'

The man cleared his throat and began.

'On the morning following the client's request, my operative waited close to the entrance of the underground car park beneath ManCon House. He was lucky, in that the subject, whom he had noted the day before arriving back there by taxi from his interview at Sloane Avenue with our client, arrived by car. The operative got a clear view of him as he swung into the car-park tunnel entrance. It was beyond doubt the subject. He was at the wheel of a Chevrolet Corvette. The operative took the number as the car went down the ramp. Enquiries were later made with a contact at the Licensing Department at County Hall. The vehicle is registered in the name of one Simon John Endean, resident in South Kensington.' The man paused. 'Do you want the address, Mr Brown?'

'Not necessarily,' said Shannon. 'Do you know what this man Endean does at ManCon House?'

'Yes,' said the private agent. 'I checked up with a friend who's a City journalist. He is the personal aide and right-hand man of Sir James Manson, chairman and managing director of Manson Consolidated.'

'Thank you,' said Shannon and put the phone down.

'Curiouser and curiouser,' he murmured as he left the hotel lobby and strolled down to Jermyn Street to cash a cheque and buy some shirts. It was the first of April, All Fools' Day, the sun was shining and daffodils covered the grass around Hyde Park Corner.

Simon Endean had also been busy while Shannon was away. The results of his labours he imparted to Sir James Manson that afternoon in the penthouse over Moorgate.

'Colonel Bobi,' he told his chief, as he entered the office. The mining boss furrowed his brow.

'Who?'

'Colonel Bobi. The former commander of the army of Zangaro. Now in exile, banished forever by President Jean Kimba. Who, incidentally, has sentenced him to death by presidential decree for high treason. You wanted to know where he was.'

Manson was at his desk by this time, nodding in recollection. He had still not forgotten the Crystal Mountain.

'All right, where is he?' he asked.

'In exile in Dahomey,' said Endean. 'It took a hell of a job to trace him without being too obvious about it. But he's taken up residence in the capital of Dahomey. Place called Cotonou. He must have a little money, but probably not much, or he'd be in a walled villa outside Geneva with all the other rich exiles. He has a small rented villa, and lives very quietly, probably because it is the safest way of ensuring the Dahomey government doesn't ask him to leave. It's believed Kimba has asked for his extradition back home, but no one has done anything about it. Besides, he's far enough away for Kimba to assume he'll never present a threat.'

'And Shannon, the mercenary?' asked Manson.

'Due back sometime today or tomorrow,' said Endean. 'I booked him into the Lowndes from yesterday onwards to be on the safe side. He hadn't arrived this morning at nine. I'm due to try again tomorrow at the same time.'

'Try now,' said Manson.

The hotel confirmed to Endean that Mr Brown had indeed arrived, but that he was out. Sir James Manson listened on the extension.

'Leave a message,' he growled at Endean. 'Ring him tonight at seven.'

Endean left the message and the two men put the phones down.

'I want his report as soon as possible,' said Manson. 'He should finish it at noon tomorrow. You meet him first and read the report. Make sure it covers every point I told you I wanted answered. Then bring it to me. Put Shannon on ice for two days to give me time to digest it.'

Shannon got Endean's message just after five, and was in his room to take the call at seven. He spent the rest of the evening between supper and bed making up his notes and the memorabilia he had brought back from Zangaro – a series of sketches done freehand on a pad of cartridge paper he had bought in the airport in Paris to while away the time, some scale-drawings done from measurements between fixed points in Clarence that he had paced out stride by stride, a local guide-book showing 'points of interest' of which the only interesting one was titled 'The residence of His Excellency the Governor of the Colony' and dated from 1959, and an official and highly flattering portrait of Kimba, one of the few items not in short supply in the republic.

The next day he strolled down Knightsbridge just as the shops opened, bought himself a typewriter and a block of paper, and spent the morning writing his report. It covered three subjects: a straight narrative of his visit, a detailed description of the capital, building by building and accompanied by the diagrams, and an equally detailed description of the military situation. He mentioned the fact that he had seen no signs of either an air force or a navy, and Gomez's confirmation that neither existed. He did not mention his stroll down the peninsula to the native shanty towns where he had seen the clustered shacks of the poorer Caja and beyond them the shanties of the thousands of immigrant workers and their families, chattering to each other in their native tongue, brought with them from many miles away.

He finished the report with a summary:

'The essence of the problem of toppling Kimba has been simplified by the man himself. In all respects the majority of the republic's land area, the Vindu country beyond the river, is of nil political or economic value. If Kimba should ever lose control of the coastal plain producing the bulk of the nation's few resources, he must lose the country. To go one step further, he and his men could not hold this plain in the face of the hostility and hatred of the entire Caja population, which, although muted by fear, exists beneath the surface, if he had once lost the peninsula. Again, the peninsula is untenable by Vindu forces if once the town of Clarence is lost. And lastly, he has no strength within the town of Clarence if he and his forces have lost the palace. In short, his policy of total centralization has reduced the number of targets necessary to be subdued for a takeover of the state to one – his palace complex, containing himself, his guards, the armoury, treasury and radio station.

'As to means of taking and reducing this palace and compound, they have been reduced to one, by virtue of the wall surrounding the entire place. It has to be stormed.

'The main gate could perhaps be rammed down by a very heavy truck or bulldozer driven straight at it by a man prepared to die in the attempt. I saw no evidence of any such spirit present among the citizenry or the Army, nor signs of a suitable truck. Alternatively, self-sacrificing courage by hundreds of men with scaling ladders could overwhelm the palace walls and take the place. I saw no signs of such spirit either. More realistically, the palace and grounds could be taken with little life loss after being first pulverized with mortar fire. Against a weapon like this the encircling wall, far from being a protection, becomes a death-trap to those inside. The door could be taken apart by a bazooka rocket. I saw no signs of either of these weapons, nor any sign of one single person capable of using them. The unavoidable conclusion reached from the above has to be as follows:

'Any section or faction within the republic, seeking to topple Kimba and take over, must destroy him and his Praetorian guards inside the palace compound. To achieve this they would require expert assistance at a technical level which they have not achieved, and such assistance would have to arrive, complete with all necessary equipment, from outside the country. With these conditions fulfilled, Kimba could be destroyed and toppled in a firefight lasting no longer than one hour.'

'Is Shannon aware that there is no faction inside Zangaro that has indicated it wants to topple Kimba?' asked Sir James Manson the following morning when he read the report.

'I haven't told him so,' said Endean. 'I briefed him as you told me. Just said there was an army faction inside, and that the group I represented, as interested businessmen, were prepared to pay for a military assessment of their chances of success. But he's no fool. He must have seen for himself there's no one there capable of doing the job anyway.'

'I like the sound of this Shannon,' said Manson, closing the military report. 'He's obviously got nerve, to judge by the way he dealt with the soldier. He writes quite well, he's short and to the point. Question is, could he do the whole of this job himself?'

'He did mention something significant,' interjected Endean. 'He said when I was questioning him that the calibre of the Zangaran Army was so low that any assisting force of technicians would have to do practically the whole job anyway, then hand over to the new men when it was done.'

'Did he now? Did he?' mused Manson. 'Then he suspects already the reason for his going down there was not the stated one.'

He was still musing when Endean asked.

'May I put a question, Sir James?'

'What is it?' asked Manson.

'Just this: what did he go down there for? Why do you need a military report on how Kimba could be toppled and killed?'

Sir James Manson stared out of the window for some time. Finally he said, 'Get Martin Thorpe up here.' While Thorpe was being summoned, Manson walked to the window and gazed down, as he usually did when he wanted to think hard.

He knew he had personally taken Endean and Thorpe as young men and promoted them to salaries and positions beyond their years. It was not simply because of their intelligence, although they had plenty of it. It was because he recognized an unscrupulousness in each of them that matched his own, a preparedness to ignore so-called moral principles in pursuit of the goal – success. Like Shannon, like himself, they too were mercenaries. Only the degree of success and the question of public respectability separated the four of them. He had made them his team, his hatchet-men, paid by the company, but serving him personally in all things. The problem was: could he trust them with this one, the big one? As Thorpe entered the office, he decided he had to. He thought he knew how to guarantee their loyalty.

He bade them sit down, and, remaining standing with his back to the window, he told them:

'I want you two to think this one over very carefully, then give me your reply. How far would you be prepared to go to be assured of a personal fortune in a Swiss bank of five million pounds each?'

The hum of the traffic ten floors down was like a buzzing bee, accentuating the silence in the room. Endean stared back at his chief and nodded slowly.

'A very, very long way,' he said softly.

Thorpe made no reply. He knew this was what he had come to the City for, joined Manson for, absorbed his encyclopaedic knowledge of company business for. The big one, the once-in-a-decade grand slam. He nodded assent.

'How?' breathed Endean. For answer Manson walked to his wall safe and extracted two reports. The third, Shannon's, lay on his desk as he seated himself behind it.

Manson talked steadily for an hour. He started at the beginning, and soon read the final six paragraphs of Dr Chalmers's report on the samples from the Crystal Mountain. Thorpe whistled softly, and muttered 'Jesus'.

Endean required a ten-minute lecture on platinum to catch the point, then he too breathed a long sigh.

Manson went on to relate the exiling of Mulrooney to northern Kenya, the suborning of Chalmers, the second visit of Bryant to Clarence, the acceptance of the dummy report by Kimba's Minister. He stressed the Russian influence on Kimba, and the recent exiling of Colonel Bobi, who, given the right circumstances, could return as a plausible alternative in the seat of power.

For Thorpe's benefit he read much of Endean's general report of Zangaro and finished with the conclusion of Shannon's report.

'If it is to work at all, it must be a question of mounting two parallel, highly secret operations,' Manson said finally. 'In one, Shannon, stage-managed throughout by Simon, mounts a project to take and destroy that palace and all its contents, and for Bobi, accompanied by Simon, to take over the powers of state the following morning and become the new president. In the other, Martin would have to buy a shell company without revealing who had gained control or why.'

Endean furrowed his brow.

'I can see the first operation, but why the second?' he asked.

'Tell him, Martin,' said Manson. Thorpe was grinning, for his astute mind had caught Manson's drift.

'A shell company, Simon, is a company, usually very old and without assets worth talking about, which has virtually ceased trading and whose shares are very cheap, say, a shilling each.'

'So why buy one?' asked Endean, still puzzled.

'Say Sir James has control of a company, bought secretly through unnamed nominees, hiding behind a Swiss bank, all nice and legal, and the company has a million shares valued at one shilling each. Unknown to the other shareholders or the Board of Directors or the Stock Exchange, Sir James, via the Swiss bank, own 600,000 of these million shares. Then Colonel – beg his pardon – President Bobi sells that company an exclusive ten-year mining franchise for an area of land in the hinterland of Zangaro. A new mining survey team from a highly reputable company specializing in mining goes out and discovers the Crystal Mountain. What happens to the shares of Company X when the news hits the stock market?'

Endean got the message.

'They go up,' he said with a grin.

'Right up,' said Thorpe. 'With a bit of help they go from a shilling to well over £100 a share. Now do your arithmetic. Six hundred thousand shares at a shilling each cost £30,000 to buy. Sell 600,000 shares at £100 each – and that's the minimum you'd get – and what do you bring home? A cool sixty million pounds in a Swiss bank. Right, Sir James?'

'That's right,' nodded Manson grimly. 'Of course, if you sold half the shares in small packets to a wide variety of people, the control of the company owning the concession would stay in the same hands as before. But a bigger company might put in a bid for the whole block of 600,000 shares in one flat deal.'

Thorpe nodded thoughtfully.

'Yes, control of such a company bought at £60 million would be a good market deal. But whose bid would you accept?'

'My own,' said Manson. Thorpe's mouth opened.

'Your own?'

'ManCon's bid would be the only acceptable one. That way the concession would remain firmly British, and ManCon would have gained a fine asset.'

'But,' queried Endean, 'surely you would be paying yourself sixty million quid?'

'No,' said Thorpe quietly, 'ManCon's shareholders would be paying Sir James sixty million quid, without knowing it.'

'What's that called, in financial terms of course?' asked Endean.

'There *is* a word for it, on the Stock Exchange,' Thorpe admitted.

Sir James Manson tendered them each a glass of whisky. He reached round and took his own.

'Are you on, gentlemen?' he asked softly. Both younger men looked at each other and nodded.

'Then here's to the Crystal Mountain.'

They drank.

'Report to me here tomorrow morning at nine sharp,' Manson told them, and they rose to go. At the door to the back stairs Thorpe turned.

'You know, Sir James, it's going to be bloody dangerous. If one word gets out . . .'

Sir James Manson stood again with his back to the window, the westering sun slanting onto the carpet by his side. His legs were astride, his fists on his hips.

'Knocking off a bank or an armoured truck,' he said, 'is merely crude. Knocking off an entire republic has, I feel, a certain style.'

CHAPTER SEVEN

'What you are saying in effect is that there is no dissatisfied faction within the Army, that, so far as you know, has ever thought of toppling President Kimba?'

Cat Shannon and Simon Endean were sitting in Shannon's room at the hotel taking mid-morning coffee. Endean had phoned Shannon by agreement at nine, and told him to wait for a second call. He had been briefed by Sir James Manson and had called Shannon back, to make the eleven o'clock appointment.

Endean nodded. 'That's right. The information has changed in that one detail. I can't see what difference it makes. You yourself said the calibre of the Army was so low that the technical assistants would have to do all the work themselves in any case.'

'It makes a hell of a difference,' said Shannon. 'Attacking the palace and capturing it is one thing. Keeping it is quite another. Destroying the palace and Kimba simply creates a vacuum at the seat of power. Someone has to step in and take over that power. The mercenaries must not even be seen by daylight. So who takes over?'

Endean nodded again. He had not expected a mercenary to have any political sense at all.

'We have a man in view,' he said cautiously.

'He's in the republic now, or in exile?'

'In exile.'

'Well, he would have to be installed in the palace and broadcasting on the radio that he has conducted an internal *coup d'état* and taken over the country, by midday of the day following the night of the attack on the palace.'

'That could be arranged.'

'There's one more thing.'

'What's that?' asked Endean.

'There must be troops loyal to the new régime, the same troops who ostensibly carried out the coup of the night before, visibly present and mounting the guard by sunrise of the day after the attack. If they don't show up, we would be stuck – a group of white mercenaries holed up inside the palace, unable to show themselves for political reasons, and cut off from retreat in the event of a counter-attack. Now your man, the exile, does he have such a back-up force he could bring in with him when the coup comes? Or could he assemble them quickly once inside the capital?'

'I think you have to let us take care of that,' said Endean stiffly. 'What we are asking from you is a plan in military terms to mount the attack and carry it through.'

'That I can do,' said Shannon without hesitation. 'But what about the preparations, the organization of the plan, getting the men, the arms, the ammo?'

'You must include that as well. Start from scratch and go right through to the capture of the palace and the death of Kimba.'

'Kimba has to get the chop?'

'Of course,' said Endean. 'Fortunately he has long since destroyed anyone with enough initiative or brains to become a rival. Consequently, he is the only man who might re-group his forces and counter-attack. With him dead, his ability to mesmerise the people into submission will also end.'

'Yeah. The juju dies with the man.'

'The what?'

'Nothing. You wouldn't understand.'

'Try me,' said Endean coldly.

'The man has a juju,' said Shannon, 'or at least the people believe he has. That's a powerful protection, given him by the spirits, protecting him against his enemies, guaranteeing him invincibility, guarding him from attack, ensuring him against death. In the Congo the Simbas believed their leader, Pierre Mulele, had a similar juju. He told them he could pass it on to his supporters and make them immortal. They believed him. They thought bullets would run off them like water. So they came at us in waves, bombed out of their minds on dagga and whisky, died like flies and still kept coming. It's the same with Kimba. So long as they think he's immortal, he is. Because they'll never lift a finger against him. Once they see his corpse, the man who killed him becomes the leader. He has the stronger juju.'

Endean stared in surprise. 'It's really that backward?'

'It's not so backward. We do the same with lucky charms, holy relics, the assumption of divine protection for our own particular cause. But we call it religion in us, savage superstition in them.'

'Never mind,' snapped Endean. 'If that's the way it is, all the more reason why Kimba has to die.'

'Which means he must be in that palace when we strike. If he's up-country it's no good. No one will support your man if Kimba is still alive.'

'He usually is in the palace, so I'm told.'

'Yes,' said Shannon, 'but we have to guarantee it. There's one day he never misses. Independence Day. On the eve of Independence Day he will be sleeping in the palace, sure as eggs is eggs.'

'When's that?'

'Three and a half months away.'

'Could a project be mounted in that time?' asked Endean.

'Yes, with a bit of luck. I'd like at least a couple of weeks longer.'

'The project has not been accepted yet,' observed Endean.

'No, but if you want to install a new man in that palace, an attack from outside is the only way of doing it. Do you want me to prepare the whole project from start to finish, with estimated costings and time schedule?'

'Yes. The costing is very important. My ... er ... associates will want to know how much they are letting themselves in for.'

'All right,' said Shannon. 'It will cost you £500.'

'You've already been paid,' said Endean coldly.

'I've been paid for a mission into Zangaro and a report on the military situation there,' replied Shannon. 'What you're asking for is a new report right outside the original briefing you gave me.'

'Five hundred is a bit steep for a few sheets of paper with writing on them.'

'Rubbish. You know perfectly well if your firm consults a lawyer, architect, accountant or any other technical expert, you pay him a fee. I'm a technical expert in war. What you pay for is the knowledge and the experience – where to get the best men, the best arms, how to ship them, etc. That's what costs £500, and the same knowledge would cost you double if you tried to research it yourself in twelve months, which you couldn't anyway because you haven't the contacts.'

Endean rose. 'All right. It will be here this afternoon by special messenger. Tomorrow is Friday. My partners would like to read your report over the weekend. Please have it prepared by tomorrow afternoon at three. I'll collect it here.'

He left and as the door closed behind him Shannon raised his coffee cup in mock toast. 'Be seeing you, Mr Walter Harris oblique stroke Simon Endean,' he said softly.

Not for the first time he thanked his stars for the amiable and garrulous hotel-keeper Gomez. During one of their long nightly conversations Gomez had mentioned the affair of Colonel Bobi, now in exile. He had also mentioned that without Kimba, Bobi was nothing, being hated by the Caja for his army's cruelties against them on the orders of Kimba, and not able to command Vindu troops either. Which left Shannon with the problem of a back-up force with black faces to take over on the morning after.

Endean's brown manila envelope containing fifty £10 notes arrived just after three in a taxi cab and was delivered to the reception desk of the Lowndes Hotel. Shannon counted the notes, stuffed them into the inside pocket of his jacket and began work. It took him the rest of the afternoon and most of that night.

He worked at the writing desk in his room, poring over his own diagrams and maps of the city of Clarence, its harbour, port area and the residential section that included the presidential palace and the army lines.

The classical military approach would have been to land a force on the side of the peninsula near the base with the main coastline, march the short distance inland and take the road from Clarence to the interior, with guns covering the T-junction. That would have sealed off the peninsula and the capital from reinforcement. It would also have lost the element of surprise.

Shannon's talent was that he understood Africa and the African soldier, and his thinking was unconventional, the same kind of thinking that had branded Hoare with the nickname of Mad Mike, although the Congo mercenary's tactics were exactly suited to African terrain and opposition, which are almost the exact opposite of the European situation.

Had Shannon's plans ever been seen by a European military mind, thinking in conventional terms, they would have been styled as reckless and without hope of success. He was banking on Sir James Manson's not having been in the British Army – there was no reference in *Who's Who* to indicate that he had – and accepting the plan. Shannon knew it was workable, and the only one that was.

He based his plan on three facts about war in Africa that he had learned the hard way. One was that the European soldier fights well and with precision in the dark, provided he has been well briefed on the terrain he can expect, while the African soldier, even on his own terrain, is sometimes reduced to near helplessness by his fear of the hidden enemy in the surrounding darkness. The second was that the speed of reaction of the African soldier, once wholly disoriented, his ability to recover, re-group and counter-attack, is longer than the European soldier's speed, exaggerating the normal effects of surprise. The third was that firepower and hence noise are the qualities that can bring African soldiers to fear, panic and headlong flight, without consideration of the smallness of the actual numbers of their opponents.

So Shannon based his plan on a night attack of total surprise in conditions of deafening noise and concentrated firepower.

He worked slowly and methodically, and, being a poor writer with a machine, tapped out the words with two forefingers. At two in the morning the occupant of the bedroom next door could stand no more of it, and banged on the wall to ask plaintively for a bit of peace so that he could get to sleep. Shannon concluded what he was doing five minutes later and packed up for the night. There was one other sound that disturbed the man next door, apart from the clanking of the typewriter. As he worked, and later as he lay in bed, the writer kept whistling a plaintive little tune. Had the insomniac next door known more of music he would have recognized 'Spanish Harlem'.

Martin Thorpe was also lying awake that night. He knew he had a long weekend ahead, two and half days of monotonous and time-consuming poring over cards, each bearing the basic details of one of the 4500 public companies registered at Companies House in the City of London.

There are two agencies in London who provide their subscribers with such an information service about British companies. These are Moodies and the Exchange Telegraph, known as Extel. In his office in ManCon House Thorpe had the set of cards provided by Extel, the agency whose service ManCon took as a necessary part of its commercial activities. But for the business of searching for a shell company, Thorpe had decided to buy the Moodies service and have it sent to his home, partly because he thought Moodies did a better information job on the smaller companies registered in the United Kingdom, and partly for security reasons.

That Thursday he had heard his briefing from Sir James Manson and gone straight to a firm of lawyers. Acting for him, and keeping his name to themselves, the law practice had ordered a complete set of Moodies cards. He had paid the lawyer the £260 for the cards, plus £50 for the three grey filing cabinets in which they would arrive, plus the lawyer's fee for doing it. He had also engaged a small removers' firm to send a van round to Moodies after being told the set of cards would be ready for pick-up on Friday afternoon.

As he lay in bed in his elegant detached house in Hampstead Garden Suburb, he too was planning his campaign; not in detail like Shannon, for he had too little information, but in general terms, using nominee shareholders and parcels of voting stock as Shannon used sub-machine guns and mortars.

Shannon handed his completed project to Endean at three on the Friday afternoon. It contained fourteen pages, four of them diagrams and two of them lists of equipment. He had finished it after breakfast, confident that the sleepless one in the next bedroom would be gone, and had enclosed it in a brown folder. He was tempted to put 'For Sir James Manson's Eyes Only' on the cover, but had resisted. There was no need to blow the affair wantonly, and he could sniff a good contract in the offing if the mining baron offered the job to him.

So he continued to call Endean Harris, and to refer to 'your associates' instead of 'your boss'. After taking the folder, Endean told him to stay in town over the weekend and to be available from Sunday midnight onwards.

Shannon went shopping during the rest of the afternoon, but his mind was on the references he had already seen in *Who's Who* to the man he now knew employed him, Sir James Manson, self-made millionaire and tycoon.

He had an urge, partly from curiosity, partly from the feeling that one day he might need the information, to learn more about Sir James Manson, about the man himself, and about why he had hired a mercenary to make war in Zangaro on his behalf.

The reference from *Who's Who* that stuck in his mind was the mention of a daughter Manson had, a girl who would now be in her late teens or just turned twenty. In the middle of the afternoon he stepped into a phone box off Jermyn Street and called the private enquiry agents who had traced Endean from their first meeting in Chelsea and identified him as Manson's aide.

The head of the agency was cordial when he heard his former client on the phone. Previously, he knew, Mr Brown had paid promptly and in cash. Such customers were valuable. If he wished to remain on the end of a telephone, that was his affair.

'Do you have access to a fairly comprehensive newspaper cuttings library?' Shannon asked.

'I could have,' the agency chief admitted.

'I wish to get a brief description of a young lady of whom there has probably at one time been a reference in society gossip columns somewhere in the London Press. I need very little, simply what she does and where she lives. But I need it quickly.'

There was a pause on the other end.

'If there are such references, I could probably do it by phone,' said the enquiry agent. 'What is the name?'

'Miss Julie Manson, daughter of Sir James Manson.'

The enquiry agent thought it over. He recalled that this client's previous assignment had concerned a man who turned out to be Sir James Manson's aide. He also knew he could find out what Mr Brown wanted to know within an hour.

The two men agreed the fee, a modest one, and Shannon promised to mail it in cash by registered post within the hour. The enquiry agent decided to accept the promise, and asked his client to call him back just before five.

Shannon completed his shopping and called back on the dot of five. Within a few seconds Shannon had what he wanted. He was deep in thought as he walked back to his hotel and phoned the writer who had originally introduced him to 'Mr Harris'.

'Hi,' he said gruffly down the phone, 'it's me, Cat Shannon.'

'Oh hallo, Cat,' came the surprised reply. 'Where have you been?'

'Around,' said Shannon. 'I just wanted to say thanks for recommending me to that fellow Harris.'

'Not at all. Did he offer you a job?'

Shannon was cautious. 'Yeah, a few days' worth. It's over now. But I'm in funds. How about a spot of dinner?'

'Why not?' said the writer.

'Tell me,' said Shannon, 'are you still going out with that girl you used to be with when we met last?'

'Yeah. The same one. Why?'

'She's a model, isn't she?'

'Yes.'

'Look,' said Shannon, 'you may think this crazy, but I very much want to meet a girl who's also a model but I can't get an introduction to. Name of Julie Manson. Could you ask your girl if she ever met her in the modelling world?'

The writer thought it over.

'Sure. I'll call Carrie and ask her. Where are you now?'

'In a call box. I'll call you back in half an hour.'

Shannon was lucky. His friend told him the two girls knew each other, and had been at model school together. They were also handled by the same agency. It took another hour before Shannon, by then speaking directly to the writer's girl-friend, learned that Julie Manson had agreed to a dinner date, provided it was a foursome with Carrie and her boy-friend. They agreed to meet at Carrie's flat just after eight, and that she would have Julie Manson there.

Shannon and the writer turned up within a few minutes of each other at Carrie's flat off Maida Vale, and the four of them went off to dinner. The writer had booked a table at a small cellar restaurant called the Baker and Oven in Marylebone, and the meal was the kind Shannon liked, enormous portions of English roast meats and vegetables, washed down with two bottles of Piat de Beaujolais. He liked the food and he liked Julie.

She was quite short, a little over five feet, and to give herself the impression of more height she wore high heels and carried herself well. She said she was nineteen, and she had a pert round face that could be innocently angelic when she wanted, or extremely sexy when she thought no one else was looking.

She was evidently spoiled and too accustomed to getting things her own way, probably, Shannon estimated, the result of an over-indulgent upbringing. But she was amusing and pretty, and Shannon had never asked more of a girl. She wore her dark brown hair loose so that it fell to her waist, and beneath her dress she evidently had a very curved figure. She also seemed to be intrigued by her blind date.

Although Shannon had asked his friend not to mention what he did for a living, Carrie had nevertheless let it slip that he was a mercenary. But the conversation managed to avoid the question during dinner. As usual Shannon did less talking than anyone, which was not difficult because Julie and the tall auburn-haired Carrie did enough for four between them.

As they left the restaurant and climbed back into the cool night air of the streets, the writer mentioned that he and his girl-friend were taking the car back to his flat. He hailed a taxi for Shannon, asking him if he would take Julie home before going on to his hotel. As the mercenary climbed in, the writer gave him a slow wink. 'I think you're on,' he whispered. Shannon grunted.

Outside her Mayfair flat Julie suggested he might like to come in for a coffee, so he paid off the taxi and accompanied her up to the evidently expensive apartment. Only when they were seated on the settee drinking the appalling coffee Julie had prepared did she refer to the way he earned his living.

He was leaning back in the corner of the settee, she was perched on the edge of the seat, turned towards him.

'Have you killed people?' she asked.

'Yes.'

'In battle?'

'Sometimes. Mostly.'

'How many?'

'I don't know. I never counted.'

She savoured the information and swallowed several times.

'I've never known a man who had killed people.'

'You don't know that,' countered Shannon. 'Anyone who has been in a war has probably killed people.'

'Have you got any scars from wounds?' It was another of the usual questions. In fact Shannon carried over a score of marks on his back and chest, legacies of bullets, fragments of mortar and shards of grenade. He nodded.

'Some.'

'Show me,' she said.

'No.'

'Go on, show me. Prove it.'

She stood up. He grinned up at her.

'I'll show you mine, if you'll show me yours,' he taunted, mimicking the old kindergarten challenge.

'I haven't got any,' Julie said indignantly.

'Prove it,' said Shannon shortly, and turned to place his empty coffee cup on the table behind the sofa. He heard a rustle of cloth. When he turned back he nearly choked on the last mouthful of coffee. It had taken her less than a second to unzip her dress at the back and let the whole lot slip to a pool of crumpled cloth round her ankles. Beneath it she wore a pair of grip-top stockings and a thin gold waist-chain.

'See,' she said softly, 'not a mark anywhere.'

She was right. Her small, nubile teenager's body was an unblemished milky white from the floor to the mane of dark hair that hung round her shoulders and almost touched the waist-chain. Shannon swallowed.

'I thought you were supposed to be Daddy's sweet little girl,' he said.

She giggled. 'That's what they all think, especially Daddy,' she said. 'Now it's your turn.'

Sir James Manson sat at the same hour in the library of his country mansion not far from the village of Notgrove in the rolling Gloucestershire countryside, Shannon's file on his knee and a brandy and soda at his elbow. It was close to midnight and Lady Manson had long since gone up to bed. He had saved the Shannon project to read alone in his library, resisting the temptation to open it in the car on the way down, or to slip away early from dinner. When he wanted to concentrate hard he preferred the night hours, and on this document he wanted to concentrate hard.

He flicked the cover open and set on one side the maps and sketches. Then he started on the narrative. It read:

PREAMBLE. The following plan has been prepared on the basis of the report on the republic of Zangaro written by Mr Walter Harris, my own visit to Zangaro and my own report on that visit, and the briefing given by Mr Harris on what is desired to achieve. It cannot take into account elements known to Mr Harris but undisclosed by him to me. Notable among these must be the aftermath of the attack and the installation of the successor government. Nevertheless, this aftermath may well require preparations built in to the planning of the attack, and these I have obviously not been able to make.

OBJECT OF THE EXERCISE. To prepare, launch and carry out an attack on the presidential palace at Clarence, capital of Zangaro, to storm and capture that palace, and to liquidate the president and his personal guards living inside. Also, to take possession of the bulk of the weapons and armoury of the republic, its national treasury and broadcasting radio station, also inside the palace. Lastly, to create such conditions that any armed survivors of the guard unit or the army are scattered outside the town and in no position to mount a viable counter-attack.

METHOD OF ATTACK. After studying the military situation of Clarence there is no doubt the attack must be from the sea, and launched directly from the sea at the palace itself. I have studied the idea of an airborne landing at the airport. It is not feasible. Firstly, the authorities at the airport of takeoff would not permit the necessary quantity of arms and men to board a charter aircraft without suspecting the nature of the flight. Such authorities, even if a set could be found to permit such a takeoff, would constitute a serious risk of arrest, or a breach of security.

Secondly, a land attack offers no extra advantages, and many disadvantages. To arrive in an armed column over the northern border would only mean the men and arms would have to be smuggled into the neighbouring republic, which has an efficient police and security system. The risk of premature discovery and arrest would be extremely high, unacceptably so. To land elsewhere on the coast of Zangaro and march to Clarence would be no more realistic. For one thing most of the coast is of tangled mangrove swamp impenetrable by boats, and such tiny coves as there are would be unfindable in darkness. For another, being without motor transport, the attacking force would have a long march to the capital, and the defenders would be forewarned. For a third, the paucity of the numbers of the attacking force would be visible in daylight, and would hearten the defenders to put up a stiff resistance.

Lastly, the idea was examined to smuggle the arms and the men into the republic clandestinely and hide them out until the night of the attack. This too is unreal, partly because the quantity of weapons would be too great in weight terms, partly because such quantities and so many unaccustomed visitors would inevitably be spotted and betrayed, and partly because such a plan would require an assisting organization on the ground inside Zangaro, which does not exist.

In consequence it is felt the only realistic plan must be for an attack by light boats, departing from a larger vessel moored out at sea, straight into the harbour of Clarence, and an attack on the palace immediately on landing.

REQUIREMENTS FOR THE ATTACK. The force should be not less than a dozen men, armed with mortars, bazookas and grenades, and all carrying as well sub-machine carbines for close quarters use. The men should come off the sea between two and three in the morning, giving ample time for all in Clarence to be asleep, but sufficiently before dawn for no visible traces of white mercenaries to be available by sunrise of the same day.

The report continued for six more pages to describe exactly how Shannon proposed to plan the project, engage the necessary personnel, the arms and ammunition he would need, the ancillary equipment of radio sets, assault craft, outboard engines, flares, uniforms, webbing, food and victuals; how each item could be costed, and how he would destroy the palace and scatter the Army.

On the question of the ship to carry the attacking force he said: 'Apart from the arms, the acquisition of the ship will prove the most difficult part. On reflection I would be against chartering a vessel, since this involves crew who may turn out to be unreliable, a captain who could at any time change his mind, and the security hazard that vessels of a kind likely to undertake such a charter are probably notorious to the authorities of the countries bordering on the Mediterranean. I advocate spending more money to buy outright a small freighter, crew it with men paid by and loyal to the patrons, and with a legal reputation in shipping circles. Such a boat would in any case be a returnable asset and might work out cheaper in the long run.'

Shannon had also stressed the necessity of security at all times. He pointed out: 'Since I am unaware of the identity of the patrons, with the exception of Mr Harris, it is recommended that in the event of the project being accepted, Mr Harris remain the sole link between the patrons amd me. Payments of the necessary money should be made to me by Mr Harris, and my accounting of expenditure returned the same way. Similarly, although I would need four subordinate operatives, none would know the nature of the project, and certainly not the destination, until all are well out to sea. Even the coastal charts should only be handed over to the captain after sailing. The above plan takes in the security angle, since wherever possible the purchases may be made legally on the open market, and only the arms an illegal purchase. At each stage there is a cut-out at which any investigator comes up against a blank wall, and also at each stage the equipment is being bought separately in different countries by different operatives. Only myself, Mr Harris and the patrons would know the whole plan, and in the worst event I could not identify the patrons, nor, probably, Mr Harris.'

Sir James Manson nodded and grunted in approval several times as he read. At one a.m. he poured himself another brandy and turned to the costings and timings, which were on separate sheets. These read:

Reconnaissance visit to Zangaro. Two reports	*Completed*	£2500
Project commander's fee		£10,000
Engagement all other personnel and their salaries		£10,000
Total administrative costs, travelling, hotels, etc., for CO and all subordinates		£10,000
Purchase of arms		£25,000
Purchase of vessel		£30,000
Purchase of ancillary equipment		£5000
Reserve		£7500
	Total	£100,000

The second sheet bore the estimated timings.

Preparatory Stage:	Recruitment and assembly of personnel. Setting up of bank account. Purchase of foreign based company.	20 days
Purchasing Stage:	Period to cover purchase of all items in sections.	40 days
Assembly Stage:	Assembly of equipment and personnel onto the vessel, culminating in sailing day.	20 days
Shipment Stage:	Transporting entire project by sea from embarkation port to point off coast of Clarence.	20 days

Sir James Manson read the report twice, and spent a long hour steadily smoking one of his Upman Coronas while he stared at the rich panelling and Moroccan-bound books that lined his walls. Finally he locked the project file in his wall safe and went upstairs to bed.

Cat Shannon lay on his back in the darkened bedroom and ran his hand idly over the girl's body that lay half across his own. It was a small but highly erotic body, as he had discovered during the previous hour, and whatever Julie had spent her time learning in the two years since she left school it had not had much to do with shorthand-typing. Her appetite and taste for sexual variety were equalled only by her energy and almost constant stream of chatter between meals.

As he stroked her she stirred and began to play with him.

'Funny,' he said reflectively, 'it must be a sign of the times. We've been screwing half the night, and I don't know a thing about you.'

She paused for a second, said 'Like what?' and resumed.

'Where your home is,' he said. 'Apart from this pad.'

'Gloucestershire,' she mumbled.

'What does your old man do?' he asked softly. There was no answer. He took a handful of her hair and pulled her face round to him.

'Ow, you're hurting. He's in the City. Why?'

'Stockbroker?'

'No, he runs some company to do with mining. That's his speciality, and this is mine. Now, watch.'

Half an hour later she rolled off him and asked, 'Did you like that, darling?'

Shannon laughed and she caught a flash of teeth in the darkness as he grinned.

'Oh yes,' he said softly, 'I enjoyed that enormously. Tell me about your old man.'

'Daddy? Oh he's a boring old businessman. Spends all his day in a stuffy office in the City.'

'Some businessmen interest me. So tell me what he's like . . .'

*

Sir James Manson was enjoying his mid-morning coffee in the sun-lounge on the south side of his country mansion that Saturday morning when the call came through from Adrian Goole. The Foreign Office was speaking from his own home in Kent.

'I hope you won't mind my calling you over the weekend,' he said.

'Not at all, my dear fellow,' said Manson quite untruthfully. 'Any time.'

'I would have called at the office last night but I got held up at a meeting. Recalling our conversation some time ago about the results of your mining survey down in that African place. You remember?'

Manson supposed Goole felt obliged to go through the security rigmarole on an open line.

'Yes indeed,' he said. 'I took up your suggestion made at that dinner. The figures concerned were slightly changed, so that the quantities revealed were quite unviable from a business standpoint. The report went off, was received, and I've heard no more about it.'

Goole's next words jerked Sir James Manson out of his weekend relaxation.

'Actually, we have,' said the voice down the line. 'Nothing really disturbing, but odd all the same. Our ambassador in the area, although accredited to that country and three other small republics, doesn't live there, as you know. But he sends in regular reports, gleaned from a variety of sources, including normal liaison with other friendly diplomats. A copy of a section of his latest report, concerned with the economic side of things out there, landed on my desk yesterday at the office. It seems there's a rumour out there that the Soviet government has secured permission to send in a mining survey team of their own. Of course, they may not be concerned with the same area as your chaps . . .'

Sir James Manson stared at the telephone as Goole's voice twittered on. In his head a pulse began to hammer close to his left temple.

'I was only thinking, Sir James, that if these Russian chaps go over the same area your man went over, their findings might be somewhat different. Fortunately, it's only a question of minor quantities of tin. Still, I thought you ought to know. Hello? Are you there . . . ?'

Manson jerked himself out of his reverie. With a massive effort he made his voice appear normal.

'Yes indeed. Sorry, I was just thinking. Very good of you to call me, Goole. I don't suppose they'll be in the same area as my man. But damn useful to know, all the same.'

He went through the usual pleasantries before hanging up, and walked slowly back to the sun terrace, his mind racing. Coincidence? Could be, it just could be. If the Soviet survey team were going to cover an area miles away from the Crystal Mountain range, it would be purely a coincidence. On the other hand, if they went straight towards the Crystal Mountain without having done any aerial survey work to notice the differences in vegetation in that area, then that would be no coincidence. That would be bloody sabotage. And there was no way he could find out, no way of being absolutely certain, without betraying his own continuing interest. And that would be fatal.

He thought of Chalmers, the man he was convinced he had silenced with money. His teeth ground. Had he talked? Wittingly? Unwittingly? He had half a mind to let Endean, or one of Endean's friends, take care of Dr Chalmers. But that would change nothing. And there was no proof of a security leak.

He could shelve his plans at once, and think no more of them. He considered this, then considered again the pot of pure gold at the end of this particular rainbow. James Manson was no softy: he was not where he was because he had the habit of backing down on account of an increased element of risk, most of all an unproven one.

He sat down in the deck chair next to the now cold coffee pot and thought hard. He intended to go forward as planned, but he had to assume the Russian mining team would touch on the area Mulrooney had visited, and he had to assume they too would notice the vegetation changes. Therefore there was now a new element, a time limit. He did some mental calculation and came up with the figure of three months. If the Russians learned the content of the Crystal Mountain, there would be a 'technical aid' team in there like a dose of salts, and a big one at that. Over half the members, he knew, would be hard men from the KGB.

Shannon's shortest schedule had been a hundred days, but he had originally told Endean that another fortnight added to the timetable would make the whole project that much more feasible. Now they did not have that fortnight. In fact, if the Russians moved faster than usual, they might not even have a hundred days.

He returned to the telephone and called Simon Endean. His own weekend had been disturbed; there was no reason why Endean should not start doing a bit of work.

Endean called Shannon at the hotel on Monday morning and set up a rendezvous for two p.m. at a small block of flats in St John's Wood. He had hired the flat on the instructions of Sir James Manson that morning, after having had a long briefing at the country mansion on the Sunday afternoon. He had taken the flat for a month in the name of Harris, paying cash and giving a fictitious reference which no one checked. The reason for the hiring was simple: the flat had a telephone that did not go through a switchboard.

Shannon was there on time and found the man he still called Harris already installed. The telephone was hung in a desk microphone set that would enable a telephone conference between one or more people in the room and the person on the other end of the line to be held.

'The chief of the consortium has read your report,' he told Shannon, 'and wants to have a word with you.'

At two-thirty the phone rang. Endean threw the 'speak' switch on the machine and Sir James Manson's voice came on the line. Shannon already knew who it would be, but gave no sign.

'Are you there, Mr Shannon?' asked the voice.

'Yes, sir.'

'Now, I have read your report, and I approve your judgement and conclusions. If offered this contract, would you be prepared to go through with it?'

'Yes, sir, I would,' said Shannon.

'There are a couple of points I want to discuss. I notice in the budget you award yourself the sum of ten thousand pounds.'

'Yes, sir. Frankly, I don't think anyone would do the job for less, and most would ask more. Even if a budget were prepared by another person which quoted a lower sum, I think that person would still pass a minimum of ten per cent to himself, simply by hiding the sum in the prices of purchases that could not be checked out.'

There was a pause, then the voice said:

'All right. I accept it. What does this salary buy me?'

'It buys you my knowledge, my contacts, my acquaintanceship with the world of arms dealers, smugglers, gun-runners and mercenaries. It also buys my silence in the event of anything going wrong. It pays me for three months' damned hard work, and the constant risk of arrest and imprisonment. Lastly, it buys the risk of my getting killed in the attack.'

There was a grunt.

'Fair enough. Now as regards financing. The sum of £100,000 will be transferred into a Swiss account which Mr Harris will open this week. He will pay you the necessary money in slices, as and when you need it over the forthcoming two months. For that purpose you will have to set up your own communications system with him. When the money is spent, he will either have to be present or to receive receipts.'

'That will not always be possible, sir. There are no receipts in the arms business, least of all in black market deals, and most of the men I shall be dealing with would not have Mr Harris present. He is not in their world. I would suggest the extensive use of travellers cheques and credit transfers by banks. At the same time, if Mr Harris has to be present to counter-sign every banker's draft or cheque for £1000, he must either follow me around everywhere, which I would not accept on grounds of my own security, or we could never do it all inside a hundred days.'

There was another long pause.

'What do you mean by your own security?' asked the voice.

'I mean, sir, that I don't know Mr Harris. I could not accept that he be in a position to know enough to get me arrested in a European city. You have taken your security precautions. I have to take mine. These are that I travel and work alone and unsupervised.'

'You're a cautious man, Mr Shannon.'

'I have to be. I'm still alive.'

There was a grim chuckle.

'And how do I know you can be trusted with large sums of money to handle on your own?'

'You don't, sir. Up to a point Mr Harris can keep the sums low at each stage. But the payments for the arms have to be made in cash and by the buyer alone. The only alternatives are to ask Mr Harris to mount the operation personally, or hire another professional. And you would not know if you could trust him either.'

'Fair enough, Mr Shannon. Mr Harris . . .'

'Sir?' answered Endean immediately.

'Please return to see me at once after leaving where you are now. Mr Shannon, you have the job. You have one hundred days, Mr Shannon, to steal a republic. One hundred days.'

PART TWO
THE HUNDRED DAYS

Chapter Eight

For several minutes after Sir James Manson had rung off, Simon Endean and Cat Shannon sat and stared at one another. It was Shannon who recovered first.

'Since we're going to have to work together,' he told Endean, 'let's get this clear. If anyone, anyone at all, gets to hear about this project, it will eventually get back to one or other of the secret services of one of the main powers. Probably the CIA, or at least the British SIS or maybe the French SDECE. And they will screw, but good. There'll be nothing you or I could do to prevent them ending the affair stone dead. So we keep security absolute.'

'Speak for yourself,' snapped Endean. 'I've got a lot more tied up in this than you.'

'OK. First thing has to be money. I'll fly to Brussels tomorrow and open a new bank account somewhere in Belgium. I'll be back by tomorrow night. Contact me then, and I'll tell you where, in which bank and in what name. Then I shall need a transfer of credit to the tune of at least £10,000. By tomorrow night I'll have a complete list of where it has to be spent. Mainly, it will be in salary cheques for my assistants, deposits, etc.'

'Where do I contact you?' asked Endean.

'That's point number two,' said Shannon. 'I'm going to need a permanent base, secure for telephone calls and letters. What about this flat? Is it traceable to you?'

Endean had not thought of that. He considered the problem.

'It's hired in my name. Cash in advance for one month,' he said.

'Does it matter if the name Harris is on the tenancy agreement?' asked Shannon.

'No.'

'Then I'll take it over. That gives me a month's tenancy – seems a pity to waste it – and I'll take up the payments at the end of that time. Do you have a key?'

'Yes, of course. I let myself in by it.'

'How many keys are there?'

For answer Endean reached into his pocket and brought out a ring with four keys on it. Two were evidently for the front door of the block and two for the flat door. Shannon took them from his hand.

'Now for communications,' he said. 'You can contact me by phoning here any time. I may be in, I may not. I may be away abroad. Since I assume you will not want to give me your phone number, set up a *poste restante* mailing address in London somewhere convenient either to your home or office, and check twice daily for telegrams. If I need you urgently I'll telegram with the phone number of where I am, and a time to phone. Understood?'

'Yes. I'll have it by tomorrow night. Anything else?'

'Only that I'll be using the name of Keith Brown throughout the operation. Anything signed as coming from Keith is from me. When ringing a hotel ask for me as Keith Brown. If ever I reply by saying "This is Mister Brown", get off the line fast. It means trouble. Explain that you have the wrong number, or the wrong Brown. That's all for the moment. You'd better get back to the office. Ring me here at eight tonight and I'll give you the progress to date.'

A few minutes later Endean found himself on the pavements of St John's Wood looking for a taxi.

Luckily Shannon had not banked the £500 he had received from Endean before the weekend for his attack project, and he still had £450 of it left. There was his hotel bill in Knightsbridge to settle, but that could come later.

He rang BEA and booked an economy class return on the morning flight to Brussels, returning at 1600 hours, which would get him back in his flat by six. Following that he telephoned four telegrams abroad, one to Paarl, Cape Province, South Africa, one to Ostende, one to Marseilles and one to Munich. Each said simply, 'URGENT YOU PHONE ME LONDON 507–0041 ANY MIDNIGHT OVER NEXT THREE DAYS STOP SHANNON'. Finally he summoned a taxi and had it take him back to the Lowndes Hotel. He checked out, paid his bill and left as he had come, anonymously.

At eight Endean rang him as agreed and he told Manson's aide what he had done so far. They agreed Endean would ring again at ten the following evening.

Shannon spent a couple of hours exploring the block he was now living in, and the surrounding area. He spotted several small restaurants including a couple not far away in St John's Wood High Street, and ate a leisurely supper at one of them. He was back home by eleven.

He counted his money – there was over £400 left – put £300 on one side for the air fare and expenses the following day, and checked over his effects. The clothes were unremarkable, all of them less than three months old, most bought in the last ten days in London. He had no gun to bother about, and for safety destroyed the typewriter ribbon he had used to type his reports, replacing it with one of his spares.

Though it was dark early in London that evening, it was still light on a warm, sunny summer evening in Cape Province as Janni Dupree gunned his car past Seapoint and on towards Cape Town. He too had a Chevrolet, older than Endean's, but bigger and flashier, bought second-hand with some of the dollars with which he had returned from Paris four weeks earlier. After spending the day swimming and fishing from a friend's boat at Simonstown, he was driving back to his home in Paarl. He always liked to come home to Paarl after a contract, but inevitably it bored him quickly, just as it had when he left it ten years before.

As a boy he had been raised in the Paarl Valley and had spent his pre-school years scampering through the thin and poor vineyards owned by people like his parents. He had learned to stalk birds and shoot in the valley with Pieter, his klonkie, the coloured playmate white boys are allowed to play with until they grow too old and learn what skin colour is all about.

Pieter, with his enormous brown eyes, tangled mass of black curls and mahogany skin, had been two years older than he, and supposed to look after him. In fact they had been the same size, for Janni was physically precocious and had quickly taken the leadership of the pair. On summer days like this one, twenty years ago, the two barefoot boys used to take the bus along the coast to Cape Agulhas, where the Atlantic and the Indian oceans finally meet, and fish for yellowtail, galjoen and red steenbras off the point.

After Paarl Boys' High, Janni had been a problem, too big, aggressive, restless, getting into fights with those big, scything fists and ending up twice in front of the magistrates. He could have taken over his parents' farm, tending with his father the stubby little vines that produced such thin wine. The prospect appalled him, of becoming old and bent trying to make a living from the smallholding with only four coloured boys working with him. At eighteen he volunteered for the Army, did his basic training at Potchefstroom and transferring to the paratroops at Bloemfontein. It was here he had found the thing he wanted to do most in life, here and in the counter-insurgency training in the harsh bushveld around Pietersburg. The Army had agreed with him about his suitability, except on one point, his propensity for going to war while pointing in the wrong direction. In one fist-fight too many, Corporal Dupree had beaten a sergeant senseless and the commanding officer had busted him down to private.

Bitter, he went AWOL, was taken in a bar in East London, battered two MPs before they held him down, and did six months in the stockade. On release he saw an advertisement in an evening newspaper, reported to a small office in Durban, and two days later was flown out of South Africa to Kamina base in Katanga. He had become a mercenary at twenty-two, and that had been six years ago.

As he drove along the winding road through Franshoek towards the Paarl Valley, he wondered if there would be a letter from Shannon or one of the boys with news of a contract. But when he got there, there was nothing waiting at the post office. Clouds were blowing up from the sea, and there was the hint of thunder in the air.

It would rain that evening, a nice cooling shower, and he glanced up towards the Paarl Rock, the phenomenon that had given the valley and the town its name long ago when his ancestors first came into the valley. As a boy he had stared in wonderment at the rock, a dull grey when dry, but which after rain glistened like an enormous pearl in the moonlight. Then it became a great, glistening, gleaming thing, dominating the tiny town beneath it. Although the town of his boyhood could never offer him the kind of life he wanted, it was still home; and when he saw the Paarl Rock glistening in the light, he always knew he was back home again. That evening he wished he were somewhere else, heading towards another war.

What he did not know was that by the following morning Shannon's telegram, summoning him to another war, would be in Paarl post office.

Tiny Marc Vlaminck leaned on the bar counter and downed another foaming schooner of Flemish ale. Outside the front windows of the place his girl-friend managed, the streets of Ostende's red-light district were almost empty. A chill wind was blowing off the sea and the summer tourists had not started to arrive yet. He was bored already.

For the first month since his return from the tropics it had been good to be back, good to take hot baths again, to chat with his mates who had dropped in to see him. Even the local press had taken an interest, but he had told them to get lost. The last thing he needed was trouble from the authorities, and he knew they would leave him alone if he did or said nothing to embarrass them with the African embassies in Brussels.

But after weeks the inactivity had palled. A few nights back it had been enlivened when he thumped a seaman who had tried to fondle Anna's bottom, an area he regarded as entirely his own preserve. The memory had started a thought running through his mind. He could hear a low thump-thump from upstairs where Anna was doing the housework in the small flat that they shared above the bar. He heaved himself off his bar-stool, drained the tankard and called, 'If anyone comes in, serve 'em yourself.'

Then he lumbered up the back stairs. As he did so the door opened and a telegram boy came in.

It was a clear spring evening with just a touch of chill in the air and the water of the Old Port of Marseilles was like glass. Across its centre, a few moments ago a mirror for the surrounding bars and cafés, a single home-coming trawler cut a swathe of ripples that wandered across the harbour and died chuckling under the hull of the fisher boats already moored. The cars were locked solid along the Canebière, smells of cooking fish emanated from a thousand windows, the old men sipped their anisette and the heroin sellers scuttled through the alleys on their lucrative missions. It was an ordinary evening.

In the multi-national, multi-lingual cauldron of seething humanity that called itself Le Panier, where only a policeman is illegal, Jean-Baptiste Langarotti sat at a corner table in a small bar and sipped a long cool Ricard.

He was not as bored as Janni Dupree or Marc Vlaminck. Years in prison had taught him the ability to keep himself interested in even the smallest things, and long periods of inactivity he could survive better than most.

Moreover, he had been able to get himself a job of work and earn a living, so that his savings were still intact. He saved steadily, his economies mounting up in a bank in Switzerland that no one knew about. One day it would buy him the little bar in Calvi that he wanted.

A month earlier a good friend of his from the Algerian days had been picked up for a small matter of a suitcase containing twelve former French Army Colt Forty-fives and from Les Baumettes had sent Jean-Baptiste a message asking him to 'mind' the girl off whose earnings the imprisoned friend normally lived. He knew he could trust the Corsican not to cheat him. She was a good girl, a broad-beamed hoyden called Marie-Claire who went under the name of Lola and did her nightly stint in a bar in the Tubano district. She had taken quite a fancy to Langarotti, perhaps because of his size, and her only complaint was that he did not knock her about the way her boyfriend in prison had done. Being small was no hindrance to being a minder, because the rest of the underworld, who might have made a claim for Lola, needed no education about Langarotti.

So Lola was happy to be the best-minded girl in town, and Jean-Baptiste content to while away the days until another contract to fight came up. He was in contact with a few people in the mercenary business, but being new to it was relying more on Shannon to hear of something first. He was more the sort clients would come to.

Shortly after returning to France, Langarotti had been contacted by Charles Roux from Paris, who had proposed that the Corsican sign on with him in exclusivity, in exchange for first choice if and when a contract turned up. Roux had talked largely of the half-dozen projects he had brewing at the time, and the Corsican had remained non-committal. Later he had checked up and found Roux was mostly talk, for he had set up no projects of his own since his return from Bukavu in the autumn of '67 with a hole through his arm.

With a sigh Langarotti glanced at his watch, finished his drink and rose to go. It was time to fetch Lola from their apartment and escort her to the bar for work, and then drop in at the all-night post office to see if there was a telegram from Shannon offering a prospect of a new war.

In Munich it was even colder than in Marc Vlaminck's Ostende, and Kurt Semmler, his blood thinned by years in the Far East, Algeria and Africa, shivered in his knee-length black leather coat as he headed towards the all-night post office. He made a regular check-call at the counter every morning and evening, and each time hoped for some letter or telegram bearing news or an invitation to meet someone for an interview for possible selection for a mercenary assignment.

The period from his return from Africa had been one of idleness and boredom. Like most army veterans he disliked civilian life, wore the clothes badly, despised the politics and longed again for some form of routine combined with action. The return to his birth-city had not been encouraging. Everywhere he saw long-haired youths, sloppy and ill-disciplined, waving their banners and screaming their slogans. There seemed to be none of the sense of purpose, of commitment to the ideal of the greatness of the Fatherland and its leader that had so completely absorbed his own childhood and youth, nor the sense of order that characterized the army life.

Even the smuggling life in the Mediterranean, although it had been free and easy, at least could offer the sense of activity, the scent of danger, the feeling of a mission planned, executed and accomplished. Easing a fast launch in towards the Italian coast with two tons of American cigarettes on board, he had at least been able to imagine himself back on the Mekong, going into action with the Legion against the Xoa Binh river pirates.

Munich offered him nothing. He had drunk too much, smoked too much, whored a bit and become thoroughly disgruntled.

At the post office there was nothing for him that evening. But next morning it would be a different story, for Shannon's telegram was on its way across a darkened Europe.

At midnight Marc Vlaminck phoned in from Ostende. The Belgian telegram delivery services are excellent and deliver up to ten at night. Shannon told Vlaminck simply to meet him in front of Brussels National airport the following morning with a car and gave him his flight number.

Belgium has, from the point of view of those wishing to operate a discreet but legal bank account, many advantages that outweigh those offered by the much better publicized Swiss banking system. Not nearly as rich or powerful as Germany, nor neutral like Switzerland, Belgium nevertheless offers the facility of permitting unlimited quantities of money to pass in and out without government control or interference. The banks are also just as discreet as those of Switzerland, which is why they and the banks of Luxembourg and Lichtenstein have been steadily increasing their volume of business at the expense of the Swiss.

It was to the Kredietbank in Brugge, seventy minutes' driving time from Brussels airport, that Shannon had himself driven by Marc Vlaminck the following morning.

The big Belgian was evidently full of curiosity, but he kept it to himself. When they were on the road to Brugge Shannon mentioned briefly that he had been given a contract, and there was room for four helpers. Was Vlaminck interested?

Tiny Marc indicated that of course he was. Shannon told him he could not say what the operation was, other than that it was a job that not merely had to be fought, but set up from scratch. He was prepared to offer normal rates of 1250 dollars a month plus expenses for the next three months, and that the job, although not requiring absence from home until the third month, would require a few hours' risk inside Europe. That, of course, was not strictly mercenary work, but it had to be done. Marc grunted.

'I'm not knocking off banks,' he said. 'Not for that kind of money.'

'It's nothing like that. I need some guns taken on board a boat. We have to do it ourselves. After we sail, it's all set for Africa and a nice little firefight.'

Marc grinned.

'A long campaign, or a quick in-and-out job?'

'An attack,' said Shannon. 'Mind you, if it works, there could be a long contract in the offing. Can't promise, but it looks like that. And a fat success bonus.'

'OK, I'm on,' said Marc, and they drove into the main square at Brugge.

The Kredietbank head office is situated at Number 25 in the Vlamingstraat, a narrow thoroughfare flanked by house after house in the distinctive style of eighteenth-century Flemish architecture, and all in a perfect state of preservation. Most of the ground floors have been converted into shops, but upwards from the ground floors the façades resemble something from a painting by one of the old masters.

Inside the bank Shannon introduced himself to the head of the foreign accounts' section, Mr Goossens, and proved his identity as Keith Brown by tendering his passport. Within forty minutes he had opened a current account with a deposit of £100 sterling in cash, informed Mr Goossens that a sum of £10,000 in the form of a transfer from Switzerland could be expected any day, and left instructions that of this sum £5000 was to be transferred at once to his account in London. He left several examples of his Keith Brown signature and agreed on a method of establishing his identity over the phone by reeling off the twelve numbers of his account in reverse order followed by yesterday's date. On this basis verbal instructions for transfers and withdrawals could be made without his coming to Brugge again. He signed an indemnity form protecting the bank from any risks of using this method of communication, and agreed to write his account number in red ink under his signature on any written instruction to the bank, again to prove authenticity.

By half past twelve he was finished, and joined Vlaminck outside. They ate a lunch of solid food accompanied by the inevitable chips at the Café des Arts on the main square before the Town Hall, and then Vlaminck drove him back to Brussels airport. Before parting from the Fleming, Shannon gave him £50 in cash and told him to take the Ostende–Dover ferry the next day and be at the London flat at six in the evening. He had to wait an hour for his plane and was back in London by tea-time.

Simon Endean had also had a busy day. He had caught the earliest flight of the day to Zürich and had landed at Kloten airport by just after ten. Within an hour he was standing at the counter of the Handelsbank of Zürich's head office at 58, Talstrasse, and opened a current account in his own name. He too left several specimen signatures, and agreed with the bank official who interviewed him on a method of signing all written communications to the bank simply by writing the account number at the bottom of the letter and under the number the day of the week on which the letter had been written. The day would be written in green ink, while the account number would inevitably be in black. He deposited the £500 in cash that he had brought, and informed the bank the sum of £100,000 would be transferred into the account within the week. Lastly he instructed the Union Bank that as soon as the credit had been received, they were to remit £10,000 to an account in Belgium which he would give them later by letter. He signed a long contract which exonerated the bank from anything and everything including culpable negligence and left him no protection whatever in law. Not that there was any point in contesting a Swiss bank before a Swiss court, as he well knew.

Taking a taxi from Talstrasse he dropped a wax-sealed letter through the door of the Zwingli Bank and headed back to the airport.

The letter, which Dr Martin Steinhofer had in his hand within thirty minutes, was from Sir James Manson. It was signed in the approved manner by which Manson signed all his correspondence with his Zürich bank. It requested Dr Steinhofer to transfer £100,000 to the account of Mr Simon Endean at the Union Bank forthwith, and informed him that Sir James would be calling on him at his office the following day, Wednesday.

Endean was in London airport just before six.

Martin Thorpe was exhausted when he came into the office that Tuesday afternoon. He had spent the two days of the weekend and Monday going methodically through the 4500 cards in the Moodies index of companies quoted on the London Stock Exchange.

He had been concentrating on finding a suitable shell company, and had sought out the small companies, preferably founded many years ago, largely run-down and with few assets, companies which over the past three years had traded at a loss, or broken even, or made a profit below £10,000. He also wanted companies with a market capitalization of under £200,000.

Martin Thorpe had come up with two dozen companies that fitted the bill, and these he showed to Sir James Manson. He had listed them provisionally in order from One to Twenty-Four on the basis of their apparent suitability.

He still had more to do, and by mid-afternoon he was at Companies House, in City Road, EC2.

He sent up to the archivists the list of his first eight companies and paid his statutory fee for each name on the list, giving him, as any other member of the public, the right to examine the full company documents. As he waited for the eight bulky folders to come back to the reading room, he glanced through the latest Stock Exchange Official List and noted with satisfaction that none of the eight was quoted at over three shillings a share.

When the files arrived he started with the first on his list and began to pore over the records. He was looking for three things not given in the Moodies cards, which are simply a synopsis. He wanted to study the distribution of the ownership of the shares, to ensure that the company he sought was not controlled by the combined board of directors, and to be certain there had not been a recent build-up of shareholdings by another person or associated group, which would have indicated that another City predator was looking for a meal.

By the time Companies House closed for the evening, he had been through seven of the eight files. He would cover the remaining seventeen the following day. But already he was intrigued by the third on his list and mildly excited. On paper it looked great, from his point of view, even too good, and that was the rub. It looked so good, he was surprised no one had snapped it up ages ago. There had to be a flaw somewhere, but with Martin Thorpe's ingenuity there might even be a way of overcoming it. If there was such a way . . . it was perfect.

Simon Endean phoned Cat Shannon at the latter's flat at ten that evening. Shannon reported what he had done, and Endean gave a resumé of his own day. He told Shannon the necessary £100,000 should have been transferred to his new Swiss account before closing time that afternoon, and Shannon told Endean to have the first £10,000 sent to him under the name of Keith Brown at the Kredietbank in Brugge, Belgium.

Within a few minutes of hanging up, Endean had written his letter of instruction to the Handelsbank, stressing that the transferred sum should be sent at once but that under no condition was the name of the Swiss account holder to become known to the Belgian bank. The account number alone should be quoted on the transfer, which should be by telex. He mailed the letter express rate from the all-night post office in Trafalgar Square just before midnight.

At eleven-forty-five the phone rang again in Shannon's flat. It was Semmler on the line from Munich. Shannon told him he had work for all of them if they wanted it, but that he could not come to Munich. Semmler should take a single ticket by air to London the following day and be there by six. He gave his address and promised to repay the German his expenses in any case, and pay his fare back to Munich if he declined the job. Semmler agreed to come, and Shannon hung up.

The next on the line was Langarotti from Marseilles. He had checked his *poste restante* box and found Zangaro's cable waiting for him. He would be in London by six and would report to the flat.

Janni Dupree's call was late, coming through at half past midnight. He too agreed to pack his bags and fly the 8000 miles to London, though he could not be there for a day and a half. He would be at Shannon's flat on the Friday evening instead.

With the last call taken, Shannon read for an hour and switched off the light. It was the end of Day One.

Sir James Manson did not fly economy class; he went first, and on the businessman's Trident Three to Zürich ate a hearty breakfast that Wednesday morning. Shortly before noon he was ushered respectfully into the panelled office of Dr Martin Steinhofer.

The two men had known each other for ten years and during this time the Zwingli Bank had several times carried out business on Manson's behalf in situations where he had needed a nominee to buy shares which, had it become known that the name of Manson was behind the purchase, would have trebled in value. Dr Steinhofer valued his client, and rose to shake hands and usher the English knight into a comfortable armchair.

The Swiss offered cigars, and coffee was brought along with small glasses of Kirschwasser. Only when the male secretary had gone did Sir James broach his business.

'Over the forthcoming weeks I shall be seeking to acquire a controlling interest in a small British company, a public company. At the moment I cannot give the name of it, because a suitable vehicle for my particular operation has not yet come to light. I hope to know it fairly soon.'

Dr Steinhofer nodded silently and sipped his coffee.

'At the start it will be quite a small operation, involving relatively little money. Later, I have reason to believe news will hit the Stock Exchange that will have quite an interesting effect on the share value of that company,' he went on.

There was no need for him to explain to the Swiss banker the rules that apply in share dealings on the London Stock Exchange, for he was as familiar with them as Manson, as he was also with the rules of all the main exchanges and markets throughout the world.

Under British company law, any person acquiring ten per cent or more of the shares of a public quoted company must identify himself to the directors within fourteen days. The aim of the law is to permit the public to know who owns what, and how much, of any public company.

For this reason, a reputable London stockbroking house, buying on behalf of a client, will also abide by the law and inform the directors of their client's name, unless the purchase is less than ten per cent of the company's stock, in which case the buyer may remain anonymous.

One way round this rule is for a tycoon seeking to gain secret control of a company to use nominee buyers. But again, a reputable firm on the Stock Exchange will soon spot if the real buyer of a big block of shares is in fact one man operating through nominees, and will obey the law.

But a Swiss bank, not bound by the laws of Britain, abiding by its own laws of secrecy, simply refuses to answer questions about who stands behind the names they present as their clients, nor will they reveal anything else, even if they privately suspect that the front-men do not exist at all.

Both of the men in Dr Steinhofer's office that morning were well aware of all the finer points involved.

'In order to make the necessary acquisition of shares,' Sir James went on, 'I have entered into association with six partners. They will purchase the shares on my behalf. They have all agreed they would wish to open small accounts with the Zwingli Bank and to ask you to be so kind as to make the purchases on their behalf.'

Dr Steinhofer put down his coffee cup and nodded. As a good Swiss he agreed there was no point in breaking rules where they could be legally bent, with the obvious proviso that they were not Swiss rules, and he could also see the point in not wantonly sending the share price upwards, even in a small operation. One started by saving pfennigs, and one became rich after a lifetime of application.

'That presents no problem,' he said carefully. 'These gentlemen will be coming here to open their accounts?'

Sir James exhaled a stream of aromatic smoke.

'It may well be they will find themselves too busy to come personally. I have myself appointed my financial assistant to stand in for me. To save time and trouble, you understand. It may well be the other six partners will wish to avail themselves of the same procedure. You have no objection to that?'

'Of course not,' murmured Dr Steinhofer. 'Your financial assistant is who, please?'

'Mr Martin Thorpe.' Sir James Manson drew a slim envelope from his pocket and handed it to the banker.

'This is my power of attorney, duly notarised and witnessed, and signed by me. You have my signature for comparison of course. In it you will find Mr Thorpe's full name and the number of his passport, by which he will identify himself. He will be visiting Zürich in the next week or ten days to finalise arrangements. From then on he will act in all matters on my behalf and his signature will be as good as mine. Is that acceptable?'

Dr Steinhofer scanned the single sheet in the envelope and nodded.

'Certainly, Sir James. I see no problems.'

Manson rose and stubbed out his cigar.

'Then I'll bid you good-bye, Dr Steinhofer, and leave further dealings in the hands of Mr Thorpe, who of course will consult with me on all steps to be taken.'

They shook hands and Sir James Manson was ushered down to the street. As the solid oak door clicked quietly shut behind him he pulled up his coat collar against the still chilly air of the north Swiss town, stepped into the waiting hired limousine and gave instructions for the Baur au Lac for lunch. One ate well there, he reflected, but otherwise Zürich was a dreary place. It did not even have a good brothel.

Assistant Under-Secretary Sergei Golon was not in a good humour that morning. The mail had brought a letter to his breakfast table to notify him that his son had failed the entrance examination for the Civil Service Academy, and there had been a general family row. In consequence his perennial problem of acid indigestion had elected to ensure him a day of unrelenting misery and his secretary was away sick.

Beyond the windows of his small office in the West Africa section of the Foreign Ministry the canyons of Moscow's windswept boulevards were still covered with snow slush, a grimy grey in the dim morning light, waiting tiredly for the thaw of spring.

'Neither one thing nor the other,' the attendant had remarked as he had berthed his Moskvitch in the car park beneath the ministry building.

Golon had grunted agreement as he took the lift to his eighth floor to begin the morning's work. Devoid of a secretary, he had taken the pile of files brought for his attention from various parts of the building, and started to go through them, an antacid tablet revolving slowly in his mouth.

The third file had been marked for his attention by the office of the Under-Secretary, and the same clerkish hand had written on the cover-sheet 'Assess and Instigate Necessary Action'. Golon perused it gloomily. He noted that the file had been started on the basis of an inter-departmental memorandum from Foreign Intelligence, and that his Ministry had, on reflection, given Ambassador Dobrovolsky certain instructions which, according to the latest cable from Dobrovolsky, had been carried out. The request had been granted, the ambassador reported, and he urged prompt action.

Golon snorted. Passed over for an ambassadorship, he held firmly to the view that men in diplomatic posts abroad were far too prone to believe their own parishes were of consummate importance.

'As if we have nothing else to bother about,' he grunted. Already his eye had caught the folder beneath the one he was reading. He knew it concerned the Republic of Guinea, where a constant stream of telegrams from the Soviet ambassador reported the growth of Chinese influence in Conakry. Now that, he mused, was something of concern. Compared to this, he could not see the importance of whether there was, or was not, tin in commercial quantities in the hinterland of Zangaro. Besides, the Soviet Union had enough tin.

Nevertheless, action had been authorized from above, and as a good civil servant he took it. To a secretary borrowed from the typing pool he dictated a letter to the Director of the Sverdlovsk Institute of Mining requiring him to select a small team of survey geologists and engineers to carry out an examination of a suspected mineral deposit in West Africa, and to inform him in due course that the team and its equipment were ready to depart.

Privately he thought he would have to tackle the question of their transportation to West Africa through the appropriate directorate, but pushed the thought to the back of his mind. The painful burning in the back of his throat subsided, and he observed that the scribbling stenographer had rather pretty knees.

Cat Shannon had a quiet day. He rose late and went into the West End to his bank, where he withdrew most of the £1000 his account contained. He was confident the money would be replaced and more when the transfer came through from Belgium.

After lunch he rang his friend the writer, who seemed surprised to hear from him.

'I thought you'd left town,' said the scribe.

'Why should I?' asked Shannon.

'Well, little Julie has been looking for you. You must have made an impression. Carrie says she has not stopped talking. But she rang the Lowndes, and they said you had left, address unknown.'

Shannon promised he'd ring. He gave his own phone number, but not his address. With the small talk over, he requested the information he wanted.

'I suppose I could,' said the friend dubiously. 'But honestly, I ought to ring him first and see if it's OK.'

'Well, do that,' said Shannon. 'Tell him it's me, that I need to see him, and am prepared to go down there for a few hours with him. Tell him I wouldn't trouble him if it wasn't important in my opinion.'

The writer agreed to put through the call and ring Shannon back with the telephone number and address of the man Shannon wished to talk to, if the man agreed to speak to Shannon.

In the afternoon he wrote a letter to Mr Goossens at the Kredietbank to tell him that he would in the future give two or three business partners the Kredietbank as his mailing address, and would keep in contact by phone with the bank to check whether any mail was waiting for collection. He would also be sending some letters to business associates via the Kredietbank, in which case he would mail an envelope to Mr Goossens from wherever he happened to be. He requested Mr Goossens to take the enclosed envelope which would be inside, addressed but not stamped, and forward it from Brugge to its destination. Lastly he bade Mr Goossens deduct all postal and bank charges from his account.

At five p.m. Endean rang him at the flat and Shannon gave him a progress report, omitting to mention his contact with his writer friend, whom he had never mentioned to Endean. He told him however that he expected three of his four chosen associates to be in London for their separate briefings that evening, and the fourth to arrive on Friday evening at the latest.

Martin Thorpe had his fifth tiring day, but at least his search was over. He had perused the documents of another seventeen companies in the City Road, and had drawn up a second short list, this time of five companies. Top of the list was the company that had caught his eye the previous day. He finished his reading by the mid-afternoon and as Sir James Manson had not returned from Zürich, Thorpe decided to take the rest of the day off. He could brief his chief in the morning and later begin his private inquiries into the set-up of his chosen company, a series of inquiries to determine why such a prize was still available. By the late afternoon he was back in Hampstead Garden Suburb and mowing the lawn.

Chapter Nine

The first of the mercenaries to arrive at London's Heathrow airport was Kurt Semmler, on the Lufthansa flight from Munich. He tried to reach Shannon by phone soon after clearing customs, but there was no reply. He was early for his check-in call, so he decided to wait at the airport, took a seat in the restaurant window overlooking the apron of Number Two Building. He chain-smoked nervously as he sat over coffee and watched the jets leaving for Europe.

Marc Vlaminck phoned to check in with Shannon just after five. The Cat glanced down the list of three hotels in the neighbourhood of his apartment and read out the name of one. The Belgian took it down in his Victoria Station phone booth, letter by letter. A few minutes later he hailed a taxi outside the station and showed the paper to the driver.

Semmler was ten minutes after Vlaminck. He too received from Shannon the name of a hotel, wrote it down and took a mini-cab from the front of the airport building.

Langarotti was the last, checking in just before six from the Air Terminal in Cromwell Road. He too hired a taxi to take him to his hotel.

At seven Shannon rang them all, one after the other, and bade them assemble at his flat within thirty minutes.

When they greeted each other, it was the first indication any of them had that the others had been invited. The broad grins with which they learned the others were also present came partly from the pleasure of meeting friends, partly from the knowledge that Shannon's investment in bringing them all to London with a guarantee of a reimbursed air fare could only mean he had money. If they wondered who the patron might be, they knew better than to ask.

Their first impression was strengthened when Shannon told them that he had instructed Dupree to fly in from South Africa on the same terms. A £500 air ticket meant Shannon was not playing games. They settled down to listen.

'The job I've been given,' he told them, 'is a project that has to be organized from scratch. It has not been laid on, and the only way to set it up is to do it ourselves. The object is to mount an attack, a short, sharp attack, commando-style, on a town on the coast of Africa. We have to shoot the shits out of one building, storm it, capture it, knock off everyone in it, and pull back out again.'

The reaction was what he had confidently expected. The men exchanged glances of approval. Vlaminck gave a wide grin and scratched his chest; Semmler muttered '*Klasse*' and lit a fresh cigarette from the stub of the old one. He offered one to Shannon, who regretfully shook his head. Langarotti remained deadpan, his eyes on Shannon, the knife blade slipping smoothly across the black leather round his left fist.

Shannon spread a map out on the floor in the centre of the circle and the men eyed it keenly. It was a hand-drawn map, depicting a section of seashore and a series of buildings on the landward side. It was not even accurate, for it excluded the two curving spits of shingle that were the identifying marks of the harbour of Clarence. But it sufficed to indicate the kind of operation required.

The mercenary leader talked for twenty minutes, outlining the kind of attack he had already proposed to his patron as the only feasible way of taking the objective, and the three men concurred. None of them asked the name of the destination. They knew he would not tell them, and that they did not need to know. It was not a question of lack of trust, simply of security. If a leak was sprung in the secret, they did not want to be among the possible suspects.

Shannon spoke in French, his own strongly accented grasp of the language, which he had picked up in the Sixth Commando in the Congo. He knew Vlaminck had a reasonable grasp of English, as a barman in Ostende must have, and that Semmler commanded a vocabulary of about two hundred words. But Langarotti knew very little indeed, so French was the common language, except when Dupree was present, when everything had to be translated.

'So that's it,' said Shannon as he finished. 'The terms are that you all go on salary of 1250 dollars a month from tomorrow morning, plus expenses for living and travelling while in Europe. The budget is ample for the job. Only two of the tasks that have to be done in the preparation stages are illegal, because I've planned to keep the maximum of the preparations strictly legal. Of these tasks one is a border crossing from Belgium to France, the other a problem of loading some cases onto a ship somewhere in southern Europe. We'll all be involved in both jobs.

'You get three months' guaranteed salary, plus 5000 dollars each bonus for success. So what do you say?'

The three men looked at each other. Vlaminck nodded.

'I'm on,' he said. 'Like I said yesterday. It looks good.'

Langarotti stropped his knife.

'Is it against French interests?' he asked. 'I don't want to be an exile.'

'You have my word it is not against the French in Africa.'

'*D'accord*,' said the Corsican simply.

'Kurt?' asked Shannon.

'What about insurance?' asked the German. 'It doesn't matter for me, I have no relatives, but what about Marc?'

The Belgian nodded.

'Yes, I don't want to leave Anna with nothing,' he said.

Mercenaries on contract are usually insured by the contractor for 20,000 dollars for loss of life and 6000 for loss of a major limb.

'You have to take out your own, but it can be as high as you want to go. If anything happens to anyone, the rest swear blind he was lost overboard at sea by accident. If anyone gets badly hurt and survives, we all swear the injury was caused by shifting machinery on board. You all take out insurance for a sea trip from Europe to South Africa as passengers on a small freighter. OK?'

The three men nodded.

'I'm on,' said Semmler.

They shook on it, and that was enough. Then Shannon went into the jobs he wanted each man to do.

'Kurt, you'll get first salary cheque and £1000 expenses on Friday. I want you to go down to the Mediterranean and start looking for a boat. I need a small freighter with a clean record. Get that, it must be clean. Papers in order, ship for sale. One hundred to two hundred tons, coaster or converted trawler, possibly converted Navy vessel if needs be, but not looking like an MTB. I don't want speed, but reliability. The sort that can pick up a cargo in a Mediterranean port without exciting attention, even an arms cargo. Registered as a general freighter, owned by a small company or its own skipper. Price not over £25,000 including the cost of any work that needs doing on it. Absolute latest sailing date, fully fuelled and victualled for a trip to Cape Town, not later than sixty days from now. Got it?'

Semmler nodded, and began to think at once of his contacts in the shipping world.

'Jean-Baptiste. Which city do you know best in the Mediterranean?'

'Marseilles,' said Langarotti without hesitation.

'OK. You get salary and £500 on Friday. Get to Marseilles, set up in a small hotel, and start looking. Find me three large inflatable semi-rigid craft of the same kind as Zodiac make. The sort developed for water sports from the basic design of the Marine Commando assault craft. Buy them at separate suppliers, then book them into the bonded warehouse of a respectable shipping agent for export to Morocco. Purpose – water-skiing and sub-aqua diving at a holiday resort. Colour black. Also three powerful outboard engines, battery-started. The boats should take up to a ton of payload. The engines should move such a craft and that weight at not less than ten knots, with a big reserve. You'll need about 60 horsepower. Very important – make sure they are fitted with underwater exhausts for silent running. If they can't be got in that condition, get a mechanic to make you three exhaust-pipe extensions with the necessary outlet valves, to fit the engines. Store them at the same export agent's bonded warehouse, for the same purpose as the dinghies. Water-sports in Morocco. You won't have enough money in the £500. Open a bank account and send me the name and number, by mail, to this address. I'll send the money by credit transfer. Buy everything separately, and submit me the price lists, by mail, here. OK?'

Langarotti nodded and resumed his knife-stropping.

'Marc. You remember you mentioned once that you knew a man in Belgium had knocked off a German store of a thousand brand-new Schmeisser submachine pistols in 1945 and still had half of them in store? I want you to go back to Ostende on Friday with your salary and £500 and locate that man. See if he'll sell. I want a hundred, and in first-class working order. I'll pay 100 dollars each, which is way over the rate. Contact me by letter only, here at this flat, when you have found the man and can set up a meeting between him and me. Got it?'

By nine-thirty they were through, the instructions memorized, noted and understood.

'Right, what about a spot of dinner?' Shannon asked his colleagues. The suggestion was met with noisy agreement, for the men had had little but airline lunches and snacks, and all were hungry. Shannon took them round the corner to the Paprika for a meal. They still spoke in French, but no one else took much notice, exept to glance over when a loud burst of laughter came from the group of four. Evidently they were excited at something, though none of the diners could have surmised that what elated the group in the corner was the prospect of going once again to war under the leadership of Cat Shannon.

Across the Channel another man was thinking hard about Carlo Alfred

Thomas Shannon, and his thoughts were not charitable. He paced the sitting room of his apartment in one of the residential boulevards near the Place de la Bastille, and considered the information he had been gathering for the previous week, and the snippet from Marseilles that had reached him several hours earlier.

If the writer who had originally recommended Charles Roux to Simon Endean as a second possible mercenary for Endean's project had known more about the Frenchman, his description would not have been so complimentary. But he knew only the basic facts of the man's background, and little about his character. Nor did he know, and thus was unable to tell Endean, of the vitriolic hatred that Roux bore for the other man he had recommended, Cat Shannon.

After Endean had left Roux, the Frenchman had waited a full fortnight for a second contact to be made. When it never came, he was forced to the conclusion either that the project in the mind of the visitor who had called himself Walter Harris had been abandoned or that someone else had got the job.

Pursuing the latter line of inquiry, he had looked for any one among the other possible selections that the English businessman could have made. It was while he was making these inquiries, or having them made for him, that he had learned Cat Shannon had been in Paris, staying under his own name at a small hotel in Montmartre. This had shaken him, for he had lost trace of Shannon after their parting at Le Bourget airport, and had thought the man had left Paris.

At this point, over a week earlier, he had briefed one of the men he knew to be loyal to him to make intensive inquiries about Shannon. The man was called Henri Alain, and was a former mercenary.

Alain had reported back within twenty-four hours that Shannon had left his Montmartre hotel and not reappeared. He had also been able to tell Roux two other things: that Shannon's disappearance had taken place the morning after Roux had received the London businessman in his own apartment, and secondly that Shannon had also received a visitor the same afternoon. The hotel clerk, with a little currency persuasion, had been able to decribe Shannon's visitor, and privately Roux had no doubt the visitor in Montmartre had been the same man who came to him.

So Mr Harris from London had seen two mercenaries in Paris, although he needed only one. As a result Shannon had disappeared while he, Roux, had been left on the shelf. That it was Shannon of all people who seemed to have got the contract made his rage even worse, for there was no one the man in the flat in the 11th arrondissement hated more.

He had had Henri Alain stake out the hotel for four days, but Shannon had not come back. Then he tried another tack. He recalled that newspaper reports had linked Shannon with the Corsican Langarotti in the fighting in the last days of the enclave. Presumably if Shannon was back in circulation, so was Langarotti. So he had sent Henri Alain to Marseilles to find the Corsican and discover where Shannon might be. Alain had just arrived back, bearing the news that Langarotti had left Marseilles that same afternoon. Destination, London.

Roux turned to his informant. '*Bon*, Henri. That's all. I'll contact you when I need you. Meantime, the clerk in the Montmartre place will let you know if Shannon returns?'

'Sure,' said Alain as he rose to go.

'Then ring me immediately if you hear.'

When Alain had gone, Roux thought things over. For him the disappearance of Langarotti to London of all places meant the Corsican had gone to join Shannon there. That in turn meant Shannon was recruiting, and that could only mean he had got a contract. Roux had no doubt it was Walter Harris's contract, one he felt he personally should have had. It was an impertinence, compounded by the recruiting of a Frenchman and on French territory, which Roux regarded as being his own exclusive perserve.

There was another reason why he wanted the Harris contract. He had not worked since the Bukavu affair, and his ability to keep his hold over the French mercenary community was likely to slip unless he could produce some form of work for them. If Shannon were unable to continue, if for instance he were to disappear permanently, Mr Harris would presumably have to come back to Roux, and engage him as he should have done in the first place.

Without further delay he made a local Paris phone call.

Back in London the dinner was nearing its end. The men had drunk a lot of carafe wine, for like most mercenaries they preferred it the rougher the better. Tiny Marc raised his glass and proposed the often-heard toast of the Congo.

'Vive la Mort, vive la guerre,
Vive le sacré mercenaire.'

Sitting back in his chair, clear-headed while the rest got drunk, Cat Shannon wondered idly how much havoc would be wreaked when he let slip this group of dogs on Kimba's palace. Silently he raised his own glass and drank to the dogs of war.

Charles Roux was forty-eight and several parts mad, although the two facts were quite unconnected. He could never have been certified insane, but most psychiatrists would at least have held him to be mentally unstable. The basis for such a diagnosis would have been the presence of a fair degree of megalomania, but this is present in many people outside lunatic asylums and is usually more kindly interpreted, at least when present in the rich and famous, as merely exaggerated egocentricity.

The same psychiatrists would probably have detected a tinge of paranoia and a severe examiner might have gone so far as to suggest there was a streak of the psychopath in the French mercenary. But as Roux had never been examined by a skilled psychiatrist and as his instability was usually well camouflaged beneath an exterior of some intelligence and considerable cunning, these questions were never raised.

The only exterior clues to his make-up lay in his capacity to impute a status and importance to himself that was wholly illusory, a quality for self-pity that insisted he had never once been at fault but that all others who disagreed with him were wholly in the wrong, and the capacity for vicious hatreds towards those he felt had wronged him.

Often the victims of his hatreds had done little or nothing beyond frustrating Roux, but in Shannon's case there were at least grounds for the dislike.

Roux had been a top sergeant in the French Army until his late thirties when he was dismissed after an affair involving certain missing funds.

In 1961, at a loose end, he had paid his own fare to Katanga and proposed himself as a well-qualified adviser to the secessionist movement of the then Katangese leader, Moise Tshombe. That year was the height of the struggle to tear the mineral-rich province of Katanga out of the union with the sprawling, anarchic and newly independent Congo. Several of the men who later became mercenary chieftains began their freelance careers in the imbroglio in Katanga. Hoare, Denard, and Schramme were among them. Despite his claims to greater things, Roux was permitted only a small role in the Katangese events, and when the mighty United Nations finally managed to vanquish the small bands of freebooting pistoleros, which had to be done politically since it could not be done militarily, Roux was among those who got out.

That was in 1962. Two years later, with the Congo falling like a set of skittles to the Communist-backed Simbas, Tshombe was recalled from exile to take over not Katanga but the whole Congo. He in turn sent for Hoare, and Roux was among those who flew back to enter service under Hoare. As a Frenchman, his natural unit would have been the French-speaking Sixth Commando, but as he had been in South Africa at the time, it was to the Fifth that he went. Here he was put in charge of a company, and one of his section commanders six months later was a young Anglo-Irishman called Shannon.

Roux's break with Hoare came three months later. Already becoming convinced of his own superiority as a military commander, Roux was entrusted with the job of knocking out a Simba road-block. He devised his own plan of attack and it was a total disaster. Four white mercenaries were killed and over a score of his Katangese levies. Part of the reason was the plan of attack, part of the fact that Roux had been blind drunk. Behind the drunkenness was the secret certainty that, for all his bombast, Roux did not like combat.

Colonel Hoare called for a report from Roux and got it. Parts of it did not tally with the known facts. Hoare sent for the only surviving section commander, Carlo Shannon, and questioned him closely. From what emerged, he sent for Roux and dismissed him on the spot.

Roux went north and joined the Sixth Commando under Denard at Paulis, explaining his defection from the Fifth as being due to racial dislike of a superb French commander by the inferior British, a reason Denard found little difficulty in believing. He posted Roux as second-in-command of a smaller commando, nominally dependent on the Sixth but in fact almost independent. This was the Fourteenth Commando at Watsa, ruled by Commandant Tavernier.

By 1966 Hoare had retired and gone home, and Tavernier had left. The Fourteenth was commanded by Commandant Wautier, like Tavernier a Belgian. Roux was still second-in-command and hated Wautier. Not that the Belgian had done anything; the reason for the loathing was that Roux had expected the command after Tavernier's departure. He had not got it. So he hated Wautier.

The Fourteenth, heavily staffed by Katangese levies, was the spearpoint of the 1966 mutiny against the Congolese government. It had been planned, and well so, by Wautier, and would probably have succeeded. Black Jack Schramme was holding his own predominantly Katangese Tenth Commando in check only to see how things went. Had Wautier led the revolt, it might well have succeeded; Black Jack would probably have brought his Tenth into the affair had it been successful, and the Congolese government might well have fallen. To launch the revolt, Wautier had brought his Fourteenth to Stanleyville, where on the left bank of the Congo river the vast arsenal stood, containing enough munitions to enable anyone holding it to rule the central and eastern Congo for years.

Two hours before the attack, Commandant Wautier was shot dead. His death was never fully proved, but in fact it was Roux who murdered him with a shot in the back of the head. A wiser man might have called off the attack. Roux insisted on taking command, and the mutiny was a disaster. His forces never got across the river to the left bank, the Congolese Army rallied on learning the armoury was still theirs, and Roux's unit was wiped out to the last man. Schramme thanked his stars he had kept his own men out of the fiasco. On the run and terrified, Roux sought refuge with John Peters, new commander of the English-speaking Fifth, who were also not involved. Peters smuggled the desperate Roux out of the country, swathed in bandages and masquerading as an Englishman.

The only plane out was heading for South Africa, and that was where Roux went. Ten months later, Roux flew back into the Congo, this time accompanied by five South Africans. He had heard wind of the coming July 1967 revolt, and came to join Schramme at the headquarters of the Tenth Commando near Kindu. He was in Stanleyville again when mutiny broke out, this time with Schramme and Denard participating. Within hours Denard was out of action, hit in the head by a ricochet bullet loosed off in error by one of his own men. At a crucial point the leader of the joint forces of the Sixth and Tenth was out of the fight. Roux, claiming that as a Frenchman he should take precedence over the Belgian Schramme, maintaining he was the best commander present and the only one who could command the mercenaries, put himself forward for overall command.

The choice fell on Schramme, not because he was the best man to command the whites, but because he was the only man who could command the Katangese, and without these levies the small band of Europeans would have been too badly outnumbered.

Roux's claim failed on two fronts. The Katangese loathed and distrusted him, remembering the unit of their own people he had led to annihilation the previous year. And at the mercenaries' council, held the night Denard was flown out on a stretcher to Rhodesia, one of those who spoke against Roux's nomination was one of Denard's company commanders, Shannon, who had left the Fifth eighteen months earlier and joined the Sixth rather than serve under Peters.

A second time the mercenaries failed to take the arsenal, and Schramme opted for the long march from Stanleyville to Bukavu, a resort town on Lake Bukavu, abutting the neighbouring republic of Rwanda and offering some form of retreat if things went wrong.

By this time Roux was gunning for Shannon, and to keep them apart Schramme gave Shannon's company the hazardous job of point unit, breaking trail up front as the column of mercenaries, Katangese and thousands of camp followers fought their way through the Congolese towards the lake. Roux was given a job at the rear of the convoy, so the two never met.

They finally met in Bukavu town after the mercenaries had settled in, and the Congolese had surrounded them on all sides except the lake behind the town. It was September 1967 and Roux was drunk. Over a game of cards he lost through lack of concentration he accused Shannon of cheating. Shannon replied that Roux made as big a mess of his poker as he had of attacks on Simba roadblocks and for the same reason – he had no nerve. There was dead silence among the group round the table, as the other mercenaries edged back towards the walls. But Roux backed down. Glaring at Shannon he let the younger man get up and walk towards the door. Only when the Irishman had his back turned did Roux reach for the Colt .45 they all carried and take aim.

Shannon reacted first. He turned, pulled his own automatic and fired down the length of the long hall. The slug was a lucky one for a shot from the hip on a half-turn. It took Roux high in the right arm, tore a hole through the biceps and left his arm hanging limp from his side, the fingers dripping blood onto the useless Colt on the floor by his side.

'There's one other thing I remember,' Shannon called down the room, 'I remember what happened to Wautier.'

Roux was finished after the shoot-out. He evacuated himself across the bridge into Rwanda, had himself driven to Kigali, the capital, and flew back to France. Thus he missed the fall of Bukavu when finally the ammunition ran out in November, and the five months in an internment camp in Kigali. He also missed a chance to settle scores with Shannon.

Being the first back into Paris from Bukavu, Roux had given several interviews in which he spoke glowingly of himself, his battle wound and his desire to get back and lead his men. The fiasco at Dilolo when a recuperated

Denard tried a badly planned invasion of the Congo from Angola in the south, as a diversion to take the strain off his men in Bukavu, and the virtual retirement of the former leader of the Sixth, gave Roux the impression he had every right to claim leadership over the French mercenaries. He had made quite a lot of money from looting in the Congo, and had salted it away.

With the money, he was able to make a splash among the barflies and street-corner bums who like to style themselves mercenaries, and from them he still retained a certain degree of loyalty, but of the bought kind.

Henry Alain was one such, and so was Roux's next visitor, who came in answer to his telephoned summons. He was another mercenary, but of a different type.

Raymond Thomard was a killer by instinct and profession. He too had been in the Congo once, when on the run from the police, and Roux had used him as a hatchet man. For a few small handouts and in the mistaken view that Roux was a bigshot, Thomard was as loyal as a paid man can ever be.

'I've got a job for you,' Roux told him. 'A contract worth five thousand dollars. Are you interested?'

Thomard grinned.

'Sure, Patron. Who's the bugger you want knocked off?'

'Cat Shannon.'

Thomard's face dropped. Roux went on before he could reply.

'I know he's good. But you're better. Besides, he knows nothing. You'll be given his address when he checks into Paris next time. You just have to wait till he leaves, then take him at your own convenience. Does he know you by sight?'

Thomard shook his head.

'We never met,' he said.

Roux clapped him on the back.

'Then you've got nothing to worry about. Stay in touch, I'll let you know when and where you'll find him.'

Chapter Ten

Simon Endean's letter sent on the Tuesday night arrived at ten on Thursday morning at the Handelsbank in Zürich. According to the instructions in it, they telexed £10,000 to the account of Mr Keith Brown at the Kredietbank in Brugge.

By noon Mr Goossens had seen the telex, and wired £5000 to Mr Brown's account in the West End of London. Shortly before four that afternoon, Shannon made a check call to his bank and learned the credit was there waiting for him. He asked the manager personally to give him drawing facilities in cash up to £3500 the following morning. He was told it would be available for collection by eleven-thirty.

Shortly after nine the same morning Martin Thorpe presented himself in Sir James Manson's office with the file containing his findings since the previous Saturday.

The two men went over the short list together, studying the pages of photostat documents acquired at Companies House on Tuesday and Wednesday. When they finished, Manson sat back in his chair and gazed at the ceiling.

'There's no doubt you are right about Bormac, Martin,' he said, 'but why the hell hasn't the major stockholder been bought out long ago?'

It was the question Martin Thorpe had been asking himself all the previous night and day.

The Bormac Trading Company Limited had been founded in 1904 to exploit the output of a series of vast rubber plantations that had been created during the last years of the previous century on the basis of slave labour by Chinese coolies.

The founder of the estates had been an enterprising and ruthless Scot by the name of Ian Macallister, later created Sir Ian Macallister in 1921, and the estates were situated in Borneo, hence the name of the company.

More of a builder than a businessman, Macallister had agreed in 1903 to enter into partnership with a group of London businessmen and the following year Bormac was created and floated with an issue of half a million ordinary shares. Macallister, who had married a 17-year-old girl the previous year, received 150,000 shares, a place on the Board, and managership during his lifetime of the rubber estates.

Ten years after the company's founding, the London businessmen had clinched a series of lucrative contracts with companies, supplying the British war effort with rubber, and the share price had climbed from its issue price of four shillings to over £2. The war profiteers' boom lasted until 1918. There was a slump for the company just after the First World War, until the motor-car craze of the twenties boosted the need for rubber tyres, and again shares rose. This time there was a one-for-one new issue, raising the total amount of the company's shares on the market to a million and Sir Ian's block to 300,000. There had been no more share issues after that.

The slump of the Depression sent prices and shares down again, and they were recovering by 1937. In that year one of the Chinese coolies finally ran amok and performed an unpleasantness on the sleeping Sir Ian with a heavy-bladed parang. Ironically he died of blood poisoning. The under-manager took over, but lacked the drive of his dead master, and production fell as prices rose. The Second World War could have been a boon to the company, but the Japanese invasion of 1941 disrupted supplies.

The death knell of the company was finally sounded by the Indonesian nationalist movement which wrested control of the Dutch East Indies and Borneo from Holland in 1948. When the border between Indonesian Borneo and British North Borneo was finally drawn, the estates were on the Indonesian side, and were promptly nationalized without compensation.

For over twenty years the company had staggered on, its assets unrecoverable, fruitless lawsuits with President Soekarno's régime eating away at the cash, the prices falling. By the time Martin Thorpe went over the company's books, the shares stood at a shilling each, and their highest price over the previous year had been one shilling and threepence.

The Board was composed of five directors, and the company rules stipulated that two of them made a quorum for the purpose of passing a resolution. The company office's address was given and turned out to be the premises of an old-established firm of City solicitors, one of whose partners acted as company secretary and was also on the board. The original offices had long since been given up due to rising costs. Board meetings were rare, and usually consisted of the chairman, an elderly man living in Sussex, who was the younger brother of Sir Ian's former under-manager. He had died in Japanese hands during the war, and his shares had passed to the younger brother. Sitting with the chairman was the company secretary, the City solicitor, and occasionally one of the other three, who all lived a long way from London. There was seldom any business to discuss, and the company income consisted mainly of the occasional belated compensation payments now being made by the Indonesian government under General Suharto.

The combined five directors controlled no more than eighteen per cent of the million shares, and fifty-two per cent were distributed between six and a half thousand shareholders scattered across the country. There seemed to be a fair proportion of married women and widows. No doubt portfolios of long-forgotten shares sat in deed boxes in banks and solicitors' offices up and down the land, and had done for years.

But that was not what interested Thorpe and Manson. If they had tried to acquire a controlling interest by buying through the market, it would firstly have taken years and secondly have become quickly plain to other City-watchers that someone was at work on Bormac. Their interest was held by the one single block of 300,000 shares held by the widowed Lady Macallister.

The puzzle was why no one had not long since bought the entire block from her and taken over the shell of the once-flourishing rubber company. In every other sense it was ideal for the purpose, for its memorandum of association was widely drawn, permitting the company to operate in any field of exploitation of any country's natural assets outside the United Kingdom.

'She must be eighty-five if she's a day,' said Thorpe at last. 'Lives in a vast dreary old block of flats in Kensington, guarded by a long-serving lady companion, or whatever they are called.'

'She must have been approached,' mused Sir James, 'so why does she cling to them?'

'Perhaps she just doesn't want to sell,' said Thorpe, 'or didn't like the people who came to ask her to let them buy. Old people can be funny.'

It is not simply old people who are illogical about buying and selling stocks and shares. Most stockbrokers have long since had the experience of seeing a client refuse to do business when proposed a sensible and advantageous offer, solely and simply for the reason that they did not like the stockbroker.

Sir James Manson shot forward in his chair and planted his elbows on the desk.

'Martin, find out about that old woman. Find out who she is, what she thinks, what she likes and hates, what are her tastes, and, above all, find out where her weak spot is. She has to have one, some little thing that would be too big a temptation for her, and for which she would sell her holding. It may not be money, probably isn't, for she's been offered money before now. But there has to be something. Find it.'

Thorpe rose to go. Manson waved him back to his chair. From his desk drawer he drew six printed forms, all identical and all application forms for a numbered account at the Zwingli Bank in Zürich.

He explained briefly and concisely what he wanted done, and Thorpe nodded.

'Book yourself on the morning flight, and you can be back tomorrow night,' said Manson as his aide left.

Simon Endean rang Shannon at his flat just after two, and was given an up-to-date report on the arrangements the mercenary was making. Manson's assistant was pleased by the precision of Shannon's reporting, and he noted the details on a scratch pad, so that he could later make up his own report for Sir James.

When he had finished, Shannon put forward his next requirements.

'I want £5000 telexed direct from your Swiss bank to my credit as Keith Brown at the head office of the Banque de Luxembourg in Luxembourg by next Monday noon,' he told Endean, 'and another £5000 telexed direct to my credit at the head office of the Landesbank in Hamburg by Wednesday morning.'

He explained tersely how the bulk of the £5000 he had imported to London was already spoken for, and the other £5000 was needed as a reserve in Brugge. The two identical sums required in Luxembourg and Hamburg were mainly so that he could show his contacts there a certified cheque to prove his credit before entering into purchasing negotiations. Later most of the money would be remitted to Brugge, and the balance fully accounted for.

'In any case, I can write you out a complete accounting of money spent to date or committed for spending,' he told Endean. 'but I have to have your mailing address.'

Endean gave him the name of a professional accommodation address where he had opened a box that morning in the name of Walter Harris, and promised to get the instructions off to Zürich within the hour to have both sums of £5000 awaiting collection by Keith Brown in Luxembourg and Hamburg.

*

Big Janni Dupree checked in from London airport at five. His had been the longest journey; from Cape Town to Johannesburg the previous day, an overnight stop at the Holiday Inn and then the long SAA flight through Luanda in Portuguese Angola and the Isla do Sol stopover which avoided overflying the territory of any black African country. Shannon ordered him to take a taxi straight to the flat.

While he was on his way, Shannon called up the other three mercenaries from their hotels and had them come round to his place.

At six there was a second reunion when they all greeted the South African and listened in silence as Shannon gave Dupree the same briefing they had received the night before. When he heard the terms Janni's face cracked into a grin.

'We going to go fighting again, Cat? Count me in.'

'Good man. So here's what I want from you. Stay here in London, find yourself a small bedsitter flat. I'll help you do that tomorrow. We'll go through the *Evening Standard* and get you fixed up by nightfall.

'I want you to buy all our clothing. We need fifty sets of tee-shirts, fifty sets of underpants, fifty pairs of light nylon socks. Then a spare set for each man, making a hundred. I'll give you the list later. After that, fifty sets of combat trousers, preferably in jungle camouflage and preferably matching the jackets. Next, fifty combat blouses, zip-fronted and in the same jungle camouflage.

'You can get all these quite openly at camping shops, sports shops and army surplus stores. Even the hippies are beginning to wear combat jackets about towns, and so do people who go shooting in the country.

'You can get all the vests, socks and underpants at the same stockist, but get the trousers and blouses at different ones. Then fifty green berets, and fifty pairs of boots. Get the trousers on the large size, we can shorten them later; get the blouses half in large size, half in medium. Get the boots from a camping equipment shop. I don't want heavy British Army boots, I want the green canvas jackboots with front-lacing and water-proofed.

'Now for the webbing. I need fifty webbing belts, ammo pouches, knapsacks and campers' haversacks, the ones with the light tubular frame to support them. These will carry the bazooka rockets with a bit of reshaping. Lastly, fifty light nylon sleeping bags. OK? I'll give you the full written list later.'

Dupree nodded.

'OK. How much will that lot cost?'

'About a thousand pounds. This is how you buy it. Take the Yellow pages telephone directory and under Surplus Stores you'll find over a dozen shops and stockists. Get the jackets, blouses, belts, berets, webbing harnesses, knapsacks, haversacks, and boots at different shops, placing one order at each. Pay cash and take the purchase away with you. Don't give your real name – not that anyone should ask for it – and don't leave a real address.

'When you have bought the stuff, store it in a normal storage warehouse, have it crated for export, and contact four separate freight agents accustomed to handling export shipments. Pay them to send it in four separate consignments in bond to a shipping freight agent in Marseilles for collection by Mr Jean-Baptiste Langarotti.'

'Which agent in Marseilles?' asked Dupree.

'We don't know yet,' said Shannon. He turned to the Corsican.

'Jean, when you have the name of the shipping agent you intend to use for the export of the boats and engines, send the full name and address by mail to London, one copy to me there at the flat, and a second copy to Jan Dupree, Poste Restante, Trafalgar Square Post Office, London. Got it?'

Langarotti noted the address while Shannon translated the instructions for Dupree.

'Janni, go down there in the next few days and get yourself *poste restante* facilities. Then check in every week or so until Jean's letter arrives. Then instruct the freight agents to send the crates to the Marseilles agent in a bonded shipment for export by sea from Marseilles onwards, in the ownership of Langarotti. Now for the question of money. I just heard the credit came through from Brussels.'

The three Europeans produced slips of paper from their pockets while Shannon took Dupree's airline ticket stub. From his desk Shannon took four letters, each of them from him to Mr Goossens at the Kredietbank. Each letter was roughly the same. It required the Kredietbank to transmit a sum of money in US dollars from Mr Keith Brown's account to another account for the credit of Mr X.

In the gaps Shannon filled in the sum equivalent to the return air fare to and from London, starting at Ostende, Marseilles, Munich and Cape Town. The letters also bade Mr Goossens transmit 1250 dollars to each of the named men in the named banks on the day of receipt of the letter, and again on the 5th of May and again on the 5th of June. Each mercenary dictated to Shannon the name of his bank, usually in Switzerland, and Shannon typed in the gaps.

When he had finished, each man read his own letter, and Shannon signed them at his desk, sealed them in separate envelopes, and gave each man his own envelope for posting.

Lastly he gave them each £50 in cash to cover their 48-hour stay in London, and told them to meet him outside the door of his London bank at eleven the following morning.

When they had gone he sat down and wrote a long letter to a man in Africa. He rang the writer who, having checked by phone that it was in order to do so, gave him the African's mailing address. That evening Shannon mailed his letter, express rate, and dined alone.

Martin Thorpe got his interview with Dr Steinhofer at the Zwingli Bank just before lunch. Being previously announced by Sir James Manson, Thorpe received the same red carpet treatment.

He presented the banker with the six application forms for numbered accounts. Each had been filled out in the required manner and signed. Separate cards carried the required two specimen signatures of the men seeking to open the accounts. They were in the names of Messrs Adams, Ball, Carter, Davies, Edwards and Frost.

Attached to each form were two other letters. One was a signed power of attorney, in which Messrs Adams, Ball, Carter, Davies, Edwards and Frost separately gave power of attorney to Mr Martin Thorpe to operate the accounts in their names. The other was a letter signed by Sir James Manson requesting Dr Steinhofer to transfer to the account of each of his associates the sum of £50,000 from Sir James's account.

Dr Steinhofer was neither as gullible nor as new to the business of banking as not to suspect that the fact the names of the six 'business associates' all began with the first six letters of the alphabet was a remarkable coincidence. But he was quite able to believe that the possible non-existence of the six nominees was not his business. If a wealthy British businessman chose to get round the tiresome rules of his own Companies Act, that was his own business. Besides, Dr Steinhofer knew certain things about quite a number of City businessmen that would have created enough Department of Trade inquiries to keep that London ministry occupied for the rest of the century.

There was another good reason why he should stretch out his hand and take the application forms from Thorpe. If the shares of the company Sir James was going to try and buy secretly shot up from their present level to astronomic heights – and Dr Steinhofer could see no other reason for the operation – there was nothing to prevent the Swiss banker from buying a few of those shares for himself.

'The company we have our eye on is called Bormac Trading Company,' Thorpe told him quietly. He outlined the position of the company, and the fact that old Lady Macallister held 300,000 shares, or thirty per cent of the company.

'We have reason to believe attempts may already have been made to persuade this old lady to sell her holding,' he went on. 'They appear to have been unsuccessful. We are going to have another try. Even should we fail, we will still go ahead and choose another shell company.'

Dr Steinhofer listened quietly as he smoked his cigar.

'As you know, Dr Steinhofer, it would not be possible for one purchaser to buy these shares without declaring his identity. Therefore the four buyers will be Mr Adams, Mr Ball, Mr Carter and Mr Davies, who will each acquire seven and a half per cent of the company. We would wish you to act on behalf of all four of them.'

Dr Steinhofer nodded. It was standard practice.

'Of course, Mr Thorpe.'

'I shall attempt to persuade the old lady to sign the share transfer certificates with the name of the buyer left out. This is simply because some people in England, especially old ladies, find Swiss banks rather, how shall I say? – secretive organizations.'

'I am sure you mean sinister,' said Dr Steinhofer smoothly. 'I completely understand. Let us leave it like this then. When you have had an interview with this lady, we will see how best it can be arranged. But tell Sir James to have no fear. The purchase will be by four separate buyers, and the rules of the Companies Act will not be affronted.'

As Sir James Manson had predicted, Thorpe was back in London by nightfall to begin his weekend.

The four mercenaries were waiting on the pavement when Shannon came out of his bank just before twelve. He had in his hand four brown envelopes.

'Marc, here's yours. There's £500 in it. Since you'll be living at home, your expenses will be the smallest. So within that £500 you have to buy a van and rent a lock-up garage. There are other items to be bought. You'll find the list inside the envelope. Trace the man who has the Schmeissers for sale and set up a meeting between me and him. I'll be in touch with you by phone at your bar in about ten days.'

The giant Belgian nodded and hailed a taxi at the kerbside to take him to Victoria Station and the boat train back to the Ostende ferry.

'Kurt, this is your envelope. There's £1000 inside it, because you'll have to do much more travelling. Find that ship, and inside forty days. Keep in touch by phone and cable, but be very discreet and brief when using either. You can be frank in written letters to my flat. If my mail is on intercept we're finished anyway.

'Jean-Baptiste, here's £500 for you. It has to keep you for forty days. Stay out of trouble and avoid your old haunts. Find the boats and engines and let me know by letter. Open a bank account and tell me where it is. When I approve the type and price of the stuff, I'll transmit you the money. And don't forget the shipping agent. Keep it nice and legal all down the line.'

The Frenchman and the German took their money and instructions and looked for a second taxi to get them to London airport, Semmler bound for Naples and Langarotti for Marseilles.

Shannon took Dupree's arm and they strolled down Piccadilly together. Shannon passed Dupree his envelope.

'I've put £1500 in there for you, Janni. The £1000 should cover all the purchases and the storage, crating and shipping costs to Marseilles, with something to spare. The £500 should keep you easily for the next month to six weeks. I want you to get straight into the buying first thing Monday morning. Make your list of shops and warehouses with the Yellow Pages and a map over the weekend. You have to finish the buying in thirty days, because I want the stuff in Marseilles in forty-five.'

He stopped and bought an evening paper, opened it at the 'Properties to Let' page and showed Dupree the columns of adverts for flats and flatlets for rent, furnished and unfurnished.

'Find yourself a small flat by tonight and let me know the address tomorrow.'

They parted just short of Hyde Park Corner.

Shannon spent the evening writing out a complete statement of accounts for Endean. He pointed out that the total had eaten up the bulk of the £5000 transferred from Brugge, and that he would leave the few hundreds left over from that sum in the London account as a reserve.

Lastly, he pointed out that he had not taken any part of his own £10,000 fee for the job, and proposed either that Endean transfer it straight from Endean's Swiss account into Shannon's Swiss account, or remit the money to the Belgian bank for credit to Keith Brown.

He mailed his letter that Friday evening.

The weekend was free, so he called Julie Manson and suggested taking her out to dinner. She had been about to set off for a weekend at her parents' country house, but rang up and told them she was not coming. As it was late by the time she was ready, she came to collect Shannon, looking pert and spoilt at the wheel of her pillar-box red MGB.

'Have you booked anywhere?' she asked.

'Yes. Why?'

'Let's go and eat at one of my places,' she suggested. 'Then I can introduce you to some of my friends.'

Shannon shook his head.

'Forget it,' he said. 'That's happened to me before. I am not spending the whole evening being stared at like a zoo animal and asked damn-fool questions about killing people. It's sick.'

She pouted.

'Please, Cat darling.'

'Nope.'

'Look, I won't say what you are and what you do. I'll just keep it a secret. Come on. No one will know you by your face.'

Shannon weakened.

'One condition,' he said. 'My name is Keith Brown. Got it? Keith Brown. That's all. Nothing else do you say about me or where I come from. Nor about what I do. Understood?'

She giggled.

'Great,' she said. 'Great idea. Mystery Man himself. Come on then, Mr Keith Brown.'

She took him to Tramps where she was evidently well known. Johnny Gold rose from his doorside table as they entered and greeted her effusively with a kiss on both cheeks. He shook hands with Shannon as she introduced him.

'Nice to see you, Keith. Have a good time.'

They dined at the long row of tables running parallel to the bar, and started by ordering the house lobster cocktail from a hollowed-out pineapple. Seated facing the room, Shannon glanced round at the diners; most, from their long hair and casual dress, could be placed in show business or on its fringes. Others were evidently young generation businessmen trying to be trendy or make a model girl or small actress. Among the latter he spotted someone he knew, seated across the room with a group, out of vision by Julie.

After the lobster Shannon ordered 'bangers and mash', and excusing himself got up. He strolled slowly out of the door and into the centre lobby as if on his way to the men's room. Within seconds a hand fell on his shoulder and he turned to face Simon Endean.

'Are you out of your mind?' grated the City hard boy.

Shannon looked at him in mock surprise, a wide-eyed innocent.

'No. I don't think so. Why?' he asked.

Endean was about to tell him, but checked himself in time. His face was white with anger. He knew his boss well enough to know how Manson doted on his supposedly innocent little girl, and knew roughly what his reaction would be should he ever hear about Shannon taking her out, let alone climbing into bed with her.

But he was check-mated. He assumed Shannon was still unaware of his own real name, and certainly of Manson's existence. To bawl him out for going dining with a girl called Julie Manson would 'blow' both his own concern and Manson's name, together with both their roles as Shannon's employer. Nor could he tell Shannon to leave her alone, for fear Shannon would consult the girl and she would tell him who Endean was. He choked back his anger.

'What are you doing here?' he asked lamely.

'Having dinner,' said Shannon, appearing puzzled. 'Look, Harris, if I want to go out and have dinner, that's my affair. There's nothing to be done over the weekend. I have to wait till Monday to fly to Luxembourg.'

Endean was even angrier. He could not explain that Shannon slacking on the job was not what concerned him.

'Who's the girl?' he asked.

Shannon shrugged.

'Name's Julie. Met her in a café two days ago.'

'Picked her up?' asked Endean in horror.

'Yes, you might say that. Why?'

'Oh, nothing. But be careful about girls, all girls. It would be better if you left them alone for a while, that's all.'

'Harris, don't worry about my security. There won't be any indiscretions, in bed or out. Besides, I told her my name was Keith Brown; I'm on leave in London and I'm in the oil business.'

For answer Endean spun round, snapped at Paolo to tell the group he was with that he had been called away, and headed for the stairs to the street before Julie Manson could recognize him. Shannon watched him leave.

'Up yours,' he said quietly, 'with Sir Bloody James Manson's biggest drill.'

On the pavement outside, Endean swore quietly. Apart from that he could only pray that Shannon had been telling the truth about the Keith Brown business, and that Julie Manson would not tell her father about her new boy-friend.

Shannon and his girl danced until shortly before three and had their first row on the way back to Shannon's flat. He had told her it would be better if she did not tell her father she was going out with a mercenary, or even mention his name.

'From what you have already told me about him, he seems to dote on you. He'd probably send you away somewhere, or have you made a ward of court.'

Her response had been to start teasing, keeping a straight face and saying she would be able to handle her father, as she always had, and in any case being made a ward of court would be fun, and would get her name in all the papers. Besides, she argued, Shannon could always come and get her, fight his way out, and elope with her.

Shannon was not sure how serious she was, and thought he might have gone too far in provoking Endean that evening, although he had not planned on meeting him anyway. They were still arguing when they reached the sitting room of the flat.

'Anyway, I'm not being told what I'll do and what I won't do,' said the girl as she dropped her coat over the armchair.

'You will by me,' growled Shannon. 'You'll just keep damn silent about me when you're with your father. And that's flat.'

For answer the girl stuck her tongue out at him.

'I'll do what I damn well like,' she insisted, and to emphasize her words, stamped her foot. Shannon got angry. He picked her up, spun her round, marched her to the armchair, sat down and pulled her over his knee. For five minutes there were two conflicting sounds in the sitting room, the girl's protesting squeals and the crack of Shannon's hand. When he let her up she scuttled into the bedroom sobbing loudly and slammed the door.

Shannon shrugged. The die was cast one way or the other, and there was nothing he could do about it. He went into the kitchen, made a coffee and drank it slowly by the window, looking out at the backs of the houses across the gardens, almost all darkened as the respectable folk of St John's Wood slept.

When he entered the bedroom it was in darkness. In the far corner of the double bed was a small hump, but no sound, as if she were holding her breath. Half-way across the floor his foot scuffed her fallen dress and two paces further he kicked one of her discarded shoes. He sat on the edge of the bed and as his eyes grew accustomed to the darkness he made out her face on the pillow, eyes watching him.

'You're rotten,' she whispered.

He leaned forward and slipped a hand into the angle of her neck and jaw, stroking slowly and firmly.

'No one's ever hit me before.'

'That's why you've turned out the way you have,' he murmured.

'How is that?'

'A spoiled little girl.'

'I'm not.' There was a pause. 'Yes I am.'

He continued caressing her.

'Cat.'

'Yes.'

'Did you really think Daddy might take me away from you if I told him?'

'Yes. I still do.'

'And do you think I'd really tell him?'

'I thought you might.'

'Is that why you got angry?'

'Yes.'

'Then you only smacked me because you love me?'

'I suppose so.'

She turned her head and he felt her tongue busily licking the inside of his palm.

'Get into bed, Cat, darling. I'm so randy I can't wait any more.'

He was only half out of his clothes when she threw the bedsheets back and knelt on the mattress, running her hands over his chest and muttering 'Hurry, hurry' between kisses.

'You're a lying bastard, Shannon,' he thought as he lay on his back feeling this avid and infatuated young girl go to work on him.

There was a light grey glow in the east over Camden Town when they lay still two hours later and he wished he had a cigarette. Julie was curled up in the crook of his arm, her varied appetites for the moment satisfied.

'Tell me something,' she said.

'What?'

'Why do you live the way you do? Why be a mercenary and go around making wars on people?'

'I don't make wars. The world we live in makes wars, led and governed by men who pretend they are creatures of morality and integrity, whereas most of them are self-seeking bastards. They make the wars, for increased profits or increased power. I just fight the wars, because it's the way I like to live.'

'But why for money? Mercenaries fight for money, don't they?'

'Not only the money. The bums do, but when it comes to a crunch the bums who style themselves mercenaries usually don't fight. They scarper. Most of the best ones fight for the same reason I do; they enjoy the life, the hard living, the combat.'

'But why do there have to be wars? Why can't they all live in peace?'

He stirred and in the darkness scowled at the ceiling.

'Because there are only two kinds of people in this world: the predators and the grazers. And the predators always get to the top, because they're prepared to fight to get there and consume people and things that get in their way. The others haven't the nerve, or the courage, or the hunger or the ruthlessness. so the world is governed by the predators, who become the potentates. And the potentates are never satisfied. They must go on and on seeking more of the currency they worship.

'In the Communist world – and don't ever kid yourself into thinking the Communist leaders are peace-loving – the currency is power. Power, power and more power, no matter how many people have to die so they can get it. In the capitalist world the currency is money. More and more money. Oil, gold, stocks, and shares, more and more, are the goals, even if they have to lie, steal, bribe and cheat to get it. These make the money, and the money buys the power. So really it all comes back to the lust for power. If they think there's enough of it to be taken, and it needs a war to grab it, you get a war. The rest, the so-called idealism, is a load of cock.'

'Some people fight for idealism. The Vietcong do. I've read it in the papers.'

'Yeah, some people fight for idealism, and ninety-nine out of a hundred of them are being conned. So are the ones back home who cheer for war. We're always right and they're always wrong. In Washington and Peking, London and Moscow. And you know what? They're being conned. Those GIs in Vietnam, do you think they died for life, liberty and the pursuit of happiness? They died for the Dow Jones Index in Wall Street, and always have done. And the British soldiers who died in Kenya, Cyprus, Aden. You really think they rushed into battle shouting for God, King and Country? They were in those lands because their colonel ordered them there, and he was ordered by the War Office, and that was ordered by the Cabinet, to keep British control over the economies. So what? They went back to the people who owned them in the first place, and who cared about the bodies the British Army left behind? It's a big con, Julie Manson, a big con. The difference with me is that no one tells me to go and fight, or where to fight, or which side to fight on. That's why the politicians, the establishments, hate mercenaries. It's not that we are more lethal than they are; in fact we're a damn sight less so. It's because they can't control us; we don't take their orders. We don't shoot the ones they tell us to shoot, and we don't start when they say "start" or stop when they say "stop". That's why we're outlaws; we fight on contract and we pick our own contracts.'

Julie sat up and ran her hands over the hard, scarred muscles of his chest and shoulders. She was a conventionally raised girl and could not, like so many of her generation, understand even a tiny fraction of the world she saw about her.

'What about the wars when people fight for what they know is right?' she asked. 'I mean, what about fighting against Hitler? That was right, wasn't it?'

Shannon sighed and nodded.

'Yes, that was right. He was a bastard all right. Except that they, the bigshots in the Western world, sold him steel up to the outbreak of war and then made more fortunes making more steel to crush Hitler's steel. And the Communists were no better. Stalin signed a pact with him and waited for capitalism and Nazism to destroy each other so he could take over the rubble. Only when Hitler struck Russia did the world's so-idealistic Communists decide Nazism was naughty. Besides, it cost thirty million lives to kill Hitler. A mercenary could have done it with one bullet costing less than a shilling.'

'But we won, didn't we? It was the right thing to do, and we won.'

'We won, my little darling, because the Russians, British and Americans had more guns, tanks, planes and ships than Adolf. That's why, and that's the only reason why. If he had had more, he'd have won, and you know what? History would have written that he was right and we were wrong. Victors are always right. There's a nice little adage I heard once: "God is on the side of the big battalions." It's the gospel of the rich and powerful, the cynical and the gullible. Politicians believe in it, the so-called equality newspapers preach it. The truth is, the Establishment is on the side of the big battalions, because it created and armed them in the first place. It never seems to occur to the millions of readers of that garbage that maybe God, if there is one, has something to do with truth, justice and compassion rather than sheer brute force, and that truth and justice might possibly be on the side of the little platoons. Not that it matters. The big battalions always win, and the "serious" Press always approves, and the grazers always believe it.'

'You're a rebel, Cat,' she murmured.

'Sure. Always have been. No, not always. Since I buried six of my mates in Cyprus. That was when I began to question the wisdom and integrity of all our leaders.'

'But apart from killing people, you could die yourself. You could get killed in one of these futile wars.'

'Yes, and I could live on, like a battery hen in one of these futile cities. Filling in futile forms, paying futile taxes to enable futile politicians and state managers to fritter it away on electorally useful white elephants. I could earn a futile salary in a futile office and commute futilely on a train, morning and evening, until a futile retirement. I prefer to do it my way, live my way and die my way.

'Do you ever think of death?' she asked him.

'Of course. Often. Don't you?'

'Yes. But I don't want to die. I don't want you to die.'

'Death's not so bad. You get used to the idea when it has come very close, and passed by, many times. Let me tell you something. The other day I was clearing out the drawers in this place. There was some newspaper, a year old, at the bottom of one. I saw a piece of news and began to read it. It dated from the winter before last. There was this old man, see? He lived alone in a basement. They found him dead one day. A week or so after he died. The coroner was told no one ever came to see him, and he couldn't get out much. The pathologist said he had been undernourished for at least a year. You know what they found in his throat? Bits of cardboard. He had been nibbling bits of cardboard from a cereal packet to try and get nourishment. Well, not me, baby. When I go, I'll go my way. I'd prefer to go with a bullet in my chest, and blood in my mouth, and a gun in my hand; with defiance in my heart and shouting "Sod the lot of you", than to flicker out in a damp basement with a mouth full of cardboard.

'Now go to sleep, love, it's dawn already.'

Chapter Eleven

Shannon arrived in Luxembourg just after one p.m. on the following Monday and from the airport took a taxi to the Banque de Credit. He identified himself as Keith Brown by using his passport, and asked for the £5000 that should be waiting for collection by him.

After a delay while the telex room was checked, the credit was discovered. It had just come through from Zürich. Instead of drawing the whole sum in cash, Shannon took the equivalent in Luxembourg francs of £1000 and signed a form making over the balance of £4000 to the bank. In exchange for this he was given a certified bank cheque for the equivalent of £4000.

He had time for a quick lunch before making his way to the Hougstraat where he had an appointment with the firm of accountants Lang & Stein.

Luxembourg, like Belgium and Liechtenstein, maintains a system of offering to the investor a highly discreet and even secretive service in banking and the operation of companies, into whose affairs a foreign police force has the greatest difficulty in trying to pry. By and large, unless a company registered in Luxembourg can be shown to have broken the laws of the Archduchy, or can be proved beyond doubt to have been involved in international illegal activities of a highly unpleasant nature, foreign police inquiries as to who owns or controls such a company will be met with a stoic refusal to cooperate. It was this kind of facility that Shannon sought.

His interview, arranged by phone three days earlier, was with Mr Emil Stein, one of the partners in the highly respectable firm. For the occasion Shannon wore a newly acquired charcoal-grey suit, white shirt and school tie. He carried a briefcase and *The Times* under one arm. For some reason, the carrying of this newspaper always seems to impress Europeans that the bearer is a respectable Englishman.

'Over the forthcoming few months,' he told the grey-haired Luxembourger, 'a group of British associates, of whom I am one, wish to engage in commercial activities in the Mediterranean area, possibly Spain, France and Italy. For this purpose we would like to establish a holding company in Luxembourg. As you may imagine, being British citizens and residents, and doing business in several European countries with differing financial laws could prove very complicated. From a tax standpoint alone a holding company in Luxembourg seems to be advisable.'

Mr Stein nodded, for the request was no surprise. Many such holding companies were already registered in his tiny country, and his firm received such requests every day.

'That should present no problem, Mr Brown,' he told his visitor. 'You are aware of course that all the procedures required by the Archduchy of Luxembourg must be complied with. Once that is done, the holding company may hold the majority of shares in an array of other companies registered elsewhere, and after that the company affairs remain entirely private from foreign tax investigations.'

'That's very kind of you. Perhaps you would outline the essentials of starting such a company in Luxembourg,' said Shannon.

The accountant could reel off the requisites in a few seconds.

'Unlike in Britain, all limited liability companies in Luxembourg must have a minimum of seven share holders and a minimum of three directors. However, quite often the accountant asked to help in setting the company up takes the chairmanship of the directors, his junior partners form the other two, and his staff become shareholders, each with a purely nominal number of shares. In this manner the person wishing to establish the company is merely the seventh shareholder although by virtue of his greater number of shares he controls the company.

'Shares will normally be registered and the names of the shareholders also, but there is the provision for the issue of bearer shares, in which case no registration of the identity of the majority holder is necessary. The snag to that is that the bearer shares are exactly what they mean, and the bearer of the majority controls the company. Should one man lose them, or have them stolen, the new owner would automatically become the controller without needing a vestige of proof as to how he acquired them. Do you follow me, Mr Brown?'

Shannon nodded. This was the arrangement he hoped to establish, in order to have Semmler buy the boat behind the cover of an uncheckable company.

'A holding company,' said Mr Stein, 'as its name implies, may not trade in any form. It may only hold stock in other companies. Does your group of associates hold shares in other companies which it would like to have taken over and held in Luxembourg?'

'No, not yet,' said Shannon. 'We hope to acquire existing companies in the area of chosen operations, or found other limited liability companies and transfer the majority shareholdings to Luxembourg for safe keeping.'

By the end of an hour the agreement had been reached. Shannon had shown Mr Stein his £4000 banker's cheque to prove his solvency, and had paid a deposit of £500 in cash.

Mr Stein had agreed to proceed at once with the foundation and registration of a holding company to be called Tyrone Holdings SA, after searching through the bulky list of already registered companies to ensure that no such name existed on the register. The total share capital would be £40,000 of which only £1000 would be issued immediately, and this would be issued in 1000 bearer shares of £1 each. Mr Stein would accept one share and the chairmanship of the board. One share each would go to his partner Mr Lang and a junior partner in the firm. These three men would form the board. Three other staff members of the firm – they turned out later to be secretaries – would be issued with one bearer share each, and the remaining 994 shares would be held by Mr Brown, who would thus control the company and whose wishes the board would have to implement.

A general meeting to float the company was fixed for twelve days thence, or any time after that if Mr Brown would let them know in writing when he could be in Luxembourg to attend it. On that note Shannon left.

Before closing time he was back at the bank, returned the cheque and had the £4000 transferred to the account at Brugge. He checked into the Excelsior and spent the night in Luxembourg. He already had his onward booking the next morning for Hamburg, and he had the hotel ring up to confirm it. It was to Hamburg that he flew the following morning. This time, he was looking for arms.

The trade in lethal weapons is the world's most lucrative after narcotics, and not surprisingly the governments of the world are deeply involved in it. Since 1945 it has become almost a point of national prestige to have one's own native arms industry, and they have flourished and multiplied to the point where by the early seventies it was estimated there existed one military firearm for every man, woman and child on the face of the planet. Arms manufacture simply cannot be kept down to arms consumption except in case of war, and the logical response has to be either to export the surplus or encourage war or both. As few governments want to be involved in a war themselves, but also do not wish to run down their arms industry just in case, the accent has for years been on the exporting of arms. To this end, all the major powers operate highly paid teams of salesmen to trot the globe persuading any potentate with whom they can secure an interview that he does not have enough weapons, or that those he does possess are not modern enough and should be replaced.

It is of no concern to the sellers that ninety-five per cent of all the hardware on the face of, for example, Africa is not used to protect the owner-country from external aggression but to keep the populace in subjection to the dictator. Arms sales have logically started as a product of the profits rivalry between competing Western nations, the entry of Russia and China into the arms manufacturing and exporting business has equally logically transferred the salesmanship into an extension of the power rivalry.

The interaction of the profit desirability and political desirability has produced a tangled web of calculations that continue daily in the capitals of the major world powers. One power will sell arms to republic A, but not to B. At which a rival power will rush to sell weapons to B but not to A. This is called establishing a power balance and therefore keeping the peace. The profit desirability of selling arms is permanent; it is always profitable. The only constraints are imposed by political desirability in this or that country having certain arms in its possession at all, and from this shifting quicksand of expediency versus profit has evolved the intimate link between Foreign Affairs departments and Defence departments all over the world.

To establish an indigenous arms industry is not difficult, provided it is kept basic. It is relatively simple to manufacture rifles and submachine guns, ammunition for both, along with hand grenades and hand guns. The level of technology, industrial development and the variety of the raw materials is not large, but the smaller countries usually buy their weaponry ready-made from the larger ones, because their internal requirements are too small to justify the necessary industrialization, and they know their technical level would not put them into the export market with a chance.

Nevertheless, a very large and growing number of medium-sized countries have in the past two decades gone ahead and established their own native, if basic, arms factories. The difficulties increase, and therefore the number of participating nations decreases, with the complexity of the weapon to be made. It is easy to make small arms, harder to make artillery, armoured cars and tanks, very difficult to create an entire shipbuilding industry to build modern warships, and the hardest of all to turn out modern jet fighters and bombers. The level of development of a local arms industry can be judged by the point at which local weaponry reaches its technical limits, and imports have to be made for anything above those limits.

The main world arms makers and exporters are the United States, Canada, Britain, France, Italy, West Germany (with certain banned manufacturers under the 1954 Paris treaty), Sweden, Switzerland, Spain, Belgium, Israel and South Africa in the Western world. Sweden and Switzerland are neutral but still make and export very fine weaponry, while Israel and South Africa built up their arms industries because of their peculiar situations, because they did not wish to be dependent on anyone in the event of a crisis, and both export very little indeed. The others are all NATO countries and linked by a common defence policy. They also operate an ill-defined degree of cooperation on foreign policy as it relates to arms sales, and an application for an arms purchase made to any of them habitually undergoes a close scrutiny before it is granted and the arms are sold. In the same vein, the small buyer country always has to sign a written undertaking not to pass weaponry sold to itself to another party without express written permission from the supplier. In other words, a lot of questions are asked before a sale is agreed by the Foreign Affairs office rather than the Weapons Sales office, and sales thus made are almost inevitably deals made government-to-government.

Communist arms are largely standardized and come mainly from Russia and Czechoslovakia. The newcomer, China, now also produces weaponry up to a sufficiently high level of sophistication for Mao's guerrilla war theory's requirements. For Communists the sales policy is different. Political influence, not money, is the overriding factor, and many Soviet arms shipments are made as gifts to curry favour, not as commercial deals. Being committed to the adage that power grows out of the barrel of a gun, and obsessed with power, the Communist nations will not merely sell weapons to other sovereign governments, but also to 'liberation' organizations that they politically favour. In most cases these are not sales, but gifts. Thus a Communist, Marxist, extreme left-wing or revolutionary movement almost anywhere in the world can be reasonably assured of not running short of the necessary hardware for guerrilla war.

In the middle, the neutral Swiss and Swedes operate their own self-imposed inhibitions on whom they will sell to, and thus curtail their arms export by their own volition on moral grounds. No one else does.

With the Russians selling or giving their hardware from governmental source to non-governmental recipients, and the West being too shy to do so, the private arms dealer enters into the picture. The Russians have no private arms dealers, so this creature fills the gap for the West. He is a businessman who may be used as a source of weaponry by someone seeking to buy, but in order to stay in business he must liaise closely with the defence department of his own country or the department will see that he goes out of business. It is in his interest to abide by his native country's wishes anyway; that country may be the source of his own purchases, which could be cut off if he causes displeasure, apart from his fear of being put out of business by other less pleasant means.

Thus the licensed arms dealer, usually a national and resident of his native country, sells arms to buyers after consulting his own government that the sale is acceptable to them. Such dealers are usually large companies, and hold stocks.

This is at the highest level of the private enterprise arms business. Lower in the pond are more dubious fish. Next down the scale is the licensed dealer who does not hold a stock of weapons in a warehouse but is licensed to hold a franchise by one of the large, often government-owned or -controlled arms manufacturing companies. He will negotiate a deal on behalf of a client, and take his cut. His licence depends on his toeing the line with the government whose franchise to operate he holds. This does not prevent some licensed arms dealers occasionally pulling a fast one, though two well-established arms dealers have been put out of business by their governments when discovered doing it.

Down in the mud at the bottom sit the black market arms dealers. These are self-styled, since they hold no licence. They may not therefore legally hold any stocks of weapons at all. They remain in business by being of value to the secret buyer, a man or organization who, not being a government or representing one, cannot clinch an inter-governmental deal; who would not be tacitly approved of by a Western government as desirable to receive arms; who cannot persuade a Communist government to support his cause on the grounds of political ideology; but who needs arms.

The vital document in an arms deal is called the end user certificate. This certifies that the weapons purchase is being made by, or on behalf of, the End User, who almost without exception in the Western world has to be a sovereign government. Only in the case of a flat gift by a secret service organization to an irregular army or of a pure black market deal does the question of an end user certificate not apply. Examples of the former were the arming, without payment, by the CIA of the anti-Castro forces of the Bay of Pigs, and the arming of the Congo mercenaries also by the CIA. An example of the latter is the shipment to Ireland from various European and US private sources of arms for the Provisional IRA.

The end user certificate, being an international document, has no specific form, shape or size, or specific wording. It is a written affirmation from a certified representative of a national government that either he the bearer or

Mr X the dealer is authorized to apply to the supplier government for permission to purchase *and export* a quantity of arms.

The vital point about the end user certificate is that some countries carry out the most rigorous checks to ensure the authenticity of this document, while others come under the heading of 'no questions asked' suppliers. Needless to say, end user certificates, like anything else, can be forged. It was into this world that Shannon carefully entered when he flew to Hamburg.

He was aware that he could certainly not make a direct application for permission to buy arms to any European government with a chance of success. Nor would Communist governments be kind enough to donate the weapons; indeed, their reaction would be totally opposed to the toppling of Kimba. By the same token, any direct application would firstly 'blow' the entire operation, and thus lead to its being frustrated.

He was also not in a position, for the same reasons, to approach one of the leading government-owned arms makers, such as Fabrique Nationale of Belgium, for any request put to a government-owned combine in the arms-making and -selling business would be passed on to the government; similarly, he could not approach a large private arms dealer, like Cogswell and Harrison of London or Parker Hale of Birmingham. In the same category Bofors of Sweden, Oerlikon of Switzerland, CETME of Spain, Werner and the others in Germany, Omnipol of Czechoslovakia and Fiat of Italy were ruled out.

He also had his own peculiar buying circumstances to consider. The amount he had to spend was too small to interest the big legitimate licensed dealers who habitually dealt in millions. He could not have interested the erstwhile king of the private arms dealers, Sam Cummings of Interarmco, who for two decades after the war ran a private arms empire from his penthouse suite in Monaco and had retired to enjoy his wealth; nor Dr Strakaty of Vienna, the licensee franchise holder for Omnipol across the border at Washington Street 11, Prague; nor Dr Langenstein in Munich; nor Dr Peretti in Rome; nor M Cammermundt in Brussels.

He had to go further down the scale to the men who dealt in smaller sums and quantities. He knew the names of Günther Leinhauser, the German, former associate of Cummings; in Paris, of Pierre Lorez, Maurice Herscu and Paul Favier. But on consideration he had decided to go and see two men in Hamburg.

The trouble with the packet of arms he sought was that it looked like what it was: a single packet of arms for a single job, and it would not need a keen military mind to realize that job had to be the taking of one building within a short period. There was not enough leeway in the quantities to kid any professional soldier that a defence ministry, even a small one, was behind the order.

Shannon had therefore decided to split the packet even smaller, so that at least the items sought from each dealer were consistent. A mixed package would be a giveaway.

From one of the men he was going to see he wanted 400,000 rounds of standard 9 mm ammunition, the sort that fits into automatic pistols and also submachine carbines. Such a consignment was too large and too heavy to be bought on the black market and shipped without a large amount of complicated smuggling to get it on board. But it could well be the kind of consignment needed by the police force of any small country, and was not suspicious in that there were no matching guns in the same packet and it could therefore pass under scrutiny as an order designed simply to replenish stocks.

To get it, he needed a licensed arms dealer who could slip such a small order through the procedures among a batch of bigger orders. Although licensed to trade in arms, the dealer must nevertheless be prepared to do a bent deal with a forged end user certificate. This was where an intimate knowledge of the no-questions-asked countries came in useful.

Ten years earlier there had been vast quantities of superfluous weaponry lying about Europe in private hands, 'black', i.e., illegally held, arms leftovers from colonial wars like those of the French in Algeria and the Belgians in the Congo.

But a series of small irregular operations and wars throughout the sixties had used them up, notably in the Yemen and Nigeria. So he would have to find a man who would use a bent end user certificate and present it to a supplier government that asked no or few questions. Only four years earlier the most noted of these was the Czech government, which, although Communist, had continued the old Czech tradition of selling arms to all comers. Four years earlier one could have walked into Prague with a suitcase full of dollars, gone to the Omnipol headquarters, selected one's hardware and a few hours later have taken off from the airport in one's chartered plane with the stuff on board. It was that simple. But since the Soviet takeover of 1968, the KGB had taken to vetting all such applications, and far too many questions were being asked.

Two other countries had earned a reputation of asking few questions about where the presented end user certificates really came from. One was Spain, traditionally interested in earning foreign currency, and whose CETME factories produced a wide range of weapons which were then sold by the Spanish Army ministry to almost all comers. The other, a newcomer, was Yugoslavia.

Yugoslavia had only begun manufacturing her own arms a few years earlier, and inevitably had reached a point where her own armed forces were equipped with domestic arms. The next step was over-production (because factories cannot be run down a few years after they have been most expensively started), and hence the desire to export. Being a newcomer to the arms market, with weapons of unknown quality, and eager for foreign currency, the Yugoslavs had adopted the 'ask no questions and you'll get told no lies' attitude to applicants for her weaponry. She produced a good light company mortar and a useful bazooka, the latter based heavily on the Czech RPG-7.

Because her goods were new, Shannon estimated a dealer could persuade Belgrade to sell a tiny quantity of these arms, consisting of two 60 mm mortar tubes and 100 bombs, plus two bazooka tubes and forty rockets. The excuse could well be that the customer was a new one, wishing to make some tests with the new weaponry, and then come back with a far larger order.

For the first of his orders, Shannon intended to go to a dealer licensed to trade with CETME in Madrid, but known also not to be above putting through a phoney end user certificate. For the second, Shannon had heard the name of another man in Hamburg who had skilfully cultivated the baby Yugoslav arms makers at an early stage and had established a good relationship with them, although he was unlicensed.

Normally there is no point in going to an unlicensed dealer. Unless he can fulfil the order out of illegally held stocks of his own, which means no export licence, his only use can be in securing a bent but plausible end user certificate for those who cannot find their own, and then persuading a licensed dealer to accept this piece of paper. The licensed dealer can then fulfil it, with government approval, from his own legally held stocks and secure an export licence, or put the phoney certificate to a government with his name and guarantee backing it up. But occasionally he has one other use which makes him employable; his intimate knowledge of the state of the market, and where to go at any given moment with any given requirement to have the best chance of success. It was for this quality that Shannon was visiting the second man on his Hamburg list.

When he arrived in the Hansa city Shannon stopped by the Landesbank to find his £5000 was there already. He took the lot in the form of a banker's cheque made out to himself, and went on to the Atlantic Hotel where his room was booked. Deciding to give the Reeperbahn a miss, and being tired, he dined early and went to bed.

Johann Schlinker, when Shannon confronted him in his small and modest office the next morning, was short, round and jovial. His eyes sparkled with bonhomie and welcome, so much so that it took Shannon ten seconds to realize the man could be trusted as far as the door. The pair of them spoke in English, but talked of dollars, the twin languages of the arms market place.

Shannon thanked the arms dealer for agreeing to see him, and offered his passport in the name of Keith Brown as identification. The German flicked through it and handed it back.

'And what brings you here?' he asked.

'You were recommended to me, Herr Schlinker, as a businessman with a high reputation for reliability in the business of military and police hardware.'

Schlinker smiled and nodded, but the flattery made no impression.

'By whom, may I ask?'

Shannon mentioned the name of a man in Paris, closely associated with African affairs on behalf of a certain French governmental but clandestine service. The two had met during one of Shannon's previous African wars, and a month earlier Shannon had looked him up in Paris for old times' sake. A week ago Shannon had rung the man again, and he had indeed recommended Shannon to Schlinker for the kind of merchandise he wanted. Shannon had told the man he would be using the name Brown.

Schlinker raised his eyebrows.

'Would you excuse me a minute?' he asked, and left the room. In an adjoining booth Shannon could hear the chatter of a telex. It was thirty minutes before he came back. He was smiling.

'I had to call a friend of mine in Paris on a business matter,' he said brightly. 'Please go on.'

Shannon knew perfectly well he had telexed to another arms dealer in Paris, asking the man to contact the French agent and get a confirmation that Keith Brown was all right. Apparently the confirmation had just come back.

'I want to buy a quantity of 9 mm ammunition,' he said bluntly. 'I know it is a small order, but I have been approached by a group of people in Africa who need this ammunition for their own affairs, and I believe if those affairs go well, there would be further and much larger shipments in the future.'

'How much would the order be?' asked the German.

'Four hundred thousand rounds.'

Schlinker made a move.

'That is not very much,' he said simply.

'Certainly. For the moment the budget is not large. One is hoping a small investment now might lead to greater things later on.'

The German nodded. It had happened in the past. The first order was usually a small one.

'Why did they come to you? You are not a dealer in arms or ammunition.'

'They happened to have retained me as a technical adviser on military matters of all kinds. When the question of seeking a fresh supplier for their needs arose, they asked me to come to Europe for them,' said Shannon.

'And you have no end user certificate?' the German asked.

'No, I'm afraid not. I hoped that sort of thing could be arranged.'

'Oh, yes, it can,' said Schlinker. 'No problem there. It takes longer, and costs more. But it can be done. One could supply this order from stocks, but they are held in my Vienna office. That way there would be no requirement for an end user certificate. Or one could obtain such a document and make the application normally through legal channels.'

'I would prefer the latter,' said Shannon. 'The delivery has to be by ship, and to bring that sort of quantity through Austria and into Italy, then on board a boat, would be hazardous. It enters an area I am not familiar with. Moreover, interception could mean long terms in prison for those found in possession. Apart from that, the cargo might be identified as coming from your stocks.'

Schlinker smiled. Privately he knew there would be no danger of that, but Shannon was right about the border controls. The newly emergent menace of the Black September terrorists had made Austria, Germany and Italy highly nervous about strange cargoes passing through the borders.

Shannon for his part did not trust Schlinker not to sell them the ammunition one day and betray them the next. With a phoney end user certificate, the

German would have to keep his side of the bargain; it would be he who presented the bent certificate to the authorities.

'I think you are perhaps right,' Schlinker said at last. 'Very well. I can offer you 9 mm standard ball at sixty-five dollars per thousand. There would be a surcharge of ten per cent for the certificate, and another ten per cent free on board.'

Shannon calculated hastily. Free on board meant a cargo complete with export licence, cleared through customs and loaded onto the ship, with the ship itself clearing the harbour mouth. The price would be 26,000 dollars for the ammunition, plus 5200 dollars surcharge.

'How would payment be made?' he asked.

'I would need the 5200 dollars before starting work,' said Schlinker. 'That has to cover the certificate, which has to be paid for, plus all personal travelling and administrative costs. The full purchase price would have to be paid here in this office when I am able to show you the certificate; but before purchase. As a licensed dealer I would be buying on behalf of my client, the government named on the certificate. Once the stuff had been bought, the selling government would be extremely unlikely to take it back and repay the money. Therefore I would need total payment in advance. I would also need the name of the exporting vessel, to fill in the application for export permit. The vessel would have to be a scheduled liner or freighter, or a general freighter owned by a registered shipping company.'

Shannon nodded. The terms were steep, but beggars cannot be choosers. If he had really represented a sovereign government he would not be here in the first place.

'How long from the time I give you the money until shipment?' he asked.

'Madrid is quite slow in these matters. About forty days at the outside,' said the German.

Shannon rose. He showed Schlinker the banker's cheque to prove his solvency, and promised to be back in an hour with 5200 US dollars in cash, or the equivalent in German marks. Schlinker opted for German marks, and when Shannon returned gave him a standard receipt for the money.

While Schlinker had been writing out the receipt, Shannon glanced through a series of brochures on the coffee table. They covered the items put on sale by another company, which evidently specialized in non-military pyrotechnic goods of the kind that are not covered by the classification of 'arms', and a wide variety of items used by security companies, including riot sticks, truncheons, walkie-talkies, riot-gas canisters and launchers, flares, rockets and the like.

As Schlinker handed him his receipt, Shannon asked, 'Are you associated with this company, Herr Schlinker?'

Schlinker smiled broadly.

'I own it,' he said. 'It is what I am best known for to the general public.'

'And a damn good cover for holding a warehouse full of crates labelled "Danger of Explosion",' thought Shannon. But he was interested. Quickly he wrote out a list of items and showed them to Schlinker.

'Could you fulfil this order, for export, out of your stocks?' he asked.

Schlinker glanced at the list. It included two rocket-launching tubes of the type used by coastguards to send up distress flares, ten rockets containing magnesium flares of maximum intensity and duration attached to parachutes, two penetrating fog-horns powered by compressed gas canisters, four sets of night-binoculars, three fixed-crystal walkie-talkie sets with a range of not less than five miles, and five wrist compasses.

'Certainly,' he said. 'I stock all of these things.'

'I'd like to place an order for the list. Being off the classification of arms, I assume there would be no problems with exporting them?'

'None at all. I can send them anywhere I want, particularly to a ship.'

'Good.' said Shannon. 'How much would that lot cost, with freight in bond to an exporting agent in Marseilles?'

Schlinker went through his catalogue and priced the list, adding on ten per cent for freight.

'Four thousand eight hundred dollars,' he said.

'I'll be in touch with you in twelve days,' said Shannon. 'Please have the whole lot ready crated for freighting. I will give you the name of the exporting agent in Marseilles, and mail you a banker's cheque in your favour for 4800 dollars. Within thirty days I expect to be able to give you the remaining 26,000 dollars for the ammunition deal, and the name of the ship.'

He met his second contact for dinner that night at the Atlantic. Alan Baker was an expatriate, a Canadian who had settled in Germany after the war and married a German girl. A former Royal Engineer during the war, he had got himself involved during the early post-war years in a series of border-crossing operations into and out of the Soviet Zone, running nylons, watches and refugees. From there he had drifted into arms running into the scores of tiny nationalist or anti-Communist bands of maquis who, left over from the war, still ran their resistance movements in Central and Eastern Europe – with the sole difference that during the war they had been resisting the Germans, while after it they were resisting the Communists.

Most of them had been paid for by the Americans, but Baker was content to use his knowledge of German and commando tactics to slip quantities of arms to them, and take a hefty salary cheque from the Americans for doing so. When these groups finally petered out, he found himself in Tangier in the early fifties, using the smuggling talents he had learned in the war and after it to bring cargoes of perfume and cigarettes into Italy and Spain from the then international and free port on the north coast of Morocco. Finally put out of business by the bombing and sinking of his ship in a gangland feud, he had returned to Germany and gone into the business of wheeler-dealing in any commodity that had a buyer and a supplier. His most recent feat had been to negotiate a deal in Yugoslav arms on behalf of the Basques in northern Spain.

He and Shannon had met when Baker was running guns into Ethiopia, and Shannon had been at a loose end after returning from Bukavu in April 1968. He knew Shannon under his real name.

He listened quietly while Shannon explained what he wanted, a short wiry man, his eyes flickering from his food to the other mercenary.

'Yes, it can be done,' he said when Shannon had finished. 'The Yugoslavs would accept the idea that a new customer wanted a sample set of two mortars and two bazookas for test purposes before placing a larger order if they were satisfied. It's plausible. There's no problem from my side in getting the stuff from them. My relations with the men in Belgrade are excellent. And they are quick. Just at the moment I have to admit I have one other problem, though.'

'What's that?'

'End user certificate,' said Baker. 'I used to have a man in Bonn, diplomat for a certain East African country, who would sign anything for a price, and a few nice big German girls laid on at a party, the sort he liked. He was transferred back to his own country two weeks ago. I'm a bit stuck for a replacement at the moment.'

'Are the Yugoslavs particular about end users?'

Baker shook his head.

'Nope. So long as the documentation is in order, they don't check further. But there has to be a certificate, and it must have the right governmental stamp on it. They can't afford to be too slack, after all.'

Shannon thought for a moment. He knew of a man in Paris who had once boasted he had a contact in an embassy there who could make out end user certificates.

'If I could get you one, a good one, from an African country? Would that work?' he asked.

Baker inhaled on his cigar.

'No problem at all,' he said. 'As for the price, a 60 mm mortar tube would run you 1100 dollars each. Say, 2200 for the pair. The bombs are twenty-four dollars each. The only problem with your order is that the sums are really too small. Couldn't you up the number of mortar bombs from a hundred to three hundred? It would make things much easier. No one throws off just a hundred bombs, not even for test purposes.'

'All right,' said Shannon, 'I'll take three hundred, but no more. Otherwise I'll go over budget, and that comes off my cut.'

It did not come off his cut, for he had allowed a margin for over-expenditure, and his own salary was secure. But he knew Baker would accept the argument as final.

'Good,' said Baker. 'So that's 7200 dollars for the bombs. The bazookas cost 1000 dollars each, two thousand for the pair. The rockets are forty-two dollars and fifty cents each. The forty you want come out at ... let's see ...'

'Seventeen hundred dollars,' said Shannon. 'The whole packet comes out at 13,100 dollars.'

'Plus ten per cent for getting the stuff free on board your ship, Cat. Without the end user certificate. If I could have got one for you, it would have been twenty per cent. Let's face it, it's a tiny order, but the travelling and out-of-pocket expenses for me are constants. I ought to charge you fifteen per cent for such a small order. So the total is 14,400 dollars. Let's say fourteen and a half, eh?'

'We'll say 14,400,' said Shannon. 'I'll get the certificate and mail it to you, along with a fifty per cent deposit. I'll pay another twenty-five per cent when I see the stuff in Yugoslavia crated and ready to go, and twenty-five per cent as the ship leaves the quay. Travellers cheques in dollars, OK?'

Baker would have liked the lot in advance, but not being a licensed dealer he had no offices, warehouses, or business address as Schlinker had. He would act as broker, using another dealer he knew to make the actual purchase on his behalf. But being a black market man, he had to accept these terms, the lower cut and less in advance.

One of the oldest tricks in the book is to promise to fulfil an arms order, show plenty of confidence, assure the customer of the broker's absolute integrity, take the maximum in advance and disappear. Many a black and brown seeker after arms in Europe has had that happen to them. He knew Shannon would never fall for the trick; besides, fifty per cent of 14,400 dollars was too small a sum to disappear for.

'OK. The moment I get your end user certificate I'll get straight on to it.

They rose to leave.

'How long from the time you make your first approach until shipping date?' asked Shannon.

'About thirty to thirty-five days,' said Baker. 'By the way, have you got a ship?'

'Not yet. You'll need the name, I suppose. I'll let you have it with the certificate.'

'If you haven't, I know a very good one for charter. Two thousand German marks a day and all found. Crew, victuals, the lot. Take you and the cargo anywhere and discreet as you like.'

Shannon thought it over. Twenty days in the Mediterranean, twenty days out to target and twenty days back. A hundred and twenty thousand marks, or £15,000. Cheaper than buying one's own ship. Tempting. But he objected to the idea of one man outside the operation controlling part of the arms deal, the ship, and being aware of the target as well. It would involve making Baker, or the man he would have to go to for the charter, virtually a partner.

'Yes,' he said cautiously. 'What's she called?'

'The *San Andrea*,' said Baker.

Shannon froze. He had heard Semmler mention that name.

'Registered in Cyprus?' asked Shannon.

'That's right.'

'Forget it,' he said shortly.

As they left the dining room Shannon caught a swift glimpse of Johann Schlinker, dining in an alcove. For a moment he thought the German dealer might have followed him, but the man was dining with a second man, evidently a valued customer. Shannon averted his head and strode past.

On the doorstep of the hotel he shook hands with Baker.

'You'll be hearing from me,' he said. 'And don't let me down.'

'Don't worry, Cat. You can trust me,' said Baker.

He turned and hurried off down the street. 'In a pig's ear I can,' muttered Shannon, and went back into the hotel.

On the way up to his room the face of the man he had seen dining with the German arms merchant stayed in his memory. He had seen the face somewhere, but could not place it. As he was falling asleep it came to him. The man was the chief of staff of the IRA.

The next morning, Wednesday, he flew back to London. It was the start of Day Nine.

Chapter Twelve

Martin Thorpe stepped into Sir James Manson's office about the time Cat Shannon was taking off from Hamburg.

'Lady Macallister,' he said by way of introduction, and Sir James waved him to a seat.

'I've been into her with a fine toothcomb,' Thorpe went on. 'As I suspected, she has twice been approached by people interested in buying her thirty per cent holding in Bormac trading. It would seem each person used the wrong approach, and got turned down. She's eighty-six, half-way senile, and very tetchy. At least, that's her reputation. She's also broad Scottish and has all her affairs handled by a solicitor up in Dundee. Here's my full report on her.'

He handed Sir James a buff folder, and the head of Manson Consolidated read it within a few minutes. He grunted several times, and muttered 'Bloody hell' once. When he had finished, he looked up.

'I still want those 300,000 shares in Bormac,' he said. 'You say the others went about it the wrong way. Why?'

'She would appear to have one obsession in life, and it's not money. She's rich in her own right. When she married she was the daughter of a Scottish laird with more land than ready cash. The marriage was no doubt arranged between the families. After her father died she inherited the lot, mile after mile of desolate moorland. But over the past twenty years the fishing and hunting rights have brought in a small fortune from city-dwelling sportsmen, and parcels of land sold off for industry have made even more. It's been invested by her broker, or whatever they call them up there. She has a nice income to live on. I suspect the other bidders offered a lot of money but nothing else. That would not interest her.'

'Then what the hell would?' asked Sir James.

'Look at paragraph two on the second page, Sir James. See what I mean? The notices in *The Times* every anniversary, the attempt to have a statue erected, which was refused by the London County Council. The memorial she had put up in his home town. I think that's her obsession – the memory of the old slave-driver she married.'

'Yes, yes, you may be right. So what do you propose?'

Thorpe outlined his idea and Manson listened thoughtfully.

'It might work,' he said eventually. 'Stranger things have happened. The trouble is, if you try it and she still refuses, you can hardly go back again with another offer couched in a different vein. But then I suppose a pure cash offer would in any case get the same reaction the previous two proposals met. All right, play it your way. Just get her to sell those shares.'

With that, Thorpe was on his way.

Shannon was back in his London flat shortly after twelve. Lying on the mat was a cable from Langarotti in Marseilles. It was signed simply 'Jean' and addressed to Keith Brown. Its message was simply an address, a hotel in a street a little way out of the centre of the town where the Corsican had checked in under the name of Lavallon. Shannon approved the precaution. Checking into a French hotel requires the filling out of a form which is later collected by the police. They might have wondered why their old friend Langarotti was staying so far out of town from his usual haunts.

Shannon spent ten minutes extracting the number of the hotel from Continental Directory Enquiries, and placed a call. When he asked the hotel for M Lavallon, he was told the monsieur was out. He left a message asking M Lavallon to call Mr Brown in London on his return. He had already given each of the four his own telephone number and made them commit it to memory.

Still using the telephone he sent a telegram to the *poste restante* address of Endean under the name of Walter Harris, advising the project manager that he was back in London and would like to discuss something. Another telegram went to Janni Dupree at his bedsitter instructing him to report to Shannon as soon as he received the cable.

He rang his own Swiss bank and learned that of the salary for himself of £10,000, half that amount had been transferred to him, the credit having come from an unnamed account holder at the Handelsbank. This he knew to be Endean. He shrugged. It was normal for half the salary only to be paid at this early date. He was confident from the sheer size of ManCon, and their evident eagerness to see Kimba fall from power, that the other £5000 would be his as the operation progressed.

Through the afternoon he typed out a full report of his Luxembourg and Hamburg trip, excluding the names of the firm of accountants in Luxembourg, and the two arms dealers. To these sheets he attached a full statement of expenditure.

It was past four when he finished, and he had not eaten since the mid-morning snack provided by Lufthansa on the flight from Hamburg. He found half a dozen eggs in the fridge, made a complete mess of an omelette, threw it away and had a nap.

The arrival of Janni Dupree at the door just after six woke him, and five minutes later the phone rang. It was Endean who had picked up the telegram in the post office.

Endean soon noticed that Shannon was not in a position to talk freely.

'Is there someone with you?' asked Endean down the phone.

'Yes.'

'Is it connected with business?'

'Yes.'

'Do you want to meet?'

'I think we ought,' said Shannon. 'What about tomorrow morning?'

'OK. About eleven suit you?'

'Sure,' said Shannon.

'Your place?'

'Suits me fine.'

'I'll be there at eleven,' said Endean and hung up.

Shannon turned to the South African.

'How are you getting on, Janni?' he asked.

Dupree had made a little progress in the three days he had been working. The hundred pairs of socks, singlets and underpants were on order and would be ready for collection by Friday. He had found a supplier for the fifty combat tunics, and had placed the order. The same firm could have provided trousers to match, but according to his orders Dupree was seeking another firm to supply the trousers, so that no one supplier would realize he was providing complete sets of uniforms. Dupree mentioned that no one seemed suspicious in any case, but Shannon decided nevertheless to stick to the original idea.

Janni said he had tried several footwear stores, but had not found the canvas boots he was looking for. He would go on trying for the rest of the week, and start searching for berets, haversacks, knapsacks, a variety of webbing and sleeping bags next week. Shannon advised him to contact his first export agent and get the first consignment of underwear and tunics off to Marseilles as soon as possible. He promised Dupree to get from Langarotti the name and address of a consignee agent in Marseilles within the next forty-eight hours.

Before the South African left, Shannon typed out a letter to Langarotti and addressed it to him under his real name at the main post office of Marseilles. In the letter he reminded the Corsican of a conversation they had had six months earlier beneath the palm trees when the talk had turned to the buying of arms. The Corsican had mentioned that he knew a man in Paris who could get end user certificates from a diplomat in one of the Paris embassies of an African republic. Shannon needed to know the name of the man and where he could be contacted.

When he had finished he gave Dupree the letter and ordered him to post it express rate that same evening from Trafalgar Square. He explained he would have done it himself but he had to wait in the flat for Langarotti himself to ring from Marseilles.

He was getting very hungry by eight when Langarotti finally called, his voice crackling down a telephone line that must have been created personally by the inventor of that antique masterpiece, the French telephone network.

Shannon asked him, in guarded terms, how he had been getting on. Before any of the mercenaries had left him he had warned them all that under no circumstances was a telephone line to be used to talk openly about what they were doing.

'I checked into a hotel and sent you a telegram with my address on it,' said Langarotti.

'I know. I got it,' shouted Shannon.

'I hired a scooter and toured all the shops that deal in the kind of merchandise we are looking for,' came the voice. 'There are three manufacturers in each category. I got the addresses and names of the three boat-makers and wrote off to each for their brochures. I should get them in a week or so. Then I can order the best-suited from the local dealers, quoting the maker's name and brand name of the article,' said Langarotti.

'Good idea,' said Shannon. 'What about the second articles?'

'They depend on the kind we pick from the brochures I shall get. One depends on the other. But don't worry. Of the second thing we need there are thousands of every kind and description in the shops along this coast. With spring coming, every shop in every port is stocking up with the latest models.'

'OK. Fine,' Shannon shouted. 'Now listen. I need the name of a good export agent for shipping. I need it earlier than I thought. There will be a few crates to be sent from here in the near future, and another from Hamburg.'

'I can get that easy enough,' said Langarotti from the other end. 'But I think it would be better in Toulon. You can guess why.'

Shannon could guess. Langarotti could use another name at his hotel, but for exporting goods from the port on a small freighter, he would have to identify himself with his identity card. Moreover, in the past year or so Marseilles police had tightened up considerably in their watch on the port and a new Customs chief had been drafted in, who was believed to be a holy terror. The aim of both operations was to clamp down on the heroin traffic that made Marseilles the start of the French connection with New York, but a search of a boat for drugs could just as easily turn up arms instead. It would be the worst irony to be caught because of something one was not even involved in.

'Fair enough, you know that area best,' said Shannon. 'Cable me the name and address as soon as you have it. There is one other thing. I have sent a letter, by express rate tonight, to you personally at the main post office in Marseilles. You'll see what I want when you read it. Cable me the man's name at once, when you get the letter, which should be Friday morning.'

'OK,' said Langarotti. 'Is that all?'

'Yes, for the moment. Send me those brochures as soon as you get them, with your own comments and the prices. We must stay in budget.'

'Right. Bye-bye,' called Langarotti, and Shannon hung up. He had a dinner alone at the Bois de St Jean and slept early.

Endean called at eleven the next morning and spent an hour reading the report and accounts, and discussing both with Shannon.

'Fair enough,' he said at length. 'How are things going?'

'Well,' said Shannon. 'It's early days yet, of course. I've only been on the job for ten days, but a lot of ground has been covered. I want to get all the orders placed by Day Twenty, which will leave forty days for them to be fulfilled. After that there must be an allowance of twenty days to collect all the component parts and get them safely and discreetly aboard the ship. Sailing date should be Day Eighty, if we are to strike on schedule. By the way, I shall need more money soon.'

'You have three and a half thousand in London, and seven thousand in Belgium,' objected Endean.

'Yes, I know. But there is going to be a spate of payments soon.'

He explained he would have to pay 'Johann', the Hamburg arms dealer, the outstanding 26,000 dollars within twelve days to allow him forty days to get the consignment through the formalities in Madrid and ready for shipment; then there would be 4800 dollars also to Johann for the ancillary gear he needed for the attack. When he had the end user certificate in Paris, he would have to send it to 'Alan', along with a credit transfer of 7200 dollars, being fifty per cent of the Yugoslav arms price.

'It all mounts up,' he said. 'The big payments, of course, are the arms and the boat. They form over half the total budget.'

'All right,' said Endean. 'I'll consult and prepare a draft to your Belgian account for another £20,000. Then the transfer can be made on a telephone call from me to Switzerland. In that way it will only take a matter of hours, when you need it.'

He rose to go.

'Anything else?'

'No,' said Shannon. 'I'll have to go away again at the weekend for another trip. I should be away most of next week. I want to check on the search for the boat, the choice of dinghies and outboards in Marseilles and the submachine guns in Belgium.'

'Cable me at the usual address when you leave and when you get back,' said Endean.

The drawing room in the sprawling apartment above Cottesmore Gardens, not far from Kensington High Street, was gloomy in the extreme, with heavy drapes across the windows to shut out the spring sunshine. A gap a few inches wide between them allowed a little daylight to filter in through thick net curtains. Between the four formally placed and overstuffed chairs, each of them late Victorian pieces, a myriad of small tables bore assorted bric-à-brac. There were buttons from long-punctured uniforms, medals won in long-past skirmishes with long-liquidated heathen tribes. Glass paperweights nudged Dresden china dolls, cameos of once-demure Highland beauties and fans that had cooled faces at balls whose music was no longer played.

Round the walls of discoloured brocades hung portraits of ancestors,

Montroses and Monteagles, Farquhars and Frazers, Murrays and Mintoes. Surely such a gathering could not all be the ancestors of one old woman? Still, you never knew with the Scots.

Bigger than them all, in a vast frame above the fire that, clearly, was never lit, stood a man in a kilt, a painting evidently much more recent than the other blackened antiques, but still discoloured by age. The face, framed by two bristling ginger muttonchop whiskers, glared down into the room, as if its owner had just spotted a coolie impudently collapsing from overwork at the other end of the plantation. Sir Ian Macallister, KBE, read the motto beneath the portrait.

Martin Thorpe dragged his eyes back to Lady Macallister, slumped in a chair and fiddling as she constantly did with the hearing aid that hung on her chest. He tried to make out from the mumblings and ramblings, sudden digressions and difficult accent, what she was saying.

'People have come before, Mr Martin,' she was saying; she insisted on calling him Mr Martin, although he had introduced himself twice. 'But I don't see why I should sell. It was my husband's company, don't you see. He founded all these estates that they make their money from. It was all his work. Now people come and say they want to take the company away and do other things with it ... build houses and play around with other things. I don't understand it all, not at all, and I will not sell ...'

'But Lady Macallister ...'

She went on as if she had not heard him, which indeed she had not, for her hearing aid was up to its usual tricks through her constant fiddling with it. Thorpe began to understand why other suitors had eventually gone elsewhere for their shell companies.

'You see, my dear husband, God rest his poor soul, was not able to leave me very much, Mr Martin. When those dreadful Chinese killed him, I was in Scotland on furlough, and I never went back. I was advised not to go. But they told me the estates belonged to the company, and he had left me a large part of the company. So that was his legacy to me, don't you see. I could not sell his own legacy to me ...'

Thorpe was about to say that the company was worthless, but realized that would not have been the right thing to say.

'Lady Macallister ...' he began again.

'You'll have to speak directly into the hearing aid. She's deaf as a post,' said Lady Macallister's companion.

Thorpe nodded his thanks to her, and noticed her properly for the first time. In her late sixties, she had the careworn look of those who once had their own independence, but who, through the strange turns of fortune, have fallen on harder times and to survive have to put themselves in bond to others, often to cantankerous, troublesome, exhausting employers, whose money enables them to hire others to serve them.

Thorpe rose and approached the senile old woman in the armchair. He spoke closer to the hearing aid.

'Lady Macallister, the people I represent do not want to change the company. On the contrary, they want to put a lot of money into it and make it rich and famous again. We want to start up the Macallister estates, just like when your husband ran them ...'

For the first time since the interview had started an hour before, something like a glimmer of light awoke in the old woman's eyes.

'Like when my husband ran them ... ?' she queried.

'Yes, Lady Macallister,' bawled Thorpe. He pointed up at the figure of the tyrant on the wall. 'We want to create all his life's work again just the way he would have wanted it, and make the Macallister estates a memorial to him and his work.'

But she was gone again.

'They never put up a memorial to him,' she quavered. 'I tried, you know. I wrote to the authorities. I said I would pay for the statue, but they said there was no room. No room. They put up lots of statues, but not to my Ian.'

'They will put up a memorial to him if the estates and the company become rich again,' Thorpe shouted into the hearing aid. 'They'll have to. If the company was rich, it could insist on a memorial. It could found a scholarship, or a foundation, called the Sir Ian Macallister Trust, so that people would remember him ...'

He had already tried that ploy once, but no doubt she had not heard him, or not grasped what he was saying. But she heard him this time.

'It would cost a lot of money,' she quavered. 'I am not a rich woman ...'

She was in fact extremely rich, but probably unaware of it.

'You don't have to pay for it, Lady Macallister,' he said. 'The company would pay for it. But the company would have to expand again. And that means money. The money would be put into the company by my friends ...'

'I don't know, I don't know,' she wailed and began to sniff, reaching for a cambric handkerchief in her sleeve. 'I don't understand these things. If only my dear Ian were here. Or Mr Dalgleish. I always ask him what would be for the best. He always signs the papers for me. Mrs Barton, I'd like to go back to my room.'

'It's time enough,' said the housekeeper-companion brusquely. 'Now come along, it's time for your nap. And your medicine.'

She helped the old woman to her feet and assisted her out of the sitting room and down the corridor. Through the open door Thorpe could hear her businesslike voice commanding her charge to get onto the bed, and the old woman's protests as she took her medicine.

After a while Mrs Barton came back into the sitting room.

'She's on the bed, she'll rest for a while,' she said.

Thorpe smiled his most rueful smile.

'It looks as if I've failed,' he said sadly. 'And yet, you know, the stock she holds is quite valueless unless the company is rejuvenated with fresh management and some hard cash, quite a lot of it, which my partners would be prepared to put in.'

He prepared to leave for the door.

'I'm sorry if I put you to inconvenience,' he said.

'I'm quite used to inconvenience,' said Mrs Barton, but her face softened. It had been a long time since anyone apologized for putting her to trouble. 'Would you care for a cup of tea? I usually make one at this hour.'

Some instinct at the back of Thorpe's mind prompted him to accept. As they sat over a pot of tea in the back kitchen which was the housekeeper-companion's domain, Martin Thorpe felt almost at home. His mother's kitchen in Battersea had not been dissimilar. Mrs Barton told him about Lady Macallister, her whining and her tantrums, her obstinacy and the constant strain of competing with her all-too-convenient deafness.

'She can't see all your fine arguments, Mr Thorpe, not even when you offered to put up a memorial to that old ogre in the sitting room.'

Thorpe was surprised. Evidently the tart Mrs Barton had a mind of her own when her employer was not listening.

'She does what you tell her,' he said.

'Would you like another cup of tea?' she asked. As she poured it, she said quietly, 'Oh yes, she does what I tell her. She depends on me, and she knows it. If I went, she'd never get another companion. You can't nowadays. People aren't prepared to put up with that sort of thing these days.'

'It can't be much of a life for you, Mrs Barton?'

'It's not,' she said shortly, 'but I have a roof over my head, and food and some clothes. I get by. It's the price one pays.'

'For being a widow?' asked Thorpe gently.

'Yes.'

There was a picture of a young man in the uniform of a pilot of the Royal Air Force, propped on the mantelpiece next to the clock. He wore a sheepskin jacket, a polkadotted scarf and a broad grin. Seen at one angle, he looked not unlike Martin Thorpe.

'Your son?' said the financier, with a nod.

Mrs Barton nodded and gazed at the picture.

'Yes. Shot down over France in 1943.'

'I'm sorry.'

'It was a long time ago. One becomes accustomed.'

'So he won't be able to look after you when she's dead and gone.'

'No.'

'Then who will?'

'I'll get by. She'll no doubt leave me something in her will. I've looked after her for sixteen years.'

'Yes, of course she will. She'll see you all right – no doubt of it.'

He spent another hour in the back kitchen, and when he left he was a much happier man. It was nearly closing time for shops and offices, but from a corner phone booth he made a call to the head office of ManCon, and within ten minutes Endean had done what his colleague asked.

In the West End an insurance broker agreed to stay late in his office that night and receive Mr Thorpe at ten the next morning.

That Thursday evening Johann Schlinker flew into London from Hamburg. He had arranged his evening appointment by telephone from Hamburg the same morning, phoning his contact at his home rather than the office.

He met the diplomat from the Iraqi embassy for dinner at nine. It was an expensive dinner, even more so when the German arms dealer handed over an envelope containing the equivalent in German marks of £1000. In return he took an envelope from the Arab and checked the contents. They took the form of a letter on crested embassy notepaper. The letter was addressed to whom it might concern, and stated that the undersigned, being a diplomat on the staff of the London embassy of the Republic of Iraq, had been required and requested by the Interior and Police Ministry of his country to authorize Herr Johann Schlinker to negotiate the purchase of 400,000 rounds of standard 9 mm ball for shipment to Iraq to replenish the stocks of the police forces of the country. It was signed by the diplomat, and bore the stamp and seal of the Republic of Iraq, which would normally be on the desk of the ambassador.

The letter further stated that the purchase would be wholly and exclusively for the use of the Republic of Iraq and would under no circumstances be passed, in whole or in part, to any other party. It was an end user certificate.

When they parted, it was too late for the German to return home, so he spent the night in London and left the following morning.

At eleven on the Friday morning Cat Shannon phoned Marc Vlaminck at his flat above the bar in Ostende.

'Did you find that man I asked you to trace?' he inquired after introducing himself. He had already warned the Belgian to talk very carefully on the telephone.

'Yes, I found him,' replied Tiny Marc. He was sitting up in bed, while Anna snored gently beside him. The bar usually closed between three and four in the morning, so midday was the habitual rising time for both of them.

'Is he prepared to talk business about the merchandise?' asked Shannon.

'I think so,' said Vlaminck. 'I haven't raised the matter with him yet, but a business friend here says he will normally do business after a suitable introduction through a mutual acquaintance.'

'He still has the goods I mentioned to you at our last meeting?'

'Yes,' said the voice from Belgium. 'He still has them.'

'Fine,' said Shannon. 'Get a meeting and introduction with him yourself first, and tell him you have a customer who has approached you and would like to talk business. Ask him to be available for a meeting next weekend with the customer. Tell him the customer is good and reliable, and is an Englishman called Brown. You know what to say. Just get him interested in a business deal. Tell him the customer would wish to examine one example of the goods at the meeting, and if it is up to standard, discuss terms and delivery. I'll ring you towards the weekend and let you know where I am, and when I could come to see you and him together. Understand?'

'Sure,' said Marc, 'I'll get on with it over the next couple of days and set the meeting up for some time to be confirmed later, but during next weekend.'

They exchanged the usual good wishes and hung up.

At half past two, a cable arrived at the flat from Marseilles. It bore the name of a Frenchman and an address. Langarotti said he would telephone the man and introduce Shannon with a personal recommendation. The cable concluded by saying inquiries regarding the shipping agent were under way, and he expected to be able to give Shannon a name and address within five days.

Shannon picked up the phone and rang the offices of UTA Airlines in Piccadilly, to book himself a seat on the flight on the following Sunday midnight to Africa from Le Bourget, Paris. From BEA he reserved a ticket to Paris on the first flight the next morning, Saturday. By the late afternoon he had paid for both of them in cash.

He put £2000 of the money he had brought back from Germany into an envelope and slipped it into the lining at the bottom of his handgrip, for London airport representatives of the Treasury by and large disapprove of British citizens strolling out of the country with more than the permitted £25 in cash and £300 in travellers cheques.

Just after lunch Sir James Manson summoned Simon Endean to his office. He had finished reading Shannon's report and was agreeably surprised at the speed with which the mercenary's proposed plan of twelve days earlier was being carried out. He had checked the accounts and approved the expenditure. What pleased him even more was the long telephone call he had had from Martin Thorpe, who had spent half the night and most of the morning with an insurance broker.

'You say Shannon will be abroad for most of next week,' he told Endean when his aide entered the office.

'Yes, Sir James.'

'Good. There's a job that has to be done sooner or later, and it might as well be now. Get one of our standard contracts of employment, the kind we use for the engagement of African representatives. Paste over the name of ManCon with a strip of white paper and fill in the name of Bormac in its place. Make it out for a one-year's engagement for the services as West African representative of Antoine Bobi at a salary of £500 a month. When you've got it done, show it to me.'

'Bobi?' queried Endean. 'You mean Colonel Bobi?'

'That's the one. I don't want the future president of Zangaro running off anywhere. Next week, starting Monday, you are going down to Cotonou to interview the colonel and persuade him that Bormac Trading Company, whose representative you are, has been so impressed by his mental and business acumen that it would like to engage his services as a West African consultant. Don't worry, he'll never check to see who or what Bormac is, or that you are its representative. If I know anything about these lads, the hefty salary will be what interests him. If he's short of the ready, it ought to be manna from heaven.

'You are to tell him his duties will be communicated to him later, but the sole condition of employment for the moment is that he remain where he is at his house in Dahomey for the next three months or until you visit him again. Persuade him there will be a bonus in salary if he waits where he is. Tell him the money will be transferred to his local account in Dahomean francs. On no account is he to receive any hard currency. He might vamoose. One last thing. When the contract is ready, have it photocopied to hide the traces of the change of name of the employing company, and only take with you photo-copies. As for the date on it, make sure the last figure for the year is blurred. Smudge it yourself.'

Endean absorbed the instructions and left to begin setting up the employment under false pretences of Colonel Antoine Bobi.

That Friday afternoon, just after four, Thorpe emerged from the gloomy Kensington apartment with the four share transfer deeds he needed, duly signed by Lady Macallister and witnessed by Mrs Barton. He also bore a letter of authority signed by the old woman instructing Mr Dalgleish, her attorney in Dundee, to hand over to Mr Thorpe the share certificates upon presentation of the letter and proof of identity, and the necessary cheque.

The name of the recipient of the shares had been left blank on the transfer deeds, but Lady Macallister had not noticed. She had been too distraught at the thought of Mrs Barton packing her bags and leaving. Before nightfall the name of the Zwingli bank's nominee company, acting on behalf of Messrs Adams, Ball, Carter and Davies, would be written into the vacant space. After a visit to Zürich the following Monday the bank stamp and counter-signature of Dr Steinhofer would complete the form, and four certified cheques, one drawn against the account of each of the four nominees buying seven and a half per cent of the stock of Bormac, would be brought back from Switzerland.

It had cost Sir James Manson two shillings to buy each of the 300,000 shares, then quoted at one shilling and one penny on the Stock Exchange, or a total of £30,000. It had also cost him another £30,000, shunted that morning through three bank accounts, withdrawn once in cash and re-paid into a fresh account an hour later to purchase a life annuity which would assure a comfortable and worry-free end to her days to an elderly housekeeper-companion.

All in all, Thorpe reckoned it was cheap at the price. Even more important, it was untraceable. Thorpe's name appeared nowhere on any document, the annuity had been paid for by a solicitor and solicitors are paid to keep their mouths shut; Thorpe was confident Mrs Barton would have enough sense to do the same. And to cap it all, it was even legal.

Chapter Thirteen

Benoit Lambert, known to friends and police as Benny, was a small-fry member of the underworld and self-styled mercenary. In point of fact, his sole appearance in the mercenary-soldier field had occurred when, with the police looking for him in the Paris area, he had taken a plane for Africa and signed on in the Sixth Commando in the Congo under the leadership of Denard.

For some strange reason the mercenary leader had taken a liking to the timorous little man and had given him a job at headquarters, which kept him well away from combat. He had been useful in his job, because it enabled him to exercise to good effect the one talent he really did possess. He was a wizard at obtaining things. He seemed to be able to conjure up eggs where there were no chickens and whisky where there was no still. In the headquarters of any military unit, such a man is always useful, and most units have one. He had stayed with the Sixth Commando for nearly a year, until May 1967 when he spotted trouble brewing in the form of a pending revolt by Schramme's Tenth Commando against the Congolese government. He felt, rightly as it turned out, that Denard and the Sixth might be drawn into this fracas, and there would be an opportunity for all, including headquarters staff, to see some real combat. For Benny Lambert this was the moment to move briskly in the other direction.

To his surprise he had been allowed to go.

Back in France he had cultivated the notion of himself as a mercenary and later had called himself an arms dealer. The first he certainly was not, but as for arms, with his variety of contacts he had occasionally been able to provide an item of weaponry here and there, usually hand guns for the underworld, occasionally a case of rifles. He had also come to know an African diplomat who was prepared, for a price, to provide a moderately serviceable end user certificate in the form of a letter from the ambassador's personal desk, complete with embassy stamp. Eighteen months earlier, he had mentioned this in a bar to a Corsican called Langarotti.

Nevertheless, he was surprised on the Friday evening to hear the Corsican on the phone, calling long distance, to tell him he would be visited at his home the next day or Sunday by Cat Shannon. He had heard of Shannon, but even more so he was aware of the vitriolic hatred Charles Roux bore for the Irish mercenary, and he had long since heard on the grapevine that circulated among the mercenaries of Paris that Roux was prepared to pay money for anyone who would tip him off as to Shannon's whereabouts, should the Irishman ever turn up in Paris. After consideration, Lambert agreed to be at home to see Shannon.

'Yes, I think I can get that certificate,' he said when Shannon had finished explaining what he wanted. 'My contact is still in Paris. I deal with him fairly frequently, you know.'

It was a lie, for his dealings were very infrequent, but he was sure he could swing the deal.

'How much?' asked Shannon shortly.

'Fifteen thousand francs,' said Benny Lambert.

'Bollocks,' said Shannon, and he said it in French. It was one of the numerous phrases he had picked up in the Congo, even though it was not to be found in the best of Larousse's French dictionaries. 'I'll pay you a thousand pounds, and that's over the rate.'

Lambert calculated. The sum was just over eleven thousand francs at the current rate.

'OK,' he said.

'You let out one word of this, and I'll slit your gizzard like a chicken,' said Shannon. 'Even better, I'll get the Corsican to do it, and he'll start at the knee.'

'Not a word, honest,' protested Benny. 'A thousand pounds, and I'll get you the letter in four days. And not a word to anyone.'

Shannon put down five hundred pounds.

'You'll take it in sterling,' he said. 'Half now, half when I pick it up.'

Lambert was about to protest, but realized it would be no good. The Irishman did not trust him.

'I'll call you here on Wednesday,' said Shannon. 'Have the letter here, and I'll hand over the other five hundred.'

When he had gone Benny Lambert thought over what he would do. Finally he decided to get the letter, collect the remainder of his fee, and tell Roux later.

The following evening Shannon flew to Africa on the midnight flight, arriving at dawn on Monday morning.

It was a long drive upcountry. The taxi was hot and rattled abominably. It was still the height of the dry season, and the sky above the oil-palm plantations was robin's-egg blue, without a cloud. Shannon did not mind. It was good to be back in Africa again for a day and a half, even after a six-hour flight without sleep.

It was familiar to him, more so than the cities of western Europe. Familiar were the sounds and the smells, the villagers walking along the edge of the road to market, columns of women in Indian file, their gourds and bundles of wares balanced on their heads, unwaveringly steady.

At each village they passed, the usual morning market was set out beneath the shade of the palm-thatch roofs of the rickety stalls, the villagers bargaining and chattering, buying and selling, the women tending the stalls while the men sat in the shade and talked of important matters that only they could understand, and the naked brown children scampering through the dust between the legs of their parents and the stalls.

Shannon had both windows open. He sat back and sniffed the moisture and the palms, the woodsmoke and the brown stagnant rivers they crossed. From the airport he had already telephoned the number the writer had given him, and he knew he was expected. He arrived at the villa set back from the road in a private, if small, park just before noon.

The guards checked him at the gate, frisking him from ankles to armpits, before letting him pay off the taxi and enter the gate. Inside, he recognized a face, one of the personal attendants of the man he had come to see. The servant grinned broadly and bobbed his head. He led Shannon to one of the three houses in the grounds of the park and ushered him into an empty sitting room. He waited alone for half an hour.

Shannon was staring out of the windows, feeling the cool of the air conditioner dry out his clothes, when he heard the creak of a door and the soft sound of a sandal on tiles behind him. He turned round.

The general was much the same as when they had last met on the darkened airstrip, the same luxuriant beard, the same deep bass voice.

'Well, Major Shannon, so soon. Couldn't you stay away?'

He was bantering, as he usually did. Shannon grinned as they shook hands.

'I've come down because I need something, sir. And because there is something I think we ought to talk over. An idea in the back of my head.'

'There's not much that an impoverished exile can offer you,' said the general, 'but I'll always listen to your ideas. If I remember rightly, you used to have some fairly good ones.'

Shannon said, 'There's one thing you have, even in exile, that I could use. You still have your people's loyalty. And what I need is men.'

The two men talked through the lunch hour and through the afternoon. They were still discussing when darkness fell, Shannon's freshly drawn diagrams spread out on the table. He had brought nothing with him but clean white paper and a variety of coloured felt-nib pens. Just in case of a skin-search at Customs.

They reached agreement on the basic points by sundown and elaborated the plan through the night. Only at three in the morning was the car summoned to drive Shannon back to the coast and the airport for takeoff on the dawn plane to Paris.

As they parted on the terrace above the waiting car and its sleepy chauffeur, they shook hands again.

'I'll be in touch, sir,' said Shannon.

'And I'll have to send my emissaries immediately,' replied the general. 'But in sixty days the men will be there.'

Shannon was dead tired. The strain of the constant travelling was beginning to tell, the nights without sleep, the endless succession of airports and hotels, negotiations and meetings, had left him drained. In the car to the south he slept for the first time in two days, and dozed again on the plane trip back to Paris. The flight stopped too many times to enable a proper sleep, an hour at Ouagadougou, another at a God-forsaken strip in Mauretania, and again at Marseilles. He reached Le Bourget just before six in the afternoon. It was the end of Day Fifteen.

While he was landing in Paris, Martin Thorpe was boarding the overnight sleeper train to Glasgow, Stirling and Perth. From there he could make a connecting train to Dundee, where were situated the old-established offices of Dalgleish and Dalgleish, attorneys-at-law. He carried in his briefcase the document signed before the weekend by Lady Macallister and witnessed by Mrs Barton, along with the cheques issued by the Zwingli Bank of Zürich, four of them, each in the sum of £7500 and each enough to purchase 75,000 of Lady Macallister's shares in Bormac.

'Twenty-four hours,' he thought as he drew down the blinds of his first-class sleeper compartment, blotting out the sights of the scurrying platform of King's Cross station. Twenty-four hours should see it through, and they would be home and dry, and three weeks later a new director on the board, a nominee responding to the strings pulled by him and Sir James Manson. Settling himself on the bunk, his briefcase under the pillow, Martin Thorpe enjoyed the feel of it and gazed up at the ceiling.

Later that Tuesday evening Shannon was settled into a hotel not far from the Madeleine in the heart of Paris's 8th arrondissement. He had had to forsake his regular Montmartre hideout, where he was known as Carlo Shannon, because he was now using the name of Keith Brown. But the Plaza-Surene was a good substitute. He had bathed and shaved and was about to go out for dinner. He had telephoned to book a table at his favourite eating place in the quarter, the Restaurant Mazagran, and Madame Michelle had promised him a filet mignon the way he liked it, with a tossed lettuce salad by the side and a Pot de Chirouble to wash it down.

The two person-to-person calls he had booked came through almost together. First on the line was a certain M Lavallon from Marseilles, whom he knew better as Jean-Baptiste Langarotti.

'Do you have that shipping agent yet?' asked Shannon when they had exchanged greetings.

'Yes,' said the Corsican. 'It's in Toulon. A very good one, very respectable and efficient. They have their own bonded warehouse on the port.'

'Spell it out,' said Shannon. He had pencil and paper ready.

'Agence Maritime Duphot,' spelled Langarotti, and dictated the address. 'Send the consignments to the agency, clearly marked as the property of Monsieur Langarotti.'

Shannon hung up, and the hotel operator came on the line immediately to say a Mr Dupree was calling from London.

'I just got your cable,' bawled Janni Dupree.

Shannon dictated the name and address of the Toulon agents to him, letter by letter, and Dupree took it down.

'Fine,' he said at length. 'I've got the first of the four crates ready and bonded over here. I'll tell the London agents to get the stuff on its way as soon as possible. Oh, by the way, I've found the boots.'

'Good,' said Shannon, 'well done.'

He placed one more call, this time to a bar in Ostende. There was a fifteen-minute delay before Marc's voice came through.

'I'm in Paris,' said Shannon. 'That man with the sample of merchandise I wanted to examine ...'

'Yes,' said Marc. 'I've been in touch. He's prepared to meet you and discuss prices and terms.'

'Good. I'll be in Belgium Thursday night or Friday morning. Tell him I propose Friday morning over breakfast in my room at the Holiday Inn Hotel near the airport.'

'I know it,' said Marc. 'All right, I'll put it to him and call you back.'

'Call me tomorrow between ten and eleven,' said Shannon and hung up.

Only then did he slip on his jacket and head for a long-awaited dinner and a long-desired full night's sleep.

While Shannon slept, Simon Endean was also winging his way southwards to Africa on the overnight flight. He had arrived in Paris by the first flight on Monday and taken a taxi immediately to the embassy of Dahomey in the Avenue Victor Hugo. Here he had filled out a lengthy pink form requesting a six-day tourist visa. It was ready for collection just before the closure of the consular office on the Tuesday afternoon, and he had caught the midnight flight to Cotonou via Niamey. Shannon would not have been particularly surprised to know that Endean was going to Africa, for he assumed the exiled Colonel Bobi had to play some part in Sir James Manson's scheme of things, and that the former commander of the Zangaran Army was cooling his heels somewhere along the mangrove coast. But if Endean had known Shannon had just returned from a secret visit to the general in the same area of Africa, it would have quite ruined his sleep aboard the UTA DC-8 that night, despite the pill he had taken to ensure an uninterrupted slumber.

Marc Vlaminck rang Shannon at his hotel at ten-fifteen the next day.

'He agrees to the meeting, and he'll bring the sample,' said the Belgian. 'Do you want me to come too?'

'Certainly,' said Shannon. 'When you get to the hotel ask at reception for the room of Mr Brown. One other thing. Have you bought that van I asked you to get?'

'Yes, why?'

'Has this gentleman seen it yet?'

There was a pause while Vlaminck thought.

'No.'

'Then don't bring it to Brussels. Hire a car and drive yourself. Pick him up on the way. Understood?'

'Yes,' said Vlaminck, still perplexed. 'Anything you say.'

Shannon, who was still in bed but feeling a sight better, rang for breakfast and had his habitual five minutes under the shower, four of them in steaming hot water and sixty seconds under a stream of ice-cold. The coffee and rolls were on the side table when he emerged. He placed two calls from the bedside phone, to Benny Lambert in Paris and Mr Stein of Lang & Stein in Luxembourg.

'Have you got that letter for me?' he asked Lambert.

The little crook's voice sounded strained.

'Yes. I got it yesterday. Luckily my contact was on duty on Monday and I saw him that night. He produced the letter of introduction yesterday evening. When do you want it?'

'This afternoon,' said Shannon.

'All right. Have you got my fee?'

'Don't worry, I've got it right here.'

'Then come to my place about three,' said Lambert.

Shannon thought for a moment.

'No, I'll meet you here,' he said, and gave Lambert the name of his hotel. He preferred to meet the little man in a public place. Rather to his surprise Lambert agreed to come round to the hotel, with what sounded like elation in his voice. There was something not quite right about this deal, but Shannon cold not put his finger on it. What he did not realize was that he had given the Paris crook the information he would later sell to Roux.

Mr Stein was engaged on the other phone when the call came, so rather than wait Shannon said he would ring back. This he did an hour later.

'About the meeting to launch my holding company, Tyrone Holdings,' he began.

'Ah yes, Mr Brown,' said Stein's voice down the line. 'Everything is in order. When would you suggest?'

'Tomorrow afternoon,' replied Shannon. It was agreed the meeting would be in Stein's office at three. Shannon got the hotel to book him a reserved place on the express from Paris to Luxembourg just after nine the next morning.

'I must say, I find it all very strange, very strange indeed.'

Mr Duncan Dalgleish Senior in appearance and manner matched his office, and his office looked as if it had been the scene for the reading of the will of Sir Walter Scott.

He examined the four share transfer deals, signed by Lady Macallister and witnessed by Mrs Barton, carefully and at length. He had muttered 'Aye' in sorrowful tones several times, and the glances he shot at the younger man from London were disapproving. He was evidently quite unused to handling certified cheques from a bank in Zürich, and he had held them between forefinger and thumb as he read them. He was examining the four deeds again as he spoke.

'Ye'll understand, Lady Macallister has been approached before, concerning the sale of these shares. In the past she has always seen fit to consult the firm of Dalgleish, and I have always seen fit to advise her against selling the stock,' he went on.

Thorpe thought privately that no doubt other of Mr Duncan Dalgleish's clients were holding on to piles of valueless stock on the basis of his advice, but he kept his face polite.

'Mr Dalgleish, you must agree the gentlemen whom I represent have paid Lady Macallister close to twice the face value of the stock. She for her part has freely signed the deeds and empowered me to collect the shares on presentation of cheque or cheques totalling £30,000. Which you now hold in your hand.'

The old man sighed again.

'It's just so strange that she should not have consulted me first,' he said sadly. 'I usually advise her on all her financial matters. For this I hold her general power of attorney.'

'But her own signature is still perfectly valid,' insisted Thorpe.

'Yes, yes, my power of attorney in no way invalidates her own power to sign on her behalf.'

'Then I would be grateful if you would let me have the share certificates so that I can return to London,' said Thorpe.

The old man rose slowly.

'Would you excuse me, Mr Thorpe,' he said with dignity, and withdrew into an inner sanctum. Thorpe knew he was going to telephone London, and prayed Lady Macallister's hearing aid would make it necessary for Mrs Barton to intercept for the pair of them on the telephone. It was half an hour before the old attorney came back. He held a large wad of old and discoloured share certificates in his hand.

'Lady Macallister has confirmed what you say, Mr Thorpe. Not, of course, that I doubted your word, ye understand. I felt obliged to speak with my client before completing such a large transaction.'

'Of course,' said Thorpe, rose and held out his hand. Dalgleish parted with the shares as if they had been his own.

An hour later Thorpe was in his train, rolling through the spring-lit countryside of Angus County on his way back to London.

Six thousand miles away from the heather-clad hills of Scotland Simon Endean was seated with the hulking form of Colonel Bobi in a small rented villa in the residential district of Cotonou. He had arrived on the morning plane and cheked into the Hotel du Port, whose Israeli manager had helped him trace the house where the exiled Zangaran army officer lived in the straitened circumstances of exile.

Bobi was a lumbering giant of a man with a brooding brutishness and massive hands. The combination pleased Endean. It was of no consequence to him with what disastrous effects Bobi might rule Zangaro in succession to the equally disastrous Jean Kimba. What he had come to find was a man who would sign away the mineral rights of the Crystal Mountain range to Bormac Trading Company for a pittance and a hefty bribe to his personal account. He had found what he sought.

In exchange for a salary of £500 a month the colonel would be delighted to accept the post of West Africa consultant to Bormac. He had pretended to study the contract Endean had brought, but the Englishman noted with pleasure that when he turned to the second page, which Endean had stapled upside down between the first and third pages, Bobi's expression did not flicker. He was illiterate, or the next best thing to it.

Endean explained the terms of the contract slowly in the mishmash of language they had been using, a mixture of basic French and Coast-Pidgin English. Bobi nodded soberly, his small eyes, much flecked with bloodshot vessels around the whites, studying the contract intently. Endean stressed that Bobi was to remain in his villa or near it for the next two to three months, and that Endean would return to see him again in that time.

The Englishman elicited that Bobi had still got a valid Zangaran diplomatic passport, a legacy of a visit he had once made outside Zangaro at the side of the Defence Minister, Kimba's cousin.

Shortly before sundown he scrawled what could pass for a signature on the bottom of the document. Not that a signature really mattered. Only later would Bobi be told that Bormac was putting him back into power in exchange for mining rights. Endean surmised that if the price was right, Bobi would not quibble.

The following morning at dawn Endean was on another plane heading back to Paris and London.

The meeting with Benny Lambert took place as agreed in the hotel. It was short and to the point. Lambert handed over an envelope, which Shannon flicked open. From it he took two pieces of paper, both identical and both bearing the printed crest and letterhead of the stationery of the ambassador in Paris of the republic of Togo.

One of the sheets was blank, except for a signature on the bottom and an embassy seal. The other sheet was a letter, in which the author stated that he had been authorized by his government to engage the services of ... to apply to the government of... for the purchase of the military weapons listed on the attached sheet. The letter concluded with the usual assurance that the weapons were intended solely for use by the armed forces of the republic of Togo, and would not be given or sold to any third party. This too was signed and decorated with the seal of the republic.

Shannon nodded. He was confident Alan Baker would be able to insert his own name as the authorized agent and the Federal Republic of Yugoslavia as the vendor government in such a way as to leave no trace of the insertion. He handed to Lambert the £500 he owed him and left the café.

Like most weak men, Lambert was indecisive. He had for three days been on the verge of ringing Charles Roux and telling him that Shannon was in town and seeking an end user certificate. He knew the French mercenary would be more than interested in the news, but he did not know why. He assumed it was because Roux regarded Paris and its resident mercenaries as his private preserve. He would not take kindly to a foreigner coming there to set up an operation in either arms or men without cutting Roux in on the deal as equal partner, or, more desirably, as the 'patron', the boss of the project. It would never occur to Roux that no one would want to finance him to set up an operation because he had blown far too many already, taken too many bribes to kill a project and cheated too many men of their salary.

But Lambert was afraid of Roux and felt he ought to tell him. He had been on the verge of doing so that afternoon, and would have done if Shannon had not had the balance of £500 with him. But to have warned Roux in those circumstances would have cost the little crook that £500 and he was sure Roux would not have made up such a large sum to him, simply for a tip-off. What Lambert did not know was that Roux had placed a killing contract on the Irishman. So in his state of ignorance he worked out another idea.

He was not very bright, was Benny Lambert, but he felt he had hit on the perfect solution. He could collect his full thousand pounds from Shannon, and tell Roux the Irishman had approached him with a request for an end user certificate, which he had promptly refused. There was just one snag. He had heard enough of Shannon to be afraid of him also, and he feared that if Roux was in contact with the Irishman too soon after Lambert's own meeting at the hotel, Shannon would guess from whom the tip-off came. He decided to wait until the following morning.

When he finally gave Roux the tip-off, it was too late. Roux telephoned the hotel at once under another name, and asked if a Mr Shannon was staying there. The chief desk clerk replied quite truthfully that there was no one of that name at the hotel.

Cross-examined, a thoroughly frightened Lambert claimed he had not actually visited the hotel, but had simply received a call from Shannon who had given that hotel as the place where he was staying.

Shortly after nine, Roux's man Henri Alain was at the reception desk of the Plaza-Surene, and established that the only Englishman or Irishman who had stayed in the hotel the previous night exactly corresponded in description to Cat Shannon; that his name and passport had been that of Keith Brown, and that he had booked through the reception desk a ticket on the nine a.m. express train to Luxembourg. Henri Alain learned one more thing; of a meeting that M Brown had had in the residents' lounge the previous afternoon, and a description of the Frenchman with whom he had been seen speaking. All this he reported back to Roux at midday.

In the French mercenary leader's flat Roux, Henri Alain and Raymond Thomard held a conference of war. Roux made the final decision.

'Henri, we've missed him this time, but the chances are that he still knows nothing about it. So he may well return to that hotel next time he has to overnight in Paris. I want you to get friendly, real friendly, with someone on the staff there. The next time that man checks in there, I want to know, but at once. Understand?'

Alain nodded.

'Sure, *patron*. I'll have it staked out from the inside, and if he even rings to make a booking, we'll know.'

Roux turned to Thomard.

'When he comes again, Raymond, you take the bastard. In the meantime, there's one other little job. That shit Lambert lied his head off. He could have tipped me off last night and we'd have been finished with this affair. So he probably took money off Shannon, then tried to take some more off me for out-of-date information. Just make sure Benny Lambert doesn't do any walking for the next six months.'

The floating of the company to be known as Tyrone Holdings was shorter than Shannon could have thought possible. It was so quick it was over almost before it had begun. He was invited into Mr Stein's private office, where Mr Lang and a junior partner were already seated. Along one wall were three secretaries, as it turned out the secretaries of the three accountants present. With the required seven stockbrokers on hand, Mr Stein set up the company within five minutes. Shannon handed over the balance of £500 and the thousand shares were issued. Each person present received one and signed for it, then passed them to Mr Stein who agreed to keep them in the company safe. Shannon received 994 shares in a block constituted by one sheet of paper and signed for them. His own shares he pocketed. The articles and memorandum of association were signed by the chairman and company secretary, and copies of each would later be filed with the Registrar of Companies for the Archduchy of Luxembourg. The three secretaries were then sent back to their duties, the board of three directors met and approved the aims of the company, the minutes were noted on one sheet of paper, read out by the secretary and signed by the chairman. That was it. Tyrone Holdings SA existed in law.

The other two directors shook hands with Shannon, calling him Mister Brown as they did so, and left. Mr Stein escorted him to the door.

'When you and your associates wish to buy a company in the chosen field of operations, to be owned by Tyrone Holdings,' he told Shannon, 'you will then need to come here, present us with a cheque for the appropriate amount, and buy the new issue at £1 per share. The formalities you can leave to us.'

Shannon understood. Any inquiries would stop at Mr Stein as company chairman. Two hours later he caught the evening plane for Brussels and checked into the Holiday Inn just before eight.

The man who accompanied Tiny Marc Vlaminck when they knocked at Shannon's room the following morning just after ten was introduced as M Boucher. The pair of them, standing on the threshold when he opened the door, looked like a comic turn. Marc was bulky, towering over his companion, and he was beefy in every place. The other man was fat, extremely fat, the sort of fatness associated with vaudeville funny men and fairground sideshows. He seemed almost circular, balanced like one of those children's plastic toys that cannot be overturned because they are spherical. Only on closer examination was it apparent there were two tiny feet in brilliantly polished shoes beneath the mass, and that the bulk constituting the lower half was divided into two legs. In repose it looked like one single unit.

M Boucher's head appeared to be the only object to mar the contour of the otherwise uniformly globular mass. It was small at the top and flowed downwards to engulf his collar and hide it from view, the flesh of the jowls resting thankfully on the shoulders. After several seconds Shannon conceded that he also had arms, one each side, and that one held a sleek document case some five inches thick.

'Please come in,' said Shannon and stepped back.

Boucher entered first, turning slightly sideways to slip through the door, like a large ball of grey worsted suiting on castors. Marc followed, giving Shannon a wink as he caught his eye. Introductions followed and they all shook hands. Shannon gestured to an armchair, but Boucher chose the edge of the bed. He was wise, and experienced. He might never have got out of the armchair.

Shannon poured them all coffee, and went straight into business, Tiny Marc sat and stayed silent.

'M Boucher, my associate and friend may have told you that my name is Brown, I am English by nationality, and I am here representing a group of friends who would be interested in acquiring a quantity of submachine carbines or machine pistols. M Vlaminck kindly mentioned to me that he was in a position to introduce me to someone who might have a quantity of machine pistols for sale. I understand from him that these are Schmeisser 9 mm machine pistols, of wartime manufacture, but never used. I also understand and accept that there can be no question of obtaining an export licence for them, but this is accepted by my people and they are prepared to accept all responsibility in this regard. Is that a fair assessment?'

Boucher nodded slowly. He could not nod fast.

'I am in a position to make available a quantity of these pieces,' he said carefully. 'You are right about the impossibility of an export licence. For that reason the identity of my own people has to be protected. Any business arrangement we might come to would have to be on a cash basis, and with security arrangements for my own people.'

'He's lying,' thought Shannon. 'There are no people behind Boucher. He is the owner of this stuff, and works alone.'

In fact M Boucher in his younger years and slimmer days had been a Belgian SS man, and had worked as a cook in the SS barracks at Namur. His extreme fondness, not to mention obsession, with food had taken him into cooking, and before the war he had lost several jobs because he tasted more than he served through the hatch. In the starving conditions of wartime Belgium he had opted for the cookhouse of the Belgian SS unit, one of the several local SS groups the Nazis recruited in the occupied countries. In the SS, surmised the young Boucher, one could eat. In 1944, when the Germans pulled back from Namur towards the frontier, a lorry-load of unused Schmeissers from the armoury had been on their way east when the lorry broke down. There was no time to repair the lorry, so the cargo was shifted into a nearby bunker and the entrance dynamited. Boucher watched it happen. Years later he had returned, shovelled away the rubble and removed the thousand weapons.

Since then they had reposed beneath a trap-door built into the floor of the garage of his country cottage, a building left him by his parents who died in the mid-fifties. He had sold job lots of Schmeissers at various times, and had 'unloaded' half of his reserve.

'If these guns are in good working order, I would be interested in buying a hundred of them,' said Shannon. 'Of course, payment would be by cash, in any currency. All reasonable conditions imposed by you would be adhered to in the handing over of the cargo. We also would expect complete discretion.'

'As for their condition, monsieur, they are all brand new. Still in their maker's grease and each still wrapped in its sachet of grease-proof paper with seals unbroken. As they came from the factory thirty years ago and, despite their age, still possibly the finest machine pistol ever made.'

Shannon needed no lectures about the Schmeisser 9 mm. Personally he would have said the Israeli Uzi was better, but it was heavy. The Schmeisser was way ahead better than the Sten, and certainly as good as the much more modern British Sterling. He thought nothing of the American grease-gun, nor the Soviet and Chinese burp-guns. However, Uzis and Sterlings are almost unobtainable and never in mint condition.

'May I see?' he asked.

Wheezing heavily, Boucher pulled the black case he carried onto his knees and flicked open the catches after twirling the wheels of the combination lock. He lifted the lid and held the case forward without attempting to get up.

Shannon rose, crossed the room and took the case from him. He laid it on the bedside table and lifted out the Schmeisser.

It was a beautiful piece of weaponry. Shannon slid his hands over the smooth blue-black metal, gripped the pistol-grip and felt the lightness of it. He pulled back and locked the folding stock and operated the breech mechanism several times and squinted down the barrel from the foresight end. The inside was untouched, unmarked.

'That is the sample model,' wheezed Boucher. 'Of course it has had the maker's grease removed and carries only a light film of oil. But the others are identical. Unused.'

Shannon put it down.

'It takes standard 9 mm ammunition, which is easy to come by,' said Boucher helpfully.

'Thank you, I know,' said Shannon. 'What about magazines? They can't be picked up just anywhere, you know.'

'I can supply five with each weapon,' said Boucher.

'Five?' Shannon queried in feigned amazement. 'I need more than five. Ten at least.'

The bargaining had begun, Shannon complaining about the arms dealer's inability to provide enough magazines, the Belgian protesting that was the limit he could provide for each weapon without beggaring himself. Shannon proposed 75 dollars for each Schmeisser on a deal for 100 guns; Boucher claiming he could only allow that price for a deal of not less than 250 weapons, and that for 100 he would have to demand 125 dollars each. Two hours later they settled for a hundred Schmeissers at a 100 dollars each. They fixed time and place for the following Wednesday evening after dark, and agreed the method for the handover. When it was finished Shannon offered Boucher a lift back in Vlaminck's car to where he had come from, but the fat man chose to call a taxi and be taken to Brussels city centre to make his own way home. He was not prepared to assume that the Irishman, who he was certain was from the IRA, would not take him somewhere quiet and work on him until he had learned the location of the secret hoard. Boucher was quite right. Trust is a silly and superfluous weakness in the black market arms business.

Vlaminck escorted the fat man with his lethal briefcase down to the lobby and saw him away in his taxi. When he returned Shannon was packing.

'Do you see what I mean about the van you bought?' he asked Tiny.

'No,' said the other.

'We will have to use that van for the pick-up on Wednesday,' Shannon pointed out. 'I saw no reason why Boucher should see the real number plates. Have a spare set ready for Wednesday night, will you? It's only for an hour, but if Boucher does want to tip off anyone, they'll have the wrong van.'

'OK, Cat, I'll be ready. I got the lock-up garage two days ago. And the other stuff is on order. Is there anywhere I can take you? I have the hire car for the rest of the day.'

Shannon had Vlaminck drive him westwards to Brugge and wait in a café while Shannon went to the bank. M Goossens was at lunch, so the pair ate their own lunch in the small restaurant on the main square and Shannon returned to the bank at two-thirty.

There was still £7000 in the Keith Brown account, but a debit of £2000 for the four mercenaries' salaries was due in nine days. He drew a banker's cheque in favour of Johann Schlinker and placed it in an envelope containing a letter from him to Schlinker that he had written in his hotel room late the previous night. It informed Schlinker that the enclosed cheque for 4800 dollars was in full payment for the assorted marine and life-saving articles he had ordered a week earlier, and gave the German the name and address of the Toulon shipping agent to whom the entire consignment should be sent in bond for export, for collection by M Jean-Baptiste Langarotti. Lastly he informed Schlinker he would be telephoning him the coming week to inquire if the end user certificate for the ordered 9 mm ammunition was in order.

The other letter was to Alan Baker, addressed to his home in Hamburg. The cheque it contained was in Baker's favour for 7200 dollars, and Shannon's letter stated that the sum was in full settlement of the required fifty per cent advance for the purchase of the goods they had discussed over dinner at the Atlantic a week earlier. He included the end user certificate from the government of Togo and the spare sheet from the same source. Lastly he instructed Baker to get straight on with the purchase, and promised he would be in touch by phone regularly to check on progress.

Both letters were mailed from Brugge post office, express rate and registered.

When they were in the posting box, Shannon had Vlaminck drive him onwards to Ostende, had a couple of beers with the Belgian in a local bar near the seaport, and bought himself a single fare on the evening ferry to Dover.

The boat train deposited him at Victoria station at midnight and he was in bed and asleep by one in the morning of that Saturday. The last thing he did before sleeping was to send a telegram to Endean's *poste restante* address to say he was back and he felt they ought to meet.

The Saturday morning post brought a letter mailed at express rate from Malaga in the south of Spain. It was addressed to Keith Brown but began 'Dear Cat'. It came from Kurt Semmler and stated briefly that he had found a boat, a converted motor fishing vessel built twenty years earlier in a British shipyard, owned by a British citizen and registered in London. It flew a British flag, was ninety feet overall and eighty tons deadweight, with a large central hold amidships and a smaller one aft. It was classed as a private yacht, but could be re-registered as a coaster.

Semmler went on to say the vessel was for sale at a price of £20,000 and that two of the crew would be worth engaging under the new management. He was certain he could find good replacements for the other two crew members.

He finished by saying he was staying at the Malaga Palacio Hotel and asked Shannon to contact him there with his own date of arrival to inspect the boat.

The boat was called the M.Y. *Albatross*.

Shannon checked with BEA and booked himself a flight to Malaga on Monday morning, an open-dated return for which he would pay in cash at the airport. Then he cabled Semmler at his hotel to advise him of his arrival time and flight number.

Endean phoned Shannon that afternoon after checking his mail and receiving the telegram. They met around dinner time that evening at the flat, and Shannon presented Endean with his third lengthy progress report and statement of accounts and expenditure.

'You'll have to make further transfers of money if we are to move ahead in the forthcoming weeks,' Shannon told him. 'We are entering the areas of major expenditure now – the arms and the ship.'

'How much do you need at once?' Endean asked.

Shannon said: 'Two thousand for salaries, four thousand for boats and engines, four thousand for submachine guns and over ten thousand for 9 mm ammunition. That's over twenty thousand. Better make it thirty thousand, or I'll be back next week.'

Endean shook his head.

'I'll make it twenty thousand,' he said. 'You can always contact me if you need more. By the way, I would like to see some of this stuff. That will be £50,000 you'll have gone through inside a month.'

'You can't,' said Shannon. 'The ammunition is not yet bought, nor the boats, engines and so forth. Nor are the mortars and bazookas, nor the submachine pistols. All these deals have to be put through cash on the barrelhead or in advance. I explained that in my first report to your associates.'

Endean eyed him coldly.

'There had better be some purchases being made with all this money,' he grated.

Shannon stared him out.

'Don't threaten me, Harris. A lot of people have tried it; it costs a fortune in flowers. By the way, what about the boat?'

Endean rose.

'Let me know which boat and from whom it is being bought. I'll make the credit transfer direct from my Swiss account.'

'Please yourself,' said Shannon.

He dined alone and well that evening, and had an early night. Sunday would be a free day and he had found Julie Manson was already at home with her parents in Gloucestershire. As he sat over his brandy and coffee he was lost in thought, planning the weeks ahead and trying to visualize the attack on the palace of Zangaro.

It was in the middle of Sunday morning that Julie Manson decided to ring her new lover's flat in London and see if he was there. Outside, the spring rain fell in a steady curtain on the Gloucestershire countryside. She had hoped to be able to saddle up the handsome new gelding her father had given her a month earlier and gallop through the parkland surrounding the family mansion. She had hoped it would be a tonic to the feeling that flooded through her when she thought of the man she had fallen for. But the rain had washed out the idea of riding. Instead she was confined to wandering round the old house, listening to her mother's chit-chat about charity bazaars and orphan relief committees, or staring at the rain falling on the garden.

Her father had been working in his study, but she had seen him go out to the stables to talk to the chauffeur a few minutes earlier. As her mother was within earshot of the telephone in the hallway, she decided to use the extension in the study.

She had lifted the telephone beside the desk in the empty room when her eye caught the sprawl of papers lying across the blotter. On top of them was a single folder. She noted the title and idly lifted the cover to glance at the first page. A name on it caused her to freeze, the telephone still buzzing furiously in her ear. The name was Shannon.

Like most young girls she had her fantasies, seeing herself as she lay in the darkness of the dormitory at boarding school in the role of heroine of a hundred hazardous exploits, usually saving the man she loved from a terrible fate, to be rewarded by his undying devotion. Unlike most girls she had never completely grown up. From Shannon's persistent questioning about her father, she had already half managed to translate herself into the role of a girl agent on her lover's behalf. The trouble was, most of what she knew about her father was either personal, in his role of indulgent daddy, or very boring. Of his business affairs she knew nothing. And then here, on a rainy Sunday morning, lay her chance.

She flicked her eyes down the first page of the folder, and understood nothing. There were figures, costings, a second reference to the name Shannon, a mention of several banks by name and two references to a man called Clarence. She got no further. The turning of the door handle interrupted her.

With a start she dropped the cover of the folder, stood back a yard and began to babble into the unhearing telephone. Her father stood in the doorway.

'All right, Christine, that will be marvellous, darling. I'll see you on Monday then. 'Bye now,' she chattered into the telephone and hung up.

Her father's set expression had softened as he saw the person in the room was his daughter, and he walked across the carpet to sit behind his desk.

'Now, what are you up to?' he said with mock gruffness.

For answer she twined her soft arms round his neck from behind and kissed him on the cheek.

'Just phoning a friend in London, Daddy,' she said in her small, little-girl voice. 'Mummy was fussing about in the hall, so I came in here.'

'Humph. Well, you've got a phone in your own room. So please use that for private calls.'

'All right, Daddikins.' She cast her glance over the papers lying under the folder on the desk, but the print was too small to read, and was mostly columns of figures. She could make out the headings only. They concerned mining prices. Then her father turned to look up.

'Why don't you stop all this boring old work and come and help me saddle up Tamerlane?' she asked him. 'The rain will stop soon, and I can go riding.'

He smiled up at the girl who was the apple of his eye.

'Because this boring old work happens to be what keeps us all clothed and fed,' he said. 'But I will anyway. Give me a few more minutes and I'll join you in the stable.'

Outside the door, Julie Manson stopped and breathed deeply. Mata Hari, she was sure, could not have done better.

Chapter Fourteen

The Spanish authorities are far more tolerant to tourists than is generally thought. Bearing in mind the millions of Scandinavians, Germans, French and British who pour into Spain each spring and summer, and given that the law of averages must provide that a certain percentage of them are up to no good, the authorities have quite a lot to put up with. Irrelevant breaches of regulations such as importing two cartons of cigarettes rather than the permitted one carton, which would be pounced on at London airport, are shrugged off in Spain.

The attitude of the Spanish authorites has always tended to be that a tourist really has to work at it to get into trouble in Spain, but once he has made the effort the Spaniards will oblige and make it extremely unpleasant for him. The four items they object to finding in passenger luggage are arms and/or explosives, drugs, pornography and Communist propaganda. Other countries may object to two bottles of duty-free brandy but permit *Penthouse* magazine. Not Spain. Other countries have different priorities, but as any Spaniard will cheerfully admit, Spain is different.

The customs officer at Malaga airport that brilliant Monday afternoon cast a casual eye over the bundle of £1000 in used £20 notes he found in Shannon's travel bag and shrugged. If he was aware that to get it to Malaga Shannon must have carried it with him through London airport customs, which is forbidden, he gave no sign. In any case, that was London's problem. He found no copies of *Sexy Girls* or *Soviet News*, and waved the traveller on.

Kurt Semmler looked fit and tanned from his three weeks orbiting the Mediterranean looking for ships for sale. He was still rake-thin and chain-smoked nervously, a habit that belied his cold nerve when in action. But the suntan gave him an air of health and set off with startling clarity his close-cropped pale hair and icy blue eyes.

As they drove from the airport into Malaga town in the taxi Semmler had had waiting, he told Shannon he had been in Naples, Genoa, Valletta, Marseilles, Barcelona and Gibraltar, looking up old contacts in the world of small ships, checking the lists of perfectly respectable shipping brokers and agents for ships for sale, and looking some of them over as they lay at anchor. He had seen a score, but none of them suitable. He had heard of another dozen in ports he had not visited, and had rejected them because he knew from the names of their skippers they must have suspect backgrounds. From all his inquiries he had drawn up a list of seven, and the *Albatross* was the third. Of her qualities, all he would say was that she looked all right.

He had reserved Shannon a room in the Malaga Palacio in the name of Brown, and Shannon checked in there first. It was just after four when they strolled through the wide gates on the south face of the Acera de la Marina square and into the docks.

The *Albatross* was drawn up alongside a quay at the far end of the port. She was as Semmler had described her, and her white paint glistened in the sun and heat. They went aboard and Semmler introduced Shannon to the owner and captain, George Allen, who showed him over the vessel. Before very long Shannon had come to the conclusion it was too small for his purposes. There was a master cabin to sleep two, a pair of single cabins, and a saloon where mattresses and sleeping bags could be laid on the floor.

The after hold could, at a pinch, be converted into a sleeping area for another six men, but with the crew of four and Shannon's five, they would be cramped. He cursed himself for not warning Semmler there were six more men expected, who would also have to be fitted in.

Shannon checked the ship's papers, which appeared to be in order. She was registered in Britain and her Board of Trade papers confirmed it.

Shannon spent an hour with Captain Allen, discussing methods of payment, examining invoices and receipts showing the amount of work that had been done on the *Albatross* over recent months, and checking the ship's log.

He left with Semmler just before six and strolled back to the hotel, deep in thought.

'What's the matter?' asked Semmler. 'She's clean.'

'It's not that,' said Shannon. 'She's too small. She's registered as a private yacht. She doesn't belong to a shipping company. The thing that bugs me is that she might not be accepted by the exporting authorities as a fit vessel to take on board a load of arms.'

It was too late back at the hotel to make the calls he wanted to make, so they waited till the following morning. Shortly after nine Shannon called Lloyd's of London and asked for a check of the Yacht List. The *Albatross* was there all right, listed as an auxiliary ketch of 74 tons NRT with her home port given as Milford and port of residence as Hooe, both of them in Britain.

'Then what the hell's she doing here?' he wondered, and then recalled the method of payment that had been demanded. His second call, to Hamburg, clinched it.

'*Nein*, not a private yacht, please,' said Johann Schlinker down the telephone. 'There would be too great a possibility she would not be accepted to carry freight on a commercial basis.'

'OK. When do you need to know the name of the ship?' asked Shannon.

'As soon as possible. By the way, I have received your credit transfer for the articles you ordered in my office. These will now be crated and sent in bond to the address in France you supplied. Secondly, I have the paperwork necessary for the other consignment, and as soon as I receive the balance of the money owing, I will go ahead and place the order.'

'When is the latest you need to know the name of the carrying vessel?' Shannon bawled into the phone.

There was a pause while Schlinker thought.

'If I receive your cheque within five days, I can make immediate application for permission to buy. The ship's name is needed for the export licence. In about fifteen days after that.'

'You will have it,' said Shannon and replaced the receiver. He turned to Semmler and explained what had happened.

'Sorry, Kurt. It has to be a registered company in the maritime freighting business, and it has to be a licensed freighter, not a private yacht. You'll have to keep on searching. But I want the name within twelve days and no later. I have to provide the man in Hamburg with the ship's name in twenty days or less.'

The two men parted that evening at the airport, Shannon to return to London and Semmler to fly to Madrid and thence to Rome and Genoa, his next port of call.

It was late when Shannon reached his flat again. Before turning in he called BEA and booked a flight on the noon plane to Brussels. Then he called Marc Vlaminck and asked him to be present at the airport to pick him up on arrival, to take him first to Brugge for a visit to the bank and then to the rendezvous with Boucher for the handover of the equipment.

It was the end of Day Twenty-Two.

Mr Harold Roberts was a useful man. Born sixty-two years earlier of a British father and a Swiss mother, he had been brought up in Switzerland after the premature death of his father, and retained dual nationality. Entering banking at an early age, he had spent twenty years in the Zürich head office of one of Switzerland's largest banks, before being sent to their London branch as an assistant manager.

That had been just after the war, and over the second twenty-year period of his career he had risen to become the manager of the investment accounts section and later overall manager of the London branch, retiring at the age of sixty. By then he had decided to take his retirement and his pension in Swiss francs in Britain.

Since retirement he had been available for several delicate tasks on behalf not only of his former employers, but also of other Swiss banks. He was engaged on such a task that Wednesday afternoon.

It had taken a formal letter from the Zwingli Bank to the chairman and the secretary of Bormac to achieve the introduction to them of Mr Roberts, and he had been able to present letters corroborating his engagement as agent of the Zwingli Bank in London.

Two further meetings had taken place between Mr Roberts and the secretary of the company, the second one attended by the chairman, Major Luton, younger brother of the deceased under-manager to Sir Ian Macallister in the Far East.

The extraordinary Board meeting had been agreed on, and was called in the City offices of the secretary of Bormac. Apart from the solicitor and Major Luton, one other director had agreed to come to London for the meeting, and was present. Although two directors made up a working board, three gave an outright majority. They considered the resolution put by the company secretary and the documents he placed before them. The four unseen shareholders whose interests were being looked after by the Zwingli Bank undoubtedly did now own between them thirty per cent of the stock of the company. They certainly had empowered the Zwingli Bank to act on their behalf, and the bank had incontrovertibly appointed Mr Roberts to represent it.

The argument that clinched the discussion was the simple one that if a consortium of businessmen had agreed together to buy up such a large amount of Bormac stock, they could be believed when their bank said on their behalf that their intention was to inject fresh capital into the company and rejuvenate it. Such a course of action could not be bad for the share price, and all three directors were shareholders. The resolution was proposed, seconded and passed. Mr Roberts was taken onto the Board as a nominee director representing the interests of the Zwingli Bank. No one bothered to change the company rule stipulating that two directors constituted a quorum with power to pass resolutions, although there were now six and no longer five directors.

Mr Keith Brown was becoming a fairly regular visitor to Brugge and a valued customer at the Kredietbank. He was received with the usual friendliness by M Goossens and the latter confirmed that a credit of £20,000 had arrived that morning from Switzerland. Shannon drew 10,000 dollars in cash and a certified bank cheque for 26,000 dollars in favour of Johann Schlinker of Hamburg.

From the nearby post office he mailed the cheque to Schlinker by registered post, accompanied by a letter from himself asking the arms dealer to go ahead with the Spanish purchase.

He and Marc Vlaminck had nearly four hours to kill before the rendezvous with Boucher and they spent two of them taking a leisurely pot of tea in a café in Brugge before setting off just before dusk.

There is a lonely stretch of road between Brugge and Ghent, which lies forty-four kilometres to the east. Because the road twists and winds through flat farmland, most motorists prefer to take the new motorway E5 which also links the two Flemish towns as it runs from Ostende to Brussels. Half-way along the old road the two mercenaries found the abandoned farm that Boucher had described, or rather they found the faded notice-board pointing down the track to the farm, which was hidden from view by a clump of trees.

Shannon drove on past the spot and parked, while Marc got out and went to check the farm over. He came back twenty minutes later to confirm the farm was indeed deserted, and there were no signs anyone had been there for quite a time. Nor were there any preparations in progress to provide an unpleasant reception committee for the two buyers.

'Anyone in the house or outbuildings?' asked Shannon.

'The house is locked front and back. No signs of interference. I checked out the barns and stables. No one there.'

Shannon glanced at his watch. It was dark already and there was still an hour to go.

'Get back there and keep a watch from cover,' he ordered. 'I'll watch the front entrance from here.'

When Marc had gone Shannon checked the van once again. It was old and rattled, but it was serviceable and the engine had been looked over by a good mechanic. Shannon took the two false number plates from the facia and whipped them onto the real number plates with sticky insulating tape. They could be ripped off easily enough once the van was well away from the farm, but he saw no reason why Boucher should be able to note the real number plates. On each side of the van was a large publicity sticker that gave the vehicle a distinctive air, but which could also come off in a hurry. In the back were the six large sacks of potatoes he had ordered Vlaminck to bring with him, and the broad wooden board, sawn to make an internal tailgate when slotted into place. Satisfied, he resumed his vigil by the roadside.

The van he was expecting turned up at five to eight. As it slowed and swung down the track to the farm, Shannon could make out the form of the driver hunched over the wheel and beside him the blob surmounted by a pimple of a head that could only be M Boucher. The red tail-lights of the vehicle disappeared down the track and went out of sight behind the trees. Apparently Boucher was playing it straight.

Shannon gave him three minutes, then he too pulled his van off the hard road and onto the track. When he got to the farmyard Boucher's van was standing with side-lights on in the centre. He cut his engine and climbed down, leaving his own side-lights on, the nose of his van parked ten feet from the rear of Boucher's.

'Monsieur Boucher,' he called into the gloom. He stood in darkness himself, well to one side of the glow of his own lights.

'Monsieur Brown,' he heard Boucher wheeze, and the fat man waddled into view. He had evidently brought his 'helper' along with him, a big beefy-looking type, whom Shannon assessed as being good at lighting things but slow-moving. Marc, he knew, could move like a ballet dancer when he wished. He saw no problems if it came to trouble.

'You have the money?' asked Boucher as he came close. Shannon gestured to the driving seat of his van.

'In there. You have the Schmeissers?'

Boucher waved a pudgy hand at his own van.

'In the back.'

'I suggest we get both our consignments out onto the ground between the vans,' said Shannon. Boucher turned and said something to his helper in Flemish, which Shannon could not follow. The man moved to the back of his own van and opened it. Shannon tensed. If there were to be any surprises, they would come when the doors opened. There were none. The dull glim from his own van's lights showed ten flat, square crates and an open-topped carton.

'Your friend is not here?' asked Boucher. Shannon whistled. Tiny Marc joined them from behind a nearby barn. There was silence. Shannon cleared his throat.

'Let's get the handover done,' he said. He reached into the driving compartment and pulled out the fat brown envelope. 'Cash, as you asked for. Twenty-dollar bills. Bundles of fifty. Ten bundles.'

He stayed close to Boucher as the fat man flicked through each bundle, counting with surprising speed for such plump hands and stuffing the bundles into his side pockets. When he had reached the last he pulled all the bundles back out and selected a note at random from each. By the light of a pencil torch he scanned them closely, the samples, checking for forgeries. There were none. At last he nodded.

'All in order,' he said, and called something to his helper. The man moved aside from the van doors. Shannon nodded to Marc, who went to the van and heaved the first crate onto the grass. From his pocket he produced a tyre lever and prised up the lid. By the light of his own torch he checked the ten Schmeissers lying side by side in the crate. One of them he took out and checked for firing mechanism, pin and breech movement. He replaced the machine pistol and smacked the loose lid back down tight.

It took him twenty minutes to check all ten cases. While he did so the big helper brought by M Boucher stood nearby. Shannon stood at Boucher's elbow twelve feet away. Finally Mark looked into the open-topped crate. It contained 500 magazines for the Schmeissers. He tested one sample magazine to ensure it fitted, and that the magazines were not for a different model of pistol. Then he turned to Shannon and nodded.

'All in order,' he called.

'Would you ask your friend to help mine load them up?' asked Shannon of Boucher. The fat man passed the instruction to his assistant. Within another five minutes the ten flat crates and the carton of magazines were loaded in Marc's van. Before loading, the two beefy Flemings removed the potato sacks and Shannon heard them discussing something in Flemish. Then Boucher's helper laughed.

When the crates of arms were loaded, Marc placed the board of wood in position as a tailgate which came half-way up the back of the van. Taking a knife he slit the first sack, hefted it onto his shoulder and emptied the contents into the back of the van. The loose potatoes rolled about furiously, finding the cracks between the edges of the crates and the sides of the van and filling them up. With a laugh the other Belgian started to help him.

The quantity of potatoes they had brought more than covered every trace of the ten crates of guns and the carton of magazines. Anyone looking in the back would be confronted with a sea of loose potatoes. The sacks were thrown in the hedge.

When they were finished both men came round from the back of the van together.

'OK, let's go,' said Marc.

'If you don't mind, we'll leave first,' said Shannon to Boucher. 'After all, we now have the incriminating evidence.'

He waited till Marc had started the engine and turned the van round so that it was facing the drive back to the road before he left Boucher's side and leaped aboard. Half-way down the track there was a particularly deep pothole, over which the van had to move with great care and very slowly. At this point Shannon muttered something to Marc, borrowed his knife and jumped from the van to hide in the bushes by the side of the lane.

Two minutes later Boucher's van came along. It too slowed almost to a halt to negotiate the pothole. Shannon slipped from the bushes as the van went past, caught it up, stooped low and jammed the knife point into the rear offside tyre. He heard it hiss madly as it deflated, then he was back in the bushes. He rejoined Tiny Marc on the main road, where the Belgian had just ripped the stickers from the sides of their vehicle and the false number plates off front and back. Shannon had nothing against Boucher; he just wanted a clear half-hour's start.

By ten-thirty the pair were back in Ostende, the van loaded with spring potatoes was garaged in the lock-up Vlaminck had hired on Shannon's instructions, and the pair were in Marc's bar on Kleinstraat toasting each other in foaming steins of ale while Anna prepared a meal. It was the first time he had met the well-built woman who was his friend's mistress, and as is the tradition with mercenaries when meeting each other's womenfolk, he treated her with elaborate courtesy.

Vlaminck had booked him a room at a hotel in the town centre, but they drank until late, talking about old battles and skirmishes, recalling incidents and people, fights and narrow escapes, alternately laughing at the things that seemed hilarious in retrospect and nodding glumly at the memories that still rankled. The bar stayed open as long as Tiny Marc drank, and the lesser mortals sat around and listened.

It was almost dawn when they got to bed.

Tiny Marc called for him at his hotel in the middle of the morning and they had a late breakfast together. He explained to the Belgian that he wanted the Schmeissers packaged in such a way that they could be smuggled over the Belgian border into France for loading onto the ship in a southern French port.

'We could send them in crates of spring potatoes,' suggested Marc. Shannon shook his head.

'Potatoes are in sacks, not crates,' he said. 'The last thing we need is for a crate to be tipped over in transit or loading, so that the whole lot falls out. I've got a better idea.'

For half an hour he told Vlaminck what he wanted done with the submachine pistols and the Belgian nodded.

'All right,' he said when he understood exactly what was wanted. 'I can work mornings in the garage before the bar opens. When do we run them south?'

'About May 15th,' said Shannon. 'We'll use the champagne route. I'll bring Jean-Baptiste up here to help, and we'll change to a French-registered van at Paris. I want you to have everything packed and ready for shipment by May 15th.'

Marc accompanied him down to the port in a taxi, for the van would not be used again until it made its last run from Ostende to Paris with its cargo of illegal arms. There was no problem buying a single ticket on the car ferry to Dover, even though Shannon was on foot. He was back in London by early evening.

He spent what remained of the day writing a full report for Endean, omitting to mention from whom he had bought the guns or where they were stored. He attached to the report a statement of expenditure and a tally of what was left in the Brugge account. This he mailed to the *poste restante* address through which he communicated with Sir James Manson's organizer.

The first morning post of that Friday brought a large packet from Jean-Baptiste Langarotti. It contained a sheaf of brochures from three European firms who manufactured the rubberized inflatable semi-rigid boats of the kind he wanted. They were variously advertised as being capable of use as sea-rescue launches, power-boats, speed-craft for towing water-skiers, pleasure boats, launching vessels for sub-aqua diving, runabouts and fast tenders for yachts and suchlike. No mention was made of the fact that they had all been developed from an original design produced to give marine commandos a fast and manoeuvrable type of assault craft.

Shannon read each brochure with interest. Of the three firms, one was Italian, one British and one French. The Italian firm, with six stockists along the Côte D'Azur, seemed to be the best-suited for Shannon's purpose and to have the best delivery capability. Of their largest model, a five-and-a-half-metre launch, there were two available for immediate delivery. One was in Marseilles and the other in Cannes. The brochure from the French manufacturer showed a picture of their largest example, a five-metre craft, speeding through a blue sea, tail-down, nose-up.

Langarotti said in his letter there was one of these available at a shop for marine equipment in Nice. He added that all the British-made models needed to be ordered specially, and lastly that although there were several more of each type available in a brilliant orange colour, he was only concerning himself with those in black. He added that each could be powered by any outboard engine above fifty horse-power, and that there were seven different makes of engine available locally and immediately which would suit.

Shannon replied with a long letter instructing Langarotti to buy the two models made by the Italian firm that were available for immediate delivery, and the third of French manufacture. He stressed that on receipt of the letter the Corsican should ring the stockists at once and place a firm order, sending each shopkeeper a ten per cent deposit by registered mail. He should also buy three engines of the best make, but at separate shops.

He noted the prices of each item and that the total came to just over £4000. This meant he would overrun on his estimated budget of £5000 for ancillary equipment, but he was not worried by that. He would be under budget on the arms and, he hoped, the ship. He told Langarotti he was transferring to the Corsican's account the equivalent of £4500, and with the balance he should buy a serviceable second-hand 20-hundredweight van, making sure it was licensed and insured.

With this he should motor along the coast and buy his three crated inflatable assault craft and his three outboard engines, delivering them himself to his freight agent in Toulon to be bonded for export. The whole consignment had to be in the warehouse and ready for shipment by May 15th. On the morning of that day Langarotti was to rendezvous with Shannon in Paris at the hotel Shannon usually used. He was to bring the van with him.

The mercenary leader sent another letter that day. It was to the Kredietbank in Brugge requiring the transfer of £2500 in French francs to the account of M Jean-Baptiste Langarotti at the head office of the Société Générale bank in Marseilles. Both letters were posted express rate the same afternoon.

When he got back to his flat Cat Shannon lay on his bed and stared at the ceiling. He felt tired and flat; the strain of the past thirty days were taking its toll. On the credit side things seemed to be going according to plan. Alan Baker should be setting up the purchase of the mortars and bazookas from Yugoslavia for pick-up during the early days of June; Schlinker should be in Madrid buying enough nine-millimetre ammunition to keep the Schmeissers firing for a year. The only reason he had ordered such an excessive amount of rounds was to make the purchase plausible to the Spanish authorities. Clearance for their export should be obtained for mid to late June, provided he could let the German have the name of the carrier by the middle of May, and provided the ship and its company were acceptable to the officials in Madrid.

Vlaminck should already have the machine pistols stowed for transporting across Belgium and France to Marseilles, and loaded by June 1st. The assault craft and engines should be loaded at the same time in Toulon, along with the other ancillary gear he had ordered from Schlinker.

Apart from smuggling the Schmeissers, everything was legal and above board. That did not mean things could not still go wrong. Perhaps one of the two governments would make problems by taking over-long or refusing to sell on the basis of the provided documentation.

Then there were the uniforms, which Dupree was presumably still buying in London. They too should be in a warehouse in Toulon by the end of May at the latest.

But the big problem still to be solved was the ship. Semmler had to find the right ship, and he had been searching in vain for almost a month.

Shannon rolled off his bed and telephoned a telegram to Dupree's bedsitter in Bayswater ordering him to check in. As he put the phone down it rang again.

'Hi, it's me.'

'Hallo, Julie,' he said.

'Where have you been, Cat?'

'Away. Abroad.'

'Are you going to be in town this weekend?' she asked.

'Yes. Should be.' In fact there was nothing more he could do and nowhere he could go until Semmler contacted him with news of a ship for sale. He did not even know where the German was by this time.

'Good,' said the girl on the phone. 'Let's spend the weekend doing things.'

It must have been the tiredness. He was getting slow on the uptake.

'What things?' he asked.

She began to tell him in precise and clinical detail until he interrupted her and told her to come straight round and prove it.

Although she had been bubbling with her news a week earlier, in the thrill of seeing her lover again Julie had forgotten the news she had for him. It was not until nearly midnight that she remembered. She bent her head low over the face of the half-asleep mercenary and said, 'Oh, by the way, I saw your name the other day.'

Shannon grunted.

'On a piece of paper,' she insisted. Still he showed no interest, his face buried in the pillow between crossed forearms.

'Shall I tell you where?'

His reaction was disappointing. He grunted again.

'In a folder on my Daddy's desk.'

If she had meant to surprise him, she succeeded. He came off the sheet like in one movement, facing her, gripping both her upper arms hard. There was an intensity about his state that frightened her.

'You're hurting me,' she said irrelevantly.

'What folder on your father's desk?'

'A folder,' she sniffed, on the verge of tears. 'I only wanted to help you.'

He relaxed visibly and his expression softened.

'Why did you go looking?' he asked.

'Well, you're always asking about him, and when I saw this folder, I just sort of looked. Then I saw your name.'

'Tell me about it, from the beginning,' he said gently.

When she had finished she reached forward and coiled her arms round his neck.

'I love you, Mister Cat,' she whispered. 'I only did it for that. Was it wrong?'

Shannon thought for a moment. She already knew far too much and there were only two ways of ensuring her silence.

'Do you really love me?' he asked.

'Yes. Really.'

'Would you want anything bad to happen to me, because of something you did or said?'

She pulled herself back from him, staring deep into his face. This was much more like the scenes in her schoolgirl dreams.

'Never,' she said soulfully, 'I'd never talk. Whatever they did to me.'

Shannon blinked several times in amazement.

'Nobody's going to do anything to you,' he said. 'Just don't tell your father that you know me, or went through his papers. You see, he employs me to gather information for him about the prospects of mining in Africa. If he learned we knew each other, he'd fire me. Then I'd have to find another job. There is one that's been offered to me, miles away in Africa. So you see, I'd have to go and leave you if he ever found out about us.'

That struck home, hard. She did not want him to go. Privately he knew one day soon he would have to go, but there was no need to tell her yet.

'I won't say anything,' she promised.

'A couple of points,' said Shannon. 'You said you saw the title on the sheets with mineral prices on them. What was the title?'

She furrowed her brow, trying to recall the word.

'That stuff they put in fountain pens. They mention it in the adverts for the expensive ones.'

'Ink?' asked Shannon.

'Platignum,' she said.

'Platinum,' he corrected, his eyes pensive. 'Lastly, what was the title on the folder?'

'Oh, I remember that,' she said happily. 'Like something out of a fairy tale. The Crystal Mountain.'

Shannon sighed deeply.

'Go and make me a coffee, there's a love.'

When he heard her clattering cups in the kitchen he leaned back against the bedhead and stared out over London.

'You cunning bastard,' he breathed. 'But it won't be that cheap, Sir James, not that cheap at all.'

Then he laughed into the darkness.

That same Saturday night Benny Lambert was ambling home towards his lodgings after an evening drinking with friends in one of his favourite cafés. He had been buying a lot of rounds for his cronies, using the money, now changed into francs, that Shannon had paid him. It made him feel good to be able to talk of the 'big deal' he had just pulled off, and buy the admiring bar girls champagne. He had had enough, more than enough, himself, and took no notice of the car that cruised slowly behind him, two hundred yards back. Nor did he think much of it when the car swept up to him as he came abreast of a plot of waste ground half a mile short of his home.

By the time he took notice and started to protest, the giant figure who had emerged from the car was hustling him across the lot and behind a hoarding that stood ten yards from the road.

His protests were silenced when the figure spun him round and, still holding him by the scruff, slammed a fist into the solar plexus. Benny Lambert sagged, and when the grip on his collar was removed, slumped to the ground. Standing above him, face shadowed in the obscurity behind the hoarding, the figure drew a two-foot iron bar from his belt. Stooping down the big man grabbed the writhing Lambert by the left thigh and jerked it upwards. The iron bar made a dull 'whumph' as it crashed down with all the assailant's force into the exposed kneecap, shattering it instantly. Lambert screamed once, shrilly, like a skewered rat and fainted. He never felt the second kneecap broken at all.

Twenty minutes later Thomard was phoning his employer from the booth in a late-night café a mile away. At the other end Roux listened and nodded.

'Good,' he said. 'Now I have some news for you. The hotel where Shannon usually stays. Henri Alain has just informed me they have received a letter from Mr Keith Brown. It reserved a room for him on the night of the 15th. Got it?'

'The 15th,' he said. 'Yes. He will be there then.'

'And so will you,' said the voice down the phone. 'Henri will keep in touch with his contact inside the hotel, and you will remain on stand-by not far from the hotel from noon of that day onwards.'

'Until when?' asked Thomard.

'Until he comes out, alone,' said Roux. 'And then you will take him. For five thousand dollars.'

Thomard was smiling slightly when he came out of the booth. As he stood at the bar sipping his beer, he could feel the pressure of the gun under his left armpit. It made him smile even more. In a few more days it would earn him a small fortune. He was quite sure of it. It would, he told himself, be simple and straight-forward to take a man, even Cat Shannon, who had never even seen him and did not know he was there.

It was in the middle of Sunday morning that Kurt Semmler phoned. Shannon was lying naked on his back on the bed while Julie pottered round the kitchen making breakfast.

'Mr Keith Brown?' asked the operator.

'Yes. Speaking.'

'I have a personal call for you from a Mr Semolina in Genoa.'

Shannon swung himself off the bed and crouched on the edge, the telephone up to his ear.

'Put him on the line,' he ordered.

The German's voice was faint but reception was reasonably clear.

'Carlo?'

'Yes. Kurt?'

'I'm in Genoa.'

'I know. What news?'

'I have it. This time I am sure. She is just what you wanted. But there is someone else would like to buy her also. We may have to outbid them if we want the boat. But she is good. For us very good. Can you come out and see her?'

'You're quite sure, Kurt?'

'Yes. Quite sure. Registered freighter, property of a Genoa-based shipping company. Made to order.'

Shannon considered.

'I'll come tomorrow. What hotel are you staying at?'

Semmler told him.

'I'll be there on the first available plane. I don't know when that will be. Stay at the hotel in the afternoon and I'll contact you when I get there. Book me a room.'

A few minutes later he was speaking to BEA reservations and learned the first plane would be the Alitalia flight to Milan at 0905 the following morning, making a connection from Milan to Genoa and arriving at the port just after one in the afternoon. He booked himself a single ticket on the flight.

He was grinning when Julie returned with the coffee. If the ship was the right one he could conclude the deal over the next twelve days and be in Paris on the 15th for his rendezvous with Langarotti, secure in the knowledge that Semmler would prepare the ship ready for sea with a good crew and fully fuelled and victualled by the first of June.

'Who was that?' asked the girl.

'A friend.'

'Which friend?'

'A business friend.'

'What did he want?'

'I have to go and see him.'

'When?'

'Tomorrow morning. In Italy.'

'How long will you be gone?'

'I don't know. A fortnight. Maybe more.'

She pouted over her coffee cup.

'So what am I supposed to do all that time?' she asked.

Shannon grinned.

'You'll find something. There's a lot of it about.'

'You're a shit,' she said conversationally. 'But if you have to go, I suppose you must. It only leaves us till tomorrow morning, so I, my dear Tom Cat, am going to make the best of it.'

As his coffee was spilled over the pillow Shannon reflected that the fight for Kimba's palace was going to be a holiday compared with trying to satisfy Sir James Manson's sweet little daughter.

Chapter Fifteen

The port of Genoa was bathed in late afternoon sunshine when Cat Shannon and Kurt Semmler paid off their taxi and the German led his employer along the quays to where the Motor Vessel *Toscana* was moored. The old coaster was dwarfed by the two 3000-ton freighters that lay either side of her, but that was no problem. To Shannon's eye she was big enough for his purposes.

There was a tiny forepeak and a four-foot drop to the main deck, in the centre of which was the large square hatch to the only cargo hold set amidships. Aft was the tiny bridge and below it evidently the crew quarters and the captain's cabin. She had a short stubby mast from which a single loading derrick was attacked, rigged almost vertical. Right aft, above the stern, the ship's single lifeboat was slung.

She was rusty, her paint blistered by the sun in many places, flayed off by salt spray in others. Small and old and dowdy, she had the quality Shannon looked for – she was anonymous. There are thousands of such small freighters plying the coastal inshore trade from Haifa to Gibraltar, Tangier to Dakar, Monrovia to Simonstown. They all look much the same, attract no attention and are seldom suspected of being up to anything beyond carrying small cargoes from port to port.

Semmler took Shannon on board. They found their way aft to where a companionway led down to the darkness of the crew quarters, and Semmler called. Then they went on down. They were met at the bottom by a muscular, hard-faced man in his mid-forties who nodded at Semmler and stared at Shannon.

Semmler shook hands with him and introduced him to Shannon.

'Carl Waldenberg, the first mate.'

Waldenberg nodded abruptly and shook hands.

'You have come to look her over, our old *Toscana*?' he asked.

Shannon was pleased to note he spoke good if accented English and looked as if he might be prepared to run a cargo that did not appear on the manifest, if the price was right. He could understand the German seaman's interest in him. Semmler had already briefed him on the background, that he had told the crew his employer would be coming to look the ship over, with a view to buying. For the first mate the new owner was an interesting person. Apart from anything else, Waldenberg had to be concerned about his own future.

The Yugoslav engineer was ashore somewhere, but they met the deckhand, a teenage Italian boy reading a girlie magazine on his bunk. Without waiting for the Italian captain's return, the first mate showed them both over the *Toscana*.

Shannon was interested in three things: the ability of the boat to accommodate another twelve men somewhere, even if they had to sleep out on deck in the open, the main hold and the possibility of secreting a few crates below the flooring down in the bilges, and the trustworthiness of the engines to get them as far as South Africa.

Waldenberg's eyes narrowed slightly as Shannon asked his questions, but he answered them civilly. He could work out for himself that no fare-paying passengers were coming on board the *Toscana* for the privilege of sleeping wrapped in blankets on the hold-cover under the summer stars; nor was the *Toscana* going to pick up much freight for a run to the other end of Africa. Cargo sent that distance will be shipped in a bigger vessel. The advantage of a small coaster is that she can often load a cargo at very short notice and deliver it two days later a couple of hundred miles away. Big ships spend longer in port while turning round. But on a long run like that from the Mediterranean to South Africa, a bigger ship makes up in extra speed what she spent in port before setting out. For the exporter the *Toscanas* of the sea have little attraction over 500 miles.

After seeing the boat they went topsides and Waldenberg offered them bottles of beer, which they drank in the shade of the canvas awning set up behind the bridge. That was when the negotiations really started. The two Germans rattled away in their own language, the seaman evidently putting the questions and Semmler answering. At last Waldenberg looked keenly at Shannon, looked back at Semmler and nodded slowly.

'Possibly,' he said in English.

Semmler turned to Shannon and explained.

'Waldenberg is interested why a man like yourself who evidently does not know the charter cargo business wants to buy a freighter for general cargo. I said you were a businessman and not a seaman. He feels the general cargo business is too risky for a rich man to want to hazard money on it, unless he has something specific in mind.'

Shannon nodded.

'Fair enough. Kurt, I want a word with you alone.'

They went aft and leaned over the rail while Waldenberg drank his beer.

'How do you reckon this guy?' muttered Shannon.

'He's good,' said Semmler without hesitation.

'The captain is the owner also, and he is an old man and wants to retire. For this he has to sell the boat and retire on the money. That leaves a place vacant as captain. I think Waldenberg would like it, and I agree with that. He has his master's ticket and he knows this boat inside out. He also knows the sea. That leaves the question of whether he would run a cargo with a risk attached. I think he would, if the price is right.'

'He suspects something already?' asked Shannon.

'Sure. Actually he thinks you are in the business of running illegal immigrants into Britain. He would not want to get arrested, but if the price is right I think he would take the risk.'

'Surely, the first thing is to buy the ship. He can decide whether to stay on later. If he wants to quit, we can find another captain.'

Semmler shook his head.

'No. For one thing we would have to tell him enough beforehand for him to know roughly what the job was. If he quit then, it would be a breach of security.'

'If he learns what the job is, and then quits, he only goes out one way,' said Shannon, and pointed his forefinger down at the oil-slicked water beneath the stern.

'There's one other point, Cat. It would be an advantage to have him on our side. He knows the ship, and if he decides to stay on, he will try to persuade the captain to let us have the *Toscana*, rather than the local shipping company that is sniffing around. His opinion counts with the captain, because the old boy wants the *Toscana* to be in good hands, and he trusts Waldenberg.'

Shannon considered the logic. It appealed to him. Time was running short and he wanted the *Toscana*. The first mate might help him get it, and could certainly run it. He could also recruit his own first mate and make sure he was a kindred spirit. Apart from that, there is one useful precept about bribing people. Never try to bribe them all; just buy the man who controls his own subordinates, and let him keep the rest in line. Shannon decided to make an ally of Waldenberg if he could. They strolled back to the awning.

'I'll be straight with you, Mister,' he told the German. 'It's true if I bought the *Toscana* she would not be used for carrying peanuts. It's also true there would be a slight element of risk as the cargo went on board. There would be no risk as the cargo went ashore, because the ship would be outside territorial waters. I need a good skipper, and Kurt Semmler tells me you're good. So let's get down to basics. If I get the *Toscana* I'll offer you the post of captain. You get a six-month guaranteed salary at double your present one, plus a 500-dollar bonus for the first shipment, which is due ten weeks from now.'

Waldenberg listened without saying a word. Then he grinned and uncoiled himself from where he sat. He held out his hand.

'Mister, you just got yourself a captain.'

'Fine,' said Shannon. 'Except the first thing is to buy the boat.'

'No problem,' said Waldenberg. 'How much would you spend for her?'

'What's she worth?' countered Shannon.

'What the market will take,' answered Waldenberg. 'The opposition has fixed its own ceiling at £25,000 and not a penny more.'

'I'll go to £26,000,' said Shannon. 'Will the captain take that?'

'Sure. Do you speak Italian?'

'No.'

'Spinetti speaks no English. So let me interpret for you. I'll fix it with the old man. With the price, and me as captain, he'll let you have her. When can you meet him?'

'Tomorrow morning?' asked Shannon.

'Right. Tomorrow at ten, here on board.'

They shook hands again and the two mercenaries left.

Tiny Marc Vlaminck was contentedly at work in the garage he had rented, while the locked van stood outside the door in the mews alley. Marc had closed and locked the garage door also, in case he be disturbed while he worked. It was his second afternoon alone in the garage and he had almost finished the first part of the job.

Along the rear wall of the garage he had erected a work bench of solid timber baulks, and equipped it with what he needed, the tools bought with Shannon's £500, as was also the van and the rest of the necessary items. Along one wall stood five large drums. They were bright green and bore the trading mark of the Castrol oil company. They were empty, which was the way Marc had bought them, quite cheaply, from one of the big shipping firms in the port, and they had once contained heavy lubricating oil, which was also plainly marked on each barrel.

From the first in the line, Marc had cut a circular disc out of the bottom, and the barrel stood upended with the gaping hole showing upwards and the screw-cap at the top of the barrel on the floor. Round the hole was a one-and-a-half-inch flange, all that was left of the original base of the drum.

From the van Marc had taken two crates of Schmeissers, and the twenty machine pistols were almost ready to enter their new hiding place. Each gun had been carefully mummified from end to end in sticky masking tape, and each had five magazines taped to the weapon itself. Following the wrapping process, each machine pistol had been slipped into a stout polythene envelope, which Marc had then sucked empty of air and tied securely at the neck with twine. After that each had gone into a second and outer envelope of polythene, which was again tied at the neck. Such wrapping, he reckoned, should keep each weapon dry until it was next brought out into the air.

He took the twenty stubby packages and with two stout webbing straps rolled them all into one large bundle. This he inserted into the hole at the top of the drum and lowered it to the bottom. The drums were the usual forty-four-gallon or two-hundred-litre type, and there was enough room in each for twenty Schmeissers and their accompanying magazines, with a little room to spare round the walls.

When the first bundle was secreted, Marc began the process of re-sealing the barrel. He had had fresh tinplate discs cut at a machine-shop in the port, and the first of these he fitted on to the top of the opened drum. It took half an hour of filing and rasping before the disk finally settled tight and neatly on to the drum-head, running right up to the rim in all places, and nicely covering the inch-and-a-half overlap that remained of the previous end of the drum. Turning on his steam jet, powered by a gas bottle and burner, and taking a stick of soft solder, he began to 'sweat' the tinplate to tinplate.

Metal can be welded to metal, and to get the hardest join, it usually is. But a barrel that has once contained oil or ignitable fuel always retains a residue film on the inner surface of the metal. When heated, as it must be by welding, the film turns to fumes, and can easily explode very dangerously. 'Sweating' a piece of tinplate onto another piece does not give the same strenth of join, but can be done with steam heat at a lower temperature. Provided the drums were not laid on their sides and juggled about, which would have produced a powerful surge inside, they would hold together against a fair amount of handling.

When he had finished, Marc packed any remaining crevices with solder, and when all was cool spray-painted the whole area with a colour the exact replica of Castrol oil drums the world over. Leaving the paint to dry, he later eased the drum gently on to its new base, and removing the screw-cap at the top, he took one of several large jerry-cans standing ready and began to pour in the lubricating oil.

The emerald-green liquid, thick, sticky, viscous, flowed into the open aperture and gurgled its way to the bottom of the drum. Slowly it filled up the air spaces between the sides of the drum and the bundle of machine pistols inside, slid noiselessly into every nook and cranny between the individual weapons and impregnated the webbing and twine. Despite Marc's sucking before twisting the ends of each polythene bag tight shut, there were still bubbles of air inside the bags, trapped in magazines, barrels and breeches. These offset the weight of the metal, so that as the barrel filled, the cumbersome bundle of guns became almost weightless, bobbing in the heavy oil like a body on the tide and finally sinking slowly below the surface.

The Belgian used two jerry-cans, and when the drum was full to the brim he estimated seven-tenths of the interior was taken up by the bundle, three-tenths by oil. He had poured sixty litres into the two-hundred-litre drum. Finally he took a pencil torch and scanned the surface of the liquid. It gleamed back at him in the light, slick and green, with hints of gold. Of what lay at the bottom of the drum there was not a sign. He waited another hour before he checked round the base. Nothing had leaked, the new base of the barrel was sealed tight.

There was a jauntiness to him as he rolled open the garage doors and ran the van back inside. He still had the wood of two flat crates with German markings to destroy, and a disc of now useless tinplate to throw away. The latter would go into the harbour, the former on to a bonfire. He knew now that the system worked, and that he could convert one barrel every two days. He would be ready for Shannon by May 15th as promised. It was good to be back at work.

Doctor Ivanov was incensed, not for the first time and doubtless not for the last.

'The bureaucracy,' he snapped at his wife across the breakfast table, 'the sheer, incompetent, stultifying bureaucracy in this country is bloody unbelievable.'

'I'm sure you're right, Mikhail Mikhailovich,' his wife said soothingly, pouring two more cups of tea, strong, dark and bitter as she knew her husband liked it. A placid and contented woman, she wished her volatile scientist husband would be careful with his outbursts, or at least confine them to the house.

'If the capitalist world knew how long it takes to get a couple of nuts and bolts in this country, they'd fall about laughing.'

'Shush, dear,' she told him, stirring in the sugar for herself. 'You must be patient.'

It had been weeks since the Director had summoned him to the pine-panelled office in the heart of the vast complex of laboratories and living quarters that made up the Institute in the heart of the Siberian New Lands to inform him that he would be in charge of a survey team being sent to West Africa, and that he should take charge of the details himself.

It had meant forsaking a project that interested him deeply, and doing the same to two of his junior colleagues. He had indented for the necessary equipment for an African climate, sending off his requirements to the half-dozen different supply directorates concerned, answering the petty queries as politely as he could, and waiting, always waiting, for the equipment to arrive and be crated. He knew from his membership of a survey team in Ghana while Nkrumah was in power there what working in the deep bush could entail.

'Give me the snow any time,' he had told his team leader at the time. 'I'm a cold-weather man.'

But he had done it, on orders and on time. His team was ready, his equipment prepared and crated, down to the last water-purification tablet and camp-bed. With luck, he had thought, he could be there, do the survey, and be back with his rock samples before the brief and glorious days of the Siberian summer had been eaten by the bitter autumn. The letter in his hand told him it was not to be.

It came from his Director personally, and he bore the man no animosity, for he knew he was only passing on instructions from Moscow. Unfortunately the Transport Directorate there had ruled that the confidential nature of the survey forbade the use of public transport, but the Foreign ministry did not feel able to instruct Aeroflot to put an airliner at the team's disposal. In view of continuing Middle East developments, neither would it be possible to use one of the military's Antonov freighters.

In consequence, ran the instructions from Moscow, it had been felt necessary, in view of the volume of equipment required for the survey, and the even greater volumes of samples that would have to be brought back from West Africa, to use maritime transport. It was decided that the team could be best transported by a Soviet freighter heading past the coast of West Africa towards the Far East. On their return, they would simply notify Ambassador Dobrovolsky that they had completed their survey, and on instructions from him a freighter heading back towards home would divert to take the three-man team and its crates of samples on board. Notification would be made in due course of the date and port of departure, and vouchers authorizing the use of state transport to the port of embarkation would be provided.

'The whole summer,' shouted Ivanov as his wife helped him into his fur-collared coat and fur hat. 'I'm going to miss the whole bloody summer. And it'll be in the rainy season down there.'

Cat Shannon and Kurt Semmler were at the ship again the following morning and met Captain Alessandro Spinetti for the first time. He was a gnarled old man with a face like a walnut, a tee-shirt over what was still a barrel of a chest, and a white-topped peaked cap aslant on his head.

The negotiating started then and there, before they adjourned to the office of the captain's lawyer, a certain Giulio Ponti, who ran his practice from one of the narrow side streets that lead backwards and upwards from the brawling, riotous Via Gramschi. To be fair to the Signor, he was at least at the better end of the Via Gramschi and the tarts in the bars they passed became progressively more presentable and expensive as they neared the lawyer's office.

Nothing to do with the business of the law moves at faster than a snail's pace in Italy, and usually that of an arthritic snail.

The terms had been agreed already. With Carl Waldenberg translating Captain Spinetti had accepted the package deal Shannon offered; £26,000 cash for the ship, to be paid in any currency or country the captain cared to name; his own first mate to be offered a minimum six-month contract as the new skipper, at a salary double that he had received as first mate; the chance for the other two men, the engineer and the deckhand, to stay on for six months at existing salary, or part company with severance pay of £500 for the deckhand and £1000 for the engineer.

Privately Shannon had already decided to persuade the deckhand to leave, but to do all he could to keep the engineer, a surly Serbian who Waldenberg said could coax those engines to hell and back, who said nothing and asked less, and best of all whose papers were probably not in order and who therefore needed the job.

For taxation reasons the captain had long ago invested £100 in forming a small private company, Spinetti Maritimo Shipping Company. It had 100 ordinary shares of which he held ninety-nine and his lawyer, Signor Ponti, held one, plus the post of company secretary. The sale of the ship MV *Toscana*, the company's only asset, was therefore linked to the sale of the shipping company Spinetti Maritimo which suited Shannon perfectly.

What did not suit him so well was that it took five days of meetings with the lawyer before the details were in order. And that was only for the first stage.

It was a week into May and Day Thirty-One of Shannon's private calendar of 100 days before Ponti could start drawing up the contracts. As the deal was going through in Italy, and the *Toscana* was an Italian registered and resident vessel, the contract had to comply with Italian law, which is complex. There were three contracts, that for the sale of Spinetti Maritimo and all her assets to Tyrone Holdings of Luxembourg, that which contracted Tyrone Holdings to offer Carl Waldenberg the post of captain for six months at the agreed salary, and the third guaranteeing the two other crewmen their existing salaries or severance pay. This process took four days, and Ponti's attitude was evidently that he was breaking all speed records, although all participant parties were anxious to complete the sale as soon as possible.

Big Janni Dupree was content with life that bright May morning when he emerged from the camping goods store having placed the last of his orders. He had put down a deposit for the required number of haversacks and sleeping bags. Delivery had been promised for the next day, and that same afternoon he intended to pick up two large cardboard boxes full of military-style knapsacks and berets from a warehouse in the east end of London.

Three bulky consignments of miscellaneous equipment were already on their way to Toulon. The first should have arrived, he estimated, and the other two should be in transit. The fourth would be crated and put in the hands of the shipping agent the following afternoon, which left him a week in hand. The day before, he had received a letter from Shannon telling him to vacate his London flatlet and fly to Marseilles on May 15th. He was to check into a given hotel in the French port and wait there to be contacted. He liked precise instructions; they left little room for errors, and if anything did go wrong it could not be his fault. He had booked his ticket and was eager for the remaining week to pass so that he could be off. It was good to be going into action again.

When Signor Ponti had finally drawn up the necessary paperwork, Cat Shannon despatched a series of letters from his Genoa hotel. The first was to Johann Schlinker to tell him that the ship that would be engaged to carry the ammunition from Spain would be the MV *Toscana*, owned by Spinetti Maritimo Shipping Company of Genoa. He himself would need from

Schlinker details of where the arms shipment was supposed to be heading, so that the captain could draw up the appropriate manifest.

He included in his letter full details of the *Toscana*, and had already checked with Lloyd's Shipping List, a copy of which he was able to study in the office of the British vice-consul in Genoa, to ensure the *Toscana* was listed there. He told Schlinker he would be contacting him within the next fifteen days.

Another letter went to Alan Baker, so that he too could inform the Yugoslav authorities of the name and details of the carrying vessel for the export licence to be granted. He already knew what the manifest would have to read. It would say the vessel was proceeding with her cargo from the Yugoslav port of embarkation to Lome, the capital of Togo.

He wrote a long letter to Mr Stein as Chairman of Tyrone Holdings instructing him to prepare the papers for a board meeting of the company in his office four days hence, with two resolutions on the agenda. One would be for the company to buy Spinetti Maritimo and all its assets for £26,000 and the other would be to issue a further 26,000 £1 bearer shares to Mr Keith Brown in exchange for a certified cheque for £26,000.

He dashed off a line to Marc Vlaminck telling him the pick-up of the cargo in Ostende would have to be delayed until May 20th and another to Langarotti putting back the Paris rendezvous to the 19th.

Lastly he sent Simon Endean a letter in London asking him to meet Shannon in Luxembourg four days hence and to have at his disposal funds amounting to £26,000 for the purchase of the ship to carry the whole operation to the target area.

The evening of the 13th was soft and cool, and several hundred miles along the same coastline Jean-Baptiste Langarotti was driving his van westwards from Hyères on the last stretch into Toulon. He had the window down and sniffed the smell of conifer and maquis coming off the hills to his right. Like Dupree in London, preparing that evening to fly to Marseilles, like Vlaminck in Ostende putting the final touches to his fifth and last oil drum of guns, Langarotti was content with life.

He had in the back of the van the last two outboard engines, bought for cash, and equipped with underwater exhaust attachments for silent running. He was on his way back to Toulon to deliver them to the bonded warehouse. Already in the warehouse of Maritime Duphot were three black inflatable dinghies, each crated and unopened, and the third engine. Also there were four large crates of assorted clothing that had arrived over the past fortnight from London in his own name. He too would be ready on time.

It was a pity he had had to move from his hotel. A chance encounter with an old underworld friend as he left the doorway three days ago had forced him to make a quick excuse and move out the following morning. He was now in a new hotel, and would have informed Shannon of this except he did not know where Shannon was. It made no matter. In forty-eight hours, on the 15th, he would keep his rendezvous with his chief at the Plaza Surene hotel in Paris.

*

The meeting in Luxembourg on May 14th was surprisingly short. Shannon was not present. He had met Mr Stein earlier in his office and handed over to him the documents for the sale of the Spinetti Shipping Company and its vessel the *Toscana*, along with a certified cheque for £26,000, payable to Tyrone Holdings SA.

Thirty minutes later Mr Stein emerged from the board meeting and handed Shannon 26,000 ordinary bearer shares in Tyrone Holdings. He also showed him an envelope which contained the documents concerning the sale of the ship to Tyrone, and Tyrone Holdings' cheque in favour of Signor Alessandro Spinetti. He sealed the envelope, which was addressed to Signor Giulio Ponti at his Genoa office, and gave it to Shannon. The last document he handed over was a board decision to appoint Herr Kurt Semmler managing director of Spinetti Maritimo Shipping Company.

Two days later in the Italian lawyers' office the deal was finalized. The cheque for the purchase of the *Toscana* had been cleared and Tyrone Holdings legally owned one hundred per cent of Spinetti Maritimo. In respect of this, Signor Ponti despatched by registered post the one hundred ordinary shares in Spinetti Maritimo to the company office of Tyrone in Luxembourg. As a separate matter Signor Ponti accepted a package from Shannon and locked it in his vault for safe-keeping. He took two sample signatures from Shannon, in the name of Keith Brown, to be able to certify the authenticity of any letter from Shannon regarding disposal of the package. Unknown to Ponti the package contained the 26,994 controlling shares of Tyrone.

Carl Waldenberg received his captaincy and his six-month contract, as did the Serbian engineer. One month's salary was paid to each man in cash and the remaining five months' for each was placed in escrow in the hands of Signor Ponti.

The Italian deckhand was persuaded without difficulty to take his £500 severance pay, plus a bonus of £100, and left the crew. Semmler was installed as managing director.

Shannon had had a further £5000 transferred from Brugge to his credit in Genoa, and with this he had covered the two salaries of the crewmen who were remaining with the *Toscana*. Before he left Genoa on the 18th, he handed the rest over to Semmler and gave him his briefing.

'How about the two replacement crew?'

'Waldenberg is seeing to it already,' Semmler told him. 'He reckons this port is crawling with men available for recruitment. He knows the place inside out. He also knows what we need. Good hard men, the sort who ask no questions and do what they are told, particularly if they know there is a bonus at the end of it. Don't worry, he'll get a good pair before the end of the week.'

'Right. Fine. This is what I want. Get the *Toscana* ready for sea. A complete engine overhaul and servicing. Port dues paid up, papers in order with the new captain's name. Manifest prepared for Toulon to pick up general cargo for Morocco. Get her fuelled and victualled. Take on enough stores for the crew plus a further dozen men. Extra fresh water, beer, wine, cigarettes. When she's ready, take her to Toulon. You have to be there by June 1st, at the latest. I'll be there with Marc, Jean-Baptiste and Janni. Contact me through the shipping agent, Agence Maritime Duphot. They're in the port area. I'll see you then. Good luck.'

Chapter Sixteen

Jean-Baptiste Langarotti was alive in part at least due to his ability to sense danger before it came looking for him. The first day he reported to the Paris hotel he just sat quietly at the appointed hour in the residents' lounge and read a magazine. He gave Shannon two hours, but the mercenary leader did not show up.

On the off-chance, the Corsican inquired at the reception desk, for although Shannon had said nothing about staying the night, it might be he had arrived early and taken a room. The reception clerk checked the register and informed Langarotti there was no Monsieur Brown from London in the hotel. Langarotti assumed Shannon had been delayed, and would make the rendezvous at the same hour on the next day.

So the Corsican was there, sitting in the residents' lounge at the same hour on the 16th. There was still no Shannon, but there was something else. Twice the same staff member of the hotel peeked into the room and vanished as soon as Langarotti looked up. After another two hours, Shannon still not having come, he left the hotel again. As he passed down the street he had a glimpse of a man in the corner doorway showing a bizarre interest in the window into which he was staring with such fixed intensity. The shop window was full of women's corsets. Langarotti had the feeling the man was one component that did not fit into the pattern of that quiet back street on a spring morning.

Over the next twenty-four hours the Corsican began to sniff the wind in the bars of Paris where mercenaries foregather, using his old contacts of the Corsican Union in the Paris underworld. He continued to go to the hotel each morning, and on the fifth morning, that of the 19th, Shannon was there.

He had arrived the previous evening by plane from Genoa and Milan, and had stayed the night at the hotel. He seemed in good spirits, and told his colleague over coffee in the lounge that he had bought a ship for their operation.

'No problem?' asked Langarotti. Shannon shook his head.

'No problems.'

'But here in Paris we have a problem.'

Unable to strop his knife in such a public place, the small Corsican sat with his hands idle in his lap. Shannon put down his coffee cup. He knew if Langarotti referred to problems that meant trouble.

'Such as?' he asked softly.

'There's a contract on you,' said Langarotti.

The two men sat in silence for a while, as Shannon considered the news. His friend did not interrupt. He usually answered questions only when they were asked.

'Do you know who placed it?' asked Shannon.

'No. Nor who has taken it up. But it's expensive, about 5000 dollars.'

'Recently?'

'The word is, the contract was placed some time in the past six weeks. It seems uncertain whether the contractor, who must be Paris-based, is the one who placed it, or whether he is acting for someone behind the scenes. The word is, only a good hit-man would take a contract on you, or a stupid one. But someone has taken it. Inquiries are being made about you.'

Shannon cursed slightly. He had little doubt the Corsican was right. He was too careful a man to go bandying unchecked information like that around. He tried to think back to any incident that might give rise to the placing of a contract on his head. The trouble was, there were so many possible reasons, some of which he knew he could not even guess.

Methodically he began to go over the possibilities he could envisage. Either the contract stemmed from something to do with the present operation, or it came from a motive that lay further back. He considered the first option first.

Had there been a leak? Had some government agency received a whiff of intelligence that he was mounting a coup in Africa and decided to stop it permanently by snuffing out the operations commander? The thought even crossed his mind that Sir James Manson had learned of the multiple deflowering – if that was the word for such an experienced Lolita – of his daughter. He rejected them all. It could be that he had offered someone in the murky world of the black market arms dealers who had decided to settle the score the hard way while remaining in the background. But such a move would have been preceded by an argument over a deal, a squabble over money, a stand-up row, or threats. There had been none.

He turned his memory further back, to the wars and the fights gone by. The trouble was, one never knew if one might, at some time, have angered a big organization without meaning to. Perhaps one of the men he had gunned down had secretly been an agent of the CIA or the KGB. Both organizations bore long grudges, and being peopled by the world's most savagely unprincipled men, insisted on settling scores even when there was no pragmatic motive, but simply revenge. He was aware the CIA still had an open-ended hit contract out on Bruce Rossiter who had shot an American in a bar in Leopoldville because the man was staring at him. The American, it had later turned out, was one of the horde of local CIA men, though Rossiter had not known this. It did not help him. The contract still went out, and Rossiter was still running.

The KGB were as bad. They sent assassins across the world to liquidate fugitives, foreign agents who had hurt them and been blown for all to see, and were thus unprotectable by their own former employers; and the Russians needed no practical motive, like the information in the man's head that he had not yet spilled. They did it just for revenge.

That left the French SDECE, and the British SIS. The French could have taken him a hundred times over the past two years, and made sure it happened in the jungles of Africa. Moreover, they would not place the deal with a Paris contractor and risk a leak. They had their own men, good ones, on the staff. The British were even less likely. Legalistic to the end, they would have to get permission from almost Cabinet level for a hit, and only used the method in the direst emergency, to prevent a vital leak, to create a nasty example to encourage others to have confidence in the service, or occasionally to even a score where one of their own men had been knowingly knocked over by an identifiable killer. Shannon was sure he had never hit a blue-carded Britisher, and that left the motive of preventing an embarrassment. The Russians and French would kill for that reason, but not the British. They had left Stephen Ward alive to stand trial and nearly ruin the Macmillan government; they had left Philby alive after he was blown, and Blake too; in France or Russia both traitors would have entered the road accident statistics.

That left a private firm. The Corsican Union? No, Langarotti could not have stuck by him if it had been the Union. So far as he knew he had never upset the Mafia in Italy or the Syndicate in America. That took the matter back to a private individual with a private grudge. If it was not a government agency, and not a big private firm, it had to be an individual. But who, for God's sake?

Langarotti was still watching him, waiting for his reaction. Shannon kept his face still, his air bored.

'Do they know I'm here in Paris?'

'I think so. I believe they know about this hotel. You always stay here. It's a mistake. I was here four days ago, as you had said ...'

'Didn't you get my letter, putting the meeting back to today?'

'No. I had to move from my Marseilles hotel a week ago.'

'Oh. Go on.'

'There was someone watching the hotel the second time I came. I had already asked for you by the name of Brown. So I think the leak came from inside this hotel. The man was watching yesterday and today.'

'So I move hotels,' said Shannon.

'You might shake him. You might not. Someone knows the name of Keith Brown. They could find you elsewhere. How much do you have to be in Paris over the next few weeks?'

'Quite a bit,' admitted Shannon. 'I have to stage through several times, and we have to bring Marc's stuff down from Belgium to Toulon through Paris in two days.'

Langarotti shrugged.

'They might not find you. We don't know how good they are, or how many of them. Or who. But they might find you a second time. Then there would be problems, perhaps with the police.'

'I can't afford that. Not now. Not with Marc's consignment sitting in the van,' said Shannon.

He was a reasonable man, and would much prefer to have negotiated with the one who had placed the contract on him. But whoever it was, he had chosen to do it the other way.

Shannon would still have tried to talk to the man, but first he had to identify him. There was only one man who could do that for him. The man who had taken the contract to kill him. He put this to the Corsican, who nodded sombrely.

'Yes, *mon ami*, I think you're right. We have to take the hit-man. But first he must be lured out.'

'Will you help me, Jean-Baptiste?'

'Of course,' said Langarotti. 'Whoever it is, it is not the Union. It is not my people, so I am your man.'

They spent close to an hour with a street map of Paris on the table in front of them. Then Langarotti left.

During the day he parked his Marseilles-registered van at a prearranged spot. In the late afternoon Shannon went to reception and asked the way to a well-known restaurant a mile away. He was within earshot of the hotel clerk who had been described to him by Langarotti. The chief receptionist told him where the restaurant was.

'Within walking distance?' asked Shannon.

'But certainly, m'sieu. About fifteen minutes, maybe twenty.'

Shannon thanked him and used the desk telephone to make a reservation in the name of Brown for ten o'clock that night. He did not leave the hotel all day.

At nine-forty exactly, carrying his overnight grip in one hand and a light raincoat over the other arm, he left the hotel and turned up the street in the direction for the restaurant. The route he took was not direct. It led down two streets even smaller than the one in which the hotel was situated. As he walked, he left the other pedestrians behind and entered streets in the First Arrondissement which were dimly lit and where no passers-by came his way. He dawdled, passing the time staring into lighted shop windows, killing time until the hour of his restaurant reservation was long past. He never looked back. Sometimes, in the quiet, he thought he could hear the soft slap of a moccasin somewhere up the dim-lit streets behind him. Whoever was there, it was not Langarotti. The Corsican could move without disturbing the dust.

It was past eleven when he reached the dark, black alley he had been told was there. It led to his left and had no lights in it all. The far end was blocked by a row of bollards, making it into a cul-de-sac. On each side the walls were blank and tall. Any light that might have entered the alley from the other end was muted by the bulk of the French van that stood parked there, empty but with its rear doors open. Shannon walked towards the van's gaping back and when he reached it, turned.

Like most fighting men he always preferred to face danger than know it was somewhere behind. He knew from past experience that even when moving backwards, it is safer always to face the danger source. At least, then, you can watch it. Moving up the alley with his back to the entrance he had felt the hairs on his neck prickling. If the psychology was wrong, he could be very dead. But the psychology had been right. Keeping to empty streets the man behind him had stayed well back, hoping for just such an opportunity as now presented itself.

Shannon tossed his bag and raincoat to the ground and stared at the hulking shadow that blocked the vertical streak of lamplight from the end of the alley. He waited patiently. He hoped there would be no sound, not in the centre of Paris. The shadow paused, assessed the situation, and evidently checked Shannon for a gun. But the sight of the open van reassured the hit-man. He assumed Shannon had simply parked it there for discretion's sake, and had been all this time returning to it.

The shadow in the alley moved softly forward. Shannon could make out the right arm, out of the raincoat pocket now, held forward, holding something. The face was in shadow, the whole man was a silhouette, but he was big. His form stood dead centre of the cobbled cul-de-sac, stopped now, raising his gun. He paused for several seconds as he aimed, then slowly lowered it again, straight-armed, down to his side. It was almost as if he changed his mind.

Still staring at Shannon from the shadow-black face, the man slowly leaned forward and went onto his knees. Some shots do this to steady themselves. The gunman cleared his throat, leaned forward again and placed both his hands, knuckles down, on the cobbles in front of him. The metal of the Colt .45 clattered on the stones. Slowly, like a Moslem facing Mecca at the hour of prayer, the gunman bowed his head, staring for the first time in twenty seconds not at Shannon but at the cobbles. There was a light splashing sound as of a liquid running fast onto cobbles, and finally the man's arms and thighs gave out. He slumped forward into a puddle of his own aortic blood and went to sleep, quite gently, like a child.

Shannon was still standing against the doors of the van. With the man down, a shaft of lamplight came from the lit end of the alley. It glistened on the polished black sheen of the four-inch bone knife-handle that protruded upwards from the mackintoshed back of the man on the pavement, slightly left of centre, between the fourth and fifth rib.

The Cat looked up. There was another figure against the lamplight, small, spare, motionless, still standing fifteen yards from the body at the point where he had made his throw. Shannon hissed and Langarotti padded noiselessly down the cobbles.

'I thought you'd left it too late,' grunted Shannon.

'*Non.* Never too late. He could not have squeezed the trigger of the Colt at any time since you emerged from the hotel.'

The rear of the van was already laid with a large sheet of tough industrial polythene over a canvas tarpaulin. The tarpaulin had loopholes all round the edge for easy lashing into a bundle, and plenty of cord and bricks were stacked at the far end. Each taking an arm and a leg, the two men swung the body up and inwards. Langarotti climbed in to retrieve his knife, while Shannon shut the doors. He heard them securely locked from the inside.

Langarotti climbed into the front seat and started up. Slowly he backed out, down the alley and into the street. As he swung the van round before driving off, Shannon approached the driver's window.

'Have you had a good look at him?'

'Sure.'

'You know him?'

'Yes. Name of Thomard, Raymond. In the Congo once for a short period, more of a city type. Professional hit-man. But not quality. Not the sort one of the big contractors would use. More likely to work for his own boss.'

'Who's that?' asked Shannon.

'Roux,' said Langarotti. 'Charles Roux.'

Shannon swore quietly and viciously.

'That bastard, that stupid, ignorant, incompetent fool. He could have fouled up a whole operation just because he wasn't invited to come in on it.'

He fell silent and thought for a while. Roux had to be discouraged, but in a way that would keep him out of the Zangaro affair once and for all.

'Hurry up,' said the Corsican, the engine still running. 'I want to get this customer put to bed before anyone comes along.'

Shannon made up his mind and spoke urgently and rapidly for several seconds. Langarotti nodded.

'All right. Actually, I like it. It should fix that bugger for a long time. But it will cost extra. Five thousand francs.'

'Done,' said Shannon. 'Get moving, and meet me outside the Porte de la Chapelle métro station in three hours.'

They met Marc Vlaminck for lunch in the small south Belgian town of Dinant by agreement. Shannon had called him the previous day and given him the instructions and the rendezvous. Tiny Marc had kissed Anna goodbye that morning and she had given him his lovingly packed suitcase of clothes and his snack box with half a loaf, some butter and a hunk of cheese for mid-morning break. As usual she had told him to take care of himself.

He had driven the van, carrying in the back five 200-litre drums of engine oil by Castrol, across Belgium without being stopped. There was no reason why he should be. His licence was in order, as was the permit for the van and the insurance.

As the three men sat over lunch at a main-street café, Shannon asked the Belgian:

'When do we go over?'

'Tomorrow morning, just before sun-up. It's the quietest time. Did you two sleep last night?'

'Nope.'

'You'd better get some rest,' said Marc. 'I'll watch over both vans. You can have till midnight.'

Charles Roux was another one who was tired that day. All the previous evening, since he had received his telephone call from Henri Alain about Shannon walking to his restaurant meal, he had waited for news. There had been none by midnight, when there should have been a call from Thomard to say it was all over. There had been none by three in the morning and none by sunrise.

Roux was unshaven and puzzled. He knew Thomard was no match for Shannon on equal terms, but he was sure the Irishman would be taken in the back as he walked through one of the quieter streets on his way to the evening meal.

At mid-morning, as Langarotti and Shannon in their empty van were passing without trouble into Belgium north of Valenciennes, Roux finally slipped on a pair of trousers and a shirt and took the lift the five floors down to the lobby to check his mailbox.

There did not seem to be anything wrong with the lock of his mailbox, a container some twelve inches tall, nine wide and nine deep, screwed to the wall of the lobby along with a score more for the other tenants.

There was no indication that it had been opened, and if so, the burglar must have picked the lock. But opened it most certainly had been.

Roux used his personal key to unlock the door and swung it open.

He stood for about ten seconds without moving. Nothing changed about him except the normal ruddy colour of his face, which slid into a chalky grey. Still staring mesmerized, he began to mutter, '*Mon Dieu, O mon Dieu...*' over and over again like an incantation. His stomach turned over, he felt like the moment in the Congo when he had heard the Congolese soldiers questioning his identity inside the bandages as he lay on a stretcher while John Peters smuggled him out from certain death. He felt he wanted to urinate, run, but could only sweat with fear. With an air of almost sleepy sadness, eyes half-closed, lips gummed together, the head of Raymond Thomard gazed back at him from inside the mail-box.

Roux was not squeamish, but he was no lion heart either. He closed the box, went back to his flat, and started into the brandy bottle, for medicinal purposes only. He needed a lot of medicine.

Alan Baker emerged from the office of the Yugoslav State arms company into the bright sunshine of Belgrade feeling well pleased with the way things were going. On receiving Shannon's down payment of 7200 dollars and the end user certificate, he had gone to a licensed arms dealer for whom he had occasionally done work in the past on a sub-contractual level. As in the case of Schlinker, the man had felt the amount of weaponry and money involved in the proposed deal to be derisory, but he had yielded to Baker's argument that if the buyers were satisfied with the first consignment they might well return for more, a lot more.

So he had given Baker his fiat to fly to Belgrade and make application for the purchase, using the certificate from Togo, duly filled out with the appropriate names, and with a letter of authority from the dealer appointing Baker his representative.

It meant Baker would lose a part of his cut, but it was the only way he could be received in Belgrade, and for such a small deal he had in any case allowed a mark-up of a hundred per cent on the buying price of the arms.

His five days of talks with Mr Pavlovic had been fruitful and had included a visit to the state warehouse in which he had selected the two mortar tubes and two bazookas. The ammunition for both was standard and supplied in crates of twenty bazooka rockets and ten mortar bombs.

The Yugoslavs had accepted the Togolese end user certificate without demur, and although Baker, the licensed dealer, and probably Mr Pavlovic must be aware the certificate was just a piece of paper, the air was maintained that the government of Togo was eagerly awaiting the chance to buy Yugoslavia's weaponry for testing. Mr Pavlovic had also required full payment in advance, and Baker had needed to pay over what remained of the 7200 dollars Shannon had given him, after his travel costs, plus a thousand dollars of his own. He was confident Shannon's balance of another 7200 dollars would reimburse him, and even after the licensed dealer had taken his cut, leave 4000 dollars for Baker's pocket.

His morning's talks had confirmed that the goods would be granted an export licence and sent by army lorries to a bonded warehouse at the port of Ploce in the north-west, close to the holiday resorts of Dubrovnik and Split.

It was here that the *Toscana* should dock to take the shipment aboard, any time after June 10th. With a light heart Baker took the next flight for Munich and Hamburg.

Johann Schlinker was in Madrid that morning, May 20th. He had telexed the full details of the deal in 9 mm ammunition that he wanted to put through to his Madrid partner, a Spanish national, a full month earlier, and had later flown to the Spanish capital himself with his Iraqi end user certificate as soon as he had received Shannon's 26,000 dollars in full payment.

The Spanish formalities were more complicated than those Alan Baker had discovered in Belgrade. Two applications were necessary, the first to buy the hardware, the second to export it. The application to buy had been made three weeks earlier, and over the past twenty days had been vetted by the three departments of state in Madrid who concern themselves with such matters. First the Finance Ministry had been needed to confirm that the full purchase price of 18,000 dollars had been received into the appropriate bank in hard currency. A few years earlier only US dollars had been acceptable, but more recently Madrid was more than happy to take German marks.

The second department was the Foreign Ministry. Their job had been to confirm that the buyer country was not a state to whom Spain was opposed. There was no problem with Iraq, since the great bulk of Spanish arms exports habitually go to the Arabs, with whom Spain has always maintained close and friendly relations. The Foreign Ministry had no hesitation in confirming its approval of Iraq as a recipient of Spanish 9 mm ball ammunition.

Lastly the Defence Ministry had been required to confirm that nothing in the proposed sale was on the secret list, or among the categories of arms not for export. With simple small-arms ammunition, this too had been no problem.

Although there had been no sticky problems with such a consignment, it had taken eighteen days for the papers to pass through the three departments, accumulating more paperwork as they went, until the final dossier emerged with the stamp of approval. At this point the crates of ammunition were taken from the CETME factory and stored in a warehouse of the Spanish Army on the outskirts of Madrid. From this point the Army Ministry took over, and notably the head of its arms export section, Colonel Antonio Salazar.

Schlinker had come to Madrid to present personally the application for export licence. He had been in possession of the full details of the MV *Toscana* on his arrival, and the seven-page questionnaire had been filled out and presented. Back in his room in the Hotel Mindanao, the German expected no problems here either. The *Toscana* was a clean ship, small but belonging to a registered shipping company, Spinetti Maritimo, as Lloyd's Shipping List confirmed. According to the application form, she would wish to berth in Valencia between June 16th and June 20th, take the shipment on board, and proceed straight to Latakia on the coast of Syria, where the consignment would be handed over to the Iraqis for trucking to Baghdad. The export licence should take no longer than another two weeks, and then application would be made for a movement order, permitting the crates to be taken from the army warehouse and detailing an army officer to mount escort with ten soldiers as far as Valencia quayside. The latter precaution, brought into force over the previous three years, was to prevent any risk of hi-jacking by the Basque terrorists. The last thing the government of the Caudillo wanted was to see Madrid's bullets being used against the Guardia Civil in Coruna.

As Schlinker prepared to leave for Hamburg, he reflected that his Madrid partner was perfectly capable of ensuring the liaison with the Army Ministry remained at a cordial level and the crates were waiting in Valencia for the arrival of the *Toscana* on time.

In London a third and seemingly unconnected meeting took place. Over the past three weeks Mr Harold Roberts, the nominee director of Bormac Trading Company, controlling thirty per cent of the company stock, had been cultivating the chairman, Major Luton. He had several times taken him to lunch and once visited him at his Guildford home. They had become quite friendly.

Throughout their talks Roberts had made it clear that if the company were to get off the ground and go back into business, whether in rubber or some other area of trading, a large injection of fresh capital would be needed. Major Luton could well see that. When the time was ripe, Mr Roberts proposed to the chairman that the company should make a new one-for-two issue of shares, a total therefore of half a million of new stock.

At first the major was aghast at the boldness of the move, but Mr Roberts assured him that the bank, whose nominee he was, would find the necessary fresh finance. Mr Roberts added that in the event of any of the new shares not being taken up by existing shareholders or new shareholders, the Zwingli Bank would take up the rest at full value on behalf of its customers.

The clinching argument was that when news of the fresh share issue broke on the market the price of Bormac ordinaries would be bound to rise, perhaps by as much again as their present value, which then stood at one shilling and threepence. Major Luton thought of his own 100,000 shares and agreed. As is so often the case when a man has once weakened, he then went along with Mr Robert's proposal without further demur.

The new director pointed out that the pair of them could form a quorum and hold a directors' meeting able to pass a resolution binding on the company. At the major's insistence a letter was still sent to the other four directors, simply stating that it was intended to hold a board meeting to discuss company business including the possibility of making a share issue.

In the event only the company secretary, the City solicitor, turned up. The resolution was passed, and the announcement of the new share issue posted. There was no need for a meeting of shareholders as in the long-distant past an increase in capital had been authorized but never carried out.

Existing shareholders were given the first choice to buy the stock and were sent allotment letters for the appropriate number of new shares. They were also given the right to apply for any shares not subscribed by those to whom they were originally offered.

Within a week papers and cheques signed by Messrs Adams, Ball, Carter and Davies, forwarded by the Zwingli Bank, were in the company secretary's hands. Each man opted to buy 50,000 of the new shares, including those originally allotted to them because of their existing holdings.

The shares had to be issued at par, which was four shillings each, and with the existing shares standing at less than a third of that price it was an unattractive offer. Two City speculators noticed the press announcement and tried to offer to underwrite the issue, assuming there had to be something in the wind. They would have succeeded, but for Mr Roberts. His own bid on behalf of the Zwingli Bank was already in, wishing to buy any shares remaining at the closure of the offer that had not been bought by existing shareholders of Bormac.

Some idiot in Wales agreed to buy a thousand shares, even at the too-high price, and another three thousand were bought by eighteen other shareholders scattered round the country, who apparently could not do basic arithmetic or were clairvoyant. Mr Roberts, as a nominee director, was not in a position to buy for himself, since he owned no stock. But for the remaining unsold shares at three in the afternoon of May 20th, the closing date of the offer, he subscribed for all the 296,000 in the name of the Zwingli Bank, who in turn was buying these on behalf of two of its customers. Their names happened to be Edwards and Frost. Again the bank used designated accounts of its nominee company.

In no case were the rules of the Companies Act regarding disclosure broken. Messrs Adams, Ball, Carter and Davies each owned 75,000 of the shares from their first purchase, and 50,000 from their second. But as the number of shares now in circulation had risen from a million to one and a half million, each man held less than ten percent and was able to remain anonymous. Messrs Edwards and Frost each owned 148,000 shares, just under the ten per cent limit.

What did not appear in public or even to the directors was that Sir James Manson owned 796,000 shares in Bormac, an overwhelming majority. He controlled, through Martin Thorpe, the six non-existent shareholders who had bought so heavily. They could, through Martin Thorpe, direct the Zwingli Bank in its dealings with the company, and the bank controlled his contracted servant Mr Roberts. Using their proxies, the six invisible men behind the Zwingli Bank, operating through Harold Roberts, could make the company do anything they wished.

It had cost Sir James Manson £60,000 to buy the original 300,000 shares, and £100,000 to buy up the bulk of the new issue of half a million. But when the shares reached the predicted £100 each, which he was sure they would do after the chance 'discovery' of the Crystal Mountain in the heart of Bormac's Zangaran franchise, he stood to make £80 million.

Mr Roberts was a contented man when he left the Bormac offices after hearing how many shares his six Swiss-based stockholders had been allotted. He knew that when he placed the share certificates in the hands of Dr Martin Steinhofer, there would be a handsome bonus for him. Although not a poor man, his retirement in comfort was secured.

In Dinant Shannon and Langarotti woke from their slumbers shortly after dark had fallen to find Marc shaking them. Both were stretched out in the back of the empty French van.

'Time to be going,' said the Belgian.

Shannon looked at his watch.

'I thought you said before sunrise,' he grumbled.

'That's when we go over,' said Marc. 'We ought to get these vans out of town before they become too noticeable. We can park by the roadside for the rest of the night.'

They did park, but none of the men slept any more. Instead they smoked and played cards with the pack Vlaminck kept in the glove compartment of his van. Sitting under the trees by the Belgian roadside in the darkness, waiting for the dawn, feeling the night air on their faces, each could almost think he was back in the African bush again, about to go into action, except for the flashing lights through the trees where cars headed south on the road to France.

As they sat through the wee small hours, tired of playing cards, too tensed to sleep, each fell back into his old habits. Tiny Marc munched the remnants of the bread and cheese his girl Anna had made for him. Langarotti stropped his knife blade a little sharper. Shannon gazed at the stars and whistled softly.

Chapter Seventeen

There is no great technical difficulty in running an illegal consignment across the Belgian–French border in either direction, and that includes a quantity of black market arms.

Between the sea at La Panne and the junction with Luxembourg near Longwy, this border sprawls for miles, and most of it in the south-east corner is through heavily wooded hunting country. Here the border is crossed by scores of side roads and tracks through the forest, and by no means all of them are manned.

Both governments seek to establish some kind of control, using what they call '*douanes volantes*', or flying Customs. These are units of Customs men who pick a track or side road at random and set up a border post. By using the existing Customs points, one may reasonably assume that one vehicle in ten is likely to be stopped and examined. On the unmanned roads, if the flying customs of either side happen to be sitting there for the day, every vehicle going through gets a check. One can take one's choice.

The third alternative is to pick a road where there is definitely no Customs post set up, and drive straight through. This method of running cargoes through the frontier is particularly favoured by the smugglers of French champagne, who see no reason why this drink connected with mirth and gaiety should receive the attentions of the very unhumorous Belgian import duty. As a bar owner, Marc Vlaminck knew about this route. It is called the Champagne Run.

Running south from Namur, the old fortress town of Belgium, following the line of the river Meuse, one comes first to Dinant, and from here the road runs almost due south over the border to the first French town, called Givet. along this road there is a finger of French territory that juts upwards into Belgium's underbelly, and this corridor of France is surrounded on three sides by Belgian territory. It is also a hunting forest and intersected by scores of tracks and paths. The main road from Dinant to Givet has a customs post on it – in fact, one Belgian post and one French, set four hundred yards apart but in sight of each other.

Shortly before dawn Marc got out his maps and briefed Shannon and Jean-Baptiste on what he needed to be sure of getting across the border unspotted. When both men understood exactly what was required, they set off in convoy, the Belgian van in front driven by Marc, the other two in the French van two hundred yards behind.

South from Dinant the road is fairly well built up, with a series of villages whose outskirts almost connect with each other. In the pre-dawn darkness these hamlets were quiet and obscure. At kilometre six, south of Dinant, there is a side road leading to the right, and this Marc took. It was the last they saw of the river Meuse. For four and a half kilometres they ran through undulating country of even-sized, rounded hills, thickly wooded and covered in the lush leafage of late May. The run was parallel to the border and into the heart of hunting country. Without warning Vlaminck swung his van off to the left, heading again towards the frontier, and after three to four hundred yards he pulled to the side. He climbed down and walked back to the French van.

'Make it snappy,' he said, 'I don't want to wait here for long. It's too obvious where I'm heading for, with Ostende number plates.' He pointed down the road.

'The border is down there at one and a half kilometres exactly. I'll give you twenty minutes while I pretend to change a tyre. Then I get back to Dinant and we meet at the café.'

The Corsican nodded and let in the clutch. The drill is, if either the Belgian or French Customs men have set up a flying barricade, the first vehicle stops and allows itself to be searched. Being clean, it then proceeds south to rejoin the main road, heads into Givet, turns north again and returns via the fixed Customs post to Dinant. If either Customs post is in operation, it cannot return back up the road within twenty minutes.

At kilometre one and a half Shannon and Langarotti saw the Belgian post. At each side of the road a vertical steel upright had been placed, embedded in concrete. Beside the right-hand one was a small glass and wooden booth, where the Customs men could shelter while drivers passed their papers through the window. If in occupation, there would be a red and white striped sole supported by both uprights, blocking the road. There was none.

Langarotti cruised slowly past, while Shannon scanned the booth. Not a sign. The French side was trickier. For half a kilometre the road wound between the flanks of the hills, lost to sight from the Belgian posts. Then came the French border. No posts, no booth. Just a lay-by on the left, where the French Customs van always parked. There was nothing there. They had been gone five minutes. Shannon gestured to the Corsican to go round two more corners, but there was nothing in sight. A glimmer of light showed in the east over the trees.

'Turn her round,' snapped Shannon. '*Allez.*'

Langarotti pulled the van into a tight turn, almost made it, backed up, and was off towards Belgium like a cork from a bottle of the very best champagne. From then on time was precious. They shot past the French lay-by, through the Belgian posts, and 1500 metres later saw the bulk of Marc's waiting van. Langarotti flashed his lights, two short, one long, and Marc gunned his engine into life. A second later he was past them, racing through to France.

Jean-Baptiste turned round more leisurely and followed. If Marc drove fast, he could be through the danger area within four minutes, even heavily laden with a ton of cargo. If any Customs men hove in sight in those vital five minutes, it was bad luck. Marc would try to bluff it out, say he had got lost, hope the oil barrels stood up to a thorough checking.

There were no officials there, even on the second run. South of the French lay-by is a five-kilometre stretch with no turnings. Even here the French gendarmerie sometimes patrol, but there was nothing that morning. Langarotti caught up with the Belgian van and followed it at two hundred metres. After five kilometres Marc turned off to the right at another lay-by, and for six more kilometres wended his way through more back-roads until he finally emerged onto a sizeable main road. There was a signpost by the roadside. Shannon saw Marc Vlaminck wave his arm out of the window and point to it. The sign said 'Givet' in the direction from which they had come, and pointed the way they were going with the word 'Reims'. A muted cheer came wafting back from the van in front.

They did the swap-over on a hard concrete car park next to a transport café just south of Soisson. The two vans, open-doored, were backed up tight against each other, and Marc eased the five barrels from the Belgian van to the French one. It would have taken Shannon and Langarotti together all their strength, the more so as the loaded van was squashed on its springs so the floors of the two vehicles were not at the same height. There was a six-inch step-up to get into the empty van. Marc managed it on his own, gripping each barrel at the top in huge hands and swinging it in arcs while balanced on its lower rim.

Jean-Baptiste went to the café and returned with a breakfast of long, crisp baguette loaves, cheese, fruit and coffee. Shannon had no knife, so they all used Marc's. Langarotti would never use his knife for eating. He had his finer feelings. It would dishonour the knife to use it on orange peel.

Just after ten they set off again. The drill was different. The Belgian van, being old and slow, was soon driven into a gravel pit and abandoned, the licence plates and windscreen sticker being taken off and thrown into a stream. The van was originally of French make anyway. After that the three proceeded together. Langarotti drove. It was legally his van. He was licensed. If stopped he would say he was driving five barrels of lubricating oil south to his friend who owned a farm and three tractors outside Toulon. The other two were hitchhikers he had picked up.

They left the A1 autoroute, took the peripheral road round Paris, and picked up the A6 south to Lyon, Avignon, Aix and Toulon.

Just south of Paris they saw the sign to the right pointing to Orly airport. Shannon climbed out and they shook hands.

'You know what to do?' he asked.

They both nodded.

'Keep her under cover and safe till you get to Toulon. Don't worry, no one will find this little baby when I've hidden her,' said Langarotti.

'The *Toscana* is due in by June 1st at the latest, maybe before. I'll be with you before then. You know the rendezvous? Then good luck.'

He hefted his grip and walked away as the van headed south. At the nearby garage he used the telephone, called a cab from the airport and was driven there an hour later. Paying cash he bought his single ticket to London and was home in St John's Wood by sundown. Of his hundred days, he had used up forty-six.

Although he sent Endean a telegram on his arrival home, it was a Sunday, and twenty-four hours before Endean rang him at the flat. They agreed to meet on the Tuesday morning.

It took him an hour to explain to Endean all that had happened since they last met. He also explained that he had used up all the money both in the cash sum he had retained in London, and the Belgian account.

'What's the next stage?' asked Endean.

'I have to return to France within five days at the latest and supervise the loading of the first section of the cargo onto the *Toscana*,' said Shannon. 'Everything about the shipment is legal except what's in those oil barrels. The four separate crates of assorted uniforms and webbing should pass without any problem on board, even if examined by Customs. The same goes for the non-military stuff bought in Hamburg. Everything in that section is the sort of stuff a ship might normally take on as ship's stores; distress flares, night glasses and so forth.

'The inflatable dinghies and outboard engines are for shipping to Morocco, at least that's what the manifest will say. Again, it's perfectly legal. The five oil drums have to go aboard as ship's stores. The quantity is rather excessive, but there shouldn't be any problem despite that.'

'And if there is?' asked Endean. 'If Toulon Customs men examine those barrels too closely?'

'We're busted,' said Shannon simply. 'The ship impounded unless the captain can show he hadn't a clue what was going on. The exporter arrested. The operation wrecked.'

'Bloody expensively,' observed Endean.

'What do you expect? The guns have got to go on board somehow. The oil barrels are about the best way possible. There was always that risk involved.'

'You could have bought the submachine guns legally, through Spain,' said Endean.

'I could,' Shannon conceded, 'but there would then have been a good chance the order would have been refused. The guns and the ammo together make a matching pair. That would have looked like a special order to outfit one company of men; in other words, a small operation. Madrid might have turned it down on those grounds, or examined the end user certificate too thoroughly. I could have ordered the guns from Spain and bought the ammunition on the "black". Then I would have had to smuggle the ammo on board, and it would have been a much bigger consignment. Either way, there has to be an element of smuggling, and hence of risk. So if it all goes wrong, it'll be me and my men who go down, not you. You're protected by a series of cut-outs.'

'I still don't like it,' snapped Endean.

'What's the matter?' Shannon mocked. 'Losing your nerve?'

'No.'

'So cool it. All you have to lose is a bit of money.'

Endean was on the verge of telling Shannon just how much he and his employer stood to lose, but thought better of it. Logic dictated that if the mercenary was going to face prison, he would be as careful as possible.

They talked finance for another hour. Shannon explained that the payment of Johann Schlinker in full, and half to Alan Baker, along with the mercenaries' second month's salary, the £5000 he had transformed to Genoa to fit out the *Toscana*, and his own travelling, had emptied the Brugge account.

'Also,' he added, 'I want my second half of salary.'

'Why now?' asked Endean.

'Because the risks of arrest start next Monday and I shall not be returning to London after that. If the ship is loaded without fuss, she sails for Brindisi while I arrange the pick-up of the Yugoslav arms. After that, Valencia and the Spanish ammunition. Then we head for the target. If I'm ahead of schedule, I'd prefer to kill the extra time on the high seas rather than wait in a port. From the moment that ship has hardware on board, I want her in port as little as possible.'

Endean digested the argument.

'I'll put it to my associates,' he said.

'I want the stuff in my Swiss account before the weekend,' countered Shannon, 'and the rest of the agreed budget transferred to Brugge.'

They worked out that with Shannon's salary paid in full, there would be £20,000 left in Switzerland of the original money.

Shannon explained why he needed the lot.

'From now on I need a wad of big-denomination travellers cheques in US dollars on me all the time. If anything goes wrong from now, it can only be of a nature where a fat bribe on the spot might sort out the problem. I want to tidy up all the remaining traces, so that if we all get the chop, there are no clues left. Also, I may need to make cash bonuses on the spot to the ship's crewmen to persuade them to go ahead when they find out what the job really is, as they must when we are at sea. With the last half-payment for the Yugoslav arms still to come, I could need up to £20,000.'

Endean agreed to report all this to 'his associates' and let Shannon know.

The following day he rang back to say that both transfers of the money had been authorized and the letters instructing the Swiss bank had been sent.

Shannon booked his ticket from London to Brussels for the following Friday and a Saturday-morning flight from Brussels to Paris to Marseilles.

He spent that night with Julie, and Thursday as well and Thursday night. Then he packed his bags, mailed the flat keys with an explanatory letter to the estate agents and left. Julie drove him to the airport in her red MGB.

'When are you coming back?' she asked him as they stood outside the

'Departing Passengers Only' entrance to the Customs area of Number Two Building.

'I won't be coming back,' he said, and gave her a kiss.

'Then let me come with you.'

'No.'

'You will come back. I haven't asked where you are going, but I know it has to be dangerous. It's not just business, not ordinary business. But you will come back. You must.'

'I won't be coming back,' he said quietly. 'Go find someone else, Julie.'

She began to sniffle.

'I don't want anybody else. I love you. You don't love me. That's why you're saying you won't see me again. You've got another woman, that's what it is. You're going to see another woman ...'

'There's no other woman,' he said, stroking her hair. An airport policeman looked discreetly away. Tears in the departure lounge are not uncommon anywhere. There would be, Shannon knew, no other woman in his arms. Just a gun, the cool comforting caress of the blued steel against his chest in the night. She was still crying when he kissed her on the forehead and walked through into passport control.

Thirty minutes later the Sabena jet made its last turn over south London and headed for its home in Brussels. Below the starboard wing the county of Kent was spread out in the sunshine. Weatherwise, it had been a beautiful month of May. From the portholes one could see the acres of blossom where the apple, pear and cherry orchards covered the land in pink and white.

Along the lanes that trickle through the heart of the Weald, the maythorn would be out, the horse-chestnut trees glowing with green and white, the pigeons clattering among the oaks. He knew the country well from the time years ago when he had been stationed at Chatham and had bought an old motor cycle to explore the ancient country pubs between Lamberhurst and Smarden. Good country, good country to settle down in, if you were the settling type.

Ten minutes later one of the passengers further back summoned the stewardess to complain about someone up front who was whistling a monotonous little tune.

It took Cat Shannon two hours on Friday afternoon to withdraw the money transferred from Switzerland and close his account. He took two certified bank cheques, each for £5000, which could be converted into a bank account somewhere else, and from that into more travellers cheques; and the other £10,000 in fifty 500-dollar cheques that needed only counter-signature to be used as cash.

He spent that night in Brussels and flew the next morning to Paris and Marseilles.

A taxi from the airport brought him to the small hotel in the outskirts where Langarotti had once lived under the name of Lavallon, and where Janni Dupree, still following orders, was in residence. He was out at the time, so Shannon waited until he returned that evening, and together they drove in a hire-car Shannon had engaged to Toulon. It was the end of Day Fifty-Two, and the sprawling French naval port was bathed in warm sunshine.

During Sunday the shipping agent's office was not open, but it made no matter. The rendezvous spot was the pavement in front of it, and here Shannon and Dupree met Marc Vlaminck and Langarotti on the dot of nine o'clock. It was the first time they had been together for weeks, and only Semmler was missing. He should be a hundred miles or so along the coast, steaming offshore in the *Toscana* towards Toulon.

At Shannon's suggestion Langarotti telephoned the harbourmaster's office from a nearby café and ascertained that the *Toscana*'s agents in Genoa had cabled that she was due in on Monday morning and that her berth was reserved.

There was nothing more to do that day, so they went in Shannon's car along the coast road towards Marseilles and spent the day swimming at the cobbled fishing port of Sanary. Despite the heat and the holiday atmosphere of the picturesque little town, Shannon could not relax. Only Dupree bought himself a pair of swimming trunks and dived off the end of the mole of the yacht harbour. He said later the water was still damn cold. It would warm up later, through June and July when the tourists began to pour south from Paris. By then they would all be preparing to strike at another harbour town, not much larger and many miles away.

Shannon sat for most of the day with the Belgian and Corsican on the terrace of Charley's bar, the Pot D'Etain, soaking up the sunshine and thinking of the morning. The Yugoslav or the Spanish shipment might not turn up, or might be late, or might be blocked for some as yet unknown bureaucratic reason, but there would be no reason for them to be arrested in Yugoslavia or Spain. They might be held for a few days while the boat was searched, but that would be all. The following morning was different. If anyone insisted on peering deep into those oil barrels, there would be months, maybe years, spent sweating in Les Baumettes, the great forbidding fortress prison he had passed on Saturday as he drove from Marseilles to Toulon.

The waiting was always the worst, he reflected as he settled the bill and called his three colleagues to the car.

It turned out to be smoother than they thought. Toulon is known as an enormous navy base, and the skyline at the harbour is dominated by the superstructures of the French Navy warships lying at anchor. The centre of attraction for the tourists and the strollers of Toulon that Monday was the battle cruiser *Jean Bart*, home from a voyage to the French Caribbean territories, full of sailors with back-pay to spend and looking for girls.

Along the broad sweep of esplanade fronting the leisure harbour the cafés were full of people indulging the favourite pastime of every Mediterranean country – watching life go by. They sat in brightly coloured hordes gazing from the shaded awnings across the half-mile of bobbing yachts, from little outboard-powered runabouts to the sleek sea greyhounds of the very rich.

Up against the eastward quay were the dozen fisher boats that had elected not to go to sea, and behind these were the long, low customs sheds, warehouses and harbour offices.

It was beyond these, in the small and hardly observed commercial port, that the *Toscana* slipped into her berth just before noon.

Shannon waited till she was tied up, and from his seat on a bollard fifty metres away he could see Semmler and Waldenberg moving about the decks. There was no sign of the Serbian engineer, probably still in his beloved engine room, but two other figures were also on deck, making fast the coiling ropes. These had to be the two new crewmen recruited by Waldenberg.

A small Renault buzzed along the quay and came to a halt by the gangway. A rotund Frenchman in a dark suit emerged and went aboard the *Toscana*. The representative of Agence Maritime Duphot. Before long he came back down, followed by Waldenberg, and the two strolled over to the Customs shed. It was nearly an hour before the two men emerged, the shipping agent to return to his car and drive away into the town, the German captain to get back to his ship.

Shannon gave them another thirty minutes, then he too strolled up the gangway and onto the *Toscana*. Semmler beckoned him into the companionway that led down to the crew's saloon.

'So, what's been going on?' Shannon asked, when he and Semmler were seated below. Semmler grinned.

'All smooth and easy,' he said. 'I got the papers changed to show the new captain, had a complete engine service done, bought an unnecessarily large amount of blankets and a dozen foam-rubber mattresses. No one asked any questions, and the captain still thinks we are going to run immigrants into Britain.

'I used the *Toscana*'s usual shipping agent in Genoa to book us in here and the manifest says we are taking on a mixed cargo of sporting goods and leisure equipment for a holiday camp on the coast of Morocco.'

'What about the engine lubricating oil?'

Semmler grinned.

'It was all ordered, then I called and cancelled it. When it didn't arrive, Waldenberg wanted to delay for a day and wait for it. I vetoed that and said we would get it here in Toulon.'

'Fine,' said Shannon, 'don't let Waldenberg order it. Tell him you've done it yourself. Then when it arrives he'll be expecting it. That man who came on board ...'

'The shipping agent. He has all the stuff still in bond, and the papers prepared. He's sending it down this afternoon in a couple of vans. The crates are so small we can load them ourselves with the derrick.'

'Good. Let him and Waldenberg sort out the paperwork. An hour after the stuff is all aboard, the fuel company van will arrive with the oil. Driven by Langarotti. You have enough money left to pay for it?'

'Yes.'

'Then pay for it in full, cash, and get a signed receipt. Just make sure no one bangs it about too hard as it goes aboard. The last thing we need is for the bottom of one of the barrels to fall out. The quay will be waist-deep in Schmeissers.'

'When do the men come aboard?'

'Tonight after dark. One by one. Just Marc and Janni. I'm leaving Jean-Baptiste here for a while. He has the van, and there's one more job to be done at this end. When can you sail?'

'Any time. Tonight. I can fix it. Actually, it's rather nice being the managing director.'

'Don't get too accustomed to it. It's only a front.'

'OK, Cat. Incidentally, where are we going when we leave?'

'Brindisi. Know it?'

'Sure I know it. I've run more cigarettes into Italy from Yugoslavia than you've had hot dinners. What do we pick up there?'

'Nothing. You wait for my telegram. I'll be in Germany. I'll cable you through the port office at Brindisi with the next destination and the day you have to arrive. Then you must get a local agent to cable the Yugoslav port in question and reserve a berth. Are you OK to go to Yugoslavia?'

'I think so. Anyway, I won't get off the ship. We pick up more arms?'

'Yes. At least, that's the plan. I just have to hope my arms dealer and the Yugoslav officals have not cocked it up. Do you have all the charts you need?'

'Yes, I bought them all in Genoa as you told me. You know, Waldenberg will have to realize what we are taking on board in Yugoslavia. Then he'll know we aren't running illegal immigrants. He accepts the speedboats and the engines, the walkie-talkies and the clothing as quite normal, but arms are something else again.'

'I know,' said Shannon. 'It will cost a bit of money. But I think he'll get the message. There'll be you and me, Janni and Marc, on board. Besides, by then we can tell him what's in the oil drums. He'll be so far in by then, he'll have to go along. What are the two new crewmen like?'

Semmler nodded and stubbed out his fifth cigarette. The air was a blue haze in the small saloon.

'Good. Two Italians. Hard boys, but obedient. I think they're both wanted by the carabinieri for something. They were so pleased to get on board and under cover. They couldn't wait to get to sea.'

'Fine. Then they won't want to be put ashore in a foreign country. That would mean they'd be picked up without papers and repatriated, straight into the hands of their own police.'

Waldenberg had done well. Shannon met both men briefly and short nods were exchanged. Semmler simply introduced him as a man from head office, and Waldenberg translated. The men, Norbiatto the first mate and Cipriani the deckhand, evinced no further interest. Shannon exchanged a few instructions with Waldenberg and left.

In mid-afternoon the two vans from Agence Maritime Duphot rolled to a stop by the *Toscana*, accompanied by the same man who had appeared that morning. A French Customs officer, clipboard in hand, emerged from the Customs house and stood by as the crates were swung inboard by the ship's derrick. Four crates of assorted rough clothing, belts, boots and caps, for the Moroccan workers at the holiday village; three crated large-size inflatable dinghies for sporting and leisure purposes – three outboard engines for same; two crates assorted flares, binoculars, ship's gas-powered foghorn, radio parts and magnetic compasses. The last crates were listed under ship's stores.

The Customs officer ticked them off as they went aboard and confirmed with the shipping agent that they were either bonded for re-export, having arrived from Germany or Britain, or they were locally bought and carried no export duty. The Customs man did not even want to look inside the crates. He knew the agency well, dealing with them every day.

When it was all aboard, the Customs man stamped the ship's cargo manifest. Waldenberg said something to Semmler in German, and the latter translated. He explained to the agency that Waldenberg needed lubricating oil for his engines. It had been ordered in Genoa, but had not been delivered in time.

The agency man noted in his book.

'How much do you need?'

'Five drums,' said Semmler. Waldenberg did not understand the French.

'That's a lot,' said the agent.

Semmler laughed. 'This old bucket uses as much oil as diesel. Besides, we might as well get it here and have enough for a long time to come.'

'When do you need it?' asked the agent.

'Five this afternoon be all right?' asked Semmler.

'Make it six,' said the agency man, noting the type and quantity in his notebook, along with the hour of delivery. He looked up at the Customs man. The official nodded. He was uninterested, and strolled away. Shortly after, the agency man left in his car, followed by the two vans.

At five o'clock Semmler left the *Toscana*, went to a phone in a café on the waterfront, rang the agency and cancelled the oil order. The skipper, he said, had discovered a full barrel at the rear of the stores locker and would not be needing any more for several weeks. The agency man was disgruntled but agreed.

At six a van drove carefully along the quay and stopped opposite the *Toscana*. It was driven by Jean-Baptiste Langarotti in a bright green overall suit with the word Castrol on the back.

Opening the back of the van, he carefully rolled five large oil drums down the plank he had fitted to the rear step. From the window of the Customs house the duty officer peered out.

Waldenberg caught his eye and waved. He pointed to the barrels and back to his ship.

'OK?' he called, adding with a thick accent, '*Ça va*?'

From the window the Customs man nodded and withdrew to make a note on his clipboard. At Waldenberg's orders the two Italian crewmen slipped cradles under the barrels and one by one winched them aboard. Semmler was uncommonly eager to help, steadying the drums as they swung over the ship's rail, shouting in German to Waldenberg on the winch to let them down easily. They slid out of sight into the dark, cool hold of the *Toscana* and soon the hatch was back in place and clamped down.

Langarotti, having made his despatch, had long since left in his van. A few minutes later the overall suit was at the bottom of a waste bin in the heart of the town. From his bollard at the other end of the quay Shannon had watched the loading with bated breath. He would have preferred to be involved, like Semmler, for the waiting was almost physically painful, worse than going into action.

When it was over, things quietened down on the *Toscana*. The captain and his three men were below decks, the engineer having taken one turn of the ship to sniff the salt air and then having gone back to his diesel fumes. Semmler gave them half an hour, then slipped down to the quay and came to join Shannon. They met up round three corners and out of sight of the harbour.

Semmler was grinning.

'I told you. No problems.'

Shannon nodded, and grinned back with the relief. He knew better than Semmler what was at stake, and unlike the German he was not familiar with port procedures.

'When can you take the men aboard?'

'The Customs office closes at nine. They should come between twelve and one in the morning. We sail at five. It's fixed.'

'Good,' said Shannon, 'let's go and find them and have a drink. I want you back there quickly in case there are any inquiries still to come.'

'There won't be.'

'Never mind. We'll play safe. I want you to watch that cargo like a mother hen. Don't let anyone near those barrels till I say so, and that will be in a harbour in Yugoslavia. Then we tell Waldenberg what he's carrying.'

They met the other three mercenaries at a prearranged café and had several beers to cool down. The sun was setting and the sea within the vast bowl of land that forms the anchorage and rods of Toulon was ruffled by only a slight breeze. A few yachts pirouetted like ballerinas far out on the stage as their crews brought them about, to catch the next gust. Semmler left them at eight and returned to the *Toscana*.

Janni Dupree and Marc Vlaminck slipped quietly aboard between midnight and one, and at five, watched from the quay by Shannon and Langarotti, the *Toscana* slipped back to the sea.

Langarotti ran Shannon to the airport in the mid-morning to catch his plane. Over breakfast Shannon had given the Corsican his last set of instructions and enough money to carry them out.

'I'd prefer to be going with you,' Jean-Baptiste said, 'or with the ship.'

'I know,' said Shannon. 'But I need someone good to do this part of it. It's vital. Without it we can't go through. I need someone reliable, and you have the added advantage of being French. Besides, you know two of the men well, and one speaks a smattering of French. Janni couldn't go in there with a South African passport. Marc I need to intimidate the crew if they cut up rough. I know you're better with a knife than he is with his hands, but I don't want a fight, just enough to persuade the crew to do what they're told. And I need Kurt to check the navigation, in case Waldenberg chickens out. In fact, if the worst comes to the worst, and Waldenberg goes over the side, Kurt has to skipper the ship. So it has to be you.'

Langarotti agreed to go on the mission.

'They're good boys,' he said with a little more enthusiasm. 'It will be good to see them again.'

When they parted at the airport, Shannon reminded him. 'It can all fall through if we get there and have no back-up force. So it depends on you to do it right. It's all set up. Just do what I said and cope with the small problems as they arise. I'll see you in a month.'

He left the Corsican, walked through Customs and boarded his plane for Paris and Hamburg.

Chapter Eighteen

'My information is that you can pick up the mortars and bazookas any time after June 10th, and that was re-confirmed yesterday by telex,' Alan Baker told him.

It was the day after Shannon's arrival in Hamburg, and they had met in a restaurant for lunch after a mid-morning telephone call to fix a rendezvous.

'What port?' asked Shannon.

'Ploce.'

'Where?'

'Ploce. Spelt P–l–o–c–e, pronounced Plochay. It's a small port almost exactly half-way between Split and Dubrovnik.'

Shannon thought. He had ordered Semmler while in Genoa to pick up the necessary sea charts to cover the whole Yugoslav coast, but he had supposed the pick-up would be at one of the larger ports. He hoped the German had got a chart covering the sea approaches to Ploce, or could get one at Brindisi.

'How small?'

'Quite small. Very discreet. Half a dozen wharves and two large warehouses. The Yugoslavs usually use it for their arms exports. The last shipment out of Yugoslavia I did by plane, but I was told at that time if it was to be by sea, it would be from Ploce. It's better if it's a small port. There's usually a berth, and loading facilities are quicker. Moreover, the Customs there must be a very small unit, probably with one lowly man in charge, and if he gets his present, he'll see everything on board within a few hours.'

'OK, Ploce. On June 11th,' said Shannon. Baker noted the date.

'The *Toscana* is OK?' he asked. He still wished he could have clinched the deal for his friend who ran the *San Andrea*, but decided to bear the *Toscana* in mind for later use. Shannon, he was sure, would have little use for her after whatever operation he was mounting was finished, and Baker was always on the lookout for a good boat for running his cargoes into deserted coves.

'She's fine,' said Shannon. 'She's running for an Italian port now, where I have to let her know by telex or letter where to head for. Any problems at your end?'

Baker shifted slightly.

'One,' he said. 'The price.'

'What about it?'

'I know I quoted you fixed prices, totalling 14,400 dollars. But the system inside Yugoslavia has changed over the past six months. To get the paperwork through on time, I had to engage a Yugoslav partner. At least, that's what he is called, though in fact he's another middleman.'

'So?' asked Shannon.

'So he has to get a fee or salary for getting the paperwork through the Belgrade office. On balance, I supposed it was worth it to you to have the shipment ready on time, and no bureaucratic hang-ups. So I agreed to engage him. He's the brother-in-law of the official in the Trade Ministry. It's another way of taking a kickback. But what can you expect these days? The Balkans are still the Balkans, and they've got wised up.'

'How much extra will he cost?'

"A thousand pounds sterling.'

'In dinars or dollars?'

'In dollars.'

Shannon thought it over. It might be the truth, or it might be that Baker was trying to squeeze a bit more out of him. If it was the truth, refusing to pay would simply force Baker to pay the Yugoslav out of his own cut. That would reduce Baker's margin to such a small amount, he might lose interest in the deal, not caring whether it went through or not. And he still needed Baker, and would need him until he saw the white wake of the *Toscana* heading out of Ploce harbour on her way to Spain.

'All right,' he said. 'Who is this partner?'

'Fellow called Ziljak. He's out there now, taking care of the shipment right up to Ploce and into the warehouse there. When the ship comes in, he'll get the stuff from the warehouse, through Customs and onto the boat.'

'I thought that was your job.'

'It is, but now I have to engage a Yugoslav as partner. Honestly, Cat, they let me no alternative.'

'Then I'll pay him personally, in travellers cheques.'

'I wouldn't,' said Baker.

'Why not?'

'The buyers of this shipment are supposed to be the government of Togo, right? Black men. Another white turns up, obviously the paymaster, and they might begin to smell a rat. We can go to Ploce if you like, or I can go alone.

But if you want to come with me, you'll have to come ostensibly as my assistant. Besides, travellers cheques have to be cashed at a bank, and in Yugoslavia that means they take the man's name and identity card number. If someone cashing them in is a Yugoslav, there are questions asked. It would be better if Ziljak got cash as he has asked.'

'All right. I'll cash some cheques here in Hamburg and I'll pay him in dollar bills,' said Shannon. 'But you get yours in cheques. I'm not carrying vast sums of dollars in cash around. Not to Yugoslavia. They get sensitive about that sort of thing. Security gets interested. They think you're funding a spy operation. So we go as tourists with travellers cheques.'

'Fine by me,' said Baker. 'When do you want to go?'

Shannon glanced at his watch. The next day would be the first of June.

'Day after tomorrow,' he said. 'We'll fly to Dubrovnik and have a week in the sun. I could do with a rest anyway. Or you can join me on the 8th or 9th, but not a day later. I'll hire a car and we can motor up the coast to Ploce on the 10th. I'll have the *Toscana* come in that night or early on the morning of the 11th.'

'You go on alone,' said Baker. 'I have work to do in Hamburg. I'll join you on the 8th.'

'Without fail,' said Shannon. 'If you don't turn up, I'll come looking. And I'll be hopping mad.'

'I'll come,' said Baker. 'I still want the balance of my money, don't forget. So far, I'm out of pocket on this deal. I want it to go through just as much as you.'

That was the way Shannon wanted him to feel.

'You do have the money, I suppose,' asked Baker, fingering a lump of sugar.

Shannon flicked through a booklet of large-denomination dollar cheques under Baker's nose. The arms dealer smiled.

They left the table and on the way out used the restaurant telephone to ring a Hamburg charter company specializing in package tours for the thousands of Germans who holiday along the Adriatic coast. From this company they learned the names of the three best hotels in the Yugoslav resort. Baker was told he would find Shannon in one of them under the name of Keith Brown.

Johann Schlinker was as confident as Baker that he could fulfil his arms deal, though he had no idea that Baker was also doing business with Shannon. No doubt the men knew of each other, might even be acquainted, but there would not be a question of discussing each other's business together.

'The port should be Valencia, though this has yet to be fixed and is in any case the choice of the Spanish authorities,' he told Shannon. 'Madrid tells me the dates have to be between the 16th and 20th of June.'

'I'd prefer the 20th for loading,' said Shannon. 'The *Toscana* should be permitted to berth on or during the night of the 19th and load in the morning.'

'Good,' said Schlinker. 'I'll inform my Madrid partner. He habitually handles the transporting and loading side of things, and employs a first-class freight agent in Valencia who knows all the Customs personnel very well. There should be no problem.'

'There must be no problem,' growled Shannon. 'The ship has been delayed already once, and by loading on the 20th I have enough sailing time but no margin to fulfil my own contract.'

It was not true, but he saw no reason why Schlinker should not believe it was true.

'I shall want to watch the loading also,' he told the arms dealer.

Schlinker pursed his lips. 'You may watch it from afar, of course,' he said. 'I cannot stop you. But as the customers are supposed to be an Arab government, you cannot propose to be an Arab government, you cannot propose yourself as the buyer of the merchandise.'

'I also want to board the ship at Valencia,' said Shannon.

'That will be even harder. The whole port area is sealed off inside a chain-link fence. Entry is by authority only. To board the ship you would have to go through passport control. Also, as she will be carrying ammunition, there will be a Guardia Civil at the bottom of the gangplank.'

'Supposing the captain needed another crewman. Could he engage a seaman locally?'

Schlinker thought it over.

'I suppose so. Are you connected with the company owning the vessel?'

'Not on paper,' said Shannon.

'If the captain informed the agent on arrival that he had permitted one of his crewmen to leave the vessel at its last port of call to fly home and attend his mother's funeral, and that the crewman would be rejoining the vessel at Valencia, I suppose there would be no objection. But you would need a merchant seaman's card to prove you were a seaman. And in the same name as yourself, Mr Brown.'

Shannon thought for a few minutes.

'OK. I'll fix it,' he said.

Schlinker consulted his diary.

'As it happens I shall be in Madrid on the 19th and 20th,' he said. 'I have another business deal to attend to. I shall be at the Mindanao Hotel. If you want to contact me, you can find me there. If loading is for the 20th, the chances are the convoy and escort from the Spanish Army will run the shipment down to the coast during the night of the 19th to arrive at crack of dawn. If you are going to board the ship at all, I think you should do so before the military convoy arrives at the docks.'

'I could be in Madrid on the 19th,' said Shannon. 'Then I could check with you that the convoy had indeed left on time. By driving fast to Valencia, I could be there ahead of it, and board the *Toscana* as the rejoining seaman before the convoy arrives.'

'That is entirely up to you,' said Schlinker. 'For my part, I will have my agents arrange the freighting, transportation and loading, according to all the normal procedures, for dawn of the 20th. That is what I contracted to do. If there is any risk attached to your boarding the vessel in harbour, that must be your affair. I cannot take responsibility for that. I can only point out that ships carrying arms out of Spain are subjected to scrutiny by the Army and Customs authorities. If anything goes wrong with the loading and clearance of the ship to sail, because of you, that is not my responsibility. One other thing. After loading arms a ship must leave a Spanish port within six hours, and may not re-enter Spanish waters until the cargo has been off-loaded. Also, the manifest must be in perfect order.'

'It will be,' said Shannon. 'I'll be with you in Madrid on the morning of the 19th.'

Before leaving Toulon Kurt Semmler had given Shannon a letter to post. It was from Semmler to the *Toscana*'s shipping agents in Genoa. It informed them there had been a slight change of plan, and that the *Toscana* would be proceeding from Toulon not directly to Morocco but first to Brindisi to pick up further cargo. The order, Semmler informed the agents, had been secured locally by him in Toulon and was lucrative, since it was a rush order, whereas the consignment of mixed cargo from Toulon to Morocco was in no hurry. As managing director of Spinetti Maritimo, Semmler's instructions were those of the boss. He required the Genoa agents to cable Brindisi reserving a berth for June 7th and 8th, and to instruct the port office to hold any mail addressed to the *Toscana* for collection when she berthed.

Such a letter was what Shannon wrote and despatched from Hamburg. It was to Signor Kurt Semmler, MV *Toscana*, c/o The Post Office, Brindisi, Italy.

In it he told Semmler that from Brindisi he should proceed to Ploce on the Adriatic coast of Yugoslavia, and that if he had no charts to negotiate the tricky straits north of Korcula Island, he should get them locally. He had to get the *Toscana* there on the evening of June 10th, and his berth would be reserved. There was no need to inform the agents in Genoa of the extra leg from Brindisi to Ploce.

His last instruction to Semmler was important. He told the German ex-smuggler he wanted him to acquire a merchant seaman's card for a deckhand called Keith Brown, stamped and up to date, and issued by the Italian authorities. The second thing the ship would need was a cargo manifest showing the *Toscana* had proceeded straight from Brindisi to Valencia to Latakia, Syria, after taking cargo aboard in Valencia without a halt, and would be heading from Valencia. Semmler would have to use his old Brindisi contacts to obtain these documents.

Before leaving Hamburg for Yugoslavia, Shannon's last letter was to Simon Endean in London. It required Endean to meet Shannon at a rendezvous in Rome on the 16th of June, and to bring certain maritime charts with him.

About the same time, the MV *Toscana* was chugging steadily through the Bight of Bonifacio, the narrow channel of limpid blue water that separates the southern tip of Corsica from the northern end of Sardinia. The sun was blistering, but mellowed by a light wind. Marc Vlaminck was stretched out, stripped to the waist, on the hatch cover of the main hold, a wet towel beneath him, his torso like a pink hippopotamus covered in suntan oil. Janni Dupree, who always went a brick red in the sun, was propped up against the wall of the after structure, under the awning, swigging from his tenth bottle of beer of the morning. Cipriani, the deckhand, was painting part of the rail round the forepeak white, and the first mate, Norbiatto, was snoozing on his bunk down below after taking the night watch.

Also down below, in the stinking heat of the engine room, was the engineer, Grubic, oiling some piece of machinery that only he could understand but which no doubt was vital to keep the *Toscana* steady on her eight knots through the Mediterranean. In the wheelhouse Kurt Semmler and Carl Waldenberg were sipping cold beer and exchanging reminiscences of their respective careers.

Jean-Baptiste Langarotti would have liked to be there. From the port rail he could have watched the grey-white, sun-bleached coast of his homeland slipping past barely four miles across the water. But he was many miles away, in West Africa, where the rain season was already begun and where, despite the fever heat, the clouds were leaden grey.

Alan Baker came into Shannon's hotel in Dubrovnik just as the mercenary was returning from the beach on the evening of June 8th. He looked tired and dusty.

Cat Shannon by contrast was looking and feeling better. He had spent his week in the Yugoslav holiday resort behaving like any other tourist, sunbathing and swimming several miles each day. He looked thinner, but fit and tanned. He was also optimistic.

After settling into his hotel he had sent Semmler a cable at Brindisi requesting confirmation of the arrival of the vessel and receipt of the waiting letter mailed from Hamburg. That morning he had got Semmler's telegrammed reply. The *Toscana* had arrived safely in Brindisi, the letter had been received and acted on, and they would depart on the morning of the 9th to make destination by midnight of the 10th.

Over drinks on the terrace of their hotel, where Shannon had booked Baker a room for the night, he told the dealer from Hamburg the news. Baker nodded and smiled.

'Fine. I got a cable forty-eight hours ago from Ziljak in Belgrade. The crates have arrived in Ploce and are in the government warehouse near the quay under guard.'

They spent the night in Dubrovnik and the following morning hired a taxi to take them the hundred kilometres up the coast to Ploce. It was a boneshaker of a car, that appeared to have square wheels and cast-iron suspension, but the drive along the coast road was agreeable, mile upon mile of unspoilt coastline, with the small town of Slano at the half-way mark, where they stopped for a cup of coffee and to stretch their limbs.

They were established in their hotel by lunchtime, and waited in the shade of the terrace until the port office opened again at four in the afternoon.

The port was set on a broad sweep of deep blue water, shielded to its seaward side by a long peninsula of land called Peliesac, which curved out of the main coast to the south of Ploce and ran northwards parallel to the coast. Up to the north the gap between the tip of the peninsula and the coast was almost blocked by the rocky island of Hvar, and only a narrow gap gave access to the sea lagoon on which Ploce stood. This lagoon, nearly thirty miles long, surrounded on nine-tenths of its perimeter by land, was a paradise for swimming, fishing and sailing.

As they approached the port office a small and battered Volkswagen squealed to a halt a few yards away and hooted noisily. Shannon froze. His first instinct said trouble, something he had been fearing all along, some slip-up in the paperwork, a sudden block put on the whole deal by the authorities, and an extended stay under questioning in the local police station.

The man who climbed out of the small car and waved cheerily might have been a policeman, except that the police in most totalitarian states of East or West seemed to be banned from smiling by Standing Orders. Shannon glanced at Baker and saw his shoulders sag in relief.

'Ziljak,' he muttered through closed mouth, and went to meet the Yugoslav. He was a big, shaggy man, like an amiable black-haired bear, and he embraced Baker with both arms. When he was introduced, his first name turned out to be Kemal, and Shannon supposed there was more than a touch of Turk in the man. That suited Shannon fine; he liked the type, normally good fighters and comrades, with a healthy dislike of bureaucracy.

'My assistant,' said Baker, and Ziljak shook hands and muttered something in what Shannon assumed to be Serbo-Croat. Baker and Ziljak communicated in German, which many Yugoslavs speak a little. He spoke no English.

With Ziljak's assistance, they knocked up the head of the Customs office and were taken off to inspect the warehouse. The Customs man jabbered a few words at the guard on the door, and in the corner of the building they found the crates. There were thirteen of them; one apparently contained the two bazookas, and two others contained one mortar including the base-plates and sighting mechanisms in each. The rest were of ammunition, four of them with ten bazooka rockets in each, and the other six containing the ordered three hundred mortar bombs. The crates were in new timber, unmarked with any description of contents, but stencilled with serial numbers and the word *Toscana*.

Ziljak and the Customs chief babbled away in their own dialect, and it appeared they were using the same one, which was helpful because there are dozens in Yugoslavia including seven major languages, and difficulties have been known to occur.

Eventually Ziljak turned to Baker and said several sentences in his halting German. Baker replied and Ziljak translated for the Customs Man. He smiled and they all shook hands and parted. Outside the sunshine struck like a sledgehammer.

'What was all that about?' asked Shannon.

'Kemal was asked by the Customs man if there was a little present in it for him,' explained Baker. 'Kemal told him there would be a nice one if the paperwork could be kept trouble-free and the ship was loaded on time tomorrow morning.'

Shannon had already given Baker the first half of Ziljak's £1000 bonus for helping the deal go through, and Baker drew the Yugoslav to one side to slip it to him. The man's all-embracing bonhomie became even more embracing for both of them, and they adjourned to the hotel to celebrate with a little slivovits. A little was the word Baker had used. Ziljak may have used the same word. He did not mean it. Happy Yugoslavs never drink a little slivovits. With £500 under his belt, Ziljak ordered a bottle of the fiery plum liquor and bowl after bowl of almonds and olives. As the sun went down and the Adriatic evening slipped through the streets, he relived again his years in the war, hunting and hiding in the Bosnian hills to the north with Tito's partisans.

Baker was hard put to it to translate as the exuberant Kemal related his forays behind Dubrovnik in Montenegro, in the mountains behind where they sat, the coast of Herzogovina, and among the cooler, richer, wooded countryside north of Split in Bosnia. He relished the thought that he would once have been shot out of hand for venturing into any of the towns where now he drove on behalf of his brother-in-law who was in the government. Shannon asked if he was a committed Communist, having been a partisan, and Ziljak listened while Baker translated, using the word 'good' for 'committed'. Ziljak thumped his chest with his fist.

'*Guter Kommunist*,' he exclaimed, eyes wide, pointing at himself. Then he ruined the effect by giving a broad wink, throwing back his head and roaring with laughter as he tossed another glass of slivovits down the hatch. The folded notes of his first £500 bonus made a bulge under his waistband, and Shannon laughed too, and wished the giant was coming along to Zangaro with them. He was that kind of man.

They had no supper, but at midnight wandered unsteadily back to the quay to watch the *Toscana* come in. She was rounding the harbour wall, and an hour later was tied up alongside the single quay of hewn local stone. From the forepeak Semmler looked down in the half-light cast by the dock lamps. Each nodded slowly at the other and Waldenberg stood at the top of the gangplank consulting with his first mate. He had already been instructed, following Shannon's letter, that he should leave the talking to Semmler.

After Baker had headed back to the hotel with Ziljak, Shannon slipped up the gangplank and into the captain's tiny cabin. No one on the quay took any notice. Semmler brought Waldenberg in and they locked the door.

Slowly and carefully Shannon told Waldenberg what he had really brought the *Toscana* to Ploce to take on board. The German captain took it well. He kept his face expressionless until Shannon had finished.

'I never carried arms before,' he said. 'You say this cargo is legal. How legal?'

'Perfectly legal,' said Shannon. 'It has been bought in Belgrade, trucked up here, and the authorities are of course aware what the crates contain. Otherwise there would be no export licence. The licence has not been forged, nor has anyone been bribed. It's a perfectly legal shipment under the laws of Yugoslavia.'

'And the laws of the country it's going to?' asked Waldenberg.

'The *Toscana* never enters the waters of the country where these arms are due to be used,' said Shannon. 'After Ploce, there are two more ports of call. In each case only to take on board cargoes. You know ships are never searched for what they are carrying when they arrive in a port to take on more cargo only, unless the authorities have been tipped off.'

'It has happened all the same,' said Waldenberg. 'If I have these things on board and the manifest doesn't mention them, and there is a search, and they are discovered, the ship gets impounded and I get imprisoned. I didn't bargain on arms. With the Black September and the IRA about these days, everyone's looking for arms shipments.'

'Not at the port of embarkation of fresh cargo,' said Shannon.

'I didn't bargain for arms,' repeated Waldenberg.

'You bargained for illegal immigrants to Britain,' Shannon pointed out.

'They're not illegal until their feet touch British soil,' the captain pointed out. 'And the *Toscana* would be outside territorial waters. They could go inshore in fast boats. Arms are different. They are illegal on this ship if the manifest says there aren't any. Why not put it on the manifest? Just say these arms are being legally transported from Ploce to Togo. No one can prove we later deviate from course.'

'Because if there are arms already on board, the Spanish authorities will not allow the ship to stay in Valencia, or any other Spanish port. Even in transit. Certainly not to take on more arms. So they have to remain unmentioned on the manifest.'

'So where did we come from to reach Spain?' asked Waldenberg.

'From Brindisi,' replied Shannon. 'We went there to take on cargo, but it was not ready in time. Then the owners ordered you to Valencia to pick up a new cargo for Latakia. Of course, you obeyed.'

'Supposing the Spanish police search the boat?'

'There's not the slightest reason why they should,' said Shannon. 'But if they do, the crates have to be below decks in the bilges.'

'If they find them there, there's not a hope for us,' Waldenberg pointed out. 'They'd think we were bringing the stuff to the Basque terrorists. We'd be inside for ever.'

The talk went on till three in the morning. It cost Shannon a flat bonus of £5000, half before loading and half after sailing from Valencia. There was no extra charge for the stopover in the African port. That would present no problem.

'You'll take care of the crew?' Shannon asked.

'I'll take care of the crew,' said Waldenberg with finality. Shannon knew he would, too.

Back in his hotel Shannon paid Baker the third quarter of his bill for the arms, 3600 dollars, and tried to get some sleep. It was not easy. The sweat rolled off him in the heat of the night, and he had an image of the *Toscana* lying down there in the port, the arms in the customs shed, and prayed there would be no problems. He felt he was so close now, just three short ceremonies away from the point where no one could stop him whatever they tried.

The loading started at seven, and the sun was already well up. With a customs man, armed with a rifle, walking beside the crates, they were wheeled on trolleys down to the dockside and the *Toscana* hoisted them aboard with her own jumbo derrick. None of the crates were very large, and down in the hold Vlaminck and Cipriani swung them easily into position before they were roped down across the floor of the hold. By nine in the morning it was over, and the hatches went on.

Waldenberg had ordered the engineer to make steam and the latter needed no second bidding. Shannon learned later he had suddenly become very voluble when he learned three hours out from Brindisi that they were heading for his native country. Apparently he was wanted there for something or other. He stayed well hidden in his engine room, and no one went looking for him.

As he watched the *Toscana* chugging out of the port, Shannon slipped Baker the remaining 3600 dollars and the second £500 for Ziljak. Unbeknown to either, he had had Vlaminck quietly prise up the lids on five of the crates, taken at random, as they came aboard. Vlaminck had verified the contents, waved up to Semmler on the deck above him, and Semmler had blown his nose, the signal Shannon wanted. Just in case the crates contained scrap iron. It has been known, quite frequently, in the arms world.

Baker, having received his money, gave the £500 to Ziljak as if it came from himself, and the Yugoslav saw the customs chief did not go without supper. Then Alan Baker and his British 'assistant' quietly left town.

On Shannon's calendar of a hundred days, given him by Sir James Manson to bring off his coup, it was Day Sixty-Seven.

No sooner was the *Toscana* out to sea than Captain Waldenberg began to organize his ship. One by one the three other crewmen were brought into his cabin for a quiet interview. Although none of them knew it, had they refused to continue to serve aboard the *Toscana*, there would have been some unfortunate accidents on board. Few places are quite as well suited for a complete disappearing act as a ship on a dark night at sea, and Vlaminck and Dupree between them could have pitched anyone else on board a long way from the ship's side before he touched the water. Perhaps their presence did the trick. In any case, no one objected.

Waldenberg dispensed a thousand pounds of the two and a half he had received in travellers cheques from Shannon. The Yugoslav engineer, delighted to be out of his own country again, took his £250, stuffed it into his pocket and went back to his engines. He made no comment one way or the other. The first mate, Norbiatto, became quite excitable at the thought of a Spanish jail, but pocketed his £600 in dollars and thought of the difference that could make to his chances of his own ship one day. The crewman, Cipriani, seemed almost happy at the prospect of being on a vessel full of contraband, took his £150, said an ecstatic 'Thank you', and left muttering 'This is the life'. He had little imagination and knew nothing about Spanish jails.

With this done, the crates were broken open and all afternoon the contents were examined, wrapped in polythene and stowed deep in the bilges, below the floor of the hold and inside the curvature of the ship's hull. The planks which had been removed to make this possible were replaced and covered with the innocent cargo of clothing, dinghies and outboard engines.

Finally Semmler told Waldenberg he had better put the Castrol oil drums to the back of the stores locker, and when he told his fellow countryman why, Waldenberg finally did lose his composure. He lost his temper as well, and used some expressions that could best be described as regrettable.

Semmler calmed him down and they sat having beer as the *Toscana* ploughed her away south for the Otranto Channel and the Ionian Sea. Finally Waldenberg began to laugh.

'Schmeissers,' he said. 'Bloody Schmeissers. *Mensch*, it's a long time since they've been heard in the world.'

'Well, they're going to be heard again,' said Semmler. Waldenberg looked wistful.

'You know,' he said at length, 'I wish I was going ashore with you.'

Chapter Nineteen

When Shannon arrived, Simon Endean was reading a copy of *The Times*, bought that morning in London before he left for Rome. The lounge of the Excelsior Hotel was almost empty, for most of those taking late morning coffee were on the outside terrace watching the chaotic traffic of Rome inch past and trying to make themselves heard above the noise.

Shannon had only picked the place because it was in easy reach of Dubrovnik to the east and in line with Madrid to the west. It was the first time he had ever been to Rome, and he wondered what the ecstatic guide books were talking about. There were at least seven separate strikes in progress, one of them being among the garbage workers, and the city stank in the sun from the uncleared fruit and other rubbish on the pavements and down every back alley.

He eased himself into a seat beside the man from London and savoured the cool of the inner room after the heat and frustration of the taxi in which he had been stuck for the past hour. Endean eyed him.

'You've been out of touch a long time,' he said coldly. 'My associates were beginning to think you had scarpered. That was unwise.'

'There was no point in my making contact until I had something to say. That ship doesn't exactly fly across the water. It takes time to get her from

Toulon to Yugoslavia, and during that time there was nothing to report,' said Shannon. 'By the way, did you bring the charts?'

'Of course.'

Endean pointed to his bulging attaché case beside his chair.

On receiving Shannon's letter from Hamburg, he had spent several days visiting three of the top maritime chart companies in Leadenhall Street, London, and in separate lots had acquired inshore charts for the entire African coast from Casablanca to Cape Town.

'Why the hell do you need so many?' he asked in annoyance. 'One or two would suffice.'

'Security,' said Shannon briefly. 'If you or I were searched at Customs, or if the ship were boarded and searched in port, one single chart showing the area of the ship's destination would be a give-away. As it is, no one, including the captain and crew, can discover which section of the coast really interests me. Until the last moment, when I have to tell them. Then's it's too late. Do you have the slides as well?'

'Yes, of course.'

Another of Endean's jobs had been to make up slides of all the photographs Shannon had brought back from Zangaro, along with others of the maps and sketches of Clarence and the rest of Zangaro's coastline.

Shannon himself had already sent a slide projector, bought duty-free at London airport, onto the *Toscana* in Toulon.

He gave Endean a complete progress report from the moment he had left London, mentioning the stay in Brussels, the loading of the Schmeissers and other equipment onto the *Toscana* in Toulon, the talks with Schlinker and Baker in Hamburg and the Yugoslav shipment a few days earlier in Ploce.

Endean listened in silence, making a few notes for the report he would later have to give to Sir James Manson.

'Where's the *Toscana* now?' he asked at length.

'She should be south and slightly west of Sardinia, *en route* for Valencia.'

Shannon went on to tell him what was planned in three days' time, the loading of the 400,000 rounds of 9 mm ammunition for the machine pistols in Valencia, and then departure for the target. He made no mention of the fact that one of his men was already in Africa.

'Now there's something I need to know from you,' he told Endean. 'What happens after the attack? What happens at dawn? We can't hold on for very long before some kind of new régime takes over, establishes itself in the palace, and broadcasts news of the coup and the new government.'

'That's all been thought of,' said Endean smoothly. 'In fact, the new government is the whole point of the exercise.'

From his briefcase he withdrew three foolscap sheets of paper covered with close typing.

'These are your instructions, starting the moment you have possession of the palace and the Army and guards have been destroyed or scattered. Read, memorize, and destroy these sheets before we part company, here in Rome. You have to carry the lot in your head.'

Shannon ran his eye quickly over the first page. There were few surprises for him. He had already suspected the man Manson was boosting into the presidency had to be Colonel Bobi, and although the new president was referred to simply as X, he did not doubt Bobi was the man in question. The rest of the plan was simple, from his point of view.

He glanced up at Endean.

'Where will you be?' he asked.

'A hundred miles north of you,' said Endean.

Shannon knew Endean meant he would be waiting in the capital of the republic next door to Zangaro on its northern side, the one with a road route straight along the coast to the border and thence to Clarence.

'Are you sure you'll pick up my message?' he asked.

'I shall have a portable radio set of considerable range and power. The Braun, the best they make. It will pick up anything within that range, provided it's broadcast on the right channel and frequency. A ship's radio should be powerful enough to send in clear over at least twice that distance.'

Shannon nodded and read on. When he had finished he put the sheets on the table.

'Sounds all right,' he said. 'But let's get one thing clear. I'll broadcast on that frequency at those hours from the *Toscana*, and she'll be hove-to somewhere off the coast, probably at five or six miles. But if you don't hear me, if there's too much static, I can't be responsible for that. It's up to you to hear me.'

'It's up to you to broadcast,' said Endean. 'The frequency is one that has been tested before by practical use. From the *Toscana*'s radio it must be picked up by my radio set at a hundred miles. Not first time, perhaps, but if you repeat for thirty minutes, I have to hear it.'

'All right,' said Shannon. 'One last thing. The news of what has happened in Clarence should not have reached the Zangaran border post. That means it'll be manned by Vindu. It's your business to get past them. After the border, and particularly nearer Clarence, there may be scattered Vindu on the roads, running for the bush but still dangerous. Supposing you don't get through?'

'We'll get through,' said Endean. 'We'll have help.'

Shannon supposed, rightly, that this would be provided by the small operation in mining that he knew Manson had going for him in that republic. For a senior company executive they could provide a truck or jeep and maybe a couple of repeater hunting rifles. For the first time he supposed Endean might have some guts to back up his nastiness.

Shannon memorized the code-words and the radio frequency he needed and burned the sheets with Endean in the men's lavatory. They parted an hour later. There was nothing else to say.

Five floors above the streets of Madrid, Colonel Antonio Salazar, head of the exporting office of the Spanish Army Ministry (Foreign Arms Sales) sat at his desk and perused the file of papers in front of him. He was a grey-haired, grizzled man, a simple man, whose loyalties were uncomplicated and uncompromising. His fidelity was towards Spain, his beloved Spain, and for him all that was right and proper, all that was truly Spanish, was embodied in one man, the short and aged generalissimo who sat in the Pardo. Antonio Salazar was a Franquist to his boot-heels.

Two years from retirement at the age of fifty-eight, he had been one of those who stepped ashore on the sand of Fuengirola with Francisco Franco many years ago when the Caudillo of modern Spain had been a rebel and outcast, returning against orders to launch war against the Republican government in Madrid. They had been few then, and condemned to death by Madrid, and they had nearly died.

Sergeant Salazar was a good soldier. He carried out his orders, whatever they were, went to mass between the battles and the executions, and believed, deeply, in God, the Virgin, Spain and Franco.

In another army, at another time, he would have retired as a sergeant-major. He emerged from the civil war a full captain, one of the ultras, the inner circle. His background was solid working class, peasant, his education next to nil. But he had made full colonel, and he was grateful. He was also trusted with one of the jobs that in Spain is unmentionable and top secret. No Spaniard ever, under any circumstances, learns that Spain exports arms, in large quantities, to almost all comers. Publicly, Spain regrets the international arms trade as unethical and conducive to further warfare in a world already torn by war. Privately, she makes a lot of money out of it. Antonio Salazar could be trusted to check the paperwork, decide whether to grant or refuse permission for export licences, and keep his mouth shut.

The dossier in front of him had been in his hands for four weeks. Individual papers from the dossier had been checked out by the Defence Ministry, who had confirmed, without knowing why the question was being asked, that 9 mm bullets were not on the secret list; by the foreign Ministry, who had confirmed, without knowing why, that the possession by the Republic of Iraq of 9 mm ammunition was not contrary to established foreign policy; and by the Finance Ministry, which had confirmed simply that a sum of money in dollars, paid into a certain account in the Banco Popular, had been received and cleared.

The top paper on the file was an application for movement order, to shift a quantity of crates from Madrid to Valencia and export them on a vessel called the MV *Toscana*. Beneath this sheet was the export licence, granted by his own signature.

He glanced up at the civil servant in front of him.

'Why the change?' he asked.

'Colonel, it is simply that there is no berth available in Valencia port for two weeks. The place is crowded to capacity.'

Colonel Salazar grunted. The explanation was feasible. In the summer months Valencia was always crowded, with millions of oranges from the nearby Gancia area being exported. But he did not like changes. He liked to play things by the book. Nor did he like this order. It was small, too small, for an entire national police force. Target practice alone for a thousand policemen would use it up in an hour. Nor did he trust Schlinker, whom he knew well and who had slipped the order through his ministry with a batch of other orders, including over 10,000 artillery shells for Syria.

He glanced through the papers again. Outside, a church bell struck the hour of one. The hour of lunch. There was still nothing wrong with the papers, including the end user certificate. Everything bore the right stamp. If only he could have found one discrepancy, in the certificate, in the carrying ship of the company that owned it. But everything was clean. Making a final decision he scrawled his signature across the bottom of the movement order and handed the file back to the civil servant.

'All right,' he growled. 'Castellon.'

'We've had to change the port of embarkation from Valencia to Castellon,' said Johann Schlinker two nights later. 'There was no choice if the loading date of the 20th was to be adhered to. Valencia was full up for weeks.'

Cat Shannon was sitting on the bed in the German arms dealer's room in the Mindanao Hotel.

'Where's Castellon?' asked Shannon.

'Forty miles up the coast. It's a smaller port, and quieter. Probably better than Valencia for you. The turnaround of your ship is likely to be quicker. The cargo agent in Valencia has been informed and will personally go north to Castellon to supervise the loading. As soon as the *Toscana* checks in with Valencia harbour authorities by radio, she will be advised of the change of port. She will only have a couple of hours' extra steaming if she diverts at once.'

'What about my going aboard?'

'Well, that's your business,' said Schlinker. 'However, I have informed the agent that a seaman from the *Toscana* who was left behind ten days ago in Brindisi is due to rejoin, and given him the name of Keith Brown. How are your papers?'

'Fine,' said Shannon. 'They're in order, passport and merchant seaman's card.'

'You'll find the agent at the Customs office in Castellon as soon as it opens on the morning of the 20th,' Schlinker told him. 'His name is Señor Moscar.'

'What about the Madrid end of things?'

'The movement order provides for the lorry to be loaded under Army supervision between eight and midnight on the 19th, tomorrow. It will set off with escort at midnight, timing its arrival at Castellon harbour gates at six a.m., the hour they open. If the *Toscana* is on time, she should have docked during the night. The lorry carrying the crates is a civilian one, from the same freight firm I always employ. They're very good and very experienced. I have given the transport manager instructions to see the convoy depart from the warehouse and to phone me here immediately.'

Shannon nodded. There was nothing he could think of that might go wrong.

'I'll be here,' he said, and left.

That afternoon he hired a powerful Mercedes from one of the internationally known hire-car agencies who have offices in Madrid.

At half past ten the following evening he was back in the Mindanao with Schlinker while they waited for the telephone call. Both men were nervous, as men must be when a carefully laid plan rests for its success or catastrophic failure in the hands of others. Schlinker was as concerned as Shannon but for different reasons. He knew that if anything went badly wrong, a complete investigation into the end user certificate he had supplied could be ordered, and that certificate would not stand up to a complete investigation, which must include a check with the Interior Ministry in Baghdad. If he were exposed on that one, other, and for him far more lucrative, deals with Madrid would be forfeit. Not for the first time he wished he had not taken the order in the first place, but like most arms dealers he was a man so greedy that no offer of money could be turned down. It would almost be physical pain to do it.

Midnight came, and still there was no call. Then half past midnight. Shannon paced the room, snarling his anger and frustration at the fat German who sat drinking whisky. At twelve-forty the phone rang. Schlinker leapt at it. He spoke several words in Spanish, and waited.

'What is it?' snapped Shannon.

'*Moment*,' replied Schlinker and waved his hand for silence. Then someone else came on the phone and there was more Spanish, which Shannon could not understand. Finally Schlinker grinned and said '*Gracias*' down the phone several times.

'It's on its way,' he said when he put the phone down. 'The convoy left the depot fifteen minutes ago under escort for Castellon.'

But Shannon was gone.

The Mercedes was more than a match for the convoy, even though on the long motorway from Madrid to Valencia the convoy could keep up a steady 100 kilometres per hour. It took Shannon forty minutes to find his way out of the sprawling suburbs of Madrid, and he supposed the convoy would know the way much better. But on the motorway he could take the Mercedes to 180 kph. He kept a careful eye open as he sped past hundreds of lorries roaring through the night towards the coast, and found what he was looking for just past the town of Requena, forty miles west of Valencia.

His lights picked up the army jeep keeping station to a covered eight-ton truck and as he swept past he noted the name on the lorry's side. It was the name of the trucking company Schlinker had given him. Driving ahead of the lorry was another army vehicle, a four-door saloon, evidently with an officer sitting alone in the back. He touched the accelerator and the Mercedes sped past towards the coast.

At Valencia he took the ring road round the sleeping city, following the pointing to the E26 highway to Barcelona. The motorway ran out just north of Valencia, and he was back to crawling behind orange lorries and early farm vehicles, past the miraculous Roman fortress of Sagunto, hacked by the legionaries out of the living rock and later converted by the Moors into a citadel of Islam. He drove into Castellon just after four, and followed the signs labelled 'Puerto'.

The port of Castellon lies five kilometres from the main town, down a narrow, arrow-straight road that leads from the city to the sea. At the end of the road it is impossible to miss the port and harbour, for there is nothing else there.

As usual with Mediterranean ports, there are three separate harbours, one for freighters, one for yachts and pleasure craft and one for fishing vessels. In Castellon the commercial port lies to the left as one faces the sea, and like all Spanish ports is ringed by a fence and the gates are manned day and night by armed Guardia Civil. In the centre lies the harbourmaster's office and beside it the splendid yacht club, with a dining room looking out over the commercial port on one side, and the yacht basin and fish harbour on the other. Landward side of the harbour office is a row of warehouses.

Shannon turned to the left and parked the car by the roadside, climbed out and started walking. Half-way round the perimeter fence of the port area he found the main gate, with a sentry dozing in a box inside it. The gate was locked. Further on he peered through the chain-links and with a surge of relief spotted the *Toscana* berthed against the far side of the basin. He settled to wait till six o'clock.

He was at the main gate at quarter to six, smiled and nodded at the Guardia Civil sentry, who stared coldly back. In the rising sunlight he could see the army staff car, lorry and jeep, with seven or eight soldiers milling round them, parked a hundred yards away. At six-ten a civilian car arrived, parked next to the gate and sounded its horn. A small, dapper Spaniard climbed out. Shannon approached him.

'Señor Moscar?'

'*Si.*'

'My name's Brown. I'm the seaman who's got to join his ship here.'

The Spaniard puckered his brow.

'*Por favor? Que?*'

'Brown,' insisted Shannon. '*Toscana.*'

The Spaniard's face lightened.

'*Ah, si. El marinero.* Come, please.'

The gate had been opened, and Moscar showed his pass. He babbled for several seconds at the guard and the Customs man who had opened the gate, and pointed at Shannon. Cat caught the word 'marinero' several times, and his passport and merchant seaman's card were examined. Then he followed Moscar to the Customs office. An hour later he was on board the *Toscana*.

The search started at nine. There was no warning. The captain's manifest had been presented and checked out. It was perfectly in order. Down on the quay the truck from Madrid was parked, along with the car and the jeep. The army escort captain, a thin, sallow man with a face like a Moor and a lipless mouth, consulted with two Customs officers. Then the latter came aboard. Moscar followed. They checked the cargo to make sure it was what the manifest said, and no more. They peered in nooks and crannies, but not under the floorboards of the main hold. They looked in the store locker, gazed at the tangle of chains, oil drums and paint cans, and closed the door. It took an hour. The main thing that interested them was why Captain Waldenberg needed seven men on such a small ship. It was explained that Dupree and Vlaminck were company employees who had missed their ship in Brindisi and were being dropped off at Malta on the way to Latakia. They had no seaman's cards with them because they had left their gear on board their own ship. Asked for a name, Waldenberg gave the name of a ship he had seen in Brindisi harbour. There was silence from the Spaniards, who looked at their chief for advice. He glanced down at the army captain, shrugged, and left the ship. Twenty minutes later, loading began.

At half past noon the *Toscana* slipped out of Castellon harbour and turned her helm south to Cape San Antonio. Cat Shannon, feeling sick now that it was all over, knowing that from then on he was virtually unstoppable, was leaning against the after rail, watching the flat green orange groves south of Castellon slip away as they headed for the sea. Carl Waldenberg came up behind him.

'That's the last stop?' he asked.

'The last where we have to open our hatches,' said Shannon. 'We have to pick up some men on the coast of Africa, but we'll moor in the roads. The men will come out by launch. Deck cargo native workers. At least, that's what they'll be shipped as.'

'I've only got charts as far as the Straits of Gibraltar,' objected Waldenberg.

Shannon reached into his zip-up windbreaker and pulled out a sheaf of charts, half of the number Endean had handed him in Rome.

'These,' he said, handing them to the skipper, 'will get you as far as Freetown, Sierra Leone. That's where we anchor and pick up the men. Please give me an arrival time at noon on July 2nd. That is the rendezvous.'

As the captain left to return to his cabin and start to plot his course and speed, Shannon was left alone at the rail. Seagulls wheeled around the stern, seeking morsels dropped from the galley where Cipriani was preparing lunch, squealing and cawing as they dipped towards the foaming wake to snatch up a scrap of bread or vegetable.

Anyone listening would have heard another sound amid their screaming, the sound of a man whistling 'Spanish Harlem'.

Far away to the north another ship slipped her moorings and under the guidance of a port pilot eased her way out of the harbour of Archangel. The Motor Vessel *Komarov* was only ten years old and something over 5000 tons.

Inside her bridge the atmosphere was warm and cosy. The captain and the pilot stood side by side staring forward as the quays and warehouses slipped past to her port side and watched the channel ahead to the open sea. Each man held a cup of steaming coffee. The helmsman kept the vessel on the heading given him by the pilot and to his left the radar screen gleamed and died endlessly, its iridescent sweep arm picking up on each turn the dotted ocean ahead and beyond it the fringe of the ice that would never melt, even in high summer.

In the stern two men leaned over the rail beneath the flag with the hammer and sickle emblem and watched the Russian arctic port slip past. Dr Ivanov clipped the crushed cardboard filter of his black cigarette between his teeth and sniffed the crisp, salt-caked air. Both men were wrapped against the cold, for even in June the wind off the White Sea is no invitation to shirt sleeves. By his side one of his technicians, younger, eager for his first trip abroad, turned to him.

'Comrade Doctor,' he began.

Ivanov took the stump of the *papiross* from his teeth and flicked it into the foaming wake.

'My friend,' he said, 'I think as we are now aboard you can call me Mikhail Mikhailovich.'

'But at the Institute . . .'

'We are not at the Institute. We are on board a ship. And we will be in fairly close confinement either here or in the jungle for months to come.'

'I see,' said the younger man, but he was not to be repressed. 'Have you ever been to Zangaro before?'

'No,' said his superior.

'But to Africa,' insisted the younger man.

'To Ghana, yes.'

'What is it like?'

'Full of jungle, swamps, mosquitoes, snakes and people who don't understand a damn thing you say.'

'But they understand English,' said the assistant. 'We both speak English.'

'Not in Zangaro, they don't.'

'Oh.' The junior technician had read all he could find about Zangaro, which was not much, in the encyclopaedia borrowed from the vast library at the Institute.

'The captain told me if we make good time, we should arrive at Clarence in twenty-two days. That will be their Independence Day.'

'Bully for them,' said Ivanov, and walked away.

Past Cape Spartel, nosing her way from the Mediterranean into the Atlantic, the MV *Toscana* radioed a ship-to-shore telegram to Gibraltar for on-passing to London. It was to Mr Walter Harris at a London address. It said simply, 'Pleased announce your brother completely recovered.' It was the sign meaning the *Toscana* was on her way and on schedule. Slight variations of the message about Mr Harris's brother's health could have meant she was on course but late, or in some kind of trouble. No telegram of any kind meant she had not been cleared from Spanish territorial waters.

That afternoon there was a conference in Sir James Manson's office.

'Good,' said the tycoon, when Endean broke the news. 'How much time has she got to reach target?'

'Twenty-two days, Sir James. It is now Day Seventy-Eight of the hundred estimated for the project. Shannon had allowed Day Eighty for his departure from Europe, and that would have left him twenty days. He estimated the time at sea between sixteen and eighteen days, allowing for adverse weather or a two-day breakdown. He had four days in hand, even on his own estimate.'

'Will he strike early?'

'No, sir. Strike day is still Day One Hundred. He'll kill time hove-to at sea if he has to.'

Sir James Manson paced up and down his office.

'How about the rented villa?' he asked.

'It has been arranged, Sir James.'

'Then I don't see any point in your waiting around London any longer. Get over to Paris again, get a visa for Cotonou, fly down there and get our new employee, Colonel Bobi, to accompany you to this place next to Zangaro. If he seems shifty, offer him more money.

'Get settled in, get the truck and the hunting guns ready, and when you receive Shannon's signal that he is going in for the attack that evening, break the news to Bobi. Get him to sign that mining concession as President Bobi, date it one month later, and send all three copies by registered post in three different envelopes to me here.

'Keep Bobi virtually under lock and key until Shannon's second signal to say he has succeeded. Then in you go. By the way, that bodyguard you are taking with you. Is he ready?'

'Yes, Sir James. For the kind of money he's getting, he's good and ready.'

'What's he like?'

'As nasty as they come. Which is what I was looking for.'

'You could still have problems, you know. Shannon will have all his men round him, at least those who survive the battle. He could prove troublesome.'

Endean grinned.

'Shannon's men will follow Shannon,' he said. 'And I can handle him. Like all mercenaries, he's got his price. I'll just offer it to him – but in Switzerland and out of Zangaro.'

When he had gone Sir James Manson stared down at the City below him and wondered if any man had not got his price. Either in money, or in the inspiration of fear. He had never met one. 'They can all be bought, and if they can't, they can be broken,' one of his mentors had once said to him. And after years as a tycoon, watching politicians, generals, journalists, editors, businessmen, ministers, entrepreneurs and aristocrats, workers and union leaders, blacks and whites, at work and play, he was still of that view.

Many years ago a Spanish seafarer, looking from the sea towards the land, had seen a mountain, which, with the sun behind it in the east, appeared to him to have the shape of a lion's head. He called the land Lion Mountain, and passed on. The name stuck, and the country became known as Sierra Leone. Later another man, seeing the same mountain in a different light, or through different eyes, called it Mount Aureole. That name also stuck. Even later, and in a more whimsical bout of fantasy, a white man named the town founded in its shadow Freetown, and it still bears the name today. It was just after noon on July 2nd, Day Eighty-Eight in Shannon's private calendar, that the Motor Vessel *Toscana* dropped anchor a third of a mile out from the shore off Freetown, Sierra Leone.

On the voyage from Spain, Shannon had insisted that the cargo remain just where it was, untouched and unopened. This was just in case there was a search at Freetown, although, with nothing to discharge and no cargo to take on board, that would have been most unusual. The ammunition crates had been scrubbed clean of their Spanish markings and sanded down with a disc sander to the bright white wood. Stencilled markings showing the crates contained drilling bits for the oil rigs off the Cameroon coast had been painted on.

Only one job had he allowed to be done on the way south. The bundles of mixed clothing had been sorted and the one containing the haversacks and webbing had been opened. With canvas needle and palm, Cipriani, Vlaminck and Dupree had passed the days cutting the haversacks to pieces and transforming them into back-packs fitted with a score of long, narrow pouches, each capable of taking one bazooka rocket. These now shapeless and inexplicable bundles were stored in the paint locker among the cleaning rags.

The smaller knapsacks had also been altered. The packs had been cut away so that only the shoulder straps remained, with braces across the chest and round the waist. Dog-clips had been fastened atop each shoulder strap, with others at the belt, and later these frames would accommodate an entire crate of mortar bombs, enabling up to twenty to be carried at one time.

The *Toscana* had announced her presence while six miles off-shore to the harbourmaster's office of Freetown, and had been given permission to enter port and anchor out in the bay. As she had no cargo to load or unload, there was no need for her to take up room at the port's precious Queen Elizabeth II Quay. She had only come to take on deck crew.

Freetown is one of the favourite ports along the West African coast for taking aboard these brawny labourers who, trained in the use of tackle and winches, are used by the tramp steamers frequenting the smaller timber ports along the coast. They board at Freetown on the outward voyage and are discharged with their pay on the way back. In a hundred coves and creeks along the coast, where cranes and jetties are at a premium, ships have to use their own jumbo derricks to load cargo. It is grindingly hard work, sweating in the tropical fever heat, and white seamen are paid to be seamen, not stevedores. Locally recruited labour might not be available, and probably would not know how to handle cargo, so Sierra Leonians are brought along. They sleep in the open on the ship's deck for the voyage, brewing up their food and performing their ablutions over the stern. It caused no surprise in Freetown when the *Toscana* gave this as her reason for calling.

When the anchor cable rattled down, Shannon scanned the shoreline right round the bay, almost all of it taken up by the outer shanty town of the country's capital.

The sky was overcast, no rain fell, but beneath the clouds the heat was like a greenhouse, and he felt the sweat clamping his shirt to his torso. It would be like this from here on. His eyes riveted on the central area of the city's waterfront, where a large hotel stood looking out over the bay. If anywhere, this was where Langarotti would be waiting, staring out to sea. Perhaps he had not arrived yet. But they could not wait for ever. If he was not there by sundown, they would have to invent a reason for staying on, like a broken refrigerator. It would be unthinkable to sail without the cold store working. He took his eyes away from the hotel and watched the tenders plying round the big Elder Dempster ship tied up at the quay.

On shore the Corsican had already seen the *Toscana* before she dropped anchor, and was heading back into the town. He had been there for a week, and had all the men Shannon wanted. They were not the same tribal group as the Leonians, but no one minded. Men of mixed tribes were available as stevedores and deck cargo.

Just after two, a small pinnace came out from the Custom House with a uniformed man standing in the back. When he came aboard, he was the assistant chief Customs officer, white socks a-gleam, khaki shorts and tunic pressed, epaulettes sparkling and stiff peaked cap set dead straight. Between the regalia a pair of ebony knees and a beaming face could be distinguished. Shannon met him, introduced himself as the owner's representative, shook hands profusely, and led the Customs man to the captain's cabin.

The three bottles of whisky and two cartons of cigarettes were waiting. The officer fanned himself, sighed gustily with pleasure at the cool of the air conditioning, and sipped his beer. He cast an incurious eye over the new manifest, which said the *Toscana* had picked up machine parts at Brindisi and was taking them to the AGIP oil company's offshore concessions near the Cameroon coast. There was no mention of Yugoslavia or Spain. Other cargo was listed as power boats (inflatable), engines (outboard) and tropical clothing (assorted), also for the oil drillers. On the way back, she would wish to load cocoa and some coffee at Sam Pedro, Ivory Coast, and return to Europe. He exhaled on his official stamp to moisten it, and placed his approval on the manifest. An hour later he was gone, his presents in his tucker bag.

Just after six, as the evening cooled, Shannon made out the longshore boat moving away from the beach. Amidships the two local men who ran passengers out to the waiting vessels in the bay heaved at their oars. Aft sat seven other Africans, clutching bundles on their knees. In the prow sat a lone European. As the craft swung expertly into the side of the *Toscana*, Jean-Baptiste Langarotti came nimbly up the ladder that hung to the water.

One by one the bundles were heaved from the bobbing rowing boat up to the rail of the freighter, then the seven Africans followed. Although it was indiscreet to do so in sight of land Vlaminck, Dupree and Semmler started to clap them on the back and shake hands. The Africans, grinning from ear to ear, seemed as happy as the mercenaries. Waldenberg and his mate looked on in surprise. Shannon signed to the captain to take the *Toscana* back to sea.

After dark, sitting in groups on the main deck, taking with gratitude the cooling breeze off the sea as the *Toscana* rolled on to the south, Shannon introduced his recruits to Waldenberg. The mercenaries knew them all, as they did the mercenaries. Six of the Africans were young men, called Johnny, Patrick, Jinja (nicknamed Ginger), Sunday, Bartholomew and Timothy.

Each of them had fought with the mercenaries before, each of them had been personally trained by one of the European soldiers, each of them had been tried and tested in battle many times, and would stick it out however hard the firefight. And each of them was loyal to his leader. The seventh was an older man, who smiled less, bore himself with a confident dignity and was addressed by Shannon as 'Doctor'. He too was loyal to his leader and his people.

'How are things at home?' Shannon asked him.

Doctor Okoye shook his head sadly. 'Not well,' he said.

'Tomorrow we start work,' Shannon told him. 'We start preparing tomorrow.'

PART THREE
THE BIG KILLING

Chapter Twenty

For the remainder of the sea voyage, Cat Shannon worked his men without pause. Only the middle-aged African whom he called 'Doctor' was exempt. The rest were divided into parties, each with a separate job to do.

Marc Vlaminck and Kurt Semmler broke open the five green Castrol oil drums by hammering off the false bottoms, and from each plucked the bulky package of twenty Schmeissers and a hundred magazines that were inside. The superfluous lubricating oil was poured into smaller containers and saved for the ship's use.

Aided by the six African soldiers, the pair stripped the masking tape from each of the hundred submachine guns, which were then individually wiped clean of oil and grease. By the time they had finished, the six Africans had already learned the operating mechanisms of the Schmeisser in a way that was as good if not better than any weapon-familiarization course that they could have undergone.

Breaking open the first ten boxes of 9 mm ammunition, the eight of them sat around the decks slotting the shells into the magazines, thirty to each, until the first 15,000 rounds from their store had gone into the 500 magazines at their disposal. Eighty of the Schmeissers were then set aside while Jean-Baptiste Langarotti prepared sets of uniforms from the bales stored in the hold. These sets consisted of two tee-vests, two pairs of pants, two pairs of socks, one pair of boots, one set of trousers, one beret, one combat blouse, and one sleeping bag. When these were ready, the bundle was wrapped up, one Schmeisser and five full magazines were wrapped in an oily cloth, slipped into a polythene bag, and the whole lot stuffed into the sleeping bag. Tied at the top and ready for handling like a sack, each sleeping bag comprised the necessary clothing and weaponry for one future soldier.

Twenty sets of uniforms and twenty Schmeissers with five magazines per carbine were set aside. These were for the attack force itself, although the force only numbered eleven, with spares for the crew if necessary. Langarotti, who had learned while in the Army and in prison to handle a needle and thread, altered and sewed eleven sets of uniform for the members of the attack party until each man was fitted out.

Dupree and Cipriani, the deckhand, who turned out to be a useful carpenter, stripped down several of the packing crates that had once contained ammunition and turned their attention to the outboard engines. All three were Johnson sixty-horsepower units. The two men built wooden boxes to fit neatly over the top of each engine, and lined the boxes with foam rubber from the mattresses they had brought along. With the exhaust noise of the engines muffled by the underwater exhausts, the mechanical noise emanating from the engine casings could also be reduced to a low murmur by the muffling boxes they thus prepared.

When Vlaminck and Dupree had finished these tasks, each turned his attention to the weapon he would be using on the night of the strike. Dupree uncrated his two mortar tubes and familiarized himself with the aiming mechanisms. He had not used the Yugoslav model of mortar before, but was relieved to see it was helpfully simple. He prepared seventy mortar bombs, checking and arming the primers in the nose-cone of each bomb.

Re-packing the prepared bombs into their boxes, he clipped two boxes, one above the other, to the webbing harness that had already been prepared from the army-style knapsacks he had bought in London two months earlier.

Vlaminck concentrated on his two bazookas, of which only one would be used on the night of the attack. Again, the main limitation on what he could take with him was the weight factor. Everything had to be carried on a human back. Standing on the forepeak, using the tip of the flagpole sticking above the stern as a fixed point, his aiming disc slotted to the end of the bazooka, he carefully adjusted the sights to the weapon until he was certain he could take a barrel at two hundred metres with no more than two shots. He had already picked Patrick as his back-up man, for they had been together before and knew each other well enough to make a good team. With his backpack, the African would be carrying ten bazooka rockets as well as his own Schmeisser. Vlaminck added another two rockets as his personal load, and Cipriani sewed him two pouches to hang from his belt, which could contain the extra rockets.

Shannon concentrated on the ancillary gear, examining the magnesium-flare rockets and explaining to Dupree how they worked. He distributed one compass to each mercenary, tested the gas-powered foghorn and checked the portable radio sets.

Having time in hand, Shannon had the *Toscana* heave to for two days well out at sea in an area where the ship's radar told them there was no other shipping within twenty miles. As the ship lay almost stationary, heaving slightly on the swell, each man tested his personal Schmeisser. The whites had no problems; they had each in their time used half a dozen different submachine guns, and these weapons vary but slightly. The Africans took longer to get used to them, for most of their experience had been with bolt-action 7.92 mm Mausers or the standard 7.62 NATO self-loading rifle. One of the German carbines jammed repeatedly, so Shannon threw it overboard and gave the man another. Each African fired off nine hundred rounds, until he was accustomed to the feel of the Schmeisser in his hands, and each man had been cured of the annoying habit African soldiers tend to adopt, of closing their eyes while they fire.

The five empty and open-topped oil barrels had been stored for later use, and these were now streamed astern of the *Toscana* for target practice. At a hundred metres all of the men, black and white, could riddle a barrel before they had ceased their practice. Four barrels were destroyed and sunk in this manner, and the fifth was used by Marc Vlaminck. He let it stream to two hundred metres, then planted himself in the stern of the *Toscana*, feet apart and braced, the bazooka across his right shoulder, right eye applied to the sight. Judging the gentle heave of the deck, he waited until he was sure, and fired off his first rocket. It screamed over the top of the barrel and exploded with a spout of spray into the ocean. His second rocket took the barrel in the centre. There was a crash and the boom of the explosion echoed back over the water to the watching mercenaries and crew. Fragments of tin-plate spattered the water close to where the barrel had been and a cheer came from the watchers. Grinning widely, Vlaminck turned to Shannon, ripped off the glasses he had used to protect his eyes and wiped the specks of smut from his face.

'You said you wanted a door taken off, Cat?'

'That's right, a bloody great wooden gate, Tiny.'

'I'll give it to you in matchsticks, and that's a promise,' said the Belgian.

Because of the noise they had made, Shannon ordered the *Toscana* to move on the next day, and two days later he called his second halt. In the period under way, the men had hauled out the three assault craft and inflated them. They lay side by side along the main deck. Each, despite being a deep, dark grey in colour, had a brilliant orange nose and the name of the manufacturer in the same luminous colour down each side. These were painted out with black paint from the ship's store.

When they were hove-to for the second time, they tested all three. Without the muffling boxes placed over the top of each engine, the Johnsons made an audible mutter even when four hundred yards away from the *Toscana*. With the boxes in place and the engines throttled back to less than quarter-power, there was hardly a sound at thirty yards. They tended to overheat after twenty minutes at half-power, but this could be stretched to thirty minutes if power was reduced. Shannon took one of the craft out for two hours, checking throttle settings for speed-against-noise, to get the best combination. As the powerful outboards gave him a large reserve, he elected never to push them beyond one-third full power, and advised his men to close down to less than one-quarter power for the last two hundred yards as they approached the landing beaches of the target area.

The walkie-talkies were also tested at up to four miles, and despite the heavy atmospherics and the hint of thunder in the stifling air, messages could still be heard if read over clearly and slowly. To get them used to the motion, the Africans were also given trips in the powercraft, at a varying range of speeds, in daylight and at night.

The night exercises were the most important. For one of them Shannon took the other four whites and the six Africans three miles out from the *Toscana*, which burned one small light at her masthead. On the journey away from the ship, the ten men had their eyes bandaged. When the masks were taken off, each was given ten minutes to accustom his vision to the blackness of the sky and the ocean, before the move back to the boat began. With the engine throttled down and dead silence maintained aboard, the assault craft moved quietly back towards the light that represented the *Toscana*. Sitting with the tiller bar in his hand, holding the power setting steady at one third, then cutting back to less than a quarter for the final run-in, Shannon could feel the tension of the men in front of him. They knew this was what it would be like when they struck, and there would be no second chances.

Back on board, Carl Waldenberg came up to Shannon as the two men watched the crew winch the vessel inboard by torchlight.

'I hardly heard a sound,' he said. 'Not until you were a couple of hundred metres away, and I was listening hard. Unless they have very alert guards posted, you should be able to make the beach, wherever you are going. Incidentally, where are you going? I need more charts if I have to proceed much further.'

'I think you'd all better know' said Shannon. 'We'll spend the rest of the night going through the briefing.'

Until dawn, the crew (with the exception of the engineer who still slept with his engines), the seven Africans and the four mercenaries listened to Shannon in the main saloon while he went through the entire plan of attack. He had prepared and set up his projector and slide transparencies, some of which were pictures he had taken while in Zangaro, others of which were the maps and charts he had bought or drawn for himself.

When he had finished, there was dead silence in the stifling cabin, the blue wreaths of cigarette smoke trickling out through the open portholes into the equally clammy night outside.

Finally Waldenberg said, *'Gott in Himmel!'* Then they all started. It took an hour before the questions were answered. Waldenberg wanted reassurance that if anything went wrong the survivors would be back on board and the *Toscana* well over the horizon before sunrise. Shannon gave it to him.

'We only have your word for it they have no navy, no gunboats,' he said.

'Then my word will have to do,' said Shannon. 'They have none.'

'Just because you did not see any ...'

'They have none,' snapped Shannon. 'I spent hours talking with people who have been there for years. There are no gunboats, no navy.'

The six Africans had no questions. They would each stick close to the mercenary who would lead them, and trust that he knew what he was doing. The seventh, the doctor, asked briefly where he would be, and accepted that he would remain on board the *Toscana.* The four mercenaries had a few purely technical questions, which Shannon answered in technical terms.

When they came back up on deck the Africans stretched themselves out on their sleeping bags and went to sleep. Shannon had often envied their ability to sleep at any time, in any place, in almost any circumstances. The doctor retired to his cabin, as did Norbiatto who would take the next watch. Waldenberg went into his wheelhouse and the *Toscana* began to move again towards her destination, just three days away.

The five mercenaries grouped themselves on the after deck behind the crew quarters and talked until the sun was high. They all approved of the plan of attack and accepted that Shannon's reconnaissance had been accurate and precise. If anything had changed since then, if there had been an unforeseen addition to the town's defences or improvements to the palace, they knew they could all die. They would be very few, dangerously few, for such a job, and there was no margin for things going wrong. But they accepted that either they had to win within twenty minutes or they would have to get back to their boats and leave in a hurry, those that could leave. They knew that no one was going to come looking for wounded, and that anyone finding one of his colleagues badly hurt and unmovable would be expected to give him one mercenary's last gift to another, the quick clean way out, preferable to capture and the slow death. It was part of the rules, and they had all had to do it before.

Just before noon they parted company and turned in.

They all woke early on the morning of Day Ninety-Nine. Shannon had been up half the night, watching beside Waldenberg as the coastline loomed out of the perimeter of the tiny radar screen at the rear of the wheelhouse.

'I want you to come within visual range of the coast to the south of the capital,' he had told the captain, 'and spend the morning steaming northwards, parallel to the shore, so that at noon we are off the coast here.'

His finger jabbed the sea off the coast of the country to Zangaro's northern side. During the twenty days at sea he had come to trust the German captain. Waldenberg, having taken his money in Ploce port, had stuck by his side of the bargain, giving himself completely to making the operation as successful as he could. Shannon was confident the seamen would hold his ship at readiness four miles off the coast, a bit to the south of Clarence, while the firefight went on, and if the distress call came over the walkie-talkie, that he would wait until the men who had managed to escape rejoined the *Toscana* in their speedboats, before making at full power for the open sea. There was no spare man Shannon could leave behind to ensure this, so he had to trust Waldenberg.

He had already found the frequency on the ship's radio on which Endean wanted him to transmit his first message, and this was timed for noon.

The morning passed slowly. Through the ship's telescope Shannon watched the estuary of the Zangaro River move past, a long, low line of mangrove trees along the horizon. At mid-morning he could make out the break in the green line where the town of Clarence lay, and passed the telescope to Vlaminck, Langarotti, Dupree and Semmler. Each studied the off-white blur in silence and handed the glass to the next man. They smoked more than usual and mooched around the deck, tense and bored with the waiting, wishing, now they were so close, that they could go straight into action.

At noon Shannon began to transmit his message. He read it in clear into the radio speaker. It was just one word, 'Plantain'. He gave it every ten seconds for five minutes, then broke for five minutes, then gave it again. Three times within thirty minutes, each time over a five-minute period, he broadcast the word, and hoped that Endean would hear it somewhere on the mainland. It meant that Shannon and his men were on time and in position, and that they would strike Clarence and Kimba's Palace in the small hours of the following morning.

Twenty-two miles away across the water, Simon Endean heard the word on his Braun transistor radio, folded the long wasp-antenna, left the hotel balcony and withdrew into the bedroom. Then he began, slowly and carefully, to explain to the former colonel of the Zangaran Army that within twenty-four hours he, Antoine Bobi, would be President of Zangaro. At four in the afternoon the colonel, grinning and chuckling at the thought of the reprisals he would take against those who had assisted in his ousting, struck his deal with Endean. He signed the document granting Bormac Trading Company a ten-year exclusive mining concession in the Crystal Mountains for a flat annual fee, a tiny profits-participation by the Zangaran government, and watched Endean place in an envelope and seal a cheque certified by a Swiss bank for a half a million dollars in favour of Antoine Bobi.

In Clarence preparations went ahead through the afternoon for the following day's independence celebrations. Six prisoners, lying badly beaten in the cells beneath the former colonial police station, listened to the cries of the Kimba Patriotic Youth marching through the streets above them, and knew that they would be battered to death in the main square as part of the celebrations Kimba had prepared. Photographs of the president were prominently hung on every public building and the diplomatic wives prepared their migraines so they would be excused attendance at the ceremonies.

In the shuttered palace, surrounded by his guards, President Jean Kimba sat alone at his desk contemplating the advent of his sixth year of office.

During the afternoon the *Toscana* and her lethal cargo put about and began to cruise slowly back down the coast from the north.

In the wheelhouse Shannon sipped his coffee and explained to Waldenberg how he wanted the *Toscana* placed.

'Hold her just north of the border until sundown,' he told his captain. 'After nine p.m., start her up again and move diagonally towards the coast. Between sundown and nine, we will have streamed the three assault craft astern of the ship, each loaded with its complement. That will have to be done by torchlight, but well away from the land, at least ten miles out.

'When you start to move, around nine, keep her really slow, so you end up here, four miles out from the shore and one mile north of the peninsula at two a.m. You'll be out of sight of the city in that position. With all lights doused, no one should see you. So far as I know there's no radar on the peninsula, unless a ship is in port.'

'Even if there is, she should not have a radar on,' growled Waldenberg. He was bent over his inshore chart of the coast, measuring his distances with dividers and parallel rule. 'When does the first craft set free and move inshore?'

'At two. That will be Dupree and his mortar crew. The other two boats cast adrift and head for the beach one hour later, OK?'

'OK,' said Waldenberg, 'I'll have you there.'

'It has to be accurate,' insisted Shannon. 'We'll see no lights in Clarence, even if there are any, until we round the headland. So we'll be on compass heading only, calculating by speed and heading, until we see the outline of the shore, which might be no more than a hundred metres. It depends on the sky; cloud, moon and stars.'

Waldenberg nodded. He knew the rest. After he heard the firefight begin, he was to ease the *Toscana* across the mouth of the harbour, four miles out, and heave-to again two miles to the south of Clarence, four miles out from the tip of the peninsula. From then on he would listen on his walkie-talkie. If all went well, he would stay where he was until sun-up. If things went badly he would turn on the lights at the masthead, the forepeak and the stern, to guide the returning force back to the *Toscana*.

Darkness that evening came early, for the sky was overcast and the moon would not rise until the small hours of the morning. The rains had already started, and twice in the previous three days they had weathered drenching downpours as the skies opened. The weather report, listened to avidly on the radio, indicated there would be scattered squalls along the coast that night, but no tornadoes, and they could only pray there would be no torrential rains while the men were in their open boats or while the battle for the palace was on.

Before sundown the tarpaulins were hauled off the equipment, piled in rows along the main deck, and when darkness fell Shannon and Norbiatto began organizing the departure of the assault craft. The first over the side was the one Dupree would use. There was no point in using the derrick; the sea was only eight feet beneath the deck at the lowest point. The men lowered the fully-inflated craft into the water manually, and Semmler and Dupree went down into it as it bobbed against the *Toscana*'s side in the slow swell.

The two of them hoisted the heavy outboard engine into place over the stern and screwed it tight to the backboard. Before placing the muffler on top of it, Semmler started the Johnson up and ran her for two minutes. The Serbian engineer had already given all three engines a thorough check-over, and it ran like a sewing machine. With the muffling box on top, the noise died to a low hum.

Semmler climbed out and the equipment was lowered to Dupree's waiting hands. There were baseplates and sighting gear for both mortars, then the two mortar tubes. Dupree was taking forty mortar bombs for the palace and twelve for the barracks. To be on the safe side, he took sixty bombs, all primed and fused for detonation on impact.

He also took both flare-launching rockets and the ten flares, one of the gas-powered fog horns, one walkie-talkie and his night glasses. Slung over his shoulder he had his personal Schmeisser and stuck in his belt were five full magazines. The two Africans who were going with him, Timothy and Sunday, were the last into the assault craft.

When it was ready, Shannon stared down at the three faces that looked back up at him in the dim torchlight.

'Good luck,' he called softly. For answer Dupree raised one thumb and nodded. Holding the painter of the assault craft, Semmler moved back along the rail while Dupree fended off from down below. When the craft was streamed astern of the *Toscana* in complete darkness, Semmler tied her painter to the after-rail, leaving the three men to bob up and down on the swell.

The second boat took less time to let into the water, for the men had got the hang of it. Marc Vlaminck went down with Semmler to set the outboard engine in position, for this was their boat. Vlaminck was taking one bazooka and twelve rockets, two on his own body, the other ten carried by his back-up man, who was Patrick. Semmler had his personal Schmeisser and five magazines, each in easy-extraction pouches hung around his belt. He had a set of night glasses round his neck and the second walkie-talkie strapped to one thigh. As he was the only man who could speak German, French and reasonable English, he would double as the main attack party's radio operator. When the two whites were ensconced in their craft, Patrick and Jinja, who would be Semmler's back-up man, slid down the jacob's ladder from the *Toscana* and took their places.

The two were streamed astern of the ship, and Dupree's painter was passed to Semmler, who made it fast to his own assault craft. The two inflatable vessels bobbed behind the *Toscana* in line astern, separated by the length of rope, but none of their occupants said a word.

Langarotti and Shannon took the third and last boat. They were accompanied by Bartholomew and Johnny, the latter a big, grinning fighter who had been promoted to captain at Shannon's insistence when they last fought together, but who had refused to take his own company as his new rank entitled him, preferring to stick close to Shannon and look after him.

Just before Shannon, who was the last man into the boats, descended the ladder, Captain Waldenberg appeared from the direction of the bridge and tugged at his sleeve. The German pulled the mercenary to one side and muttered quietly, 'We may have a problem.'

Shannon was immobile, frozen by the thought that something had gone seriously wrong.

'What is it?' he asked.

'There's a ship. Lying off Clarence, further out than us.'

'How long since you saw it?'

'Some time,' said Waldenberg, 'but I thought it must be cruising south down the coast, like us, or moving northwards. But it's not, it's riding-to.'

'You're sure? There's no doubt about it?'

'None at all. When we came down the coast we were moving so slowly that if the other had been steaming in the same direction, she'd be well away by now. If northwards, she'd have passed us by now. She's immobile.'

'Any indication of what she is, who she belongs to?' The German shook his head.

'The size of a freighter. No indication who she is, unless we contact her.'

Shannon thought for several minutes.

'If she were a freighter, bringing cargo to Zangaro, would she anchor till morning before entering harbour?' he asked.

Waldenberg nodded.

'Quite possible. Entry by night is frequently not allowed in some of the smaller ports along this coast. She's probably riding out until the morning before asking permission to enter port.'

'If you've seen her, presumably she's seen you?' Shannon suggested.

'Bound to,' said Waldenberg. 'We're on her radar all right.'

'Could her radar pick up the dinghies?'

'Unlikely,' said the captain, 'too low in the water most probably.'

'We go ahead,' said Shannon. 'It's too late now. We have to assume she's just a freighter waiting out the night.'

'She's bound to hear the fire fight,' said Waldenberg.

'What can she do about it?'

The German grinned.

'Not much. If you fail, and we're not out of here before sunrise, she'll recognize the *Toscana* through binoculars.'

'We mustn't fail then. Carry on as ordered.'

Waldenberg went back to his bridge. The middle-aged African doctor, who had watched the proceedings in silence, stepped forward.

'Good luck, Major,' he said in perfectly modulated English. 'God go with you.'

Shannon felt like saying that he would have preferred a Wombat recoilless rifle, but held his tongue. He knew these people took religion very seriously. He nodded, said 'Sure' and went over the side.

Out of the darkness, looking up at the dim blob of the *Toscana*'s stern above him, there was complete silence but for the slop of the water against the rubberized hulls of the boats. Occasionally it gurgled behind the ship's rudder. From the landward side there was not a sound, for they were well out of earshot of the shore, and by the time they came close enough to hear shouts and laughter, it would be well past midnight, and with luck everyone would be asleep. Not that there was much laughter in Clarence, but Shannon was aware how far a single, sharp sound can travel over water at night, and everyone in his party, in the boats and on the *Toscana*, was sworn to silence and no smoking.

He glanced at his watch. It was quarter to nine. He sat back to wait.

At nine the hull of the *Toscana* emitted a low rumble, and the water beneath her stern began to churn and bubble, the phosphorescent white wake running back to slap against the snub nose of Shannon's assault craft. Then they were under way, and by dipping his fingers over the side he could feel the caress of the passing water. Five hours to cover twenty-eight nautical miles.

The sky was still overcast and the air was like that inside an old greenhouse, but a hole in the cloud cover let a little dim starlight through. Astern he could make out the craft of Vlaminck and Semmler at the end of the twenty feet of rope, and somewhere behind them Janni Dupree was moving along in the wake of the *Toscana*.

The five hours went by like a nightmare. Nothing to do but watch and listen, nothing to see but the darkness and the glitter of the sea, nothing to hear but the low thump of the *Toscana*'s old pistons moving inside her rusted hull. No one could sleep, despite the mesmeric rocking of the light craft, for the tensions were building up in every man in the operation.

But they did pass, somehow. Shannon's watch said five past two when the noise of the *Toscana*'s engines died, and she slowed to idle in the water. From above the after-rail a low whistle came through the darkness; Waldenberg letting him know they were in position for cast-off. Shannon turned his head to signal Semmler, but Dupree must have heard the whistle, for a few seconds later they heard his engine cough into life and begin to move away towards the shore. They never saw him go, just heard the low buzz of the engine under its muffler vanishing into the darkness.

At the helm of his assault craft Big Janni checked his power setting on the twist-grip he held in his right hand and held his left arm, with the compass as steady as he could under his eyes. He knew he should have four and a half miles to cover, angling in towards the coast, trying to make landfall on the outer side of the northern arm that curved round the harbour of Clarence. At that power setting, on that course, he should make it in thirty minutes. At twenty-five minutes he would shut the engine almost closed and try to make out his landfall by eyesight. If the others gave him one hour to set up his mortars and flare-rockets, they should move past the tip of the point towards their own beach landing just about the time he was ready. But for that hour, he and his two Africans would be the only ones on the shore of Zangaro. That was all the more reason why they should be completely silent as they set up their battery.

Twenty-two minutes after he left the *Toscana*, Dupree heard a low 'pssst' from the bow of his dinghy. It was Timothy, whom he had posted as a lookout. Dupree glanced up from his compass and what he saw caused him to throttle back quickly. They were already close to a shoreline, little more than three hundred yards, and the dim starlight from the hole in the clouds above them made out a line of deeper darkness right ahead. Dupree squinted hard, easing the craft another two hundred yards inshore. It was mangrove, he could hear the water chuckling among the roots. Far out to his right he could discern the line of vegetation end and the single line of the horizon between sea and night sky run away to the end of vision. He had made landfall three miles into the northern coast of the peninsula.

He brought his boat about, still keeping the throttle very low and virtually silent, and headed back out towards the sea. He set the tiller to keep the shoreline of the peninsula in vision at half a mile until he reached the limit of the strip of land at whose end the town of Clarence stood, then again headed slowly inshore. At two hundred metres he could make out the long, low spit of gravel that he was seeking, and in the thirty-eighth minute after leaving the *Toscana*, he cut the engine and let the assault craft drift on its own momentum towards the spit. It grounded with a soft grating of fabric on gravel.

Dupree stepped lightly down the boat, avoiding the piles of equipment, swung a leg over the prow and dropped onto the sand. He felt for the painter and kept it in his hand to prevent the boat drifting away. For five minutes all three men remained immobile, listening for the slightest sound from the town they knew lay over the low hammock of gravel and scrub in front of them, and four hundred yards to the left. But there was no sound. They had arrived without causing any alarm.

When he was certain, Dupree slipped a marlin spike out of his belt and rammed it deep into the shingle of the shore, tying the painter securely to it. Then he rose to a crouch and ran lightly up the hammock ahead of him. It was barely fifteen feet above sea level at its top, and covered in knee-high scrub that rustled against his boots. The rustling was no problem; it was drowned by the slap of the sea on the shingle and far too soft to be heard away in the town. Crouching at the spine of the strip of land that formed one arm of the harbour, Dupree looked over the top. To his left he could make out the spit running away into the darkness, and straight ahead lay more water, the flat, mirror-calm of the protected harbour. The end of the spit of gravel was ten yards to his right.

Returning to the assault craft he whispered to the two Africans to begin unloading the equipment in complete silence. As the bundles came on to the shore he picked them up and carried them one by one up to the top of the rise. Each metallic piece was covered in sacking to prevent noise if two should knock together.

When the whole of his weaponry was assembled, Dupree began to set it up. He worked fast and quietly. At the far end of the spit, where Shannon had told him there was a round, flat area, he set up his main mortar. He knew, if Shannon's measurements were accurate, and he trusted they would be, that the range from the tip of the land to the centre of the palace courtyard was 721 metres. Using his compass he pointed the mortar on the exact compass bearing Shannon had given him from the point he stood to the presidential palace and carefully adjusted his mortar's elevation to drop his first range-finding bomb as near to the centre of the palace courtyard as possible.

He knew when the flares went up that he would not see the whole palace, but just the top storey, so he could not watch the bomb hit the ground. But he would see the upward flash of the explosion over the brow of the ground behind the warehouse at the other end of the harbour, and that would be enough.

When he was finished with the first, he set up the second mortar. This was pointing at the barracks, and he put the baseplate ten yards away from the first, down the spine of the land on which he stood. He knew both range and bearing from this mortar to the barracks, and that the accuracy of the second mortar was not vital, since its intent was to drop bombs at random into the acreage of the former police lines and scatter the Zangaran army men through panic. Timothy, who had been his sergeant on mortars the last time they fought, would handle the second mortar on his own.

He established a pile of a dozen mortar bombs next to the second tube, settled Timothy beside it and whispered a few last instructions into his ear.

Between the two mortars he established the two flare-launching rockets and jammed one rocket down each launcher, leaving the other eight lying handy. Each flare was reputed to have a life of twenty seconds, so if he was to operate both his own mortar and the illuminations, he knew he would have to work fast and skilfully. He needed Sunday to pass him his mortar bombs from the stack he had built beside the emplacement.

When he was finished he looked at his watch. Three twenty-two in the morning. Shannon and the other two boys must be off the shore somewhere, heading for the harbour. He took his walkie-talkie, extended the aerial to its full length, switched on and waited the prescribed thirty seconds for it to warm up. From then on, it would not be switched off again. When he was ready he pressed the 'blip' button three times at one-second intervals.

A mile off the shore, Shannon was at the helm of the leading assault craft, eyes straining into the darkness ahead. To his lefthand side Semmler kept the second craft in formation order, and it was he who heard the three buzzes from the walkie-talkie on his knee. He steered his boat softly into the side of Shannon's, so the two rounded sides scuffed each other. Shannon looked towards the other boat. Semmler hissed and pulled his boat away again, to maintain station at two metres. Shannon was relieved. He knew Semmler had heard Dupree's signal across the water, and that the rangy Afrikaner was set up and waiting for them. Two minutes later, a thousand metres off the shore, Shannon caught the quick flash from Dupree's torch, heavily masked and blinkered to a pinpoint of light. It was off to his right, so he knew that he was heading too far north. In unison the two craft swung to starboard, Shannon trying to recall the exact point from which the light had come, and to head for a point a hundred metres to the right of it. That would be the harbour entrance. The light came again when Dupree caught the low buzz of the two outboard engines as they were three hundred metres from the tip of the point. Shannon spotted the light and changed course a few degrees.

Two minutes later, shut down to less than a quarter power and making no noise louder than a bumble-bee, the two assault craft went by the tip of the spit where Dupree was crouching, fifty metres out. The South African caught the glitter of the wake, the bubbles from the exhausts rising to the surface, then they were gone into the harbour entrance and across the still water towards the warehouse on the other side.

There was still no sound from the shore when Shannon's straining eyes made out the bulk of the warehouse against the marginally lighter skyline, steered to the right and grounded on the shingle of the fishing beach among the natives' dug-out canoes and hanging fish-nets.

Semmler brought his own boat to the shore a few feet away, and both engines died together. Like Dupree, all the men remained motionless for several minutes waiting for an alarm to be called. They tried to make out the difference between the humped backs of the fishing canoes and the shape of an awaiting ambush party. There was no ambush. Shannon and Semmler stepped over the side, each jabbed a marlin spike into the sand and tethered the boats to it. The rest followed. With a low, muttered, 'Come on, let's go,'

Shannon led the way across the beach and up the sloping incline of the two-hundred-yard-wide plateau between the harbour and the sleeping palace of President Jean Kimba.

Chapter Twenty-One

The eight men ran in a low crouch, up through the scrubland of the hillside and out onto the plain at the top. It was after half past three, and no lights were burning in the palace. Shannon knew that half-way between the top of the rise and the palace two hundred yards away they would meet the coast road, and standing at the junction would be at least two palace guards. He expected he would not be able to take them both silently, and that after the firing started they would have to crawl the last hundred yards to the palace wall. He was right.

Out across the water, waiting in his lonely vigil, Big Janni Dupree waited for the shot that would send him into action. He had been briefed that whoever fired the shot, or however many there were, the first one would be his signal. He crouched close to the flare-rocket launchers, waiting to let the first one go. In his spare hand was his first mortar bomb.

Shannon and Langarotti were out ahead of the other six when they made the road junction in front of the palace, and already both were wet with sweat. Their faces, blackened with sepia-dye, were streaked by the running perspiration. The rent in the clouds above them was larger, and more stars showed through, so that although the moon was still hidden, there was a dim light across the open area in front of the palace. At a hundred yards Shannon could make out the line of the roof against the sky, though he missed the guards until he stumbled over one. The man was seated on the ground, snoozing.

He was too slow and clumsy with the Commando knife in his right hand. After stumbling he recovered, but the Vindu guard rose with equal speed and emitted a brief yell of surprise. The call attracted his partner, also hidden in the uncut grass a few feet away. The second man rose, gurgled once as the Corsican's knife opened his throat from carotid artery to jugular vein, and went back down again, choking out his last seconds. Shannon's man took the swipe with the Bowie knife in the shoulder, let out another scream and ran.

A hundred yards in front, close to the palace gate, there was a second cry, and the sound of a bolt operating in the breech of a rifle. It was never quite certain who fired first. The wild shot from the palace gate and the snarling rip of Shannon's half-second burst that sliced the running man almost in two, blended with each other. From far behind them there was a whoosh and a scream in the sky, two seconds later the sky above them exploded in blistering white light. Shannon caught a brief impression of the palace in front of him, two figures in front of its gate, and the feeling of his other six men fanning out to right and left of him. Then the eight of them were face-down in the grass and crawling forwards.

Janni Dupree stepped away from the rocket-launcher the instant he had torn the lanyard off the first rocket, and was slipping his mortar bomb down the tube as the rocket screamed upwards. The smack-thump of the mortar bomb departing on its parabola towards the palace blended with the crash of the magnesium flare exploding away towards the land, over the spot he hoped his colleagues would have reached. He took his second bomb and, squinting into the light from the palace, waited to watch the first one fall. He had given himself four sighting shots, on an estimate of fifteen seconds for each bomb in flight. After that he knew he could keep up a fire-rate of one every two seconds, with Sunday feeding him the ammunition singly but fast and in rhythm.

His first sighting bomb hit the front right-hand cornice of the palace roof, high enough for him to see the impact. It did not penetrate, but blew the tiles off the roof just above the gutter. Stooping, he twirled the traverse knob of the directional aiming mechanism a few mills to the left, and slipped in his second bomb just as the flare fizzled out. He had stepped across to the other rocket-launcher, ripped off the firing lanyard of the rocket, sent it on its way and stuffed a fresh pair into the two launchers before he needed to look up again. The second flare burst into light above the palace and four seconds later the second bomb landed. It was dead centre, but short, for it fell onto the tiles directly above the main door.

Dupree was also pouring sweat and the grub-screw was slick between his fingers. He brought the angle of elevation slightly down, lowering the nose of the mortar a whisker towards the ground for extra range. Working the opposite way to artillery, mortars have to be lowered for extra range. Dupree's third mortar was on its way before the flare fizzled out, and he had a full fifteen seconds to send up the third flare, trot down the spit a short way to actuate the foghorn and be back in time to watch the mortar explode. It went clean over the palace roof and into the courtyard behind. He saw the red glow for a split second, then it was gone. Not that it mattered. He knew he had got his range and direction exactly right. There would be no shortfalls to endanger his own men in front of the palace.

Shannon and his men were face down in the grass as the three flares lit up the scene around them and Janni's ranging shots went in. No one was prepared to raise his head until the Afrikaner was sending the hardware over the top of the palace and into the rear courtyard.

Between the second and third explosions Shannon risked putting his head up. He knew he had fifteen seconds until the third mortar went home. He saw the palace in the glare of the third magnesium flare, and two lights had gone on in the upper rooms. After the reverberations of the second mortar bomb died away, he heard a variety of screams and shouts from inside the fortress. These were the first and last sounds the defenders made before the roar of explosives blotted out all else.

Within five seconds the foghorn had gone on, the long maniacal scream, howling across the water from the harbour spit, filling the African night with a wail like a thousand released banshees. The crash of the mortar going into the palace courtyard was almost drowned out, and he heard no more screams. When he raised his head again he would see no further damage to the front of the palace, and assumed Janni had dropped the bomb over the top. By agreement, Janni would use no more testing shots after his first on target, but go straight into the faster rhythm. From the sea behind him, Shannon heard the thud of mortars begin, steady, pulsing like a heartbeat in the ears, backed by the low monotonous wail of the foghorn that had a life of seventy seconds on its gas canister.

To get rid of forty bombs, Janni would need eighty seconds, and it was agreed that if there were a ten-second pause at any point after half-way he would cease the bombardment so his colleagues would not run forward and be blown apart by a late-comer. Shannon had few doubts Janni would not muff it.

When the main barrage began to hit the palace fifteen seconds after the thumps of their firing were heard, the eight men in the grass had a grandstand view. There was no more need for flares; the roaring crash of the mortar bombs going into the flagstone-covered courtyard behind the palace threw up gobbets of red light every two seconds. Only Tiny Marc Vlaminck had anything to do.

He was out to the left of the line of men, almost exactly in front of the main gate. Standing foresquare to the palace he took careful aim and sent off his first rocket. A twenty-foot long tongue of flame whirled out of the rear of the bazooka, and the pineapple-sized warhead sped for the main gate. It exploded high to the right-hand edge of the double-doors, ripping a hinge out of the masonry and leaving a yard-square hole in the woodwork.

Kneeling by his side, Patrick slipped the rockets out of his back-pack, spread on the ground, and passed them upwards. The second shot began to topple in mid-air and exploded against the stonework of the arch above the door. The third hit the centre lock. Both doors seemed to erupt upwards under the impact, then they sagged on the twisted hinges, fell apart and swung inwards.

Janni Dupree was half-way through his barrage and the red glare from behind the roof of the palace had become constant. Something was burning in the courtyard, and Shannon supposed it was the guard houses. When the doors swung open, the men crouching in the grass could see the red glare through the archway, and two figures swayed in front of it and fell down before they could emerge.

Marc sent four more rockets straight through the open gate into the furnace beyond the archway, which apparently was a through-passage to the courtyard behind. It was Shannon's first glimpse of what lay beyond the gate.

The mercenary leader screamed to Vlaminck to stop firing, for he had used seven of his dozen rockets, and for all Shannon knew there might be an armoured vehicle somewhere in the town, despite what Gomez had said.

But the Belgian was enjoying himself. He sent another four rockets through the front wall of the palace at ground level and the first floor, finally standing exultantly waving both his bazooka and his last rocket at the palace in front, while Dupree's mortar bombs whirred overhead.

At that moment the foghorn whined away to a whisper and died. Ignoring Vlaminck, Shannon shouted to the others to move forward, and he, Semmler and Langarotti began to run at a crouch through the grass, Schmeissers held forward, safety catches off, fingers tense on the triggers. They were followed by Johnny, Jinja, Bartholomew and Patrick, who, having no more bazooka rockets to carry, unslung his submachine gun and joined the others.

At twenty metres, Shannon stopped and waited for Dupree's last bombs to fall. He had lost count of how many were still to come, but the sudden silence after the last bomb fell told him it was over. For a second or two the silence itself was deafening. After the foghorn and the mortars, the roar and crash of Tiny's bazooka rockets, the absence of sound was almost uncanny. So much so, that it was almost impossible to realize the entire operation had lasted less than five minutes.

He wondered for a second if Timothy had sent off his dozen mortar bombs to the army barracks, if the soldiers had scattered as he surmised they would, and what the other citizens of the town had thought of the inferno that must have nearly deafened them. He was jerked into wakefulness when the next two magnesium flares exploded over him, one after the other, and without waiting longer he leapt to his feet, screamed 'Come on!' and ran the last twenty metres to the smouldering main gate.

He was firing as he went through sensing more than seeing the figure of Jean-Baptiste Langarotti to his left and Kurt Semmler closing up on his right. Through the gate and inside the archway the scene was enough to stop anybody in their tracks. The arch went straight through the main building and into the courtyard. Above the courtyard the flares still burned with a stark brilliance that lit the scene behind the palace like something from the Inferno.

Kimba's guards had been caught asleep by the first sighting shots, which had brought them out of their lean-to barracks huts and into the centre of the paved area. That was where the third shot, and the succeeding forty quick-succession bombs, had found them. Up one wall ran a ladder, and four mangled men hung from its rungs, caught in the back as they tried to run to the top of the enclosing wall. The rest had taken the full force of the mortars, exploding on stone flag and scattering lethal shards of steel in all directions.

There were piles of bodies, some still half alive, most very dead. Two army trucks and three civilian vehicles, one the presidential Mercedes, were standing shredded from end to end against the rear wall. Several palace servants, about to flee the horror in the rear, had apparently been grouped behind the main gate when Vlaminck's mortars came through. They were strewn all over the undercover area beneath the archway.

To right and left were further arches, each leading to what seemed to be a set of stairs to the upper floors. Without waiting to be asked, Semmler took the right-hand set, Langarotti the left. Soon there were bursts of submachine carbine fire from each side as the two mercenaries laundered the upper floor.

Just beyond the stairs to the upper floors were doors at ground level, two on each side. Shouting to make himself heard above the screams of the maimed Vindu and the chattering of Semmler's Schmeisser upstairs, Shannon ordered the four Africans to take the ground floor. He did not have to tell them to shoot everything that moved. They were waiting to go, eyes rolling, chests heaving.

Slowly, cautiously, Shannon moved through the archway, into the threshold to the courtyard at the rear. If there was any opposition left in the palace guards, it would come from there. As he stepped outside, a figure with a rifle ran screaming at him from his left. It could be a panic-stricken Vindu was making a break for safety, but there was no time to find out. Shannon whirled and fired, the man jack-knifed and blew a froth of blood from an already dead mouth onto Shannon's blouse front. The whole area and palace smelt of blood and fear, sweat and death, and over it all the greatest intoxicant smell in the world for mercenaries, the reek of cordite.

He sensed rather than felt the scuff of footsteps in the archway behind him and swung round. From one of the side doors into which Johnny had run to start mopping up the remaining Vindu alive inside the palace, a man had emerged. What happened when he reached the centre of the flagstones, under the arch, Shannon could only recall later as a kaleidoscope of images. The man saw Shannon the same time Shannon saw him, and snapped off a shot from the gun he clenched in his right hand at hip level.

Shannon felt the slug blow softly on his cheek as it passed. He fired half a second later, but the man was agile. After firing he went to the ground, rolled and came up in the fire position a second time. Shannon's Schmeisser had let off five shots but they went above the gunman's body as he went to the flagstones, then the magazine ran out. Before the man in the hallway could take another shot, Shannon stepped aside and out of sight behind a stone pillar, snapped out the old magazine and slapped in a new one. Then he came round the corner firing. The man was gone.

It was only then he became fully conscious that the gunman, stripped to the waist and barefoot, had not been an African. The skin of his torso, even in the dim light beneath the arch, had been white, and the hair dark and straight.

Shannon swore and ran back towards the embers of the gate on their hinges. He was too late.

As the gunman ran out of the shattered palace, Tiny Marc Vlaminck was walking towards the archway. He had his bazooka cradled in both hands across his chest, the last rocket fitted into the end. The gunman never even stopped. Still running flat out, he loosed off two fast shots that emptied his magazine. They found the gun later in the long grass. It was a Makarov 9 mm, and it was empty.

The Belgian took both shots in the chest, one of them in the lungs. Then the gunman was past him, dashing across the grass for safety beyond the reach of the light cast by the flares Dupree was still sending up. Shannon watched as Vlaminck, moving in a kind of slow motion, turned to face the running man, raised his bazooka and slotted it carefully across his right shoulder, took steady aim and fired.

Not often does one see a bazooka the size of the warhead on the Yugoslav RPG-7 hit a man in the small of the back. Afterwards, they could not even find more than a few pieces of cloth from his trousers.

Shannon had to throw himself flat again to avoid being broiled by the backlash of flame from the Belgian's last shot. He was still on the ground, eight yards away, when Tiny Marc dropped his weapon and crashed forward, arms outspread, across the hard earth before the gateway.

Then the last of the flares went out.

Big Janni Dupree straightened up after sending off the last of his ten magnesium flares and yelled 'Sunday'.

He had to shout three times before the African standing ten yards away could hear him. All three men were partly deaf from the pounding their ears had taken from the mortar and the foghorn. He shouted to Sunday to stay behind and keep watch over the mortars and the boat, then signalling to Timothy to follow him, he began to jogtrot through the scrub and bushes along the spit of sand towards the mainland. Although he had loosed off more firepower than the other four mercenaries put together, he saw no reason why he should be denied all the action.

Besides, his job was still to silence the army barracks and he knew from his memory of the maps on board the *Toscana* roughly where it was. It took the pair of them ten minutes to reach the road that ran across the end of the peninsula from side to side, and instead of turning right towards the palace, Dupree led the way left towards the barracks. Janni and Timothy had slowed to a walk, one on each side of the laterite road, their Schmeissers pointing forwards, ready to fire the moment trouble showed itself.

The trouble was round the first bend in the road. Scattered twenty minutes earlier by the first of the mortar bombs despatched by Timothy falling between the hutments that made up the barracks lines, the two hundred encamped men of Kimba's army had fled into the night. But about a dozen of them had re-grouped in the darkness, and were standing at the edge of the road muttering in low whispers among themselves. If they had not been so deaf, Dupree and Timothy would have heard them sooner. As it was, they were almost on the group before they saw them, shadows in the shadows of the palm trees. Ten of the men were naked, having been roused from sleep. The other two had been on guard duty, and were clothed and armed.

The previous night's torrential rain had left the ground so soft that most of Timothy's dozen mortar bombs had embedded themselves too deeply in the earth to have their full intended impact. The Vindu soldiers they found waiting round that corner still had something of their wits about them. One of them also had a hand grenade.

It was the sudden movement of the soldiers when they saw the white gleam of Dupree's face, from which the dye had long since run away with his sweat, that alerted the South African. He screamed 'Fire' and opened up at the group. Four of them were cut apart by the stream of slugs from the Schmeisser. The other eight ran, two more falling as Dupree's fire pursued them into the trees. As he ran, one of them turned and hurled the thing he carried in his hand. He had never used one before, nor ever seen one used. But it was his pride and joy, and he had always hoped to use it one day.

The grenade went high in the air, out of sight, and when it fell it hit Timothy full in the chest. In instinctive reaction the African veteran clutched at the object as he went over backwards, and sitting on the ground recognized it for what it was. He also saw that the fool who had thrown it had forgotten to take the pin out. Timothy had seen a mercenary catch a grenade once. He had watched as the man hurled it straight back at the enemy. Rising to his feet Timothy whipped the pin out of the grenade and threw it as far as he could after the retreating Vindu soldiers.

It went high into the air a second time, but this time it hit a tree. There was a dull clunk and the grenade fell short of where it was intended to go. At that moment Janni Dupree started in pursuit, a fresh magazine in his carbine. Timothy shouted a warning, but Dupree must have thought it was a scream of elation. He ran eight paces forward into the trees, still firing from the hip, and was two yards from the grenade when it exploded.

He did not remember much more. He remembered the flash and the boom, the sensation of being picked up and tossed aside like a rag doll. Then he must have passed out. He came to, lying out on the laterite road, and there was someone kneeling in the road beside him, cradling his head. He could feel that his throat was very warm, like the time he had had a fever as a boy, a comfortable, drowsy feeling, half awake and half asleep. He could hear a voice talking to him saying something repeatedly and urgently but he could not make out the words, 'Sorry, Janni, so sorry, sorry ...'

He could understand his own name, but that was all. This language was different, not his own language, but something else. He swivelled his eyes round to the person who was holding him and made out a dark face in the half-light beneath the trees. He smiled and said quite clearly in Afrikaans 'Hallo, Pieter.'

He was staring up at the gap between the palm fronds when finally the clouds shifted to one side and the moon came out. It looked enormous, as it always does in Africa, brilliant white and shining. He could smell the rain in the vegetation beside the road, and see the moon sitting up there glistening like a giant pearl, like the Paarl rock after the rain. It was good to be back home again, he thought. Janni Dupree was quite content when he closed his eyes again and died.

It was half past five when enough natural daylight filtered over the horizon for the men at the palace to be able to switch off their torches. Not that the daylight made the scene in the courtyard look any better. But the job was done.

They had brought Vlaminck's body inside and laid it out straight in one of the side rooms off the ground floor hallway. Beside him lay Janni Dupree, brought up from the seashore road by three of the Africans. Johnny was also dead, evidently surprised and shot by the white bodyguard who had seconds later stopped Vlaminck's last bazooka rocket. The three of them were side by side.

Semmler had summoned Shannon to the main bedroom on the first floor and showed him by torchlight the figure he had gunned down as he tried to clamber out of the window.

'That's him,' said Shannon.

There were six survivors from among the dead president's domestic staff. They had been found cowering in one of the cellars, which they had found, more by instinct than logic, to be the best security from the rain of fire from the skies. These were being used as forced labour to tidy up. Every room in the main part of the palace was examined, and the bodies of all the other friends of Kimba and palace servants who had been lying around the rooms were carried down and dumped in the courtyard at the back. The remnants of the door could not be replaced, so a large carpet taken from one of the staterooms was hung over the entrance to mask the view inside.

At five o'clock Semmler had gone back to the *Toscana* in one of the speedboats, towing the other two behind him. Before leaving he had contacted the *Toscana* on his walkie-talkie to give them the code-word meaning all was in order.

He was back by six-thirty with the African doctor and the same three boats, this time loaded with stores, the remaining mortar bombs, the eighty bundles containing the remaining Schmeissers, and nearly a ton of 9 mm ammunition.

At six, according to a letter of instruction Shannon had sent to Captain Waldenberg, the *Toscana* had begun to broadcast three words on the frequency to which Endean was listening. The words, Paw-paw, Cassava and Mango, meant respectively: The operation went ahead as planned, it was completely successful, and Kimba is dead.

When the African doctor had viewed the scene of carnage at the palace, he sighed and said, 'I suppose it was necessary.'

'It was necessary,' affirmed Shannon, and asked the older man to set about the task he had been brought to do.

By nine nothing had stirred in the town and the clearing-up process was almost complete. The burial of the Vindu would have to be done later. Two of the speedboats were back at the *Toscana*, slung aboard and stowed below, while the third was hidden in a creek not far from the harbour. All traces of the mortars on the point had been removed, the tubes and baseplates brought inside, the rocket-launchers and packing crates dropped out at sea. Everything and everyone else had been brought inside the palace, which although battered to hell from the inside, bore only two areas of shattered tiles, three broken windows in the front and the destroyed door to indicate from the outside that it had taken a beating.

At ten Semmler and Langarotti joined Shannon in the main dining room, where the mercenary leader was finishing off some jam and bread that he had found in the presidential kitchen. Both men reported on the result of their searches. Semmler told Shannon the radio room was intact, apart from several bullet-holes in the wall, but the transmitter would still send. Kimba's private cellar in the basement had yielded at last to the persuasion of several magazines of ammunition. The national treasury was apparently in a safe at the rear of the cellar, and the national armoury was stacked round the walls – enough guns and ammunition to keep an army of two or three hundred men going for several months in action.

'So now what?' asked Semmler when Shannon had heard him out.

'So now we wait,' said Shannon.

'Wait for what?'

Shannon picked his teeth with a spent match. He though of Janni Dupree and Tiny Marc lying below on the floor, and of Johnny who would not liberate another farmer's goat for his evening supper. Langarotti was slowly stropping his knife on the leather band round his left fist.

'We wait for the new government,' said Shannon.

The American-built one-ton truck carrying Simon Endean arrived just after one in the afternoon. There was another European at the wheel, and Endean sat beside him clutching a large-bore hunting rifle. Shannon heard the growl of the engine as the truck left the shore road and came slowly up to the front entrance of the palace, where the carpet hung lifeless in the humid air, covering the gaping hole where the main gate had been.

He watched from an upper window as Endean climbed suspiciously down, looked at the carpet and the other pock marks on the front of the building, and examined the eight black guards at attention before the gate.

Endean's trip had not been completely without incident. After hearing the *Toscana*'s radio call that morning, it had taken him two hours to persuade Colonel Bobi that he was actually going back into his own country within hours of the coup. The man had evidently not won his colonelcy by personal courage. Endean himself had a private motive for his bravado, a pot of gold that awaited him when the platinum in the Crystal Mountain was 'discovered' in two or three months' time.

They had set off from the neighbouring capital by road at nine-thirty on the hundred-mile drive to Clarence. In Europe that distance may take two hours; in Africa it is more. They arrived at the border in the mid-morning, and the haggle began to bribe their way past the Vindu guards, who had still not heard of the night's coup in the capital. Colonel Bobi, hiding behind a pair of large and very dark glasses, and dressed in a white flowing robe, in aspect like a nightshirt, posed as their car-boy, a personal servant who, in Africa, never requires papers to cross a border. Endean's papers were in order, like those of the man he brought with him, a hulking strong-arm from

London's East End, who had been recommended to Endean as one of the most feared protectors in Whitechapel and a former enforcer for the Kray Gang. Ernie Locke was being paid a very handsome fee to keep Endean alive and well, and was carrying a gun under his shirt, acquired locally through the offices of ManCon's mining enterprise in the republic. Tempted by the money offered, he had already made the mistake of thinking, like Endean, that a good hard-man in the East End will automatically make a good hard-man in Africa.

After crossing the frontier the truck had made good time until it blew a tyre ten miles short of Clarence. With Endean mounting guard with his rifle, Locke had changed the tyre while Bobi cowered under the canvas in the back. That was when the trouble started. A handful of Vindu troops, fleeing from Clarence, had spotted them and loosed off half a dozen shots. They all went wide except one, which hit the tyre Lock had just replaced. The journey was finished in first gear on a flat tyre.

Shannon leaned out of the window and called down to Endean. The latter looked up.

'Everything OK?' he called.

'Sure,' said Shannon. 'But get out of sight. No one seems to have moved yet, but someone is bound to start snooping soon.'

Endean led Colonel Bobi and Locke through the curtain and they mounted to the first floor where Shannon was waiting. When they were seated in the presidential dining room Endean asked for a full report on the previous night's battle. Shannon gave it to him.

'Kimba's palace guard?' asked Endean.

For answer Shannon led him to the rear window whose shutters were closed, pushed one open and pointed down into the courtyard from which a ferocious buzzing of flies mounted. Endean looked out and drew back.

'The lot?' he asked.

'The lot,' said Shannon. 'Wiped out.'

'And the army?'

'Twenty dead, the rest scattered. All left their arms behind except perhaps a couple of dozen with bolt-action Mausers. No problem. The arms have been gathered up and brought inside.'

'The presidential armoury?'

'In the cellar, under our control.'

'And the national radio transmitter?'

'Downstairs on the ground floor. Intact. We haven't tried the electricity circuits yet, but the radio seems to have a separate diesel-powered generator.'

Endean nodded, satisfied.

'Then there's nothing for it but for the new president to announce the success of his coup last night, the formation of a new government, and to take over control,' he said.

'What about security?' asked Shannon. 'There's no army left intact until they filter back, and not all the Vindu may want to serve under the new man.'

Endean grinned.

'They'll come back when the word spreads that the new man has taken over, and they'll serve under him just so long as they know who is in charge. And they will. In the meantime, this group you seem to have recruited will suffice. After all, they're black, and no European diplomats here are likely to recognize the difference between one black and another.'

'Do you?' asked Shannon.

Endean shrugged.

'No,' he said, 'but it doesn't matter. By the way, let me introduce the new president of Zangaro.'

He gestured towards the Zangaran colonel, who had been surveying the room he already knew well, a broad grin on his face.

'Former commander of the Zangaran Army, successful operator of a *coup d'état* as far as the world knows, and new president of Zangaro. Colonel Antoine Bobi.'

Shannon rose, faced the colonel and bowed. Bobi's grin grew even wider. Shannon gestured to the door at the end of the dining room.

'Perhaps the president would like to examine the presidential office,' he said. Endean translated.

Bobi nodded and lumbered across the tiled floor and through the door. It closed behind him. Five seconds later there came the crash of a single shot.

After Shannon reappeared, Endean sat for a moment staring at him.

'What was that?' he asked unnecessarily.

'A shot,' said Shannon.

Endean was on his feet, across the room and standing in the open doorway to the study. He turned round, ashen-faced, hardly able to speak.

'You shot him,' he whispered. 'All this bloody way, and you shot him. You're mad, Shannon, you're fucking crazy.'

His voice rose with his rage and bafflement.

'You don't know what you've done, you stupid, blundering maniac, you bloody mercenary idiot . . .'

Shannon sat back in the armed chair behind the dining table gazing at Endean with scant interest. From the corner of his eye he saw the bodyguard's hand move under his floppy shirt. The second crash seemed louder to Endean for it was nearer. Ernie Locke went back out of his chair in a complete somersault and sprawled across the tiles, varying the pattern of the old colonial marquetry with a thin filament of blood that came from his midriff. He was quite dead, for the soft bullet had gone through to shatter his spine. Shannon brought his hand out from under the oak table and laid the Makarov 9 mm automatic on the table. A wisp of blue smoke wriggled out of the end of the barrel.

Endean seemed to sag at the shoulders, as if the knowledge of the certain loss of his personal fortune, promised by Sir James Manson when Bobi was installed, had suddenly been compounded by the realization that Shannon was the most completely dangerous man he had ever met. But it was a bit late to realize that.

Semmler appeared in the doorway of the study behind Endean, and Langarotti slipped quietly through the dining room door from the corridor. Both held Schmeissers, catch off, very steady, pointing at Endean. Shannon rose.

'Come on,' he said, 'I'll drive you back to the border. From there you can walk.'

The single unpunctured tyre from the two Zangaran trucks in the courtyard had been fitted to the vehicle that had brought Endean into the country. The canvas behind the cab had been taken away and three African soldiers crouched in the back with submachine carbines. Another twenty, fully uniformed and equipped, were being marshalled into a line outside the palace.

In the hallway close to the shattered door they met a middle-aged African in civilian clothes. Shannon nodded to him and exchanged a few words.

'Everything OK, Doctor?'

'Yes. So far. I have arranged with my people to send a hundred volunteer workers to clean up. Also another fifty will be here this afternoon for fitting out and equipping. Seven of the Zangaran men on the list of notables have been contracted at their homes and have agreed to serve. They will meet this evening.'

'Good. Perhaps you had better take time off to draft the first bulletin from the new government. It should be broadcast as soon as possible. Ask Mr Semmler to try to get the radio working. If it can't be done, we'll use the ship, Anything else?'

'One more thing,' said the Doctor. 'Mr Semmler reports that the ship lying off the shore is a Russian vessel, the *Komarov*, which has been making repeated requests for permission to enter harbour.'

Shannon thought for several moments.

'Ask Mr Semmler to have conveyed from the shore to the *Komarov*, the following: "REQUEST DECLINED STOP INDEFINITELY STOP",' he said.

They parted and Shannon took Endean back to his lorry. He took the wheel himself and swung the truck back on the road to the hinterland and the border.

'Who was that?' asked Endean sourly as the truck sped along the peninsula, past the shanty town of the immigrant workers, where all seemed to be bustle and activity. With amazement Endean noticed that each crossroads had an armed soldier with a submachine carbine standing on point duty.

'The man in the hallway?' asked Shannon.

'Yes.'

'That was Dr Okoye.'

'A witch doctor, I suppose.'

'Actually he's a PhD of Oxford.'

'Friend of yours?'

'Yes.'

There was no more conversation until they were on the highway towards the north.

'All right,' said Endean at last, 'I know what you've done. You've ruined one of the biggest and richest coups that has ever been attempted. You don't know that, of course. You're too bloody thick. What I'd like to know is, why? In God's name, why?'

Shannon thought for a moment, keeping the truck steady on the bumpy road that had deteriorated to a dirt track.

'You made two mistakes, Endean,' he said carefully. Endean started at the sound of his real name.

'You assumed that because I'm a mercenary, I'm automatically stupid. It never seemed to occur to you that we are both mercenaries, along with Sir James Manson and most of the people who have power in this world. The second mistake was that you assumed all black people were the same, because to you they look the same.'

'I don't follow you.'

'You did a lot of research on Zangaro, you even found out about the tens of thousands of immigrant workers who virtually keep this place running. It never occurred to you that those workers form a community of their own. They're a third tribe, the most intelligent and hard-working one in the country. Given half a chance they can play a part in the political life of the country. What's more you failed to recognize that the new army of Zangaro and therefore the power in the country might be recruited from among that third community, in fact, it just has been. Those soldiers you saw were neither Vindu nor Caja. There were fifty in uniform and armed when you were in the palace, and by tonight there'll be another fifty. In five days there will be over four hundred new soldiers in Clarence, untrained of course, but looking efficient enough to keep law and order. They'll be the real power in this country from now on. There was a *coup d'état* last night, all right, but it wasn't conducted for or on behalf of Colonel Bobi.'

'For whom then?'

'For the general.'

'Which general?'

Shannon told him the name. Endean faced him, mouth open in horror.

'Not *him*. He was defeated, exiled.'

'For the moment, yes. Not necessarily for ever. Those immigrant workers are his people. They call them the Jews of Africa. There are one and a half million of them scattered over this continent. In many areas they do most of the work and have most of the brains. Here in Zangaro, they live in the shanty town behind Clarence.'

'That stupid great idealistic bastard ...'

'Careful,' warned Shannon.

'Why?'

Shannon jerked his head over his shoulder.

'They're the general's soldiers too.'

Endean turned and looked at the three impassive faces above the three Schmeisser barrels.

'They don't speak English all that well, do they?'

'The one in the middle,' said Shannon mildly, 'was a chemist once. Then he became a soldier, then his wife and four children were wiped out by a Saladin armoured car. They're made by Alvis in Coventry, you know. He doesn't like the people who were behind that.'

Endean was silent for a few more miles.

'What happens now?' he asked.

'The Committee of National Reconciliation takes over,' said Shannon. 'Four Vindu members, four Caja and two from the immigrant community. But the army will be made up of the people behind you. And this country will be used as a base and a headquarters. From here the newly trained men will go back one day to avenge what was done to them. Maybe the general will come and set up residence here, in effect to rule it.'

'You expect to get away with that?'

'You expected to impose that slobbering ape, Bobi, and get away with it. At least the new government will be moderately fair. That mineral deposit, which I happen to know is platinum, buried somewhere in the Crystal Mountains. No doubt the new government will find it, eventually. And no doubt it wil be exploited. But if you want it you will have to pay for it. A fair price, a market price. Tell Sir James that when you get back home.'

Round the corner they came within view of the border post. News travels fast in Africa, even without telephones, and the Vindu soldiers on the border post had gone. Shannon stopped the truck and pointed ahead.

'You can walk the rest,' he said.

Endean climbed down. He looked back at Shannon in the cab with undiluted hatred.

'You still haven't explained why,' he said. 'You've explained what and how, but not why.'

Shannon stared ahead up the road.

'For nearly two years,' he said musingly, 'I watched between half a million and a million small kids starved to death because of people like you and Manson. It was done basically so that you and your kind can make bigger profits through a vicious and totally corrupt dictatorship, and it was done in the name of law and order, of legality and constitutional justification. I may be a fighter, I may be a killer, but I am not a bloody sadist. I worked out for myself how it was done and why it was done, and who were the men behind it. Visible up front were a bunch of politicians and Foreign Office men, but they are just a cage full of posturing apes, neither seeing nor caring past their inter-departmental squabbles and their re-election. Invisible behind them were profiteers like your precious James Manson. That's why I did it. Tell Manson when you get back home. I'd like him to know. Personally. From me. Now get walking.'

Ten yards on, Endean turned round.

'Don't ever come back to London, Shannon,' he called. 'We can deal with people like you there.'

'I won't,' yelled Shannon. Under his breath he murmured, 'I won't ever have to.' Then he turned the truck round and headed for the peninsula and Clarence.

EPILOGUE

The new government was duly installed, and at the last count was ruling humanely and well. There was hardly a mention of the coup in the European newspapers, just a brief piece in *Le Monde* to say that dissident units of the Zangaran Army had toppled the president on the eve of Independence Day and that a governing council had taken over the administration pending national elections. But there was nothing in the newspaper to report that the Soviet mining survey team would not be permitted to land in the republic and that new arrangements for surveying the area would be made in due course.

Big Janni Dupree and Tiny Marc Vlaminck were buried down on the point, beneath the palm trees where the wind blows off the Gulf. The graves were left unmarked at Shannon's request. The body of Johnny was taken by his own people who keened over him and buried him according to their own ways.

Simon Endean and Sir James Manson kept quiet about their parts in the affair. There was really nothing they could say publicly.

Shannon gave Jean-Baptiste Langarotti the £5000 remaining in his money belt from the operation's budget, and the Corsican went back to Europe. He was last heard of heading for Burundi where he wanted to train the Hutu partisans who were trying to oppose the Tutsi-dominated dictatorship of Micombero. As he told Shannon when they parted on the shore, 'It's not really the money. It was never for the money.' Shannon wrote out letters to Signor Ponti in Genoa in the name of Keith Brown ordering him to hand over the bearer shares controlling the ownership of the *Toscana* in equal parts to Captain Waldenberg and Kurt Semmler. A year later Semmler sold out his share to Waldenberg, who raised a mortgage to pay for it. Then he went off to another war. He died in South Sudan, when he, Ron Gregory and Rip Kirby were laying a mine to knock out a Sudanese Saladin armoured car. The mine went off, killing Kirby instantly and badly injuring Semmler and Gregory. Gregory got home via the British Embassy in Ethiopia, but Semmler died in the bush.

The last thing Shannon did was to send letters to his bank in Switzerland through Langarotti, ordering the bank to make a credit transfer of £5000 to the parents of Janni Dupree, in Paarl, Cape Province, and another in the same sum to a woman called Anna who ran a bar in the Kleinstraat in Ostende's red-light quarter.

He died a month after the coup, the way he told Julie he wanted to go, with a gun in his hand, and blood in his mouth and a bullet in the chest. But it was his own gun and his own bullet. It was not the risks or the danger or the fighting that destroyed him, but the little white sticks with the filter tips. That was what he had learned from Dr Dunois in the Paris surgery.

Up to a year if he took things easy, less than six months if he pushed himself, and the last month would be bad. So he went out alone when the coughing got worse and walked into the jungle with his gun and a fat envelope full of typescript, which was sent to a friend in London some weeks later.

The natives who saw him walking alone, and later brought him back to the town for burial, said he was whistling when he went. Being simple peasants, growers of yams and cassava, they did not know what the whistling was. It was a tune called 'Spanish Harlem'.

THE END

WILBUR SMITH
WILD JUSTICE

Once again this book is for my wife
Danielle Antoinette

There were only fifteen joining passengers for the British Airways flight at Victoria Airport on the island of Mahé in the oceanic republic of the Seychelles.

Two couples formed a tight group as they waited their turn for departure formalities. They were all young, all deeply tanned and they seemed still carefree and relaxed by their holiday in that island paradise. However, one of them made her three companions seem insignificant by the sheer splendour of her physical presence.

She was a tall girl, with long limbs and her head set on a proud, shapely neck. Her thick, sun-gilded blonde hair was twisted into a braid and coiled high on top of her head, and the sun had touched her with gold and brought out the bloom of youth and health upon her skin.

As she moved with the undulating grace of one of the big predatory cats, bare feet thrust into open sandals, so the big pointed breasts joggled tautly under the thin cotton of her tee-shirt and tight round buttocks strained the faded denim of her hacked-off shorts.

Across the front of her tee-shirt was blazoned the legend 'I AM A LOVE NUT' and below it was drawn the suggestive outline of a coco-de-mer.

She smiled brilliantly at the dark-skinned Seychellois immigration officer as she slid the green United States passport with its golden eagle across the desk to him, but when she turned to her male companion she spoke in quick fluent German. She retrieved her passport and led the others through into the security area.

Again she smiled at the two members of the Seychelles Police Force who were in charge of the weapons search, and she swung the net carry bag off her shoulder.

'You want to check these?' she asked, and they all laughed. The bag contained two huge coco-de-mer; the grotesque fruit, each twice the size of a human head, were the most popular souvenirs of the Islands. Each of her three companions carried similar trophies in net bags, and the police officer ignored such familiar objects and instead ran his metal detector in a perfunctory manner over the canvas flight bags which made up the rest of their hand luggage. It buzzed harshly on one bag and the boy who carried it shamefacedly produced a small Nikkormat camera. More laughter and then the police officer waved the group through into the final Departure Lounge.

It was already crowded with transit passengers who had boarded at Mauritius, and beyond the lounge windows the huge Boeing 747 Jumbo squatted on the tarmac, lit harshly by floodlights as the refuelling tenders fussed about her.

There were no free seats in the lounge and the group of four formed a standing circle under one of the big revolving punkah fans, for the night was so close and humid – and the mass of humanity in the closed room sullied the air with tobacco smoke and the smell of hot bodies.

The blonde girl led the gay chatter and sudden bursts of laughter, standing inches above her two male companions and a full head above the other girl, so that they were a focus of attention for the hundreds of other passengers. Their manner had changed subtly since they entered the lounge, there was a sense of relief as though a serious obstacle had been negotiated, and an almost feverish excitement in the timbre of their laughter. They were never still, shifting restlessly from foot to foot, hands fiddling with hair or clothing.

Although they were clearly a closed group, quarantined by an almost conspiratorial air of camaraderie, one of the transit passengers left his wife sitting and stood up from his seat across the lounge.

'Say, do you speak English?' he asked, as he approached the group.

He was a heavy man in his middle fifties with a thick thatch of steel-grey hair, dark horn-rimmed spectacles, and the easy confident manner of success and wealth.

Reluctantly the group opened for him, and it was the tall blonde girl who answered, as if by right.

'Sure, I'm American also.'

'No kidding?' The man chuckled. 'Well, what do you know.' And he was studying her with open admiration. 'I just wanted to know what those things are.' He pointed to the net bag of nuts that lay at her feet.

'They are coco-de-mer,' the blonde answered.

'Oh yeah, I've heard of them.'

'They call them "love nuts",' the girl went on, stooping to open the heavy bag at her feet. 'And you can see why.' She displayed one of the fruit for him.

The double globes were joined in an exact replica of a pair of human buttocks.

'Back end.' She smiled, and her teeth were so white they appeared as translucent as fine bone china.

'Front end.' She turned the nut, and offered for his inspection the perfect *mons veneris* complete with a feminine gash and a tuft of coarse curls, and now it was clear she was flirting and teasing; she altered her stance, thrusting her hips forward slightly, and the man glanced down involuntarily at her own plump *mons* beneath the tight blue denim, its deep triangle bisected by the fold of material which had rucked up into the cleft.

He flushed slightly and his lips parted with a small involuntary intake of breath.

'The male tree has a stamen as thick and as long as your arm.' She widened her eyes to the size and colour of blue pansies, and across the lounge the man's wife stood up and came towards them, warned by some feminine instinct. She was much younger than her husband and very heavy and awkward with child.

'The Seychellois will tell you that in the full moon the male pulls up its roots and walks around to mate with the females –'

'As long and as thick as your arm –' smiled the pretty little dark-haired girl beside her, '– wow!' She was also teasing now, and both girls dropped their gaze deliberately down the front of the man's body. He squirmed slightly, and the two young men who flanked him grinned at his discomfort.

His wife reached him and tugged at his arm. There was a red angry rash of prickly heat on her throat and little beads of perspiration across her upper lip, like transparent blisters.

'Harry, I'm not feeling well,' she whined softly.

'I've got to go now,' he mumbled with relief, his poise and confidence shaken, and he took his wife's arm and led her away.

'Did you recognize him?' asked the dark-haired girl in German, still smiling, her voice pitched very low.

'Harold McKevitt,' the blonde replied softly in the same language. 'Neurosurgeon from Fort Worth. He read the closing paper to the convention on Saturday morning.' She explained. 'Big fish – very big fish,' and like a cat she ran the pink tip of her tongue across her lips.

Of the four hundred and one passengers in the final Departure Lounge that Monday evening three hundred and sixty were surgeons, or their wives. The surgeons, including some of the most eminent in the world of medicine, had come from Europe and England and the United States, from Japan and South America and Asia, for the convention that had ended twenty-four hours previously on the island of Mauritius, five hundred miles to the south of Mahé island. This was one of the first flights out since then and it had been fully booked ever since the convention had been convoked.

'British Airways announces the departure of Flight BA 070 for Nairobi and London; will transit passengers please board now through the main gate.' The announcement was in the soft singsong of the Creole accent, and there was a massed movement towards the exit.

'Victoria Control this is Speedbird Zero Seven Zero request push back and start clearance.'

'Zero Seven Zero you are cleared to start and taxi to holding point for runway Zero One.'

'Please copy amendment to our flight plan for Nairobi. Number of Pax aboard should be 401. We have a full house.'

'Roger, Speedbird, your flight plan is amended.'

The gigantic aircraft was still in its nose-high climb configuration and seat-belt and no-smoking lights burned brightly down the length of the first-class cabin. The blonde girl and her companion sat side by side in the roomy seats 1a and 1b directly behind the forward bulkhead that partitioned off the command area and the first-class galley. The seats that the young couple occupied had been reserved many months previously.

The blonde nodded to her companion and he leaned forward to screen her from the passengers across the aisle while she slipped one of the coco-de-mer from its net bag and held it in her lap.

Through its natural division the nut had been carefully sawn into two sections to allow removal of the milk and the white flesh, then the two sections had been glued together again just as neatly. The joint was only apparent after close inspection.

The girl inserted a small metal instrument into the joint and twisted it sharply, and with a soft click the two sections fell apart like an Easter egg.

In the nests formed by the double husk of the shells, padded with strips of plastic foam, were two smooth, grey, egg-like objects – each the size of a baseball.

They were grenades of East German manufacture, with the Warsaw Pact command designation MK IV (C). The outer layer of each grenade was of armoured plastic, of the type used in landmines to prevent discovery by electronic metal detectors. The yellow stripe around each grenade indicated that it was not a fragmentation type, but was designed for high impact concussion.

The blonde girl took a grenade in her left hand, unlatched her lap belt and slipped quietly from her seat. The other passengers paid her only passing interest as she ducked through the curtains into the galley area. However, the purser and the two stewardesses, still strapped into their fold-down seats, looked up sharply as she entered the service area.

'I'm sorry, madam, but I must ask you to return to your seat until the Captain extinguishes the seat-belt lights.'

The blonde girl held up her left hand and showed him the shiny grey egg.

'This is a special grenade, designed for killing the occupants of a battle tank,' she said quietly. 'It could blow the fuselage of this aircraft open like a paper bag or kill by concussion any human being within fifty yards.'

She watched their faces, saw the fear bloom like an evil flower.

'It is fused to explode three seconds after it leaves my hand.' She paused again, and her eyes glittered with excitement and her breath was quick and shallow.

'You –' she selected the purser, '– take me to the flight deck; you others stay where you are. Do nothing, say nothing.'

When she ducked into the tiny cockpit, hardly large enough to contain the members of the flight crew and its massed banks of instruments and electronic equipment, all three men turned to look back at her in mild surprise – and she lifted her hand and showed them what she carried.

They understood instantly.

'I am taking command of this aircraft,' she said, and then to the flight engineer, 'Switch off all communications equipment.'

The engineer glanced quickly at his captain, and when he nodded curtly, began obediently to shut down his radios – the very high frequency sets, then the high frequency, the ultra high frequency –

'And the satellite relay,' the girl commanded. He glanced up at her, surprised by her knowledge.

'And don't touch the bug.' He blinked at that. Nobody, but nobody, outside the company should have known about the special relay which, when activated by the button beside his right knee, would instantly alert Heathrow Control to an emergency and allow them to monitor any conversation on the flight deck. He lifted his hand away.

'Remove the fuse to the bug circuit.' She indicated the correct box above his head, and he glanced at the captain again, but her voice stung like the tail of a scorpion.

'Do what I tell you.'

Carefully he removed the fuse and she relaxed slightly.

'Read your departure clearance,' she instructed.

'We are cleared to radar departure on track for Nairobi and an unrestricted climb to cruise altitude of thirty-nine thousand feet.'

'When is your next "operations normal" due?'

Operations normal was the routine report to Nairobi Control to assure them that the flight was proceeding as planned.

'In eleven minutes and thirty-five seconds.' The engineer was a young dark-haired, rather handsome man with a deep forehead, pale skin and the quick, efficient manner instilled by his training.

The girl turned to the captain of the Boeing and their gazes locked as they measured each other. The captain's hair was more grey than black and cropped close to his big rounded skull. He was bull-necked, and had the beefy, ruddy face of a farmer or of a butcher – but his eyes were steady and his manner calm and unshakeable. He was a man to watch, the girl recognized instantly.

'I want you to believe that I am committed entirely to this operation,' she said, 'and that I would welcome the opportunity to sacrifice my life to my cause.' Her dark blue eyes held his without fear, and she read the first growth of respect in him. That was good, all part of her careful calculations.

'I believe that,' said the pilot, and nodded once.

'Your duty is to the four hundred and seventeen lives aboard this aircraft,' she went on. He did not have to reply. 'They will be safe, just as long as you follow my commands implicitly. That I promise you.'

'Very well.'

'Here is our new destination.' She handed him a small white typewritten card. 'I want a new course with forecast winds, and a time of arrival. Your turn on to the new heading to commence immediately after your next "operations normal" report in –' She glanced back at the engineer for the time.

'Nine minutes fifty-eight seconds,' he said promptly.

'– and I want your turn to the new heading to be very gentle, very balanced. We don't want any of the passengers to spill their champagne – do we?'

In the few minutes that she had been on the flight deck she had already established a bizarre rapport with the captain; it was a blend of reluctant respect and overt hostility and of sexual awareness. She had dressed deliberately to reveal her body, and in her excitement her nipples had hardened and darkened, pushing out through the thin cotton shirt with its suggestive legend, and the musky woman's smell of her body again intensified by her excitement filled the confined cockpit.

Nobody spoke again for many minutes, then the flight engineer broke the silence.

'Thirty seconds to "operations normal".'

'All right, switch on the H F and make the report.'

'Nairobi Approach this is Speedbird Zero Seven Zero.'

'Go ahead Speedbird Zero Seven Zero.'

'Operations normal,' said the engineer into his headset.

'Roger, Zero Seven Zero. Report again in forty minutes.'

'Zero Seven Zero.'

The blonde girl sighed with relief. 'All right, shut down the set.' Then to the captain, 'Disengage the flight director and make the turn to the new heading by hand, let's see how gentle you can be.'

The turn was a beautiful exhibition of flying, two minutes to make a change of 76° of heading, the needles of the turn-and-balance indicator never deviating a hair's breadth, and when it was completed, the girl smiled for the first time.

It was a gorgeous sunny flash of very white teeth.

'Good,' she said, smiling directly into the captain's face. 'What is your name?'

'Cyril,' he replied after a moment's hesitation.

'You can call me Ingrid,' she invited.

There was no set routine to the days in this new command of Peter Stride's, except the obligatory hour on the range with pistol and automatic weapons. No member of Thor Command – not even the technicians – were spared daily range practice.

The rest of Peter's day had been filled with unrelenting activity, beginning with a briefing on the new electronic communications equipment that had just been installed in his command aircraft. This had taken half the morning, and he had been only just in time to join his striker force in the main cabin of the Hercules transport for the day's exercise.

Peter jumped with the first stick of ten men. They jumped from five hundred feet, the parachutes seeming to snap open only seconds before they hit the ground. However, the crosswind had been strong enough to spread them out a little even from that height. The first landing had not been tight enough for Peter. They had taken two minutes fifty-eight seconds from jump to penetration of the deserted administration block standing forlornly in one of the military zones of Salisbury plain.

'If they had been holding hostages in here, we'd have arrived just in time to start mopping up the blood,' Peter told his men grimly. 'We'll do it again!'

This time they had cut one minute fifty seconds off their time, falling in a tightly steered pattern about the building – beating the time of Colin Noble's No 2 striker team by ten seconds.

To celebrate Peter had scorned the military transports and they had run the five miles to the airstrip, each man in full combat kit and carrying the enormous bundle of his used parachute silk.

The Hercules was waiting to fly them back to base, but it was after dark before they landed and taxied into Thor Command's security compound at the end of the main runway.

For Peter the temptation to leave the de-briefing to Colin Noble had been strong indeed. His driver would have picked up Melissa-Jane at East Croydon Station and she would already be waiting alone in the new cottage, only half a mile from the base gates.

He had not seen her for six weeks, not since he had taken command of Thor, for in all that time he had not allowed himself a single day's respite. He felt a tickle of guilt now, that he should be allowing himself this indulgence, and so he lingered a few minutes after the briefing to transfer command to Colin Noble.

'Where are you going for the weekend?' Colin demanded.

'She's taking me to a pop concert tomorrow night – The Living Dead, no less,' Peter chuckled. 'Seems I haven't lived until I hear the Dead.'

'Give M.J. my love, and a kiss,' Colin told him.

Peter placed high value on his new-found privacy. He had lived most of his adult life in officers' quarters and messes, constantly surrounded by other human beings. However, this command had given him the opportunity to escape.

The cottage was only four and a half minutes' drive from the compound but it might have been an island. It had come furnished and at a rental that surprised him pleasantly. Behind a high hedge of dog rose, off a quiet lane, and set in a sprawling rather unkempt garden, it had become home in a few weeks. He had even been able to unpack his books at last. Books accumulated over twenty years, and stored against such an opportunity. It was a comfort to have them piled around his desk in the small front room or stacked on the tables beside his bed, even though there had been little opportunity to read much of them yet. The new job was a tough one.

Melissa-Jane must have heard the crunch of gravel under the Rover's tyres, and she would certainly have been waiting for it. She came running out of the front door into the driveway, directly into the beam of the headlights, and Peter had forgotten how lovely she was. He felt his heart squeezed.

When he stepped out of the car she launched herself at him and clung with both arms around his chest. He held her for a long moment, neither of them able to speak. She was so slim and warm, her body seeming to throb with life and vitality.

At last he lifted her chin and studied her face. The huge violet eyes swam with happy tears, and she sniffed loudly. Already she had that old-fashioned

English porcelain beauty, there would never be the acne and the agony of puberty for Melissa-Jane.

Peter kissed her solemnly on the forehead. 'You'll catch your death,' he scolded fondly.

'Oh Daddy, you are a real fusspot.' She smiled through the tears and on tiptoe she reached up to kiss him full on the mouth.

They ate lasagne and cassata at an Italian restaurant in Croydon, and Melissa-Jane did most of the talking. Peter watched and listened, revelling in her freshness and youth. It was hard to believe she was not yet fourteen, for physically she was almost fully developed, the breasts under the white turtle-neck sweater no longer merely buds; and she conducted herself like a woman ten years older, only the occasional gleeful giggle betraying her or the lapse as she used some ghastly piece of Roedean slang – 'grotty' was one of these.

Back at the cottage she made them Ovaltine and they drank it beside the fire, planning every minute of the weekend ahead of them and skirting carefully around the pitfalls, the unwritten taboos of their relationship which centred mostly on 'Mother'.

When it was time for bed she came and sat in his lap and traced the lines of his face with her fingertip.

'Do you know who you remind me of?'

'Tell me,' he invited.

'Gary Cooper – only much younger, of course,' she added hurriedly.

'Of course,' Peter chuckled. 'But where did you ever hear of Gary Cooper?'

'They had *High Noon* as the Sunday movie on telly last week.'

She kissed him again and her lips tasted of sugar and Ovaltine, and her hair smelled sweet and clean.

'How old are you, anyway, Daddy?'

'I'm thirty-nine.'

'That isn't really so terribly old.' She comforted him uncertainly.

'Sometimes it's as old as the dinosaurs –' and at that moment the bleeper beside his empty cup began its strident, irritating electronic tone, and Peter felt the slide of dread in his stomach.

'Not now,' he thought. 'Not on this day when I have been so long without her.'

The bleeper was the size of a cigarette pack, the globe of its single eye glared redly, insistent as the audio-signal. Reluctantly Peter picked it up and, with his daughter still in his lap, he switched in the miniature two-way radio and depressed the send button.

'Thor One,' he said.

The reply was tinny and distorted, the set near the limit of its range.

'General Stride, Atlas has ordered condition Alpha.'

Another false alarm, Peter thought bitterly. There had been a dozen Alphas in the last month, but why on this night. Alpha was the first stage of alert with the team embarked and ready for condition Bravo which was the GO.

'Inform Atlas we are seven minutes from Bravo.'

Four and a half of those would be needed for him to reach the compound, and suddenly the decision to rent the cottage was shown up as dangerous self-indulgence. In four and a half minutes innocent lives can be lost.

'Darling,' he hugged Melissa-Jane swiftly, 'I'm sorry.'

'That's all right.' She was stiff and resentful.

'There will be another time soon, I promise.'

'You always promise,' she whispered, but she saw he was no longer listening. He dislodged her and stood up, the heavy jawline clenched and thick dark brows almost meeting above the narrow, straight, aristocratic nose.

'Lock the door when I'm gone, darling. I'll send the driver for you if it's Bravo. He will drive you back to Cambridge and I will let your mother know to expect you.'

He stepped out into the night, still shrugging into his duffle coat, and she listened to the whirl of the starter, the rush of tyres over gravel and the dwindling note of the engine.

The controller in Nairobi tower allowed the British Airways flight from Seychelles to run fifteen seconds past its reporting time. Then he called once, twice and a third time without reply. He switched frequencies to the channels reserved for information, approach, tower and, finally, emergency, on one at least of which 070 should have been maintaining listening watch. There was still no reply.

Speedbird 070 was forty-five seconds past 'operations normal' before he removed the yellow slip from his approach rack and placed it in the emergency 'lost contact' slot, and immediately search and rescue procedures were in force.

Speedbird 070 was two minutes and thirteen seconds past 'operations normal' when the telex pull sheet landed on the British Airways desk at Heathrow Control, and sixteen seconds later Atlas had been informed and had placed Thor Command on condition Alpha.

The moon was three days short of full, its upper rim only slightly indented by the earth's shadow. However, at this altitude it seemed almost as big as the sun itself and its golden light was certainly more beautiful.

In the tropical summer night great silver cloud ranges towered into the sky, and mushroomed into majestic thunderheads, and the moonlight dressed them in splendour.

The aircraft fled swiftly between the peaks of cloud, like a monstrous black bat on backswept wings it bored into the west.

Under the port-side wing a suddenly dark chasm opened in the clouds like the mouth of hell itself, and deep in its maw there was the faint twinkle of far light, like a dying star.

'That will be Madagascar,' said the captain, his voice overloud in the quiet cockpit. 'We are on track.' And behind his shoulder the girl stirred and carefully transferred the grenade into her other hand before she spoke for the first time in half an hour.

'Some of our passengers might still be awake and notice that.' She glanced at her wristwatch. 'It's time to wake up the others and let them know the good news.' She turned back to the flight engineer. 'Please switch on all cabin lights and the seat-belt lights and let me have the microphone.'

Cyril Watkins, the captain, was reminded once again that this was a carefully planned operation. The girl was timing her announcement to the passengers when their resistance would be at its lowest possible ebb; at two o'clock in the morning after having been awoken from the disturbed rest of intercontinental flight their immediate reaction was likely to be glum resignation.

'Cabin and seat-belt lights are on,' the engineer told her, and handed her the microphone.

'Good morning, ladies and gentlemen.' Her voice was warm, clear and bright. 'I regret having to waken you at such an inconvenient hour. However, I have a very important announcement to make and I want all of you to pay the most careful attention.' She paused, and in the cavernous and crowded cabins there was a general stir and heads began to lift, hair tousled and eyes unfocused and blinking away the cobwebs of sleep. 'You will notice that the seat-belt lights are on. Will you all check that the persons beside you are fully awake and that their seat belts are fastened. Cabin staff please make certain that this is done.'

She paused again, the belts would inhibit any sudden movement, any spontaneous action at the first shock. Ingrid noted the passage of sixty seconds on the sweep hand of her wristwatch before going on.

'First let me introduce myself. My name is Ingrid. I am a senior officer of the Action Commando for Human Rights –' Captain Watkins curled his lip cynically at the pompous self-righteous title, but kept silent, staring ahead into the starry, moonlit depths of space '– and this aircraft is under my command. Under no circumstances whatsoever will any of you leave your seats without the express permission of one of my officers – if this order is disobeyed, it will lead directly to the destruction of this aircraft and all aboard by high explosive.'

She repeated the announcement immediately in fluent German, and then in less proficient but clearly intelligible French before reverting to English once again.

'Officers of the Action Commando will wear red shirts for immediate identification and they will be armed.'

As she spoke her three companions in the front of the first-class cabin were stripping out the false bottoms from their canvas flight bags. The space was only two inches deep by fourteen by eight, but it was sufficient for the broken-down twelve-bore pistols, and ten rounds of buckshot cartridges. The barrels of the pistols were fourteen inches long, the bores were smooth and made of armoured plastic. This material would not have withstood the passage of a solid bullet through rifling or any of the newer explosive propellants but it had been designed for use with the lower velocity and pressures of multiple shot and cordite.The breech piece was of plastic as were the double pistol grips, and these clipped swiftly into position. The only metal in the entire weapon was the case-steel firing pin and spring, no bigger than one of the metal studs in the canvas flight bag, so they would not have activated the metal detectors of the security check at Mahé airport. The ten cartridges contained in each bag had plastic cases and bases, again only the percussion caps were of aluminium foil, which would not disturb an electrical field. The cartridges were packed in looped cartridge belts which buckled around the waist.

The weapons were short, black and ugly, they required reloading like a conventional shotgun, the spent shells were not self-ejecting and the recoil was so vicious that it would break the wrists of the user who did not bear down heavily on the pistol grips. However, at ranges up to thirty feet the destructive power was awesome, at twelve feet it would disembowel a man and at six feet it would blow his head off cleanly – yet it did not have the penetrating power to hole the pressure hull of an intercontinental airliner.

It was the perfect weapon for the job in hand, and within a few seconds three of them had been assembled and loaded and the two men had slipped on the bright scarlet shirts that identified them over their tee-shirts and moved to their positions – one in the back of the first-class cabin and one in the back of the tourist cabin, they stood with their grotesque weapons ostentatiously displayed.

The slim, pretty, dark-haired German girl stayed in her seat a little longer, working swifly and neatly as she opened the remaining coco-de-mer and transferred their contents into two of the netting bags. These grenades differed only from the one carried by Ingrid in that they had double red lines painted around the middle. This signified that they were electronically fused.

Now Ingrid's clear young voice resumed over the cabin address system, and the long rows of passengers – all fully awake now – sat rigid and attentive, their faces reflecting an almost uniform expression of shock and trepidation.

'– The officer of the Action Commando who is moving down the cabin at this time is placing high explosive grenades –' The dark-haired girl started down the aisle, and every fifteen rows she opened one of the overhead lockers and placed a grenade in it, closed the locker and moved on. The passengers' heads revolved slowly in unison as they watched her with the fascination of total horror. 'A single one of those grenades has the explosive power to destroy this aircraft – they were designed to kill by concussion the crew of a battle tank protected by six inches of armour – the officer is placing fourteen of these devices along the length of this aircraft. They can be detonated simultaneously by an electronic transmitter under my control –' The voice contained a hint of mischief now, a little undercurrent of laughter. '– and if that happened they'd hear the bang at the North Pole!'

The passengers stirred like the leaves of a tree in a vagrant breeze, somewhere a woman began to weep. It was a strangled passionless sound and nobody even looked in her direction.

'But don't worry yourselves. That isn't going to happen. Because everybody is going to do exactly as they are told, and when it's all over you are going to be proud of your part in this operation. We are all partners in a noble and glorious mission, we are all warriors for freedom and for the dignity of man. Today we take a mighty step forward into the new world – a world purged and cleansed of injustice and tyranny and dedicated to the welfare of all its peoples.'

The woman was still weeping, and now a child joined her on a higher, more strident note.

The dark-haired girl returned to her seat and now she retrieved the camera that had activated the metal detector at Mahé airport. She slung it around her neck and crouched again to assemble the two remaining shot pistols, carrying them and the cartridge belts she hurried forward to the flight deck where the big blonde kissed her delightedly and unashamedly on the lips.

'Karen, *Liebling*, you were wonderful.' And then she took the camera from her and slung it around her own neck.

'This –' she explained to the captain '– is not what it appears to be. It is the remote radio detonator for the grenades in the fuselage.'

He nodded without replying, and with obvious relief Ingrid disarmed the grenade that she had carried for so long by replacing the safety pin. She handed it to the other girl.

'How much longer to the coast?' she asked as she strapped and buckled the cartridge belt around her waist.

'Thirty-two minutes,' said the flight engineer promptly, and Ingrid opened the breech of the pistol, checked the load and then snapped it closed again.

'You and Henri can stand down now,' she told Karen. 'Try and sleep.'

The operation might last many days still, and exhaustion would be the most dangerous enemy they would have to contend with. It was for this reason alone that they had employed such a large force. From now on, except in an emergency, two of them would be on duty and two would be resting.

'You have done a very professional job,' said the pilot, Cyril Watkins, '– so far.'

'Thank you.' Ingrid laughed, and over the back of his seat placed a comradely hand on his shoulder. 'We have practised very hard for this day.'

Peter Stride dipped his lights three times as he raced down the long narrow alley that led to the gates of the compound without slowing the Rover, and the sentry swung the gate open just in time for him to roar through.

There were no floodlights, no bustling activity – just the two aircraft standing together in the echoing cavern of the hangar.

The Lockheed Hercules seemed to fill the entire building, that had been built to accommodate the smaller bombers of World War II. The tall vertical fin of its epinage reached to within a few feet of the roof girders.

Beside it the Hawker Siddeley HS 125 executive jet seemed dainty and ineffectual. The differing origins of the machines emphasized that this unit was a cooperative venture between two nations.

This was underscored once more when Colin Noble hurried forward to meet Peter as he cut the Rover's engine and lights.

'A grand night for it, Peter.' There was no mistaking the drawl of mid-Western America, although Colin looked more like a successful used-car salesman than a colonel in the US Marines. In the beginning Peter had believed that this strict apportioning of material and manpower on equal national lines might weaken the effectiveness of Atlas. He no longer had those doubts.

Colin wore the nondescript blue overalls and cloth cap, both embroidered with the legend 'THOR COMMUNICATIONS' which deliberately made him look more of a technician than a soldier.

Colin was Peter's second in command. They had known each other only the six weeks since Peter had assumed command of Thor – but after a short period of mutual wariness the two men had formed one of those fast bonds of liking and mutual respect.

Colin was of medium height, but none the less a big man. First glance might have given the impression that he was fat, for his body had a certain toad-like spread to it. There was no fat upon his frame, however, it was all muscle and bone. He had boxed heavyweight for Princeton and the marines, and his nose above the wide laughing mouth had been broken just below the bridge, it was lumped and twisted slightly.

Colin cultivated the boisterous bluff manner of a career athlete, but his eyes were the colour of burned toffee and were brightly intelligent and all-seeing. He was tough and leery as an old alley cat. It was not easy to earn the respect of Peter Stride. Colin had done so in under six weeks.

He stood now between the two aircraft, while his men went about their Alpha preparation with quick understated efficiency.

Both aircraft wre painted in commercial airline style, blue and white and gold, with a stylized portrait of the Thunder God on the tail fin and the 'THOR COMMUNICATIONS' title down the fuselage. They could land at any airport in the world without causing undue comment.

'What is the buzz, Colin?' Peter Stride demanded as he slammed the Rover's door and hurried to meet the American. It had taken him some time and conscious effort to adapt his language and mode of address to fit in with his new second-in-command. He had learned very early not to expect that, merely because he was the youngest major-general in the British army, Colonel Colin Noble was going to call him 'Sir' every time he spoke.

'Missing Aircraft.' It could have been a train, an embassy, even an ocean liner, Peter realized. 'British Airways. For Chrissake let's get out of the cold.' The wind was flapping the legs of Colin's overalls and tugging at his sleeves.

'Where?'

'Indian Ocean.'

'Are we set for Bravo?' Peter asked as they climbed into his command plane.

'All set.'

The interior of the Hawker had been re-styled to make it a compact headquarters and communications centre.

There was comfortable seating for four officers directly behind the flight deck. Then the two electronics engineers and their equipment occupied a separate rear compartment, beyond which were the small toilet and galley in the extreme rear.

One of the technicians looked through the communicating door as Peter stooped into the cabin. 'Good evening, General Stride – we have a direct link with Atlas established.'

'Put him on the screen,' he ordered as he sank into the padded leather of his chair behind the small working desk.

There was a single fourteen-inch main television screen in the panel directly facing Peter, and above it four smaller six-inch screens for conference communication. The main screen came alive, and the image of the big noble leonine head firmed.

'Good afternoon, Peter.' The smile was warm, charismatic, compelling.

'Good evening, sir.'

And Dr Kingston Parker tilted his head slightly to acknowledge the reference to the time difference between Washington and England.

'Right at this moment we are in the dark completely. All we have is that BA 070 with four hundred and one passengers and sixteen crew on a flight from Mahé to Nairobi has not reported for thirty-two minutes.'

Parker was Chairman of the Intelligence Oversight Board, among other duties, and he reported directly to the President of the United States in that capacity. He was the President's personal and trusted friend. They had been in the same class at Annapolis, both of them had graduated in the top twenty but, unlike the President, Parker had gone directly into government.

Parker was an artist, a talented musician, the author of four scholarly works of philosophy and politics, and a grand master of chess. A man of overwhelming presence, of vast humanity and towering intelligence. Yet also he was a secret man, avoiding the glaring scrutiny of the media, hiding his ambitions, if ambitions he had – although the presidency of the United States would not be an impossible dream to such a man – only taking up with rare skill and strength any burden that was thrust upon him.

Peter Stride had met him personally on half a dozen occasions since being seconded to Thor. He had spent a weekend with Parker at his New York home, and his respect for the man had become boundless. Peter realized that he was the perfect head for such a complex concept as Atlas, it needed the philosopher's tempering influence over trained soldiers, it needed the tact and charisma of the diplomat to deal directly with the heads of two governments, and it needed that steely intellect to make the ultimate decision that could involve hundreds of innocent lives and incur fearsome political consequences.

Now swiftly and incisively he told Peter what little they knew of Flight 070 and what search and rescue routine was already in force, before going on, 'Without being alarmist, this does seem to be the perfect target. The flight carries most of the world's leading surgeons, and the convention was public knowledge eighteen months ago. Doctors have the necessary image to appeal to public sentiment and their nationalities are nicely mixed – American, British, French, Scandinavian, German, Italian – three of those countries have notoriously *soft* records with militant activity. It's a British aircraft, and the final destination would probably have been chosen to further complicate the issue and inhibit any counter-action.'

Parker paused, and a small crease of worry appeared for a moment in the broad smooth forehead.

'I have put Mercury on condition Alpha as well – if this is a strike the final destination could just as easily be eastwards of the aircraft's last reported position.'

Atlas's offensive arm comprised three identical units. Thor would be used only in Europe or Africa. Mercury was based on the American Naval base in Indonesia and covered Asia and Australasia, while Diana was in Washington itself and ready for counter-action in either of the American continents.

'I have Tanner of Mercury on the other relay now. I will be back to you in a few seconds, Peter.'

Very well, sir.'

The screen went blank, and in the chair beside him Colin Noble lit one of his expensive Dutch cheroots and crossed his ankles on the desk in front of him.

'Seems the great god Thor came down to earth for a little poontang. When he'd finished pleasuring one of the vestal virgins he thought he'd let her know the honour she'd been given. "I'm Thor," he told her. "Tho am I," she agreed, "but it wath loth of fun.".'

Peter shook his head sorrowfully. 'That's funny?' he asked.

'Helps to while away the time.' Colin glanced at his wristwatch. 'If this is another false alarm, it's going to make it thirteen straight.' He yawned. There was nothing to do. It had all been done before. Everything was in the ultimate state of readiness. In the huge Hercules transport, every item of a comprehensive arsenal of equipment was ready for instant use. The thirty highly trained soldiers were embarked. The flight crews of both aircraft were at their stations, the communications technicians had set up their links with satellites and through them to the available intelligence computers in Washington and London. It remained only to wait – the greater part of a soldier's life was spent waiting, but Peter had never become hardened to it. It helped now to have the companionship of Colin Noble.

In a life spent in the company of many men it was difficult to form close relationships. Here in the smaller closed ranks of Thor in shared endeavour they had achieved that and become friends, and their conversation was relaxed and desultory, moving casually from subject to subject, but without relaxing the undercurrent of alertness that gripped both men.

At one stage Kingston Parker came on the screen again to tell them that search and rescue aircraft had found no indications at the last reported position of 070, and that a photographic run by the 'Big Bird' reconnaissance satellite had been made over the same area, but that film would not be ready for appraisal for another fourteen hours. Speedbird 070 was now one hour six minutes past 'operations normal' and suddenly Peter remembered Melissa-Jane. He asked communications for a telephone line and dialled the cottage. There was no reply, so the driver would have collected her already. He hung up and rang Cynthia in Cambridge.

'Damn it, Peter. This really is most inconsiderate of you.' Freshly aroused from sleep, her voice was petulant, immediately awakening only antipathies. 'Melissa has been looking forward to this –'

'Yes, I know, and so have I.'

'– and George and I had arranged –' George, her new husband, was a political history don; despite himself Peter quite liked the man. He had been very good to Melissa-Jane.

'The exigencies of the service,' Peter cut in lightly – and her voice took on a bitter edge.

'How often I had to listen to that – I hoped never to hear it again.' They were on the same futile old treadmill, and he had to stop it.

'Look, Cynthia. Melissa is on her way –'

In front of him the big television screen lit and Kingston Parker's eyes were dark with regret, as though he mourned for all mankind.

'I have to go,' Peter told the woman whom once he had loved, and broke the connection, leaning forward attentively towards the image on the screen.

'The South African radar defences have painted an unidentified target approaching their airspace,' Kingston Parker told him. 'Its speed and position correspond with those of 070. They have scrambled a Mirage flight to intercept – but in the meantime I'm assuming that it's a militant strike and we'll go immediately to condition Bravo, if you please, Peter.'

'We are on our way, sir.'

And beside him Colin Noble took his feet off the desk and thumped them together on to the floor. The cheroot was still clamped between his teeth.

The target was live and the pilot of the leading Mirage F.1 interceptor had his flight computer in 'attack' mode and all his weaponry – missiles and cannon – were armed. The computer gave him a time to intercept of thirty-three seconds, and the target's heading was constant at 210° magnetic and its ground speed at 483 knots.

Ahead of him the dawn was rising in wildly theatrical display. Avalanches of silver and pink cloud tumbled down the sky, and the sun, still below the horizon, flung long lances of golden light across the heavens. The pilot leaned forward against his shoulder straps and lifted the Polaroid visor of his helmet with one gloved hand, straining ahead for the first glimpse of the target.

His trained gunfighter's eye picked out the dark speck against the distracting background of cloud and sunlight and he made an almost imperceptible movement of the controls to avoid the direct head-on approach to the target.

The speck swelled in size with disturbing rapidity as they converged at combined speeds of nearly fifteen hundred miles per hour, and at the instant he was certion of his identification the leader took his flight, still in a tight 'fingers five', up into a vertical climb from which they rolled out neatly five thousand feet above the target and on the same heading, immediately reducing poweer to conform in speed to the big aircraft far below.

'Cheetah, this is Diamond Leader – we are visual, and target is a Boeing 747 bearing British Airways markings.'

'Diamond Leader, this is Cheetah, conform to target, maintain five thousand feet separation and avoid any threatening attitudes. Report again in sixty seconds.'

Major-General Peter Stride's executive jet was arrowing southwards and leaving its enormous protégé lumbering ponderously along in its wake. Every minute increased the distance between the two aircraft, and by the time they reached their ultimate destination – wherever that might be – there would probably be a thousand miles or more separating them.

However, the big Hercules's slow speed became a virtue when the need arose to take its heavy load of men and equipment into short unsurfaced strips in unlikely corners of the earth – perhaps in the 'hot and high' conditions that a pilot most dreads.

It was the Hawker's job to get Peter Stride to the scene of terrorist activity as swiftly as possible, and the General's job once there to stall and procrastinate and bargain until Colin Noble's assault team caught up with him.

The two men were still in contact, however, and the small central television screen in front of Peter was permanently lit with a view of the interior of the Hercules's main hold. When he lifted his head from his work, Peter Stride could see a picture of his troops, all in the casual Thor overalls, lounging or sprawled in abandoned attitudes of relaxation down the central aisle of the Hercules. They also were veterans at the hard game of waiting, while in the foreground Colin Noble sat at his small work desk, going through the voluminous check list for 'condition Charlie' which was the next state of alert when terrorist activity was confirmed.

Watching Colin Noble at work, Peter Stride found a moment to ponder once again the enormous cost of maintaining Atlas, most of it paid by the United States intelligence budget, and the obstacles and resistance that had been overcome to launch the project in the first place. Only the success of the Israelis at Entebbe and of the Germans at Mogadishu had made it possible, but there was still violent opposition in both countries to maintaining a dual national counter-action force.

With a preliminary click and hum the central screen of Peter's communications console came alive and Dr Parker spoke before his image had properly hardened.

'I'm afraid it's condition Charlie, Peter,' he said softly, and Peter was aware of the rush of his blood through his veins. It was natural for a soldier whose entire life had been spent in training for a special moment in time to welcome the arrival of that moment – yet he found contempt for himself in that emotion; no sane man should anticipate violence and death, and all the misery and suffering which attended them.

'– the South Africans have intercepted and identified 070. It entered their airspace forty-five seconds ago.'

'Radio contact?' Peter asked.

'No.' Parker shook his great head. 'It is declining contact, and we must assume that it is under the control of militants – so now I'm going to be at this desk until this thing is settled.' Kingston Parker never used the emotive word 'terrorist' and he did not like to hear it from his subordinates either.

'Never hate your adversary blindly,' he had told Peter once. 'Understand his motives, recognize and respect his strengths – and you will be better prepared to meet him.'

'What cooperation can we expect?' Peter asked.

'All African States that we have so far been able to contact have offered full cooperation, including overflight, landing and refuelling facilities – and the South Africans are being helpful. I have spoken to their defence minister and he has offered the fullest possible cooperation. They will refuse 070 landing clearance, of course, and I anticipate that it will have to go to one of the black states farther north, which is probably the militants' intention anyway. I think you know my views about South Africa – but in this instance I must say they are being very good.'

Parker brought into the television shot a black briar pipe with a big round bowl, and began to stuff it with tobacco. His hands were large, like the rest of his body, but the fingers were long and supple as those of a pianist – which of course he was. And Peter remembered the scented smell of the tobacco he smoked. Even though he was a non-smoker, Peter had not found the odour offensive. Both men were silent, deep in thought, Parker frowning slightly as he seemed to concentrate on his pipe. Then he sighed and looked up again.

'All right, Peter. Let's hear what you have.'

Peter shuffled through the notes he had been making. 'I have prepared four tentative scenarios and our responses to each, sir. The most important consideration is whether this is a strike "á l'allemande" or "á l'italienne" –'

Parker nodded, listening; although this was well-travelled ground they must go over it again. A strike in the Italian fashion was the easier to resolve, a straight demand for cash. The German tradition involved release of prisoners, social and political demands that crossed national boundaries. They worked on for another hour before they were interrupted again.

'Good God.' It was a measure of Kingston Parker's astonishment that he used such strong language. 'We have a new development here –'

It was only when 070 joined the eastern airway and began to initiate a standard approach and let down, without however obtaining air traffic control clearance, that South African Airforce Command suddenly realized what was about to happen.

Immediately emergency silence was imposed on all the aviation frequencies while the approaching flight was bombarded by urgent commands to immediately vacate national airspace. There was no response whatsoever, and one hundred and fifty nautical miles out from Jan Smuts International Airport the Boeing reduced power and commenced a sedate descent to enter controlled airspace.

'British Airways 070 this is Jan Smuts Control, you are expressly refused clearance to join the circuit. Do you read me, 070?'

'British Airways 070 this is Airforce Command. You are warned that you are in violation of national airspace. You are ordered to climb immediately to thirty thousand feet and turn on course for Nairobi.'

The Boeing was a hundred nautical miles out and descending through fifteen thousand feet.

'Diamond Leader, this is Cheetah. Take the target under command and enforce departure clearance.'

The long sleek aircraft in it mottled green and brown battle camouflage dropped like a dart, rapidly overhauling the huge multi-engined giant, diving down just behind the tailplane and then pulling up steeply in front of the gaily painted red, white and blue nose.

Skilfully the Mirage pilot stationed his nimble little machine one hundred feet ahead of the Boeing and rocked his wings in the 'Follow me' command.

The Boeing sailed on serenely as though it had not seen or understood. The Mirage pilot nudged his throttles and the gap between the two aircraft narrowed down to fifty feet. Again he rocked his wings and began a steady rate-one turn on to the northerly heading ordered by Cheetah.

The Boeing held rock steady on its standard approach towards Johannesburg, forcing the Mirage leader to abandon his attempts to lead her away.

He edged back alongside, keeping just above the jet-blast of the Boeing's port engines until he was level with the cockpit and could stare across a gap of merely fifty feet.

'Cheetah, this is Diamond One. I have a good view into target's flight deck. There is a fourth person in the cockpit. It's a woman. She appears to be armed with a machine pistol.'

The faces of the two pilots were white as bone as they turned to watch the interceptor. The woman leaned over the back of the left-hand seat, and lifted the clumsy black weapon in an ironic salute. She smiled and the Mirage pilot was close enough to see how white her teeth were.

'– a young woman, blonde hair, *mooi, baie mooi* –' the Mirage pilot reported. 'Pretty – very pretty.'

'Diamond One, this is Cheetah. Position for head-on attack.'

The Mirage thundered instantly ahead and climbed away swiftly, the other four aircraft of the flight sweeping in to resume their tight 'finger five' formation as they went out in a wide turn ahead of the Boeing.

'Cheetah. We are in position for a head-on attack.'

'Diamond Flight. Simulate. Attack in line astern. Five-second intervals. Minimum separation. Do not, I say again, do not open fire. This is a simulated attack. I say again, this is a simulated attack.'

'Diamond One – understands simulated attack.'

And the Mirage F.1 winged over and dived, its speed rocketing around the mach scale, booming through the sonic barrier in a fearsomely aggressive display.

Cyril Watkins saw him coming from seven miles ahead.

'Jesus,' he shouted. 'This is real,' and he lunged forward to take manual control of the Boeing, to pull her off the automatic approach that the electronic flight director was performing.

'Hold her steady.' Ingrid raised her voice for the first time. 'Hold it.' She swung the gaping double muzzles of the shot pistol on to the flight engineer. 'We don't need a navigator now.'

The captain froze, and the Mirage howled down on them, seemed to grow until it filled the whole view through the windshield ahead. At the last possible instant of time the nose lifted slightly and it flashed only feet overhead, but the supersonic turbulence of its passage struck and tossed even that huge machine like a piece of thistledown.

'Here comes another,' Cyril Watkins shouted.

'I mean it.' Ingrid pressed the muzzles so fiercely into the back of the flight engineer's neck that his forehead struck the edge of his computer console, and there was the quick bright rose of blood on the pale skin.

The jet blasts struck the Boeing one after the other as the Mirages attacked. Ingrid clutched wildly for support with her free hand, but kept the pistol jammed into the navigator's neck. 'I mean it,' she kept shouting. 'I'll kill him,' and they could hear the screams of the passengers even through the bulkhead of the flight deck.

Then the last Mirage was past and gone and the Boeing's flight director recovered from the battering of close separation and quickly realigned the aircraft on the the radio navigational beacons of Jan Smuts Airport.

'They won't buzz us again.' Ingrid stepped back from the flight engineer, allowing him to lift his head and wipe away the trickle of blood on the sleeve of his shirt. 'They can't come again. We are into controlled airspace.' She pointed ahead. 'Look!'

The Boeing was down to five thousand feet, but the horizon was obscured by the haze of smog and summer heat. To the right rose the smooth silhouette of the Kempton Park Power Station cooling towers and, closer at hand, the poisonous yellow tablelands of the mine dumps squatted on the flat and featureless plain of the African highveld. Around them human habitation was so dense that hundreds of windowpanes caught the early morning sun and glittered like beacons.

Closer still was the long, straight, blue streak of the main runway of Jan Smuts Airport.

'Take her straight in on runway twenty-one,' Ingrid ordered.

'We can't –'

'Do it,' snapped the girl. 'Air traffic control will have cleared the circuit. They can't stop us.'

'Yes, they can,' Cyril Watkins answered. 'Just take a look at the runway apron.'

They were close enough now to count five fuel tenders, to see the Shell company insignia on the tanks.

'They are going to block the runway.'

With the tankers were five brilliant red vehicles of the fire service and two big white ambulances. They bumped wildly over the grass verge of the runway and then, one after the other, tenders and fire control vehicles and ambulances parked at intervals of a few hundred yards down the white-painted centre line of the runway.

'We can't land,' said the captain.

'Take her off automatic and fly her in by hand.' The girl's voice was different, hard, cruel.

The Boeing was sinking through a thousand feet, lined up for runway twenty-one and directly ahead the revolving red beacons on top of the fire vehicles seemed to flash a direct challenge.

'I can't pile into them,' Cyril Watkins decided, and there was no longer hesitation nor doubt in his tone. 'I'm going to overshoot and get out of here.'

'Land on the grass,' the girl shrieked. 'There is open grass on the left of the runway – put her down there.'

But Cyril Watkins had leaned forward in his seat and rammed the bank of throttles forward. The engines howled and the Boeing surged into a nose-high climb.

The young flight engineer had swivelled his stool and was staring ahead through the windscreen. His whole body was rigid, his expression intense and the smear of blood across his forehead was in vivid contrast to the pallor of his skin.

With his right hand he gripped the edge of his desk, and the knuckles of his fist were white and shiny as eggshell.

Without seeming to move the blonde girl had pinned the wrist of that rigid right hand, pressing the muzzles of the pistol into it.

There was a crash of sound, so violent in the confines of the cabin that it seemed to beat in their eardrums. The weapon kicked up as high as the girl's golden head and there was the immediate acrid stench of burned cordite.

The flight engineer stared down incredulously at the desk top. There was a hole blown through the metal as big as a teacup, and the edges were jagged with bright bare metal.

The blast of shot had amputated his hand cleanly at the wrist. The severed member had been thrown forward into the space between the pilots' seats, with the shattered bone protruding from the mangled meat. It twitched like a crushed and maimed insect.

'Land,' said the girl. 'Land or the next shot is through his head.'

'You bloody monster,' shouted Cyril Watkins, staring at the severed hand.

'Land or you will be responsible for this man's life.'

The flight engineer clutched the stump of his arm against his belly and doubled over it silently, his face contorted by the shock.

Cyril Watkins tore his stricken gaze from the severed hand and looked ahead once more. There was wide open grass between the runway markers and the narrow taxiway. The grass had been mown knee-high, and he knew the ground beneath it would be fairly smooth.

Cyril's hand on the throttle bank pulled back smoothly, almost of its own volition, the engine thunder died away and the nose dropped again.

He held his approach aligned with the main runway until he was well in over the threshold lights. He did not want to alert the drivers of the blocking vehicles to his intention while they still had time to counter it.

'You murderous bitch,' he said under his breath. 'You filthy murderous bitch.'

He banked the Boeing steeply, realigned it with the long strip of open grass and cut the throttles completely, bringing her in nose-high and just a fraction above the stall, flaring out deliberately low and banging the Boeing down into the grass for positive touch down.

The huge machine settled to the rough strip, jolting and lurching wildly as Cyril Watkins fought the rudders to keep them lined up, holding his nose wheel off with the control yoke, while his co-pilot threw all her giant engines into reverse thrust and trod firmly down on the main landing gear brakes.

The fire engines and fuel tankers flashed past the starboard wing tip. The startled faces of their crews seemed very close and white – then 070 was past, her speed bleeding off sharply so her nose wheel dropped and she rocked and swayed gradually to a dead stop just short of the brick building which housed the approach and landing beacons, and the main radar installation.

It was 7.25 a.m. local time and Speedbird 070 was down.

'Well, they are down,' intoned Kingston Parker. 'And you can well understand the extreme efforts that were made to prevent them. Their choice of final destination settles one of your queries, Peter.'

'A l'allemand –' Peter nodded. 'It's got to be political. I agree, sir.'

'And you and I must now face in dreadful reality what we have discussed only in lofty theory –' Parker held a taper to his pipe and puffed twice before going on '– morally justifiable militancy.'

'Again we have to differ, sir,' Peter cut in swiftly, 'There is no such thing.'

'Is there not?' Parker asked, shaking his head. 'What of the German officers killed in the streets of Paris by the French resistance?'

'That was war,' Peter exclaimed.

'Perhaps the group that seized 070 believes that they are at war –'

'With innocent victims?' Peter shot back.

'The *Haganah* took innocent victims – yet what they were fighting for was right and just.'

'I'm an Englishman, Dr Parker – you cannot expect me to condone the murder of British women and children.' Peter had stiffened in his chair.

'No,' Parker agreed. 'So let us not speak of the Mau-Mau in Kenya, nor of present-day Ireland then – but what of the French Revolution or the spreading of the Catholic faith by the most terrible persecution and tortures yet devised by man – were those not morally justifiable militancy?'

'I would prefer to call it understandable but reprehensible. Terrorism in any form can never be morally justifiable.' Provoked himself, Peter used the word deliberately to provoke and saw the small lift of Parker's thick bushy eyebrows.

'There is terrorism from above – as well as from below.' Parker picked up the word and used it deliberately. 'If you define terrorism as extreme physical or physiological coercion used to induce others to submit to the will of the terrorist – there is the legal terror threat of the gallows, the religious terror threat of hell fire, the paternal terror threat of the cane – are those more morally justifiable than the aspiration of the weak, the poor, the politically oppressed, the powerless victims of an unjust society? Is their scream of protest to be strangled –'

Peter shifted uncomfortably in his chair.

'Protest outside the law –'

'Laws are made by man, almost always by the rich and the powerful – laws are changed by men, usually only after militant action. The women's suffragette movement, the civil rights campaign in this country –' Parker broke off and chuckled. 'I'm sorry, Peter. Sometimes I confuse myself. It's often more difficult to be a liberal than it is to be a tyrant. At least the tyrant seldom has doubts.' Parker lay back in his chair, a dismissive gesture. 'I propose to leave you in peace for an hour or two now. You will want to develop your plans in line with the new developments. But I personally have no doubts now that we are dealing with politically motivated militants, and not merely a gang of old-fashioned kidnappers after a fast buck. Of one other thing I am certain, before we see this one through we will be forced to examine our own consciences very closely.'

'Take the second right,' said Ingrid quietly, and the Boeing swung off the grass on to the taxiway. There seemed to be no damage to her landing gear, but now that she had left her natural element, the aircraft had lost grace and beauty and became lumbering and ungainly.

The girl had never been on the flight deck of a grounded Jumbo before, and the height was impressive. It gave her a feeling of detachment, of being invulnerable.

'Now left again,' she instructed, and the Boeing turned away from the main airport buildings towards the southern end of the runway. The observation deck of the airport's flat roof was already lined with hundreds of curious spectators, but all activity on the apron was suspended. The waiting machines and tenders were deserted, not a single human being on the tarmac.

'Park there.' She pointed ahead to an open area four hundred yards from the nearest building, midway between the terminal and the cluster of service hangars and the main fuel depot. 'Stop on the intersection.'

Grimly silent, Cyril Watkins did as he was ordered, and then turned in his seat.

'I must call an ambulance to get him off.'

The co-pilot and a stewardess had the flight engineer stretched out on the galley floor, just beyond the door to the flight deck. They were using linen table napkins to bind up the arm and try and staunch the bleeding. The stench of cordite still lingered and mingled with the taint of fresh blood.

'Nobody leaves this aircraft.' The girl shook her head. 'He knows too much about us already.'

'My God, woman. He needs medical attention.'

'There are three hundred doctors aboard –' she pointed out indifferently. 'The best in the world. Two of them may come forward and attend to him.'

She perched sideways on the flight engineer's blood-splattered desk, and thumbed the internal microphone. Cyril Watkins noticed even in his outrage that it needed only a single demonstration and Ingrid was able to work the complicated communications equipment. She was bright and very well trained.

'Ladies and gentlemen, we have landed at Johannesburg Airport. We will be here for a long time – perhaps days, even weeks. All our patience will be tried, so I must warn you that any disobedience will be most severely dealt with. Already one attempt at resistance has been made – and in consequence a member of the crew has been shot and gravely wounded. He may die of this wound. We do not want a repetition of this incident. However, I must again warn you that my officers and I will not hesitate to shoot again, or even to detonate the explosives above your heads – if the need arises.'

She paused and watched a moment as two selected doctors came forward and knelt on each side of the flight engineer. He was shaking like a fever victim with shock, his white shirt splashed and daubed with blood. Her expression showed no remorse, no real concern, and her voice was calm and light as she went on.

'Two of my officers will now pass down the aisles and they will collect your passports from you. Please have these documents ready.'

Her eyes flicked sideways, as movement caught her eye. From beyond the service hangars a line of four armoured cars emerged in line ahead. They were the locally manufactured version of the French Panhard with heavily lugged tall tyres, a raked turret and the disproportionately long barrels of the cannons trained forward. The armoured vehicles circled cautiously and parked three hundred yards out, at the four points – wing tips, tail and nose – around the aircraft, with the long cannon trained upon her.

The girl watched them disdainfully until one of the doctors pushed himself in front of her. He was a short chubby little man, balding – but brave.

'This man must be taken to a hospital immediately.'

'That is out of the question.'

'I insist. His life is in danger.'

'All our lives are in danger, doctor.' She paused and let that make its effect. 'Draw up a list of your requirements. I will see that you get them.'

'They have been down for sixteen hours now and the only contact has been a request for medical supplies and for a power link-up to the electrical mains.'

Kingston Park had removed his jacket and loosened the knot of his tie, but was showing no other ill effects of his vigil.

Peter Stride nodded at the image on the screen. 'What have your medics made of the supplies?' he asked.

'Looks like a gunshot casualty. Whole blood type AB Positive, that's rare but one of the crew is cross-matched AB Postive on his service record. Ten litres of plasmalyte B, a blood-giving set and syringes, morphine and intravenous penicillin, tetanus toxoid – all the equipment needed to treat massive physical trauma.'

'And they are on mains power?' Peter asked.

'Yes, four hundred people would have suffocated by now without the air-conditioning. The airport authority has laid a cable and plugged it into the external socket. All the aircraft's support system – even the galley heating – will be fully functional.'

'So we will be able to throw the switch on them at any time.' Peter made a note on the pad in front of him. 'But no demands yet? No negotiator called for?'

'No, nothing. They seem fully aware of the techniques of bargaining in this type of situation – unlike our friends, the host country. I am afraid we are having a great deal of trouble with the Wyatt Earp mentality –' Parker paused. 'I'm sorry, Wyatt Earp was one of our frontier marshals –'

'I saw the movie, and read the book,' Peter answered tartly.

'Well, the South Africans are itching to storm the aircraft, and both our ambassador and yours are hard pressed to restrain them. They are all set to kick the doors of the saloon open and rush in with six-guns blazing. They must also have seen the movie.'

Peter felt the crawl of horror down his spine. 'That would be a certain disaster,' he said quickly. 'These people are running a tight operation.'

'You don't have to convince me,' Parker agreed. 'What is your flying time to Jan Smuts now?'

'We crossed the Zambesi River seven minutes ago.' Peter glanced sideways through the perspex bubble window, but the ground was obscured by haze and cumulus cloud. 'We have another two hours ten minutes to fly – but my support section is three hours forty behind us.'

'All right, Peter. I will get back on to them. The South African Government has convened a full cabinet meeting, and both our ambassadors are sitting in as observers and advisers. I think I am going to be obliged to tell them about the existence of Atlas.'

He paused a moment. 'Here at last we are seeing Atlas justified, Peter. A single unit, cutting across all national considerations, able to act swiftly and independently. I think you should know that I have already obtained the agreement of the President and of your Prime Minister to condition Delta – at my discretion.'

Condition Delta was the kill decision.

'– but again I emphasize that I will implement Delta only as a last possible resort. I want to hear and consider the demands first, and in that respect we are open to negotiation – fully open –'

Parker went on speaking, and Peter Stride shifted slightly, dropping his chin into the cup of his hand to hide his irritation. They were into an area of dispute now – and once again Peter had to voice disagreement.

'Every time you let a militant walk away from a strike you immediately create the conditions for further strikes, to free the captive.'

'I have the clearance for condition Delta,' Parker reiterated with a trace of acid in his tone now, 'but I am making it clear that it will be used only with the greatest discretion. We are not an assassination unit, General Stride.' Parker nodded to an assistant off-screen. 'I am going through to the South Africans now to explain Atlas.' The image receded into darkness.

Peter Stride leapt up abruptly and tried to pace the narrow aisle between the seats, but there was insufficient headroom for his tall frame and he flung himself angrily into the seat again.

Kingston Parker stood up from his communications desk in the outer office of his suite in the west wing of the Pentagon. The two communications technicians scurried out of his way and his personal secretary opened the door to his inner office.

He moved with peculiar grace for such a large man, and there was no excess weight on his frame, his big heavy bones lean of flesh. His clothes were of fine cloth, well cut – the best that Fifth Avenue could offer – but they were worn almost to the point of shoddiness, the button-down collar slightly frayed, the Italian shoes scuffed at the toes as though material trappings counted not at all with him. Nevertheless he wore them with a certain unconscious panache, and he looked ten years younger than his fifty-three, only a few silver strands in the thick bushy mane of hair.

The inner office was spartan in its furnishings, all of it US Government issue, utilitarian and impersonal, only the books that filled every shelf and the grand piano were his own. The piano was a Bechstein grand and much too large for the room. Parker ran his right hand lightly across the keyboard as he passed it – but he went on to the desk.

He dropped into the swivel chair and shuffled through the dozen intelligence folders on his desk. Each of them contained the latest computer print-outs that he had requested. There were personal histories, appraisals, and character studies of all the personalities that had so far become involved in the taking of Speedbird 070.

Both the ambassadors – their pink files signified the highest security ratings, and were marked 'Heads of Departments only'. Four other files in lower echelon green were devoted to the South African Government personalities with decision-making capabilities in the emergency. The thickest file was that of the South African Prime Minister – and once again Parker noted wryly that the man had been imprisoned by the pro-British government of General Jan Smuts during World War II as a militant opponent of his country's involvement in that war. He wondered just how much sympathy he would have for other militants now.

There were files for the South African Ministers of Defence and of Justice, and still slimmer green files for the Commissioner of Police and for the Assistant Commissioner who had been given the on-site responsibility of handling the emergency. Of them all only the Prime Minister emerged as a distinct personality – a powerful bulldog figure, not a man easily influenced or dissuaded, and instinctively Kingston Parker recognized that ultimate authority rested here.

There was one other pink file at the bottom of the considerable stack, so well handled that the cardboard cover was splitting at the hinge. The original print-out in this file had been requisitioned two years previously, with quarterly up-dates since that time.

'STRIDE PETER CHARLES' it was headed – and reclassified 'Head of Atlas only'.

Kingston Parker could probably have recited its contents by heart – but he untied the ribbons now, and opened it in his lap.

Puffing deliberately at his pipe he began to turn slowly through the loose pages.

There were the bare bones of the subject's life. Born 1939, one of twin war-time babies of a military family, his father killed in action three years later when the armoured brigade of guards he commanded was overrun by one of Erwin Rommel's devastating drives across the deserts of North Africa. The elder twin brother had inherited the baronetcy and Peter followed the well-travelled family course, Harrow and Sandhurst, where he must have disconcerted the family by his academic brilliance and his reluctance to participate in team sports – preferring the loner activities of golf and tennis and long-distance running.

Kingston Parker pondered that a moment. They were pointers to the man's character that had disconcerted him as well. Parker had the intellectual's generalized contempt for the military, and he would have preferred a man who conformed more closely to his ideal of the brass-headed soldier.

Yet when the young Stride had entered his father's regiment, it seemed that the exceptional intelligence had been diverted into conventional channels and the preference for independent thought and action held in check, if not put aside completely – until his regiment was sent to Cyprus at the height of the unrest in that country. Within a week of arrival the young Stride had been seconded, with his commanding officer's enthusiastic approval, to central army intelligence. Perhaps the commanding officer had already become aware of the problems involved in harbouring a wonder-boy in the tradition-bound portals of his officers' mess.

For once the military had made a logical, if not an outright brilliant, choice. Stride in the sixteen years since then had not made a single mistake, apart from the marriage which had ended in divorce within two years. Had he remained with his regiment that might have affected his career – but since

Cyprus Stride's progress had been as unconventional and meteoric as his brain.

In a dozen different and difficult assignments since then, he had honed his gifts and developed new talents; rising against the trend of reduced British expenditure on defence, he had reached staff rank before thirty years of age.

At NATO Headquarters he had made powerful friends and admirers on both sides of the Atlantic, and at the end of his three-year term in Brussels he had been promoted major-general and been transferred to head British Intelligence in Ireland, bringing his own particular dedication and flair to the job.

A great deal of the credit for containing the sweep of Irish terrorism through Britain was his, and his in-depth study of the urban guerrilla and the mind of the militant, although classified departmentally, was probably the definitive work on the subject.

The Atlas concept was first proposed in this study, and so it was that Stride had been on the short list to head the project. It seemed certain the appointment would be made – the Americans had been impressed with his study and his friends from NATO had not forgotten him. His appointment was approved in principle. Then at the last moment there had developed sudden and intense opposition to the appointment of a professional soldier to head such a sensitive agency. The opposition had come from both Whitehall and Washington simultaneously, and had prevailed.

Kingston Parker knocked out his pipe, and carried the file across the room and laid it open on the music rack of the piano. He seated himself at the keyboard and, still studying the printout sheets, began to play.

The stream of music, the lovely ethereal strains of Liszt, did not interrupt his thoughts but seemed to buoy them brightly upwards.

Parker had not wanted Stride, had considered from the very first that he was dangerous, sensing in him ambitions and motivations which would be difficult to control. Parker would have preferred his own nominees – Tanner, who now commanded the Mercury arm of Atlas, or Colin Noble – and had expected that Stride would have declined a command so far below his capability.

However, Stride had accepted the lesser appointment and headed Thor. Parker suspected that there was unusual motivation in this, and had made every effort to study the man at first hand. On five separate occasions he had ordered Stride to Washington, and focused upon him the full strength of his charisma and personality. He had even invited him to stay with him in his New York home, spending many hours with him in deep far-ranging discussions – from which he had developed a prudent respect for the man's mind, but had been able to reach no firm conclusions as to his future in Atlas.

Parker turned a page of the character appraisal. When he looked for the weakness in an opponent, Parker had long ago learned to start at the groin. With this man there was no evidence of any unnatural sexual leanings. Certainly he was not homosexual, if anything too much the opposite. There had been at least a dozen significant liaisons with the opposite sex since his divorce. However, all of these had been discreet and dignified. Although three of the ladies had been married, none of them were the wives of his subordinates in the armed services, nor of brother officers or of men who might be able to adversely affect his career.

The women he chose all had certain qualities in common – they all tended to be tall, intelligent and successful. One was a journalist who had her own syndicated column, another was a former fashion model who now designed and marketed her clothes through her own prestigious outlets in London and on the continent. Then there was an actress who was a leading female member of the Royal Shakespeare Company – Parker skimmed the list impatiently, for Parker himself had no sympathy nor patience with a man who succumbed to the dictates of his body.

Parker had trained himself to be totally celibate, channelling all his sexual energies into pursuits of the mind, while this man Stride, on the other hand, was not above conducting two or three of his liaisons concurrently.

Parker moved on to the second area of weakness. Stride's inheritance had been decimated by the punitive British death duties – yet his private income even after savage taxation was still a little over twenty thousand pounds sterling a year, and when this was added to his salary and privileges as a general officer, it enabled him to live in good style. He could even indulge in the mild extravagance of collecting rare books – and, Parker observed acidly, the greater extravagance of collecting rare ladies.

However, there was no trace of any illicit hoard – no Swiss bank accounts, no deposits of gold bullion, no foreign properties, no shares in off-shore companies held by nominees – and Parker had searched diligently for them, for they would have indicated payments received, perhaps from foreign governments. A man like Stride had much to sell, at prices he could set himself – but it seemed he had not done so.

Stride did not smoke; Parker removed the old black briar from his own mouth, regarded it affectionately for a moment. It was his one indulgence, a harmless one despite what the surgeon-general of the United States had determined, and he took the stem firmly between his teeth again.

Stride took alcohol in moderation and was considered knowledgeable on the subject of wine. He raced occasionally, more as a social outing than as a serious punter, and the odd fifty pounds he would well afford. There was no evidence of other gambling. However, he did not hunt, nor did he shoot – traditional pursuits of the English gentleman. Perhaps he had moral objections to blood sports, Parker thought, though it seemed unlikely, for Stride was a superlative marksman with rifle, shotgun and pistol. He had represented Britain at the Munich Olympics as a pistol shot, winning a gold in the fifty metre class, and he spent at least an hour every day on the range.

Parker turned to the page of the print-out that gave the man's medical history. He must be superbly fit as well – his body weight at the age of thirty-nine was one pound less than it had been at twenty-one, and he still trained like a front-line soldier. Parker noticed that he had logged sixteen parachute jumps the previous month. Since joining Atlas he had no opportunity or time for golf, though when he was with NATO Stride had played off a handicap of three.

Parker closed the folder and played on softly, but neither the sensual polished feel of cool ivory beneath his fingertips nor the achingly lovely lilt of the music could dispel his sense of disquiet. Exhaustive as the report was, yet it left unanswered questions, like why Stride had downgraded himself to accept the command of Thor – he was not the kind of man who acted ill-advisedly. Yet the most haunting questions that nagged at Parker were just how strong were his qualities of resilience and independent thought, just how strongly was he driven by his ambitions and that penetrating intellect – and just how great a threat such a man would present to the evolution of Atlas into its ultimate role.

'Doctor Parker, sir –' his assistant knocked lightly and entered, '– there are new developments.'

Parker sighed softly. 'I'm coming,' he said, and let the last sad and beautiful notes fall from his long, powerful fingers before he stood up.

The Hawker slid almost silently down the sky. The pilot had closed down power at five thousand feet and made his final approach without touching the throttles again. He was ten knots above the stall as he passed over the boundary fence and he touched down twenty feet beyond the chevron markings of the threshold of runway One Fife, instantly applying maximum safe braking. One Fife was the secondary cross-wind runway and the Hawker's roll-out was so short that every part of the landing had been screened by the building of the main airport terminal from where Speedbird 070 stood at the southern intersection of the main taxiway.

The pilot swung the Hawker through 360° and back-tracked sedately up runway fifteen, using just enough power to keep her rolling.

'Well done,' grunted Peter Stride, crouching behind the pilot's seat. He was almost certain that nobody aboard 070 had remarked their arrival.

'They've prepared a slot for us, with hook up to the electrical mains at the north –' Peter broke off as he saw the apron marshal waving them in with the bats, and beyond him a tight group of four men waiting. Three of them wore camouflage battledress and the other the trim blue uniform, cap and gold insignia of a senior South African police officer.

The uniformed officer was the first to greet Peter as he came down the Hawker's fold-out air-stairs.

'Prinsloo.' He shook hands. 'Lieutenant-General.'

He ranked Peter, but it was a police, not a military appointment. He was a stocky man, with steel-rimmed spectacles, a little paunchy, and not less than fifty-five years of age. He had the rather heavy features, the fleshiness of jowl and lips, that Peter had noticed so often in Belgian and Dutch peasants during his NATO tour in the Netherlands. A man of the earth, dour and conservative.

'Let me introduce Commandant Boonzaier.' This was a military rank, equivalent to that of colonel, and he was a younger man, but with the same thick accent and his features cast in the same mould. A tall man, however, only an inch or so shorter than Peter – but both of the South Africans were suspicious and resentful, and the reason was immediately apparent.

'I have been instructed to take my orders from you, General,' and there was a subtle shift of position, the two officers ranging themselves beside Peter, but facing each other, and he was aware instantly that not all the hostility was directed at him. There had been friction between police and military already – and the basic value of Atlas was underlined yet again.

A single clean-cut line of command and of responsibility was absolutely essential – Peter's mind flicked back to the shoot-out at Larnaca Airport between Egyptian commandos and Cypriot national guardsmen, from which the hijackers of the grounded jet emerged unscathed while the airfield was littered with the burning wreckage of the Egyptian transport aircraft and dozens of dead and dying Cypriots and Egyptians.

The first principle of terrorist strategy was to strike at the point where national responsibilities were blurred. Atlas cut through that.

'Thank you.' Peter accepted command without flaunting it. 'My back-up team will land in just over three hours' time. We will, of course, use force only as a last resort – but if it comes to that, I will use exclusively Atlas personnel in any counterstrike. I would like to make that quite clear immediately.' And he saw the line of the soldier's mouth harden with disappointment.

'My men are the élite –'

'It's a British aircraft, most of the hostages are British or American nationals – it's a political decision, Colonel. But I would value your help in other areas.' Peter turned him aside tactfully.

'Firstly, I want you to suggest a position where I can place my surveillance equipment – and then we will go over the ground together.'

Peter had no difficulty selecting his forward observation post. The service manager's roomy, sparsely furnished office on the third floor of the terminal building overlooked the entire service area and the southern portion of the taxiway where the Boeing stood.

The windows had been left open when the offices were evacuated, so there was no need to change the external appearance of the room.

The overhang of the observation balcony on the floor above shaded the interior, and the office was deep enough to ensure that an observer out there in the bright glare of sunshine would not be able to see into the room, even with a powerful lens. The militants would expect surveillance from the glass control tower high above – any deception, however trivial, was worthwhile.

The surveillance equipment was lightweight and compact, the television cameras were neither of them bigger than a Super 8-mm home movie camera and a man could carry in one hand both of the aluminium extension tripods. However, the cameras could zoom to 800-mm focal length, and they repeated on the screens of the command console in the cabin of the Hawker, while the image was simultaneously stored on video tape.

The audio intensifier was more bulky, but no heavier. It had a four-foot dish antenna, with the sound collector in the centre. The telescopic sight could aim the intensifier at a sound source with the accuracy of a sniper's rifle – could focus on the lips of a human being at eight hundred yards distance and clearly record normal conversation at that range, passing sound directly to the command console and at the same time storing it on the big magnetic tape spools.

Two of Peter's communications team were posted here, with a plentiful supply of coffee and doughnuts, and Peter, accompanied by the South African colonel and his staff, went up in the elevator to the glass house of the control tower.

From the air traffic control tower there was an unobstructed view across the airfield and over the apron and service areas around the terminal. The observation platform below the tower had been cleared of all but military personnel.

'– I have road blocks at all the main entrances to the airfield. Only passengers with confirmed reservations and current tickets are being allowed through – no thrill seekers – and we are using only the northern section of the terminal for traffic.'

Peter nodded and turned to the senior controller. 'What is the state of your traffic pattern?'

'We have refused clearance to all private flights, incoming and departing. All domestic scheduled flights have been re-routed to Lanseria and Germiston airports, and we are landing and despatching only international scheduled flights – but the backlog has delayed departures by three hours.'

'What separation are you observing from 070?' Peter asked.

'Fortunately the international departures terminal is the farthest from the aircraft, and we are not using the taxiways or the apron of the southern section. As you see, we have cleared the entire area – except for those three SA Airways aircraft which are undergoing overhaul and servicing, there are no other aircraft within a thousand yards of 070.'

'I may have to freeze all traffic, if –' Peter paused, 'or should I say, when we have an escalation.'

'Very well, sir.'

'In the meantime, you may continue as you are at present.' Peter lifted his binoculars and once again very carefully examined the huge Boeing.

It stood in stately isolation, silent and seemingly abandoned. The bright, almost gaudy marking gave her a carnival air. Red and blue and crisp sparkling white in the brilliant sunlight of the highveld. She was parked fully broadside to the tower, and all her hatches and doors were still armed and locked.

Peter traversed slowly along the line of perspex windows down the length of the fuselage – but over each of them the sunshades had been firmly closed from the interior, turning them into the multiple eyes of a blinded insect.

Peter lifted his scrutiny slightly on to the windshield and side panels of the flight deck. These again had been screened with blankets, hung over them from inside, completely thwarting any glimpse of the crew or their captors – and certainly preventing a shot into the flight deck, although the range from the nearest corner of the terminal was not more than four hundred yards, and with the new laser sights one of Thor's trained snipers could pick through which eye of the human head he would put a bullet.

Snaking across the open tarmac of the taxiway was the thin black electrical cable that connected the aircraft to the mains supply, a long, vulnerable umbilical cord. Peter studied it thoughtfully, before turning his attention to the four Panhard armoured cars. A little frown of irritation crossed his forehead.

'Colonel, please recall those vehicles.' He tried not to let the irritation come through in his tone. 'With the turrets battened down, your crews will be roasting like Christmas geese.'

'General, I feel it my duty –' Boonzaier began, and Peter lowered the glasses and smiled. It was a charming, friendly grin that took the man by surprise, after the previous stern set of features – and yet the eyes were devoid of humour, cracking blue and hard in the craggy granite of the face.

'I want to de-fuse the atmosphere as much as possible.' The necessity to explain irked Peter, but he maintained the smile. 'Somebody with four great cannons aimed at him is more likely to make a bad decision, and pull the trigger himself. You may keep them in close support, but get them out of sight into the terminal car park, and let your men rest.'

With little grace the colonel passed the order over the walkie-talkie on his belt, and as the vehicles started up and slowly pulled away behind the line of hangars, Peter went on remorselessly.

'How many men have you got deployed?' He pointed to the line of soldiers along the parapet of the observation balcony, and then to the heads visible as specks between the soaring blue of the African sky and the silhouette of the service hangars.

'Two hundred and thirty.'

'Pull them out,' Peter instructed, 'and let the occupants of the aircraft see them go.'

'All of them?' incredulously.

'All of them,' Peter agreed, and now the smile was wolfish, 'and quickly, please, Colonel.'

The man was learning swiftly, and he lifted the miniaturized walkie-talkie to his mouth again. There were a few moments of scurrying and confusion amongst the troops on the observation deck below before they could be formed up and marched away in file. Their steel helmets, like a bobbing line of button mushrooms, and the muzzles of their slung weapons would show above the parapet, and would be clearly visible to an observer in the Boeing.

'If you treat these people, these animals –' the colonel's voice was choked slightly with frustration, '– if you treat them soft –'

Peter knew exactly what was coming, '– and if you keep waving guns in their faces, you will keep them alert and on their toes, Colonel. Let them settle down a little and relax, let them get very confident.' He spoke without lowering the binoculars. With a soldier's eye for ground he was picking the site for his four snipers. There was little chance that he would be able to use them – they would have to take out every single one of the enemy at the same instant – but a remote chance might just offer itself, and he decided to place one gun on the service hangar roof, there was a large ventilator which could be pierced and would command the port side of the aircraft, two guns to cover the flight deck from both sides – he could use the drainage ditch down the edge of the main runway to get a man into the small hut that housed the approach radar and ILS beacons. The hut was in the enemy's rear. They might not expect fire from that quarter – point by point from his mental checklist Peter planned his dispositions, scribbling his decisions into the small leather-covered notebook, poring over the large-scale map of the airport, converting gradients and angles into fields of fire, measuring 'ground to cover' and 'time to target' for an assault force launched from the nearest vantage points, twisting each problem and evaluating it, striving for novel solutions to each, trying to think ahead of an enemy that was still faceless and infinitely menacing.

It took him an hour of hard work before he was satisfied. Now he could pass his decisions to Colin Noble on board the incoming Herc, and within four minutes of the big landing wheels hitting tarmac his highly trained team with their complex talents and skills would be in position.

Peter straightened up from the map and tucked the notebook under the flap of his button-down breast pocket. Once again he scrutinized every inch of the silent, battened-down aircraft through his glasses – but this time he allowed himself the luxury of gut emotion,.

He felt the anger and the hatred rise from some hidden depth of his soul and flush his blood and tighten the muscles of his belly and thighs.

Once again he was confronted by the many-headed monster. It crouched out there in ambush, waiting for him as it had so often before.

He remembered suddenly the shards of splintered glass littering the cobbles of a Belfast street and glittering like diamond chips in the arc lamps, the smell of explosives and blood thick in the air.

He remembered the body of a young woman lying in the gutted interior of a fashionable London restaurant. Her lovely young body stripped by the blast of all but a flimsy pearl-coloured pair of French lace panties.

He remembered the smell of a family, father, mother and three small children, burning in the interior of their saloon car, the bodies blackening and twisting in a slow macabre ballet as the flames scorched them. Peter had not been able to eat pork since that day.

He remembered the frightened eyes of a child, through a mask of blood, a dismembered arm lying beside her, the pale fingers still clutching a grubby little rag doll.

The images flashed in disjointed sequences across his memory, feeding his hatred until it pricked and stung behind his eyes and he had to lower the binoculars and wipe his eyes with the back of his hand.

It was the same enemy that he had hunted before, but his instincts warned him that it had grown even stronger and more inhuman since last he had met and fought it. He tried to suppress the hatred now, lest it cloud his judgement, lest it handicap him during the difficult hours and days that he knew lay ahead – but it was too powerful, had been too long nurtured.

He recognized that hatred was the enemy's vice, that from it sprang their twisted philosophy and their monstrous actions, and that to descend to hatred was to descend to their sub-human levels – yet still the hatred persisted.

Peter Stride understood clearly that his hatred was not only for the ghastly death and mutilation that he had witnessed so often. More it was fostered by the threat that he recognized to an entire society and its civilized rule of law. If this evil should be allowed to triumph, then in the future laws would be made by the wild-eyed revolutionary, with a gun in his fist – the world would be run by the destroyers instead of the builders, and Peter Stride hated that possibility even more than the violence and the blood, and those he hated as a soldier hates. For only a soldier truly knows the horror of war.

His soldier's instinct now was to immediately engage the enemy and destroy him – but the scholar and philosopher in him warned that this was not the moment, and with an enormous effort of will he held that fighting man's instinct in check.

Yet still he was deeply aware that it was for this moment, for this confrontation of the forces of evil, that he had jeopardized his whole career.

When command of Atlas had been plucked away and a political appointee named in his place, Peter should have declined the offer of a lesser position in Atlas. There were other avenues open to him, but instead he had elected to stay with the project – and he hoped that nobody had guessed at the resentment he felt. God knows, Kingston Parker had no cause for complaint since then. There was no harder working officer on Atlas, and his loyalty had been tested more than once.

Now all that seemed worthwhile, and the moment for which he had worked had arrived. The enemy waited for him out there on the burning tarmac under an African sun, not on a soft green island in the rain nor in the grimy streets of a crowded city – but still it was the same old enemy, and Peter knew his time would come.

His communications technicians had Colin Noble on the main screen as Peter ducked into the Hawker's cabin that was now his command headquarters, and settled into his padded seat. On the top right screen was a panoramic view of the southern terminal area, with the Boeing squatting like a brooding eagle upon its nest in the centre of the shot. On the next screen beside it was a blow-up through the 800-mm zoom lens of the Boeing's flight deck. So crisp was the detail that Peter could read the maker's name on the tab of the blanket that screened the windshield. The third small screen held a full shot of the interior of the air traffic control tower. In the foreground the controllers in shirt sleeves sitting over the radar repeaters, and beyond them through the floor to ceiling windows still another view of the Boeing. All these were being shot through the cameras installed an hour earlier in the terminal building. The remaining small screen was blank, and Colin Noble's homely, humorous face filled the main screen.

'Now if only it had been the cavalry instead of the US marines,' Peter said, 'you'd have been here yesterday –'

'What's your hurry, pal. Doesn't look like the party has started yet.' Colin grinned at him from the screen and pushed his baseball cap to the back of his head.

'Damned right,' Peter agreed. 'We don't even know who is throwing the party. What's your latest estimate on arrival time?'

'We've picked up a good wind – one hour twenty-two minutes to fly now,' Colin told him.

'Right, let's get down to it,' Peter said, and he began his briefing, going carefully over the field notes he had taken. When he wanted to emphasize a point, Peter called for a change of shot from his cameramen, and they zoomed in or panned to his instruction, picking up the radar shed or the service hangar ventilator where Peter was siting his snipers. The image was repeated not only on the command console but in the cavernous body of the approaching Hercules so that the men who would be called to occupy those positions could study them now and prepare themselves thoroughly for the moment. The same images were hurled across the stratosphere to the circling satellite and from there bounced down to appear, only slightly distorted, on the screen of Atlas Command in the west wing of the Pentagon. Sagging like an old lion in his armchair, Kingston Parker followed every word of the briefing, rousing himself only when a long telex message was passed to him by his assistant, then he nodded a command to have his own televised image superimposed on Peter's command console.

'I'm sorry to interrupt you, Peter, but we've got a useful scrap here. Assuming that the militant group boarded 070 at Mahé, we asked the Seychelles Police to run a check on all joining passengers. There were fifteen of them, ten of whom were Seychelles residents. A local merchant and his wife, and eight unaccompanied children between nine and fourteen years of age. They are the children of expatriate civil servants employed on contract by the Seychelles Government, returning to schools in England for the new term.'

Peter felt the weight of dread bearing down upon him like a physical burden. Children, the young lives seemed somehow more important, somehow more vulnerable. But Parker was reading from the telex flimsy in his left hand, the right scratching the back of his neck with the stem of his pipe.

'There is one British businessman, Shell Oil Company, and well-known on the island, and there are four tourists, an American, a Frenchman, and two

Germans. These last four appeared to be travelling in a group, the immigration and security officers remember them well. Two women and two men, all young. Names Sally-Anne Taylor, twenty-five years, American, Heidi Hottschauser, twenty-four and Gunther Retz, twenty-five, the two Germans, and Henri Larousse, twenty-six, the Frenchman. The police have run a back check on the four. They stayed two weeks at the Reef Hotel outside Victoria, the women in one double room and the two men in another.They spent most of the time swimming and sunbathing – until five days ago when a small ocean-going yacht called at Victoria. Thirty-five foot, single-hander around the world, skippered by another American. The four spent time on board her every day of her stay, and the yacht sailed twenty-four hours before the departure of 070.'

'If the yacht delivered their arms and munitions, then this operation has been planned for a long time,' Peter pondered, 'and damn well planned.'

Peter felt the tingling flush of his blood again, the form of the enemy was taking shape now, the outline of the beast becoming clearer, and always it was uglier and more menacing.

'You have run the names through the computer?' he asked.

'Nothing.' Parker nodded. 'Either there is no intelligence record of them, or the names and passports are false –'

He broke off as there was sudden activity on the screen that monitored the air traffic control tower, and another voice boomed out of the secondary speaker; the volume was set too high, and the technician at the control board adjusted it swiftly. It was a female voice, a fresh, clear young voice speaking English with the lilt and inflection of the west coast of America in it.

'Jan Smuts tower, this is the officer commanding the task force of the Action Commando for Human Rights that has control of Speedbird 070. Stand by to copy a message.'

'Contact!' Peter breathed. 'Contact at last.'

On the small screen Colin Noble grinned and rolled his cheroot expertly from one side of his mouth to the other. 'The party has begun,' he announced, but there was the razor edge in his voice not entirely concealed by his jocular tone.

The three-man crew had been moved back from the flight deck, and were held in the first class seats vacated by the group of four.

Ingrid had made the cockpit of the Boeing her headquarters, and she worked swiftly through the pile of passports, filling in the name and nationality of each passenger of the seating plan spread before her.

The door to the galley was open, and except for the hum of the air-conditioning, the huge aircraft was peculiarly silent. Conversation in the cabins was prohibited, and the aisles were patrolled by the red-shirted commandos to enforce this edict.

They also ordered the use of the toilets, a passenger must return to his seat before another was allowed to rise. The toilet doors had to remain open during use, so that the commandos could check at a glance.

Despite the silence, there was a crackling atmosphere of tension down the full length of the cabin. Very few of the passengers, mostly the children, were asleep, but the others sat in rigid rows, their faces taut and strained – watching their captors with a mixture of hatred and of fear.

Henri, the Frenchman, slipped into the cockpit.

'They are pulling back the armoured cars,' he said. He was slim, with a very youthful face and dreaming poet's eyes. He had grown a drooping blond gunfighter's moustache, but the effect was incongruous.

Ingrid looked up at him. 'You are so nervous, chéri.' She shook her head. 'It will all be all right.'

'I am not nervous,' he answered her stiffly.

She chuckled fondly, and reached up to touch his face. 'I did not mean it as an insult.' She pulled his face down and kissed him, thrusting her tongue deeply into his mouth. 'You have proved your courage – often,' she murmured.

He dropped his pistol on to the desk with a clatter and reached for her. The top three buttons of her red cotton shirt were unfastened, and she let him grope and find her breasts.

They were heavy and pointed and his breathing went ragged as he teased out her nipples. They hardened erect like jelly beans – but when he reached down with his free hand for the zipper of her shorts, she pushed him away roughly.

'Later,' she told him brusquely, 'when this is over. Now get back into the cabin.' And she leaned forward and lifted a corner of the blanket that screened the side window of the cockpit. The sunlight was very bright but her eyes adjusted swiftly and she saw the row of helmeted heads above the parapet of the observation deck. So they were pulling back the troops as well. It was nearly time to begin talking – but she would let them stew in their own juice just a little longer.

She stood up, buttoned her shirt and adjusted the camera on its strap around her neck, paused in the galley to rearrange the shiny mass of golden hair – and then walked slowly back down the full length of the central aisle, pausing to adjust the blanket over a sleeping child, to listen attentively to the complaints of the pregnant wife of the Texan neuro-surgeon.

'You and the children will be the first off this plane – I promise you.'

When she reached the prone body of the flight engineer, she knelt beside him.

'How is he?'

'He is sleeping now. I shot him full of morphine.' The fat little doctor muttered, not looking at her, so she could not read the hatred in his expression. The injured arm was elevated to control the bleeding, sticking up stiffly in its cocoon of pressure bandages. Oddly foreshortened with the bright ooze of blood through the dressing.

'You are doing good –' She touched his arm. 'Thank you.' And now he glanced at her startled, and she smiled – such a radiant lovely smile, that he began to melt.

'Is that your wife?' Ingrid dropped her voice, so that he alone could hear –

and he nodded, glancing at the plump little Jewish woman in the nearest seat. 'I will see she is amongst the first to leave,' she murmured, and his gratitude was pathetic. She stood and went on down the aircraft.

The red-shirted German stood at the head of the tourist cabin, beside the curtained entrance to the second galley. He had the intense drawn face of a religious zealot, dark burning eyes, long black hair falling almost to his shoulders – a white scar twisted the corner of his upper lip into a perpetual smirk.

'Kurt, everything is all right?' she asked in German.

'They are complaining of hunger.'

'We will feed them in another two hours – but not as much as they expect –' and she ran a contemptuous glance down the cabin. 'Fat,' she said quietly, '– big fat bourgeoisie pigs,' and she stepped through the curtains into the galley and looked at him in invitation. He followed her immediately, drawing the curtains behind them.

'Where is Karen?' Ingrid asked, as he unbuckled his belt. She needed it very badly, the excitement and the blood had inflamed her.

'She is resting – at the back of the cabin.'

Ingrid slipped the button that held the front of her shorts together and drew down the zipper. 'All right, Kurt,' she whispered huskily, 'but quickly, very quickly.'

Ingrid sat in the flight engineer's seat, at her shoulder stood the dark-haired girl. She wore the cartridge belt across the shoulder of her bright red skirt, like a bandolier – and she carried the big ugly pistol on her hip.

Ingrid held the microphone to her lips, and combed the fingers of her other hand through the thick golden tangle of her tresses as she spoke.

'– One hundred and ninety-eight British subjects. One hundred and forty-six American nationals –' She was reading the list of her captives. 'There are one hundred and twenty-two women on board, and twenty-six children under the age of sixteen years.' She had been speaking for nearly five minutes and now she broke off and shifted in her seat, turning to smile at Karen over her shoulder. The dark-haired girl smiled in return and reached across to caress the fine mass of golden hair with a narrow bony hand, before letting it drop back to her side.

'We have copied your last transmission.'

'Call me Ingrid.' She spoke into the mike with the smile turning into a wicked grin. Then there was a moment's silence as the controller in the tower recovered from his shock.

'Roger, Ingrid. Do you have any further messages for us?'

'Affirmative, Tower. As this is a British aircraft and as three hundred and forty-four of my passengers are either British or American, I want a spokesman, representing the embassies of those countries. I want him here in two hours' time to hear my terms for the release of passengers.'

'Stand by, Ingrid. We will be back to you immediately we have been able to contact the ambassadors.'

'Don't horse around, Tower.' Ingrid's voice snapped. 'We both know damned well they are breathing down your neck. Tell them I want a man here in two hours – otherwise I am going to be forced to put down the first hostage.'

Peter Stride was stripped down to a pair of bathing trunks, and he wore only canvas sneakers on his feet. Ingrid had insisted on a face-to-face meeting, and Peter had welcomed the opportunity to assess at close range.

'We'll be covering you every inch of the way there and back,' Colin Noble told Peter, fussing over him like a coach over his fighter before the gong. 'I'm handling the gunners, personally.'

The snipers were armed with specially hand-built .222 magnums with accurized barrels that threw small light bullets with tremendous velocity and striking power. The ammunition was match-grade, each round lovingly hand finished and polished. The infra-red telescopic sights were readily interchangeable with the laser sights, making the weapon deadly accurate either in daylight or at night. The bullet had a clean, flat trajectory up to seven hundred yards. They were perfectly designed mankillers, precision weapons that reduced the danger to bystanders or hostages. The light bullet would slam a man down with savage force, as though he had been hit by a charging rhinoceros, but it would break up in his body, and not over-penetrate to kill beyond the target.

'You're getting into a lather,' Peter grunted. 'They want to talk, not shoot – not yet, anyway.'

'The female of the species –' Colin warned, '– that one is real poison.'

'More important than the guns are the cameras, and sound equipment.'

'I went up there and kicked a few arses. You'll get pictures that will win you an Oscar – my personal guarantee.' Colin checked his wristwatch. 'Time to go. Don't keep the lady waiting.' He punched Peter's shoulder lightly. 'Hang loose,' he said, and Peter walked out into the sunshine, lifting both hands above his shoulders, palms open, fingers extended.

The silence was as oppressive as the dry fierce heat, but it was intentional. Peter had frozen all air traffic, and had ordered the shut down of all machinery in the entire terminal area. He did not want any interference with his sound equipment.

There was only the sound of his own footfalls, and he stepped out briskly – but still it was the longest walk of his life, and the closer he got to the aircraft, the higher it towered above him. He knew that he had been required to strip almost naked, not only to ensure that he carried no weapons, but to place him at a disadvantage – to make him feel ill at ease, vulnerable. It was an old trick – the Gestapo always stripped the victim of an interrogation – so he held himself proud and tall, pleased that his body was so lean and hard and muscled like an athlete's. He would have hated to drag a big, pendulous gut and sagging old-man's tits across those four hundred yards.

He was half-way there when the forward door, just behind the cockpit, slid back and a group of figures appeared in the square opening. He narrowed his eyes, there were two uniformed figures, no, three – British Airways uniforms, the two pilots and between them the shorter slimmer feminine figure of a stewardess.

They stood shoulder to shoulder, but beyond them he could make out another head, a blonde head – but the angle and the light were against him.

Closer, he saw that the older pilot was on the right, short-cropped grey curls, ruddy round face – that would be Watkins, the commander. He was a good man, Peter had studied his service record. He ignored the co-pilot and stewardess and strained for a glimpse of the figure beyond them, but it was only when he stopped directly below the open hatch that she moved to let him get a clear view of her face.

Peter was startled by the loveliness of that golden head, by the smooth gloss of young sun-polished skin and the thundering innocence of wide-set, steady, blue eyes – for a moment he could not believe she was one of them, then she spoke.

'I am Ingrid,' she said. Some of the most poisonous flowers are the loveliest, he thought.

'I am the accredited negotiator for the British and American Governments,' he said, and switched his gaze to the beefy red face of Watkins. 'How many members of your commando are aboard?' he asked.

'No questions!' Ingrid snapped fiercely, and Cyril Watkins extended four fingers of his right hand down his thigh without a change of expression.

It was vital confirmation of what they already suspected, and Peter felt a rush of gratitude towards the pilot.

'Before we discuss your terms,' Peter said, 'and out of common humanity, I would like to arrange for the well being and comfort of your hostages.'

'They are well cared for.'

'Do you need food or drinking water?'

The girl threw back her head and laughed delightedly. 'So you can dope it with laxative – and have us knee deep in shit? Stink us out, hey?'

Peter did not pursue it. The doped trays had already been prepared by his doctor.

'You have a gunshot casualty on board?'

'There are no wounded aboard,' the girl denied flatly, cutting her laughter short – but Watkins made the circular affirmative sign of thumb and forefinger, effectively contradicting her, and Peter noticed the spots of dried blood on the sleeves of his white shirt. 'That's enough,' Ingrid warned Peter. 'Ask one more question and we'll break off –'

'All right,' Peter agreed quickly. 'No more questions.'

'The objective of this commando is the ultimate downfall of the brutally fascist, inhuman, neo-imperialistic regime that holds this land in abject slavery and misery – denying the great majority of the workers and the proletariat their basic rights as human beings.'

'And that,' thought Peter bitterly, 'even though it's couched in the garbled jargon of the lunatic left, is every bit as bad as it can be.' Around the world hundreds of millions would have immediate sympathy, making Peter's task just that little bit more difficult. The hijackers had picked a soft target.

The girl was still speaking, with an intense, almost religious fervour, and as he listened Peter faced the growing certainty that the girl was a fanatic, treading the thin line which divided sanity from madness. Her voice became a harsh screech as she mouthed her hatred and condemnation, and when she had finished he knew that she was capable of anything – no cruelty, no baseness was beyond her. He knew that she would not stop even at suicide, the final act of destroying the Boeing, its passengers and herself – he suspected she might even welcome the opportunity of martyrdom, and he felt the chill of it tickle up along his spine.

They were silent now, staring at each other, while the hectic flush of fanaticism receded from the girl's face and she regained her breath, and Peter waited, controlling his own misgivings, waiting for her to calm herself and continue.

'Our first demand –' the girl had steadied and was watching Peter shrewdly now, '– our first demand is that the statement I have just made be read on every television network in Britain and the United States, and also here upon the South African network.' Peter felt his loathing of that terrible little box rise to the surface of his emotions. That mind-bending electronic substitute for thought, that deadly device for freezing, packaging and distributing opinion. He hated it, almost as much as the violence and sensation it purveyed so effectively. 'It must be read at the next occurrence of seven p.m. local time in Los Angeles, New York, London and Johannesburg –' Prime time, of course, and the media would gobble it up hungrily, for this was their meat and their drink – the pornographers of violence!

High above him in the open hatch the girl brandished a thick buff envelope. 'This contains a copy of the statement for transmission – it contains also a list of names. One hundred and twenty-nine names, all of them either imprisoned or placed under banning orders by this monstrous police regime. The names on this list are the true leaders of South Africa.' She flung the envelope, and it landed at Peter's feet.

'Our second demand is that every person on that list be placed aboard an aircraft provided by the South African Government. Aboard the same aircraft there will be one million gold Kruger Rand coins also provided by the same government. The aircraft will fly to a country chosen by the freed political leaders. The gold will be used by them to establish a government in exile, until such time as they return to this country as the true leaders of the people.'

Peter stooped and picked up the envelope. He was calculating swiftly. A single Kruger Rand coin was worth $170 at the very least. The ransom demand was, therefore, worth one hundred and seventy million dollars.

There was another calculation. 'One million Krugers will weigh well over forty tons,' he told the girl. 'How are they going to get all that on one aircraft?'

The girl faltered. It was a little comfort to Peter to realize that they hadn't thought out everything perfectly. If they made one small mistake, then they were capable of making others.

'The government will provide sufficient transport for all the gold and all the prisoners,' the girl said sharply. The hesitation had been momentary only.

'Is that all?' Peter asked; the sun was stinging his naked shoulders and a cold drop of sweat trickled down his flank. He had never guessed it could be this bad.

'The aircraft will depart before noon tomorrow, or the execution of hostages will begin then.' Peter felt the crawl of horror. 'Execution.' She was using the jargon of legality, and he realized at that moment that what she promised she would deliver.

'When those aircraft arrive at the destination chosen by the occupants, a prearranged code will be flashed to us, and all women and children aboard this aircraft will immediately be released.'

'And the men?' Peter asked.

'On Monday the sixth – three days from now, a resolution is to be tabled before the General Assembly of the United Nations in New York. It will call for immediate total mandatory economic sanctions on South Africa – including withdrawal of all foreign capital, total oil and trade embargoes, severance of all transport and communications links, blockade of all ports and air borders by a UN peacekeeping force – pending free elections under universal suffrage supervised by UN inspectors –'

Peter's mind was racing to keep ahead of the girl's demands. He knew of the UN motion, of course, it had been tabled by Sri Lanka and Tanzania. It would be vetoed in the Security Council. That was a certainty – but the girl's timing brought forward new and frightening considerations. The beast had changed shape again, and what he had heard sickened him. It surely could not be merely coincidence that the resolution was to be tabled within three days of this strike – the implications were too horrible to contemplate. The connivance, if not the direct involvement, of world leaders and governments in the strategy of terror.

The girl spoke again deliberately. 'If any member of the Security Council of the UN – America, Britain or France – uses the veto to block the resolution of this General Assembly, this aircraft and all aboard her will be destroyed by high explosive.'

Peter had lost the power of speech. He stood gaping up at the lovely blonde child, for child she seemed, so young and fresh.

When he found voice again, it croaked hoarsely. 'I don't believe you could have got high explosive aboard this aircraft to carry out that threat,' he challenged her.

The blonde girl said something to somebody who was out of sight, and then a few moments later she tossed a dark round object down to Peter.

'Catch!' she shouted, and he was surprised by the weight of it in his hands. It took only a moment to recognize it.

'Electronically fused!' The girl laughed. 'And we have so many I can afford to give you a sample.'

The pilot, Cyril Watkins, was trying to tell him something, touching his own chest – but Peter was occupied with the explosive in his hands. He knew that a single one of these would be fully capable of destroying the Boeing and all aboard her.

What was Watkins trying to tell him? Touching his neck again. Peter transferred his attention to the girl's neck. She wore a small camera slung around her neck. Something connecting camera and grenade – perhaps? Is that what the pilot was trying to tell him?

But now the girl was speaking again. 'Take that to your masters, and let them tremble. The wrath of the masses is upon them. The revolution is here and now,' she said, and the door of the hatchway was swung closed. He heard the lock fall into place.

Peter turned and began the long walk back, carrying an envelope in one hand, a grenade in the other, and sick loathing in his guts.

Colin Noble's rugged frame almost filled the hatchway of the Hawker, and for once his expression was deadly serious, no trace of laughter in his eyes or at the corners of the wide friendly mouth.

'Doctor Parker is on the screen.' He greeted Peter who was still buttoning his overalls as he hurried to the command plane. 'We copied every word, and he was hooked into the system.'

'Christ, it's bad, Colin,' Peter grunted.

'That was the good news,' Colin told him. 'When you have finished with Parker, I've got the bad news for you.'

'Thanks, pal.' Peter shouldered his way past him into the cabin and dropped into his leather command chair.

On the screen Kingston Parker was hunched over his desk, poring over the teleprinter sheet on which the entire conversation between Ingrid and Peter had been recorded, the cold empty pipe gripped between his teeth, the broad brow creased with the weight of his responsibility as he studied the demands of the terrorist commando.

The communications director's voice from off-screen alerted Parker.

'General Stride, sir.' And Parker looked up at the camera.

'Peter. This is you and me alone. I have closed the circuit and we will restrict to single tape recording. I want your first reaction, before we relay to Sir William and Constable –' Sir William Davies was the British Ambassador and Kelly Constable was the United States Ambassador to Pretoria.

'I want your first reaction.'

'We are in serious trouble, sir,' Peter said, and the big head nodded.

'What is the militant capability?'

'I am having my explosives team take down the grenade – but I have no doubt that they have the physical capability to destroy 070, and all aboard. I reckon they have an overkill potential of at least ten.'

'And the psychological capability.'

'In my view, she is the child of Bakunin and Jean-Paul Sartre –' again Parker nodded heavily and Peter went on. 'The anarchist conception that destruction is the only creative act, that violence is man re-creating himself. You know Sartre said that when the revolutionary kills, a tyrant dies and a free man emerges.'

'Will she go all the way?' Parker insisted.

'Yes, sir.' Peter answered without hesitation. 'If she is pressed she'll go all the way – you know the reasoning. If destruction is beautiful, then self-destruction is immortality. In my view, she'll go all the way.'

Parker sighed and knocked the stem of his pipe against his big white teeth. 'Yes, it squares with what we have on her.'

'You have read her?' Peter asked eagerly.

'We got a first-class voice print, and the computer cross-matched with her facial structure print.'

'Who is she?' Peter cut in impatiently; he did not have to be told that the sound intensifier and the zoom video cameras had been feeding her voice and image into the intelligence computer even as she issued her demands.

'Her born name is Hilda Becker. She is a third-generation American of German extraction. Her father is a successful dentist widowed in 1959. The girl is thirty-one years old –' Peter had thought her younger, that fresh young skin had misled him. '– IQ 138. University of Columbia 1965–68, Master's degree in Modern Political History. Member of SDS – that's Students for a Democratic Society –'

'Yes.' Peter was impatient. 'I know.'

'– Activist in Vietnam war protests. Worker for the draft evasion pipeline to Canada. One arrest for possession of marijuana 1967, not convicted. Implicated with Weathermen – and one of the leaders of on-campus rioting in the spring of 1968. Arrested for bombing of Butler University and released. Left America in 1970 for further study at Dusseldorf. Doctorate in Political Economics 1972. Known association with Gudrun Ensslin and Horst Mahler of the Baader-Meinhof. Went underground in 1976 after suspicion of implication in the abduction and murder of Heinrich Kohler, the West German industrialist –' Her personal history was an almost classical development of the modern revolutionary, Peter reflected bitterly, a perfect picture of the beast. 'Believed to have received advanced training from the PFLP in Syria during 1976 and 1977. No recorded contact since then. She is a habitual user of cannabis-based drugs, reported voracious sexual activity with members of both sexes –' Parker looked up. 'That's all we have,' he said.

'Yes,' Peter repeated softly. 'She'll go all the way.'

'What is your further assessment?'

'I believe that this is an operation organized at high level – possibly governmental –'

'Substantiate!' Parker snapped.

'The coordination with UNO proposals sponsored by the unaligned nations points that way.'

'All right, go on.'

'For the first time we have a highly organized and heavily supported strike that is not seeking some obscure, partisan object. We've got demands here about which a hundred million Americans and fifty million Englishmen are going to say in unison, "Hell, these aren't unreasonable." '

'Go on,' said Parker.

'The militants have picked a soft target which is the outcast pariah of Western civilization. That UN resolution is going to be passed a hundred to nil, and those millions of Americans and Englishmen are going to have to ask themselves if they are going to sacrifice the lives of four hundred of their most prominent citizens to support a government whose racial policies they abhor.'

'Yes?' Parker was learning forward to stare into the screen. 'Do you think they'll do a deal?'

'The militants? They might.' Peter paused a moment and then went on. 'You know my views, sir. I oppose absolutely dealing with these people.'

'Even in these circumstances?' Parker demanded.

'Especially now. My views of the host country's policies are in accord with yours, Doctor Parker. This is the test. No matter how much we personally feel the demands are just, yet we must oppose to the death the manner in which they are presented. If these people win their objects, it is a victory for the gun – and we place all mankind in jeopardy.'

'What is your estimate for a successful counterstrike?' Parker demanded suddenly, and even though he had known the question must come, still Peter hesitated a long moment.

'Half an hour ago I would have put the odds at ten to one in our favour that I could pull off condition Delta with only militant casualties.'

'And now?'

'Now I know that these are not fuddle-headed fanatics. They are probably as well trained and equipped as we are, and they have had years to set this operation up.'

'And now?' Parker insisted.

'We have a four to one in our favour of getting them out with a Delta strike, with say less than ten casualties.'

'What is the next best chance?'

'I would say there is no middle ground. If we failed, we would be into a situation with one hundred per casualties – we would lose the aircraft and all aboard, including all Thor personnel involved.'

'All right then, Peter.' Parker leaned back in his chair, the gesture of dismissal. 'I am going to speak with the President and the Prime Minister, they are setting up the link now. Then I will brief the ambassadors – and be back to you within the hour.'

His image flickered into darkness, and Peter realized that all his hatred was suppressed. He felt cold, and functional as the surgeon's blade. Ready to do the job for which he had trained so assiduously, and yet able to assess and evaluate the enemy and the odds against success.

He pressed the call button. Colin had been waiting beyond the soundproof doors of the command cabin, and he came through immediately.

'The explosives boys have taken down the grenade. It's a dandy. The explosive is the new Soviet CJ composition, and the fusing is factory manufacture. Professional stuff – and it will work. Oh, baby, will it ever work.'

Peter hardly needed this confirmation, and Colin went on as he flung himself untidily in the chair opposite Peter.

'We put the list of names and the text of the militant statement on the teleprinter for Washington –' He leaned forward and spoke into the cabin intercom. 'Run that loop – without sound first.' Then he told Peter grimly. 'Here's the bad news I promised.'

The loop of video tape began to run on the central screen. It had clearly been shot from the observation post in the office overlooking the service area.

It was a full shot of the Boeing, the background flattened by the magnification of the lens and swimming and wavering with heat mirage rising from the tarmac of the main runway beyond the aircraft.

In the foreground were Peter's own naked back and shoulders as he strode out towards the aircraft. The lens had again flattened the action so that Peter appeared to be marking time on the same spot without advancing at all.

Suddenly the forward hatch on the Boeing changed shape as the door was slid aside, and the cameraman instantly zoomed in for the closer shot.

The two pilots and the air hostess in the doorway, the camera checked for a few frames and then zoomed closer. The aperture of the lens adjusted swiftly, compensating for the gloom of the interior, and the shot was close and tight on the blonde girl's head for a heart beat, then the head turned slightly and the lovely line of her lips moved as she spoke – it seemed like three words – before she turned back full face to the camera.

'Okay,' Colin said. 'Run it again – with neutral balance on the sound.'

The entire loop re-ran, the cabin door opened, there were the three hostages, the fine golden head turned, and then the words 'Let's slide,' from Ingrid, but there was background hiss and clutter.

'"Let's slide"?' Peter asked.

'Run it again with the bass density filter on the sound,' Colin ordered.

The same images on the screen, the golden head turning on the long neck.

'"It's slide."' Peter could not quite catch it.

'Okay,' Colin told the technician. 'Now with full filter and resonance modulation.'

The repetitive images, the girl's head, the full lips parting, speaking to somebody out of sight in the body of the aircraft.

Very clearly, unmistakably, she said, 'It's Stride.' And Peter felt it jolt in his belly like a fist.

'She recognized you,' said Colin. 'No, hell, she was expecting you!'

The two men stared at each other, Peter's handsome craggy features heavy with foreboding. Atlas had one of the highest security classifications. Only twenty men outside the close ranks of Atlas itself were privy to its secrets. One of those was the President of the United States – another was the Prime Minister of Great Britain.

Certainly only four or five men knew who commanded the Thor arm of Atlas – and yet there was no mistaking those words the girl had spoken.

'Run it again,' Peter ordered brusquely.

And they waited tensely for those two words, and when they came they were in the clear lilt of that fresh young voice.

'It's Stride,' said Ingrid, and the screen went blank.

Peter massaged his closed eyelids with thumb and forefinger. He realized with mild surprise that he had not slept for nearly forty-eight hours, but it was not physical weariness that assailed him now but the suddenly overwhelming knowledge of treason and betrayal and of undreamed-of evil.

'Somebody has blown Atlas,' said Colin softly. 'This is going to be a living and breathing bastard. They'll be waiting for us at every turn of the track.'

Peter dropped his hand and opened his eyes. 'I must speak to Kingston Parker again,' he said. And when Parker's image reappeared on the main screen he was clearly agitated and angry.

'You have interrupted the President.'

'– Doctor Parker –' Peter spoke quickly. '– Circumstances have altered. In my opinion the chances of a successful Delta strike have dropped. We have no better than an even chance.'

'I see.' Parker checked the anger. 'That's important. I will inform the President.'

The lavatories were all blocked by this time, the bowls almost filled, and the stench permeated all the cabins despite the air-conditioning.

Under the strict rationing of food and water most of the passengers were suffering from the lethargy of hunger, and the children were petulant and weepy.

The terrible strain was beginning to show on the hijackers themselves. They were standing a virtual watch and watch, four hours of broken rest followed by four of ceaseless vigil and activity. The red cotton shirts were rumpled and sweat-stained at the armpits, the sweat of nervous and physical strain, eyes bloodshot and tempers uncertain.

Just before nightfall, the dark-haired girl, Karen, had lost her temper with an elderly passenger who had been slow to respond to her command to return to his seat after using the toilet. She had worked herself up into an hysterical shrieking rage, and repeatedly struck the old man in the face with the short barrel of her shot pistol, laying his cheek open to the bone. Only Ingrid had been able to calm her, leading her away to the curtained tourist galley where she pampered and hugged her.

'It will be all right, *Liebchen*.' She stroked her hair. 'Only a little longer now. You have been so strong. In a few more hours we will all take the pills. Not long now.' And within minutes Karen had controlled the violent trembling of her hands, and although she was pale, she was able to take her position at the rear of the tourist cabin again.

Only Ingrid's strength seemed without limits. During the night she passed slowly down the aisles, pausing to talk quietly with a sleepless passenger, comforting them with the promise of imminent release.

'Tomorrow morning we will have an answer to our demands, and all the women and children will be free – it's going to be all right, you just wait and see.'

A little after midnight the little roly-poly doctor sought her out in the cockpit.

'The navigator is very ill,' he told her. 'Unless we get him to a hospital immediately we will lose him.'

Ingrid went back and knelt beside the flight engineer. His skin was dry and burning hot and his breathing rasped and sawed.

'It's renal failure,' said the doctor, hovering over them. 'Breakdown of the kidneys from delayed shock. We cannot treat him here. He must be taken to hospital.'

Ingrid took the semi-conscious flight engineer's uninjured hand. 'I'm sorry, but that's impossible.'

She went on holding his hand for another minute.

'Don't you feel anything?' the doctor demanded of her bitterly.

'I feel pity for him – as I do for all mankind,' she answered quietly. 'But he is only one. Out there are millions.'

The towering flat-topped mountain was lit by floodlights. It was high holiday season and the fairest cape in all the world was showing her beauty to the tens of thousands of tourists and holidaymakers.

On the penthouse deck of the tall building, named for a political mediocrity as are so many buildings and public works in South Africa, the cabinet and its special advisers had been in session for most of the night.

At the head of the long table brooded the heavily built figure of the Prime Minister, bulldog-headed, powerful and unmovable as one of the granite kopjes of the African veld. He dominated the large panelled room, although he had hardly spoken, except to encourage the others with a nod or a few gruff words.

At the far end of the long table sat the two ambassadors, shoulder to shoulder, to emphasize their solidarity. At short intervals the telephones in front of them would ring, and they would listen to the latest reports from their embassies or instructions from the heads of their governments.

On the Prime Minister's right hand sat the handsome moustached Minister of Foreign Affairs, a man with enormous charisma and a reputation for moderation and common sense – but now he was grim and hard faced.

'Your own governments have both pioneered the policy of non-negotiation, of total resistance to the demands of terrorists – why now do you insist that we take the soft line?'

'We do not insist, minister, we have merely pointed out the enormous public interest that this affair is generating in both the United Kingdom and in my own country.' Kelly Constable was a slim, handsome man, intelligent and persuasive, a democratic appointee of the new American administration. 'It is in your government's interest even more than ours to see this through to a satisfactory conclusion. We merely suggest that some accommodation to the demands might bring that about.'

'The Atlas Commander on the spot has assessed the chances of a successful counter-strike as low as fifty-fifty. My government considers that risk unacceptable.' Sir William Davies was a career diplomat approaching retirement age, a grey, sere man with gold-rimmed spectacles, his voice high-pitched and querulous.

'My men think we can do better than that ourselves,' said the Minister of Defence, also bespectacled, but he spoke in the thick blunt accent of the Afrikaaner.

'Atlas is probably the best equipped and most highly trained anti-terrorist group in the world,' Kelly Constable said, and the Prime Minister interrupted harshly.

'At this stage, gentlemen, let us confine ourselves to finding a peaceful solution.'

'I agree, Prime Minister.' Sir William nodded briskly.

'However, I think I should point out that most of the demands made by the terrorists are directly in line with the representations made by the government of the United States –'

'Sir, are you expressing sympathy with these demands?' the Prime Minister asked heavily, but without visible emotion.

'I am merely pointing out that the demands will find sympathy in my country, and that my government will find it easier to exercise its veto on the extreme motion of the General Assembly on Monday if some concessions are made in other directions.'

'Is that a threat, sir?' the Prime Minister asked, a small humourless smile hardly softening the question.

'No, Prime Minister, it's common sense. If that UN motion was carried and implemented, it would mean the economic ruin of this country. It would be plunged into anarchy and political chaos, a ripe fruit for further Soviet encroachment. My government does not desire that – however, nor does it wish to endanger the lives of four hundred of its citizens.' Kelly Constable smiled. 'We have to find a way out of our mutual predicament, I'm afraid.'

'My Minister of Defence has suggested a way out.'

'Prime Minister, if your military attack the aircraft without the prior agreement of both the British and American heads of state, then the veto will be withheld in the Security Council and regretfully we will allow the majority proposal to prevail.'

'Even if the attack is successful?'

'Even if the attack is successful. We insist that military decisions are made by Atlas only,' Constable told him solemnly; and then, more cheerfully, 'Let us examine the minimum concessions that your government would be prepared to make. The longer we can keep open the lines of communication with the terrorists, the better our chances of a peaceful solution. Can we offer to fulfil even one small item on the list of demands?'

Ingrid supervised the serving of breakfast personally. Each passenger was allowed one slice of bread and one biscuit with a cup of heavily sweetened coffee. Hunger had lowered the general resistance of the passengers, they were apathetic and listless once they had gobbled their meagre meal.

Ingrid went amongst them again, passing out cigarettes from the duty-free store. Talking gently to the children, stopping to sympathize with a mother – smiling and calm. Already the passengers were calling her 'the nice one'.

When Ingrid reached the first-class galley she called her companions to her one at a time, and they each ate a full breakfast of eggs and buttered toast and kippers. She wanted them as strong and alert as the arduous ordeal would allow. She could not begin to use the stimulants until midday. The use of drugs could only be continued for seventy-two hours with the desired effects. After that the subject would become unpredictable in his actions and decisions. Ratification of the sanctions vote by the Security Council of the United Nations would take place at noon New York time on the following Monday – that was seven p.m. local time on Monday night.

Ingrid had to keep all her officers alert and active until then, she dared not use the stimulants too early and risk physical disintegration before the decisive hour, and yet she realized that lack of sleep and tension were corroding even her physical reserves; she was jumpy and nervous, and when she examined her face in the mirror of the stinking first-class toilets, she saw how inflamed her eyes were, and for the first time noticed the tiny lines of ageing at the corners of her mouth and eyes. This angered her unreasonably. She hated the thought of growing old, and she could smell her own unwashed body even in the overpowering stench from the lavatory.

The German, Kurt, was slumped in the pilot's seat, his pistol in his lap, snoring softly, his red shirt unbuttoned to the waist and his muscular hairy chest rising and falling with each breath. He was unshaven and the lank, black hair fell over his eyes. She could smell his sweat, and somehow that excited her, and she studied him carefully. There was an air of cruelty and brutality about him, the machismo of the revolutionary, which always attracted her strongly – had perhaps been the original reason for her radical leanings so many years ago. Suddenly she wanted him very badly. However, when she woke him with a hand down the front of his thin linen slacks, he was bleary-eyed and foul-breathed, not even her skilful kneading could arouse him, and in a minute she turned away with an exclamation of disgust.

As a displacement activity, she picked up the microphone, switched on the loudspeakers of the passenger cabins. She knew she was acting irrationally, but she began to speak.

'Now listen to me everybody, I have something very important to tell you.' Suddenly she was angry with them. They were of the class that had devised and instituted the manifestly unjust and sick society against which she was in total rebellion. They were the fat, complacent bourgeoisie. They were like her father and she hated them as she hated her father. As she began to speak she realized that they would not even understand the language she was using, the language of the new political order, and her anger and frustration against them and their society mounted. She did not realize she was raving, until suddenly she heard as from afar the shriek of outrage in her own voice, like the death wail of a mortally wounded animal – and she stopped abruptly.

She felt giddy and light-headed, so she had to clutch at the desk top for support and her heart banged wildly against her ribs. She was panting as though she had run a long way, and it took nearly a full minute for her to bring herself under control.

When she spoke again, her tone was still ragged and breathless.

'It is now nine o'clock,' she said. 'If we do not hear from the tyrant within three hours I shall be forced to begin executing hostages. Three hours –' she replied ominously, '– only three hours.'

Now she prowled the aircraft like a big cat paces along the bars of its cage as feeding time approaches.

'Two hours,' she told them, and the passengers shrank away from her as she passed.

'One hour.' There was a bright sadistic splinter of anticipation in her voice. 'We will choose the first hostages now.'

'But you promised,' pleaded the fat little doctor as Ingrid pulled his wife out of her seat and the Frenchman hustled her forward towards the flight deck.

Ingrid ignored him, and turned to Karen. 'Get children, a boy and a girl –' she instructed, '– oh yes, and the pregnant one. Let them see her big belly. They won't be able to resist that.'

Karen herded the hostages into the forward galley and forced them at pistol point to sit in a row upon the fold-down air-crew seats.

The door to the flight deck was open and Ingrid's voice carried clearly to the galley, as she explained to the Frenchman Henri, speaking in English.

'It is of the utmost importance that we do not allow a deadline to pass without retaliating strongly. If we miss one deadline, then our credibility is destroyed. It will only be necessary once, we must show the steel at least once. They must learn that every one of our deadlines are irrevocable, not negotiable –'

The girl began to cry. She was thirteen years old, able to understand the danger. The plump doctor's wife put her arm around her shoulders and hugged her gently.

'Speedbird 070 –' the radio squawked suddenly, '– we have a message for Ingrid.'

'Go ahead, Tower, this is Ingrid.' She had jumped up to take the microphone, pushing the door to the flight deck closed.

'The negotiator for the British and American governments has proposals for your consideration. Are you ready to copy?'

'Negative.' Ingrid's voice was flat and emphatic. 'I say again negative. Tell the negotiator I will talk only face to face – and tell him we are only forty minutes to the noon deadline. He had better get out here fast,' she warned. She hooked the microphone and turned to Henri.

'All right. We will take the pills now – it has truly begun at last.'

It was another cloudless day, brilliant sunlight that was flung back in piercing darts of light from the bare metal parts of the aircraft. The heat came up through the soles of his shoes and burned down upon Peter's bare neck.

The forward hatch opened, as it had before, when Peter Stride was halfway across the tarmac.

This time there were no hostages on display, the hatchway was a dark empty square. Suppressing the urge to hurry, Peter carried himself with dignity, head up, jaw clenched firmly.

He was fifty yards from the aircraft when the girl stepped into the opening. She stood with indolent grace, her weight all on one leg, the other cocked slightly, long, bare, brown legs. She carried the big shot pistol on one hip, and the cartridge belt emphasized the narrow waist.

She watched Peter come on, with a half smile on her lips. Suddenly a medallion of light appeared on her chest, a dazzling speck like a brilliant insect and she glanced down at it contemptuously.

'This is provocation,' she called. Clearly she knew that the bright speck was the beam thrown by the laser sight of one of the marksmen covering her from the airport building. A few ounces more of pressure on the trigger would send a .222 bullet crashing precisely into that spot, tearing her heart and lungs to bloody shreds.

Peter felt a flare of anger at the sniper who had activated his laser sight without the order, but his anger was tempered by the reluctant admiration for the girl's courage. She could sneer at that mark of certain death upon her breast.

Peter made a cut-out sign with his right hand, and almost immediately the speck of light disappeared as the gunner switched off his laser sight.

'That's better,' the girl said, and she smiled, running her gaze appraisingly down Peter's body.

'You've a good shape, baby,' she said, and Peter's anger flared again under her scrutiny.

'Nice flat belly –' she said, '– good legs, and you didn't get those muscles sitting at a desk and pushing a pen.' She pursed her lips thoughtfully. 'You know I think you're a cop or a soldier. That's what I think, baby. I think you're a goddamned pig.' Her voice had a new harsh quality, and the skin seemed drier and drawn – older than it had been before.

He was close enough now to see the peculiar diamantine glitter in her eyes, and he recognized the tension that seemed to rack her body, the abrupt restless gestures. She was on to drugs now. He was certain of it. He was dealing with a political fanatic, with a long history of violence and death, whose remaining humane traits would be now entirely suppressed by the high of stimulant drugs. He knew she was more dangerous now than a wounded wild animal, a cornered leopard, a man-eating shark with the taste of blood exciting it to the killing frenzy.

He did not reply, but held her gaze steadily, keeping his hands in view, coming to a halt below the open hatchway.

He waited quietly for her to begin, and the itch of the drug in her blood would not allow her to stand still, she fidgeted with the weapon in her hands, touched the camera still hanging from around her neck. Cyril Watkins had tried to tell him something about that camera – and suddenly Peter realized what it was. 'The trigger for the fuses?' he pondered, as he waited. 'Almost certainly,' he decided, that was why it was with her every moment. She saw the direction of his eyes, and dropped her hand guiltily, confirming his conclusion.

'Are the prisoners ready to leave?' she demanded. 'Is the gold packed? Is the statement ready for transmission?'

'The South African Government has acceded to urgent representations by the governments of Great Britain and the United States of America.'

'Good.' She nodded.

'As an act of common humanity the South Africans have agreed to release all the persons on your list of detainees and banned persons –'

'Yes.'

'They will be flown to any country of their choice.'

'And the gold?'

'The South African Government refuses categorically to finance or to arm an unconstitutional foreign-based opposition. They refuse to provide funds for the persons freed under this agreement.'

'The television transmission?'

'The South African Government considers the statement to be untrue in substance and in fact and to be extremely prejudicial to the maintenance of law and order in this country. It refuses to allow transmission of the statement.'

'They have accepted only one of our demands –' The girl's voice took on an even more strident tone, and her shoulders jerked in an uncontrolled spasm.

'The release of political detainees and banned persons is subject to one further condition –' Peter cut in swiftly.

'And what is that –' the girl demanded, two livid burning spots of colour had appeared in her cheeks.

'In return for the release of political prisoners, they demand the release of all hostages, not only the women and children, all persons aboard the aircraft – and they will guarantee safe passage for you and all members of your party to leave the country with the released detainees.'

The girl flung back her head, the thick golden mane flying wildly about her head as she screeched with laughter. The laughter was a wild, almost maniacal sound, and though it went on and on, there was no echo of mirth in her eyes. They were fierce as eagles' eyes, as she laughed. The laughter was cut off abruptly, and her voice was suddenly flat and level.

'So they think they can make demands, do they? They think they can draw the teeth from the UN proposals, do they? They think that without hostages to account for, the fascist governments of Britain and America can again cast their veto with impunity?'

Peter made no reply.

'Answer me!' she screamed suddenly. 'They do not believe we are serious, do they?'

'I am a messenger only,' he said.

'You're not,' she screamed in accusation. 'You're a trained killer. You're a pig!' She lifted the pistol and aimed with both hands at Peter's face.

'What answer must I take back?' Peter asked, without in any way acknowledging the aim of the weapon.

'An answer –' Her voice dropped again to an almost conversational level. 'Of course, an answer.' She lowered the pistol and consulted the stainless steel Japanese watch on her wrist. 'It's three minutes past noon – three minutes past the deadline, and they are entitled to an answer, of course.'

She looked around her with an almost bewildered expression.

The drug was having side effects, Peter guessed. Perhaps she had overdosed herself, perhaps whoever prescribed it had not taken into account the forty-eight sleepless hours of strain that preceded its use.

'The answer,' he prodded her gently, not wanting to provoke another outburst.

'Yes. Wait,' she said, and disappeared abruptly into the gloom of the interior.

Karen was standing over the four hostages on the fold-down seats. She looked around at Ingrid with smouldering dark eyes. Ingrid nodded once curtly, and Karen turned back to her prisoners.

'Come,' she said softly, 'we are going to let you go now.' Almost gently she lifted the pregnant woman to her feet with a hand on her shoulder.

Ingrid left her and passed swiftly into the rear cabins. She nodded again to Kurt, and with a toss of his head he flicked the lank locks of hair from his eyes and thrust the pistol into his belt.

From the locker above his head he brought down two of the plastic grenades. Holding one in each fist he pulled the pins with his teeth and held the rings hooked over his little fingers.

With his arms spread like a crucifix, he ran lightly down the aisle.

'These grenades are primed. Nobody must move, nobody must leave their seats – no matter whatever happens. Stay where you are.'

The fourth hijacker took up the cry from him, holding primed grenades in both hands above his head.

'Nobody move. No talking. Sit still. Everybody still.' He repeated in German and in English and his eyes had the same hard, glossy glitter of the drug high.

Ingrid turned back towards the flight deck.

'Come, sweetheart.' She placed an arm round the girl's shoulder, shepherding her towards the open hatchway – but the child shrank away from her with dread.

'Don't touch me,' she whispered, and her eyes were huge with terror. The boy was younger, more trusting. He took Ingrid's hand readily.

He had thick curly hair, and honey-brown eyes as he looked up at her. 'Is my daddy here?' he asked.

'Yes, darling.' Ingrid squeezed his hand. 'You be a good boy now, and you'll see your daddy very soon.'

She led him to the open hatchway. 'Stand there,' she said.

Peter Stride was uncertain what to expect, as the boy stepped into the open hatchway high above him. Then next to him appeared a plump middle-aged woman in an expensive but rumpled, high-fashion silk dress, probably a Nina Ricci, Peter decided irrelevantly. The woman's elaborate lacquered hair style was coming down in wisps around her ears, but she had a kindly humorous face and she placed a protective arm about the boy-child's shoulders.

The next person was a taller and younger woman, with a pale sensitive skin; her nostrils and eyelids were inflamed pink from weeping or from some allergy and there were blotches of angry prickly heat on her throat and upper arms. Under the loose cotton maternity dress her huge belly bulged grotesquely, throwing her off balance; she stood with her thin white legs knock-kneed awkwardly and blinked in the brilliant sparkling sunshine, her eyes still attuned to the shaded gloom of the cabin.

The fourth and last person was a young girl, and with a sudden blinding stab of agony below the ribs Peter thought it was Melissa-Jane. It took a dozen racing beats of the heart before he realized it was not her – but she had the same sweet Victorian face, the classical English skin of rose petals, the finely bred body of almost woman with delicate breast-buds and long coltish legs below narrow boyish hips.

There was naked terror in her huge eyes, and almost instantly she seemed to realize that Peter was her hope of salvation. The eyes turned on him pleading, hope starting to awaken.

'Please,' she whispered. 'Don't let them hurt us.' So softly that Peter could hardly catch the words. 'Please, sir. Please help us.'

But Ingrid was there, her voice rising stridently.

'You must believe that what we promise, we mean. You and your evil capitalist masters must understand completely that we will not let a single deadline pass without executions. We have to prove that for the revolution we are without mercy. You must be made to understand that our demands must be met in full, that they are not negotiable. We must demonstrate the price for missing a deadline.' She paused. 'The next deadline is midnight tonight. If our demands are not met in full by then – you must know the price you will be made to pay.' She halted again, and then her voice rose into that hysterical shriek. 'This is the price!' and she stepped back out of sight.

Helpless with dread, Peter Stride tried to think of some way to prevent the inevitable.

'Jump!' he shouted, lifting both hands towards the girl. 'Jump, quickly. I will catch you!'

But the child hesitated, the drop was almost thirty feet, and she teetered uncertainly.

Behind her, ten paces back, the dark-haired Karen and the blonde lion-maned girl stood side by side, and in unison they lifted the short, big bored pistols, holding them in the low double-handed grip, positioning themselves at the angle and range which would allow the mass of soft heavy beads with which the cartridges were packed to spread sufficiently to sweep the backs of the four hostages.

'Jump!' Peter's voice carried clearly into the cabin, and Ingrid's mouth convulsed in a nervous rictus, an awful parody of a smile.

'Now!' she said, and the two women fired together. The two shots blended in a thunderous burst of sound, a mind-stopping roar, and blue powder smoke burst from the gaping muzzles, flying specks of burning wadding hurled across the cabin, and the impact of lead shot into living flesh sounded like a handful of a watermelon pips thrown against a wall.

Ingrid fired the second barrel a moment before Karen, so this time the two shots were distinct stunning blurts of sound, and in the dreadful silence that followed, the two men in the passenger cabins were screaming wildly.

'Nobody move! Everybody freeze!'

For Peter Stride those fractional seconds seemed to last for long hours. They seemed to play on endlessly through his brain, like a series of frozen frames in a grotesque movie. Image after image seemed separated from the whole, so that forever afterwards he would be able to re-create each of them entire and undistorted and to experience again undiluted the paralysing nausea of those moments.

The pregnant woman took the full blast of one of the first shots. She burst open like an overripe fruit, her swollen body pulled out of shape by the passage of shot from spine to navel, and she was flung forward so she somersaulted out into space. She hit the tarmac in a loose tangle of pale thin limbs, and was completely still, no flicker of life remaining.

The plump woman clung to the boy beside her, and they teetered in the open doorway – around them swirled pale blue wisps of gunsmoke. Though she kept her balance, the tightly stretched beige silk of her dress was speckled with dozens of tiny wounds, as though she had been stabbed repeatedly with a sharpened knitting needle.The same wounds were torn through the boy's white school shirt, and little scarlet flowers bloomed swiftly around each wound, spreading to stain the cloth. Neither of them made any sound, and their expressions were startled and uncomprehending. The next blasts of sound and shot struck them solidly, and they seemed boneless and without substance as they tumbled forward, still locked together. Their fall seemed to continue for a very long time, and then they sprawled together over the pregnant woman's body.

Peter ran forward to catch the girl-child as she fell, and her weight bore him to his knees on the tarmac. He came to his feet, carrying her like a sleepy baby, one arm under her knees and the other around her shoulders. Her lovely head bumped against his shoulder, and the fine silken hair blew into his face, half blinding him.

'Don't die,' he found himself grunting the words in time to his pounding feet. 'Please don't die.' But he could feel the warm wet leak of blood down his belly, soaking into his shorts, and dribbling down the front of his thighs.

At the entrance to the terminal buildings Colin Noble ran out a dozen paces and tried to take the child from his arms, but Peter resisted him fiercely.

Peter relinquished the frail, completely relaxed body to the Thor doctor, and he stood by without word or expression of regret as the doctor worked swiftly over her. Peter's face was stony and his wide mouth clamped in a hard line when the doctor looked up at last.

'I'm afraid she's dead, sir.'

Peter nodded curtly and turned away. His heels cracked on the echoing marble of the deserted terminal hall and Colin Noble fell in silently beside him. His face was as bleak and expressionless as Peter's, as they climbed into the cabin of the Hawker command aircraft.

'Sir William, you point at us for holding enemies of the State without trial.' The Foreign Minister leaned forward to point the accuser's finger. 'But you British discarded the citizen's right of Habeas Corpus when you passed the Prevention of Terrorism Act, and in Cyprus and Palestine you were holding prisoners without trial long before that. Now your H block in Ulster – is that any better than what we are forced to do here?'

Sir William, the British Ambassador, gobbled indignantly, while he collected his thoughts.

Kelly Constable intervened smoothly. 'Gentlemen, we are trying to find common ground here – not areas of dispute. There are hundreds of lives at stake –'

A telephone shrilled in the air-conditioned hush of the room and Sir William lifted the receiver to his ear with patent relief, but as he listened, all blood drained from his face, leaving it a jaundiced, putty colour.

'I see,' he said once, and then, 'very well, thank you,' and replaced the receiver. He looked down the length of the long polished imbuia wood table to the imposing figure at the end.

'Prime Minister –' His voice quavered a little. '– I regret to inform you that the terrorists have rejected the compromise proposals offered by your government, and that ten minutes ago they murdered four hostages –'

There was a gasp of disbelief from the attentive circle of listening men.

'– The hostages were two women and two children – a boy and a girl – they were shot in the back and their bodies thrown from the aircraft. The terrorists have set a new deadline – midnight tonight – for the acceptance of their terms. Failing which there will be further shootings.'

The silence lasted for almost a minute as head after head turned slowly, until they were all staring at the big hunched figure at the end of the table.

'I appeal to you in the name of humanity, sir.' It was Kelly Constable who broke the silence. 'We must save the women and children at least. The world will not allow us to sit by as they are murdered.'

'We will have to attack the aircraft and free the prisoners,' said the Prime Minister heavily.

But the American Ambassador shook his head. 'My government is adamant, sir – as is that of my British colleague –' He glanced at Sir William, who nodded support. '– We cannot and will not risk a massacre. Attack the aircraft and our governments will make no attempt to moderate the terms of the UN proposals, nor will we intervene in the Security Council to exercise the veto.'

'Yet, if we agree to the demands of these – these animals –' The last words were said fiercely, '– we place our nation in terrible danger.'

'Prime Minister, we have only hours to find a solution – then the killing will begin again.'

'You yourself have placed the success chances of a Delta strike as low as even,' Kingston Parker pointed out, staring grimly at Peter Stride out of the little square screen. 'Neither the President nor I find those odds acceptable.'

'Doctor Parker, they are murdering women and children out there on the tarmac.' Peter tried to keep his tone neutral, his reasoning balanced.

'Very strong pressure is being brought to bear on the South African Government to accede to the terms for release of the women and children.'

'That will solve nothing.' Peter could not restrain himself. 'It will leave us with exactly the same situation tomorrow night.'

'If we can secure the release of the women and children, the number of lives at risk will be reduced, and in forty hours the situation might have changed – we are buying time, Peter, even if we have to pay for it with a heavy coin.'

'And if the South Africans do not agree? If we come to the midnight deadline without an agreement with the hijackers, what happens then, Doctor Parker?'

'This is a difficult thing to say, Peter, but if that happens –' Parker spread those long graceful hands in a gesture of resignation, '– we may lose another four lives, but that is better than precipitating the massacre of four hundred. And after that the South Africans will not be able to hold out. They will have to agree to free the women and children – at any cost.'

Peter could not truly believe what he had heard. He knew he was on the very brink of losing his temper completely, and he had to give himself a few seconds to steady himself. He dropped his eyes to his own hands that were interlocked on the desk top in front of him. Under the fingernails of his right hand were black half moons, the dried blood of the child he had carried back from the aircraft. Abruptly he unlocked his fingers and thrust both hands deeply into the pockets of his blue Thor overalls. He took a long deep breath, held it a moment, then let it out slowly.

'If that was difficult to say, Doctor Parker – console yourself that it was a bloody sight harder to listen to.'

I understand how you feel, Peter.'

'I don't think you do, sir.' Peter shook his head slowly.

'You are a soldier –'

'– and only a soldier knows how to really hate violence,' Peter finished for him.

'Our personal feelings must not be allowed to intrude in this.' Kingston Parker's voice had a sharp edge to it now. 'I must once again forcibly remind you that the decision for condition Delta has been delegated to me by the President and your Prime Minister. No strike will be made without my express orders. Do you understand that, General Stride?'

'I understand, Doctor Parker,' Peter said flatly. 'And we hope to get some really good video tapes of the next murders. I'll let you have copies for your personal collection.'

The other 747 had been grounded for servicing when the emergency began, and it was parked in the assembly area only a thousand yards from where Speedbird 070 stood, but the main service hangars and the corner of the terminal buildings effectively screened it from any observation by the hijackers.

Although it wore the orange and blue of South African Airways with the flying Springbok on the tail, it was an almost identical model to its sister ship. Even the cabin configurations were very close to the plans of Speedbird 070, which had been teleprinted from British Airways Headquarters at Heathrow. It was a fortunate coincidence, and an opportunity that Colin Noble had seized immediately. He had already run seven mock Deltas on the empty hull.

'All right, you guys, let's try and get our arses out of low gear on this run. I want to better fourteen seconds from the "go" to penetration –' His strike team glanced at one another as they squatted in a circle on the tarmac, and there were a few theatrical rollings of eyes. Colin ignored them. 'Let's go for nine seconds, gang,' he said and stood up.

There were sixteen men in the actual assault group – seventeen when Peter Stride joined them. The other members of Thor were technical experts – electronics and communications, four marksmen snipers, a weapons quartermaster, and a bomb disposal and explosives sergeant, doctor, cook, three engineering NCOs under a lieutenant, the pilots and other flight personnel – a big team, but every man was indispensable.

The assault group wore single-piece uniforms of close-fitting black nylon, for low night visibility. They wore their gas masks loosely around their necks, ready for instant use. Their boots were black canvas lace-ups, with soft rubber soles for silence. Each man wore his specialized weapons and equipment either in a back pack or on his black webbing belt. No bulky bullet-proof flak jackets to impede mobility or to snag on obstacles, no hard helmets to tap against metal and tell tales to a wary adversary.

Nearly all the group were young men, in their early twenties, hand picked from the US marine corps or from the British 22. SAS regiment that Peter Stride had once commanded. They were superbly fit, and honed to a razor's edge.

Colin Noble watched them carefully as they assembled silently on the marks he had chalked on the tarmac, representing the entrances to the air terminal and the service hangars nearest to 070. He was searching for any sign of slackness, any deviation from the almost impossible standards he had set for Thor. He could find none. 'All right, ten seconds – to flares,' he called. A Delta strike began with the launching of phosphorus flares across the nose of the target aircraft. They would float down on their tiny parachutes, causing a diversion which would hopefully bunch the terrorists in the flight deck of the target aircraft as they tried to figure out the reason for the lights. The brilliance of the flares would also sear the retina of the terrorists' eyes and destroy night vision for many minutes afterwards.

'Flares!' shouted Colin, and the assault group went into action. The two 'stick' men led them, sprinting out directly under the gigantic tail of the deserted aircraft. Each of them carried a gas cylinder strapped across his shoulder, to which the long stainless steel probes were attached by flexible armoured couplings – these were the 'sticks' that gave them their name.

The leader carried compressed air in the tank upon his back at a pressure of 250 atmospheres, and on the tip of his twenty-foot probe was the diamond cutting bit of the air-drill. He dropped on one knee under the belly of the aircraft ten feet behind the landing gear and reached up to press the point of the air-drill against the exact spot, carefully plotted from the manufacturer's drawing, where the pressure hull was thinnest and where direct access to the passenger cabins lay just beyond the skin of alloy metal.

The whine of the cutting drill would be covered by the revving of the jet engines of aircraft parked in the southern terminal. Three seconds to pierce the hull, and the second stick man was ready to insert the tip of his probe into the drill hole.

'Power off,' Colin grunted; at that moment electrical power from the mains would be cut to kill the air-conditioning.

The second man simulated the act of releasing the gas from the bottle on his back through the probe and saturating the air in the aircraft's cabins. The gas was known simply as FACTOR V. It smelled faintly of newly dug truffles, and when breathed as a five per cent concentration in air would partially paralyse a man in under ten seconds – loss of motor control of the muscles, uncoordinated movement, slurred speech and distorted vision, were initial symptoms.

Breathed for twenty seconds the symptoms were total paralysis, for thirty seconds loss of consciousness; breathed for two minutes, pulmonary failure and death. The antidote was fresh air or, better still, pure oxygen, and recovery was rapid with no long-term after-effects.

The rest of the assault group had followed the 'stick' men and split into four teams. They waited poised, squatting under the wings, gas masks in place, equipment and weapons ready for instant use.

Colin was watching his stopwatch. He could not chance exposing the passengers to more than ten seconds of Factor V. There would be elderly people, infants, asthma sufferers aboard; as the needle reached the ten-second mark, he snapped:

'Power on.' Air-conditioning would immediately begin washing the gas out of the cabins again, and now it was 'Go!'

Two assault teams poured up the aluminium scaling ladders on to the wing roots, and knocked out the emergency window panels. The other two teams went for the main doors, but they could only simulate the use of slap-hammers to tear through the metal and reach the locking device on the interior – nor could they detonate the stun grenades.

'Penetration.' The assault leader standing in for Peter Stride on this exercise signalled entry of the cabins, and Colin clicked his stopwatch.

'Time?' asked a quiet voice at his shoulder, and he turned quickly. So intent on his task, Colin had not heard Peter Stride come up behind him.

'Eleven seconds, sir.' The courteous form of address was proof of Colonel Colin Noble's surprise. 'Not bad – but sure as hell not good either. We'll run it again.'

'Rest them,' Peter ordered. 'I want to talk it out a bit.'

They stood together at the full windows in the south wall of the air traffic control tower, and studied the big red, white and blue aircraft for the hundredth time that day.

The heat of the afternoon had raised thunderheads, great purple and silver mushroom bursts of cloud that reached to the heavens. Trailing grey skirts of torrential rain they marched across the horizon, forming a majestic backdrop that was almost too theatrical to be real, while the lowering sun found the gaps in the cloud and shot long groping fingers of golden light through them, heightening the illusion of theatre.

'Six hours to deadline,' Colin Noble grunted, and groped for one of his scented black cheroots. 'Any news of concessions by the locals?'

'Nothing. I don't think they will buy it.'

'Not until the next batch of executions.' Colin bit the end from the cheroot and spat it angrily into a corner. 'For two years I break my balls training for this, and now they tie our hands behind our backs.'

'If they gave you Delta, when would you make your run?' Peter asked.

'As soon as it was dark,' Colin answered promptly.

'No. They are still revved up high on drugs,' Peter demurred. 'We should give them time to go over the top, and start downing. My guess is they will dope again just before the next deadline. I would hit them just before that –' He paused to calculate. '– I'd hit them at fifteen minutes before eleven – seventy-five minutes before the deadline.'

'If we had Delta,' Colin grunted.

'If we had Delta,' Peter agreed, and they were silent a moment. 'Listen,

Colin, this has been wearing me down. If they know my name, what else does that gang of freaks know about Thor? Do they know our contingency planning for taking an aircraft?'

'God, I hadn't worked it out that far.'

'I have been looking for a twist, a change from the model, something that will give us the jump even if they know what to expect.'

'We've taken two years to set it up tightly –' Colin looked dubious. 'There is nothing we can change.'

'The flares,' said Peter. 'If we went, we would not signal the Delta with the flares, we would go in cold.'

'The uglies would be scattered all through the cabins, mixed up with passengers and crew –'

'The red shirt Ingrid was wearing. My guess is, all four of them will be uniformed to impress their hostages. We would hose anything and everybody in red. If my guess is wrong, then we would have to do it Israeli style.'

Israeli style was the shouted command to lie down, and to kill anyone who disobeyed or who made an aggressive move.

'The truly important one is the girl. The girl with the camera. Have your boys studied the video tapes of her?'

'They know her face better than they do Fawcett Majors',' Colin grunted, and then, 'the bitch is so goddamned lovely – I had to run the video of the executions three times for them, twice in slow motion, to wipe out a little of the old chivalry bit.' It is difficult to get a man to kill a pretty girl, and a moment of hesitation would be critical with a trained fanatic like Ingrid. 'I also made them take a look at the little girl before they put her in a basket and took her down to the morgue. They're in the right mood.' Colin shrugged. 'But what the hell, Atlas isn't going to call Delta. We're wasting our time.'

'Do you want to play make believe?' Peter asked, and then without waiting for an answer, 'Let's make believe we have a Delta approval from Atlas. I want you to set up a strike timed to "go" at exactly 10.45 local time tonight. Do it as though it was the real thing – get it right in every detail.'

Colin turned slowly and studied his commander's face, but the eyes were level and without guile and the strong lines of jaw and mouth were unwavering.

'Make believe?' Colin Noble asked quietly.

'Of course.' Peter Stride's tone was curt and impatient, and Colin shrugged.

'Hell, I only work here,' and he turned away.

Peter lifted the binoculars and slowly traversed the length of the big machine from tail to nose, but there was no sign of life, every port and window still carefully covered – and reluctantly he let his binoculars sink slightly until he was staring at the pitiful pile of bodies that still lay on the tarmac below the forward hatch.

Except for the electrical mains hook-up, the delivery of medicines and the two occasions when Peter himself had made the long trip out there, nobody else had been allowed to approach the machine. No refuelling, no refuse nor sanitary removals, no catering – not even the removal of the corpses of the murdered hostages. The hijackers had learned the lesson of previous hijacking attempts when vital information had been smuggled off the aircraft in refuse and sewerage at Mogadishu, and at Lod where the storming party had come disguised as caterers.

Peter was still gazing at the bodies, and though he was accustomed to death in its most obscene forms, these bodies offended him more deeply than any in his life before. This was a contemptuous flaunting of all the deepest rooted taboos of society. Peter was grimly content now with the decision of the South African police not to allow any television teams or press photographers through the main gates of the airport.

Peter knew that the world media were howling outrage and threats, protesting in the most extreme terms against the infringement of their god-given rights to bring into the homes of all civilized people images of dreadful death and mutilation, lovingly photographed in gorgeous colour with meticulous professional attention to all the macabre details.

Without this enthusiastic chronicling of their deeds, international terrorism would lose most of its impetus and his job would be a lot easier. For sneaking moments he envied the local police the powers they had to force irresponsibles to act in the best interests of society, then as he carried the thought a step further, he came up hard once again against the question of who was qualified to make such decisions on behalf of society. If the police made that decision and exerted it, was it not just another form of the terrorism it was seeking to suppress? 'Christ,' thought Peter angrily, 'I'm going to drive myself mad.'

He stepped up beside the senior air traffic controller.

'I want to try again,' Peter said, and the man handed him the microphone.

'Speedbird 070 this is the tower. Ingrid, do you read me? Come in, Ingrid.'

He had tried a dozen times to make contact in the last few hours, but the hijackers had maintained an ominous silence.

'Ingrid, come in please.' Peter kept trying, and suddenly there was the clear fresh voice.

'This is Ingrid. What do you want?'

'Ingrid, we request your clearance to have an ambulance remove the bodies,' Peter asked.

'Negative, Tower. I say again, negative. No one is to approach this aircraft.' There was a pause. 'We will wait until we have a round dozen bodies for you to remove –' The girl giggled, still on the drug high, '– wait until midnight, and we'll make it really worth your while.' And the radio clicked into silence.

'We are going to give you dinner now,' Ingrid shouted cheerfully, and there was a stir of interest down the length of the cabin. 'And it's my birthday today. So you're going to have champagne – isn't that great!'

But the plump little Jewish doctor rose suddenly to his feet. His grey sparse hair stood up in comical wisps, and his face seemed to have collapsed, like melting wax, ravaged and destroyed by grief. He no longer seemed to be aware of what had been said or what was happening. 'You had no right to kill her.' His voice sounded like a very old man. 'She was a good person. She never hurt anyone –' He looked about him with a confused, unfocused look, and ran the fingers of one hand through his disordered hair. 'You should not have killed her,' he repeated.

'She was guilty,' Ingrid called back at him. 'Nobody is innocent – you are all the cringing tools of international capitalism –' Her face twisted, in an ugly spasm of hatred. '– You are guilty, all of you, and you deserve to die –' She stopped short, controlled herself with an obvious effort of will, and then smiled again; going forward to the little doctor, she put an arm around his shoulders. 'Sit down,' she said, almost tenderly, 'I know just how you feel, please believe me, I wish there had been another way.'

He sank down slowly, his eyes vacant with sorrow and his fingers plucking numbly at themselves.

'You just sit there quietly,' Ingrid said gently. 'I'm going to bring you a glass of champagne now.'

'Prime Minister –' Kelly Constable's voice was husky with almost two days and nights of unceasing tension, '– it's after ten o'clock already. We must have a decision soon, in less than two hours –'

The Prime Minister lifted one hand to silence the rest of it.

'Yes, we all know what will happen then.'

An airforce jet had delivered a copy of the video tape from Johannesburg, a thousand miles away, and the cabinet and the ambassadors had watched the atrocity in detail, recorded by an 800-mm lens. There was not a man at the table who did not have children of his own. The toughest right-wingers amongst them wavered uncertainly, even the puckish little Minister of Police could not meet the ambassador's eyes as he swept the table with a compelling gaze.

'And we all know that no compromise is possible, we must meet the demands in full or not at all.'

'Mister Ambassador –' the Prime Minister broke the silence at last, '– if we agree to the terms, it will be only as an act of humanity. We will be paying a very high price indeed for the lives of your people – but if we agree to that price, can we be absolutely assured of your support – the support of both Britain and the United States – in the Security Council the day after tomorrow at noon?'

'The President of the United States has empowered me to pledge his support in return for your cooperation,' said Kelly Constable.

'Her Britannic Majesty's Government has asked me to assure you of the same support,' intoned Sir William. 'And our governments will make good the 170 million dollars demanded by the hijackers.'

'Still I cannot make the decision on my own. It is too onerous for one man,' the Prime Minister sighed. 'I am going to ask my ministers, the full cabinet –' he indicated the tense, grim faces around him, '– to vote. I am going to ask you gentlemen to leave us alone now for a few minutes while we decide.'

And the two ambassadors rose together and bowed slightly to the brooding, troubled figure before leaving the room.

'Where is Colonel Noble?' Kingston Parker asked.

'He is waiting –' Peter indicated with a jerk of his head the soundproof door of the Hawker's command cabin.

'I want him in on this, please,' Parker said from the screen, and Peter pressed the call button.

Colin Noble came in immediately, stooping slightly under the low roof, a chunky powerful figure with the blue Thor cap pulled low over his eyes.

'Good evening, sir.' He greeted the image on the screen and squeezed into the seat beside Peter.

'I'm glad Colonel Noble is here.' Peter's voice was crisp and businesslike. 'I think he will support my contention that the chances of a successful Delta counterstrike will be greatly enhanced if we can launch our attack not later than ten minutes before eleven o'clock.' He tugged back the cuff of his sleeve, and glanced at his watch. 'That is forty minutes from now. We reckon to catch the militants at the moment when the drug cycle is at its lowest, before they take more pills and begin to arouse themselves to meet their deadline. I believe that if we strike then, we will have an acceptable risk –'

'Thank you, General Stride –' Parker interrupted him smoothly, '– but I wanted Colonel Noble present so there could be no misunderstanding of my orders. Colonel Noble –' Parker's eyes shifted slightly as he changed the object of his attention. 'Commander of Thor has requested an immediate Delta strike against Speedbird 070. I am now, in your presence, disapproving that request. Negotiations with the South African Government are at a critical state, and under no circumstances must there be either overt or covert hostile moves towards the militants. Do I make myself entirely clear?'

'Yes, sir.' Colin Noble's expression was stony.

'General Stride?'

'I understand, sir.'

'Very well. I want you to stand by, please. I am going to confer with the ambassadors. I will re-establish contact as soon as I have further concrete indications.'

The image receded rapidly, and the screen went dark. Colonel Colin Noble turned slowly and looked at Peter Stride, his expression changed slightly at what he saw, and quickly he pressed the censor button on the command console, stopping all recording tapes, killing the video cameras so there would be no record of his words now.

'Listen, Peter, you're in line for that NATO command, everybody knows that. From there the sky is the limit, pal. Right up there to the joint chiefs – just as far as you want to go.'

Peter said nothing, but glanced once more at the gold Rolex wristwatch. It was seventeen minutes past ten o'clock.

'Think, Peter. For God's sake man. It's taken you twenty heartbreaking years of hard work to get where you are. They would never forgive you, buddy. You'd better believe it. They'll break you and your career. Don't do it, Peter. Don't do it. You're too good to waste yourself. Just stop and think for one minute.'

'I'm thinking,' said Peter quietly. 'I haven't stopped thinking since –' he checked, '– always it comes back to this. If I let them die – then I am as guilty as that woman who pulls the trigger.'

'Peter, you don't have to beat your head in. The decision is made by someone else –'

'It would be easier to believe that, wouldn't it,' Peter snapped, 'but it won't save those people out there.'

Colin leaned across and placed a large hairy paw on Peter's upper arm. He squeezed slightly. 'I know, but it eats me to see you have to throw it all away. In my book, you're one of the tops, buddy.' It was the first time he had made any such declaration, and Peter was fleetingly moved by it.

'You can duck this one, Colin. It doesn't have to touch you or your career.'

'I never was very hot at ducking.' Colin dropped his hand away. 'I think I'll go along for the ride –'

'I want you to record a protest – no sense us all getting ourselves fired,' said Peter, as he switched on the recording equipment, both audio and video; now every word would be recorded.

'Colonel Noble,' he said distinctly, 'I am about to lead an immediate Delta assault on Flight 070. Please make the arrangements.'

Colin turned to face the camera. 'General Stride, I must formally protest at any order to initiate condition Delta without express approval from Atlas Command.'

'Colonel Noble, your protest is noted,' Peter told the camera gravely, and Colin Noble hit the censor button once again, cutting tapes and camera.

'Okay, that's enough crap for one day.' He came nimbly to his feet. 'Let's get out there and take the bastards.'

Ingrid sat at the flight engineer's desk, and held the microphone of the on-board loudspeaker system to her lips. There was a greyish tone beneath the sun-gilded skin, she frowned a little at the throbbing pulse of pain behind her eyes and the hand that held the microphone trembled slightly. She knew these were all symptoms of the drug hangover. She regretted now having increased the initial dosage beyond that recommended on the typed label of the tablet phial – but she had needed that extra lift to be able to carry out the first executions. Now she and her officers were paying the price, but in another twenty minutes she would be able to issue another round of tablets. This time she would stay exactly within the recommended dosage, and she anticipated the rush of it through her blood, the heightened vision and energy, the tingling exhilaration of the drug. She even anticipated the thought of what lay head; to be able to wield absolute power, the power of death itself, was one of life's most worthwhile experiences. Sartre and Bakunin and Most had discovered one of the great truths of life – that the act of destruction, of total destruction, was a catharsis, a creation, a reawakening of the soul.

She looked forward, even through the staleness and ache of the drug let down, she looked forward to the next executions.

'My friends –' she spoke into the microphone, '– we have not heard from the tyrant. His lack of concern for your lives is typical of the fascist imperialist. He does not concern himself with the safety of the people, though he sucks and bloats himself on the blood and sweat –'

Outside the aircraft the night was black and close. Thunderheads blotted out half the sky, and every few minutes lightning lit the clouds internally. Twice since sundown abrupt fierce downpours of torrential rain had hammered briefly against the Boeing hull, and now the airport lights glinted on the puddled tarmac.

'– We have to show the face of unrelenting courage and iron purpose to the tyrant. We cannot afford to show even a moment's hesitation. We must now choose four more hostages. It will be done with the utmost impartiality – and I want you all to realize that we are now all part of the revolution together, you can proud of that –'

Lightning exploded suddenly, much closer, a crackling greenish, iridescent flaming of the heavens that lit the field in merciless light, and then the flail of thunder beat down on the aircraft. The girl Karen exclaimed involuntarily and sprang nervously to her feet and crossed quickly to stand beside Ingrid. Her dark eyes were now heavily underscored by the dark kohl of fatigue and drug withdrawal, she trembled violently, and Ingrid caressed her absently the way she might calm a frightened kitten as she went on speaking into the microphone.

'– We must all of us learn to welcome death, to welcome the opportunity to take our place and add our contribution, no matter how humble it might be, to man's great reawakening.'

Lightning burst in fierce splendour once again, but Ingrid went on talking into the microphone, the senseless words somehow hypnotic and lulling so that her captives sat in quietly lethargic rows, not speaking, unmoving, seeming no longer capable of independent thought.

'I have drawn lots to choose the next martyrs of the revolution. I will call out the seat numbers and my officers will come to fetch you. Please cooperate by moving quickly forward to the first-class galley.' There was a pause, and then Ingrid's voice again. 'Seat number 63B. Please stand up.'

The scarred German in the red shirt and with the lank black hair hanging over his eyes had to force the thin, middle-aged man to his feet, twisting his wrist up between his shoulder blades. The man's white shirt was crumpled and he wore elastic braces over his shoulders and old-fashioned narrow trousers.

'You can't let them,' the man pleaded with his fellow passengers, as Henri pushed him up the aisle. 'You can't let them kill me, please.' And they looked down at their laps. Nobody moved, nobody spoke.

'Seat number 43F.' It was a handsome dark-haired woman in her middle thirties, and her face seemed to dissolve slowly as she read the number above her seat, and she covered her mouth with one hand to prevent herself crying out – but from the seat exactly across the aisle from her a sprightly old gentleman with a magnificent mane of silver-grey hair rose swiftly to his feet and adjusted his tie.

'Would you care to change seats with me, madam?' he said softly in a clipped English accent, and strode down the aisle, on long, thin, stork-like legs, contemptuously brushing past the blond moustached Frenchman who came hurrying forward to escort him. Without a glance to either side, and with thin shoulders thrown back, he disappeared through the curtains into the forward galley.

The Boeing had a blind spot that extended back from the side windows of the flight deck at an angle of 20° to the tail, but the hijackers were so well equipped and seemed to have considered every eventuality in such detail that there was no reason to fear that they had worked out some arrangement to keep the blind spot under surveillance.

Peter and Colin discussed the possibility quietly as they stood in the angle of the main service hangar, and both of them carefully studied the soaring shape of the Boeing tailplane and the sagging underbelly of the fuselage for the glint of a mirror or some other device. They were directly behind the aircraft and there was a little over four hundred yards to cover, half of that through knee-high grass and the rest over tarmac.

The field was lit only by the blue periphery lights of the taxi-way, and the glow of the airport buildings.

Peter had considered dousing all the airport lights, but discarded the idea as self-defeating. It would certainly alert the hijackers, and would slow the crossing of the assault team.

'I can't see anything,' Colin murmured.

'No,' agreed Peter and they both handed their night glasses to a hovering NCO – they wouldn't need them again. The assault team had stripped all equipment down to absolute essentials.

All that Peter carried was a lightweight eleven-ounce VHF transceiver for communicating with his men in the terminal building – and in a quick-release holster on his right hip a Walther P 38 automatic pistol.

Each member of the assault team carried the weapon of his choice. Colin Noble, the only fickle one amongst them, vacillated between the Browning Hi-power 9-mm parabellum which he liked for its thirteen-shot magazine and the Colt Commander .45 ACP for its lighter weight and massive killing power – Peter on the other hand favoured the pinpoint accuracy and light recoil of the Walther with which he could be sure of a snap head-shot at twenty metres.

One item was standard equipment for all members of the assault team. Every one of their weapons was loaded with Super Velex explosive bullets which trebled the knock-down power at impact, breaking up in the human body and thereby reducing the risk of over-penetration and with it the danger to innocents. Peter never let them forget they would nearly always be working with terrorist and victim closely involved.

Beside Peter, Colin Noble unclipped the thin gold chain from around his neck which held the tiny Star of David, twinkling gold on the black bush of his chest hair. He slipped the ornament into his pocket and buttoned down the flap.

'I say, old chap –' Colin Noble gave an atrocious imitation of a Sandhurst accent '– shall we toddle along then?'

Peter glanced at the luminous dial of his Rolex. It was sixteen minutes to eleven o'clock. The exact moment at which my career ends, he thought grimly, and raised his right arm with clenched first, then pumped it up and down twice, the old cavalry signal to advance.

Swiftly the two stick men raced out ahead, absolutely silent on soft rubber soles, carrying their probes at high port to prevent them clattering against the tarmac or against the metal parts of the aircraft, dark hunchbacked figures under the burden of the gas cylinders they carried.

Peter gave them a slow count of five, and while he waited he felt the adrenalin charge his blood, every nerve and muscle of his body coming under tension, and he heard his own words to Kingston Parker echo in his ears like the prophecy of doom.

'There is no middle ground. The alternative is one hundred per cent casualties. We lose the aircraft, the passengers and all the Thor personnel aboard her.'

He thrust the thought aside, and repeated the signal to advance. In two neat files, bunched up close and well in hand, the assault teams went out, at the run. Three men carrying each of the aluminium alloy scaling ladders, four with the sling bags of stun grenades, others with the slap-hammers to tear out the door locks, and each with his chosen weapon – always a big-calibre handgun – for Peter Stride would trust nobody with an automatic weapon in the crowded interior of a hijacked aircraft, and the minimum requirement for every member of the assault teams was marksmanship with a pistol that would enable him to pick a small moving target and hit it repeatedly and quickly without endangering innocents.

They ran in almost total silence; the loudest sound was Peter's breathing in his own ears, and he had time now for a moment's regret. It was a gamble which he could never win, the best that could happen was the utter ruin of his life's work, but he steeled himself brutally and thrust aside the thought. He ran on into the night.

Just ahead of him now, silhouetted by the lights of the terminal building, the dark figures of the stick men were in position under the bulging silver belly; and lightning flared suddenly, so that the tall silver thunderheads rippled with intense white fire, and the field was starkly lit, the double column of black-clad figures standing out clearly against the paler grass. If they were observed, it would come now, and the crash of thunder made Peter's nerves jump, expecting detonation and flame of a dozen percussion grenades.

Then it was dark again, and the sponginess of wet grass beneath his feet gave way to flat hard tarmac. Then suddenly they were under the Boeing fuselage, like chickens under the protective belly of the hen, and the two columns split neatly into four separate groups and still in tight order every man dropped on to his left knee, and at the same moment, with the precision of repeated rehearsals, every member of the team lifted his gas mask to cover his nose and mouth.

Peter swept one quick glance at them, and then depressed the transmit button on his transceiver. He would not speak a word from now until it was over, there was always a remote possibility that the hijackers were monitoring his frequency.

The click of the button was the signal to the members of his team in the terminal – and almost immediately, there was a rising whistling howl of jet engines running up.

Even though the aircraft were parked up in the northern international departures area, they had been turned so the jet exhausts were pointed at the service area, and there were five intercontinental jet liners cooperating. The combined sound output of twenty big jet engines was deafening even at that range – and Peter gave the open hand signal.

The stick man was waiting poised, and at the signal he reached up and placed the drill bit against the belly of the fuselage. Any sound of the compressed air spinning the drill was effectively drowned, and there was only the slight jerk of the long probe as it went through the pressure hull. Instantly the second stick man placed the tip of his probe into the tiny hole, and glanced at Peter. Again the open hand signal, and the gas was spurting into the hull. Peter was watching the sweep hand of his watch.

Two clicks on the transmit button, and the lights behind the row of shaded portholes blinked out simultaneously as the mains power was cut – and the air-conditioning in the Boeing's cabins with it.

The howl of combined jet engines continued a few seconds longer and Peter signalled the ladder men forward.

Gently the rubber padded tops of the ladders were hooked on to the leading edges of the wings and into the door sills high above them by black-costumed, grotesquely masked figures working with deceptively casual speed.

Ten seconds from discharge of the Factor V gas into the hull, and Peter clicked thrice. Instantly mains power to the Boeing was resumed and the lights flicked on. Now the air-conditioning was running again, washing the gas swiftly from the cabins and flight deck.

Peter drew one long, slow deep breath and tapped Colin's shoulder. They went up the ladders in a concerted silent rush, Peter and Colin leading the teams to each wing surface.

'Nine minutes to eleven,' said Ingrid to Karen. She lifted her voice slightly above the din of jet engines howling somewhere out there in the night. Her throat was dry and sore from the drug withdrawal and a nerve jumped involuntarily in the corner of her eye. Her headache felt as though a knotted rope was being twisted slowly tighter around her forehead. 'It looks as though Caliph miscalculated. The South Africans aren't going to give in –' She glanced with a small anticipatory twist of her lips back through the open door of the flight deck at the four hostages sitting in a row on the fold-down seats. The silver-haired Englishman was smoking a Virginia cigarette in a long ivory holder, and he returned her gaze with disdain, so that Ingrid felt a prickle of annoyance and raised her voice so he could hear her next words. 'It's going to be necessary to shoot this batch also.'

'Caliph has never been wrong before.' Karen shook her head vehemently. 'There is still an hour to deadline –' and at that instant the lights flickered once and then went out. With all the portholes shaded the darkness was complete, and the hiss of the air-conditioning faded into silence before there was a murmur of surprised comment.

Ingrid groped across the control for the switch which transferred the flight deck on to the power from the aircraft's own batteries, and as the soft ruddy glow of the panel lights came on her expression was tense and worried.

'They've switched off the main,' she exclaimed. 'The air-conditioning – this could be Delta.'

'No.' Karen's voice was shrill. 'There are no flares.'

'We could be – ' Ingrid started but she could hear the drunken slur in her own voice. Her tongue felt too large for her mouth, and Karen's face started to distort before her eyes, the edges blurring out of focus.

'Karen –' she said, and now in her nostrils the unmistakable aroma of truffles and on her tongue the taste of raw mushrooms.

'Christ!' she screamed wildly and lunged for the manual oxygen release. Above each seat the panels dropped open and the emergency oxygen masks dangled down into the cabins on their corrugated hoses.

'Kurt! Henri!' Ingrid shrieked into the cabin intercom. 'Oxygen! Take oxygen! It's Delta. They are going to Delta.'

She grabbed one of the dangling oxygen masks and sucked in deep pumping breaths, cleansing the numbing paralysing gas from her system. In the first-class galley one of the hostages collapsed slowly forward and tumbled on to the deck, another slumped sideways.

Still breathing oxygen, Ingrid unslung the camera from around her neck, and Karen watched her with huge terrified dark eyes, lifted the oxygen mask from her face to ask:

'You're not going to blow, Ingrid?'

Ingrid ignored her and used the oxygen in her lungs to shout into the microphone.

'Kurt! Henri! They will come as soon as the mains are switched on again. Cover your eyes and ears for the stun grenades and watch the doors and wing windows.' Ingrid slapped the oxygen mask back over her mouth and panted wildly.

'Don't blow us up, Ingrid,' Karen pleaded around her mask. 'Please, if we surrender Caliph will have us free in a month. We don't have to die.'

At that moment the lights of the cabin came on brightly, and there was the hiss of the air-conditioning. Ingrid took one last breath of oxygen and ran back into the first-class cabin, jumping over the unconscious figures of the hostages and of two air hostesses. She grabbed another of the dangling oxygen masks above a passenger seat and looked down the long fuselage.

Kurt and Henri had obeyed her orders. They were breathing oxygen from the roof panels. The German was ready at the port wing panel, and Henri waited at the rear doorway hatch – both of them had the short big-mouthed shot pistols ready, but their faces were covered with the yellow oxygen masks, so Ingrid could not see nor judge their expressions.

Only a small number of the passengers had been quick enough and sensible enough to grab the dangling oxygen masks and remain conscious – but hundreds of others slumped in their seats or had fallen sideways into the aisles.

A thicket of dangling, twisting, swinging oxygen hoses filled the cabin like a forest of lianas, obscuring and confusing the scene, and after the darkness the cabin lights were painfully bright.

Ingrid held the camera in her free hand, for she knew that they must continue breathing oxygen. It would take the air-conditioning many minutes longer to cleanse the air of all trace of Factor V, and she held a mask over her mouth and waited.

Karen was beside her, with her shot pistol dangling from one hand and the other pressing a mask to her mouth.

'Go back and cover the front hatch,' Ingrid snapped at her. 'There will be –'

'Ingrid, we don't have to die,' Karen pleaded, and with a crash the emergency exit panel over the port wing burst inwards, and at the same instant two small dark objects flew through the dark opening into the cabin.

'Stun grenades!' Ingrid howled. 'Get down!'

Peter Stride was light and jubilant as an eagle in flight. His feet and hands hardly seemed to touch the rungs of the ladder, now in the swift all-engulfing rush of action there were no longer doubts, no more hesitations – he was committed, and it was a tremendous soaring relief.

He went up over the smooth curved leading edge of the wing with a roll of his shoulders and hips, and in the same movement was on his feet, padding silently down the broad glistening metal pathway. The raindrops glittered like diamonds under his feet, and a fresh wind tugged at his hair as he ran.

He reached the main hull, and dropped into position at the side of the panel, his fingertips finding the razor-tight joint while his number-two man knelt swiftly opposite him. The grenade men were ready facing the panel, balanced like acrobats on the curved slippery upper surface of the great wing.

'Under six seconds.' Peter guessed at the time it had taken them to reach this stage from the 'go'. It was as swift and neat as it had never been in training, all of them armed by the knowledge of waiting death and horror.

In unison Peter and his number two hurled their combined strength and weight on to the releases of the emergency escape hatch, and it flew inwards readily, for there was no pressurization to resist, and at exactly the same instant the stun grenades went in cleanly, thrown by the waiting grenade men, and all four members of Peter's team bowed like Mohammedans in prayer to Mecca, covering eyes and ears.

Even outside the cabin, and even with ears and eyes covered, the thunder of the explosions was appalling, seeming to beat in upon the brain with oppressive physical force, and the glare of burning phosphorus powder painted an x-ray picture of Peter's own fingers on the fleshy red of his closed eyelids. Then the grenade men were shouting into the interior, 'Lie down! Everybody down!' They would keep repeating that order Israeli style as long as it lasted.

Peter was a hundredth of a second slow, numbed by the blast, fumbling slightly at the butt of the Walther, thumbing the hammer as it snapped out of the quick-release holster, and then he went in – feet first through the hatch, like a runner sliding for the home base. He was still in the air when he saw the girl in the red shirt running forward brandishing the camera, and screaming something that made no sense, though his brain registered it even in that unholy moment. He fired as his feet touched the deck and his first shot hit the girl in the mouth, punching a dark red hole through the rows of white teeth and snapping her head back so viciously that he heard the small delicate bones of her neck crackle as they broke.

Ingrid used both arms to cover eyes and ears, crouching forward into the appalling blast of sound and light that swept through the crowded cabins like a hurricane wind, and even when it had passed she was reeling wildly clutching for support at a seat back, trying to steady herself and judge the moment when the attackers were into the hull.

Those outside the hull would escape the direct force of the explosives she was about to detonate, there was a high survival chance for them. She wanted to judge the moment when the entire assault team penetrated the hull, she wanted maximum casualties, she wanted to take as many with her as possible, and she lifted the camera above her head with both hands.

'Come on!' she shrieked, but the cabin was thick with swirling clouds of white acrid smoke, and the dangling hoses twisted and writhed like the head of the Medusa. She heard the thunder of a shot pistol and somebody screamed, voices were chanting, 'Lie down! Everybody down!'

It was all smoke and sound and confusion, but she watched the dark opening of the emergency hatchway, waiting for it, finger on the detonator button of the camera. A supple black-clad figure in a grotesque face mask torpedoed feet first into the cabin, and at the same instant Karen shrieked beside her.

'No, don't kill us,' and snatched the camera from Ingrid's raised hands, jerking it away by the strap, leaving Ingrid weaponless. Karen ran down the aisle through the smoke, still screaming, 'Don't kill us!' holding the camera like a peace offering. 'Caliph said we would not die.' She ran forward screaming frantically. 'Caliph –' and the black-clad and masked figure twisted lithely in the air, arching his back to land feet first in the centre of the aisle; as his feet touched the deck so the pistol in his right hand jerked up sharply but the shot seemed muted and unwarlike after the concussion of the stun grenades.

Karen was running down the aisle towards him, screaming and brandishing the camera, when the bullet took her in the mouth and wrenched her head backwards at an impossible angle. The next two shots blended into a single blurt of sound, fired so swiftly as to cheat the hearing, and from such close range that even the Velex explosive bullets ripped the back out of Karen's shirt and flooded it with a brighter wetter scarlet as they erupted from between her shoulder blades. The camera went spinning high across the cabin, landing in the lap of an unconscious passenger slumped in one of the central seats between the aisles.

Ingrid reacted with the instinctive speed of a jungle cat, diving forward, flat on the carpet aisle below the line of fire; shrouded by the sinking white smoke of the grenades she wriggled forward on her belly to reach the camera.

It was twenty feet to where the camera had landed, but Ingrid moved with the speed of a serpent; she knew that the smoke was hiding her, but she knew also that to reach the camera she would have to come to her feet again and reach across two seats and two unconscious bodies.

Peter landed in balance on the carpeted aisle, and he killed the girl swiftly, and danced aside, clearing space for his number two to land.

The next man in landed lightly in the space Peter had made for him, and the German in the red shirt jumped out from the angle of the rear galley and hit him in the small of the back with a full charge of buckshot. It almost blew his body into two separate parts, and he seemed to break in the middle like a folding penknife as he collapsed against Peter's legs.

Peter whirled at the shot, turning his back on Ingrid as she crawled forward through the phosphorus smoke.

Kurt was desperately trying to pull down the short, thick barrel of the pistol, for the recoil had thrown it high above his head. His scarlet shirt was open to the navel, shiny hard brown muscle and thick whorls of black body hair, mad glaring eyes through a greasy fringe of black hair, the scarred lip curled in a fixed snarl.

Peter hit him in the chest, taking no chance, and as he reeled backwards still fighting to aim the pistol, Peter hit again, in the head through the temple just in front of the left ear; the eyelids closed tightly over those wild eyes, his features twisted out of shape like a rubber mask and he went down face first into the aisle.

'Two.' Peter found that, as always in these desperate moments, he was functioning very coldly, very efficiently. His shooting had been as reflexively perfect as if he were walking a combat shoot with jump-up cardboard targets.

He had even counted his shots, there were four left in the Walther.

'And two more of them,' he thought, but the smoke was still so thick that his visibility was down to under fifteen feet, and the swirling forest of dangling oxygen hoses still agitated by the grenade blasts cut down his visibility further.

He jumped over the broken body of his number two, the blood squelching under his rubber soles, and suddenly the chunky black figure of Colin Noble loomed across the cabin. He was in the far aisle, having come in over the starboard wing. In the writhing smoke he looked like some demon from the pit, hideous and menacing in his gas mask. He dropped into the marksman's crouch, holding the big Browning in a double-handed grip, and the clangour of the gun beat upon the air like one of the great bronze bells of Notre Dame.

He was shooting at another scarlet-shirted figure, half seen through the smoke and the dangling hoses, a man with a round boyish face and drooping sandy moustache. The big Velex bullets tore the hijacker to pieces with the savagery of a predator's claws. They seemed to pin him like an insect to the central bulkhead, and they smashed chunks of living flesh from his chest and splinters of white bone from his skull.

'Three,' thought Peter. 'One left now – and I must get the camera.'

He had seen the black camera in the hands of the girl he had killed, had seen it fall, and he knew how deadly important it was to secure the detonator before it fell into the hands of the other girl, the blonde one, the dangerous one.

It had been only four seconds since he had penetrated the hull, yet it seemed like a dragging eternity. He could hear the crash of the slap-hammers tearing out the door locks, both fore and aft, within seconds there would be Thor assault teams pouring into the Boeing through every opening, and he had not yet located the fourth hijacker, the truly dangerous one.

'Get down! Everybody down!' chanted the grenade men, and Peter spun lightly, and ran for the flight deck. He was certain the blonde girl would be there at the control centre.

Then, in front of him lay the girl he had shot down, the long, dark hair spread out around her pale, still terrified face. Her hair was already sodden with dark blood, and the black gap in her white teeth made her look like an old woman. She blocked the aisle with a tangle of slim boneless limbs.

The forward hatch crashed open as the lock gave way, but there were still solid curtains of white smoke ahead of him. Peter gathered himself to jump over the girl's body, and at that instant the other girl, the blonde girl, bounded up from the deck, seeming to appear miraculously from the smoke, like some beautiful but evil apparition.

She dived half across the block of central seating, groping for the camera, and Peter was slightly off balance, blocking himself in the turn to bring his gun hand on to her. He changed hands smoothly, for he was equally accurate with either, but it cost him the tenth part of a second, and the girl had the strap of the camera now and was tugging desperately at it. The camera seemed to be snagged, and Peter swung on her, taking the head shot for she was less than ten paces away, and even in the smoke and confusion he could not miss.

One of the few passengers who had been breathing oxygen from his hanging mask, and was still conscious, ignored the chanted orders 'Get down! Stay down!' and suddenly stumbled to his feet, screaming, 'Don't shoot! Get me out of here! Don't shoot!' in a rising hysterical scream. He was directly between Peter and the red-shirted girl, blocking Peter's field of fire, and Peter wrenched the gun off him at the moment that he fired. The bullet slammed into the roof, and the passenger barged into Peter, still screaming.

'Get me out! I want to get out!'

Peter tried desperately to clear his gun hand, for the girl had broken the strap of the camera and was fumbling with the black box. The passenger had an arm around Peter's gun arm, was shaking him wildly, weeping and screaming.

From across the central block of seats, Colin Noble fired once. He was still in the starboard aisle and the angle was almost impossible, for he had to shoot nine inches past Peter's shoulder, and through the forest of dangling hose.

His first shot missed, but it was close enough to flinch the girl's head violently, and she stumbled backwards, groping with clumsy fingers for the detonator.

Peter chopped the hysterical passenger in the throat with the stiffened fingers of his right hand and hurled him back into his seat, trying desperately to line up for a shot at the girl – knowing he must get the brain and still her fingers instantly.

Colin fired his second shot, one hundredth of a second before Peter, and the big bullet flung the girl aside, jerking her out of the track of Peter's shot.

Peter saw the strike of Colin's bullet, it hit her high in the right shoulder, almost in the joint of the scapula and the humerus, shattering the bone with such force that her arm was flung upwards in a parody of a communist salute, twisting unnaturally and whipping above her head; once again the camera was flung aside and the girl's body was thrown violently backwards down the aisle as though she had been hit by a speeding automobile.

Peter picked his shot, waiting for a clean killing hit in the head as the girl tried to drag herself upright – but before he could fire a mass of black-costumed figures swarmed out of the smoke, and covered the girl, pinning her kicking and screaming on the carpet of the aisle. The Thor team had come in through the forward hatch, just in time to save her life, and Peter clipped the Walther into his holster and stooped to pick up the camera gingerly. Then he pulled off his mask with his other hand.

'That's it. That's all of them,' he shouted. 'We got them all. Cease fire. It's all over.' Then into the microphone of the transceiver. 'Touch down! Touch down!' The code for total success. Three of his men were holding the girl down, and despite the massive spurting wound in her shoulder, she fought like a leopard in a trap.

'Get the emergency chutes down,' Peter ordered, and from each exit the long plastic slides inflated and drooped to the tarmac – already his men were leading the conscious passengers to the exits and helping them into the slide.

From the terminal building a dozen ambulances with sirens howling, gunned out across the tarmac. The back-up members of Thor were running out under the glare of the floodlights, cheering thinly. 'Touch down! Touch down!'

Like prehistoric monsters the mechanical stairways lumbered down from the northern apron, to give access to the body of the Boeing.

Peter stepped up to the girl, still holding the camera in his hands, and he stood looking down at her. The icy coldness of battle still gripped him, his mind felt needle sharp and his vision clear, every sense enhanced.

The girl stopped struggling, and looked back at him. The image of a trapped leopard was perfect. Peter had never seen eyes so fierce and merciless, as she glared at him. Then she drew her head back like a cobra about to strike, and spat at him. White frothy spittle splattered down the front of Peter's legs.

Colin Noble was beside Peter now, pulling off his gas mask.

'I'm sorry, Peter. I was going for the heart.'

'You'll never hold me,' shrieked the girl suddenly. 'I'll be free before Thanksgiving!'

And Peter knew she was right. The punishment that a befuddled world society meted out to these people was usually only a few months' imprisonment, and that often suspended. He remembered the feel of the dying child in his arms, the warm trickle of her blood running over his belly and legs.

'My people will come for me,' the girl spat again, this time into the face of one of the men who held her down. 'You will never hold me. My people will force you to free me.'

Again she was right, her capture was a direct invitation for further atrocity, the wheel of vengeance and retribution was set in motion. For the life of this trapped and vicious predator, hundreds more would suffer, and dozens more would die.

The reaction was setting in now, the battle rage abating, and Peter felt the nausea cloying his bowels. It had been in vain, he thought, he had thrown away a lifetime's strivings and endeavour to win only a temporary victory. He had checked the forces of evil, not beaten them – and they would regroup and attack again, stronger and more cunning than ever, and this woman would lead them again.

'We are the revolution.' The girl lifted her uninjured arm in the clenched fist salute. 'We are the power. Nothing, nobody can stop us.'

When this woman had fired a load of buckshot through the swollen body of the pregnant woman it had distorted her shape completely. The image was recaptured entire and whole in Peter's memory, the way she had burst open like the pod of a ripe fruit.

The blonde woman shook the clenched fist into Peter's face.

'This is only the beginning – the new era has begun.'

There was a taunt and a sneering threat in her voice, uttered in complete confidence – and Peter knew it was not misplaced. There was a new force unleashed in the world, something more deadly than he had believed possible, and Peter had no illusion as to the role that blind fortune had played in his small triumph. He had no illusion either that the beast was more than barely wounded, next time it would be more powerful, more cunning, having learned from this inconsequential failure – and with the reaction from battle came a powerful wave of dread and despair that seemed to overwhelm his soul. It had all been in vain.

'You can never win,' taunted the woman, splattered with her own blood, but undaunted and unrepentant, seeming to read his very thoughts.

'And we can never lose,' she shrieked.

'Gentlemen.' The South African Prime Minister spoke with painful deliberation. 'My cabinet and I are firmly of the opinion that to accede to the terrorists' demands is to take a seat on the back of the tiger, from which we will never be able to dismount.' He stopped, hung his great granite-hewn head for a moment and then looked up at the two ambassadors. 'However, such is the duty we owe to humanity and the dignity of human life, and such is the pressure which two great nations can bring to bear upon one much smaller, that we have decided unanimously to agree in full to all the conditions necessary for the release of the women and children –'

A telephone on the tabletop in front of the American Ambassador began to shrill irritatingly, and the Prime Minister paused, frowned slightly.

'However, we place complete faith in the undertaking given by your governments –' He stopped again for the telephone insisted, '– you had best answer that, sir –' he told Kelly Constable.

'Excuse me, Prime Minister.' The American lifted the receiver, and as he listened an expression of utter disbelief slowly changed his features. 'Hold the line,' he said into the receiver, and then, covering the mouthpiece with his hand, he looked up. 'Prime Minister – it is a very great pleasure to inform you that three minutes ago the Thor assault team broke into Flight 070 and killed three of the terrorists – they wounded and captured a fourth terrorist, but there were no casualties amongst the passengers. They got them all out, every last one of them. Safe and sound.

The big man at the head of the table sagged with relief in his seat, and as the storm of jubilation and self-congratulation broke about him, he started to smile. It was a smile that transformed his forbidding features, the smile of an essentially fatherly and kindly man. 'Thank you, sir,' he said, still smiling. 'Thank you very much.'

'You are guilty of blatant dereliction of your duty, General Stride,' Kingston Parker accused grimly.

'My concern was entirely with the lives of hostages and the force of moral law.' Peter answered him quietly, it was less than fifteen minutes since he had penetrated the hull of the Boeing in a blaze of fire and fury. His hands were still shaking slightly and the nausea still lay heavily on his guts.

'You deliberately disobeyed my specific orders.' Parker was an enraged lion, the mane of thick shot-silver hair seemed to bristle, and he glowered from the screen; the vast power of his personality seemed to fill the command cabin of the Hawker. 'I have always had grave reservations as to your suitability for the high command with which you have been entrusted. I have already expressed those reservations in writing to your superiors, and they have been fully justified.'

'I understand by all this that I have been removed from command of Thor,' Peter cut in brusquely, his anger seething to the surface, and Parker checked slightly.

Peter knew that even Kingston Parker could not immediately fire the hero of such a successful counterstrike. It would take time, a matter of days, perhaps, but Peter's fate was sealed. There could be no doubt of that, and Parker went on to confirm this.

'You will continue to exercise command under my direct surveillance. You will make no decision without referring directly back to me, no decision whatsoever. Do you understand that, General Stride?'

Peter did not bother to reply, he felt a wildly reckless mood starting to buoy his sagging spirits, a sense of freedom and choice of action such as he had never known before. For the first time in his career he had deliberately disobeyed a superior officer and, luck or not, the outcome had been a brilliant success.

'Your first duty now will be to withdraw all Thor units, and swiftly and in as good an order as possible. The militant you have taken will be returned to London for questioning and trial –'

'Her crimes were committed here. She should be tried here for murder – I have already had demands from the local –'

'Arrangements are being made with the South African authorities.' Parker's anger had not abated but he had it better under control. 'She will return to Britain aboard your command aircraft, with the Thor doctor in attendance.'

Peter remembered what had happened to the terrorist Leila Khaled, dragged from the El Al airliner where she was being held by Israeli security agents. As a guest of the British police, she had spent six short days in captivity, and then been released in a blaze of publicity and glory, heroine of the communications media, Joan of Arc of terror – released to plan and execute the death and destruction of hundreds more innocents, to lead the attack on the foundations of civilization, to shake the columns that held aloft the rule of law and society.

'I want this woman in London within twenty-four hours. She is to be strictly guarded at all times against retaliation. We cannot afford another bloodbath – like the one you led on 070.'

Peter Stride walked very erect, very tall into the echoing, marble-columned domestic departures hall of the airport, and his men called to him as he came.

'Well done, sir.'

'Great stuff, General.'

'Way to go –'

They were tending the released passengers, re-assembling their scattered gear, dismantling the security and communications equipment and packing it away – within the hour they would be ready to pull out – but now they left their tasks to crowd about him, competing to shake his hand.

The passengers realized that this must be the architect of their salvation and they cheered him as he passed slowly through the hall, and now he was smiling, acknowledging their pitiful gratitude, stopping to talk with an old lady, and submitting to her tearful embrace.

'God bless you, my boy. God bless you.' And her body trembled against him. Gently Peter set her aside, and went on, and though he smiled it was with his lips only, for there was steel in his heart.

There were Thor guards on the main administrative offices on the mezzanine floor armed with submachine guns, but they stood aside for him and Peter went through.

Colin Noble was still in his black skin-tight assault suit with the big .45 on his hip, and a cheroot clamped between his teeth.

'Take a look at this lot,' he called to Peter. The desk was covered with explosives and weapons. 'Most of it's iron-curtain stuff – but God alone knows where they got these.' He indicated the double-barrelled shot pistols. 'If they had these custom built, it would have cost them plenty.'

'They have got plenty,' Peter answered drily. 'The ransom for the OPEC ministers was one hundred and fifty million dollars, for the Braun brothers twenty-five million, for Baron Altmann another twenty million – that's the defence budget for a nation.' He picked up one of the shot pistols and opened the breech. It had been unloaded.

'Is this the one she used to gun down the hostages?'

Colin shrugged. 'Probably, it's been fired through both barrels.' Colin was right, there were black specks of burned powder down the short smooth bores.

Peter loaded it with buckshot cartridges from the pile on the desk, and walked on down the long office with the covered typewriters on the deserted desks and the airline travel posters decorating the wall.

Along one wall the three bodies of the hijackers were laid out in a neat row, each encapsuled in its separate translucent plastic envelope.

Two Thor men were assembling the contents of their pockets – personal jewellery, meagre personal effects – and they were packing them into labelled plastic bags.

The body of Peter's number two was against the far wall, also in his plastic body-bag, and Peter stooped over him. Through the plastic he could make out the features of the dead man's face. The eyes were wide and the jaw hung open slackly. Death is always so undignified, Peter thought, and straightened up.

Still carrying the shot pistol, Peter went on into the inner office, and Colin Noble followed him.

They had the girl on another stretcher, a plasma drip suspended above her, and the Thor doctor and his two orderlies were working over her quietly, but the young doctor looked up irritably as Peter pushed open the door, then his expression changed as he recognized Peter.

'General, if we are going to save this arm, I have to get her into theatre pretty damned quickly. The joint of the shoulder is shattered –'

The girl rolled the lovely head towards Peter. The thick springing golden hair was matted with drying blood, and there was a smear of it across one cheek.

Now her face was completely drained of all colour, like the head of an angel carved out of white marble. The skin had a waxen, almost translucent, lustre and only the eyes were still fierce, not dulled by the painkilling drugs they had injected into her.

'– I have asked the South Africans for cooperation –' the doctor went on, '– they have two top orthopaedic surgeons standing by, and they have offered a helicopter to fly her into the Central Hospital at Edenvale.'

Already she was being treated, even by Thor, as the major celebrity she was. She had taken her first step along the rose-strewn pathway to glory, and Peter could imagine how the media would extol her beauty – they had gone berserk with extravagant praise for the swarthy ferrety-eyed Leila Khaled with her fine dark moustache – they would go over the top for this one.

Peter had never known any emotion so powerful as the emotion that gripped him now.

'Get out,' he said to the doctor.

'Sir?' The man looked startled.

'Get out,' Peter repeated, 'all of you.' And he waited until the opaque glass door closed behind them, before he spoke to the girl in conversational tones.

'You have made me abandon my own principles, and descend to your level.'

The girl watched him uncertainly, her eyes flickered to the shot pistol that Peter held dangling from his right hand.

'You have forced me, a career soldier, to disobey the orders of a superior officer in the face of the enemy.' He paused. 'I used to be a proud man, but when I have done what I must do now I will no longer have much of which to be proud.'

'I demand to see the American Ambassador,' said the girl huskily, still watching the pistol. 'I am an American citizen. I demand the protection –'

Peter interrupted her, again speaking quickly. 'This is not revenge. I am old and wise enough to know that revenge has the most bitter taste of all human excess.'

'You cannot do it –' The girl's voice rose, the same strident tones, but now shriller still with fear. 'They will destroy you.'

But Peter went on as though she had not spoken. 'It is not revenge,' he repeated. 'You, yourself, gave the reason clearly. If you continue to exist, they will come to get you back. As long as you live, others must die – and they will die stripped of all human dignity. They will die in terror, the same way you murdered –'

'I am a woman. I am wounded. I am a prisoner of war,' screamed the girl, trying to struggle upright.

'Those are the old rules,' Peter told her. 'You tore up the book, and wrote a new one – I am playing to your rules now. I have been reduced to your level.'

'You cannot kill me,' the girl's voice rang wildly. 'I still have work –'

'Colin,' Peter said quietly, without looking at the American. 'You'd better get out now.'

Colin Noble hesitated, his right hand on the butt of the Browning, and the girl rolled her head towards him imploringly.

'You can't let him do it.'

'Peter –' Colin said.

'You were right, Colin,' Peter spoke quietly. 'That kid did look a lot like Melissa-Jane.'

Colin Noble dropped his hand from the pistol and turned to the door. Now the girl was shrieking obscenity and threat, her voice incoherent with terror and hatred.

Colin closed the door softly and stood with his back to it. The single crash of shot was shockingly loud, and the stream of filthy abuse was cut off abruptly. The silence was even more appalling than the harrowing sounds which had preceded it. Colin did not move. He waited four, five seconds before the door clicked open and General Peter Stride came out into the main office. He handed the shot pistol to Colin and one barrel was hot in his hand.

Peter's handsome aristocratic features seemed ravaged, as though by a long wasting disease. The face of a man who had leapt into the abyss.

Peter Stride left the glass door open, and walked away without looking back. Despite the terrible expression of despair, he still carried himself like a soldier and his tread was firm.

Colin Noble did not even look through the open door.

'All right,' he called to the doctor. 'She's all yours now.' And he followed Peter Stride down the broad staircase.

There was a long hard gallop over good going and open pasture to the crest of the ridge, with only one gate. Melissa-Jane led on her bay filly, her Christmas gift from Uncle Steven. She was in the midst of the passionate love affair that most pubescent girls have with horses, and she looked truly good astride the glistening thoroughbred. The cold struck high colour into her cheeks and the braid of honey-coloured hair thumped gaily down her back at each stride. She had blossomed even in the few weeks since last Peter had seen her – and he realized with some awe and considerable pride that she was fast becoming a great beauty.

Peter was up on one of Steven's hunters, a big rangy animal with the strength to carry his weight, but the gelding was slogging hard to hold the flying pair that danced ahead of him.

At the hedge, Melissa-Jane scorned the gate, gathered the filly with fine strong hands and took her up and over. Her little round bottom lifted out of the saddle as she leaned into the jump, and clods of black earth flew from the filly's hooves.

As soon as she was over she swivelled in the saddle to watch him, and Peter realized that he was under challenge. The hedge immediately appeared to be head-high and he noticed for the first time how the ground fell away at a steep angle beyond. He had not ridden for almost two years, and it was the first time he had been up on this gelding – but the horse went for the jump gamely, and they brushed the top of the hedge, landed awkwardly, stumbled with Peter up on his neck for an appalling instant of time in which he was convinced he was to take a toss in front of his daughter's critical eye; caught his balance, held the gelding's head up and they came away still together.

'Super-Star!' Melissa-Jane shouted laughing, and by the time he caught her she had dismounted under the yew tree at the crest, and was waiting for him with her breath steaming in the crisp calm air.

'Our land once went right as far as the church –' Peter pointed to the distant grey needle of stone that pricked the belly of the sky. '– and there almost to the top of the downs.' He turned to point in the opposite direction.

'Yes.' Melissa-Jane slipped her arm through his as they stood close together under the yew. 'The family had to sell it when grandfather died. You told me. And that's right too. One family shouldn't own so much.'

Peter glanced down at her, startled. 'My God, a communist in the family. An asp in the bosom.'

She squeezed his arm. 'Don't worry, Daddy darling. It's Uncle Steven who is the bloated plutocrat. You're not a capitalist – you aren't even employed any more –' And the instant she had said it, her laughter collapsed around her and she looked stricken. '– Oh, I didn't mean that. I truly didn't.'

It was almost a month now since Peter's resignation had been accepted by the War Office, but the scandal had not yet run out of steam.

The first heady paeans of praise for the success of Thor's Delta strike had lasted only a few days. The glowing editorials, the full front pages, the lead news item on every television channel, the effusive messages of congratulations from the leaders of the Western governments, the impromptu triumph for Peter Stride and his little band of heroes, had quickly struck an odd note, a sudden souring of the ecstasies.

The racist Government of South Africa had actually agreed to the release of political prisoners *before* the assault, one of the hijackers had been taken alive, and died of gunshot wounds received in the terminal building. Then one of the released hostages, a freelance journalist who had been covering the medical convention in Mauritius and was returning aboard the hijacked aircraft, published a sensational eye-witness account of the entire episode, and a dozen other passengers supported his claims that there had been screams from the fourth hijacker, screams for mercy, before she was shot to death after her capture.

A storm of condemnation and vilification from the extreme left of the British Labour Government had swept through the Westminster parliament, and had been echoed by the Democrats in the American Congress. The very existence of the Thor Command had come under scrutiny and been condemned in extravagant terms. The Communist parties of France and Italy had marched, and the detonation of an M.26 hand grenade – one of those stolen by the Baader-Meinhof gang from the American base in Metz – amongst the crowd leaving the Parc des Princes football stadium in Paris had killed one and injured twenty-three. A telephone call to the offices of *France Soir* by a man speaking accented French claimed that this fresh atrocity was revenge for the murder of four hijackers by the Imperialist execution squad.

Pressure for Peter's discharge had come initially from the Pentagon, and there was very little doubt that Dr Kingston Parker was the accuser, though, as head of Atlas, he was never identified, total secrecy still surrounding the project. The media had begun to demand an investigation of all the circumstances surrounding Thor. '– And if it is ascertained that criminal irregularities did indeed exist in the conduct of the operation, that the person or persons responsible be brought to trial either by a military tribunal or the civil courts.' Fortunately the media had not yet unravelled the full scope of Atlas Command. Only Thor was under scrutiny; they did not yet suspect the existence of either Mercury or Diana.

Within the War Office and the governments of both America and Britain, there had been much sympathy and support for Peter Stride – but he had made it easier for his friends and for himself by tendering his resignation. The resignation had been accepted, but still the left was clamouring for more. They wanted blood, Peter Stride's blood.

Now Melissa-Jane's huge pansy violet eyes flooded with the tears of mortification. 'I didn't mean that. I truly didn't.'

'One thing about being out of a job – I have more time to be with my favourite girl.' He smiled down at her, but she would not be mollified.

'I don't believe the horrible things they are saying. I know you are a man of honour, Daddy.'

'Thank you.' And he felt the ache of it, the guilt and the sorrow. They were silent a little longer, still standing close together, and Peter spoke first.

'You are going to be a palaeontologist –' he said.

'No. That was last month. I've changed my mind. I'm not interested in old bones any more. Now I'm going to be a doctor, a child specialist.'

'That's good.' Peter nodded gravely. 'But let's go back to old bones for a moment. The age of the great reptiles. The dinosaurs – why did they fade into extinction?'

'They could not adapt to a changing environment.' Melissa-Jane had the answer promptly.

Peter murmured, '– A concept like honour. Is it outdated in today's world, I wonder?' Then he saw the puzzlement, the hurt in her eyes, and he knew they had wandered on to dangerous ground. His daughter had a burning love for all living things, particularly human beings. Despite her age, she had a developed political and social conscience, distinguished by total belief in shining ideals and the essential beauty and goodness of mankind. There would be time in the years ahead for the agony of disillusion. The term 'man or woman of honour' was Melissa-Jane's ultimate accolade. No matter that it could be applied to any of her current heroes or heroines – the Prince of Wales, or the singer of popular songs with an outrageous name that Peter could never remember, to Virginia Wade, the former Wimbledon champion, or to the Fifth Form science teacher at Roedean who had aroused Melissa-Jane's interest in medicine – Peter knew that he should feel proper gratitude for being included in this exalted company.

'I will try to live up to your opinion of me.' He stooped and kissed her, surprised at the strength of his love for this child-woman. 'And now it's too cold to stand here any longer, and Pat will never forgive us if we are late for lunch.'

They clattered over the stone cobbles of the stable yard, riding knee to knee, and before he dismounted, Peter indulged himself in the pleasure of his favourite view of the house that had always been home, even though it belonged now, together with the title, to Steven, the older brother, older by three hours only, but older none the less.

The house was red brick with a roof that ran at fifty different unlikely angles. It missed being hideous by a subtle margin and achieved a fairytale enchantment. Peter could never grudge it to Steven, who loved the sprawling edifice with something close to passion.

Perhaps the desire to own the house and to restore it to its former magnificence was the goad which had pricked Steven to the superhuman effort that a British resident must make against taxation and socialist restrictions in order to amass anything like a fortune.

Steven had made that effort and now Abbots Yew stood immaculate and well-beloved in glorious gardens, and Sir Steven kept baronial style.

His affairs were so complicated, spread over so many continents that even the British tax man must have been daunted. Peter had once skirted this subject with his twin brother, and Steven had replied quietly.

'When a law is patently unjust, such as our tax law is, it's the duty of an honest man to subvert it.'

Peter's old-fashioned sense of rightness had baulked at such logic, but he let it pass.

It was strange that it had worked this way for the two brothers, for Peter had always been the brilliant one, and the family had always referred to 'Poor Steven'. Nobody was very surprised when Steven left Sandhurst amid dark whispers half-way through his final year – but two years later Steven was already a millionaire while Peter was a lowly second lieutenant in the British Army. Peter grinned without rancour at the memory. He had always been particularly fond of his elder brother – but at that moment his train of thought was interrupted as his eye caught the mirror-like finish of the silver limousine parked at the end of the stable yard. It was one of those long Mercedes-Benz favoured by pop stars, Arab oil men, or Heads of State. The chauffeur was uniformed in sober navy-blue and was busy burnishing the paintwork to an even higher gloss. Even Steven did not run to that sort of transportation, and Peter felt mildly intrigued. House guests at Abbots Yew were always interesting. Steven Stride did not concern himself with those who did not wield either power, wealth or extraordinary talent. Beyond the Mercedes 600 was parked another smaller model; this one was black and the two men in it had the hard closed faces that marked them as bodyguards.

Melissa-Jane rolled her eyes at the automobile. 'Another bloated plutocrat, I expect,' she muttered. It was the currently favoured term of extreme disapproval, a great advance on 'grotty' which had preceded it, Peter could not help thinking as he helped his daughter unsaddle and then rub down the horses. They went up through the rose garden, arm in arm, and then laughing together into the main drawing-room.

'Peter old boy!' Steven came to meet him, as tall as his brother, and once he had been as lean, but good living had thickened his body while at the same time the strains of being a professional deal maker had greyed his hair at the temples and laced his moustache with silver bristles. His face was not quite a mirror image of Peter's, slightly more fleshy and florid – but the twin resemblance was still strongly marked, and now his face was alive with pleasure.

'Thought you'd broken your bloody neck, what!' Steven carefully cultivated the bluff manner of the country squire to shield his quick and shrewd intelligence.

Now he turned to Melissa-Jane and hugged her with barely a touch of incestuous pleasure. 'How did Florence Nightingale go?'

'She's a darling, Uncle Steven. I will never be able to thank you.'

'Peter, I would like you to meet a very charming lady –'

She had been talking to Patricia Stride, Steven's wife, and now as she turned, the winter sunshine through the bay windows behind lit her with a soft romantic aura.

Peter felt as though the earth had tilted under his feet, and a fist closed around his ribs constricting his breathing and inhibiting the action of his heart.

He recognized her immediately from the photographs in the official file during the long-drawn-out kidnapping and subsequent murder of her husband. At one stage it seemed that the kidnappers had crossed the Channel with their victim, and Thor had gone to condition Alpha for almost a week. Peter had studied the photographs that had been assembled from a dozen sources, but even the glossy coloured portraits from *Vogue* and *Jours de France* had not been able to capture the magnificence of the woman.

Surprisingly, he saw his own immediate recognition reflected. There was no change in her expression, but it flared briefly like dark-green emerald fire in her eyes. There was no question in Peter's mind but that she had recognized him, and as he stepped towards her he realized she was tall, but the fine proportion of her body had not made that immediately apparent. Her skirt was of a fine wool crêpe which moulded the long, stately legs of a dancer.

'Baroness, may I present my brother. General Stride.'

'How do you do, General.' Her English was almost perfect, a low husky voice, the slight accent very attractive, but she pronounced his rank as three distinct syllables.

'Peter, this is Baroness Altmann.'

Her thick glossy black hair was scraped back severely from the forehead with a perfect arrowhead of widow's peak at the centre, emphasizing the high Slavic cheekbones and the unblemished perfection of her skin – but her jawline was too square and strong for beauty, and the mouth had an arrogant determined line to it. Magnificent, but not beautiful – and Peter found himself violently attracted. The breathless wholesale feeling he had not experienced for twenty years.

She seemed to epitomize everything he admired in a woman.

Her body was in the condition of a trained athlete. Beneath the oyster silk of her blouse her arms were delicately sculpted from toned muscle, the waist narrow, the breasts very small and unfettered, their lovely shape pressing clearly through fine material, her clean lightly tanned skin glowed with health and careful grooming. All this contributed to his attraction.

However, the greater part was in Peter's own mind. He knew she was a woman of extraordinary strength and achievement, that was pure aphrodisiac for him, and she exuded also the challenging air of being unattainable. The regal eyes mocked his evident masculinity with the untouchable aloofness of a queen or a goddess. She seemed to be smiling inwardly, a cool patronizing smile at his admiration, which she realized was no more than her due. Quickly Peter reviewed what he knew of her.

She had begun her association with the Baron as his private secretary, and in five years had become indispensable to him. The Baron had recognized her ability by rapidly elevating her to the boards of directors, first of some of the group's lesser subsidiaries, and finally to that of the central holding company. When the Baron's physical strength had begun to decline in his losing battle with an inexorable cancer, he came to rely more upon her, trust well placed as it soon turned out. For she ran the complex empire of heavy industrial companies, of electronics and armaments corporations, of banking and shipping and property developments, like the son he never had. When he married her he was fifty-eight years of age, almost thirty years her senior, and she had been a perfect wife as she had been a perfect business partner.

She had assembled and personally delivered the massive ransom demanded by his abductors, against the advice of the French police, going alone and unguarded to a meeting with merciless killers, and when they had returned the Baron's fearfully mutilated corpse to her, she had mourned him and buried him and continued to run the empire she had inherited with vision and strength so far beyond her years.

She was twenty-nine years old. No, that had been two years ago, Peter realized, as he bowed over her hand, not quite touching the smooth cool fingers with his lips. She would be thirty-one years old now. She wore a single ring on her wedding finger, a solitaire diamond, not a particularly large diamond, not more than six carats but of such a perfect whiteness and fire that it seemed to be endowed with its own life. It was the choice of a woman of immense wealth and even greater style.

As Peter straightened, he realized that she was appraising him as carefully as he was her. It seemed that he would be unable to conceal anything from those slanted emerald eyes, but he returned her gaze steadily, knowing without conceit that he could withstand any such scrutiny; still intrigued, however, with the certainty that she had known him.

'Your name has been much in the news recently,' she said, as if in explanation.

There were sixteen for lunch, including Steven and Pat's three children and Melissa-Jane. It was a happy, relaxed meal, but the Baroness was seated at a distance that made it impossible for Peter to speak directly to her, and though he strained to follow her conversation, her voice was low and addressed mostly to Steven and the editor of one of the national daily newspapers who flanked her. Peter found himself fully occupied in fending off the breathless attention of the pretty but featherbrained blonde on his left. She was a starlet who had married well and divorced better. She had been handpicked by Pat Stride. Peter's sister-in-law was indefatigable in her efforts to find him a suitable replacement for Cynthia. Twelve years of straight failures had not daunted her in the least.

There was still time for Peter to notice that though the Baroness sipped once or twice at her wine, the level in the glass never fell, and she picked only lightly at her plate.

Though Peter watched her covertly, the Baroness never glanced once in his direction. It was only as they went through for coffee that she came directly and unaffectedly to his side.

'Steven tells me there are Roman ruins on the estate,' she said.

'I could show them to you. It is a lovely walk up through the woods.'

'Thank you. I do have some business to discuss with Steven before that; shall we meet at three o'clock?'

She had changed into a loose tweed skirt and jacket that would have looked bulky on a shorter or plumper woman, and high boots in the same lavender-tinted brown. Under it she wore a cashmere rollneck jersey, and a scarf of the same fine wool hung down her back. A wide-brimmed hat with a bright feather in the band was pulled down over her eyes.

She walked in silence, hands thrust deeply into the big pockets of her jacket, making no effort to protect the expensive boots from mud, thorns or damp bracken. She moved with a flowing, long-legged grace, swinging from the hips so that her shoulder and head seemed to float beside Peter, at not much lower level than his own. Had she not been a world leader in finance and industry, she might have made a great model, he decided. She had a talent for making clothes look important and elegant, while treating them with indifference.

Peter respected her silence, pleased to be able to step out to match her pace, as they went up through the dark dripping woods that smelt of leaf mould and cold rain, the oaks bare and moss-pelted, seeming to beseech a purple-grey sky with arthritic limbs held high.

They came out on the higher open ground without having stopped once, although the path had been steep and the ground soft underfoot.

She was breathing deeply but evenly, and she had coloured just sufficiently to flatter the high Slavic cheeks. She must be in peak physical condition, he thought.

'Here they are.' Peter indicated the barely discernible grass-covered ditch that circled the hill top. 'They are not very impressive, but I didn't want to warn you in advance.'

She smiled now. 'I have been here before,' she said in that intriguing husky accent.

'Well, we are off to a flying start. We have both deceived each other at our first meeting –' Peter chuckled.

'I came all the way from Paris,' she explained. 'It was most inconvenient really – the business I had to discuss with Sir Steven could have been completed by telephone in five minutes. What I had to discuss with you could only be done face by face –' she corrected herself immediately. 'I am sorry, face to face.' It was a rare slip. Steven had been strangely insistent that Peter spend this particular weekend at Abbots Yew, and was certainly party to this encounter.

'I am flattered by the interest of such a beautiful lady –'

Instantly she frowned, and with a gesture of irritation cut short the compliment as frivolous.

'Very recently you were approached by the Narmco section of Seddler Steel with an offer to head their Sales Division,' she said, and Peter nodded. Since his resignation had been accepted by the War Office, there had been many offers. 'The terms of employment offered were extraordinarily generous.'

'That is true.'

'You prefer the cloistered academic life, perhaps?' she asked, and though Peter's expression did not change, he was taken off balance. It seemed impossible that she could know of the offer of the Chair of Modern Military History that he had been offered by a leading American university, an offer with which he was still toying idly.

'There are some books I want to read and write,' Peter said.

'Books. You have an important collection, and I have read those you have written. You are an interesting contradiction, General Stride. The man of direct action, and at the same time of deep political and social thought.'

'I confuse myself at times,' Peter smiled. 'So what chance do you have to understand me?'

She did not rise to the smile. 'A great deal of your writing coincides with my own conviction. As for your action, if I had been a man and in your position, I might have acted as you did.'

Peter stiffened, resenting any allusion to the taking of Flight 070, and again she seemed to understand instinctively.

'I refer to your entire career, General. From Cyprus to Johannesburg, and including Ireland.' And he relaxed slightly.

'Why did you refuse the Narmco offer?' she asked.

'Because it was presented with the unstated conviction that I could not refuse. Because the terms were so generous that they left a strange unsatisfying odour in my nostrils. Because I believe that I would have been required to perform duties in line with the reputation I seem to have acquired since the taking of Flight 070.'

'What reputation is that?' She leaned slightly towards him, and he smelled her particular aroma. The way perfume reacted upon that petally smooth skin, heated by the exertion of the climb up the hill. She smelled faintly of crushed lemon blossom and clean healthy mature woman. He felt himself physically aroused by it, and had an almost undesirable impulse to reach out and touch her, to feel the warmth and glossiness of her skin.

'A man who makes accommodations, perhaps,' he answered her.

'What did you think you might have been asked to do?'

This time he shrugged. 'Perhaps carry bribes to my one-time colleagues in NATO Command, to induce them to consider favourably the products of Narmco.'

'Why would you believe that?'

'I was once a decision-making officer in that Command.'

She turned away from him and looked out across the special greens of an English winter landscape, the orderly fields and pastures, the dark wedges and geometrical shapes of the woods and copses.

'Do you know that through Altmann Industries and other companies I control a majority shareholding in Seddler Steel, and naturally in Narmco?'

'No,' Peter admitted. 'But I cannot say I am surprised.'

'Did you know that the offer from Narmco was in reality from me personally?'

This time he said nothing.

'You are quite right, of course, your contacts with the upper echelon of NATO and with the British and American high commands would have been worth every centime of the extravagant salary you were offered. As for bribes –' She smiled then suddenly, and it altered her face entirely, making her seem many years younger, and there was a warmth and a sense of fun that he would not have suspected, '– this is a capitalist society, General. We prefer to talk about commissions and introducer's fees.'

He found himself smiling back at her, not because of what she had said, but simply because her smile was irresistible.

'However, I give you my solemn word that you would never have been expected to offer or carry – no, since Lockheed were indiscreet, it has changed. Nothing disreputable could ever be traced back to Narmco, and certainly not to the top men there. Certainly not to you.'

'It's all academic now,' Peter pointed out. 'I've refused the offer.'

'I disagree, General Stride.' The brim of the hat covered her eyes as she looked down. 'I hope that when you hear what I had hoped to achieve you may reconsider. I made the error of trying to keep us at arms' length to begin with. I relied on the generosity of the offer to sway you. I do not usually misjudge people so dismally –' and she looked up and smiled again, and this time reached out and touched his arm. Her fingers were like her limbs, long and slim, but they were delicately tapered, and the nails were shaped and lacquered to a glossy fleshy pink. She left them on his arm as she went on speaking.

'My husband was an extraordinary man. A man of vast vision and strength and compassion. Because of that they tortured and killed him –' her voice had sunk to a hoarse catchy whisper, '– they killed him in the most vile manner –' She stopped, but made no attempt to turn her head away, she was unashamed of the tears that filled both eyes but did not break over the lower lids. She did not even blink, and it was Peter who looked away first. Only then she moved her hand, slipping it lightly into the crook of Peter's elbow and coming beside him so her hip almost touched his.

'It will rain soon,' she said, her voice level and controlled. 'We should go down.' And as they started, she went on talking.

'The butchers who did that to Aaron went free, while an impotent society looked on. A society which has systematically stripped itself of defence against the next attack. America has virtually disbanded its intelligence system, and so shackled and exposed what is left that it is powerless. Your own country is concerned only with its own particular problems, as we are in the rest of Europe – there is no international approach to a problem that is international in scope. Atlas was a fine concept, limited as it was by the fact that it was a force that could only be used in retaliation and then only in special circumstances. However, if they ever suspect that it exists, the denizens of the left will mass to tear it down like a hunting pack of hyena.' She squeezed his arm lightly, and looked sideways at him with a solemn slant of the emerald eyes. 'Yes, General, I do know about Atlas – but do not ask me how.'

Peter said nothing, and they entered the forest, stepping carefully, for the path was slick and steep.

'After the death of my husband, I began to think a great deal about how we could protect the world that we know, while still remaining within the laws which were first designed to do that. With Altmann Industries I had inherited a comprehensive system of international information-gathering, naturally it was attuned almost entirely to commercial and industrial considerations –' She went on talking in that low intense voice that Peter found mesmeric, describing how she had gradually used her massive fortune and influence to reach across borders closed to most to gain the overall view of the new world of violence and intimidation. '– I was not tied by considerations such as that of Interpol, forbidden by suicidal laws to involve itself in any crime that has political motivation. It was only when I was able to pass on what I had learned that I found myself coming up against the same self-destructive state of mind that masquerades as democracy and individual freedom. Twice I was able to anticipate a terrorist strike and to warn the authorities, but intention is not a crime, I was told, and both the culprits were quietly escorted to the border and turned free to prepare themselves almost openly for the next outrage. The world must wait and cringe for the next stroke, prohibited from making any pre-emptive strike to prevent it, and when it comes they are hampered by confused national responsibilities and by the complicated concept of minimum force –' The Baroness broke off. 'But you know all this! You have written in depth of the same subject.'

'It's interesting to hear it repeated.'

'I will come soon enough to the interesting part – but we are almost back at the house.'

'Come,' Peter told her, and led her past the stables to the swimming pool pavilion. The surface of the heated pool steamed softly, and lush tropical plants were in odd contrast to the wintry scene beyond the glass walls.

They sat side by side on a swing seat, close enough to be able to talk in subdued tones, but the intense mood was broken for the moment. She took off her hat, scarf and jacket, and tossed them on to the cane chair opposite, and she sighed as she settled back against the cushions.

'I understand from Sir Steven that he wants you to go into the bank.' She slanted her eyes at him. 'It must be difficult to be so sought after.'

'I don't think I have Steven's reverence for money.'

'It's a readily acquired taste, General Stride,' she assured him.' One that can become an addiction.'

At that moment the children of both Stride brothers arrived in a storm of shouted repartee and laughter, which moderated only marginally when they realized that Peter and the Baroness were in the swing seat.

Steven's youngest son, bulging over the top of his costume with puppy-fat and with silver braces on his front teeth, rolled his eyes in their direction and in a stage whisper told Melissa-Jane,

'Je t'aime, ma chérie. Swoon! Swoon!' His accent was frighteningly bad and he received a hissed rebuke and a shove in the small of the back that hurled him into the deep end of the pool.

The Baroness smiled. 'Your daughter is very protective –' she turned slightly to examine Peter's face again '– or is it merely jealousy?' Without waiting for an answer she went straight on to ask another question. Against the background of shouts and splashes, Peter thought he had misheard.

'What did you say?' he asked carefully, certain that his expression had revealed nothing, and she repeated.

'Does the name Caliph mean anything to you?'

He frowned slightly, pretending to consider, while his memory darted back to the terrible micro-seconds of mortal combat, of smoke and flame and gunfire and a dark-haired girl in a scarlet shirt screaming:

'Don't kill us! Caliph said we would not die. Caliph –' And his own bullets stopping the rest of it, smashing into the open mouth. The word had haunted him since then, and he had tried a thousand variations, looking for sense and meaning, considering the possibility that he had misheard. Now he knew he had not.

'Caliph?' he asked, not knowing why he was going to deny it, merely because it seemed vital that he keep something in reserve, that he were not carried headlong on the torrent of this woman's presence and personality. 'It's a Mohammedan title – I think it literally means the heir of Mohammed, the successor to the prophet.'

'Yes.' She nodded impatiently. 'It's the title of a civil and religious leader – but have you heard it used as a code name?'

'No. I am sorry, I have not. What is the significance?'

'I am not sure, even my own sources are obscure and confused.' She sighed, and they watched Melissa-Jane in silence. The child had been waiting for Peter's attention, and when she had it she ran lightly out along the springboard and launched herself, light as a swallow in flight, into a clean one-and-a-half somersault, entering the water with hardly a ripple and surfacing immediately with fine pale hair slick down across her face, immediately looking again for Peter's approval.

'She's a lovely child,' said the Baroness. 'I have no children. Aaron wanted a son – but there was not one.' And there was real sorrow in the green eyes that she masked quickly. Across the pool Melissa-Jane climbed from the pool and quickly draped a towel around her shoulders, covering her bosom which was not large enough and yet so novel as to provide her with a constant source of embarrassment and shy pride.

'Caliph,' Peter reminded the Baroness quietly, and she turned back to him.

'I first heard the name two years ago, in circumstances I shall never forget –' She hesitated. 'May I take it that you are fully aware of the circumstances surrounding my husband's kidnapping and murder? I do not wish to repeat the whole harrowing story – unless it is necessary.'

'I know it,' Peter assured her.

'You know that I delivered the ransom, personally.'

'Yes.'

'The rendezvous was a deserted airfield near the East German border. They were waiting with a light twin-engined aircraft, a Russian-built reconnaissance machine with its markings sprayed over –' Peter remembered the meticulous planning and the special equipment used in the hijacking of 070. It all tallied. '– There were four men, masked. They spoke Russian, or rather two of them spoke Russian. The other two never spoke at all. It was bad Russian –' Peter remembered now that the Baroness spoke Russian and five other languages. She had a Middle European background, Peter wished he had studied her intelligence file more thoroughly. Her father had escaped with her from her native Poland when she was a small child. '– Almost certainly, the aircraft and the Russian were intended to cover their real identity,' she mused. 'I was with them for some little time. I had forty-five million Swiss francs to deliver and even in notes of large denomination it was a bulky and heavy cargo to load aboard the aircraft. After the first few minutes, when they realized that I had no police escort, they relaxed and joked amongst themselves as they worked at loading the money. The word "Caliph" was used in the English version, in a Russian exchange that roughly translates as "He was right again" and the reply "Caliph is always right". Perhaps the use of the English word made me remember it so clearly –' She stopped again, grief naked and bleak in the green eyes.

'You told the police?' Peter asked gently, and she shook her head.

'No. I don't know why not. They had been so ineffectual up to that time. I was very angry and sad and confused. Perhaps even then I had already decided that I would hunt them myself – and this was all I had.'

'That was the only time you heard the name?' he asked, and she did not reply immediately. They watched the children at play – and it seemed fantasy to be discussing the source of evil in such surroundings, against a background of laughter and innocent high spirits.

When the Baroness answered, she seemed to have changed direction completely.

'There had been that hiatus in international terrorism. The Americans seemed to have beaten the hijacking problem with their Cuban agreement and the rigorous airport searches. Your own successful campaign against the Provisional wing of the IRA in this country, the Entebbe raid and the German action at Mogadishu were all hailed as breakthrough victories. Everybody was beginning to congratulate themselves that it was beaten. The Arabs were too busy with the war in the Lebanon and with inter-group rivalries. It had been a passing thing.' She shook her head again. 'But terrorism is a growth industry – the risks are less than those of financing a major movie. There is a proven sixty-seven per cent chance of success, the capital outlay is minimal, with outrageous profits in cash and publicity, with instant results – and potential power not even calculable. Even in the event of total failure, there is still a better than fifty per cent survival rate for the participants.' She smiled again, but now there was no joy and no warmth in it. 'Any businessman will tell you it's better than the commodity markets.'

'The only thing against it is that the business is run by amateurs,' Peter said, 'or by professionals blinded by hatred or crippled by parochial interests and limited goals.'

And now she turned to him, wriggling around in the canvas swing seat, curling those long legs up under her in that double-jointed woman's manner, impossible for a man.

'You are ahead of me, Peter.' She caught herself. 'I am sorry, but General Stride is much to say, and I have the feeling I have known you so long.' The smile now was fleeting but warm. 'My name is Magda,' she went on simply. 'Will you use it?'

'Thank you, Magda.'

'Yes.' She picked up the thread of conversation again. 'The business is in the hands of amateurs – but it is too good to stay that way.'

'Enter Caliph,' Peter guessed.

'That is the whisper that I have heard; usually there is no name. Just that there was a meeting in Athens, or Amsterdam or East Berlin or Aden – only once have I heard the name Caliph again. But if he exists already he must be one of the richest men in the world, and soon he will be the most powerful.'

'One man?' Peter asked.

'I do not know. Perhaps a group of men – perhaps even a government. Russia, Cuba, an Arab country? Who knows yet?'

'And the goals?'

'Money, firstly. Wealth to tackle the political objectives – and finally power, raw power.' Magda Altmann stopped herself, and made a self-deprecating gesture. 'This is guesswork again, my own guessing – based only on past performance. They have the wealth now, provided by OPEC and – myself amongst others. Now he or they have started on the political objectives, a soft target first. An African racist minority government unprotected by powerful allies. It should have succeeded. They should have won an entire nation – a mineral-rich nation – for the price of a dozen lives. Even had they failed to gain the main prize, the consolation prize was forty tons of pure gold. That's good business, Peter. It should have succeeded. It *had* succeeded. The Western nations actually put pressure on the victims, and forced them to accede to the demands – it was a trial run, and it worked perfectly, except for one man.'

'I am afraid,' said Peter softly, 'as afraid as I have ever been in my life.'

'Yes. I am also, Peter. I have been afraid ever since that terrible phone call on the night they took Aaron, and the more I learn the more afraid I become.'

'What happens next?'

'I do not know – but the name he has chosen has the hint of megalomania, perhaps a man with visions of godlike domination –' She spread her fine narrow hands and the diamond flashed white fire. '– We cannot hope to fathom the mind of a man who could embark on such a course. Probably he believes that what he is doing is for the eventual good of mankind. Perhaps he wants to attack the rich by amassing vast wealth, to destroy the tyrant with universal tyranny, to free mankind by making it a slave to terror. Perhaps he seeks to right the wrongs of the world with evil and injustice.'

She touched his arm again, and this time the strength of those long fingers startled Peter. 'You have to help me find him, Peter. I am going to put everything into the hunt, there will be no reservations, all the wealth and influence that I control will be at your disposal.'

'You choose me because you believe that I murdered a wounded prisoner?' Peter asked. 'Are those my credentials?' And she recoiled from him slightly, and stared at him with the slightly Mongolian slant of eyes, then her shoulders slumped slightly.

'All right, that is part of it, but only a small part of it. You know I have read what you have written, you must know that I have studied you very carefully. You are the best man available to me, and finally you have proved that your involvement is complete. I know that you have the strength and skill and ruthlessness to find Caliph and destroy him – before he destroys us and the world we know.'

Peter was looking inwards. He had believed that the beast had a thousand heads, and for each that was struck off a thousand more would grow – but now for the first time he imagined the full shape of the beast, it was still in ambush, not clear yet, but there was only a single head. Perhaps, after all, it was mortal.

'Will you help me, Peter?' she asked.

'You know I will,' he answered quietly. 'I do not have any choice.'

She flew in the brilliance of high sunlight reflected from snowfields of blazing white, jetting through her turns with flowing elegance, carving each turn with a crisp rush of flying snow, swaying across the fall line of the mountain in an intricate ballet of interlinked movement.

She wore a slim-fitting skin suit of pearly grey, trimmed in black at the shoulders and cuffs, she was shod with gleaming black Heierling snowbirds, and her skis were long, narrow, black Rossignol professionals.

Peter followed her, pressing hard not to lose too much ground, but his turns were solid Christies without the stylish fallback unweighting of the jet turn which gave her each time a fractional gain.

The dun he ran like a stag of ten
But the mare like a new roused fawn.

Kipling might have been describing them, and she was a hundred yards ahead of him as they entered the forest.

The pathway was barred with the shadows of the pines, and sugary ice roared under his skis as he pushed the narrow corners dangerously fast. Always she was farther ahead, flickering like a silver-grey wraith on those long lean legs, her tight round buttocks balancing the narrow waist and swinging rhythmically into the turns, marvellous controlled broadsides where the icy roadway denied purchase, coming out fast and straight, leaning into the rush of the wind, and her faint sweet laughter came back to Peter as he chased. There is an expertise that must be learned in childhood, and he remembered then that she was Polish, would probably have skied before she was weaned, and suppressed the flare of resentment he always felt at being outclassed by another human being, particularly by the woman who was fast becoming his driving obsession.

He came round another steeply banked turn, with the sheer snow wall rising fifteen feet on his right hand and on his left the tops of the nearest pines at his own level, so steep the mountain fell away into the valley.

The ice warning signs flashed past, and there was a wooden bridge, its boards waxen, opalescent with greenish ice. He felt control go as he hit the polished iron-hard surface. The bridge crossed a deep sombre gorge, with a frozen waterfall skewered to the black mountain rock by its own cruel icicles, like crucifixion nails.

To attempt to edge in, or to stem the thundering rush across the treacherous going, would have invited disaster, to lean back defensively would have brought him down instantly and piled him into the sturdy wooden guide rails. At the moment he was lined up for the narrow bridge Peter flung himself forward so that his shins socked into the pads of his boots, and in a swoop of terror and exhilaration he went through, and found that he was laughing aloud though his heart leaped against his ribs and his breathing matched the sound of the wind in his own ears.

She was waiting for him where the path debouched on to the lower slopes. She had pushed her goggles to the top of her head, and stripped off her gloves, both sticks planted in the snow beside her.

'You'll never know how much I needed that.' She had flown into Zurich that morning in her personal Lear jet. Peter had come in on the Swissair flight from Brussels, and they had motored up together. 'You know what I wish, Peter?'

'Tell me,' he invited.

'I wish that I could take a whole month, thirty glorious days, to do what I wish. To be ordinary, to be like other people and not feel a moment's guilt.'

He had seen her on only three occasions in the six weeks since their first meetings at Abbots Yew. Three too brief and, for Peter, unsatisfying meetings.

Once in his new office suite at the Narmco headquarters in Brussels, again at La Pierre Bénite, her country home outside Paris, but then there had been twenty other guests for dinner. The third time had been in the panelled and tastefully decorated cabin of her Lear jet on a flight between Brussels and London.

Though they had made little progress as yet in the hunt for Caliph, Peter was still exploring the avenues that had occurred to him and had cast a dozen lines, baited and hooked.

During their third meeting Peter had discussed with her the need to restructure her personal safety arrangements. He had changed her former bodyguards, replacing them with operatives from a discreet agency in Switzerland which trained its own men. The Director of the agency was an old and trusted friend.

They had come to this meeting now so that Peter might report back on his progress to Magda. But for a few hours the snow had seduced them both.

'There is still another two hours before the light goes.' Peter glanced across the valley at the village church. The gold hands of the clock showed a little after two o'clock. 'Do you want to run the Rheinhorn?'

She hesitated only a moment. 'The world will keep turning, I'm sure.' Her teeth were very white, but one of them was slightly crooked, a blemish that was oddly appealing as she smiled up at him. 'Certainly it will wait two hours.'

He had learned that she kept unbelievable hours, beginning her day's work when the rest of the world still slept, and still hard at it when the offices of Altmann Industries in Boulevard Capucine were deserted, except her own office suite on the top floor. Even during the drive up from Zurich she had gone through correspondence and dictated quietly to one of her secretaries.

He knew that the chalet across the valley her two secretaries would be waiting already, while a pile of telex flimsies for her consideration and the line held open for her replies.

'There are better ways to die than working yourself to death.' He was suddenly out of patience with her single-mindedness, and she laughed easily with high colour in her cheeks and the sparkle of the last run in the green eyes.

'Yes, you are right, Peter. I should have you near to keep reminding me of that.'

'That's the first bit of sense I've had from you in six weeks.' He was referring to her opposition to his plans for her security. He had tried to persuade her to change established behaviour-patterns, and though the smile was still on her lips, her eyes were deadly serious as she studied his face.

'My husband left me a trust –' she seemed suddenly sad beneath the laughter '– a duty that I must fulfil. One day I should like to explain that to you – but now we only have two hours.'

It was snowing lightly, and the sun had disappeared behind the mountains of rock and snow and cloud as they walked back through the village. The lights were burning in the richly laden shop windows and they were part of the gaily clad stream returning from the slopes, clumping along the frozen sidewalks in their clumsy ski boots, carrying skis and sticks over one shoulder and chattering with the lingering thrill of the high piste that even the lowering snow-filled dusk could not suppress.

'It feels good to be free of my wolves for a while.' Magda caught his arm as her snowbirds skidden on dirty ridged ice, and after she had regained her balance she left her gloved hand there.

Her wolves were the bodyguards that Peter had provided, the silent vigilant men who followed her either on foot or in a second car. They waited outside her offices while she worked, and others guarded the house while she slept.

That morning, however, she had told Peter, 'Today I have as a companion a gold medal Olympic pistol champion, I don't need my wolves.'

Narmco marketed its own version of the 9-mm parabellum pistol. It was called 'Cobra', and after a single morning in the underground range Peter had taken a liking to the weapon. It was lighter and flatter than the Walther he was accustomed to, easier to carry and conceal, and the single action mechanism saved a flicker of time with the first shot, for there was no need to cock the action. He had had no trouble obtaining a permit to carry one as a trade sample, although it was necessary to check it before every commercial flight, but it carried neatly in a rigid moulded Allessi quick-release holster.

He had felt theatrical and melodramatic at first, but with a little sober thought had convinced himself that to follow on Caliph's tracks unarmed was shortening the odds against himself.

Now it was becoming a habit, and he was barely aware of the comforting shape and weight in his armpit, until Magda spoke.

'I am close to dying from thirst,' she went on, and they racked their skis and went into the jovial warmth and clouds of steam that billowed from one of the coffee shops that lined the main street.

They found a seat at a table already crowded with young people, and they ordered glasses of steaming hot *Glühwein.*

Then the four-piece band thumped out a popular dance tune and their table companions swarmed on to the tiny dance floor.

Peter raised a challenging eyebrow at her and she asked with amusement, 'Have you ever danced in ski boots?'

'There has to be a first time for everything.'

She danced like she did everything else, with complete absorption, and her body was strong and hard and slim against his.

It was completely dark as they climbed the narrow track above the village and went in through the electronically controlled gate in the protective wall around the chalet.

It was somehow typical of her that she had avoided the fashionable resorts, and that externally the chalet seemed not much different from fifty others that huddled in the edge of the pine forest.

There was patent relief amongst her entourage at her return, and she seemed almost defiant at their concern as though she had just proved something to herself – but still she did not change from her sports clothes before disappearing into the office suite on the first floor with her two male secretaries. 'I work better with men,' she had explained to Peter once. As Peter dressed in slacks, blazer and silk rollneck after a scalding shower, he could still hear the clatter of the telex machine from the floor below, and it was an hour later when she called him on the house telephone.

The entire top floor was her private domain and she was standing at the windows looking out over the snow-fuzzed lights of the valley as he entered.

She wore green slacks tucked in après-ski boots, and a blouse of the same colour, a perfect match for her eyes. The moment Peter entered, she pressed a concealed switch and the curtains slid silently closed, then she turned to him.

'A drink, Peter?' she asked.

'Not if we are going to talk.'

'We are going to talk,' she said positively, and indicated the soft squashy leather armchair across from the fireplace. She had resisted the traditional Swiss cuckoo-clock and knotty pine décor, and the carpeting was thick Wilton to match the curtains, the furniture low and comfortable but modern, sporty and good fun, the very best made to appear natural and unaffected, blending easily with the modern art on the walls and abstract sculpture in marble and grained wood.

She smiled suddenly at him. 'I had no idea that I had found myself a gifted Sales Director for Narmco – I really am impressed with what you have done in so short a time.'

'I had to establish a plausible cover –' Peter deprecated the compliment. 'And I used to be a soldier – the job interests me.'

'You English!' she told him with mock exasperation. 'Always so modest.'

She did not seat herself but moved about the room; although never at rest, neither did she give the feeling of restlessness. 'I am informed that there is to be a definite NATO testing of Kestrel – after almost two years of procrastination.'

Kestrel was Narmco's medium-range ground-to-ground infantry portable missile.

'I am further informed that the decision was made to test after you had met with some of your former colleagues.'

'The whole world runs on the old boy system –' Peter chuckled, '– you should know that.'

'And you are on old boy terms with the Iranians?' She cocked her head at him.

'That was a small stroke of luck. Five years ago I was on a staff college course with their new military adviser.'

'Luck again.' She smiled. 'Isn't it strange that luck so often favours those who are clever and dedicated and who move faster than the pack?'

'I have had less luck in other directions,' Peter pointed out, and immediately there was no trace of laughter left upon her lips nor in the emerald eyes, but Peter went on. 'So far I have been unsuccessful with the contact we spoke about on our last meeting –'

They had discussed the possibility of access to the Atlas computer link, of requisitioning a print-out on 'Caliph' from the central intelligence bank, if there was one programmed.

'As I explained, there was the one remote possibility of access, somebody who owed me a favour. He was of no help. He believes that if there is a "Caliph" listing, it's blocked and buzzed.' Which meant that any unauthorized requisition would sound an alarm in intelligence control. 'We'd trigger a Delta condition in Atlas if we put in a print-out requisition.'

'You did not give him the name?' Magda asked sharply.

'No. No names, just a general discussion over dinner at Brooks's – but all the implications were there.'

'Do you have any further avenues –?'

'I think so. One more, but it's a last resort,' Peter said. 'Before we come to that, though, perhaps you can tell me if you have anything further from your sources.'

'My sources –' Magda had never made more explicit descriptions, and Peter had instinctively known not to pry. There was a certain finality to the way she said it. 'My sources have been mostly negative. The seizure of the Netherlands Embassy in Bonn was unconnected with Caliph. It was exactly what it purported to be – South Moluccan extremists. The hijackers of Cathay Airlines and Transit Airlines were both enthusiastic amateurs, as evidence the methods and the outcome –' She smiled drily and drifted back across the room to touch the Hundedwasser collage that hung on the side wall, rearranging the hang of the frame in an essentially feminine gesture. '– There is only one recent act that has the style of Caliph.'

'Prince Hassied Abdel Hayek?' Peter asked, and she turned to face him, thrusting out one hip with her hand upon it, the nails very red against the light-green cloth and the marquise cut diamond sparkling.

'What did you make of it?' she asked. The Prince had been shot dead, three bullets of .22 calibre in the back of the head while asleep in his rooms on the Cambridge campus. A nineteen-year-old grandson of King Khalid of Saudi Arabia, not one of the particular favourites of the king, a bespectacled scholarly youth who seemed content to remain outside the mainstream of palace power and politics. There had been no attempt at abduction, no sign of a struggle, no evidence of robbery – the young Prince had no close friends nor apparent enemies.

'It does not seem to have reason or motive,' Peter admitted. 'That's why I thought of Caliph.'

'The deviousness of Caliph –' Magda turned away and her haunches rippled under the elastic of her green slacks. There was no ruck line of panties, and her buttocks were perfect spheres, with the shadow of the deep cleft between them showing through the thin material. Peter watched her legs as she paced, realizing for the first time that her feet were long and narrow as her hands, fine and graceful bones in perfect proportion.

'If I told you that Saudi Arabia last week made clear to the other members of OPEC that, far from supporting a rise in the price of crude, she will press for a *five per cent* reduction in the world price at the organization's next meeting –'

Peter straightened up in his chair slowly and Magda went on softly – 'if I told you that, what would you think?'

'The King has other, more favoured grandchildren – grandsons and sons as well, brothers, nephews –'

'Seven hundred of them,' Magda agreed, and then went on musing. 'And the King of Saudi Arabia is an Arab. You know how Mohammedans are about sons and grandsons.' Magda came to stand so close to him that he could feel the warmth of her flesh through the narrow space between them, and her perfume subtly underlined the ripe sweet woman's smell of her body, disturbing him, but strangely heightening his awareness. 'Perhaps King Khalid has also been reminded of his own mortality.'

'All right.' Peter hunched his shoulders and frowned in concentration. 'What are we suggesting? That Caliph has struck another easy formula? A man who controls the economic destiny of the Western world? A man who makes decisions at the personal level, who is not answerable to cabinets or causes or governments?'

'A man who is therefore vulnerable to personal terrorism, who has a record of appeasement to terrorist pressure.' Magda paused. 'The old truths are still good. "Uneasy lies the head that wears a crown." The King will be no stranger to the fear of the assassin's blade. He will understand the law of the knife, because he has always lived by it.'

'Hell, you have to admire it.' Peter shook his head. 'There is no need to take and hold hostages. No need for exposure. You kill one obscure member of a large royal family, and you promise that there will be others, each one more important, closer to the head.'

'The King's family has a high profile – any time you want to drop into the Dorchester you'll find one of his sons or grandsons sipping coffee in the public lounge. They are soft targets, and there are plenty of them. You might even have to kill two princelings or three – but secretly the world will feel that they had it coming to them anyway. There will not be oceans wept for men who have themselves held the world to ransom.'

Peter's frown smoothed away, and he grinned wryly. 'Not only do you have to admire it – you've got to have a sneaking sympathy for the object. A dead brake to the crippling inflation of the world, a slowing of disruptive imbalance in trade.'

And Magda's expression was fierce as he had never seen it before. 'That is the trap, Peter. To see the end only, and to harden yourself to the means. That was the trap that Caliph set with the taking of 070. His demands coincided with those of the Western powers, and they placed additional pressure on the victim. Now, if we are correct and Caliph is pressuring the oil dictators for a moderation of their demands, how much more support can he expect from the Western capitalist powers?'

'You are a capitalist,' Peter pointed out. 'If Caliph succeeds you will be one of the first to benefit.'

'I'm a capitalist, yes. But before that I am a human being, and a thinking human being. Do you really believe that if Caliph succeeds now that this will be the last we hear of him?'

'Of course not.' Peter spread his hands in resignation. 'Always his demands will be harsher – with each success he must become bolder.'

'I think we can have that drink now,' Magda said softly, and turned away from him. The black onyx top of the coffee table slid aside at her touch to reveal the array of bottles and glasses beneath.

'Whisky, isn't it?' she asked, and poured a single malt Glenlivet into one of the cutglass tumblers. As she handed it to him their fingers touched and he was surprised at how cool and dry her skin felt.

She poured half a flute glass of white wine and filled it with Perrier water. As she replaced the wine bottle in the ice bucket, Peter saw the label. It was le Montrachet 1969. Probably the greatest white wine in the world, and Peter had to protest at the way in which she had desecrated it.

'Alexandre Dumas said it should be drunk only on bended knee and with head reverently bared –'

'– He forgot the mineral water,' Magda purred with throaty laughter. 'Anyway you can't trust a man who employed other people to write his books for him.' She lifted the adulterated wine to him. 'Long ago I decided to live my life on my own terms. To hell with Messrs Dumas and Caliph.'

'Shall we drink to that?' Peter asked, and they watched each other over the rims. The level of Magda's glass had not lowered and she set the glass aside, moving across to adjust the bowl of hot-house tulips in the chunky free form crystal bowl.

'If we are right. If this is Caliph at work – then it disturbs the instinctive picture I had formed of him.' Peter broke the silence.

'How?' she asked without looking up from the flowers.

'Caliph – it's an Arabic name. He is attacking the leader of the Arab world.'

'The deviousness of Caliph. Was the name deliberately chosen to confuse the hunters – or perhaps there are other demands apart from the oil price – perhaps pressure is also being put on Khalid for closer support of the Palestinians, or one of the other extremist Arab movements. We do not know what else Caliph wants from Saudi Arabia.'

'But then, the oil price. It is Western orientated. Somehow it has always been accepted that terrorism is a tool of the far left,' Peter pointed out, shaking his head. 'The hijacking of 070 – even the kidnapping of your husband – were both aimed against the capitalist society.'

'He kidnapped Aaron for the money, and killed him to protect his identity. The attack on the South African Government, the attack on the oil cartel, the choice of name, all point to a person with godlike pretensions.' Magda broke the head off one of the tulips with an abrupt, angry gesture, and crushed it in her fist. She let the petals fall into the deep onyx ashtray. 'I feel so helpless, Peter. We seem to be going round in futile circles.' She came back to him as he stood by the curtained windows. 'You said earlier that there was one sure way to flush out Caliph?'

'Yes,' Peter nodded.

'Can you tell me?'

'There was an old trick of the Indian shikari. When he got tired of following the tiger in thick jungle without a sight of the beast, he used to stake out a goat and wait for the tiger to come to it.'

'A goat?'

'My Zodiacal sign is Capricorn – the goat.' Peter smiled slightly.

'I don't understand.'

'If I were to put the word out that I was hunting Caliph –' He smiled again. 'Caliph knows me. The hijacker spoke my name clearly, unmistakably. She had been warned. So I believe that Caliph would take me seriously enough to consider it necessary to come after me.'

He saw the lingering colour drain dramatically from her high cheeks, and the sudden shadow in the depths of her eyes.

'Peter –'

'That's the only way I'm going to get close to him.'

'Peter –' She placed her hand on his forearm, but then she could not go on. Instead she stared at him silently and her eyes were green and dark and unfathomable. He saw there was a pulse that throbbed softly in her long graceful neck, just below the ear. Her lips parted, as though she were about to speak. They were delicately sculptured lips, and she touched them with the pink tip of her tongue, leaving them moist and soft and somehow defenceless. She closed them, without speaking, but the pressure of her fingers on his arm increased, and the carriage of her whole body altered. Her back arched slightly so her lower body swayed towards him and her chin lifted slightly

'I have been so lonely,' she whispered. 'So lonely, for so very long. I only realized how lonely today – while I was with you.'

Peter felt a choking sensation in his throat, and the prickle of blood behind his eyes.

'I don't want to be lonely again, ever.'

She had let her hair come down. It was very thick and long. It fell in a straight rippling curtain shot through with glowing lights, to her waist.

She had parted it in the centre; a thin straight line of white scalp divided the great black wings and they framed her face, making it appear pale and childlike with eyes too large and vulnerable, and as she came towards where Peter lay the glossy sheets of hair slid silently across the brocade of her gown.

The hem of the gown swept the carpet, and her bare toes peeped out from under it with each step. Narrow finely boned feet, and the nails were trimmed and painted with a colourless lacquer. The sleeves of the gown were wide as batwings and lined internally with satin, the collar buttoned up in a high Chinese style.

Beside the bed she stopped and her courage and poise seemed to desert her, her shoulders slumped a little and she clasped the long narrow fingers before her in a defensive gesture.

'Peter, I don't think I am going to be very good at this.' The throaty whisper was barely audible, and her lips trembled with the strength of her appeal. 'And I want so badly to be good.'

Silently he reached out one hand towards her, palm upwards. The bedclothes covered him to the waist, but his chest and arms were bare. Lightly tanned and patterned with dark wiry body hair. As he reached for her the muscle bunched and expanded beneath the skin, and she saw that there was no surplus flesh on his waist, nor on his shoulders and upper arms. He looked lean and hard and tempered, yet supple as the lash of a bullwhip, and she did not respond immediately to the invitation, for his masculinity was overpowering.

He folded back the thick down-filled duvet between them, and the sheet was crisp and smoothly ironed in the low rosy light.

'Come,' he ordered gently, but she turned away and with her back to him she undid the buttons of the embroidered gown, beginning at the throat and working downwards.

She slipped the gown from her shoulders, and held it for a moment in the crook of her elbows. The smooth pale flesh gleamed through the fall of dark hair, and she seemed to steel herself like a diver bracing for the plunge into unknown depths.

She let the gown drop with a rustling slide down the full length of her body, and it lay around her ankles in a shallow puddle of peacock colours.

She heard him gasp aloud, and she threw the hair back from her shoulders with a toss of the long, swan-like neck. The hair hung impenetrably to the small of her back; just above the deep cleft of her lower body it ended in a clean line and her buttocks were round and neat and without blemish, but even as he stared the marble smoothness puckered into a fine rash of gooseflesh as though his eyes had physically caressed her, and she had responded with an appealingly natural awareness that proved how her every sense must be aroused and tingling. At the knowledge Peter felt his heart squeezed. He wanted to rush to her and sweep her into his arms, but instinct warned him that she must close the last gap herself, and he lay quietly propped on one elbow, feeling the deep ache of wanting spread through his entire body.

She stooped to pick up the gown, and for a moment the long legs were at an awkward coltish angle to each other and the spheres of her buttocks altered shape. No longer perfectly symmetrical, but parted slightly, and in the creamy niche they formed with her thighs there was an instant's heart-stopping glimpse of a single dense tight curl of hair and the light from beyond tipped the curl with glowing reddish highlights, then she had straightened again, once more lithe and tall, and she dropped the robe across the low couch and in the same movement turned back to face Peter.

He gasped again and his sense of continuity began to break up into a mosaic of distinct, seemingly unconnected images and sensations.

Her breasts were tiny as those of a pubescent child, but the nipples were startlingly prominent, the colour and texture of ripening young berries, dark red wine, already fully erect and hard as pebbles.

The pale plain of her belly, with the deep pit of the navel at its centre, that ended at last on the plump darkly furred mound pressed into the deep wedge between her thighs, like a small frightened living creature crouching from the stoop of the falcon.

The feel of her face pressed to his chest, and the tickle of her quick breath stirring his body hair, the almost painful grip of slim powerful arms locked with desperate strength around his waist.

The taste of her mouth as her lips parted slowly, softly, to his and the uncertain flutter of her tongue becoming bolder, velvety on top and slick and slippery on the underside.

The sound of her breathing changing to a deep sonorous pulse in his ears, seeming to keep perfect time with his own.

The smell of her breath, heavy with the aromatic musk of her arousal, and blending with the orangy fragrance of her perfume and the ripe woman smell of her body.

And always the feel of her – the warmth and the softness, the hardness of toned muscle and the running ripple of long dark hair about his face and down his body, the crisp electric rasp of tight, dense curls parting to unbearable heat and going on for ever to depths that seemed to reach beyond the frontier of reality and reason.

And then later the stillness of complete peace that reached out from the centre where she lay against his heart and seemed to spread to the farthest corners of his soul.

'I knew that I was lonely,' she whispered. 'But I did not realize just how terribly deeply.' And she held him as though she would never relinquish her grip.

Magda woke him in the cold utter darkness three hours before dawn, and it was still dark when they left the chalet. The headlights of the following Mercedes that carried her wolves swept the interior of their saloon through each bend in the steep twisting road down from the mountains.

On take off from Zurich Magda was in the Lear jet's left-hand seat, flying as pilot-in-command, and she handled the powerful machine with the sedate lack of ostentation which marks the truly competent aviator. Her personal pilot, a grizzled and taciturn Frenchman, who was flying now as her co-pilot, evidently held her skill in high regard and watched over her with an almost fatherly pride and approval as she cleared Zurich controlled air space and levelled out at cruise altitude for Paris Orly before she left him to monitor the autopilot and came back to the main cabin. Though she sat beside Peter in the black calfskin armchairs, her manner was unchanged from the way it had been during their last flight together in this machine – reserved and polite – so that he found it difficult to believe the wonders they had explored together the previous night.

She worked with the two dark-suited secretaries opposite her, speaking her fluent rippling French with the same enchanting trace of accent that marked her English. In the short time since he had joined Narmco, Peter had been forced to make a crash revision of his own French. Now once again he could manage, if not with éclat, at least with competence, in technical and financial discussion. Once or twice Magda turned to him for comment or opinion, and her gaze was serious and remote, seeming as impersonal and efficient as an electronic computer – and Peter understood that they were to make no show of their new relationship before employees.

Immediately she proved him wrong, for her co-pilot called her over the cabin speaker.

'We will join the Orly circuit in four minutes, Baroness.'

And she turned easily and naturally and kissed Peter's cheek, still speaking French.

'Pardon me, chéri. I will make the landing. I need the flying time in my logbook.'

She greased the sleek swift aircraft on to the runway as though she was spreading butter on hot toast. The co-pilot had radioed ahead so that when she parked in the private hangar there were a uniformed immigration *policier* and a *douanier* already waiting.

As they came aboard, they saluted her respectfully and then barely glanced at her red diplomatic passport. They took a little longer with Peter's blue and gold British passport, and Magda murmured to Peter with a trace of a smile.

'I must get you a little red book. It's so much easier.' Then to the officials: 'It is a cold morning, gentlemen, I hope you will take a glass.' And her white-jacketed steward was hovering already. They left the two Frenchmen removing their kepis and pistol belts, settling down comfortably in the leather armchairs to make a leisurely selection of the cigars and cognac that the steward had produced for their approval.

There were three cars waiting for them, parked in the back of the hangar with drivers and guards. Peter's lip curled as he saw the Maserati.

'I told you not to drive that thing,' he said gruffly. 'It's like having your name in neon lights.'

They had argued about this vehicle while Peter was reorganizing her personal security, for the Maserati was an electric silver-grey, one of her favourite colours, a shimmering dart of metal. She swayed against him with that husky little chuckle of hers.

'Oh, that is so very nice to have a man being masterful again. It makes me feel like a woman.'

'I have other ways of making you feel like that.'

'I know,' she agreed, with a wicked flash of green eyes. 'And I like those even better, but not now – please! What in the world would my staff think!' Then seriously, 'You take the Maserati, I ordered it for you, anyway. Somebody may as well enjoy it. And please do not be late this evening. I have especially made it free for us. Try and be at La Pierre Bénite by eight o'clock – will you please.'

By the time Peter had to slow for the traffic along the Pont Neuilly entrance to Paris, he had accustomed himself to the surging power and acceleration of the Maserati, and, as she had suggested, he was enjoying himself. Even in the mad Parisian traffic he used the slick gear box to knife through the merest suspicion of an opening, bulling out of trouble or overtaking with the omnipotent sense of power that control of the magnificent machine bestowed upon its driver.

He knew then why Magda loved it so dearly, and when he parked it at last in the underground garage on the Champs Elysées side of Concorde he grinned at himself in the mirror.

'Bloody cowboy!' he said, and glanced at his Rolex. He had an hour before his first appointment, and at a sudden thought unclipped the holster of the Cobra and, with the pistol still in it, locked it in the glove compartment of the Maserati. He grinned again as he pondered the inadvisability of marching into French Naval Headquarters armed to the teeth.

The drizzle had cleared, and the chestnut trees in the Elysée gardens were popping their first green buds as he came out into Concorde. He used one of the call boxes in the Concorde Metro station to make a call to the British Embassy. He spoke to the Military Attaché for two minutes, and when he hung up he knew the ball was probably already in play. If Caliph had penetrated the Atlas Command deeply enough to know him personally as the commander of Thor – then it would not be too long before he knew that the former commander had picked up the spoor. The Military Attaché at the Paris Embassy had other more clandestine duties than kissing the ladies' hands at diplomatic cocktail parties.

Peter reached the main gates of the Marine Headquarters on the corner of the rue Royale with a few minutes to spare, but already there was a secretary waiting for him below the billowing Tricolour. He smoothed Peter's way past the sentries, and led him to the armaments committee room on the third floor overlooking a misty grey view of the Seine and the gilded arches of the Pont Neuf. Two of Peter's assistants from Narmco were there ahead of him with their briefcases unpacked and the contents spread upon the polished walnut table.

The French Flag Captain had been in Brussels, and on one unforgettable evening he had conducted Peter on a magic carpet tour of the brothels of that city. He greeted him now with cries of Gallic pleasure and addressed him as 'tu' and 'toi' – which all boded very well for the meeting ahead.

At noon precisely, the French Captain moved that the meeting adjourn across the street to a private room on the first floor of Maxim's, blissful in the certainty that Narmco would pick up the tab, if they were really serious about selling the Kestrel rocket motors to the French Navy.

It required all Peter's tact not to make it obvious that he was taking less than his share of the Clos de Vougeot or of the Rémy Martin, and more than once he found that he had missed part of the discussion which was being conducted at a steadily increasing volume. He found that he was thinking of emerald eyes and small pert bosoms.

From Maxim's back to the Ministry of Marine, and later it required another major act of diplomacy on Peter's part when the Captain smoothed his moustache and cocked a knowing eye at Peter. 'There is a charming little club, very close and wonderfully friendly –'

By six o'clock Peter had disentangled himself from the Frenchman's company, with protestations of friendship and promises to meet again in ten days' time. An hour later Peter left his two sales assistants at the Hôtel Meurice after a quick but thorough summation of the day's achievements. They were, all three, agreed that it was a beginning but a long, long road lay ahead to the ending.

He walked back along Rivoli; despite the frowsiness of a long day of endless talk and the necessity for quick thinking in a language which was still strange on the tongue, despite a slight ache behind the eyes from the wine and cognac and despite the taste of cigar and cigarette smoke he had breathed, he was buoyed by a tingling sense of anticipation, for Magda was waiting, and he stepped out briskly.

As he paused for traffic lights, he caught a glimpse of his own reflection in a shop window. He was smiling without realizing it.

While he waited on the ramp of the parking garage for his turn to pay and enter the traffic stream, with the Maserati engine whispering impatiently, he glanced in the rear view mirror. He had acquired the habit long ago when one of the captured Provo death-lists had begun with his name; since then he had learned to look over his shoulder.

He noticed the Citroën two back in the line of vehicles because the windshield was cracked and there was a scrape which had dented the mudguard and exposed a bright strip of bare metal.

He noticed the same black Citroën still two back as he waited for pedestrian lights in the Champs Elysées, and when he ducked his head slightly to try and get a look at the driver, the headlights switched on as though to frustrate him and at that moment the lights changed and he had to drive on.

Going around the Étoile, the Citroën had fallen back four places in the grey drizzling dusk of early autumn, but he spotted it once again when he was halfway down the Avenue de la Grande Armée, for by now he was actively searching for it. It was immediately lost in the maze of side streets and Peter should have been able to forget it and concentrate on the pleasure of controlling the Maserati, but there lingered a sense of foreboding and even after he had shot the complicated junction of roads that got him on to the periphery route and eventually out on the road to Versailles and Chartres, he found himself changing lanes and speed while he scanned the road behind in the mirror.

Only when he left Versailles and was on the Rambouillet road did he have a clear view back a mile down the straight avenue of plane trees, and he was certain there was no other vehicle on the road. He relaxed completely and began to prepare himself for the final turn off that would bring him at last to La Pierre Bénite.

The shiny wet black python of road uncoiled ahead of him and then humped abruptly. Peter came over the rise at 150 kilometres an hour and instantly started to dance lightly on brake and clutch, avoiding the temptation of tramping down hard and losing adhesion on the slippery uneven tarmac. Ahead of him there was a gendarme in a shiny white plastic cape, wet with rain, brandishing a torch with a red lens; there were reflective warning triangles bright as rubies, a Peugeot in the ditch beside the road with headlights glaring at the sky, a dark blue police Kombi van half blocking the road, and in the stage lit by the Kombi's headlights two bodies were laid out neatly, and all of it hazed by the soft insistent mantle of falling rain – a typical roadside accident scene.

Peter had the Maserati well in hand, bringing her neatly down through the gears to a crawl, and as he was lowering the side window, the electric motor whining softly and the icy gust of night air into the heated interior, the gendarme gestured with the flashlight for him to pull over into the narrow gap between hedge and the parked Kombi, and at that moment unexpected movement caught Peter's eye. It was one of the bodies lying in the roadway under the headlights. The movement was the slight arch of the back that a man makes before rising from the prone position.

Peter watched him lift his arm, not more than a few inches, but it was just enough for Peter to realize he had been holding an object concealed down the outside of his thigh, and even in the rain and the night Peter's trained eye recognized the perforated air-cooled sleeve enclosing the short barrel of a fold-down machine pistol.

Instantly his brain was racing so that everything about him seemed to be taking place in dreamy slow motion.

The Maserati! he thought. They're after Magda.

The gendarme was coming round to the driver's side of the Maserati, and he had his right hand under the white plastic cape, at the level of his pistol belt.

Peter went flat on the gas pedal, and the Maserati bellowed like a bull buffalo shot through the heart. The rear wheels broke from the wet surface, and with a light touch Peter encouraged the huge silver machine to swing like a scythe at the gendarme. It should have cut him down, but he was too quick. As he dived for the hedge, Peter saw that he had brought the pistol out from under his cape but was too busy at that moment to use it.

The side of the Maserati touched the hedge with a fluttering rustle of foliage, and Peter lifted his right foot, caught the enraged charge of the machine and swung her the other way. The moment she was lined up he hit the gas again, and the Maserati howled. This time she burned blue rubber smoke off her rear wheels.

There was a driver at the wheel of the blue police Kombi, and he tried to pull across to block the road completely, but he was not fast enough.

The two vehicles touched, with a crackle and scream of metal that jarred Peter's teeth, but what concerned him was that the two bodies in the headlights were no longer flat. The nearest was on one knee and he was swinging the short stubby machine pistol – it looked like a Czech Skorpion or the German VP70 burst fire shoulder-stock pistol, but he was using the fold-down wire butt, wasting vital fractions of a second to get the weapon to his shoulder. He was also blocking the field of fire of the man who crouched behind him with another machine pistol pinned to his hip, pointing with index finger and forearm, ready to trigger with his second finger – 'That's the way it should be done.' Peter recognized professional skill, and his brain was running so swiftly that he had time to applaud it.

The Maserati cannoned off the police Kombi, and Peter lifted his right foot to take traction off the rear wheels, and spun the wheel the hard lock to the right. The Maserati swung her tail with a screech of rubber and went into a left side slide towards the two figures in the road, and Peter ducked down below the level of the door. He had deliberately induced the left-hand slide, so that he had some little protection from the engine compartment and bodywork.

As he ducked he heard the familiar sound, like a giant ripping heavyweight canvas, an automatic weapon throwing bullets at a cyclic rate of almost two thousand rounds a minute, and the bullets tore into the side of the Maserati, beating in the metal with an ear-numbing clangour, while glass exploded in upon Peter like the glittering spray as a storm-driven wave strikes a rock. Glass chips pelted across his back, and stung his cheek and the back of his neck. They sparkled like a diamond tiara in his hair.

Whoever was doing the shooting had certainly emptied the magazine in those few seconds, and now Peter bobbed up in his seat, slitting his eyes against the cloud of glass splinters. He saw a looming nightmare of dark hedges and spun the wheel back to hold the Maserati. She swayed to the limits of her equilibrium and Peter had a glimpse of the two gunmen in the road rolling frantically into the half-filled ditch, but at that moment his off rear wheel hit the lip and he was slammed up short against his safety belt with a force that drove the air from his lungs, and the Maserati reared like a stallion smelling the mare and tail-walked, swinging in short vicious surges back and forth across the road, as he desperately fought for control with gear and brake and wheel. He must have spun full circle, Peter realized, for there was a giddy dazzle of light beams and of running and rolling figures, everything was hazy and indistinct in the rain, then the open road ahead again, and he sent the car at it with a great howling lunge, at the same moment glancing up at his mirror.

In the headlights he saw the burned blue clouds of smoke and steam thrown up by his own tyres, and through it the figure of the second gunman obscured from the waist by the ditch. He had the machine pistol at his waist, and the muzzle flash bloomed about him.

Peter heard the first burst hit the Maserati and he could not duck again, for there was a bend ahead in the rain, coming up at dazzling speed and he clenched his jaws waiting for it.

The next burst hit the car, like the sound of hail on a tin roof, and he felt the rude tugging, numbing jerk in his upper body.

'Tagged!' he realized. There was no mistaking it, he had been hit before. The first time when he had led a patrol into an EOKA ambush a very long time ago, and at the same moment he was evaluating the hit calmly finding he still had use of both of his hands and all his senses. Either it was a ricochet, or the bullet had spent most of its force in penetrating the rear windshield and seat back.

The Maserati tracked neatly into the bend, and only then he felt the engine surge and falter. Almost immediately the sharp stink of gasoline filled the cab of the Maserati.

'Fuel line,' he told himself, and there was the warm, uncomfortable spread of his own blood down his back and side, and he placed his wound low in the left shoulder. If it had penetrated it would be a lung hit, and he waited for the coppery salt taste of blood in his throat or the bubbling froth of escaping air in his chest cavity.

The engine beat checked again, surged and checked, as it starved for fuel. That first traversing burst of automatic fire must have ripped through the engine compartment, and Peter throught wryly that in the movies the Maserati would have immediately erupted in spectacular pyrotechnics like a miniature Vesuvius – though in reality it didn't happen like that, still gasoline from the severed lead would be spraying over plugs and points.

One last glance backwards, before the bend hid it and he saw three men running for the police van – three men and the driver, that was lousy odds. They would be after him immediately, and the crippled machine made a final brave leap forward that carried them five hundred yards more, and then it died.

Ahead of him, at the limits of the headlight beam, Peter saw the white gates of La Pierre Bénite. They had set the ambush at the point where they could screen out most extraneous traffic, and gather only the silver Maserati in their net.

He cast his mind back swiftly, recalling the lie of the land beyond the main gates of the estate. He had been here only once before, and it had been dark then also – but he had the soldier's eye for ground, and he remembered thick forest on both sides of the road, down to a low bridge over a narrow fast flowing stream with steep banks, a hard left hander and a climb up to the house. The house was half a mile beyond the gates, a long way to go with a body hit and at least four armed men following, and no guarantee that he would be safe there either.

The Maserati was coasting down the slight incline towards the gates, slowing as it ran out of momentum, and now there was the hot smell of oil and burning rubber. The paintwork of the engine hood began to blister and discolour. Peter switched off the ignition to stop the electric pump spraying more fuel on to the burning engine and he slipped his hand into his jacket. He found the wound there he had expected it – low and left. It was beginning to sting and his hand came away sticky and slick with blood. He wiped it on his thigh.

Behind him was the reflected glow of headlights in the rain, a halo of light growing stronger. At any moment they would come through the bend, and he opened the glove compartment.

The 9-mm Cobra gave some little comfort as he slipped it from its holster and thrust it into the front of his belt. There was no spare magazine and the breech was empty, a safety consideration which he now regretted, for it left him with only nine rounds in the magazine – one more might make a lot of difference.

Pretty little fingers of bright flame were waving at him from under the bonnet of the engine compartment, finding the hinge and joint, probing the ventilation slot on the top surface. Peter released his seat belt, held open the door and steered with his other hand for the verge. Here the road was banked and dropped away steeply.

He flicked the wheel back the opposite way and let the change of direction eject him neatly, throwing him clear, while the Maserati swerved back into the centre of the road and rolled away, slowing gradually.

He landed as though from a parachute drop, feet and knees together cushioning the impact and then rolled into it. Pain flared in his shoulder and he felt something tear. He came up in a crouch and ran doubled over for the edge of the woods, and the burning auto lit the dark trees with flickering orange light.

The fingers of his left hand felt swollen and numb as he pumped a round into the chamber of the Cobra, and at that moment the headlights beyond the bend flared with shocking brilliance and Peter had the illusion of being caught in front stage centre of the Palladium. He went down hard on his belly in the soft rain-sodden earth, but still his wound jarred and he felt the warm trickle of running blood under his shirt as he crawled desperately for the treeline.

The police van roared down the stretch of road. Peter flattened and pressed his face to the earth, and it smelled of leaf mould and fungus. The van roared past where he lay.

Three hundred yards down the road the Maserati had coasted to a halt, two wheels still on the road, the offside wheels over the verge so she stood at an abandoned angle, burning merrily.

The van pulled up at a respectful distance from it, aware of the danger of explosion, and a single figure, the gendarme in his plastic cape, ran forward, took one look into the cab and shouted something. The language sounded like French, but the flames were beginning to drum fiercely and the range too long to hear clearly.

The van locked into a U-turn, bumped over the verge, and then started back slowly. The two erstwhile accident victims, still carrying their machine pistols, running ahead like hounds on leash, one on each side of the road, heads down as they searched for signs in the soft shoulders of the road. The white-caped gendarme rode on the runningboard of the van, calling encouragement to the hunters.

Peter was up again, doubled over, heading for the edge of the forest, and he ran into the barbed wire fence at full stretch. It brought him down heavily. He felt the slash of steel through the cloth of his trousers, and as he gathered himself again, he thought bitterly.

'One hundred and seventy guineas.' The suit had been tailored in Savile Row. He crawled between the strands of barbed wire, and there was a shout behind him. They had picked up his spoor, and as he dodged across the last few yards of open ground, another sharper, more jubilant shout.

They had spotted him in the towering firelight of the blazing Maserati, and again there was a tearing rip of automatic fire; but it was extreme range for the short barrel and low velocity ammunition. Peter heard passing shot like a whisper of bats' wings in the darkness above him and then he reached the first trees and ducked behind one of them.

He found he was breathing deeply, but with a good easy rhythm. The wound wasn't handicapping him yet, and he was into the cold reasoning rage that combat always instilled in him.

The range to the barbed wire fence was fifty metres, he judged, it was one of his best distances – International pistol standard out-of-hand with a 50-mm X circle – but there were no judges out here and he took a double-handed grip, and let them run into the fence just as he had done.

It brought two of them down, and the cries of angry distress were definitely in French; as they struggled to their feet again they were precisely backlit by the flames, and the Cobra had a luminous foresight. Peter went for midsection of one of the machine gunners.

The 9-mm had a vicious whipcrack report, and punched into flesh and bone with 385 foot pounds of energy. The strike of the bullet sounded like a watermelon hit with the full swing of a baseball bat. It lifted the man off his feet, and threw him backwards, and Peter swung on to the next target, but they were pros. Even though the fire from the edge of the woods had come as a complete surprise, they reacted instantly, and disappeared flat against the dark earth. They gave him no target, and Peter was too low on ammunition to throw down holding fire.

One of them fired a burst of automatic and it tore bark and wood and leaves along the edge of the trees. Peter fired at the muzzle flash only once as a warning and then he ducked away and, keeping his head down to avoid lucky random fire, sprinted back into the woods.

They would be held up for two or three minutes by the fence and by the threat of coming under fire again, and Peter wanted to open some ground between them during that time.

The glow of the burning Maserati kept him well orientated and he moved quickly towards the river; however, before he had covered two yards he was starting to shiver uncontrollably. His two-piece city suit was soaked by the persistent drizzle and by the shower from each bush he brushed against. His shoes were light calf leather soles and he had stepped in puddles of mud, and the knee-high grass was sodden. The cold struck through his clothing; he could feel his wound stiffening agonizingly and the first nauseating grip of shock tightened his belly, but he paused every fifty yards or so and listened for sounds of pursuit. Once he heard the sound of a car engine from the direction of the road, passing traffic probably, and he wondered what they would make of the abandoned police vehicle and the blazing Maserati. Even if it was reported to the real police, it would be all over before a patrol arrived and Peter discounted the chance of assistance from that quarter.

He was beginning now to be puzzled by the total lack of any sign of further pursuit, and he looked for and found a good stance in which to wait for it. There was a fallen oak tree and he wriggled in under the trunk, with a clear avenue of retreat, good cover and a low position from which any pursuer would be silhouetted against the sky glow of the burning Maserati. There were only three pursuers now, and seven cartridges in the Cobra. If it were not for the cold and the demoralizing ache through his upper body, he might have felt more confident, but the nagging terror of the hunted animal was still on him.

He waited five minutes, lying completely still, every sense tuned to its finest, the Cobra held out in extended double grip, ready to roll left or right and take the shot as it came. There was no sound but the drip and plop of the rain-soaked woods.

Another ten minutes passed before it occurred to him suddenly that the pursuers must now realize that the wrong quarry had sprung their trap. They were setting for Magda Altmann, and it must be clear to them that they had a man, and an armed one at that. He pondered their reaction. Almost certainly they would pull out now, had already done so.

Instead of a lady worth twenty or thirty million dollars in ransom money, they must realize they had one of her employees, probably an armed bodyguard, who was driving the Maserati either as a decoy or merely as delivery driver. Yes, he decided, they would pull out – take their casualty and melt away, and Peter was sure they would leave no clues to their identity.

He would have enjoyed the opportunity to question one of them, he thought, and grimaced at a new lance of pain in the shoulder.

He waited another ten minutes, utterly still and alert, controlling the spasms of cold and reaction that shook him, then he rose quietly and moved back towards the river. The Maserati must have burned out completely now for the sky was black again and he had to rely on his own sense of direction to keep orientated. Even though he knew he was alone, he paused every fifty yards to listen and look.

He heard the river at last. It was directly ahead and very close. He moved a little faster and almost walked off the bank in the dark. He squatted to rest for a moment, for the shoulder was very painful now, and the cold was draining his energy.

The prospect of wading the river was particularly uninviting. The rain had fallen without a break for days now, and the water sounded powerful and swift – it would certainly be icy cold, and probably shoulder deep rather than waist deep. The bridge must be only a few hundred yards downstream, and he stood up and moved along the bank.

Cold and pain can sap concentration very swiftly, and Peter had to make a conscious effort to keep himself alert, and he felt for every foothold before transferring his weight forward. He held the Cobra hanging at full stretch of his right arm, but ready for instant use, and he blinked his eyes clear of the fine drizzle of rain and the cold sweat of pain and fear.

Yet it was his sense of smell that alerted him. The rank smell of stale Turkish tobacco smoke on a human body, it was a smell that had always offended him, and now he picked it up instantly, even though it was just one faint whiff.

Peter froze in mid stride while his brain raced to adjust to the unexpected. He had almost convinced himself that he was alone.

Now he remembered the sound of a car engine on the main road, and he realized that men who had set up such an elaborate decoy – the faked motor accident, the police van and uniform – would certainly have taken the trouble to plot and study the ground between the ambush point and the victim's intended destination.

They would know better than Peter himself the layout of woods and river and bridge, and would have realized immediately they had taken their first casualty the futility of blundering pursuit through the dark. It was the smart thing to circle back and wait again, and they would choose the river bank or the bridge itself.

The only thing that troubled Peter was their persistence. They *must* know it was not Magda Altmann, and then even in this tense moment of discovery he remembered the Citroën that had followed him down the Champs Elysées – nothing was what it appeared to be, and slowly he completed the step in which he had frozen.

He stood utterly still, poised, every muscle and every nerve screwed to its finest pitch, but the night was black and the rush of the river covered all sound. Peter waited. The other man will always move if you wait long enough, and he waited with the patience of the stalking leopard, although the cold struck through to his bones and the rain slid down his cheeks and neck.

The man moved at last. The squelch of mud and the unmistakable brush of undergrowth against cloth, then silence. He was very close, within ten feet, but there was no glimmer of light, and Peter shifted his weight carefully to face the direction of the sound. The old trick was to fire one shot at the sound and use the muzzle flash to light the target for the second which followed it in almost the same instant of time – but there were three of them and at ten feet that machine pistol could cut a man in half. Peter waited.

Then from upstream there was the sound of a car engine again, still faint but fast approaching. Immediately somebody whistled faintly, a rising double note in the night up towards the bridge, clearly some prearranged signal. A car door banged shut, much closer than the sound of the approaching engine and a starter whirred, another harsher engine roared into life, headlights flared through the rain, and Peter blinked as the whole scene ahead of him lit up.

A hundred yards ahead the bridge crossed the stream, the surface of the water was shiny and black as new-mined coal as it flowed about the supporting piles.

The blue van had parked on the threshold of the bridge, obviously to wait for Peter, but now it was pulling out, probably alarmed by the approach of the other more powerful engine from the direction of La Pierre Bénite. The driver was heading back towards the main road, the phoney gendarme scrambling alongside with his cape flapping as he tried to scramble through the open offside door – and out of the darkness, close to Peter, a voice cried out with alarm.

'Attendez!' The third man had no desire to be left by his companions, and he ran forward, abandoning all attempt at concealment. He had his back to Peter now, waving the machine pistol frantically, clearly outlined by the headlights of the van, and the range was under ten feet. It was a dead shot, and Peter went for it instinctively – and only at the very instant of trigger pressure that would have sent a 125-grain bullet between his shoulder blades was Peter able to check himself.

The man's back was turned and the range would make it murder, Peter's training should have cured him of such nice gentlemanly distinctions. However, what really held his trigger finger was the need to know. Peter had to know who these people were and who had sent them, and what they had been sent to do, who they were after.

Now that the man was being deserted, he had abandoned all stealth and was running as though he were chasing a bus, and Peter saw the chance to take him. Roles had been exchanged completely, and Peter darted forward, transferring the Cobra to his injured left hand.

He caught the man in four paces, keeping low to avoid his peripheral vision, and he whipped his good right arm around the throat, going for the half nelson and the spin that would disorientate the man before he slammed the barrel of the Cobra against the temple.

The man was quick as a cat, something warned him – perhaps the squelch of Peter's sodden shoes, and he ducked his chin on to his chest, rolling his shoulders and beginning to turn back into the line of Peter's attack.

Peter missed the throat and caught him high, the crook of his elbow locking about the man's mouth, and the unexpected turn had thrown him slightly off balance. If he had had full use of his left arm, he could still have spun his victim, but in an intuitive flash he realized that he had lost the advantage, already the man was twisting his head out of the armlock, bulking his shoulders, and by the feel of him, Peter knew instantly that he was steel-hard with muscle.

The barrel of the machine pistol was short enough to enable him to press the muzzle into Peter's body just as soon as he completed his turn, it would tear Peter to pieces like a chain saw.

Peter changed his grip slightly, no longer opposing the man's turn, but throwing all his weight and the strength of his right arm into the same direction; they spun together like a pair of waltzing dancers, but Peter knew that the moment they broke apart the man would have the killing advantage again.

The river was his one chance, he realized that instinctively, and before the advantage passed back from him to his adversary, he hurled himself backwards, keeping his grip on the man's head.

They went out into black space, falling together in a short gut-swooping drop with Peter underneath. If there was rock below the steep bank of the river, he realized he would be crushed by the other's weight.

They struck the surface of the fast black water, and freezing cold struck like a club so that Peter almost released the air from his lungs as a reflex.

The shock of cold water seemed to have stunned the man in his grip momentarily, and Peter felt the whoosh of air from his lungs as he let go. Peter changed his grip, wedging his elbow under the chin, but not quite able to get at the throat – immediately the man began the wild panic-stricken struggles of somebody held under icy water with empty lungs.

He had lost the machine pistol, for he was tearing at Peter's arms and face with both hands as the water swirled them both end over and down towards the bridge.

Peter had to keep him from getting air, and as he held his own precious single breath, he tried to get on top and stay there.

Fingers hooked at his closed eyes, and then into his mouth as the man reached back desperately over his own shoulders. Peter opened his mouth slightly and the other man thrust his fingers deeply in, trying to tear at his tongue. Immediately Peter locked his teeth into the fingers with a force that made his jaw ache at the hinges, and his mouth filled with the sickening warm spurt of the other man's blood.

Fighting his own revulsion, he hung on desperately with teeth and arms. He had lost his own weapon, dropping it into the black flood from numbed and crippled fingers, and the man was fighting now with the animal strength of his starved lungs and mutilated fingers; every time he tried to yank his hand out of Peter's mouth the flesh tore audibly in Peter's ears and fresh blood made him gag and choke.

They came out on the surface and through streaming eyes Peter had one glimpse of the bridge looming above him. The blue van had disappeared, but Magda Altmann's Mercedes limousine was parked in the centre of the bridge, and in the wash of its headlights he recognized her two bodyguards. They were leaning far out over the guardrail, and Peter had a moment's dread that one of them might try a shot – then they were flung into the concrete piles of the bridge with such force that they lost the deathlock they had upon each other.

The back eddy beyond the bridge swung them in towards the bank. Gasping and swallowing with cold and exhaustion and pain, Peter fought for a footing on gravel and rock. The machine-gunner had found bottom also and was stumbling desperately towards the bank. In the headlights of the limousine Peter saw Magda's two bodyguards racing back across the bridge to head him off.

Peter realized that he would not be able to catch the man before he reached the bank.

'Carl!' he screamed at the bodyguard who was leading. 'Stop him. Don't let him get away.'

The bodyguard vaulted over the guardrail, landing cat-like in complete balance, with the pistol double-handed at the level of his navel.

Below him the machine-gunner dragged himself waist deep towards the bank. It was only then that Peter realized what was going to happen.

'No!' He choked on blood and water. 'Take him alive. Don't kill him, Carl!'

The bodyguard had not heard, or had not understood. The muzzle blast seemed to join him and the wallowing figure in the river below him, a blood-orange rope of flame and thunderous explosion. The bullets smacked into the machine-gunner's chest and belly like an axeman cutting down a tree.

'No!' Peter yelled helplessly. 'Oh Jesus, no! No!'

Peter lunged forward and caught the corpse before it slid below the black water, and he dragged it by one arm to the bank. The bodyguards took it from him and hauled it up, the head lolling like an idiot's, and the blood diluted to pale pink in the reflected headlights.

Peter made three attempts to climb the bank, each time slithering back tiredly into the water, then Carl reached down and gripped his wrist.

Peter knelt on the muddy bank, still choking with the water and blood he had swallowed, and he retched weakly.

'Peter!' Magda's voice rang with concern, and he looked up and wiped his mouth on the back of his forearm. She had slipped out of the back door of the limousine and was running back along the bridge, long-legged in black boots and ski-pants, her face dead white with concern and her eyes frantic with worry.

Peter pushed himself on to his feet and swayed drunkenly. She reached him and caught him, steadying him as he teetered.

'Peter, oh God, darling. What happened –'

'This beauty and some of his friends wanted to take you for a ride – and they got the wrong address.'

They stared down at the corpse. Carl had used a .357 magnum and the damage was massive. Magda turned her head away.

'Nice work,' Peter told the bodyguard bitterly. 'He's not going to answer any questions now, is he?'

'You said to stop him.' Carl growled as he reloaded the pistol.

'I wonder what you would have done if I'd said to really clobber him.' Peter began to turn away with disgust, and pain checked him. He gasped.

'You're hurt.' Magda's concern returned in full strength. 'Take his other arm,' she ordered Carl, and they helped him over the parapet to the limousine.

Peter stripped off the torn and sodden remains of his clothing and Magda wrapped him in the Angora wool travel rug before examining his wound under the interior light of the cab.

The bullet hole was a perfect little blue puncture, and the bullet was trapped between his ribs and the sheet of flat, hard trapezium muscles. She could see the outline of it quite clearly, the size of a ripe acorn in his flesh, swollen out angry purple.

'Thank God –' she whispered, and unwound the Jean Patou scarf from her long pale throat. She bound the wound carefully. 'We'll take you directly to the hospital at Versailles. Drive fast, Carl.'

She opened the walnut-fronted cocktail cabinet in the bodywork beside her and poured half a tumbler of whisky from the crystal decanter.

It washed the taste of blood from Peter's mouth and then went warmly all the way down his throat to soothe the cramps of cold and shock in his belly.

'What made you come? ' he asked, his voice still rough with the fierce spirit, the timely arrival nagged at his sense of rightness.

'The police at Rambouillet had a report of a car smash – they knew the Maserati, and the inspector rang La Pierre Bénite immediately. I guessed something bad –'

At that moment they reached the gates at the main road. The remains of the Maserati lay smouldering on the side of the road, around it like boy scouts around a camp fire were half a dozen gendarmes in their white plastic capes and pillbox kepis. They seemed uncertain of what they should do next.

Carl slowed the limousine and Magda spoke tersely through the window to a sergeant, who treated her with immense respect. 'Oui, madame la Baronne, d'accord. Tout à fait vrai –' She dismissed him with a final nod, and he and his men saluted the departing limousine.

'They will find the body at the bridge –'

'There may be another one on the edge of the forest there –'

'You are very good, aren't you?' She slanted her eyes at him.

'The really good ones don't get hit,' he said, and smiled at her. The whisky had taken some of the sting and stiffness out of the wound and unknotted his guts. It was good to still be alive, he started to appreciate that again.

'You were right about the Maserati then – they were waiting for it.'

'That's why I burned it,' he told her, but she did not answer his smile.

'Oh, Peter. You'll never know how I felt. The police told me that the driver of the Maserati was still in it and had been burned. I thought – I felt as though part of me had been destroyed. It was the most terrifying feeling –' She shivered. 'I nearly did not come, I didn't want to see it. I nearly sent my wolves, but then I had to know – Carl saw you in the river as we turned on to the bridge. He said it was you, I just couldn't believe it –' She stopped herself and shuddered at the memory. 'Tell me what happened, tell me all of it,' she demanded and poured more whisky into his tumbler.

For some reason that he was not sure of himself, Peter did not mention the Citroën that had followed him out of Paris. He told himself that it could not have been relevant. It must have been a coincidence, for if the driver of the Citroën had been one of them he would have been able to telephone ahead and warn the others that Baroness Magda Altmann was not in the Maserati, so that would have meant that they were not after her – but after him, Peter Stride, and that didn't make sense because he had only set himself up as bait that very morning, and they would not have had time yet. He stopped the giddy carousel of thoughts – shock and whisky, he told himself. There would be time later to think it all out more carefully. Now he would simply believe that they were waiting for Magda, and he had run into their net. He told it that way, beginning from the moment that he had seen the police van parked in the road. Magda listened with complete attention, the huge eyes clinging to his face, and she touched him every few moments as if to reassure herself.

When Carl parked under the portico of the emergency entrance of the hospital, the police had radioed ahead and there were an intern and two nurses waiting for Peter with a theatre trolley.

Before she opened the door to let them take Peter, Magda leaned to him and kissed him full on the lips.

'I'm so very glad to have you still,' she whispered, and then with her lips still very close to his ear she went on. 'It was Caliph again, wasn't it?'

He shrugged slightly, grimaced at the stab of pain, and answered.

'I can't think of anyone else off-hand that would do such a professional job.'

Magda walked beside the trolley as far as the theatre doors, and she was beside his bed in the curtained cubicle as he struggled up through the deadening, suffocating false death of anaesthetic.

The French doctor was with her, and he produced the gruesome blood-clotted souvenir with a magician's flourish.

'I did not have to cut,' he told Peter proudly. 'Probe only.' The bullet had mushroomed impressively, had certainly lost much of its velocity in penetrating the bodywork of the Maserati. 'You are a very lucky man,' the doctor went on. 'You are in fine condition, muscles like a race horse that stopped the bullet going deep. You will be well again very soon.'

'I have promised to look after you, so he is letting you come home now.' Magda hovered over him also. 'Aren't you, doctor?'

'You will have one of the world's most beautiful nurses.' The doctor bowed gallantly towards Magda with a certain wistfulness in his expression.

The doctor was right, the bullet wound gave him less discomfort than the tears in his thighs from the barbed wire, but Magda Altmann behaved as though he were suffering from an irreversible and terminal disease.

When she did have to go up to her office suite in the Boulevard des Capucines the next day, she telephoned three times for no other reason than to make sure he was still alive and to ask for his size in shoes and clothing. The cavalcade of automobiles carrying her and her entourage were back at La Pierre Bénite while it was still daylight.

'You are keeping civil service hours,' he accused when she came directly to the main guest suite overlooking the terraced lawns and the artificial lake.

'I knew you were missing me,' she explained, and kissed him before beginning to scold him. 'Roberto tells me you have been wandering around in the rain. The doctor said you were to stay in bed. Tomorrow I will have to stay here to take care of you myself.'

'Is that a threat?' he grinned at her. 'For that sort of punishment I would let Caliph shoot another hole –'

Swiftly she laid her fingers on his lips. 'Peter, chéri, don't joke like that.' And the shadow that passed across her eyes was touched with fear, then immediately she was smiling again. 'Look what I have bought you.'

Peter's valise had been in the trunk of the Maserati, and she had replaced it with one in black crocodile from Hermes. To fill it she must have started at the top end of the Faubourg St Honoré and worked her way down to the Place Vendôme.

'I had forgotten how much fun it is to buy presents for one who you –' She did not finish the sentence, but held up a brocade silk dressing-gown. '– Everybody in St Laurent knew what I was thinking when I chose this.'

She had forgotten nothing. Shaving gear, silk handkerchiefs and underwear, a blue blazer, slacks and shoes from Gucci, even cufflinks in plain gold, each set with a small sapphire.

'You have such blue eyes,' she explained. 'Now I will go and make myself respectable for dinner. I told Roberto we would eat here, for there are no other guests tonight.'

She had changed from the gunmetal business suit and turban into floating cloud-light layers of gossamer silk, and her hair was down to her waist, more lustrous than the cloth.

'I will open the champagne,' she said. 'It needs two hands.'

He wore the brocade gown, with his left arm still in a sling, and they stood and admired each other over the top of the champagne glasses.

'I was right.' She nodded comfortably. 'Blue is your colour. You must wear it more often.' And he had to smile at the quaint compliment, and touched her glass with his. The crystal pinged musically and they saluted each other before they drank. Immediately she set the glass aside, and her expression became serious.

'I spoke with my friends in the Sûreté. They agree that it was a kidnap attempt against me, and because I asked it, they will not trouble you to make a statement until you feel better. I told them to send a man tomorrow to speak to you. There was no sign of the second man you shot at on the edge of the woods, he must have been able to walk or been carried by his friends .'

'And the other man?' Peter asked. 'The dead one.'

'They know him well. He had a very ugly past. Algeria with the paras. The mutiny.' She spread her hands eloquently. 'My friends were very surprised that he had not killed you when he tried to do so. I did not say too much about your own past. It is better, I think?'

'It's better,' Peter agreed.

'When I am with you like this, I forget that you also are a very dangerous man.' She stopped and examined his face carefully. 'Or is it part of the reason I find you so –' she searched for the word '– so compelling? You have such a gentle manner, Peter. Your voice is so soft and –' She shrugged. 'But there is something in the way you smile sometimes, and in certain light your eyes are so blue and hard and cruel. Then I remember that you have killed many men. Do you think that is what attracts me?'

'I hope it is not.'

'Some women are excited by blood and violence – the bull fight, the prize ring, there are always as many women as men at these, and I have watched their faces. I have thought about myself, and still I do not know it all. I know only that I am attracted by strong men. Aaron was such a man. I have not found many others since then.'

'Cruelty is not strength,' Peter told her.

'No, a truly strong man has that streak of gentleness and compassion. You are so strong, and yet when you make love to me it is with extreme gentleness, though I can always feel the strength and cruelty there, held in bate, like the falcon under the hood.'

She moved away across the room furnished in cream and chocolate and gold, and she tugged the embroidered bell-pull that dangled from the corniced ceiling with its hand-painted panels, pastoral scenes of the type that Marie Antoinette had so admired. Peter knew that much of the furnishing of La Pierre Bénite had been purchased at the auction sales with which the revolutionary committee dispersed the accumulated treasures of the House of Bourbon. With the other treasures there were flowers, wherever Magda Altmann went there were flowers.

She came back to him as Roberto, the Italian butler, supervised the entry of the dinner trolley, and then Roberto filled with wine glasses himself, handling the bottles with white gloves as though they were part of the sacrament, and stationed himself ready to serve the meal, but Magda dismissed him with a curt gesture and he bowed himself out silently.

There was a presentation-wrapped parcel at Peter's place setting, tissue paper and an elaborately tied red ribbon. He looked up at her inquiringly as she served the soup into fragile Limoges bowls.

'Once I began buying presents, I could not stop myself,' she explained. 'Besides, I kept thinking that bullet might have been in my back.' Then she was impatient. 'Are you not going to open it?'

He did so carefully, and then was silent.

'Africa, it is your speciality, is it not?' she asked anxiously. 'Nineteenth-century Africa?'

He nodded, and reverently opened the cover of the volume in its bed of tissue paper. It was fully bound in maroon leather, and the state of preservation was quite extraordinary, only the dedication on the fly leaf in the author's handwriting was faded yellow.

'Where on earth did you find this?' he demanded. 'It was at Sotheby's in 1971. I bid on it then.' He had dropped out of the bidding at five thousand pounds.

'You do not have a first edition of Cornwallis Harris?' she asked again anxiously, and he shook his head, examining one of the perfectly preserved colour plates of African big game.

'No, I do not. But how did you know that?'

'Oh, I know as much about you as you do yourself,' she laughed. 'Do you like it?'

'It is magnificent. I am speechless.' The gift was too extravagant, even for someone of her fortune. It troubled him, and he was reminded of the comedy situation of the husband who brings home flowers unexpectedly and is immediately accused by his wife. 'Why do you have a guilty conscience?'

'Do you truly like it? I know so little about books.'

'It is the one edition I need to complete my major works,' he said. 'And it is probably the finest specimen left outside the British Museum.'

'I'm so glad.' She was genuinely relieved. 'I was truly worried.' And she put down the silver soup ladle and lifted both arms to welcome his embrace.

During the meal she was gay and talkative, and only when Roberto had wheeled away the trolley and they settled side by side on the down-filled couch before the fire did her mood change again.

'Peter, today I have been unable to think of anything but this business – you and me and Caliph. I have been afraid, and I am still afraid. I keep thinking of Aaron, what they did to him – and then I think of you and what nearly happened.'

They were silent, staring into the flames and sipping coffee from a demi-tasse, then suddenly she had changed direction again. He was growing accustomed to these mercurial switches in thought.

'I have an island – not one island, but nine little islands – and in the centre of them is a lagoon nine kilometres wide. The water is so clear you can see the fish fifty feet down. There is an airstrip on the main atoll. Just under two hours' flying time to Tahiti. Nobody would ever know we were there. We could swim all day, walk in the sand, make love under the stars. You would be king of the islands, and I would be your queen. No more Altmann Industries – I would find somebody as good or better than myself to run it. No more danger. No more fear. No more Caliph – no more –' She stopped abruptly, as though she had been about to commit herself too far, but she went on quickly. 'Let's go there, Peter. Let's forget all this. Let's just run away and be happy together, for ever.'

'It's a pretty thought.' He turned to her, feeling deep and genuine regret.

'It would work for us. We would make it work.'

And he said nothing, just watching her eyes, until she looked away and sighed.

'No.' She mirrored his regret. 'You are right. Neither of us could ever give up living like that. We have to go on – but, Peter, I am so afraid. I am afraid of what I know about you and of what I do not know. I am afraid of what you do not know about me, and what I can never tell you – but we must go on. You are right. We have to find Caliph, and then destroy him. But, oh God, I pray we do not destroy ourselves, what we have found together – I pray we will be able to keep that intact.'

'The best way to conjure up emotional disaster is to talk about it.'

'All right, let's play riddles instead. My turn first. What is the most miserable experience ever known to the human female?'

'I give up.'

'Sleeping alone on a winter's night.'

'Salvation is at hand,' he promised her.

'But what about your poor shoulder?'

'If we combine our vast talents and wisdom, I am sure we will manage something.'

'I think you are right,' she purred and nestled against him like a sleek and silken cat. 'As always.'

There is always a delightfully decadent feeling about buying underwear for a beautiful woman, and Peter was amused by the knowing air of the middle-aged sales lady. She clearly had her own ideas about the relationship, and slyly produced a tray filled with filmy lace and iniquitously expensive wisps of silk.

'Yes,' Melissa-Jane approved rapturously. 'Those are exactly –' She held one of them to her cheek, and the sales lady preened at her own foresight. Peter hated to disillusion her, and he played the role of sugar daddy a few moments longer as he glanced up at the mirror behind her head.

The tail was still there, a nondescript figure in a grey overcoat, browsing through a display of brassieres across the hall with the avid interest and knowledgeable air of a closet queen.

'I don't really think your mother will approve, darling,' Peter said, and the sales woman looked startled.

'Oh, please, Daddy. I will be fourteen next month.'

They had had a tail on him since he had arrived at Heathrow the previous afternoon, and Peter could not decide who they were. He began to regret he had not yet replaced the Cobra he had lost in the river.

'I think we'd better play it safe –' Peter told his daughter, and both Melissa-Jane and the sales lady looked crestfallen.

'Not bloomers!' Melissa-Jane wailed. 'Not elastic legs.'

'Compromise,' Peter suggested. 'No elastic legs – but no lace, not until you're sixteen. I think painted fingernails is enough for right now.'

'Daddy, you can be so medieval, honestly!'

He glanced at the mirror again, and they were changing the guard across the sales hall. The man in the shabby grey overcoat and checked woollen scarf drifted away and disappeared into one of the lifts. It would take some little time for Peter to spot his replacement – and then he grinned to himself, no it would not. Here he came now. He wore a tweed sports jacket in a frantic hounds' tooth pattern, above Royal Stewart tartan trews and a grin like an amiable toad.

'Son of a gun. This is a surprise.' He came up behind Peter and hit him an open-handed blow between the shoulder blades that made Peter wince. At least he knew who they were at last.

'Colin.' He turned and took the massive paw with its covering of wiry black hair across the back. 'Yes, it is a surprise. I've been falling over your gorillas since yesterday.'

'Oafs,' Colin Noble agreed amiably. 'All of them, oafs!' And turned to seize Melissa-Jane. 'You're beautiful,' he told her and kissed her with more than avuncular enthusiasm.

'Uncle Colin. You came straight from heaven.' Melissa-Jane broke from the embrace and displayed the transparent panties. 'What do you think of these?'

'It's you, honey. You've just got to have them.'

'Tell my father, won't you.'

Colin looked around the Dorchester suite and grunted. 'This is really living. You don't get it this good in this man's army.'

'Daddy is truly becoming a bloated plutocrat – just like Uncle Steven,' Melissa-Jane agreed.

'I notice that you and Vanessa and the other comrades all wear lace panties.' Peter counter-attacked his daughter.

'That's different.' Melissa-Jane backtracked swiftly, and hugged the green Harrod's package defensively. 'You can have a social conscience without dressing like a peasant, you know.'

'Sounds like a good life.' Peter threw his overcoat across the couch and crossed to the liquor cabinet. 'Bourbon?'

'On the rocks,' said Colin.

'Is there a sweet sherry?' Melissa-Jane asked.

'There is Coke,' Peter answered. 'And you can take it through to your own room, young lady.'

'Oh Daddy, I haven't seen Uncle Colin for ages.'

'Scat,' said Peter, and when she had gone, 'sweet sherry, forsooth.'

'It's a crying bastard when they start growing up – and they look like that.' Colin took the glass from Peter and rattled the ice cubes together as he lay back in the armchair. 'Aren't you going to congratulate me?'

'With pleasure.' Peter took his own glass and stood at the windows, against the backdrop of bare branches and grey misty skies over Hyde Park. 'What did you do?'

'Come on, Pete! Thor – they gave me your job, after you walked out.'

'Before they fired me.'

'After you walked out,' Colin repeated firmly. He took a sip of the Bourbon and gargled it loudly. 'There are a lot of things we don't understand – "Ours not to reason why, ours but to do and die." Shakespeare.'

He was still playing the buffoon, but the small eyes were as honey bright and calculating as those of a brand new teddy bear on Christmas morning. Now he waved his glass around the suite.

'This is great. Really it's great. You were wasted in Thor – everybody knew that. You must be pulling down more than all the joint-chiefs put together now.'

'Seven gets you five that you've already seen a Xeroxed copy of my contract of employment with Narmco.'

'Narmco!' Colin whistled. 'Is that who you're working for? No kidding, Pete baby, that's terrific!'

And Peter had to laugh, it was a form of capitulation. He came across and took the seat opposite Colin.

'Who sent you, Colin?'

'That's a lousy question –'

'That's just an opener.'

'Why should somebody have sent me? Couldn't I just bust to chew the fat with an old buddy?'

'He sent you because he worked it out that I might just bust the jaw of anybody else.'

'Sure now and everybody knows we love each other like brothers.'

'What's the message, Colin?'

'Congratulations, Peter Baby, I am here to tell you that you have just won yourself a return ticket to the Big Apple.' He placed one hand across his heart and sang with a surprisingly mellow baritone. 'New York, New York, it's a wonderful town.'

Peter sat staring impassively at Colin, but he was thinking swiftly. He knew he had to go. Somehow he was certain that something was surfacing through muddied waters, the parts were beginning to click together. This was the sort of thing he had hoped for when he put the word on the wind.

'When?'

'There is an airforce jet at Croydon right now.'

'Melissa-Jane?'

'I've got a driver downstairs to take her home.'

'She's going to hate you.'

'Story of my life,' Colin sighed. 'Only the dogs love me.'

They played gin-rummy and drank teeth-blackening airforce coffee, all the way across the Atlantic. Colin Noble did most of the talking, around the stub of his cheroot. It was shop, Thor shop, training and personnel details, small anecdotes about men and things they both knew well – and he made no effort to question Peter about his job and Narmco, other than to remark that he would have Peter back in London for the series of Narmco meetings he had arranged starting on the following Monday. It was a deliberate and not very subtle intimation of just how much Atlas knew about Peter and his new activities.

They landed at Kennedy a little after midnight, and there was an army driver to take them to a local Howard Johnson for six hours' sleep, that kind of deep black coma induced by jetlag.

Peter still felt prickly-eyed and woollen-headed as he watched with a feeling of disbelief as Colin devoured one of those amazing American breakfasts of waffles and maple syrup, wieners and bacon and eggs, sugar cakes and sticky buns, washed down with countless draughts of fruit juice and coffee. Then Colin lit his first cheroot and announced.

'Hell, now I know I'm home. Only now I realize I've been slowly fading away with malnutrition for two years.'

The same army driver was waiting for them at the front entrance of the motel. The Cadillac was an indication of their status in the military hierarchy. Peter looked out with detachment from the air-conditioned and padded interior on to the brooding ghettoes of Harlem. From the elevated highway along the East River, it reminded Peter of a deserted battle ground – where a few survivors lurked in the cold misty morning. Only the graffiti that adorned the bare brick walls had passion and vitality.

Their drive caught the junction of Fifth and One Hundred and Eleventh Street, and ran south down the park past the Metropolitan Art Museum in the thickening rush-hour traffic, then slipped off and into the cavernous mouth of a parking garage beneath one of the monolithic structures that seemed to reach to the grey cold heavens.

The garage entrance was posted 'Residents Only', but the doorman raised the electronically controlled grid and waved them through. Colin led Peter to the bank of elevators and they rode up with the stomach-dropping swoop while the lights above the elevator door recorded their ascent to the very top of the building.

There they stepped out into a reception area protected by ornamental, but none the less functional, screens.

A guard in military police uniform and wearing a side-arm surveyed them through the grille and checked Colin's Atlas pass against the register before allowing them through.

The apartment occupied the entire top level of the building, for there were hanging gardens beyond the sliding glass panels and a view across the sickening canyons of space to the other tall structures farther down Island – the Pan Am building and the twin towers of the World Trade Center.

The décor was Oriental, stark interiors in which were displayed works of art that Peter knew from his previous visit were of incalculable value – antique Japanese brush paintings on silk panels, carvings in jade and ivory, a display of tiny netsuke – and in an atrium through which they passed was a miniature forest of Bonsai trees in their shallow ceramic bowls, the frozen contortions of their trunks and branches a sign of their great age.

Incongruously, the exquisite rooms were filled with the thunder of Von Karajan leading the Berlin Philharmonic Orchestra through the glories of the Eroica.

Beyond the atrium was a plain door of white oak, and Colin Noble pressed the buzzer beside the lintel and almost immediately the door slid open.

Colin led into a long carpeted room, the ceiling of which was covered with acoustic tiles. The room contained besides the crowded bookshelves and work table an enormous concert piano, and down the facing wall an array of hi fi turntables and loudspeakers that would have been more in place in a commercial recording studio.

Kingston Parker stood beside the piano, a heroic figure, tall and heavy in the shoulder, his great shaggy head hanging forward on to his chest, his eyes closed and an expression of almost religious ecstasy glowing upon his face.

The music moved his powerful frame the way the storm wind sways a giant of the forest. Peter and Colin stopped in the doorway, for it seemed an intrusion on such a private, such an intimate moment, but it was only a few seconds before he became aware of them and lifted his head. He seemed to shake off the spell of the music with the shudder that a spaniel uses to shake itself free of water when it reaches dry land, and he lifted the arm of the turntable from the spinning black disc.

The silence seemed to tingle after the great crashing chords of sound.

'General Stride,' Kingston Parker greeted him. 'Or may I still call you Peter?'

'Mister Stride will do very nicely,' said Peter, and Parker made an eloquent little gesture of regret, and without offering to shake hands indicated the comfortable leather couch across the room.

'At least you came,' he said, and as Peter settled into the couch, he nodded.

'I have always had an insatiable curiosity.'

'I was relying on that,' Kingston Parker smiled. 'Have you breakfasted?'

'We've had a snack,' Colin cut in but Peter nodded.

'Coffee then,' said Parker, and spoke quietly into the intercom set, before turning back to them.

'Where to begin?' Parker combed the thick greying hair back with both hands, leaving it even more tousled than it had been.

'Begin at the beginning,' Peter suggested. 'As the King of Hearts said to Alice.'

'At the beginning –' Parker smiled softly. '– All right, at the beginning I opposed your involvement with Atlas.'

'I know.'

'I did not expect that you would accept the Thor command, it was a step backwards in your career. You surprised me there, and not for the first time.'

A Chinese manservant in a white jacket with brass buttons carried in a tray. They were silent as he offered coffee and cream and coloured crystal sugar and then, when he had gone, Parker went on.

'At that time, my estimate of you, General Stride, was that although you had a record of brilliance and solid achievement, you were an officer of rigidly old-fashioned thought. The Colonel Blimp mentality more suited to trench warfare than to the exigencies of war from the shadows – the kind of wars that we are fighting now, and will be forced to fight in the future.'

He shook the great shaggy head and unconsciously his fingers caressed the smooth cool ivory keyboard, and he settled down on the stool before the piano.

'You see, General Stride, I saw the role of Atlas to be too limited by the original terms of reference placed upon it. I did not believe that Atlas could do what it was designed for if it was only an arm of retaliation. If it had to wait for a hostile act before it could react, if it had to rely entirely on other organizations – with all their internecine rivalries and bickerings – for its vital intelligence. I needed officers who were not only brilliant, but who were capable of unconventional thought and independent action. I did not believe you had those qualities, although I studied you very carefully. I was unable to take you fully into my confidence.'

Parker's slim fingers evoked a fluent passage from the keyboard as though to punctuate his words, and for a moment he seemed completely enraptured by his own music, then he lifted his head again.

'If I had done so, then the conduct of your rescue operation of Flight 070 might have been completely different. I have been forced radically to revise my estimate of you, General Stride – and it was a difficult thing to do. For by demonstrating those qualities which I thought you lacked, you upset my judgement. I admit that personal chagrin swayed my reasoned judgement – and by the time I was thinking straight again you had been provoked into offering your resignation –'

'I know that the resignation was referred to you personally, Doctor Parker – and that you recommended that it be accepted.' Peter's voice was very cold, the tone clipped with controlled anger – and Parker nodded.

'Yes, you are correct. I endorsed your resignation.'

'Then it looks as though we are wasting our time here and now.' Peter's lips were compressed into a thin, unforgiving line, and the skin across his cheeks and over the finely chiselled flare of his nostrils seemed tightly drawn and pale as porcelain.

'Please, General Stride – let me explain first.' Parker reached out one hand to him as though to physically restrain him from rising, and his expression was earnest, compelling. Peter sank back into the couch, his eyes wary and his lips still tight.

'I have to go back a little first, in order to make any sense at all.' Parker stood up from the piano and crossed to the rack of pipes on the work table between the hi fi equipment. He selected one carefully, a meerschaum mellowed to the colour of precious amber. He blew through the empty pipe and then tramped back across the thick carpet to stand in front of Peter.

'Some months before the hijacking of 070 – six months to be precise, I had begun to receive hints that we were entering a new phase in the application of international terrorism. Only hints at first, but these were confirmed and followed by stronger evidence.' Parker was stuffing the meerschaum from a leather wallet as he spoke, now he zipped this closed and tossed it on to the piano top. 'What we were looking at was a consolidation of the forces of violence under some sort of centralized control – we were not sure what form this control was taking.' He broke off and studied Peter's expression, seemed to misinterpret it for utter disbelief, for he shook his head. 'Yes, I know it sounds far-fetched, but I will show you the files. There was evidence of meetings between known militant leaders and some other shadowy figures, perhaps the representatives of an Eastern government. We were not sure then, nor are we now. And immediately after this a complete change in the conduct and apparent motivation of militant activity. I do not really have to detail this for you. Firstly the systematic accumulation of immense financial reserves by the highly organized and carefully planned abduction of prominent figures, starting with the ministers of OPEC, then leading industrialists and financial figures –' Parker struck a match and puffed on his pipe and perfumed smoke billowed around his head. '– So that it appeared that the motivation had not really changed and was still entirely self gain or parochial political gain. Then there was the taking of 070. I had not confided in you before and once you were on your way to Johannesburg it was too late. I could do nothing more than try to control your actions by rather heavy-handed commands. I could not explain to you that we suspected that this was the leading wave of the new militancy, and that we must allow it to reveal as much as possible. It was a terrible decision, but I had to gamble a few human lives for vital information – and then you acted as I had believed you were incapable of acting.' Parker removed his pipe from his mouth and he smiled, when he smiled you could believe anything he said and forgive him for it, no matter how outrageous. 'I admit, General Stride, that my first reaction was frustrated rage. I wanted your head, and your guts too. Then suddenly I began using my own head instead. You had just proved you were the man I wanted, my soldier capable of unconventional thought and action. If you were discredited and cast adrift, there was just a chance that this new direction of militancy would recognize the same qualities in you that I had been forced to recognize. If I allowed you to ruin your career, and become an outcast – an embittered man, but one with vital skills and invaluable knowledge, a man who had proved he could be ruthless when it was necessary –' Parker broke off and made that gesture of appeal. '– I am sorry, General Stride, but I had to recognize the fact that you would be very attractive to –' he made an impatient gesture '– I do not have a name for them, shall we just call them "the enemy". I had to recognize the fact that you would be of very great interest to the enemy. I endorsed your resignation.' He nodded sombrely. 'Yes, I endorsed your resignation, and without your own knowledge you became an Atlas agent at large. It seemed perfect to me. You did not have to act a role – you believed it yourself. You were the outcast, the wronged and discredited man ripe for subversion.'

'I don't believe it,' Peter said flatly, and Parker went back to the work table, selected an envelope from a Japanese ceramic tray and brought it back to Peter.

It took Peter a few moments to realize that it was a Bank Statement – Crédit Suisse in Geneva – the account was in his name, and there were a string of deposits. No withdrawals or debits. Each deposit was for exactly the same amount, the net salary of a Major-General in the British Army.

'You see,' – Parker smiled – 'you are still drawing your Atlas salary. You are still one of us, Peter. And all I can say is that I am very sorry indeed that we had to subject you to the pretence – but it seems it was all worthwhile.'

Peter looked up at him again, not entirely convinced, but with the hostility less naked in his expression.

'What do you mean by that, Doctor Parker?'

'It seems that you are very much back in play again.'

'I am Sales Director for Northern Armaments Company,' he said flatly.

'Yes, of course, and Narmco is part of the Altmann Industrial Empire – and Baron Altmann and his lovely wife are, or rather were, an extraordinarily interesting couple. For instance, did you know that the Baron was one of the top agents of Mossad in Europe?'

'Impossible,' Peter shook his head irritably. 'He was a Roman Catholic. Israeli intelligence does not make a habit of recruiting Catholics.'

'Yes,' Parker agreed. 'His grandfather converted to Catholicism – and changed the name of the family home to La Pierre Bénite. It was a business decision, that we are certain of, there was not much profit in being Jewish in nineteenth-century France. However, the young Altmann was much influenced by his grandmother and his own mother. He was a Zionist from a very early age, and he unswervingly used his enormous wealth and influence in that cause – right up until the time of his murder. Yet he did it so cunningly, with such subtlety that very few people were aware of his connections with Judaism and Zionism. He never made the mistake of converting back to his ancestral religion, realizing that he could be more effective as a practising Christian.'

Peter was thinking swiftly. If this was true, then it all had changed shape again. It must affect the reasons for the Baron's death – and it would change the role of Magda Altmann in his life.

'The Baroness?' he asked. 'Was she aware of this?'

'Ah, the Baroness!' Kingston Parker removed his pipe from between his teeth, and smiled with reluctant admiration. 'What a remarkable lady. We are not certain of very much about her – except her beauty and her exceptional talents. We know she was born in Warsaw. Her father was a professor of medicine at the University there, and he escaped to the West when the Baroness was still a child. He was killed a few years later, a traffic accident in Paris. Hit and run driver, while the professor was leaving his faculty in the Sorbonne. A small mystery still hangs around his death. The child seems to have drifted from family to family, friends of her father, distant relatives. She already was showing academic leanings, musical talent, at thirteen a chess player of promise – then for a period there is no record of her. She seems to have disappeared entirely. The only hint is from one of her foster mothers, a very old lady now, with a fading memory. "I think she went home for a while – she told me she was going home."' Parker spread his hands. 'We do not know what that means. Home? Warsaw? Israel? Somewhere in the East?'

'You have researched her very carefully,' Peter said. What he had heard had left him uneasy.

'Of course, we have done so to every contact you have made since leaving Atlas Command. We would have been negligent not to do so – but especially we have been interested in the Baroness. She has been the most fascinating, you understand that, I am sure.'

Peter nodded, and waited. He did not want to ask for more. Somehow it seemed disloyal to Magda, distrustful and petty – but still he waited and Parker went on quietly.

'Then she was back in Paris. Nineteen years of age now – a highly competent private secretary, speaking five languages fluently, beautiful, always dressed in the height of fashion, soon with a string of wealthy, influential and powerful admirers – the last of these was her employer, Baron Aaron Altmann.' Parker was silent then, waiting for the question, forcing Peter to come to meet him.

'Is she Mossad also?'

'We do not know. It is possible – but she has covered herself very carefully. We are rather hoping you will be able to find that out for us.'

'I see.'

'She must have known that her husband was a Zionist. She must have suspected that it had something to do with his abduction and murder. Then there are the missing six years of her life – from thirteen to nineteen, where was she?'

'Is she Jewish?' Peter asked. 'Was her father Jewish?'

'We believe so, although the professor showed no interest in religion and did not fill in the question on his employment application to the Sorbonne. His daughter showed the same lack of religious commitment – we know only that her marriage to the Baron was a Catholic ceremony followed by a civil marriage in Rambouillet.'

'We have drifted a long way from international terrorism,' Peter pointed out.

'I do not think so.' Kingston Parker shook his big shaggy head. 'The Baron was a victim of it, and almost as soon as you – one of the world's leading experts on militancy and urban warfare – as soon as you are associated with her there is an assassination attempt, or an abduction attempt made on the Baroness.'

Peter was not at all surprised that Parker knew of that night on the road to La Pierre Bénite – it was only a few days since Peter's arm had been out of the sling.

'Tell me, Peter. What was your estimate of that affair? I have seen an excerpt of the statement that you made to the French police – but what can you add to that?'

Peter had a vivid cameo memory of the Citroën that had followed him out of Paris, and then almost simultaneously the tearing sound of automatic fire in the night.

'They were after the Baroness,' Peter said firmly.

'And you were driving her car?'

'That's right.'

'You were at the place at the time that the Baroness usually passed?'

'Right.'

'Who suggested that? You?'

'I told her that the car was too conspicuous.'

'So you suggested taking it down to La Pierre Bénite that night.'

'Yes.' Peter lied without knowing why he did so.

'Did anybody else know that the Baroness would not be driving?'

'Nobody.' Except her two bodyguards, the two chauffeurs who had met them on their return from Switzerland, Peter thought.

'You are certain?' Parker persisted.

'Yes,' Peter snapped. 'Nobody else.' Except Magda, only Magda. He pushed the thought aside angrily.

'All right, so we must accept that the Baroness was the target – but was it an assassination or an abduction attempt? That could be significant. If it was assassination, it would indicate that it was the elimination of a rival agent, that the Baroness was probably also a Mossad agent, recruited by her husband. On the other hand, an abduction would suggest that the object was monetary gain. Which was it, Peter?'

'They had blocked the road –' he said, but not completely, he remembered. 'And the police impersonator signalled me to stop –' or at least to slow down, he thought, slow down sufficiently to make an easy target before they started shooting '– and they did not open fire until I made it clear that I was not going to stop.' But they had been ready to begin shooting at the instant Peter made the decision to send the Maserati through the roadblock. The intention of the two machine-gunners had seemed evident. '– I would say the object was to seize the Baroness alive.'

'All right,' Parker nodded. 'We will have to accept that for the time being.' He glanced at Colin. 'Colonel Noble? You had a question?'

'Thank you, Doctor. We haven't heard from Peter in what terms he was approached by Narmco or the Baroness. Who made the first contact?'

'I was approached by a London firm who specializes in making top executive placements. They came directly from the Narmco Board –' And I turned them down flat, he thought. 'It was only later at Abbots Yew –'

'I see.' Colin frowned with disappointment. 'There was no question of a meeting with the Baroness?'

'Not at that stage.'

'You were offered the sales appointment – no mention of any other duties, security, industrial intelligence –'

'No, not then.'

'Later?'

'Yes. When I met the Baroness, I realized her personal security arrangements were inadequate. I made changes.'

'You never discussed her husband's murder?'

'Yes, we did.'

'And?'

'And nothing.' Peter was finding it difficult to improvise answers, but he used the old rule of telling as much of the truth as possible.

'There was no mention by the Baroness of a hunt for her husband's murderers? You were not asked to use your special talents to lead a vendetta?'

Peter had to make a swift decision. Parker would know of his leak to the British military attaché in Paris – the bait he had so carefully placed to attract Caliph. Of course Parker would know: he was head of Atlas with access to the Central Intelligence computer. Peter could not afford to deny it.

'Yes, she asked me to relay any information which might point to her husband's murderers. I asked G.2 in Paris for any information he might have. He couldn't help me.'

Parker grunted. 'Yes. I have a note that G.2 filed a routine report – but I suppose her request was natural enough.' He wandered back to his work table to glance at a pad on which was scribbled some sort of personal shorthand.

'We know of eight sexual liaisons that the Baroness formed prior to her marriage, all with politically powerful or wealthy men. Six of them married men –'

Peter found himself trembling with anger so intense that it surprised him. He hated Parker for talking like this of Magda. With a huge effort he kept his expression neutral, the hand in his lap was relaxed and the fingers spread out naturally, though he felt a driving desire to bunch it and drive it into Parker's face.

'– all these affairs were conducted with utmost discretion. Then during her marriage there is no evidence of any extra-marital activity. Since the Baron's murder there have been three others, a minister in the French Government, an American businessman – head of the world's second largest oil company –' He dropped the pad back on the desk and swung back to face Peter with a bright penetrating gaze. 'The lady certainly believes in mixing business with pleasure. All her partners have been men who are able to deliver very concrete proof of their affections. I think this rule probably applies to her latest choice of sexual partner.'

Colin Noble coughed awkwardly, and shifted in his chair, but Peter did not even glance at him, he went on staring impassively at Kingston Parker. He and Magda had made very little secret of their relationship – still it was bitterly distasteful to have to discuss it with anybody else.

'I think that you are in a position now to gather vital intelligence. I think that you are very near the centre of this nameless and formless influence – I think that you will be able to make some sort of contact with the enemy, even if it is only another military brush with them – the only question is whether or not you find any reason, emotional or otherwise, that might prevent you fulfilling this duty?' Kingston Parker cocked his head on one side, making the statement into a question.

'I have never let my private life interfere with my duty, Doctor,' Peter said quietly.

'No,' Kingston Parker agreed. 'That is true. And I am sure that now you know a little more about Baroness Altmann you will appreciate just how vital is our interest in that lady.'

'Yes, I do.' Peter had his anger under control completely. 'You want me to use a privileged relationship to spy on her. Is that correct?'

'Just as we can be sure she is using the same relationship to her own ends—' Parker broke off as an odd thought seemed to occur. 'I do hope I have not been too blunt, Peter, I haven't destroyed some cherished illusion.' Now Parker's attitude was dismissive. The interview was over.

'At my age, Doctor – a man has no more illusions.' Peter rose to his feet. 'Do I report to you direct?'

'Colonel Noble will make the arrangements for all communications.' Kingston Parker held out his hand. 'I would not have asked this of you if I had a choice.'

Peter did not hesitate, but took the hand. Parker's hand was cool and dry. Although he made no show of it, Peter could sense the physical power in those hard pianist's fingers.

'I understand, sir,' said Peter – and he thought grimly, and even if that is also a lie, I'm going to understand pretty damned soon.

Peter made the excuse of tiredness to avoid the gin-rummy game, and pretended to sleep during most of the long trans-Atlantic flight. With his eyes closed he tried to marshal his thoughts into some sort of pattern, but always they seemed to come around full circle and leave him chasing his tail. He could not even achieve any certainty about his feelings and loyalties to Magda Altmann. They seemed to keep changing shape every time he examined them, and he found himself brooding on irrelevancies. 'Sexual liaisons' – what a ridiculously stilted expression Parker had used, and why had it angered Peter so much. Eight liaisons before marriage, six with married men, two others since marriage – all wealthy or powerful. He found himself trying to flesh out these bare statistics, and with a shock of bitter resentment imagined those faceless, formless figures with the slim smooth body, the tiny, perfectly shaped breasts, and the long smoky fall of shimmering hair. He felt somehow betrayed, and immediately scorned himself for this adolescent reaction.

There were other more dire questions and chances that Kingston Parker had raised, the Mossad connection, the six missing years in Magda's life – and yet he came back again to what had happened between them. Was she capable of such skilful deception, or was it not deception? Was he merely suffering from hurt pride now, or somehow unbeknown to him had she been able to force him into a more vulnerable position? Had she succeeded in making him fall in love with her?

How did he feel about her? At last he had to face that question directly and try to answer it, but when they landed again he still had no answer, except that the prospect of seeing her again pleased him inordinately and the thought that she had deliberately used him to her own ends and was capable of discarding him as she had done those others left him with an aching sense of dismay. He dreaded the answer for which he had to search, and suddenly he remembeed her suggestion of an island to which they could escape together. He realized then that she was a victim of the same dread, and with a clairvoyant shudder he wondered if they were somehow preordained to destroy each other.

There were three separate messages from her at the Dorchester. She had left the Rambouillet number, each time. He telephoned immediately he reached the suite.

'Oh, Peter. I was so worried. Where were you?' And it was hard to believe her concern was faked, and it was even harder to discount the pleasure when the following noon, she met him at Charles de Gaulle Airport herself instead of sending a chauffeur.

'I needed to get out of the office for an hour,' she explained, and then she tucked her hand into the crook of his elbow and pressed herself against him. 'That's a lie, of course. I came because I couldn't wait the extra hour to see you.' Then she chuckled huskily. 'I am behaving shamelessly, I can't imagine what you must think of me!'

They were with a party of eight that evening, dinner at Le Doyen and then the theatre at the Palais de Chaillot. Peter's French was still not up to Molière, so he took his pleasure in surreptitiously watching Magda, and for a few hours he succeeded in suppressing all those ugly questions, only on the midnight drive back to La Pierre Bénite did he begin the next move in the complicated game.

'I couldn't tell you on the telephone –' he said in the intimate darkness and warmth of her limousine. 'I had an approach from Atlas. The head of Atlas summoned me to New York. That's where I was when you called. They are also on to Caliph.'

She sighed then, and her hand stole into his. 'I was waiting for you to tell me, Peter,' she said simply, and she sighed again. 'I knew you'd gone to America, and I had a terrible premonition that you were going to lie to me. I don't know what I would have done then.' And Peter felt a lance of conscience driven up under his ribs, and with it the throb of concern – she had known of his journey to New York, but how? Then he remembered her 'sources'.

'Tell me,' she said, and he told her – everything, except the nagging question marks which Kingston Parker had placed after her name. The missing years, the Mossad connection with the Baron, and those ten nameless men.

'They don't seem to know that Caliph uses that name,' Peter told her. 'But they seem to be pretty certain that you are hunting him, and that you've hired me for that purpose.'

They discussed it quietly as the small cavalcade of cars rushed through the night, and later when she came to his suite, they went on talking, holding each other as they whispered in the night, and Peter was surprised that he could act so naturally, that the doubts seemed to evaporate so easily when he was with her.

'Kingston Parker still has me as a member of Atlas,' Peter explained. 'And I did not deny it, nor protest. We want to find Caliph, and if I still have status with Atlas it will be useful, of that I am certain.'

'I agree. Atlas can help us – especially now that they are also aware that Caliph exists.'

They made love in the dawn, very deeply satisfying love that left bodies and minds replete, and then keeping her discretion she slipped away before it was light, but they met again an hour later for breakfast together in the Garden Room.

She poured coffee for him, and indicated the small parcel beside his plate.

'We aren't quite as discreet as we think we are, chéri.' She chuckled. 'Somebody seems to know where you are spending your evenings.'

He weighed the parcel in his right palm; it was the size of a roll of 35-mm film, wrapped in brown paper, sealed with red wax.

'Apparently it came special delivery yesterday evening.' She broke one of the crisp croissants into her plate, and smiled at him with that special slant of her green eyes.

The address was typed on a stick-on label, and the stamps were British, franked in south London the previous morning.

Suddenly Peter was assailed with a terrifying sense of foreboding; the presence of some immense overpowering evil seemed to pervade the gaily furnished room.

'What is it, Peter?' Her voice cracked with alarm.

'Nothing,' he said, 'It's nothing.'

'You suddenly went deadly pale, Peter. Are you sure you are all right?'

'Yes. I'm all right.'

He used his table knife to lift the wax seal and then unrolled the brown paper.

It was a small screw-topped bottle of clear glass, and the liquid it contained was clear also. Some sort of preservative, he realized immediately, spirits or formaldehyde.

Hanging suspended in the liquid was a soft white object.

'What is it?' Magda asked.

Peter felt cold tentacles of nausea closing around his stomach.

The object turned slowly, floating free in its bottle, and there was a flash of vivid scarlet.

'Does your mother allow you to wear nail varnish now, Melissa-Jane?' He heard the question echoed in his memory, and saw his daughter flirt her hands, and the scarlet flash of her nails. The same vivid scarlet.

'Oh yes – though not to school, of course. You keep forgetting I'm almost fourteen, Daddy.'

The floating white object was a human finger. It had been severed at the first joint, and the preservative had bleached the exposed flesh a sickly white. The skin had puckered and wrinkled like that of a drowned man. Only the painted fingernail was unaltered, pretty and festively gay.

The nausea caught Peter's throat, choking him and he heaved and retched drily as he stared at the tiny bottle.

The telephone rang three times before it was answered.

'Cynthia Barrow.' Peter recognized his ex-wife's voice, even though it was ragged with strain and grief.

'Cynthia, it's Peter.'

'Oh, thank God, Peter. I have been trying to find you for two days.'

'What is it?'

'Is Melissa-Jane with you, Peter?'

'No.' He felt as though the earth had lurched under his feet.

'She's gone, Peter. She's been gone for two nights now. I'm going out of my mind.'

'Have you informed the police?'

'Yes, of course.' The edge of hysteria was in her voice.

'Stay where you are,' Peter said. 'I'm coming to England right now, but leave any message for me at the Dorchester.' He hung up quickly, sensing that her grief would overflow at any moment and knowing that he could not handle it now.

Across the ormolu Louis Quatorze desk Magda was pale, tense, and she did not have to ask the question, it was in the eyes that seemed too large for her face.

He did not have to reply to that question. He nodded once, an abrupt jerky motion, and then he dialled again and while he waited he could not take his eyes from the macabre trophy that stood in its bottle in the centre of the desk.

'Colin Noble.' Peter snapped into the mouthpiece. 'Tell him it's General Stride and it's urgent.'

Colin came on within the minute. 'Peter, is that you?'

'They've taken Melissa-Jane.'

'Who? I don't understand.'

'The enemy. They've taken her.'

'Jesus God! Are you sure?'

'Yes, I'm sure. They sent me her finger in a bottle.'

Colin was silent for a few seconds, and then his voice was subdued. 'That's sick, Christ that's really sick.'

'Get on to the police. Use all your clout. They must be keeping quiet on it. There has been no publicity. I want to be in on the hunt for these animals. Get Thor involved, find out what you can. I'm on my way now. I'll let you know what flight I am on.'

'I'll keep a listening watch at this number round the clock,' Colin promised. 'And I'll have a driver meet you.' Colin hesitated. 'Peter, I'm sorry. You know that.'

'Yes, I know.'

'We will all be with you, all the way.'

Peter dropped the receiver on to its arm, and across the desk Magda stood up resolutely.

'I'll come with you to London,' she said, and Peter reached out and took her hand.

'No,' he said gently. 'Thank you, but no. There will be nothing for you to do.'

'Peter, I want to be with you through this terrible thing. I feel as though it's all my fault.'

'That's not true.'

'She's such a lovely child.'

'You will be more help to me here,' said Peter firmly. 'Try through all your sources, any little scrap of information.'

'Yes, very well.' She accepted the decision, without further argument. 'Where can I find you if I have anything?'

He gave her Colin Noble's private number at Thor, scribbling it on the pad beside the telephone. 'Either there or the Dorchester,' he said.

'At least I will come with you as far as Paris,' she said.

The news had broken by the time Peter landed at Heathrow Airport. It was on the front page of the *Evening Standard* and Peter snatched a copy off the news stand and read it avidly during the drive up to London.

> The victim was abducted at the front gate of her home in Leaden Street, Cambridge at eleven o'clock on Thursday. A neighbour saw her speak to the occupants of a maroon Triumph saloon car, and then enter the back door of the vehicle, which drove off immediately.
>
> 'I thought there were two people in the car,' Mrs Shirley Callon, 32, the neighbour, told our correspondent, 'and Melissa-Jane did not seem alarmed. She appeared to enter the Triumph quite willingly. I know that her father, who is a senior officer in the army, often sends different cars to fetch her or bring her home. So I thought nothing about it.'
>
> The alarm was not raised for nearly twenty-four hours, as the missing girl's mother also believed that she might be with her ex-husband.
>
> Only when she was unable to contact Major-General Stride, the

girl's father, did she inform the police. The Cambridge police found a maroon Triumph abandoned in the car park at Cambridge railway station. The vehicle had been stolen in London the previous day, and immediately a nationwide alert was put in force for the missing girl.

Chief-Inspector Alan Richards is the police officer in charge of the investigation and any person who may be able to provide information should telephone ...

There followed a London number and a detailed description of Melissa-Jane and the clothes she was wearing at the time she disappeared.

Peter crumpled the newspaper and dropped it on the seat. He sat staring ahead, cupping his anger to him like a flame, husbanding it carefully – because the heat was infinitely more bearable than the icy despair which waited to engulf him.

Chief-Inspector Alan Richards was a wiry little man, more like a jockey than a policeman. He had a prematurely wizened face, and he had combed long wisps of hair across his balding pate to disguise it. Yet his eyes were quick and intelligent, and his manner direct and decisive.

He shook hands when Colin Noble introduced them. 'I must make it very clear that this is a police matter, General. However, in these very special circumstances I am prepared to work very closely with the military.'

Swiftly Richards went over the ground he had already covered. He had mounted the investigation from the two offices set aside for him on the third floor of Scotland Yard, with a view over chimney pots of the spires of Westminster Abbey and the Houses of Parliament.

Richards had two young policewomen answering the telephone calls coming in through the number they had advertised in the Press and on television. So far they had accepted over four hundred of these. 'They range from long shots to the completely crazy, but we have to investigate all of them.' For the first time his expression softened. 'It's going to be a long, slow process, General Stride, but we have a few more leads to follow – come through.'

The inner office was furnished in the same nondescript Public Works Department furniture, solid and characterless, but there was a kettle boiling on the gas ring, and Richards poured the tea as he went on.

'Three of my men are taking the kidnap car to pieces. We are sure it is the right car. Your ex-wife has identified a purse found on the floor of the vehicle. It is you daughter's. We have lifted over six hundred fingerprints, and these are being processed. It will take some time until we can isolate each and hope for an identification of any alien prints. However, two of these correspond to prints lifted from your daughter's room – Sugar? Milk?'

Richards brought the cup to Peter as he went on.

'– The neighbour, Mrs Callon, who saw the pick-up, is working on an identikit portrait of the driver, but she did not get a very good view of him. That is a very long shot.'

Richards sipped his tea. 'However, we will show the final picture on television and hope for another lead from it. I am afraid that in cases like this, this is all we can do. Wait for a tip, and wait for the contact from the kidnappers. We do not expect the contact will be made through your ex-wife but of course we have a tap on her telephone and men watching over her.' Richards spread his hands. 'That's it, General Stride. Now it's your turn. What can you tell us? Why should anybody want to snatch your daughter?'

Peter exchanged a glance with Colin Noble, and was silent as he collected his thoughts, but Chief-Inspector Richards insisted quietly.

'I understand you are not a very wealthy man, General – but your family. Your brother?'

Peter dismissed the idea with a shake of his head. 'My brother has children of his own. They would be the more logical targets.'

'Vengeance? You were very active against the Provos in Ireland. You commanded the recapture of Flight 070.'

'It's possible.'

'You are no longer connected with the army, I understand.'

Peter was not going to be drawn further in that direction. 'I do not think this type of guesswork will profit us much. We will know the motive as soon as the kidnappers make their demands known.'

'That is true.' Richards rattled his teacup, a little nervous gesture. 'They could not have sent you her—' He broke off as he saw Peter's expression change. '– I'm sorry, General. It is horrible and terribly distressing, but we have to accept the finger as proof that your daughter is still alive and that the contact, when it comes, will be made to you. It was an expression of their earnest intention, and a threat – but—'

The telephone on his desk rang shrilly and Richards snatched it up.

'Richards!' he snapped, and then listened at length, occasionally grunting encouragement to the caller. When he hung up the receiver he did not speak immediately, but offered Peter a rumpled pack of cigarettes. When Peter refused, the policeman lit one himself and his voice was diffident.

'That was the laboratory. You know your daughter was a white cell donor, don't you?'

Peter nodded. It was part of Melissa-Jane's social commitment. If she had not been tactfully dissuaded, she would have donated her blood and marrow by the bucketful.

'We were able to get a tissue typing from the Cambridge hospital. The amputated finger matches your daughter's tissue type. I'm afraid we must accept that it is hers – I cannot imagine that the kidnappers would have gone to the lengths of finding a substitute of the same type.'

Peter had been secretly cherishing the belief that it was a bluff. That he had been sent the fingertip from a corpse, from a medical sample, from the casualty ward of a city hospital – and now as that hope died he was assailed by the cold spirit-sapping waves of despair. They sat in silence for fully a minute, and now it was Colin Noble who broke it.

'Inspector, you are aware of the nature of the Thor Command?'

'Yes, of course. There was great deal of publicity at the time of the Johannesburg hijacking. It is an anti-terrorist unit.'

'We are probably the most highly trained specialists in the world at removing hostages safely from the hands of militants—'

'I understand what you are trying to tell me, Colonel,' Richards murmured drily. 'But let us track down our militants first, and then any rescue attempts will be entirely under the control of the Commissioner of Police.'

It was after three o'clock in the morning when Peter Stride checked in with the night receptionist at the Dorchester Hotel in Park Lane.

'We have been holding your suite since midday, General.'

'I'm sorry.' Peter found himself slurring his words, exhaustion and nervous strain, he realized. He had only left Police Headquarters when he could convince himself that everything possible was being done, and that he could place complete trust in Chief-Inspector Richards and his team. He had Richards's solemn undertaking that he would be informed, no matter at what time of day or night, as soon as there was any new development.

Now he signed the register, blinking at the gritty swollen feeling of his eyelids.

'There are these messages for you, General.'

'Thank you again, and goodnight.'

In the elevator he glanced at the mail the clerk had given him.

The first was a telephone slip.

'Baroness Altmann asks you to return her call to either Paris or Rambouillet number.'

The second was another telephone slip.

'Mrs Cynthia Barrow called. Please call her at Cambridge 699–313.'

The third was a sealed envelope, good-quality white paper, undistinguished by crest or monogram.

His name had been printed in capitals, very regular lettering, an old-fashioned copperplate script. No stamp, so it would have been delivered by hand.

Peter split the flap with his thumb, and withdrew a single sheet of lined writing paper, again good but undistinguished. There would be a stack of these sheets in any stationery department throughout the United Kingdom.

The writing was the same regular, unnatural script, so that Peter realized that the writer had used a stencil to form each letter, one of those clear plastic cutout stencils obtainable from any toy store or stationery department. A completely effective method of disguising handwriting.

> A finger you have already, next you will have the hand, then another hand, then a foot, then another foot – and at last the head.
>
> The next package will arrive on 20th April, and there will be another delivery every seven days.
>
> To prevent this you must deliver a life for a life. The day Dr Kingston

> Parker dies, your daughter will return to you immediately, alive and suffering no further harm.
>
> Destroy this letter and tell nobody, or the head will be delivered immediately.

The letter was signed with the name which had come to loom so largely in Peter's life:

'CALIPH'

The shock of it seemed to reach to the extremities of his soul. To see the name written. To have complete confirmation of all the evil that they had suspected, to see the mark of the beast deeply printed and unmistakable.

The shock was made greater, almost unbearable, by the contents of the letter. Peter found that such cruelty, such utter ruthlessness, tested his credibility to its limits.

The letter was fluttering in his hands, and he realized with a start of surprise that he was shaking like a man in high fever. The porter carrying his black crocodile valise was staring at him curiously, and it required a huge physical effort to control his hands and fold the sheet of white paper.

He stood rigidly, as though on the parade ground, until the elevator door opened and then he marched stiffly down the passage to his suite. He gave the porter a banknote, without glancing at it, and the moment the latch clicked closed, he unfolded the sheet again, and standing in the centre of the living-room floor scanned the stilted script again, and then again until the words seemed to melt together and lose coherence and meaning.

He realized that for the first time in his life he was in complete panic, that he had lost all resolution and direction.

He took a deep breath and closed his eyes, counting slowly to one hundred, emptying his mind completely, and then giving himself the command:

'Think!'

All right, Caliph knew his movements intimately. Even to when he was expected at the Dorchester. Who knew that? Cynthia, Colin Noble, Magda Altmann and the secretary at Rambouillet who had made the reservation, Colin's secretary at Thor, the Dorchester staff, and anybody else who had made even an idle study of Peter's movements would know he always stayed at the Dorchester. That was a cul-de-sac.

'Think!'

Today was April fourth. There were sixteen days before Caliph sent him Melissa-Jane's severed hand. He felt the panic mounting again, and he forced it back.

'Think!'

Caliph had been watching him, studying him in detail, assessing his value. Peter's value was that he could move unsuspected in high places. He could reach the head of Atlas by simply requesting an audience. More than that, he could probably get access to any head of state if he wanted it badly enough.

For the first time in his life Peter felt the need for liquor. He crossed quickly to the cabinet and fumbled with the key. A stranger's face stared at him out of the gilt-framed mirror above it. The face was pale, haggard, with deep parentheses framing the mouth. There were plum-coloured bruises of fatigue below the eyes, and the gaunt, bony jaw was gun-metal blue with new beard – and the sapphire blue of the eyes had a wild deranged glitter. He looked away from his own image. It only increased his sense of unreality.

He poured half a tumbler of Scotch whisky, and drank half of it straight off. He coughed at the sting of the liquor and a drop of it broke from the corner of his mouth and trickled down his chin. He wiped it away with his thumb, and turned back to study the sheet of white paper again. It was crumpled already, where he had gripped it too hard. He smoothed it carefully.

'Think!' he told himself. This was how Caliph worked, then. Never exposing himself. Picking his agents with incredible attention to detail. Fanatics, like the girl, Ingrid who had led the taking of Flight 070. Trained assassins, like the man he had killed in the river at La Pierre Bénite. Experts in high places, like General Peter Stride. Studying them, assessing them and their capabilities, and finally finding their price.

Peter had never believed the old law that every man has his price. He had believed himself above that general rule. Now he knew he was not – and the knowledge sickened him.

Caliph had found his price, found it unerringly. Melissa-Jane, suddenly Peter had a vivid memory of his daughter on horseback, swivelling in the saddle to laugh and call back to him.

'Super-Star!' And the sound of her laughter on the wind.

Peter shivered, and without realizing it he crumpled the sheet of paper to a ball in his fist.

Ahead of him he saw the road that he was destined to follow. With a new flash of insight, he realized that he had already taken his first steps along the road. He had done so when he had put the gun to the blonde killer in the terminal of Johannesburg Airport, when he had made himself judge and executioner.

Caliph had been responsible for that first step on the road to corruption, and now it was Caliph who was driving him farther along it.

With a sudden prophetic glimpse ahead, Peter knew it would not end with the life of Kingston Parker. Once he was committed to Caliph, it would be for ever – or until one of them, Peter Stride, or Caliph, was completely destroyed.

Peter drank the rest of the whisky in the tumbler.

Yes, Melissa-Jane was his price. Caliph had made the correct bid. Nothing else would have driven him to it.

Peter picked the booklet of matches off the liquor cabinet and like a sleepwalker moved through to the bathroom. He twisted the sheet of paper into a taper and lit the end of it, holding it over the toilet bowl. He held it until the flame scorched his fingers painfully, then dropped it into the bowl and flushed the ash away.

He went back into the lounge, and refilled the glass with whisky. He picked the comfortable armchair below the window and sank into it. Only then did he realize how very weary he was. The nerves in his thighs quivered and twitched uncontrollably.

He thought about Kingston Parker. A man like that had an incalculable amount to offer mankind. It will have to look like an assassination attempt aimed at me, Peter thought. One that finds the wrong victim.

'A bomb,' Peter thought. He hated the bomb. Somehow it seemed to be the symbol of the senseless violence which he hated. He had seen it used in Ireland and in London town, and he hated it. The undirected destruction, mindless, merciless.

'It will have to be a bomb,' he decided, and with surprise he found that his hatred had found a new target. Again for the first time ever, he hated himself for what he was going to do.

Caliph had won. He knew that against an adversary of that calibre there was no chance they would find where Melissa-Jane was hidden. Caliph had won, and Peter Stride sat the rest of the night planning an act which he had dedicated his life, until then, to prevent.

'I cannot understand why we haven't had the demand contact yet.' Chief-Inspector Richards ran his hand distractedly across his pate, disturbing the feathery wisps that covered it and leaving them standing out at a startled angle. 'It's five days now. Still no demands.'

'They know where to contact Peter,' Colin Noble agreed. 'The interview he gave covered that.'

Peter Stride had appeared on BBC TV to broadcast an appeal to the kidnappers not to maim his daughter further, and to the general public to offer any information that might lead to her rescue.

On the same programme they had displayed the police identikit portrait of the driver of the maroon Triumph prepared by the one witness.

The response had been overwhelming, jamming the switchboard at Chief-Inspector Richards's special headquarters, and a mixed bag had fallen into the net.

A fourteen-year-old runaway had the police barge into the Bournemouth apartment where she was in bed with her thirty-two-year-old lover. She was returned weeping bitterly to the bosom of her family, and had again disappeared within twenty-four hours.

In North Scotland the police sadly bungled a raid on a remote cottage hired by a man with the same lank dark hair and gunfighter's moustache as the identikit portrait. He turned out to be a cottage-industry manufacturer of LSD tablets, and he and his four assistants, one of them a young girl who vaguely fitted the description of Melissa-Jane in that she was female and blonde, had scattered across the Highlands before being overtaken and borne to earth by sweating pounding members of the Scottish Constabulary.

Peter Stride was furious. 'If it had been Melissa-Jane, they would have had fifteen minutes in which to put her down—' He raged at Richards. 'You've got to let Thor go in to the next raid.'

Through the Thor communications net he spoke directly to Kingston Parker on the video screens.

' – We'll put all our influence into it,' Parker agreed, and then with deep compassion in his eyes, 'Peter, I'm living every minute of this with you. I cannot escape the knowledge that I have placed you into this terrible situation. I did not expect the attack would come through your daughter. I think you know that you can call on me for any support you need.'

'Thank you, sir,' said Peter and for a moment felt his resolve weaken. In ten days he would have to execute this man. He steeled himself by thinking of a puckered dead-white finger floating in its tiny bottle.

Kingston Parker's influence worked immediately. Six hours later the order came down from Downing Street via the Commissioner of Police, that the next raid on a suspect hideout would be conducted by Thor Command.

The Royal Air Force placed two helicopters at Thor's disposal for the duration of the operation, and Thor's assault unit went into intensive training for penetration and removal under urban conditions. Peter trained with them, he and Colin swiftly re-establishing the old rapport of concerted action.

When they were not practising and refining the exit and assembly from the hovering helicopters, Peter spent much of his time in the enclosed pistol range, trying to drown his awareness in the crash of gunfire, but the days passed swiftly in a series of false alarms and misleading clues.

Each night when Peter examined his face in the mirror above the liquor cabinet, it was more haggard, the blue eyes muddied by fatigue and terrible gut-eroding terror of what the next day might bring forth.

There were six days left when Peter left the hotel room before breakfast, caught the tube at Green Park and left it again at Finsbury Park. In a garden supplies shop near the station he purchased a twenty-pound plastic bag of ammonium nitrate garden fertilizer. He carried it back to the Dorchester in a locked Samsonite suitcase and stored it in the closet behind his hanging trenchcoat.

That night, when he spoke to Magda Altmann, she pleaded once again to be allowed to come to London.

'Peter, I know I can be of help to you. Even if it's just to stand beside you and hold your hand.'

'No. We've been over that.' He could hear the brutal tone in his own voice, but could not control it. He knew that he was getting very close to the edge. 'Have you heard anything?'

'I'm sorry, Peter. Nothing, absolutely nothing. My sources are doing all that is possible.'

Peter bought the dieseline from a pump at the Lex Garage in Brewer Street. He took five litres in a plastic screw-topped container that had contained a household detergent. The pump attendant was a pimply teenager in dirty overalls. He was completely uninterested in the transaction.

In his bathroom Peter worked on the dieseline and the nitrate from the garden shop. He produced twenty-one pounds of savagely weight-efficent high explosive that was, none the less, docile until activated by a blasting cap – such as he had devised with a flashlight bulb.

It would completely devastate the entire suite, utterly destroying everybody and everything in it. However, the damage should be confined to those three rooms.

It would be a simple matter to lure Kingston Parker to the suite under the pretence of having urgent information about Caliph to deliver, information so critical it could only be delivered in person and in private.

That night the face in the mirror above the liquor cabinet was that of a man suffering from a devouring terminal disease, and the whisky bottle was empty. Peter broke the seal on a fresh bottle, it would make it easier to sleep, he told himself.

The wind came off the Irish Sea like the blade of a harvester's scythe, and the low lead-coloured cloud fled up the slopes of the Wicklow hills ahead of it.

There were weak patches in the cloud layer through which a cold and sickly sun beamed swiftly across the green forested slopes. As it passed so the rain followed – icy grey rain slanting in on the wind.

A man came up the deserted street of the village. The tourists had not yet begun the annual invasion, but the 'Bed and Breakfast' signs were already out to welcome them on the fronts of the cottages.

The man passed the pub, in its coat of shocking salmon pink paint – and lifted his head to read the billboard above the empty car park. 'Black is Beautiful – drink Guinness' it proclaimed, and the man did not smile but lowered his head and trudged on over the bridge that divided the village in two.

On the stone balustrades of the bridge a midnight artist had used an aerosol paint can to spray political slogans in dayglo colours.

'BRITS OUT' on the left-hand balustrade and 'STOP H BLOCK TORTURE' on the other. This time the man grimaced sourly.

Below him the steely grey water boiled about the stone piers before hissing on down towards the sea.

The man wore a cyclist's plastic cape and a narrow-brimmed tweed cap pulled down over his eyes. The wind dashed at him, flogging the skirts of the cape against his Wellington boots.

He seemed to cringe to the wind, hunching down against its cold fury, as he trudged on past the few buildings of the village. The street was deserted, though the man knew that he was being watched from curtained windows.

This village on the lower slopes of the Wicklow hills, a mere thirty miles from Dublin, would not have been his choice. Here isolation worked against them, making them conspicuous. He would have preferred the anonymity of the city. However, his preferences had never been asked for.

This was only the third time he had left the house since they had arrived. Each time it had been for some emergency provision, something that a little more forethought might have prevented, which should have been included when the old house was stocked for their stay. That came from having to rely on a drinking man, but here again he had not been consulted.

He was discontented and in a truculent, smouldering mood. It had rained most of the time, and the oil-fired central heating was not working, the only heating was the smoking peat fires in the small fireplaces in each of the two big rooms they were using. The high ceilings and sparse furnishings had made the rooms more difficult to warm – and he had been cold ever since they had arrived. They were using only the two rooms, and had left the rest of the house locked and shuttered. It was a gloomy building, with the smell of damp pervading it. He had only the company of a whining alcoholic, day after cold rainy day. The man was ripe and over-ripe for trouble, for any diversion to break the grinding monotony – but now he was reduced to errand boy and house servant, roles for which he was unsuited by temperament and training, and he scowled darkly as he trudged over the bridge towards the village store, with its row of petrol pumps standing before it like sentries.

The storekeeper saw him coming, and called through into the back of the shop.

'It's himself from down at the Old Manse.'

His wife came through, wiping her hands on her apron, a short plump woman with bright eyes and ready tongue.

'City people have no more sense than they need, out in this weather.'

'Sure and it's not baked beans nor Jamieson whisky he's after buying.'

Speculation about the new occupant of the Old Manse had swiftly become one of the village's main diversions, with regular bulletins broadcast by the girl on the local telephone exchange – two overseas telephone calls, by the postman – no mail deliveries, by the dustman – the disposals into the dustbins were made up mainly of empty Heinz baked beans cans and Jamieson whisky bottles.

'I still think he's from the trouble up north,' said the shopkeeper's wife. 'He's got the look and the sound of an Ulster man.'

'Hush, woman.' Her husband cautioned her. 'You'll bring bad luck upon us. Get yourself back into the kitchen now.'

The man came in out of the rain and swept the tweed cap off his head, beating the water from it against the jamb of the door. He had black straight hair, cut into a ragged fringe above the dark Irish visage and fierce eyes, like those of a falcon when first the leather hood is slipped.

'The top of the morning to you, Mr Barry,' the shopkeeper greeted him heartily. 'Like as not it will stop raining, before it clears.'

The man they knew as Barry grunted, and as he slipped the waterproof cape from his shoulders, swept the cluttered interior of the little general dealer's store with a quick, all-embracing glance.

He wore a rough tweed jacket over a cable-stitched jersey and brown corduroys tucked into the top of the Wellington boots.

'You finished writing on your book, have you?' Barry had told the milkman that he was writing a book about Ireland. The Wicklow hills were a stronghold of the literary profession, there were a dozen prominent or eccentric writers living within twenty miles, taking advantage of Ireland's tax concessions to writers and artists.

'Not yet,' Barry grunted, and went across to the shelves nearest the till. He made a selection of half a dozen items and laid them on the worn counter top.

'When it's good and wrote I'm going to ask the library to keep a copy for me,' the shopkeeper promised, as though that was exactly what a writer would want to hear, and began to ring up the purchases on his register.

Barry's upper lip was still unnaturally smoother and paler than the rest of his face. He had shaved away the dark droopy moustache the day before arriving in the village, and at the same time had cut the fringe of hair that hung almost to his eyes.

The shopkeeper picked up one of the purchases and looked inquiringly at Barry, but when the dark Irish face remained impassive and he volunteered no explanation, the shopkeeper dropped his eyes self-consciously and rang up the package with the other purchases and dropped it into a paper carrier.

'That will be three pounds twenty pence,' he said, and closed the cash drawer with a clang, waiting while Barry slung the cape over his shoulders and adjusted the tweed cap.

'God be with you then, Mr Barry.'

There was no reply and the shopkeeper watched him set off back across the bridge before he called his wife again.

'He's a surly one, all right, he is.'

'He's got him a girlfriend down there.' The shopkeeper was bursting with the importance of his discovery. 'He's up to a nice little bit of hanky-panky.'

'How do you know that?'

'He was after buying woman's things – you know.' He hooded a knowing eye.

'No, I don't know.' His wife insisted.

'For the curse – you know. Women's things,' and his wife glowed with the news and began to untie her apron.

'You're sure now?' she demanded.

'Would I ever be lying to you?'

'I think I'll go across to Mollie for a cuppa tea,' said his wife eagerly; the news would make her the woman of the hour throughout the village.

The man they knew as Barry trudged into the narrow, high-walled lane that led up to the Old Manse. It was only the heavy boots and voluminous cape that gave him a clumsy gait, for he was a lithe, lean man in prime physical condition, and under the brim of his cap the eyes were never still, hunter's eyes probing and darting from side to side.

The wall was twelve feet high, the stonework blotched with silver-grey lichen, and although it was cracked and sagging at places, yet it was still substantial and afforded complete privacy and security to the property beyond.

At the end of the lane there was a pair of rotten and warping double doors, but the lock was a bright new brass Yale and the cracks in the wood and the gaping seams had been covered with fresh white strips of pine so that it was impossible to see into the interior of the garage.

Barry unlocked the brass Yale lock and slipped through, pulling the latch closed behind him.

There was a dark-blue Austin saloon car parked facing the doors for immediate departure. It had been stolen in Ulster two weeks before, resprayed and fitted with a roof rack to alter its appearance, and with new licence plates. The engine had been tuned and checked and Barry had paid nearly twice its market value.

Now he slipped behind the wheel and turned the key in the ignition. The engine fired and caught immediately. He grunted with satisfaction, seconds could mean the difference between success and failure, and in his life failure and death were synonymous. He listened to the engine beat for half a minute, checking the oil pressure and fuel gauges before switching off the engine again and going out through the rear door of the garage into the overgrown kitchen yard.

The old house had the sad unloved air of approaching dereliction. The fruit trees in the tiny orchard were sick with fungus diseases and surrounded by weed banks.

The thatch roof was rotten-green with moss, and the windows were blindman's eyes, unseeing and uncaring.

Barry let himself in through the kitchen door and dropped his cape and cap on the scullery floor and set the carrier on the draining board of the sink. Then he reached into the cutlery drawer and brought out a pistol. It was British officer's service pistol, had in fact been taken during a raid on a British Army arsenal in Ulster three years previously.

Barry checked the handgun with the expertise of long familiarity and then thrust it into his belt. He had felt naked and vulnerable for the short time that he was without the weapon – but he had reluctantly decided not to risk carrying it in the village.

Now he tapped water into the kettle, and at the sound a voice called through from the dim interior.

'Is that you?'

'None other,' Barry answered drily, and the other man came through and stood in the doorway to the kitchen.

He was a thin, stooped man in his fifties with the swollen inflamed face of the very heavy drinker.

'Did you get it?' his voice was husky and rough with whisky, and he had a seedy run-down air, a day's stubble of grey hairs that grew at angles on the blotchy skin.

Barry indicated the package on the sink.

'It's all there, doctor.'

'Don't call me that, I'm not a doctor any more,' the man snapped irritably.

'Oh, but you are a damned fine one. Ask the girls who dropped their bundles—'

'Leave me alone, damn you.'

Yes, he had been a damn fine doctor. Long ago, before the whisky, now however it was the abortions and the gunshot wounds of fugitives, and jobs like this one. He did not like to think about this one. He crossed to the sink and sorted through the packages.

'I asked you for adhesive tape,' he said.

'They had none. I brought the bandage.'

'I cannot—' the man began, but Barry whirled on him savagely, his face darkening with angry blood.

'I've had a gutsful of your whining. You should have brought what you needed, not sent me to get it for you.'

'I did not expect the wound—'

'You didn't expect anything but another dram of Jamiesons, man. There is no adhesive tape. Now get on with it and tie the bitch's hand up with the bandage.'

The older man backed away swiftly, picked up the packages and shuffled through into the other room.

Barry made the tea and poured it into the thick china mug, spooned in four spoons of sugar and stirred noisily, staring out of the smeared panes. It was raining again. He thought that the rain and the waiting would drive him mad.

The doctor came back into the kitchen, carrying a bundle of linen soiled with blood and the yellow ooze of sepsis.

'She is sick,' he said. 'She needs drugs, antibiotics. The finger—'

'Forget it,' said Barry.

From the other room there was a long-drawn-out whimper, followed by the incoherent gabble of a young girl deep in the delirium induced by fever and hypnotic drugs.

'If she is not taken to proper care, I won't be responsible.'

'You'll be responsible,' Barry told him heavily. 'I'll see to that.'

The doctor dropped the bundle of linen into the sink and let the water run over it.

'Can I have a drink now?' he asked.

Barry made a sadistic display of consulting his watch.

'No. Not yet,' he decided.

The doctor poured soapflakes into the sink.

'I don't think I can do the hand,' he whispered, shaking his head. 'The finger was bad enough – but I can't do the hand.'

'You'll do the hand,' said Barry. 'Do you hear me, you whisky-guzzling old wreck? You'll do the hand, and anything else I tell you to do.'

Sir Steven Stride offered a reward of fifty thousand pounds to anyone giving information that led to the recovery of his niece, and the offer was widely reported on television and in the press with reprints of the identikit portrait. It led to a revival of the flagging public interest in the case.

Chief-Inspector Richards had been able to reduce his telephone answering staff to one the last few days, but with the renewed spate of informers and speculators, he had to ask for the other policewoman to return to the third floor, and he had two sergeants processing the material that flowed in.

'I feel like Littlewoods,' he growled to Peter. 'Everybody taking a ticket on the pools, or getting his threepence worth of advertising.' He picked up another message slip. 'Here is another claim for responsibility – The Democratic People's Party for the Liberation of Hong Kong – have we ever heard of them before?'

'No, sir.' The senior sergeant looked up from his lists. 'But that makes one hundred and forty-eight confessions or claims for responsibility so far.'

'And 'Enry the Eighth was on again half an hour ago.' One of the girls at the switchboard turned and smiled around her mouthpiece. 'Hasn't missed a day.'

'Enry the Eighth was a sixty-eight-year-old pensioner who lived in a council estate in South London. His hobby was confessing to the latest spectacular crime from rape to bank robbery, and he called regularly every morning.

'Come and get me,' he challenged each time. 'But I warn you I won't come peaceful like—' When the local constable had made a courtesy call, while on his regular beat, 'Enry the Eighth had his suitcase packed and ready to go. His disappointment was heartrending when the bobby tactfully explained that they weren't going to arrest him, but when the bobby assured him that they would be keeping him under close surveillance as the Commissioner considered him a very dangerous man, he brightened up considerably and offered the constable a cup of tea.

'The trouble is we dare not dismiss any of it, even the real loonies, it all has to be checked out,' Richards sighed, and motioned Peter to go through to the inner office.

'Still nothing?' Richards asked. It was an unnecessary question. They had a tap on his telephone, at the hotel and at Thor Headquarters, to record any contact from the kidnappers.

'No, nothing,' Peter lied, but the lie had become easy now – just as he had learned to accept whatever else was necessary for Melissa-Jane's release.

'I don't like it, General. I really don't like the fact that there has been no attempt to contact you. I don't want to be despondent, but every day of silence makes it look more like an act of vengeance—' Richards broke off and covered his embarrassment by lighting a cigarette. 'Yesterday the Deputy-Commissioner telephoned me. He wanted my opinion as to how much longer I thought it necessary to maintain this special unit.'

'What did you tell him?' Peter asked.

'I told him that if we did not have some firm evidence within ten days, at least some sort of demand from the kidnappers – then I would have to believe that your daughter was no longer alive.'

'I see.' Peter felt a fatalistic calm. He knew. He was the only one who knew. There were four days to Caliph's deadline, he had worked out his timetable. Tomorrow morning he would request his urgent meeting with

Kingston Parker. He expected it would take less than twelve hours to arrange it, he would make it too attractive for Parker to refuse.

Parker would have to come, but against the remote possibility that he did not, Peter had left himself three clear days before the deadline in which to put into action his alternative plan. This would mean going to Kingston Parker. The first plan was the better, the more certain – but if it failed, Peter would accept any risk.

Now he realized that he had been standing in the centre of Richards's office, staring vacantly at the wall above the little inspector's head. He started as he realized the Richards was staring at him with a mingling of pity and concern.

'I am sorry, General. I understand how you feel – but I cannot keep this unit functioning indefinitely. We just do not have enough people—'

'I understand.' Peter nodded jerkily, and wiped his face with an open hand. It was a weary, defeated gesture.

'General, I think you should see your doctor. I really do.' Richards's voice was surprisingly gentle.

'That won't be necessary – I'm just a little tired.'

'A man can take just so much.'

'I think that's what these bastards are relying on,' Peter agreed. 'But I'll be all right.'

From the next door office there was the almost constant tinkle of telephone bells, and the murmur of female voices as the two policewomen answered the incoming stream of calls. It had become a steady background effect, so that when the call for which they had prayed and pleaded and waited finally came, neither of the two men was aware of it, and there was no excitement on the switchboard.

The two girls sat side by side on swivel stools in front of the temporary switchboard. The blonde girl was in her middle twenties, she was pretty and pert, with big round breasts buttoned primly under her blue uniform jacket. The blonde hair was twisted into a bun at the back of her neck to free her ears, but the headset made her appear older and businesslike.

The bell pinged and a panel lit in front of her, she plugged in the switch and spoke into the headset.

'Good morning. This is the Police Special Information Unit—' She had a pleasant middle-class accent, but was unable to keep the trace of boredom out of it. She had been on this job for twelve days now. There was the warning tone of a public telephone and then the click of small change fed into the slot.

'Can you hear me?' The accent was foreign.

'Yes, sir.'

'Listen carefully. Gilly O'Shaughnessy has her—' No, it was an imitation, the foreign accent slipped a little with the pronunciation of the name.

'Gilly O'Shaughnessy,' the police girl repeated.

'That's right. He's holding her at Laragh.'

'Spell that, please.' Again the accent slipped as the man spelled the name.

'And where is that, sir?'

'County Wicklow, Ireland.'

'Thank you, sir. What is your name, please?'

There was the click of a broken connection and the hum of the dialling tone. The girl shrugged, and scribbled the message on the pad before her, glancing at her wristwatch simultaneously.

'Seven minutes to tea time,' she said. 'Roll on death, battle with the angels.' She tore the sheet off the pad and passed it over her shoulder to the burly, curly-headed sergeant who sat behind her.

'I'll buy you a sticky bun,' he promised.

'I'm on a diet,' she sighed.

'That's daft, you look a treat—' The sergeant broke off. '—Gilly O'Shaughnessy. Why do I know that name?'

The older sergeant looked up sharply.

'Gilly O'Shaughnessy?' he demanded. 'Let me see that.' And he snatched the sheet, scanning it swiftly, his lips moving as he read the message. Then he looked up again.

'You know the name because you've seen it on the wanted posters, and heard it on telly. Gilly O'Shaughnessy, strewth man, he's the one who bombed the Red Lion at Leicester, and shot the Chief Constable in Belfast.'

The curly-headed policeman whistled softly. 'This looks like a hot one. A real hot one—' But his colleague was already barging into the inner office without the formality of knocking.

Richards had the connection to the Dublin police within seven minutes.

'Impress upon them that there must be no attempt—' Peter fretted, while they waited, and Richards cut him short.

'All right, General. Leave this to me. I understand what has to be done—' At that moment the Dublin connection was made, and Richards was transferred quickly to a Deputy-Commissioner. He spoke quietly and earnestly for nearly ten minutes before he replaced the receiver.

'They will use the local constabulary, not to waste time in sending a man down from Dublin. I have their promise that no approach will be made if a suspect is located.'

Peter nodded his thanks. 'Laragh,' he said. 'I have never heard of it. It cannot have a population of more than a few hundred.'

'I've sent for a map.' Richards told him, and when it came they studied it together.

'It's on the slopes of the Wicklow hills – ten miles from the coast—' And that was about all there was to learn from the large-scale map.

'We'll just have to wait for the Dublin police to call back—'

'No,' Peter shook his head. 'I want you to call them again, and ask them to contact the surveyor-general. He must have trig maps of the village, aerial photographs, street layouts. Ask them to get them down with a driver to Enniskerry Airfield—'

'Should we do that now? What if this turns out to be another false alarm?'

'We'll have wasted a gallon of petrol and the driver's time—' Peter was no longer able to sit still, he jumped out of the chair and began to pace restlessly about the office, it was too small for him suddenly, he felt as though he were on the point of suffocation. 'I don't think it is, however. I have the smell of it. The smell of the beast.'

Richards looked startled and Peter deprecated the exaggerated phrase with a dismissive gesture. 'A manner of speech,' he explained, and then stopped as a thought struck him. 'The helicopters will have to refuel, they haven't got the range to make it in one hop, and they are so bloody slow!' He paused and reached a decision, then leaned across Richards's desk to pick up the telephone and dialled Colin Noble's private number at Thor.

'Colin.' He spoke curtly with the tension that gripped him like a mailed fist. 'We've just had a contact. It's still unconfirmed, but it looks the best yet.'

'Where?' Colin broke in eagerly.

'Ireland.'

'That's to hell and gone.'

'Right, what's the flight time for the whirly birds to reach Enniskerry?'

'Stand by.' Peter heard him talking to somebody else – probably one of the RAF pilots. He came back within the minute.

'They will have to refuel en route—'

'Yes?' Peter demanded impatiently.

'Four and a half hours,' Colin told him.

'It's twenty past ten now – almost three o'clock before they reach Enniskerry. With this weather it will be dark before five.' Peter thought furiously; if they sent the Thor team all the way to Ireland on a false trail – and while they were there the correct contact was made in Scotland, or Holland or—

'It's got the smell. It's got to be right,' he told himself, and took a deep breath. He could not order Colin Noble to go to Bravo. Peter was no longer commander of Thor.

'Colin,' he said. 'I think this is it. I have the deep-down gut feel for it. Will you trust me and go to Bravo now? If we wait even another half hour we'll not get Melissa-Jane out before nightfall – if she is there.'

There was a long silence, broken only by Colin Noble's light quick breath.

'Hell, it can only cost me my job,' he said easily at last. 'Okay, Pete Baby, it's Bravo, we'll be airborne in five minutes. We'll pick you up from the helipad in fifteen minutes; be ready.'

The cloud was breaking up, but the wind was still bitter and spiteful, and up on the exposed helipad it cut cruelly through Peter's trench coat, blazer and rollneck jersey. They looked out across the churned surface of the Thames River, eyes watering in the wind, for the first glimpse of the helicopters.

'What if we have a confirmation before you reach Enniskerry?'

'You can reach us on the RAF frequencies, through Biggin Hill,' Peter told him.

'I hope I don't have bad news for you.' Richards was holding his bowler hat in place with one hand, the skirts of his jacket slapping around his skinny rump and his face blotchy with the cold.

The two ungainly craft came clattering in, low over the rooftops, hanging on the whirling silver coins of their rotors.

At a hundred feet Peter could plainly recognize the broad shape of Colin Noble in the open doorway of the fuselage, just forward of the brilliant RAF roundels, and the downdraught of the rotors boiled the air about them.

'Good hunting.' Richards raised his voice to a shout. 'I wish I was coming with you.'

Peter ran forward lightly, and jumped before the helicopter gear touched the concrete pad. Colin caught him by the upper arm and helped to swing him aboard without removing the cheroot from his wide mouth.

'Welcome aboard, buddy. Now let's get this circus on the road.' And he hitched the big .45 pistol on his hip.

'She's not eating.' The doctor came through from the inner room and scraped the plate into the rubbish bin below the sink. 'I'm worried about her. Very worried.'

Gilly O'Shaughnessy grunted but did not look up from his own plate. He broke a crust off the slice of bread and very carefully wiped up the last of the tomato ketchup. He popped the bread into his mouth and followed it with a gulp of steaming tea, and while he chewed it all together, he leaned back on the kitchen chair and watched the other man.

The doctor was on the verge of cracking up. He would probably not last out the week before his nerve went completely, Gilly O'Shaughnessy had seen better men go to pieces under less strain.

He realized then that his own nerves were wearing away.

It was more than just the rain and the waiting that was working on him. He had been the fox for all of his life, and he had developed the instincts of the hunted animal. He could sense danger, the presence of the pursuers, even when there was no real evidence. It made him restless to stay longer in one place than was necessary, especially when he was on a job. He had been here twelve days, and it was far too long. The more he thought about it the more uneasy he became. Why had they insisted he bring the brat to this isolated, and therefore conspicuous, little dead-end? There was only one road in and out of the village, a single avenue of escape. Why had they insisted that he sit and wait it out in this one place? He would have liked to keep moving. If he had had the running of it, he would have bought a second-hand caravan, and kept rolling from one park to another – his attention wandered for a few moments as he thought how he would have done it – if he had been given the planning of it.

He lit a cigarette and gazed out of the rain-blurred window panes, hardly aware of the muttered complaints and misgivings of his companion. What they should have done was crop the brat's fingers and bottle all of them to send to her father at intervals, and then they should have held a pillow over her face and buried her in the vegetable garden or weighted her and dumped her out beyond the hundred-fathom line of the Irish Sea – that way they would not have had to bother with a doctor, and the nursing—

Everything else had been done with professional skill, starting with the contact they had made with him in the *favela* of Rio de Janeiro, where he was hiding out in a sleazy one-room shack with the halfcaste Indian woman, and down to his last fifty quid.

That had given him a real start, he thought he had covered his tracks completely, but they had him made. They had the passport and travel papers in the name of Barry, and they did not look like forgeries. They were good papers, he was sure of it, and he knew a lot about papers.

Everything else had been as well planned, and swiftly delivered. The money – a thousand pounds in Rio, another five thousand the day after they grabbed the brat, and he was confident that the final ten would be there as it was promised. It was better than an English gaol, the 'Silver City' as the Brits called their concentration camp at the Maze. That was what Caliph had promised, if he didn't take the job.

Caliph, now that was a daft name, Gilly O'Shaughnessy decided for the fiftieth time as he dropped the stub of his cigarette into the dregs of his teacup and it was extinguished with a sharp hiss. A real daft name, but somehow it had the ability to put a chill on the blood, and he shivered not only from the cold.

He stood up and crossed to the kitchen window. It had all been done with such speed and purpose and planning – everything so clearly thought out, that when there was a lapse it was more troubling.

Gilly O'Shaughnessy had the feeling that Caliph did nothing without good reason – then why had they been ordered to back themselves into this dangerously exposed bottle neck, without the security of multiple escape routes, and to sit here and wait?

He picked up the cyclist cape and tweed cap. 'Where are you going?' the doctor demanded anxiously. 'I'm going to take a shufti,' Gilly O'Shaughnessy grunted as he pulled the cap down over his eyes.

'You're always prowling around,' the doctor protested. 'You make me nervous.'

The dark Irishman pulled the pistol from under his jacket and checked the load before thrusting it back into his belt. 'You just go on playing nursemaid,' he said brusquely. 'And leave the man's work to me.'

The small black Austin crawled slowly up the village street, and the rain hammered on the cab and bonnet in tiny white explosions that blurred the outline, giving the machine a softly focused appearance, and the streaming windscreen effectively hid the occupants. It was only when the Austin parked directly in front of Laragh's only grocery store and both front doors opened that the curiosity of watchers from behind the curtained windows all down the street was satisfied.

The two members of the Irish constabulary wore the service blue winter uniform with darker epaulettes. The soft rain speckled the patent leather peaks of their caps as they hurried into the shop.

'Good morning, Maeve, me old love,' the sergeant greeted the plump red-faced lady behind the counter.

'Owen O'Neill, I do declare—' She chuckled as she recognized the sergeant – there had been a time, thirty years before, when the two of them had given the priest some fine pickings at the confessional. 'And what brings you all the way up from the big city?'

That was a generous description of the quaint seaside resort town of Wicklow, fifteen miles down the road.

'The sight of your blooming smile—'

They chatted like old friends for ten minutes, and her husband came through from the little storeroom when he heard the rattle of teacups.

'So what is new in Laragh, then?' the sergeant asked at last. 'Any new faces in the village?'

'No, all the same faces. Nothing changes in Laragh, bless the Lord for that.' The shopkeeper wagged his head. 'No, indeed – only new face is the one down at the Old Manse, he and his lady friend –' he winked knowingly ' – but seeing as how he's a stranger, we aren't after counting him.'

The sergeant ponderously delved for his notebook, opened it and extracted a photograph from it, it was the usual side view and full face of police records. he held the name covered with his thumb as he showed it to them.

'No.' The woman shook her head positively. 'Himself down at the Manse is ten years older than that, and he does not have a moustache.'

'This was taken ten years ago,' said the sergeant.

'Oh, well, why didn't you say so.' She nodded. 'Then that's him. That's Mr Barry for certain sure.'

'The Old Manse, you say.' The sergeant seemed to inflate visibly with importance, as he put the photograph back into his notebook. 'I'm going to have to use your telephone now, dear.'

'Where will you be after telephoning?' the shopkeeper asked suspiciously.

'Dublin,' the sergeant told him. 'It's police business.'

'I'll have to charge you for the call,' the shopkeeper warned him quickly.

'There,' said the wife as they watched the sergeant making his request to the girl on the village switchboard. 'I told you he had the look of trouble, now didn't I. The first time I laid eyes on him I knew he was from up in the North, and carrying trouble like the black angel.'

Gilly O'Shaughnessy kept close in under the stone wall, keeping out of the slanting rain and out of the line of sight of a casual watcher on the slope beyond the river. He moved carefully and quietly as a tomcat on his midnight business, stopping to examine the earth below the weakened or tumbled places in the wall where a man could have come over, studying the wet drooping weeds for the brush marks where a man might have passed.

At the farthest corner of the garden, he stepped up on to the leaning main stem of an apple tree to see over the wall, wedging himself against the lichen-encrusted stone, so that the silhouette of his head did not show above the wall.

He waited and watched for twenty minutes, with the absolute animal patience of the predator, then he jumped down and went on around the perimeter of the wall, never for a moment relaxing his vigilance, seemingly oblivious to the discomfort of the cold and the insistent rain.

There was nothing, not the least sign of danger, no reason for the nagging disquiet – but still it was there. He reached another vantage point, the iron gate that led into the narrow walled alley, and he leaned against the stone jamb, cupping his hands to protect match and cigarette from the wind, and then shifting slightly so he could see through the crack between wall and gate and cover the walled lane, and the road beyond as far as the bridge.

Once again he assumed the patient watching role, closing his mind against physical discomfort and letting his eyes and his brain work at their full capacity.

Not for the first time he pondered the unusual system of signals and exchanges of material that Caliph had insisted upon.

The payments had been made by bearer deposit certificates, in Swiss francs, sent through the post to his Rio address and then to his collection address in London.

He had made one delivery to Caliph, the bottle and its contents – and two telephone calls. The delivery had been made within two hours of grabbing the girl, while she was still under the effects of the initial shot of the drug. The doctor – Dr Jamieson – as Gilly O'Shaughnessy liked to think of him, had done the job in the back of the second car. It had been waiting in the car park at Cambridge railway station, a little green Ford delivery van with a completely enclosed rear compartment. They had moved the girl from the maroon Triumph to the Ford in the covering dusk of the autumn evening, and they had parked again in the lot of a roadside café on the A.10 while Dr Jamieson did the job. All the instruments had been ready for him in the van, but he had botched it badly, his hands shaking with nerves and the need for liquor. The brat had bled copiously, and now the hand was infected.

Gilly O'Shaughnessy felt his irritation rising sharply when he thought of the doctor. Everything he touched seemed to turn to disaster.

He had delivered the bottle to a pickup car that had been exactly where he was told it would be, and it had dipped its headlights in the prearranged signal. Gilly had hardly stopped, but merely drawn up alongside and handed the bottle across, then driven straight into the West, and caught the early morning ferry long before any general alarm was out for the girl.

Then there were the telephone calls. They worried Gilly O'Shaughnessy as much as anything else in this whole bloody business. He had made the first call immediately they reached Laragh. It was an international call, and he had to say one sentence:

'We arrived safely.' And then hang up. A week later a call to the same number, and again only one sentence:

'We are enjoying ourselves.' And then immediately break the connection.

Gilly remembered how each time the girl on the local exchange had called him back to ask if the contact had been satisfactory – and each time she had sounded puzzled and intrigued.

It was not the way Caliph had worked up until then, it was leaving a trail for the hunters to follow and he would have protested – if there had been somebody to protest to, but there was only the international telephone number, no other way of contacting Caliph. He decided as he stood by the gate that he would not make the next telephone call to that number which was due in four days' time.

Then he remembered that was the day the hand was due – and he would probably receive his orders for delivery of the hand when he made the call – but he didn't like it. Not even for the money – and suddenly his mind went back to an incident long ago.

They had wanted to pass false information to the English, details of an intended operation – which would in fact take place at a different place and a different time. They had fed the detailed but duff information to a young unreliable Provo, one who they knew would not hold out under interrogation, and they had put him in a safe house in the Shankill Road – and that was where the English took him.

Gilly O'Shaughnessy felt a little electric prickle run down his spine like ghost-fire, and that feeling had never let him down before – never. He looked at his cheap Japanese wristwatch, it was almost four o'clock, and evening was lowering on the hills of grey and cold green. When he looked up again, there was movement on the road.

From the top of the hill a vehicle was following the curve of the road, down towards the bridge. It was a small black saloon car, and it went out of sight behind the hedge.

Gilly O'Shaughnessy watched for it to reappear without particular interest, still worrying about those two telephone calls. Trying to find the need for them, why Caliph should want to take that chance.

The small black car turned on to the bridge, and came directly down towards the Manse, but the light was wrong and Gilly could make out only the shape of two heads beyond the rhythmically flogging windscreen wipers.

The car began to slow up, coming down almost to walking speed, and Gilly straightened up instinctively, suddenly completely alert as he peered throught the slit. There was the pale blur of faces turned towards him, and the car slowed almost to a halt. The nearest side window was lowered slowly and for the first time he could see clearly into the interior. He saw the peak of the uniform cap, and the silver flash of a cap badge above the straining white face. The ghost-fire flared up Gilly O'Shaughnessy's spine and he felt his breath suddenly scalding his throat.

The small black car disappeared beyond the corner of the stone wall, and he heard it accelerate away swiftly.

Gilly O'Shaughnessy whirled with the cape ballooning around him and he ran back to the house. He felt very cold and sure and calm now that the moment of action had come.

The kitchen was empty and he crossed it in half a dozen strides, and threw open the door to the second room.

The doctor was working over the bed and he looked up angrily.

'I've told you to knock.'

They had argued this out before. The doctor still retained some bizarre vestige of professional ethics in his treatment of his patient. He might surgically mutilate the child for the money he so desperately needed, but he had protested fiercely when Gilly O'Shaughnessy had lingered at the doorway to ogle the maturing body whenever the doctor stripped it for cleansing, treatment or for the performance of its natural functions.

The dark Irishman had half-heartedly attempted to force him to back down, but when he had encountered surprisingly courageous opposition he had abandoned his voyeuristic pleasures and had returned to the inner room only when called to assist.

Now the child lay face down on the soiled sheets. Her blonde hair was matted and snarled into greasy tresses; the doctor's attempts at cleanliness were as bumbling and ineffectual as his surgery.

The infection and use of drugs had wasted the flesh off the tender young body, each knuckle of her spine stood out clearly and her naked buttocks seemed pathetically vulnerable, shrunken and pale.

Now the doctor pulled the grubby sheet up to her shoulders, and turned to stand protectively over her. It was an absurd gesture, when you looked at the untidy, stained dressing that bound up her left hand – and Gilly O'Shaughnessy snarled at him fiercely.

'We are getting out.'

'You can't move her now,' protested the doctor. 'She's really sick.'

'Suit yourself,' Gilly agreed grimly. 'Then we'll leave her.' He reached under the dripping cape, and brought out the pistol. He thumbed back the hammer and stepped up to the bed. The doctor grabbed at his arm, but Gilly pushed him away easily, sending him reeling back against the wall.

'You are right, she'll be a nuisance,' he said, and placed the muzzle of the pistol against the base of the child's skull.

'No,' shrieked the doctor. 'No, don't do that. We'll take her.'

'We are leaving as soon as it's dark.' Gilly stepped back and uncocked the pistol. 'Be ready by then,' he warned.

The two helicopters flew almost side by side, with the number two only slightly behind and higher than the leader; below them the Irish Sea was a sheet of beaten lead flecked with feathers of white water.

They had refuelled at Caernarvon and had made good time since leaving the Welsh coast, for the wind drove them on, but still the night was overtaking them and Peter Stride fretted, glancing at his wristwatch every few seconds.

It was only ninety miles of open water to cross, but to Peter it seemed like the entire Atlantic. Colin slumped beside him on the bench that ran the length of the hold, with the cold stump of a cheroot in the corner of his mouth in deference to the 'No smoking' light that burned on the bulkhead behind the flight deck. The rest of the Thor team had adopted their usual attitudes of complete relaxation, some of them sprawled on the deck using their equipment as pillows, the others stretched out full length on the benches.

Peter Stride was the only one tensed up, as though his blood fizzed with nervous energy. He stood up once again to peer through the perspex window, checking the amount of daylight and trying to judge the height and position of the sun through the thick cloud cover.

'Take it easy,' Colin counselled him as he dropped back into his seat. 'You will give yourself an ulcer.'

'Colin, we've got to decide. What are our priorities on this strike?' he had to shout above the racket of wind and motor.

'There are no priorities. We have only one object – to get Melissa-Jane out, and out safely.'

'We aren't going to try for prisoners to interrogate?'

'Peter Baby, we are going to hit anything and everything that moves in the target area, and we are going hit them hard.'

Peter nodded with satisfaction. 'They will only be goons anyway, you can be certain that their paymaster will not let them connect to him – but what about Kingston Parker, he would want prisoners?'

'Kingston Parker?' Colin removed the stub of cheroot from his mouth. 'Never heard of him – around here it's Uncle Colin makes the decisions.' And he grinned at Peter, that friendly lopsided grin, and at that moment the flight engineer crossed the cabin and yelled at Colin.

'Irish coast ahead – We'll be landing at Enniskerry in seven minutes, sir.'

Air traffic control at Enniskerry had been apprised of the emergency. They stacked the other traffic in holding pattern above circuit altitude and cleared the two RAF helicopters for immediate landing.

They came clattering out of the low grey cloud and rain, and settled on the hangar apron. Immediately a police car, with headlights burning in the gloom, sped out from between the hangars and parked beside the leading machine. Before the rotors had stopped turning, two members of the Irish Constabulary and a representative of the surveyor general's office were scrambling up into the camouflaged fuselage.

'Stride.' Peter introduced himself quickly, he was dressed now in Thor assault gear, the one-piece fitted black suit and soft boots, the pistol on its webbing belt strapped down to his right thigh.

'General, we've had a confirmation,' the police inspector told him while they were still shaking hands. 'Local people have identified O'Shaughnessy from a police photograph. He is staying in the area all right.'

'Have they found where?' Peter demanded.

'They have, sir. It's an old rambling building on the edge of the village –'

He motioned the bespectacled surveyor to come forward with the file he was clutching to his chest. There was no chart table in the stripped-out hull of the helicopter, and they spread the survey map and photographs on the deck.

Colin Noble ordered across the team from the second helicopter, and twenty men crowded into a huddle about the maps. 'There, that's the building.' The surveyor placed a circle on the map with a blue pencil.

'Right,' grunted Colin. 'We've got good fixes – we pick up either the river or the road and follow it to the bridge and the church. The target is between them.'

'Haven't we got a blow-up of the building, a plan of the interior?' one of the Thor team asked.

'Sorry, there wasn't time to do a proper search,' the surveyor apologized.

'The local police reported again a few minutes ago, and we got a relay on the radio. They say the house is enclosed by a high stone wall and that there are no signs of activity.'

'They haven't been near it?' Peter demanded. 'They were strictly ordered not to approach the suspects.'

'They drove past once on the public road.' The inspector looked slightly abashed. 'They wanted to make certain that –'

'If it's O'Shaughnessy, he needs only one sniff and he'll be gone –' Peter's expression was stony, but his eyes sparked blue with anger. '– Why can't these people do what they are told?' He turned quickly to the helicopter pilot in his yellow life jacket and helmet with its built-in microphone and earphones.

'Can you get us in?'

The pilot did not answer immediately but glanced up at the nearest window; a fresh gout of rain splashed against the pane.

'It will be dark in ten minutes, or even earlier, and the ceiling is down to the deck now, we only got down here using the airport VOR beacons –' He looked dubious. '– There is nobody aboard who will recognize the target, hell – I don't know – I could get you in at first light tomorrow.'

'It has to be tonight, now. Right now.'

'If you could get the local police to mark the target –' the pilot suggested, '– with torches or a flare.'

'There is no chance of that – we have to go in cold, and the longer we sit here talking the less our chances. Will you give it your best shot?' Peter was almost pleading, the go decision is one that cannot be forced on a pilot, even air traffic control cannot force a pilot-in-command to operate beyond his personal judgement.

'We will have to try and keep ground contact all the way, it's classic conditions for trouble, rising terrain and deteriorating weather –'

'Try it –' Peter said, '– please.'

The pilot hesitated five second longer.

'Let's go!' he said abruptly, and there was a concerted rush for the hatchway as the second Thor team made for the other machine, and the police and surveyor made certain they were not included on the passenger list.

Turbulence slogged the helicopter like the punches of a heavyweight prize fighter, and she dipped and staggered to them with a nauseatingly giddy action.

The ground flickered past under them, very close, and yet darkly insubstantial in the wild night. The headlights of a solitary vehicle on a lonely country road, the cluttered lights of a village, each a distinct yellow rectangle they were so close, these were the only landmarks with any meaning – the rest was dark patches of woods, the threads of hedges and stone walls drawn lightly across sombre fields, and every few minutes even that was gone as a fresh squall of grey clouds and rain washed away all vision, and the pilot concentrated all his attention on the dull glow of the flight instruments arranged in their distinctive T layout in front of him.

Each time they emerged from cloud, the light seemed to have diminished and the dark menace of earth loomed more threateningly as they were forced lower and lower to keep contact.

Peter was squeezed into the jump seat of the helicopter's flight deck, between the two pilots, and Colin crowded in behind him, all of them peering ahead, all silent and tense as the ungainly machines lumbered low and heavy over the earth, groping for the shoreline.

They hit the coast, the ghostly white line of surf flared with phosphorescence only fifty feet below them, and the pilot swung them to run south with it – and seconds later another brighter field of lights appeared below them.

'Wicklow,' said the pilot, and his co-pilot called the new heading, now they had made a fix they could head for Laragh directly.

They swung on to the new heading, following the road inland.

'Four minutes to target,' the co-pilot shouted at Peter, stabbing ahead with his finger, and Peter did not try to answer in the clatter and roar of the rotors, but he reached down and checked the Walther in its quick-release holster; it came out cleanly in his fist.

Gilly O'Shaughnessy threw his few personal possessions into the blue canvas airways grip, a change of underclothing and his shaving gear. Then he pulled the iron bedstead away from the wall, ripped back the skirting board and cleared out the hiding place he had made there by removing a single brick.

There were the new papers and passports. Caliph had even provided papers for the brat – Helen Barry – his daughter. Caliph had thought of everything. With the papers was six hundred pounds sterling in travellers' cheques, and a package of spare ammunition for the pistol. He thrust these into the pocket of his jacket, and took one last look around the bare bleak room. He knew that he had left nothing to lead the hunters, because he never carried anything that could be used to identify him. Yet he was obsessed by the need to destroy all sign of his passing. He had long ago ceased to think of himself by the name of Gilly O'Shaughnessy. He had no name, and only one purpose – that purpose was destruction. The magnificent passion to reduce all life to decay and mortification.

He could recite by heart most of Bakunin's *The Revolutionary Catechism*, especially the definition of the true revolutionary:

> The lost man, who has no belongings, no outside interests, no personal ties of any sort – not even a name. Possessed of but one thought, interest and passion – the revolution. A man who has broken with Society, broken with its laws and conventions. He must despise the opinions of others, and be prepared for death and torture at any time. Hard towards himself, he must be hard to others, and in his heart there must be no place for love, friendship, gratitude or even honour.

As he stood now in the empty room, he saw himself in a rare moment of revelation, as the man he had set out to become – the true revolutionary, and his head turned for a moment to indulge in the vanity of regarding his own image in the mirror screwed to the peeling wallpaper above the iron bedstead.

It was the dark cold face of the lost man, and he felt proud to belong to that élite class, the cutting edge of the sword, that was what he was.

He picked up the canvas grip, and strode through into the kitchen.

'Are you ready?' he called.

'Help me.'

He dropped the grip and stepped to the window. The last of the light was fading swiftly, glowing pink and mother of pearl within the drooping, pregnant belly of the sky. It seemed so close he could reach out and touch it. Already the trees of the unkempt orchard were melting into the darkness as the night encroached.

'I cannot carry her on my own,' the doctor whined, and he swung away from the window. It was time to go again. In his life there was always the moving onwards, and always the hunters baying hard upon his scent. It was time to run again, run like the fox.

He went through into the second room. The doctor had the child wrapped in a grey woollen blanket, and he had tried to lift her from the bed, but had failed. She was sprawled awkwardly, half on to the floor.

'Help me,' repeated the doctor.

'Get out of the way.' Gilly O'Shaughnessy pushed him roughly aside, and stooped over the girl. For a second their faces were within inches of each other.

Her eyes were opened, half-conscious, although the pupils were widely dilated by the drug. The lids were pink-rimmed and there were little butter-yellow lumps of mucus in the corners. Her lips were dried to white scales, and cracked through to the raw flesh at three places.

'Please tell my daddy,' she whispered. 'Please tell him I'm here.'

His nostrils flared at the sick sour smell of her body, but he picked her up easily with an arm under her knees and the other under her shoulders, and carried her out across the kitchen, kicking open the door so the lock burst and it slammed back against its hinges.

Quickly he carried her across the yard to the garage, with the doctor staggering along after them carrying a carton of medical supplies and equipment against his chest, cursing miserably at the cold, and sliding and slipping in the treacherous footing.

Gilly O'Shaughnessy waited while the doctor opened the rear door of the car, and then he bundled her in so roughly that the child cried out weakly. He ignored her and went to the double garage doors and dragged them open. It was so dark now that he could not see as far as the bridge.

'Where are we going?' bleated the doctor.

'I haven't decided yet,' Gilly told him brusquely. 'There is a safe house up North, or we might go back across the sea to England –' He thought of the caravan again, that was a good one –

'But why are we leaving now, so suddenly?'

He did not bother to reply but left the garage and ran back into the kitchen. Always he was obsessed by the need to cover his tracks, to leave no sign for the hunters.

Though he had brought little with him, and was taking that now, yet he knew the old house contained signs, even if it was only his fingerprints. There was also the single remaining appetite for destruction to assuage.

He ripped the wooden doors off the kitchen cupboards and smashed them to splinters under his heel, piled them in the centre of the wood floor. He crumpled the newspapers piled on the table and added them to the pile, threw the table and chairs upon it.

He lit a match, and held it to the crumpled newsprint. It flared readily, and he straightened and opened the windows and doors. The flames fed on the cold fresh air and climbed greedily, catching on the splintered doors.

Gilly O'Shaughnessy picked up the canvas grip and stepped out into the night, crouching to the wind and the rain – but halfway to the garage he straightened again abruptly and paused to listen.

There was a sound on the wind, from the direction of the coast. It might have been the engine note of a heavy truck coming up the hills, but there was a peculiar thin whistling sound mingled with the engine beat, and the volume of sound escalated too sharply to be that of a lumbering truck. It was coming on too swiftly, the sound seemed to fill the air, to emanate from the very clouds themselves.

Gilly O'Shaughnessy stood with his face lifted to the fine silver drizzle, searching the belly of the clouds, until a throbbing regular glow began to beat like a pulse in the sky, and it was a moment until he recognized it as the beacon light of a low-flying aircraft, and at the same moment he knew that the shrill whistle was the whirling of rotors bringing the hunters.

He cried aloud in the certainty of betrayal and onrushing death. 'Why? God, why?' He called to the God he had so long ago denied, and began to run.

'It's no good.' The pilot twisted his neck to shout at Peter without taking his eyes from the flight instruments which kept the great ungainly machine level and on course. They had lost contact with the other machine.

'We are socked in, blind.' The cloud frothed over the canopy like boiling milk over the lip of the pot. 'I'm going to have to climb out, and head back for Enniskerry before we run into my number two.'

The risk of collision with the other helicopter was now real and imminent.

The beacon light throbbed above them, reflected off the impenetrable press of soft cloud – but the other pilot would not see it until too late.

'Hold on. Just another minute,' Peter shouted back at him, his expression tortured in the glow of the instrument panel. The entire operation was disintegrating about him, would soon end in tragedy or in fiasco, but he must go on.

'It's no good –' the pilot began, and then shouted with fright and hurled the helicopter over on to its side, as the same instant altering pitch and altitude so the machine shuddered and lurched as though she had run into a solid obstruction, and then bounded upwards, gaining a hundred feet in a swoop.

The spire of a church had leapt at them out of the cloud, like a predator from ambush, and now it flickered by only feet from where they crouched in the flight deck, but it had disappeared again instantly as they roared past.

'The church!' Peter yelled. 'That's it! Turn back.'

The pilot checked the machine, hovering blindly in the chaos of rain and cloud churned to a fury by the downdraught of their own rotor.

'I can't see a damned thing,' shouted the pilot.

'We've got one hundred and seventy feet on the radio altimeter,' his co-pilot called; that was actual height from the ground and still they could see nothing below them.

'Get us down. For God's sake, get us down,' Peter pleaded.

'I can't take the chance. We don't have any idea of what is under us.' The pilot's face was sickly orange in the instrument glow, his eyes the dark pits of a skull. 'I'm climbing out and heading back –'

Peter reached down and the butt of the Walther jumped into his hand, like a living thing. He realized coldly that he was capable of killing the pilot, to force the co-pilot to land – but at the moment there was a hole in the cloud, just enough to make out the dark loom of the earth below them.

'Visual,' Peter shouted. 'We've visual, get us down!' And the helicopter sank swiftly, breaking out suddenly into the clear.

'The river.' Peter saw the glint of water. 'And the bridge –'

'There's the churchyard –' Colin roared eagerly. '– and that's the target.'

The thatched roof was a black oblong, and light spilled from the windows of one side of the building, so they could see the high enclosing wall. The pilot spun the helicopter on its axis like a compass needle, and dived towards the building.

Colin Noble scrambled down into the cabin, shouting to his team. 'Delta! We are going to Delta –' And the flight engineer slid the cabin hatch cover open. Immediately a fine swirling mist filled the cabin as the downdraught of the rotors churned the rain-filled air.

The Thor team were on their feet, forming up on each side of the open hatch, while Colin towered over the flight engineer as he took lead position – 'point' as he always called it.

The dark earth rushed up to meet them, and Colin spat out the cheroot stub and braced himself in the doorway.

'Hit anything that moves,' he yelled. 'But for Chrissake watch out for the kid. Let's go, gang. Let's go!'

Peter was jammed into the jump seat by the swooping drop of the machine, unable to follow, wasting precious seconds – but he had a clear view ahead through the canopy.

The light in the windows of the building wavered unnaturally, and Peter realized that it was burning. Those were flames, and his concern was heightened by the knowledge, but he did not have a chance to ponder this new development. In the shadows of the walled yard he saw movement, just the dark blur of it in the glow of the flames, and what was left of the daylight – but it was the shape of a man, running, crouched low, disappearing almost immediately into one of the outbuildings that flanked the narrow stone-walled lane.

Peter dragged himself out of the seat against the G force, scrambled awkwardly down into the cabin as the helicopter dropped the last few feet, and then hung, swaying slightly, suspended ten feet above the open yard at the rear of the house – and black-clad figures spilled out of her, dropping lightly on to their feet and racing forward as they touched ground, seeming to disappear again miraculously through the doors and windows of the building. Even in the grinding tension of the moment Peter felt the flare of pride in the way it was done, instant and seemingly effortless penetration, the lead man using sandbags to break in glass and wooden shutters and the man behind him going in with a clean controlled dive.

Peter was the last man left aboard, and something made him check in the open hatchway before jumping. Perhaps it was that glimpse of movement outside the main building that he had been given; he looked back that way, and suddenly lights leapt in solid white lances down the walled lane – the headlights of a motor vehicle, and at the same moment the vehicle launched itself from the dark derelict outbuilding and rocketed away down the lane.

Peter teetered in the open hatch, for he had been in the very act of jumping, but he caught his balance now, grabbing wildly at the nylon line above the door. The vehicle slowed for the turn into the main road at the bridge – and Peter caught the flight engineer and shook his shoulder violently, pointing after the escaping vehicle. His lips were inches from the man's face.

'Don't let it get away!' he screamed, and the flight engineer was quick and alert, he spoke urgently into his microphone, directly to the pilot in the flight deck above them, and obediently the helicopter swung around and the beat of the engines changed as the rotors altered pitch and roared in forward thrust – the machine lunged forward, skimming the garage roof by mere feet and then hammered out into the night in pursuit of the dwindling glow of headlights.

Peter had to hang out of the hatchway to see ahead, and the wind clamoured around his head and tore at his body, but they were swiftly overhauling the vehicle as it raced down the twisting narrow road towards the coast.

It was two hundred yards ahead, and the dark tree tops seemed to rush by at the same level as the hatch in which Peter stood. A hundred yards ahead, the headlights blazing through the drizzle of rain, etching fleeting cameos of hedges and starkly lit stone walls from the night.

They were close enough now for Peter to make out that it was a smallish vehicle with an estate car body, not quite large enough to be a station wagon – the driver was throwing it through the curves and twists of the road with reckless skill, but the helicopter crept up behind him.

'Tell him to switch off the beacon light.' Peter swung inboard to shout in the flight engineer's ear. He did not want to warn the driver that he was being followed, but as the engineer lifted the microphone to his mouth the headlights snapped out into darkness. The driver had become aware, and after the brilliance of the headlights the night seemed totally dark, and the car disappeared into it.

Peter felt the helicopter lurch, as the pilot was taken by surprise, and his own dismay was a lance.

'We have lost them,' he thought, and he knew that it was suicide to fly on in darkness only a few feet above the tree tops, but the pilot of the helicopter steadied the craft and then suddenly the earth below them was lit by a blaze of stark white light that startled Peter until he realized that the pilot had switched on his landing lights. There were two of them, one on each side of the fuselage; they were aimed down and slightly forward.

The escaping car was caught fairly in their brilliance.

The helicopter dropped lower, edging in between the telegraph poles and trees that lined the narrow road.

Now Peter could see that the car was a dark blue Austin, with a carrying rack bolted to the long roof. It was that carrying rack which decided him. Without it no human being could have hoped for purchase on the smooth rounded roof of the lurching, swaying car.

The doctor in the back seat of the Austin had been the one who spotted the helicopter. The engine noise and the drumming of the wind had covered the whistling whine of the rotors, and Gilly O'Shaughnessy had chuckled with grim triumph and self-congratulation. He had deliberately waited for the helicopter to discharge its load of fighting men before he had switched on his headlights and roared out of the garage into the lane.

He knew it would be many minutes before the assault team realized that the burning house was empty and that it would take as long again to regroup and board the helicopter to continue the hunt – and by that time he would be clear; there was a safe house in Dublin – or there had been, four years previously. Perhaps it was blown now; in that case he would have to get rid of the brat and Dr Jamieson, a bullet each in the back of the head, and drive the Austin into the Irish Sea.

The wild exhilaration of danger and death was upon him again, the waiting was over at last and he was living again the way he had chosen – the fox running ahead of the hounds, he was alive again, with his right foot thrust flat to the floor boards and the Austin rocketing through the night.

The girl was screaming weakly from the back seat, in pain and panic; the doctor was trying to quiet her, and Gilly laughed aloud. The tyres screeched wildly as he skidded out in the turn, brushing the hedge with the side before he was through.

'They are following,' screamed the doctor, as he straightened the car into the next stretch, and Gilly glanced back over his shoulder. He could see nothing through the rear windows.

'What?'

'The helicopter –'

Gilly lowered his window and, driving with one hand, thrust his head out. The flashing aircraft beacon was close behind and above, and he ducked back in and looked ahead to make sure that the road ran straight, then he switched off the headlights.

In total darkness he did not diminish speed, and now when he laughed it was a wild and reckless sound.

'You're mad,' the doctor shrieked. 'You'll kill us all!'

'Right you are, doctor!' But his night vision was clearing and he caught the Austin before she wandered into the stone wall on the left-hand side, and at the same moment he jerked the pistol from under his cape and laid it on the seat beside him.

'There is not going to be –' he began and then broke off as the blinding light burst over them. The helicopter had switched on its landing lights – the road ahead was brightly lit, and he skidded into the next turn with rubber squealing.

'Stop!' the doctor pleaded, trying to hold the semi-conscious child from being hurled about in the swaying cab. 'Let's give up now, before they kill us.'

'They've got no fighting men on board,' Gilly yelled back at him. 'There's nothing they can do.'

'Give up,' the doctor whined. 'Let's get out of this alive.' And Gilly O'Shaughnessy threw back his head and roared with laughter.

'I'm keeping three bullets, doctor, one for each of us –'

'They're right on top of us.'

Gilly snatched up the pistol and once again thrust his head and right shoulder out, twisting to look upwards.

The eye-searing lights beamed down upon him, very close above. It was all he could see and he fired at them, the crash of the shots lost in the clattering whistling roar of the rotors and the tearing rush of the wind.

Poised in the hatchway, Peter counted the bright orange spurts of gunfire. There were three of them, but there was no sound of passing shot, no thump of the strike.

'Get lower!' he shouted at the engineer, reinforcing the order with urgent hand signals, and obediently the big machine sank down upon the racing Austin.

Peter gathered himself, judging his moment carefully, and when it came he launched himself clear of the hatchway, and his guts seemed to cram into his throat as he dropped.

He dropped with all four limbs spread and braced to land together, but for a moment he thought he had misjudged it and would fall behind the Austin, into the metalled roadway, to be crushed and shredded by the forward impetus of the low-flying helicopter.

Then the Austin swerved and checked slightly and Peter crashed into its roof with stunning force; he felt the metal buckle and sag under him, and then he was rolling and slipping sideways. His whole left side was numbed by the force of impact, and he clutched wildly with his right hand, his fingernails tearing at the paintwork, but still he slid towards the edge, his legs kicking wildly in dark rushing space.

At the last instant before he was hurled into the roadway, his clawed fingers hooked in the framework of the roof rack, and he hung bat-like from his one arm. It had taken only a small part of a second, and immediately the driver of the Austin realized that there was a man on the roof. He slewed the little car from one side of the road to the other, short wrenching turns that brought her over on two outside wheels before slamming back and twisting the other way. The tyres squealed harsh protest, and Peter was flung brutally back and forth, the muscle and tendons of his right arm popping and creaking with the strain of holding on – but feeling was flooding swiftly back into his numbed left side.

He had to move quickly, he could not survive another of those wrenching swerves, and he gathered himself, judged the Austin's momentum, and used it to roll and grab with his free hand; at the same moment the toes of his soft boots found purchase on one of the struts of the roof carrier, and he pressed himself belly down, clinging with both arms and legs to the wildly swinging machine.

The Austin checked and steadied as a steep turn appeared ahead in the arc lights of the helicopter which still hung over them. The driver shot the car into the corner, and ahead of them was a long extended drop as the road twisted down the hills towards the coast.

Peter half lifted himself and was about to slide forward when the metal six inches in front of his nose exploded outwards, leaving a neatly punched hole through the roof, and tiny fragments of flying metal stung his cheek; at the same moment the concussion of the pistol shot beat in upon his eardrums. The driver of the Austin was firing blindly up through the coachwork, and he had misjudged Peter's position above him by inches. Peter threw himself desperately to one side, for an instant almost losing his grip on the struts of the carrier – and another pistol bullet clanged out through the metal roof, that one would have taken him through the belly, and Peter had a fleeting image of the kind of wound that it would have inflicted, the bullet would have been mushroomed and deformed by the roof and would have broken up inside his body.

Desperately Peter threw himself back the opposite way, trying to outguess the gunman below him, and once again the crash of the shot and the metal roof erupted in a little jagged pockmark, flecking the paintwork away so the rim of the bullet hole shone like a polished silver shilling. Again it would have hit him, if he had not moved.

Peter rolled again, tensing his belly muscles in the anticipation of the tearing, paralysing impact, expecting the gun shot – which did not come. Only then he remembered the wasted pistol fire the driver had thrown up at the hovering helicopter. He had emptied his pistol and as the realization dawned on Peter there was another completely compelling sound, very faint in the drumming rush of the wind and the engine roar – but unmistakable. It was the sound of a young girl screaming and it galvanized Peter as nothing else, even the threat of death, could have done.

He came up on toes and fingers, like a cat, and he went forward and to the right, until he was directly above the driver's seat.

The girl screamed again, and he recognized Melissa-Jane's voice. There was no question of it, and he slipped the Walther from its quick-release holster and cocked the hammer with the same movement, one glance ahead and they were rushing down on another turn in the narrow road. The driver would be using both hands to control the swaying and bucking little machine.

'Now!' he told himself, and dropped forward, so that he was peering backwards and upside-down through the windshield directly into the driver's pale face and at a distance of only eighteen inches.

In the thousandth part of a second Peter recognized the dark, wolfish features and the cold, merciless eyes of the killer. He had hunted this man for many years and studied his photograph endlessly when the hunting of the Provo terrorists had been his life's work.

Gilly O'Shaughnessy was driving with both hands, the pistol still gripped in one of them and the chamber open for reloading. He snarled at Peter like an animal through the bars of its cage, and Peter fired with the muzzle of the Walther touching the glass of the windshield.

The glass starred into a glittering sheet, white and opaque, and then it collapsed inwards with the force of the wind, filling the interior of the Austin with flying diamond chips of sparkling glass.

Gilly O'Shaughnessy had thrown up both hands to his face, but bright blood burst from between them, spattering his chest and soaking swiftly into the lank black hair.

Still hanging upside down across the Austin's cab, Peter thrust the Walther in through the shattered windscreen until it almost touched the man's body and he fired twice more into his chest, where the explosive Velex bullets would break up against bone, and would not overpenetrate to harm anybody else in the interior. Melissa-Jane's screams still rang clearly in his ears, as he killed Gilly O'Shaughnessy. He did it as coldly as a veterinary surgeon would put down a rabid dog, and with as little pleasure, and the bullets punched

Gilly O'Shaughnessy back on the bucket seat, head lolling from side to side, and Peter expected the howl of the engine to cut out now as the dead man's foot slipped from the accelerator.

It did not happen. There was no change in the engine beat, the body had slid forward and jammed, the knee under the dashboard, bearing down fully on the pedal, and the little car flew down the slope of the hill, the stone walls on each side blurring past as though down a tunnel in the depths of the earth.

Peter wriggled forward and thrust both arms through the shattered windshield and caught the untended wheel as it began to spin aimlessly. He checked the Austin and swung her back into the road, but she had been driven to her limits, rocking and swaying crazily before she righted herself and flew down the hill.

It was almost impossible to judge the control needed to keep her on the road.

Peter was hanging head down, gripping only with knees and toes, and he had to manipulate the wheel from this inverted position with his upper arms sawing across the teeth of jagged glass still remaining in the frame of the windshield.

The wind whipped and clawed him, and Gilly O'Shaughnessy's body flopped forward bonelessly on to the wheel, jamming it at a critical moment, so that while Peter used one hand to shove him backwards, the side of the Austin touched the stone wall with a screech of rending metal and a shower of orange sparks. Peter wrenched her back into the road, and she began a series of uncontrolled broadsides, swinging wildly from side to side, touching the wall with another jarring shock, then swinging back sideways to bounce over the verge, then back again.

She was going over, Peter knew it, and he would be crushed under the metal roof and smeared along the abrasive surface of the macadam road. He should jump now, and take his chances – but grimly he stayed with the crazed machine, for Melissa-Jane was in her and he could not leave.

She survived one more skid, and ahead Peter had the glimpse of a barred wooden gate in the wall. Deliberately he turned the front wheels into the direction of the next skid, no longer trying to counteract it, but aggravating it – steering directly for the gate, and the Austin smashed into it.

A wooden beam cartwheeled over Peter's head, and a scalding cloud of steam from the shattered radiator stung his face and hands, and then the Austin was into the open field, bouncing and thudding over the rocks that studded it, the drag of soft muddy earth slowing her, and the steep slope of the hillside against her – within fifty feet the front end dropped heavily into a drainage ditch, and the little car shuddered to a halt, canted at an abandoned angle.

Peter slipped over the side and landed on his feet. He jerked open the rear door and a man half fell from the cab. He dropped on to his knees in the mud, blubbering incoherently and Peter drove his right knee into his face. Bone and cartilage crunched sharply and there was the crackle of breaking teeth. His voice was cut off abruptly and, as he dropped, Peter chopped him with the stiffened blade of his right hand, a controlled blow – judged finely to immobilize but not to kill, and before the unconscious body dropped, Peter had gone in over it.

He lifted his daughter out of the Austin, and the frail wasted body felt insubstantial in his arms, and the heat of fever and infection burned against his chest.

He was possessed by an almost uncontrollable desire to crush her body to him with all the strength of his arms, but instead he carried her as though she was made of some precious and fragile substance, stepping carefully over the uneven rocky surface of the field to where the helicopter was settling cumbersomely out of the darkness.

The Thor doctor was still aboard her; he jumped clear before the helicopter touched and ran towards Peter in the brilliant glare of the landing lights.

Peter found he was crooning softly.

'It's all right now, darling. It's all over now. It's all finished, my baby – I'm here, little one –'

Then Peter made another discovery. It was not sweat running down his cheeks and dripping from his chin, and he wondered unashamedly when last it was he had wept. He could not remember, and it did not seem important, not now, not with his daughter in his arms.

Cynthia came down to London, and Peter relived some of those horrors from their marriage.

'Everybody around you always has to suffer, Peter. Now it's Melissa-Jane's turn.'

He could not avoid her, nor her martyred expression, for she was always at Melissa-Jane's bedside. While he bore her recriminations and barbed accusations, he wondered that she had ever been gay and young and attractive. She was two years younger than he was but she already had the shapeless body and grey mind that made her seem twenty years older.

Melissa-Jane responded almost miraculously to the antibiotics, and although she was still weak and skinny and pale, the doctor discharged her on the third day, and Peter and Cynthia had their final degrading haggling and bargaining session which Melissa-Jane settled for them.

'Mommy, I'm still so afraid. Can't I go with Daddy – just for a few days?'

Finally Cynthia agreed with sighs and the pained airs that left them both feeling a little guilty. On the drive down to Abbots Yew, where Steven had invited them for as long as was necessary for Melissa-Jane's convalescence, she sat very quietly beside Peter, her left hand still in the sling and the finger wearing a small neat white turban. She spoke only after they had passed the Heathrow turn off on the M.4.

'All the time I knew you were going to come. I can't remember much else. It was always dark and giddy-making – things kept changing, I'd look at a face and it would fade away, and then we'd be somewhere else –'

'It was the drug they were giving you,' Peter explained.

'Yes, I know that. I remember the prick of the needle –' Reflexively she rubbed her upper arm, and shivered briefly. 'But even with the drug I always knew you were going to come. I remember lying in the darkness listening for your voice –'

There was the temptation to try to pretend it had never happened, and Melissa-Jane had not spoken about it until now – but Peter knew she must be allowed to talk it out.

'Would you like to tell me about it?' he invited gently, knowing that it was essential to the healing process. He listened quietly as she spilled out drug-haunted memories, disjointed scraps of conversation and impressions. The terror was back in her voice when she spoke of the dark one.

'He looked at me sometimes. I remember him looking at me –' And Peter remembered the cold killer's eyes.

'He is dead now, darling.'

'Yes, I know. They told me.' She was silent for a moment, and then went on. 'He was so different from the one with grey hair. I liked him, the old one. His name was Doctor Jamieson.'

'How did you know that?' Peter asked.

'That's what the dark one called him.' She smiled. 'Doctor Jamieson, I remember he always smelled like cough mixture and I liked him –'

The one who had done the amputation, and would have taken her hand as well, Peter thought grimly.

'I never saw the other one. I knew he was there, but I never saw him.'

'The other one?' Peter turned to her sharply. 'Which other one, darling?'

'There was another one – and even the dark one was afraid of him. I knew that, they were all afraid of him.'

'You never saw him?'

'No, but they were always talking about him, and arguing about what he would do –'

'Do you remember his name?' Peter asked, and Melissa-Jane frowned in concentration.

'Did he have a name?' Peter prompted.

'Usually they just talked about *him*, but, yes, I remember now. The dark one called him "Casper".'

'Casper?'

'No, not that, not Casper. Oh, I can't remember.' Her voice had risen, a shrill note in terror that ripped at Peter's nerves.

'Don't worry about it.' He tried to soothe her, but she shook her head with frustration.

'Not Casper, a name like that. I knew he was the one who really wanted to hurt me – they were just doing what he told them. He was the one I was truly afraid of.' Her voice ended with a sob, and she was sitting bolt upright in the seat.

'It's over now, darling.' Peter swung into the verge of the road and braked to a halt. He reached for her but she was rigid in his arms and at his touch she began to shake uncontrollably. Peter's alarm flared, and he held her to his chest.

'Caliph!' she whispered. 'That's his name. Caliph.' And she relaxed against him softly, and sighed. The shaking stopped slowly. Peter went on holding her, trying to control the terrible consuming waves of anger that engulfed him, and it was some little time before he realized suddenly that Melissa-Jane had fallen asleep.

It was as though uttering the name had been a catharsis for her terror, and now she was ready to begin the healing inside.

Peter laid her gently back in the seat and covered her with the angora rug before he drove on, but every few seconds he glanced across to make sure she was at peace.

Twice Peter called Magda Altmann from Abbots Yew, both times to her private number, but she was unobtainable and there was no message for him. That was five days he had not been able to reach her, not since the Delta Strike which had freed Melissa-Jane. She seemed to have disappeared completely, and Peter pondered the implications during the quiet days when he was almost always alone with his daughter.

Then Dr Kingston Parker arrived at Abbots Yew, and Sir Steven Stride was delighted to have as his guest such a distinguished statesman.

Kingston Parker's giant personality seemed to fill the beautiful old home. When he put himself out, his graciousness was irresistible. Steven was delighted with him, particularly when he discovered that despite Parker's image as a liberal and his well-known concern for human rights, he was also a champion of the capitalist system, and determined that his country should take more seriously its responsibilities as leader of the Western world. They both deplored the loss of the B1 bomber and the delaying of the neutron bomb programme, and the restructuring of America's intelligence agencies. They spent much of the first afternoon in Steven's redwood-panelled study exploring each other's views, and came out of it fast friends.

When they emerged, Parker completed his conquest of the Stride household by showing he shared with Patricia Stride a scholarly knowledge and love of antique porcelain. His concern and warmth for Melissa-Jane and his relief at her safety were too spontaneous not to be entirely genuine. His conquest of that young lady's affections was complete when he went down with her to the stables to meet Florence Nightingale and prove that he was also a fair judge of horseflesh.

'He's a lovely man. I think he is truly an honourable man,' Melissa-Jane told Peter, when he went up to her bedroom to bid her goodnight. '– And he's so kind and funny –' Then, lest there be any question of disloyalty, 'But you are still my most favourite man in all the world.'

Her cure and convalescence seemed almost complete, and as Peter went down to rejoin the company he marvelled again at the resilience of young flesh and young minds.

As usual at Abbots Yew there was glittering and stimulating company at dinner, with Kingston Parker at its centre, but afterwards he and Peter exchanged a single glance down the length of Pat Stride's silver- and candle-decorated table and they left them to the port and cognac and cigars and slipped out unobtrusively into the walled rose garden.

While they paced side by side on the crunching gravel pathway, Kingston Parker stoked his meerschaum and then began to talk quietly. Once his bodyguard coughed in the shadows where he waited just out of range of their subdued voices, but that was the only intrusion and the spring night was still and balmy. Their conversation seemed utterly incongruous in these surroundings, talk of death and violence, the use and abuse of power, and the manipulations of vast fortunes by a single mysterious figure.

'It's been five days since I arrived in England –' Kingston Parker shrugged. 'One does not rush through the echoing passages of Whitehall. There was much to discuss –' Peter knew that he had met with the Prime Minister on two separate occasions. '– And it wasn't just Atlas business, I'm afraid –' Parker was one of the President's confidants. They would have taken full advantage of his visit to exchange views with the British Government. 'However, we did discuss Atlas in depth and detail. You know very well that Atlas has opponents and critics on both sides of the Atlantic. They tried very hard to squash it, and when they could not they saw to it that its powers and duties were severely curtailed –' Parker paused and his pipe gurgled. He flicked out the juices from the mouthpiece on to the gravel path. 'The opponents of Atlas are all highly intelligent concerned and informed men. Their motives and their reasoning in opposing Atlas are laudable. I find myself a little in sympathy despite myself. If you create a strike force such as Atlas, where enormous powers are placed in the hands of a single man or a small élite leadership, you could very well be creating a Frankenstein – a monster more frightening than you are setting out to destroy.'

'That depends on the man who controls it, Dr Parker. I believe that you have the right man.'

'Thank you, Peter.' Parker turned his big shaggy head and smiled. 'Won't you please call me Kingston.'

Peter nodded agreement, while Parker went on. 'Atlas has had some spectacular successes – at Johannesburg and now in Ireland – but that makes it more dangerous. There will be a readier acceptance of the whole concept by the public; if Atlas asks for wider powers, it is more likely they would be granted. And, believe me, if it is to do the job it needs wider powers, Peter. I find myself torn down the centre –'

'And yet,' Peter pointed out, 'we cannot take on the most dangerous animal in the world, man the killer, we cannot do it without arming ourselves in every possible way.'

Kingston Parker sighed. 'And if Atlas achieves those powers, who can say when they will be abused, when will the rule of force supersede the rule of law?'

'The rules have changed. The rule of law is so often powerless in the face of those who have no respect for the law.'

'There is another aspect, Peter. One that I have thought about half my life. What about the rule of unjust law? The laws of oppression and greed. A law that enslaves or deprives a man because of the colour of his face or the God he worships? If a duly constituted parliament makes racial laws – Or if the General Assembly of the United Nations declares that Zionism is a form of Imperialism and must be outlawed. What if a handful of men gain control of the world's resources and legally manipulate them in a manner dictated by personal greed to the detriment of all mankind, such as the Committee of the OPEC, and the King of Saudi Arabia –' Kingston Parker made a helpless gesture, spreading those long sensitive fingers. 'Must we respect those laws? The rule of law, even unjust law, is it sacrosanct?'

'Balance,' said Peter. 'There has to be a balance between law and force.'

'Yes, but what is the balance, Peter?' He abruptly closed his hands into fists. 'I have asked for greater powers for Atlas, wider scope for its use, and I think these will be granted. When they are, we will have need of good men, Peter.' Kingston Parker reached out and took Peter's shoulder in a surprisingly powerful grip. 'Just men, who can recognize when the rule of law has either failed or is unjust, and who have the courage and the vision to act to restore the balance that you spoke of a moment ago.'

His hand was still on Peter's shoulder and he left it there. It was a natural gesture, without affectation.

'I believe you are one of those men.' He let the hand drop, and his manner changed. 'Tomorrow I have arranged that we meet with Colonel Noble. He has been busy breaking down and examining the entire Irish operation, and I hope he will have come up with something for us to get our teeth into. Then there is much else to discuss. Two o'clock at Thor Command, will it suit you, Peter?'

'Of course.'

'Now let's go in and join the company.'

'Wait.' Peter stopped him. 'I have something I must tell you, Kingston. It's been tearing at my guts, and after you have heard it you may alter your opinion of me – my suitability for my role at Atlas.'

'Yes?' Parker turned back and waited quietly.

'You know that the people who kidnapped my daughter made no demands for her return, made no attempt to contact me or the police to negotiate.'

'Yes,' Parker answered. 'Of course. It was one of the puzzling things about the whole business.'

'It was untrue. There was a contact and a demand.'

'I don't understand.' Parker frowned and thrust his face closer to Peter's as though trying to study his expression in the poor light from the windows.

'The kidnappers contacted me. A letter which I destroyed –'

'Why?' Parker shot at him.

'Wait. I'll explain,' Peter replied. 'There was a single condition for my daughter's release, and a deadline of two weeks. If I did not meet the condition by that time, they would have sent me parts of my daughter's body – her hands, her feet, and finally her head.'

'Diabolical,' Parker whispered. 'Inhuman. What was the condition?'

'A life for a life,' said Peter. 'I was to kill you in exchange for Melissa-Jane.'

'Me!' Parker started, throwing back his head with shock. 'They wanted me?'

Peter did not reply, and they stood staring at each other, until Parker raised his hand and combed at his hair, a distracted gesture.

'That changes it all. I will have to think it out carefully – but it makes a whole new scenario.' He shook his head. 'Me. They were going for the head of Atlas. Why? Because I was the champion of Atlas, and they opposed its formation? No! That's not it. There seems only one logical explanation. I told you last time I saw you that I suspected the existence of a central figure – the puppetmaster who was taking control of all known militant organizations and welding them into a single cohesive and formidable entity. Well, Peter, I have been hunting this figure. I have learned much to confirm my suspicions since last we met. I believe this person, or assembly of persons, does in fact exist – part of the new powers I have asked for Atlas were to be used to hunt and destroy this organization before it does grave damage – before it succeeds in so terrifying the nations of the world that it becomes itself a world power – ' Parker stopped as though to gather his thoughts, and then went on in quieter more measured tones. 'I think now that this is absolute proof that it does exist, and that it is aware of my suspicions and intentions to destroy it. When I set you up as Atlas agent at large, I believed you would make contact with the enemy – but, God knows, I did not expect it to come like this.'

He paused again, considering it. 'Incredible!' He marvelled. 'The one person whom I would never have suspected, you, Peter. You could have reached me at any time, one of the few people who could. And the leverage! Your daughter – the protracted mutiliations – I may have just misjudged the cunning and ruthlessness of the enemy.'

'Have you ever heard the name Caliph?' Peter asked.

'Where did you hear that?' Parker demanded harshly.

'The demand letter was signed Caliph, and Melissa-Jane heard her captors discussing it.'

'Caliph.' Parker nodded. 'Yes, I have heard the name, Peter. Since I last spoke to you. I have heard the name. Indeed I have.' He was silent again, sucking distractedly on his pipe, then he looked up. 'I will tell you how and when tomorrow when we meet at Thor, but now you have given me much to keep me awake tonight.'

He took Peter's arm and led him back towards the house. Warm yellow light and laughter spilled out from the downstairs windows, welcoming and gay, but both of them were withdrawn and silent as they trudged up the smoothly raked path.

At the garden door Kingston Parker paused, holding Peter back from entering.

'Peter, would you have done it?' he asked gruffly.

Peter answered him levelly without attempting to avoid his eyes. 'Yes, Kingston, I would have done it.'

'How?'

'Explosives.'

'Better than poison,' Parker grunted. 'Not as good as the gun.' And then angrily, 'We have to stop him, Peter. It is a duty that supersedes every other consideration.'

'What I have just told you does not alter our relationship?' Peter asked. 'The fact that I would have been your assassin – does not change it?'

'Strangely enough, it merely confirms what I have come to believe of you, Peter. You are a man with the hard ruthless streak we need, if we are to survive.' He smiled bleakly. 'I might wake up sweating in the night – but it doesn't alter what we have to do – you and I.'

Colin Noble with his cheroot, and opposite him Kingston Parker with the amber meerschaum, seemed to be in competition as to who could soonest render the air in the room incapable of supporting human life. It was already thick and blue, and the temporary headquarters of Thor Command lacked air-conditioning – but within minutes Peter had become so immersed in what he was hearing that the discomfort was forgotten.

Colin Noble was going over the details of the Irish operation, and all that had been gleaned from it.

'The house, the Old Manse, was burned to the ground, of course, the Irish constabulary had twenty men sifting through the ashes –' He spread his hands. 'A big nix. Nothing at all.

'Next the contents of the Austin and its – provenance – how do you like that word, Peter Baby? Provenance, that's a classy word.'

Parker smiled indulgently. 'Please go on, Colin.'

'The Austin was stolen in Dublin, and resprayed and fitted with the roof carrier. It contained nothing, no papers, nothing in the glove compartment or boot, it had been stripped and cleaned out by an expert –'

'The men,' Parker prompted him.

'Yes, sir. The men. The dead one first. Name of Gerald O'Shaughnessy, also known as "Gilly", born Belfast 1946 –' As he spoke Colin picked up the file that lay on the table in front of him. It was five inches thick. '– Do we want to read all of it? It's a hell of a story. The guy had a track record –'

'Only as far as it concerns Atlas,' Parker told him.

'There is no evidence as to when or how he became involved with this business –' Colin sketched the facts swiftly and succinctly. '– So we end with the contents of his pockets. Six hundred pounds sterling, thirty-eight rounds of .38 ammunition, and papers in the name of Edward and Helen Barry – forged, but beautifully forged.' Colin closed the file with a snap. 'Nothing,' he repeated. 'Nothing we can use. Now the other man. Morrison – Claude Bertram Morrison – celebrated abortionist and dedicated alcoholic. Struck off the medical rolls in 1969 –' Again he recounted the sordid history swiftly and accurately. '– His price for the digital surgery was three thousand pounds – half in advance. Hell, that's cheaper than Blue Cross.' Colin grinned but his eyes were black and bright with anger. 'I am pleased to report that he can expect a sentence of approximately fifteen years. They are going to throw the book at him. There is only one item of any possible interest which he could give us. Gilly O'Shaughnessy was the leader from whom he took his orders, O'Shaughnessy in turn took his orders from somebody called –' He paused dramatically. 'Yes, that's right. The name we have all heard before. Caliph.'

'Just one point here,' Kingston Parker interrupted. 'Caliph likes to use his name. He signs it on his correspondence. Even his lowliest thugs are given the name to use. Why?'

'I think I can answer that.' Peter stirred and raised his head. 'He wants us to know that he exists. We must have a focal point for our fear and hatred. When he was merely a nameless, faceless entity he was not nearly as menacing as he is now.'

'I think you are right.' Parker nodded his head gravely. 'By using the name he is building up a store of credibility which he will draw upon later. In future when Caliph says he will kill or mutilate we know he is in deadly earnest, there will be no compromise. He will do exactly as he promises. The man, or men, are clever psychologists.'

'There is just one aspect of the Irish operation we have not yet considered,' Peter broke in, frowning with concentration. 'That is – who was it that tipped us off, and what was the reason for that telephone call?'

They were all silent, until Parker turned to Colin.

'What do you think of that one?'

'I have discussed it with the police, of course. It was one of the first things that puzzled us. The police believe that Gilly O'Shaughnessy picked his hideout in Ireland because he was familiar with the terrain, and had friends there. It was his old stamping ground when he was with the Provos. He could move and disappear, get things fixed.' Colin paused and saw the sceptical expression on Peter's face. 'Well, look at it this way, Peter Baby. He had a woman negotiate the lease on the Old Manse – Kate Barry, she called herself and signed it on the lease – so that was one ally, there must have been others, because he was able to buy a stolen and reworked automobile – he would have had difficulty doing that in Edinburgh or London without the word getting about.'

Peter nodded reluctantly. 'All right, having the Irish connection helped him –'

'– But there was the other side of the coin. O'Shaughnessy had enemies, even in the Provos. He was a ruthless bastard with a bloody record. We can only believe that one of those enemies saw the chance to make a score – the one who sold him the stolen auto, perhaps. We have had the recording of the tip-off call examined by language experts and had a run against the voice prints on the computer. Nothing definite. The voice was disguised, probably through a handkerchief and nose plugs, but the general feeling is that it was an Irishman who made the call. The boffins from the telephone department were able to test the loading of the line and guess that it was a call from a foreign country – very likely Ireland, although they cannot be certain of that.'

Peter Stride raised one eyebrow slightly, and Colin chuckled weakly and waved the cheroot at him in a wide gesture of invitation.

'Okay. That's my best shot,' he said. 'Let's hear you do better. If you don't like my theories, you must have one of your own.'

'You are asking me to believe it was all a coincidence; that O'Shaughnessy just happened to run into an old enemy who just happened to tip us off twenty-four hours before the deadline for Melissa-Jane's hand to be amputated. Then it just so happened that we reached Laragh at exactly the same moment as O'Shaughnessy was pulling out and making a run for it. Is that what you want me to believe?'

'Something like that,' Colin admitted.

'Sorry, Colin. I just don't like coincidence.'

'Shoot!' Colin invited. 'Let's hear how it really happened.'

'I don't know,' Peter grinned placatingly. 'It is just that I have this feeling that Caliph doesn't deal in coincidence either. I have this other feeling that somehow Gilly O'Shaughnessy had the death mark on his forehead from the beginning. I have this feeling it was all part of the plan.'

'It must be great fun to have these feelings.' Colin was prickling a little. 'But they sure as hell aren't much help to me.'

'Take it easy.' Peter held up one hand in surrender. 'Let's accept tentatively that it happened your way, then –'

'But?' Colin asked.

'No buts – not until we get some more hard evidence –'

'Okay, Buster.' There was no smile on Colin's face now, the wide mouth clamped in a grim line. 'You want hard evidence, try this one for size –'

'Hold it, Colin,' Parker shot in quickly, authoritatively. 'Wait for a moment before we come to that.' And Colin Noble deflated with a visible effort, the cords in his throat smoothing out and the line of mouth relaxed into the old familiar grin as he deferred to Kingston Parker.

'Let's backtrack here a moment,' Parker suggested. 'Peter came up with the name Caliph. In the meantime we had picked up the name – but from an entirely different source. I promised Peter I would tell him about our source – because I think it gives us a new insight into this entire business.' He paused and tinkered with his pipe, using one of those small tools with folding blades and hooks and spikes with which pipe smokers arm themselves. He scraped the bowl and knocked a nub of half-burned tobacco into the ashtray, before peering into the pipe the way a rifleman checks the bore of his weapon. Peter realized that Parker used his pipe as a prop for his performances, the way a magician distracts his audience with flourishes and mumbojumbo. He was not a man to underestimate, Peter thought again for the hundredth time. Kingston Parker looked up at him and smiled, a conspiratorial smile as if to acknowledge that Peter had seen through his little act.

'Our news of Caliph comes from an unlikely direction – or rather, considering the name, a more likely direction. East. Riyadh to be precise. Capital city of Saudi Arabia, seat of King Khalid's oil empire. Our battered and beleaguered Central Intelligence Agency has received an appeal from the King following the murder of one of his grandsons. You recall the case, I'm sure –' Peter had a strange feeling of *déjà-vu* as he listened to Kingston Parker confirming exactly the circumstances that he and Magda Altmann had discussed and postulated together, was it only three weeks before? '– You see the King and his family are in a very vulnerable position really. Did you know that there are at least seven hundred Saudi princes who are multi-millionaires, and who are close to the King's affections and power structure? It would be impossible to guard that many potential victims adequately. It's really damned good thinking – you don't have to seize a hostage with all the attendant risks. There is virtually an unlimited supply of them walking around, ripe for plucking, and an inexhaustible supply of assassins to be either pressured or paid to do the job, just as long as you have the information and leverage, or just enough money. Caliph seems to have all that.'

'What demand has been made upon Khalid?' Peter asked.

'We know for certain that he had received a demand, and that he has appealed to the CIA for assistance to protect and guard his family. The demand came from an agency or person calling himself Caliph. We do not know what the demand is – but it may be significant that Khalid has agreed that he will not support a crude oil price increase at the next pricing session of OPEC, but on the contrary he will push for a five per cent decrease in the price of crude.'

'Caliph's thinking has paid off again,' Peter murmured.

'It looks like it, doesn't it.' Parker nodded, and then chuckled bitterly. 'And once again you get the feeling, as with his demands to the South African Government, that his final objective is desirable – even if the way he goes about procuring it is slightly unconventional, to say the least.'

'To say the very least,' Peter agreed quietly, remembering the feel of Melissa-Jane's fever-racked body against his chest.

'So there is no doubt now that what we feared, is fact. Caliph exists –' said Parker.

'Not only exists, but flourishes,' Peter agreed.

'Alive and well with a nice house in the suburbs.' Colin lit the stub of his cheroot before going on. 'Hell! He succeeded at Johannesburg. He is succeeding at Riyadh – where does he go from there – why not the Federation of Employers in West Germany? The Trade Union leaders in Great Britain? – Any group powerful enough to affect the fate of nations, and small enough to be terrorized as individuals.'

'It's a way to sway and direct the destiny of the entire world – you just cannot guard all the world's decision-makers from personal attack,' Peter agreed. 'And it's no argument to point out that because his first two targets have been South Africa and the oil monopoly, then the long term results will be to the benefit of mankind. His ultimate target will almost certainly be the democratic process itself. I don't think there can be any doubt that Caliph sees himself as a God. He sees himself as the paternal Tyrant. His aim is to cure the ills of the world by radical surgery, and to maintain its health by unrestrained force and fear.'

Peter could remain seated no longer. He pushed back his chair and crossed to the windows, standing there in the soldier's stance, balanced on the balls of his feet with both hands clasped lightly behind his back. There was an uninspiring view of the high barbed-wire fence, part of the airfield and the corrugated sheet wall of the nearest hangar. A Thor sentry paced before the gates with a white MP helmet on his head and side arm strapped to his waist. Peter watched him without really seeing him, and behind him the two men at the table exchanged a significant glance. Colin Noble asked a silent question and Parker answered with a curt nod of affirmation.

'All right, Peter,' Colin said. 'A little while back you asked for hard facts. I promised to give you a few.'

Peter turned back from the window and waited.

'Item One. During the time that Gilly O'Shaughnessy held Melissa-Jane in Laragh, two telephone calls were made from the Old Manse. They were both international calls. They both went through the local telephone exchange. The first call was made at seven p.m. local time on the first of this month. That would have been the first day that they could have reached the hideout. We have to guess it was an "All Well" report to the top management. The second call was exactly seven days later again at seven o'clock local time precisely. To the same number. We have to guess that it was another report, "All is still well." Both calls were less than one minute in duration. Just time enough to pass a prearranged code message –' Colin broke off and looked again at Kingston Parker.

'Go on,' Parker instructed.

'The calls were to a French number. Rambouillet 47-87-47.'

Peter felt it hit him in the stomach, a physical blow, and he flinched his head. For a moment closing both his eyes tightly. He had called that number so often, the numerals were graven on his memory.

'No.' He shook his head, and opened his eyes. 'I'm not going to believe it.'

'It's true, Peter,' Parker said gently.

Peter walked back to his seat. His legs felt rubbery and shaky under him. He sat down heavily.

The room was completely silent. Neither of the other two looked directly at Peter Stride.

Kingston Parker made a gesture to Colin and obediently he slid the red box file, tied with red tapes, across the cheap vinyl-topped table.

Parker untied the tapes and opened the file. He shuffled the papers, scanning them swiftly. Clearly he was adept at speed reading and was able to assimilate each typed double-spaced page at a glance – but now he was merely waiting for Peter to recover from the shock. He knew the contents of the red file almost by heart.

Peter Stride slumped in the steel-framed chair with its uncushioned wooden seat, staring sightlessly at the bulletin board on the opposite wall on which were posted the Thor rosters.

He found it hard to ride the waves of dismay that flooded over him. He felt chilled and numbed, the depth of this betrayal devastated him, and when he closed his eyes again he had a vivid image of the slim, tender body with the childlike breasts peeping through a silken curtain of dark hair.

He straightened in his seat, and Kingston Parker recognized the moment and looked up at him, half closing the file and turning it towards him.

The cover bore the highest security gradings available to Atlas Command – and below them was typed:

ALTMANN MAGDA IRENE. Born KUTCHINSKY.

Peter realized that he had never known her second name was Irene. Magda Irene. Hell, they were really ugly names – made special only by the woman who bore them.

Parker turned the file back to himself and began to speak quietly.

'When last you and I met, I told you of the special interest we had in this lady. That interest has continued, unabated, since then, or rather it has gathered strength with every fresh item of information that has come to us.' He opened the file again and glanced at it as if to refresh his memory. 'Colin has been very successful in enlisting the full cooperation of the intelligence agencies of both our countries, who in turn have been able to secure that of the French and – believe it or not – the Russians. Between the four countries we have been able to at last piece together the woman's history –' He broke off. 'Remarkable woman,' and shook his head in admiration. 'Quite incredible really. I can understand how she is able to weave spells around any man she chooses. I can understand, Peter, your evident distress. I am going to be utterly blunt now – we have no time nor space in which to manoeuvre tactfully around your personal feelings. We know that she has taken you as a lover. You notice that I phrase that carefully. Baroness Altmann takes lovers, not the other way around. She takes lovers deliberately and with careful forethought. I have no doubt that once she has made the decision, she accomplishes the rest of it with superb finesse.'

Peter remembered her coming to him and the exact words she had used. 'I am not very good at this, Peter, and I want so badly to be good for you.'

The words had been chosen with the finesse that Kingston Parker had just spoken of. They were exactly turned to make herself irresistible to Peter – and afterwards she had given the gentle lie to them with the skill and devilish cunning of her hands and mouth and body.

'You see, Peter. She had special and expert training in all the arts of love. There are probably few women in the Western world who know as much about reading a man, and then pleasing him. What she knows she did not learn in Paris or London or New York –' Kingston Parker paused and frowned at Peter. 'This is all theory and hearsay, Peter. You are in a better position to say just how much of it is false?'

The ultimate skill in pleasing a man is to fuel his own belief in himself, Peter thought, as he returned Parker's inquiring gaze with expressionless eyes. He remembered how with Magda Altmann he had felt like a giant, capable of anything. She had made him feel like that with a word, a smile, a gift, a touch – that was the ultimate skill.

He did not answer Parker's question. 'Go on please, Kingston,' he invited. Externally, he had himself completely under control now. His right hand lay on the table top, with the fingers half open, relaxed.

'I told you that even as a child she showed special talents. In languages, mathematics – her father was an amateur mathematician of some importance – chess and other games of skill. She attracted attention. Especially she attracted attention because her father was a member of the Communist Party –' Parker broke off as Peter lifted his head in sharp inquiry. '– I'm sorry, Peter. We did not know that when last we met. We have learned it since from the French, they have access to the party records in Paris it seems, and it was confirmed by the Russians themselves. Apparently the child used to accompany her father to meetings of the party, and soon showed a precocious political awareness and understanding. Her father's friends were mostly party members, and after his death – there still remains a mystery around his death. Neither the French nor the Russians are forthcoming on the subject. – Anyway, after his death, Magda Kutchinsky was cared for by these friends. It seemed she was passed on from family to family –' Kingston Parker slid a postcard-sized photograph from a marbline envelope and passed it across the table to Peter. '– from this period.'

It showed a rather skinny little girl in short skirts and dark stockings, wearing the yoked collar and straw bonnet of the French schoolgirl. Her hair was in two short braids, tied with ribbons, and she held a small fluffy white dog in her arms. The background was a Parisian summer park scene, with a group of men playing *boule* and chestnut trees in full leaf.

The child's face was delicately featured with huge beautiful eyes, somehow wise and compassionate beyond her age, and yet still imbued with the fresh innocence of childhood.

'You can see she already had all the markings of spectacular beauty.' Kingston Parker grunted, and reached across to take back the photograph. For a moment Peter's fingers tightened instinctively, he would have liked to have kept it, but he relaxed and let it go. Parker glanced at it again and then slipped it back into the envelope.

'Yes. She attracted much interest, and very soon an uncle from the old country wrote to her. There were photographs of her father and the mother she had never known, anecdotes of her infancy and her father's youth. The child was enchanted. She had never known she had an uncle. Her father had never spoken of his relatives, but now at last the little orphan found she had family. It took only a few more letters, exchanges of delight and affection, and then it was all arranged. The uncle came to fetch her in person – and

Magda Kutchinsky went back to Poland.' Parker spread his hands. 'It was easy as that.'

'The missing years,' Peter said, and his voice sounded strange in his own ears. He cleared his throat and shifted uncomfortably under Parker's piercing but understanding gaze.

'No longer missing, Peter. We have been fed a little glimmering of what happened during those years – and we have been able to fill in the rest of it from what we knew already.'

'The Russians?' Peter asked, and when Parker nodded, Peter went on with a bitter tang to his voice. 'They seem to be very forthcoming, don't they? I have never heard of them passing information – at least not valuable information – so readily.'

'They have their reasons in this case,' Parker demurred. 'Very good reasons as it turns out – but one will come to those in due course.'

'Very well.'

'The child returned with her uncle to Poland, Warsaw. And there was an extravagant family reunion. We are not certain if this was her real family, or whether the child was provided with a foster family for the occasion. In any event, the uncle soon announced that if Magda would submit to examination there was an excellent chance that she would be provided with a scholarship to one of the élite colleges of the USSR. We can imagine that she passed her examination with great distinction and her new masters must have congratulated themselves on their discovery.

'The college is on the shores of the Black Sea near Odessa. It does not have a name, nor an old school tie. The students are very specially selected, the screening is rigorous and only the brightest and most talented are enrolled. They are soon taught that they are an élite group and are streamed in the special direction that their various talents dictate. In Magda's case it was languages and politics, finance and mathematics. She excelled and at the age of seventeen graduated to a higher, more specialized branch of the Odessa college. There she was trained in special memory techniques, the already bright mind was honed down to a razor edge. I understand that one of the less difficult exercises was to be given access to a list of a hundred diverse items for sixty seconds. The list had to be repeated from memory, in the correct order, twenty-four hours later.' Parker shook his head again, expressing his admiration.

'At the same time she was also trained to fit naturally into upper-class international Western society. Dress, food, drink, cosmetics, manners, popular music and literature, cinema, theatre, democratic politics, business procedures, the operation of stocks and commodities markets, the more mundane secretarial skills, modern dancing, the art of lovemaking and pleasuring men – that and much else, all of it taught by experts – flying, skiing, weapons, the rudiments of electronics and mechanical engineeering and every other skill that a top-class agent might have to call upon.

'She was the star of her course and emerged from it much as the woman you know. Poised, skilled, beautiful, motivated – and deadly.

'At the age of nineteen she knew more, was capable of more, than most other human beings, male or female, twice her age. The perfect agent, except for a small flaw in her make-up that only showed up later. She was too intelligent and too personally ambitious.' Kingston Parker smiled for the first time in twenty minutes. '– Which of course is a pseudonym for Greed. Her masters did not recognize it in her, and perhaps at that age it was only latent greed. She had not yet been fully exposed to the attractions of wealth – nor of unlimited power.'

Kingston Parker broke off, leaned across the table towards Peter. He seemed to change direction then, smiling an inward knowledgeable smile, as though pondering a hidden truth.

'Greed for wealth alone belongs essentially to the lower levels of human intelligence. It is only the developed and advanced mind that can truly appreciate the need for power –' He saw the protest in Peter's expression. '– No, no, I don't mean merely the power to control one's own limited environment, merely the power of life and death over a few thousand lives – not that, but true power. Power to change the destiny of nations, power such as Caesar or Napoleon wielded, such as the President of the United States wields – that is the ultimate greed, Peter. A magnificent and noble greed.'

He was silent a moment, as though glimpsing some vision of splendour. Then he went on:

'I digress. Forgive me,' and turned to Colin Noble. 'Do we have some coffee, Colin? I think we could all do with a cup now.'

Colin went to the machine that blooped and gurgled and winked its red eye in the corner, and while he filled the cups, the charged atmosphere in the room eased a little, and Peter tried to arrange his thoughts in some logical sequence. He looked for the flaws and weak places in the story but could find none – instead he remembered only the feel of her mouth, the touch of her hands on his body. Oh God, it was a stab of physical pain, a deep ache in the chest and groin, as he remembered how she had coursed him like a running stag, driving and goading him on to unvisited depths of his being. Could such skills be taught, he wondered, and if so, by whom? He had a horrifying thought of a special room set on the heights above the Black Sea, with that slim, vulnerable tender body practising its skills, learning love as though it were cookery or small arms practice – and then he shut his mind firmly against it, and Kingston Parker was speaking again, balancing his coffee cup primly with his pinky finger raised, like an old maid at a tea party.

'So she arrived back in Paris and it fell at her feet. It was a triumphant progress.' Kingston Parker prodded in the file with his free hand, spilling out photographs of Magda – Magda dancing in the ballroom of the Elysée Palace, Magda leaving a Rolls Royce limousine outside Maxim's in the rue Royale, Magda skiing, riding, beautiful, smiling, poised – and always there were men. Rich, well-fed, sleek men.

'I told you once there were eight sexual liaisons.' Kingston Parker used that irritating expression again. 'We have had reason to revise that figure.

The French take a very close interest in that sort of thing, they have added to the list.' He flicked over the photographs. 'Pierre Hammond, Deputy Minister of Defence –' And another. 'Mark Vincent, head of mission at the American Consulate –'

'Yes,' Peter cut in short, but still there was a sickly fascination in seeing the faces of these men. He had imagined them accurately, he realized, without particular relish.

'Her masters were delighted – as you can imagine. With a male agent it is sometimes necessary to wait a decade or more for results while he moles his way into the system. With a young and beautiful woman she has her greatest value when those assets are freshest. Magda Kutchinsky gave them magnificent value. We do not know the exact extent of her contributions – our Russian friends have not bared everything to us, I'm afraid, but I estimate that it was about this time they began to realize her true potential. She had the magical touch, but her beauty and youth could not last for ever –' Kingston Parker made a deprecating gesture with the slim pianist's hands. '– We do no know if Aaron Altmann was a deliberate choice by her masters. But it seems likely. Think of it – one of the richest and most powerful men in Western Europe, one who controlled most of the steel and heavy engineering producers, the single biggest armaments complex, electronics – all associated and sensitive secondary industries. He was a widower, childless, so under French law his wife could inherit his entire estate. He was known to be fighting a slowly losing battle with cancer, so his life term was limited – and he was also a Zionist and one of the most trusted and influential members of Mossad. It was beautiful. Truly beautiful,' said Kingston Parker. 'Imagine being able to undermine a man of that stature, perhaps being able to double him! Though that seemed an extravagant dream – not even the most beautiful siren of history could expect to turn a man like Aaron Altmann – He is a separate study on his own, another incredible human being with the strength and courage of a lion – until the cancer wore him out. Again I digress, forgive me. Somebody, either the Director of the NKVD in Moscow, or Magda Kutchinsky's control at the Russian Embassy in Paris, who was, incidentally, the Chief NKVD Commissar for Western Europe, such was her value, or Magda Kutchinsky herself, picked Aaron Altmann. Within two years she was indispensable to him. She was cunning enough not to use her sexual talents upon him immediately. Altmann could have any woman who took his fancy, and he usually did. His sexual appetites were legendary, and they probably were the cause of his remaining childless. A youthful indiscretion resulted in venereal disease with complications. It was later completely cured, but the damage was irreversible, he never produced an heir.'

He was a man who would have toyed with her and cast her aside as soon as he tired of her, if she had been callow enough to make herself immediately available to him.

First, she won his respect and admiration. Perhaps she was the first woman he had ever met whose brain and strength and determination matched his own –

Kingston Parker selected another photograph and passed it across the table. Fascinated, Peter stared at the black and white image of a heavily built man with a bull neck, and a solid thrusting jaw. Like so many men of vast sexual appetite, he was bald except for a Friar Tuck frill around the cannonball dome of his skull. But there were humorous lines chiselled about his mouth, and his eyes, though fierce, looked as though they too could readily crinkle with laughter lines. Portrait of Power, Peter thought.

'When at last she gave him access to her body, it must have been like some great electrical storm.' Kingston Parker seemed to be deliberately dwelling on her past love affairs, and Peter would have protested had not the information he was receiving been so vital. 'This man and woman must have been able to match each other once again. Two very superior persons, two in a hundred million probably – it is interesting to speculate what might have happened if they had been able to produce a child.' Kingston Parker chuckled. 'It would probably have been a mongolian idiot – life is like that.'

Peter moved irritably, hating this turn in the conversation, and Parker went on smoothly.

'So they married, and the NKVD had a mole in the centre of Western industry. Narmco, Altmann's armaments complex, was manufacturing top-secret American, British and French missile hardware for NATO. The new Baroness was on the Board, was in fact Deputy Chairman of Narmco. We can be sure that armaments blueprints were passed, not by the sheet but by the truckload. Every night, the leaders and decision-makers of the Western world sat at the new Baroness's board and swilled her champagne. Every conversation, every nuance and indiscretion was recorded by that specially trained memory, and slowly, inevitably, the Baron's strength was whittled away. He began to rely more and more upon her. We do not know exactly when she began to assist him with his Mossad activities – but when it happened the Russians had succeeded in their design. In effect they had succeeded in turning Baron Aaron Altmann, they had his right hand and his heart – for by this time the dying Baron was completely besotted by the enchantress. They could expect to inherit the greater part of Western European heavy industry. It was all very easy – until the latent defect in the Baroness's character began to surface. We can only imagine the alarm of her Russian masters when they detected the first signs that the Baroness was working for herself alone. She was brighter by far than any of the men who had up until that time controlled her, and she had been given a taste of real power. The taste seemed very much to her liking. We can only imagine the gargantuan battle of wills between the puppet masters and the beautiful puppet that had suddenly developed a mind of her very own – quite simply her ambition now was to be the most wealthy and powerful woman since Catherine of Russia, and the makings were almost within her pretty hands – except –'

Kingston Parker stopped; like a born storyteller, he knew instinctively how to build up the tension in his audience. He rattled his coffee cup.

'This talking is thirsty business.' Colin and Peter had to rouse themselves with a physical effort. They had been mesmerized by the story and personality of the storyteller. When Parker had his cup refilled, he sipped at it, then went on speaking.

'There was one last lever her Russian masters had over her. They threatened to expose her. It was quite a neat stroke, really. A man like Aaron Altmann would have acted like an enraged bull if he had known how he had been deceived. His reaction was predictable. He would have divorced Magda immediately. Divorce is difficult in France – but not for a man like the Baron. Without his protection Magda was nothing, less than nothing, for her value to the Russians would have come to an end. Without the Altmann Empire her dreams of power would disappear like a puff of smoke. It was a good try – it would have worked against an ordinary person, but of course they were not dealing with an ordinary person –'

Parker paused again; it was clear he was as wrapped up by the story as they were, and he was drawing out the pleasure of the telling it.

'I have been doing a lot of talking,' he smiled at Peter. 'I'm going to let you have a chance now, Peter. You know her a little, you have learned a lot more about her in the last hour. Can you guess what she did?'

Peter began to shake his head – and then it crashed in upon him with sickening force, and he stared at Parker, the pupils of his eyes dilating with the strength of his revulsion.

'I think you have guessed.' Parker nodded. 'Yes, we can imagine that by this stage she was becoming a little impatient herself. The Baron was taking a rather long time to die.'

'Christ, it's horrible.' Peter grunted, as though in pain.

'– From one point of view, I agree.' Parker nodded. 'But if you look at it like a chess player, and remember she is a player of Grand Master standard, it was a brilliant stroke. She arranged that the Baron be kidnapped. There are witnesses to the fact that she insisted on the Baron accompanying her that day. He was feeling very bad, and he did not want to go sailing, but she insisted that the sun and fresh air would be good for him. He never took his bodyguard when he went sailing. There were just the two of them. A very fast cruiser was waiting offshore –' He spread his hands. '– You know the details?'

'No,' Peter denied it.

'The cruiser rammed the yacht. Picked the Baron out of the water, but left the Baroness. An hour later there was a radio message to the coastguard, they went out and found her still clinging to the wreckage. The kidnappers were very concerned that she survived.'

'They may have wanted a loving wife to bargain with,' Peter suggested swiftly.

'That is possible, of course, and she certainly played the role of the bereaved wife to perfection. When the ransom demand came it was she who forced the Board of Altmann Industries to ante up the twenty-five million dollars. She personally took the cash to the rendezvous – alone.' Parker paused significantly.

'She didn't need the money.'

'Oh, but she did,' Parker contradicted. 'The Baron was not in his dotage, you know. His hands were still very firmly on the reins – and the purse strings. Magda had as much as any ordinary wife could wish for, furs, jewellery, servants, clothes, cars, boats – pocket money, around two hundred thousand dollars a year, paid to her as a salary from Altmann Industries. Any ordinary wife would have been well content – but she was not an ordinary wife. We must believe she had already planned how to carry forward her dreams of unlimited power – and it needed money, not thousands but millions. Twenty-five million would be a reasonable stopgap, until she could get her pretty little fingers on the big apple. – She drove the cash, in thousand-Swiss-franc bills, I understand; she drove alone to some abandoned airfield and had a plane come and pick it up and fly it out to Switzerland. Damned neat.'

'But –' Peter searched for some means of denial. '– But the Baron was mutilated. She couldn't –'

'Death is death, mutilation may have served some obscure purpose. God knows, we are dealing with an Eastern mind, devious, sanguinary – perhaps the mutilation was merely to make any suspicion of the wife completely far-fetched – just as you immediately used it to protect her.'

He was right, of course. The mind that could plan and execute the rest of such a heinous scheme would not baulk at the smaller niceties of execution. He had no more protest to make.

'So let us review what she had achieved by this stage. She was rid of the Baron, and the restrictions he placed upon her – an example of these restrictions, for we will find it significant later. She was very strongly in favour of Narmco banning the sale of all weapons and armaments to the South African Government. The Baron, ever the businessman, looked upon that country as a lucrative market. There was also the South African sympathy for Zionism. He overruled her, and Narmco continued to supply aircraft, missiles and light armaments to that country right up until the official UN resolution to enforce a total arms embargo, with France ratifying it. Remember the Baroness's anti-South African attitude. We come to it again later.

'She was rid of the Baron. She was rid of her Russian control, well able to maintain a small army to protect herself. Even her former Russian masters would hesitate to take revenge on her. She was a French Grande Dame now. She had gained significant working capital – twenty-five million for which she was not accountable to another living human being. She had gained an invincible power base at Altmann Industries. Although she was still under certain checks and safeguards from the Board of Directors, yet she had access to all its information-gathering services, to its vast resources. As the head of such a colossus she had the respect of and sympathy of the French Government, and as a fringe benefit – limited but significant access to their intelligence systems. Then there was the Mossad connection, was she not the heir to Aaron Altmann's position –'

Peter suddenly remembered Magda speaking of her 'sources' – and never identifying them. Was she really able to use the French and Israeli intelligence as her own private agencies? It seemed impossible. But he was learning swiftly that when dealing with Magda Altmann, anything was possible – as Kingston Parker had pointed out, she was not an ordinary person – but Parker was speaking again.

'There was a period then of consolidation, a time when she gathered up the reins that Aaron had dropped. There were changes amongst the top management throughout Altmann Industries as she replaced those who might oppose her with her own minions. A time of planning and organizing, and then the first attempt to govern and prescribe the destiny of nations. She chose the nation which most offended her personal view of the new world she was going to build. We will never know what made her choose the name of Caliph –'

'You have to be wrong.' Peter squeezed his eyelids closed with thumb and forefinger. 'You just don't know her.'

'I don't think anybody knows her, Peter,' Kingston Parker murmured, and fiddled with his pipe. 'I'm sorry, we are going pretty fast here. Do you want to back up and ask any questions?'

'No, it's all right.' Peter opened his eyes again. 'Go on, will you, Kingston?'

'One of the most important lessons that Baroness Altmann had learned was the ease with which force and violence can be used, and their tremendous effect and profitablity. Bearing this lesson in mind, the Baroness chose her first act as the new ruler of mankind, and the choice was dictated by her early political convictions, those convictions formed at her father's knee and at the Communist Party meetings that she had attended as a precocious child in Paris. There is a further suggestion that the choice was reinforced by the Altmann banking corporation's interests in South African gold sales, for by this time the Baroness had tempered her socialist and communist leanings with a good healthy dollop of capitalistic self-interest. We can only guess, but if the scheme to bring out forty tons of gold – and a black-based government-in-exile – had succeeded, it would not have taken very long for Caliph to gain control of both government and gold –' Parker shrugged. '– We just cannot say how ambitious, even grandiose, those plans were. But we can say that Caliph, or the Baroness, recruited her team for the execution of the plan with the skill she brought to anything she handled.' He broke off, and smiled. 'I think all three of us remember the taking of Flight 070 vividly enough not to have to go once more over the details. Let me just remind you that it would have succeeded, in fact it had actually succeeded, when Peter here made his unscheduled move that brought it all down. But it succeeded. That was the important thing. Caliph could afford to congratulate herself. Her information was impeccable. She had chosen the right people for the job. She even knew the name of the officer who would command the anti-terrorist force which would be sent to intervene, and her psychology had been excellent. The execution of the four hostages had so shocked and numbed the opposition that they were powerless – the cup had been dashed from her lips by one man alone. Inevitably her interest in that man was aroused. Possibly with feminine intuition she was able to recognize in him the qualities which could be turned to her own purpose. She had that indomitable streak in her make-up that is able to recognize even in the dust of disaster that material for future victory –' Parker shifted his bulk, and made a small deprecatory gesture. '– I hope it will not seem immodest if I bring myself into the story at this stage. I had been given the hint that something like Caliph existed. In fact this may not have been her first act after the killing of Aaron Altmann. Two other successful kidnappings have her style – one of them the OPEC ministers in Vienna – but we cannot be sure. I had been warned and I was waiting for Caliph to surface. Dearly I would have loved a chance to interrogate one of the hijackers –'

'They would have had nothing to tell you,' Peter interjected brusquely. 'There were merely pawns, like the doctor we captured in Ireland.'

Parker sighed. 'Perhaps you are right, Peter. But at the time I believed that our only lead to Caliph had been severed. Later when the thing had been done and I had recovered from the shock of it, it suddenly occurred to me that the lead was still there – stronger than ever. You were that lead, Peter. That was why I recommended that your resignation be accepted. If you had not resigned, I would have forced you out anyway, but you played along superbly by resigning –' He smiled again. '– I have never thanked you for that.'

'Don't mention it,' said Peter grimly. 'I like to be of service.'

'And you were. Almost immediately you were on the loose, the Baroness began making her approach. First she collected every known fact about you. Somehow she even got a computer run on you. That's a fact. An unauthorized run was made on the Central Intelligence computer four days after your resignation. She must have liked what she got, for there was the Narmco offer – through conventional channels. Your refusal must have truly excited her interest, for she used her connections to have herself invited down to Sir Steven's country house.' Parker chuckled. 'My poor Peter, you found yourself without warning in the clutches of one of history's most accomplished enchantresses. I know enough about the lady to guess that her approach to you was very carefully calculated from the complete information that she had on you. She knew exactly what type of woman attracted you. Fortunately, she fitted the general physical description –'

'What is that?' Peter demanded. He was unaware that he had a specific type of physical preference.

'Tall, slim and brunette,' Parker told him promptly. 'Think about it,' he invited. 'All your women have been that.'

He was right, of course, Peter realized. Hell, even at thirty-nine years of age it was still possible to learn something about yourself.

'You're a cold-blooded bastard, Kingston. Did anybody ever tell you that?'

'Frequently.' Kingston smiled. 'But it's not true, and compared to Baroness Altmann I am Father Christmas.' And he became serious again. 'She wanted to find out what we at Atlas know about her activities. She knew by this stage that we had our suspicions, and through you she had an inside ear. Of course, your value would deteriorate swiftly the longer you were out of Thor – but you could still be useful in a dozen other ways. As a bonus you could be expected to do a good job at Narmco. All her expectations were fulfilled, and exceeded. You even thwarted an assassination attempt on her life –'

Peter lifted an eyebrow in inquiry.

'– On the road to Rambouillet that night. Here we are only guessing, but it's a pretty well-informed guess. The Russians had by this time despaired of returning her to the fold. They had also suspicions as to her role as Caliph. They decided on a radical cure for their one-time star agent. They either financed and organized the assassination attempt themselves, or they tipped off Mossad that she had murdered Aaron Altmann. I would be inclined to believe that they hired the killers themselves – because the Mossad usually do their own dirty work. Anyway, with NKVD or Mossad as paymasters, an ambush was set up on the Rambouillet road and you drove into it. I know you don't like coincidence, Peter, but I believe it was merely coincidence that you were driving the Baroness's Maserati that night.'

'All right,' Peter murmured. 'If I swallow the rest of the hog, that little crumb goes down easily enough.'

'That attempt severely alarmed the Baroness. She was not certain who had been the author. I think she believed it was Atlas Command, or at the very least that we had something to do with it. Almost immediately after that you were able to confirm our interest in her, and our knowledge that Caliph existed. I invited you to America, Colin brought you to meet me, and when you returned you either told her about it, or in some way confirmed her suspicions of Atlas Command and Kingston Parker. I am guessing again – but how close am I, Peter? Be honest.'

Peter stared at him, trying to keep his face expressionless while his mind raced. That was exactly how it had happened.

'We were all hunting Caliph. You saw no disloyalty in discussing it with her.' Parker prompted him gently, and Peter nodded once curtly.

'You believed that we had common goals,' Parker went on with deep understanding and compassion. 'You thought we were all hunting Caliph. That is right.'

'She knew I had been to America to see you before I told her. I don't know how – but she knew,' Peter said stiffly. He felt like a traitor.

'I understand,' Parker said simply. He reached across the table and once again placed his hand on Peter's shoulder. He squeezed it while he looked into Peter's eyes, a gesture of affirmation and trust. Then he laid both hands on top of the table.

'She knew who was the hunter then, and she knew enough about me to know I was dangerous. You were probably the only man in the world who could reach me and do the job – but you had to be motivated. She picked the one and only lever that would move you. She picked it unerringly – just as she had done everything else. It would have worked – in one stroke she would have gotten rid of the hunter, and she would have acquired a top-class assassin. When you had done the job, you would have belonged to Caliph for all time. She would have used you to kill again and again, and each time you killed you would be more deeply enmeshed in her net. You really were a very valuable prize, Peter. Valuable enough for her to find it worthwhile to use her sexual wiles upon you.'

He saw the lumps of clenched muscle at the corner of Peter's jaw, and the fire in his eyes.

'You are also a very attractive man, and who knows but she felt the need to combine business and pleasure? She is a lady with strongly developed sexual appetites.'

Peter felt a violent urge to punch him in the face. He needed some outlet for his rage. He felt belittled, soiled and used.

'She was clever enough to realize that sex was not enough of a hold to force you to commit murder. So she took your daughter, and immediately had her mutilated – just as at Johannesburg she had executed hostages without hesitation. The world must learn to fear Caliph.'

There was no smile on Parker's face now.

'I truly believe that if you had not been able to deliver my head by deadline, she would not have hesitated to carry out the next mutilation, and the one after that.'

Again Peter was assailed by a wave of nausea as he remembered that the shrivelled white lump of flesh with the scarlet fingernail floating horribly in its tiny bottle.

'We were saved from that by the most incredible piece of luck. The Provo informer,' said Parker. 'And again the understandable eagerness of the Russians to cooperate with us. It is a wonderful opportuntiy for them to hand us their problem. They have let us have an almost full account of the lady and her history.'

'But what are we going to do about it?' Colin Noble asked. 'Our hands are tied. Do we just have to wait for the next atrocity – do we have to hope we will get another lucky break when Caliph kills the next Arab prince?'

'That will happen – unless they push through the OPEC decision,' Parker predicted levelly. 'The lady has converted very easily to the capitalist system now that she owns half of Europe's industry. A reduction in the oil price would benefit her probably more than any other individual on earth – and at the same time it will also benefit the great bulk of humanity. How nicely that squares all her political and personal interests.'

'But if she gets away with it—' Colin insisted. ' – What will be her next act of God?'

'Nobody can predict that,' Parker murmured, and they both turned their heads to look at Peter Stride.

He seemed to have aged twenty years. The lines at the corners of his mouth were cut in deeply like the erosion of weathered granite. Only his eyes were blue and alive and fierce as those of a bird of prey.

'I want you to believe what I am going to say now, Peter. I have not told you all this to put pressure on you,' Parker assured him quietly. 'I have told you only what I believe is necessary for you to know – to protect yourself if you should elect to return into the lion's den. I am not ordering you to do so. The risks involved cannot be overestimated. With a lesser man I would term it suicidal. However, now that you are forewarned, I believe you are the one man who could take Caliph on her own ground. Please do not misunderstand what I mean by that. I am not for a moment suggesting assassination. In fact I expressly forbid you even to think in that direction. I would not allow it, and if you acted independently, I would do my utmost to see that you were brought to justice. No, all I ask is that you keep close to Caliph and try to outguess her. Try to expose her so we can lawfully act to take her out of action. I want you to put out of your mind the emotional issues – those hostages at Johannesburg, your daughter – try to forget them, Peter. Remember we are neither judge nor executioner—' Parker went on speaking quietly and insistently, and Peter watched his lips with narrowed eyes, hardly listening to the words, trying to think clearly and see his course ahead – but his thoughts were a children's carousel, going around and around with fuss and fury but returning with every revolution to the one central conclusion.

There was only one way to stop Caliph. The thought of attempting to bring someone like Baroness Magda Altmann to justice – in a French Court – was laughable. Peter tried to force himself to believe that vengeance had no part in his decisions, but he had lived too long with himself to be able to pull off such a deceit. Yes, vengeance was part of it – and he trembled with the rage of remembrance, but it was not all of it. He had executed the German girl Ingrid, and Gilly O'Shaughnessy – and he had not regretted the decision to do so. If it was necessary for them to die – then surely Caliph deserved to die a thousand times more.

And there is only one person who can do it, he realized.

Her voice was quick and light and warm, with just that fascinating trace of accent; he remembered it so well, but had forgotten the effect it could have upon him. His heart pounded as though he had run a long way.

'Oh Peter. It's so good to hear your voice. I have been so worried. Did you get my cable?'

'No, which cable?'

'When I heard that you had freed Melissa-Jane, I sent you a cable from Rome.'

'I didn't get it – but it doesn't matter.'

'I sent it to you via Narmco – in Brussels.'

'It's probably waiting for me there. I haven't been in touch.'

'How is she, Peter?'

'She is fine now—' He found it strangely difficult to use her name, or any form of endearment. He hoped that the strain would not sound in his voice. 'But we went through a hell of a time.'

'I know. I understand. I felt so helpless. I tried so hard, that's why I was out of contact, Peter chéri, but day after day there was no news.'

'It's all over now,' Peter said gruffly.

'I don't think so,' she said swiftly. 'Where are you calling from?'

'London.'

'When will you come back?'

'I telephoned Brussels an hour ago. Narmco wants me back urgently. I am taking a flight this afternoon.'

'Peter, I have to see you. I've been too long without you – but, oh mon Dieu, I have to be in Vienna tonight. Wait, let me see, if I sent the Lear to fetch you now we could meet, even for an hour. You could take the late flight from Orly to Brussels and I could go on to Vienna with the Lear – please, Peter. I missed you so. We could have an hour together.'

One of the airport sub-managers met Peter as he disembarked from the Lear and led him to one of the VIP lounges above the main concourse.

Magda Altmann came swiftly to meet him as he stepped into the lounge – and he had forgotten how her presence could fill a room with light.

She wore a tailored jacket over a matching skirt, severe gun-metal grey and tremendously effective. She moved like a dancer on long graceful legs which seemed to articulate from the narrow waist – and Peter felt awkward and heavy-footed, for the awareness that he was in the presence of evil sat heavily upon him, weighing him down.

'Oh, Peter. What have they done to you?' she asked with quick concern flaring in those huge compassionate eyes. She reached up to touch his cheek.

The strain and horror of the last days had drawn him out to the edge of physical endurance. His skin had a greyish, sickly tone against which the dark new beard darkening his jaws contrasted strongly. There were more fine silver threads at his temples, gull's wings against the thicker darker waves of his hair, and his eyes were haunted. They had sunk deeply into their sockets.

'Oh darling, darling,' she whispered, low enough so that the others in the room could not hear her, and she reached up with her mouth for his.

Peter had carefully schooled himself for this meeting. He knew how important it was that he should not in any way betray the knowledge he had. Magda must never guess that he had found her out. That would be deadly dangerous. He must act completely naturally. It was absolutely vital, but there was just that instant's remembrance of his daughter's pale wasted fever-racked features, and then he stooped and took Magda's mouth.

He forced his mouth to soften, as hers was soft and warm and moist, tasting of ripe woman and crushed petals. He made his body welcoming as hers was melting and trusting against his – and he thought he had succeeded completely until she broke gently from his embrace and leaned back, keeping those slim strong hips still pressed against his. She studied his face again, a swift probing, questioning gaze, and he saw it change deep in her eyes. The flame going out of them leaving only a cold merciless green light, like the beautiful spark in the depths of a great emerald.

She had seen something, no there had been nothing to see. She had sensed something in him, the new awareness. Of course, she would have been searching for it. She needed only the barest confirmation – the quirk of expression on his mouth, the new wariness in his eyes, the slight stiffness and reserve in his body – all of which he thought he had been able to control perfectly.

'Oh I am glad you are wearing blue now.' She touched the lapel of his casual cashmere jacket. 'It does suit you so well, my dear.'

He had ordered the jacket with her in mind, that was true – but now there was something brittle in her manner. It was as though she had withdrawn her true self, bringing down an invisible barrier between them.

'Come.' She turned away, leading him to the deep leather couch below the picture windows. Some airport official had been able to find flowers, yellow tulips, the first blooms of spring, and there was a bar and coffee machine.

She sat beside him on the couch, but not touching him, and with a nod dismissed her secretary. He moved across the room to join the two bodyguards, her grey wolves, and the three of them remained out of earshot, murmuring quietly amongst themselves.

'Tell me, please, Peter.' She was still watching him, but the cold green light in her eyes had been extinguished – she was friendly and concerned, listening with complete attention as he went step by step over every detail of Melissa-Jane's kidnapping.

It was an old rule of his to tell the complete truth when it would serve – and it served now, for Magda would know every detail. He told her of Caliph's demand for Kingston Parker's life, and his own response.

'I would have done it,' he told her frankly, and she hugged her own arms and shuddered once briefly.

'God, such evil can corrupt even the strongest and the best—' and now there was an understanding softening her lips.

Peter went on to tell her of the lucky tip-off and the recovery of Melissa-Jane. He went into details of the manner in which she had been abused, of her terror and the psychological damage she had suffered – and he watched Magda's eyes carefully. He saw something there, emphasized by the tiny frown that framed them. He knew that he could not expect feelings of guilt. Caliph would be far beyond such mundane emotion – but there was something there, not just stagey compassion.

'I had to stay with her. I think she needed those few days with me,' he explained.

'Yes. I am glad you did that, Peter.' She nodded, and glanced at her wristwatch. 'Oh, we have so little time left,' she lamented. 'Let's have a glass of champagne. We have a little to celebrate. At least Melissa-Jane is alive, and she is young and resilient enough to recover completely.'

Peter eased the cork and when it popped he poured creaming pale yellow Dom Perignon into the flutes, and smiled at her over the glass as they saluted each other.

'It's so good to see you, Peter.' She was truly a superb actress, she said it with such innocent spontaneity that he felt a surge of admiration for her despite himself. He crushed it down and thought that he could kill her now and here. He did not really need a weapon. He could use his hands if he had to, but the Cobra parabellum was in the soft chamois leather holster under his left armpit. He could kill her, and the two bodyguards across the room would gun him down instantly. He might take one of them, but the other would get him. They were top men. He had picked them himself. They would get him.

'I'm sorry we will not be together for very long,' he countered, still smiling at her.

'Oh, chéri. I know, so am I.' She touched his forearm, the first touch since the greeting embrace. 'I wish it were different. There are so many things that we have to do, you and I, and we must forgive each other for them.'

Perhaps the words were meant to have a special significance; there was a momentary flash of the warm green fire in her eyes, and something else – perhaps a deep and unfathomable regret. Then she sipped the wine, lowered the long curled lashes across her eyes, shielding them from his scrutiny.

'I hope we will never have anything terrible to forgive—'

For the first time he faced the act of killing her. Before it had been something clinical and academic, and he had avoided considering the deed itself. But now he imagined the impact of an explosive Velex bullet into that smooth sweet flesh. His guts lurched, and for the first time he doubted if he were capable of it.

'Oh, Peter, I hope so. More than anything in life, I hope that.' She lifted her lashes for a moment, and her eyes seemed to cling to his for an instant, pleading for something – forgiveness, perhaps. If he did use the gun, then how would he do it, he wondered. Could he stand the feeling of cartilage and bone snapping and cracking under his fingers, could he hold the blade of a knife into her flat hard belly and feel her fight it like a marlin fights the gleaming curved hook of the gaff?

The telephone on the bar buzzed, and the secretary picked it up on the second ring. He murmured into it.

'Oui, oui. D'accord.' And hung up. 'Ma Baronne, the aircraft is refuelled and ready to depart.'

'We will leave immediately,' she told him, and then to Peter, 'I am sorry.'

'When will I see you?' he asked.

She shrugged, and a little shadow passed over her eyes. 'It is difficult. I am not sure – I will telephone you. But now I must go, Peter. Adieu, my darling.'

When she had gone, Peter stood at the windows overlooking the airfield. It was a glorious spring afternoon, the early marguerites were blooming wild along the grass verges of the main runways, like scattered gold sovereigns, and a flock of black birds hopped amongst them, probing and picking for insects, completely undisturbed by the jet shriek of a departing Swissair flight.

Peter ran his mind swiftly over the meeting. Carefully identifying and isolating the exact moment when she had changed. When she had ceased to be Magda Altmann and become Caliph.

There was no doubt left now. Had there ever been, he wondered, or had it merely been his wish to find doubt?

Now he must harden himself to the act. It would be difficult, much more difficult than he had believed possible. Not once had they been alone, he realized then – always the two grey wolves had hovered around them. It was just another sign of her new wariness. He wondered if they would ever be alone together again – now that she was alerted.

Then abruptly he realized that she had not said 'Au revoir, my darling' but instead she had said, 'Adieu, my darling'.

Was there a warning in that? A subtle hint of death – for if Caliph suspected him, he knew what her immediate reaction must be. Was she threatening, or had she merely discarded him, as Kingston Parker had warned that she would?

He could not understand the desolate feeling that swamped him at the thought that he might never see her again – except through the gunsight.

He stood staring out of the window, wondering how his career and his life had begun to disintegrate about him since first he had heard the name Caliph.

A polite voice at his shoulder startled him and he turned to the airport sub-manager. 'They are calling the KLM flight to Brussels now, General Stride.'

Peter roused himself with a sigh and picked up his overcoat and the crocodile-skin Hermés briefcase that had been a gift from the woman he must kill.

There was such a volume of correspondence and urgent business piling the long desk in his new office that Peter had excuse to put aside the detailed planning of the pre-emptive strike against Caliph.

To his mild surprise he found himself enjoying the jostle and haggle, the driving pace and the challenge of the market place. He enjoyed pitting wits and judgement against other sharp and pointed minds, he enjoyed the human interaction – and for the first time understood the fascination which this type of life had exerted over his brother Steven.

Three days after arriving back at his desk, the Iranian Air Force made their first order of the Narmco Kestrel missiles. One hundred and twenty units, over a hundred and fifty million dollars' worth. It was a good feeling, and could grow stronger, could finally become addictive, he realized.

He had always looked upon money as rather a nuisance, those degrading and boring sessions with bank managers and clerks of the income tax department, but now he realized that this was a different kind of money. He had glimpsed the world in which Caliph existed, and realized how once a human being became accustomed to manipulating this kind of money, then dreams of godlike power became believable, capable of being transmuted into reality.

He could understand, but could never forgive, and so at last, seven days after his return to Brussels, he forced himself to face up to what he must do.

Magda Altmann had withdrawn. She had made no further contact since that brief and unsatisfactory hour at Orly Airport.

He must go to her, he realized. He had lost his special inside position which would have made the task easier.

He could still get close enough to kill her, of that he was certain. Just as he had the opportunity to do so at Orly. However, if he did it that way it would be suicidal. If he survived the swift retribution of her guards, there would be the slower but inexorable processes of the law. He knew without bothering to consider it too deeply that he would be unable to use the defence of the Caliph story. No court would believe it. It would sound like the rantings of a maniac without the support of Atlas or the intelligence systems of America and Britain. That support would not be forthcoming – of that he was certain. If he killed Caliph they would be delighted, but they would let him go to the guillotine without raising a voice in his defence. He could imagine the moral indignation of the civilized world if they believed that an unorthodox organization such as Atlas was employing assassins to murder the prominent citizens of a foreign and friendly nation.

No. He was on his own, completely. Parker had made that quite clear. And Peter realized that he did not want to die. He was not prepared to sacrifice his life to stop Caliph – not unless there was no other way. There had to be another way, of course.

As he planned it he thought of the victim only as Caliph – never as Magda Altmann. That way he was able to bring a cold detachment to the problem. The where, the when, and the how of it.

He had complicated the task by replanning her personal security, and his major concern when he did so had been to make her movements as unpredictable as possible. Her social calendar was as closely guarded as a secret of state, there were never any forward press reports of attendance at public or state events.

If she were invited to dine at the Élysée Palace, the fact was reported the day after, not the day before – but there were some annual events that she would never miss. Together they had discussed these weaknesses in her personal security.

'Oh, Peter – you cannot make a convict of me.' She had laughed in protest when he mentioned them. 'I have so few real pleasures – you would not take them from me, would you?'

The first seasonal showing of Yves St Laurent's collections, that she would never miss – or the Grande Semaine of the spring racing season which culminates with the running of the Grand Prix de Paris at Longchamp. This year she had high hopes of victory with her lovely and courageous bay mare, Ice Leopard. She would be there. It was absolutely certain.

Peter begun to draw up the list of possible killing grounds, and then crossed off all but the most likely. The estate of La Pierre Bénite, for instance. It had the advantage of being familiar ground for Peter. With a soldier's eye he had noticed fields of fire across the wide terraced lawns that dropped down to the lake; there were stances for a sniper in the forests along the far edge of the lake, and in the little wooded knoll to the north of the house which commanded the yard and stables. However, the estate was well guarded and even there the victim's movements were unpredictable. It would be possible to lie in ambush for the week when she was in Rome or New York. Then again the escape route was highly risky, though a sparsely populated area with only two access roads – both easily blocked by swift police action. No. La Pierre Bénite was crossed from the list.

In the end Peter was left with the two venues that had first sprung to mind – the members' enclosure at Longchamp or Yves St Laurent's premises, at 46 Avenue Victor Hugo.

Both had the advantages of being public and crowded, circumstances favouring pickpockets and assassins, Peter thought wryly. Both had multiple escape routes, and crowds into which the fugitive could blend. There were good stances for a sniper in the grandstands and buildings overlooking the members' enclosure and the saddling paddock at Longchamp or in the multi-storeyed buildings opposite No. 46 in the Avenue Victor Hugo.

It would probably be necessary to rent an office in one of the buildings – with the attendant risks, even if he used a false name, which put the probability slightly in favour of the racecourse. However, Peter delayed the final decision until he had a chance to inspect each site critically.

There was one last advantage in doing it this way. It would be a stand-off kill. He would be spared the harrowing moments of a kill at close range with handgun or knife or garrotte.

There would be a detached view of Caliph through the lens of a telescopic sight. The flattened perspectives and the altered colour balances always made for a feeling of unreality. The intervening distance obviated the need for confrontation. He would never have to watch the green light go out in those magnificent eyes, nor hear the last exhalation of breath through the soft and perfectly sculptured lips that had given him so much joy – quickly he thrust those thoughts aside. They weakened his resolve, even though the rage and the lust for vengeance had not abated.

If he could get one of the Thor .222 sniper rifles it would be the perfect tool for this task. With the extra long, accurized barrels designed for use with match grade ammunition and the new laser sights, the weapon could throw a three-inch group at seven hundred yards.

The sniper had only to depress the button on the top of the stock with the forefinger of his left hand. This activated the laser and the beam swept precisely down the projected flight of the bullet. It would show as a bright white coin the size of a silver dime. The sniper looked for the spot of light through the telescopic lens of the sight, and the moment it was exactly on the target he pressed the trigger. Even an unskilled marksman could hardly miss with this sight, in Peter's hands it would be infallible – and Colin Noble would give him one. Not only would Colin give him one, hell, he would probably have it delivered with the compliments of the American Marine Corps by the senior military attaché of the US Embassy in Paris.

Yet Peter found himself drawing out the moment of action, going over his plans so often and with such a critical eye that he knew he was procrastinating.

The sixteenth day after his return to Brussels was on a Friday. Peter spent the morning on the NATO range north of the city at a demonstration of the new electronic shield that Narmco had developed to foil the radar guidance on short-range anti-tank missiles. Then he helicoptered back with the three Iranian officers who had attended the demonstration and they lunched at Epaule de Mouton, a magnificent and leisurely meal. Peter still felt guilty spending three hours at the lunch table, so he worked until eight o'clock that evening, on the missile contracts.

It was long after dark when he left through the rear entrance, taking all his usual precautions against the chance that Caliph had an assassin waiting for him in the dark streets. He never left at the same time nor followed the same route, and this evening he bought the evening papers from a *marchand du tabac* in the Grand'Place and stopped to read them at one of the outdoor cafés overlooking the square.

He began with the English papers, and the headlines filled the page from one side to the other; black and bold, they declared:

DROP IN PRICE OF CRUDE OIL

Peter sipped the whisky thoughtfully as he read the article through, turning to Page Six for the continuation.

Then he crumpled the newsprint in his lap, and stared at the passing jostle of spring tourists and early evening revellers.

Caliph had achieved her first international triumph. From now on there would be no bounds to her ruthless rampage of power and violence.

Peter knew he could delay no longer. He made the go decision then, and it was irrevocable. He would arrange to visit London on Monday morning, there was excuse enough for that. He would ask Colin to meet him at the airport, and it would be necessary to tell him of his plan. He knew he could expect full support. Then he could move on to Paris for the final reconnaissance and the choice of killing ground. There was still two weeks until the showing of the spring collections – two weeks to plan it so carefully that there would be no chance of failure.

He felt suddenly exhausted, as though the effort of decision had required the last of his reserves. So exhausted that the short walk back to the hotel seemed daunting. He ordered another whisky and drank it slowly before he could make the effort.

Narmco maintained two permanent suites at the Hilton for their senior executives and other important visitors. Peter had not yet made the effort of finding private accommodation in the city, and he was living out of the smaller of the two suites. It was merely a place to wash and sleep and leave his clothes, for he could not shake off the feeling of impermanence, of swiftly changing circumstances, by which he found himself surrounded.

My books are in storage again, he thought with a little chill of loneliness. His collection of rare and beautiful books had been in storage for the greater part of his life, as he roamed wherever his duty took him, living out of barracks and hotel rooms. His books were his only possessions, and as he thought about them now he was filled with an unaccustomed longing to have a base, a place that was his own – and immediately he thrust it aside, smiling cynically, at himself as he strode through the streets of another foreign city, alone again.

It must be old age catching up with me, he decided. There had never been time for loneliness before – but now, but now? Unaccountably he remembered Magda Altmann coming into his arms saying quietly:

'Oh, Peter, I have been alone for so long.'

The memory stopped him dead, and he stood in the light of one of the street lamps, a tall figure in a belted trench coat with a gaunt and haunted face.

A blonde girl with lewdly painted lips sauntered towards him down the sidewalk, pausing to murmur a proposition, and it brought Peter back to the present.

'Merci.' He shook his head in curt refusal and walked on.

As he passed the bookstall in the lobby of the Hilton, a rack of magazines caught his attention and he stopped at the shelf of women's magazines. There would be announcements of the Paris haute couture showings soon, and he thumbed the pages of *Vogue* looking for mention of Yves St Laurent's show – instead he was shocked by the image of a woman's face that leapt out of the page at him.

The elegant cheekbone structure framing the huge slanted Slavic eyes. The shimmering fall of dark hair, the feline grace of movement frozen by the camera flash.

In the photograph she was in a group of four people. The other woman was the estranged wife of a pop singer, the sulky expression, slightly skew eyes and bee-stung lips a landmark on the Parisian social scene. Her partner was a freckled, boyish-faced American actor in a laid-back velvet suit with gold chains around his throat, more famous for his sexual exploits than his film roles. They were not the type of persons with whom Magda Altmann habitually associated, but the man beside her, on whose arm she leaned lightly, was much more her style. He was fortyish, dark and handsome in a fleshy heavily built way, with dense wavy hair, and he exuded the special aura of power and confidence that befitted the head of the biggest German automobile manufacturing complex.

The caption below the photograph had them attending the opening of an exclusive Parisian discotheque – again this was not Magda Altmann's habitual territory, but she was smiling brilliantly at the tall handsome German, so obviously enjoying herself that Peter felt a stinging shaft of emotion thrust up under his ribs. Hatred or jealousy – he was not certain – and he slapped the magazine closed and returned it to his rack.

In the impersonal antiseptically furnished suite he stripped and showered, and then standing naked in the small lounge of the suite he poured himself a whisky. It was his third that evening.

Since the kidnapping he had been drinking more than ever before in his life, he realized. It could exert an insidious hold when a man was lonely and in grave doubt. He would have to begin watching it. He took as sip of the smoky amber liquid and turned to look at himself in the mirror across the room.

Since he had been back in Brussels, he had worked out each day in the gymnasium at the NATO officers' club where he still had membership, and his body was lean and hard with a belly like a greyhound's – only the face was ravaged by the strain and worry – and, it seemed, by some deep unutterable regret.

He turned back towards the bedroom of the suite, and the telephone rang.

'Stride,' he said into the mouthpiece, standing still naked with the glass in his right hand.

'Please hold on, General Stride. We have an international call for you.'

The delay seemed interminable with heavy buzzing and clicking on the line, and the distant voices of other operators speaking bad French or even worse English.

Then suddenly her voice, but faint and so far away that it sounded like a whisper in a vast and empty hall.

'Peter, are you there?'

'Magda?' He felt the shock of it, and his voice echoed back at him from the receiver; there was a click before she spoke again, that switch of carrier wave that told him they were on a radio telephone link.

'I have to see you, Peter. I cannot go on like this. Will you come to me, please, Peter?'

'Where are you?'

'Les Neuf Poissons.' Her voice was so faint, so distorted, that he asked her to repeat it.

'Les Neuf Poissons – The Nine Fishes,' she repeated. 'Will you come, Peter?'

'Are you crying?' he demanded, and then the silence echoed and clicked and hummed so he thought they had lost contact, and he felt a flare of alarm so his voice was harsh as he asked again. 'Are you crying?'

'Yes.' It was only a breath, he might have imagined it.

'Why?'

'Because I am sad and frightened, Peter. Because I am alone, Peter. Will you come, please will you come?'

'Yes,' he said. 'How do I get there?'

'Ring Gaston at La Pierre Bénite. He will arrange it. But come quickly, Peter. As quickly as you can.'

'Yes. As soon as I can – but where is it?'

He waited for her reply, but now the distances of the ether echoed with the sound of utter finality.

'Magda? Magda?' He found himself shouting desperately, but the silence taunted him and reluctantly he pressed a finger down on the cradle of the telephone.

'Les Neuf Poissons,' he repeated softly, and lifted the finger. 'Operator,' he said, 'please get me a call to France Rambouillet 47-87-47.' And while he waited he was thinking swiftly.

This was what he had been subconsciously waiting for, he realized. There was a feeling of inevitability to it, the wheel could only turn – it could not roll sideways. This was what had to happen.

Caliph had no alternative. This was the summons to execution. He was only surprised that it had not come sooner. He could see why Caliph would have avoided the attempt in the cities of Europe or England. One such attempt well planned and executed with great force had failed that night on the road to Rambouillet. It would have been a warning to Caliph not to underestimate the victim's ability to retaliate – for the rest, the problems would have been almost the same as those that Peter had faced when planning the strike against Caliph herself.

The when and the where and the how – and Caliph had the edge here. She could summon him to the selected place – but how incredibly skilfully it had been done. As he waited for the call to Rambouillet, Peter marvelled at the woman afresh. There seemed no bottom to her well of talent and accomplishments – despite himself, knowing full well that he was listening to a carefully rehearsed act, yet his heart had twisted at the tones of despair in her voice, the muffled weeping perfectly done, so he had only just been able to identify it.

'This is the residence of Baroness Altmann.'

'Gaston?'

'Speaking, sir.'

'General Stride.'

'Good evening, General. I was expecting your call. I spoke to the Baroness earlier. She asked me to arrange your passage to Les Neufs Poissons. I have done so.'

'Where is it, Gaston?'

'Les Neuf Poissons – it's the Baroness's holiday island in the Îles sous le Vent – it is necessary to take the UTA flight to Papeete-Faaa on Tahiti where the Baroness's pilot will meet you. It's another hundred miles to Les Neuf Poissons and unfortunately the airstrip is too short to accommodate the Lear jet – one has to use a much smaller aircraft.'

'When did the Baroness go to Les Neuf Poissons?'

'She left seven days ago, General,' Gaston answered, and immediately went on in the smooth, efficient secretarial voice to give Peter the details of the UTA flight. ' – The ticket will be held at the UTA check-in counter for you, General, and I have reserved a non-smoking seat at the window.'

'You think of everything. Thank you, Gaston.'

Peter replaced the receiver, and found that his earlier exhaustion had left him – he felt vital and charged with new energy. The elation of a trained soldier facing the prospect of violent action, he wondered, or was it merely the prospect of an end to the indecision and the fear of unknown things? Soon, for good or for evil, it would be settled and he welcomed that.

He went through into the bathroom and pitched the whisky that remained in his glass into the handbasin.

The UTA DC 10 made its final approach to Tahiti-Faaa from the east, slanting down the sky with the jagged peaks of Moorea under the port wing. Peter remembered the spectacularly riven mountains of Tahiti's tiny satellite island as the backdrop of the musical movie *South Pacific* that had been filmed on location here. The volcanic rock was black and unweathered so that its crests were as sharp as sharks' fangs.

They arrowed down across the narrow channel between the two islands, and the runway seemed to reach out an arm into the sea to welcome the big silver machine.

The air was heavy and warm and redolent with the perfume of frangipani blossoms, and there were luscious brown girls swinging and swaying gracefully in a dance of welcome. The islands reached out with almost overpowering sweetness and friendliness – but as Peter picked his single light bag out of the luggage hold and started for the exit doors, something unusual happened. One of the Polynesian customs officers at the gate exchanged a quick word with his companion and then politely stepped into Peter's path.

'Good afternoon, sir.' The smile was big and friendly, but it did not stretch as far as the eyes. 'Would you be kind enough to step this way.' The two customs men escorted Peter into the tiny screened office.

'Please open your bags, sir.' Swiftly but thoroughly they went through his valise and crocodile-skin briefcase; one of them even used a measuring stick to check both cases for a hidden compartment.

'I must congratulate you on your efficiency,' said Peter, smiling also, but his voice was tight and low.

'A random check, sir.' The senior officer answered his smile. 'You were just unlucky to be the ten thousandth visitor. Now, sir, I hope you won't object to a body search?'

'A body search?' Peter snapped, and would have protested further, but instead he shrugged and raised both arms. 'Go ahead.'

He could imagine that Magda Altmann was as much the Grande Dame here as she was in mother France. She owned an entire island group, and it would need only a nod to have an incoming visitor thoroughly searched for weapons of any sort.

He could imagine also that Caliph would be very concerned that the intended victim should be suitably prepared for execution, lest he should inadvertently become the executioner.

The one customs officer checked his arms and flanks from armpit to waist, while the other knelt behind him and checked inside and outside of his legs from crotch to ankle.

Peter had left the Cobra in the safe deposit box in the Hilton in Brussels. He had anticipated something like this, it was the way Caliph would work.

'Satisfied?' he asked.

'Thank you for your cooperation, sir. Have a lovely stay on our island.'

Magda's personal pilot was waiting for Peter in the main concourse, and hurried forward to shake his hand.

'I was worried that you were not on the flight.'

'A small delay in customs,' Peter explained.

'We should leave immediately, if we are to avoid a night landing on Les Neuf Poissons – the strip is a little difficult.'

Magda's Gates Lear was parked on the hardstand near the service area, and beside it the Norman Britten Trislander looked small and ungainly, a storklike ugly aircraft capable of the most amazing performance in short take-off and landing situations.

The body of the machine was already loaded with crates and cartons of supplies, everything from toilet rolls to Veuve Cliquot champagne, all tied down under a wide-meshed net.

Peter took the right hand seat, and the pilot started up and cleared with control, then to Peter:

'One hour's flying. We will just make it.'

The setting sun was behind them as they came in from the west and Les Neuf Poissons lay like a precious necklace of emeralds upon the blue velvet cushion of the ocean.

There were nine islands in the characteristic circular pattern of volcanic formation, and they enclosed a lagoon of water so limpid that every whirl and twist of the coral outcrops showed through as clearly as if they were in air.

'The islands had a Polynesian name when the Baron purchased them back in 1945,' the pilot explained in the clearly articulated, rather pedantic French of the Midi. 'They were given by one of the old kings as a gift to a missionary he favoured and the Baron purchased them from his widow. The Baron could not pronounce the Polynesian name so he changed it—' The pilot chuckled. ' – The Baron was a man who faced the world on his own terms.'

Seven of the islands were merely strips of sand and fringes of palms, but the two to the east were larger with hills of volcanic basalt glittering like the skin of a great reptile in the rays of the lowering sun.

As they turned on to their downwind leg, Peter had a view through the window at his elbow of a central building with its roof of palm thatch elegantly curved like the prow of a ship in the tradition of the islands, and around it half-hidden in luscious green gardens were the other smaller bungalows. Then they were over the lagoon and there were a clutter of small vessels around the long jetty which reached out into the protected waters – Hobie-cats with bare masts, a big powered schooner which was probably used to ship the heavy stores such as dieseline down from Papeete, power boats for skiing and diving and fishing. One of them was out in the middle of the lagoon, tearing a snowy ostrich feather of wake from the surface as it ran at speed, a tiny figure towed on skis behind it lifted an arm and waved a greeting. Peter thought it might be her, but at that moment the Trislander banked steeply on to its base leg and he was left with only a view of cumulus cloud bloodied by the setting sun.

The runway was short and narrow, hacked from the palm plantation on the strip of level land between beach and hills. It was surfaced with crushed coral. They made their final approach over a palisade of palm trees. Peter saw that the pilot had not exaggerated by calling it a little difficult. There was a spiteful crosswind rolling in and breaking over the hills, and it rocked the Trislander's wings sickeningly. The pilot crabbed her in, heading half into the wind, and as he skimmed in over the palm tops, closed the throttles, kicked her straight with the rudders, lowered a wing into the wind to hold her from drifting and dropped her neatly fifty feet over the threshold, perfectly aligned with the short runway so she kissed and sat down solidly; instantly the pilot whipped the wheel to full lock into the crosswind to prevent a ground loop and brought her up short.

'Parfait!' Peter grunted with involuntary admiration, and the man looked slightly startled as though the feat deserved no special mention. Baroness Altmann employed only the very best.

There was an electric golf cart driven by a young Polynesian girl waiting at the end of the strip amongst the palm trees. She wore only a pareo wrapped around her body below the armpits, a single length of crimson and gold-patterned cloth that fell to mid thigh. Her feet were bare, but around her pretty head she wore a crown of fresh flowers – the maeva of the islands.

She drove the golf cart at a furious pace along narrow winding tracks through the gardens that were a rare collection of exotic plants, skilfully laid out, so that there was an exquisite surprise around each turn of the path.

His bungalow was above the beach with white sand below the verandah, and the ocean stretching to the horizon, secluded as though it were the only building on the island. Like a child the island girl took his hand, a gesture of perfect innocence, and led him through the bungalow, showing him the controls for the air-conditioning, lighting and the video screen, explaining it all in lisping French patois, and giggling at his expression of pleasure.

There was a fully stocked bar and kitchenette, the small library contained all the current bestsellers, and the newspapers and magazines were only a few days old. The offerings on the video screen included half a dozen recent successful features and Oscar winners.

'Hell, Robinson Crusoe should have landed here,' Peter chuckled, and the girl giggled and wriggled like a friendly little puppy in sympathy.

She came to fetch him again two hours later, after he had showered and shaved and rested and changed into a light cotton tropical suit with open shirt and sandals.

Again she held his hand and Peter sensed that if a man had taken the gesture as licence the girl would have been hurt and confused. By the hand she led him along a path that was demarcated by cunningly concealed glow lights, and the night was filled with the murmur of the ocean and the gentle rustle and clatter of palm fronds moving in the wind.

Then they came to the long ship-roofed building he had seen from the air.

There was soft music and laughter, but when he stepped into the light the laughter stopped and half a dozen figures turned to him expectantly.

Peter was not sure what he had expected, but it was not this gay, social gathering, tanned men and women in expensive and elegant casual wear, holding tall frosted glasses filled with ice and fruit.

'Peter!' Magda Altmannn broke from the group, and came to him with that gliding hip-swinging walk.

She wore a soft, shimmering, wheaten gold dress, held high at the throat with a thin gold chain, but completely nude across the shoulders and down her back to within an inch of the cleft of her buttocks. It was breathtaking for her body was smooth as a rose petal and tanned to the colour of new honey. The dark hair was twisted into a rope as thick as her wrist and piled up on to the top of her head, and she had touched her eyes with shadows so they were slanting and green and mysterious.

'Peter,' she repeated, and kissed him lightly upon the lips, a brush like a moth's wing, and her perfume touched him as softly, the fragrance of Quadrille flowering with the warmth and magic of her body.

He felt his senses tilt. With all he knew of her, yet he was still not hardened to her physical presence.

She was cool and groomed and poised as she had ever been, there was no trace at all of the confusion and fearsome loneliness that he had heard in those muffled and choked-down sobs from halfway across the world – not until she stepped back to tilt her head on one side, surveying him swiftly, smiling lightly.

'Oh, chéri, you are looking so much better. I was so worried about you when last I saw you.'

Only then he thought he was able to detect the shadows deep in her eyes, and the tightness at the corners of her mouth.

'And you are more beautiful than I remembered.'

It was true, so he could say it without reserve, and she laughed, a single soft purr of pleasure.

'You never said that before,' she reminded him, but still her manner was brittle. Her show of affection and friendliness might have convinced him at another time, but not now. 'And I am grateful.'

Now she took his arm, her fingers in the crook of his elbow, and she led him to the waiting group of guests as though she did not trust herself to be alone with him another moment lest she reveal some forbidden part of herself.

There were three men and their wives: an American Democrat senator of considerable political influence, a man with a magnificent head of silver hair, eyes like dead oysters, and a beautiful wife at least thirty years his junior who looked at Peter the way a lion looks at a gazelle and held his hands seconds longer than was necessary.

There was an Australian, heavy in the shoulder and big in the gut. His skin was tanned leathery and his eyes were framed in a network of wrinkles. They seemed to be staring through dust and sun glare at distant horizons. He owned a quarter of the world's known uranium reserves, and cattle stations whose area was twice the size of the British Isles. His wife was as tanned and her handshake was as firm as his.

The third man was a Spaniard whose family name was synonymous with sherry, an urbane and courtly Don, but with that fierce Moorish rake to his thin features. Peter had read somewhere that the sherry and cognac ageing in this man's cellars was valued at over five hundred million dollars, and that formed only a small part of his family's investments. His wife was a darkly brooding Spanish beauty with an extraordinary streak of chalk white through the peak of her otherwise black hair.

As soon as the group had assimilated Peter, the talk turned back easily to the day's sport. The Australian had boated a huge black marlin that morning, a fish over one thousand pounds in weight and fifteen feet from the point of its bill to the tip of the deep sickle tail, and the company was elated.

Peter took little part in conversation. but watched Magda Altmann covertly. Yet she was fully aware of his scrutiny, he could see it the way she held her head, and the tension in her whole long slim body, but she laughed easily with the others and glanced at Peter only once or twice, each time with a smile, but the shadows were in the green depths of her eyes.

Finally she clapped her hands. 'Come, everybody, we are going to open the feast.' She linked arms with the senator and the Australian and led them down on to the beach. Peter was left to cope with the senator's wife, and she pushed her bosom against his upper arm and ran her tongue lightly over her lips as she clung to him.

Two of the Polynesian servants were waiting beside a long mound of white beach sand, and at Magda's signal they attacked it with shovels, swiftly exposing a thick layer of seaweed and banana leaves from which poured columns of thick and fragrant steam. Below that was a rack of banyan wood and palm fronds which suspended the feast over another layer of seaweed and live coals.

There were exclamations of delight as the aroma of chicken and fish and pork mingled with those of bread-fruit and plantains and spices.

'Ah, a success,' Magda declared gaily. 'If any air is allowed to enter the bake we lose it all. It burns, poof! And we are left with only charcoal.'

While they feasted and drank the talk and laughter became louder and less restrained, but Peter made the single drink last the evening and waited quietly – not joining the conversation and ignoring the blandishments of the senator's wife.

He was waiting for some indication of when and from what direction it would come. Not here, he knew, not in this company. When it came it would be swift and efficient as everything else that Caliph did. And suddenly he wondered at his own conceit, that had allowed him to walk, entirely unarmed and unsupported, into the arena selected and prepared by his enemy. He knew his best defence was to strike first, perhaps this very night if the opportunity offered. The sooner the safer, he realized, and Magda smiled at him across the table set under the palm trees and laden with enough food to feed fifty. When he smiled back at her, she beckoned with a slight inclination of her head, and then while the men argued and bantered loudly, she murmured an apology to the women and slipped unobtrusively into the shadows.

Peter gave her a count of fifty before he followed her. She was waiting along the beach. He saw the flash of her bare smooth back in the moonlight and he went forward to where she stood staring out across the wind-ruffled waters of the lagoon.

He came up behind her, and she did not turn her head but her voice was a whisper.

'I am so glad you came, Peter.'

'I am so glad you asked me to.'

He touched the back of her neck, just behind her ear. The ear had an almost elfin point to it that he had not noticed before and the upswept hair at her nape was silken under his fingertips. He could just locate the axis, that delicate bone at the base of the skull which the hangman aims to crush with the drop. He could do it with the pressure of the thumb and it would be as quick as the knot.

'I am so sorry about the others,' she said. 'But I am getting rid of them – with almost indecent haste, I'm afraid.' She reached up over her shoulder and took his hand from her neck, and he did not resist. Gently she spread the hand, and then pressed the open palm to her cheek. 'They will leave early tomorrow. Pierre is flying them back to Papeete, and then we will have Les Neuf Poisssons to ourselves – just you and I—' And then the husky little chuckle. ' – And thirty-odd servants.'

He could understand exactly why it would be that way. The only witnesses would be the faithful retainers of the Grande Dame of the islands.

'Now we must go back. Unfortunately my guests are very important, and I cannot ignore them longer – but tomorrow will come. Too slowly for me, Peter – but it will come.'

She turned in the circle of his arms and kissed him with a sudden startling ferocity, so his lips were crushed against his teeth, and then she broke from him and whispered close to his ear.

'Whatever way it goes, Peter, we have had something of value, you and I. Perhaps the most precious thing I have had in my life. They can never take that from me.'

And then she was out of his arms with that uncanny speed and grace of movement and gliding back along the path towards the lights. He followed her slowly, confused and uncertain as to what she had meant by those last words, concluding finally that the purpose had been exactly that – to confuse and unbalance him, and at that moment he sensed rather than heard movement behind him, and instantly whirled and ducked.

The man was ten paces behind him, had come like a leopard, silently from the cover of a fall of lianas and flowering creepers beside the path; only some animal instinct had warned Peter – and his body flowed into the fighting stance, balanced, strung like a nocked arrow, at once ready both to attack and meet attack.

'Good evening, General Stride.' Peter only just managed to arrest himself, and he straightened slowly, but with each hand still extended stiffly at his side like the blade of a meat cleaver, and as lethal.

'Carl!' he said. So the grey wolves had been close, within feet of them, guarding their mistress even in that intimate moment.

'I hope I did not alarm you,' said the bodyguard – and though Peter could not see the man's expression, there was a faint mockery in his voice. If there was confirmation needed, complete and final, this was it. Only Caliph would have need of a guard on a romantic assignment. Peter knew then beyond any doubt that either he or Magda Altmannn would be dead by sunset the following evening.

Before going into the bungalow he made a stealthy prowling circuit of the bushes and shrubs that surrounded it. He found nothing suspicious but in the interior the bed had been prepared and his shaving gear cleaned and neatly rearranged. His soiled clothing had been taken for cleaning and the other clothing had been pressed and rearranged more neatly than his own unpacking. He could not therefore be certain that his other possessions had not been searched, but it was safe to presume they had. Caliph would not neglect such an elementary precaution.

The locks on doors and windows were inadequate, had probably not been used in years, for there had been no serpents in this paradise, not until recently. So he placed chairs and other obstacles in such a way that an intruder should stumble over them in the dark, and then he rumpled the bed and arranged the pillows to look like a sleeping figure, but took a single blanket to the long couch in the private lounge. He did not really expect an attempt before the other guests left the island, but if it came he would confuse Caliph's scenario as much as possible.

He slept fitfully, jerking awake when a falling palm frond rattled across the roof, or the moon threw picture shadows on the wall across the room. Just before dawn he fell into a deeper sleep and his dreams were distorted and nonsensical, only the sharp clear image of Melissa-Jane's terrorstricken face and her silent screams of horror remained with him when he woke. The memory roused in him the cold lust for vengeance which had abated a little in the weeks since her rescue, and he felt reaffirmed, possessed of a steely purpose once more, determined to resist the softening, fatal allure of Caliph.

He rose in the slippery pearl light of not yet dawn, and went down to the beach. He swam out a mile beyond the reef, and had a long pull back against a rogue current, but he came ashore feeling good and hard and alert as he had not been in weeks.

All right, he thought grimly. Let it come. I'm as ready as I'll ever be.

There was a farewell breakfast for the departing guests, on the sugary sands of the beach that had been swept smooth by the night tide – pink Laurent Perrier champagne and hot-house strawberries flown in from Auckland, New Zealand.

Magda Altmann wore brief green pants that showed off her long shapely legs to perfection, and a matching 'boob tube' across her small neat breasts – but her belly and shoulders and back were bare. It was the body of a finely trained athlete, but drawn by a great artist.

She seemed unnaturally elated to Peter, her gaiety was slightly forced and the low purring laughter just a little too ready – and with a saw edge to it. It was almost as though she had made some hard decision, and was steeling herself to carry it through. Peter thought of them as true opponents who had trained carefully for the coming confrontation – like prize fighters at the weigh-in.

After the breakfast they rode up in a cavalcade of electric carts to the airfield. The Senator, revved up with pink champagne and sweating lightly in the rising heat, gave Magda an over-affectionate farewell, but she skillfully avoided his hands and shunted him expertly into the Trislander after the other passengers.

Pierre, Magda's pilot, stood on the brakes at the end of the runway while he ran all three engines up to full power. Then he let her go, and the moment she had speed he rotated her into a nose-high obstacle-clearance attitude. The ungainly machine jumped into the sky and went over the palms at the end of the short strip with five hundred feet to spare – and Magda turned to Peter ecstatically.

'I hardly slept last night,' she admitted, as she kissed him.

'Neither did I,' Peter told her – and then he added silently '– for the same reasons, I'm sure.'

'I've planned a special day for us,' she went on. 'And I don't want to waste another minute of it.'

The head boatman had Magda's big forty-five-foot Chriscraft Fisherman singled up at the end of the jetty. It was a beautiful boat, with long low attacking lines that made it seem to be flying even when on its mooring lines, and loving care had very obviously been lavished upon it. The paintwork was unmarked and the stainless steel fittings were polished to a mirror finish. The boatman beamed happily when Magda commended him with a smile and a word.

'Tanks are full, Baronne. The scuba bottles are charged and the light rods are rigged. The water-skis are in the main racks, and the chef came down himself to check the ice box.'

However, his wide white smile faded when he learned that Magda was taking the boat out alone.

'Don't you trust me?' she laughed.

'Oh, of course, Baronne –' But he could not hide his chagrin at having to give over his charge – even to such a distinguished captain.

He handled the lines himself, casting her off, and calling anxious last-minute advice to Magda as the gap between jetty and vessel opened.

'Ne t'inquiet pas!' she laughed at him, but he made a dejected figure standing on the end of the jetty as Magda slowly opened up both diesels and the Chris-craft came up on the plane and seemed almost to break free of the surface. Her wake was scored deep and clean and straight through the gin-clear water of the lagoon, a tribute to the design of her hull, and then it curved out gracefully behind them as Magda made the turn between the channel markers and lined her up for the passage through the reef, and out into the open Pacific.

'Where are we going?'

'There is an old Japanese aircraft carrier lying in a hundred feet of water beyond the reef. Yankee aircraft sank her back in 'forty-four – it is a beautiful site for scuba diving. We will go there first —'

How? Peter wondered. Perhaps one of the scuba bottles had been partially filled with carbon monoxide gas. It was simply done, with a hose from the exhaust of the diesel generator, simply pass the exhaust gases through a charcoal filter to remove the taste and smell of unconsumed hydrocarbons and the remaining carbon monoxide gas would be undetectable. Fill the bottle to 30 atmospheres of pressure then top it up with clean air to its operating pressure of 110 atmospheres. It would be swift, but not too swift to alarm the victim, a gentle long sleep. When the victim lost his mouthpiece, the bottles would purge themselves of any trace of the gas. That would be a good way to do it.

'After that we can go ashore on Île des Oiseaux. Since Aaron stopped the islanders stealing the eggs to eat, we've got one of the biggest nesting colonies of terns and noddies and frigate birds in the Southern Pacific —'

Perhaps a spear-gun. That would be direct and effective. At short range, say two feet, even below the surface, the spear arrow would go right through a human torso – in between the shoulder blades and out through the breast bone.

'– Afterwards we can water-ski —'

With an unsuspecting skier in the water, awaiting the pick-up, what could be more effective than opening up both those tremendously powerful diesels to the gates and running the victim down? If the hull did not crush him, the twin screws turning at 500 revolutions per minute would cut him up as neatly as a loaf of pre-sliced bread.

Peter found himself intrigued with the guessing-game. He found himself regretting the fact that he would never know what she intended, and he looked back from where they stood side by side on the tall flying bridge of the Chris-craft. The main island was lowering itself into the water, already they were out of sight of anybody who did not have a pair of powerful binoculars.

Beside him Magda pulled the retaining ribbon out of her hair, and shook loose a black rippling banner that streamed in the wind behind her.

'Let's do this for ever,' she shouted above the wind and the boom of the engines.

'Sold to the lady with the sexy backside,' Peter shouted back, and he had to remind himself that she was one of the most carefully trained killers he would ever meet. He must not allow himself to be lulled by the laughter and the beauty – and he must not allow her to make the first strike. His chances of surviving that were remote.

He glanced back again at the land. Any minute now, he thought, and moved as though to glance over the side, getting slightly into her rear, but still in the periphery of her vision; she shifted slightly towards him still smiling.

'At this state of the tide there are always amberjack in the channel. I promised the chef I would bring him a couple of them kicking fresh,' she explained. 'Won't you go down and get two of the light rods ready, chéri? The feather lures are in the forward starboard locker.'

'Okay,' he nodded.

'I'll throttle back to trolling speed when I make the turn into the channel – put the lines in then.'

'D'accord.' And then on an impulse. 'But kiss me first.'

She held up her face to him, and he wondered why he had said that. It was not to take farewell of her. He was sure of that. It was to lull her just that fraction, and yet as their lips met he felt the deep ache of regret that he had controlled for so long and as her mouth spread slowly and moistly open under his, he felt as though his heart might break then. For a moment he felt that he might die himself before he could do it, dark waves of despair poured over him.

He slid his hand over her shoulder to the nape of her neck and her body flattened against his, he caressed her lightly, feeling for the place, and then settling thumb and forefinger – a second, another second passed, and then she pulled back softly.

'Hey, now!' she whispered huskily. 'You stop that before I pile us on the reef.'

He had not been able to do it with his bare hands. He just could not do it like that – but he had to do it quickly, very quickly. Every minute delayed now led him deeper and deeper into deadly danger.

'Go!' she ordered, and struck him a playful blow on the chest. 'We've got time for that later – all the time in the world. Let's savour it, every moment of it.'

He had not been able to do it, and he turned away. It was only as he went down the steel ladder into the cockpit of the Chris-craft that it suddenly occurred to him that during the lingering seconds of that kiss the fingers of her right hand had cupped lovingly under his chin. She could have crushed his larynx, paralysing him with a thumb driven up into the soft vulnerable arch of his throat at the first offensive pressure of his thumb and forefinger.

As his feet hit the deck of the cockpit another thought came to him. Her other hand had lain against his body, stroking him softly under the ribs. That hand could have struck upwards and inwards to tear through his diaphragm – his instincts must have warned him. She had been poised for the strike, more so than he was; she had been inside the circle of his arms, inside his defences, waiting for him – and he shivered briefly in the hot morning sun at the realization of how close he had been to death.

The realization turned instantly to something else, that slid down his spine cold as water down a melting icicle. It was fear, not the crippling fear of the craven, but fear that edged him and hardened him. Next time he would not hesitate – he could not hesitate.

He was instinctively carrying out her instructions as his mind raced to catch up with the problem. He lifted the lid of the seat locker. In the custom-fitted interior were arranged trays of fishing gear, swivels of brass and stainless steel in fifty different sizes; sinkers shaped for every type of water and bottom; lures of plastic and feathers, of enamel and bright metal; hooks for gigantic bill fish or for fry – and in a separate compartment in the side tray a bait knife.

The knife was a fifty-dollar Ninja with a lexan composition handle, chequered and moulded for grip. The blade was seven inches of hollow ground steel, three inches broad at the hilt and tapering to a stiletto point. It was a brutal weapon, you could probably chop through an oak log with it, as the makers advertised. Certainly it would enter human flesh and go through bone as though it were Cheddar cheese.

It balanced beautifully in Peter's fist as he made one testing slash and return cut with it. The blade hissed in the air, and when he tested the edge too hurriedly it stung like a razor and left a thin line of bright blood across the ball of his thumb.

He kicked off his canvas sneakers, so the rubber soles did not squeak on the deck. He was dressed now in only a thin cotton singlet and boxer-type swimming trunks, stripped down for action.

He went up the first three rungs of the ladder on bare silent feet, and lifted his eyes above the level of the flying bridge.

Magda Altmann stood at the controls of the Chris-craft, conning the big vessel into the mouth of the channel, staring ahead in complete concentration.

Her hair still flew in the wind, snaking and tangling into thick shimmering tresses. Her naked back was turned to him, the deeply defined depression running down her spine and the crest of smooth hard muscle rising on each side of it.

One leg of her pants had rucked up slightly exposing a half moon of round white buttock, and her legs were long and supple as a dancer's as she balanced on the balls of her narrow feet, raising herself to see ahead over the bows.

Peter had been gone from the bridge for less than ten seconds, and she was completely unaware, completely unsuspecting.

Peter did not make the same mistake again, he went up the ladder in a single swift bound, and the bellow of the diesels covered any sound he might have made.

With the knife you never take the chance of the point turning against bone, if you have a choice of target.

Peter picked the small of the back, at the level of the kidneys where there was no bone to protect the body cavity.

It is essential to put the blade in with all possible power; this decreases the chance of bone deflection and it peaks the paralysing effect of impact-shock.

Peter put the full weight of his rush behind the thrust.

The paralysis is total if the blade is twisted a half turn at the same instant that the blade socks in hilt-deep.

The muscles in Peter's right forearm were bunched in anticipation of the moment in which he would twist the blade viciously in her flesh, quadrupling the size and the trauma of the wound.

The polished stainless steel fascia of the Chris-craft's control panel reflected a distorted image, like those funny mirrors of the fairground. Only at the moment that Peter had committed himself completely, at the moment when he had thrown all his weight into the killing stroke, did he realize with a sickening flash that she was watching him in the polished steel control panel, she had been watching him from the moment he reappeared at the head of the ladder.

The curved surface of the steel distorted her face, so that it appeared to consist only of two enormous eyes, it distracted him in that thousandth part of a second before the point of the blade entered flesh. He did not see her move.

Blinding, numbing agony shot down his right flank and arm, from a point in the hollow where his collar bone joined the upper arm, while at the same instant something hit him on the inside of his forearm just below the elbow. The knife stroke was flung outwards, passing an inch from her hip, and the point of the blade crashed into the control panel in front of her, scoring the metal with a deep bright scratch, but Peter's numbed fingers could not keep hold on the hilt. The weapon spun from his grip, ringing like a crystal wine glass as it struck the steel handrail and rebounded over the side of the bridge into the cockpit behind him. He realized that she had struck backwards at him, not turning to face him but using only the reflection in the control panel to judge her blow with precision into the pressure point of his shoulder.

Now pain had crippled him and the natural reaction was to clutch at the source of it. Instead with some reflexive instinct of survival he flung up his left hand to protect the side of his neck and the next blow, also thrown backwards, felt as though it had come from a full-blooded swing of a baseball bat. He hardly saw it, it came so fast and hard there was just the flicker of movement across his vision, like the blur of a humming bird's wing, and then the appalling force of it crushing into the muscle of his forearm.

Had it taken him in the neck where it was aimed, it would have killed him instantly; instead it paralysed his other arm, and she was turning into him now effortlessly, matching his bull strengh with a combination of speed and control.

He knew he must try and keep her close, smother her with his weight and size and strength and he hooked at her with the clawed crippled fingers of his knife hand; they caught for a moment and then she jerked free. He had ripped away the flimsy strip of elasticized cloth that covered her breasts, and she spun lightly under and out of the sweep of his other arm as he tried desperately to club her down with his forearm.

He saw that her face was bone-white with the adrenalin overdose coursing her blood. Her lips were drawn back into a fixed snarl of concentration and fury and her teeth seemed as sharp as those of a female leopard in a trap.

It was like fighting a leopard, she attacked with an unrelenting savagery and total lack of fear, no longer human, dedicated only to his total destruction.

The long hair swirled about him, at one moment flicking like a whiplash into his eyes to blind and unbalance him, and she weaved and dodged and struck like a mongoose at the cobra, every movement flowing into the next, her taunting red-tipped breasts dancing and jerking with each blow she hurled at him.

With a jar of disbelief, Peter realized that she was beating him down. So far he had managed barely to survive each blow that he caught on arm and shoulder; each time her bare feet crashed into his thigh or lower belly, each time her knees drove for his groin and jarred against the bone of his pelvis, he felt a little more of his strength dissipate, felt his reactions becoming more rubbery, just that instant slower. He had countered her attack with luck and instinct, but any instant she must land solidly and drop him, for she was never still, cutting him with hands and feet, keeping him off balance – and he had not hurt her yet, had not touched her with any of his counterstrokes. Still there was no feeling in his hands and fingers. He needed respite, he needed a weapon, and he thought desperately of the knife that had fallen into the cockpit behind him.

He gave ground to her next attack, and the bridge rail caught him in the small of the back; at the same moment another of her strokes – aimed at the soft of his throat – deflected off his arm and crunched into his nose. Instantly his eyes flooded with tears, and he felt the warm salt flood of blood over his upper lip and down the back of his throat; he doubled over swiftly, then in the same movement he threw himself backwards, like a diver making a one-and-a-half from the three-metre board. The rail behind him helped his turn in the air, and he had judged it finely. He landed like a cat on both feet on the deck of the cockpit ten feet below the bridge, flexing at the knees to absorb the shock, and flicking the tears from his eyes, wringing his arms to return blood and feeling.

As he spun into a crouch he saw the knife. It had slid down the cockpit into the stern scuppers. He went for it.

The dive had taken her by surprise, just as she was poised for the final killing stroke to the back of his exposed neck, but she swirled to the head of the ladder and gathered herself while below her Peter launched himself across the cockpit for the big ugly Ninja knife.

She went for him feet first, dropping from ten feet, and the bare soles of her feet hit him together, the impetus of her falling body enhanced by the stabbing kick that she released at the moment that she hit him.

She caught him high in the back, hurling him forward so that the top of his head cracked into the bulkhead and darkness rustled through his head. He felt his senses going, and it required all of his resolve to roll over and pull his knees swiftly to his chest, to guard himself against the next killing stroke. He caught it on his shins, and once again launched himself after the knife.

His fingers felt swollen and clumsy on the rough chequered surface of the hilt, and at the moment they touched he unwound his doubled-up body like a steel coil spring, lashing out with both feet together. It was a blind stroke, delivered in complete desperation.

It was the first solid blow he had landed, it caught her at the moment when she had already launched herself into her next onslaught; both his feet slammed into her belly just below the ribs, and had the flesh there been soft or yielding it would have ended it; but she was just able to absorb the force of it with flat hard muscle – though it hurled her backwards across the cockpit with the breath hissing from her lungs and the long slim body doubling over in an agonized convulsion.

Peter realized that this was the only chance that he had had, and the only one he would ever have – yet his body was racked with such pain that he could hardly drag himself up on to his elbow, and his vision swam and blurred with tears and blood and sweat.

He did not know how he had managed it, some supreme exertion of will, but he was on his feet with the knife in his hand, instinctively extending the blade down the back of his right thigh to keep it protected until the moment it had to be used, crouching as he went in, left arm raised as a shield – and knowing that now he had to end it swiftly, he could not go on longer. This was his last effort.

Then she had a weapon also. Moving so swiftly that it had happened before she was halfway across the cockpit, she had knocked the retaining clip off the boat hook that stood in the rack beside the cabin entrance.

It was eight feet of heavy varnished ash, with an ornate but vicious brass head, and she cut at him with it, a low swinging warning blow to hold him off while she forced air back into her empty lungs.

She was recovering swiftly, much more swiftly than Peter himself. He could see the cold killing light rekindle in her eyes. He knew he could not go on much longer, he must risk it all in one last total effort.

He threw the knife, aiming at her head. The Ninja was not designed as a throwing weapon, it rolled out of line of flight, hilt foremost – but still it forced her to lift the staff of the boat hook and deflect it. It was the distraction he had wanted.

Peter used the momentum of his throw to go in under the swinging staff, and he hit her with his shoulder while her arms were raised.

Both of them reeled backwards into the cabin bulkhead, and Peter groped desperately for a grip. He found it in the thick lustrous tresses of her hair, and he wove his fingers into it.

She fought like a dying animal with strength and fury and courage that he could never have believed possible, but now at last he could pit his superior weight and strength directly against hers.

He smothered her against his chest, trapping one arm between their bodies, while he was able to pull her head backwards at an impossible angle, exposing the long smooth curve of her throat.

And then he scissored his thighs across hers, so that those lethal feet and legs were unable to reach him, and they crashed over on to the deck.

She managed with an incredible effort to swing her weight so that she landed on top of him, her breasts sliding against his chest, lubricated by sweat and the blood that had dribbled down from his nose, but Peter heaved all his remaining strength into his shoulders and rolled back on top of her.

They were locked breast to chest and groin to groin in some bizarre parody of the act of love, only the stock of the boat hook between them.

Peter twisted down hard on the rope of hair in his left hand, pinning her head to the deck so that her eyes were only six inches from his and blood from his nose and mouth dripped on to her upturned face.

Neither of them had spoken a word, the only sound the hiss and suck of laboured breathing, the explosive grunt of a blow delivered or the involuntary gasp of pain as it landed.

They glared into each other's eyes, and at that moment neither of them was a human being, they were two animals fighting to the death, and Peter shifted quickly so the stock of the boat hook fell across her unprotected throat. She had not been ready for that and she ducked her chin too late.

Peter knew he could not dare to release his grip on her hair, nor the arm around her body, nor the scissors that enfolded her legs. He could feel the steely tension of her whole body, that required all his own strength to hold. If he relaxed his grip in the slightest, she would twist away, and he would not have the strength to go on after that.

With the elbow of the hand that held the hair, he began to bear down on the ash staff of the boat hook, slowly it crushed down into her throat.

She knew it was over then, but still she fought on. As she weakened Peter was able to transfer more and more of his weight on to the stock of the boat hook. Slowly blood suffused her face, turning it dark mottled plum, her lips quivered with each painful rasping breath and a little frothy saliva broke from the corners of her mouth and ran back down her cheek.

Watching her die was the most horrible thing Peter had ever had to do. He shifted cautiously, going for the few extra ounces of weight which would force the heavy wooden stock down that last eighth of an inch and crush in her throat, and she recognized the moment in his eyes.

She spoke for the first time. It was a croak slurred through swollen and gaping lips.

'They warned me.' He thought he had misheard her, and he checked the final thrust downwards which would pinch out the last spark of life. 'I couldn't believe it.' The faintest whisper, only just intelligible. 'Not you.'

Then the last resistance went out of her, her body relaxed, the complete acceptance of death at last. The fierce green light went out in her eyes, replaced at the very end with a sadness so heavy that seemed to acknowledge the ultimate betrayal of all goodness and trust.

Peter could not force himself to make the final thrust downwards that would end it. He rolled off her and flung the heavy wooden stock across the cockpit. It crashed into the bulkhead and he sobbed as he crawled painfully across the deck, turning his back to her completely, knowing that she was still alive and therefore still as dangerous as she had ever been – yet no longer caring. He had gone as far as he could go. It didn't matter any more if she killed him, something in him even welcomed the prospect of release.

He reached the rail and tried to drag himself on to his feet, expecting at any moment the killing blow into the nape of his neck as she attacked him again.

It did not come, and he managed to get on to his knees, but his whole body was trembling violently so that his teeth chattered to his jaws and every strained and bruised tendon and muscle screamed for surcease. Let her kill me, he thought, it doesn't matter. Nothing matters now.

Half supporting himself on the rail, he turned slowly and his vision swam and flickered with patches of darkness and little shooting stars of crimson and white flame.

Through the swirl of senses at the end of their usefulness, he saw that she was kneeling in the centre of the cockpit, facing him.

Her naked torso was splattered and smeared with his blood and the smooth tanned skin oiled with slippery sweat of near death. Her face was still swollen and inflamed, wreathed in a great tangle of matted and disordered hair. There was a flaming livid weal across her throat where the stock had crushed her, and as she fought for breath her small pert breasts lifted and dropped to the painful pumping of her chest.

They stared at each other, far beyond speech, driven to the very frontiers of their existence.

She shook her head, as though trying desperately to deny the horror of it all, and at last she tried to speak, no sound came and she licked her lips and lifted one slim hand to her throat as though to ease the pain of it.

She tried again, and this time she managed one word. 'Why?'

He could not reply for fully half a minute, his own throat seemed to have closed, grown together like an old wound. He knew that he had failed in his duty and yet he could not yet hate himself for it. He formed the words in his own mind, as though he were trying to speak a foreign language, and when he spoke his voice was a stranger's broken and coarsened by the knowledge of failure.

'I couldn't do it,' he said.

She shook her head again, and tried to frame the next question. But she could not articulate it, only one word came out, the same word again.

'Why — ?'

And he had no answer for her.

She stared at him, then slowly her eyes filled with tears, they ran down her cheeks and hung from her chin like early morning dew on the leaf of the vine.

Slowly she pitched forward on to the deck, and for many seconds he did not have the strength to go to her, and then he lurched across the deck and dropped to his knees beside her; he lifted her upper body in his arms suddenly terrified that he had succeeded after all, that she was dead.

His relief soared above the pain of his battered body as he felt her breathing still sawing through her damaged throat, and as her head lolled against his shoulder he realized that fat oily tears still welled out from between her closed eyelids.

He began to rock her like a child in his arms, a completely useless gesture, and only then did her words begin to make any sense to him.

'They warned me,' she had whispered.

'I couldn't believe it,' she had said.

'Not you.'

He knew then that had she not spoken he would have gone through with it. He would have killed her and weighted her body and dropped it beyond the 1,000-fathom line – but the words, although they did not yet make sense, had reached deep into some recess of his mind.

She stirred against his chest. She said something, it sounded like his name. It roused him to reality. The big Chris-craft was still roaring blindly through the channels and reefs of the outer passage.

He laid her back gently on the deck, and scrambled up the ladder to the flying bridge. The whole of that horrific conflict had taken less than a minute, from his knife-stroke to her collapse under him.

The steering of the Chris-craft was locked into the automatic pilot and the vessel had run straight out through the channel into the open sea. It reinforced his knowledge that she had been ready for his attack. She had been acting that total concentration in steering the vessel, luring him into the attack while the Chris-craft was on automatic pilot and she was ready to throw that backward blow at him.

It did not make sense, not yet. All that he knew was that he had made some terrible miscalculation. He threw out the switch of the automatic steering, and shut down both throttles to the idle position before disengaging the main drive. The diesels burbled softly, and she rounded up gently into the wind and wallowed beam-on to the short steep blue seas of the open ocean.

Peter took one glance back over the stern. The island were just a low dark smudge on the horizon, and then he was stumbling back to the ladder.

Magda had dragged herself into a half-sitting position, but she recoiled swiftly as he came to her and for the first time he saw fear pass like cloud shadow across her eyes.

'It's all right,' he told her, his own voice still ragged. Her fear offended him deeply. He did not want her ever to be afraid of him again.

He took her up in his arms, and her body was stiff with uncertainty, like that of a cat picked up against its will, but too sick to resist.

'It's all right,' he repeated awkwardly, and carried her down into the saloon of the Chris-craft. His own body felt battered as though his very bones were bruised and cracked, but he handled her so tenderly that slowly the resistance went out of her and she melted against him.

He lowered her on to the leather padded bench, but when he tried to straighten up she slid one arm around his neck and restrained him, clinging to him.

'I left the knife there,' she whispered huskily. 'It was a test.'

'Let me get the medicine chest.' He tried to pull away.

'No.' She shook her head and winced at the pain in her throat. 'Don't go away, Peter. Stay with me. I am so afraid. I was going to kill you if you took the knife. I nearly did, oh, Peter, what is happening to us, are we both going mad?'

She held him desperately and he sank to his knees on the deck and bowed over her.

'Yes,' he answered her, holding her to his chest. 'Yes, we must be going mad. I don't understand myself or any of it any more.'

'Why did you have to take the knife, Peter? Please – you must tell me. Don't lie, tell me the truth, I have to know why.'

'Because of Melissa-Jane – because of what you had done to her –'

He felt her jerk in his arms as though he had struck her again. She tried to speak but now her voice was only a croak of despair, and Peter went on to explain it to her.

'When I discovered that you were Caliph, I had to kill you.'

She seemed to be gathering herself for some major effort, but then when she spoke it was still in that scratchy broken whisper.

'Why did you stop yourself, Peter?'

'Because –' He knew the reason then. '– Because suddenly I knew that I loved you. Nothing else counted.'

She gasped and was silent again for nearly a minute.

'Do you still think that I am Caliph?' she asked at last.

'I don't know. I don't know anything any more – except that I love you. That's all that matters.'

'What happened to us, Peter?' She lamented softly. 'Oh God, what has happened to us?'

'Are you Caliph, Magda?'

'But Peter, you tried to kill me. That was the test with the knife. You are Caliph.'

Under Magda's direction Peter took the Chris-craft in through a narrow passage in the coral reef that surrounded Île des Oiseaux, while the seabirds wheeled about them in a raucous cloud, filling the air with their wingbeats.

He anchored in five fathoms in the protected lee, and then called the main island on the VHF radio, speaking to the head boatman.

'The Baronne has decided to sleep on board overnight,' he explained. 'Don't worry about us.'

When he went down to the saloon again Magda had recovered sufficiently to be sitting up. She had pulled on one of the terry towelling track suits from the clothes locker, and she had wound a clean towel around her throat to protect it and to hide the fierce fresh bruise that was already staining her skin like the squeezed juice of an over-ripe plum.

Peter found the medicine box in a locker above the toilet bowl of the heads, and she protested when he brought two Temprapain capsules for the pain, and four tablets of Brufin for the swelling and bruising of her throat and body.

'Take them,' he commanded and held the glass while she did so.

Then he carefully unwrapped the towel from her throat and lightly rubbed a creamy salve into the bruise with his fingertips.

'That feels better already,' she whispered, but now she had lost her voice almost entirely.

'Let's have a look at your stomach.' He pushed her down gently on her back on the long padded bench and unzipped the top of the towelling suit to the waist. The bruise where he had kicked her had spread from just below her small pale breasts to the tiny sculpted navel in the flat hard plane of her belly, again he massaged the soothing cream into her skin and she sighed and murmured with the comfort of it. When he finished she was able to hobble, still painfully doubled over, to the heads. She locked herself in for fifteen minutes while Peter tended his own injuries, and when she emerged again she had bathed her face and combed out her hair.

He poured two crystal old-fashioned glasses half full of Jack Daniel's Bourbon and he handed one to her as she sank on to the padded bench beside him. 'Drink it. For your throat,' he ordered, and she drank and gasped at the sting of the liquor and set the glass aside.

'And you, Peter?' She husked with sudden concern. 'Are you all right?'

'Just one thing,' he said. 'I'd hate you to get really mad at me.' Then he smiled, and she started to chuckle but choked on the pain and ended up clinging to him.

'When can we talk?' he asked her gently. 'We have to talk this out.'

'Yes, I know, but not yet, Peter. Just hold me for a while.' And he was surprised at the comfort that it afforded him. The warm woman shape pressed to him seemed to ease the pain of body and of mind, and he stroked her hair as she nuzzled softly against his throat.

'You said you loved me,' she murmured at last, making it a question. Seeking reassurance, as lovers always must.

'Yes. I love you. I think I knew it all along, but when I learned that you were Caliph, I had to bury it deep. It was only there at the end I had to admit to myself.'

'I'm glad,' she said simply. 'Because you see I love you also. I thought I would never be able to love. I had despaired of it, Peter. Until you. And then they told me you would kill me. That you were Caliph. I thought then I would die – having found you and then lost you. It was too cruel, Peter. I had to give you the chance to prove it wasn't true!'

'Don't talk,' he commanded. 'Just lie there and listen. There is nothing wrong with my voice, so I will tell it first. The way it was with me, and how I knew you were Caliph.'

And he told it to her, holding her to him and speaking softly, steadily.

The only other sounds in the cabin were the slap of the wavelets against the hull and the subdued hum of the air-conditioning unit.

'You know everything up to the day Melissa-Jane was taken, all of it. I told you all of it, without reservation and without lying, not once –' He started, and then he went on to tell her in detail of the hunt for Melissa-Jane.

'– I think something must have snapped in my mind during those days. I was ready to believe anything, to try anything to get her back. I would wake up in the night and go to the toilet and vomit with the thought of her hand in a glass jar.'

He told her how he had planned to kill Kingston Parker to meet Caliph's demands, exactly how he intended doing it, the detailed how and where, and she shuddered against him.

'The power to corrupt even the best,' she whispered.

'Don't talk –' he admonished her, and went on to tell her of the tip-off that had led them at last to the Old Manse in Laragh.

'When I saw my daughter like that, I lost what little was left of my reason. When I held her and felt the fever and heard her scream with lingering terror, I would have killed –' He broke off and they were silent until she protested with a small gasp and he realized that his hand had closed on her upper arm and his fingers were biting into her flesh with the force of his memories.

'I'm sorry.' He relaxed his grip, and lifted the hand to touch her cheek. 'Then they told me about you.'

'Who?' she whispered.

'The Atlas Command.'

'Parker?'

'Yes, and Colin Noble.'

'What did they tell you.'

'They told me how your father brought you to Paris when you were a child. They told me that even then you were bright and pretty and special –' He began to recite it for her. '– When your father was killed –' And she moved restlessly against his chest as he said it. '– You went to live with foster parents, all of them members of the party, and in the end you were so special that they sent somebody to take you back to Poland. Somebody who posed as your uncle –'

'I believed he was –' She nodded. '– for ten years I believed it. He used to write to me –' She stopped herself with an effort, was silent a moment and then '– he was all I ever had after Papa.'

'You were selected to go to Odessa,' Peter went on, and felt her go very still in his arms, so he repeated it with the harshness unconcealed in his tone '– to the special school in Odessa.'

'You know about Odessa?' she whispered. 'Or you think you know – but nobody who has never been there could ever really know.'

'I know they taught you to –' he paused, imagining again a beautiful young girl in a special room, overlooking the Black Sea, learning to use her body to trap and beguile a man, any man. '– They taught you many things.' He could not make the accusation.

'Yes,' she murmured. 'Many, many things.'

'Like how to kill a man with your hands.'

'I think that subconsciously I could not bring myself to kill you, Peter. God knows you should not have survived. I loved you, even though I hated you for betraying me, I could not really do it –'

She sighed again, a broken gusty sound.

'– And when I thought that you were going to kill me – it was almost a relief. I was ready to accept that, against living on without the love that I thought I had found.'

'You talk too much.' He stopped her. 'You'll damage your throat further.' He touched her lips with his fingers, to silence her, and then went on. 'And at Odessa you became one of the chosen, one of the élite.'

'It was like entering the church, a beautiful mystic thing –' she whispered. 'I cannot explain it. I would have done everything or anything for the State, for what I knew was right for "Mother Russia".'

'All of this is true?' He marvelled that she made no effort to deny it.

'All of it,' she nodded painfully. 'I will never lie to you again, Peter. I swear it.'

'Then they sent you back to France – to Paris?' he asked, and she nodded.

'You did your job, even better than they expected you to do it. You were the best, the very best. No man could resist you.'

She did not answer, but she did not lower her eyes from his. It was not a defiance but merely a total acceptance of what he was saying.

'There were men. Rich and powerful men –' His voice was bitter now. He could not help himself. 'Many, many men. Nobody knows how many, and from each of them you gathered harvest.'

'Poor Peter,' she whispered. 'Have you tortured yourself with that?'

'It helped me to hate you,' he said simply.

'Yes, I understand that. There is nothing that I can give you for your comfort – except this. I never loved a man until I met you.'

She was keeping her word. There were no more lies nor deceptions now. He was certain of it.

'Then they decided that you could be used to take over control of Aaron Altmann and his empire –'

'No,' she whispered, shaking her head. 'I decided on Aaron. He had been the only one man who I had not been able to –' Her voice pinched out and she took a sip of the bourbon and let it trickle slowly down her throat before she went on. 'He fascinated me. I had never met a man like that before. So strong, such raw power.'

'All right,' Peter agreed. 'You might even have grown tired of the other role by then –'

'It's hard work being a courtesan –' She smiled for the first time since he had begun speaking, but it was a sad self-mocking smile.

'You went about it exactly the right way. First you made yourself indispensable to him. Already he was a sick man, beginning to need a crutch, somebody he could trust entirely. You gave him that –'

She said nothing, but memories passed across her eyes, changing the green shadows like sunlight through a deep still pool.

'– And when he trusted you there was nothing you could not supply to your masters. Your value had increased a hundredfold.'

He went on talking quietly while outside the day died in a fury of crimsons and royal purples, slowly altering the light in the cabin and dimming it down so that her face was all that existed in the soft gloom. A pale intense expression, listening quietly to the accusations, to the recitation of betrayals and deceits. Only occasionally she made a little gesture of denial, a shake of her head or the pressure of fingers on his arms. Sometimes she closed her eyes briefly as though she could not accept some particularly cruel memory, and once or twice an exclamation was wrung from her in that strained and tortured whisper.

'Oh God, Peter! It's true!'

He told her how she had gradually developed the taste for the power she was able to wield as Aaron Altmann's wife, and how that flourished as Aaron's strength declined. How she at last even opposed the Baron on some issues.

'Like that of supplying arms to the South African Government,' Peter said, and she nodded and made one of her rare comments.

'Yes. We argued. That was one of the few times we argued.' And she smiled softly, as though at a private memory that she could not share even with him.

He told her how the taste of power and the trappings of power gradually eroded her commitment to her earlier political ideals, how her masters slowly realized they were losing their hold over her and of the pressures they attempted to apply to force her back into the fold. 'But you were too powerful now to respond to the usual pressures. You had even succeeded in penetrating Aaron's Mossad connections, and had that protection.'

'This is incredible!' she whispered. 'It's so close, so very close that it is the truth.' He waited for her to elaborate, but instead she motioned him to continue.

'When they threatened to expose you to the Baron as a communist agent, you had no choice but to get rid of him – and you did it in such a way that you not only got rid of the threat to your existence but you also achieved control of Altmann Industries, and to put the cherry on top of the pie you got yourself twenty-five million in operating capital. You arranged the abduction and killing of Aaron Altmann, you paid yourself the twenty-five million and personally supervised its transfer, probably to a numbered account in Switzerland –'

'Oh God, Peter!' she whispered, and in the dark of the cabin her eyes were fathomless and huge as the empty cavities of a skull.

'Is it true?' Peter asked for confirmation for the first time.

'It's too horrible. Go on please.'

'It worked so well that it opened up a new world of possibilities for you. Just about this time you truly became Caliph. The taking of Flight 070 was possibly not the first stroke after the kidnapping of Aaron Altmann – there may have been others. Vienna and the OPEC ministers, the Red Brigade activities in Rome – but 070 was the first time you used the name Caliph. It worked, except for the dereliction of duty by a subordinate officer.' He indicated himself. 'That was all that stopped it – and that was how I attracted your attention originally.'

Now it was almost totally dark in the cabin and Magda reached across and switched on the reading light beside them, adjusting the rheostat down to a soft golden glow. In its light she studied his face seriously as he went on.

'– By this time you were aware through your special sources, probably the Mossad connection and almost certainly through the French SID, that somebody was on to Caliph. That somebody turned out to be Kingston Parker and his Atlas organization, and I was the ideal person to firstly confirm that Parker was the hunter – and secondly, to assassinate him. I had the special training and talents for the job, I could get close to him without arousing his suspicions, and I needed only to be sufficiently motivated –'

'No,' she whispered, unable to take her eyes from his face.

'It holds together,' he said. 'All of it.' And she had no reply.

'When I received Melissa-Jane's finger, I was ready for anything –'

'I think I am going to be sick.'

'I'm sorry.' He gave her the glass and she drank the finger of dark liquor it contained, gagging a little on it. Then she sat for a few moments with her eyes closed and her hand on her bruised throat.

'All right?' he asked at last.

'Yes. All right now. Go on.'

'It worked perfectly – except for the tip-off to the hideout in Ireland. But nobody could have foreseen that, not even Caliph.'

'But there was no proof!' she protested. 'It was all conjecture. No proof that I was Caliph.'

'There was,' he told her quietly. 'O'Shaughnessy, the head of the gang that kidnapped Melissa-Jane, made two telephone calls. They were traced to Rambouillet 47-87-47.'

She stared at him wordlessly.

'He was reporting to his master – to Caliph, you see.' And he waited for her reply. There was none, so after a minute of silence he went on to tell her the arrangements he had made for her execution – the sites he had chosen at Longchamp race course and in the Avenue Victor Hugo, and she shuddered as though she had felt the brush of the black angels' wings across her skin.

'I would have been there,' she admitted. 'You chose the two best sites. Yves has arranged a private showing for me on the sixth of next month. I would have gone to it.'

'– Then you saved me the trouble. You invited me here. I knew that it was an invitation to die, that you knew I had become aware, that I had learned you were Caliph. I saw it in your eyes during that meeting at Orly Airport, I saw it proven by the way you were suddenly avoiding me, the way you were giving me no opportunity to do the job I had to do.'

'Go on.'

'You had me searched when I landed at Tahiti-Faaa.'

She nodded.

'You had the grey wolves search my room again last night, and you set it up for today. I knew I had to strike first, and I did.'

'Yes,' she murmured. 'You did.' And rubbed her throat again.

He went to recharge the glasses from the concealed liquor cabinet behind the bulkhead, and came back to sit beside her.

She shifted slightly, moving inside the circle of his arm, and he held her in silence. The telling of it had exhausted him, and his body ached relentlessly, but he was glad it was said, somehow it was like lancing a malignant abscess – the release of poisons was a relief, and now the healing process could begin.

He could feel his own exhaustion echoed in the slim body that drooped against him, but he sensed that hers was deeper, she had taken too much already – and when he lifted her in his arms again she made no protest, and he carried her like a sleeping child through to the master cabin and laid her on the bunk.

He found pillows and a blanket in the locker below. He slid into the bunk with her, under the single blanket, and she fitted neatly into the curve of his body, pressing gently against him, her back against his chest, her hard round buttocks against the front of his thighs, and her head pillowed under the crook of his arm, while with his other arm he cuddled her close and his hand naturally cupped one of her breasts. They fell asleep like that, pressing closely, and when he rolled over she moved without waking, reversing their positions, moulding herself to his back and pressing her face into the nape of his neck, clasping him with one arm and with a leg thrown over his lower body as though to enfold him completely.

Once he woke and she was gone, and the strength of his alarm surprised him, a hundred new doubts and fears assailed him from the darkness, then he heard the liquid purr in the bowl of the heads and he relaxed. When she returned to the bunk, she had stripped off the terry towelling track suit and her naked body felt somehow very vulnerable and precious in his arms.

They woke together with sunlight pouring into the cabin through one porthole like stage lighting.

'My God – it must be noon.' She sat up, and tossed back the long mane of dark hair over her tanned bare shoulders – but when Peter tried to rise, he froze and groaned aloud.

'Qu'a tu, chéri?'

'I must have got caught in a concrete mixer,' he moaned. His bruises had stiffened during the night, torn muscle and strained sinews protested his lightest movement.

'There is only one cure for both of us,' she told him. 'It's in three parts.'

And she helped him off the bunk as though he was an old man. He exaggerated the extent of his injuries a little to make her chuckle. The chuckle was a little hoarse, but her voice was stronger and clearer and she favoured her own bruises only a little as she led him up on to the deck. Her powers of recuperation were those of a young and superbly fit thoroughbred animal.

They swam from the diving platform over the Chris-craft's stern.

'It's working,' Peter admitted as the support of warm salt water soothed his battered body. They swam side by side, both naked, slowly at first and then faster, changing the sedate breaststroke for a hard overarm crawl, back as far as the reef, treading water there and gasping at the exertion.

'Better?' she panted with her hair floating around her like the tendrils of some beautiful water plant.

'Much better.'

'Race you back.'

They reached the Chris-craft together and clambered up into the cockpit, cascading water and laughing and panting, but when he reached for her, she allowed only a fleeting caress before pulling away.

'First Phase Two of the cure.'

She worked in the galley with only a floral apron around her waist which covered the dark bruises of her belly.

'I never thought an apron could be provocative before.'

'You are supposed to be doing the coffee,' she admonished him and gave him a lewd little bump and grind with her bare backside.

Her omelettes were thick and golden and fluffy, and they ate them in the early sunlight on the upper deck. The trade wind was sheepdogging a flock of fluffy silver cloud across the heavens, and in the gaps the sky was a peculiar brilliant blue.

They ate with huge appetites, for the bright new morning seemed to have changed the mood of doom that had overpowered them the previous night. Neither of them wanted to break this mood, and they chattered inconsequential nonsense, and exclaimed at the beauty of the day and threw bread crusts to the seagulls, like two children on a picnic.

At last she came to sit in his lap, and made a show of taking his pulse.

'The patient is much improved,' she announced; 'is now probably strong enough for Phase Three of the cure.'

'Which is?' he asked.

'Peter chéri, even if you *are* English, you are not that dense.' And she wriggled her bottom in his lap.

They made love in the warm sunlight, on one of the foam mattresses, with the trade wind teasing their bodies like unseen fingers.

It began in banter and with low gurgles of laughter, little gasps of rediscovery, and murmurs of welcome and encouragement – then suddenly it changed, it became charged with almost unbearable intensity, a storm of emotion that sought to sweep away all the ugliness and doubt. They were caught up in the raging torrent that carried them helplessly beyond mere physical response into an unknown dimension from which there seemed no way back, a total affirmation of their bodies and their minds that made all else seem unconsequential.

'I love you,' she cried at the very end, as though to deny all else that she had been forced to do. 'I have loved only you.' It was a cry torn from the very depths of her soul.

It took a long time for them to return from the far place to which they had been driven, to become two separate people again, but when they did somehow they both sensed that they would never again be completely separated; there had been a deeper more significant union than just that of their two bodies, and the knowledge sobered them and yet, at the same time, gave them both new strength and a deep elation that neither had to voice – it was there, and they both simply knew it.

They slid the big inflatable Avon S 650 dinghy over the stern, and went ashore, pulling the rubber craft above the high-water level and mooring it to one of the slanting palm boles.

Then they wandered inland, picking their way hand in hand between the seabird nests that had been crudely scraped in the earth. Half a dozen different species of birds were breeding together in one sprawling colony that covered most of the twenty-acre island. Their eggs varied from cool pale blue as big as that of a goose's, to others the size of a pullet's and speckled and spotted in lovely free-form designs. The chicks were either grotesquely ugly with bare parboiled bodies or were cute as Walt Disney animations. The entire island was pervaded by an endless susurration of thousands of wings and the uproar of squawking, screeching, feuding and mating birds.

Magda knew the zoological names of each species, its range and its habits, and its chances of survival or extinction in the changing eco-systems of the oceans.

Peter listened to her tolerantly, sensing that behind this chatter and studied gaiety she was steeling herself to answer the accusations that he had levelled at her.

At the far end of the island was a single massive takamaka tree, with dense green foliage spreading widely over the fluffy white sand. By now the sun was fiercely bright and the heat and humidity smothered them like a woollen blanket dipped in hot water.

They sought the shade of the takamaka gratefully, and sat close together on the sand staring out across the unruffled waters of the lagoon to the silhouette of the main island, five miles away. At this range and angle there was no sign of the buildings nor of the jetty, and Peter had an illusion of the primeval paradise with the two of them the first man and woman on a fresh and innocent earth.

Magda's next words dispelled that illusion entirely.

'Who ordered you to kill me, Peter? How was the command given? I must know that before I tell you about myself.'

'Nobody,' he answered.

'Nobody? There was no message like the one you received ordering you to kill Parker?'

'No.'

'Parker himself or Colin Noble? They did not order you to do it – or suggest it?'

'Parker expressly ordered me not to do it. You were not to be touched – until you could be taken in jeopardy.'

'It was your own decision?' she insisted.

'It was my duty.'

'To avenge your daughter?'

He hesitated, would have qualified it, then nodded with total self-honesty. 'Yes, that was the most part of it. Melissa-Jane, but I saw it also as my duty to destroy anything evil enough to envisage the taking of 070, the abduction of Aaron Altmann and the mutilation of my daughter.'

'Caliph knows about us. Understands us better than we understand ourselves. I am not a coward, Peter, but now I am truly afraid.'

'Fear is the tool of his trade,' Peter agreed, and she moved slightly, inviting physical contact. He placed one arm about her bare brown shoulders and she leaned lightly against him.

'All that you told me last night was the truth, only the inferences and conclusions were false. Papa's death, the lonely years with strangers as foster parents – of that period my clearest memories are of lying awake at night and trying to muffle the sound of my weeping with a false blanket. The return to Poland, yes, that was right, and the Odessa school – all of that. I will tell you about Odessa one day, if you truly want to hear it – ?'

'I don't think I do,' he said.

'Perhaps you are wise; do you want to hear about the return to Paris?'

'Only what is necessary.'

'All right, Peter. There were men. That was what I had been selected and trained for. Yes, there were men –' She broke off, and reached up to take his face between her hands, turning it so she could look into his eyes. 'Does that make a difference between us, Peter?'

'I love you,' he replied firmly.

She stared into his eyes for a long time looking for evidence of deceit, and then when she found none, 'Yes. It is so. You really mean that.'

She sighed with relief and laid her head against his shoulder, speaking quietly with just that intriguing touch of accent and the occasional unusual turn of phrase.

'I did not like the men, either, Peter. I think that was why I chose Aaron Altmann. One man, yes I could still respect myself –' She shrugged lightly. 'I chose Aaron, and Moscow agreed. It was, as you said, delicate work. First I had to win his respect. He had never respected a woman before. I proved to him I was as good as any man, at any task he wished to set me. After I had his respect, all else followed –' She paused and chuckled softly. '– Life plays naughty tricks. I found firstly that I liked him, then I grew to respect him also. He was a great ugly bull of a man, but the power ... A huge raw power, like some cosmic force, became the centre of my existence.' She lifted her head to touch Peter's cheek, with her lips in reassurance. 'No. Peter, I never came to love him. I never loved before you. But I stood in vast awe of him, like a member of a primitive tribe worships the lightning and the thunder. It was like that. He dominated my existence – more than a father, more than a teacher, as much as a god – but less, very much less than a lover. He was crude and strong. He did not make love, he could only rut and tup like the bull he was.'

She broke off and looked seriously at him. 'Do you understand that, Peter? Perhaps I explained it badly?'

'No,' he assured her. 'You explained it very well.'

'Physically he did not move me, his smell and the hairiness. He had hair on his shoulders and like a pelt down his back. His belly was bulging and hard as iron –' She shivered briefly. '– But I had been trained to be able to ignore that. To switch off something in the front of my brain. Yet in all other ways he fascinated me. He goaded me to think forbidden thoughts, to open vaults of my mind that my training had securely locked. All right, he taught me about power and its trappings. You accused me of that, Peter, and I admit it. The flavour of power and money was to my taste. I like it very much indeed. Aaron introduced me to that. He showed me how to appreciate fine and beautiful things, for he was only physically a bull and he had a wonderful appreciation of the refinements of life – he made me come completely alive. Then he laughed at me. God, I can still hear the bellow of his laughter, and see that great hairy belly shaking with it.'

She paused to remember it, almost reverently, and then she chuckled her own husky little laugh.

' "My fine little communist lady," he mocked me. Yes, Peter, it was I who was deceived, he had known from the beginning who I was. He also knew about the school at Odessa. He had accepted me as a challenge, certainly he loved me – or his version of love, but he took me knowingly and corrupted my pure ideological convictions. Only then did I learn that all the information which I had been able to pass to Moscow had been carefully screened by Aaron. He doubled me, as I had been sent to double him. He was Mossad, but of course you know that. He was a Zionist, you know that also. And he made me realize that I was a Jewess, and what it meant to be that. He showed me every fatal flaw in the doctrine of Universal Communism, he convinced me of democracy and the Western Capitalist system and then he recruited me to Mossad –'

She stopped again, and shook her head vehemently.

'– To believe that I could have wished to destroy such a one. That I could have ordered his abduction and mutilation – Towards the end, when he was getting weak, when the pain was very bad, that was the closest I ever came to loving him, the way a mother loves a child. He became pathetically dependent upon me, he used to say the only thing that could lull the pain was my touch. I used to sit for hours rubbing that hairy belly – feeling that awful thing growing bigger inside him each day, like a cauliflower or a grotesque foetus. He would not let them cut it. He hated them, "butchers" he called them. "Butchers with their knives and rubber tubes –"'

She broke off and Peter realized that her eyes were filled with tears. He hugged her a little more firmly and waited for her to recover.

'It must have been about this time that Caliph made contact with Aaron. Thinking back I can remember the time when he became suddenly terribly agitated. It made little sense to me then, but he held long diatribes about right-wing tyranny being indistinguishable from tyranny of the left. He never mentioned the name Caliph, I do not think Caliph had yet used that name – and I do believe that Aaron would eventually have told me of the contact in detail, if he had lived. It was the way he was, even with me, he could be as wary and subtle as he could be overpowering. He would have told me of Caliph – but Caliph saw to it that he did not.'

She pulled away from Peter's arm so she could again see his face.

'You must understand, chéri, that much of this I have learned only recently – in the last few weeks. Much of it I can only piece together like a jig puzzle – pardon, a jigsaw puzzle.' She corrected herself swiftly. 'But this is what must have happened. Caliph contacted Aaron with a proposition. It has a very simple proposition. He was invited to become a partner of Caliph. Aaron was to make a substantial financial contribution to Caliph's war-chest, and to place his privileged knowledge and lines of influence at Caliph's disposal. In return he would have a hand in engineering Caliph's brave new world. It was a miscalculation on Caliph's part, perhaps the only mistake he has made up to now. He had misjudged Aaron Altmann. Aaron turned him down flat – but much more dangerously Caliph had made the mistake of revealing his identity to Aaron. I expect that he had to do that in an effort to convince Aaron. You see, Aaron was not a man who would indulge in a game of code names and hidden identities. That much Caliph had divined correctly. So he had to confront Aaron face to face, and when he discovered that Aaron would not join in a campaign to murder and extortion – no matter how laudable the ultimate ends – Caliph had no choice. He took Aaron, killed him after torturing him hideously for information that could have been useful, mainly information about his Mossad connection I imagine. Then he persuaded me to pay the ransom. He won two major tricks with a single card. He silenced Aaron and he gained the twenty-five million for his war-chest.'

'How did you learn this? If only you had explained to me before –' Peter heard the bitterness in his own voice.

'I did not know it when we first met, chéri, please believe me. I will tell you how I learned it, but please be patient with me. Let me tell it as it happened.'

'I am sorry,' he said simply.

'The first time I heard the name, "Caliph" was the day I delivered the ransom. I told you about that, didn't I?'

'Yes.'

'So we come now to your part. I heard of you for the first time with the

Johannesburg hijacking of Flight 070. I thought that you might be the one to help me hunt down Caliph. I found out about you, Peter. I was even able to have a computer print-out on you –' She paused, and there was a mischievous flash in her eye again. '– I will admit to being very impressed with the formidable list of your ladies.'

Peter held up both hands in a gesture of surrender.

'Never again,' he pleaded. 'Not another word – agreed?'

'Agreed.' She laughed, and then, 'I'm hungry, and my throat is sore again with all this talking.'

They crossed the island again, with their bare feet baking on the sun-heated sand, and went back on board the Chris-craft.

The chef had stocked the refrigerator with a cornucopia of food, and Peter opened a bottle of Veuve Cliquot champagne.

'You've got expensive tastes,' he observed. 'I dont know if I can afford to keep you – on my salary.'

'I'm sure we could arrange a raise from your boss,' she assured him with the twinkle in her eyes. In tacit agreement they did not mention Caliph again until they had eaten.

'– There is one other thing you must understand, Peter. I am of Mossad, but I do not control them. They control me. It was the same with Aaron. Both of us were and are very valuable agents, possibly amongst the most valuable of all their networks, but I do not make decisions, nor am I able to have access to all their secrets.

'Mossad's singleminded goal is the safety and security of the state of Israel. It has no other reason for existence. I was certain that Aaron had made a full report to Mossad of Caliph's identity, that he had detailed the proposition that Caliph had proposed – and I suspect that Mossad had ordered Aaron to cooperate with Caliph –'

'Why?' Peter demanded sharply.

'I do not know for certain – but I can think of two reasons. Caliph must have been such a powerful and influential man that his support would have been valuable. Then again I suspect that Caliph had pro-Israeli leanings, or professed to have those leanings. Mossad finds allies where it can, and does not question their morals. I think they ordered Aaron to cooperate with Caliph – but –'

'But?' Peter prompted her.

'But you do not order a man like Aaron to go against his deepest convictions, and under that forbidding exterior Aaron Altmann was a man of great humanity. I think that the reason for his agitation was the conflict of duty and belief that he was forced to endure. His instinct warned him to destroy Caliph, and his duty –'

She shrugged, and picked up her fluted champagne glass, twisting it between those long slim fingers and studying the pinpricks of bubbles as they rose slowly through the pale golden wine. When she spoke again she had changed direction disconcertingly.

'A thousand times I had tried to discover what was so different between you and me than with the other men I have known. Why none of them could move me – and yet with you it was almost instantaneous –' She looked up at him again as though she was still seeking the reason. '– Of course, I knew so much about you. You had the qualities I admire in another human being, so I was disposed favourably – but there are other qualities you cannot detail on a computer print-out nor capture in a photograph. There was something about you that made me –' She made a helpless gesture as she searched for the word. '– You made me tingle.'

'That's a good word,' Peter smiled.

'And I had never tingled before. So I had to be very sure. It was a new experience to want a man merely because he is gentle and strong and –' She chuckled. '– just plain sexy. You are sexy, you know that, Peter, but also you are something else –' She broke off. 'No, I am not going to flatter you any more. I do not want you to get swollen ankles –' mixing the French idiom quaintly with the English, and this time not correcting herself. She went straight on. 'Caliph must have realized that I had recruited a dangerous ally. He made the attempt to kill you that night on the Rambouillet road –'

'They were after you,' Peter cut in.

'Who, Peter? Who was after me?'

'The Russians – by that time they knew you were a double agent.'

'Yes, they knew —' She cocked her head and narrowed her eyes. 'I had thought about it, of course, and there had been two previous attempts on me, but I do not think the attempt on the Rambouillet road was Russian.'

'All right, Caliph then, but after you – not me,' Peter suggested.

'Perhaps, but again I do not think so. My instinct tells me they had the right target. They were after you.'

'I would have to agree,' Peter said. 'I think I was followed when I left Paris that evening —' and he told her about the Citroën. '– I think they knew that I was alone in the Maserati.'

'Then we accept it was Caliph,' she stated flatly.

'— or Mossad,' Peter murmured, and her eyes slowly widened, turning a darker thoughtful green as Peter went on.

'What if Mossad did not want an Atlas man getting close to their star agent, they didn't want you to have an ally in your hunt for Caliph? What if they just didn't want me cluttering up the carefully rehearsed scenario?'

'Peter, it's very deep water —'

'— and there are packs of sharks.'

'Let's leave that night on the Rambouillet road for the moment,' she suggested. 'It merely complicates the story I am trying to tell you.'

'All right,' Peter agreed. 'We can come back to it, if we have to.'

'The next significant move was the abduction of Melissa-Jane,' she said, and Peter's expression changed, becoming flat and stony.

'The choice of the victim was genius-inspired,' she said. 'But it required no special knowledge of you or your domestic arrangements. There was no secret that you had an only child, and it needed but a casual appraisal of your character to understand how powerful a lever she could be –' Magda dipped the tip of her finger into the champagne and then sucked it thoughtfully, pursing her lips and frowning slightly.

'You must understand that by this time I had faced the fact that I was in love with you. The gift was supposed to affirm that —' She flushed slightly under her honey tan, and it was appealing and childlike. He had never seen her blush before and it twisted something in his chest.

'The book,' he remembered. 'The Cornwallis Harris first edition.'

'My first love gift ever. I bought it when I finally admitted it to myself – but I was determined that I would not admit it to you. I am old-fashioned enough to believe the man must speak first.'

'I did.'

'God, I'll never forget it,' she said fervently, and they both thought of the savage confrontation the previous day which had ended incongruously in a declaration of love.

'I try to be unconventional,' he said, and she shook her head smiling.

'You succeed, mon amour, oh how you succeed.' Then she sobered again. 'I was in love with you. Your distress was mine. The child was a lovely girl, she had captivated me when we met – and on top of all that I felt deadly responsible for her plight. I had inveigled you into joining my hunt for Caliph, and because of that you had lost your daughter.'

He bowed his head slightly, remembering how he had believed that she had engineered it. She recognized the gesture.

'Yes, Peter. For me it was the cruellest stroke. That you should believe it of me. There was nothing that I would not have done to give her back to you – and yet there seemed nothing that I could do. My contacts with French intelligence had nothing for me. They had no inkling of how or where the child was being held – and my control at Mossad was unaccountably evasive. Somehow I had the feeling that Mossad had the key to the kidnapping. If they were not directly involved they knew more than anybody else. I have already explained that I believed Aaron had given them the identity of Caliph. If that was so, then they must know something that could have helped you to recover your child – but from Paris I was powerless to gather that information. I had to go in person to Israel and confront my control there. It was the one chance that I could get them to cooperate. They might believe my value as an agent was worth enough to give me a lead to Melissa-Jane —'

'You threatened Mossad with resignation?' Peter asked wonderingly. 'You would have done that for me?'

'Oh Peter, don't you understand, I loved you – and I had never been in love before. I would have done anything for you.'

'You make me feel humble,' he said.

She did not reply, but let the statement stand as though she were savouring it, then she sighed contentedly and went on. 'I left everything in Paris. I have an established routine for disappearing when it is necessary. Pierre took me to Rome in the Lear; from there I telephoned you but I could not tell you what I was going to do. Then I switched identity and took a commerical flight to Tel Aviv. My task in Israel was difficult, much more difficult than I had bargained for. It was five days before my control would see me. He is an old friend. No! perhaps not a friend, but we have known each other a long time. He is the deputy director of Mossad. That is how highly they value my services, to give me such an important controller, but still it took five days before he would see me, and he was cold. There was no help they could give me, he said. They knew nothing.' She chuckled. 'You have never seen me when I want something really badly, Peter. Ha! – What a battle. There is much I knew that would embarrass Mossad with her powerful allies of the West – with France and Great Britain and the USA – I threatened to hold a Press conference in New York. He became less cold, he told me that the security of the State took precedence over all personal feelings, and I said something very rude about the security of the State, and reminded him of some outstanding business which I would happily leave outstanding. He became warmer – but all this was taking time, days, many days. I was going crazy. I remembered how they had found Aaron's body, and I could not sleep at night for worrying about that lovely child. And you, oh, Peter, you will never know how I prayed to a God that I was not too sure of. You will never know how I wanted to be with you to comfort you. I wanted so desperately just to hear your voice – but I could not break my cover from Tel Aviv. I could not even telephone you, nor send you a letter —' She broke off. '– I hoped you would not believe bad things of me. You would not believe that I did not care. That I was not prepared to help you. I could only hope that I would be able to bring you some information of value to prove it was not true – but I never dreamed that one day you would believe that it was I who had taken your daughter and tortured her.'

'I am sorry,' he said quietly.

'No, do not say you are sorry. We were both Caliph's playthings. There is no blame on you.' She laid her hand upon his arm and smiled at him. 'It was not you alone who believed bad things. For at last I had prevailed on my Mossad control to give me some little scraps of information. At first he denied completely that they had ever heard of Caliph, but I risked lying to him. I told him that Aaron had told me he had reported the Caliph contact. He gave ground. Yes, he admitted. They knew of Caliph, but they did not know who he was. I hammered on, demanding to see my controller each day, driving him as mad as I was – until he threatened to have me deported even. But each time we met I wheedled and bullied a little more from him.

'At last he admitted, "All right, we know Caliph but he is very dangerous, very powerful – and he will become more powerful – God willing, he will become one of the most powerful men in the world, and he is a friend of Israel. Or rather we believe he is a friend of Israel."

'I bullied some more and he told me, "We have put an agent close to Caliph, very close to him, and we cannot jeopardize this agent. He is a valuable agent, very valuable but very vulnerable to Caliph. We cannot take the chance that Caliph could trace information back to him. We have to protect our man."

'Now I threatened, and he told me the agent's code name to protect both of us should we ever have to make contact. The code name is "CACTUS FLOWER".'

'That was all?' Peter asked, with evident disappointment.

'No, my control gave me another name. As a sop – and as a warning. The name they gave me was so close to Caliph as to be virtually the same. Again he warned me that he was giving me the name for my own protection.'

'What was it?' Peter demanded eagerly.

'Your name,' she said softly. 'Stride.'

Peter made an irritable gesture of dismissal. 'My name is nonsensical. Why would I kidnap and mutilate my own daughter – and Cactus Flower. He might as well have said, "Kentucky Fried Chicken".'

'Now it's my turn to say I'm sorry.'

Peter caught himself, realizing suddenly that he had been too quick to dismiss these scraps of information. He stood up and paced the deck of the Chris-craft with choppy, agitated steps, frowning heavily. 'Cactus Flower,' he repeated. 'Have you ever heard it before?'

'No,' she shook her head.

'Since then?'

'No,' again.

He searched his memory, trying for a sympathetic echo. There was none.

'All right.' He accepted that as having no immediate value. 'We'll just remember it for now. Let's come to my name – Peter Stride. What did you make of that?'

'It didn't mean anything then, except as a shock. Strangely enough I did not immediately think of you, but I thought of confusion between the kidnapper and the victim.'

'Stride?' he asked. 'Peter Stride? I don't understand.'

'No, well – Melissa-Jane is a Stride also.'

'Yes, of course. They didn't give you the name Peter Stride then?'

'No. Just Stride.'

'I see.' Peter stopped in mid-pace as an idea struck him – and stared out thoughtfully to where the ocean met a blue horizon.

'But they gave me your full name later,' she interrupted his thoughts.

'When?'

'After we received the news that Melissa-Jane had been rescued. Of course, I wanted to return to Paris immediately – to be with you. I was able to get on to a flight from Ben-Gurion Airport six hours after we heard the news. My heart was singing, Peter. Melissa-Jane was safe, and I was in love. I was going to be with you very soon. At the airport, while I was going through the security check before departure, the policewoman took me aside – to the security office. My control was waiting for me there. He had rushed out from Tel Aviv to catch me before I left for home, and he was very worried. They had just received an urgent message from Cactus Flower. General Peter

Stride was now definitely Caliph-motivated, and would assassinate me at the first opportunity, he told me. And I laughed at him – but he was deadly serious. "My dear Baroness, Cactus Flower is a first-class man. You must take this warning seriously," he kept repeating.'

Magda shrugged. 'I still did not believe it, Peter. It was impossible. I loved you, and I knew you loved me – although perhaps you had not yet realized that yourself. It was crazy. But on the aircraft I had time to think. My control at Mossad has never been wrong before. Can you imagine my dilemma now – how dearly I wanted to be with you, and yet I was now terrified – not that you would kill me. That did not seem important – but that you would truly turn out to be Caliph. That was what really frightened me. You see, I had never loved a man before. I don't think I could have stood it.'

She was quiet for a while, remembering the pain and confusion, and then she shook her head so that the thick fall of dark shimmering hair rustled around her shoulders.

'Once I reached Paris, my first concern was to learn that you and Melissa-Jane were safe at Abbots Yew, and then I could begin to try and find out how much substance there was in Cactus Flower's warning – but until I could decide on how safe it was I could not take the chance of being alone with you. Every time you attempted to contact me, I had to deny you, and it felt as though some little part of me was dying.'

She reached across and took his hand now, opened the fingers and bowed her head to kiss the palm and then hold it to her cheek as she went on.

'A hundred times I convinced myself that it could not be true, and I was on the point of going to you. Oh, Peter – finally I could take it no longer. I decided to meet you at Orly that day and find out one way or the other, end the terrible uncertainty. I had the grey wolves with me, as you remember, and they had been warned to expect trouble – I didn't tell them to watch you,' she explained quickly, as if trying to dispel any memory of disloyalty, 'but if you had tried to get at me they would have —' She broke off, and let his hand fall away from her cheek. 'The moment you walked into the private lounge at Orly, I saw it was true. I could sense it, there was an aura of death around you. It was the most frightening and devastating moment of my life, you looked like a different man – not the Peter Stride I knew – your whole face seemed to be altered and restructured by hatred and anger. I kissed you goodbye, because I knew we could never meet again.' Remembering it her face darkened with sadness, as though a cloud shadow had passed over them. 'I even thought that I had to protect myself by —' She gagged the words. '– You were part of Caliph, you see, and it would have been the wise thing to do. I admit that I thought of it, Peter. Have you killed, before you could kill me – but it was only a thought and it did not go farther than that. Instead I went on with the business of living, work has always been an opiate for me. If I work hard enough I can forget anything – but this time it didn't turn out that way. I've said it before, but it explains so much that I will say it again. I had never been in love before,

Peter, and I could not turn it off. It tormented me, and I cherished doubts – about Cactus Flower's warning and what I had seen so clearly in the lounge at Orly Airport. It couldn't be, it just couldn't be true – I loved you and you loved me, and you just couldn't be plotting to kill me. I almost convinced myself of that.'

She laughed curtly, but it had no humour in the sound, only the bitterness of disillusion.

'I came out here –' she made a gesture that embraced sea and sky and islands '– to be away from the temptation of going to you. A sanctuary where I could recover from my wounds and begin to get over you. But it didn't work, Peter. It was worse here. I had more time to think, to torture myself with wild speculation and grotesque theories. There was only one way. Finally I recognized that. I would bring you out here and give you the chance to kill me.' She laughed again, and now there was the old husky warmth in it. 'It was the most crazy thing I have ever done in my life – but thank God, I did it.'

'We went right to the very brink,' Peter agreed.

'Peter, why didn't you ask me outright if I was Caliph?' she wanted to know.

'The same reason you didn't ask me outright if I was plotting to kill you.'

'Yes,' she agreed. 'We were just caught up in the web that Caliph had spun for us. I have only one more question, Peter chéri. If I was Caliph, do you truly believe that I would have been so stupid as to give my telephone number at Rambouillet to the man who kidnapped Melissa-Jane, and instruct him to ring me for a friendly chat whenever he felt like it?'

Peter looked startled. 'I thought —' he began, then stopped. '– No, I didn't think. I wasn't thinking clearly at all. Of course, you wouldn't have done that – and yet, even the cleverest criminals make the most elementary mistakes.'

'Not those who have been trained at the Odessa school,' she reminded him, and seemed immediately to regret the words, for she went on quickly. 'So there is my side of the story, Peter. I may have left something out – if you can think of anything, then ask me, darling, and I'll try to fill in any missing pieces.'

And so they started once again at the very beginning, and went over the ground minutely, searching for anything they might have overlooked at the first telling of it, this time exhaustively re-examining each fact from every angle, both of them applying their trained minds to the full without being able to come up with more than they already had.

'One thing we must never let out of sight for a moment is the quality of the opposition.' Peter summed it up as the sun began lowering itself towards the western horizon, its majestic progress flanked by cohorts of cumulonimbus cloud rising into towering anvil heads over the scattered islands, like silent nuclear explosions.

'There are layers upon layers, reasons behind reasons, the kidnapping of Melissa-Jane was not merely to force me to assassinate Kingston Parker, but you as well – the proverbial two birds – with a third bird to follow. If I had succeeded I would have been hooked into Caliph for ever.'

'Where do you and I go from here, Peter?' she asked, tacitly transferring, ultimate decision-making to him.

'How about home right now,' he suggested. 'Unless you fancy another night out here.'

Peter found that his possessions had been discreetly moved from the guest bungalow to the magnificent owner's private quarters on the north tip of the island.

His toilet articles had been laid out in the mirrored master bathroom, which flanked that of the mistress. His clothing, all freshly cleaned and pressed, was in the master's dressing room where there was one hundred and fifty-five feet of louvred hanging space – Peter paced it out and calculated it would take three hundred suits of clothing. There were specially designed swinging shelves for another three hundred shirts and racks for a hundred pairs of shoes though all were empty.

His light cotton suit looked as lonely as a single camel in the midst of the Sahara desert. His shoes had been burnished to a gloss that even his batman had never been able to achieve. Despite himself he searched the dressing room swiftly for the signs of previous occupancy – and was ridiculously relieved to find none.

'I could learn to rough it like this,' he told his reflection in the mirror as he combed the damp, darkly curling locks off his forehead.

The sitting room off the suite was on three levels, and had been decorated with cane furniture and luxuriant tropical plants growing in ancient Greek wine amphoras or in rockeries that were incorporated into the flowing design of the room. The creepers and huge glossy leaves of the plants toned in artistically with jungle-patterned curtaining and the dense growth of exotic plants beyond the tall picture windows – yet the room was cool and inviting, although the sound of air-conditioning was covered by the tinkle of a waterfall down the cunningly contrived rock face that comprised one curved wall of the room. Tropical fish floated gracefully in the clear pools into which the waterfall spilled, and the perfume of growing flowers pervaded the room, and their blooms glowed in the subdued lighting.

One of the little golden Polynesian girls brought a tray of four tall frosted glasses for Peter to choose from. They were all filled with fruit and he could smell the sweet warm odour of rum mingled with the fruit. He guessed they would be almost lethal and asked for a whisky, then relented when the girl's eyes flooded with disappointment.

'I make them myself,' she wailed.

'In that case –' He sipped while she waited anxiously.

'Parfait!' he exclaimed, and she giggled with gratification, and went off wriggling her bottom under the brief pareo like a happy puppy.

Magda came then in a chiffon dress so gossamer-light that it floated about her like a fine green sea mist, through which her limbs gleamed as the light caught them.

He felt the catch in his breathing as she came towards him, and he wondered if he would ever accustom himself to the impact of her beauty.

She took the glass from his hand and tasted it.

'Good,' she said, and handed it back. But when the girl brought the tray she refused with a smile.

They moved about the room, Magda on his arm as she pointed out the rarer plants and fishes.

'I built this wing after Aaron's death,' she told him, and he realized that she wanted him to know that it contained no memories of another man. It amused him that she should find that important – and then he remembered his own furtive search of the dressing room for signs of a lover before him, and the amusement turned inward.

One wall of the private dining room was a single sheet of armoured glass, beyond which the living jewels of coral fish drifted in subtly lit sea caverns and the fronds of magnificent sea plants waved in gentle unseen currents.

Magda ordered the seating changed so they could be side by side in the low lovers' seat facing the aquarium.

'I do not like you to be far away any more,' she explained, and she picked special titbits from the serving dishes for his plate.

'This is a speciality of Les Neuf Poissons. You will eat it nowhere else in the world.' She selected small deep-sea crustaceans from a steaming creole sauce of spices and coconut cream and at the end of the meal she peeled chilled grapes from Australia with those delicate fingers, using the long shell-pink nails with the precision of a skilled surgeon to remove the pips and then placing them between his lips with thumb and forefinger.

'You spoil me,' he smiled.

'I never had a doll when I was a little girl,' she explained, smiling.

A circular stone staircase led to the beach fifty feet below the dining room and they left their shoes on the bottom step and walked barefooted on the smooth, damp sand, compacted as hard as cement by the receding tide. The moon was a few days past full, and its reflection drew a pathway of yellow light to the horizon.

'Caliph must be made to believe that he has succeeded,' Peter said abruptly, and she shivered against him.

'I wish we could forget Caliph for one night.'

'We cannot afford to forget him for a monent.'

'No, you are right. How do we make him believe that?'

'You have to die –' He felt her stiffen.

'— or at least appear to do so. It has to look as though I killed you.'

'Tell me,' she invited quietly.

'You told me that you have special arrangements for when you want to disappear.'

'Yes, I do.'

'How would you disappear from here if you had to do so?'

She thought for only a moment. 'Pierre would fly me to Bora-Bora. I have friends there. Good friends. I would take the island airline to Tahiti-Faaa on another passport – and then a scheduled airline in the same name to California or New Zealand.'

'You have other papers?' he demanded.

'Yes, of course.' She sounded so surprised by the question, that he expected her to ask '– doesn't everybody?'

'Fine,' he said. 'And we'll arrange a suspicious accident here. A scuba diving accident, shark attack in deep water, no corpse.'

'What is the point of all this, Peter?'

'If you are dead – Caliph is not going to make another attempt to have you killed.'

'Good!' she agreed.

'So you stay officially dead until we flush Caliph out,' Peter told her, and it sounded like an order but she did not demur as he went on. 'And if I carry out Caliph's evident wishes by killing you, it's going to make me a very valuable asset. I will have proved myself, and so he will cherish me. It will give me another chance to get close to him. At least it will give me a chance to check out a few wild hunches.'

'Don't let's make my death too convincing, my love. I am a great favourite of the police on Tahiti,' she murmured. 'I'd hate to have you end up under the guillotine at Tuarruru.'

Peter woke before her and raised himself on one elbow over her to study her face, delighting to find new planes and angles to her high broad cheekbones, gloating in the velvety texture of her skin, so fine that the pores were indefinable from farther than a few inches. Then he transferred his attention to the curve of her eyelashes that interlocked into a thick dark palisade seeming to seal her eyelids perpetually in sleep – yet they sprang open suddenly, the huge black pools of her pupils shrinking rapidly as she focused, and for the first time he realized that the irises were not pure green but were flecked and shot through with gold and violet.

The surprise of finding him over her changed slowly to pleasure, and she stretched her arms out over her head and arched her back, the way a lazy panther does when it rouses itself. The satin sheet slid down to her waist, and she prolonged the stretch a little longer than was necessary, a deliberate display of her body.

'Every other morning of my life that I woke without you there was wasted,' she murmured huskily, and raised her arms still at full stretch to him, folding them gracefully around his neck, still holding her back arched so that the prominent dark-red nipples brushed lightly against the crisp dark mat of curls that covered his own chest.

'Let's pretend this will last for ever,' she whispered, with her lips an inch from his, and her breath was rich as an overblown rose, heavy with the smell of vital woman and rising passion; then her lips spread softly, warmly against his and she sucked his tongue deeply into her mouth, with a low moan of wanting – and the hard slim body began to work against his, the hands breaking from his neck and hunting down his spine, long curved nails pricking and goading him just short of pain. His own arousal was so swift and so brutally hard that she moaned again, and the tension went out of her body, it seemed to soften and spread like a wax figure held too close to the flame, her eyelids trembling closed and her thighs falling apart.

'So strong—' she whispered, deep in her throat and he reared up over her, feeling supreme, invincible.

'Peter, Peter,' she cried. 'Oh yes like that. Please like that.'

Both of them striving triumphantly for the moment of glory when each was able to lose self and become for a fleeting instant part of the godhead.

Long afterwards they lay side by side in the enormous bed, both of them stretched out flat upon their backs, not touching except for the fingers of one hand intertwined as their bodies had been.

'I will go away– ' she whispered ' – because I have to, but not now. Not yet.'

He did not reply, the effort was beyond him, and her own voice was languorous with a surfeit of pleasure.

'I will make a bargain with you. Give me three days more. Only three days, to be happy like this. For me it is the first time. I have never known this before, and it may be the last time—'

He tried to rouse himself to deny it, but she squeezed his fingers for silence and went on.

' – It may be the last,' she repeated. 'And I want to have it all. Three days, in which we do not mention Caliph, in which we do not think of the blood and striving and suffering out there. If you give me that I will do everything that you want me to do. Is it a bargain, Peter? Tell me we can have that.'

'Yes. We can have that.'

'Then tell me you love me again, I do not think I can hear you say it too often.'

He said it often during those magic days, and he had spoken the truth, each time he told her she accepted with as much joy as the last time, and always each seeemed to be within touching distance of the other.

Even when tearing side by side across the warm flat waters of the lagoon, leaning back with straight arms on the tow lines, skis hissing angrily and carving fiercely sparkling wings of water from the surface as they wove back and forth in a *pas de deux* across the streaming, creaming water, laughing together in the wind and the engine roar of the Chris-craft, Hapiti the Polynesian boatman on the flying bridge looking back with a great white grin of sympathy for their joy.

Finning gently through mysterious blue and dappled depths, the only sound the wheezing suck and blow of their scuba valves and the soft clicking and the eternal echoing susurration that is the pulse beat of the ocean, holding hands as they sank down to the long abandoned hull of the Japanese aircraft carrier, now overgrown with a waving forest of sea growth and populated by a teeming fascinating multitude of beautiful and bizarre creatures.

Flying silently down the sheer steel cliff of the canted flight deck, which seemed to reach down into the very oceanic depths, so that there was the eerie fear of suddenly being deprived of support and falling down to where the surface light blued out in nothingness.

Pausing to peer through their glass face-plates into the still gaping wounds rent into the steel by aerial bombs and high explosive, and then entering through those cruel caverns cautiously as children into a haunted house and emerging victoriously with carrier nets of trophies, coins and cutlery, brass and porcelain.

Strolling on the secluded beaches of the outer islands, still hand in hand, naked in the sunlight.

Fishing the seething tide-race through the main channel at full spring tide, and shouting with excitement as the big golden amberjack came boiling up in the wake, bellies flashing like mirrors, to hit the dancing feather lures, and send the Penn reels screeching a wild protest, and the fibreglass rods nodding and kicking.

Out in the humbling silences of the unrestricted ocean, when even the smudge of the islands disappeared beyond the wave crests for minutes at a time, with only the creak and whisper of the rigging, the trembling pregnancy of the main sail, and the rustle as the twin hulls of the big Hobie cat knifed the tops off the swells.

Strolling the long curving beaches in the moonlight, searching for the heavenly bodies that so seldom show through the turbid skies of Europe – Orion the hunter and the Seven Sisters – exclaiming at the stranger constellations of this hemisphere governed by the great fixed cross in the southern heavens.

Each day beginning and ending in the special wonder and mystery of the circular bed, in loving that welded their bodies and their souls together each time more securely.

Then on the fourth day Peter woke to find her gone, and for a moment experienced an appalling sensation of total loss.

When she came back to him he did not recognize her for a breath of time.

Then he realized that she had cut away the long dark tresses of her hair, cropped it down short so that it curled close against her skull, like the petals of a dark flower. It had the effect of making her seem even taller. He neck like the stem of the flower, longer, and the curve of the throat accentuated so that it became delicate and swan-like.

She saw his expression, and exclaimed in a matter-of-fact tone.

'I thought some change was necessary, if I am to leave under a new identity. It will grow again, if you want it that way.'

She seemed to have changed completely herself, the languid amorous mood given way to the brisk businesslike efficiency of before. While they ate a last breakfast of sweet yellow papaya and the juice of freshly squeezed limes she explained her intentions, as she went swiftly through the buff envelope that her secretary had silently laid beside her plate.

There was a red Israeli diplomatic passport in the envelope.

'I will be using the name Ruth Levy – ' and she picked up the thick booklet of airline tickets, ' – and I have decided to go back to Jerusalem. I have a house there. It's not in my name, and I do not think anybody else outside of Mossad is aware of it. It will be an ideal base, close to my control at Mossad. I will try to give you what support I can, try to get further information to assist you in the hunt—'

She passed him a typed sheet of notepaper.

' – That is a telephone number at Mossad where you can get a message to me. Use the name Ruth Levy.'

He memorized the number while she went on talking, and then shredded the sheet of paper.

'I have modified the arrangements for my departure,' she told him. 'We will take the Chris-craft across to Bora-Bora. It's only a hundred miles. I will radio ahead. My friends will meet me off the beach after dark.'

They crept in through a narrow passage in the coral with all the lights on the Chris-craft doused, Magda's boatman using only what was left of the waning moon and his own intimate knowledge of the islands to take her in.

'I wanted Hapiti to see me go ashore alive,' she whispered quietly, leaning against Peter's chest to draw comfort from their last minutes together. 'I did not exaggerate the danger you might be in if the local people thought what we want Caliph to think. Hapiti will keep his mouth shut – ' she assured him, ' – and will back up your story of a shark attack, unless you order him to tell the truth.'

'You think of everything.'

'I have only just found you, monsieur,' she chuckled. 'I do not want to lose you yet. I have even decided to speak a word to the Chief of Police on Tahiti, when I pass through. He is an old friend. When you get back to Les Neuf Poissons, have my secretary radio Tahiti—'

She went on quietly, covering every detail of her arrangements, and he could find no omissions. She was interrupted by a soft hail from out of the darkness and Hapiti throttled the diesels back to idle. They drifted down closer to the loom of the island. A canoe bumped against the side, and Magda turned quickly in his arms, reaching up for his mouth with hers.

'Please be careful, Peter,' was all that she said, and then she broke away and stepped down into the canoe as Hapiti handed down her single valise. The canoe pushed away immediately, and was lost in the dark. There was nothing to wave at, and Peter liked it better that way, but still he stared back over the stern into the night as the Chris-craft groped blindly for the channel again.

There was a hollow feeling under his ribs, as though part of himself was missing; he tried to fill it with a memory of Magda that had amused him because it epitomized for him her quick and pragmatic mind.

' – When the news of your death hits the market, the bottom is going to drop out of Altmann stock.' He had realized this halfway through their final discussion that morning. 'I hadn't thought of that.' He was troubled by the complication.

'I had,' she smiled serenely. 'I estimate it will lose a hundred francs a share within the first week after the news breaks.'

'Doesn't that worry you?'

'Not really.' She gave that sudden wicked grin. 'I telexed a buying order to Zurich this morning. I expect to show a profit of not less than a hundred million francs when the stock bounces back.' Again the mischievous flash of green eyes. 'I do have to be recompensed for all this inconvenience, tu ne penses pas?'

And although he still smiled at the memory, the hollow place remained there inside him.

Pierre flew the Tahitian police out to Les Neuf Poissons in the Trislander, and there followed two days of questions and statements. Nearly every member of the community wished to make a statement to the police, there had seldom been such entertainment and excitement available on the islands.

Nearly all of the statements were glowing eulogies to 'La Baronne' delivered to the accompaniment of lamentation and weeping. Only Hapiti had first-hand information and he made the most of this position of importance, embroidering and gilding the tale. He was even able to give a positive identification of the shark as a 'Dead White' – the English name startled Peter until he remembered that the movie *Jaws* was in the island's cassette video library and was undoubtedly the source of the big boatman's inspiration. Hapiti went on to describe its fangs as long and sharp as cane knives, and to give a gruesome imitation of the sound they made as they closed on 'La Baronne' – Peter would willingly have gagged him to prevent those flights of imagination, which were not supported by Peter's own statement, but the police sergeant was greatly impressed and encouraged Hapiti to further acts of creation with cries of astonishment.

On the last evening there was a funeral feast on the beach for Magda. It was a moving ritual, and Peter found himself curiously affected when the women of the island, swaying and wailing at the water's edge, cast wreaths of frangipani blooms on to the tide to be carried out beyond the reef.

Peter flew back to Tahiti-Faaa with the police the following morning, and they stayed with him, flanking him discreetly, on the drive to the headquarters of gendarmerie in the town. However, his interview with the Chief of Police was brief and courteous, clearly Magda had been there before him; and if there was no actual exchange of winks and nudges, the commissioner's handshake of farewell was firm and friendly.

'Any friend of La Baronne is a friend here.' And he used the present tense, then sent Peter back to the airport in an official car.

The UTA flight landed in California through that sulphurous eye-stinging layer of yellow air trapped between sea and mountains. Peter did not leave the airport, but after he had shaved and changed his shirt in the men's room he found a copy of the *Wall Street Journal* in the first-class Pan Am Clipper lounge. It was dated the previous day, and the report of Magda Altmann's death was on Page Three. It was a full column, and Peter was surprised by the depth of the Altmann Industries involvement in the American financial scene. The complex of holdings was listed, followed by a resumé of Baron Aaron Altmann's career and that of his widow. The cause of death as given by the Tahitian police was 'Shark Attack' while scuba diving in the company of a friend – General Peter Stride – Peter was grimly satisfied that his name was mentioned. Caliph would read it, wherever he was, and draw the appropriate conclusion. Peter could expect something to happen now; he was not quite sure what, but he knew that he was being drawn closer to the centre like a fragment of iron to the magnet.

He managed to sleep for an hour, in one of the big armchairs, before the hostess roused him for the Pan Am Polar flight to London's Heathrow.

He called Pat Stride, his sister-in-law, from Heathrow Airport. She was unaffectedly delighted to hear his voice.

' – Steven is in Spain, but I am expecting him home tomorrow before lunch, that is if his meetings go the way he wants them. They want to build a thirty-six-hole golf course at San Istaban – ' Steven's companies owned a complex of tourist hotels on the Spanish coast ' – and Steven had to go through the motions with the Spanish authorities. But, why don't you come down to Abbots Yew tonight? Alex and Priscilla are here, and there will be an amusing house party for the weekend—' He could hear the sudden calculating tone in Pat's voice as she began instinctively to run through the shortlist of potential mates for Peter.

After he had accepted and hung up, he dialled the Cambridge number and was relieved that Cynthia's husband, George Barrow, answered.

'Give me a Bolshevik intellectual over a neurotic ex-wife any day,' he thought as he greeted Melissa-Jane's stepfather warmly. Cynthia was at a meeting of the Faculty Wives Association, and Melissa-Jane was auditioning for a part in a production of Gilbert and Sullivan by the local drama society.

'How is she?' Peter wanted to know.

'I think she is well over it now, Peter. The hand is completely healed. She seems to have settled down—' They spoke for a few minutes more, then ran out of conversation. The two women were all they had in common.

'Give Melissa-Jane my very best love,' Peter told him, and picked up a copy of the *Financial Times* from a news stand on his way to the Avis desk. He hired a compact and while waiting for it to be delivered he searched swiftly through the newspaper for mention of Magda Altmann. It was on an inside page, clearly a follow-up article to a previous report of her death. There had been a severe reaction on the London and European stock exchanges – the hundred-franc drop in Altmann stock that Magda had anticipated had already been exceeded on the Bourse – and again there was a brief mention of his own name in a repetition of the circumstances of her death. He was satisfied with the publicity, and with Magda's judgement in buying back her own stock. Indeed it all seemed to be going a little too smoothly. He became aware of the fateful prickle of apprehension down his spine, his own personal barometer of impending danger.

As always Abbots Yew was like coming home, and Pat met him on the gravel of the front drive, kissed him with sisterly affection and linked her arm through his to lead him into the gracious old house.

'Steven will be delighted,' she promised him. 'I expect he will telephone this evening. He always does when he is away.'

There was a buff envelope propped on the bedside table of the guest room overlooking the stables that was always reserved for Peter. The message originated at Ben-Gurion Airport, Tel Aviv, and was a single word – the code he had arranged with Magda to let him know that she arrived safely and without complication. The message gave him a sharp pang of wanting, and he lay in a deep hot bath and thought about her, remembering small details of conversation and shared experience that suddenly were of inflated value.

While he towelled himself he regarded his image in the steamed mirror with a critical eye. He was lean and hard and burned dark as a desert Arab by the Pacific sun. He watched the play of muscle under the tanned skin as he moved, and he knew that he was as fit and as mentally prepared for action as he had ever been, glad that Magda was safely beyond the reach of Caliph's talons so that he could concentrate all his energies on what his instincts told him must be the final stage of the hunt.

He went through to his bedroom with the towel around his waist and stretched out on the bed to wait for the cocktail hour in Pat Stride's rigidly run household.

He wondered what made him so certain that this was the lead which would carry him to Caliph, it seemed so slim a chance and yet the certainty was like a steel thread, and the steel was in his heart.

That made him pause. Once again he went carefully over the changes which had taken place within him since his first exposure to Caliph's malignant influence; the fatal miasma of corruption that seemed to spread around Caliph like the poisonous mists from some evil swamp seemed to have engulfed Peter entirely.

He thought again of his execution of the blonde girl at Johannesburg what seemed like a thousand years before, but with mild surprise realized was months not years ago.

He thought of how he had been prepared to kill both Kingston Parker and Magda Altmann – and realized that contact with violence was brutalizing, capable of eroding the principles and convictions which he had believed inviolate after almost forty years of having lived with them.

If this was so, then after Caliph – if he succeeded in destroying him – what was there after Caliph? Would he ever be the same man again? Had he advanced too far beyond the frontiers of social behaviour and conscience? Would he ever go back? He wondered. Then he thought about Magda Altmann and realized she was his hope for the future, after Caliph there would be Magda.

These doubts were weakening, he told himself. There must be no distractions now, for once again he was in the arena with the adversary. No distraction, no doubts – only total concentration on the conflict ahead.

He stood up from the bed and began to dress.

Steven was delighted to have Peter at Abbots Yew again, as Pat had predicted.

He also was tanned from the short stay in Spain, but he had again put on weight, only a few pounds, but it would soon be a serious problem, good food and drink were two of the occupational hazards of success: the most evident but not the most dangerous temptations that face a man who has money enough to buy whatever idly engages his fancy.

Peter watched him covertly during the lunch, studying the handsome head which was so very much like his own, the same broad brow and straight aristocratic nose, and yet was so different in small but significant details, and it was not only Steven's thick dark moustache.

'All right, it's easy to be wise afterwards,' Peter told himself, as he watched his twin brother. Seeing again the little marks, which only now seemed to have meaning. The narrower set of eyes, slightly too close together, so that even when he laughed that deep bluff guffaw of his they seemed still to retain a cold cruel light, the mouth that even in laughter was still too hard, too determined, the mouth of a man who would brook no check to his ambitions, no thwarting of his desires. Or am I imagining it now? Peter wondered. It was so easy to see what you looked for expectantly.

The conversation at lunch dwelt almost exclusively on the prospects for the flat-racing season which had opened at Doncaster the previous weekend, and Peter joined it knowledgeably; but as he chatted he was casting back along the years, to the incidents that might have troubled him more if he had not immediately submerged them under an instinctive and unquestioning loyalty to his twin brother.

There was Sandhurst when Steven had been sent down, and Peter had known unquestioningly that it was unjust. No Stride was capable of what Steven had been accused of, and he had not even had to discuss it with his brother. He had affirmed his loyalty with a handshake and a few embarrassed muttered words.

'Thank you, Peter. I'll never forget that,' Steven had told him fervently, meeting Peter's gaze with steady clear eyes.

Since then Steven's rise had been meteoric through the post-war years in which it seemed almost impossible for even the most able man to amass a great fortune, a man had to have special talents and take terrible risks to achieve what Steven had.

Now sitting at his brother's board, eating roast saddle of lanb and the first crisp white asparagus shoots of the season flown in from the Continent, Peter was at last covering forbidden ground, examining loyalties which until then had been unquestioned. Yet they were straws scattered by the winds of time, possibly without significance. Peter transferred his thoughts to the present.

'Stride,' Magda's control at Mossad in Tel-Aviv had said. Just the two names: 'Cactus Flower' and 'Stride'. That was fact and not conjecture.

Down the length of the luncheon table Sir Steven Stride caught his brother's eye.

'Wine with you, my dear fellow.' Steven lifted the glass of claret in the old salute.

'Enchanted, I'm sure.' Peter gave the correct reply, a little ritual between them, a hangover from Sandhurst days, and Peter was surprised at the depth of his regret. Perhaps Caliph has not yet succeeded in corrupting me entirely, Peter thought, as he drank the toast.

After lunch there was another of their brotherly rituals. Steven signalled it with a jerk of the head and Peter nodded agreement. Peter's old army duffle coat was in the cupboard below the back staircase with his Wellingtons, and he and Steven changed into rough clothing sitting side by side on the monk's bench in the rear entrance hall as they had so often before.

Then Steven went through into the gunroom, took down a Purdey Royal shotgun from the rack, and thrust a handful of cartridges in his coat pocket.

'Damned vixen has a litter of cubs somewhere in the Bottoms, playing merry hell with the pheasant chicks – ' he explained as Peter asked a silent question. 'It goes against the grain a bit to shoot a fox but I must put a stop to her – haven't had a chance at her yet—' and he led the way out of the back door through the orchard towards the stream.

It was almost a formal beating of the bounds, the leisurely circuit of the estate boundaries that the two brothers always made on Peter's first day at Abbots Yew, another old comfortable tradition which allowed them time to have each other's news and reaffirm the bond between them.

They sauntered along the river bank, side by side, moving into single file with Steven leading when the path narrowed and turned away from the stream and went up through the woods.

Steven was elated by the success of his visit to Spain, and he boasted of his achievements in obtaining another parcel of prime seafront property on which to build the new golf course and to extend the hotel by another five hundred rooms.

'Now's the time to buy. Mark my words, Peter – we are on the verge of another explosion.'

'The cut-back in oil price is going to help, I'd expect,' Peter agreed.

'That's not the half of it, old boy.' Steven turned to glance back over his shoulder and he winked knowingly at Peter. 'You can expect another five per cent cut in six months, take my word on it. The Arabs have come to their senses.' Steven went on swiftly, picking out those types of industry which would benefit most dramatically from the reduction in crude prices, then selecting the leading companies in those sectors. ' – If you have a few pounds lying idle, that's where to put it.' Steven's whole personality seemed to change when he spoke like this of power and great wealth. Then he came out from behind the façade of the English country squire which he was usually at such pains to cultivate; the glitter in his eyes was now undisguised and his bushy moustache bristled like the whiskers of some big dangerous predator.

He was still talking quietly and persuasively as they left the woods and began to cross the open fields towards the ruins of the Roman camp on the crest of the low hills.

' – These people have still to be told what to do, you know. Those damned shop stewards up in Westminster may have thrown the Empire away, but we still have our responsibilities.' Steven changed the Purdey shotgun from one arm to the other, carrying it in the crook of the arm, the gun broken open and the shining brass caps of the Eley Kynoch cartridges showing in the breeches. ' – Government only by those fit to govern.' Steven enlarged on that for a few minutes.

Then suddenly Steven fell silent, almost as though he had suddenly decided that he had spoken too much, even to somebody as trusted as his own younger twin. Peter was silent also, trudging up the curve of the hill with his boots squelching in the soft damp earth. There was something completely unreal about the moment, walking over well-remembered ground in the beautiful mellow sunlight of an English spring afternoon with a man he had known from the day of his birth – and yet perhaps had never known at all.

It was not the first time that he had heard Steven talk like this, and yet perhaps it was the first time he had ever listened. He shivered and Steven glanced at him.

'Cold.'

'Goose walked over my grave,' Peter explained, and Steven nodded as they clambered up the shallow earth bank that marked the perimeter of the Roman camp.

They stood on the lip under the branches of a lovely copper beech, resplendent in its new spring growth of russet.

Steven was breathing hard from the pull up the hill, that extra weight was already beginning to tell. There was a spot of high unhealthy colour in each cheek, and little blisters of sweat speckled his chin.

He closed the breech of the shotgun with a metallic clash, and leaned the weapon against the trunk of the copper beech as he struggled to regain his breath.

Peter moved across casually and propped his shoulder against the copper beech, but his thumbs were hooked into the lapels of the duffle coat, not thrust into pockets, and he was still in balance, weight slightly forward on the balls of his feet. Although he seemed to be entirely relaxed and at rest he was in fact coiled like a spring, poised on the brink of violent action and the shotgun was within easy reach of his right hand.

He had seen that Steven had loaded with number four shot. At ten paces it would disembowel a man. The safety catch on the top of the pistol grip of the butt engaged automatically when the breech was opened and closed again, but the right thumb would instinctively slip the catch forward as the hand closed on the grip.

Steven took a silver cigarette case from the side pocket of his coat and tapped down a cigarette on the lid.

'Damned shame about Magda Altmann,' he said gruffly, not meeting Peter's eyes.

'Yes,' Peter agreed softly.

'Glad they handled it in a civilized fashion. Could have made it awkward for you, you know.'

'I suppose they could have,' Peter agreed.

'What about your job at Narmco?'

'I don't know yet. I will not know until I get back to Brussels.'

'Well, my offer still stands, old boy. I could do with a bit of help. I really could. Somebody I could trust. You'd be doing me a favour.'

'Damned decent of you, Steven.'

'No, really, I mean it.' Steven lit the cigarette with a gold Dunhill lighter and inhaled with evident pleasure, and after a moment Peter asked him.

'I hope you were not in a heavy position in Altmann stock. I see it has taken an awful tumble.'

'Strange that.' Steven shook his head. 'Pulled out of Altmann's a few weeks ago, actually. Needed the money for San Istaban.'

'Lucky,' Peter murmured, or much more than luck. He wondered why Steven admitted the share transaction so readily. 'Of course,' he realized, 'it would have been very substantial and therefore easily traced.'

He studied his brother now, staring at him with a slight scowl of concentration. Was it possible? he asked himself. Could Steven really have masterminded something so complex, where ideology and self-interest and delusions of omnipotence seemed so inextricably snarled and entwined.

'What is it, old boy?' Steven asked, frowning slightly in sympathy.

'I was just thinking that the whole concept and execution has been incredible, Steven. I would never have suspected you were capable of it.'

'I'm sorry, Peter. I don't understand. What are you talking about?'

'Caliph,' Peter said softly.

It was there! Peter saw it instantly. The instant of utter stillness, like a startled jungle animal – but the flinch of the eyes, followed immediately by the effort of control.

The expression of Steven's face had not altered, the little frown of polite inquiry held perfectly, then turning slowly, deeper into puzzlement.

'I'm afraid you just lost me there, old chap.'

It was superbly done. Despite himself Peter was impressed. There were depths to his brother which he had never suspected – but that was his own omission. No matter which way you looked at it, it took an extraordinary ability to achieve what Steven had achieved in less than twenty years, against the most appalling odds. No matter how he had done it, it was the working of a particular type of genius.

He was capable of running Caliph, Peter accepted the fact at last – and immediately had a focal point for the corroding hatred he had carried within him for so long.

'Your only mistake so far, Steven, was to let Aaron Altmann know your name,' Peter went on quietly. 'I suspect you did not then know that he was a Mossad agent, and that your name would go straight on to the Israeli intelligence computer. Nobody, nothing, can ever wipe it from the memory rolls, Steven. You are known.'

Steven's eyes flickered down to the shotgun, it was instinctive, uncontrollable, the final confirmation if Peter needed one.

'No, Steven. That's not for you.' Peter shook his head. 'That's my work. You're fat and out of condition, and you have never had the training. You must stick to hiring others to do the actual killing. You wouldn't even get a hand on it.'

Steven's eyes darted back to his brother's face. Still the expression on his face had not altered.

'I think you've gone out of your head, old boy.'

Peter ignored it. 'You of all people should know that I am capable of killing anybody. You have conditioned me to that.'

'We are getting into an awful tangle now,' Steven protested. 'What on earth should you want to kill anybody for?'

'Steven, you are insulting both of us. I know. There is no point in going on with the act. We have to work out between us what we are going to do about it.'

He had phrased it carefully, offering the chance of compromise. He saw the waver of doubt in Steven's eyes, the slight twist of his mouth, as he struggled to reach a decision.

' – But please do not underestimate the danger you are in, Steven.' As he spoke Peter produced an old worn pair of dark leather gloves from his pocket and began to pull them on. There was something infinitely menacing in that simple act, and again Steven's eyes were drawn irresistibly.

'Why are you doing that?' For the first time Steven's voice croaked slightly.

'I haven't yet touched the gun,' Peter explained reasonably. 'It has only your prints upon it.'

'Christ, you'd never get away with it, Peter.'

'Why, Steven? It is always dangerous to carry a loaded shotgun over muddy and uneven ground.'

'You couldn't do it, not in cold blood.' The edge of terror was in Steven's voice.

'Why not? You had no such qualms with Prince Hassied Abdel Hayek.'

'I am your brother – he was only a bloody wog—' Steven choked it off, staring now at Peter with stricken eyes, the expression of his face beginning at last to crack and crumble as he realized that he had made the fateful admission.

Peter reached for the shotgun without taking his eyes from his brother's.

'Wait!' Steven cried. 'Wait, Peter!'

'For what?'

'You've got to let me explain.'

'All right, go ahead.'

'You can't just say go ahead, like that. It's so complicated.'

'All right, Steven. Let's start at the beginning – with Flight 070. Tell me why?'

'We had to do it, Peter. Don't you see? There is over four billions of British investment in that country, another three billions of American money. It's the major world producer of gold and uranium, chrome and a dozen other strategic minerals. My God, Peter. Those ham-handed oafs in control now are on a suicide course. We had to take it away from them, and put in a controllable government. If we don't do that the Reds will have it all within ten years – probably much less.'

'You had an alternative government chosen?'

'Of course,' Steven told him urgently, persuasively, watching the shotgun that Peter still held low across his hips. 'It was planned in every detail. It took two years.'

'All right.' Peter nodded. 'Tell me about the murder of Prince Hassied.'

'It wasn't murder, for godsake man, it was absolutely essential. It was a matter of survival. They were destroying Western civilization with their childlike irresponsibility. Drunk with power, they were no longer amenable to reason, like spoiled children in a sweet shop – we had to put a stop to it, or face a breakdown of the capitalist system. They have probably done irreparable damage to the prestige of the dollar, they have taken sterling hostage and hold it in daily jeopardy with the threat of withdrawing those astronomic balances from London. We had to bring them to their senses, and look how small a price. We can reduce the price of crude oil gradually to its 1970 level. We can restore sanity to the currencies of the Western world and secure real growth and prosperity for hundreds of millions of peoples – all at the cost of a single life.'

'And anyway, he was only a bloody wog. Wasn't he?' Peter agreed reasonably.

'Look here, Peter. I said that but I didn't mean it. You are being unreasonable.'

'I will try not to be,' Peter assured him mildly. 'Tell me where it goes from here. Who do you bring under control next – the British Trade Union movement, perhaps?'

And Steven stared at him wordlessly for a moment.

'Damn it, Peter. That was a hell of a guess. But could you imagine if we had a five-year wage freeze, and no industrial action during that time. It's them or us, Peter. We could get back to being one of the major industrial powers of the Western world. Great Britain! We could be that again.'

'You are very convincing, Steven,' Peter acknowledged. 'There are only a few details that worry me a little.'

'What are they, Peter?'

'Why was it necessary to arrange the murder of Kingston Parker and Magda Altmann—'

Steven stared at him, his jaw unhinging slightly and the hard line of his mouth going slack with astonishment. 'No,' he shook his head. 'That's not so.'

'—and why was it necessary to kill Baron Altmann, and torture him to death?'

'That was not my doing – all right, it was done. And I knew it was done – but I had nothing to do with it, Peter. Not the murder at least, oh God, all right I knew it had to be done, but —' His voice tailed off, and he stared helplessly at Peter.

'From the beginning again, Steven. Let's hear it all—' Peter spoke almost gently.

'I cannot, Peter. You don't understand what might happen, what will happen if I tell you—'

Peter slid the safety catch off the Purdey shotgun. The click of the mechanism was unnaturally loud in the silence, and Steven Stride stared and stepped back a pace, blinking at his brother, fastening all his attention on Peter's eyes.

'God,' he whispered. 'You would do it too.'

'Tell me about Aaron Altmann.'

'Can I have another cigarette?'

Peter nodded and Steven lit it with hands that trembled very slightly.

'You have to understand how it worked, before I can explain.'

'Tell me how it worked,' Peter invited.

'I was recruited—'

'Steven, don't lie to me – you are Caliph.'

'No, God no, Peter. You have it all wrong,' Steven cried. 'It's a chain. I am only a link in Caliph's chain. I am not Caliph.'

'You are a part of Caliph, then?'

'Only a link in the chain,' Steven repeated vehemently.

'Tell me,' Peter invited with a small movement of the shotgun barrel that drew Steven's eyes immediately.

'There is a man I have known a long time. We have worked together before. A man with greater wealth and influence than I have. It was not an immediate thing. It grew out of many discussions and conversations over a long time, years, in which we both voiced our concern with the way that power had shifted to blocks of persons unfit to wield it—'

'– All right,' Peter nodded grimly. 'I understand your political and ideological sentiments. Leave them out of the account.'

'Very well,' Steven agreed. ' – Well, finally this man asked me if I would be prepared to join an association of Western world political and industrial leaders dedicated to restoring power to the hands of those fitted by training and upbringing to govern.'

'Who was this man?'

'Peter, I cannot tell you.'

'You have no choice,' Peter told him, and there was a long moment as they locked eyes and wills; then Steven sighed in capitulation.

'It was—' The name was that of a mining magnate who controlled most of the free world supply of nuclear fuel and gold and precious stones.

'So he is the one who would have been in control of the new South African government with which you intended replacing the present regime in that country, if the taking of 070 had succeeded?' Peter demanded, and Steven nodded wordlessly.

'All right,' Peter nodded. 'Go on.'

'He had been recruited as I was,' Steven explained. 'But I was never to know by whom. In my turn I was to recruit another desirable member – but I would be the only one who knew who that was. It was how the security of the chain was to be maintained. Each link would know only the one above and below him, the man who had recruited him and the one who he recruited in his turn—'

'Caliph?' Peter demanded. 'What about Caliph?'

'Nobody knows who he is.'

'Yet he must know who you are.'

'Yes of course.'

'Then there must be some way for you to get a message to Caliph,' Peter insisted. 'For instance, when you recruit a new member, you must be able to pass on the information? When he wants something from you, he must be able to contact you.'

'Yes.'

'How?'

'Christ, Peter. It's more than my life is worth.'

'We'll come back to it.' said Peter impatiently. 'Go on, tell me about Aaron Altmann.'

'That was a disaster. I chose Aaron as the man I would recruit. He seemed exactly the kind of man we needed. I had known him for years. I knew he could be very tough when it was necessary. So I approached him. He seemed very eager at first, leading me on. Getting me to explain the way Caliph would work. I was delighted to have recruited such an important man. He intimated that he would contribute twenty-five million dollars to the funds of the association, so I passed a message to Caliph. I told him that I had almost succeeded in recruiting Baron Altmann—'

Steven stopped nervously, and dropped the stub of his cigarette on to the damp turf, grinding it out under his heel.

'What happened then?' Peter demanded.

'Caliph responded immediately. I was ordered to break off all contact with Aaron Altmann at once. I realized I must have chosen a potentially dangerous person. You tell me now he was Mossad. I did not know that – but Caliph must have known it. I did as I was told and dropped Aaron like a hot chestnut – and four days later he was abducted. I had nothing to do with it, Peter. I swear to you. I liked the man immensely. I admired him—'

'Yet he was abducted and horribly tortured. You must have known that Caliph had done it, and that you were responsible?'

'Yes.' Steven said the word flatly, without evasion. Peter felt a small stir of admiration for that.

'They tortured him to find out if he had passed the information you had given him about Caliph to Mossad,' Peter insisted.

'Yes. I expect so. I do not know.'

'If the picture I have of Aaron Altmann was correct they received no information from him.'

'No. He was like that. They must have lost patience with him in the end – to do what they did to him. It was my first moment of disillusionment with Caliph,' Steven muttered sombrely.

They were both silent now, until Peter burst out angrily.

'My God, Steven, can't you see what a disgusting business you are mixed up in?' And Steven was mute. 'Couldn't you see it?' Peter insisted, the anger raw in his voice. 'Couldn't you realize it from the beginning?'

'Not at the beginning.' Steven shook his head miserably. 'It seemed a brilliant solution for all the diseases of the Western world – and then once I began it was like being on board a speeding express train. It was just impossible to get off again.'

'All right. So then you tried to have me assassinated on the Rambouillet road?'

'Good God, no.' Steven was truly appalled. 'You're my brother, good God—'

'Caliph did it to stop me getting close to Aaron's widow who was out to avenge him.'

'I didn't know a thing about it, I swear to you. If Caliph did it, he knew better than to let me in on it.' Steven was pleading now. 'You must believe that.'

Peter felt a softening of his resolve, but forced back the knowledge that this man was his brother, someone who had been very dear over a lifetime.

'What was your next operation for Caliph then?' He asked without allowing the softness to reach his voice.

'There wasn't—'

'Damn you, Steven, don't lie to me.' Peter's voice cracked like a whiplash. 'You knew about Prince Hassied Abdel Hayek!'

'All right. I arranged that. Caliph told me what to do and I did it.'

'Then you kidnapped Melissa-Jane and had her mutilated—'

'Oh God! No!' Steven's voice was a sob.

' – To force me to assassinate Kingston Parker—'

'No, Peter. No!'

' – And then to kill Magda Altmann—'

'Peter, I swear to you. Not Melissa-Jane. I love her like one of my own daughters. You must know that. I had no idea it was Caliph.'

Steven was pleading wildly now.

' – You have to believe me. I would never have allowed that to happen. That is too horrible.'

Peter watched him with a steely merciless glint of blue in his eyes, cold and cutting as the edge of the executioner's blade.

'I will do anything to prove to you I had nothing to do with Melissa-Jane. Anything you say, Peter. I'll take any chance to prove it to you. I swear it to you.'

Steven Stride's dismay and sincerity were beyond question. His face was drained of all colour and his lips were marble white and trembling with the strength of his denial.

Peter handed the shotgun to his brother without a word. Startled, Steven held it for a moment at arm's length.

'You are in bad trouble, Steven,' Peter said quietly. He knew that from now on he needed Steven's unreserved and wholehearted commitment. He could not be forced to do what he must do at the point of a shotgun.

Steven recognized the gesture, and slowly lowered the gun. With his thumb he pushed across the breech-locking mechanism, and the weapon hinged open. He pulled the cartridges from the double eyes of the breeches and dropped them into the pocket of his shooting jacket.

'Let's get down to the house,' Steven said. his voice still unsteady with the trauma of the last minutes. 'I need a stiff whisky—'

There was a log fire burning in the deep walk-in fireplace of Steven's study. The portals were magnificently carved altar surrounds from a sixteenth-century German church, salvaged from the ruins of World War II Allied bombing and purchased by Steven from a Spanish dealer, after having been smuggled out through Switzerland.

Opposite the fireplace, bow windows with leaded panes and ancient wavy glass looked out over the rose garden. The other two walls housed Steven's collection of rare books, each boxed in its individual leather-bound container and lettered in gold leaf. The shelves reached from floor to the high moulded ceiling. It was a passion that the brothers shared.

Steven stood now in the fireplace with his back to the flames, one hand clasped in the small of his back, hoisting up the skirts of his tweed jacket to warm his backside. In the other hand he held a deep crystal tumbler, still half-filled with whisky, hardly diluted by the soda he had dashed into it from the syphon.

Steven still looked shaken and pale, and every few minutes he shivered uncontrollably, although the room was oppresively heated by the blazing fire and all the windows were closed tightly.

Peter sprawled in the brocade-upholstered Louis Quatorze chair across the room, his legs thrust out straight and crossed at the ankles, hands thrust deeply into his pockets, and his chin lowered on his chest in deep thought.

'How much was your contribution to Caliph's war chest?' Peter asked abruptly.

'I was not in the same class as Aaron Altmann,' Steven answered quietly. 'I pledged five millions in sterling over five years.'

'So we must imagine a network extending across all international boundaries. Powerful men in every country, each contributing enormous sums of money – and almost unlimited information and influence—'

Steven nodded and took another swallow of his dark-toned whisky.

' – There is no reason to believe that it was only one man in each country. There may be a dozen in England, another dozen in Western Germany, fifty in the United States—'

'It's possible,' Steven agreed.

'So that Caliph could very easily have arranged the kidnapping of Melissa-Jane through another of his chain in this country.'

'You must believe I had nothing to do with it, Peter.'

Peter dismissed this new protestation impatiently, and went on thinking out aloud.

'It is still possible that Caliph is a committee of the founder members – not one man at all.'

'I don't think so—' Steven hesitated. ' – I had a very strong impression that it all was one man. I do not think a committee would be capable of such swift and determined action.' He shook his head, trying to cast his mind back for the exact words which had formed his impressions. ' – You must remember that I have only discussed Caliph with one other person, the man who recruited me. However, you can be certain that we discussed it in depth and over an extended period. I was not about to put out five million on something that didn't satisfy me entirely. No, it was one man who would make the decision for all of us – but the decisions would be in the interest of all.'

'Yet there was no guarantee that any individual member of the chain would be informed of every decision?'

'No. Of course not. That would have been madness. Security was the key to success.'

'You could trust somebody you had never met, whose identity was hidden from you – you could trust him with vast sums of money, and the destiny of the world as we know it?'

Steven hesitated again as if seeking the right words. 'Caliph has an aura that seems to envelop all of us. The man who recruited me – ' Steven seemed reluctant to repeat the name again, proof to Peter of the influence that Caliph exerted ' – is a man whose judgement I respect tremendously. He was convinced, and this helped to convince me.'

'What do you think now?' Peter asked abruptly. 'Are you still convinced?'

Steven drained the whisky glass, and then smoothed his moustache with a little nervous gesture.

'Come on, Steven,' Peter encouraged him.

'I still think Caliph had the right idea—' he said reluctantly. ' – The rules have changed, Peter. We were fighting for survival of the world as we know it. We were merely playing to the new morality—'

He crossed to the silver tray on the corner of his desk and refilled the whisky glass.

' – Up to now we have had one hand tied behind our backs, while the Reds and the extreme left and the members of the Third World have had both hands to fight with and a dagger in each one. All Caliph did was to take off our shackles.'

'What has made you change your mind then?' Peter asked.

'I'm not sure that I have changed my mind.' Steven turned back to face him. 'I still think it was the right idea—'

' – But?' Peter insisted.

Steven shrugged. 'The murder of Aaron Altmann, the mutilation of Melissa-Jane—' He hesitated. ' – Other acts of which I suspect Caliph was the originator. They were not for the common good. They were merely to protect Caliph's personal safety, or to satisfy what I am beginning to believe is vaunted and unbridled lust for power.' Steven shook his head again. 'I believed Caliph to be noble and dedicated – but there is no nobility in some of the things he has done. He has acted like a common criminal. He has acted for personal advantage and glorification. I believe in the concept of Caliph – but I know now we have chosen the wrong man. He has been corrupted by the power that we placed in his hands.'

Peter listened to him carefully, his head cocked to one side, his blue eyes clear and quietly searching.

'All right, Steven. So we discover that Caliph is not a deity – but a man with a man's petty greed and self-interest.'

'Yes, I suppose I do.' Steven's handsome florid face was heavy with regret. 'Caliph is not what I believed he might be.'

'Do you accept now that he is evil – truly evil?'

'Yes, I accept that.' Then, fiercely, 'But God, how I wish Caliph had been what I believed he was at the beginning.'

Peter could understand that and he nodded.

'It was what this crazy world of ours needed—' Steven went on bitterly. ' – We need somebody, a strong man to tell us what to do. I thought it was Caliph. I wanted it so badly to be him.'

'So now, do you accept that Caliph was not that man?'

'Yes,' said Steven simply. 'But if there was a man like that I would follow him again, unquestioningly.'

'You said you would do anything to prove to me that you had nothing to do with Melissa-Jane – will you help me to destroy Caliph?'

'Yes.' Steven did not hesitate.

'There will be great personal risk.' Peter pointed out, and now Steven met his eyes steadily.

'I know that. I know Caliph better than you.'

Peter found that his affection for his brother was now reinforced with admiration. Steven lacked very few of the manly virtues, he thought. He had strength and courage and brains, perhaps his major vice was that he had too much of each.

'What do you want me to do, Peter?'

'I want you to arrange a meeting with Caliph – face to face.'

'Impossible.' Steven dismissed it immediately.

'You said that you had means of getting a message to him?'

'Yes, but Caliph would never agree to a meeting.'

'Steven, what is the single – the only weakness that Caliph has shown so far?'

'He has shown no weakness.'

'Yes, he has,' Peter denied.

'What is it?'

'He is obsessed with protecting his personal identity and safety,' Peter pointed out. 'As soon as that is threatened, he immediately reverts to abduction and torture and murder.'

'That isn't a weakness—' Steven pointed out. 'It's a strength.'

'If you can get a message to him – that his identity is in jeopardy. That somebody, an enemy, has penetrated his security screen and has managed to get close to him,' Peter suggested, and Steven considered it long and carefully.

'He would react very strongly,' Steven agreed. 'But it would not take him very long to find out that I was lying. That would immediately discredit me, and as you said earlier I would be at grave risk for no good reason.'

'It isn't a lie,' Peter told him grimly. 'There is a Mossad agent close to Caliph. Very close to him.'

'How do you know that?' Steven asked sharply.

'I cannot tell you,' Peter said. 'But the information is ironclad. I even know the agent's code name. I give you my word that the information is genuine.'

'In that case—' Steven thought it out again ' – Caliph would probably already be suspicious and would be prepared to accept my warning. However, all he would do would be to ask me to give him the name – pass it to him along his usual communications channel. That would be it.'

'You would refuse to pass the information – except face to face. You will protest that the information is much too sensitive. You would protest that your personal safety was at stake. What would be his reaction?'

'I would expect him to put pressure on me to divulge the name—'

'If you resisted?'

'I suppose he would have to agree to a meeting. As you have pointed out, it is his major obsession. But, if he met me face to face, his identity would be revealed anyway.'

'Think, Steven. You know how his mind works.'

It took a few seconds, then Steven's expression changed, consternation twisting his lips as though he was in pain.

'Good God – of course. If I forced him to a face-to-face meeting, I would be highly unlikely to survive it.'

'Exactly,' Peter nodded. 'If we baited it with something absolutely irresistible, Caliph would have to agree to meet you – but he would make arrangements to have you silenced immediately, before you had a chance to pass on his identity to anyone else.'

'Hell, Peter, this is creepy. As you told me earlier today, I am fat and out of condition. I wouldn't be much of a match against Caliph.'

'Caliph would take that into consideration when deciding whether to meet you or not,' Peter agreed.

'It sounds like suicide,' Steven persisted.

'You just signed on to be tough,' Peter reminded him.

'Tough is one thing, stupid is another.'

'You would be in no danger until you delivered the message. Caliph would not dare dispose of you until you delivered your message,' Peter pointed out. 'And I give you my word that I will never call on you to go to an assignation with Caliph.'

'I can't ask for more than that, I suppose.' Steven threw up his hands. 'When do you want me to contact him?'

'How do you do it – the contact?'

'Advert in the Personal column,' Steven told him, and Peter grinned with reluctant admiration. Neat, efficient and entirely untraceable.

'Do it as soon as you can,' Peter instructed.

'Monday morning,' Steven nodded, and went on studying his brother with a peculiarly intent expression.

'What is it, Steven?'

'I was just thinking. If only Caliph had been somebody like you, Peter.'

'Me?' For the first time Peter was truly startled.

'The warrior king – utterly ruthless in the pursuit of the vision of justice and rightness and duty.'

'I am not like that.' Peter denied it.

'Yes, you are,' Steven said positively. 'You are the type of man that I hoped Caliph might be. The type of man we needed.'

Peter had to presume that Caliph was watching him. After his murder of Baroness Altmann, Caliph's interest would be intense. Peter had to act predictably.

He caught the early Monday flight back to Brussels, and before midday was at his desk in Narmco headquarters. Here also he was the centre of much interest and power play. Altmann Industries had lost its chief executive and there were strong undercurrents and court intrigues already afoot, Despite a number of subtle approaches Peter stayed aloof from the struggle.

On Tuesday evening Peter picked up the newspaper from the news stand in the Hilton lobby. Steven's contact request was in the small-ads section.

> The children of Israel asked counsel of the Lord, saying, shall I go up again to battle?
> Judges XX; 23.

The quotation that Caliph had chosen seemed to epitomize his view of himself. He saw himself as godlike, set high above his fellow men.

Steven had explained to Peter that Caliph took up to forty-eight hours to answer.

Steven would wait each day after the appearance of the personal announcement at his desk in his office suite in Leadenhall Street, from noon until twenty minutes past the hour. He would have no visitors nor appointments for that time, and he would make certain that his direct unlisted telephone line was unengaged to receive the incoming contact.

There was no contact that Wednesday, but Steven had not expected one. On the Thursday Steven paced restlessly up and down the antique silk Kirman carpet as he waited for the call. He was already wearing the jacket of his suit, and his bowler and rolled umbrella were on the corner of the ornate French ormolu desk that squatted like some benign monster beneath the windows which looked across the street at Lloyd's Exchange.

Steven Stride was afraid. He acknowledged the fact with direct self-honesty. Intrigue was part of his existence, had been for nearly all of his life – but always the game had been played to certain rules. He knew he was entering a new jungle, a savage wilderness where those few rules ceased entirely to exist. He was going in over his head; Peter had pointed out to him that this was not his way, and he knew Peter was right. Peter was right, and Steven was afraid as he had never been in his life. Yet he knew that he was going ahead with it. He had heard that it was the mark of true courage – to be able to meet and acknowledge fear, and yet control it sufficiently to be able to go ahead and do what duty dictated must be done.

He did not feel like a brave man.

The telephone rang once, too loud, too shrill – and every nerve in his body jumped taut and he found himself frozen, paralysed with fear in the centre of the beautiful and precious carpet.

The telephone rang again, the insistent double note sounded in his ears like the peal of doom, and he felt his bowels filled with the hot oily slime of fear, hardly to be contained.

The telephone rang the third time, and with an enormous effort he forced himself to take the three paces to his desk.

He lifted the telephone receiver, and heard the sharp chimes of the interference from the public telephone system.

'Stride,' he said. His voice was strained, high and almost shrill, and he heard the drop of the coin.

The voice terrified him. It was an electronic drone, inhuman, without gender, without the timbre of living emotion, without either high nor low notes.

'Aldgate and Leadenhall Street,' said the voice.

Steven repeated the rendezvous and immediately the connection was broken.

Steven dropped the receiver on to its cradle and snatched up his bowler and umbrella as he hurried to the door.

His secretary looked up at him and smiled expectantly. She was a handsome grey-haired woman who had been with Steven for fifteen years.

'Sir?' She still called him that.

'I'm popping out for half an hour, May,' Steven told her. 'Look after the shop, there is a dear.' And he stepped into his private elevator and rode swiftly to the underground garage where his Rolls was kept, together with the private vehicles of his senior executives.

In the elevator mirror he checked the exact angle of his bowler, a slightly raffish tilt over the right eye, and rearranged the bloom of the crimson carnation in the buttonhole of the dark-blue Savile Row suit with its faint and elegant chalk stripe. It was important that he looked and acted entirely naturally during the next few minutes. His staff would remark on any departure from the normal.

In the garage he did not approach the dark-maroon Rolls-Royce which glowed in the subdued lighting like some precious gem. Instead he went towards the wicket gate in the steel roll-up garage door, and the doorman in his little glassed cubicle beside the door looked up from his football pools coupons, recognized the master and leaped to his feet.

'Afternoon, Guv.'

'Good day, Harold. I won't be taking the car. Just stepping out for a few minutes.'

He stepped over the threshold of the gate, into the street and turned left, down towards the junction of Leadenhall Street and Aldgate. He walked fast, without seeming to hurry. Caliph spaced his intervals very tight to make it difficult for the subject to pass a message to a surveillance unit. Steven knew he had only minutes to get from his office to the call box on the corner. Caliph seemed to know exactly how long it would take him.

The telephone in the red-framed and glass call box started to ring when he was still twenty paces away. Steven ran the distance.

'Stride,' he said, his voice slightly puffed with exertion, and immediately the coin dropped and the same electronic droning voice gave him the next contact point. It was the public call box at the High Street entrance to Aldgate tube station. Steven confirmed and the voice troubled him deeply, it sounded like that of a robot from some science fiction movie. It would not have been so bad if he had felt human contact.

The two receiving stations, neither of which was predictable, and the distances between them, had been carefully calculated to make it only just possible to reach them in time, to make it impossible for the call to be traced while the line was still open. Caliph or his agent was clearly moving from one call box to the next in another part of the city. Tracing them even a minute after he had left would be of no possible use in trying to establish identity.

The voice distorter that Caliph was using was a simple device no bigger than a small pocket calculator. Peter had told Steven that it could be purchased from a number of firms specializing in electronic surveillance, security and counter-measure equipment. It cost less than fifty dollars, and so altered the human voice – phasing out all sound outside the middle range – that even the most sophisticated recording device would not be able to lift a usable voice print to compare with a computer bank memory. It would not even be able to determine whether the speaker was a man, a woman or a child.

Steven had an unusually clear path to the station, and found himself waiting outside the call box in the crowded entrance to the station while a young man in paint-speckled overalls, with long greasy blond hair, finished his conversation. Caliph's system allowed for prior use of the chosen public telephone, and as soon as the scruffy youth finished his leisurely chat, Steven pushed into the booth and made a show of consulting the directory.

The phone rang, and even though he was expecting it, Steven jumped with shock. He was perspiring now, with the walk and the tension, and his voice was ragged as he snatched the receiver.

'Stride,' he gulped.

The coin dropped and Caliph's impersonal tones chilled him again.

'Yes?'

'I have a message.'

'Yes?'

'There is danger for Caliph.'

'Yes?'

'A government intelligence agency has put an agent close to him, close enough to be extremely dangerous.'

'Say the source of your information.'

'My brother. General Peter Stride.' Peter had instructed him to tell the truth, as much as was possible.

'Say the government agency involved.'

'Negative. The information is too sensitive. I must have assurance that Caliph receives it personally.'

'Say the name or position of the enemy agent.'

'Negative. For the same reasons.'

Steven glanced at his gold Cartier tank watch with its black alligator strap. They had been speaking for fifteen seconds – he knew the contact would not last longer than thirty seconds. Caliph would not risk exposure beyond that time. He did not wait for the next question or instruction.

'I will pass the information only to Caliph, and I must be certain it is him, not one of his agents. I request a personal meeting.'

'That is not possible,' droned the inhuman voice.

'Then Caliph will be in great personal danger.' Steven found courage to say it.

'I repeat, say the name and position of enemy agent.'

Twenty-five seconds had passed.

'I say again, negative. You must arrange a face-to-face meeting for transfer of this information.'

A single droplet of sweat broke the hairline of Steven's temple and ran down his cheek. He felt as though he were suffocating in the claustrophic little telephone box.

'You will be contacted,' droned the voice and the line clicked dead.

Steven took the white silk handkerchief from his top pocket and dabbed at his face. Then he carefully rearranged the scrap of silk in his pocket, not folded into neat spikes but with a deliberately casual drape.

He squared his shoulders, lifted his chin and left the booth. Now for the first time he felt like a brave man. It was a feeling he relished, and he stepped out boldly swinging the rolled umbrella with a small flourish at each pace.

Peter had been within call of the telephone all that week, during the hours of involvement with the series of Narmco projects which he had put in train before his departure for Tahiti, and which all seemed to be maturing simultaneously. There were meetings that began in the morning and lasted until after dark, there were two separate day journeys, one to Oslo and another to Frankfurt, catching the early businessman's plane and back in the Narmco office before evening. Always he was within reach of a telephone and Steven Stride knew the number; even when he was in the NATO Officers Club gymnasium, sharpening his body to peak physical condition, or practising until after midnight in the underground pistol range until the 9-mm Cobra was an extension of his hands – either hand, left or right, equally capable of grouping the X circle at fifty metres, from any position, standing, kneeling or prone, always he was within reach of the telephone.

Peter felt like a prize fighter in training camp, concentrating all his attention on the preparations for the confrontation he knew lay ahead.

At last the weekend loomed, with the prospect of being boring and frustrating. He refused invitations to visit the country home of one of his Narmco colleagues, another to fly down to Paris for the Saturday racing – and he stayed alone in the Hilton suite, waiting for the call from Steven.

On Sunday morning he had all the papers sent up to his room, English and American and French – German which he could read better than he spoke, and even the Dutch and Italian papers which he could stumble through haltingly, missing every third word or so.

He went through them carefully, trying to find a hint of Caliph's activity. New abductions, hijackings or other acts which might give him a lead to some new Caliph-dominated pressures.

Italy was in a political uproar. The confusion so great that he could only guess at how much of it was from the left and how much from the right. There had been an assassination in Naples of five known members of the Terrorist Red Brigade, all five taken out neatly with a single grenade. The grenade type had been determined as standard NATO issue, and the execution had been in the kitchen of a Red Brigade safe apartment in a slum area of the city. The police had no leads. It sounded like Caliph. There was no reason to believe that his 'chain' did not include prominent Italian businessmen. A millionaire Italian living in his own country had to be the earth's most endangered species after the blue whale, Peter thought wryly, and they might have called on Caliph to go on the offensive.

Peter finished the Continental papers, and turned with relief to the English and American. It was a little before Sunday noon, and he wondered how he could live out the desolate hours until Monday morning. He was certain that there would be no reply to Steven's request for a meeting before then.

He started on the English-language newspapers, spinning them out to cover the blank time ahead.

The British Leyland Motor Company strike was in its fifteenth week – with no prospect of settlement. Now there was a case for Caliph, Peter smiled wryly, remembering his discussion with Steven. Knock a few heads together for their own good.

There was only one other item of interest in his morning's reading. The President of the United States had appointed a special negotiator in another attempt to find a solution to the Israeli occupation of the disputed territories in the Middle East. The man he had chosen was Dr Kingston Parker, who was described as a personal friend of the President and one of the senior members of his inner circle of advisors, a man well thought of by all parties in the dispute, and an ideal choice for the difficult job. Again Peter found himself in agreement. Kingston Parker's energies and resources seemed bottomless.

Peter dropped the last paper and found himself facing a void of boredom that would extend through until the following day. There were three books he should read beside his bed, and the Hermes crocodile case was half-filled with Narmco material, yet he knew that he would not be able to concentrate – not with the prospect of the confrontation with Caliph overshadowing all else.

He went through into the mirrored bathroom of the suite, and found the package that he had purchased the previous day in the cosmetic section of Galeries Anspach, one of the city's largest departmental stores.

The wig was of good-quality human hair, not the obviously shiny nylon substitute. It was in his own natural colour, but much longer than Peter wore his hair. He arranged it carefully along his own hairline, and then set to work with a pair of scissors, trimming and tidying it. When he had it as close to his liking as possible, he began to tint the temples with 'Italian Boy' hair silvering.

It took him most of the afternoon, for he was in no hurry, and he was critical of his own work. Every few minutes he consulted the snapshot which Melissa-Jane had taken with her new Polaroid camera, Peter's Christmas present to her, at Abbots Yew on New Year's Day. It was a good likeness of both the Stride brothers, Peter and Steven, standing full face and smiling indulgently at Melissa-Jane's command to do so.

It highlighted the resemblances of the two brothers, and also pointed out their physical differences. The natural hair colouring was identical but Steven's was fashionably longer, curling on his collar at the back, and appreciably greyer at the temples and streaked at the front.

Steven's face was heavier, with the first trace of jowls, and his colour was higher, perhaps the first ruddy warnings of heart malfunction or merely the banner of good living in his cheeks. Yet with the wig on his head, Peter's own face seemed much fuller.

Next Peter shaped the moustache, trimming it down into the infantry officer model that Steven favoured. There had been a good selection of artificial moustaches to choose from in the cosmetic section, amongst a display of artificial eyelashes and eyebrows, but none had been exactly right. Peter had to work on it carefully with the scissors, and then tint it with a little silver.

When he fastened it in place with the special adhesive gum, the result was quite startling. The moustache filled out his face even further, and of course the eyes of the twins were almost exactly the same shape and colour. Their noses were both straight and bony. Peter's mouth was a little more generous, and did not have the same hard relentless line of lip – but the moustache concealed much of that.

Peter stood back and examined himself in the full-length mirror. He and Steven were within a quarter of an inch in height, they had the same breadth of shoulder. Steven was heavier in the gut, and his neck was thickening, giving him a thrusting bull-like set to his head and shoulders. Peter altered his stance slightly. It worked. He doubted that anybody who did not know both of them intimately would be able to detect the substitution. There was no reason to believe that Caliph or any of his closest lieutenants would have seen either Steven or Peter in the flesh.

He spent an hour practising Steven's gait, watching himself in the mirror, trying to capture the buoyant cockiness of Steven's movements, searching for little personal mannerisms, the way Steven stood with both hands clasped under the skirts of his jacket; the way he brushed his moustache with one finger, from the parting under his nose – left and right.

Clothing was not a serious problem. Both brothers had used the same tailor since Sandhurst days, and Steven's dress habits were invariable and inviolable. Peter knew exactly what he would wear in any given situation.

Peter stripped off wig and moustache and repacked them carefully in their Galeries Anspach plastic packets, then buttoned them into one of the interior divisions of the Hermes case.

Next he removed the Cobra parabellum from another division. It was still in the chamois leather holster, and he bounced the familiar weight of the weapon in the palm of his hand. Reluctantly he decided he coud not take it with him. The meeting would almost certainly be in England. The contact that Steven had had on Thursday had clearly originated in London. He had to believe the next contact would be in the same city. He could not take the chance of walking through British customs with a deadly weapon on his person. If he was stopped, there would be publicity. It would instantly alert Caliph. He would be able to get another weapon from Thor Command once he was in England. Colin Noble would supply him, just as soon as Peter explained the need, he was certain of that.

Peter went down and checked the Cobra pistol into the safe deposit box of the hotel reception office, and returned to his room to face the wearying and indefinite wait. It was one of a soldier's duties to which he had never entirely accustomed himself – he always hated the waiting.

However, he settled down to read Robert Asprey's *War in the Shadows*, that definitive tome on the history and practice of guerrilla warfare down the ages. He managed to lose himself sufficiently to be mildly surprised when he glanced at his watch and saw it was after eight o'clock. He ordered an omelette to be sent up by room service, and ten seconds after he replaced the receiver, the telephone rang. He thought it might be a query from the kitchen about his dinner order.

'Yes, what is it?' he demanded irritably.

'Peter?'

'Steven?'

'He has agreed to a meeting.'

Peter felt his heart lunge wildly.

'When? Where?'

'I don't know. I have to fly to Orly tomorrow. There will be instructions for me at the airport.

Caliph covering and backtracking. Peter should have expected it. Desperately he cast his mind back to the layout of Orly Airport. He had to find a private place to meet Steven and make the changeover. He discarded swiftly the idea of meeting in one of the lounges or washrooms. That left one other location.

'What time will you be there?' Peter demanded.

'Cooks have got me on to the early flight. I'll be there at eleven fifteen.'

'I'll be there before you,' Peter told him. He knew the Sabena timetable by heart and all senior Narmco executives had special VIP cards which assured a seat on any flight.

'I will book a room at the Air Hotel on the fourth floor of Orly South terminal in your name,' he told Steven now. 'I'll wait in the lobby. Go directly to the reception desk and ask for your key. I will check behind you to make certain you are not followed. Do not acknowledge me in any way. Have you got that, Steven?'

'Yes.'

'Until tomorrow, then.'

Peter broke the connection, and went through into the bathroom. He studied his own face in the mirror.

'Well, that takes care of getting a weapon from Thor.' Caliph had not set the meeting in England. It was clear now that Paris was only a staging point, and that in his usual careful fashion Caliph would move the subject on from there – perhaps through one or more staging points, to the final rendezvous.

The subject would go in unarmed, and unsupported – and Peter was certain that afterwards Caliph would take his usual pains to ensure that the subject would be unable to carry back a report of the meeting.

I am drawing two cards inside for a straight flush, and Caliph is the dealer from a pack that he has had plenty of time to prepare, Peter thought coldly, but at least the waiting was over. He began to pack his toilet articles into the waterproof Gucci bag.

*

Sir Steven Stride marched into the lobby of Orly South Air Hotel at five minutes past noon, and Peter smiled to himself in self-congratulation. Steven was wearing a blue double-breasted blazer, white shirt and cricket-club tie, above grey woollen slacks and black English handmade shoes – none of your fancy Italian footwear for Steven.

It was Steven's standard informal dress, and Peter had only been wrong about the tie – he had guessed that it would be an I Zingari pattern. Peter himself wore a double-breaster and grey slacks under his trench coat and his shoes were black Barkers.

Steven's eyes flickered around the lobby, passing over Peter sitting in a far corner with a copy of *Le Monde*, then Steven moved authoritatively to the reception desk.

'My name is Stride, do you have a reservation for me?' Steven spoke slowly, in rich plummy tones, for very few of these damned people spoke English. The clerk checked swiftly, nodded, murmured a welcome and gave Steven the form and the key.

'Four One Six.' Steven checked the number loudly enough for Peter to hear. Peter had been watching the entrance carefully; fortunately there had been very few guests entering the lobby during the few minutes since Steven's arrival, and none of those could possibly have been Caliph surveillance. Of course, if this was a staging point, as Peter was certain it was, then Caliph would have no reason to put surveillance on Steven – not until he got much closer to the ultimate destination.

Steven moved to the elevator with a porter carrying his single small valise, and Peter drifted across and joined the small cluster of guests waiting at the elevators.

He rode up shoulder to shoulder with Steven in the crowded elevator, neither of them acknowledging the other's existence, and when Steven and the porter left at the fourth stage Peter rode on up three floors, walked the length of the corridor and back, then took the descending elevator to Steven's floor.

Steven had left the door to 416 off the catch, and Peter pushed it open and slipped in without knocking.

'My dear boy.' Steven was in his shirt sleeves. He had switched on the television, but now he turned down the sound volume and hurried to greet him with both affection and vast relief.

'No problems?' Peter asked.

'Like clockwork,' Steven told him. 'Would you like a drink? I got a bottle in the duty-free.'

While he hunted for glasses in the bathroom, Peter checked the room swiftly. A view down towards the square functional buildings of the market that had replaced the picturesque Les Halles in central Paris, matching curtains and covers on the twin beds, television and radio sets between the beds, modern soulless furniture – it was a room, that was the most and the least that could be said for it.

Steven carried in the glasses and handed one to Peter.

'Cheers!'

Peter tasted his whisky. It was too strong and the Parisian tap water tasted of chlorine. He put it aside.

'How is Caliph going to get instructions to you?'

'Got them already.' Steven went to his blazer, hanging over the back of the chair, and found a long white envelope in the inside pocket. 'This was left at the Air France information desk.'

Peter took the envelope and as he split the flap he sank on to one of the armchairs. There were three items in the envelope.

A first-class Air France airline ticket, a voucher for a chauffeur-driven limousine and a hotel reservation voucher.

The air ticket could have been purchased for cash at any Air France outlet or agency, the limousine and hotel bookings could have been made equally anonymously. There was no possibility of a trace back from any of these documents.

Peter opened the Air France ticket and read the destination. Something began to crawl against his skin., like the loathsome touch of body vermin. He closed the ticket and checked the two vouchers; now the sick feeling of betrayal and evil spread through his entire body, numbing his fingernails and coating the back of his tongue with a bitter metallic taste like copper salts.

The air ticket was for this evening's flight from Orly to Ben-Gurion Airport in Israel, the hired-car voucher was good for a single journey from there to Jerusalem, the hotel voucher was for a room in the King David Hotel in that ancient and holy city.

'What is it, Peter?'

'Nothing,' said Peter, only then aware that the sickness must have shown on his face. 'Jerusalem,' he went on. 'Caliph wants you in Jerusalem.'

There was one person in Jerusalem at that moment. Somebody who had been in his thoughts almost unceasingly since last he had embraced her in the darkness of Bora-Bora Island – so very long ago.

Caliph was in Jerusalem, and Magda Altmann was in Jerusalem – and the sickness was heavy in the pit of his stomach.

The deviousness of Caliph.

'No,' he told himself firmly. 'I have travelled that road already. It cannot be Magda.'

The genius of Caliph, evil and effortless.

'It is possible.' He had to admit it then. 'With Caliph, anything is possible.' Every time Caliph shook the dice box the numbers changed, different numbers, making different totals – but always completely plausible, always completely believable.

It was one of the basic proven theorems of his trade that a man, any man, was blinded and deafened and rendered senseless by love. Peter was in love, and he knew it.

'All right. So now I have to try and free my mind and think it out all over again, as though I were not besotted.'

'Peter, are you all right?' Steven demanded again, now with real concern. It was impossible to think with Steven hovering over him. He would have to put it aside.

'I am going to Jerusalem in your place,' Peter said.

'Come again, old boy?'

'We are changing places – you and I.'

'You won't get away with it.' Steven shook his head decidedly. 'Caliph will take you on the full toss.'

Peter picked up his Hermes case and went through into the bathroom. He worked quickly with the wig and artificial moustache and then called.

'Steven, come here.'

They stood side by side and stared at themselves in the mirror.

'Good God!' Steven grunted. Peter altered his stance slightly, conforming more closely to his brother.

'That's incredible. Never knew you were such a good-looking blighter,' Steven chuckled, and wagged his head wonderingly. Peter imitated the gesture perfectly.

'Damn it, Peter.' The chuckle dried on Steven's lips. 'That's enough. You're giving me the creeps.'

Peter pulled the wig off his head. 'It will work.'

'Yes,' Steven conceded. 'It will work – but how the hell did you know I would be wearing a blazer and greys?'

'Trick of the trade,' Peter told him. 'Don't worry about it. Let's go through the paperwork now.'

In the bedroom they laid out their personal documents in two piles, and went swiftly through them.

The passport photographs would pass readily enough.

'You have to shave your soup strainer,' Peter told him, and Steven stroked his moustache with one finger, left and right – lingeringly, regretfully.

'Is that absolutely necessary? I'd feel like I was walking around in public with no trousers on.'

Peter took the slim gold ballpoint from his inside pocket and a sheaf of hotel stationery from the drawer. He studied Steven's signature in the passport for a minute, and dashed it off on the top sheet.

'No.' He shook his head, and tried again. It was like Steven's walk, cocky and confident, the 'T' was crossed with a flourishing sword stroke of the pen. In sixty seconds he had it perfected.

'With that wig on your head you could walk into my bank any day and sign for the whole damned bundle,' Steven muttered uneasily. 'Then go home and climb into bed with Pat.'

'Now, *there* is an idea,' Peter looked thoughtful.

'Don't joke about it,' Steven pleaded.

'Who's joking?' Peter went through the credit cards, club membership cards, driver's licence and all the other clutter of civilized existence.

Steven's mastery of his brother's signature was not nearly as effective, but after twenty minutes' practice was just adequate for hotel registration purposes.

'Here is the address of a hotel on the left bank. Magnificent restaurant, and the management are very understanding if you should want to invite a young lady up to your room for a drink.'

'Perish the thought.' Steven looked smug at the prospect.

'It should only be for a few days, Steven. Just keep very low. Pay cash for everything. Keep clear of the George V or the Meurice, Le Doyen and Maxim's – all the places where they know you.'

They went carefully over the last details of the exchange of identity, while Steven shaved off the moustache and anointed the bare patch tenderly with Eau de Sauvage.

'You'd better move now,' Peter told him at last. 'Wear this –' It was Peter's buff trenchcoat that would cover his blazer. '– And let's change ties.'

Steven was ready, and he stood rather awkwardly by the door, in the tightly fitting trenchcoat.

'Steven, can I ask you a question?' Peter did not know why he had to know now, it had been buried so deeply for so long and yet at this moment it was deadly important to know.

'Of course, old boy.' Steven seemed to welcome the postponement of the moment of parting.

'Sandhurst.' Peter tried to keep the embarrassment out of his voice. 'I never asked you before – but you didn't do it, did you, Steven?'

Steven met his eyes calmly, steadily. 'No, Peter. I did not do it. My word on it.'

Peter took his brother's proffered right hand and squeezed it hard. It was ridiculous to feel so relieved.

'I'm glad, Steven.'

'Take care of yourself, old boy.'

'I will,' Peter nodded. 'But if anything happens,' Peter hesitated, '– Melissa-Jane –'

'Don't worry. I'll take care of it.'

Why do Englishmen have such difficulty talking to each other, Peter wondered, let alone communicating affection and gratitude?

'Well, I'll be getting along then,' said Steven.

'Take a guard on your middle stump, and don't be caught in the slips,' Peter cautioned him with the old inanity.

'Count on it,' said Steven, and went out into the passage, closing the door behind him firmly, leaving his brother to think about Jerusalem.

Only the name had changed from Lod to Ben-Gurion – otherwise the Arrivals Hall was as Peter remembered it. One of the few airports on the globe which has sufficient luggage trolleys, so that the passengers do not have to fight for possession.

In the Arrivals Hall there was a young Israeli driver with the name:

printed in white chalk on a schoolboy's black slate.

The driver wore a navy-blue cap with a black patent-leather peak. It was his only item of uniform, otherwise he was dressed in sandals and a white cotton shirt. His English had the usual strong American turn to it, and his attitude was casual and friendly – he might be driving the limousine today, but tomorrow he could be at the controls of a Centurion tank, and he was as good a man as his passenger any day.

'Shalom, Shalom,' he greeted Peter. 'Is that all your luggage?'

'Yes.'

'Beserder. Let's go.' He did not offer to push Peter's trolley, but chatted amicably as he led him out to the limousine.

It was a stretched-out 240 D Mercedes Benz – almost brand new, lovingly polished – but somebody had painted a pair of squinting eyes on each side of the chrome three-pointed star on the boot of the vehicle.

They had hardly pulled out through the airport gates when one of the characteristic aromas of Israel filled the cab of the Mercedes – the smell of orange blossom from the citrus orchards that lined each side of the road.

For some reason the smell made Peter feel uneasy, a sensation of having missed something, of having neglected some vital aspect. He tried to think it all out again, from the beginning, but the driver kept up a running commentary as they pulled up the new double highway, over the hills through the pine forests towards Jerusalem, and the voice distracted him.

Peter wished he had kept the list that he had drawn up in the hotel room at Orly instead of destroying it. He tried to reconstruct it in his mind.

There were a dozen items on the plus side. The third was:

'Magda told me about Cactus Flower. Would she have done so if she was Caliph?'

And then directly opposite, in the 'minus' column:

'If Magda is Caliph, then "Cactus Flower" does not exist. It was an invention for some undisclosed reason.'

This was the item that pricked him like a burr in a woollen sock. He kept coming back to it, there was a link missing from the logic of it and he tried to tease it loose. It was there just below the surface of his mind, and he knew instinctively that if he missed it the consequences would be dire.

The driver kept chatting, turning to glance back at him every few minutes with a cheerful demand for recognition.

'That's right, isn't it?'

Peter grunted. The man was irritating him – the missing item was there, just beginning to surface. He could see the shape of it. Why had the smell of orange blossom worried him? The smell of flowers? Cactus flower? There was something there, something missing from the list.

'If Magda is not Caliph then –' Was that it? He was not certain.

'– Will that be all right, then?' The driver was insisting again.

'I'm sorry – what was that?'

'I said, I had to drop a parcel off at my mother-in-law,' the driver explained again. 'It's from my wife.'

'Can't you do that on your way back?'

'I'm not going back tonight –' The driver grinned winningly over his shoulder. '– My mother-in-law lives right on our way. It won't take five minutes.I promised my wife I'd get it to her mother today.'

'Oh, very well then,' Peter snapped. There was something about the man he did not like, and he had lost track of the item that had been worrying him.

He felt as though he was in a chess game with a vastly superior opponent, and he had overlooked a castle on an open file, or a knight in a position to fork simultaneous check on his king and queen.

'We turn off here,' the driver explained, and swung off into a section of new apartment blocks, all of them built of the custard-yellow Jerusalem stone, row upon row of them, Israel's desperate attempt to house its new citizens. At this time of evening the streets were deserted, as families gathered for the evening meal.

The driver jinked through the maze of identical-seeming streets with garrulous confidence and then braked and parked in front of one of the square, boxlike, yellow buildings.

'Two minutes,' he promised, and jumped out of the Mercedes, scampered around to the rear and opened the boot. There was a scratching sound, a small bump and then the lid of the boot slammed and the driver came back into Peter's line of vision – carrying a brown paper parcel.

He grinned at Peter, with the ridiculous cap pushed on to the back of his head, mouthed another assurance through the closed window:

'Two minutes –' and went into the main door of the apartment.

Peter hoped he might be longer. The silence was precious. He closed his eyes, and concentrated.

'If Magda is not Caliph then – then –' There was the ticking sound of the engine cooling, or was it the dashboard clock? Peter thrust the sound to the back of his mind.

'– then – then Cactus Flower exists. Yes, that was it!' 'Cactus Flower exists, and if he exists he is close enough to Caliph to know of Sir Steven Stride's threat to expose him –'

Peter sat upright, rigid in his seat. He had believed that Steven Stride would be perfectly safe – until after the meeting with Caliph. That was the terrible mistake.

'– Cactus Flower must stop Steven Stride reaching Caliph!' Yes, of course. Christ, how had he not seen it before. Cactus Flower was Mossad, and Peter was sitting in a street of Jerusalem – Mossad's front yard – dressed as Steven Stride.

'Christ!' He felt the certainty of mortal danger. 'Cactus Flower probably made the arrangements himself. If Magda Altmann is not Caliph, then I am walking right into Cactus Flower's sucker punch!'

The damned clock kept ticking, a sound as nerve-racking as a leaky faucet.

'I am in Cactus Flower's city – in Cactus Flower's limo —'

The ticking. Oh God! It was not coming from the dashboard. Peter turned his head. It was coming from *behind him*; from the boot which the driver had opened and in which he had moved something. Something that was now ticking away quietly.

Peter wrenched the door handle and hit the door with his shoulder, instinctively grabbing the Hermes case with his other hand.

They would have stripped out the metal partition between the boot and the back seat to allow the blast to cut through. There was probably only the leather upholstery between him and whatever was ticking. That was why he had heard it so clearly.

Time seemed to have slowed, so he was free to think it out as the seconds dropped as lingeringly as spilled honey.

Infernal machine, he thought. Why that ridiculously nineteenth-century term should occur to him now, he could not guess, a relic from the childhood days when he read *Boy's Own Paper* perhaps.

He was out of the Mercedes now, almost losing his balance as his feet hit the unsurfaced and broken sidewalk.

It is probably plastic explosive with a clockwork timer on the detonator, he thought, as he started to run. What delay would they use? Thirty seconds? No, the driver had to get well away. He had said two minutes, said it twice –

The thoughts raced through his mind, but his legs seemed to be shackled, dragging against an enormous weight. Like trying to run waist deep in the sucking surf of a sandy beach.

'– It will be two minutes, and he has been gone that long —'

Ten paces ahead of him there was a low wall that had been built as a flower box around the apartment block. It was knee high, a double brick wall with the cavity filled with dry yellow earth and precariously sustaining the life of a few wizened oleander bushes.

Peter dived head first over the wall, breaking his fall with shoulder and forearm, and rolling back hard under the protection of the low wall.

Above his head were the large windows of the ground-floor apartments. Lying on his side, peering up at them, Peter saw the reflection of the parked Mercedes as though in a mirror.

He covered his ears with the palms of both hands. The Mercedes was only fifty feet away. He watched it in the glass, his body braced, his mouth wide open to absorb blast shock in his sinuses.

The Mercedes erupted. It seemed to open quite sedately, like one of those time-elapse movies of a rose blooming. The shining metal spread and distorted like grotesque black petals, and bright white flame shot through it – that was all Peter saw, for the row of apartment windows disappeared, blown away in a million glittering shards by the blast wave, leaving the windows gaping like the toothless mouths of old decrepit men, and at the same moment the blast smashed into Peter.

Even though it was muted by the thick wall of the flower box, it crushed him, seemed to drive in his ribs, and the air whooshed from his lungs. The fearsome din of the explosion clamoured in his head, filling his skull with little bright chips of rainbow light.

He thought he must have lost consciousness for a moment, then there was the patter of falling debris raining down around him and something struck him a painful blow in the small of his back. It spurred him.

He dragged himself to his feet, struggling to refill his empty lungs. He knew he had to get away before the security forces arrived, or he could expect intensive interrogation which would certainly disclose the fact that he was not Sir Steven.

He started to run. The street was still deserted, although he could hear the beginning of the uproar which must follow. The cries of anguish and of fear.

He reached the corner and stopped running. He walked quickly to the next alley behind an apartment block. There were no street lights and he paused in the shadows. By now a dozen figures shouting questions and conjecture were hurrying towards the smoke and dust of the explosion.

Peter recovered his breath and dusted down his blazer and slacks, waiting until the confusion and shouting were at their peak. Then he walked quietly away.

On the main road he joined a short queue at the bus stop. The bus dropped him off in the Jaffa Road.

He found a café opposite the bus stop and went through into the men's room. He was unmarked, but pale and strained; his hands still shook from the shock of the blast as he combed his hair.

He went back into the café, found a corner seat and ordered falafel and pitta bread with coffee.

He sat there for half an hour, considering his next move.

'If Magda Altmann is not Caliph —' he repeated the conundrum which he had solved just in time to save his life.

'Magda Altmann is not Caliph!' He knew it then with utter certainty. Cactus Flower had tried to stop Sir Steven Stride reaching Caliph with his denunciation. Therefore Magda had told him the truth. His relief flooded his body with a great warm glow – and his first instinct was to telephone her at the Mossad number she had given him. Then he saw the danger. Cactus Flower was Mossad. He dared not go near her – not yet.

What must he do then? And he knew the answer without having to search for it. He must do what he had come to do. He must find Caliph, and the only fragile thread he had to follow was the trail that Caliph had laid for him.

He left the café and found a taxi at the rank on the corner.

'King David Hotel,' Peter said, and sank back in the seat.

At least I know the danger of Cactus Flower now, he thought grimly. I won't walk into the next one blind.

Peter took one glance around the room that had been reserved for him. It was in the back of the hotel and across the road the tall bell tower of the

YMCA made a fine stance from which a sniper could command the two windows.

'I ordered a suite,' Peter snapped at the reception clerk who had led him up.

'I'm sorry, Sir Steven.' The man was immediately flustered. 'There must have been a mistake.'

Another glance around the room and Peter had noted half a dozen sites at which Cactus Flower might have laid another explosive charge to back up the one that had failed in the back of the Mercedes. He would prefer to spend a night in a pit full of cobras rather than accept the quarters that Cactus Flower had prepared for him.

Peter stepped back into the passage and fixed the clerk with his most imperious gaze. The man scampered and returned within five minutes – looking mightily relieved.

'We have one of our best suites for you.'

Number 122 commanded a magnificent view across the valley to the Jaffa Gate in the wall of the Old City, and in the centre of this vista towered the Church of the Last Supper.

The gardens of the hotel were lush with lawns and tall graceful palms, children shrieked gleefully around the swimming pool while a cool light breeze broke the heat.

The suite abutted on to the long open terrace, and the moment he was alone, Peter lowered the heavy roller shutters across the terrace door. Cactus Flower could too easily send a man in that way. Then Peter stepped out on to the private balcony.

On the tall stone battlements of the French Consulate adjoining the gardens they were lowering the Tricolour against the flaming backdrop of the sunset. Peter watched it for a moment – then concentrated again on the security of the suite.

There was possible access from the room next door, an easy step across from window to balcony. Peter hesitated – then decided to leave the balcony unshuttered. He could not bring himself to accept the claustrophobic effect of a completely shuttered room.

Instead he drew the curtains and ordered a large whisky and soda from room service. He needed it. It had been a long hard day.

Then he stripped off tie and shirt, wig and moustache and washed away some of the tensions. He was towelling himself when there was a tap on the door.

'Damned quick service,' he muttered, and clapped the wig on his head and stepped into the lounge, just as a key rattled in the lock and the door swung open. Peter lifted the towel and pretended to be still drying his face to cover the lack of moustache on his lip.

'Come in,' he gruffed through the towel, and then froze in the doorway, and a vice seemed to close around his heart and restrict his breathing.

She wore a man's open-neck shirt, with patch pockets on the breasts, and khaki combat breeches hugged her narrow hips. The long legs were thrust into soft-soled canvas boots. Yet she carried herself with the same unforced chic as if she had been dressed in the height of Parisian fashion.

'Sir Steven.' She closed the door swiftly behind her, and Peter saw her palm the slim metal pick with which she had turned the lock. 'I'm Magda Altmann, we have met before. I have come to warn you that you are in very grave danger.'

The abundant short curls formed a dark halo around her head, and her eyes were huge and green with concern.

'You must immediately leave this country. I have my private executive jet aircraft at an airfield near here –'

Peter lowered the towel enough to allow himself to speak.

'Why are you telling me this?' he interrupted her brusquely. 'And why should I believe you?'

He saw the quick roses of anger bloom in her cheeks.

'You are dabbling in things you do not understand.'

'Why should you want to warn me?' Peter insisted.

'Because —' she hesitated and then went on sharply, '— because you are Peter Stride's brother. For that reason and no other I would not want you killed.'

Peter tossed the towel back into the bathroom and with the same movement pulled off the wig and dropped it on to the chair beside him.

'Peter!' Astonishment riveted her and she stared at him, the colour that anger had painted in her cheeks fled and her eyes turned a deep luminous green. He had forgotten once again how beautiful she was.

'Well, don't just stand there,' he said, and she ran to him on those long, graceful legs and flung her arms around his neck.

They strained together silently, neither of them found words necessary for many minutes. Then she broke away.

'Peter, darling – I cannot stay long. I took a terrible chance coming here at all. They are watching the hotel and the girls on the switchboard are Mossad. That is why I could not telephone —'

'Tell me everything you can,' he ordered.

'All right, but hold me, chéri. I do not wish to waste a minute of this little time we have together.'

She hid in the bathroom when the waiter brought the whisky, then joined Peter on the couch.

'Cactus Flower reported to control that Steven had requested a meeting with Caliph, and that he intended to denounce him. That was all I knew until yesterday – but I could build on that. First of all I was amazed that Steven was the subject of the first Cactus Flower report and not you, Peter —' She caressed the smooth hard brown muscle of his chest as she spoke. '– It had never occurred to me, even when we discussed the fact that the report mentioned no Christian name.'

'It didn't occur to me either, not until I'd already left Les Neuf Poissons.'

'Then, of course, I guessed that you had taxed Steven with it, and told him the source of your information. It would have been a crazy thing to do – not your usual style, at all. But I thought that being your brother —' She trailed off.

'That is exactly what I did —'

'Peter, we could still talk if we were on the bed,' she murmured. 'I have been without you for so long.'

Her bare skin felt like hot satin, and they lay entwined with the hard smooth plain of her belly pressed to his. Her mouth was against his ear.

'– Steven's request for a meeting went directly to Caliph through a channel other than Cactus Flower. He had no chance to head it off —'

'Who is Cactus Flower, have you found that out?'

'No.' She shook her head. 'I still do not know.' And she raked her long fingernails lightly down across his belly.

'If you do that – I cannot think clearly,' he protested.

'I am sorry.' She brought her hand up to his cheek. 'Anyway, Caliph instructed Cactus Flower to arrange the meeting with Steven. I did not know what arrangements were being made – until I saw Sir Steven's name on the immigration lists this evening. I was not particularly looking for his name, but as soon as I saw it I guessed what was happening. I guessed that Cactus Flower had enticed him here to make his interception easier. It took me three hours to find where Sir Steven would be staying.'

They were both silent now, and she lowered her face and pressed it into the soft of his neck, sighing with happiness.

'Oh God, Peter. How I missed you.'

'Listen, my darling. You must tell me everything else you have.' Peter lifted her chin tenderly so he could see her face and her eyes came back into focus.

'Did you know that there was to be an assassination attempt on Steven?'

'No – but it was the logical step for Mossad to protect Cactus Flower.'

'What else?'

'Nothing.'

'You don't know if actual arrangements have been made for a meeting between Caliph and Steven?'

'No, I don't know,' she admitted.

'You still have no indication at all of Caliph's identity?'

'No, none at all.'

They were silent again, but now she propped herself on one elbow and watched his face as he spoke.

'Cactus Flower would have to make the arrangements for the meeting as Caliph instructed. He would not be able to take the chance of faking it – not with Caliph.'

Magda nodded in silent agreement.

'Therefore we have to believe that at this moment Caliph is close, very close.'

'Yes.' She nodded again, but reluctantly.

'That means that I have to go on impersonating Steven.'

'Peter, no. They will kill you.'

'They have already tried —' Peter told her grimly, and quietly outlined the destruction of the Mercedes. She touched the bruise in the small of his back where he had been struck by flying debris from the explosion.

'They won't let you get close to Caliph.'

'They may have no choice,' Peter told her. 'Caliph is so concerned for his own safety – he is going to insist on the meeting.'

'They will try and kill you again,' she implored him.

'Perhaps, but I'm betting that meeting with Caliph is arranged to take place very soon. They won't have much opportunity to set up another elaborate trap like the Mercedes, and I'll be expecting it – I've got to go ahead with it, Magda.'

'Oh Peter —' But he touched her lips, silencing the protest, and he was thinking aloud again.

'Let's suppose Mossad knew that I was not Steven Stride, that my real purpose was not to denounce Cactus Flower? What difference would that make to the thinking at Mossad?'

She considered that. 'I'm not certain.'

'If they knew it was Peter Stride impersonating Steven Stride,' he insisted, 'would that make them curious enough to let the meeting go ahead?'

'Peter, are you suggesting I turn in a report to my control at Mossad —?'

'Would you do that?'

'Sweet merciful God,' she whispered. 'I could be signing your death warrant, Peter my darling.'

'— or you could be saving my life.'

'I don't know.' She sat up erect in the bed and ran the fingers of both hands through the short dark curls, the lamplight glowed on her skin with a pale, smooth opalescence and the small fine breasts changed shape as she moved her arms. 'Oh, Peter, I don't know.'

'It could be our only chance to ever get close to Caliph,' he insisted, and the lovely face was racked with indecision.

'Caliph believes I have killed you, he believes that I have transmitted a warning to him through my brother. He will have his guard as low as ever it will be. We will never have a chance again like this.'

'I am so afraid for you, Peter. I am so afraid for myself without you —' She did not finish it, but pulled up her long naked legs and hugged her knees to her breast. It was a defensive foetal position.

'Will you do it?' he asked gently.

'You want me to tell my control your real identity, to tell him that I believe your real purpose is not to denounce Cactus Flower – but some other unknown —'

'That is right.'

She turned her head and looked at him.

'I will do it in exchange for your promise,' she decided.

'What is that?'

'If I judge from my control at Mossad that you are still in danger, and that they still intend intercepting you before you reach Caliph – then I want your promise that you will abandon the attempt. That you will immediately go to where the Lear is waiting and that you will allow Pierre to fly you out of here to a safe place.'

'You will be honest with me?' he asked. 'You will judge Mossad's reaction fairly – and even if there is a half decent chance of me reaching Caliph you will allow me to take that chance?'

She nodded, but he went on grimly, making certain of it.

'Swear it to me!'

'I would not try to prevent you – just as long as there is a chance of success.'

'Swear it to me, Magda.'

'On my love for you, I swear it,' she said quietly, and he relaxed slightly.

'And I in turn swear to you that if there is no chance of meeting Caliph – I will leave on the Lear.'

She turned against his chest, wrapping both her arms around his neck.

'Make love to me, Peter. Now! Quickly! I have to have that at least.'

As she dressed she went over the arrangements for communicating.

'I cannot come through the switchboard here – I explained why,' she told him as she laced the canvas boots. 'You must stay here, in this room where I can reach you. If there is danger I will send someone to you. It will be somebody I trust. He will say simply, "Magda sent me," and you must go with him. He will take you to Pierre and the Lear jet.'

She stood up and belted the khaki breeches around her narrow waist, crossing to the mirror to comb out the dark damp tangle of her curls.

'If you hear nothing from me it will mean that I judge there is still a chance of reaching Caliph —' Then she paused and her expression altered. '– Are you armed, Peter?' She was watching him in the mirror as she worked with her hair. He shook his head.

'I could get a weapon to you – a knife, a pistol?'

And again he shook his head. 'They will search me before I am allowed near Caliph. If they find a weapon —' He did not have to finish it.

'You are right,' she agreed.

She turned back to him from the mirror, buttoning the shirt over the nipples of her breasts, which were still swollen and dark rosy red from their loving.

'It will all happen very quickly now, Peter. One way or the other it will be over by tomorrow night. I have a feeling here —' She touched herself between the small breasts that pushed out the cotton of her shirt. 'Now kiss me. I have stayed too long already – for the safety of both of us.'

Peter slept very little after Magda left him, even though he was very tired. A dozen times he started awake during the night with every nerve strung tightly, rigid and sweating in his bed.

He was up before first light, and ordered one of those strange Israeli breakfasts of salads and hard-boiled eggs with pale green centres to be sent up to his room.

Then he settled down once more to wait.

He waited the morning out, and when there had been no message from Magda by noon, the certainty increased that Mossad had decided not to prevent the meeting with Caliph. If there had been any doubt in Magda's mind she would have sent for him. He had a light lunch sent up to the room.

The flat bright glare of noon gradually mellowed into warm butter yellow, the shadows crept out timidly from the foot of the palm trees in the garden as the sun wheeled across a sky of clear high aching blue, and still Peter waited.

When there was an hour left of daylight, the telephone rang again. It startled him, but he reached for it quickly.

'Good evening, Sir Steven. Your driver is here to fetch you,' said the girl at the reception desk.

'Thank you. Please tell him I will be down directly,' said Peter.

He was fully dressed, had been ready all that day to move immediately. He needed only to place the crocodile skin case in the cupboard and lock it, then he left the room and strode down the corridors to the elevators.

He had no way of knowing if he was going to meet Caliph, or if he was about to be spirited out of Israel in Magda's Lear jet.

'Your limousine is waiting outside,' the pretty girl at the desk told him. 'Have a nice evening.'

'I hope so,' Peter agreed. 'Thank you.'

The car was a small Japanese compact, and the driver was a woman, plump and grey-haired with a friendly, ugly face like Golda Meir – Peter thought.

He let himself into the back seat, and waited expectantly for the message, 'Magda sent me.'

Instead, the woman bade him 'Shalom Shalom' politely, started the engine, switched on the headlights and drove serenely out of the hotel grounds.

They swept sedately around the outer walls of the old city in the gathering dusk, and dropped down in the valley of Kidron. Glancing back Peter saw the elegant new buildings of the Jewish quarter rising above the tops of the walls.

When last he had been in Jerusalem that area had been a deserted ruin, deliberately devastated by the Arabs.

The resurrection of that holy quarter of Judaism seemed to epitomize the spirit of these extraordinary people – Peter thought.

It was a good conversational opening, and he remarked on the new development to his driver.

She replied in Hebrew, clearly denying the ability to speak English. Peter tried her in French with the same result.

The lady has been ordered to keep her mouth tight shut, he decided.

The night came down upon them as they skirted the lower slopes of the

Mount of Olives, and left the last straggling buildings of the Arab settlements. The lady driver settled down to a comfortable speed, and the road was almost deserted. It dropped gently down through a dark shallow valley, with the crests of a desolate desert landscape humped up on each side of the wide metalled road.

The sky was empty of cloud or haze, and the stars were brighter white and clearer, as the last of the day faded from the western sky behind them.

The road had been well signposted, ever since they had left the city. Their direction was eastwards towards the Jordan, the Dead Sea and Jericho – and twenty-five minutes after leaving the King David, Peter glimpsed in the headlights the signpost on the right-hand side of the road, declaring in English, Arabic and Hebrew that they were now descending below sea level into the valley of the Dead Sea.

Once again Peter attempted to engage the driver in conversation, but her reply was monosyllabic. Anyway, Peter decided, there was nothing she would be able to tell him. The car was from a hire company. There was a plastic nameplate fastened on to the dashboard giving the company's name, address and hire rates. All she would know was their final destination – and he would know that soon enough himself.

Peter made no further attempt to speak to her, but remained completely alert; without detectable movement he performed the pre-jump paratrooper exercises, pitting muscle against muscle so that his body would not stiffen with long inactivity but would be tuned to explode from stillness into instant violent action.

Ahead of them the warning signals of the crossroads caught the headlights, and the driver slowed and signalled the left turn. As the headlights caught the signpost, Peter saw that they had taken the Jericho road, turning away from the Dead Sea, and heading up the valley of the Jordan towards Galilee in the north.

Now the bull's horns of the new moon rose slowly over the harsh mountain peaks across the valley, and gave enough light to pick out small features in the dry blasted desert around them.

Again the driver slowed, this time for the town of Jericho itself, the oldest site of human communal habitation on this earth – for six thousand years men had lived here and their wastes had raised a mountainous tell hundreds of feet above the desert floor. Archaeologists had already excavated the collapsed walls that Joshua had brought crashing down with a blast of his ram's horns.

'A hell of a trick.' Peter grinned in the darkness. 'Better than the Nuke bomb.'

Just before they reached the tell, the driver swung off the main road. She took the narrow secondary road between the clustered buildings – souvenir stalls, Arab cafés, antique dealers – and slowed for the twisting uneven surface.

They ground up on to higher dry hills in low gear, and at the crest the driver turned again on to a dirt track. Now fine talcum dust filled the interior and Peter sneezed once at the trickle of it.

Half a mile along the track a noticeboard stood on trestle legs, blocking the right of way.

'Military Zone,' it proclaimed. 'No access beyond this point.'

The driver had to pull out on to the rocky verge to avoid the notice, and there were no sentries to enforce the printed order.

Quite suddenly Peter became aware of the great black cliff face that rose sheer into the starry night ahead of them – blotting out half the sky.

Something stirred in Peter's memory – the high cliffs above Jericho, looking out across the valley of the Dead Sea; of course, he remembered then – this was the scene of the temptation of Christ. How did Matthew record it? Peter cast for the exact quotation:

> Again, the devil taketh him up into an exceeding high mountain, and sheweth him all the kingdoms of the world, and the glory of them —

Had Caliph deliberately chosen this place for its mystical association, was it all part of the quasi-religious image that Caliph had of himself?

> He shall give his angels charge concerning thee: and in their hands they shall bear thee up —

Did Caliph truly see himself as the heir to ultimate power over all the kingdoms of the world – that power that the ancient chroniclers had referred to as 'The Sixth Order of Angels'?

Peter felt his spirits quail in the face of such monumental madness, such immense and menacing vision, compared to which he felt insignificant and ineffectual. Fear fell over him like a gladiator's net, enmeshing his resolve, weakening him. He struggled with it silently, fighting himself clear of its mesh before it could render him helpless in Caliph's all-embracing power.

The driver stopped abruptly, turned in the seat and switched on the cab light. She studied him for a moment. Was there a touch of pity in her old and ugly face, Peter wondered?

'Here,' she said gently.

Peter drew his wallet from the inner pocket of his blazer.

'No,' she shook her head. 'No, you owe nothing.'

'Toda raba.' Peter thanked her in his fragmentary Hebrew, and opened the side door.

The desert air was still and cold, and there was the sagy smell of the low thorny scrub.

'Shalom, said the woman through the open window; then she swung the vehicle in a tight turn. The headlights swept the grove of date palms ahead of them, and then turned back towards the open desert. Slowly the small car pitched and wove along the track in the direction from which they had come.

Peter turned his back on it, allowing his eyes to become accustomed to the muted light of the yellow horned moon and the whiter light of the fat desert stars.

After a few minutes he picked his way carefully into the palm grove. There was the smell of smoke from a dung fire, and the fine blue mist of smoke hung amongst the trees.

Somewhere in the grove he heard a goat bleat plaintively, and then the high thin wail of a child – there must be a Bedouin encampment in the oasis. He moved towards it, and came abruptly into an opening surrounded by the palms. The earth had been churned by the hooves of many beasts, and Peter stumbled slightly in the loose footing and then caught his balance.

In the centre of the opening was the stone parapet which guarded a deep freshwater well. There was a primitive windlass set above the parapet and another dark object which Peter could not immediately identify, dark and shapeless, crouching upon the parapet.

He went towards it cautiously, and felt his heart tumble within him as it moved.

It was a human figure, in some long voluminous robe that swept the sandy earth, so that it seemed to float towards him in the gloom.

The figure stopped five paces from him, and he saw that the head was covered by a monk's cowl of the same dark woollen cloth, so that the face was in a forbidding black hole beneath the cowl.

'Who are you?' Peter demanded, and his voice rasped in his own ears. The monk did not reply, but shook one hand free of the wide sleeve and beckoned to him to follow, then turned and glided away into the palm grove.

Peter went after him, and within a hundred yards was stepping out hard to keep the monk in sight. His light city shoes were not made for this heavy going, loose sand with scattered outcrops of shattered rock.

They left the palm grove and directly ahead of them, less than a quarter of a mile away, the cliff fell from the sky like a vast cascade of black stone.

The monk led him along a rough but well used footpath, and though Peter tried to narrow the distance between them, he found that he would have to break into a trot to do so – for although the monk appeared to be a broad and heavy man beneath the billowing robe, yet he moved lithely and lightly.

They reached the cliff, and the path zigzagged up it, at such a gradient that they had to lean forward into it. The surface was loose with shale and dry earth – becoming progressively steeper. Then underfoot the path was paved, the worn steps of solid rock.

On one hand the drop away into the valley was deeper always and the sheer cliff on the other seemed to lean out as though to press him over the edge.

Always the monk was ahead of him, tireless and quick, his feet silent on the worn steps, and there was no sound of labouring breath. Peter realized that a man of that stamina and bulk must be immensely powerful. He did not move as you might expect a man of God and prayer to move. There was the awareness and balance of a fighting man about him, the unconscious pride and force of the warrior. With Caliph nothing was ever as it seemed, he thought.

The higher they climbed, so the moonlit panorama below them became more magnificent, a soaring vista of desert and mountain with the great shield of the Dead Sea a brilliant beaten silver beneath the stars.

– All the kingdoms of the world, and the glory of them – Peter thought.

They had not paused to rest once on the climb. How high was it, Peter wondered – a thousand feet, fifteen hundred perhaps? His own breathing was deep and steady, he was not yet fully extended and the light sweat that dewed his forehead cooled in the night air.

Something nudged his memory, and he sniffed at the faintly perfumed aroma on the air. It was not steady, but he had caught it faintly once or twice during the climb.

Peter was plagued by the non-smoker's acute sense of smell, perfumes and odours always had special significance for him – and this smell was important, but he could not quite place it now. It nagged at him, but then it was lost in a host of other more powerful odours – the smell of human beings in community.

The smell of cooking smoke, of food and the underlying sickly taint of rotting garbage and primitive sewage disposal.

Somewhere long ago he had seen photographs of the ancient monastery built into the top of these spectacular cliffs, the caves and subterranean chambers honeycombed the crest of the rock face, and walls of hewn rock had been built above them by men dead these thousand years.

Yet the memory of that faint perfumed aroma lingered with Peter, as they climbed the last hundred feet of that terrifying drop and came out suddenly against the stone tower and thick fortification, into which was set a heavy timber door twelve feet high and studded with iron bolts.

At their approach the door swung open. There was a narrow stone passageway ahead of them lit by a single storm lantern in a niche at the corner of the passageway.

As Peter stepped through the gate, two other figures closed on each side of him out of the darkness and he moved instinctively to defend himself, but checked the movement and stood quiescent with his hand half raised as they searched him with painstaking expertise for a weapon.

Both these men were dressed in single-piece combat suits, and they wore canvas paratrooper boots. Their heads were covered by coarse woollen scarves wound over mouth and nose so only their eyes showed. Each of them carried the ubiquitous Uzzi submachine guns, loaded and cocked and slung on shoulder straps.

At last they stood back satisfied, and the monk led Peter on through a maze of narrow passages. Somewhere there was the sound of monks at their devotions, the harsh chanting of the Greek Orthodox service. The sound of it, and the smoky cedarwood aroma of burning incense, became stronger, until the monk led Peter into a cavernous, dimly lit church nave hewn from the living rock of the cliff.

In the gloom the old Greek monks sat like long-embalmed mummies in their tall dark wooden pews. Their time-worn faces masked by the great black bushes of their beards. Only their eyes glittered, alive as the jewels and precious metals that gilded the ancient religious icons on the stone walls.

The reek of incense was overpowering, and the hoarse chant of the office missed not a single beat as Peter and the robed monk passed swiftly amongst them.

In the impenetrable shadows at the rear of the church, the monk seemed abruptly to disappear, but when Peter reached the spot he discovered that one of the carved pews had been swung aside to reveal a dark secret opening in the rock.

Peter went into it cautiously. It was totally dark – but his feet found shallow stone steps, and he climbed a twisting stairway through the rock – counting the steps to five hundred, each step approximately six inches high.

Abruptly he stepped out into the cool desert night again. He was in a paved open courtyard, with the brilliant panoply of the stars overhead, the cliff rising straight ahead and a low stone parapet protecting the sheer drop into the valley behind him.

Peter realized that this must be one of the remotest and most easily defensible rendezvous that Caliph could have chosen – and there were more guards here.

Again they came forward, two of them, and searched him once again even more thoroughly than at the monastery gate.

While they worked Peter looked around him swiftly. The level courtyard was perched like an eagle's eyrie on the brink of the precipice, the parapet wall was five feet high. Across the courtyard were the oblong entrances to caves carved into the cliff face. They would probably be the retreats of the monks seeking solitude.

There were other men in the courtyard, wearing the same uniform with heads hidden by the Arab shawl headgear. Two of them were setting out flashlight beacons in the shape of a pyramid.

Peter realized they were beacons for an aircraft. – Not an aircraft. A helicopter was the only vehicle which would be able to get into this precarious perch on the side of the precipice.

All right then, the beacons would serve to direct a helicopter down into the level paved courtyard.

One of the armed guards ended his body search by checking the buckle of Peter's belt, tugging it experimentally to make certain it was not the handle of a concealed blade.

He stood back and motioned Peter forward. Across the courtyard the big monk waited patiently at the entrance to one of the stone cells that opened on to the courtyard.

Peter stooped through the low entrance. The cell was dimly lit by a stinking kerosene lamp set in a stone niche above the narrow cot. There was a crude wooden table against one wall, a plain crucifix above it and no other ornamentation.

Hewn from the rock wall was a ledge which acted as a shelf for a dozen heavy battered leather-bound books and a few basic eating utensils. It was also a primitive seat.

The monk motioned him towards it, but himself remained standing by the entrance to the cell with his hands thrust into the wide sleeves of his cassock, his face turned away and still masked completely by the deep hood.

There was utter silence from the courtyard beyond the doorway, but it was an electric waiting silence.

Suddenly Peter was aware of the perfumed aroma again, here in the crude stone cell, and then with a small tingling shock he recognized it. The smell came from the monk.

He knew instantly who the big man in the monk's cowl was, and the knowledge confused him utterly, for long stricken moments.

Then like the click of a well-oiled lock slipping home it all came together. He knew – oh God – he knew at last.

The aroma he had recognized was the faint trace of the perfumed smoke of expensive Dutch cheroots, and he stared fixedly at the big hooded monk.

Now there was a sound on the air, a faint flutter like moths' wings against the glass of the lantern, and the monk cocked his head slightly, listening intently.

Peter was balancing distances and times and odds in his head.

The monk, the five armed men in the courtyard, the approaching helicopter –

The monk was the most dangerous factor. Now that Peter knew who he was, he knew also that he was one of the most highly trained fighting men against whom he could ever match himself.

The five men in the yard – Peter blinked with sudden realization. *They would not be there any longer.* It was as simple as that. Caliph would never allow himself to be seen by any but his most trusted lieutenants, and by those about to die. The monk would have sent them away. They would be waiting close by, but it would take them time to get back into action.

There were only the monk and Caliph. For he knew that the dinning of rotor and engine was bringing Caliph in to the rendezvous. The helicopter sounded as though it were already directly overhead. The monk's attention was on it, Peter could see now he held his head under the cowl, he was off-guard for the first time.

Peter heard the sound of the spinning rotors change as the pilot altered pitch for the vertical descent into the tiny courtyard. The cell was lit through the doorway by the reflection of the helicopter's landing lights beating down into the courtyard with a relentless white glare.

Dust began to swirl from the downdraught of the rotors, it smoked in pale wisps into the cell and the monk moved.

He stepped to the doorway, the empty dark hole in the cowl which was his face turned briefly away from Peter as he glanced out through the entrance of the cell.

It was the moment for which Peter had waited, his whole body was charged, like the *S* in an adder's neck before it strikes. At the instant that the monk turned his head away, Peter launched himself across the cell.

He had ten feet to go, and the thunder of the helicopter's engines covered all sound – yet still some instinct of the fighting man warned the huge monk, and he spun into the arc of Peter's attack. The head under the cowl dropped defensively, so that Peter had to change his stroke. He could no longer go for the kill at the neck, and he chose the right shoulder for a crippling blow. His hand was stiff as a headsman's blade and it slogged into the monk's shoulder between the neck and the humerus joint of the upper arm. Peter heard the collarbone break with a sharp brittle crack, high above even the roar of the helicopter's engines.

With his left hand Peter caught the monk's crippled arm at the elbow and yanked it up savagely, driving the one edge of shattered bone against the other so it grated harshly, twisting it so the bone shards were razor cutting edges in their own living flesh – and the monk screamed, doubling from the waist to try and relieve the intolerable agony in his shoulder.

Shock had paralysed him, the big powerful body went slack in Peter's grasp.

Peter used all his weight and the impetus of his rush to drive the monk's head into the doorjamb of the cell; skull met stone with a solid clunk and the big man dropped face down to the paved floor.

Peter rolled him swiftly and pulled up the skirts of his cassock. Under it the man wore paratrooper boots and the blue full-length overalls of Thor Command. On his webbing belt was the blue steel and chequered walnut butt of the Browning Hi-power pistol in its quick-release holster. Peter sprang it from its steel retaining clamp and cocked the pistol with a sweep of the left hand. It would be loaded with Velex explosives.

The woollen folds of the cowl had fallen back from Colin Noble's head, the wide generous mouth now hanging open slackly, the burned toffee eyes glazed with concussion, the big crooked prizefighter's nose – all the well-remembered features, once so dearly cherished in comradeship.

Blood was streaming from Colin's thick curly hairline, running down his forehead and under his ear – but he was still conscious.

Peter put the muzzle of the Browning against the bridge of his nose. The Velex bullet would cut the top off his skull. Peter had lost his wig in those desperate seconds, and he saw recognition spark in Colin's stunned eyes.

'Peter! No!' croaked Colin desperately. '– I'm Cactus Flower!'

The shock of it hit Peter solidly, and he released the pressure on the Browning's trigger. It held him for only a moment and then he turned and ducked through the low doorway leaving Colin sprawling on the stone floor of the cell.

The helicopter had settled into the courtyard. It was a five-seater Bell Jet Ranger, painted in the blue and gold colours of Thor Command – and on its side was the Thor emblem and the words:

'THOR COMMUNICATIONS'

There was a pilot still at the controls, and one other man who had already left the cabin of the machine and was coming towards the entrance of the cell.

Even though he was doubled over to avoid the swirling rotor blades, there was no mistaking the tall powerful frame. The high wind of the rotors tumbled the thick greying leonine curls about the noble head, and the landing lights lit him starkly like the central character in some Shakespearian tragedy – a towering presence that transcended his mere physical stature.

Kingston Parker straightened as he came out from under the swinging rotor, and for an earth-stopping instant of time he stared at Peter across the stone-paved courtyard. Without the wig he recognized Peter instantly.

Kingston Parker stood for that instant like an old lion brought to bay.

'Caliph!' Peter called harshly, and the last doubt was gone as Kingston Parker whirled, incredibly swiftly for such a big man. He had almost reached the cabin door of the Jet Ranger before Peter had the Browning up.

The first shot hit Parker in the back, and flung him forward through the open door, but the gun had thrown high and right. It was not a killing shot, Peter knew it, and now the helicopter was rising swiftly, turning on its own axis, rising out over the edge of the precipice.

Peter ran twenty feet and jumped to the parapet of the hewn stone wall. The Jet Ranger soared above him, its belly white and bloated like that of a man-eating shark, the landing lights blazing down, half dazzling Peter. It swung out over the edge of the cliff.

Peter took the Browning double-handed, shooting directly upwards, judging the exact position of the fuel tank in the rear of the fuselage, where it joined the long stalk-like tail – and he pumped the big heavy explosive shells out of the gun, the recoil pounding down his outflung arms and jolting into his shoulders.

He saw the Velex bullets biting into the thin metal skin of the underbelly, the tiny wink of each bullet as it burst, but still the machine reared away above him – and he had been counting his shots. The Browning was almost empty.

Eleven, twelve – then suddenly the sky above him filled with flame, and the great whooshing concussion of air jarred the stone under his feet.

The Jet Ranger turned over on her back, a bright bouquet of flame, the engine howling its death cry, and it toppled beyond the edge of the precipice and plunged, burning savagely, into the dark void below where Peter stood.

Peter began to turn back towards the courtyard, and he saw the armed men pouring in through the stone gateway.

They were Thor men, picked fighting men, men he had trained himself. There was one bullet left in the Browning. He knew he was not going to make it – but he made a try for the entrance to the stairway, his only escape route.

He ran along the top of the stone wall like a tightrope artist, and he snapped the single remaining bullet at the running men to distract them.

The crackle of passing shot dinned in his head, and he flinched and missed his footing. He began to fall, twisting sideways away from the edge of the precipice – but then the bullets thumped into his flesh.

He heard the bullets going into his body with the rubbery socking sound of a heavyweight boxer hitting the heavy punch bag, and then he was flung out over the wall into the bottomless night.

He expected to fall for ever, a thousand feet to the desert floor below, where already the helicopter was shooting a hundred-foot fountain of fire into the air to mark Caliph's funeral pyre.

There was a narrow ledge ten feet below the parapet where a thorny wreath of desert scrub had found a precarious hold. Peter fell into it, and the curved thorns hooked into his clothing and into his flesh.

He hung there over the drop, and his senses began to fade.

His last clear memory was Colin Noble's bull bellow of command to the five Thor guards.

'Cease fire! Don't shoot again!' And then the darkness filled Peter's head.

In the darkness there were lucid moments, each disconnected from the other by eternities of pain and confused nightmare distortions of the mind.

He remembered being lifted up through the hatchway of an aircraft, lying in one of the light body-fitting Thor stretchers, strapped to it tightly, helpless as a newborn infant.

There was the memory of the inside cabin of Magda Altmann's Lear jet. He recognized the hand-painted decoration of the curved cabin roof. There were plasma bottles suspended above him, the whole blood was the beautiful ruby colour of fine claret in a crystal glass, and when he rolled his eyes downwards he saw the tubes connected to the thick bright needles driven into his arms – but he was terribly tired, an utter weariness that seemed to have bruised and crushed his soul – and he closed his eyes.

When he opened his eyes again, there was the roof of a long brightly lit corridor passing swiftly in front of his eyes. The feeling of motion, and the scratchy squeak of the wheels of a theatre trolley. Quiet voices were speaking French, and the bottle of beautiful bright blood was held above him by long slim hands that he knew so well.

He rolled his head slightly and he saw Magda's beloved face swimming on the periphery of his vision.

'I love you,' he said, but there was no sound and he realized that his lips had not moved. He could no longer support the weariness and he let his eyelids droop closed.

'How bad is it?' he heard Magda's voice speaking in that beautiful rippling French, and a man replied.

'One bullet is lying very close to the heart – we must remove it immediately.'

Then the prick of something into his flesh searching for the vein, and the sudden musty taste of Pentothal on his tongue, followed by the abrupt sinking plunge back into the darkness.

He came back very slowly out of the darkness, conscious first of the bandages that swathed his chest and restricted his breathing.

The next thing he was aware of was Magda Altmann, and how beautiful she was. It seemed that she must have been there all along while he was in darkness. He watched the joy bloom in her face as she saw that he was conscious.

'Thank you,' she whispered. 'Thank you for coming back to me, my darling.'

Then there was the room at La Pierre Bénite, with its high gilded ceilings and the view through the tall sash windows across the terraced lawns down to the lake. The trees along the edge of the water were in full leaf, and the very air seemed charged with spring and the promise of new life. Magda had filled the room with banks of flowers, and she was with him during most of each day.

'What happened when you walked back into the boardroom at Altmann Industries?' was one of the first questions he asked her.

'Consternation, chéri.' She chuckled, that husky little laugh of hers. 'They had already divided the spoils.'

The visitor came when Peter had been at La Pierre Bénite for eight days, and was able to sit in one of the brocaded chairs by the window.

Magda was standing beside Peter's chair, ready to protect him from over-exertion – physically or emotionally.

Colin Noble came into the room like a sheepish St Bernard dog. His right arm was strapped and carried in a sling across his chest. He touched it with his good hand.

'If I'd known it was you – and not Sir Steven – I'd never have turned my back on you,' he told Peter, and grinned placatingly.

Peter had stiffened, his face had transformed into a white rigid mask. Magda laid her hand upon his shoulder.

'Gently, Peter,' she whispered.

'Tell me one thing,' Peter hissed. 'Did you arrange the kidnapping of Melissa-Jane?'

Colin shook his head. 'My word on it. Parker used one of his other agents. I did not know it was going to happen.'

Peter stared at him, hard and unforgiving.

'Only after we had recovered Melissa-Jane, only then I knew that Caliph had planned it. If I had known – I would never have let it happen. Caliph must have known that. That is why he did not make me do it.' Colin was speaking quickly, urgently.

'What was Parker's object?' Peter's voice was still a vicious hiss.

'He had three separate objects. Firstly, to convince you that he was not Caliph. That's why his first order was to have you kill Parker himself. Of course, you never would have got near him. Then you were allowed to recover your daughter. It was Caliph himself who gave us O'Shaughnessy's name and where to find him. Then you were turned on to Magda Altmann —' Colin glanced at her apologetically. '– Once you had killed her, you would have been bound to Caliph by guilt.'

'When did you learn this?' Peter demanded.

'The day after we found Melissa-Jane. By then there was nothing I could do that would not expose me as Cactus Flower – all I could do was to pass a warning to Magda through Mossad.'

'It's true, Peter,' said Magda quietly.

Slowly the rigidity went out of Peter's shoulders.

'When did Caliph recruit you as his Chief Lieutenant?' he asked, his voice also had altered, softened.

'As soon as I took over Thor Command from you. He was never certain of you, Peter, that was why he opposed your appointment to head of Thor – and why he jumped at the first chance to have you fired. That was why he tried to have you killed on the Rambouillet road. Only after the attempt failed did he realize your potential value to him.'

'Are the other Atlas unit commanders Caliph's lieutenants – Tanner at Mercury Command, Peterson at Diana?'

'All three of us. Yes!' Colin nodded, and there was a long silence.

'What else do you want to know, Peter?' Colin asked softly. 'Are there any other questions?'

'Not now.' Peter shook his head wearily. 'There will be many others later.'

Colin looked up at Magda Altmann inquiringly. 'Is he strong enough yet?' he asked. 'Can I tell him the rest of it?'

She hesitated a moment. 'Yes,' she decided. 'Tell him now.'

'Atlas was to be the secret dagger in the sleeve of Western civilization – a civilization which had emasculated itself and abased itself before its enemies. For once we would be able to meet naked violence and piracy with raw force. Atlas is a chain of powerful men of many nations banded together, and Caliph was to be its executive chief. Atlas is the only agency which transcends all national boundaries, and has as its object the survival of Western society as we know it. Atlas still exists, its structure is complete – only Caliph is dead. He died in a most unfortunate air accident over the Jordan valley – but Atlas still exists. It has to go on, once that part which Caliph has perverted is rooted out. It is our hope for the future in a world gone mad.'

Peter had never heard him speak so articulately, so persuasively.

'You know, of course, Peter, that you were the original choice to command Atlas. However, the wrong man superseded you – although nobody could know he was the wrong man at that time. Kingston Parker seemed to have all the qualities needed for the task – but there were hidden defects which only became apparent much later.' Colin began enumerating them, holding up the fingers of his uninjured arm.

'Firstly, he lacked physical courage. He became obsessed with his own physical safety – grossly abusing his powers to protect himself.

'Secondly, he was a man of unsuspected and overbearing ambition, with an ungoverned lust for raw power. Atlas swiftly became the vehicle to carry him to glory. His first goal was the Presidency of the United States. He was using Atlas to destroy his political opponents. Had he succeeded in achieving the presidency, no man can tell what his next goal would have been.'

Colin dropped his hand and balled it into a fist.

'The decision to allow you to reach the rendezvous with Kingston Parker on the cliffs above Jericho was made by more than one man – in more than one country.'

Colin grinned again, boyishly, disarmingly.

'I did not even know it was you. I believed it was Steven Stride, right up until the moment I turned my back on you!'

'Tell him,' said Magda quietly. 'Get it over with, Colin. He is still very weak.'

'Yes,' Colin agreed. 'I'll do it now. Yesterday at noon, your appointment to succeed Doctor Kingston Parker as head of Atlas Command was secretly confirmed.'

For Peter it was as though a door had at last opened, a door so long closed and locked, but through it now he could see his destiny stretching out ahead of him, clearly he could see it for the first time.

'You are the man best suited by nature and by training to fill the void which Kingston Parker has left.'

Even through the weakness of his abused body, Peter could feel a deep well of strength and determination within himself which he had never before suspected. It was though it had been reserved expressly for this time, for this task.

'Will you accept the command of Atlas?' Colin asked. 'What answer must I take back with me?'

Magda's long fingers tightened on his shoulder, and they waited while he made his decision. It came almost immediately. There was no alternative open to him, Peter knew that – it was his destiny.

'Yes,' he said clearly. 'Tell them I accept the responsibility.'

It was a solemn moment, nobody smiled nor spoke for long seconds, and then,

'Caliph is dead,' Magda whispered. 'Long live Caliph.'

Peter Stride raised his head to look at her, but his voice when he replied was so cold that it seemed to frost upon his lips.

'Never,' he said, 'call me that again, ever.'

Magda made a small gesture of acquiescence, of total accord, then she stooped to kiss him on the mouth.